LIMIT

Frank Schätzing

LIMIT

Translated by Shaun Whiteside,
Jamie Lee Searle
and Samuel Willcocks

Jo Fletcher

JF

Jo Fletcher Books
An imprint of Quercus
New York • London

First published in the German language as *Limit* by Frank Schätzing
© 2009 by Verlag Kiepenheuer & Witsch GmbH & Co. KG, Cologne/ Germany
© 2009 by Frank Schätzing
Translation © 2009 by Shaun Whiteside, Jamie Searle, and Samuel Willcocks
First published in the United States by Quercus in 2013

Any member of educational institutions wishing to photocopy part or all of the work for classroom use or anthology should send inquiries to Permissions c/o Quercus Publishing Inc., 31 West 57th Street, 6th Floor, New York, NY 10019, or to permissions@quercus.com.

ISBN 978-1-62365-044-5

Library of Congress Control Number: 2013937912

Distributed in the United States and Canada by Random House Publisher Services c/o Random House, 1745 Broadway
New York, NY 10019

This book is a work of fiction. Names, characters, institutions, places, and events are either the product of the author's imagination or are used fictitiously. Any resemblance to actual persons—living or dead—events, or locales is entirely coincidental.

Manufactured in the United States

2 4 6 8 10 9 7 5 3 1

www.quercus.com

For Brigitte and Rolf who gave me life in the world

For Christine and Clive who gave me a piece of the moon

Planet Earth is blue
And there's nothing I can do

David Bowie

AUGUST 2, 2024
Prologue

EVA

I want to wake up in a city that doesn't sleep—

Good old Frankie-boy. Untroubled by urban transformation, as long as there was a stiff drink waiting for you when you woke up.

Vic Thorn rubbed his eyes.

In thirty minutes the automatic alarm signal would rouse the early shift from their beds. Strictly speaking he couldn't have cared less. As a short-term visitor he was largely free to decide how he was going to spend the day, except that even guests had to adapt to a certain formal framework. Which didn't necessarily mean getting up early, but they woke you anyway.

If I can make it there,
I'll make it anywhere—

Thorn started unfastening his belt. Because he thought staying too long in bed was degrading, he didn't trust anyone else's automatic devices to allow him to spend as little time of his life as possible asleep. Particularly since he liked to decide for himself who or what summoned him back to consciousness. Thorn loved turning his music systems up to the max. And he preferred to entrust his wake-up call to the Rat Pack: Frank Sinatra, Dean Martin, Joey Bishop, Sammy Davis Jr., the disreputable heroes of times past for whom he felt an almost romantic affection. And up here nothing, nothing at all, was conducive to the habits of the Rat Pack. Even Dean Martin's now famous observation that "You're not drunk if you can lie on the floor without holding on" was physically invalidated, and nor would the inveterate drinker have been able to indulge his predilection for falling off his bar stool and tottering out into the street. At 35,786 kilometers above the Earth's surface there were no prostitutes waiting for you outside the door, just lethal, airless space.

King of the hill, top of the heap—

Thorn hummed along with the tune, mumbling a wonky-sounding "*New York, New York.*" With a faint twitch, he pushed himself away and floated off his bunk, drifted to the small, round porthole of his cabin, and looked outside.

In the city that never slept, Huros-ED-4 was on the way to his next assignment.

He wasn't bothered by the cold of space or the total lack of atmosphere. The sequence of day and night which, at such a vast distance from the Earth, was in any case based more on general agreement than on sensory experience, held no validity for him. His alarm call was made in the language of the programmers. Huros-ED stood for *Humanoid Robotic System for Extravehicular Demands*, the 4 placed him along with another nineteen of his kind, each one two meters tall, torso and head entirely humanoid, while their exaggeratedly long arms in their resting state recalled the raptorial claws of a praying mantis. When required, they unfolded with admirable agility, and with hands that were able to perform extremely difficult operations. A second, smaller pair of arms emerged from the broad chest, packed with electronics, and these were used to provide assistance. The legs, however, were completely absent. Admittedly the Huros-ED had a waist and a pelvis, but where the hips would have been in a human being there sprouted flexible grippers with devices that allowed him to fasten himself on wherever he happened to be needed. During the breaks he looked for a sheltered niche, connected his batteries to the main supply, topped up the tanks of his navigation nozzles with fuel, and settled down to a spot of mechanical contemplation.

By now the last break was eight hours ago. Since then Huros-ED-4 had been working away industriously in the most diverse spots of the gigantic space station. In the outer zone of the roof, as the part turned toward the zenith was called, he had helped to swap ageing solar panels for new ones, in the wharf he had adjusted the floodlights for Dock 2, where one of the spaceships for the planned Mars mission was currently under construction. Then he had been dispatched a hundred meters lower to the scientific payloads fastened along the cantilevers, to remove the defective platinum parts from a measuring instrument designed to scan the surface of the Pacific Ocean off the coast of Ecuador. After this reconditioning had been successfully completed, his task was to go back inside the spaceport to investigate one of the manipulator arms that had ceased to function in the middle of a loading process.

The spaceport: that meant descending a bit further along the outside of the station, to a ring 180 meters in diameter, with eight berths for incoming and outgoing moon shuttles, and a further eight for evacuation pods. Leaving aside the fact that the ships anchored there were passing through a vacuum rather than through water, what went on around the ring was not much different from what happened in Hamburg or Rotterdam, the big terrestrial seaports, meaning that it too had cranes, huge robot arms on rails, called manipulators. One of these had packed in halfway through the loading process of a freight-and-passenger shuttle that was to start its journey to the Moon in only a few hours' time. The arm should have been working, but with mechanical stubbornness it absolutely refused to move, and instead hung, effectors spread, half inside the shuttle's loading area and half outside, which meant that the ship's opened body couldn't be closed.

On stipulated flight-paths, Huros-ED-4 passed alongside docked shuttles, airlocks and connecting tunnels, spherical tanks, containers, and masts until he reached the defective arm that glinted coldly in the unfiltered sunlight. The cameras behind the visor on his head and the ends of limbs sent pictures to the control center as he passed close by the construction and subjected every square centimeter to detailed analysis. The control constantly compared these pictures with the images located in his data storage system, until it had found the reason for the failure.

The control instructed him to clean the arm.

He stopped. Someone in his central steering module said, "Fucking shit!," prompting a query from Huros-ED-4. Although programmed to respond to the human voice, he could detect no meaningful order in the exclamation. The control room neglected to repeat the words, so at first he did nothing but examine the damage. Tiny splinters were wedged into the joint of the manipulator. A long, deep gash ran diagonally across the top of the joint's structure, gaping like a wound. At first sight the electronics seemed to be intact, meaning that the damage was purely material although serious enough to have caused the manipulator to switch off.

The control room issued an instruction to clean the joint.

Huros-ED-4 paused.

Had he been a human being, his behavior might have been described as indecisive. At length he requested further information, thus indicating in his own vague way that the task was beyond his capabilities. Revolutionary a piece of engineering though he was—sensor-based steering, sensory impression feedback, flexible and autonomous operation—robots were still machines that thought in templates. He probably knew they were there, but he didn't know *what* they were. Likewise, he recorded the tear, but was unable to match it with familiar information. As a result the defective places did not exist for him. Consequently it was hard to tell exactly what he was supposed to be cleaning, so he didn't clean anything at all.

A smattering of consciousness, and robots would have realized that their lives were mercifully free of anxiety.

But everyone else was anxious enough to be going on with. Vic Thorn had had a long shower, listened to "My Way," put on a T-shirt, sneakers, and shorts, and had just decided to spend the day in the fitness studio when the call came from headquarters.

"You could be useful to us in solving a problem," said Ed Haskin, under whose responsibility the spaceport and the systems attached to it fell.

"Right now?" Thorn hesitated. "I was planning to spend a bit of time on the treadmill."

"Right now would be better."

"What's up?"

"It looks as if there are problems with your spaceship."

Thorn bit his lower lip. A thousand alarm bells went off in his head at the idea that his take-off might be delayed. Bad, very bad! The ship was supposed to leave the port at about midday, with him and another seven astronauts on board, to relieve the crew of the American moon base who, after six months of selenic exile, were succumbing to hallucinations of tarmac roads, carpeted apartments, sausages, meadows, and a sky full of color, clouds, and rain. On top of that, Thorn was scheduled to be one of the two pilots for the two-and-a-half-day flight and, to cap it all off, to be leader of the crew, which explained why they were talking to him rather than anyone else. And there was another reason why any hesitation struck him as more than inopportune—

"What's up with the crate?" he asked, with deliberate indifference. "Doesn't it want to fly?"

"Oh, it wants to fly all right, but it can't. There was a glitch during loading. The manipulator broke down and blocked the hatches. We can't shut the freight area."

"I see." Relief flooded through Thorn. A defective manipulator could be dealt with.

"And you know why it broke down? *Debris.* A heavy fall."

Thorn sighed. Space debris, whose unwelcome omnipresence was down to an unparalleled orbital congestion, begun in the 1950s by the Soviets with their Sputnik launches. Since then, the remnants of thousands of missions had circulated at every altitude: burnt-out propulsion stages, decommissioned and forgotten satellites, wreckage from countless explosions and collisions, from complete reactors to tiny fragments of shrapnel, drops of frozen coolant, screws and wires, bits of plastic and metal, scraps of gold foil and vestiges of flaked-off paint. The constant fracturing of the splinters with each fresh collision meant that they were breeding like rodents. By now the number of objects larger than one centimeter was estimated at 900,000. Barely three percent of these were constantly monitored, and the ominous remainder, along with billions of smaller particles and micrometeorites, was on its way elsewhere—in case of doubt, with the inevitability with which insects ended up on windshields, toward wherever you happened to be.

The problem was, a wasp hurtling at a luxury limousine with the momentum of an identically sized fragment of space debris would have developed the kinetic energy of a hand-grenade and written off the vehicle in an instant. The speeds of objects moving in opposite directions became extreme in space. Even particles only micrometers across had a destructive effect in the long term: they ground away at solar panels, they destroyed the surfaces of satellites, and they roughened the outer shells of spaceships. Near-Earth debris burned up sooner or later in the upper layers of the atmosphere, but only to be replaced by new debris. With increasing altitude its lifetime extended, and it could theoretically have survived for all eternity at the level at which the space station was orbiting. The fact that several of the dangerous objects were known and their flight paths could be calculated weeks and months in advance provided a certain consolation, because it allowed the astronauts just to steer the whole station out of the way. The thing that had crashed into the manipulator plainly hadn't been one of those.

"And what can I do about it?" asked Thorn.

"I know, crew time." Haskin laughed irritably. "Tightness of resources. The robot can't sort it out all by itself. Two of us will have to go out, but at the moment I've only got one staff member available. Would you jump in?"

Thorn didn't think for long. It was very important for him to get out of there on time, and besides, he liked space walks.

"That's fine," he said.

"You'll be going out with Karina Spektor."

Even better. He'd met Spektor the previous evening in the crew cafeteria, an expert in robotics, of Russian origin, with high cheekbones and cat-green eyes, who had responded to his attempts at flirtation with seeming willingness to engage in further international understanding.

"I'm on my way!" he said.

—in a city that never sleeps—

Cities tended to generate noise. Streets in which the air seethed with acoustic activity. People drawing attention to themselves by beeping, calling, whistling, chatting, laughing, complaining, shouting. Noise as social putty, coded into cacophony. Guitarists, singers, sax players in house doorways and subway tunnels. Disgruntled crows, barking dogs. The reverberation of construction machinery, thundering jackhammers, metal on metal. Unexpected, familiar, wheedling, shrill, sharp, dark, mysterious, noises that rose and fell, that approached and fled, some that rose like a gas, others that caught you right in the pit of the stomach and the auditory canal. Background noises of traffic. The flashy bass baritone of heavy limousines vying with dainty mopeds, with the purr of electromobiles, the grandiloquence of sports cars, souped-up motorcycles, the thumping get-to-the-side of the buses. Music from boutiques, footstep concerts in pedestrian precincts, strolling, shuffling, strutting, rushing, the sky vibrating with the thunder of distant airplane turbines, the whole city one huge bell.

Outside the space city:

None of that.

Familiar as the sounds might have been inside the living modules, laboratories, control rooms, connecting tunnels, leisure areas, and restaurants distributed across an overall height of 280 meters, there was a ghostly feeling the first time you left the station for EVA, "Extravehicular Activity," the external maintenance service. Suddenly, without transition, you were out there, really out there, more out there than anywhere else. Beyond the air locks all sound stopped. Of course you didn't go entirely deaf. You could hear yourself very clearly, and you could hear the rush of the air-conditioning unit built into the space suit, and of course the walkie-talkie, but it was all being played out inside your own portable spaceship.

All around you, in the vacuum, perfect silence reigned. You saw the mighty structure of the station, peered through illuminated windows; saw the icy radiance of the floodlight batteries high above, where enormous spaceships were being assembled, spaceships that would never land on a planet and only existed in weightless suspension; you were aware of industrial activity, the turning and stretching of the cranes on the outer ring and the shuttles from the inner zone; you observed robots in free fall, so like living creatures that you felt like asking them the way—and intuitively, overwhelmed by the beauty of the architecture, the faraway Earth and the coldly staring stars, their light undispersed by the atmosphere, you expected to hear mysterious or dramatic music. But space stayed mute, its sublimity orchestrated only by your own breath.

In the company of Karina Spektor, Thorn floated through the emptiness and silence toward the defective manipulator. Their suits, fitted with steering nozzles, enabled them to navigate precisely. They slipped across the docks of the vast spaceport embraced by the tower-like construction of the space station, wide as a freeway. Three moon shuttles were currently anchored on the ring—two of them fixed to air locks, Thorn's spaceship in the parking position—and also the eight plane-like evacuation pods. Basically the whole ring was one large switching yard, around which the spaceships constantly changed location to keep the symmetrically constructed station in balance.

Thorn and Spektor had left Torus-2, the distributor module in the center of the port, and headed for one of the external locks not far from the shuttle. White and massive, with opened loading hatches, it rested in the sunlight. The frozen arm of the manipulator loomed high above them, bent abruptly at the elbow and disappearing into the cargo zone. Huros-ED-4 hung motionless by its anchor platform. With his gaze fixed on the blocked joint, there was something unsettling about his posture. Only at the very last moment did he move slightly to the side so that they could get a glimpse of the damage. Of course his behavior was not the result of cybernetic peevishness, as a Huros doesn't even have the beginning of a notion of selfhood, but his images were now surplus to requirements. From now on what mattered were the impressions that the helmet-cameras sent to the control room.

"So?" Haskin asked. "What do you think?"

"Bad." Spektor gripped the frame of the manipulator and drew herself closer to it. Thorn followed her.

"Odd," he said. "It looks to me as if something's brushed against the arm and torn this gaping hole, but the electronics seem to be undamaged."

"Then it should move," Haskin objected.

"Not necessarily," said Spektor. She spoke English with a Slavic smoothness, rather erotic, Thorn thought. A shame, in fact, that he couldn't stay another day. "The impact must have released a lot of micro-debris. Perhaps our friend is suffering from constipation. Did the Huros perform an environmental analysis?"

"Slight contamination. What about the splinters? Could they have caused the blockage?"

"It's possible. They probably come from the arm itself. Perhaps something's got twisted, and it's under tension." The astronaut studied the joint carefully. "On the other hand, this is a manipulator, not a pastry fork. The object would have been 7 or 8 millimeters long at the most. I mean it wasn't an actual collision, it should really be able to cope with something like that."

"You certainly know your way around these things," Thorn said appreciatively.

"Party trick," she laughed. "I hardly deal with anything else. Space debris is our biggest problem up here."

"And what about this?" He leaned forward and pointed to a spot where a tiny, bright shard protruded. "Could that come from a meteorite?"

Spektor followed his outstretched index finger.

"At any rate it comes from the thing that hit the arm. The analyses will tell you more."

"Exactly," said Haskin. "So get a move on. I suggest you get the thing out with the ethanol blower."

"Have we got one of those?" Thorn asked.

"The Huros does," Spektor replied. "We can use his left arm, there are tanks inside and nozzles on the effectors. But it'll take two of us, Vic. Have you ever worked with a Huros?"

"Not directly."

"I'll show you. We'll have to turn him off partially if we want to use him as a tool. That means one of us will have to help stabilize him, while the other—"

At that moment the manipulator stirred into life.

The huge arm stretched out of the loading-space, pushed backward, swiveled, grabbed the Huros-ED, and shoved it away as if it had had enough of its company. Thorn automatically pushed his companion downward and out of the collision zone, but couldn't keep the robot from striking her shoulder and whirling her around. At the last second

Spektor managed to cling on to the frame; then the manipulator crashed into Thorn, dragged him away from her and from the ring, and catapulted him into space.

Back! He had to get back!

Fingers flying, he tried to regain control over his steering nozzles. He was followed by the pirouetting torso of the Huros-ED, which was getting closer and closer, as Haskin and Spektor's shouts rang in his ear. The robot's abdomen hit his helmet. Thorn somersaulted and started circling helplessly as he was slung over the edge of the ring-level and hurtled from the space station at terrifying speed. He realized with horror that in attempting to protect his companion he had lost his only chance of saving himself. In wild panic he reached around him, found the switches for the steering nozzles, turned them on to stabilize his flight path with short blasts, to slow his circling trajectory, found he couldn't breathe, realized that his suit had been damaged, that it was all over, waved his arms around, tried to scream—

His scream froze.

Vic Thorn's body was carried out into the silent, endless night, and everything changed in the seconds of his death, everything.

MAY 19, 2025
The Island

ISLA DE LAS ESTRELLAS, PACIFIC OCEAN

The island wasn't much more than a rocky outcrop, set on the equator like a pearl on a string. Compared with other nearby islands, its charms were rather modest. In the west a quite impressive cliff rose from the sea, crowned by tropical rain forest, which clung dark and impenetrable to jagged volcanic slopes, and was inhabited almost exclusively by insects, spiders, and an unusually ugly species of bat. Streams had dug cracks and gorges, collected into waterfalls, and poured thundering into the ocean. On the eastern side, the landscape fell in terraces, intermingled with rocky elevations and largely bare. You would have looked in vain for palm-lined beaches. Black basalt sand marked the few bays that gave access to the interior. Rainbow-colored lizards sunned themselves on stone pillars amid the crashing waves. Their day consisted in catapulting themselves several meters into the air and snapping for insects, the meager climax of an otherwise anticlimactic repertoire of natural spectacles. Overall, the Isla had hardly anything to offer that didn't exist in more beautiful, bigger, and higher forms elsewhere.

On the other hand its geographical location was impeccable.

It actually lay exactly at the middle of the Earth, where the northern and southern hemispheres met, 550 kilometers west of Ecuador and thus far from any air routes. There were no storms in this part of the world. Major accumulations of cloud were a rarity, lightning never flashed. During the first half of the year it sometimes rained, violently and for hours at a time, without the air growing particularly cooler. Temperatures hardly ever fell below 71.6 degrees Fahrenheit, and usually they were significantly higher than that. Because the island was uninhabited and economically useless, the Ecuadorian parliament had been more than happy to lease it, for the next forty years in return for an invigorating boost to the state economy, to new tenants whose first job was to rename Isla Leona as Isla de las Estrellas: Stellar Island: island of the stars.

Subsequently part of the eastern slope disappeared under an accumulation of glass and steel that promptly united the fury of all animal conservationists. But the building had no effect on the island's ecology. Flocks of noisy seabirds, unperturbed by the evidence of human presence, daubed cliff and architecture alike with their guano. The creatures were untroubled by ideas of beauty, and the humans had their minds on higher things than swallow-tailed gulls and ringed plovers. In any case, not many people had set foot on the island for a long time, and everything indicated that it would remain a rather exclusive place in the future as well.

At the same time, nothing fired the imagination of the whole of humanity as much as this island.

It might have been a rough pile of bird shit, but at the same time it was considered the most extraordinary, perhaps the most hopeful place in the world. In fact the actual magic emanated from an object about two nautical miles off the coast, a gigantic platform resting on five house-sized pontoons. If you approached it on misty days, at first you couldn't see what was so special about it. You saw flat structures, generating plants and tanks, a helicopter landing pad, a terminal with a tower, aerials, and radio telescopes. The whole thing looked like an airport, except that there was no runway to be seen. Instead, a massive cylindrical construction grew from the center, a gleaming colossus with bundles of pipes meandering up its sides. Only by narrowing your eyes could you make out the black line that emerged from the cylinder and soared steeply upward. If the clouds were low, they engulfed it after a few hundred meters, and you found yourself wondering what you would see if the sky cleared. Even people who knew better—in principle, then, anyone who had managed to get through the high-security area—expected to see something where the line ended, a fixed point on which the overstretched imagination could settle.

But there was nothing.

Even in bright sunshine, when the sky was deep blue, you couldn't see the end of the line. It became thinner and thinner until it seemed to dematerialize in the atmosphere. Through field glasses it just disappeared a little higher up. You stared until your neck ached, with Julian Orley's now legendary observation in your ears, that the Isla de las Estrellas was the ground floor of eternity—and you started to sense what he had meant by it.

Carl Hanna strained his neck too, craning from the seat of the helicopter to look up stupidly into the blue, while below him two finback whales plowed the azure of the Pacific. Hanna didn't waste a glance on them. When the pilot pointed out the rare animals yet again, he heard himself murmuring that there was nothing less interesting than the sea.

The helicopter curved around and roared toward the platform. The line blurred briefly in front of Hanna's eyes, seemed to dissolve, and then it was clearly visible in the sky again, as straight as if drawn by a ruler.

A moment later it had doubled.

"There are two of them," observed Mukesh Nair.

The Indian brushed the thick black hair off his forehead. His dark face glowed with delight, the nostrils of his cucumber-shaped nose flared as if to inhale the moment.

"Of course there are two." Sushma, his wife, held up her index and middle fingers as if explaining something to a child in preschool. "Two cabins, two cables."

"I know that, I know!" Nair waved her impatiently away. His mouth twisted into a smile. He looked at Hanna. "How amazing! Do you know how wide those cables are?"

"Just over a meter, I think." Hanna smiled back.

"For a moment they were gone." Nair looked out, shaking his head. "They simply disappeared."

"That's true."

"You saw that too? And you, Sushma? They flickered like a mirage. Did you see—"

"Yes, Mukesh, I saw it too."

"I thought I was imagining it."

"No, you weren't," Sushma said benignly and rested a small, paddle-shaped hand on his knee. Hanna thought the two of them looked as if they'd been created by the painter Fernando Botero. The same rounded physiques, the same short, inflated-looking extremities.

He looked out of the window again.

The helicopter stayed an appropriate distance from the cables as it drifted past the platform. Only authorized pilots from NASA or Orley Enterprises were allowed to fly this route when they brought guests to the Isla de las Estrellas. Hanna tried to catch a glimpse of the inside of the cylinder, where the cables disappeared, but they were too far away. A moment later they had left the platform behind, and were swinging in toward the Isla. Below them, the shadow of the helicopter darted across deep blue waves.

"That cable must be really thin if you can't see it from the side," Nair reflected. "Which means it must actually be flat. Are they cables at all?" He laughed and wrung his hands. "They're more like tapes, really, aren't they? I've probably got it all wrong. My God, what can I say? I grew up in a field. In a field!"

Hanna nodded. They had fallen into conversation on the flight here from Quito, but even so he knew that Mukesh Nair had a very close relationship with fields. A modest farmer's son from Hoshiarpur in Punjab, who liked eating well but preferred a street stall to any three-star restaurant, who thought more highly of the concerns and opinions of simple people than of small talk at receptions and gallery openings, who preferred to fly Economy Class and who craved expensive clothes as much as a Tibetan bear craves a tie. At the same time Mukesh Nair, with an estimated private fortune of 46 billion dollars, was one of the wealthiest people in the world, and his way of thinking was anything but rustic. He had studied agriculture in Ludhiana and economics at Bombay University, he was a holder of the Padma Vibhushan, the

second-highest Indian order for civilian merits, and an unchallenged
market leader when it came to supplying the world with Indian fruit and
vegetables. Hanna was intimately acquainted with the CV of Mr. Tomato,
as Nair was generally known, having studied the careers of all the guests
who were traveling in for the meeting.

"Now look, just look at that!" shouted Nair. "That's not bad, is it?"

Hanna craned his neck. The helicopter hovered along the eastern
slope of the island so that they could enjoy a perfect view of the Stellar Island Hotel. Like a stranded cruise ship it lay on the slopes, seven
receding stories piled up on top of one another, overlooking a prow
with a huge swimming pool. Each room had its own sun terrace. The
highest point of the building formed a circular terrace, half covered by
a huge glass dome. Hanna could make out tables and chairs, loungers,
a buffet, a bar. Amidships lay a part that had been left level, plainly
the lobby, bounded to the north by the stern-shaped construction of a
helicopter landing pad. Architecture alternated with sections of rough
stone, as if the architects had been trying to beam up a cruise ship right
in front of the island, and had miscalculated by a few hundred meters
toward the center. It seemed to Hanna that parts of the hotel grounds
must have been blown into the mountain with explosives. A footpath,
interrupted by flights of steps, wound its way down, crossed a green plateau whose design looked too harmonious to be of natural origin, then
led further down and opened up into a path running along the coast.

"A golf course," Nair murmured in delight. "How wonderful."

"I'm sorry, but I thought you liked things simple." And when the
Indian looked at him in amazement, Hanna added, "According to
yourself. Plain restaurants. Simple people. Third-class travel."

"You're getting things muddled."

"If the media are to be trusted, you're surprisingly modest for a
public figure."

"Such nonsense! I try to keep out of public life. You can count the
number of interviews that I've given over the past few years on one
hand. If Tomato gets a good press, I'm happy. The main thing is that no
one tries to get me in front of a camera or a microphone." Nair frowned.
"By the way, you're right. Luxury isn't something I need to live. I come
from a tiny village. The amount of money you have is irrelevant. Deep
down, I'm still living in that village, it's just got a bit bigger."

"By a few continents on either side of the Indian Ocean," Hanna
teased. "Got you."

"So?" Nair grinned. "As I said, you're getting things muddled."

"What?"

"Look, it's quite simple. The platform we just flew over—things
like that occupy my heart. The fate of the entire human race may hang
on those cables. But this hotel fascinates me the way theater might

fascinate you. It's fun, so you go there from time to time. Except that most people, as soon as they get some money, start thinking theater is real life. Ideally they'd like to live on stage, dress up again every day and play a part. That makes me think, you know the joke about the psychologist who wants to catch a lion?"

"No."

"Quite easy. He goes into the desert, sets up a cage, gets in, and decides that inside is outside."

Hanna grinned. Nair shook with laughter.

"You see, I have no interest in that, it was never my thing. I don't want to sit in a cage or live out my life on a stage. Nonetheless, I shall enjoy the next two weeks, you can bet on that. Before it gets going tomorrow, I'll play a round of golf down there and love it! But once the fourteen days are over I'll go back home to where you laugh at a joke because it's good and not because a rich person's telling it. I'll eat things that taste good, not things that are expensive. I'll talk to people because I like them, not because they're important. Many of those people don't have the money to go to my restaurants, so I'll go to theirs."

"Got it," said Hanna.

Nair rubbed his nose. "At the risk of depressing you—I don't actually know anything about you at all."

"Because you've spent the whole flight talking about yourself," Sushma observed reproachfully.

"Have I? You must excuse my need to communicate."

"That's fine," Hanna said with a wave of his hand. "There isn't so much to say about me. I tend to work in silence."

"Investment?"

"Exactly."

"Interesting." Nair pursed his lips. "What fields?"

"Mostly energy. And a bit of everything." Hanna hesitated. "It might interest you to know that I was born in New Delhi."

The helicopter lowered itself toward the heliport. The landing pad had room for three helicopters that size and was marked with a fluorescent symbol, a silvery O with a stylized orange moon around it: the company logo of Orley Enterprises. At the edge of the heliport Hanna spotted people in uniform, taking reception of passengers and luggage. A slim woman in a light-colored pantsuit broke away from the group. The wind in the rotor blades tugged at her clothes, her hair glistened in the sun.

"You come from New Delhi?" Sushma Nair, visibly taken with Hanna's unexpected revelation, edged closer. "How long did you live there?"

The helicopter came gently to rest. The door swung aside and a stepladder unfolded.

"Let's talk about it by the pool," Hanna said, putting her off for the time being, then let them walk ahead of him and followed them without any great haste. Nair's smile revealed more tooth enamel. He beamed at the staff, the surroundings and life, he drew the island air into his nostrils, said, "Ah!" and "Incredible!" As soon as he caught sight of the woman in the pantsuit he started praising the grounds in the most effulgent terms. Sushma added indifferent noises of appreciation. The slim woman thanked them. Nair went on talking, without drawing breath. How wonderful everything was. How successful. Hanna practiced being patient as he appreciated her appearance. Late thirties, neat ash-blonde hair, well groomed and displaying that natural grace that is never entirely aware of itself, she could have played the glamorous lead in an advertisement for a credit company or a range of cosmetics. In fact she was in charge of Orley Travel, Orley's tourism department, which made her the second most important person in the biggest business empire in the world.

"Carl." She smiled and extended her hand. Hanna looked into sea-blue eyes, impossibly intense, the iris dark-rimmed. Her father's eyes. "Nice to have you here as our guest!"

"Thanks for the invitation." He returned her handshake and lowered his voice. "You know, I'd prepared a few nice remarks about the hotel, but I'm afraid my predecessor preempted everything I had to say."

"Haha! Ha!" Nair clapped him on the shoulder. "I'm sorry, my friend, but we have Bollywood! Your old-school charm couldn't possibly match so much poetry and pathos."

"Don't listen to him," said Lynn, without turning her eyes away. "I'm very susceptible to Canadian charm. Even its nonverbal variant."

"Then I won't allow myself to be discouraged," Hanna promised.

"I would be most offended if you did."

All around them, willing hands were busy unloading mountains of battered-looking luggage. Hanna assumed it belonged to the Nairs. Solidly built things that had been in use since Old Testament times. He himself had brought only a small suitcase and a valise.

"Come on," Lynn said cordially. "I'll show you to your rooms."

From the terrace, Tim saw his sister leaving the heliport with an Indian-looking couple and an athletically built man, and walking to the reception building. He and Amber lived in a corner room on the fifth floor, with a perfect panoramic view. Some distance away, glinting in the sunlight, was the platform that they would be going to the following morning. Another helicopter was approaching the island, its arrival heralded by the clattering noise of the rotors.

He threw his head back.

A day of rare, crystal clarity.

The sky stretched across the sea like a deep-blue dome. A single ragged cloud hung there like an ornament or a landmark, apparently motionless. It made Tim think of an old film that he'd seen years ago, a tragicomedy in which a man grew up in a small town without ever leaving it. He'd gone to school there, got married, taken a job, met up with friends he'd known since childhood—and then, in his mid-thirties, he discovered that he was the involuntary star of a television show and the town was one huge, colossal fake, stuffed full of cameras, fake walls, and stage lighting. All the inhabitants apart from him were actors with lifetime contracts, *his* lifetime, of course, and consistently enough the sky proved to be a huge, blue-painted dome.

Tim Orley narrowed one eye and held up his right index finger in such a way that the tip seemed to touch the lower edge of a cloud. It balanced on it like a piece of cotton ball.

"Do you want something to drink?" Amber called from inside.

He didn't reply, but wrapped his left hand around his wrist and tried to keep his finger as still as possible. At first nothing happened. Then, extremely slowly, the tiny cloud drifted eastward.

"The bar is full to the brim. I'll take a bitter lemon. What would you like?"

It was moving. It would drift on. For some unfathomable reason it reassured Tim to know that the cloud up there wasn't nailed on or painted up.

"What?" he asked.

"I asked what you'd like to drink."

"Yes."

"So, what?"

"No idea."

"Goodness me. I'll take a look and see if they've got any."

He returned his attention to Lynn. Amber came across the terrace toward him, swinging an open bottle of Coca-Cola seductively between thumb and forefinger. Tim mechanically accepted it, put it to his lips and drank without noticing what he was pouring down his throat. His wife watched him. Then she looked down to where Tim's sister and her little entourage were just disappearing into the lobby.

"Oh, I see," she remarked.

He said nothing.

"You're still worried?"

"You know me."

"What for? Lynn's looking good." Amber leaned against the railing and sucked noisily on her lemonade. "Really good, in fact, if you ask me."

"That's exactly what I'm worried about."

"That she looks good?"

"You know exactly what I mean. She's trying to be more perfect than perfect, all over again."

"Oh, Tim—"

"You've dealt with her before, haven't you?"

"More than anything I've experienced her having everything under control here."

"Everything here has *Lynn* under control!"

"Fine, so what should she do, in your opinion? Julian's invited a crowd of filthy-rich eccentrics that she's got to look after. He's promised them two weeks in the most exclusive hotels of all time, and Lynn's responsible for them all. Should she start letting herself go, and walk around the place looking all unwashed and with her hair in a mess, neglect her guests, just to prove that she's a human being?"

"Of course not."

"This is a circus, Tim! She's the ringmaster. She *has* to be perfect, or else the lions will eat her."

"I know that," Tim said impatiently. "That's not the issue. It's just that I can see that she's starting to get agitated again."

"She didn't seem especially agitated to me."

"That's because she deceives you. Because she deceives everybody. You know how well her personal diplomacy works."

"I'm sorry, but isn't it possible that you're dramatizing everything just a little bit?"

"I'm not dramatizing anything at all. I'm really not. Let's leave aside the question of whether it was a brilliant idea to join in all this nonsense in the first place, but fine, nothing to be done. You and Julian, you—"

"Hey!" A warning light flashed in Amber's eyes. "Don't go saying we twisted your arm again."

"What else?"

"No one twisted your arm."

"Oh, come on! You insisted like mad."

"So? How old are you? Five or something? If you really hadn't wanted—"

"I didn't. I'm here because of Lynn." Tim sighed and rubbed his eyes. "Okay, okay! She *looks* fantastic! She seems to be stable. But still."

"Tim. She *built* this hotel!"

"Sure." He nodded. "Yes, sure. And it's great! Really."

"I'm taking you seriously. I just don't want you to start blaming Lynn simply because you can't sort things out with your father."

Tim tasted the bitterness of the insult. He turned to face her and shook his head.

"That's unfair," he said quietly.

Amber turned her lemonade bottle between her fingers. Silence fell for a while. Then she put her arms around his neck and kissed him.

"I'm sorry."

"It's fine."

"Have you talked to Julian about it?"

"Yes, and I'll give you three guesses. He insists she's doing brilliantly. You say she looks as if she's in the pink. So I'm the idiot."

"Of course you are. The most lovable idiot who's ever got on anyone's nerves."

Tim grinned crookedly. He pressed Amber to him, but his gaze was fixed beyond the parapet. The helicopter that had brought the athlete and the Indian couple here hummed its way out to the open sea. The next one was hovering above the heliport and preparing to land. Below it, Lynn was leaving the lobby to welcome the new guests. Tim's eyes drifted across the steep terrain between the hotel and the cliffs, the abandoned golf course, then followed the walkway down to the coastal path. Dips and gorges had required the construction of several small bridges, with the result that you could comfortably stroll along the whole of the eastern side of the Isla de las Estrellas. He saw someone ambling along the path. A slender form came darting up from the opposite direction, its body gleaming bright in the sun.

Bright as ivory.

Finn O'Keefe saw her and stopped. The woman was running at an athletic pace. She was a curious creature, with willowy limbs, almost on the edge of anorexia, but still shapely. Her skin was snow-white, as was her long, flowing hair. She wore a skimpy mother-of-pearl-colored bathing suit and sneakers of the same color, and moved as nimbly as a gazelle. Someone who belonged on the front pages.

"Hello," he said.

The woman stopped running and approached him in springy steps.

"Hi! And who are you?"

"Finn."

"Oh, of course. Finn O'Keefe. You look somehow different on screen."

"I always look somehow different."

He held out his hand. Her fingers, long and delicate, gave a surprisingly firm handshake. Now that she was standing right in front of him he could see that her eyebrows and eyelids were the same shimmering white as her hair, while her irises were almost violet. Below her narrow, straight nose, a sensuously curving mouth arched with almost colorless lips. To Finn O'Keefe she looked like an attractive alien whose firm skin was starting to crease in places. He guessed that she was just past forty.

"And who are you?"

"I'm Heidrun," she said. "Are you part of the tour group?"

Her English sounded as if it ran on crunchy gears. He tried to guess her accent. Germans generally spoke a kind of saw-toothed English, the Scandinavian version was soft and melodious. Heidrun, he decided, wasn't German, but she wasn't Danish or Swedish either.

"Yes," he said. "I'm part of it."

"And? Fed up?"

He laughed. She didn't seem even slightly impressed to find herself bumping into him here. Exposed as he was to the wearying and universal admiration of women who would happily have ditched their husbands just to go to bed with him, not to mention the men who fancied him too, he was constantly on the run.

"Quite honestly, yes. A bit."

"Whatever. Me too."

She brushed her sweat-drenched mane from her brow, turned around, spread the thumbs and index fingers of both hands into right angles, brought the tips together, and studied the platform in the sea through the frame she had created. You could only make out the vertical black line if you looked very carefully.

"And what does he want from you?" she asked suddenly.

"Who?"

"Julian Orley." Heidrun lowered her hands and directed her violet gaze at him. "He wants something from each of us, after all."

"Really?"

"Oh, come on. Otherwise we wouldn't be here, would we?"

"Hmm."

"Are you rich?"

"I get by."

"Silly question. God, you must be rich! You're Mr. Royalties, aren't you? If you haven't somehow screwed everything up, you must be worth a few hundred million dollars." She laid her head curiously on one side. "And? Are you?"

"And you?"

"Me?" Heidrun laughed. "Forget it. I'm a photographer. With what I own he couldn't even have the platform repainted. Let's say I'm part of a job lot. It's Walo that he's after. Walo."

"Sorry, who's that?"

"Walo?" She pointed up to the hotel. "My husband. Walo Ögi."

"Doesn't ring a bell."

"I'm not surprised. Artists are incapable of thinking about money, and he doesn't do anything else." She smiled. "But he does have a lot of good ideas on how you can spend it once you've got it. You'll like him. Do you know who else is here?"

"Who's that?"

"Evelyn Chambers." Heidrun's smile assumed a mischievous quality. "Darling, she'll put you through the wringer. You can run away
from her down here, but up there—"

"I have no problem talking to her."

"Let's bet you do?"

Heidrun turned her back on him and started climbing the path
back up to the hotel. O'Keefe came after her. In fact he did have a
brontosaurus-sized problem talking to Evelyn Chambers, America's
number one talk-show host. He avoided those shows more than anything else in the world. A thousand times, perhaps more, she'd invited
him onto *Chambers*, her high-rating spiritual striptease that millions
of socially depraved Americans gathered in front of their screens to
watch every Friday evening. On every occasion he'd declined. Here,
now, without the bars between them, he was the fillet steak and she
was the lion.

Appalling!

They passed by the golf course.

"You're an albino," he said.

"Clever Finn."

"Not scared of burning? Because of—what do you call it—"

"My pronounced melanin disorder and my light-sensitive eyes," she
chanted the answer down at him. "Nope, not a problem. I wear highly
filtered contact lenses."

"And your skin?"

"How flattering," she said mockingly. "Finn O'Keefe is interested in
my skin."

"Nonsense. I really am interested."

"Of course it's entirely free of pigment. Without sun protection I'd
go up in flames. So I use Moving Mirrors."

"Moving Mirrors?"

"It's a gel with microscopic mirrors that adjust themselves according
to the heat of the sun. It means I can stay in the open for a few hours,
but of course it shouldn't become a habit. So, sporty guy, fancy a swim?"

After she'd spent most of the day accompanying guests from the heliport to the hotel and going back to wait for the next helicopter to arrive,
back and forth, back and forth, Lynn Orley was surprised she hadn't
worn a groove in the ground ages ago.

Of course she'd done other things as well. Andrew Norrington,
deputy head of security at Orley Enterprises, had turned the Isla de las
Estrellas into the kind of high-security zone that made you think you
were in the Hotel California: "You can check out any time you like, but
you can never leave!" Lynn's own idea of security included protection,
but not its visible display, while Norrington argued that you couldn't

hide the guards in the bushes like garden gnomes. She mentioned that it had been difficult enough to persuade the new arrivals against having their own bodyguards with them at all times, and referred to Oleg Rogachev, who had only reluctantly left at home the half-dozen heavies he usually arrived with, and pointed out that half of the service staff were highly trained sharpshooters. No one, when they were out jogging or playing golf, wanted to be constantly bumping into dark figures with the word Emergency practically stamped on their foreheads. Besides, she rather liked gun-toting gnomes who looked after you without tripping you up all the time.

After a stubborn battle Norrington had finally retrained his brigades and found ways of adapting them to their surroundings. Lynn knew she was making his life difficult, but he had to deal with it. Norrington was excellent at his job, highly organized and dependable, but he was also a victim of that infectious paranoia that gripped all bodyguards sooner or later.

"Interesting," she said.

Beside her, Warren Locatelli snorted like a horse.

"Yes, but you wanted to lower the price! My God, I lost it at that point. I said hang on. Hang *on*. . . ! Do you know exactly who you're dealing with here? Pimps! Monkey-brains! I didn't just climb down from the trees, you get me? You don't lure me out of the jungle with bananas. Either you play by my rules or I'll—"

And so on and so forth.

Lynn nodded sympathetically as she walked the new arrivals to reception. Warren Locatelli was such a jerk! And Momoka Omura, that silly slut beside him, not one bit better. But as long as Julian thought it was important, she would have to pay attention even to a talking dung beetle. You didn't necessarily have to understand it to have a conversation with it. It was enough to react to tone, tempo, and accompanying noises like grunts, growls, or laughter. If the torrent of words raining down on you ended in merriment, then you joined in with the laughter. If it rattled down furiously, you were always on the safe side with an "Unbelievable!" or a "No really?" If the situation called for contextual understanding, you just listened. Mockery was legitimate; it was just important not to get called out.

In Locatelli's case autopilot was sufficient. As long as he wasn't talking shop, his main topic of conversation was the state of his own awesomeness, and the fact that everyone else was a bunch of assholes. Or pimps and monkey-brains. Depending.

Who would arrive next?

Chuck and Aileen Donoghue.

Chucky, the hotel mogul. He was okay, even though he told terrible jokes. Aileen would probably turn to the kitchen first thing to see if they were cutting the meat thickly enough.

Aileen: "Chucky likes fat steaks! They've got to be fat."

Chucky: "Yes, fat! What Europeans call steaks aren't steaks at all. Hey, you know what I call European steaks? You want to know? You do? Okay—carpaccio!"

But Chuck was okay.

To Lynn's regret, on Julian's chessboard Locatelli was the queen, or at least a rook. He had managed to do something that had driven generations of physicists to despair, namely develop solar cells that converted over 60 percent of sunlight into electricity. With those, and because he was also a brilliant businessman, Locatelli's company Light-years had become market leader in the solar energy sector and made its owner so rich that Forbes put him at number five among the world's billionaires. Momoka Omura strutted indifferently along beside him, let her eye wander over the grounds and managed a grudging "nice." Lynn imagined hitting her between the eyes with her clenched fists, but instead took her arm and complimented her on her hair.

"I knew you'd like it," Momoka replied with the faintest of smiles.

No, it looks lousy, Lynn thought. Complete disaster.

"Nice to have you both here," she said.

At the same time Evelyn Chambers, sunning herself on her sixth-floor terrace, was calling up her knowledge of Russian and pricking up her ears. She was the high-society seismographer. Every tremor, however small, registered as news value on her personal Richter scale, and there had just been a big one.

The Rogachevs were in the room next door. The terraces were separated by sound-absorbing barriers, but she could still hear Olympiada Rogacheva's breathless sobs, now close by, now further away. She was obviously pacing back and forth on the sundeck, clutching a full glass, as usual.

"Why?" she wailed. "Why again?"

Oleg Rogachev's answer came dully and incomprehensibly from inside the room. Whatever he had said made Olympiada explode in a volcanic eruption.

"You complete bastard!" she yelled. "Right in front of my eyes!" Muffled sounds, gasps. "You didn't even bother to do it in secret!"

Rogachev stepped outside.

"You want me to have secrets? Then fine."

His voice was calm, uninterested, and designed to bring the surrounding temperature down a few degrees. Evelyn pictured him in front of her. A middle-sized, inconspicuous man with thin, blond hair and a foxy face, eyes set in it like little icy mountain lakes. Evelyn had interviewed Oleg Alexeyevich Rogachev the previous year, shortly after he had become majority shareholder of the Daimler company, and met a polite, quiet businessman who had willingly answered all her questions while at the same time appearing as impenetrable as a piece of armor plating.

She recapitulated what she knew about Rogachev. His father had run a Soviet steel firm, which had been privatized as a consequence of Perestroika. The usual model at the time was to give the workers voucher share certificates. For a short time, the multicellular organism of the proletariat had assumed command, except that shares in a steelworks didn't get families through the winter. So most workers had quickly been willing to turn their certificates into money, selling them to finance companies or their superiors, and receiving, on the eat-or-be-eaten principle, just a fraction of their actual value. Gradually the former state companies of the fragmented Soviet Union had fallen into the hands of investment firms and speculators. Old Rogachev had also turned up and bought enough of his workers' share certificates to purchase the company himself, which brought him into the firing line of a competing Mafia clan, unfortunately in the literal sense of that phrase: two bullets hit him in the chest, a third drilled its way into his brain. The fourth had been intended for his son, but missed. Oleg, who had until that point been more inclined toward student distractions, had immediately interrupted his studies and established an allegiance against the murderers with a clan close to the government, that led to a shoot-out about which no further documentation was available. At this point Oleg was demonstrably living abroad, but after his return he was suddenly appointed chairman of the management committee and a welcome guest at the Kremlin.

He had simply sided with the right people.

In the years that followed Rogachev set about modernizing the company, raked in considerable profits, and swallowed up a German and an English steel giant in quick succession. He invested in aluminum, signed contracts with the government relating to the extension of the Russian railway network, acquired shares in European and Asian car companies, and made a fortune in China, with its hunger for raw materials. At the same time he was painfully aware that he had to take the interests of the powerful men in Moscow into account. In return the sun shone for him: Vladimir Putin assured him of his high esteem; Dmitri Medvedev invited him to his table as an adviser. When the world market leader Arcelor Mittal was plunged into a crisis, Rogachev took over the ailing steel giant and put himself, with Rogamittal, at the top of his field.

At around this time Maxim Ginsburg, Medvedev's successor, had so permanently abolished the boundaries between private business and politics—which were eroding in any case—that the press dubbed him the "CEO of Russia PLC." Rogachev paid homage to Ginsburg in his own way. One very drunken evening, in fact, it turned out that

Ginsburg had a daughter, Olympiada, taciturn and of no apparent charm, whom the president was anxious to see married, if possible to someone of a wealthy background. Somehow Olympiada had managed to complete a course of studies in politics and economics. Now she was a Member of Parliament, expressed her love of her father in referendums and faded away without having blossomed. Rogachev did Ginsburg the favor. The marriage of these two great fortunes passed off with much pomp, except that on the wedding night Rogachev shunned her bed and went elsewhere. From then on he was, in fact, constantly elsewhere, even when Olympiada gave birth to their only son, who was entrusted to a private school and from that point onward seldom seen. Ginsburg's daughter got lonely. She didn't know how to respond to her husband's enthusiasm for martial arts, guns, and soccer, even less to his constant affairs. She complained to her father. Ginsburg thought of the 56 billion dollars that his son-in-law put on the scales, and advised Olympiada to take a lover. She did exactly that. His name was Jim Beam, and he had the advantage of being there whenever you needed him.

How on earth was the poor woman going to survive the next fourteen days?

Evelyn Chambers stretched her Latin physique. Not bad for forty-five, she thought, everything still firm, even though the inevitable muscular fatty degeneration was beginning, and signs of cellulite were appearing on her bottom and thighs. She squinted into the sun. The cry of seabirds filled the air. Only now did it strike her that there was just one single cloud in the whole sky, as if it had strayed there, a cloud-child. It seemed to be floating very high up, but then what was height? She would be traveling far above the point where clouds dwelt.

Up, down. All a matter of perspective.

In her mind she ran through the members of the traveling party, assessing them for their media usefulness. Eight couples and five singles, including her. Some of those present would not welcome her participation. Finn O'Keefe, for example, who refused to go on talk shows. Or the Donoghues: hard-line Republicans who didn't much care for the fact that America's powerful talk-show queen supported the Democrat camp. Admittedly Evelyn's only active excursion into politics, in 2017, when she had fought for the office of governor of New York, had begun in triumph and ended in disaster, but her stranglehold on public opinion remained unbroken.

Mukesh Nair? Another one who didn't like going on talk shows.

Warren Locatelli and his Japanese wife, on the other hand, had entertainment value in spades. Locatelli was vain and coarse, but he was also brilliant. There was a biography of him entitled *What if Locatelli had Created the World?*, which accurately captured his vision of the world. He sailed, and had won the America's Cup the previous year, but his chief enthusiasm was racing. Umura had for a long time appeared as an actress in indigestible big-screen experiments before enjoying a *succès d'estime* with *Black Lotus*. She was snooty and—as far as Evelyn could tell—free from any kind of empathy.

Who else? Walo Ögi, Swiss investor, art collector. Involved in every imaginable area from property, insurance, airlines, and cars via Pepsi-Cola to tropical wood and ready meals. According to rumor, he planned to build a second Monaco on behalf of that country's prince, but Evelyn was more interested in Heidrun Ögi, his third wife, who was said to have financed her photographic studies as a stripper and an actress in porn films. Also part of the group was Marc Edwards, who owed his popularity to the development of quantum chips so tiny that they were switched on and off with a single atom, and Mimi Parker, creator of intelligent fashion, whose fabrics were woven with Edwards's chips. Fun people, sporty and socially committed, moderately exciting. The Tautous might have more to give. Bernard Tautou had political ambitions and had earned billions in the water business, a subject that preoccupied the human rights organizations with monotonous regularity.

The eighth couple, finally, came from Germany. Eva Borelius was seen as the uncrowned queen of stem-cell research; her companion, Karla Kramp, worked as a surgeon. Flagship lesbians. And then there was Miranda Winter, ex-model and squeaky-voiced widow of an industrialist, as well as Rebecca Hsu, Taiwan's Coco Chanel. All four of them had already opened their hearts to Evelyn, but she didn't know the slightest thing about Carl Hanna.

She thoughtfully rubbed her belly with suntan oil.

Hanna was strange. A Canadian private investor, born in 1981 as the son of a wealthy British diplomat in New Delhi, who had moved at the age of ten with his family to British Columbia, where he later studied business. Apprentice years in India, death of his parents in an accident, return to Vancouver. He had clearly invested his inheritance cleverly enough never to have to lift a finger ever again: according to rumor he planned to invest in India's space trip, and that was that. The CV of a speculator. Of course, not everybody had to be a bighead like Locatelli. But Donoghue boxed, for example. Rogachev was trained in all kinds of martial arts and had bought Bayern Munich a few years previously. Edwards and Mimi dived, Borelius rode, Karla played chess, O'Keefe had a scandalous drug career behind him and had lived with Irish gypsies. Everyone had something that identified them as a person of flesh and blood.

Hanna owned yachts.

Originally, Gerald Palstein had been scheduled to fly instead of him: the Director of Strategy of EMCO, the third-largest mineral company in the world, was a free spirit who had, years before, thought out loud about the end of the fossil-fuel years. Evelyn would have liked to meet him, but the previous month Palstein had been victim of an attempted assassination, and injured so badly that he had had to cancel, and Hanna had stepped in.

Who was this guy?

Evelyn decided to find out, swung her legs over her lounger and walked to the balustrade of her terrace. Deep below her glittered the enormous pool of the Stellar Island Hotel. Some people were already diving into the turquoise-colored water, and Heidrun Ögi and Finn O'Keefe were arriving at that very moment. Evelyn wondered whether she should go down and join them, but suddenly the very thought of conversation made her feel ill, and she turned away.

That was happening to her more and more often. A talk-show queen who was allergic to talking. She grabbed herself a drink and waited for the attack to pass. O'Keefe followed Heidrun to the pool bar, where a stout man of about sixty was explaining something, waving his arms around as he did so. He was enjoying the attention of a sporty-looking couple who were listening agog, laughing comfortably as one, saying "Good heavens!" at the same time, and looking like the kind of people who rode around on tandems.

"It was extreme, of course," the older man said and laughed. "Completely over the top. And that's exactly why it was good!"

There was something craggily sublime about his features, powerful Roman nose, chiseled chin. His wiry dark hair, run through with silver, was greased back, his tousled mustache matched his finger-thick eyebrows.

"What was over the top?" Heidrun asked, giving him a kiss.

"The musical," the man said, and looked at O'Keefe. "And who is this, *mein Schatz*?"

Unlike Heidrun he spoke smooth, almost unaccented English. The odd thing was that he said "my darling" in German. Heidrun came and stood next to him and rested her head on his shoulder.

"Don't you ever go to the movies?" she said. "This is Finn O'Keefe."

"Finn—O'Keefe—" The wrinkles on his high forehead formed into question marks. "Sorry, but I—"

"He played Kurt Cobain."

"Oh! Ah! Brilliant! Great to meet you. I'm Walo. Heidrun's seen all your films. I haven't, but I remember *Hyperactive*. Incredible achievement!"

"I'm delighted." O'Keefe smiled. He had no particular problems meeting people, except that he always found the rigmarole of mutual introductions horribly tiring. Shaking hands. Telling someone you'd never seen before how brilliant it was to meet them here. Ögi introduced the blonde at his side as Mimi Parker, a tanned all-American girl with dark eyebrows and perfect teeth. Presumably Californian, O'Keefe thought. California seemed to have registered a patent on this kind of girl who smelled of the sun.

"Mimi designs incredible clothes," Ögi raved. "If you wear one of her pullovers you'll never need to see a doctor again."

"Really! How come?"

"Very simple." Mimi was about to say something, but Ögi talked over her. "It measures your bodily functions! Let's say you have a heart attack, it sends your medical records to the nearest hospital and calls the ambulance."

"But it can't perform the operation itself?"

"It has transistors woven into it," Mimi explained seriously. "The item of clothing is effectively a computer with a million sensors. They form connections with the wearer's body, but they can also be connected to any external system."

"Sounds scratchy."

"We weave Marc's quantum chips into them. They don't scratch at all."

"May I take the opportunity," the fair-haired man said and held out his right hand. "Marc Edwards."

"Pleased to meet you."

"Look." Mimi pointed to her bathing costume. "Even in this there are about two million sensors. Among other things they absorb my body heat and turn it into electricity. Of course you only get very small amounts of usable energy from a human power station, but it's enough to warm the costume up if necessary. The sensors react to the temperature of the air and water."

"Interesting."

"I've seen *Hyperactive*, by the way," Heidrun said in a bored voice. "Finn grew up with guitars and pianos. He even has his own band."

"Had." O'Keefe raised his hands. "I *had* a band. We don't meet up that much these days."

"I thought the film was great," said Edwards. "You're one of my favorite actors."

"Thanks."

"Your singing was great in it. What was your band called again?"

"The Black Sheep."

Edwards pulled a face as if he was inches away from remembering The Black Sheep and all their hits. O'Keefe smiled.

"Believe me, you've never heard of us."

"He hasn't, either." Ögi put his arm around his shoulders and lowered his voice. "Between ourselves, young man, they're all kids. Bet you they don't even know who Kurt Cobain *was*."

Mimi Parker looked uncertainly from one to the other.

"To be quite honest—"

"You mean he really existed?" Edwards said in amazement.

"A historical figure." Ögi took out a cigar, cut it, and set the tip thoughtfully alight. "Tragic hero of a generation infatuated with suicide. A romantic in nihilist's clothing. *Weltschmerz*, a latent longing for death, nothing you wouldn't find in Schubert and Schumann as well. Brilliant exit. How did you prepare for the part, Finn?"

"Well—"

"Did you try to be *him*?"

"He'd have had to pump himself full of drugs," said Edwards. "That guy Cobain was permanently stoned."

"Perhaps he did," said Ögi. "Did you?"

O'Keefe shook his head with a laugh. How could he explain in a few words to a pool party how you played Kurt Cobain? Or anyone else?

"Isn't that called method acting?" Mimi asked. "The actor gives up his identity for his character in the film, weeks and months before filming. He basically subjects himself to a kind of brainwashing."

"No, it's not quite like that. I have a different way of working."

"How's that?"

"More mundanely. It's a job, you understand. Just a job."

Mimi looked disappointed. O'Keefe felt Heidrun's violet gaze settling on him. He began to feel uncomfortable. Everyone was staring at him.

"You were talking about a musical," he said to Ögi, to creep away from the focus of interest. "Which one would that be?"

"*Nine Eleven*," said Ögi. "We saw it in New York last week. You?"

"Not yet."

"We're thinking of going," said Edwards.

"Do that," Ögi gave off swirls of smoke. "As I said, extreme stuff! They could have let it drown in piety, but of course the material needs a powerful production."

"The set's supposed to be amazing," Mimi raved.

"Holographic. You think you're sitting in the middle of it."

"I like the tune with the cop and the girl. It's always on the radio. 'Into Death, My Child'—"

She started humming a tune. O'Keefe hoped he wouldn't have to express an opinion on the matter. He hadn't seen *Nine Eleven*, and had no intention of doing so.

"The slushy numbers on their own don't justify a visit," Ögi snorted. "Yes, Jimeno and McLoughlin are constantly busy, and so are their wives, but it's mostly worth it for the effects. When the planes come, you can't believe it! And the guy who sings Osama bin Laden. He's really OTT."

"Bass?"

"Baritone."

"I'm going swimming," said Heidrun. "Who's coming? Finn?"
Thanks, he thought.

He went to his room and got undressed. Ten minutes later they
were competing at the crawl in the pool. Heidrun left him behind twice
in a row, and it was only the third time that they reached the edge
of the pool at the same time. She pulled herself up. Walo blew her a
Havana-smoke kiss, before carrying on with a story accompanied by
vigorous hand gestures. At that moment an athlete and a woman with
a curvy figure and a fire-red ponytail arrived near the pool.

"Do you know that guy?" he asked.

"Nope." Heidrun folded her arms on the edge of the pool. "They
must just have arrived. Maybe it's that Canadian investor. Something
with an H, Henna or Hanson. I've seen the redhead before, I think. But
I can't remember where."

"Oh, yeah! Wasn't she a murder suspect at some point?"

"For a while, yes." O'Keefe shrugged. "She's quite witty, once you've
got used to the fact that she has names for her breasts and that she's
squandering an inheritance of thirteen billion dollars pretty much at
random. No idea if there was anything to those accusations. It was in
all the papers. She got off in the end."

"Where do you meet such characters? At parties?"

"I don't go to parties."

Heidrun slipped lower into the water and lay on her back. Her hair
spread into a faded flower. O'Keefe couldn't help thinking of stories
about mermaids, seductive creatures who had risen from the depths
and dragged mariners under water to steal their breath with a kiss.

"That's right. You hate being at the center of things, don't you?"

He thought for a moment. "I don't really, no."

"Exactly. It only annoys you when there isn't at least a screen or a
barrier between you and the people who see your films. You enjoy the
cult that's organized around you, but even more than that you enjoy
making people think you couldn't care less."

He stared at her in amazement. "Is that your impression?"

"When *People* magazine voted you 'Sexiest Man Alive,' you pulled
your cap over your forehead and claimed you really couldn't understand why women cried at the sight of you."

"I don't get it," O'Keefe said. "I really don't."

Heidrun laughed. "Me neither."

She plunged under the surface of the water. Her outline fragmented
into Cubist vectors as she darted away. O'Keefe wondered for a moment
whether he liked her answer. The hammering of rotors reached him.
He looked into the sky and found himself confronted with a single
white cloud.

Lonely little cloud. Lonely little Finn.

We understand each other, you and I, he thought with amusement.

The rump of a helicopter entered his field of vision, crossed the pool, and came down.

"There are people in the water," Karla Kramp observed. She said it with analytical coolness, as if referring to the appearance of microbes under warm and damp conditions. It didn't sound as if she wanted to join them. Eva Borelius looked out of the helicopter window and saw a pale-skinned woman gliding against a turquoise-colored background.

"Perhaps it's finally time for you to learn to swim."

"I've already learned to ride for you," Karla replied expressionlessly.

"I know." Borelius leaned back and stretched her bony limbs. "You never stop learning, my jewel."

Facing her, Bernard Tautou was dozing with his head leaning back and his mouth half open. After spending the first half-hour of the flight giving an account of his exhausting everyday life, which seemed to play out between remote desert springs and intimate dinners at the Élysée Palace, he had fallen asleep, and was now giving them a view of his nasal cavities. He was short and slim, with wavy, probably dyed hair that was starting to lighten at the temples. His eyes, beneath their heavy lids, had something weary about them, which was further accentuated into melancholy by the long shape of his face. The impression vanished as soon as he laughed and his eyebrows rose clownishly, and Tautou laughed often. He delivered compliments and acted interested, just to use his interlocutor's statements as a springboard for self-reflection. Every second sentence that he directed at his wife ended in a challenging *n'est-ce pas?* Paulette's sole function was to confirm what he had said. Only after he had gone to sleep did she become more lively, talked about his friendship and hers with the French president, the country's first female head of state, and how important it was to grant humanity access to the most precious of all scarce resources. She talked about how, as head of the French water company Suez Environnement, he had contrived to take over Thames Water, which had made the resulting company a leader in global water supply and saved the world, which as good as meant her husband had saved the world. In her account plucky Bernard was tirelessly laying pipelines to the areas where the poor and wretched lived, a guardian angel in the battle against thirst.

"Isn't water a free human resource?" Karla had asked.

"Of course."

"So it can't be privatized?"

Paulette's expression had remained unfathomable. With her hooded eyelids she looked like the young Charlotte Rampling, although without the actress's class. The question just asked had been put to people in the water business with great regularity for decades.

"Oh, you know, that debate is passing out of fashion, thank God. Without privatization there would have been no supply networks, no treatment plants. What's the use of free access to a resource if you have no chance of accessing it?"

Karla had nodded thoughtfully.

"Could you actually privatize the air that we breathe?"

"Sorry? Of course not."

"I'm just trying to understand. So Suez is building supply installations, for example in—"

"Namibia."

"Namibia. Exactly. And are such planned constructions subsidized by development aid?"

"Yes, of course."

"And the plant operates on a profitable basis?"

"Yes, it has to."

"That means that Suez is privately registering profits that have been subsidized by development aid?"

At that point Paulette Tautou had assumed a tortured expression, and Borelius had said quietly, "Enough, Karla." Right now she didn't feel like getting involved in disasters as she usually did when Karla deployed the scalpel of her curiosity. After that they had exchanged harmless pleasantries and admired the platform in the sea. More precisely, her gaze and Karla's had hung spellbound on that endless line, while Paulette eyed them rather suspiciously and made no move to shake her husband awake.

"Aren't you going to wake him?" Borelius had asked. "I'm sure he'd love to see this."

"Oh, no, I'm happy for him to get some sleep. You can't imagine how hard he works."

"We'll be there in a minute. Then you'll have to wake him anyway."

"He needs every second. You know, I'd only wake him for something really *important*."

Something really important, Borelius thought. Okay . . .

Now that the helicopter was lowering itself onto the landing platform, Paulette forced herself to say "Bernard" several times in a quiet voice, until he opened his eyes in confusion and blinked.

"Are we there already?"

"We're landing."

"What?" He jerked upright. "Where's the platform? I thought we were going to see the platform."

"You were asleep."

"Oh! *Merde!* Why didn't you wake me, *chérie*? I'd have loved to see the platform!"

Borelius forbore from commenting. Before they got out, she caught a glimpse of a stately, snow-white yacht far out on the sea. Then the skids touched the ground, and the side door of the helicopter swung open.

On the yacht Rebecca Hsu left her study, crossed the huge, marble-covered drawing-room, and stepped out onto the deck, while she phoned her headquarters in Taipei.

"I don't give a damn what the French sales manager wants," she said harshly. "We're talking about a perfume for twelve-year-old girls. *They* have to like it, not *him*. If *he* starts liking the stuff, we've made a mistake."

Wild arguments came crackling down the line. Rebecca walked quickly to the stern, where the first officer, the captain, and the speed-boat were waiting for her.

"It's already clear to me that you want your own campaign," she said. "I'm not stupid, after all. You always want something of your own. These Europeans are terribly complicated. We've put the perfume on the market in Germany, Italy, and Spain, without giving anyone special treatment, and we've been successful every time. I don't see why France of all places—What? He said *what*?"

The information was repeated.

"Nonsense, I love France!" she yelled furiously. "Even the French! I'm just fed up with all that constant rebellion. They will have to learn to live with the fact that I've bought their beloved luxury company. I'll leave them in peace as far as Dior and so on are concerned, but for our own creations I expect unconditional cooperation."

She looked irritably across to the Isla de las Estrellas, which rose from the Pacific like a humpbacked sea serpent. No breeze stirred the air. The sea stretched like dark aluminum foil from horizon to horizon. She ended the conversation and turned to the two liveried men.

"And? Did you ask again?"

"I'm extraordinarily sorry, madame." The captain shook his head. "No permit."

"I'm absolutely mystified about what's going on."

"The Isla de las Estrellas and the platform can't be approached by private ships. The same applies to airspace. The whole area is one single high-security zone. If it wasn't you, we would even have to wait for their helicopter. Unusually, they have given us permission to ferry you across in our own speedboat."

Rebecca sighed. She was used to rules not applying to her. On the other hand the prospect of a trip on the speedboat was too much fun for her to insist.

"Is the luggage on board?"

"Of course, madame. I hope you have a pleasant vacation."

"Thank you. How do I look?"

"Perfect, as ever."

That would be lovely, she thought. Since she had turned fifty, she had been fighting a losing battle. It was played out on various pieces of fitness equipment, in swimming-pools with cross-current features, on private jogging paths, and her 140-meter yacht, which she had had built in such a way that you could perform a circuit of it unimpeded. Since leaving Taiwan she ran there every day. With iron discipline she had even managed to get her extreme hunger under control, but still her body went on expanding. At least the dress emphasized what was left of her waist, and was appropriately extravagant. Her trademark bird's-nest hairdo was characteristically chaotic, and her makeup was impeccable.

As soon as the speedboat cast off, she was back on the phone again.

"Rebecca Hsu is heading this way," Norrington said on the walkie-talkie.

Lynn left the kitchen of Stellar Island Hotel, gave the canapés a quick examination, issued instructions to her little group of waiters and waitresses, and stepped out into the sunlight.

"Has she brought bodyguards?" she asked.

"No. On the other hand she has checked several times to ask if we seriously intend to refuse her docking permission."

"Excuse me? Rebecca wants to park her *damned yacht* here?"

"Calm down. We refused to budge. Now she's coming in the speedboat."

"That's okay. When does she get here?"

"In about ten minutes. As long as she doesn't fall overboard on the way." An idea that Norrington seemed to find cheering. "There must be some pretty good sharks around here, don't you think? When I last saw our little darling she was fit for a banquet."

"If Rebecca Hsu gets eaten, you're dessert."

"Funny and relaxed as ever," Norrington sighed and ended the conversation.

She followed the coastal path at a walking pace, as her mind split into pieces and thousands of concerned and disembodied Lynns haunted the hotel grounds. Was there something she'd overlooked? Each of the booked suites gleamed immaculately. Even in terms of furniture the personal preferences of the guests had been taken into account: lilies, mountains of lychees, and passion fruit for Rebecca Hsu; Momoka Omura's favorite champagne; a luxury volume about the history of car racing on Warren Locatelli's pillow; reproductions of Asian and Russian art on the Ögis's walls; old tin toys for Marc Edwards; the biography of Muhammad Ali with photographs never before published for the edification of good old Chucky; chocolate-scented bath oils for Miranda Winter. Even the menu reflected likes and dislikes. Lynn's worried ghosts sighed in the saunas and Jacuzzis of the spa area, prowled icily over the golf course, streamed damply into Stellar Island Dome, the underground multimedia center, and found nothing to complain about.

Everything that was supposed to work, worked.

And besides, no one would *see* that they hadn't been ready in time. Unless the guests opened doors they had no business opening.

Tools were still lying around in most of the rooms, bags of cement were stacked up, the paintwork was only half finished. In the knowledge that she couldn't keep the official opening deadline, Lynn had put all her energy into getting the booked suites ready. Only part of the kitchen was operational, enough to spoil the group, but certainly not the three hundred visitors for whom the hotel had actually been conceived.

She stopped for a moment and looked at the gleaming cruise ship that grew out of the basalt. As if her pause was a signal, hundreds of seabirds scattered from a nearby cliff and formed a swarming cloud that drifted inland. Lynn gave a start. She imagined the creatures swooping down on the hotel grounds, shitting all over it, hacking and scratching it to pieces, and chasing the few people into the sea. She saw bodies drifting in the pool, blood mixing with water. The survivors ran up to her and screamed at her for not preventing the attack. Loudest of all was Julian.

The hotel staff were frozen. Their eyes wandered back and forth between Lynn and the hotel, visibly unsettled, since their boss suddenly gave every appearance of witnessing the Day of Judgment.

After a minute of complete stillness she pulled herself together and continued down the coastal path to the harbor.

Andrew Norrington saw her walking on. From the hill above the pool where he had taken up his post, he could look out over large sections of the eastern shore. In the harbor, a natural inlet extended by blasting, several small ships lay at anchor, most of them patrol boats and some Zodiacs, marked with the familiar O of Orley Enterprises. He could have provided plenty of room for Rebecca Hsu's yacht, but not even in his wildest dreams did Norrington imagine giving the Taiwanese woman special treatment. All the others had, as agreed, flown in on Orley's company helicopters, why not her? Rebecca could be glad that she'd been allowed to travel in by water at all.

As he walked down to the pool, he thought about Julian's daughter. Even though he didn't particularly like Lynn, he respected her authority and competence. Even at a young age she had had to shoulder a huge amount of responsibility, and in spite of all the naysayers she had put Orley Travel at the top of all tourist companies. Without a doubt,

Stellar Island Hotel was one of her *pièces de résistance,* even though there was still much to be done, but it paled into insignificance next to the OSS Grand and the Gaia! No one had ever built anything comparable. In her late thirties, Lynn was a star in the company, and those two hotels *had* been finished.

Norrington threw his head back and blinked into the sun. He absently flicked a saucer-sized spider from his shoulder, entered the pool landscape via a path overgrown with ferns and conifers, and gazed forensically around the area. By now the whole traveling party had met up by the pool. Drinks and snacks were being handed out, people were noisily introducing themselves. Julian had selected the participants very cleverly. The diverse group there was worth several hundred billion dollars: world-improvers like Mukesh Nair, oligarchs along the lines of Rogachev, and people like Miranda Winter, who had, for the first time, found her pea-brain faced with the task of spending money sensibly. Orley planned to relieve them all of part of their fortunes. At that moment Evelyn Chambers joined them, and smiled radiantly around. Still remarkably good-looking, Norrington thought. Perhaps she'd become a bit plump over time, but nothing compared to the progressive spherification of Rebecca Hsu.

He walked on, ready for anything.

"Mimi! Marc! How lovely to see you."

Evelyn had overcome her revulsion, and was once again capable of communicating. She was almost on friendly terms with Mimi Parker, and Marc was a nice guy. She waved to Momoka Omura and exchanged kisses on the cheek with Miranda Winter, who greeted every new arrival with a "Wooouuuuhhw" that sounded like a burglar alarm, followed by a saucy, "Oh yeah!" Evelyn had last seen Winter with long, steel-blue hair, and now she wore it short and bright red, which made you think of fire alarms. The ex-model's forehead was decorated with a filigree pattern. Her breasts squeezed themselves reluctantly into a dress that only just covered the planetary curve of her bottom and was so tight at the waist that it made one fear that Ms. Miranda might at any moment split in two. The youngest here, at the age of 28, she had undergone so many surgical interventions that the mere documentation of her operations kept hundreds of society reporters in employment, not to mention her extravagances, her excesses, and the aftershocks of her trial.

Evelyn pointed at the pattern on her brow.

"Pretty," she said, trying frantically to escape the massive double constellation of the Miranda cleavage, which seemed to be drawing her gaze powerfully downward. Everyone knew that Evelyn's sexual appetite was equally divided between men and women. The revelation of her private life, namely the fact that she lived with her husband and her lover in a *ménage à trois*, had cost her the candidacy in New York.

"It's Indian," Miranda replied gleefully. "Because India is in the stars, you know?"

"Really?"

"Yes! Just imagine! The stars say we're heading for an Indian age. Quite wonderful. The transformation will begin in India. Humanity will change. First India, then the whole world. There will never be war again."

"Who says that, darling?"

Olinda Brannigan was an ancient, dried-up Hollywood actress from Beverly Hills who looked like a codfish. Miranda went to her to have her cards read and her future predicted.

"And what else does Olinda have to say?"

"You shouldn't buy anything Chinese. China's going to go under."

"Because of the trade deficit?"

"Because of Jupiter."

"And what sort of dress are you wearing?"

"This? Cute, isn't it? Dolce and Gabbana."

"You should take it off."

"What, here?" Miranda looked furtively around and lowered her voice. "Now?"

"It's Chinese."

"Oh, stop! They're Italians, they—"

"It's Chinese, darling," Evelyn repeated with relish. "Rebecca Hsu bought Dolce and Gabbana last year."

"Does she have to buy everything?" For a moment Miranda looked frankly hurt. Then the sun came out once again. "Never mind. Maybe Olinda made a mistake." She spread her fingers and shook herself. "Anyway, I'm *reaaally* looking forward to the trip! I'm going to squeal the whole time!"

Evelyn didn't doubt for a moment the serious intent behind this threat. She glanced around and saw the Nairs, the Tautous, and the Locatellis in conversation. Olympiada joined the group, while Oleg Rogachev studied her, nodded to her, and went to the bar. He immediately came over with a glass of champagne, handed it to her, and assumed his familiar, sphinxlike smile.

"So we're going to be exposed to your judgment in space," he said in a strong Slavic accent. "We'll all have to be very careful what we say."

"I'm here as a private individual." She winked at him. "But if you really want to tell me anything—"

Rogachev laughed quietly, without losing his icy expression.

"I'm sure I will, not least for the pleasure of your company." He looked out to the platform. By now the sun was low over the volcano, and bathed the artificial island in warm colors. "Have you been through preparatory training? Weightlessness isn't everyone's cup of tea."

"In Orley Space Center." Evelyn took a sip. "Zero-gravity flights, simulation in the immersion tank, the whole kaboodle. You?"

"A few suborbital flights."

"Are you excited?"

"Thrilled."

"You do know what Julian is trying to do by organizing this event?"

The remark hovered in the room, waiting to be picked up. Rogachev turned to look at her.

"And now you're interested to find out my opinion on the matter."

"And you wouldn't be here if you weren't thinking seriously about it."

"And you?"

Evelyn laughed.

"Forget it. In this company I'm the church mouse. He can hardly have had his beady eyes on my savings."

"If all church mice had to reveal the state of their finances, Evelyn, mice would run the world."

"Wealth is relative, Oleg, I don't have to tell you that. Julian and I are old friends. I'd love to convince myself that it was that that persuaded him to make me a member of the group, but of course I realize that I manage capital that's more important than money."

"Public opinion," Rogachev nodded. "In his place I'd have invited you too."

"You, on the other hand, *are* rich! Almost everybody here is rich, *really* rich. If each of you throws only a tenth of his wealth into the jackpot, Julian can build a second elevator and a second OSS."

"Orley won't allow a shareholder to influence the fate of his company to any great extent. I'm a Russian. We have our own programs. Why should I support American space travel?"

"Do you really mean that?"

"You tell me."

"Because you're a businessman. Nation states may have interests, but what good is that if you lack money and know-how? Julian Orley dusted off American state space travel and at the same time sealed its fate. He's the boss now. Worth mentioning to the extent that space travel programs are now almost exclusively in private hands, and Julian's lead in the sector is astronomical. Even in Moscow people are supposed to have been saying that he doesn't give a damn for the interests of nation states. He just looks for people who think the same way as he does."

"You might say he doesn't give a damn for loyalty either."

"Julian's loyalty is to ideals, believe it or not. The fact is that he could get on perfectly well with NASA, but NASA couldn't cope with him. Last year he presented the White House with a plan for how a second elevator could be financed by the Americans, and that would have meant that he was putting himself in a highly dependent position as a supplier of know-how. But rather than using the opportunity to involve him, Congress hesitated and expressed concern. America still hasn't worked out that for Julian it's just an investor."

"And because this investor seems to lack a certain potency at the moment, he's extending the circle of his possible partners."

"Correct. He couldn't care less whether you're a Russian or a Martian."

"Even so. Why shouldn't I invest in *my* country's space travel?"

"Because you have to ask yourself whether you want to entrust your money to a state which, while it might be your homeland, is hopelessly underperforming in technological terms."

"Russian space travel is just as privatized and efficient as the American version."

"But you haven't got a Julian Orley. And there isn't one on the horizon, either. Not in Russia, not in India, not in China. Not even the French and the Germans have one. Japan is running on the spot. If you invest your money in the attempt to invent something that other people invented ages ago, just for the sake of national pride, you're not being loyal, you're being sentimental." Evelyn looked at him. "And you aren't inclined toward sentimentality. You're sticking to the rules of the game in Russia, that's all. And you feel no more connected to your country than Julian feels to anybody."

"You think you know so much about me."

Evelyn shrugged. "I just know that Julian would never pay for anyone to take the most expensive trip in the world simply out of love for his fellow man."

"And you?" Rogachev asked an athletically built man who had joined them in the course of the conversation. "What brings you here?"

"An accident." The man came closer and held out his hand to Evelyn. "Carl Hanna."

"Evelyn Chambers. You're referring to the attempt on Palstein's life?"

"He should have been flying instead of me. I know I shouldn't be pleased in the circumstances—"

"But you've been promoted and you're pleased anyway. That's completely understandable."

"Nice to meet you anyway. I watch *Chambers* whenever I can." His eyes turned to the sky. "Will you be making a program up there?"

"Don't worry, we'll keep it private. Julian wants to shoot a commercial with me, in which I praise the beauties of the universe. To stimulate space tourism. Do you happen to know Oleg Alexeyevich Rogachev?"

"Rogamittal." Hanna smiled. "Of course. I think we even share a passion."

"And that would be?" Rogachev asked carefully.

"Soccer."

"You like soccer?"

The Russian's impenetrable, foxy face grew animated. *Aha*, Evelyn thought. *First clue about Hanna.* She looked with interest at the Canadian, whose whole body seemed to consist of muscle, although without the awkwardness that bodybuilders so often had. With his close-shaven hair and beard, his thick eyebrows, and the little cleft in his chin, he could easily have played the lead in a war movie.

Rogachev was usually a little frosty with strangers, but the mention of soccer made him seem suddenly almost euphoric. Straight away they were discussing things that Evelyn didn't understand, so she took her leave and moved on. At the bar she ran into Lynn Orley, who introduced her to the Nairs, the Tautous, and Walo Ögi. She at once took a liking to the swaggering Swiss. Complacent, and with a parodic tendency to overdramatize things, he immediately proved to be open and attentive. In general, no one was talking about anything but the imminent trip. To her delight, Evelyn didn't have to try to attract Heidrun Ögi's attention, as she cheerfully waved her over to introduce her, with furtive delight, to the tormented-looking Finn O'Keefe. Over the next five minutes Evelyn didn't manage to ask him a single question, and said she presumed it would stay that way.

"Forever?" O'Keefe asked slyly.

"For the next two weeks," she confessed. "Then I'll give it another go."

Not staring at Heidrun was a far more hopeless task than escaping the gravitational pull of Miranda Winter's breasts—undulating landscapes of promised delight, but nothing in the end to lose your head over. Miranda, by and large, was a simple design. Sex with her, Evelyn guessed, would be like licking out of a honey pot, sweet and enticing, a bit ordinary after a while, eventually boring and possibly making you feel a bit sick afterward. Heidrun's pigment-free, anorexic body, on the other hand, her white hair, snow-white all over, promised an intense erotic experience.

Evelyn sighed inwardly. She couldn't afford any kind of adventure with this lot, particularly since everything about Heidrun shouted that she wasn't interested in women.

At least not that way.

A little way off she spotted Chuck Donoghue's barrel shape, with its complete lack of a neck. His chin jutted bossily forward, his thinning, reddish hair blown into a sculpture on his head. He had just launched into a noisy diatribe directed at two women, one tall and bony, with strawberry blonde hair, the other dark and delicate, looking as if she had emerged from a painting by Modigliani. Eva Borelius and Karla Kramp. At regular intervals Chuck's lecture was counterpointed by

Aileen Donoghue's maternal falsetto. With her rosy cheeks and silver hair, you might have expected to see her flitting off at any moment to serve homemade apple pie, which according to rumors she did with great enthusiasm when she wasn't helping Chuck run their hotel empire. To talk to Borelius, Evelyn would have had to put up with Chuck's teasing, so instead she went in search of Lynn, and found her in conversation with a man who looked uncannily like her. The same ash-blond hair, sea-blue eyes, Orley DNA. Lynn was saying, "Don't worry, Tim, I've never been better," as Evelyn walked in.

The man turned his head and looked at her reproachfully.

"Excuse me. Didn't mean to interrupt." She made as if to go.

"Not at all." Lynn held her back by the arm. "Do you know my brother?"

"Great to meet you. We hadn't had the pleasure."

"I'm not part of the company," Tim said stiffly.

Evelyn remembered that Julian's son had turned his back on the firm years before. The siblings were close, but there were problems between Tim and his father that had started when Tim's mother had died, in a state of total insanity, it was rumored. Lynn had never revealed any more than that, except that Amber, Tim's wife, didn't share her husband's dislike of Julian.

"You wouldn't happen to know where Rebecca is?" said Evelyn.

"Rebecca?" Lynn frowned. "She should be down at any moment. I just dropped her off at her suite."

In point of fact Evelyn couldn't have cared less where Rebecca Hsu had got to and who she was talking to on the phone. She just had a distinct feeling of being about as welcome as a case of shingles, and tried to find a reason to slope quietly off again.

"And otherwise? Do you like it?"

"Brilliant!—I heard that Julian's not getting here until the day after tomorrow?"

"He's stuck in Houston. Our American partners are causing a few problems."

"I know. Word gets around."

"But he'll be there for the show." Lynn grinned. "You know him. He loves making the big entrance."

"But it should be you in the limelight," said Evelyn. "You've sorted everything out fantastically well, Lynn. Congratulations! Tim, you should be proud of your sister."

"Thanks, Evie! Many thanks for that."

Tim Orley nodded. Evelyn felt more unwelcome than ever. Curious, she thought, he's not a nasty guy. What's his problem? Is he pissed off with me for some reason? What did I burst in on?

"Are you flying with us?" she asked.

"I'm, er . . . Of course, this is Lynn's big moment." He forced a smile, put his arm around his sister's shoulder and drew her to him. "Believe me, I'm *incredibly* proud of her."

There was so much warmth in his words that Evelyn had every reason to feel touched. But the undertone in Tim's voice said, *clear off, Evelyn.*

She went back to the party, slightly flummoxed.

The twilight phase was brief but dream-like. The sun adorned itself in blood-red and pink before drowning itself in the Pacific. Darkness fell within a few minutes. Because of the Stellar Island Hotel's location on the eastern slope, for most of those present the sun didn't disappear into the sea but slipped behind the volcanic peaks; only O'Keefe and the Ögis were able to enjoy its big farewell. They had left the party and driven up to the crystal dome, from where you had a view of the whole island including its inaccessible, jungle-covered western side.

"My goodness," said Heidrun, staring out. "Water on all sides."

"Hardly a shattering observation, darling." Ögi's voice emerged from the cloud of his cigar smoke. He had used the opportunity to get changed, and was now wearing a steel-blue shirt with an old-fashioned matching cravat.

"As you wish, jerk." Heidrun turned toward him. "We're standing on a bloody great stone in the Pacific." She laughed. "Do you know what that means?"

Ögi blew a spiral galaxy into the approaching night.

"As long as we don't run out of Havanas, it means we're in good hands here."

As they talked, O'Keefe wandered aimlessly around. The terrace was now half covered by the massive glass dome to which it owed its name. Only a few tables were set for dinner, but Lynn had told him that at peak period there was room for more than three hundred people here. He looked to the east, where the platform stood brightly lit in the sea. It was a fantastic sight. Except that the straight line was absorbed by the dark of the sky.

"Perhaps you'll wish you were standing back on this bloody great stone," he said.

"Really?" Heidrun flashed her teeth. "But maybe I'll be holding your little hand—*Perry.*"

O'Keefe grinned. After plunging lemming-like into the depths of noncommercial film, and choosing his roles in terms of their inappropriateness, he had been more surprised than anyone else when he was awarded an Oscar for his impersonation of Kurt Cobain. *Hyperactive* became the certificate of his ability. No one however could ignore the fact that the famously shy Irishman with the amber gaze, the regular features, and sensual lips was already yesterday's man, seen only in unwieldy low-budget and no-budget productions, cryptic *films d'auteur* and blurry Dogme dramas. Box-office poison had become a drug. Cleverly, he had avoided ogling blockbusters and gone on making the sort of things that he liked, except that all of a sudden everybody else liked them too. Azerbaijani directors could still book him for a pittance, if he liked the subject matter. He cultivated his origins and played James Joyce. He acted out the lives of junkies and homeless people. He did so much both in front of the camera and behind it that his past blurred: born in Galway, mother a journalist, father an operatic tenor. Learned piano and guitar as a boy, acted in theater to overcome his shyness, bit parts in TV series and advertisements. Worked his way up from minor to major roles at Dublin's Abbey Theater, shone with The Black Sheep in O'Donoghue's pub, wrote poetry and short stories. Even spent a year living with tinkers, Irish gypsies, out of a pure romantic connection with good old Éire. So convincing, finally, as a rebellious farmer's son in the TV series *Mo ghrá thú*, that Hollywood called.

Or so they said, and it sounded good, and was somehow true.

That shy Finn had been short-tempered as a child, and had knocked out his fellow pupils' teeth, that he was seen as a slow learner and, unable to decide what to be, had at first done nothing at all, was rarely mentioned. Not were his fallings-out with his parents, his immoderate alcohol consumption, the drugs. He had no memory at all of his first year with the tinkers, because he had spent most of his time drunk, or high, or both. Once he had been successfully socialized in the Abbey Theater, a German producer had had him in mind for the main role in Süskind's classic *Perfume*, but while Ben Wishaw had auditioned, O'Keefe had fallen noisily asleep on top of a Dublin prostitute and hadn't even turned up for the appointment. Not a word about losing his day job because of similar escapades and being thrown out of the TV series, followed by two more years of neglect among the traveling people, until he had finally been able to effect a reconciliation with his parents and gone into rehab.

It was only then that the myth began. From *Hyperactive* until that remarkable day in January 2017, when an unemployed screenwriter of German origins in Los Angeles got hold of a fifty-year-old pulp novel, that marked the start of an unparalleled literary phenomenon, an intergalactic soap opera that had never been published in America but which could claim to be the most successful sci-fi series of all time. Its hero was a space traveler called Perry Rhodan, whom O'Keefe played as cheerfully as ever, without worrying about success. He interpreted the role in such a way that perfect Perry became a hot-headed fool, who built Terrania, the capital of humanity, more or less by accident in the Gobi Desert, and stumbled out from there into the great expanses of the Milky Way.

The movie release beat everything that had gone before. Since then O'Keefe had played the space hero in two additional films. He had taken a training course at the Orley Space Center, and struggled against nausea on board a Boeing 727 converted to take zero-gravity flights. On that occasion he had met and liked Julian Orley, since which time they had formed a loose friendship based on their shared love of movies.

But perhaps I'll hold your little hand—

Why not, thought O'Keefe, but refrained from replying accordingly to avoid annoying Walo, because he strongly suspected Heidrun of loving the jovial Swiss. You didn't have to know the two of them any better to have a sense that that was the case. It was expressed less in what they said to each other than in the way they looked at and touched each other. Better not to flirt.

For the time being.

In space everything might look very different.

MAY 20, 2025
Paradise

Shenzhen, Guangdong Province, Southern China

Owen Jericho knew he still had a good chance of entering Paradise today, and he loathed the idea.

Other people loved it. To get there, you needed unbridled lust, the musty sweetness of a misdirected love of children, sadistic tendencies, and an ego sufficiently deformed to sentimentalize anything objectionable that you might get up to. Many of those who desired access saw themselves as champions for the sexual liberation of the very ones they were laying their hands on. Control was more important to them than anything else. At the same time most of them considered themselves perfectly normal, and saw the people who got in the way of their self-realization as the real perverts. Others claimed their legitimate right to be perverted; yet others saw themselves as businessmen. But hardly any of them had endured the shame of being described as sick and weak. It was only once they were up before the courts, when they summoned experts who testified to their inability to resist the call of their own nature, that they turned themselves into pitiably driven individuals in need of sympathy and healing. While still undiscovered, however, and in full possession of their intellectual powers, they were all too happy to withdraw to the playground of their clammy imaginations, the Paradise of the Little Emperors, which was indeed paradise from their vantage point, if not for the little emperors themselves.

For them it was hell.

Owen Jericho hesitated. He knew he shouldn't have followed Animal Ma this far. He saw him, his eyes widened by archaically fat eyeglass lenses into an expression of constant astonishment, crossing the square, elliptically swaying his bottom and hips. He owed this duck-like walk to a hip condition which created the false impression that he was easy prey. But Ma Liping, to give him his real name, hadn't been given his nickname by accident. He was considered aggressive and dangerous. In fact he pretended to have been given the name Animal at birth, a bizarre act of showing-off, not least because he also pretended it embarrassed him. Ma was cunning too. He must have been, or else he wouldn't have been able to lull the authorities into the sleepy conviction that he had forsworn pedophilia. As walking proof of the successful reintegration experiment, he worked for the police in the battle against the growing plague of child pornography in China; he provided instructions for the catching of small fry and apparently did everything he could to escape social ostracism.

Five years in jail as a child abuser, he used to say, is like five hundred years in a torture chamber.

This infectiously flourishing suburb of the urban network of Shenzhen in South China, with its boringly functional architecture, had allowed Ma, who was originally from Beijing, the chance to start again. No one knew him here, the local authorities didn't even have a file on him. In the capital they knew where he was living, but the connection had become attenuated, since the pedophile scene was in a state of constant flux, and Ma could credibly suggest that he had lost contact with its inner circle. No one paid him any attention now; there were other things that needed doing. Fresh depths granted nauseating glimpses of worlds of unbelievable human wretchedness.

Worlds like the Paradise of the Little Emperors.

Lost in a morass of mental overload as they tried to protect, check, and defraud 1.4 billion individuals all at the same time, the Chinese authorities increasingly resorted to private investigators to give them support. In hock to digitalization, they relied on cyber-detectives, specialists in all kinds of criminality and dark online practices, and Owen Jericho had the reputation of being extraordinarily gifted in the field. His portfolio was impeccable when it came to cracking web espionage, phishing, cyberterrorism, and so on. He penetrated illegal communities; infiltrated blogs, chat rooms, and virtual worlds; tracked down missing people using their digital fingerprints and advised companies on how to protect themselves against electronic attacks, Trojans, and malicious software. In England, he had dealt with several cases of child pornography so, when the hell of the "little emperors" was revealed to a team of shocked investigators, he had been asked for support by Patrice Ho, a high-ranking officer in the Shanghai Police and a friend of his. As a result of this request he was now standing here, watching Animal Ma on his way into the old, abandoned bicycle factory.

He shivered in spite of the heat. Accepting the commission had meant paying a visit to the Paradise of the Little Emperors. An experience that would leave traces in his cerebral cortex for the rest of time, even though he had had a fundamentally clear idea what he was letting himself in for. "Little emperors" was what the Chinese, with an almost Italian besottedness, called their children. But there had been no way of avoiding the journey to Paradise, he had to log in and put on the hologoggles to understand just *who* he was looking for.

Animal Ma stepped through the factory door.

After the city planners had, unusually, revealed no inclination to tear down the collection of moldy brick buildings, artists and freelancers had moved in, including a gay couple who repaired antiquated electrical devices, an ethno-metal band who vied with one another to see who could make the most noise and shake a deserted fitness studio to its foundations, and Ma Liping with his shop, buying and selling all kinds of goods, from cheap imitations of Ming vases to molting songbirds in portable bamboo cages. The investigator from Shenzhen who was working with Jericho had started observing Ma on May 20, and had not let the man out of sight for two days. He had followed him from his home to the old factory and back, he had taken photographs, followed every one of his limping steps, and drawn up a list of his customers' comings and goings. According to this list, during that time a grand total of four people had wandered into the shop, one of them Ma's wife, an ordinary-looking South Chinese woman of indeterminable age. What made the small number of customers more surprising was the fact that Ma and his wife lived in a six-story house, big and nicely presented by local standards, which Ma couldn't possibly have afforded on the small income that he got from the shop. His wife, as far as anyone knew, didn't do anything at all except cross the street to the shop several times a day and stay there for some time, perhaps to do office stuff or serve customers who never came.

Apart from two men.

For a whole series of reasons Jericho had reached the conviction that Ma, if he wasn't alone, was at least the driving force behind the Paradise of Little Emperors. Once he'd managed to narrow the circle of suspects down to a handful of child abusers who were currently rampaging on the net or had attracted attention there some time before, he had homed in on Animal Ma Liping. It was here, however, that his ideas and those of the authorities parted company. While Jericho saw a storm cloud of clues over Shenzhen, in the opinion of the police it was a man from the smoggy hell of Lanzhou who was attracting the most suspicion, and a raid was being organized there at that very minute. In Jericho's view there was no doubt that the police would find much of interest in Lanzhou, just not the thing they were looking for. In the Paradise the beast reigned, the snake, Animal Ma, he was sure of it, but he had been instructed to take no further steps for the time being.

An instruction that he basically intended to ignore.

Because apart from the fact that the case bore Ma's trademark, the fact that he was married gave Jericho food for thought. He had nothing against reformation and change, but Ma was clearly homosexual, he was a gay pedophile. It was also striking that the men who came to the shop only reappeared several hours later. Thirdly, the shop didn't seem to have anything remotely like fixed opening times, and last of all no one could have wished for a better place to carry out dark practices than the abandoned bicycle factory. All the other occupants used side-buildings with direct access to the street, leaving Ma as the only one with premises off the internal courtyard and the only one who ever set foot in it, apart from a few children who trickled in and out.

From Shanghai, Jericho had instructed the investigator to pay a visit to the shop, take a look around and buy something unimportant, if possible something that Ma stocked in his storeroom. This meant that Jericho was already familiar with the shop by the time he followed Ma across the square that morning. He waited for a few minutes in the shadow of the factory wall, passed through the gate, crossed the dusty area of the courtyard, climbed a short flight of stairs, and stepped inside the crammed shop, which was filled with shelves and tables. Behind the counter the shop's owner was busy with jewelry. A bead curtain separated the sales area from an adjacent room, and a video camera was fixed above the doorway.

"Good morning."

Ma looked up. The enlarged eyes behind the horn-rimmed glasses studied the visitor with a mixture of suspicion and interest. No one he knew.

"I heard you had something for every occasion," Jericho explained.

Ma hesitated. He set aside the jewelry, cheap, tarnished stuff, and smiled shyly.

"Who, if I might ask, says that?"

"An acquaintance. It must have been here, yesterday. He needed a birthday present."

"Yesterday—" Ma mused.

"He bought a make-up set. Art deco. Green, gold, and black. A mirror, a powder compact."

"Oh, yes!" His suspicion vanished, replaced by eagerness. "A lovely piece of work, I remember. Was the lady pleased?"

"The lady who received the present was my wife," said Jericho. "And yes, she was very pleased."

"How wonderful. What can I do for you?"

"You remember the design?"

"Of course."

"She would like more from the same series. If there are any more."

Ma widened his smile, glad to be of service since, as Jericho knew from the investigator, there were still a matching brush and a comb to buy. With his curious rolling gait he came out from behind the counter, pushed a little stepladder against one of the shelved walls, and climbed up it. Comb and brush shared a drawer quite high up, so that Ma was occupied for a few seconds while Jericho scanned his surroundings. The sales room was probably just what it looked like. The counter had a kitschy fake art nouveau front, behind which ivory-colored pearl necklaces dangled. Beyond it, barely visible, lay the second room, perhaps an office. In the midst of all the junk a surprisingly expensive-looking computer adorned the counter, its screen turned toward the wall.

Ma Liping reached up and clumsily brought down the goods. Jericho didn't risk going behind the counter. The danger was too great that the man might turn toward him at that very moment. Instead he walked a little way along the counter until the screen display appeared reflected in a glass case. The glowing surface was divided into three, one part covered with characters, the other half divided into pictures showing two rooms from the perspective of surveillance cameras. Although he couldn't make out any details, Jericho knew that one of the cameras was directed at the sales room, because he saw himself walking around in the window. The other room looked gloomy and it clearly didn't contain very much furniture.

Was it the back room?

"Two very beautiful pieces," said Ma, as he came down from the ladder and set the comb and brush down in front of him. Jericho lifted both up, one by one, ran his fingers expertly through the bristles, and inspected the teeth. Why did Ma need a camera to monitor his back room? Checking the area toward the courtyard made sense, but did he want to watch himself at work? Unlikely. Was there another means of access from outside leading to that room?

"One tooth is broken," he observed.

"Antiques," Ma lied. "The charm of imperfection."

"What do you want for it?"

Ma quoted a ridiculously high price. Jericho made a no less ridiculous counteroffer, as the situation demanded. At last they agreed upon a sum that allowed both of them to save face.

"While I'm here," Jericho said, "there's something else that occurs to me."

Antennae of alertness grew from Ma's temples.

"She has a necklace," he went on. "If only I knew something about jewelry. But I'd like to give her a suitable pair of earrings and, well, I thought—" He pointed rather helplessly to the displays in the counter case. Ma relaxed. "I have some things I could show you," he said.

"Yeah, I'm afraid it won't be much use without the chain." Jericho pretended he needed to have a think. "The thing is, I've got some meetings to get to, but this evening would be the ideal time to surprise her with them."

"If you brought me the chain—"

"Impossible, I have no time. That is, wait a moment. Do you get e-mail?"

"Of course."

"Then it's all fine!" Jericho acted relieved. "I'll send you a photograph, and you look for something suitable. Then I'd just have to collect it later. You'd be doing me a big favor."

"Hmm." Ma bit his lower lip. "When would you be coming, round about?"

"Yeah, if only I knew. Late afternoon? Early evening?"

"I've got to go out for a while too. Shall we say from six? I'd be here for another good hour after that."

Faking gratitude, Jericho left the shop, walked to his rental car two streets away, and drove to a better area in search of a jewelry shop. After a short time he found one, had them show him necklaces in the lower price range, and asked to be allowed to take a photograph of one with his cell phone, so that he could send the picture, he said, to his wife for inspection. Back in the car he wrote Ma a brief e-mail and attached the photograph, but not before he had attached a Trojan. As soon as Ma Liping opened the attachment, he would unwittingly load the spy program onto his hard drive, from where it would transmit the drive's contents. Jericho couldn't assume that Ma was stupid enough to store incriminating content on a publicly accessible computer, but that wasn't what he was concerned with in any case.

He drove back to a place near the factory and waited.

Ma had opened the attachment shortly after one o'clock, and the Trojan had started transmitting straight away. Jericho connected his cell phone to a roll-out screen and received, sharp and in detail, the impressions from the two surveillance cameras. They captured their surroundings in wide-screen mode, unfortunately without sound. On the other hand, a few moments later he received confirmation that camera two actually was monitoring the back room separated off with beads, when Ma disappeared from one window and appeared again immediately in the other one, shuffled over to a sideboard, and fiddled with a tea maker.

Jericho appraised the furniture. A massive desk with a swivel chair and worn-looking stools in front of it, obliging visitors to assume a petitioner's crouch, some ramshackle shelves, with stacks of paper on the worn plywood, files, wood carvings, and all kinds of horrors like silk flowers and industrially manufactured statues of the Buddha. Nothing to suggest that Ma placed any value on the personal note. No painting interrupted the whitewashed monotony of the walls; there were no discernible signs of that symbiotic connection produced by spouses looking at each other from little frames at work.

Ma Liping, happily married? Ludicrous idea.

Jericho's eye fell on a narrow, closed door opposite the desk. Interesting, but when Ma set down his tea and opened it, he merely revealed a view of tiles, a washbasin, and a piece of mirror. Less than half a minute later the man appeared again with his hands on his fly, and Jericho had to acknowledge that the supposed entrance was probably a toilet.

In that case why was Ma monitoring the damned room? Who did he hope or fear to see there?

Jericho sighed. He waited patiently for an hour. He watched as Ma, with the photograph of the chain in front of his eyes, assembled an assortment of more or less matching earrings and seized the unexpected appearance of a customer as the opportunity to fob off on her a remarkably ugly set of tableware. He watched Ma polishing glass jugs and ate dried chilis from a bag until his tongue burned. At about three o'clock the so-called wife entered the shop. Supposedly unobserved, in a state of married familiarity, as they both were, one might have expected to see them exchange a kiss, a tiny act of intimacy. But they met as strangers, talked to one another for a few minutes, then Ma closed the front door, turned the Open/Closed sign around, and they went together into the back room.

What followed needed no soundtrack.

Ma opened the toilet, let his wife step inside, glanced alertly in all directions again, and pulled the door closed behind him. Jericho waited tensely, but the couple didn't reappear. Not after two minutes, not after five, not even after ten. Only half an hour later did Ma suddenly come storming out, and into the sales room, where the figure of a man could now be seen outside the glass-paneled entrance. As if frozen, Jericho stared at the half-open toilet door, tried to make out reflections in the mirror, but the restroom didn't yield up its secrets. Meanwhile Ma had let in the new arrival, a bull-necked, shaven-headed man in a leather jacket, bolted the door again, and walked ahead of the new arrival into the back room where they both made for the lavatory and disappeared inside.

Amazing. Either this deadly trio liked to party in a confined space or the toilet was bigger than he thought.

What were the three of them getting up to?

Over an hour and a half went by. At ten past five the guy in the leather jacket and the woman reappeared in the office and came out to the front. This time it was she who opened the sales room, let the bald guy out, and followed him, carefully closing the door behind her. Of Ma himself there was no sign. From six o'clock onward, Jericho guessed, his efforts would be directed at customers and profit, explicitly on complementing a necklace with earrings, but until then, God alone knew what monstrous activities he was pursuing. Meanwhile Jericho thought he had understood the purpose of the second camera monitoring the office. Taking care that no one saw him when he disappeared into the miraculous world of the lavatory, Ma would be equally keen to avoid anyone waiting for him when he came back. The camera probably also supplied a picture to the toilet.

Jericho had seen enough. He would have to catch the bastard unprepared, but was Ma unprepared? Was he ever?

He quickly slipped his phone into his jacket, got out of the car, and walked the few minutes back to the factory building as he came up

with a battle plan. Perhaps he would have been better off calling the
local authorities for support, but they would want to consult further
before doing anything. If they obstructed his investigations, he might
as well drive back to Shanghai, and Jericho was firmly resolved to get
to the bottom of the mystery of the back room. His gun, an ultra-flat
Glock, was safely stowed over his heart. He hoped he wouldn't have
to use it. He had too many years drenched in sweat and blood behind
him, too much active work at the front, in the course of which he, his
adversaries, or both had needed emergency medical treatment. The
cheekbone on the cobblestones, the taste of dirt and hemoglobin in the
mouth—all in the past. Jericho didn't want to fight again. He no longer
valued the bony grin of his old partner from the hereafter, who up until
now had been involved in every shoot-out, who had stormed every
house with him, entered every snake pit with him, without being on
anyone's side; who always just reaped the harvest. One last time, in the
Paradise of the Little Emperors, he would bring Death into the equation, in the hope of winning him as an ally in spite of his unreliability.

He stepped into the factory courtyard, resolutely crossed it, and
climbed the steps. As might have been expected, the shop sign said
Closed. Jericho rang the bell, long and insistently, excited to see
whether Ma would force himself out of the toilet or play dead. In fact
he parted the bead curtain after the third ring. Limping elegantly, Ma
circled the hideous counter, opened the door, and fastened his vision-
corrected eyes on the unwelcome guest.

"My mistake I'm sure," he said in a pinched voice. "I thought I said
six o'clock, but probably—"

"You did," Jericho assured him. "I'm sorry, but I now need the earrings sooner than we agreed. Please forgive my obstinacy. Women." He
spread his arms in a gesture of impotence. "You understand."

Ma forced a smile, stepped aside, and let him in.

"I'll show you what I've found," he said. "I'm sorry you had to wait
so long, but—"

"I'm the one who should apologize."

"No, not at all. My mistake. I was in the toilet. Now, let's have a
look."

Toilet? Jericho registered with amazement that Ma had just given
him the password.

"This is very awkward," he stammered. "But—"

Ma stared at him.

"Could I use it?"

"Use it?"

"Your toilet?" Jericho added.

The man's hands developed a crawling life of their own, pushed earrings around on the threadbare velvet of the pad. A cough crept up his

throat, followed by another. Small, slimy, startled animals. Suddenly Jericho had the horrific vision of a bag in the shape of a humanoid, filled with swarming, chitinous, glittering vermin, stirring Ma Liping's husk from within and imitating humanoid gestures.

Animal Ma.

"Of course. Come with me."

He held the bead curtain open, and Jericho stepped into the back room. The second camera fastened its dark eye on him.

"But I must—" Ma paused. "I'm not equipped for this, you know. If you wait a second, I just want to sort out a fresh towel." He directed Jericho to the desk, and opened the toilet door behind him.

Jericho grabbed the handle and pulled it open.

As if in a flash he took in the scene. A restroom, sure enough, tall and narrow. The outlines of dead insects in the frosted glass of the ceiling light. The tiles cracked in certain places, mildewed grouting, the mirror stained and tarnished, a rust-yellow back to the wash-basin, the toilet itself little more than a hole in the floor. A closet on the back wall, if you could call it a wall, because it was half open, a disguised door that Ma had neglected to close in his haste to serve Jericho.

And in all this Animal Ma Liping, who seemed at that moment to consist only of his magnified eyes and the sole of a shoe darting out and colliding painfully with Jericho's sternum.

Something cracked. All the air was driven out of his lungs. The kick sent him to the floor. He saw the Chinese man, teeth bared, appear in the doorframe, drew the Glock from its holster, and took aim. Ma darted back and turned around. Jericho leaped to his feet, but not quickly enough to prevent his opponent from escaping into the darkness beyond the secret opening. The back wall swung back and forth. Without pausing, he charged through it, stopped at the top of a flight of stairs, and hesitated. A curious smell struck him, a mixture of mold and sweetness. Ma's footsteps rang out down below, then everything fell silent.

He mustn't go down there. Whatever lay hidden in that cellar, the secret of the toilet was solved. Ma was in a trap. It was better to call the police, let them take care of whatever horrors lay down there and allow himself a drink.

And what if Ma *wasn't* in a trap?

How many entrances and exits did the cellar have?

Jericho thought of the Paradise. Scattered across the organism of the World Wide Web, the pedophiles' pages were suppurating wounds that sickened society irremediably. The perfidiousness with which the "goods" were offered was unparalleled, he thought, and just then something from the vaults rose up toward him, ghostly and thin. A whimpering that stopped abruptly. Then nothing more.

He made his mind up.

Gun at the ready, he stepped slowly down. Strangely, with every step, the silence seemed to coagulate; he was moving through a medium enriched with rot and decay, a sound-swallowing ether. The stench grew more intense. The stairs wound around in a curve, led further downward, and opened out into a gloomy vault supported by brick pillars, some connected by wooden slats, crates that had been cobbled together. What they contained was impossible to make out from the foot of the stairs, but at the end of the chamber he glimpsed something that captured his attention.

A film set.

Yes, that was exactly what it was. The more his eyes grew accustomed to the gloom, the clearer it became to him that films were being made there. Phalanxes of unlit floodlights, perched on stands and hanging from the ceiling, peeled from the darkness; folding chairs, a camera on a tripod. The set seemed to be divided into parts, some furnished with equipment, others bare, possibly something like a green screen so that virtual backgrounds could be added later. Checking in all directions as he walked on, he made out little beds, furniture, toys, an artificial landscape with a children's house, meadows and trees, a dissecting table from a pathology lab. Something on the floor looked unsettlingly like a chainsaw. Cages hung from the ceiling, surrounded by various utensils and something that might have been a small electric chair; tools were mounted on the wall—no, not tools: knives, pincers, and hooks—a torture chamber.

Somewhere in all that madness Ma was hiding.

Jericho walked on, heart thumping, putting one foot in front of the other as if crossing ice that might crack at any moment. He reached the crates. Turned his head.

A boy looked at him.

He was naked and dirty, perhaps five years old. His fingers clutched the wire mesh between the slats, but his eyes looked apathetic, almost lifeless, the sort of eyes familiar in people who had withdrawn deep inside themselves. Jericho turned his head in the other direction and saw two girls in the cage opposite, barely clothed. One of them, very small, lay on the ground, clearly sleeping; the other, older, leaned with her back against the wall, hugging a cuddly toy. She lethargically turned a swollen face, and fastened sad eyes upon him. Then she seemed to understand that he was not one of the people who normally came here.

She opened her mouth.

Jericho shook his head and put his finger to his lips. The girl nodded. Holding the gun rigidly out ahead of him, he peered in all directions, checked again and again, and ventured further into the hell of the little emperors. Still more children. Only a few who saw him. He gestured to them, the ones who raised their heads, to be silent. From cage to cage it got worse and worse: dirt and degradation, apathy, fear. A baby lay on a grimy blanket. Something dark rattled against a bar and yapped at him, so that he instinctively flinched, turned around and held his breath. The sickly stench seemed to have its source right in front of him. He heard the buzzing of flies, saw something darting across the floor—

His eyes widened and he felt nauseous.

That brief moment of inattention cost him his control. Dragging footsteps echoed, a draught brushed the back of his neck, then someone jumped at him, pulled him back, laid into him, screamed incomprehensible words.

A woman!

Jericho tensed his muscles and jabbed his elbows back again and again. His attacker wailed. As they whirled around he recognized her— Ma's wife or whatever role she might have played in that nightmare— grabbed her, pressed her against one of the columns, and held the barrel of the Glock to her temple. How did she get here? He had seen her leave, but he hadn't seen her come back. Was there another entrance to the cellar? Could Ma finally have escaped him?

No, it was his fault! He had been sloppy on the way from the car to the factory. He had neglected to keep an eye on his computer. At some point during that time she must have come back here, to—

The pain!

Her heel had driven itself into his foot. Jericho reached out and slapped her in the face with the back of his hand. The woman struggled like a mad thing in his clutches. He gripped her throat and pushed her harder against the pillar. She kicked out at him and then, surprisingly, she abandoned all resistance and stared at him with hatred.

In her eyes he saw what she saw.

Alarmed, he let go of her and spun around to see Ma sailing through the air in a grotesque posture, coming straight at him, his arm outstretched, swinging a huge knife. He wouldn't have time to shoot him, to run away, he would just have time to—

Jericho ducked.

The knife came down, sliced whistling through the air and through Mrs. Ma's throat, from which a cascade of blood sprayed. Ma staggered, thrown off balance by his own momentum, stared through blood-sprinkled glasses at his collapsing wife, and flailed his arms. Jericho hammered the Glock against his wrist and the knife clattered to the floor. He kicked it away, kicked Ma in the belly and again in the shoulder, at which the child-abuser toppled forward. The man groaned, collapsed on all fours. His glasses slipped from his nose. He felt around, half blind, struggled to his feet, both hands raised, palms outward.

"I'm unarmed," he gurgled. "I'm defenseless."

"I see a few defenseless people here," Jericho panted, the Glock aimed at Ma. "So? Did that help *them* at all?"

"I have my rights."

"So do the children."

"That's different. It's something you can't understand."

"I don't *want* to understand!"

"You can't do anything to me." Ma shook his head. "I'm sick, a sick man. You can't shoot a sick man."

For a moment Jericho was too flabbergasted to reply. He kept Ma in check with the gun and saw the man's lips curling.

"You won't shoot," said Ma, with a flash of confidence.

Jericho said nothing.

"And you know why not?" His lips pulled into a grin. "Because you feel it. You feel it too. The fascination. The beauty. If you could feel what I feel, you wouldn't point a gun at me."

"You kill children," Jericho said hoarsely.

"The society you represent is so dishonest. *You* are dishonest. Pitifully so. You poor little policeman in your wretched little world. Do you actually realize that you envy people like me? We've attained a degree of freedom of which you can only dream."

"You swine."

"We're so far ahead!"

Jericho raised the gun. Ma reacted immediately. Shocked, he threw both hands in the air and shook his head again.

"No, you can't do that. I'm sick. Very sick."

"Yes, but you shouldn't have made that attempt to escape."

"What attempt?"

"This one."

Ma blinked. "But I'm not escaping."

"Yes, you're escaping, Ma. You're trying to get away. This very second. So I find myself forced—"

Jericho fired at his left kneecap. Ma screamed, doubled up, rolled on the floor, and screeched blue murder. Jericho lowered the Glock and crouched down exhaustedly. He felt miserable. He wanted to throw up. He was dog-tired, and at the same time he had a sense that he would never be able to sleep again.

"You can't do that!" Ma wailed.

"You shouldn't have tried to get away," Jericho murmured. "Asshole."

It took the police a full twenty minutes to find their way to the factory, and when they did they treated him as if he were in cahoots with the child-abuser. He was far too exhausted to get worked up about it, and just told the officers that it would be in the interest of their professional advancement to call a particular number. The duty inspector pulled a sulky face, came back as a different man, and handed him the phone with almost child-like timidity.

"Someone would like to speak to you, Mr. Jericho."

It was Patrice Ho, his high-ranking policeman friend from Shanghai. In return for the information that the raid in Lanzhou had thrown up a pedophile ring, although it hadn't been possible to prove a connection with the Paradise of the Little Emperors, Jericho improved his evening with the news that Paradise had been found and the snake defeated.

"What snake?" his friend asked, puzzled.

"Forget it," Jericho said. "Christian stuff. Could you make sure that I don't have to put down roots here?"

"We owe you a favor."

"Fuck the favor. Just get me out of here."

There was nothing he yearned for so much as the chance to leave the factory and Shenzhen as quickly as possible. He was suddenly enjoying the deference normally reserved for folk heroes and very popular criminals, but he wasn't allowed to leave until eight. He dropped the rental car off at the airport, took the next plane for Shanghai, a Mach 1 flying wing, and checked his messages in the air.

Tu Tian had been trying to contact him.

He called back.

"Oh, nothing in particular," said Tu. "I just wanted to tell you your surveillance was successful. The hostile competitors admitted to data theft. We had a talk."

"Brilliant," said Jericho without any particular enthusiasm. "And what came out of the talk?"

"They promised to stop it."

"That's all?"

"That's a lot. I had to promise to stop it too."

"Excuse me?" Jericho thought he had misheard. Tu Tian, whose company had proved to have fallen victim to Trojans, had been absolutely furious. He had spared no expense to get his hands on the, as he put it, pack of miserable blowflies and cockroaches so presumptuous as to spy on his company secrets. "You yourself wanted to—"

"I didn't know who they were."

"And excuse me, but what difference does that make?"

"You're right, absolutely none at all." Tu laughed, in great humor now. "Are you coming to the golf course the day after tomorrow? You can be my guest."

"Very kind of you, Tian, but—" Jericho rubbed his eyes. "Could I decide later?"

"What's up? Bad mood?"

Shanghai Chinese were different. More direct, more open. Practically Italian, and Tu Tian was possibly the most Italian of all of them. He could have performed a convincing version of "Nessun dorma."

"Quite honestly," Jericho said, "I'm wiped out."

"You sound it," Tu agreed. "Like a wet rag. A rag-man. We'll have to hang you out to dry. What's up?"

And because fat Tu, for all his egocentricity, was one of the few people who granted Jericho an insight into his own inner state, he told him everything.

"Young man, young man," Tu said, amazed, after a few seconds of respectful silence. "How did you do it?"

"I just told you."

"No, I mean, how did you get wise to him? How did you know it was him?"

"I didn't. It was just that everything pointed in that direction. Ma is vain, you know. The website was more than a catalogue of ready-produced horrors, with men forcing themselves on babies and women forcing little boys to have sex with them before laying into them with a hatchet. There were the usual films and photographs, but you could also put on your hologoggles and be there in 3D, and at various things happening live as well, which gives these guys a special kick."

"Revolting."

"But most importantly there was a chat room, a fan forum where these people swapped information and boasted to each other. Even a second-life sector where you could assume a virtual identity. Ma appeared there as a water spirit. I suspect most pedos aren't familiar with that kind of thing. They tend to be made of more conventional stuff, and they don't much like talking into microphones, even with voice-changer software. They'd rather type out all their bullshit on the keyboard in the old-fashioned way, and of course Ma joined in and there he was. So I got the idea of adding my own contributions."

"You must have felt like chucking!"

"I've got a switch in the back of my head and another in my belly. I usually manage to turn off at least one of them."

"And back in the cellar?"

"Tian." Jericho sighed. "If I'd managed that, I wouldn't have told you all this crap."

"I understand. Go on."

"So, every imaginable visitor to the page is online, and of course Ma, the vain swine, is on there too. He disguises himself as a visitor, but you notice that he knows too much, and he has this huge need to communicate, so that I start suspecting that this guy is at least *one* of the originators, and after a while I'm convinced that it's *him*. A little while ago, I subjected his contributions to a semantic analysis—peculiarities of expression, preferred idioms, grammar—and the computer narrows the field, but there are still about a hundred known internet pedophiles who are possible suspects in this one. So I have the guy analyzed while he's online and writing, and his typing rhythms give him away. Just about every time. That leaves four."

"One of them Ma."

"Yes."

"And you're convinced it's him."

"Unlike the police. They, of course, are convinced that Ma is the only one of the four that it *isn't*."

"Which is why you went out on your own. Hmm." Tu paused. "All due respect to your approach, but didn't you recently tell me the nice thing about i-profiling was that the only fighting you have to do is against computer viruses?"

"I've had it with brawling," Jericho said wearily. "I don't want to see any more dead, mutilated, abused people. I don't want to shoot anyone, and I don't want anyone shooting at me. I've had enough, Tian."

"Are you sure?"

"Completely. That was the last time."

Back at home—although it wasn't really a home anymore, filled as it was with moving boxes that he had spent several weeks packing, making his life look as if it came from a props store and had to be returned in its original packaging—Jericho suddenly had a creeping fear that he'd gone too far.

It was just after ten when the taxi set him down outside the high-rise building in Pudong that he would leave in a few days to move into his dream apartment, but every time he closed his eyes he saw the half-decaying baby lying in the shack, the army of organisms that had pounced upon it to consume its flesh; he saw Ma's knife flashing down at him, again he felt the moment of deadly fear, a film that would now be on constant rerun, so that his new home threatened to become a place of nightmare. Experience alone told him that thoughts were by their nature drifting clouds, and that all images eventually faded, but until that happened it could be a long and painful period of suffering.

He shouldn't have taken on that damned mission!

Wrong, he scolded himself. True despair lurked in the subjunctive, in the spinning-out of alternative plot strands that weren't alternatives because each one had only one path that it could travel down. And you couldn't even tell whether you were traveling voluntarily, or whether someone or something was impelling you—and Christ, what that something might be, there was no way of knowing! Are we just a medium for predetermined processes? Had he had a choice about whether or not to take on the mission? Of course, he could have turned

it down, but he hadn't. Didn't that invalidate any idea of choice? Had
he had a choice about whether or not to follow Joanna to Shanghai?
Whichever path you took, you took it, so there was no choice at all.

A trite acknowledgment of the bitter truth. Perhaps he should write
a self-help manual. The airport bookstores were full of self-help manuals. He himself had even seen some warning against self-help manuals.

How could you be so wide awake and at the same time so tired?

Was there anything else he needed to pack?

He turned on the monitor wall and found a BBC documentary—
unlike the bulk of the population, he was able to receive most foreign
channels without any difficulty, legal or illegal—and went in search of
a box to sit on. At first he could hardly work out what was going on,
then the subject started to interest him. Exactly right. Pleasantly far
away from everything he had had to deal with over the past few days.

"A year ago today," the commentator was saying, "on May 22, 2024, a
dramatic worsening in Chinese-American relations preoccupied the plenary meeting of the United Nations, one that would become known as:"

The Moon Crisis

Jericho grabbed a beer from the fridge and sat cross-legged on the
box. The documentary was about the ghost of the previous summer,
but began two years earlier, in 2022, a few weeks after the American
base on the North Pole of the Moon went into operation. Back then
the United States had started quarrying the noble-gas isotope helium-3
in the Mare Imbrium, setting in motion a development that had hith-
erto occupied the minds only of economic romantics and authors of
science-fiction novels. Without a doubt, the Moon had a special part to
play in the opening up of the solar system: as a springboard for Mars,
as a place of research, as a telescopic eye reaching the edges of the universe. From a purely economic point of view, compared with Mars
Luna it was a cheap date. You needed less fuel to get there, you got
there quickly, and you came back quickly too. Philosophers justified
moon travel with references to the spiritual sustenance of the enterprise, hoping for proofs or counterproofs of God's existence and, quite
generally, an insight into the status of Homo sapiens, as if it took a stone
ball 360,000 kilometers away to do it.

Having said this, the distant view of Man's shared fragile home did
seem to encourage the formation of peaceful states of mind. The only
questionable aspect was the satellite's economic productivity. There
was no gold up there, no diamond mines, no oil. But even if there
had been, the cost would have made commercial exploitation absurd.
"We may discover resources on the Moon or Mars that will boggle
the imagination, that will test our limits to dream," George W. Bush
had announced in 2004, wearing the face of a founding father, and

it had sounded exciting, naïve, and adventurous, but then who took Bush seriously? At the time America had been bogged down in wars, and had been about to ruin its economy and its international standing. Hardly anything could have seemed more inappropriate than the idea of the reawakening of a new El Dorado, and besides, NASA had no money.

And yet—

Startled by the announcement by the United States that they planned to send astronauts to the Moon again by 2020, the whole world had suddenly been galvanized into frantic activity. Whatever there was to be brought back from the Moon, the field wasn't to be left open for America again, particularly since this time it seemed to have less to do with the symbolism of flags and footprints than with a tangible policy of economic supremacy. The European Space Agency offered technological support. Germany's DLR fell in love with the idea of having its own moon base. France's ESA carthorse EADS preferred a French solution. China hinted that in a few decades moon-mining would be crucially important to the national economy, explicitly the mining of helium-3. Roskosmos was also flirting with this quarrying idea, and so were the Russian companies Energia Rocket and Space Corporation, which had announced the construction of a moon base by 2015, whereupon India had immediately sent a probe with the beautiful name of Chandrayaan-1 into the polar orbit of the satellite to see how exploitable it was. Given the clear undertone of the Bush doctrine of going it alone, representatives of Russian and Chinese space travel authorities met for discussions about joint ventures, Japan's JAXA entered the game: everyone was in a terrific hurry to court La Luna and make sure they got hold of some of her legendary treasures, as if it were enough simply to go there, dig the stuff up, and scatter it over the home territory. Each prognosis outdid the last in terms of boldness until Julian Orley set out his clear conditions.

The richest man in the world had become involved with the Americans.

The result was, to put it mildly, radical. No sooner had international competition for extraterrestrial raw materials begun than it had fizzled out again, as the victor was, thanks to Orley's decision, quite clear: a decision made less for reasons of sympathy than because the notoriously cash-strapped NASA turned out to have more money and a better infrastructure than all the other space-traveling nations put together. Apart from China, perhaps. There, during the nineties, ambitions to soar to cosmic greatness had become apparent, admittedly with a modest self-evaluation and an overall budget that came to a tenth of the United States's, but which were driven by patriotism and claims to world-power status. Then, after one Zheng Pang-Wang had begun financing Chinese space travel in 2014, their budgets and aspirations had become almost equal; there was just a lack of know-how—a shortcoming that Beijing thought it would be able to make up.

Zheng, high priest of a globally active technology company whose greatest ambition lay in putting China on the Moon even before the United States, and making the exploitation of helium-3 a possibility, was often described in the media as the Orley of the East. In fact, like the Englishman he had not only immense wealth but also an army of high-class builders and scientists. The Zheng Group went to work feverishly on the realization of a space elevator, probably in the knowledge that Orley was doing the same thing. But while Orley attained his goal, Zheng didn't solve the problem. Instead, the group managed to build a fusion reactor, but again they fell behind because Orley's model worked more safely and efficiently. China's ruling Communist Party grew nervous. Zheng was urged finally to demonstrate some success, if necessary by making long-nose an offer he couldn't refuse; so old Zheng went for dinner with Orley and told him that Beijing wanted to cooperate in the near future.

Orley said Beijing could kiss his butt. But would Zheng share another bottle of that wonderful Tignanello with him?

Why not share everything, asked Zheng.

Like what?

Well, money, a lot of money. Power, respect, and influence.

He had money of his own.

Yes, but China was hungry and extremely highly motivated, far more than slack, overweight America, which was still reeling from the financial crisis of 2009, so that there was something doddery about everything it did. If you asked an American about the future, in seventy percent of cases he would see something profoundly terrifying about it, while in China everyone faced the coming day with a cheerful heart.

That was all well and good, said Orley, but shouldn't they move on to an Ornellaia?

It was pointless, and certainly all mining plans with traditional rocket technology were economically unproductive, and condemned to throw Chinese space travel into the red. But with the defiance of a foot-stamping child, the Party decided to do just that, trusting in the hope that Zheng and the great minds of the Chinese National Space Administration would soon be back in the running. And because America had shown no scruples about letting its mining machines loose on the very part of the Moon where, according to the general geological view, there was a higher-than-average deposit of helium-3, a border area of the Mare Imbrium, the components for a mobile Chinese base and solar furnaces on caterpillar tracks were transported to that very spot, right next to their unloved competitor, and the Chinese began their own mining operation on March 2, 2023. America acted first amazed, then delighted. China was cordially welcomed to the Moon, there was talk of a global legacy and an international community, and no one worried about the newcomer's touching efforts to squeeze its pathetic portion of helium-3 out of moondust.

Until May 9, 2024.

Over the past few months both nations had successively stepped up their mining operations. On that day a rather heated discussion took place between the American moon base and Houston. Following immediately on from this, the alarming message reached the White House that Chinese astronauts had deliberately and with unambiguous intentions crossed the mining boundaries and annexed American territory, and that the Americans felt provoked and threatened. The Chinese ambassador was summoned and accused of border violations, and ordered to reestablish the status quo forthwith. The Party asked for an inquiry into what had happened, and on May 11 declared itself unaware of any guilt. Without officially negotiated borders there could be no border violation. Broadly speaking, Washington must know what the world thought of the way that America, in defiance of all clauses in the space treaty in general and the lunar treaty in particular, had invented facts; and how had anyone ever come up with the abstruse idea of crossing that heavenly body—which, according to those treaties, belonged to no one—with borders? And did they really want to have that tiresome discussion all over again, instead of contenting themselves with their own superiority, which was, after all, plainly visible to anyone with eyes to see?

The United States felt snubbed. The Moon was a long way away, no one on Earth could say exactly who was strolling about on whose territory, but on May 13 the moon base announced the arrest of the Chinese astronaut Hua Liwei. The man had been sniffing around on the territory of the American mining station, an automatized facility, which was why he could hardly have shown up there to talk about the moon weather over tea and cakes. That Hua was also commander of the Chinese base, a highly decorated officer who was given no opportunity to provide his version of events, did nothing to defuse the situation. Beijing raged and protested vehemently. At the Ministry for State Security, they outdid themselves in describing the martyrdom that Hua would have to endure in the remote polar base, and made demands for his immediate release which Washington studiously ignored, whereupon Chinese associations, officially this time, invaded American territory with vehicles and mining robots, or at least that was how it was reported. In fact, only one unfortunate small robot was involved, which accidentally rammed an American machine and completely wrote itself off. There could have been no question of manned vehicles, given the isolated Chinese Rover roaming around on its own, and on closer inspection the feared associations proved to be the clueless, disorganized remnants of the base staff, two women who had had to simulate an invasion because of political arm-twisting, while the American astronauts at the Pole didn't understand why they had had to take poor Hua prisoner, and put all their efforts into at least giving him a good time.

But no one on Earth was interested in any of that.

Instead, ghosts long thought exorcised tried to scare each other to death. Imperialism versus the Red Peril. In a sense the excitement was even justified. It wasn't at all about the few astronauts or a few square miles of terrain, but who was and would be in charge if more nations tried to take possession of the Moon. Then Washington promptly threatened sanctions, froze Chinese bank accounts, prevented Chinese ships from leaving American ports, and expelled the Chinese ambassador, prompting Beijing to threaten massive measures against American mining, if bank accounts, ships, and Hua were not released forthwith. America insisted on an apology. No one at all would be released before that. Beijing announced a plan to storm the American station. Bafflingly, no one asked the question how the completely overtaxed taikonauts could take a huge, partly subterranean base at the inaccessible, mountainous North Pole, and once Washington had threatened military strikes against the Chinese mining station and Chinese facilities on Earth, no one really felt like asking it either.

The world was beginning to get frightened.

Unimpressed, if not actually motivated by this, the aggrieved superpowers continued to tear into each other. Each accused the other of perpetrating a military build-up in space, and of having stationed weapons on the Moon, with the result that the news was full of simulations of lunar nuclear engagements, with dark hints that the conflict might be continued on Earth. While the BBC showed pictures of exploding space stations and, in happy ignorance of physics, gave them an audible bang, the moon-base crews were forbidden to talk to each other. In the end neither party knew what the other was doing and what the whole thing was really about, apart from keeping face until the United Nations ruled that enough was enough.

That old carthorse, diplomacy, was yoked up to the cart, to drag it out of the dirt. The UN plenary session met on May 22, 2024. China pointed out that because they didn't have their own space elevator they were unable to transport weapons to the Moon, while this was an easy matter for the Americans. Therefore the Americans must be seen as the aggressors, because they had very clearly stationed weapons on the Moon and broken the space treaty yet again, but then what was new?

They themselves, incidentally, were not planning to arm, but found themselves forced by continued provocations to consider a modest contingent for self-defense. The Americans expressed similar intentions. China had been the source of the aggression, and if America were ever to arm itself on the Moon, it would be the consequence of a completely unnecessary border violation.

No border had been violated.

Okay, fine. And we didn't have weapons on the Moon.

Did.

Didn't.

Did.

Didn't.

Did.

The UN General Secretary, with weary rage, condemned both the actions of the Chinese and the imprisonment of the Chinese astronaut by the United States. The world wanted peace. That much was true. Basically, Beijing and Washington wanted nothing more than peace, but face must be saved! It was not until June 4, 2024, that China, teeth gritted, backed down, without reference to the UN resolution, the power of which, once again, seemed to be more symbolic in character than anything else. The truth was that neither of the two nations was either willing or able to engage in open conflict. China withdrew from American territory, which involved the taikonauts carting away the shattered mining machine. Hua was released, along with the Chinese bank accounts and ships, and the ambassadors moved back into their offices. At first the situation was characterized by threats and suspicion. There was a political chill, which meant that the economy froze temporarily as well. Julian Orley, who had wanted to open his Moon hotel as early as 2024, had to suspend its construction for an indefinite period, and helium-3 mining suffered on both sides.

"It took until November 10, 2024," the commentator said with a serious demeanor, "for dialogue between the United States and China to resume at the World Economy Summit in Bangkok, for the first time since the outbreak of the dispute, and since then it has been marked by conciliatory tones." Her voice became more menacing and dramatic. "The world has escaped an escalation—how narrowly, no one can say." And again, in a milder tone: "The United States assured the Chinese of a stronger connection to the infrastructure of the moon base, new agreements for mutual aid in space were signed and existing ones extended, Americans and Chinese reached an understanding on trade agreements that had until then been contentious." Positive, optimistic, with a sleep-well-little-children smile: "The waves have been stilled. As ambitiously as they went at each other's throats, gestures of goodwill were now exchanged. For a very simple reason: the economies couldn't do without each other. The integration between the two trading giants, the United States and China, could not withstand a war; each party would only be destroying its own property on hostile territory. There is half-hearted talk about cooperating more strongly in the future, while only now is each of the two major world powers able to strive for dominance on the Moon. Meanwhile the space-traveling world is vying for the patents of Julian Orley, who has over the last few days broken into space with an illustrious and suspiciously multinational troop of selected guests, perhaps in order to reconsider his U.S.–exclusive attitude—but perhaps also to show them our small, fragile planet from a distance, and remind them that belligerent disputes would not be won by anyone. On that note: good night."

Jericho sucked the last bit of foam from the bottle.

Curious race, humanity. Flew to the Moon and abused little children.

He turned off the television, gave the box a kick, and went to bed in the hope of being able to sleep.

MAY 21, 2025
The Elevator

The Cave

"The Stellar Dome was originally planned for the highest point of the island, where the crystal dome with the restaurant is now," Lynn Orley explained as she walked through the lounge ahead of the group. "Until, while we were exploring the place, we discovered something that led us to abandon our previous plans. The mountain provided us with an alternative that we could barely have imagined."

On the evening of the third and last day of their stay on the Isla de las Estrellas the group was waiting for the prelude to their big adventure. Lynn led them to a wide, locked doorway set in the back wall of the lobby.

"It can't have escaped anyone that the Stellar Island Hotel looks like an cruise ship stranded in the volcano. And *officially* that volcano is extinct." Here and there she registered unease. In Momoka Omura's imagination in particular, streams of lava seemed to be flowing through the lounge and spoiling the evening once and for all. "At the summit and along the flank moderate temperatures prevail. Pleasantly cool, ideally suited for storing food and drink, for locating pumps, generators and processing plants, the laundry, janitor's office, and various other things. Just behind me," she turned her head toward the bulkheads, "offices were planned. We started drilling into the rock, but after only a few meters we found ourselves in a fault that extended into a cave, and at the end of that cave—"

Lynn rested the palm of her hand on a scanner, and the door slid open.

"—lay the Stellar Dome."

A steeply descending passageway with roughly carved walls stretched beyond the doorway and turned a corner so that it was impossible to see where it went next. Lynn saw faces filled with curiosity, excitement, and anticipation. Only Momoka Omura, once she had been reassured that she would not be burning up in liquid rock, seemed to have lost interest completely, and stared earnestly at the ceiling.

"Any more questions?" Lynn let a mysterious smile play around the corners of her mouth. "Then let's go."

A collage of sounds enveloped them, all apparently of natural origin. There were clicks, echoes, whispers and drips, and orchestral surfaces created a timeless atmosphere. Lynn's idea of turning the emotional screw without slipping into the Disneyesque was taking effect: sounds on the boundary edge of perception, as a subtle way of creating moods, which had required the building of a complicated technical installation, but the result exceeded all expectations. The two sides of the door closed behind them, and cut them off from the airy, comfortable atmosphere of the lobby.

"We laid out this section ourselves," Lynn explained. "The natural part begins just past the bend. The cave system extends through the whole of the eastern flank of the volcano. You could walk around in it for hours, but we preferred to close the passageways. Otherwise there might be a danger of you getting lost in the heart of the Isla de las Estrellas."

Past the bend, the corridor stretched out considerably. It grew darker. Shadows flitted over pitted basalt, like the shadows of strange and startled animals escaping to safety from the horde of tourists. The echoes of their footsteps seemed to the group to precede and follow them at the same time.

"How are caves like this formed?" Bernard Tautou threw his head back. "I've seen a few, but every time I've forgotten to ask."

"They can have all kinds of possible causes. Tensions in the rock, pockets of water, landslips. Volcanoes are porous structures; when they cool down they often leave cavities. In this case it's most probably lava drainage channels."

"Oh great," blustered Donoghue. "We've landed in the gutter."

The corridor turned in a curve, narrowed, and debouched into an almost circular room. The walls were lined with motifs from the dawn of humanity, some painted, some carved into the rock. Bizarre life-forms stared at the visitors from the penumbra, with fathomlessly dark eyes, horns and tails and helmets with aerial-shaped growths sprouting from them. Some of the clothes looked like space suits. They saw creatures that seemed to have merged with complicated machines. A huge, rectangular relief showed a humanoid creature in a fetal position operating levers and switches. The sound changed, becoming eerie.

"Horrible," Miranda Winter sighed with relish.

"I hope so," grinned Lynn. "After all, we've brought together the most mysterious testimonies of human creativity. Reproductions, obviously. The figures in the striped suits, for example, were discovered in Australia, and according to tradition they represent the two lightning brothers Yagjagbula and Tabiringl. Some researchers think they are astronauts. Next to them, the so-called Martian God, originally a 6-meter cave drawing from the Sahara. The creatures there on the left, the ones who seem to be holding their hands up in greeting, were found in Italy."

"And this one?" Eva Borelius had stopped in front of the relief and was looking at it with interest.

"The gem of our collection! A Mayan artifact. The gravestone of King Pakal of Palenque, an ancient pyramid city in Chiapas in Mexico.

It's supposed to depict the ruler's descent to the underworld, symbol-ized by the open jaws of a giant snake." Lynn walked over to it. "What do you recognize?"

"Hard to say, but it looks as if he's sitting in a rocket."

"Exactly!" cried Ögi, rushing over. "And you know what? It was a Swiss man who was responsible for that interpretation!"

"Oh?"

"You don't know of Erich von Däniken?"

"Wasn't he a sort of fantasist?" Borelius smiled coldly. "Someone who saw extraterrestrials everywhere?"

"He was a visionary!" Ögi corrected her. "A very great one!"

"I'm sorry." Karla Kramp gave a little cough. "But your visionary has been regularly contradicted."

"So?"

"In that case I'd just like to understand what makes him so great."

"How often do you think, my dear, that the Bible has been con-tradicted," Ögi bellowed again. "Without fantasists the world would be more boring, more average, more stale. Who cares whether he was right? Do you always have to be right to be great?"

"I'm sorry, I'm a doctor. If I'm wrong, my patients don't generally reach the conclusion that I'm great."

"Lynn, could you come over here for a moment?" Evelyn Chambers called. "Where does that come from? It looks as if they're flying."

Conversations sprouted, a little knowledge blossomed. The motifs were admired and discussed. Lynn provided explanations and hypoth-eses. This was the first time that a group of visitors had been inside the cave. Her plan to use prehistoric drawings and sculptures to get people in the mood for the mystery to come was a success. At length she drummed the group together and led them from the cave-room to the next stretch of passageway, which grew even steeper, even darker—

And warmer.

"What's that noise?" Miranda Winter wondered. "Voom, voom! Is that normal?"

And true enough, a dull rumble mingled with the soundtrack, coming from the depths of the mountain, and creating a menacing atmosphere. Reddish wisps of smoke drifted over the rock.

"There's something there," Aileen Donoghue whispered. "Some sort of light."

"God, Lynn," laughed Marc Edwards. "Where are you taking us?"

"We must be quite deep already, aren't we?" It was the first time Rebecca Hsu had spoken. Since her arrival she had been constantly on the phone, and nobody had been able to speak to her.

"Just over 80 meters," said Lynn. She stepped briskly on, toward another turn, bathed in flickering firelight.

"Exciting," O'Keefe observed.

"Oh come on, it's just theater," Warren Locatelli announced from above. "We're entering a strange world, is what they're trying to suggest. The inside of the Earth, the interior of a strange planet, some waffle like that."

"Just wait," said Lynn.

"What's she got for us this time?" Momoka Omura said, striving for disenchantment, while the tone of her voice revealed that streams of lava were starting to flow in her head again. "A cave, another cave. Brilliant."

The rumbling and roaring rose in a crescendo.

"So, I think it's—" Evelyn Chambers began, stopped in the middle of the sentence and said, "Oh, my!"

They had passed the bend. Monstrous heat came roaring at them. The passageway widened, suffused with a pulsating glow. Some of the guests came to an abrupt standstill, others ventured hesitantly forward. On the right-hand side the rock opened up, providing a glimpse into a huge, adjacent vault, from which the thundering and roaring emanated, drowning out their conversation. A glowing lake half-filled the chamber, boiling and bubbling, spitting red and yellow fountains. Basalt spikes jutted from the sluggish surge toward the domed ceiling, which flickered spectrally in the glow. With quiet delight, Lynn studied fear, fascination, astonishment; she saw Heidrun Ögi shielding herself against the heat with her raised hands. Her white hair, her skin seemed to be blazing. As she uncertainly approached, she looked for a moment as if she had just emerged from some inferno.

"What on earth is that?" she asked in disbelief.

"A magma chamber," Lynn explained calmly. "A store that keeps the volcano fed with lava and gases. Such chambers form when liquid rock rises from a great depth to the weak areas of the Earth's crust. As soon as pressure in the chamber gets out of control, the lava forces its way up, and the eruption occurs."

"But didn't you say the volcano was extinct?" Mukesh Nair said in amazement.

"Officially extinct, yes."

Suddenly everyone was talking at the same time. O'Keefe was the first to voice some suspicion. During the whole excursion he had been strolling thoughtfully along the passageway, absorbed, keeping his distance; now he walked right up to the seething cauldron.

"Hé, mon ami!" called Tautou. "Don't singe your hair."

"Pas de problème," O'Keefe turned around and grinned. "I hardly think there's anything to be afraid of. Isn't that right, Lynn?"

He held out his right hand. His fingers touched a surface. Warm, but not hot. Entirely smooth. He pressed the palm of his hand against it and smiled appreciatively.

"When was the last time it looked like this inside the mountain?"

Lynn smiled.

"According to the geologists, about a hundred thousand years ago. But not as far up. Magma chambers usually lie at a depth of 25 to 30 kilometers, and they're much bigger than this one."

"Anyway, it's the best hologram I've seen in ages."

"We do our best to please."

"A hologram?" echoed Sushma.

"More precisely, an interplay of holographic projections with sound, colored light, and thermal panels."

Sushma stepped up beside O'Keefe and tapped her finger against the surface of the screen, as if there might still be a chance that he was mistaken. "But it looks perfectly real!"

"Of course. We don't want to bore you, after all."

Everybody touched the screen now, stepped respectfully back, and yielded once more to the illusion. Chuck Donoghue forgot to wise-crack, Locatelli to prattle condescendingly. Even Momoka Omura stared into the digital lava lake and looked almost impressed.

"We're practically at our destination," said Lynn. "In a few seconds we'll be able to enter that chamber, only then it will look completely different. You will be traveling from the distant past to the future of our planet, the future of mankind."

She tapped a switch hidden in the rock. At the end of the passageway a tall, vertical crack appeared. Faint light seeped from it. The music swelled, powerful and mystical, the crack widened and provided a glimpse of the vault beyond. It really did, in appearance and dimensions, look very much like the holographic depiction, except that there was no lava sloshing about. Instead, there was a kind of theatrical arena suspended above the bottomless pit. Steel walkways led to banked rows of comfortable-looking seats, which hovered freely above the abyss. At the center there arched a transparent surface measuring at least a thousand square meters in area. Its bottom end was lost in the light-less depths, the top reached to just below the domed ceiling, its sides stretched far beyond the rows of seats.

Standing on the gallery was a lone man.

He was of medium height, slightly squat, and youthful in appearance, although his beard and his long, collar-length hair were gray, and the ash-blond color of earlier years was a thing of the distant past. He wore a T-shirt and jacket, jeans and cowboy boots. There were rings on his fingers. His eyes flashed jauntily, his grin was like a lighthouse beam.

"Here you are at last," said Julian Orley. "Okay, then: let's rock 'n'roll!"

Tim stood apart from the others, watching his father greet the guests with handshakes or hugs according to how well he knew them. Julian, the great communicator, laying friendly traps. So keen to meet people that he never doubted for a moment that those people wanted to meet him, and that was exactly what attracted them. The physics of meeting people is based on both attraction and repulsion, but it was practically impossible to escape Julian's gravitational pull. You were introduced to him and you instantly felt warm familiarity. Two, three more times and you were lost in memories of old times together that had never existed. Julian didn't do much, he came out with no quips, he didn't practice speeches in front of the mirror, he just took it for granted that in Newton's two-body system he was the planet and not the satellite.

"Carl, old man! Lovely to have you here!"

"Evelyn, you look fantastic. What idiot ever said the *circle* was the most perfect form?"

"Momoka, Warren. Welcome. Oh, and thank you for last time, I've been meaning to call for ages. To be quite honest, I have no idea how I got home."

"Olympiada Rogacheva! Oleg Rogachev! Isn't this fantastic? Here we are meeting right now for the first time, and tomorrow we'll be traveling to the Moon together."

"Chucky, old man, I've got a great joke for you, but we'll have to step aside for a minute if you're to hear it."

"Where is my Fairy Queen? Heidrun! I've finally met your husband. Did you ever buy that Chagall?—Of course I know about that, I know about all your passions, your wife has been doing nothing but rave about you!"

"Finn, young man, this is where it gets serious. You've got to go up there now. And this *isn't* a movie!"

"Eva Borelius, Karla Kramp. I've been particularly looking forward to—"

And so on, and so forth.

Julian found friendly words for everyone, then he came dashing over to Tim and Amber with a furtive grin.

"So? How do you like it?"

"Brilliant," said Amber, and put an arm around his shoulders. "The magma chamber's amazing."

"Lynn's idea." Julian beamed. He could barely utter his daughter's name without adopting a sickly tone. "And this is nothing! Wait until you see the show."

"It'll be perfect, as always," Tim stammered with barely concealed sarcasm.

"Lynn and I came up with it together." As usual, Julian pretended not to have noticed Tim's ironic tone. "The cave is a gift from heaven, I tell you. These rows of seats mightn't look like much, but we can now screen this spectacle for five hundred paying guests, and if it's more—"

"I thought the hotel only had room for three hundred?"

"Sure, but we can basically double our capacity. Put four or five decks on our cruise ship, either that or Lynn will build a second one. Not a problem either way. The main thing is that we rustle up the cash for another elevator."

"The main thing is that you don't get into difficulties."

Julian looked at Tim with his light blue eyes.

"And I'm not. Will you excuse me? Enjoy yourselves, see you later.— Oh, Madame Tautou!"

Julian darted back and forth between the visitors, a laugh here, a compliment there. Every now and again he drew Lynn to him and kissed her on the temples. Lynn smiled. She looked proud and happy. Amber sipped at her champagne.

"You could be a bit friendlier to him," she said quietly.

"To Julian?" snorted Tim.

"Who else?"

"What difference does it make if I'm friendly to him? He only sees himself anyway."

"Perhaps it makes a difference *to me*."

Tim stared at her uncomprehendingly.

"What's up?" Amber raised her eyebrows. "Are you slow-witted all of a sudden?"

"No, but—"

"Clearly you are. Then I'll put it a different way. I don't feel like spending the next two weeks constantly staring into your gloomy face, okay? I want to enjoy this trip, and you should too."

"Amber—"

"Leave your prejudices down here."

"It's not a matter of prejudices! The thing is, that—"

"It's *always* something."

"But—"

"No buts. Just be a good boy. I want to hear a yes. Just a simple yes. Do you think you can manage that?"

Tim chewed his bottom lip. Then he shrugged. Lynn walked past them, followed by the Tautous and the Donoghues. She winked at them, lowered her voice, and said behind her hand, "Hey, insider knowledge. This is confidential information for family members only. Row eight, seats thirty-two and thirty-three. Best view."

"Got it. Over and out."

Amber linked arms with the group and disappeared without another word toward the auditorium. Tim sauntered along behind her. Someone drew up beside him.

"You're Julian's son, aren't you?"

"Yes."

"Lovely to meet you. Heidrun Ögi. Your family's completely bonkers. I mean, it's not a problem, it's absolutely fine," she added when he failed to reply. "I love people with bees in their bonnets. You're far more interesting than the common run of people."

Tim stared at her. He would have expected anything from this chalk-white woman with the violet eyes and the white mane of hair: Celtic magic spells, extraterrestrial dialects, just not that kind of misplaced remark.

"Really?" he managed.

"So what sort of madman are you, then? If you take after Julian."

"You think my father's mad?"

"Of course, he's a genius. So he must be mad."

Tim said nothing. *What kind of madman are you, then?* Good question. No, he thought, what an idiotic assumption! I'm definitely the only one in the family who *isn't* mad.

"Well—"

"See you." Heidrun smiled, drew away from him, waving her fingertips, and followed the jovial Swiss chap who was clearly her husband. Slightly startled, he pushed his way to the middle of the eighth row and slumped down next to Amber.

"Who are these Ögis?" he asked.

She looked over her shoulder. "The guy with the albino wife?"

"Mmhm."

"Glittering couple. He runs a company called Swiss Performance. They're involved in all kinds of areas, but mostly he's in the construction business. I think he came up with the first pontoon estates for the flooded areas of Holland. At the moment he's in discussions with Albert over Monaco Two."

"Monaco Two?"

"Yes, just imagine! A huge floating island. It was on the news a while ago. The thing's only going to cruise in fair-weather zones."

"Ögi must be the same sort of bonkers as Julian."

"Could be. He's said to be a philanthropist. He supports needy artists, performers, and circus folk; he's started up educational institutions for underprivileged young people; he sponsors museums; he donates money like it was going out of fashion. Last year he donated a considerable part of his fortune to the Bill and Melinda Gates Foundation."

"How the hell do you know all this?"

"You should read the gossip sheets more often."

"Don't need to while I've got you. And Heidrun?"

"Yeah . . ." Amber smiled knowingly. "That's where things get interesting! Ögi's family isn't exactly over the moon about their relationship."

"Tell me more."

"She's a photographer. She's talented. She takes pictures of celebrities and ordinary people. She's published picture books about the, erm . . . red-light scene. In her wild years she's said to have gone so far off the rails that she was thrown out of her house and disinherited. After that she started funding her studies by working as a stripper, and later as an actress in posh porn films. At the start of the millennium she became a cult figure in Switzerland's smart set. I mean, you couldn't exactly claim she's not striking."

"Good God, no."

"Eyes straight ahead, Timmy. She gave up the porn films after her studies, but went on stripping. At parties, gallery openings, just for fun. At one of those events she came across Walo, and he helped boost her career as a photographer."

"Which is why she married him."

"Apparently she isn't an opportunist."

"Touching," said Tim, and was about to add something else when the lights went out. They were immediately sitting in inky blackness. A solo violin started playing. Gentle music wove threads through the dark, shimmering lines that formed elaborate structures. At the same time the space assumed a blue glow, a mysterious, gloomy ocean. From what seemed to be a long distance away—the impressive result of holographic projections on the huge, concave glass wall—something came toward them, pulsating and transparent, something that looked like an organic spaceship with a vague nucleus of alien, shadowy passengers.

"Life," said a voice, "began in the sea."

Tim turned his head. Amber's profile shone like a ghost in the blue light. Enchanted, she watched the cell growing bigger and slowly beginning to rotate. The voice spoke of primal lakes and chemical marriages contracted many years ago. The lonely cell in the infinity of blue divided, and then that division became faster and faster, more and more cells came into being, and all of a sudden something long and serpentine came wriggling toward them.

"Six hundred million years ago, the age of complex, multicellular living creatures began!" the voice announced.

Over the minutes that followed, a speeded-up version of evolution occurred. The realism was so overwhelming that Tim flinched involuntarily when a monster a meter long, with shredder teeth and thorny claws, catapulted toward him, switched direction with a flick of its powerful tail, and devoured not him, but a twitching trilobite. The Cambrian age emerged and faded before his eyes, followed by the Ordovician, the Silurian, and the Devonian. As if someone had pressed a search button on a geological remote control, life swarmed through the blue and underwent every imaginable metamorphosis. Jellyfish, worms, lancelets and crabs, giant scorpions, octopuses, sharks, and reptiles appeared in turn, an amphibian turned into a saurian, everything moved onto land, a radiant, cloud-scattered sky took the place of the depths of the sea, the Mesozoic sun shone down on hadrosaurs, brachiosaurs, tyrannosaurs, and raptors, until a huge meteorite came crashing down on the horizon and set off a wave of destruction that swept all life away. In digital perfection the inferno charged onward, taking the audience's breath away, but when the dust settled it revealed the victory parade of the mammals, and everyone was still sitting unscathed in their rows of seats. Something ape-like swung through a summery-green grove, stood upright, turned into a chattering early hominid, armed and clothed itself, changed its build, posture, and physiognomy, rode a horse, drove a car, piloted an airplane, floated waving through the interior of a space station and out through an opening—but instead of landing in space, it stretched and dived back into the waters of the ocean. Diffuse blue, once again. The human, floating in it, smiled, and they all smiled back.

"They say we are attracted to water because we come from water and we ourselves are over seventy percent water. But did we originate only in the sea?"

The blue condensed into a sphere and shrank to a tiny drop of water in a black void.

"If we go in search of our origins, we have to look a long way back into the past. Because water, which covers over two-thirds of the Earth, and which we are made of—" the voice paused significantly "—came from space!"

Silence.

To the deafening sound of an orchestra the droplet exploded into millions of glittering particles, and suddenly everything was full of galaxies, lined up like dewdrops on the threads of a spider's web. As if they were sitting in a spaceship, they approached a single galaxy, flew into it, passed a sun and floated on, toward its third planet, until it hung before them as a fiery sphere, covered with an ocean of boiling lava. Asteroids crashed noisily in as the voice explained how the water had come to Earth on meteorites from the depths of space, bringing organic matter with it. They watched a second ocean of steam settling over the sea of lava. The whole thing reached a climax when a huge planetoid came dashing by, slightly smaller than the young Earth and bearing the name of Theia. The magma chamber shook with the impact, debris flew in all directions, and the Earth survived that too, now richer in mass and water and in possession of a moon that formed from the debris and sped around the planet. The hail of projectiles eased, oceans and continents came into being.

Sitting beside Tim, Julian said quietly, "Of course the idea that you can have noises in a vacuum is total nonsense. Lynn would rather have stuck to the facts, but I thought we should think about the children."

"What children?" Tim whispered back. Only now did he notice his father sitting on his other side.

"Well, most of the people making the journey will be parents with their children! To show them the wonders of the universe. The whole show is aimed at children and adolescents. Just imagine how excited they're going to be."

"So we aren't just drawn back to the sea," the voice was saying. "An even older legacy guides our eyes to the stars. We look into the night sky and feel an unsettling closeness, almost something like homesickness, which we can barely explain to ourselves."

The imaginary spaceship had passed through the planet's new atmosphere, and was now heading toward New York. The Manhattan skyline with the illuminated Freedom Tower lay impressively beneath a fairy-tale night sky.

"And the answer is obvious. Our true home is space. We are island-dwellers. Just as people in every age have pushed their way into the unknown to expand their knowledge and find new places to live, the natural desire to explore is written in our genes. We look up to the stars and ask ourselves why our technological civilization shouldn't be able to do what the nomads of early times managed using the simplest means, with boats made of animal skins, on peregrinations that lasted for years, defying the wind and weather, impelled only by their curiosity, their endlessly inventive spirit and their yearning for knowledge, the deep desire to understand."

"And that's where I come in!" squeaked a little rocket, that stomped into the picture and clicked its fingers.

The wonderful panoramic view of New York at night, starry sky and all, disappeared. Some of the audience laughed. The rocket did actually look funny. It was silver and fat with a pointy tip: a spaceship out of a picture book, with four tailfins on which it marched around, wildly waving arms, and a rather odd-looking face.

"Kids will love this," Julian whispered with delight. "Rocky Rocket! We plan comics with this little fellow, cartoons, cuddly toys, the whole shebang."

Tim was about to reply when he saw his father arriving to stand next to the rocket in the black void. The virtual Julian Orley wore jeans too, an open white shirt, and glittering silver sneakers. The inevitable rings sparkled on his fingers as he shooed the little rocket off to the side.

"You're not needed here for the time being," he said, and spread his arms. "Good evening, ladies and gentlemen, I'm Julian Orley. A warm welcome to the Stellar Dome. Let me take you on a journey to—"

"Yes, with me," trumpeted the rocket, and came sliding into the foreground in full showbiz style, also with his arms spread, on his knees or whatever rockets called knees. "Me, the one it all started with. Follow me to—"

Julian shoved the rocket aside again, and it in turn tripped him up. The two of them squabbled for a while about who was going to lead everybody through the history of space travel, until they agreed to do it together. The auditorium was plainly amused, and Chucky's expansive laughter roared out at every trick that Rocky played. What followed was once again accompanied by images, such as a brick-built space station orbiting the Earth which, as Julian informed them, came from the science-fiction story *The Brick Moon* by the English clergyman Edward Everett Hale. Rocky Rocket dragged a startled-looking dog into orbit and explained that it was the first satellite. The scenery changed again. A huge cannon, its barrel driven into a tropical mountainside. People in old-fashioned clothes climbed onto a kind of projectile and were fired into space by the cannon.

"That was in 1865, eight years after the appearance of the Brick Moon. In his novels *De la Terre à la Lune* and *Autour de la Lune*, Jules Verne described the beginning of manned space flight with astonishing farsightedness, even though the cannon, because of the length required, would have been impossible to make. But all the same, the projectile is successfully fired from Tampa in Florida, where, and just think about this, NASA is based today. Unfortunately, over the course of the story the unfortunate dog is thrown overboard at some point and circles the spaceship for a short time, the very first satellite."

Rocky Rocket threw a bone to the puzzled creature, which tried in vain to catch it, with the result that the bone now went into orbit along with the dog.

"In novels and short stories people started speculating a long time ago about how we could travel to the stars, but it was the Russians who first managed to fire an artificial heavenly body into near-Earth orbit. On October 4, 1957, at 22.29 hours and 34 seconds they fired an aluminum sphere into orbit, just over 185 pounds in weight and with four antennae that broadcast a series of now legendary beeps as a radio signal on 15 and 7.5 meter wavelengths, all across the world: 'Sputnik 1 took the world's breath away!'"

Over the next few minutes the imaginary spaceship turned once again into a time machine, as new objects were constantly fired into space. The dogs Strelka and Belka barked cheerfully on board Sputnik 4. Alexei Leonov ventured out of his capsule and floated like an astral baby on his umbilical cord through space. They met Valentina Vladimirovna Tereshkova, the first woman in space; they saw Neil Armstrong leaving his boot-prints in the Moon's dust on July 20, 1969, and all kinds of space stations circling the Earth. Space Shuttles and Soyuz capsules carried goods and crews to the International Space Station. China started its first moon probe. A new international space race began, the Space Shuttle was mothballed, Russia revived its Soyuz program, Ares rockets now headed for the endless construction site that was ISS, the spaceship Orion brought people to the Moon again, the European Space Agency immersed itself in preparations for a flight to Mars, China started to build a space station of its own. Almost everyone fantasized about the colonization of space, via Moon landings, flights to Mars, and ventures into galaxies to which no man had ever boldly gone, as a science-fiction series of the early years had so nicely put it.

"But all these plans," Julian explained, "shared the problem that spaceships and space stations *couldn't* be built the way they ideally *should* have been built. Which was down to two unavoidable physical givens: air resistance—and gravitation."

Now Rocky Rocket made his grand entrance again, balancing on a stylized globe, with a distant, friendly lunar face hanging over it. The satellite, unambiguously female, with crater acne but pretty nonetheless, winked at Rocky and flirted so brazenly with the little rocket that he sent sparks into ether from his pointed tip. Tim slipped deeper into his seat and leaned over to Julian.

"Very child-friendly," he teased quietly.

"What's the problem?"

"The whole thing's a bit phallic. I mean, the Moon is female, so Miss Luna wants to be fucked. Or what?"

"Rockets *are* phallic," Julian complained. "What should we have done in your view? Make the Moon masculine? Would you rather have had a gay Moon? I wouldn't."

"I don't mean that."

"I don't want a gay Moon. No one wants a gay Moon. Or a gay spaceship with a glowing ass. Forget it."

"I didn't say I didn't like it. I just—"

"You're a born skeptic."

Arguing for argument's sake. Tim wondered how they would survive the next two weeks together. Meanwhile Rocky Rocket packed everything a rocket might need into his suitcase, cleanly folded a few astronauts in there too, stuffed the case into his belly, and then, blowing kisses, fired off a cute little stream of fire and leaped into the air. Immediately the Earth's surface threw out a dozen extendable arms and pulled him back down again. Rocky, extremely puzzled, tried again, but escaping the planet seemed impossible. High above him, the randy Moon fell into a mild depression.

"If someone jumps in the air, it is one hundred percent certain that he will fall back to the ground," Julian explained. "Matter exerts gravity. The more mass a body contains, the greater is its field of gravity, with which it pulls smaller objects to it."

Sir Isaac Newton appeared dozing under a tree, until an apple fell on his head and he leaped up with a knowing expression: "This is exactly," he said, "how the heavenly mechanics of all bodies works. Because I am bigger than the apple, you would imagine that the fruit would succumb to my very personal physicality. And in fact I do exert modest forces of gravity. But compared with the mass of the planet, I play a subordinate role for the apple, which is ripe for gravitational behavior. In fact this tiny apple has no chance against Earth's gravity. The more power I summon up in my attempt to throw it back up in the air, the higher it will climb, but however hard I try, it will inevitably fall back to the ground." As if to prove his remarks, Sir Isaac tried his hand at apple-throwing and wiped the sweat from his brow. "You see, the Earth pulls the apple right back down again. So how much energy would be required to sling it straight into space?"

"Thank you, Sir Isaac," Julian said affably. "That's exactly what's at issue. If we consider the Earth as a whole, a rocket is not much different from an apple, even though rockets are, of course, bigger than apples. In other words, it takes a massive amount of energy for it to be able to launch at all. And additional energy to balance out the second force that slows it as it climbs: our atmosphere."

Rocky Rocket, exhausted by his efforts to reach his celestial beloved, walked over to an enormous cylinder marked *Fuel* and drank it down, whereupon he swelled up suddenly and his eyes burst from their sockets. By now, however, he was finally in a position to produce such a massive explosion of flame that he took off and became smaller and smaller until at last he could no longer be seen.

Julian wrote up a calculation. "Leaving aside the fact that the size of the fuel tank required for interstellar spaceships becomes a problem after a certain point, in the twentieth century each new launch cost a phenomenal sum of money. Energy is expensive. In fact, the amount of energy required to accelerate a single kilogram to flight velocity sufficient to escape the Earth's gravity was on average 50,000 US dollars. Just one kilogram! But the fully crewed Apollo 11 rocket with Armstrong, Aldrin, and Collins on board weighed almost 3,000 tons! So anything you installed on the ship, anything you took with you made the costs—*astronomical*. Making spaceships safe enough against meteorites, space junk, and cosmic radiation looked like a wild fantasy. How could you ever get the heavy armor up there, when every sip of drinking water, every centimeter of legroom was already far too expensive? It was all well and good sharing a sardine tin for a few days, but who wanted to fly to Mars in such conditions? The fact that more and more people were questioning the point of this ruinous endeavor, while the bulk of the world's population was living on less than a dollar a day, was another exacerbating factor. Given all these considerations, plans such as the settlement and economic exploitation of the Moon or flights to other planets seemed an impossible dream." Julian paused.

"When in fact the solution had been sitting on the table all the time! In the form of an essay written by a Russian physicist called Konstantin Tsiolkovsky in 1895, sixty-two years before the launch of Sputnik 1."

An old man, with cobweb hair, a fuzzy beard, and metal-rimmed glasses, stepped onto the virtual stage with all the grace of an ancient Cossack. As he spoke, a bizarre grid construction rose up on the Earth's surface.

"What I had in mind was a tower," Tsiolkovsky told the audience, hands bobbing. "Like the Eiffel Tower, but much, much higher. It was to reach all the way to space, a colossal elevator shaft, with a cable hung from the top end that was to reach all the way to the Earth. With such a device, it seemed to me, it would surely be possible to put objects into a stable terrestrial orbit without the need of noisy, stinky, bulky, and expensive rockets. During the ascent, these objects, the further they go from the Earth's gravity, would be tangentially accelerated until their energy and velocity are sufficient to remain at their destination, at an altitude of 35,786 kilometers, in perpetuity."

"Great idea," cried Rocky Rocket, back from his lunar pleasure trip, and circled the half-finished tower, which immediately collapsed in on itself. Tsiolkovsky trembled, paled, and went back to join his ancestors.

"Yeah." Julian shrugged regretfully. "That was the weak point in Tsiolkovsky's plan. No material in the world seemed stable enough for such a construction. The tower would inevitably collapse under its own weight, or be torn apart by the forces exerted upon it. It was only in the fifties that the idea regained popularity, except that now people were thinking about firing a satellite into geostationary orbit and lowering a cable from there to the Earth—"

"Erm—excuse me," Rocky Rocket cleared his throat.

"Yes? What is it?"

"This is embarrassing, boss, but—" The little rocket blushed and awkwardly scraped its stubby fins. "What does geostationary mean exactly?"

Julian laughed. "No problem, Rocky, Sir Isaac, an apple please."

"Got it," said Newton, and slung another apple in the air. This time the fruit sped straight into the air, showing no signs of falling back again.

"If we imagine that the Earth and similar bodies aren't there, no gravity is exerted on the apple. According to the impulse that accelerated its mass when thrown by Sir Isaac Newton's muscles, it will fly and fly without ever coming to a standstill. We know this effect as centrifugal force. Let's put the Earth back where it was, and now gravitation, which we've already mentioned, comes into play, to some extent counteracting centrifugal force. If the apple is far enough away from the Earth, the Earth's field of gravity has become too weak to bring it back, and it will disappear into space. If it's too close, the Earth's gravity will pull it back. Now, geostationary orbit, GEO in short, is found at the exact point where the Earth's force of attraction and centrifugal force balance one another out perfectly, at an altitude of 35,786 kilometers. From there, the apple can neither escape nor fall back down. Instead, it remains forever in GEO, as long as it circles the Earth synchronously with its rotational velocity, which is why a geostationary object always seems to stand above the same point."

The Earth spun before their eyes. Newton's apple seemed to stand motionlessly above the equator, fixed to an island in the Pacific. It wasn't really standing still, of course, it was circling the planet at a speed of 11,070 kilometers per hour, while the Earth rotated below it at 1,674 kilometers per hour, measured at the equator. The effect was startling. Just as the valve of a bicycle tire always stands above the same point on the hub when the wheel is turned, the satellite stayed in place, as if nailed up above the island.

"Geostationary orbit is ideal for a space elevator. First for the stable installation of the top floor in a stable position, secondly because of the fixed position of that floor. So once it was clear that you would just need to lower a cable 35,786 kilometers long from that point and anchor it to the ground, the question arose of what loads such a cable would have to support. The greatest tension would arise at the center of gravity, in the GEO itself, which meant that a cable would have to become either broader or more resilient toward the top."

Immediately just such a cable stretched between the island and the satellite, into which the apple had suddenly transmuted. Small cabins traveled up and down it.

"In this context a further consideration arose. Why not extend the cable beyond the center of gravity? To recap: in geostationary orbit gravity and centrifugal force balance one another out. Beyond it, the relationship between the two forces alters in favor of centrifugal force. A vehicle climbing the cable from the Earth needs to use only a tiny fraction of the energy that would be required to catapult it upward on a rocket. With increasing altitude the influence of gravity declines in favor of centrifugal force, which means that less and less energy is required until hardly any at all is needed in geostationary orbit. Now, if we imagine the cable being extended to an altitude of 143,800 kilometers, the vehicle could go charging beyond the geostationary orbit: it would be continuously accelerated and would actually *gain* in energy. A perfect springboard for interstellar travel, to Mars or anywhere else!"

The cabins were now transporting construction components into orbit, to be assembled into a space station. Rocky Rocket loaded up the cabins and started visibly sweating.

"One way or another the advantages of a space elevator were quite obvious. To carry a kilo of cargo load to an altitude of almost 36,000 kilometers, you no longer needed 50,000 dollars, just 200, and you could also use the elevator 365 days a year around the clock. Suddenly the idea of building gigantic space stations and adequately armored spaceships no longer seemed like a problem. The colonization of space became a tangible possibility, and inspired the British science-fiction author Arthur C. Clarke to write his novel *The Fountains of Paradise*, in which he describes the construction of space elevators like this."

"But why does the thing have to be built at the equator, of all places?" asked Rocky Rocket, wiping the sweat from his tip. "Why not at the North Pole or the South Pole, where it's nice and cool? And why in the middle of the stupid sea and not, for example in—" his eyes gleamed, he took a few dance steps and clicked his fingers "—Las Vegas?"

"I'm not sure if you seriously want to set off for space surrounded by penguins," Julian replied skeptically. "But it wouldn't work anyway. It's only at the equator that you can exploit the Earth's rotation to achieve a maximum of centrifugal force. It's only there that geostationary objects are possible." He thought for a moment. Then he said, "Listen, I want to explain something to you. Imagine you're a hammer-thrower."

The little rocket seemed to like the idea. He threw out his chest and tensed his muscles.

"Where's the hammer?" he crowed. "Bring it here!"

"It's not a real hammer these days, idiot, that's just its name. These days the hammer is a metal ball on a steel cable." Julian conjured the object out of nowhere and pressed the handle firmly into both of Rocky's hands. "Now you have to spin on your axis with your arms outstretched."

"Why?"

"To speed up the hammer. Let it spin."

"Heavy, isn't it?" Rocky groaned and pulled on the steel cable. He started to spin around, faster and faster. The cable tightened, the sphere lifted from the ground and reached a horizontal position.

"Can I throw it now?" panted Rocky.

"In a minute. For now you've just got to imagine you're not Rocky, you're the planet Earth. Your head is the North Pole, your feet are the South Pole. In between them is the axis that you're spinning around. If that's the case, what's the middle of your body?"

"Huh? What? The equator, obviously."

"Well done."

"Can I throw it now?"

"Wait. From the middle of your body, the equator, the hammer swings out, pulled tight by centrifugal force, just as the cable of the space elevator must be pulled tight."

"I get it. Can I do it?"

"Just one moment! Your hands are, in a sense, our Pacific islands, the metal sphere is the satellite or the space station in geostationary orbit. That clear?"

"It's clear."

"Okay. Now raise your hands. Go on spinning, but lift them high above your head."

Rocky followed the instructions. The steel cable immediately lost its tension and the ball came crashing down on the little rocket. He rolled his eyes, staggered, and fell to the ground.

"Do you think you get the principle?" Julian asked sympathetically.

Rocky waved a white flag.

"Then that's all sorted out. Practically every point on the equator is suitable for the space elevator, but there are a few things you have to take into account. The anchor station, the ground floor, so to speak, should be in an area that is free of storms, strong winds, and electrical discharges, with no air traffic and a generally clear sky. Most such places are found in the Pacific. One of them lies 550 kilometers to the west of Ecuador, and is the place where we are right now—the Isla de las Estrellas!"

Suddenly Julian was standing on the viewing terrace of the Stellar Island Hotel. Far outside the floating platform could be seen, and the two cables stretching from the inside of the Earth station into the endless blue.

"As you can see, we have built not one, but two elevators. Two cables stretch in parallel to the orbit. But even a few years ago it seemed doubtful whether we would ever experience this sight. Without the research work of Orley Enterprises the solution would probably have had to wait for several more years, and all this—" Julian spread his arms out "—would not exist."

The illusion vanished; Julian floated in bible-blackness.

"The problem was to find a material from which a cable 35,786 kilometers long could be manufactured. It had to be ultra-light and at the same time ultra-stable. Steel was out of the question. Even the highest quality steel cable would break under its own weight alone after only 30 or 40 kilometers. Some people came up with the idea of spiders' silk, given that it's four times more resilient than steel, but even that wouldn't have given the cable the requisite tensile strength, let alone the fact that for 35,786 kilometers of cable you'd need one hell of a lot of spiders. Frustrating! The anchor station, the space station, the cabins, all of that seemed manageable. But the concept seemed to founder on the cable—until the start of the millennium, when a revolutionary new material was discovered: carbon nanotubes."

A gleaming, three-dimensional grid structure began to rotate in the black. Its tubal form vaguely resembled the kind of bow net that people use for fishing.

"This object is actually ten thousand times thinner than a human hair. A tiny tube, constructed from carbon atoms in a honeycomb arrangement. The smallest of these tubes has a diameter of less than one nanometer. Its density is one sixth that of steel, which makes it very light, but at the same time it has a tensile strength of about 45 gigapascals, whereas at 2 gigapascals steel crumbles like a cookie. Over the years ways were found to bundle the tubes together and spin them into threads. In 2004, researchers in Cambridge produced a thread 100 meters long. But it seemed doubtful whether such threads could be woven into larger structures, particularly since experiments showed that the tensile strength of the thread declined dramatically in comparison with individual tubes. A kind of weaving flaw was introduced by missing carbon atoms, and besides, carbon is subject to oxidation. It erodes, so the threads needed to be coated."

Julian paused.

"For many years Orley Enterprises invested in research into the question of how this flaw could be remedied. Not only were we able to replace the missing atoms, we also managed to enhance the tensile strength of the cables to 65 gigapascals through cross-connections! We found ways to layer them and protect them against meteorites, space junk, natural oscillations, and the destructive effect of atomic oxygen. They are just one meter wide but flatter than a human hair, which is why they seem to disappear when you see them from the side. At a distance of 140,000 kilometers from Earth, where they end, we have connected them to a small asteroid, which acts as a counterweight. In the future we want to accelerate spaceships along that stretch of ribbon in such a way that they could fly to Mars, or beyond, without any notable outlay of energy." He smiled. "In geostationary orbit, however, we have built a space station unlike anything that has ever existed before: the OSS, the Orley Space Station, accessible within three hours by space elevator: research station, space station, and port! All manned and unmanned transfer flights to the Moon start from there. In turn, compressed helium-3 from the mining sites comes to OSS, is loaded onto the space elevator, and sent to Earth, so that the prospect of ten billion people being provided with unlimited supplies of clean and affordable energy is becoming more and more of a reality every day. We can now say that helium-3 has supplanted the age of fossil fuels, because the necessary fusion reactors required have also been developed to market maturity by Orley Enterprises. The significance of oil and gas has dramatically declined. The plundering of our home planet is coming to an end. Oil wars will be a thing of the past. None of this would have been possible without the development of the space elevator, but we have taken to its conclusion the dream that Konstantin Tsiolkovsky dreamed—and made it reality!"

A moment later everything was back—the viewing terrace, the slope of the Isla de las Estrellas, the floating platform in the sea. Julian Orley, with waving ponytail and sparkling eyes, stretched his arms to the sky as if to receive the eleventh Commandment.

"Twenty years ago, when Orley Enterprises began thinking about the construction of space elevators, I promised the world that I would build it an elevator into the future. Into a future that our parents and grandparents would never have dared to dream of. The best future we have ever had. And we have built it! In a few days you will travel on it to the OSS. You will see the Earth as a whole, our unique and wonderful home—and you will be amazed as you turn your gaze to the stars, to our home of tomorrow."

To dramatic background music, on columns of red light, two shimmering cabins rose from the cylindrical station building on the sea platform and shot up into the sky. Julian threw back his head and gazed after them.

"Welcome," he said, "to the future."

Anchorage, Alaska, USA

Not again, thought Gerald Palstein. Not the same accusation, the same question, for the fourth time.

"Perhaps it would have been cleverer, Mr. Palstein, to keep on the people you are now throwing out of their workplaces and keep them otherwise engaged instead of digging up the last intact ecosystems on Earth in an obsessive quest for oil. Wasn't it a grave mistake by your department to install the facility in the first place, as if energy sources like helium-3 and solar power were an irrelevance?"

Suspicion, incomprehension, malice. The press conference that EMCO was holding to bury the Alaska project had assumed the character of a tribunal, with him as whipping boy. Palstein tried not to let his exhaustion show.

"From the perspective of the time we acted completely responsibly," he said. "In 2015, helium-3 was a crazy dream. The United States of America couldn't base their energy policy purely on the off-chance of a technological stroke of genius—"

"In which you now want to participate," the journalist interrupted. "A bit late, don't you think?"

"Of course, but perhaps I could refer you to a few things I thought were familiar to both of us. On the one hand I wasn't yet presiding over the strategy sector of EMCO in 2015—"

"But you were its deputy manager."

"The final decision for what was to be built was my predecessor's responsibility. But you're right. I supported the Alaska project because there was no way of telling whether either the space elevator or fusion technology would work as predicted. So the project was clearly in the interest of the American nation."

"Or in the interest of a few profiteers."

"Let's reconsider the situation. At the start of the millennium our energy policy was aimed at freeing us from dependency on the Middle East. Particularly since we were forced to accept that the one who decides to fight a war doesn't necessarily win the peace. Going into Iraq was madness. The American market couldn't profit from it nearly as much as we had hoped. We had planned to send our people down there and take over the oil business; instead we saw American soldiers coming back in coffins week after week, so we hesitated until other people had divided up the cake between themselves. Except that after even conservative Republicans had reached the conclusion that George W. Bush had been a hugely dangerous fool, who had ruined both our economy and our standing in the world, no one really felt like marching into Iran carrying guns."

"Do you mean you regret that the option of another war was off the table?"

"Of course not." Incredible! The woman just wasn't listening. "I was always vehemently opposed to war, and still am today. You just have to understand what a jam the United States was in. Asia's hunger for raw materials, Russia's gamble on resources, our disappointing performance in the Middle East, one great big disaster. Then 2015, the uprising in Saudi Arabia. The stars and stripes burning in the streets of Riyadh, the whole folklore of the Islamist seizure of power, except that we couldn't just throw those guys out because China had lent them money and arms. An official military intervention in Saudi Arabia would have amounted to a declaration of war on Beijing. You know yourself how things look down there now. Nobody might be interested in it today, but in those days it would have been reckless to depend entirely on Arab oil. We had to take alternatives into consideration. One of those lay in the sea, the other in the exploitation of oil sand and shale, the third in the resources of Alaska."

Another journalist put her hand up. Loreena Keowa, environmental activist with Native American roots, and reporter-in-chief for Greenwatch. Her reports were hugely popular on the net. She was critical, but Palstein knew that under certain circumstances he could see her as an ally.

"I don't think anyone can blame a company for declaring a corpse to be dead," she said. "Even if it means a loss of jobs. I just wonder what EMCO has to offer the people who are now losing their workplaces. Perhaps there's no point crying over spilt milk, but didn't the refusal of ExxonMobil to invest in alternative energies lead to their present disastrous situation?"

"That is correct."

"I remember Shell pointing out twenty years ago that it was an energy company and not an oil company, while ExxonMobil insisted that it didn't need a foothold in the alternative energies. The end of the oil age, which many saw on the horizon, was, literally, a *widespread misunderstanding*."

"That assessment was clearly incorrect."

"And we are feeling the aftereffects all the more painfully for that. Perhaps it's true that no one could have predicted a turnaround in the energy market on the present scale. What is clear is that EMCO isn't in a position to employ its people in alternative fields, because there are no alternative fields."

"That's exactly what we want to change," said Palstein patiently.

"I know *you* want to change it, Gerald." Keowa grinned crookedly. "But your critics see your planned involvement in Orley Enterprises as smoke and mirrors."

"Incorrect." Palstein smiled back. "You see, I don't want to make excuses for anything, but in 2005 I was responsible for drilling projects in Ecuador for ConocoPhillips, and only switched to strategic management in 2009. At that time the American oil and gas business was dominated by ExxonMobil. Prognoses about alternative energies were pretty much divided on either side of the Atlantic. ExxonMobil invested in the Arabian Gulf and tried to take over Russian oil companies, backed high growth rates as the result of rising oil prices, and disregarded things like ethics and sustainability. In Europe it looked quite different. By the end of the nineties Royal Dutch Shell had created a new commercial division for renewable energies. BP had been a bit shrewder, in opening up deep-sea projects and becoming involved in Russian projects, while at the same time using slogans like 'Beyond Petroleum' and diversifying their commercial areas wherever they could."

Palstein knew that the younger journalists in particular were short of information. He outlined how the process of consolidation had peaked immediately before the seizure of power by the Saudi Islamists, when Royal Dutch Shell was absorbed into BP, producing UK Energies, while in America ExxonMobil had merged with Chevron and ConocoPhillips into EMCO.

"In 2017 I assumed the position of deputy director within the strategic sector of EMCO. On the very first day a press release landed on my table, saying that Orley Enterprises had made a breakthrough in the development of a space elevator. I suggested entering negotiations with Julian Orley for a participation in Orley Energy. I also recommended that we purchase shares in Warren Locatelli's Light-years or, better still, buy the whole company. Locatelli's market leadership in photovoltaics didn't just come out of the blue; he would still have been open to negotiation in 2015."

He saw approval on their faces. Keowa nodded.

"I know, Gerald. You tried to steer the EMCO juggernaut in the direction of renewable energies. Everybody knows that you are highly critical about your own sector. But they also know that none of your suggestions has been taken on board."

"That is regrettably the case. The old Exxon management who still had EMCO in their clutches were only interested in our core products. It was only when the oil market went into free fall, when even the hard-liners had to step aside and the new chairman put me in charge of strategic management, that I was able to act. EMCO has been transformed in the meantime. Since 2020 we have done everything we can to make up for the shortcomings of the past. We have moved into photovoltaics, into wind and water power. Perhaps people aren't generally aware, but we are in a position to transfer our staff into future-oriented commercial sectors. Except that when mistakes have been made for decades, we can't sort them out overnight."

"Can it still be repaired?"

Palstein leaned back in his chair. Basically he didn't need to reply. Helium-3 was establishing itself as the energy source of the future, there was no doubt about that. Orley's fusion reactors were working reliably around the clock, and in terms of the balance between energy and environment everything was fine; the transport of the element from the Moon to the Earth was no longer a problem. Palstein's sector, however, seemed to be traumatized. The oil companies had reckoned with everything—except the end of the oil age, *without* oil and gas running out! Not even the boldest visionaries of Royal Dutch Shell or BP had been able to imagine that their sector could be wiped out so quickly by an alternative energy source. Only ten years before, UK Energies had calculated the market share of alternative technologies at thirty percent, nuclear energy included. Equally, it had been clear to everyone that most of those technologies could only be offered at competitive prices by companies operating on a global level. The photovoltaic sector, for example, got a good market share in sunny countries, but it required complex logistical infrastructures. And who was capable of doing that, if not the big multinational oil companies, who only had to make sure that they could make a quick getaway and switch to a different area when it came to the crunch?

That most of the companies weren't even ready to make this shift was down to prognoses about when oil and gas would actually run dry. Like Jehovah's Witnesses constantly changing the date of the end of the world, throughout the 1980s various prophets of doom had predicted that the oil age would come to an end in 2010; in the 1990s it was 2030; at the start of the new millennium, in spite of increased consumption, it was 2050. But now it was clear that the existing reserves would last until 2080, even though production had already peaked, while the resources available suggested an even longer life. There was only one point on which they had all agreed: there would never be cheap oil again. Never again.

But in fact it had become *very* cheap.

So cheap, in fact, that the sector had started to feel like the Incredible Shrinking Man, for whom a house spider represented a deadly threat. The most likely survivors were those who had invested in renewable energies early on. UK Energies had succeeded in reversing their fortunes. The French Total group had diversified enough to survive, even though personnel downsizing was rife. High-efficiency solar technology, as developed by Locatelli's Light-years, was considered the most trustworthy fuel, alongside helium-3, and there was also money to be made in wind power. On the other hand the Norwegian association

Statoil Norsk Hydro was in its death-throes, while China's CNPC and Russia's Lukoil gazed dispiritedly into an oil-free future, clearly in culpable ignorance of the now legendary statement of Ahmed al Jamanis, the former Saudi Arabian oil minister: "The Stone Age didn't end for want of stones."

The problem wasn't so much that gasoline wasn't needed anymore: it was used for plastics, fertilizers and cosmetics; in the textile industry; in food production; and in pharmaceutical research. Orley's newfangled fusion reactors were still thin on the ground; most cars ran on combustion engines, airplanes were fueled with kerosene. The United States was the chief beneficiary of the new resource. The global switch to a helium-3-based energy economy was still years away, that much was clear.

But not decades away.

The mere fact that the so-called aneutronic fusion of helium-3 with deuterium worked in reactors had sent already sickly oil prices through the floor. At the end of the first decade it had turned out that people were *not* in fact prepared to pay just any sum for oil. If it became too expensive, their ecological conscience sprang to life; they saved electricity and encouraged the development of alternative energies. The notion popular among speculators that the barrel price might be driven up by panic buying had not become reality. There was also the fact that most countries had set aside strategic reserves and had not had to make any new purchases, and that new generations of cars had batteries with generous storage capacities and filled up at sockets on environmentally friendly electricity which, thanks to helium-3, would soon be available in ample quantities. The United States of America, which had turned a deep dark green since Barack Obama's terms as president, was urging an international agreement on emission reduction, and had discovered the devil in CO_2. A few years after the first helium-3-fueled fusion reactor had gone live, it was also clear that astronomically high profits could be achieved with environmental-oriented thinking. In the course of these developments, EMCO had slipped in the ranking of the world's biggest mineral-oil companies from first place to third, while the entire sector was threatening to shrink to a micro verse. Atrophied by ignorance, EMCO increasingly found itself stumbling, like King Kong just before the fall and, dimly aware that it was doomed to failure, clutching around for something to hold on to, and grasping only air.

Now they'd lost Alaska too.

The drilling plans won through years spent battling against the environmental lobby had to be abandoned because no one was interested in the huge natural gas deposits there any longer. This press conference was barely different from the one they had had to hold in Alberta, Canada, a few weeks before, where the exploitation of oil sand was coming to an end, an expensive and environmentally harmful procedure that had given the conservationists nightmares for ages, but which had been feasible as long as the world was still crying out for oil like a baby for milk. What use was it that certain representatives of the Canadian government shared EMCO's concerns, when two-thirds of the world's oil resources were stored in this sand, 180 million barrels on Canadian soil alone? The overwhelming majority of Canadians were glad that it would soon be all over. In Alberta, mining had permanently destroyed rivers and marshes, the northern forest, the complete ecosystem. In view of this, Canada had not been able to stick to its international obligations. Greenhouse emissions had risen; the signed protocols were so much waste paper.

"It can be repaired," said Palstein firmly. "We're about to conclude negotiations with Orley Enterprises. I promise you, we will be the first oil company to be involved in the helium-3 business, and we are also in discussion about possible alliances with strategists from other companies."

"What concrete offers do Orley Enterprises have to make to you?"

"There are a few things."

The man wouldn't let go. "The problem with the multinationals is that they haven't a clue about the fusion business. I mean, some of the companies have pounced on photovoltaics, on wind and water power, bioethanol and all that stuff, but fusion technology and space travel—you'll forgive me, but that's not exactly your area of expertise."

Palstein smiled.

"I can tell you that at present Julian Orley is looking for investors for a second space elevator, not least to develop the infrastructure for the transport of helium-3. Of course we're talking about vast amounts of money here. But we've got that money. The question is how we want to use it. My sector is in a state of shock at the moment. Should have seen it coming, you might say, so what do you think we should do? Go down in flames, feeling sorry for ourselves? EMCO isn't going to achieve supremacy in solar energy, however much we might try to get a foothold in it. Other people are historically ahead of us there. So either we can watch one market after another breaking away until our funds are devoured by social programs, or we put the money into a second elevator and organize logistical processes on the Earth. As I have said, discussions are almost concluded, the contracts are about to be signed."

"When's that due?"

"At the moment Orley is staying with a group of potential investors on the Isla de las Estrellas. From there he will go on to OSS and the opening of Gaia. Yeah." Palstein shrugged in a gesture somewhere between melancholy and fatalism. "I was supposed to be there. Julian Orley isn't just our future business partner, he's also a personal friend. I'm sorry not to be able to take this journey with him, but I don't need to remind you what happened in Canada."

With these words he had rung the bell for round two. Everyone began talking at the same time.

"Have they discovered who shot you?"

"Given the state of your health, how will you get through the coming weeks? Did the injury—"

"What are we to make of conjectures that the attack might have something to do with your decision to put EMCO and Orley Enterprises—"

"Is it true that a furious oil worker—"

"You've made loads of enemies with your criticism of abuses in your sector. Might any of them have—"

"How are you generally, Gerald?" asked Keowa.

"Thanks, Loreena, not bad under the circumstances." Palstein raised his left hand until silence returned. His right arm had been in a sling for four weeks. "One at a time. I'll answer all your questions, but I would ask you to show understanding if I avoid speculation. At the moment I can say nothing more except that I myself would love to know who did it. All I know for certain is that I was incredibly lucky. If I hadn't stumbled on the steps up to the podium, the bullet would have got me in the head. It wasn't a warning, as some people thought, it was a botched execution. Without any doubt at all, they wanted to kill me."

"How are you protecting yourself at the moment?"

"With optimism." Palstein smiled. "Optimism and a bulletproof vest, to tell you the truth. But what use is that against shots to the head? Am I supposed to go into hiding? No! Peter Tschaikowsky said you can't tiptoe your way through life just because you're afraid of death."

"To put it another way," said Keowa, "who would benefit if you disappeared from the scene?"

"I don't know. If anyone wanted to stop us merging with Orley Enterprises, he would destroy EMCO's biggest and perhaps only chance of a quick recovery."

"Maybe that's the plan," a voice called out. "Destroying EMCO."

"The market's become too small for the oil companies," said someone else. "In fact the company's death would make sense in terms of economic evolution. Someone eliminating the competition in order to—"

"Or else someone wants to get at Orley through you. If EMCO—"

"What's the mood like in your own company? Whose toes did you tread on, Gerald?"

"Nobody's!" Palstein shook his head firmly. "The board approved every aspect of my restructuring model, and top of the list is our commitment to Orley. You're fumbling around in the dark with assumptions like that. Talk to the authorities. They're following every lead."

"And what does your gut tell you?"

"About the perpetrator?"

"Yes. Any suspects in mind?"

Palstein was silent for a moment. Then he said, "Personally I can only imagine it was an act of revenge. Someone who's desperate, who's lost his job, possibly lost everything, and is now projecting his hatred onto me. That I could understand. I'm fully aware of where we are right now. A lot of people are worried about their livelihoods, people who had confidence in us in better years." He paused. "But let's be honest, the better times are only just beginning. Perhaps I'm the wrong man to say this, but a world that can satisfy its energy needs with environmentally friendly and renewable resources makes the oil economy look like a thing of the past. I can only stress again and again that we will really do everything we can to secure EMCO's future. And thus the future of our workforce!"

An hour later Gerald Palstein was resting in his suite, his head cradled on his left arm, his legs stretched out as if it would have taken too much effort to cross them. Dog-tired and raddled, he lay on the bedspread and stared up at the canopy of the four-poster bed. His delegation was staying in the Sheraton Anchorage, one of the finer addresses in a city not exactly blessed with architectural masterpieces. Anything of any historical substance had fallen victim to the 1964 earthquake. The Good Friday earthquake, as it was known. The most violent hiccup that seismologists had ever recorded on American territory. Now there was just one really beautiful building, and that was the hospital.

After a while he got up, went into the bathroom, splashed cold water into his face with his free hand and looked at himself in the mirror. A droplet hung trembling on the tip of his nose. He flicked it away. Paris, his wife, liked to say she had fallen in love with his eyes, which were a mysterious earthy brown, big and doe-like, with thick eyelashes like a woman's. His gaze was filled with perpetual melancholy. Too beautiful, too intense for his friendly but unremarkable face. His forehead was high and smooth, his hair cut short. Recently his slender body had developed a certain aesthetic quality, the consequence of a lack of sleep, irregular meals, and the hospital stay in which the bullet had been removed from his shoulder four weeks previously. Palstein knew he should have eaten more, except that he barely had an appetite. Most of what was put in front of him he left. He was paralyzed by an unsettlingly stubborn feeling of exhaustion, as if a virus had taken hold of him, one that occasional snoozes on the plane weren't enough to shake.

He dried his face, came out of the bathroom, and stepped to the window. A pale, cold summer sun glittered on the sea. To the north, the snow-covered peaks of the Alaska chain loomed into the distance. Not far from the hotel he could see the former ConocoPhillips office. Now it bore the EMCO logo, in defiance of the change that was already under way. There were still office spaces to rent in the Peak Oilfield Service Company building. UK Energies had put a branch of their solar division in the former BP headquarters and rented out the rest to a travel company, and here too there were many empty spaces. Everything was going down the drain. Some logos had completely disappeared, such as Anadarko Oil, Doyon Drilling, and Marathon Oil Company. The place was threatening to lose its position as the most economically successful state in the United States. Since the seventies, more than 80 percent of all state income had flowed from the fossil fuels business into the Alaska Permanent Fund, which was supposed to benefit all the inhabitants. Support that they would soon have to do without. In the mid-term, the region was left only with metals, fishing, wood, and a bit of fur farming. Oil and gas too, of course, but only on a very limited scale, and at prices so low that the stuff would have been better off left in the ground.

The journalists and activists that he had been dealing with over the past few hours—and who reproached him now for having gotten involved in the extractions in the first place—certainly weren't representing public opinion when they cheered the end of the oil economy. In fact helium-3 had met with a very muted response in Alaska, just as enthusiasm on the Persian Gulf was notably low-key. The sheikhs imagined themselves being thrown back on the bleak desert existence of former years, their territory returning to the scorpions and sand beetles. The specter of impoverishment stripped the potentates of Kuwait, Bahrain, and Qatar of their sleep. Hardly anyone seriously wanted to go to Dubai now. Beijing had abandoned its support of the Saudi Arabian Islamists; the United States seemed to have forgotten all about North Africa; in Iraq, Sunnis and Shi'ites went on slaughtering each other in time-honored fashion; Iran provoked unease with its nuclear programs, bared its teeth in all directions, and tried to get close to China, which apart from America was the only nation in the world mining helium-3, albeit in vanishingly small quantities. The Chinese didn't have a space elevator, and didn't know how to build one either. No one apart from the Americans had such a thing, and Julian Orley sat on the patents like a broody hen, which was why China had fallen back entirely on traditional rocket technology, at devastating expense.

Palstein looked at his watch. He had to get over to the EMCO building, a meeting was about to start. It would go on until late as usual. He phoned the business center and asked to be put through to the Stellar Island Hotel on the Isla de las Estrellas. It was three hours later there, and a good 68 degrees warmer. A better place than Anchorage. Palstein would rather have been anywhere else than Anchorage.

He wanted at least to wish Julian a pleasant journey.

Isla de las Estrellas, Pacific Ocean

Going inside the volcano might have been spectacular, but coming out was a big disappointment. Once the lights had come on, they left the cave via a straight and well-lit corridor which aroused the suspicion that the whole mountain was actually made of scaffolding and paper mâché. It was wide enough to allow a hundred panicking, trampling, and thrashing people to escape. After about 150 meters it led to a side wing of the Stellar Island Hotel.

Chuck Donoghue pushed his way through to stand next to Julian.

"My respect," he bellowed. "Not bad."

"Thanks."

"And this is how you found the cave? Come on! You didn't help a bit? No demolition charges anywhere?"

"Just for the evacuation routes."

"Incredibly lucky. Of course you realize, my boy, that I'll have to steal this one! Haha! No, don't worry, I still have enough ideas of my own. My God, how many hotels have I built in my life? How many hotels!"

"Thirty-two."

"You're right," Donoghue mumbled in amazement.

"Yes, and maybe one day you might be building another one on the Moon," Julian grinned. "That's why you're here, old man."

"I see!" Donoghue laughed even louder. "And I thought you'd invited me because you liked me."

At sixty-five the hotel mogul was the oldest member of the group, five years older than Julian, although Julian looked ten years younger. The insignificant age difference didn't keep Donoghue from jovially addressing the richest man in the world as "my boy."

"Of course I like you," Julian said cheerfully as they followed Lynn to the elevators. "But more than anything else I want to show you *my* hotels so that you'll put *your* money into them.—Oh, and by the way, do you know the one about the man doing the survey?"

"Tell me!"

"A guy gets asked, what would you do if you had two possibilities?—A: You spend all night having sex with your wife. B:—B, says the man, B!"

It was a crap little joke, and thus exactly right for Chucky, who stayed behind laughing to tell Aileen. Julian didn't have to turn around to see her face, as if she'd just sucked on a lemon. The Donoghues ruled over thirty of the most imposing, expensive, and trashy hotels of all time; they had built various casinos, ran an international booking agency through which global stars passed with great regularity—artistes, singers, dancers, and animal trainers, and of course you could, if you wished, also book shows in which nothing was left to the imagination. But Aileen, good, fat, cake-baking Aileen, opted for good old southern prudery, as if dozens of showgirls weren't dancing across the stages of Las Vegas every night, breasts bouncing, girls who had contracts that bore her signature. She placed great emphasis on piety, gun ownership, good food, good deeds, and the death penalty if all else failed, and sometimes when it didn't. She put morality before everything else. Nonetheless, she would appear for dinner crammed into a little dress so tight it was embarrassing, to collect compliments from the younger men for her laser-firmed cleavage. She would launch her usual nannying campaign and pass on the silly joke with lots of tittering and snorting, before getting drinks for everyone, and her other side would fight its way through, marked by a genuinely felt concern for the welfare of all God's creatures, which made it possible not only to put up with Aileen Donoghue, but even somehow to like her.

The glass elevator cabins filled up with people and chatter. After a short trip they discharged the group onto the viewing terrace, beneath a starry sky worthy of a Hollywood movie. With regal dignity an old and beautiful lady in evening dress was directing half a dozen waiters to the guests. Champagne and cocktails were handed out, binoculars distributed. A jazz quartet played "Fly Me To The Moon."

"Everyone over here," Lynn called cheerfully. "To me! Look to the east."

The guests happily followed her instructions. Out on the platform yet more lights had been lit, glowing fingers reaching into the night sky. As tiny as ants, people were seen walking around among the structures. A big ship, apparently a freighter, lay massively on a calm sea.

"Dear friends." Julian stepped forward, a glass in his hand. "I didn't let you see the whole show earlier. In another version you would also have met the OSS and Gaia, but that one is intended for visitors without the advantage of what you will experience. Relatives of travelers, spending a few days on the island before going back home. To you, however, I wanted to demonstrate the elevator. For the rest you won't need films, because you will see it *with your own eyes*! You will never forget the two weeks ahead of you, I promise you that!"

Julian showed his perfect teeth. There was applause, scattered at first, then everyone clapped enthusiastically. Miranda Winter yelled, "Oh yeah!" Glowing with pride, Lynn went and joined her father.

"Before we invite everyone to join us for dinner, we have a little taste of your imminent trip." She glanced at her watch. "In the next few minutes the two cabins are expected back from orbit. Both will be bringing back to Earth, among other things, compressed helium-3 that was loaded onto them on OSS. I think it might be an idea to throw your heads back now, and not just to drink—"

"Although I advise you do that too," said Julian, raising his glass to everyone.

"Of course," Lynn laughed. "What he hasn't yet told you, in fact, is that on OSS we will drastically reduce alcohol consumption."

"How regrettable." Bernard Tautou pulled a face, drank his glass down in one and beamed at her. "So we should make provision."

"I thought your passion was water?" teased Mukesh Nair.

"*Mais oui!* Particularly if it's topped up with alcohol."

"'These vessels here from which we drink / When emptied their appeal does shrink,'" declaimed Eva Borelius with a superior smile.

"*Pardon?*"

"Wilhelm Busch, you wouldn't know him."

"Can you actually get a hangover in zero gravity?" Olympiada Rogacheva asked timidly, prompting her husband to turn away from her and stare pointedly up at the stars. Miranda Winter snapped her fingers like a schoolgirl:

"And what if you throw up in zero gravity?"

"Then your puke will find you wherever you are," Evelyn Chambers explained.

"Sphere formation," nodded Walo Ögi and formed a hypothetical ball of vomit with both hands. "The puke forms itself into a ball."

"I'm pretty sure it spreads," said Karla Kramp.

"Yes, so that we all get some," Borelius nodded. "Nice topic, by the way. Perhaps we should—"

"There!" cried Rebecca Hsu. "Up there!"

All eyes followed her outstretched hand. Two little points of light had started moving in the firmament. For a while they seemed to be heading to the southeast on orbital paths, except that at the same time they were getting bigger and bigger, a sight that contradicted everything that anyone had seen before. Clearly something had gone dimensionally awry. And then, all of a sudden, everyone worked out that the bodies were dropping from space in a perfect vertical. As if the stars were climbing down to them.

"They're coming," Sushma Nair whispered reverently.

Binoculars were yanked up. After a few minutes, even without magnification, two long structures could be made out, one slightly higher than the other, looking a bit like space shuttles, except that they were both standing upright and their undersides ended in broad, plate-like slabs. The conically pointed tips were brightly illuminated, and navigation lights darted evenly as heartbeats along the sides of the cylindrical bodies. The cabins approached the platform at great speed, and the lower they came the harder the air vibrated, as if stirred by giant dynamos. Julian registered with satisfaction that even his son wasn't immune to the fascination. Amber's eyes were as wide as if she were waiting for her Christmas presents.

"That's wonderful," she said quietly.

"Yes." Julian nodded. "It's technology, and it's still a miracle. 'Any sufficiently advanced technology is indistinguishable from magic.' Arthur C. Clarke. Great man!"

Tim said nothing.

And suddenly Julian was aware of the bitter taste of repressed rage in his mouth. He simply couldn't work out what was up with the boy. If Tim didn't want to take the job that awaited him at Orley Enterprises that was his business. Everyone had to go his own way, even if Julian couldn't really understand that there were other paths to take apart from a future in the company, but okay, fine. Except—*what the hell* had he actually done to Tim?

Then everything happened very quickly.

An audible gasp from all the onlookers introduced the final phase. For a moment it looked as if the cabins would crash into the circular terminal like projectiles and pull the whole platform into the sea, then they abruptly slowed down, first one, then the other, and decelerated until they entered the circle of the space terminal and disappeared into it, one after the other. Again there was applause, broken by cries of "Bravo!" Heidrun came and stood by Finn O'Keefe and whistled on two fingers.

"Still sure you want to get into one of those?" he asked.

She looked at him mockingly. "And you?"

"Of course."

"Boaster!"

"Someone will have to stand by your husband when you start clawing the walls."

"We'll just see who's scared, shall we?"

"If it's me," O'Keefe grinned, "remember your promise."

"When did I ever promise you anything?"

"A little while ago. You were going to hold my hand."

"Oh yeah." The corners of Heidrun's mouth twitched with amusement. For a moment she seemed to be thinking seriously about it. "I'm sorry, Finn. You know, I'm boring and old-fashioned. In my film the woman falls off her horse and lets the man save her from the Indians. Screaming her head off, of course."

"Shame. I've never acted in that kind of movie."

"You should have a word with your agent."

She gracefully raised a hand, ran a finger gently over his cheek and walked away. O'Keefe watched her as she joined Walo. Behind him a voice said:

"Pathetic, Finn. Total knock-back."

He turned around and found himself looking into the beautiful, haughty face of Momoka Omura. They knew each other from the parties that O'Keefe avoided like the plague. If he did have to go to one, she inevitably bumped into him, as she recently had at Jack Nicholson's eighty-eighth birthday party.

"Shouldn't you be filming?" he said.

"I didn't end up in the mass market like you did, if that's what you mean." She looked at her fingernails. A mischievous smile played around her lips. "But I could give you some lessons in flirting if you like."

"Very kind of you." He smiled back. "Except you're not supposed to get off with your teacher."

"Only theoretically, you idiot. Do you seriously think I'd let you anywhere near me?"

"You wouldn't?" He turned away. "That's reassuring."

Momoka threw her head back and snorted. The second woman to have walked away from him in the course of only a few minutes, she strutted over to Locatelli, who was noisily talking shop with Marc Edwards and Mimi Parker about fusion reactors, and linked arms with him. O'Keefe shrugged and joined Julian, who was standing with Carl Hanna, Rebecca Hsu, his daughter, and the Rogachevs.

"But how do you get the cabin all the way up there?" the Taiwanese woman wanted to know. She looked overexcited and scatterbrained. "It can hardly *float* up the cable."

"Didn't you see the presentation?" Rogachev asked ironically.

"We're just introducing a new perfume," said Rebecca, as if that explained everything. And in fact for half the show she'd been staring at the display on her pocket computer, correcting marketing plans, and had missed the explanation of the principle. At first sight it would look as if the slabs that formed the cabin sterns were sending out bright red beams, but in fact it was the other way around. The undersides of the plates were covered with photovoltaic cells, and the beams were emitted by huge lasers inside the terminal. The energy produced by the impact set the propulsion system in motion, six pairs of interconnected wheels per cabin, with the belt stretched between them. When the wheels on one side were set in motion, those on the other side joined in automatically in the opposite direction, and the elevator climbed up the belt.

"It gets faster and faster," Julian explained. "After only 100 meters it reaches—"

There was a beep from his jacket. He frowned and dug out his phone.

"What's up?"

"Forgive the disturbance, sir." Someone from the switchboard. "A call for you."

"Can't it wait?"

"It's Gerald Palstein, sir."

"Oh. Of course." Julian smiled apologetically at everybody. "Could I neglect you for a moment? Rebecca, don't run away. I'll explain the principle to you every hour, or ideally more often, if that'll make you happy."

He dashed off into a little room behind the bar, stuck his phone into a console and projected the image onto a bigger screen.

"Hi, Julian," said Palstein.

"Gerald. Where in heaven's name are you?"

"Anchorage. We've buried the Alaska project. Didn't I tell you about that?"

The EMCO manager looked exhausted. They had last seen each other a few weeks before the attempt on his life. Palstein was calling from a hotel room. A window in the background gave a glimpse of snow-covered mountains under a pale, cold sky.

"No, you did," said Julian. "But that was before you were shot. Do you really have to do this to yourself?"

"No big deal." Palstein waved the idea away. "I have a hole in my shoulder, not my head. That kind of injury lets me travel, although unfortunately not to the Moon. Regrettably."

"And how did it go?"

"Let's say Alaska's preparing itself with some dignity for the rebirth of the age of the trapper. Of all the union representatives I've met there, most of them would have liked to finish the job that gunman in Canada fluffed."

"Just don't beat yourself up! Nobody's been as hard on his sector as you have, and from now on they *will* listen to you. Did you tell them about your planned allegiance?"

"The press release is out. So yes, it came up."

"And? How was it received?"

"As an attempt to get ourselves back in action. At least most people are being kind about it."

"That's great! As soon as I get back, let's sign the contracts."

"Other people think it's a smoke screen." Palstein hesitated. "Let's not kid ourselves, Julian. It's a great help to us that you're getting us on board—"

"It's a help to *us*!"

"But it's not going to work any miracles. We've been concentrating on gasoline for far too long. Well, the main thing for us is to avoid competition. I'd rather have a future as a middle-sized company than go bankrupt as a giant. The consequences would be terrible. There's nothing you can do about your downward slide, but you may be able to prevent the crash. Or cushion it at least."

"If anyone can do it, you can. God, Gerald! It's a real shame you can't be with us."

"Next time. Who took my place, by the way?"

"A Canadian investor called Carl Hanna. Heard of him?"

"Hanna?" Palstein frowned. "To be quite honest—"

"Doesn't matter. I didn't know him either until a few months ago. One of those people who got rich on the quiet."

"Interested in space travel?"

"That's exactly what makes him so interesting! You don't have to make the subject tempting for him. He wants to invest in space travel anyway. Unfortunately he spent his youth in New Delhi and feels obliged to sponsor India's moon program because of his old connection." Julian grinned. "So I'll have to make a big effort to win the guy over."

"And the rest of the gang?"

"I'm pretty sure that Locatelli will come up with an eight-figure sum. His megalomania alone dictates that he needs a monument in space, and our facilities are equipped with his systems. Involvement would be only logical. The Donoghues and Marc Edwards have promised me major sums on the quiet, the only issue is how many zeroes there are going to be at the end. There's a really interesting Swiss guy, Walo Ögi. Lynn and I met his wife two years ago in Zermatt, she took some pictures of me. Then we have Eva Borelius on board, perhaps you know her, German stem-cell research—"

"Am I right in thinking that you've simply copied out the Forbes List?"

"It wasn't exactly like that. Borelius Pharmaceuticals was recommended to me by our strategic management team, and so was Bernard Tautou, the water tsar from Suez. Another guy whose ego just needs massaging. Or there's Mukesh Nair—"

"Ah, Mr. Tomato." Palstein raised his eyebrows appreciatively.

"Yes, nice guy. But he has no stake in space travel. It doesn't do us much good that he's rich, so we've had to bring a few extra criteria into play. Wanting to give humanity a more viable future, for example. Even the anti-space-travel brigade stand shoulder to shoulder on that one: Nair with food, Tautou with water, Borelius with medicine, me with energy. That unites us, and it's encouraging the others. And then there are privately wealthy individuals like Finn O'Keefe, Evelyn Chambers, and Miranda Winter—"

"Miranda Winter? My God!"

"What, why not? She doesn't know what to do with all her money, bless her, so I'm inviting her to find out. Believe me, the mixture is perfect. Guys like O'Keefe, Evelyn, and Miranda really loosen the gang up, it makes it really sexy, and in the end I'll have them all on my side!

Rebecca Hsu, with all her luxury brands, isn't that interested in energy, but she goes for space travel as if she'd come up with the idea all by herself. She's completely fixated on the idea that Moët et Chandon will be drunk on the Moon in the future. Did you ever look at her portfolio? Kenzo, Dior, Louis Vuitton, L'Oréal, Dolce & Gabbana, Lacroix, Hennessy, not to mention her own brands, Boom Bang and the other stuff. As far as she's concerned we're a unique and inimitable brand. I could fund half of the OSS Grand with the advertising contracts I'm signing with her alone."

"Didn't you invite that Russian, too? Rogachev?"

Julian grinned. "He's my very personal little challenge. If I manage to get him to put *his* billions into *my* projects, I'll do a cartwheel in zero gravity."

"Moscow are hardly going to let him go."

"Wrong! They'll practically force him into it if they think they can do business with me."

"Which will only be the case if you build them a space elevator. Until that happens, they'll look on Rogachev as if his money's flowing into American space travel through your project."

"Nonsense. It'll look as if it's flowing into a lucrative business, and that's exactly what it will be doing! I'm not America, Gerald!"

"*I* know that. Rogachev, on the other hand—"

"He knows it too. A guy like that isn't stupid, after all! There isn't a country in the world today that's capable of paying for space travel with its own funds. Do you really think that cheerful community of states that worked so harmoniously to set up the ISS was stirred by a spirit of international fraternity? Bullshit! None of them had the money to do it alone. It was the only way to send anything up into space without E.T. laughing himself sick. To do that they *had* to pull strings and swap information, with the result that they ended up with squat! Funds were short for everything, all kinds of crap was budgeted for, just not space travel. It was private individuals who changed that, after Burt Rutan flew the first commercial suborbital flight on Space Ship One in 2004, and who financed that? The United States of America? NASA?"

"I know," Palstein sighed. "It was Paul Allen."

"Exactly! Paul Allen, co-founder of Microsoft. Entrepreneurs showed the politicians how to get things done more quickly and efficiently. Like you, when your sector still meant something. You made presidents and toppled governments. Now it's people like me paying off that pile of bank-breakers, doomsayers, and nationalists. We have more money, more know-how, better people, a more creative climate. Without Orley Enterprises there would be no space elevator, no Moon tourism, reactor research wouldn't be where it is today, nothing would. Even though it's not exactly coming down with money, NASA would still have to justify itself to some incompetent regulatory agency or other every time it broke wind. We're not regulated at all, not by any government in the world. And why? Because we're not obliged to any government. Believe me, even Rogachev gets *that* one."

"Even so, you shouldn't just go handing him the OSS user's handbook. He might get it into his head to copy it."

Julian chuckled. Then he grew suddenly serious.

"Any news about your assassination attempt?"

"Not really." Palstein shook his head. "They're pretty sure where the shot was fired from, but that doesn't really help them much. It was just a public event. There were loads of people there."

"I still don't quite understand who would want to kill you. Your sector's running out of smoke. No one's going to change that by shooting oil managers."

"People don't think rationally." Palstein smiled. "Otherwise they'd have shot *you*. You basically invented helium-3 transport. Your elevator finished off my sector."

"You could shoot me a thousand times, the world would still switch to helium-3."

"Quite. Actions like that aren't calculated, they're the product of despair. Of blind hatred."

"Exactly. Hatred has never been used to make things better."

"But it's created more victims than anything else."

"Hmm, yes." Julian fell silent and rubbed his chin. "I'm not a hater. Hatred is alien to me. I can lose my temper. I can wish someone in hell and send him there, but only if there's a point to it. Hatred is completely pointless."

"So we're not going to find the murderer by looking for a motive." Palstein straightened the sling that held his arm. "Anyway. I just phoned you to wish you a pleasant journey."

"Next time you'll be there too! Soon as you're better."

"I'd love to see all that."

"You will see it!" Julian grinned. "You'll go walking on the Moon."

"Good luck, then. Squeeze that cash out of them."

"Take care, Gerald. I'll call you. From up at the top."

Palstein smiled. "You *are* up at the top."

Julian thoughtfully studied the empty screen. More than a decade ago, while the oil sector had still kept the Monopolies and Mergers Commission busy with their yields and price rises, Palstein had turned up in his London office one day, curious to see what sort of work went on there. There was a realization that the elevator had just suffered a sharp setback, because the optimistic new material from which the cable was to be made had apparently irreparable crystal structure flaws. The world already knew that moon dust contained huge quantities of an element that could solve all the world's energy problems. But without a plan for mining the stuff and getting it to Earth, along with the lack of appropriate reactors, helium-3 seemed like an irrelevance. Even so, Julian had gone on researching on all fronts, ignored by the oil sector, which had its hands full fighting for alternative trends like wind power and photovoltaics. Hardly anyone really took Julian's efforts seriously. It simply seemed too unlikely that he would be successful.

Palstein, on the other hand, had listened carefully to everything, and recommended to the board of his company—which had just changed its name to EMCO after its marriage to ExxonMobil—that they buy shares in Orley Energy and Orley Space. Notoriously, the company's directors hadn't gotten on board, but Palstein stayed in contact with Orley Enterprises, and Julian came to like and esteem this melancholy character, who was always gazing into the future. Even though they had barely spent three whole weeks together, usually at spontaneous lunches, now and again at events, rarely in a private context, they were bound together by something like friendship, even though the stubbornness of the one had finally consigned the other to oblivion. Lately Palstein had been forced with increasing frequency to announce the abandonment or limitation of mining projects, as he was doing currently in Alaska and as he had done three weeks previously in Alberta, where he had had to face hundreds of furious people and had promptly been shot.

Julian knew that the manager would prove to be right. A partnership with Orley Enterprises wouldn't save EMCO, but it might be useful to Gerald Palstein. He stood up, left the room behind the bar, and returned to his guests.

"—so back here for dinner in three-quarters of an hour," Lynn was saying. "You can stay and enjoy the drinks and the view, or freshen up and change. You could even do some work, if that's your drug, conditions here are ideal for that too."

"And for that you should thank my fantastic daughter," said Julian, putting his arm around her shoulder. "She's stunning. She did all this. She's the greatest as far as I'm concerned." Lynn lowered her head with a smile.

"No false modesty," Julian whispered to her. "I'm very proud of you. You can do anything. You're perfect."

A little later Tim was walking along the corridor on the fourth floor. Everything was antiseptically clean. On the way he met two security men and a cleaning robot insistently searching for the nonexistent leftovers of a world only partially inhabited. There was something profoundly disheartening about the way the machine, buzzing busily, pursued the purpose of its existence. A Sisyphus that had rolled the stone up the mountain and now had nothing left to do.

He stopped in front of her room and rang the bell. A camera transmitted his picture inside, then Lynn's voice said:

"Tim! Come in."

The door slid open. He entered the suite and saw Lynn, wearing an attractive evening dress, standing at the panoramic window with her back to him. Her hair was loose, and fell in soft waves to her shoulders. When she smiled at him over her shoulder, her pale blue eyes gleamed like aquamarines. With sudden brio she swung around and displayed her cleavage. Tim ignored it, while his sister stared so closely past him that her smile bordered on the idiotic. He walked to a spherical chair, bent down, and gave the woman who was lolling in it—scantily clothed in a silk kimono, legs bent and head thrown back—a kiss on the cheek.

"I'm impressed," he said. "Really."

"Thanks." The thing in the evening dress went on strutting around, twisted, and turned, wallowed in its transfigured ego, while the real Lynn's smile started sagging at the corners.

Tim sat down on a stool and pointed at her holographic alter ego.

"Are you planning to wear that tonight?"

"I don't know yet." Lynn frowned. "It's a bit too formal, don't you think? I mean, for a Pacific island."

"Odd idea. You've already thrown the rules of South Sea romanticism to the four winds. It looks great, put it on. Or are there alternatives?"

Lynn's thumbs slid over the remote control. Her avatar's appearance changed without transition. Hologram-Lynn was now wearing an apricot-colored catsuit, bare at the arms and shoulders, which she presented with the same empty grace as she had the evening dress. Her gaze was directed at imaginary admirers.

"Can you program her to look at you?"

"Absolutely not! Do you think I want to stare at myself the whole time?"

Tim laughed. His own avatar was a character from the days of two-dimensional animations, Wall-E, a battered-looking robot whose winning qualities bore no relation to his external appearance. Tim had seen the film as a child and immediately fallen in love with the character. Perhaps because he himself felt battered in Julian's world of shifting mountains and pulling stars down from the sky.

The avatar's magnificent flowing locks were replaced by a chignon.

"Better," said Tim.

"Really?" Lynn let her shoulders droop. "Damn, I've already had it up all day. But you're right. Unless—"

The avatar presented a tight, turquoise blouse with champagne-colored pants.

"And this?"

"What on earth kind of clothes are those?" Tim asked.

"Mimi Kri. Mimi Parker's new collection. She brought her entire range with her after I had to promise to wear some of it. Her catalogue is compatible with most of the avatar programs."

"So mine could wear them too?"

"If they could be restitched to fit caterpillar tracks and bulldozer hands, then sure. Afraid not, Tim, it only works with human avatars. And by the way, the program is ruthless. If you're too fat or too small for Mimi's creation, it won't recalculate. The problem is that most people improve their images so much for the avatar that everything fits the calculator and they look like shit afterward anyway."

"Then it's their own fault." Tim narrowed his eyes. "Hey, your avatar's butt's far too small! Half the size of your real one. No, a third. And where's your paunch? And your cellulite?"

"Idiot," Lynn laughed. "What are you doing here anyway?"

"Oh, nothing."

"Nothing? Good reason to visit me."

"Well, yeah." He hesitated. "Amber says I'm worrying about you too much."

"No, it's fine."

"I didn't want to get on your nerves back there."

"It's sweet of you to care. Really."

"Still, perhaps—" He wrung his hands. "You know, it's just that I suspect Julian of being completely blind to his surroundings. He may be able to locate individual atoms in the time-space continuum, but if you're lying dead in your grave right in front of him, he'll complain that you aren't listening to him properly."

"You exaggerate."

"But he completely failed to acknowledge your breakdown. Remember?"

"But that's more than five years ago," Lynn said softly. "And he had no experience of anything like that."

"Nonsense, he denied it! What special experience do you need to recognize a burnout, complete with anxiety and depression, for what it is? In Julian's world you don't break down, that's the point. He only knows superheroes."

"Perhaps he lacks the counterbalance. After mother died—"

"Mother died ten years ago, Lynn. Ten years! Since he noticed that at some point she'd given up breathing, talking, eating, and thinking, he's been screwing everything that moves and—"

"That's his business. Really, Tim."

"I'll shut up." He looked at the ceiling as if searching for clues to the real reason for his visit. "In fact I only came here to tell you your hotel is fantastic. And that I'm looking forward to the trip."

"That's sweet."

"Seriously! You've got everything under control. Everything's brilliantly organized!" He grinned. "Even the guests are more or less bearable."

"If one of them doesn't suit you we'll dispose of him in the vacuum." She rolled her eyes and said in a hollow, sinister voice: "In space no one can hear you scream!"

"Huh!" Tim laughed.

"I'm glad you're coming," she added quietly.

"Lynn, I promised to look after you, and that's what I'm doing." He got to his feet, bent down to her, and kissed her again. "So, see you later. Oh, and wear the pants and the blouse. And your hair looks great down."

"That's *exactly* what I wanted to hear, little brother."

Tim left. Lynn let her avatar go on modeling and trying on jewelry. Traditionally, avatars were virtual assistants, programs made form, that helped organize the networked human being's daily life and created the illusion of a partner, a butler, or a playmate. They controlled data, remembered appointments, acquired information, navigated the web, and made suggestions that matched their user's personality profile. There were no restrictions on their design, which also included virtually cloning yourself, whether out of pure self-infatuation or simply to spare yourself a trip to the shops. Five minutes later Lynn called Mimi Parker. The avatar shrank and froze, while the Californian appeared on the holoscreen, dripping wet and with a towel around her hips.

"I'm just out of the shower," she said apologetically. "Find anything nice?"

"Here," Lynn said, and sent a jpeg of the avatar, which appeared simultaneously on Mimi's display.

"Hey, good choice. Really suits you."

"Fine. I'll tell the staff. Someone will come and collect the things from you."

"Fine. See you later, then."

"Yes, see you later," Lynn smiled. "And thank you!"

The projection disappeared. At the same time Lynn's smile went out. Her gaze slipped away. Blank-faced, she stared straight ahead and recapitulated Julian's last remark, before she had left the viewing terrace:

I'm really proud of you. You're the greatest. You're perfect.

Perfect.

So why didn't she feel she was? His admiration weighed down on her like a mortgage on a house with a glorious façade and rotten pipes. Since stepping inside the suite, she had been walking as if on glass, as if the floor might collapse. She pushed herself up, dashed to the bathroom and took two little green tablets that she washed down with hasty sips of water. Then she thought for a moment and took a third.

Breathing, feeling your body. Taking a good deep breath, right into your belly.

After she had stared at her reflection for a while, her gaze wandered to her fingers. They were gripping the edge of the basin, and the sinews stood out on the back of her hands. For a moment she considered wrenching the basin from its base, which of course she wouldn't be able to do, except that it might keep her from screaming.

You're the greatest. You're perfect.

Just fuck off, Julian, she thought.

At that moment a pang of shame ran through her. Heart thumping, she slumped to the floor and performed thirty panting sit-ups. In the bar she found a bottle of champagne and tossed a glass down, even though she never normally drank alcohol. The black hole that had opened up beneath her began to close. She called room service, told them to go to Mimi Parker's suite, and went into the shower. When she stepped into the elevator a quarter of an hour later, wearing a blouse and pants and with her hair down, Aileen Donoghue was already waiting there and looked as expected. Christmas baubles dangled from her ear lobes. A necklace bit into the big valley of her bosom.

"Oh Lynn, you look—" Aileen struggled for words. "Good God, what should I say? Beautiful! Oh, what a beautiful girl you are! Let me give you a hug. Julian is rightly proud of you."

"Thanks Aileen," smiled Lynn, slightly crushed.

"And your hair! It suits you much better down. I mean, not that you should always wear it down, but it brings out your femininity. If only you weren't—Oops."

"Yes?"

"Nothing."

"Say it."

"Oh, you young things are all so thin!"

"Aileen, I weigh 128 pounds."

"Really?" That plainly wasn't the answer that Aileen wanted to hear. "So in a minute, once we're upstairs, I'll make you a plate of something. You need to eat, my dear! People have to eat."

Lynn looked at her and imagined tearing the Christmas balls out of her ears. Zip, zap, so fast that her ear lobes ripped and a fine mist of blood sprayed onto the mirrored glass of the elevator.

She relaxed. The green pills were starting to work.

"I'm hugely looking forward to tomorrow," she said brightly. "When it gets going. It'll be really lovely!"

MAY 23, 2025
The Station

Orley Space Station (OSS),
Geostationary Orbit

Evelyn Chambers was dreaming.

She was in an odd room about 4 meters high and just over 5 meters deep, and 6 meters wide. The only level surface was formed by the back wall; ceiling and floor merged into one another, leading her to conclude that she was inside an elliptical tube. In each end of it the architects had set a circular bulkhead at least 2 meters in diameter. Both bulkheads were sealed, although she didn't feel closed in, quite the opposite. It promised the certainty of being safely accommodated.

When the rooms had been furnished, the plans must have been temporarily upside down. Like a flying carpet, an expansive bed hovered just above the floor; there was a desk with seats, a computer work station, a huge display. Subdued lighting illuminated the room, a frosted glass door hid shower, washbasin, and toilet. The whole thing resembled a futuristically designed ship's cabin, except that the comfortable, red upholstered sofas hung below the ceiling—and the wrong way up.

But the most remarkable thing was that Evelyn Chambers received all these impressions without touching the room or its furniture with a single cell of her body. Just as naked as the choice combination of Spanish, Indian, and North American genes had made her, flattered by nothing but fresh air, set to a pleasant 69.8 degrees Fahrenheit, she floated above the curved, three-meter panoramic front window, and looked at a starry sky of such ineffable clarity and opulence that it *could* only have been a dream. Shimmering just under 36,000 kilometers below her was the Earth, the work of an Impressionist artist.

It *must* be a dream.

But Evelyn wasn't dreaming.

Since her arrival the previous day she couldn't get enough of her faraway home. There was nothing to obstruct the view, no looming lattice mast, no antenna, no module, not even the space elevator cable running toward the nadir. In a quiet voice she said, "Lights out," and the lights went out. There was, indeed, a manual remote control for the service systems, but she didn't want to risk changing her perfect position by waving the thing around. After fifteen hours on board the OSS she had slowly started to get used to weightlessness, even though she was deeply unsettled by the lack of up and down. She was all the more surprised not to have fallen victim to the space sickness people talked about, unlike Olympiada Rogacheva, who lay strapped tightly to her bed, whimpering and wishing she had never been born. Evelyn, on the other hand, felt pure bliss, like the memory of Christmas, pure delight distilled into a drug.

She barely dared breathe.

Staying poised over a single point wasn't easy, she noted. In a state of weightlessness you involuntarily assumed a kind of fetal position, but Evelyn had stretched her legs and crossed her arms in front of her chest like a diver propelling himself over a reef. Any hasty movement might mean that she would start spinning, or drift away from the glass. Now that all the light had gone out and the room, furniture included, had half vanished, every cell of her brain wanted to savor the illusion that there was no protecting shell surrounding her, that she was in fact floating like Kubrick's star-child, naked and alone above this wondrously beautiful planet. And suddenly she saw the tiny, shimmering little ball spinning away and realized that her eyes had filled with tears.

Was this how she had imagined the whole thing? Had she been able to imagine anything at all twenty-four hours ago, when the helicopter came down over the platform in the sea and the travelers got out, the night tugging at their coats and a magnificent sunrise failing to attract anyone's attention?

From a distance the platform looked imposing and mysterious, and even a little scary; now that they are actually there it exerts a fascination of a quite different and much deeper kind. First the feeling hits that this isn't Disneyland and there's no going back, that they will soon be swapping this world for a different, alien one. Evelyn isn't surprised to see some members of the group repeatedly looking across at the Isla de las Estrellas. Olympiada Rogacheva, for example, Paulette Tautou— even Momoka Omura casts stolen glances at the ragged cliffs, where the lights of the Stellar Island Hotel are beaming with an unexpectedly cozy radiance, as if warning them to leave this nonsense and come home, to freshly squeezed fruit juices, sunscreen, and the cries of gulls.

Why us? she asks herself irritably. Why is it always the women who get queasy at the idea of getting into the elevator? Are we really such scaredy cats? Forced by evolution into the role of worrywarts because nothing must be allowed to endanger the brood, while males— dispensable once robbed of their sperm—can advance calmly into the unknown and die there? At that moment she notices that Chuck Donoghue is sweating an unusual amount, Walo Ögi is displaying distinct signs of nerves, she sees the tense expectation on Heidrun Ögi's face, Miranda Winter's childlike enthusiasm, the intelligent interest in Eva Borelius's eyes, and is reconciled to her circumstances. Together they walk up to the multi-story cylinder of the terminal, and all of a sudden she realizes why she was getting agitated before.

Embarrassing—but even she is utterly terrified.

"To be perfectly honest," says Marc Edwards, who is walking along beside her, "I don't have a very good feeling about this."

"You don't?" Evelyn smiles. "I thought you were an adventurer."

"Hmm."

"That's what you said on my show, at least. Diving into shipwrecks, diving into caves—"

"I suspect this is going to be different from diving." Edwards stares pensively at his right index finger, its first joint missing. "Completely different."

"Incidentally, you never told me how *that* happened."

"I didn't? A puffer fish. I annoyed him, on a reef off Yucatán. If you tap them on the nose they get angry, retreat, and inflate themselves. I kept tapping him—" Edwards pesters an imaginary puffer fish "— except there was coral everywhere, he couldn't get any further back, so the next time I did it he just opened his mouth. My finger disappeared into it for a moment. Yeah. You should never try to pull your finger out of a fish's mouth, certainly not by force. By the time I pulled it out again, there was just a bone sticking out."

"You won't have to worry about things like that up there."

"No." Edwards laughs. "It'll probably be the safest vacation of our lives."

They enter the terminal. It's perfectly circular, and looks even bigger from inside than it seemed from outside. High-powered spotlights illuminate two structures, one in front of the other, identical in every detail but mirror images of one another. At the center of each the cable stretches vertically upward from its mooring in the ground, surrounded by three barrel-shaped mechanisms oscillating in appearance between cannons and searchlights, their muzzles pointing to the sky. A double grille runs around each of the structures to head height. Its mesh is wide enough for a person to slip through, but its presence indicates quite clearly that this would be a bad idea.

"And you know why?" Julian calls, in a dazzlingly good mood. "Because direct contact with the cable can cost you a body part in a fraction of a second. You must bear in mind that it's thinner than a razor blade, but incredibly hard. If I ran a screwdriver over the outside edge, I could slice it to shreds. Does anyone want to have a go with a finger? Does anyone want to get rid of their partner?"

Evelyn can't help thinking of what a journalist once said: "Julian Orley doesn't go on stage, the stage follows him around." Accurate, but the truth still looks a bit different. You actually *trust* the guy, you believe *every single word* he says, because his confidence is enough on its own to dissolve doubts, ifs and buts, nos and maybes, like sulfuric acid.

Motionless, and about 20 meters above the ground, the two elevators dangle like insects from the cables. From close up they look less like space shuttles, not least because they have no wings or tailplanes. Instead, what you notice is the wide undersides, mounted with photovoltaic cells. Compared with two days ago, when they came back from orbit, their appearance has changed slightly, in that the tanks of liquid helium-3 have been swapped for rounded, windowless passenger modules. Walkways lead from a high balustrade to open entrance hatches in the bellies of the cabins.

"Your technology?" asks Ögi, walking along beside Locatelli, eyes on the elevators' solar panels.

Locatelli stretches, becoming half an inch taller. Evelyn can't help thinking of the late Muammar al-Gaddafi. The similarity is startling, and so is the monarchical posture.

"What else?" he says condescendingly. "With the traditional junk those boxes wouldn't get ten meters up."

"They wouldn't?"

"No. Without Light-years, nothing here would work at all."

"Are you seriously trying to claim the elevator wouldn't work without you?" smiles Heidrun.

Locatelli peers at her as if she is a rare species of beetle. "What do you know about these things?"

"Nothing. It just looks to me as if you're standing there with an electric guitar around your neck claiming that an acoustic would produce nothing but crap. Who are you again?"

"But *mein Schatz*." Ögi's bushy mustache twitches with amusement. "Warren Locatelli is the Captain America of alternative energies. He's tripled the yield from solar panels."

"Okay," murmurs Momoka Omura, who is walking along beside him. "Don't expect too much of her."

Ögi raises his eyebrows. "You may not believe it, my little lotus blossom, but my expectations of Heidrun are exceeded again every day."

"In what respect?" Momoka gives a mocking grimace.

"You couldn't even imagine. But nice of you to ask."

"Anyway, with traditional energy those things on the cable would *creep* up at best," says Locatelli, as if the bickering isn't going on around him. "It would take us days to get there. I can explain it to you if you're interested."

"I'm not sure, my dear. Look, we're Swiss, and we do everything very slowly. That's why we built that particle accelerator all those years ago."

"To produce faster Swiss people?"

"Exactly."

"Doesn't it keep breaking down?"

"Yes, quite."

Evelyn stands close behind them, absorbing it all like a bee sucking nectar. She likes this kind of thing. It's always the way: put a lot of birds of paradise in a cage, and the feathers will fly.

The get-up gives a hint of what's to come. First everyone is dressed in silver and orange coats, the colors of Orley Enterprises; then the whole group heads up to the gallery from which the walkways descend to the elevators. Next they make the acquaintance of a powerfully built black man, whom Julian introduces as Peter Black.

"Easy to remember," Black says cheerfully, and shakes everyone's hand. "But just call me Peter."

"Peter's one of our two pilots and expedition leaders," Julian explains. "He and Nina—ah, here she is!"

A blonde woman with a short haircut and a freckled snub nose climbs out of the elevator hatch and joins them. Julian puts an arm around her muscular shoulders. Evelyn screws up her eyes and bets that Nina turns up in Julian's bedroom from time to time.

"May I introduce you: Nina Hedegaard from Denmark."

"Hey!" Nina waves to everybody.

"Same role as Peter: pilot, expedition leader. They will both be by your side over the next two weeks, whenever you're traveling vast distances. They will show you the most beautiful parts of our satellite, and protect you from weird space creatures such as the Chinese. Apologies, Rebecca—the red Chinese of course!"

With a start, Rebecca Hsu looks up from the display of her phone.

"I have no network," she says pleadingly.

It's cramped inside the elevator cabin. You have to climb. Six rows of five seats are arranged vertically, connected by a ladder. The luggage has been stowed in the other elevator. Evelyn Chambers sits in the same row as Miranda Winter, Finn O'Keefe, and the Rogachevs. She leans back and stretches her legs. In terms of comfort, the seats are easily a match for first class in any airline.

"Ooohh, how nice," Miranda says, delighted. "A Dane."

"You like Denmark?" Rogachev asks with cool politeness, while Olympiada stares straight ahead.

"Excuse me!" Miranda opens her eyes wide. "I *am* a Dane."

"You must forgive my ignorance, I work in the steel sector." Rogachev's mouth curls into a smile. "Are you an actress?"

"Hmm. Opinions vary on that one." Miranda gives a loud, dirty laugh. "What am I, Evelyn?"

"The entertainment factor?" Evelyn suggests.

"Well, okay, I'm actually a model. So I've done pretty much everything. Of course I wasn't always a model, I used to be a salesgirl at the cheese counter and I was responsible for the fries at McDonald's, but then I was discovered on this kind of casting show? And then Levi's took me on straight away. I caused car accidents! I mean, six foot tall, young, pretty, and boobs, genuine boobs, you understand, the real thing. Hollywood was bound to give me a call sooner or later."

O'Keefe, slouching in his seat, raises an eyebrow. Olympiada
Rogacheva seems to have worked out that you can't deny reality just
by looking away.

"So what kinds of parts have you played?" she asks flatly.

"Oh, I had my breakthrough with *Criminal Passion*, an erotic
thriller." Miranda gives a sugary smile. "I even got a prize, but let's not
go into that."

"Why? That's very—that's great."

"Not really, they gave me the Golden Raspberry for the worst performance." Miranda laughs and throws her hands in the air. "But hey! Then
came comedies, but I didn't have much luck with that. No hits, so I just
started drinking. Bad stuff! For a while I looked like a Danish pastry with
raisins for eyes, until one night there I am careening along Mulholland
Drive and I go over this homeless guy, my God, poor man!"

"Terrible."

"Yeah, but actually not because, between ourselves, he survived and
made a lot of money out of it. Not that I'm trying to whitewash anything! But I swear, that's what happened, and I had my whole stay in
jail filmed from the very first second to the last; they were even able
to get into the shower. Prison on prime time! And I was back on top
again." She sighs. "Then I met Louis Burger. Do you know him?"

"No, I—sorry, but—"

"Oh right. You're from the steel sector, or your husband is, where
you don't know people like that.—Although Louis Burger, industrialist, investment magnate—"

"Really not—"

"No, I'm sure I do," Rogachev says thoughtfully. "Wasn't there a
swimming accident?"

"That's right. Our happiness lasted only two years." Miranda stares
straight ahead. Suddenly she sniffs and rubs something from the corner of her eye. "It happened off the coast of Miami. Heart attack, when
swimming, and now can you imagine what his children have done,
the revolting brats? Not ours, we didn't have any, the ones from Louis's
previous marriage. They only go and sue me!—Me, his wife? They're
saying I contributed to his death, can you believe it?"

"And did you?" O'Keefe asks innocently.

"Idiot!" For a moment Miranda looks deeply hurt. "Everybody
knows I was acquitted. What can I do about it if he leaves me thirteen
billion? I could never harm anyone, I couldn't hurt a fly! You know
what?" She looks Olympiada deep in the eyes. "As a matter of fact I
can't do anything at all. But I do it really well! Hahaha! And you?"

"Me?" Olympiada looks as if she's been ambushed.

"Yes. What do you do?"

"I—" She looks pleadingly at Oleg. "We're—"

"My wife is a member of the Russian Parliament," says Rogachev without looking at her. "She's the daughter of Maxim Ginsburg."

"Hey! Oh, my God! Wooaahh! Ginsburg, wooooww!" Miranda claps her hands, winks conspiratorially at Olympiada, thinks for a moment, and asks greedily: "And who's that?"

"The Russian president," Rogachev explains. "Until last year at least. The new one's called Mikhail Manin."

"Oh yeah. Hasn't he done it before?"

"He hasn't, in fact." Rogachev smiles. "Maybe you mean Putin."

"No, no, it's longer ago, something with an 'a' and 'in' at the end." Miranda searches through the nursery of her education. "Nope, it's not coming."

"Maybe you mean Stalin?" O'Keefe asks slyly.

The PA system puts an end to all their speculation. A soft, dark, woman's voice issues safety instructions. Almost everything she says sounds to Evelyn like a perfectly normal airplane safety routine. They fasten their seatbelts, like horse harnesses. In front of each row of seats, monitors light up and transmit vivid camera pictures of the outside world, giving the illusion that you're looking through windowpanes. They see the inside of the cylinder, increasingly illuminated by the rising sun. The hatch closes, life-support systems spring to life with a hum, then the seats tip backward so that they're all lying as if they're at the dentist's.

"Tell me, Miranda," whispers O'Keefe, turning his head toward Miranda. "Do you still have names for them?"

"Who?" she asks back, just as quietly. "Oh, right. Of course." Her hands become display units. "This one's Huey. That other one's Dewey."

"What about Louie?"

She looks at him from under lowered eyelids.

"For Louie we'll have to get to know each other better."

At that moment a jolt runs through the cabin, a tremor and a vibration. O'Keefe slips lower in his seat. Evelyn holds her breath. Rogachev's face is blank. Olympiada has her eyes shut. Somewhere someone laughs nervously.

What happens next is nothing, but nothing, like the launch of a plane.

The elevator accelerates so quickly that Evelyn feels momentarily as if she has merged with her seat. She is pressed into the plump upholstery until arms and armrests seem to have become one. The vehicle shoots vertically out of the cylinder. Below them, from the perspective of a second camera, the Isla de las Estrellas shrinks to a long, dark scrap with a turquoise dot inside it: the pool. Was it really only yesterday that she was lying down there, critically eyeing her belly, bewailing the extra 9 pounds that had recently driven her from bikini to one-piece, while everyone around her was constantly insisting that her weight increase suited her and stressed her femininity? Forget the 9 pounds she thinks. Now she could swear she weighs tons. She feels so heavy that she's afraid she might at any moment crash through the floor of the elevator and plop down in the sea, causing a medium-sized tsunami.

The ocean becomes an even, finely rippling surface; early sunlight pours in gleaming lakes across the Pacific. The elevator climbs the cable at incredible speed. They hurtle through high-altitude fields of vapor, and the sky becomes bluer, dark blue, deep blue. A display on the monitor informs her that they are traveling at three times, no, four times, eight times the speed of sound! The earth curves. Clouds scatter to the west, like fat snowflakes on water. The cabin accelerates further to 12,000 kilometers an hour. Then, very slowly, the murderous pressure eases. The seat begins to heave Evelyn back up again, and she completes the transformation back from dinosaur to human being, a human being who cares about an extra 9 pounds.

"Ladies and gentlemen, welcome on board OSS Space Elevator One. We have now reached our cruising speed and passed through the Earth's lower orbit, the one in which the International Space Station, ISS, circles. In 2023, operation of the ISS was officially halted, and since then it has served as a museum featuring exhibits from the early days of space travel. Our journey time will be about three hours, the space debris forecast is ideal, so everything suggests that we will arrive at OSS, Orley Space Station, in good time. At present we are starting to pass through the Van Allen radiation belt, a shell of highly charged particles around the Earth, caused by solar eruptions and cosmic radiation. On the Earth's surface we are protected from these particles; above an altitude of 1,000 kilometers, however, they are no longer deflected by the Earth's magnetic field, and flow directly into the atmosphere. Around here, or more precisely at an altitude of 700 kilometers, the inner belt begins. It essentially consists of high-energy protons, and reaches its highest densities at an altitude of between 3,000 and 6,000 kilometers. The outer belt extends from altitudes of 15,000 to 25,000 kilometers, and is dominated by electrons."

Evelyn is startled to note that the pressure has completely disappeared. No, more than that! For a brief moment she thinks she's falling, until she realizes where she has had this strange feeling of being released from her own body before. She experienced it briefly during the zero-gravity flights. She is weightless. In the main monitor she sees the starry sky, diamond dust on black satin. The voice from the speaker assumes a conspiratorial tone.

"As many of you may have heard, critics of manned space travel see the Van Allen belts as an impassable obstacle on the way to space because of the high concentration of radiation. Conspiracy theorists even see them as proof that man was never on the Moon. Supposedly it would only be possible to pass through them behind steel walls 2 meters thick. Be assured, none of this is true. The fact is that the intensity of the radiation fluctuates greatly according to variations in solar activity. But even under extreme conditions, the dosage, as long as you are surrounded by aluminum 3 millimeters thick, is half of what is considered safe under general radiation protection regulations for professional life. Generally it's less than 1 percent of that! In order to protect your health to the optimum degree, the passenger cabins of this elevator are armored accordingly, which is, incidentally, the chief reason for the lack of windows. As long as you don't feel an urge to get out, we can guarantee you complete safety as you pass through the Van Allen belt. Now enjoy your trip. In the armrests of your seats you will find headphones and monitors. You have access to eight hundred TV channels, video films, books, games—"

The whole kaboodle, then. After a while Nina Hedegaard and Peter Black come floating over, handing out drinks in little plastic bottles that you have to suck on to get anything out of them, finger food, and refreshment towels.

"Nothing that could spill or crumble," Hedegaard says, with a Scandinavian sibilance on the S. Miranda Winter says something to her in Danish, Hedegaard replies, they both grin. Evelyn leans back and grins too, even though she didn't understand a word. She just feels like grinning. She is flying into space, to Julian's faraway city . . .

. . . in which she felt now as if she were alone with the Earth. It lay so far below her, so small, that it looked as if she would just have to reach out and the planet would slip softly into the palm of her hand. Gradually the darkness faded toward the west and the Pacific began to glow. China still slept, while staff in North America were already hurrying to their lunch breaks, talking on their phones, and Europe was spinning toward the end of the working day. She was astonished to realize that three more earths would have fit in the space between her and the blue and white sphere, although it would have been a bit of a tight squeeze. Almost 36,000 kilometers above her home, the OSS drifted in space. That in itself stretched her imagination to its limits, and yet to reach the Moon they would have to travel ten times as far.

After a while she pushed herself away from the window and floated over to one of the upside-down sofas. She clambered rather inelegantly into it. Strictly speaking, there was no point in even having furniture in a place like this. Under water, buoyancy compensated for gravitation to allow you to float, but you were still subject to influences such as water density and current, while in zero gravity no forces at all affected the body. You didn't weigh anything, you didn't tend to move in any particular direction, you didn't need a chair to keep you from falling on your behind, or the comfort of soft cushions, or a bed to stretch out on. Basically you needed only to float in void with your legs and forearms bent, except that even the tiniest motor impulses, a twitch of a muscle, were enough to set the body drifting, so that you were in constant danger of cracking your head in your sleep. Millions of years of genetic predisposition also required you to lie *on* something, even if it was vertical or stuck to the ceiling. At the same time concepts such as "vertical" were irrelevant in space, but people were used to systems of reference. Investigations had shown that space travelers found the idea of an earth at their feet more natural than one floating above their heads, which was why psychologists encouraged the so-called gravity-oriented style of construction, to create the illusion of a floor. You just strapped yourself firmly to the bed, in the chair you acted as if you were sitting down, and in the end it felt almost homey.

She stretched, did a somersault and decided to go—float, rather—to breakfast. In the concave wall that seemed to conceal the life-support system, there was a closet from which she chose a pair of dark three-quarter-length pants and a matching T-shirt, and tight-fitting slippers. She paddled over to the bulkhead and said, "Evelyn Chambers. Open."

The computer tested pressure, atmosphere, and density; then the module opened to reveal a tube several meters across. Many miles of such tubes stretched all the way across the station, connecting the modules to one another and with the central structure, and creating lines of communication and escape routes. Everything was subject to the redundancy principle. There were always at least two possible ways of leaving a module, each computer system had matching mirror systems, there were several copies of the life-support systems. Months before the trip, Evelyn had tried to imagine the massive construction by studying it using models and documents, before establishing, as she had now, that her fantasy had been blinding her to the reality. In the isolation of the cell in which she was staying, she could hardly imagine the colossus that loomed above it, its size, its complex ramifications. The only thing that was certain was that next to it the good old ISS looked like a toy out of a blister pack.

She was on board the biggest structure in space ever created by human beings.

In homage to the concept of the space elevator, the designers had built the OSS on a vertical. Three massive steel masts, each one 280 meters high, arranged at an equal angle to each other, formed the spine, connected at the base and the head, producing a kind of tunnel through which the cables of the elevator passed. Like the stories of a building, ring-shaped elements called tori stretched around the masts, defining the five levels of the facility. At the bottom level lay the OSS Grand, the space hotel. Torus-1 housed comfortable living rooms, a snack and coffee bar, a room with a holographic fireplace, a library, and a rather desperate-looking crèche, which Julian stubbornly planned to extend: "Because children will come, they will love it!" In fact, since its opening two years previously, although the OSS Grand had been well booked, there had so far been no families. Very few people were willing to entrust their offspring to the weightless state, a fact that Julian defiantly dismissed by saying, "Nothing but prejudice! People are so silly. It's no more dangerous up here than it is in the stupid Bahamas, quite the contrary. There's nothing up here to bite you, you can't drown, you don't get jaundice, the natives are friendly, so what is there to worry about? Space is *paradise* for children!"

Perhaps it was just that people had always had a twisted relationship with paradise.

Like a predatory shark, Evelyn snaked her way along the pipe. You could move incredibly quickly in zero gravity if you put your mind to it. On her way she passed numbered side tunnels, with suites similar to her own behind them. Every unit consisted of five modules, each divided into two living units and arranged in such a way that all the guests enjoyed an unimpeded view of the Earth. The connection to the torus branched off to the right, but Evelyn fancied breakfast, and continued along the course of the tunnel. It opened out into the Kirk, one of the two most spectacular modules of the OSS. Disc-shaped, these protruded far above the accommodation areas, so that Earth could be seen through the glass floor. The Kirk served as a restaurant; its counterpart to the north, appropriately christened the Picard, alternated between lounge, nightclub, and multimedia center.

"Making this glass floor stretched us to the limits," Julian never tired of stressing. "What a struggle! I can still hear the builders' complaints in my ears. So? said I. Since when have we cared about limits? Astronauts have always yearned for windows, lovely great big panoramic windows, except that the walls weren't strong enough on the flying sardine cans of the past. The problem was solved with the elevator. We need mass? Send it up there. We want windows? Let's put some in." And then, as he always did, he lowered his voice and whispered almost reverently. "Building them like that was Lynn's idea. Great girl. She's pure rock 'n'roll! I tell you."

The communication hatch leading to the Kirk was open. Evelyn remembered the hazards of her newly won freedom too late, clutched at the frame of the lock to halt her flight, missed it, and flew through, flailing her arms, past a not especially startled waiter. Someone grabbed her ankle.

"Trying to get to the Moon all by yourself?" she heard a familiar voice say.

Evelyn gave a start. The man drew her down to eye level.

His eyes—

Of course she knew him. Everyone knew him. She'd had him on her show at least a dozen times, but she still couldn't get used to those eyes. "What are you doing here?" she exclaimed, bewildered.

"I'm the evening entertainment." He grinned. "What about you?"

"Morale booster for space grouches. Julian and the media, you know . . ." She shook her head and laughed. "Incredible. Has anyone seen you?"

"Not yet. Finn's here, I heard."

"Yeah, he was suitably dismayed to bump into me here. He's become quite trusting now, though."

"No pose is a pose in itself. Finn enjoys playing the part of the out-sider. The less you ask him, the more answers you'll get. You up for breakfast?"

"Definitely."

"Great, me too. And then?"

"To the multimedia center. Lynn's giving us an introduction to the station. They've divided us up. Some people are having the scientific aspect explained to them, the others are going out to play."

"And you aren't?"

"No, I am, but later. They can only take six people out at any one time. You fancy coming?"

"I'd love to, but I've got no time. We're shooting a video in Torus-4."

"Oh really, you're doing something new? Seriously?"

"Not another word." He smiled, putting a finger to his lips. His eyes whisked her off to another galaxy. "Remember, someone has to take care of the old folks."

Lynn smiled, answered questions, smiled again.

She was proud of the multimedia space, just as she was intensely proud of the whole OSS Grand, of the Stellar Island Hotel, and the faraway Gaia. At the same time they all filled her with terrible anxiety, as if she had built Venice on matchstick foundations. Everything she did was affected by that awareness. She tortured herself with apocalyptic scenarios, and catharsis was possible only if her worst fears proved to be well-founded. She was trapped in a terrible internal struggle, in which she tirelessly pursued another version of herself. The more arguments she produced to quell her anxieties, the bigger they became, as if she were approaching a Black Hole.

I'm going to lose my mind, she thought. Just like Mom. I'm definitely going insane.

Smile. Smile.

"Lots of people see OSS as a mushroom," she said. "Or a parasol, or a tree with a flat crown. A bar table. Other people see a medusa."

"What's a medusa again, darling?" asked Aileen, as if talking about some kind of fashionable gewgaw that teenagers might be interested in.

"It's a sort of jellyfish thing," Ed Haskin replied. "You've got this gooey umbrella thing at the top, with tentacles and other sorts of gooey stuff dangling from the bottom."

Lynn bit her lips. Haskin, previously a director of the spaceport and for a few months now responsible for the whole technical sector, was a nice man, very competent, and sadly equipped with the sensitivity of a Neanderthal.

"They're also very beautiful creatures," she added.

They were both orbiting a 4-meter-tall holographic model of OSS, projected into the center of Picard. Drifting in their wake through the virtual space came Walo Ögi, Aileen and Chuck Donoghue, Evelyn Chambers, Tim, and some recently arrived French scientists. The Picard had a different design from the Kirk, which was closer to classical restaurant style. Here floating islands of conviviality were arranged on different levels, bathed in muted light and overlooked by a long bar that cried out to be populated by Barbarellas with heavy eye liner. At the touch of a button, everything could be reconfigured, so that tables and seats grouped themselves into an atrium.

"Jellyfish, table, or parasol; such associations are due to the vertical construction and symmetry of the station," said Haskin. "We mustn't forget that space stations aren't buildings with fixed foundations. In fact they don't actually need foundations at all, but they are exposed to the constant redistribution of mass and all kinds of possible impact, from joggers on treadmills to moon shuttles attaching themselves to the outer ring. All of these things set the structure vibrating independently, and a symmetrical construction is ideally suited to the redistribution of vibration energies. The vertical alignment contributes to the stabilization, and matches the principle of the space elevator. As you can see, the smallest moment of inertia is directed toward the Earth."

Right at the bottom the torus with the hotel in it could be seen, with its outrigger suites, and Kirk and Picard protruding above them. Along the lattice masts, modules containing fitness centers, staff accommodation, storerooms, and offices were stacked all the way up to Torus-2, at the center of which the space elevator came to a halt. Retractable gangways linked the bagel-shaped module with the cabins.

"This is where we arrived yesterday," Lynn explained. "Torus-2 serves as the reception area for the OSS Grand, and also as a terminal for passengers and freight. As you see, corridors radiate in a spoke arrangement from there to a larger, surrounding ring." Her hand passed through a lattice structure that stretched generously around the torus. "Our spaceport. Those things that look like airplanes are evacuation pods, the little cans are moon shuttles. In one of them, the Charon, we'll be heading for the satellite tomorrow."

"I should have gone on a diet," Aileen said excitedly to Chuck. "How am I going to fit in one of those? My butt's the size of Halley's Comet."

Lynn laughed.

"Oh no, they're very spacious. Very comfortable. The Charon is over 30 meters long."

"And that thing there?" Ögi had spotted crane-like structures on the top side of the ring and along the mast. He floated over to them, passed through the projection beam for a moment, and looked like a huge cosmic monster attacking the OSS.

"Manipulators," said Haskin. "Robot arms on tracks. They unload the arriving cargo shuttles, take out the tanks of condensed helium-3, bring them inside the torus, and anchor them to the elevators."

"What happens exactly when one of those shuttles docks?"

"There's a big bang," said Haskin.

"But doesn't that mean that the station has too much weight on one side? There isn't always the same number of ships at anchor."

"That isn't a problem. All the docking sites are transferable, we can always right the balance. Well spotted, by the way." Haskin looked impressed. "Are you an architect?"

"An investor. But I've built various things. Residential modules for cities: you click them into already existing structures or put them on high-rise roofs, and when you move, your little house simply goes with you. The Chinese love it. Flood-resistant estates on the North Sea. You know that Holland's being flooded; are they all supposed to move to Belgium? The houses are fixed to jetties and float when the water rises."

"He's also building a second Monaco," said Evelyn.

"Why do we need a second Monaco?" asked Tim.

"Because the first one's filled to bursting," Ögi explained. "The Monégasques are stacking up like the Alps, so Albert and I flicked through our Jules Verne. Have you heard of Propeller Island?"

"Isn't that the story of the mad captain in that weird underwater boat?" Donoghue asked.

"No, no!" One of the Frenchmen dismissed the idea. "That was the Nautilus! Captain Nemo."

"Bullshit! I've seen that one. It's by Walt Disney."

"No! Not Walt Disney! Mon Dieu!"

"Propeller Island is a mobile city state," Ögi explained. "A floating island. You can't extend Monaco indefinitely, not even with offshore islands, so we hit on the idea of building a second one that will cruise the South Sea."

"A second Monaco?" Haskin scratched his head. "You mean a ship?"

"Not a ship. An island. With mountains and coasts, a pretty capital city and a wine cellar for old Prince Ernst August. But artificial."

"And it works?"

"*You* of all people are asking me that?" Ögi laughed and spread his arms out as if to press the OSS to his heart. "Where's the problem?"

"There isn't one," Lynn laughed. "Or do *we* look as if we've got problems?"

Her eye rested on Tim. Was he actually aware of what was wrong with her? His unease touched and shamed her in equal measure, as he had had every reason to be uneasy since that day, that terrible moment five years before, that was to change their lives, just before six in the evening . . .

. . . Lynn is in the middle of the traffic jam, ten lanes of pumping, over-heated metal chugging its way along the M25 to Heathrow with the pace of a glacier, under a ruthless, cold February sun gleaming down from a yellowish, cloudy Chernobyl sky, and suddenly it happens. She has to go to Paris for a meeting; she's always going to some sort of meeting or other, but all of a sudden someone turns off the light in her head, just like that, and everything sinks into a morass of hopelessness. Profound grief sweeps over her, followed by 10,000 volts of pure panic. Later she's unable to say how she got to the airport, but she isn't flying, she's just sitting in the terminal, robbed of all certainties but one, which is that she will not be able to bear her own existence for a second longer, because she doesn't want to go on living with so much sadness and anxiety. But at that point her memory stops until the morning, when she finds herself fully dressed on the floor of her penthouse apartment in Notting Hill, mailbox, e-mail, and answering machine spilling over with other people's excitement. She walks out onto the terrace, into the icy rain that has started falling diagonally, and wonders whether the twelve stories will be enough. Then she changes her mind and calls Tim, thus sparing the sensibilities of anyone who might have been passing by.

Henceforth, whenever the topic turns to her illness, Julian invokes various baleful viruses and protracted colds as a way of explaining to himself and others what it is that is so terribly afflicting his daughter, his shining light; Tim, on the other hand, is always talking in terms of therapies and psychiatrists. Her condition is a mystery to Julian, and he represses what he perhaps guesses at, just as he has repressed the memory of Crystal's death. It is ten years since Lynn's and Tim's mother died in a state of mental derangement, but Julian develops a remark-able capacity for denial. Not because he is traumatized, but because he is actually incapable of making a connection between the two.

It's Tim and Amber who come to her rescue. When she feels nothing but naked terror at the loss of all sensation, Tim walks around the block with her, in sunshine and in pouring rain, for hours; he forces her mind back into the present until she is able once again at least to feel the cold and wet, and to become aware of the metallic taste of her fear on her tongue. When she thinks she'll never be able to sleep again, or keep down a bite of food; when seconds stretch into infinities and everything around her—light, colors, smells, music—emits shock waves of menace; when every roof, every parapet, every bridge invites her to leap; when she fears going mad as Crystal did, running amok, killing people, he makes it clear to her that no demon has taken possession of her; that no monsters are after her; that she wouldn't hurt anyone, not even herself, and very gradually she starts to believe him.

Things get better, and Tim bugs her. Forces her to take professional help at last, to lie down on the couch. Lynn refuses, plays down the nightmare. Examining the causes? What for? She isn't even slightly willing to show respect to this miserable phase of her otherwise perfect life. Her nerves have been going haywire, exhaustion, crashing synapses, biochemical mayhem, whatever. Reason to be ashamed, but not to go rummaging for the source of her distress. Why should she? To find what? She is glad and grateful that the company has camouflaged her condition with a series of explanations—flu, very bad flu, bronchitis—now that she's up and smiling and shaking hands again. The crisis has been survived, the broken doll repaired. Again she sees herself as Julian sees her, a perspective that she temporarily lost. Who cares whether she likes herself? Julian loves her! Seeing herself through his eyes solves all her problems. The stale familiarity of self-debasement, she could live with that.

"—are the dining and common rooms for the scientific operations," she heard herself saying.

She worked her way further up the hologram, from Torus-3 to the sports facilities in Torus-4, to dozens of accommodation and laboratory modules, which Julian had rented out to private and state research establishments from all over the world: NASA, ESA, and Roskosmos, his own subsidiaries Orley Space, Orley Travel, and Orley Energy. Cheeks aglow, she talked about the vegetable gardens and animal breeding facilities in the domed biospheres above Torus-4, allowed a glimpse into the observatories, workshops, control, and meeting rooms of the fifth and final Torus, from which the elevator cable led back out and into infinity or what the temporary residents imagined infinity to be. She described the disc-shaped roof, hundreds of meters across, with its wharfs in which moon shuttles and interplanetary spaceships were built, robots dashed busily through the vacuum and solar panels inhaled sunlight, so that the station could feed on the homemade kind during its hours in the Earth's shadow. Laughing on the brink of the abyss, she presented the OSS, the Orley Space Station, whose builder and owner NASA had so yearned to be. But such a proposition would have required political responsibility, and by their nature politicians were voluble, slippery creatures, and tended to criticize the decisions of their predecessors rather than anything else. Hence, in the end, a private investor had taken the dream of the settlement of space that bit further and, *en passant*, established the necessary conditions to set off a landslide in the energy sector, which threw up the question of . . .

". . . whose interests we are actually subsidizing if we decide to join forces with Orley Enterprises."

"Well, ideally ours," said Locatelli. "Don't you think?"

"I completely agree," Rogachev replied. "I'd just like to know who else I'm benefiting."

"As long as Light-years remains market leader, I couldn't give a rat's ass about anyone else who might be getting anything out of it, if I may be so bold out here in geostationary isolation."

"*Ryba ishchet gde glubzhe, a chelovek gde luchshe.*" Rogachev smiled thinly. "The fish seeks the deepest place, man the best. For my part, I'd prefer a bit more of an overview."

Locatelli snorted. "You're not going to get that by looking at everything from outside. Perspective comes from position."

"Which is?"

"My company's, in my case. I know you're scared of indirectly benefiting Washington and NASA by giving Julian money. But so what? The main thing is that the figures add up at the end of the year."

"I'm not sure if you can really see it like that," said Marc Edwards, then realized the vacuousness of his observation and turned his attention to the pairs of boots that Nina was handing out.

"*I* can see it like that. *He* can't." Locatelli pointed at the Russian with his thumbs outstretched and laughed broadly. "You see, he's married to politics."

Finn O'Keefe exchanged a glance with Heidrun Ögi. Rogachev and Locatelli were really getting on his nerves. They were having discussions which, in his opinion, really belonged at the end of the trip. And perhaps he just didn't know enough about how the sector worked, but in any case, he planned to do nothing over the coming days but enjoy himself as best he could, and obediently shoot the little film clip that he had promised Julian he would do: Perry Rhodan on the *real* Moon, singing the wonders of the *real* experience. Investor outpourings had no place, he thought, in "EVA's closet," the dressing area for Extravehicular Activities.

"And what about you?" Locatelli stared at him. "What's the view like from Hollywood?"

O'Keefe shrugged. "Relaxed."

"He wants your money too."

"No, he wants my face, so that I can tell moneybags like you that they've absolutely got to get to the Moon. You're right to that extent." O'Keefe rubbed his index finger and thumb together. "I get hold of money for him. But not mine."

"Very clever," Locatelli observed to Rogachev. "He probably even gets some for himself as well."

"Not a cent."

"And what do you *really* think about it? Space tourism, private flights to the Moon?"

O'Keefe looked around. He had expected to see complete space suits hanging here, like limp and motionless astronauts, but the section, with its sterile lighting, felt more like a boutique. Folded coats of all sizes, helmets, gloves, and boots lined up side by side, sections of rigid armor.

"No idea," he said. "Ask me again in two weeks."

Their little group—Rogachev, Locatelli, Edwards, Mimi, Heidrun Ögi, and himself—had herded around Nina Hedegaard, trying not to spin chaotically away. O'Keefe was mastering the art of space ballet better by the hour, and so was Rogachev, who had allowed himself to be dragged along by the excitement of the evening conversation; in addition to soccer, his love of martial arts was now revealed to the world. The Russian now seemed to possess his body only to subject it to reptilian control. His feelings, in so far as he had any, lay hidden beneath the ice of his pale blue eyes. Marc Edwards and Mimi Parker, both passionate divers, held their position tolerably well. Heidrun strove for control, while Locatelli's impetuosity had the potential to injure someone.

"Could I ask you to come closer?" called Nina.

"So, between ourselves—" Mimi Parker lowered her voice. "There are rumors going around. No idea if there's anything to it, but some people are suggesting that Julian's running out of smoke."

"Meaning?"

"He's as good as broke."

"That's nothing," Heidrun whispered. "You know who really is running out of smoke?"

"Sure." Mimi leaned forward. "Out with it."

"You lot, you bunch of chatterboxes. And you'll be running out of smoke out there if you don't stop talking nonsense."

Rogachev studied her with the amusement of a cat being growled at by mice.

"There's something refreshing about you, Mrs. Ögi."

She beamed at him as if he'd just crowned her Miss Moscow. The Russian twitched his eyebrows with amusement and floated closer to Nina. Heidrun followed him clumsily. Her limbs seemed to have grown even longer and more unwieldy in zero gravity. The Dane waited until they had all formed a semicircle around her, then clapped her hands and flashed her perfect teeth to the assembled group.

"So!" A hissed Scandinavian S. "You're about to embark on your first space walk. Everyone excited?"

"Sure!" Edwards and Mimi cried simultaneously.

"With reservations," Rogachev smiled. "As we are now under your charming care."

Locatelli flared his nostrils. Excitement was clearly beneath his dignity. Instead he lifted his specially made, vacuum-resistant camera aloft and took a photograph. Nina received the answers and reactions with dimples of delight.

"You should be a bit excited, because Extravehicular Activities are one of the most demanding aspects of manned space travel. Not only will you be entering a vacuum, you will also be exposed to extreme variations in temperature."

"Oh," Mimi marveled. "I always thought it was just cold in space."

"From the purely physical point of view, there is no prevalent temperature in space. What we describe as temperature is the degree of energy with which the molecules of a body, a fluid, or a gas move. Small example: in boiling water they're charging about all over the place, in ice they're almost motionless, so we experience one as hot and the other as cold. In empty space, on the other hand—"

"Yeah, yeah," Locatelli murmured impatiently.

"—we find practically no molecules at all. So there's nothing to measure. Theoretically this brings us to zero degrees on the Kelvin scale, or minus 273 degrees Celsius, absolute zero. However, we record the so-called cosmic background radiation, a kind of afterglow from the time of the Big Bang, when the universe was still unimaginably dense and hot. That comes to just 3 degrees. Doesn't exactly warm things up. Nonetheless, you can burn up or freeze out there, depending."

"We all know that already," Locatelli pressed. "I'm more interested in where—"

"Well *I* don't know it." Heidrun turned her head toward him. "But I'd *like* to know. As you might imagine, I'm vulnerable to sunburn."

"But what she's telling us is all general knowledge!"

Heidrun stared at him. Her eyes said, fuck you, smart-ass. Nina gave a conciliatory smile.

"So, in empty space anybody, whether it's a spaceship, a planet, or an astronaut, assumes the temperature that matches its environment. That's based on the factors of solar radiation and reflection into space.

That's why space suits are white, to reflect as much light as possible, which means they don't heat up as much. Even so, temperatures of over 248 degrees Fahrenheit have been measured on space suits on the side facing the sun, while the temperature on the shaded side was minus 149.8 degrees Fahrenheit."

"Brrr," said Mimi.

"Don't worry, you won't notice it. Space suits are temperature controlled. Inside they're a bearable 71.6 degrees Fahrenheit. Of course only if the suit has been put on right. Negligence can mean death. Later on the Moon you'll find similar conditions: in the polar regions there are craters which, at minus 382 degrees Fahrenheit, are among the coldest areas in the whole solar system! Light never enters them. On average the daytime temperature on the Moon's surface is 266 degrees Fahrenheit; at night it falls to minus 256 degrees—which is, incidentally, a reason why the Apollo landings took place in the Moon morning, when the sun is low and it's not quite so hot. Still, when Armstrong passed into the shadow of his moon module, the temperature of his space suit dropped all of a sudden from 149 degrees to minus 148 degrees Fahrenheit, in one single step! Any further questions?"

"About the vacuum," said Rogachev. "I gather our bodies will explode if we're exposed to an airless space without protection?"

"It's not quite as dramatic as that. But you would die whatever happened, so it's a good idea to keep your helmet on nicely at all times. Most of you are familiar with the old space suits in which you looked like a marshmallow. So inflated that the astronauts literally had to go hopping about because their pant legs didn't bend. For short missions and occasional space outings that was fine. But in continuously inhabited space cities, on the Moon or on Mars, monster suits like that wouldn't make any sense at all."

Nina pointed to the tight-fitting coat that she herself was wearing. It was made of a thick neoprene-like material and was covered with a network of dark lines. Her elbows and knees were protected by hard shells. Even though she looked as if she'd put on three diving suits one over the other, the ensemble seemed somehow sexy on her.

"That's why they've recently started using suits like these. Biosuits, developed by a beautiful woman, Professor Dava Newman of MIT. They're pretty, don't you think?" Nina turned slowly on her axis. "You're going to ask me how the required pressure is created. Very simple. Instead of gas, a huge number of fixed metal braces create a mechanical counterpressure. It's only where the skin is highly mobile that the material is kept flexible; in all other areas it's rigid, it's practically an exoskeleton."

Nina took a torso-shaped shell from the nearest shelf.

"All armor and applications fit the basic unit, as this carbon-fiber torso protector reveals. A backpack full of life-support systems is connected to attachment points on the back, and air is pumped into the helmet and guided along pipes to the boots and gloves, the only areas in which there is gas pressure. The traditional, noisy cooling system has been replaced by a temperature-controlling nano-layer. There are additional protectors for the limbs, like the ones you'll know from medieval suits of armor, except much lighter and harder. In space you're exposed to cosmic radiation, there are micrometeorites flying about, and on the Moon you'll be exposed to regolith, moon dust. While the movements of your feet in space don't really matter much, on planetary surfaces they're crucially important. To do justice to all that, bio-suits are conceived as construction sets. Dozens of elements can be combined at will, quickly and with only a few rapid maneuvers. You breathe the same oxygen-nitrogen mixture as you do on Earth and here on board, and now you no longer have to wait for ages in the pressure chamber."

She started pulling on her boots and gloves, attached the backpack with the life-support systems to the back plate of the suit, and linked the connectors to one another.

"Child's play, Dava Newman would say, but be careful. Don't try to do it on your own. Don't make me have to come and pick you up, all dried up and twisted. Okay? Fine! Bio-suits are low-maintenance, and one more thing while we're on the subject: if anyone feels a certain physical need—just let it flow. Your valuable pee is trapped in a thick layer of polyacrylate, so don't worry that it's going to splash down your legs. These—" and Nina pointed to two consoles under the wrist "—are controls for a total of sixteen thrust nozzles in the shoulder and hip areas. Astronauts no longer dangle like newborn babies from umbilical cords, they navigate by recoil. The blasts are short, and they can be manually released or left up to computer calculation. That option's a new one. When the electronics decide that you've lost control, you're automatically stabilized. Your computers are connected to mine, and remote-controlled as well, so strictly speaking you can't get lost. Here—" her hand slipped over another console along her forearm "—you'll find thirty little buttons, each one with the option of speaking and receiving. With these you'll decide who you want to communicate with. 'Talk to all' means you're talking to everybody, 'Listen to all' means you're receiving everybody. To get your declarations of love out of the way, choose the individual connection and switch the rest off." Nina grinned. "Anyone worried about me seeing you in your underwear? Nobody? Then off with your clothes! Let's get ready to go out there."

"What about the chickens?" asked Mukesh Nair.

"A crackpot idea," Julian objected. "There are four left. Two are even still laying eggs, little spherical things with the nutritional value of golf balls. The pelvic muscles of the others have regressed so far that they can't push anything out."

"So much for births in space," said Eva Borelius. "Push, push! But what with?"

"And what about the chicken poo?" Karla Kramp seemed weirdly fascinated by the subject.

"Oh, they crap more than we'd like them to," said Julian. "We tried to siphon it off, but you have to be careful that you don't suck the feathers off the poor creatures' butts. The whole thing's pretty tricky. Quite honestly, I don't know how to raise chickens in zero gravity. They don't like it. They're always bumping into each other, you have to put them on leashes, they look baffled. Unlike fish, by the way! They don't seem to care, they live in a kind of floating state anyway. We could look into fish breeding next, if you like."

"We haven't tried everything yet," announced Kay Woodthorpe, a squat woman with the face of a Chihuahua, who worked for the bioregenerative systems research group. "If the worst comes to the worst, we'll try artificial gravity."

"How would you do that?" asked Carl Hanna. "By making the OSS rotate?"

"No," Julian shook his head. "Just the breeding module, uncoupled and stored a few kilometers away. A structure like OSS isn't suited to spinning. You'd need a wheel for that."

"Like in science-fiction movies?"

"Exactly."

"But you've got one here," said Tautou. "Not a wheel, perhaps, but axial symmetric elements—"

"You're talking about a Bernal sphere, my friend. That's something else. A wheel whose rotational element corresponds to the speed of the Earth's rotation." Julian frowned. "Imagine a car tire or a cylindrical body. When it turns, centrifugal forces arise at the internal wall, opposite the axis. Then something like gravity comes into being. You can walk along a self-enclosed surface, excellent jogging route, by the way, while the gravity decreases toward the axis. Feasible in principle. The problem is the requisite size and stability of such a structure. A wheel with a diameter of—let's say—100 meters would have to complete a rotation every fourteen seconds, and the gravity at your feet would probably be stronger than the gravity at your head, because your body accelerates to different degrees. And besides, if you set something like that in motion—you know that from driving: when one of your tires isn't properly balanced, it lurches like mad; and now imagine a rotating station starting to career. You've got people walking about. How are you going to ensure that they're evenly distributed at all times? You couldn't begin to calculate the vibrations produced, everyone would be nauseous, the thing might explode—"

"But you've left the era of lightweight construction behind," said Hanna. "With the elevator you can put unlimited mass in orbit. Just build a bigger, more stable one."

"Would such a thing be possible?" Tautou said in amazement. "Like the one in *2001?*"

"Sure." Julian nodded. "I knew Kubrick. The old guy had thought very carefully about that, or let's say he'd had other people think about it for him. I've always dreamed of copying his space station—that massive wheel turning to the sounds of waltz music, which you can walk around. But it would have to be huge. Four kilometers in diameter. High orbit, highly armored. So you could fit a whole city inside, with residential areas, parks, maybe a river—"

"I think this is quite fascinating enough," Sushma Nair said to her husband and, glowing with enthusiasm, touched his arm. "Look at that, Mukesh. Spinach. Zucchinis!"

They were floating along a glass wall several meters high. Behind it all kinds of greenery curled and sprouted, fruits dangled from trees.

"Pioneering work, Julian," Mukesh agreed. "You've managed to impress a simple peasant."

"Just as you have impressed the world," Julian smiled.

False modesty, Nair, thought Hanna.

While a brave little group explored the vacuum outside, he, Eva Borelius, Karla Kramp, Bernard Tautou, and the Nairs were, under the expert guidance of Julian and Kay Woodthorpe, viewing the two biospheres, the huge, spherical modules in which the bioregenerative life-support system department was experimenting with agriculture and animal rearing. Over six floors, Biosphere A brought together zucchinis, cabbage, spinach, tomatoes, paprika, and broccoli, a real Little Italy of vegetables, as well as kiwifruit and strawberries, the whole thing populated by a fauna of bustling robots, constantly planting, fertilizing, hoeing, cutting, and harvesting. Hanna wouldn't have been surprised to see carbon-fiber-reinforced rabbits with radio-telescope ears gnawing at the lettuce and suddenly floating away at their approach. He threw back his head. One level up, apple trees stretched knotty branches resplendent with cudgel-hard fruits.

At first, Woodthorpe told them, there had been massive problems. The predecessors of the greenhouses, called salad machines, had been little more than standard racks in which tomatoes and lettuce flourished in competition. As plants took their bearings from gravity like almost all living creatures, and thus knew where to stretch and in which direction to send their roots, the loss of up and down had led to the formation of terrible thickets—unfortunately at the expense of the fruits, which led a wretched guerrilla lifestyle in the middle of the kraken-like root monster. Thrown into confusion, even spinach had produced only woody stalks in a desperate bid to cling onto something, until it occurred to someone to subject the fields to artificial tremors, brief shakes as a result of which their fruit and vegetable plants finally sought support down below, where the vibrations came from.

"Since then we've had the rank growth under control, and you can see the quality," Woodthorpe explained. "Certainly, it is and will always be greenhouse produce. The strawberries taste a bit watery, you wouldn't necessarily win any prizes with the red peppers—"

"But the zucchinis are great," said Julian.

"Yeah, and so is the broccoli, and amazingly the tomatoes too. We don't really know yet why one works better than the other. At any rate the greenhouses give us cause to hope that we may in the future be able to close life-support systems that are presently open. On the Moon we've nearly got there."

"What do you mean 'close'?" asked Karla.

"Just like on Earth. Nothing gets lost there. The Earth is a self-enclosed system, everything is constantly being processed. Just look on the space station as a small copy of our planet with proportionately limited resources of water, air, and fuel, except that in the past we couldn't rework all those resources. We were constantly forced to maintain supplies. Carbon dioxide, for example, got completely out of hand. Today we can split it in reactors, use the liberated oxygen again to breathe, or combine it with hydrogen to form water, and the remaining carbon can be synthesized with methane to form fuel. Just a bit of sludge gets lost in the process, and it's hardly worth mentioning. The problem is more one of bringing the size and consumption of the reactors into a convincing relationship with their effectiveness. So we try to do that with natural regeneration processes. Plants can also serve that purpose. Our own little rain forest, if you like. On the Moon we have bigger greenhouses, and we're on the brink of completely closing all the cycles."

"No market for a water supplier, then," laughed Tautou.

"No, the OSS is on the way to complete self-reliance."

"Hmm, self-reliance." Karla thought for a moment. "So you could soon be declaring independence, could you? Or the whole Moon. By the way, who does the Moon actually belong to?"

"Nobody," said Julian. "According to the lunar treaty."

"Interesting." Karla's Modigliani eyebrows raised, arches of amazement, her face an oval full of ovals. "Given that it doesn't belong to anyone, it's not short of people."

"That's right. The treaty urgently needs to be rewritten."

"Perhaps to say that the Moon belongs to everybody?"

"Correct."

"So the people who got there first. Or who are already up there. America and China."

"By no means. Anyone else can follow them."
"*Can* anyone follow them?" she asked slyly.
"That, my dear Karla," smiled Julian, "is exactly the point."

Finn O'Keefe tried to find solace in physics.

The dressing process had gone on for ages, until at last the group hung, packed and helmeted, in the hermetic seclusion of the airlock, a clinically illuminated, empty room with rounded edges. Handgrips ran along the walls; a display provided information about pressure, temperature, and atmospheric composition. Nina explained that this chamber was considerably larger than the other hatches distributed around the OSS. Once Peter Black had joined them, the group now comprised eight people. A hiss, growing quieter and finally fading away, indicated that the air was being sucked out, then the outer bulk-heads glided silently open.

O'Keefe gulped.

In thrall to early human fears of plunging into the abyss, and with butterflies in his stomach, he stared outside. Part of the roof extended before his eyes. He didn't know what he had expected, an outlet, a balcony, a gangway, regardless of the fact that none of it made any sense up here. The circular level had no floor—it was an open structure with a diameter of 400 meters, surrounded by a steel ring, massive enough that railway lines could have passed through it, and fitted with pay-loads and manipulators. A radial arrangement of supporting construc-tions led from the torus to the other areas. Beyond that solar park, glittering in the sunlight, radiators circulated and spherical tanks hung from crane-like cantilevers. Batteries of floodlights illuminated huge hangars, the birthplaces of future spaceships. Tiny astronauts floated below the belly of a steel giant, overseeing the installation of rows of seats by robot arms. Bizarre machine-creatures, half man, half insect, crisscrossed the area, carried parts in locust arms, crawled with seg-mented grasping claws around the scaffolding and girders, carried out soldering work and riveted prefabricated components. Their android faces seemed to have been inspired by the character Boba Fett, the always helmeted contract killer from *Star Wars*, leading inevi-tably to the conclusion that Julian Orley had been involved in their development—Orley with his enthusiasm for science-fiction films, who always managed to transform quotations into innovations.

Beyond the hatch a chasm yawned.

The vertical structure of the OSS stretched almost 300 meters below O'Keefe, and below it lay the Earth, an unimaginable distance away. He hesitated, felt his heart thundering. Although he knew about the irrelevance of his weight, it seemed sheer madness to pass beyond the edge, like leaping from a skyscraper.

Physics, he thought. Trust in the law of God.

But he didn't believe in God anyway.

Beside him, Nina Hedegaard and Peter Black sailed sedately outside, turned around and presented the mirrored fronts of their helmets. "The first time is always a breakthrough," he heard the Danish woman say. "But you can't fall. Just try to adjust your way of thinking."

Got me, thought O'Keefe.

A moment later he was given a push, slipped out over the edge toward the two guides and right past them. Startled, he gasped for air and braced himself as he flew, but there was nothing there to stop him. Dispatched on a journey of no return, he drifted away. The idea of being lost in space, of being slung out into the void, flashed through his mind and he started flailing wildly, which only made him look all the more ridiculous.

"Look," Laura Lurkin said. "It's the ladies' program."

Amber thought she could physically feel the corrosive effect of the mockery. She knew from Lynn that the fitness trainer, a menacingly sculpted block of humanity with a wrestler's crotch, a troll's arms, and a soothing voice, didn't particularly care for space tourists. Her attitude was based on her conviction that private individuals had no business being anywhere higher up than the current passenger flight paths. Lurkin was a former Navy Seal, hardened in the fire of geopolitical conflicts. When Olympiada, Miranda, Rebecca, Momoka, and Amber turned up at the spa area like a delegation of fun-hungry First Ladies, Lurkin's initial reaction had been, quite reasonably, to make fun of them, albeit in a moderately affable tone. After all, it was her job to keep orbital travelers fit, not to depress them.

"You've *got* to go, Amber! Please! We've got the EVA, the guided tour through the scientific area, the multimedia performance: I'd have been happy if we could have distributed the silly women across the three groups, but they wanted their beauty program. I'm glad we don't have to deal with Paulette, but—"

"I'd actually rather come to your presentation, Lynn."

"I know. I'm sorry, believe me! But someone has to give those four the feeling that we're making them just as welcome as all the others, who want more from an orbital trip than a bit of sweating and peeling and having their spots squeezed. I'd do the job myself, but I can't!"

"Oh, Lynn. Does it have to be like that? Tim and I—"

"They accept you as a representative, as a hostess."

"But I'm not the hostess."

"No, but you are in their eyes. You're an Orley. Please, Amber!"

That pleading tone!

"Okay, fine, whatever. But put me on the second space walk this afternoon!"

"Oh, Amber, let me kiss you! You can walk all the way to Jupiter, I'll make the sandwiches myself! Thank you!"

So here it was, the ladies' program.

The fitness center occupied two modules, elliptically flattened like the accommodation tubes. In the upper part there was a real sauna, without wooden benches, admittedly, but with straps for the hands and feet and generously sized windows, as well as a steam sauna, whose rounded walls copied the stars in the form of hundreds of tiny electric bulbs. In the crystal cave you could drift through droplets of ice-cold water that was sprayed into the room and then sucked back out again; in the quiet zone you could listen to celestial music, read, or snooze. A floor further down, various fitness devices, massage rooms, and strong hands waited for the stressed-out part-time astronauts.

"—indispensable in space!" Lurkin was saying. "Zero gravity is all well and good, but it contains a lot of dangers that shouldn't be under-estimated if you're exposed to it over a long period. You'll already have noticed certain changes in yourself. Warming in the head and chest, for example. Immediately after the start of zero gravity, more than half a liter of blood rises from the lower regions of the body to the thorax and head. You'll get apple cheeks and what astronauts call a 'puffy face.' It's a nice effect, by the way, because it compensates for wrinkles and makes you look younger. But not in the long term, unfortunately. Once you get back to Earth, gravity will tug at your tissues just as it always has done, so enjoy the moment."

"My legs are freezing," Rebecca Hsu said suspiciously, inflated in her dressing gown until she looked like a globe made of terry toweling. "Is that normal?"

"Quite normal. In accordance with the redistribution of your bodily fluids your legs will feel rather cold. You'll get used to that, as you will to your outbreaks of sweating and temporary disorientation. I heard that one of you suffered quite badly from that?"

"Madame Tautou," Miranda Winter nodded. "Wow! The poor woman keeps—" She lowered her voice. "Well, it's coming out every-where, in fact."

"Space sickness." Lurkin nodded. "No reason to be ashamed, even experienced astronauts suffer from it. Who else has any other symptoms?"

Olympiada Rogacheva hesitantly raised her hand. After a few sec-onds Momoka Omura pointed an index finger, before immediately retracting it again.

"Nothing important," she said.

"Well, with me it's like this," Rebecca said. "My sense of balance is a bit confused. Even though I'm actually used to sailing."

"I'm just happy if I can keep everything down," Rogacheva sighed.

Lurkin smiled. Of course she had been informed that the oligarch's wife had a breakdown-related alcohol problem. Strictly speaking, Olympiada Rogacheva shouldn't even have been here, but during the two-week training program she had drunk nothing but tea, confounding all the skeptics. She could clearly manage without vodka and champagne, after all.

"Never mind, ladies. By the day after tomorrow you'll be immune to space sickness. But what affects everybody are physiological long-term changes. In zero gravity your muscle mass declines. Your calves will shrink to chicken legs, your heart and circulation will be overtaxed. That's why daily exercise is the chief duty of every astronaut, meaning exercise machine, gymnastics, weight-lifting, all nicely strapped in, of course. On long-term missions a considerable decline in bone substance has also been observed, particularly in the spine and leg areas. The body loses up to ten percent of its calcium over six months in space, immune disorders appear, wounds heal more slowly, all concomitant effects that *Perry Rhodan* shamefully fails to mention. You'll only be spending a few days in zero gravity, but I urge you to get some exercise. So what shall we start with? Rowing, cycling, jogging?"

Momoka stared at Lurkin as if she had lost her mind.

"No way. I want to go to the steam room!"

"And you'll get to the steam room," said Lurkin, as if talking to a child. "But first we'll do a spot of fitness training, okay? That's how it is on board space stations. The instructor's word is final."

"Okay." Amber stretched. "I'm going on the exercise machine."

"And I'm going on the bike," Miranda cried with delight.

"An exercise machine *is* a bike." Momoka pulled a face as if being subjected to a serious injustice. "Can we at least swim here?"

"Of course." Lurkin spread her muscle-bound arms. "If you can find a way of keeping water in the pool in zero gravity, we can talk about it."

"And what about that?" Rebecca looked at a device on the ceiling just above her head. "It looks like a step machine."

"Bingo! It trains up your bottom and your thighs."

"Exactly right." The Taiwanese woman peeled herself out of her dressing gown. "You should never miss an opportunity to fight against physical decay. It's dramatic enough! I feel as if it's only my tight underwear that's keeping me from exploding!"

Amber, who knew Rebecca from the media, raised an eyebrow. Without a doubt, the queen of luxury had put on a fair bit of weight over the past few years, but her skin looked as smooth and tight as a balloon. What was it that Lurkin had said about "puffy faces"? Why should the effect be restricted to the face alone? It was obvious that upper arms shouldn't wobble in zero gravity, that breasts were lifted because they weren't being drawn toward the Earth's core, that everything was deliciously rounded and firm. The whole of Rebecca Hsu looked somehow puffy.

"Don't worry," she said. "You look great."

"For your age," Momoka added smugly.

With Lurkin's help, Rebecca wedged herself onto the step machine, allowed herself to be belted in and smiled down at Amber.

"Thanks, but when the paparazzi need helicopters to get all of you into shot, it's time to face the facts. I'm starting to turn to jelly. I distribute anticellulite miracle cures by some of the most famous cosmetic brands in the world, but slap me on the butt and you have to wait for a quarter of an hour until the waves have subsided."

And she started jogging like a peasant treading grapes, while Miranda Winder doubled up with laughter and Amber joined in. Momoka's gestures passed through various stages of human development, then she laughed as well. Something was dissolved, a deep-seated, unconfessed anxiety, and they all rolled around cackling and panting.

Lurkin waited with an indulgent expression on her face and her arms folded.

"Glad we all agree," she said.

"Out you go!"

Heidrun's words were followed by a boisterous chortle.

It was the last thing O'Keefe heard before he drifted out of the airlock. Heidrun, that bitch! Frank Poole, the unlucky astronaut from *2001*, had fallen victim to a paranoid computer, now he to a homicidal Swiss woman. His fingers grasped the thruster controls. The first stimulus stopped his flight; the second, intended to turn him back toward the air lock, instead sent him into a spin.

"Very good," he heard Nina say, as if she were sitting in the corner of his helmet with fairy wings. "Wonderful reaction speeds for a beginner."

"Don't start," he snarled.

"No, I'm serious. Can you stop the spinning too?"

"Why should he?" laughed Heidrun. "It looks good. Hey, Finn, you should catch yourself a moon to orbit around you."

He rotated clockwise. Into the spin.

And it worked. Suddenly he was hanging there motionless, watching the others spin out of the air lock like space debris. The new, close-fitting generation of space suits had the advantage of not making everyone who wore them look exactly the same. They let you have an idea of who was in front of you, even if their face was barely recognizable through the mirrored visor. Heidrun, clad like a Star Warrior, was given away by her anorexic, elf-like figure. He longed to give her a good kick.

"I'll get you for that," he mumbled, but couldn't stop himself grinning.

"Oh, *Perry*! My hero."

She carried on giggling, then got into difficulties and began to turn upside down. Someone else, it might have been Locatelli, Edwards, or Mimi, started to retreat back inside the air lock. A third flailed his arms about. Nothing about the movement suggested it was happening voluntarily. Apart from Nina and Peter, only one member of the group displayed any signs of controlled movement, turning in a neat half circle and coming down to rest next to the two leaders. O'Keefe had no doubt it was Rogachev. Then, suddenly, they all floated back toward each other as if by magic.

"A bit treacherous, isn't it!" laughed Peter. "Navigating in a vacuum is like nothing else. There's no friction, no current to carry you, no resistance. Once you're in motion you carry on that way until an adequate counterimpulse occurs, either that or you'll drift into the sphere of some celestial body and end up as a meteor or make some pretty little crater. Using a thruster properly takes practice; practice you haven't had. So that's why, from now on, you don't need to do anything. The remote control will take over. For the next twenty minutes we're putting you on control beam, which means you can just sit back and enjoy the view."

They set off and flew rapidly out over the artificial platform, toward the half-built spaceship. They hovered weightlessly between the floodlight masts.

"We try to limit EVAs to the absolute minimum of course," Nina explained. "By now, sun-storm forecasts have become accurate enough for us to take them into account during the planning stages of a mission. And in any case, no astronaut goes outside without a dosimeter. If an unexpected eruption takes place there's still plenty of time to get back inside the station, and there are dozens of armored storm shelters all around the outer walls of the OSS if it ever gets tight. But then again, even the most high-tech suit doesn't provide long-lasting protection against radiation damage, so we're increasingly reliant on robots."

"The flying things over there?" said Locatelli in a shaky voice, pointing in the direction of two machines with arms but no legs, crossing their path a short distance away. "They look like goddamn aliens."

"Yes, it's astonishing. Now that reality has emancipated itself from science fiction, it's picking up its ideas. We've realized, for example, that humanoid machines accommodate their creators' needs in all kinds of ways."

"Creation in our own image," said Mimi Parker. "Just like the boss did it six thousand years ago."

Something in those crudely chosen words made O'Keefe stop and think, but he decided to worry about it later. They flew in a wide curve and headed for the spaceship. One of the automatons had anchored itself onto the outer shell like a tick. His two main extremities disappeared inside an open shutter, where they were clearly in the process of installing something; two smaller arms around the machine's upper body were holding components at the ready. The front side of its helmet-like head was adorned with black glassy peepholes.

"Can they think?" asked Heidrun.

"They can count," said Nina. "They're Huros-ED series robots, *Humanoid Robotic System for Extravehicular Demands*. Incredibly precise and utterly reliable. So far there's only been one incident involving a Huros-ED, and it wasn't actually caused by it. But after that their circuit board was extended to include a life-saving program. We use them for everything you can think of: servicing, maintenance, construction. If you end up in outer space, you have a very good chance of being picked up by a Huros and brought back safely."

Their route led them straight up over one of the floodlight masts and over the back of the spaceship.

"It takes two to three days to get to the Moon by shuttle. They're spacious, but just for fun try imagining during the flight that you're on your way to Mars. Six months in a box like that, the sheer horror of it! Human beings aren't machines; they need social contact, private lives, space, music, good food, beautiful design, food for the senses. That's why the spaceship being created here isn't like any conventional ship. Once it's completed it will be an astonishing size; here you're only seeing the main body, almost 200 meters in length. To put it more precisely, it's constructed from individual elements which are linked up with one another: partly burned-out tanks from old space shuttles, partly new, larger models. Together they form the working and command area. There will be laboratories and conference rooms, greenhouses and processing plants. The sleep and training modules rotate on centrifugal outriggers around the main body of the ship to allow the presence of a weak artificial gravity, similar to the gravity on Mars. The next construction stage will be to extend it at the front and back, using masts several hundred meters in length."

"Several hundred meters?" echoed Heidrun. "Good grief! How long is the ship going to be?"

"About a kilometer, or so I've heard. And that's excluding the sun wings and generators. Around two-thirds of them are situated on the front mast, at the peak of which there will be a nuclear reactor to provide the power. Hence the unconventional design: the living quarters have to be at least 700 meters away from the source of radiation."

"And when will the flight be?" Edwards inquired.

"Realists have their sights set on 2030, but Washington would prefer it to be earlier. After all, it's not just a race to get to the Moon. The United States will do everything they possibly can, even if it means . . ."

". . . occupying the Red Planet," completed Rogachev. "We get the picture. Has Orley rented the entire hangar to the Americans?"

"Part of it," said Nina. "Other areas of the station have been rented to the Americans, Germans, French, Indian, and Japanese. Russians too. They're all running research stations up here."

"But not the Chinese?"

"No, not the Chinese."

Rogachev dropped the subject. Their flight led over the hangar toward the outer ring with its workstations and manipulators. Nina pointed out the far ends of the masts, which sprouted spherical objects: "The site and orbit regulation system. Orb-like tanks feed into the thrusters, which can be used to sink, lift, or move the station."

"But why?" asked O'Keefe. "I thought it had to stay at exactly this height?"

"In principle, yes. On the other hand, if a meteorite or a particularly big lump of space debris were to come rushing toward us, we would need to be able to adjust the station's position a little. Generally speaking we would know about things like that weeks in advance. A vertical shift would usually suffice, but sometimes it makes more sense to get out of the way by moving slightly to the side."

"That's why the anchor station is a swimming island!" called Mimi Parker. "So it can be moved around in synchrony with the OSS!"

"Exactly," said Nina.

"That's crazy! And does it happen often? That kind of bombardment?"

"Rarely."

"And you'd know the path of all objects like that?" O'Keefe dug deeper.

"Well." Peter hesitated. "The large ones, yes. But small odds and ends pass through here a million times without us needing to know about it: nanoparticles, micrometeorites."

"And what if something like that hits my suit?" Edwards suddenly sounded as if he was longing to be back inside the station.

"Then you'd have one more hole," said Heidrun, "and a nicely positioned one, hopefully."

"No, the suit can take that. The armored plating absorbs nanoparticles, and if a pinprick-sized hole really did appear, it wouldn't have any immediate impact. The fabric is interfaced with a polymer layer; its molecular chains close up as soon as the material reaches its melting point. And the friction heat from the impact of a micrometeorite alone would be enough to do that. You might end up with a small wound, but nothing more than you'd get from stepping on a sea urchin or having a run-in with your cat. The chance of crossing paths with a micrometeorite is far less than, let's say, your chances of getting eaten by a shark."

"How reassuring," said Locatelli, his voice sounding strained.

The group had crossed the outer edge of the ring and were now following the course of another pylon. O'Keefe would have liked ideally to turn around and go back. There should have been a fantastic view over the roof to the torus from here. But his space suit was like a horse that knew the way and went off all on its own. In front of him the pennons spread like a flock of dark glistening birds with mythical wingspans, keeping watch over these curious patches of civilization in space. And beyond the solar panels that supplied the station with energy, there was only open space.

"This section should be of particular interest to you, Mr. Locatelli. It's your stuff!" said Peter. "We'd have needed four to five times as many panels using conventional solar technology."

Locatelli said something along the lines of that being entirely true. Then he added a few other things. O'Keefe thought he picked up the words *revolution* and *humanity*, followed by *millstone*, which was probably supposed to be *milestone*. Either way, for some reason it all jumbled up and sounded like guttural porridge.

"You should be really proud of it, sir," said Peter. "Sir?"

The object of his praise lifted both arms as if he were about to conduct an orchestra. A few syllables escaped from his throat.

"Is everything okay, sir?"

Locatelli groaned. Then they heard eruptive retching.

"B-4, abort," said Nina calmly. "Warren Locatelli. I'll accompany him back to the air lock. The group will continue on as planned."

One day, Mukesh Nair told them, back when he was still a boy in the small village of Loni Kalbhor, they had cut his uncle down from the roof beam of his hut, where he had hanged himself. Suicides among farmers were a part of daily life back then, the bitter harvest of the Indian agricultural crisis. Mukesh had wandered through the fallow sugarcane fields, wondering what could be done to stem the flood of cheap imports from the so-called developed nations, whose agriculture lounged around in a feather bed of generous subsidies as it deluged the world with dirt-cheap fruit and vegetables, while Indian farmers saw no other way out of their debt than to take their own life.

He had realized back then that you couldn't misinterpret globalization as a process which politicians and companies initiated, accelerated, and controlled as they pleased. It wasn't something that could be turned off and on, not a cause, but the symptom of an idea that was as old as humanity itself: the exchange of culture and wares. Rejecting that would have been as naïve as suing the weather for crop failures. From the day human beings had first ventured into other humans' territories to trade or make war, it had always been about doing it in such a way that they could participate and profit from it as much as possible. Nair realized that the farmers' misery couldn't be blamed on some sinister pact between the First World states, but came down to the failure of the rulers in New Delhi to play to India's strengths. And one of those strengths—even though, historically, the country had always been synonymous with hunger—was nourishing the world.

Back then, Nair and a group of others had led the Green Revolution. He went to the villages, encouraging the farmers to switch from sugarcane to chilis, tomatoes, eggplants, and zucchinis. He provided them with seeds and fertilizer, introduced them to new technologies, secured them cheap credit to relieve their debt, pledged minimum purchases, and gave them shares in the profit of his supermarket chain, which he built from scratch by utilizing modern refrigeration technology, naming it Tomato after his favorite vegetable. Thanks to sophisticated logistics, the perishable goods found their way so quickly from the fields to the counters of the Tomato supermarkets that all the imported products looked old and rotten in comparison. Desperate farmers, who until recently had been faced with the choice of either going into the city as day laborers or stringing themselves up in the attic, became entrepreneurs. Tomato boomed. More and more branches opened, more and more farmers joined forces with Nair's entourage in the new, emerging India.

"The inhabitants of our hot, microbe-contaminated metropolises loved our air-conditioned, clean fresh-food markets from the word go," said Nair. "We had competitors pursuing similar concepts, of course, partly with the support of foreign multi-corporate giants. But I only ever saw my competitors as allies. When it mattered most, we were a hair's breadth ahead of the rest."

By now, there were branches of Tomato all over the world. Nair had swallowed up most of his competitors. While India's agricultural products were now being exported to the most remote corners of the world, Nair had long since gone on to explore a new field of activity, branching out into genetics and blessing the flood-prone coastal areas of his country with a saltwater-resistant rice.

"And that," said Julian, "is the very thing that unites us."

They watched a small harvest robot plucking cherry tomatoes from the vines with its intricate claws, sucking them up inside itself before they had the chance to roll away.

"We will occupy outer space, colonize the Moon and Mars. Perhaps a little less quickly than we imagined, but it will happen, if only because there are a number of sound reasons why we should. We are standing on the threshold of an era in which the Earth will be only one of the many places where we can live and develop industries."

Julian paused.

"But you won't be able to make a fortune with fruit and vegetables beyond the Earth just yet, Mukesh. The journey toward establishing Tomato branches on the Moon will be a long one! Bernard, you could supply the Moon with water of course—it's vital for any new development—but you'll barely make a cent in the process. And as far as your work is concerned, Eva: long-term stays in outer space, on the Moon and on the surface of other planets, will all present medicine with totally new challenges. And yet research will remain a loss-making business initially, just as I subsidize America's space travel to help promote the most important resource for a clean and lasting energy supply, and the way I subsidized the development of the necessary reactors. If you want to change the world and be a pioneer, the first thing you need to do is *spend money*. Carl, you made your fortune through clever investments in oil and gas, then switched sides to solar technology, but in space these new technologies wouldn't yet make any decent turnover. So why should you invest in Orley Enterprises?"

He looked at each of them in turn.

"I'll tell you why. Because we're united by something more than just what we produce, finance and research, and that's our concern for the well-being of mankind. Take Eva for example, who has successfully cultivated synthetic skin, nerves, and cardiac muscle cells. Incredibly significant work, reliable, highly lucrative, but that's only the half of it, because above all it provides *hope* for coronary-risk patients, cancer patients, and burn victims! And Bernard, a man who has provided the poorest of the poor around the globe with access to clean water. Or Mukesh, who opened up a new way of life for India's farmers and fed the world. Carl, whose investment in renewable energies helps to make its actual use possible. And what's my dream? You already know. You know why we're here. Ever since experts began to think about clean, risk-free fusion technology, about how the fuel of the future, helium-3, can be transported from the Moon to Earth, I've been obsessed with the idea of providing our planet with this new, inexhaustible source of energy. I've gone through many years of deficit to develop reactors until they were ready for production and to build the first functioning space elevator so we could give mankind a springboard into outer space. And do you know what?"

He smiled contentedly and paused for several seconds.

"All that idealism has paid off. Now I *want to* and I *will* make money from it! And you should all join me in doing so! In Orley Enterprises, the most important technology experts in the world. It's people like us who move or stop this wonderful planet 36,000 kilometers beneath us. It's up to *us*. It may not increase your sales of vegetables, water, or medication if we join forces, but you'll be part of the biggest conglomerate in the world. Tomorrow, Orley Energy will become world market leader in the energy sector with its fusion reactors and environmentally friendly power. With the help of more space elevators and spacestations, Orley Space will accelerate the conquest of the solar system for mankind's use, and, together with Orley Travel, expand space tourism too. Believe me, all of that put together will *pay off*! Everyone wants to go into orbit, everyone wants to go to the Moon, to Mars and beyond, both humans and nations. At the beginning of the century we thought the dream was over, but it's only just begun, my friends! And yet only very few countries possess the technologies the whole world needs, and Orley Technologies are way ahead of the game on this one. And everyone, everyone without exception, will pay the price!"

"Yes," said Nair in awe. "Yes!"

Hanna smiled and nodded.

Everyone will pay the price—

Everything Julian had said, with his usual eloquence and persuasiveness, reduced down to this last sentence in his ears. He had voiced what had been left behind by rulers retreating from the globalization process, the attempt for economy to become independent, the privatization of politics: a vacuum that had been filled with businessmen. He defined the future as a product. Even the days ahead wouldn't change that, quite the opposite in fact. The world would be sold yet again.

Just very differently to how Julian Orley imagined.

"I'm back," chirped Heidrun.

"Oh, my darling!" Ögi's mustache bristled with delight. "Safely and in one piece too, I see. How was it?"

"Great! Locatelli threw up when he saw his solar panels."

She floated over and gave him a kiss. The action led to repulsion. She slowly retreated again, reached out to grasp the back of a chair, and made her way back, hand over hand.

"Did Warren get spacesick or something?" asked Lynn.

"Yes, it was great!" Heidrun beamed. "Nina took him off with her, and after that it was all really nice."

"I'm not so sure." Donoghue pursed his lips. Red-cheeked and bloated, he rested grandly back against an imaginary throne like Falstaff, his hair so bouffant it looked as though an animal had died on his scalp. "It sounds dangerous to me, someone throwing up in their helmet."

"Well *you* don't have to go out there," said Aileen sharply.

"Poppycock! I wasn't saying that . . ."

"You're sixty-five, Chucky. You don't have to join in on everything."

"I said, it *sounds* dangerous!" blustered Donoghue. "I didn't say I was scared. I'd still go out there even if I were a hundred. And on the subject of age, have you heard the one about the really old couple and the divorce judge?"

"Divorce judge!" Haskin was starting to laugh already. "Let's hear it."

"So they go to the divorce judge, and he looks at the woman and says: 'My dear, how old are you?' 'Let's see,' says the woman, 'I'm ninety-five.' 'Okay, and you?' The man thinks for a second: ninety-eight! 'God Almighty,' says the judge, 'I don't believe it. Why on earth would you want to get divorced at your age?' 'Well, it's like this, your honor . . .'"

Tim snarled. It was hardly bearable. Chucky had been relentlessly setting off comedy firecrackers, one after the other, for the past two hours.

"'. . . we wanted to wait until the children had passed away.'"

Haskin did a somersault. Everyone laughed, of course. The joke wasn't that bad, at least not bad enough for Tim to blame Donoghue alone for his apocalyptic mood. But at that moment he noticed Lynn sitting there as if she'd been turned to stone, as if she were somewhere else entirely. She was gazing straight ahead and was clearly clueless of what was going on around her. Then, all of a sudden, she laughed too.

I could be wrong, he thought. It doesn't necessarily mean that it's starting all over again.

"So what did you get up to while we were gone?" Heidrun looked around curiously. "Have you been to look around the model station?"

"Yes, I could recreate it right now from memory," bragged Ögi. "Amazing building. To tell you the truth I was surprised by the safety standards."

"Why?" asked Lynn.

"Well, the privatization of space travel adds to the fear that it's all been cobbled together too quickly."

"But would you be here if you were seriously concerned about that?"

"That's true." Ögi laughed. "But in any case, it was quick. Extraordinarily quick. Aileen and Chuck here could certainly tell you a thing or two about building regulations, surveys, and restrictions."

"Just one or two?" growled Chucky. "I could go on for days."

"When we were designing the Red Planet, they thought the project would be impossible to complete," Aileen confirmed. "What a bunch of cowards! It took a decade to get from the initial design stage to the start of the construction, and even after that they never left us in peace."

The Red Planet was Donoghue's pièce de résistance, a luxury resort in Hanoi modeled on the landscape of Mars.

"It's now known as the pièce de résistance of structural engineering," she added triumphantly. "There's never been an incident with any of our hotels! But what happens? Whenever you start planning something new, they swarm over you like zombies and try to eat you alive, your enthusiasm, your ideas, even the creative power given to you by the almighty Creator himself. You might think that building up a good record over the years would earn you some credit, but it's like they take no notice whatsoever of what you've achieved so far. Their eyes are dead, their skulls stuffed with regulations."

Oh man, thought Tim.

"Yes, yes." Ögi rubbed his chin thoughtfully. "I know exactly what you mean. In this respect, my dear Lynn, I can't help but water down all this adulation with a bit of skepticism. As I said, you made the station into a reality extremely quickly. You might even say suspiciously quickly compared to the ISS, which is smaller yet took a lot longer."

"Would you like to hear an explanation for that?"

"At the risk of annoying you . . ."

"You're not annoying me in the slightest, Walo. Pressure from competition has always encouraged sloppiness in the race to be first. But Orley Space doesn't have any competitors. So we never needed to be quicker than anyone else."

"Hmm."

"The reason we were quick was perfect planning, which ultimately meant the OSS built itself. We didn't need to accommodate dozens of notoriously hard-up space authorities, nor wade through bureaucratic quicksand. We only had one partner, the United States of America, and they would even have sold the Lincoln Memorial to break out of the commodity trap. Our agreement fit on the back of a gasoline receipt. America builds up its moon base and supplies technology for mining helium-3, while we bring in marketable reactors, an inexpensive, quick transport system to the Moon and, last but not least, a great deal of money! Getting authorization from Congress was a walk in the park! It was a win-win situation! One gets to monopolize the reactor trade, the other returns to the peak of space-traveling nations and gets the solution to all their energy problems. Believe me, Walo, with prospects like those on the table, any other option but *quickly* is completely out of the question."

"Well, she's certainly right about that!" said Donoghue, his voice like thunder. "When has it ever been about whether someone *can* build something or not? Nowadays it's always about the damn money."

"And the zombies," nodded Aileen vigorously. "The zombies are everywhere."

"Sorry." Evelyn Chambers raised her hand. "I'm sure you're right, but on the other hand we're not here to inflate each other's egos. This is about investment. And my investment in you is very much linked to trust, so we should put all our cards on the table, don't you think?"

Tim looked at his sister. She looked open and interested, clearly unaware of what Evelyn Chambers was alluding to.

"Of course. What's on your mind?"

"Slipups."

"Such as?"

"Vic Thorn."

"Of course. That's on the agenda." Lynn winced, but without batting an eyelid. "I was planning to talk about him later, but we can bring it forward."

"Thorn?" Donoghue wrinkled his forehead. "Who's he?"

"No idea." Ögi shrugged. "But I'm happy to hear about slipups. Even if only to make my peace with my own."

"We don't have any secrets," said Haskin. "It was all over the news last year. Thorn was part of the first long-term crew on the American moon station. He did an excellent job, so he was recommended for a further six months, as well as being offered a leadership position. He agreed and traveled to the OSS to fly on to the base from there."

"That's right, it rings a bell," said Heidrun.

"Same here." Walo nodded. "Wasn't there some kind of problem with an EVA?"

"With one of the manipulators to be precise. It was blocking the hatch of the shuttle which was supposed to take Thorn's people to the Moon. It was paralyzed mid-movement after being hit by a piece of space debris. So we sent a Huros up . . ."

"A what?" asked Aileen.

"A humanoid robot. It discovered a splinter in one of the joints, which had apparently caused the manipulator to shut itself down."

"Well, that sounds sensible."

"Machines don't concern themselves with concepts of reason." Haskin gave her a look as if she'd just suggested never sending robots outside without warm socks on. "We agreed to have the joint cleaned, which the Huros wasn't able to do, so that's why we sent Thorn and an astronaut up. Except that the manipulator hadn't turned itself off after all. It had just temporarily fallen into a kind of electro-coma. Suddenly, it woke up and hurled Thorn into space, and it seems his life-support systems were damaged in the process. We lost contact with him."

"How awful," whispered Aileen, ashen.

"Well." Haskin went silent for a moment. "He probably wouldn't have suffered for long. It's possible that his visor took a lot of the damage."

"Probably? So you didn't manage to . . . ?"

"Unfortunately not."

"I always thought you could just dash out after them." Aileen spread out the thumb and fingers on her right hand to make the shape of airplane wings and glided it through the air. "Like in the movies."

"Well sure, in the movies," said Haskin deprecatingly.

"But we should also mention that the new generation of the Huros series would probably have been able to save him," said Lynn. "And the space suit's remote control has been developed further too. With that, we could at least have gotten Thorn back."

"If I remember correctly," said Evelyn, "there was an investigation."

"That's right." Lynn nodded. "Which resulted in a case being brought against a Japanese robotics company. They built the manipulator. Clearly it was a case of third-party negligence. Thorn's death was a tragedy, but the operators of the OSS, that is to say, we, were cleared of any responsibility."

"Thanks, Lynn." Evelyn looked around at the others. "That's enough of an explanation for me. Don't you think?"

"Pioneers have to make sacrifices," grumbled Donoghue. "The early bird catches the worm, but sometimes he gets eaten by it."

"Let's look around a little more though," said Ögi.

"You're not convinced?" asked Lynn.

He hesitated.

"Yes, I think I am."

And that was it! A barely noticeable twitch in the corner of her mouth, the meltdown of panic in Lynn's gaze as . . .

. . . she feels the pull, just as she had when she was being dragged down into the abyss, and she wonders with horror what she's let herself in for. It started weeks ago: she keeps thinking she saw weaknesses in her work where there definitely weren't any. She's willing to swear an oath that Julian's space station will survive longer than all of foolish mankind put together, but she can't help herself picturing something exploding or falling apart, and only in the lower section. And why?

Because this section is the only one that *she*, not Julian, designed, the only one that was *her* responsibility!

And yet the same designers have been working there; the same architects, engineers, construction teams. There are barely any differences between the modules in her station and the others: identical life-support systems, the same method of construction. And yet Lynn is relentlessly tormented by the idea that they might be faulty. The more Julian praises her work, the more the self-doubt eats into her thoughts. She imagines the worst incessantly. Her otherwise commendable caution has been growing into a paranoia of constant mistrust; she searches obsessively for evidence of her failure, and the less she finds, the more nervous she becomes. The OSS Grand has ballooned into a monster of her arrogance, one that will burst like a bubble, condemning dozens of people to their deaths. Cold riveting, strutting, insulation, electrolysis devices, circulation pumps, air locks, corridors: in all of it, all she sees is the reflection of her own failings. Just the mere *thought* of the hotel in space and the one on the Moon causes her overwrought brain to erode under the onslaught of adrenaline and cortisol. If, according to theological understanding, fear is the opposite of faith, the separation from the sacred, then Lynn has become the very definition of a heathen. The fear of destroying. The fear of being destroyed. They're one and the same.

At some point in the depths of her despair, the devil has infiltrated her thoughts and whispered to her that the fear of the abyss can only be overcome by entering it there and then. How do you escape the cycle of fear that something horrific *could* happen? How can you find a way out before you completely lose your mind? How can you free yourself?

By it *happening*!

The question, of course, remains what will become of her if her work proves to be transitory. Is she just one of Julian's inventions, a character in a film? What if Julian stops *thinking* her, because she proved herself to be unworthy of being thought? Will she be condemned to perpetual suffering? Eternal damnation? Disappear without a whimper? Or will she have to disappear to be born again, more vividly than ever? If everything by which she defines herself and by which others define her comes to an end, will she, the real Lynn, finally resurface? If she even exists, that is?

"Miss Orley? Are you unwell?"

"What's wrong, dear?" Aileen's maternal falsetto tones. "You're as white as a sheet."

"Lynn?" Tim was next to her. The gentle pressure of his fingers on her shoulder. They slowly began to spin, a twofold sibling star.

Lynn, oh Lynn. What have you let yourself in for?

"Hey. Lynn!" White, slender fingers stroked her forehead, violet eyes peering at her. "Is everything okay? Have you smoked something funny?"

"I'm sorry." She blinked. "You caught me."

"Caught you doing what, sweetheart?"

The smile returned to her lips. A horse that knows the way. Tim looked at her searchingly. He wanted to tell her that he knows, but he can't let himself say anything, can't ask her! Lynn pulled herself up straight, freeing herself from the suction. She's won, for now at least.

"Space sickness," she says. "Crazy, isn't it? I never thought it would happen to me, but I guess I was wrong. The lights just seemed to go out."

"Then it's okay for me to admit it," grinned Ögi. "I'm feeling a bit queasy too."

"You?" Heidrun stared at him. "You're spacesick?"

"I am, yes."

"Why didn't you say anything?"

"Be grateful I didn't. The day will come when I'll have plenty of ailments. Are you feeling better now, Lynn?"

"Yes, thank you." Lynn shrugged off Tim's hand. "Let's plan the day ahead."

Her brother looked at her fixedly. Sure, said his look, you're space-sick. And I'm the man in the Moon.

He managed to intercept Julian as he was leaving his suite, an hour before dinner. Tim's father was wearing a fashionably cut shirt with a tie, his usual jeans, and elegant slippers adorned with the emblem Mimi Kri.

"You can have a fitting with her if you like," he said cheerfully. "Mimi has developed a collection for stays in environments with zero grav-ity and reduced gravitational pull. Great, don't you think?" He spun around on his axis. "Fiber-reinforced, so nothing can flap around. Not even the tie."

"Julian, listen—"

"Oh, before I forget, she brought something along for Amber too. An evening dress. I wanted to surprise her with it, but you can see how much is going on at the moment. I'm not getting a moment's peace with this mob around. Everything okay, my boy?"

"No. I have to—"

"Evening clothes in zero gravity, just think!" Julian grinned. "Isn't it crazy? Absolutely insane! You could look up all the skirts without these reinforcements. Marilyn Monroe would have stayed just a forgotten orphan, instead of standing on that airshaft with the wind gusting up from below and everything blowing up, you know."

"No, I don't, actually."

Julian wrinkled his forehead. He seemed to notice Tim at last, taking in his crumpled coat and flushed face, which didn't seem to bode well.

"You've probably never heard of the film, right?"

"Father, I don't give a toss whose skirt is flying up. Try taking care of your daughter for a change, will you?"

"I do. And have done ever since she was born, to be precise."

"Lynn isn't well."

"Oh, that." Julian looked at the time. "Yes, she told me. Are you coming along to Kirk with me?"

"Told you about what?" asked Tim, confused.

"That she got spacesick." Julian laughed. "Although she never has been until now. That would annoy me too!"

"No, wait." Tim shook his head impatiently. "You don't understand. Lynn isn't spacesick."

"So what is it then?"

"She's overstretched. On the brink of a nervous breakdown."

"I can understand that you're concerned, but . . ."

"She shouldn't even be here, Dad! She's falling apart. For God's sake, how often do I need to tell you? Lynn is at the end of her rope. She won't make it. She's never really dealt with what happened five years ago—"

"Hey!" Julian stared at him. "Are you crazy? This is *her* hotel."

"And . . . so what?"

"It's *her work*! Good heavens, Tim! Lynn is CEO of Orley Enterprises, she *has* to be here."

"*Has* to! Exactly."

"Don't start attacking me! Have I ever forced you to do anything? Did I ever stop you from becoming a teacher and going into your shitty community politics, even though all the doors were open for you at Orley?"

"That's not what this is about."

"It never is, right? Nor is it ever about the fact that your sister is more successful than you and that, secretly, it annoys the hell out of you."

"Oh, really?"

"Too right. Lynn has no problems whatsoever. But you do! You try to make her out to be weak because you haven't sorted yourself out."

"That has to be the most ridiculous nonsense I've ever—" Tim forced himself to calm down and lower his voice. "As far as I'm concerned you can believe what you like, I don't care. Just look out for her! Don't you remember what happened five years ago?"

"Of course I do. She was exhausted back then. If you had her workload, you'd—"

"No, Julian, she wasn't exhausted. She was burned out. She was ill, psychologically ill, will you ever get that into your head? Severe depression! A suicide risk!"

Julian looked around as if the walls had ears.

"Now listen to me, Tim," he whispered. "Lynn worked hard for all of this. People admire and adore her. This is her *big moment*. I won't allow you to mess everything up for her just because you're seeing ghosts everywhere."

"God, you don't have a clue what's going on, it's unbelievable! So stupid!"

"No, you're the one who's stupid. Why did you even come?"

"To look after her."

"Oh." Julian let out a mocking laugh. "And I thought it might have had something to do with me, just a tiny bit. My apologies for the descent into sentimentality. I'll speak with her, okay? I'll tell her what a great job she did with everything, that it's perfect, that everyone thinks she's wonderful. Okay?"

Tim stayed silent as Julian, clearly annoyed, floated off toward the air lock. O'Keefe was approaching from the other side.

"Hey, Tim."

"Finn. All good?"

"Great, thanks. Are you coming to Picard for a drink?"

"No, I'll see you later at dinner." Tim thought for a moment. "I need something fiber-reinforced. A fiber-reinforced tie. You can't do anything around here without fiber reinforcement."

THE SOIRÉE

The man with the multicolored eyes was very interested in the art of cooking steaks, 36,000 kilometers above the Earth, so that they were sizzling and brown on the outside and pink on the inside, and all without a single drop of meat juices running out.

And he wanted to know what it was that drew mankind to the Moon.

"Life," said Julian. "If we find it there, it will fundamentally change our view of the world. I thought you of all people were fascinated by the idea."

"And I am. So what do the experts say? Is there life on Mars?"

"Of course," Julian grinned. "Spiders."

"Spiders from Mars." He grinned back. "You could do something with that."

A large number of people from the group, on the other hand, were interested in the man with the multicolored eyes. Walo Ögi, his greatest admirer, was unfortunately being subjected to a discussion about the economy by Bernard Tautou and Oleg Rogachev, while Miranda and Rebecca were deep in discussion, in unfathomable harmony with Momoka Omura, about the therapeutic effect of luxury on Seasonal Affective Disorder. Warren Locatelli was absent. Like Paulette Tautou, he had fallen victim to the combined forces of nervus vagus and diverse neurotransmitters, which, via the area of his brain stem known as the nausea center, had led to the torrential emptying of his stomach.

This aside, it was a wonderful dinner.

The lights had been dimmed, allowing the Earth to shine through the glass floor like a huge Chinese lantern. For the first and only time, there was alcohol: champagne from slender goblets topped with sucking teats. Just like the previous evening, the food was of astonishing quality. Julian had flown in a highly decorated Michelin-starred chef for the duration of the trip, a German from Swabia called Johannes King, who had immediately subjected the kitchen to a 300 percent increase in efficiency, conjuring up amazing culinary feats such as truffle-infused creamed vegetables, with genuine Périgord truffles, of course, a dish that had gone through endless tests to ensure it could cope with the perils of zero gravity.

"Because, obviously, sauce, or anything liquid or creamy, develops a life of its own in zero gravity." The chef was just finishing his round of the table. He was an exuberant, lively character with great coordination, and seemed to take to weightlessness like a fish to water. "Unless its consistency is created in such a way that it sticks to the fish or vegetables. But if it's too concentrated it will impair the taste, so it's a real balancing act."

Tautou suggested that the *Guide Michelin* should be extended with a chapter on "Non-Terrestrial Regions." What could be more apt than awarding their stars *up here*? But he didn't have the effrontery to pour this thin analogy into each person's ear; his enthusiasm for it would gradually tire as the game terrine with cranberries, fillet steaks, potato gratin, and an unctuous tiramisu were passed around, one after the other.

"And no garlic, no beans, or anything that causes wind! Escaping bodily gases are a real problem in close conditions like these; people have become violent for far less. Also, what you're eating here would seem overseasoned on Earth, but in space your taste buds are weakened, on the back burner so to speak. Oh yes, and make sure you eat nice and slowly. Pick up every bite carefully, lead it to your mouth with intent, put it in quickly and decisively, then chew carefully."

"Well, the steaks were works of God, anyway!" said Donoghue approvingly.

"Thank you." King made a bow, which resulted in him tipping over and doing a somersault. "In actual fact they were sterile synthetic products from the molecular kitchen. We're incredibly proud of them, if I may say so."

For the next ten minutes, Donoghue fell silent, in a state of deep contemplation.

O'Keefe suckled at the champagne.

He made an effort to maintain his peeved expression. He had noted happily that Heidrun was seated next to him, or rather that her legs were wedged into the braces provided for that purpose. As much as it pleased him, though, he was punishing her with his lack of attention, chatting pointedly with the surprise guest. For her part, she made no attempt to speak to him. It was only once the group began to compare their experiences of the day and the general conversation broke up into individual exchanges that he finally deigned to address her with a hissed remark:

"What the hell were you thinking of this morning?"

She hesitated. "What are you talking about?"

"Shoving me out of the air lock."

"Oh." Heidrun fell silent for a while. "I get it. You're angry."

"No, but I'm wondering whether you've taken leave of your senses. That was pretty dangerous."

"Nonsense, Finn. I may act like a big kid sometimes, but I'm not crazy. Nina had already told me yesterday that the suits were remote-controlled. Do you seriously think they would leave all-inclusive vacationers, people whose greatest sporting achievement was getting a badge for swimming 200 meters, to their own devices out there?"

"So you didn't want to kill me? That's comforting."

Heidrun smiled mysteriously. "Sweetheart, I just wanted to find out where Perry Rhodan stops and Finn O'Keefe begins."

"And?"

"Well, it's quite fitting that you play him as a bit of a dope."

"Now hang on a minute!" protested O'Keefe. "A heroic dope."

"Yes, of course. And it never took you long to work out whether there were any females in the vicinity who might be willing to mate with you. Pleased with yourself?"

He grinned. As he paused, he heard Eva Borelius say: "But that's not a theological question, Mimi, it's about the origins of our civilization. Why do people want to cross borders, what are they looking for in space? I sometimes feel inclined to join in the chorus of anger clamoring about the trillions of people who are starving, who have no access to fresh water—"

"By now, sure," he heard Tautou exclaim from another conversation, only to be put back in his place by a pistol-shot retort of "No you haven't!" from Karla Kramp.

"—while all the fun up here devours vast amounts of money. And yet we *have* to research. Our entire culture is based upon exchange and expansion. At the end of the day, what we're looking for in the unknown is ourselves, our meaning, our future, just like Alexander von Humboldt, like Stephen Hawking—"

"I wouldn't be here if I had anything against the spread of the human race," said Mimi Parker sharply.

"Well, it sure sounded like it just then."

"No, not at all! I'm just contesting the bigoted desire to discover something that's already obvious. I, for my part, am just here to marvel at His work."

"Which, according to you, is six thousand years old."

"Well, it could be ten thousand. Let's say up to ten thousand—after all, we're not dogmatists."

"But no more than that? Not at least a few little million?"

"Absolutely not. What I expect to find out here—"

Aha, thought O'Keefe. I knew it. *Created in our own image, just as the boss did it six thousand years ago.* Mimi was here to represent the Creationists.

"And what do *you* expect to find here?" he asked Heidrun, who was laughing at something Carl Hanna had just said.

"Me?" She turned her head. Her long white ponytail swung softly behind her. "I'm not here to expect anything."

"Then why?"

"Because my husband was invited. Whenever that happens, people get me too, whether they like it or not."

"Okay, fine, but now you're here?"

"Hmm. Regardless. I don't set much store by expectations. Expectations blind people. I prefer to be surprised. And so far it's working out great, in any case." She hesitated and leaned in a little closer. "And you?"

"Nothing. I'm just doing my job."

"I don't understand."

"What is there to understand? I'm here to do my job, and that's it."

"Your—*job*?"

"Yes."

"You mean you're just letting yourself be used by Julian?"

"That's why I'm here."

"Good God, Finn." Heidrun shook her head slowly, in disbelief. He suddenly felt embarrassed, getting the feeling he'd pressed the wrong button. "You're such a jerk! Every time I'm just starting to like you—"

"Why? What have I done this time?"

"This detachment act of yours! Nothing affects you, right? Hat pulled down over your face, standing aside from the rest. That's exactly what I meant before: Who is O'Keefe?"

"He's sitting right in front of you."

"Bullshit! You just have this vague notion of who O'Keefe is supposed be, if he wants to make everyone think he's really cool. A rebel, whose problem is that he doesn't actually have anything to rebel against, except boredom perhaps."

"Hey!" He leaned forward. "What in God's name gives you the idea I'm like that?"

"This stupid attitude."

"You said yourself that—"

"I said that I didn't have any expectations, which means I'm open to everything. That's quite a lot to be going on with. You, on the other hand, made out that it was nothing more than a job to you. That you're just buying into the story that Julian's lovely and the Moon is round, and then we'll all hold hands until the cameras get turned off and we can finally go and get pissed. That's lousy, Finn! Are you really that jaded? Do you really intend to tell me, in all seriousness, that you're just in it for the money Julian's throwing your way?"

"Nonsense. I'm not getting paid for it."

"Okay then, last chance: What are you doing up here? What do you feel when you—well, when you look down at the Earth?"

O'Keefe paused as he gave it some thought. He stared intently through the glass floor below. The problem was, he couldn't think of a convincing answer. The Earth was the Earth.

"Distance," he said finally.

"Distance." She seemed to be tasting the word. "And? Good distance? Bad distance?"

"Oh, Heidrun. Call it attitude if you really want to, but I just want to be left in peace. You think I'm some bored, arrogant type who's lost any interest in getting into a debate. Maybe you're right. Today I'm soft and compliant, the nice Finn. What are you expecting?"

"I don't know. What are *you* expecting?"

"Why are you so interested? We hardly know each other."

"Because I was—still am—interested in you."

"Well, I don't know. All I know is that there are directors who make wonderful films on minuscule budgets, against all the odds. Other people play music no one wants to listen to, apart from a few crazy types perhaps, but they're unwavering in what they do, they would die for it. Some people can barely afford the hooch that keeps them writing, but if you happen to stumble upon something of theirs online and download it, you're strangely moved by how humanity and unmarketability seem to come together, and it makes you realize that great emotions always originate in the small, the intimate, the desperate. As soon as an orchestra gets involved, it turns to pathos. If you look at it that way, even the most beautiful woman would be no match for the lousiest hooker. No luxury can give you such a feeling of being alive as getting plastered with the right people, or touching your broken nose when you've picked a fight with the wrong ones. I stay in the best hotels in the world, but being in a moldy back room with someone who has a dream, in some neighborhood no sensible person would go of their own accord, well, that moves me much more than flying to the Moon."

Heidrun thought for a moment.

"It's lovely when you can afford to romanticize poverty," she commented.

"I know what you mean. But that's not what I'm doing. I don't come from a poor background. I don't have a message, I'm not fueled by anger at society, I haven't been sent up here by some political party or other. Perhaps that means I'm not committed enough, but it really doesn't seem that way to me. We have a good time when we film *Perry Rhodan*, that's for sure. I'm not about to turn down the money, either. And, recently, I've even started to enjoy being a nice guy, a *rich* nice guy who can fly to the Moon for free. I see all that and think, hey look, that's little Finn. Then I meet women who want to be with me because they think I'm part of their life. Which is true, to some extent. I accompany them through this little, or, as far as I'm concerned, great life, I'm with them the whole time, in the movies, in magazines, on the Internet, in pictures. At night, when they lie awake, they entrust their secrets to me. During times of crisis in their lives, my films are *important* to them. They read interviews with me and after every second sentence they think: Wow, he understands me! He knows exactly what I'm about! Then when they meet me they're convinced they're standing

there with a friend, a kindred spirit. They think they know me, but I
don't know them. I mean everything to them, but they don't mean anything to me, not in the slightest. Just because my picture was hanging
on their wall when they had their first orgasm, just because they may
have been thinking about me, it doesn't mean I was there. They're not
part of my life. There's no connection between us." He paused. "And
now tell me, what was it like when you first met Walo? What did you
think? Oh man, interesting, someone I don't know. Who is he, I have
to find out. Is that how it was?"

"Yes, pretty much."

"And he thought the same. You see. The magic of the first impression. I, on the other hand, meet strangers laboring under the delusion
that they *know* me. In order to completely let go of this life I would
have to stop taking part in it, but it's just too much fun. So I sing and
dance along, but I keep my distance."

"Well, that's fame," said Heidrun. It didn't sound mocking this time,
more as if she was surprised by his list of banalities. But that's exactly
how things were. Banal. On the whole, there was nothing more banal
than fame.

"Yes" he said. "It sure is."

"So we haven't managed to come up with anything more original
than what the doctor just said. Everyone's looking for themselves in
the unknown."

He hesitated. Then he smiled his famous, shy smile.

"Perhaps we're looking for our soul mates."

Heidrun's violet eyes lingered on his, but she didn't answer. They
looked at each other, entangled in a strange, cocoon-like mood which
excited O'Keefe as much as it unsettled him. He felt a twinge of awkwardness. It looked as though he was about to fall head over heels for
a cumulative lack of melanin.

He jumped, almost relieved, as Julian clapped his hands.

"Dear friends, I didn't dare hope."

Silence fell.

"And I swear I didn't ask him to. I merely suggested keeping a guitar
handy, *just in case*! And now he's even brought his own along."

Julian smiled around at them. His gaze wandered over to the man
with the multicolored eyes.

"Back in '69, when I had just turned three years old, David went to
the movies and saw *2001: A Space Odyssey*, which would later become
my favorite film, and paid immediate tribute to its maker. Almost a
quarter of a century later I had my own opportunity to honor Kubrick,
modeling my first restaurant on the design of his space station, and
I called it Oddity, in honor of the great artist we have with us here.
Kubrick lived in Childwickbury Manor at the time, the estate near

London that he hardly ever left. He also hated airplanes. I suspect that once he moved to the United Kingdom from New York he never put any more than a hop, skip, and a jump between himself and English soil. And he was said to be very shy, so I never expected to see *him* in Oddity. But to my surprise, he turned up there one evening, when David was sitting at the bar too. We all talked, and I ended up blurting out the fact that I wanted to take them both to the Moon with me, that all they had to do was say yes and we'd be on our way. Kubrick laughed and said the lack of comfort alone would horrify him. He thought the whole thing was a joke of course. I had the presumption to claim that, by the turn of the millennium, I would have built a spaceship with all the comforts and modern conveniences, of course without the slightest idea of how I would go about achieving such a thing. I had just turned twenty-six, was producing films, more bad ones than good, and was trying my hand at being an actor. I'd brought a new production of Fritz Lang's *Woman in the Moon* to the big screen with David in the lead role, was winning favor with the critics and public alike, and was also just starting to feel my way in the field of gastronomy. Orley Enterprises was still very much in the distant future. I was, however, a passionate flyer and dreamed of the space travel that also fascinated Kubrick. So I finally managed to talk him and David into a bet: *if* I succeeded in building the promised spaceship by the year 2000, the two of them *had* to come on the flight. If not, I would finance 100 percent of Kubrick's next film and David's forthcoming album."

Julian ran his fingers through his beard, transported back to the past.

"Unfortunately, Stanley died before that could happen, and my life changed fundamentally after that evening. I only produce films as a sideline now. Orley Travel was born in a small travel bureau in Soho which I took over at the beginning of the nineties. I owned two airlines and bought an abandoned studio complex to work on the development of space vessels and space stations. With the foundation of Orley Space we pushed into the technology market. Some of the best brains from NASA and ESA worked for us—including experts from Russia, Asia, and India, and engineers from Germany—because we paid higher salaries, created better research conditions, and were more enthusiastic, speedy, and efficient than their old employers. By then, no one doubted that state space travel was in urgent need of some live-cell therapy from the private market, but I had set myself the goal of actually taking its place! I wanted to usher in the dawn of the *true* space era, without the hesitancy of the bureaucrats, the chronic lack of money, and the dependence on political change. We offered prize money for young designers, had them develop rocket-propelled aircraft, and expanded our tourism range to suborbital flights. I've flown machines like that myself many times. And maybe it wasn't yet a proper space flight, but it was a brilliant beginning. Everyone wanted to come! Space tourism promised astronomic yield, that is if we could succeed in reducing the start-up costs." He laughed softly. "Well, in spite of that I lost the bet initially. I didn't make it by the year 2000. So I offered to settle my debt with David. But he didn't want me to. All he said was: Keep your money and send me the ticket when it's ready. The only thing I can say today is that his presence on the OSS is a great honor and makes me deeply happy. And whatever one could add about his greatness, his importance to our culture and the lease of life he has given to so many generations, his music can express that much better than I ever could. So now I'll shut up and hand it over to—Major Tom."

The silence that followed was almost sacred. A guitar was passed along. The lights had been dimmed further still during Julian's speech and the Pacific was shimmering as if it had just been polished. Through the oval side window, scattered sugar glowed against a black backdrop.

Looking back later, O'Keefe saw those seconds when David Bowie launched into the opening chords of "Space Oddity"—alternating between Fmaj7 and Em, soft and muted at first, then swelling powerfully, as if one were nearing the bustle of activity around the launchpad from the indifferent silence of space, right up to the moment when ground control and Major Tom enter into their memorable dialogue—as what may have been the last, and perhaps the *only* really harmonious moment of their journey. In his naïve happiness he forgot what Orley's venture was really about: catapulting people from the globe into a hostile environment, onto a satellite which, despite having spiritualized its previous visitors, had not yet made a single one of them want to return. He was keenly aware that every search for meaning which involved leaving the Earth would only culminate in his looking around at it at every opportunity, and he suddenly pictured himself getting so far away from it that it was completely out of sight, wretched and flooded with fear.

And the stars look very different today—

And when Tom's ballad finally came to an end, and the unlucky Major had been lost to the void of his inflated expectations, he felt, instead of the enchantment he had hoped for, a strange kind of disillusionment, almost like homesickness, although they were *only* 36,000 kilometers away from home. The right-hand side of the planet had begun to darken. He saw Heidrun inhale the moment with her lips half open, her gaze alternating between Bowie and the sea of stars on the other side of the window, while his was drawn over to her as if by magic. He realized that the Swiss woman had arrived in herself a long time ago, that she would happily travel to the very edge of the universe, because she carried her home in and with her, that she had certainly reached a much higher level of freedom than him, and he found himself wishing he were upstairs above some Dublin pub, being held in someone's arms on a threadbare mattress.

It seems quite a few people had the same idea that night.

Perhaps it was the way Amber had comforted him as he'd cried on her shoulder about Julian's ignorance that had stimulated Tim physically as well as emotionally; perhaps it was her kisses, the tautness in her arms, the springy elasticity she'd acquired in the gym; perhaps it was because, after so many years of mundane married life, his fantasies still revolved exclusively around his wife to the extent that he wanted to caress no other behind but hers, glide his hand into no other delta but hers—which meant he was about as suited to infidelity as a steam engine was to leaving the tracks—and even in those moments when he was pleasuring himself, he wanted to imagine no one but her; perhaps it was because her divine looks had not been tainted by the passing of the years—praise to the genes!—and because the buoyancy of zero gravity had returned her breasts to that legendary state which, at the beginning of their relationship, had made him feel as though he were grasping ripe melons; perhaps it was the way his attempt to fumble apart the clasps on her bathrobe had resulted in his being propelled into the opposite corner of the module, which had only turned him on all the more, as she lay there laughing among the swinging folds of the open robe, like an angel ready to sin—but whatever the reason was, his body was defying all the adversity of zero gravity, the low supply of blood to the lumbar region, the disorientation and light sense of nausea, by producing a true space rocket of an erection.

He paddled over and grasped hold of her shoulders. Peeling her out of her bathrobe was one thing, but Amber's attempt to free him from his pants and T-shirt failed as they drifted apart, which they did again and again until he ended up wriggling naked above the bed, heading helplessly for the ceiling. She looked at his galactic erection with visible interest, as helpless as she was amused.

"So what do we do with that now?" she laughed.

"There must be a way." He was determined. "People must have thought about this."

"Hopefully. It'd be a shame if they hadn't."

Tim did a handstand and plowed over to her. This time, he managed to get a grip on her hips and buried his head between her legs, which she spread and then immediately closed again to keep his head in place. As a result, the blood rushed to his ears. Circling his tongue, he pressed ahead, capturing the tiny mound beneath the small forest, the density of which threatened to take his breath away as he pressed his nose inside her out of fear of ending up at the other end of the room again, becoming intoxicated by the blend of their lust and countering her first, blissful sighs—provided that his ears, packed tightly between her thighs, weren't deceiving him—with muffled agreement. An overdose of oxygen seemed to mingle with the cabin air—or was it the lack of oxygen that suddenly made him feel as high as a schoolboy? Who cared! Joyfully exhilarated, he made his way deeper inside, panting, grunting, the tip of his tongue flying dedicatedly around. At the moment when the tropical dampness of deep-lying realms opened up to him, believing he heard a declaration of love burst forth, he couldn't hold back and mumbled a "Me too, oh, me too," but got a puzzling response.

"Ow! Ouch!"

Something had clearly gone wrong. Tim looked up. In doing so, he made the mistake of loosening his grip. Amber flailed around as if she were drowning, kicking him from her. Pushed away, he saw that she was rubbing her head, and that it was in the immediate vicinity of the edge of the desk. Aha. He should have thought of that, that they would drift away in the heat of the moment. Lesson number one: it wasn't enough to clasp on to each other, they needed to fix themselves within the room too. He couldn't help but laugh. Amber wrinkled her nose and frowned, then his gaze fell on something that could offer a solution.

"Look!"

"What?" She dug the fingers of her right hand into his hair and tried to bite his nose, which resulted in her doing a somersault. Tim hopped over to the bed like a frog, pulling Amber, still head over heels, along with him.

"Buckling ourselves in?" she snorted mockingly. "How unerotic. It'd be like doing it in a car. We'll hardly be able to move—"

"No, silly, not with the sleeping belt. Look!"

Amber's expression brightened. Above the bed were some handles, mounted a little distance apart from one another.

"Wait. I think I saw something that might go with them."

She hurried over to the cupboard, opened it, rummaged around and unearthed several long bands made from a rubber-like material. They had a red, yellow, and green pattern and were adorned with a slogan.

"*Love Belt*," she read.

"So there you go," grinned Tim. "People *did* think about it." For the first time since they'd set off on the journey, he felt carefree and playful, a sensation which just an hour ago he had thought was gone for good. Lynn didn't become entirely insignificant, of course, but just retreated to an insignificant province of his cortex, one that wasn't attending to Amber's scent and the throbbing desire to fuck her. "It looks like we have to fasten you by the wrists, my darling. No, by the hands and feet. Like in the torture chambers of the Holy Inquisition."

She started to thread the bands through the handles.

"I think you misunderstood," she said. "You're the one getting tied up."

"Now just a minute! We need to talk about this first."

"Do you think he wants to talk about it?" she asked, gesturing her head at his royal member. "I think he wants to do something else, and very quickly too."

One after the other, she knotted the rubber bands around his wrists and, giggling and snorting, made her way down to fasten his feet, until he was hung in the middle of the room with his extremities stretched out. He wriggled his knees and elbows with curiosity, noticing that the bands were highly elasticized. He could move around, and generously too. It was just stopping him from flying away.

"Do you think this was Julian's idea?" he asked.

"I'd be willing to bet on it." Amber hovered toward him as if she were on a control beam, clasped his shoulders and slung her legs around his hips. For a moment, her sex balanced on his, like a trapeze artist on the nose of a sea lion.

"In my opinion, sexual positions are the most demanding maneuvers in the world," she whispered as she pressed herself against him, lowered herself, and drew him inside her.

Seemingly quite a few people had the same idea, but only a few managed to put it into action. Eva Borelius and Karla Kramp also found the straps and figured out what to do with them, as did Mimi Parker and Marc Edwards. However, Edwards found the redistribution of over half a liter of blood from the lower to upper bodily regions a little harder to handle than Tim had, while Paulette Tautou would most likely have held Bernard's head down the now-so-familiar toilet bowl if he had come near her with any intentions of that sort.

Wisely, Tautou did no such thing. Instead, in consideration of Paulette's miserable condition, he decided that they should embark on the journey home.

Suite 12 was the scene of similar suffering, the only difference being that Locatelli would never have capitulated to something as mundane as space sickness. Peaceful silence reigned in Suite 38, where the Ögis lay snuggled up to one another like field mice in winter. One floor above, Sushma and Mukesh Nair were peacefully enjoying the sight of night falling over the Isla de las Estrellas. In Suite 17, Aileen Donoghue had put in her earplugs, allowing Chuck to snore at the top of his lungs.

On the opposite side of the torus, Oleg Rogachev was staring out of the window while Olympiada Rogacheva stared straight ahead.

"Do you know what I'd like to know?" she murmured after a while.

He shook his head.

"How someone ends up like Miranda Winter."

"You don't end up like that," he said, without turning around. "You're born like it."

"I don't mean the way she looks," snorted Olympiada. "I'm not stupid. I just want to know how someone gets to be so impregnable. So completely pain-free. It's as if she's a walking immune system against every kind of problem, she's like nonchalance personified—I mean, seriously, she's even given names to her breasts!"

Rogachev turned his head slowly.

"No one's stopping you from doing the same."

"Perhaps a certain amount of it is due to stupidity," ruminated Olympiada, as if she hadn't heard him. "You know, I really do believe that Miranda is quite dumb. Oh, what am I saying, she hasn't got two brain cells to rub together. I have no doubt that she's lacking any kind of education, but perhaps that's an advantage. Perhaps it's good to be stupid, desirable even. Dumb and naïve and a little bit calculating. You feel less that way. Miranda loves only herself, whereas it seems to me that every single day I'm pouring all my feelings, all my strength into a vase that's full of holes. Your meanness would be wasted on someone like Miranda, Oleg, like a pinprick in blubber."

"I'm not mean to you."

"Oh no?"

"No. I'm just uninterested. You can't hurt someone you have no interest in."

"And you suppose that's not mean?"

"It's the truth." Rogachev glanced at her for a second. Olympiada had burrowed into her sleeping bag and was now belted in and safely out of reach. For a moment he wondered what it might be like if the sack burst open the next morning to reveal a butterfly, an astonishing feat for his rather retarded imagination. But Olympiada wasn't a caterpillar, and he had no intention of weaving her into a cocoon. "Our marriage was a strategic move. I knew it, your father knew it, and you knew it too. So please stop torturing yourself."

"One day you'll fall, Oleg," she hissed. "You'll end up like a rat. A damn rat in the gutter."

Rogachev turned to gaze again out of the window, strangely unmoved by the planet darkening below him.

"Just get on with it and take a lover," he said, tonelessly.

Miranda Winter had no intention of heading off to bed any time soon, much to the joy of Rebecca Hsu, who suffered from her inability to cope with being alone. Except that she was alone. A poor, rich woman, as she went to great pains to convince herself, twice divorced, with three daughters of whom she saw shamefully little. A woman who hung around in the company of others until even the last few closed their eyes, after which she would make calls across all the time zones thanks to the world-spanning structure of her group of companies, until even she lost the fight against tiredness. The whole day through, whenever their strictly organized schedule allowed, she had been discussing marketing plans by phone, debating campaign strategies, deliberating purchases, sales, and shares. Keeping an eye on her empire: a control freak who was tormented by the thought that she'd driven husbands and daughters away with her manic working habits.

At least she could discuss the lack of husbands with Miranda without falling head first into melancholy afterward. Besides, some of the beakers of Moët et Chandon had miraculously turned up in Miranda's cabin, which particularly pleased Rebecca, since she had owned the brand for some time now.

Finn O'Keefe didn't know what to think or feel, so he listened to music for a while and then fell asleep.

Evelyn Chambers lay awake—if it could be called lying, that is.

She didn't feel the slightest inclination to buckle herself onto the bed like some raving lunatic. She had discovered the rubber bands by chance and anchored herself to the handles near the front of the window, hoping to enjoy the sensation of zero gravity in her sleep too. But when she closed her eyes her body seemed to speed up as if it were on a roller coaster, trying to loop the loop, and she started to feel sick.

She reached up to free her shackled ankles from the bands, which was no easy task. It was only then that she noticed the inscription: *Love Belt.* Suddenly realizing what they were really intended for, a wave of regret washed over her at not being able to appropriately crown the extravagant experience of zero gravity. Intrigued, she wondered whether the others were doing it, and then—rather boldly—who *she* might be able to do it with! Her thoughts darted from Miranda Winter to Heidrun Ögi and then back again, based on the fact that Heidrun wasn't available, although admittedly neither was Miranda, if only due to lack of inclination.

Rebecca Hsu? Oh, for heaven's sake!

Her desire subsided as quickly as it had risen. And yet she had been so adamant, after her bisexuality had cost her the role of governor, that she was going to enjoy herself properly now. She was still America's most popular and influential talk-show host. In the wake of her political Waterloo she no longer felt bound to any conservative code. What had remained of her marriage barely justified professing monogamy, especially as her so-called husband was pouring their joint money into his constantly changing acquaintances. Not that that bothered her. Their love had gone down the drain years ago; but she didn't want to go to bed with anyone and everyone, even if she was consumed by lust.

Although perhaps in exceptional circumstances—

Finn O'Keefe. It was worth a try. It would certainly be fun to snare him of all people, but the thought quickly soured.

Julian?

He clearly loved flirting with her. But on the other hand Julian's job meant he flirted with everyone. Still. He was unattached, apart from the affair with Nina Hedegaard, if they were even still having one and it wasn't just her reading too much into it. If she yielded to Julian's advances there would be little danger of hurting anyone else, and they would have fun, she was sure of that. Perhaps something more might even come out of it. And if not, that was fine too.

On the spur of the moment, she dialed the number of his suite.

But no one answered, the screen stayed dark. Feeling foolish all of a sudden, like a sparrow pecking around beneath restaurant tables for food from other people's plates, she crawled hurriedly into her sleeping bag.

"You had them hanging on your every word."

"But I wasn't even the first."

Julian raised his eyebrows.

"2013," said Bowie. "Chris Hadfield—this ISS astronaut. He was the first person in the world to sing 'Space Oddity' in space."

"Correct, and it was not bad at all. But you're the original. You *had* to come up here and sing it!"

Bowie smiled. "Obviously."

"And you're quite sure?"

"Quite sure."

"Tautou told me that Madame wants them to come back to earth together. We would have room." Julian sucked at his bottle. "Oh, nonsense, forget the Tautous! We'd have room even if they did come. I've always got room for you."

They were the only ones left in the dimly lit Picard, sucking at their alcohol-free cocktails. Bowie rolled the bottle between his fingers thoughtfully.

"Thanks, Julian. But I'll pass."

"But why? It's your chance to go to the Moon. You're the star man, you're that guy in *The Man who Fell to Earth*, you're Ziggy Stardust! Who, if not you? You *have* to go to the Moon."

"Well, for a start I'm seventy-eight years old."

"And? You can't tell. You once said you wanted to live to be three hundred. Compared to that you're still a kid."

Bowie laughed.

"So?" he said, changing the subject. "Are you going to get the money together for a second elevator?"

"Of course," boomed Julian. "Shall we bet on it?"

"No more bets. What's going on with the Chinese anyway? I heard they're pestering you with offers."

"Officially they're doing nothing of the sort, but between ourselves they're kowtowing like mad. Does the name Zheng Pang-Wang mean anything to you?"

"Not off the top of my head."

"The Zheng Group."

"Ah!" Bowie wrinkled his brow. "Yes, I think it does actually. They're a technology company too, right?"

"Zheng is the driving force behind Beijing's space travel. An entrepreneur, bound to the Party, which amounts to the same thing. He never misses a single opportunity to infiltrate my ranks, but I've got my defenses up, so he tries to do it by plotting. Obviously the Chinese would love to woo me away and have me all to themselves. They've got money, more than the Americans, but they don't have the patents for the elevator, or the brainpower to build fusion reactors that don't immediately shut themselves down again. A few weeks ago I met old Pang-Wang in Paris. A nice guy really. He tried to tempt me with Chinese money, and appealed to my cosmopolitan heart by saying that clean energy supply would be of benefit to the whole world. He asked whether I didn't think it was indecent that all the money from helium-3 was going to the Americans. So I asked him what the Chinese would think of it if I went on to sell the patents to the Russians, Indians, Germans, French, Japanese, and Arabs."

"I'd be more interested to know what the Americans would think of that."

"The question is actually a little different: Who has the advantage? In my opinion, I do, but of course I would create completely new geopolitical relationships. And do I want that? For the most part, I've had a kind of symbiotic relationship with America, to our mutual advantage. Recently, since the Moon crisis, Washington has been haunted by the ghosts of the Little Depression of 2008 to 2010. They're worried things might get out of hand if they give that much power to one single company. Which is ridiculous: *I* gave *them* the power! The power to stake out their claim up there. Using my means, my know-how! But it seems the desire to have more control over companies is rampant." Julian snorted. "Instead of which the governments should be putting their energies into infrastructure, healthcare, and education. They should be building streets, schools, houses, old people's homes, but the private economy even has to help them out with that, so what do they have to crow about? Governments have proved incapable of pushing forward global processes; they only know how to squabble, hesitate, and make lazy compromises. They didn't manage to get to grips with environmental protection in that laughable treaty. They demand sanctions against corrupt and warfaring states in their shaky voices, despite the fact that no one's bothering to listen, so they just stock up on nuclear arms and impose trading blocks on each other's markets. The Russians don't have any money left for space travel now that Gazprom is hanging in the balance, but it would still be enough to give to me and the Americans for permission to use the next space elevator. Then we'd have another player on the Moon with us, and as far as I'm concerned that's a good thing."

"But America doesn't agree."

"Well no, because they've got me. The fact is, together we don't need anyone else, and in a situation like that Washington thinks they can get away with anything and demand more transparency."

"So what's your plan? Bringing the Russians over to your side without America's blessing?"

"If America doesn't want to play with them and continues to block my ideas, then yes—as you can see, I've invited some very illustrious guests. Zheng is right, but not in the way he thinks. I've had it up to here with the sponsorship failing to make headway! Competition is invigorating for business. Sure, it would be a bit shabby to run from the Americans to the Chinese now—they're all the same idiots everywhere when it comes down to it—but offering the elevator to *all* nations, now that's got a ring to it."

"And you said as much to Zheng?"

"Yes, and he thought he'd misheard. He certainly never wanted to unleash *that* kind of change in perspective, but he was overestimating his contribution. I'd had the idea for a long time already. He just made me more determined to do it."

Bowie fell silent for a while.

"Well, I'm sure you know you're playing with fire," he said.

"With the sun's fire," said Julian serenely. "With reactor fire. I'm used to fire."

"Do your American friends know about your plans?"

"They may have an idea, to a certain extent. It's no secret who I go trotting off to the Moon with."

"You sure know how to make enemies."

"I'll travel with whoever I like. It's my elevator, my space station, my hotel up there. They're far from happy about it, of course, but I don't care. They should make me better offers and stop their control games." Julian suckled noisily at his bottle and licked his lips with his tongue. "Delicious, isn't it? On the Moon we'll have wine with an alcohol substitute. Totally insane! 1.8 percent, but it tastes like really hard stuff. Are you sure you want to miss out on that?"

"You don't give up, do you?" Bowie laughed again.

"Never," grinned Julian.

"But you're too late. Don't get me wrong: I love life, and it's definitely too short, I agree with all that. Three hundred years would be wonderful, especially in times like these! But it's just that I—"

"—ended up being turned from an alien into an earthling after all," finished Julian with a smile.

"I was never anything else."

"You were the man who fell to Earth."

"No. I was just someone who tried to get to grips with his difficulties around people by disguising himself, using the line 'I'm sorry if the communication between us isn't working, I'm from Mars.'" Bowie ran his fingers through his hair. "You know, my whole life I gleefully absorbed anything that ignited the world, anything that electrified it; I collected fashions and sensitivities like other people collect art or postage stamps. Call it eclecticism, but it may have been my greatest talent. I was never really an innovator, more of a champion of the present, an architect who brought that feeling of being alive and trends together in such a way that it looked like something new. Looking back, I'd say it was my way of communicating: *Hey, people, I understand what moves you, look at me and listen up, I've made a song out of it!* Or something along those lines. But for a long time I couldn't talk to anyone about it. I simply didn't know how to do it, how a simple conversation worked. I was afraid of getting into relationships, incapable of listening to others. For someone like that, the stage, or let's say the world of the arts, is the perfect platform, it's ideally suited to giving monologues. You reach everyone, but no one reaches you. You're the messiah! A puppet of course, an idol, but for that very reason you can't let anyone get close, because then it might get out that you're actually just shy and insecure. And so, with time, you really do become an alien. You don't need to put a costume on to be one, but of course it helps. If you feel as uneasy around people as I did back then, then you just make outer space out to be your home, look for answers from a higher being, or act as though you're one yourself."

Julian tapped his bottle, let it drift away from him for a moment then grasped it again.

"You sound so terribly grown up," he said.

"I am terribly grown up," laughed Bowie, bursting with happiness. "And it's wonderful! Believe me, this whole spiritual paper chase to find out the connection between humanity and the universe, why we were born and where we go when we die, what gives us and our actions meaning, *if* there even is a meaning—I mean, I love science fiction, Julian, and I love what you've created! But all this space stuff was always just a metaphor for me. It was only ever about the spiritual search. The churches' maps were always a little too vaguely drawn for me, full of one-way streets and dead ends. I didn't want anyone else to dictate how and where I was supposed to look. You can ritualize God, or you can interpret him. The latter doesn't go down preset paths; it demands that you slip away from them. I did that, and I kept on creating new space suits for myself in order to explore this empty, endless cosmos, hoping to meet myself, as Starman, Ziggy Stardust, Aladdin Sane, Major Tom. And then, one day, you marry a wonderful woman and move to New York, and suddenly you realize: Out there, there's nothing, but on the Earth there's everything. You meet people, you talk, communicate, and what seemed difficult before now just happens, with wonderful ease. Your inflated fears shrink to become bog-standard worries; the early flirt with death, the pathos of *Rock n' Roll Suicide* reveals itself to be nothing more than the spectacularly unoriginal mood of a clueless and inexperienced young boy; you no longer wake up with the fear of going crazy; you no longer think obsessively about the misery of human existence, but about your children's future. And you ask yourself what the devil you were looking for in space! Do you see? I've landed. I've never enjoyed living on Earth so much, among other people. And if my health allows I can enjoy it for a few more years. It's bad enough that it will only be another ten or twelve, and not three hundred, so I'm looking forward to every moment. So, give me one good reason why I should fly to the Moon now, now that I've finally found my home and settled in down there."

Julian thought it over. He could think of a thousand reasons why *he* wanted to fly to the Moon, but suddenly not a single one that would have any relevance for the old man opposite him. And yet Bowie looked anything but old, more as though he had just been reborn. His eyes looked as thirsty for knowledge as ever. It wasn't the look of an extraterrestrial observer, though, but that of an earth-dweller.

That's the difference between us, he thought. I was always extremely earthly. Always on the frontier, the great communicator, untouched by fear or self-doubt. And then he wondered what it would be like if one day *he* reached the conclusion that this space opera, of which he was the director and protagonist, had only served to bring him closer to Earth, and whether he would like this realization or not.

Or was he just an egocentric alien after all, one who didn't even get what was going on with his own children. How had Tim put it?

You don't have a clue what's going on around you!

Julian pulled a face. Then he laughed too, but without any real pleasure, raised his glass and toasted Bowie.

"Cheers, old friend," he said.

A little later, Amber opened her eyes and saw that the Earth had disappeared. Fear shot through her. She had slept straight through the previous night and it had still been there in the morning, half of it in any case. But now she couldn't see even the slightest glimpse of it.

Of course she couldn't. Night had fallen over the Pacific half, and the lights of civilization weren't visible from the height of geostationary orbit. There was no cause for alarm.

She turned her head. Next to her, Tim was staring into the darkness.

"What's wrong, my hero?" she whispered. "Can't you sleep?"

"Did I wake you?"

"No, I just woke up, that's all." She crawled nearer to him and rested her head on his shoulder.

"You were wonderful," he said softly.

"No, *you* were wonderful. Is there something on your mind?"

"I don't know. Perhaps Julian was right after all. Maybe I'm just seeing ghosts."

"No, I don't think so," she said after a while. "It's good that you're keeping an eye on things. It's just that, if you continue to treat him like an enemy, he'll act like one."

"I'm not treating him like an enemy."

"Well, you're not exactly the world champion when it comes to diplomacy."

"No." He laughed softly. "I don't know, Amber. For some reason I've just got a bad feeling."

"That's just the zero gravity," she murmured, almost asleep again already. "What could go wrong?"

Tim was silent. She blinked, lifted her head and realized she'd been mistaken. You could still see a narrow blue-white crescent on the right-hand side. Everything was fine. The Earth was still in its place.

Go to sleep, my darling, she wanted to say, but the tiredness overcame her with such force that she could only think it. Before she dozed off, she was overcome by the image of a black cloth spreading out over the two of them. Then, nothing.

Carl Hanna couldn't sleep, but then again he didn't need to. He ran his possessions through his fingers one after another, looking at them searchingly, rotating them, turning them over then packing them carefully away again: the small flacon of aftershave, the bottle filled with shower gel and the one with shampoo, tubes of skin cream, shaving foam, various packages of medication for headaches, sickness, stomach upsets, cotton buds and soft, pliable earplugs, toothbrush and toothpaste. He had even packed dental floss, nail scissors and a file, a hand mirror, his electric hair trimmer, and three golf balls. There was a course in the grounds of the Gaia, Lynn had told him, Shepard's Green. Hanna played golf reasonably well, and he also placed a lot of importance on looking well groomed. Apart from that, none of all this junk was what it seemed to be. Just as the guitar wasn't really a guitar, Carl Hanna wasn't the person he pretended to be. It wasn't his real name, nor was his life story anything but complete fabrication.

He thought about Vic Thorn.

They had taken everything into account, everything except the possibility that Thorn might have an accident. The preparation for his mission had been exemplary, everything planned well in advance. Nothing should have gone wrong, but then a tiny speck of space debris had changed everything in a matter of seconds.

Hanna looked out into space.

Thorn was somewhere out there. He had joined the inventory of the cosmos, an asteroid on an unknown path. Many people believed that he must have stayed in the Earth's gravitational field, which would have meant encountering his body cyclically in orbit. But Thorn had still not been found. It was possible that he would crash into the sun one day in the far future. It was plausible that someday, in a few million years' time, he would turn up in the sphere of a planet inhabited by nonhuman intelligence and cause a great deal of surprise there.

He held up a roll-on deodorant, pulled off the cap, then put it back on and tucked it away.

This time, it would work.

MAY 26, 2025
The Mission

Xintiandi, Shanghai, China

Chen Hongbing bent forward as he entered the room, in that way typical of people whose height is in constant conflict with doorframes and low-hanging ceiling lights. He was actually extraordinarily tall for a Chinese man. On the other hand, the architect who designed the Shikumen building could hardly be accused of a lack of consideration for extravagant bodily proportions. The door was a good 3 meters high, so it hardly required him to hunch his shoulders as he did, or stretch out his chin which, as it approached his breastbone, seemed to linger hesitantly. Despite his size, Chen seemed gaunt and subservient. His gaze had a furtive nature about it, as if he were expecting to be beaten, or worse. Jericho got the impression he had spent his whole life conversing with people who towered over him while he stayed seated.

If indeed this was Chen Hongbing.

The visitor touched the doorframe fleetingly with the tips of his fingers, as if wanting to assure himself of something solid to grasp in case of a sudden collapse. Confused, he looked at the pile of removal boxes, then crossed the threshold with the caution of a tightrope walker. The white midday sun stretched across the room, a sculpture of light, broken into a billion pieces by the whirling dust. In that pale light Chen looked like a ghost, narrowing his eyes. He looked younger than Tu Tian had said he was. His skin stretched tautly over his cheekbones, forehead, and chin; a face which was deeply carved with lines. Around his eyes, though, a fine macramé pattern branched out, more like cracks than lines. To Jericho, they looked like testimonies to a difficult life.

"*Ta chi le hen duo Ku*," Tu Tian had said. "Hongbing has eaten bitterness, Owen, for many long years. Every morning it comes up, he forces it down again, and one day he will choke on it. Help him, *xiongdi*."

Eaten bitterness. Even misery was available for consumption in China.

Jericho looked indecisively at the box in his hands and wondered if he should heave it onto the desk as planned or back onto the pile. Chen's arrival was ill-timed. He hadn't expected the man to come this early. Tu Tian had said something about an afternoon visit, and it wasn't even twelve yet. His stomach was rumbling, and his brow and upper lip glistened with sweat. The more he ran his hands over his face and hair to mix the dust and sweat, the less he looked like someone who was about to move into the expensive, trendy neighborhood of Xintiandi. Three days without shaving had taken their toll. Encased in a sticky cloth of a T-shirt, which showed the 98.6 degrees Fahrenheit and what felt like

99.9 percent air humidity much more than the color it had once possessed, and having hardly eaten for twenty-four hours, Jericho wanted
nothing more than to put the move behind him as quickly as possible.
Just one more box, then off to a food stall in Taicang Lu, finish unpack-
ing, shower, shave.

That had been the plan.

But when he saw Chen standing there in the dusty light, he knew
he couldn't put his visitor off until later. Chen was the kind of person
who would stay in your mind if you sent him away, and besides, out of
respect to Tu Tian it was completely out of the question. He put the box
back on the pile and put on a B-grade smile: warm, but noncommittal.

"Chen Hongbing, I take it."

The man standing opposite him nodded and looked bewilderedly
at the boxes and piled-up pieces of furniture. He coughed slightly, then
took a small step back.

"I've come at a bad time."

"Not at all."

"It just so happened that I—I was nearby, but if it puts you out I can
come back—"

"It's no trouble at all." Jericho looked around, pulled over a chair
and put it in front of the desk. "Take a seat, honorable Chen, make
yourself at home. I'm just moving in, hence the chaos. Can I get you
anything?"

You can't, he thought, you would have needed to go shopping for
that, but you're a man. When women move into a house, they make
sure they have a full fridge before the first box even leaves the moving
van, and if there isn't a refrigerator, they buy one and plug it in. Then
he remembered the half-full bottle of orange juice. It had been on the
lounge windowsill since yesterday morning, which meant it had led
a two-day-long existence in the glaring sun and intelligent life might
even have developed inside it.

"Coffee, tea?" he asked nonetheless.

"No thank you, but thank you very much." Chen sank down onto
the edge of the chair and stared intently at his knees. If he had come
into contact with the surface of the seat, it was by an amount barely
measurable physically. "A few minutes of your time is more than I can
expect under these circumstances."

Awkward pride resonated in his words. Jericho pulled a second
chair over, placed it next to Chen's, and hesitated. There were actually
two comfortable armchairs which belonged in front of the desk, and
both were in sight, but they had mutated into misshapen clumps of
bubble wrap wrapped in packing tape.

"It's my pleasure to be able to assist you," he said, trying to stop his
smile from widening. "We'll take as much time as we need."

Chen slid back on his chair and sank cautiously against the backrest. "You're very friendly."

"And you're not comfortable. Please accept my apologies. Let me find some more comfortable seating. It's still packed, but—"

Chen lifted his head and squinted up at him. Jericho was confused for a second, then it hit him: essentially, Chen looked good. In his younger years he must have been one of those men women said were beautiful. Until the day when something had ground his well-proportioned features into a mask. Somewhat grotesquely, he now lacked a facial expression, if you didn't count his occasional nervous blinking.

"No, I won't allow you to do that on my account—"

"It would be my pleasure."

"No, I can't allow you to."

"They have to be unpacked anyway."

"Of course, but at a time of your choosing." Chen shook his head and got up again. His joints clicked. "Please, I beg of you! I'm much too early, you're in the middle of something, and I'm sure you were less than enthusiastic about my arrival."

"No, that's not the case! I'm pleased you've come to see me."

"No, I should come back later."

"My dear Mr. Chen, no moment could be better than this one. Please, stay."

"I couldn't ask that of you. If I had known—"

And so on and so forth.

Theoretically, the game could carry on forever. It wasn't that either of them harbored any doubt about the other's position. Chen knew only too well that he had caught Jericho at the wrong moment, and no assurances to the contrary would change that. Jericho, in turn, was aware that Chen would have been far more comfortable on a bed of nails than on any of his kitchen chairs. The circumstances were to blame. Chen's presence was down to a system in which favors chased one another like puppies, and he was ashamed to the core at having messed it up. It was because of one of these favors that he was even here in the first place; then he had foolishly arrived too early and stumbled into the middle of a house move, thereby shaming their mediator and putting Jericho, the mediated, into the unpleasant situation of interrupting his work on his account. Because of course Jericho wouldn't ask him to come back later. The ritual of pleasantries allowed for an open-ended succession of "No, yes, not at all, but of course, it would be an honor, no, I couldn't, yes, no, yes!" A game which, if you wanted to master it, took years of training. If you were a *peng you*, a friend in the sense of a useful go-between, it would be played differently than if you were a *xiongdi*, a close confidant. Social standing, age and gender, the context of the conversation, all of these were factored into the coordinates of decorum.

Tu Tian, for example, had shortened the game when he had rather bluntly requested the aforementioned favor, just by calling him *xiongdi*. The diplomatic walk on eggshells could be dispensed with among close friends. Perhaps it was because he was really very fond of Chen, but maybe he just didn't want to interrupt the golf match for such a long-winded process, the outcome of which was already clear either way. In any case, once he had come out with it, the yolk-yellow late afternoon sun broke through the cheerfully dispersing clouds and bathed the surroundings in the tones of an Italian Renaissance landscape painting. Two days of rain came to an end, and Mr. Tu, who had begun *comme il faut* with the words: "Owen, I know you're up to your ears in it with the move, and I wouldn't normally bother you—" looked up to the heavens, picked up his Big Bertha club and ended succinctly: "—but there's a favor you could do for me—*xiongdi*."

Tu Tian on the Tomson Shanghai Pudong golf course, two days before, deep in concentration.

Jericho waited obediently to find out what the favor might be. Tu was temporarily on another planet as he swung into a powerful drive. The rhythmic momentum came from his back, muscles, and joints working in automated harmony. Jericho was talented; for two years now he had enjoyed the honor of playing on the best courses in Shanghai, when people like Tu invited him along, and when they didn't he played in the renowned but affordable Luchao Harbor City Club. The difference between him and Tu Tian was that one of them would never get close to achieving what the other one seemed to have been given genetically. Both of them had decided relatively late in life to spend time hitting little white balls at over 200 kilometers per hour in an attempt to guide them into small holes in the ground. But on the day when Tu first walked onto a golf course, he must have felt as if he was coming home. His game was far beyond being described with attributes like accomplished or elegant. From the very beginning, Tu had played the way newborn babies swim. He *was* the game.

Jericho watched respectfully as his friend sent the ball into a perfect trajectory. Tu paused in the teeing position for a few seconds, then let Big Bertha fall with an expression of pure contentment.

"You mentioned a favor," said Jericho.

"What?" Tu wrinkled his forehead. "Oh yes, nothing major. You know."

He set off, briskly following the journey of his ball. Jericho marched behind him. He didn't know, but he had a good idea what was coming.

"What problem does he have?" he asked, taking a guess. "Or she?"

"He. A friend. His name is Chen Hongbing." Tu grinned. "But that's not the problem you need to help him with."

Jericho was familiar with the caustic element of his remark. The name was a bad joke, and one at which those it poked fun at were least able to laugh. It was likely that Chen had been born at the end of the sixties in the previous century, when the Red Guards had inflicted terror on the country, and when newborns had been given the most preposterous names in honor of the revolution and the Great Leader Mao; it was quite common for someone of the age where they could not yet control their bladder to be called "Down with America," "Honor of the Leader," or "Long March."

It was actually fear that had bestowed those names. An attempt to come to terms with things. Before the People's Revolutionary Army brought a bloody end to the Red Guards in 1969, there was uncertainty about who would rule China in the future. Three years before, on the Square of Heavenly Peace in Beijing, Mao Zedong had come down to join the mere mortals, as it were, and had a red armband tied around his sleeve, thereby symbolically becoming the leader of the Guards, a million-strong bunch of predominantly pubescent fanatics, absconding from their schools and universities, who sheared their teachers' heads, beat them, and chased them through the streets like donkeys, because anyone who knew the simplest of things and wasn't a farmer or a worker was regarded as an intellectual, and therefore subversive. The chaos didn't end until the spring of 1969—and only then because the so-called Gang of Four were rattling their chains loudly in the background. But the Red Guards walked the same path as their victims and found themselves back in reeducation camps, which, in the opinion of many of the Chinese people, made things even worse. Jiang Qing, Mao's wife, raved about cultural operas and warmed up to some of the worst atrocities in China's history. But the naming of children, at least, slowly normalized.

Chen, Jericho estimated, had come into the world sometime between 1966 and 1969: a time in which his name was about as common as caterpillars in salad. Hongbing literally meant "Red Soldier."

Tu looked at the sun.

"Hongbing has a daughter." The way he said it implied that this alone was worth telling the story for. His eyes lit up, then he got a grip of himself. "She's very pretty and unfortunately very reckless too. Two days ago, she disappeared without a trace. Generally speaking she trusts me, and I'm tempted to say she trusts me even more than her father. Anyway, it's not the first time she's taken off for a while, but before she has always let someone know, so to speak. Him, me, or at least one of her friends."

"And she forgot this time."

"Or she didn't have a chance. Hongbing is worried out of his mind, and rightly so. Yoyo has a tendency to annoy the wrong people. Or, shall we say, the right ones."

Tu had outlined the problem in his own way. Jericho pursed his lips. It was clear what was expected of him. Besides that, the name Yoyo had unleashed something inside him.

"And I'm supposed to look for the girl?"

"You would be doing me a good turn if you met with Chen Hongbing." Cheerfully, Tu spotted his ball and began to pace more briskly. "Only, of course, if you feel you're able to."

"What exactly has she done?" asked Jericho. "Yoyo, I mean."

Tu stepped over to the white object in the shortly cut grass, looked Jericho in the eyes, and smiled. His look said that he wanted to get back to putting now. Jericho smiled back.

"Tell your friend it would be an honor."

Tu nodded as if he had expected nothing less. He called Jericho *xiongdi* one more time and turned his undivided attention to the putter and ball.

The younger generation in China hardly played the game anymore. Their tone of voice had become globalized. If someone wanted something from somebody, they generally came straight to the point without wasting any time. With Chen Hongbing it was clearly a different matter. Everything about him marked him out as a representative of an older China, one in which there were a thousand ways of losing face. Jericho was indecisive for a moment, then had an idea of how he could salvage the situation for Chen. He leaned over, pulled a carpet knife from the toolbox next to the desk, and began to briskly cut the chair free from the bubble wrap.

Chen raised both hands in horror.

"I beg you! This is so embarrassing for me—"

"It doesn't have to be." said Jericho cheerfully. "To be honest I was hoping for your help. There's a second knife in the toolbox. What would you say to us joining forces and making this place a little more comfortable?"

It was an ambush. At the same time he was offering Chen a way out of the self-inflicted mess. You help me, I'll help you, then you'll be contributing to my move; we'll both be able to sit more comfortably and you can get the dust off your face. Quid pro quo.

Chen seemed uncertain. He scratched his head, rattled himself to his feet, then fished the knife out of the box, and took hold of the other chair. As he began to cut through the sticky tape, he visibly relaxed.

"I appreciate your gesture very much, Mr. Jericho. Tian unfortunately didn't have the opportunity to tell me that you were just moving in."

Which meant the idiot hadn't mentioned it. Jericho shrugged his shoulders and pulled the cover off his armchair.

"He didn't know."

That was a lie too, but in that way they had both respected Tu and could turn their attention to more important matters. One after the other, they pushed the armchairs in front of the desk.

"It doesn't look so bad after all." Jericho grinned. "Now we just need something to refuel. What do you think? I could grab us some coffee. There's a patisserie downstairs, they do—"

"No, don't worry," Chen interrupted. "I'll grab them."

Ah yes. The game.

"No, I couldn't let you."

"Of course you can."

"No, it's my pleasure. You're my guest."

"And you're receiving me unexpectedly. As I already said—"

"It's the least I can do for you. How do you like your coffee?"

"How do you like *yours*?"

"That's very kind of you, but—"

"Would you like nutmeg in yours?"

That was the latest thing: nutmeg in coffee. It had allegedly saved Starbucks from bankruptcy last winter. The whole damn world had started drinking nutmeg coffee and swore that it tasted amazing. It reminded Jericho of the Sichuan Espresso craze which had rolled across the country a few years before, transforming the taste of Italian coffee into an Asian variant of Dante's Inferno. Jericho had taken a little sip from the rim of a cup once, and even days later had still felt as though he could pull the skin from his lips.

He gave in. "A normal cappuccino would be great. The patisserie is just downstairs on the left."

Chen nodded.

And, suddenly, he was smiling too. The skin on his face stretched taut, making Jericho fear it might tear off, but it was a thoroughly lovely, friendly smile, and one which disappeared only once it reached the cracked wastelands beneath his eyes.

"Yoyo isn't her real name," explained Chen, as they sat slurping coffee together. By now the air-conditioning was on and had created a reasonably bearable temperature. Chen's posture suggested he thought the soft leather seat might throw him off at any second, but compared with the man who had skulked through the doorframe a quarter of an hour before, he made an almost normal impression.

"So what is?"

"Yuyun."

"Cloud of Jade." Jericho raised his eyebrows appreciatively. "A beautiful choice."

"Oh, I gave it a great deal of thought! I wanted it to be a light, fresh name, full of poetry, full of—" Chen's gaze clouded over and wandered off into the distance.

"Harmony," completed Jericho.

"Yes. Harmony."

"So why does she call herself Yoyo?"

"I don't know." Chen sighed. "I know far too little about her, that's the problem. Just because you have named someone, it doesn't mean you know them. The label doesn't define the content. And what are names anyway? Just rallying calls for the lost. And yet everyone hopes that their own child will be an exception, it's like being anesthetized. As if names could change anything. As if there has ever been any truth in a name!" He took a noisy gulp of his coffee.

"And Yoyo—Yuyun has disappeared?"

"Let's stick with Yoyo. Apart from me no one calls her Yuyun. Yes, I haven't seen or spoken to her for two days now. Didn't Tu Tian tell you about any of it?"

"Only a little."

For some unknown reason this seemed to please Chen. Then Jericho realized. The way Tu had said it: *I'm tempted to say that she trusts me more than her father*. Whatever it was that bound Tu and Chen together, and however close this bond was—Yoyo's preference came between them. And that's why Chen had wanted the reassurance that, this time, not even Tu knew anything.

"Well, we were supposed to meet up," he continued, "the day before yesterday, for lunch in Lianing Lu. I waited for over an hour, but she didn't show. At first I thought it was because of an argument we'd had, that perhaps she was still angry, but then—"

"You had an argument?"

"We stayed out of each other's way for a while after she confronted me with her reasons for moving out, ten days ago, out of the blue. She didn't consider it necessary to seek my advice, nor did she want my help."

"You didn't agree with her decision?"

"It seemed too hasty to me, and I told her so. Very plainly! That there wasn't the slightest reason for her to move out. That she was much better off with me than in that robber's den she's been hanging around in for years. That she's not doing herself any favor with those types of people—that it isn't clever—" Chen stared at the cup in his hand. They were silent for a while. Whole universes of dust emerged and disappeared in the sunlight. Jericho's nose was itching, but he repressed the urge to sneeze. Instead, he tried to remember where he had read the name Yoyo Chen.

"Yoyo has many talents," Chen continued softly. "Maybe I did hold her back too much. But I didn't have a choice. She incurred the displeasure of prominent circles, and it was getting increasingly dangerous. They caught up with her five years ago—because she didn't follow my advice."

"What did she do?"

"Do? She completely ignored my warnings."

"Yes, I know. But that's not a crime. Why was she arrested?"

Chen blinked distrustfully.

"I didn't say that in so many words."

Jericho frowned. He leaned over, put the tips of his fingers together, and looked Chen directly in the eyes.

"Listen to me. I don't want to push you by any means. But we won't get anywhere like this. You wouldn't be here just to say that the Party is giving Yoyo a lifetime achievement award, so let's speak plainly. What did she do?"

"She—" Chen seemed to be looking for a way of formulating it which wouldn't require definitions like "criticism of the regime."

"May I voice an assumption?"

Chen hesitated. Then he nodded.

"Yoyo is a dissident." Jericho knew this to be the case. But where on earth had he read her name? "She criticizes the system, probably on the Internet, and has been doing so for years. It drew attention on a number of occasions, but until yesterday she always got off lightly. Now something may have happened. And you're worried that Yoyo may have been imprisoned."

"She said I was the last person who could reproach her for it," whispered Chen. "But I was only trying to protect her. We argued about it, many, many times, and she shouted at me. She said it was pointless, that I don't let anyone get close to me, not even my own daughter, and how I of all people—She said I was a total hypocrite."

Jericho waited. Chen's expression hardened.

"But I didn't mean to bother you with these stories," he concluded. "The main thing is that there hasn't been any sign of life from her in two days."

"Perhaps it's less serious than you think. It wouldn't be the first time someone's son or daughter has disappeared after an argument. They lie low with friends, play dead for a while, just to teach their parents a lesson."

Chen shook his head. "Not Yoyo. She would never use an argument as cause to do something like that."

"You said yourself that you don't know your daughter well enough—"

"Well, in this respect I know her very well. We are similar in many ways. Yoyo hates that kind of childish nonsense."

"Have you checked with the authorities?"

Chen balled his hands into fists. His knuckles bulged, white, but his face remained expressionless. Jericho knew they were getting closer to the crux of the matter, the real reason why Tu had sent his friend here.

"You *have* checked, haven't you?"

"No, I haven't!" Chen seemed to chew the words before spitting them out. "I can't! I can't check with the authorities without risking putting them on Yoyo's trail."

"So it's not certain that Yoyo has been arrested?"

"Last time I was left in the dark for weeks as to which police station she was in. But the fact that she had been arrested at all, well, I found that out just a few hours after it happened. I should mention that I have managed to build up a few important contacts over the years. There are people who are willing to use their influence for Yoyo and me."

"Like Tu Tian."

"Yes, and others too. That's the only reason I knew that Yoyo had been arrested back then. I asked these—friends, but they claimed not to know Yoyo's location. It wouldn't surprise me if she has given the authorities new reasons to hunt her down, but perhaps they haven't even noticed."

"You mean that perhaps Yoyo just got scared and decided to lie low for a while?"

Chen kneaded his fingers. To Jericho, he looked like a taut bow-string. Then he sighed.

"If I go to the police," he said, "I could end up sowing mistrust into a field of ignorance. Yoyo would become a target again, whether she's done anything wrong or not. Any reason would be enough for them. Yoyo avoided provoking them for a while, and it seemed to me that she'd learned her lesson and made her peace with the past, but—" He looked at Jericho with his weary, intensely dark eyes. This time he didn't blink. "You understand my dilemma, Mr. Jericho?"

Jericho looked at him in silence. He leaned back and thought. As long as Chen continued circling the issue like a wolf around a fire, they wouldn't make any progress. So far his guest was only dropping hints. Jericho doubted Chen was even aware he was doing it. He had internalized the sidestepping in such a way that he probably thought he was walking in a straight line.

"I don't want to press you too much, Mr. Chen—but could it be that you might be the wrong person to contact the authorities when it comes to dissident activities?"

"How do you mean?"

"I'm just voicing my suspicion that Yoyo isn't only being hunted down for her own actions."

"I understand." Chen stared at him. "You're right, not everything in my past is to Yoyo's advantage. But regardless of that, I'd be doing her a disservice if I went to the police. Can we leave it at that for now?"

Jericho nodded. "You know the focus of my work?" he asked. "Did Tu Tian put you in the picture?"

"Yes."

"My hunting ground is the Internet. I imagine he recommended me because Yoyo has become active online."

"He thinks a great deal of you. He says you're the best."

"I'm honored. Do you have a photo of Yoyo?"

"Oh, I have more than that! I have films." He reached into his jacket and pulled out a cell phone. It was an older model, one that wasn't compatible with 3D projection. Chen turned his attention to it with his now familiar blinking, pressed a few buttons in succession, but nothing happened.

"May I offer my assistance?" Jericho suggested.

"Yoyo gave it to me, but I hardly ever use it." A trace of embarrassment crossed Chen's face. He handed the device to Jericho. "I know, it's laughable. Ask me something about cars. Old cars, vintage. I know all the models, but these things here—"

These things, thought Jericho, are already vintage too, in case you didn't realize.

"You're interested in cars?" he asked.

"I'm an expert! Historical Beauty, in Beijing Donglu. Haven't you been? I manage the Technical Customer Service department. You must do me the honor of a visit; we had a silver Rolls-Royce Corniche in last month, with wood and red leather seats, a splendid specimen. It came from Germany, sold by an old man. Do you like cars?"

"They have their uses."

"May I ask what you drive?"

"A Toyota."

"Hybrid?"

"Fuel cell." Jericho turned the cell phone over in his hand and glanced at the connection points. With an adapter he could have projected the contents onto his new holowall, but it wasn't being delivered until the evening. He clicked through to the folder. "May I?"

"Please. There are only three films on it, all of Yoyo."

Jericho pointed the device at the wall opposite and activated the integrated beamer. He focused the picture to the size of a standard flat screen so there would be enough clarity despite the penetrating sunlight, and started the first recording.

Tu Tian had been right.

No, he hadn't done her justice! Yoyo wasn't just pretty, she was extraordinarily beautiful. During his time in London Jericho had familiarized himself with the most differing of theories about the existence of beauty: symmetry of facial features, the shaping of particular features like the eyes or lips, proportioning of bone structure, the amount of child-like characteristics. Studies like these were used in the psychological fight against crime, and they were also used as the basis of tracking down people disguising themselves with virtual personalities. Modern studies concluded that perfect feminine beauty was defined by large, round eyes and a high, lightly curved forehead, while the nose had to be slender and the chin small but clearly defined. If you processed women's faces in a morphing program and added a certain percentage of child-like features, the rate of approval from male viewers soared spontaneously. Full lips trumped narrow ones, eyes that were too close lost against those set at a certain distance. The perfect Venus had high cheekbones, narrow, dark brows, long lashes, glossy hair, and an even hairline.

Yoyo was all of this—and yet none of it.

Chen had filmed her during a performance in some badly lit club, flanked by musicians who might or might not have been male. Nowadays, young men cultivated an increasingly androgynous style and wore their hair down to their belts. For anyone who wanted to be someone in the Mando Prog scene, the only other option was to shave their hair off and wear a skull cap. Short hair was out of the question. They could equally have been avatars, leaning over their guitars and bass: holographic simulations, even though that would have been hugely expensive. Only very successful musicians could afford avatars, like the American rapper Eminem who, now over fifty years of age and wanting to relive his heyday, had recently projected numerous versions of himself onto the stage, which played the instruments, danced, and unfortunately displayed much more agility than the master himself.

But all of this—gender, flesh and blood, bits and bytes—all of it lost any meaning next to the singer. Yoyo had combed her hair back tightly and braided it into four ponytails at the nape of her neck, which swung back and forth with each of her sinuous, powerful moves. She was singing a cover version of some ancient Shenggy track. As far as it was possible to deduce from the cell phone's mediocre recording quality, she had a good voice, if not a remarkable one. And even though the bad lighting didn't put her sufficiently in the limelight, Jericho still saw enough to know she was perhaps the most beautiful woman he had seen in the thirty-eight years of his life. It was just that Yoyo's particular kind of beauty threw all the theories about what beauty was right out of the window.

The picture blurred for a moment as Chen tried to zoom in on his daughter. Then Yoyo's eyes filled the screen—a gaze like velvet, slender eyelids, curtained by lashes which sank and then quickly lifted again. The camera wobbled, Yoyo disappeared from view, then the recording stopped.

"She sings," said Chen, as if it were necessary to point that out. Jericho played the next film. It showed Yoyo in a restaurant, sitting opposite Chen, her hair loose. She flicked through a menu, then noticed the camera and smiled.

"What are you doing?"

"Well, I hardly ever see you," answered Chen's voice. "So this way I'll at least have you preserved on film."

"Aha! Bottled Yoyo."

She laughed. Two horizontal creases formed under her eyes as she did so, which hadn't come up in the psychologists' beauty scenarios, but Jericho found them incredibly exciting.

"And besides, that way I can show you off."

Yoyo pulled a face at her father. She started to squint.

"No, don't," said Chen's voice.

The recording ended. The third one showed the restaurant again, apparently at a later date. Music blended into the cacophony of noise. In the background, waiters were hurrying between packed tables. Yoyo took a drag of her cigarette and balanced a drink in her right hand. She opened her lips and let a thin plume of smoke escape. For the duration of the entire clip, she didn't speak a single word. Her gaze rested on her father. It was one of love and noticeable sadness, so much so that Jericho wouldn't have been surprised to see tears flowing from her eyes. But nothing of the sort happened. Yoyo just lowered her eyelids from time to time, as if wanting to wipe away what she saw with her heavy lashes, sipped at her drink, dragged at her cigarette, and blew out smoke.

"I'll need these recordings," said Jericho.

Chen pushed himself out of his chair, his gaze fixed on the now empty wall as if his daughter were still visible on it. His features seemed more rigid than ever. And yet Jericho knew, without knowing the exact circumstances, that there had been times when this face had been contorted with pain. He had seen such faces in London. Victims. Families of victims. Perpetrators who had become victims themselves. Whatever it was that had hardened Chen, he hoped fervently to be far away if this rigidity ever broke down. There was no way in the world he wanted to see what would happen if it did.

"There are more you can have," said Chen tonelessly. "Yoyo enjoyed being photographed. But the films are much better. Not these ones though. Yoyo made recordings for Tian as a virtual tour guide. In high resolution, so she told me. And it's true, when you walk through the Museum of Town Planning or through the eye of the World Financial Center with one of those programs, it's as though she's there with you in the flesh. I have some of them at home, but I'm sure Tian can give you better material." He faltered. "Assuming, of course, that you're willing to find Yoyo for me."

Jericho reached for his cup, stared at the remaining puddle of cold coffee, and put it back down. Bright sunlight filled the room. He looked at Chen and knew that his visitor wouldn't ask a second time.

"I'm going to need more than the films."

JIN MAO TOWER

Around the same time, a Japanese waitress was approaching Kenny Xin's table, carrying a tray of sushi and sashimi in front of her. Xin, who saw her coming out of the corner of his eye, didn't bother turning around. His gaze was resting on the blue-gray band of the Huangpu 300 meters below him. The river was busy at this time of day. Chains of barges followed its path like sluggish water snakes, while heavy cargo ships headed for the docks to the east of the bend. Ferries, water taxis, and excursion boats forced their way between them en route for the Yangpu Bridge and the cranes of the unloading bays, past the idyllic Gongqing Park to the estuary, where the oily floods of the Huangpu mixed in a gloomy kaleidoscope with the muddy waters of the Yangtze before dispersing into the East China Sea.

It was thanks to the river's sharp, almost angular bend to the right that Shanghai's financial and economic district, Pudong, seemed like a peninsula, offering panoramic views of the coastal road Zhongshan Lu with its colonial banks, clubs, and hotels: relics from the era after the Opium Wars, when the European trade giants had divided up the country between them and erected monuments of their power on the western bank of the river. A hundred years ago, these structures must have towered over everything around them in splendor and size. Now they looked like toys against the stalagmite-like towers of glass, steel, and concrete that stretched out behind them, permeated by highways, magnetic rails and sky trains, surrounded by whirling flying machines, insectoid minicopters, and cargo-blimps. Even though the weather was unusually clear, the horizon couldn't be seen. Shanghai went up in smoke, diffused at the edges and became one with the sky. There was nothing to suggest that anything other than yet more development was beyond the development itself.

Xin looked at it all, without granting the woman who was placing the sushi before him the honor of acknowledgment. His concentration could not be divided, and right now he was concentrating on the question of where the girl he was looking for might be hiding amid this 20-million-strong moloch. She certainly wasn't at home, he'd checked there. If that student with the ridiculous name of Grand Cherokee Wang hadn't been lying, then there was still the possibility of narrowing down her location. He would have to clutch at this straw, even if the kid seemed dodgy to him: one of Yoyo's two roommates, clearly in love with the girl and even more so with money, in pursuit of which he made out he had information to offer. And yet he clearly didn't know a thing.

"Yoyo hasn't been living here that long," he had said. "She's a real party hen."

"And we're the cocks," the other had laughed immediately—showing his swinging uvula—by way of admitting it was a pretty bad joke. Hen was the Chinese term for whore, and the cocks, or cockerels, were the pimps. It seemed he had suddenly pictured what Yoyo might do to him if Xin were to pass on his tasteless little comment.

Could they pass on a message to Yoyo for him?

Xin asked when they had last seen Yoyo.

On the evening of May 23, they said. The three of them had cooked and knocked back a few bottles of beer together. Afterward, Yoyo had gone to her room, but then left the house later that same night.

At what time?

Late, Grand Cherokee seemed to remember. Around two or three in the morning. The other guy, Zhang Li, shrugged his shoulders. But since then neither of them had seen her.

Xin thought for a moment.

"Your roommate could be in trouble," he said. "I can't go into it in more detail right now, but her family is very worried."

"Are you a policeman?" Zhang wanted to know.

"No. I'm someone who was sent to help Yoyo." He gave each of them a meaningful look. "And I've also been authorized to show my gratitude for any help in an appropriate manner. Please tell Yoyo that she can reach me on this number at any time." Xin gave Grand Cherokee a card on which there was nothing but a cell phone number. "And if either of you has any more thoughts about where I might be able to find her—"

"No idea," said Zhang, clearly uninterested, and disappeared into the next room.

Grand Cherokee watched him go and shuffled from one leg to the other. Xin paused in the doorway to give Grand Cherokee the chance to take the offensive. Just as he'd expected, the boy got straight to the point—although in hushed tones—as soon as his pal was out of sight.

"I could find something out for you," he said. "For a price, of course."

"Of course," echoed Xin, smiling a little.

"Just to cover my costs, you know. I mean . . . there are a few clues, about where she is, and I could—"

Xin slid his right hand into his jacket and pulled it back out with some money.

"Could I perhaps take a quick look around her room?"

"I can't do that," said Grand Cherokee, shocked. "She would never—"

"It would be for her own safety." Xin lowered his voice. "Between you and me, the police could turn up here. I don't want them finding anything that could incriminate Yoyo."

"Oh, of course. It's just—"

"I understand." Xin moved to put the money back in his pocket.

"No, wait—I—"

"Yes?"

Grand Cherokee stared at the money and tried to tell Xin something without using words. It was clear what he wanted. The language of greed doesn't need vocabulary. Xin reached back into his jacket and increased the offer. The boy gnawed on his lower lip, then took the money and nodded his head toward the corridor.

"Last door on the right. Should I—"

"Thanks. I'll find my way. And as I said—if you should have any clues—"

"I do!" Grand Cherokee's eyes started to glisten. "I just need to make a few calls, speak to a few people. Hey, I'll take you to Yoyo as soon as I've got things sorted! Although—"

"Yes?"

"I might have to bribe a few people here and there."

"Are we talking about an advance?"

"Something like that."

Xin saw the lie in Grand Cherokee's eyes. You don't know a thing, he thought, but it's possible that your greed might lead you to find something out. You'll be in touch sooner or later. You're too sharp not to cash in on this. He pressed more money into his hand and left.

That was yesterday.

So far he had heard nothing from the boy, but Xin wasn't worried. He reckoned he would receive a call sometime in the course of the afternoon. He turned his attention to his sushi: just tuna, salmon, and mackerel, all of the highest quality. The cuisine of the Japanese restaurant on the fifty-third floor of the Jin Mao Tower left little to be desired, that is if you ignored the oversights in how the dishes were presented. The restaurant was part of the Jin Mao Grand Hyatt, which occupied the top fifty-three floors of what had once been China's tallest building. By now, the Jin Mao Tower had been outflanked a dozen times in Shanghai alone—first in 2008 by the neighboring World Financial Center, which also contained a Hyatt—and yet the aura of excess still clung to its outdated ambience. It reflected a time when China had begun to seek new self-awareness between communism, Confucius, and capital, and had found it just as much in reminiscences of the imperial past as in the art deco aesthetic of colonialism. Xin liked that, even if he had to admit that staying in the new place was a more stylish experience. He was drawn here by the idea that he could subject his presence to a concept shaped not by emotions but by cold agreement with the principles of order, ultimately, the secret formula of perfection. Kenny Xin was born in 1988, and the Jin Mao Tower surrendered itself to the number eight like the human to the genome. Deng Xiaoping had completed the design of the building at 88 years of age, and the inauguration ceremony took place on August 28, 1998. Eighty-eight flours were stacked on top of one another and formed a construction in which every segment was an eighth smaller than the base with its sixteen stories. The steel joists the tower rested on measured 80 meters. The eight could be seen in everything. By 2015 the building had 79 elevators, a flaw which was remedied by creating an elevator just for the staff.

There were, of course, a few small imperfections in the otherwise exemplary conception. For example, the tower only swung a maximum of 75 centimeters back and forth in a storm or earthquake. Xin wondered how the constructors could have overlooked that kind of mistake in its mathematical beauty. He was no architect, and perhaps there was no other way, but what were five centimeters against the priority of perfection? Compared with the order of the cosmos, even the Jin Mao Tower looked like a messy child's bedroom.

With one of his manicured fingers, Xin pushed the sushi tray away from him and a little to the left, then placed the bottle of Tsingtao beer and its accompanying glass behind it at an equal distance. It looked better to him already. He was far from subscribing to the obscene order principles of people who put everything at a right angle. Occasionally he even saw the purest order in the appearance of chaos. What could be more perfect than total homogeneity without imperfections, just as a perfectly empty spirit resembles the cosmic ideal, and every thought is a form of contamination, unless you summon it deliberately and dismiss it again at will. To control the mind is to control the world. Xin smiled as he made a few more corrections, shifting the small bowl for the soy sauce, breaking the chopsticks apart and laying them parallel in front of him. In its own way, wasn't Shanghai a wonderful chaos too? Or rather a secret plan, an ordering of capriciousness which only revealed itself to the educated observer?

Xin pushed a few clumps of rice a little further apart on the wooden board until their appearance appealed to him.

He began to eat.

XINTIANDI

When Jericho looked back, his life in China seemed like a confused succession of dangerous risks and escapes, all encircled by sound-proofed walls and building sites, in the shadow of which he had striven to improve his financial state with the industriousness of an animal burrowing a hole. In the end, the hard slog had shown results. His bank manager began to seem more like a friend. Dossiers about shares in deep-sea vessels, water treatment plants, shopping centers, and skyscrapers were presented to him. The whole world seemed intent on making him aware of all the things he could spend his money on. Clasped against the bosom of better society, respected and overworked, Jericho ended up paralyzed by his own achievements, too exhausted to add the final chapter to the story of his nomadic life by moving to the kind of area it would be worth growing old in. The step was long over-due, but the thought of packing up yet again made him go cold. So he gave priority to lying wearily on the sofa in the evenings as floodlights and construction noise leaked through the curtains, watching feature films and murmuring the mantra "I have to get out of here" to himself, then falling asleep in the process.

It was around this time that Jericho began to seriously doubt the point of his existence.

He hadn't doubted it when Joanna had lured him to Shanghai, only to leave him three months later. He hadn't doubted it when he'd realized he didn't have enough money for the flight back, nor to rebuild the life he'd left behind in London. He hadn't doubted in his first Shanghai digs on the edge of a highway, where he'd lived on damp floors and struggled to squeeze a few liters of brown water from the shower every morning, the windows of the two-story house rattling lightly from the never-relenting traffic.

He had just told himself it could only get better.

And it had.

To start with, Jericho had offered his services to foreign enter-prises that had come out to Shanghai to do business. Many felt inse-cure within the fragile framework of Chinese copyright protection legislation. They felt spied on and cheated. With time, though, the self-service mentality of the dragon had given way to great remorse. While, at the beginning of the century, China had still happily plagia-rized everything hackers unearthed from the depths of the global ideas pool, now even Chinese businesspeople were increasingly despairing about their state's inability to protect ideas. They too began to be on the receiving end of the words "It seemed worthy of imitation to us," which was a polite way of saying "Of course we stole it, but we admire you for having created it." For years, the Long-Nose accusations that Chinese companies and institutions had stolen their intellectual property had been indignantly rejected or not even acknowledged, but Jericho found that now it was Chinese companies, above all, who needed web detectives. Native entrepreneurs reacted excitedly to the fact that, during his time with Scotland Yard helping to build up the department for Cyber Crime, he had been fighting *against* them. In their opinion, it could only be advantageous to have their patents protected by someone who had previously done such an excellent job of clobbering them when they crossed the line.

Because the problem—an undulating, proliferating, all-enveloping, truly uncontrollable monster of a problem—was that China's creative elite would go on cannibalizing itself so long as a nationally and internationally accepted and implementable system for the protection of intellectual property rights remained elusive. It had always been obvious that capitalism, practically reinvented by China, was *based* upon property rights, and that an economy whose most important asset was know-how couldn't exist without the protection of brands, patents, and copyright; but it hadn't really interested anyone—not, that is, until the day when they themselves became victims of the situation. By now, the country suffering the most economic damage at the hands of Chinese espionage was China itself. Everyone was digging around in other people's front gardens, and with electronic spades wherever possible. The hunting ground was the global Internet, and Owen Jericho was one of the hunters, commissioned by other hunters as soon as they got the impression that they themselves were the quarry.

Once Jericho became part of that network without which no favors would be done and no trade negotiated in China, his career ascended like a rocket. He moved five times in five years, twice of his own free will, the other times because the houses he was living in at the time were to be pulled down for reasons he could no longer remember. He moved to better areas, wider streets, nicer houses, getting ever closer to realizing his dream of moving into one of the rebuilt Shikumen houses, with stone gateways and peaceful inner courtyards, located in the pulsating heart of Shanghai. Even though he had to make compromises along the way, he had never doubted it would happen at some point.

One day, his bank manager asked him what he was waiting for. Jericho replied that he wasn't quite there yet, but would be someday. The bank manager made him aware of his bank balance and said that "someday" was, in fact, now. With the revelation that he'd been working so hard he hadn't paid attention to the possibilities now open to him, Jericho left the bank and teetered home in a daze.

He hadn't realized he had come so far.

With the realization came the doubts. They claimed they'd always been there, but that he had avoided acknowledging them. They whispered: What the devil are you doing here anyway? How did you even get here?

How could this happen to you?

They told him that it had all been for nothing, and that the worst position anyone could ever find themselves in was that of having achieved their goals. Hope blossoms beneath the shelter of provisional arrangements, often for a whole lifetime. Now, suddenly, it had become official. He was to become a Shanghaian, but had he ever wanted that? To settle in a city he would never have moved to without Joanna?

As long as you were on the journey, said the doubts, you didn't have to think about the destination. Welcome to commitment.

In the end—he lived in a fairly prestigious high-rise in the hinterland of Pudong, the financial district, the only drawback of which was the fact that more skyscrapers were being constructed around it, causing constant noise and a fine brown dust which settled in the window-sills and airways—it took a further eviction by the city authorities to shake him from his lethargy. Two smiling men paid him a visit, let him serve them tea, and then explained that the house he was living in had to give way to an utterly amazing new building. If he so wished, they would gladly reserve an apartment in it for him. But a further move for the duration of the coming year would, much to their regret, be unavoidable. To which end, the authorities considered themselves overjoyed to be able to offer him an apartment near Luchao Harbor City, a mere 60 kilometers outside Shanghai—which, for a metropolis lovingly embracing other towns in the course of its expansion, wasn't *really* outside at all. Oh yes, and they wanted to start work in four weeks, so if he could—you know. It wasn't the first time such a thing had happened, and they said they were very sorry, but they weren't really.

Jericho had stared at the delegates as the wonderful certainty of having just awoken from a coma streamed through him. Suddenly, he could smell the world again, taste it, feel it. He shook hands with the baffled men gratefully, assuring them they had done him a great service. And that they could send whoever they wanted to Luchao Harbor City. Then he had phoned Tu Tian and, in keeping with matters of decorum, had asked whether he might know someone who knew someone who knew whether there was a renovated or newly built Shikumen house in a lively corner of Shanghai, vacant and which could be moved into at short notice. Mr. Tu, who prided himself on being Jericho's most satisfied client as well as his good friend, was the first port of call for questions such as these. He managed a mid-size technology company, was on good terms with the city's powers that be, and happily declared that he would be willing to "keep an ear to the ground."

Fourteen days later, Jericho signed the rental contract for a floor in one of the most beautiful Shikumen houses, situated in Xintiandi, one of the most popular areas of Shanghai, and which could be moved into right away. It was a new building of course. There weren't any genuine old Shikumen houses left, and there hadn't been for a long time. The last ones had been torn down shortly after the world exhibition of 2010, and yet Xintiandi could still be classified as a stronghold of Shikumen architecture just as in similar fashion the old town of Shanghai was anything but old.

Jericho didn't ask who had had to move out to make it vacant. He hoped the apartment really had been empty, put his signature on the document, and didn't give any more thought to what favor Tu Tian might ask for in return. He knew he owed Tu. So he prepared for his move and waited humbly for what was to come.

And it came sooner than expected in the form of Chen Hongbing and an unpleasant commission, which there was no way of getting out of without insulting Tu.

Shortly after Chen left, Jericho set up his computer terminal. He washed his face, combed his disheveled hair into some semblance of order and pulled on a fresh T-shirt. Making himself comfortable in front of the screen, he let the system dial the number. Two T's appeared on the screen, each one melting into the other, the symbol of Tu Technologies. The next moment, an attractive woman in her mid-forties was smiling at him. She was seated in a tastefully decorated room with lounge furniture and floor-to-ceiling windows which offered a glimpse of Pudong's skyline. She was drinking something from a tiny porcelain cup which Jericho knew to be strawberry tea. Naomi Liu would kill for strawberry tea.

"Good afternoon, Naomi."

"Good afternoon, Owen. How's the move going?"

"Fantastically, thank you."

"I'm pleased to hear it. Mr. Tu told me you're having one of our big new terminals delivered."

"Yes, this evening I hope."

"How exciting." She put the cup down on a transparent surface which seemed to sway in thin air, and looked at him from beneath her lowered lashes. "Then I'll soon be able to see you from head to toe."

"That's nothing compared to the excitement of seeing *you*." Jericho leaned forward and lowered his voice. "Anyone would swear that you're sitting right here in front of me."

"And that's enough for you?"

"Of course not."

"I'm worried it might be. It will be enough, and you'll see no reason anymore to invite me around personally. I think I'll have to convince my boss not to deliver the thing to you after all."

"No holographic program could compare to you, Naomi."

"Tell *him* that." She nodded her head in the direction of Tu's office. "Otherwise he might come up with the idea of replacing me with one."

"I would break off all business connections in an instant if he did that. Is he—"

"Yes, he's here. Take care. I'll put you through."

Jericho enjoyed their little flirting ritual. Naomi Liu was the conduit for all forms of contact with Tu Tian. Having her on his side could be useful. And Jericho wouldn't have hesitated for a second in inviting her to his apartment, but she would never have taken him up on the offer. She was happily married and the mother of two children.

The shimmering double T rotated again briefly, then Tu's huge head appeared on the screen. The little hair he had left was concentrated just above his ears, where it was gray and bristly. Narrow glasses were balanced on his nose. The left arm looked as if it was held together by transparent double-sided tape. Tu had pushed his sleeves up and was shoveling sticky-looking noodles into his mouth, fishing them out of a paper box with clattering chopsticks. The large desk behind him was full of screens and holo-projectors. In between were piles of hard disks, remote controls, brochures, cardboard boxes, and the remains of various packaging.

"No, you're not interrupting," mumbled Tu with his mouth full, as if Jericho had expressed any concern on the matter.

"I can see that. Have you ever been to your cafeteria, by the way? They make fresh food there."

"So?"

"Proper food."

"This is proper food. I poured boiling water on it and it turned into food."

"Do you even know what it's supposed to be? Does it say anything on the packaging?"

"It says something or other." Tu carried on chewing steadily. His rubbery lips moved around like copulating rubber tubes. "People with your anarchic sense of time management wouldn't understand perhaps, but there are reasons for eating in the office."

Jericho gave up. As long as he'd known Tu, he'd hardly ever seen him devour a healthy, decent meal. It seemed as though the manager had set himself the task of ruining the Chinese cuisine's reputation as the best, most varied and freshest in the world. He might be a genial inventor and a gifted golfer—but when it came to culinary matters, he made Kublai Khan look like the father of all gourmets.

"So what were you celebrating?" he asked, with a glance at the chaos in Tu's office.

"We were testing something out." Tu reached for a bottle of water, washed down the noodles in his mouth, and burped audibly.

"Holo-Cops. A commission from the traffic-control authorities. They function excellently in the dark, but sunlight is still giving them problems. It corrodes them." He chortled with laughter. "Like vampires."

"What does the city want with holographic policemen?"

Tu looked at him in amazement.

"To regulate the traffic, what else? Another one of the real ones was run over last week, didn't you read about it? He was standing in the middle of the Siping Lu crossing in Dalian Xilu when one of the furniture transporters raced right into him and distributed him evenly all over the tarmac. It was a huge mess, screaming children, angry letters! No one regulates the traffic voluntarily anymore."

"Since when did the police care whether things are voluntary?"

"They don't, Owen, but it's a question of economics. They're losing too many officers. Being a traffic policeman tops the list of most dangerous jobs right now, and most of them would rather be assigned to tracking down and catching mentally disturbed mass-murderers. And, well, there's the humane aspect too, no one wants dead policemen. It's no problem at all if a Holo-Cop gets run over, it even still manages to file a report about it. The projection sends a signal to the computer, including the car make and number plate."

"Interesting," said Jericho. "And how are the holographic tour guides coming along?"

"Ah!" Tu wiped the corner of his mouth clean with a napkin, one which had clearly had to assist with several other mealtimes too. "You had a visitor."

"Yes, I had a visitor."

"And?"

"Your friend is terribly sad. What happened to him?"

"I told you. He ate bitterness."

"And beyond that it's none of my business, I get the picture. So let's talk about his daughter."

"Yoyo!" Tu stroked his hand over his stomach. "Be honest now, isn't she sensational?"

"Without a doubt."

Jericho was intrigued as to whether Tu would talk about the girl on a public phone line. It was true that all telephone conversations were recorded by the authorities, but in reality the observation apparatus rarely followed up on the analysis, even though sophisticated programs preselected the recordings. As early as the end of the previous century, within the context of their worldwide Ecelon Program, American secret services had introduced software which was able to recognize key words, with the result that you could be arrested just for mentioning the word ice-bomb three times in succession when planning Grandma's birthday party. Modern programs by contrast were, to a certain extent, perfectly able to understand the meaning of the conversation and create priority lists. But they were still incapable of recognizing irony. Humor and double meanings were alien to them, which forced the spies themselves to listen in, just like in the old times, as soon as words like dissident or Tiananmen massacre came up. As expected, Tu merely said:

"And now you want a date with the girl, right?"

Jericho grinned cheerlessly. He knew it. There were going to be difficulties.

"If it can be arranged."

"Well, she has such high standards," said Tu craftily. "Perhaps I should give you a few useful pieces of advice, my dear boy. Will you be in the area in the next few hours at all?"

"I have things to do in Bund. I should be free around lunchtime."

"Excellent! Take the ferry. The weather's lovely, let's meet in Lujiazui Green."

PUDONG

Lujiazui Green was a picturesque park surrounded by skyscrapers, not far from Jin Mao Tower and the WFC. Tu sat on a bench on the bank of the small lake, basking in the sun. As usual, he was wearing sunglasses over his normal glasses. His crumpled shirt had worked its way almost entirely out of his waistband and was straining at the buttons. Patches of his white belly peeped through the gaps. Jericho sat down next to him and stretched out his legs.

"Yoyo is a dissident," he said.

Tu turned his head around to him lethargically. His eyes couldn't be seen behind the crooked construction of glasses and sunglasses.

"I thought you would have picked that up from our conversation on the golf course."

"That's not what I mean. What I mean is that the case is a little different to my normal ones. This time I'm supposed to look for a dissident in order to protect her."

"A former dissident."

"Her father sees that differently. Why would Yoyo have gone underground, if not out of fear? Unless she's been arrested. You said yourself that she has a tendency to aggravate the wrong people. Perhaps she crossed someone who was a little too big for her."

"And what are you planning to do?"

"You know exactly what I'm going to do," snorted Jericho. "I'm going to look for Yoyo of course."

Tu nodded. "That's very generous of you."

"No, it goes without saying. The only snag is that I'll have to work without the authorities this time. So I need any information there is about Yoyo and her world, and that's where I'm relying on your help. My impression of Chen Hongbing was that he's extremely honorable and incredibly private. Perhaps he just turns a blind eye; in any case, getting information from him was like trying to get blood from a stone."

"What did he tell you?"

"He gave me Yoyo's new address. A few films and photos. And dropped a whole load of hints."

Fumbling, Tu took the sunglasses down from his nose and tried to push the remaining glasses into a reasonably straight position. Jericho noticed that he hadn't been mistaken: the left arm really was bound with double-sided tape. He wondered, not for the first time, why Tu didn't get his eyes lasered or switch to photochromic contact lenses. Hardly anyone wore glasses for the purpose of improving their eyesight anymore. They were just eking out an existence as fashion items, and fashion was as alien to Tu Tian as the atomic age was to a Neanderthal.

They were silent for a while. Jericho blinked in the sunlight and watched an airplane pass by.

"So" said Tu. "Ask your questions."

"There's nothing to ask. Tell me something about Yoyo that I don't know yet."

"She's actually called Yuyun—"

"Chen told me that much."

"—and belongs to a group who call themselves Guardians. I bet he didn't tell you that, right?"

"Guardians." Jericho whistled softly through his teeth.

"You've heard of them?"

"I sure have. Internet guerrillas. Dedicated to human rights, raising the profile of old stories like Tiananmen, attacks on government and industry networks. They're really making the Party anxious."

"And they're right to be nervous. Guardians are of a completely different caliber to our sweet little Titanium Mouse."

Liu Di, the woman who called herself Titanium Mouse, was one of the pioneers of Internet dissidence. At the start of the millennium she had begun to publish edgy little commentaries online about the political elite, initially under the pseudonym of Stainless Steel Mouse. Realizing that it wasn't as easy to imprison virtual people as it was those of flesh and blood, Beijing's leadership began to get very nervous. These dissidents showed presence, without being present.

The head of the Beijing secret police remarked that the new threat gave cause for extreme concern and that an enemy without a face was the worst kind, a conclusion that grossly overestimated the first generation of net dissidents—most didn't even contemplate disguising their identity, and even the ones who did made other mistakes sooner or later.

The Stainless Steel Mouse, for example, had walked right into their trap when she assured the founder of a new democratic party of her support, not knowing it was an official assigned to her case. As a result of which she was dragged off to a police station and imprisoned for a year without trial. After that, however, the Party learned their next lesson: that it may be possible to make people disappear behind walls, but not on the Internet. There, Liu Di's case gained significance, made the rounds in China, and attracted the attention of the foreign media. Suddenly, the whole world was aware of this shy, twenty-one-year-old woman, who hadn't even meant any of it that seriously. And that turned out to be the powerful, faceless enemy the Party had cowered so fearfully from.

After her release, Liu Di upgraded from steel to a stronger metal. Titanium Mouse had learned something. She declared war on an apparatus that Mao couldn't have thought up in his wildest dreams: Cypol, the Chinese Internet Police. She routed Internet forums via servers abroad and created her blogs with the help of programs which filtered out incriminating words as she wrote. Others followed her example, became increasingly sophisticated in their methods, and by then the Party really *did* have cause to worry. While veterans like Titanium Mouse made no secret of their true identity, Guardians were haunting the net like phantoms. Tracking them down would have required ingenious traps, and although Beijing kept setting them, so far no one had been caught.

"Even today, the Party still has no idea how many of them there actually are. Sometimes they think they're dealing with dozens, sometimes just a few. A cancerous ulcer in any case, one which will eat away at our magnificent, happy, and healthy People's Republic from the inside." Tu hacked up some phlegm and spat it in front of his feet. "Now, we know what comes out of Beijing, predominantly rumors and very little of anything that makes sense, so how big do you think the organization really is?"

Jericho thought about it. He couldn't remember ever having heard of a Guardian being imprisoned.

"Oh sure, now and then they arrest someone and claim that person is one of them!" said Tu, as if he had read Jericho's thoughts. "But I happen to know for certain that they haven't made one successful arrest yet. Unbelievable, isn't it? I mean, they're hunting an army, so you'd think there'd be prisoners of war."

"They're hunting something that looks like an army," said Jericho.

"You're getting close."

"But the army doesn't exist. There are only a few of them, but they know how to keep slipping through the investigators' nets. So the Party exaggerates them. Makes them seem more dangerous and intelligent than they really are, to distract from the fact that the State still hasn't managed to pull a handful of hackers out of the online traffic."

"And what do you conclude from that?"

"That for one of Beijing's honorable servants you know a suspicious amount about a bunch of Internet dissidents." Jericho looked at Tu, frowning. "Is it just my imagination, or are you playing some part in the game too?"

"Why don't you just come out and ask if I'm one of them?"

"I just did."

"The answer is no. But I can tell you that the entire group consists of six people. There were never more than that."

"And Yoyo is one of them?"

"Well." Tu rubbed his neck. "Yes and no."

"Which means?"

"She's the brains behind it. Yoyo brought the Guardians to life."

Jericho smirked. In the distorting mirror of the Internet, anything was possible. The Guardians' presence suggested they were a larger group, potentially capable of spying on government secrets. Their actions were well thought out, the background research always exemplary. It all created the illusion of being an extensive network, but in actual fact that was thanks to their multitude of sympathizers, who were neither affiliated to the group nor possessed knowledge about their structure. On closer inspection the Guardians' entire activism boiled down to a small, conspiring hacker community. And yet—

"—they have to be constantly up to date," murmured Jericho.

Tu jabbed his elbow into his ribs. "Are you talking to me?"

"What? No. I mean, yes. How old is Yoyo again?"

"Twenty-five."

"No twenty-five-year-old girl is cunning enough to outmaneuver the State Security in the long term."

"Yoyo is extraordinarily intelligent."

"That's not what I mean. The State may be limping behind the hackers, but they're not completely stupid. You can't get past the Diamond Shield using conventional methods, so sooner or later you'll have the Internet Police knocking at your door. Yoyo must have access to programs which enable her to always be a step ahead of them."

Tu shrugged his shoulders.

"Which means that she knows how to use them." Jericho spun the web further. "Who are the other members?"

"Some guys. Students like Yoyo."

"And how do you know all this?"

"Yoyo told me."

"She told you." Jericho paused. "But she didn't tell Chen?"

"Well, she tried. It's just that Chen won't hear any of it. He doesn't listen to her, so she comes to me."

"Why you?"

"Owen, you don't have to know everything"

"But I want to *understand*."

Tu sighed and stroked his bald head.

"Let's just say I help Yoyo to understand her father. Or, that's what she hopes to get from me in any case." He raised a finger. "And don't ask what there is to understand. That has nothing whatsoever to do with you!"

"You speak in puzzles just as much as Chen does," boomed Jericho, aggravated.

"On the contrary. I'm showing you an excessive amount of trust."

"Then trust me more. If I'm going to find Yoyo, I need to know the names of the other Guardians. I have to find them, question them."

"Just assume the others have gone underground too."

"Or were arrested."

"Hardly. Years ago I had the opportunity to get a close look at the cogs of the State welfare services, the places where they look inside your head and declare you to be infested with all kinds of insanity. I know those types. If they had arrested the Guardians, they would have been boasting about it at the tops of their voices for a while now. It's one thing to make people disappear, but if someone's running rings around you, making you look like a fool in public, then you put their head on a spear as soon as you catch them. Yoyo has caused the Party a great deal of grief. They won't stand for it."

"How did Yoyo even get into all this?"

"The way young people always get into things like this. She identified with *zi you*, with freedom." Tu poked around between his shirt buttons and scratched his belly. "You've been living here for a good while, Owen, and I think you understand my people pretty well by now. Or, let's put it this way, you understand what you see. But a few things are still closed off from you. Everything that takes place in the Middle Kingdom today is the logical consequence of developments and breakthroughs throughout our history. I know, that sounds like something from a travel guide. Europeans always think this whole yin-and-yang business, this insistence on tradition, is just folklorist nonsense intended to disguise the fact that we're just a band of greedy imitators who want to make their stamp on the world, continually damage human rights and who, since Mao, have no more ideals. But for two thousand years, Europe was like a pot which continually had new things thrown into it; it was a patchwork of clashing identities. A patchwork of identity sensitivities trying to be a tapestry. You've all overrun each other, made your neighbors' customs and ways your own, even while you were still fighting them. Huge empires came and went as if in time-lapse. For a while it was the Romans having their say, then the French, then the Germans and the Brits. You talk of a united Europe, and yet you speak in more languages than you can possibly understand, and as if that weren't enough, you import Asia, America, and the Balkans too. You're incapable of understanding how a nation that for the most part was entirely self-sufficient and self-contained—because it felt the Middle Kingdom didn't need to know what was outside its borders—finds it hard to accept the new, especially when it's brought in from the outside."

"You guys certainly know how to brush that one under the carpet," snorted Jericho. "You drive German, French, and Korean cars; wear Italian shoes; watch American films. I can't think of any other nationality that has turned more to the outside in recent years than yours."

"Turned to the outside?" Tu laughed drily. "Nicely put, Owen. And what comes to light when you turn to the outside? Whatever's inside.

But what is it that you see? What exactly are we turning toward the outside? Only what you recognize. You wanted us to open up? We did that, in the eighties under Deng Xiaoping. You wanted to do business with us? You're doing it. Everything that Chinese emperors didn't want from you over the centuries, we've bought from you in a matter of a few years, and you *sold* it to us willingly. Now we're selling it back to you, and you *buy* it! And on top of all that you have a fancy for a good portion of authentic China. And you get that too, but you don't like it. You get all worked up about us walking all over human rights, but in essence you just don't understand how anyone can be imprisoned for his opinion in a land that drinks Coca-Cola. That doesn't compute to you. Your ethnologists lament the disappearance of the last cannibals and plead for the preservation of their living space, but woe betide them if they start to do business and wear ties. If they did, you'd want them to downgrade back to chicken and vegetables in the blink of an eye."

"Tian, with the best will in the world, I don't know—"

"Do you realize that the term *zi you* was only exported to China in the middle of the nineteenth century?" Tu continued obstinately. "Five thousand years of Chinese history weren't enough to create it, nor were they enough for *min zhu*, democracy, or *ren quan*, human rights. But what does *zi you* mean? To stay true to yourself. To make you and your point of view the starting point for everything you do, not the dogma of how the masses think and feel. You might argue that the demonization of the individual is a Maoist invention, but you'd be wrong. Mao Zedong was merely a dreadful variant on our age-old fear of being ourselves. Perhaps a just punishment, because we had cooled off in our conviction that all the people outside China were barbarians. When China was forced to open itself up to the Western powers, we were completely ignorant of what every other people with experience of colonialism knew intuitively. We wrongly believed we were the hosts, whereas in reality the guests had long since become the owners. Mao wanted to change that, but he didn't just try to turn back the wheels of history, as the Ayatollahs went on to do in Iran. His efforts were focused on undoing history and isolating China on the summit of his ignorance. That just won't work with a people who think, feel, and criticize. That only works with robots. Pu Yi wasn't our last Emperor; Mao was, if you see what I mean. He was the most horrific of them all: he stole everything from us, our language, our culture, our identity. He betrayed every ideal we had and all he left behind was a pile of rubble."

Tu Tian paused, his fleshy lips twitching. Sweat shimmered on his bald head.

"You asked how Yoyo could have become a dissident? I'll tell you, Owen. Because she doesn't want to live with the trauma that my generation and my parents' generation will never be able to come to terms with. But if she wants to help an entire people find their identity, she can't quote the spirit of the French revolution, nor the foundation of Spanish democracy, nor the end of Mussolini or Hitler, the fall of Napoleon or of the Roman Empire. History may have equipped Europe with the inconceivable eloquence it needs to formulate its demands, but we have long lacked even the simplest words to do so. Oh sure, China sparkles! China is rich and beautiful, and Shanghai is the center of the world, where everything is permitted and nothing is impossible. We've drawn even with the United States, two economic giants neck to neck, and we're on our way to becoming number one. But amid all this shine our lives are impoverished on the inside, and we're aware of this poverty. We're not turning to the outside, Owen, it just seems like that. If we did turn to the outside, you would see the emptiness, like a transparent squid. We look to abroad for examples to follow, because the last Chinese example we had betrayed us. Yoyo suffers from being a child of this hollowed-out age more than the self-satisfied critics of globalization and human rights infringements in Europe and America could ever imagine. You only see our transgressions, not the steps we're taking. Not what we've already achieved. Not the unimaginable toil necessary to stand up for ideals, to even formulate them, without any moral legacy!"

Jericho blinked in the glistening sunlight. He wanted to ask when Chen Hongbing's heart had been torn out, but he didn't say a word. Tu wheezed and swept his hand over his bald head nervously.

"That's what makes people like Yoyo bitter. If someone in England takes to the streets and demands freedom, the most that will happen is that someone might ask them what for. In China we've been laboring under the illusion that our crazy economic upturn would automatically bring freedom along with it, but we had no idea what freedom actually is.

"For over twenty years now, everything in our country has revolved around this word, everyone sings the joys of the individual way of life, but in the end all it means is the freedom to conform. People don't like talking about the other freedom because it questions by implication whether a Communist party which is no longer Communist has any right to absolute rule. The left-wing tyranny has become a right-wing one, Owen, and that in turn has become one without any substance. We live in a consumer's dictatorship, and woe betide anyone who comes and complains that there are still the issues of the farmers and the migrant workers, and the executions and the economic support of pariah states, and so on."

Jericho rubbed his chin.

"I consider myself very lucky that you would honor me with all these explanations," he said. "But I'd be much happier if you could get back to Yoyo."

"Forgive an old man, Owen." Tu looked at him, his face furrowed. "But I've been talking about Yoyo the whole time."

"Yes, but without telling me about her *personal* background."

"Owen, as I already said—"

"I know," sighed Jericho. His gaze wandered over the glass and steel panels of the Jin Mao Tower. "It's none of my business."

JIN MAO TOWER

Behind one of the panels, Xin stood staring out at the stifling sauna of the Shanghai afternoon. He had retreated to his spacious art deco suite on the seventy-third floor. It had floor-to-ceiling windows on two sides, but even from this exposed viewpoint there was nothing to see but architecture. The higher up one was, the more identical the individual blocks of apartments and offices looked, as if thousands upon thousands of termite tribes had taken up quarters alongside one another.

He dialed a tap-proof number on his cell phone.

Someone answered. The screen stayed black.

"What have you found out about the girl?" asked Xin, without wasting any time on pleasantries.

"Very little," answered the voice in his ear, the time lag barely noticeable. "Only confirmation of what we already feared. She's an activist."

"Well known?"

"Yes and no. Some of her files suggest we're dealing with a member of a group of Internet dissidents who call themselves Guardians. A faction who are becoming a real nuisance to the Party with their demands for democracy."

"You mean that Yoyo didn't intentionally seek us out?"

"We can probably rule that out. Pure coincidence. We scanned her hard drives faster than she could switch them off, which suggests the attack surprised her. We didn't manage to destroy her computer though. She must have a highly efficient security system, and unfortunately that doesn't bode well. We're now convinced that fragments—at least—of our transfer data are now in Yuyun—er, Yoyo's computer."

"She won't be able to do much with it," said Xin contemptuously. "The encoding went through the strictest of tests."

"In any other circumstances I would agree with you. But the way Yoyo's protection is set up means she could have decoding programs which are much more advanced than the norm. We wouldn't have asked you to come to Shanghai if we weren't seriously concerned about this."

"I'm as worried as you are. But what concerns me most is how sketchy your information is, if I may be so honest."

"And what have you found out?" asked the voice, without responding to Xin's comment.

"I went to her apartment. Two roommates. One knows nothing, and the other says he could take me to her. He wants money of course."

"Do you trust him?"

"Are you crazy? I have no choice but to follow every lead. He'll be in touch, but I've no idea what will come of it."

"Did she not mention any relatives to either of the roommates?"

"Yoyo doesn't exactly seem that communicative. They were having some drinks together on the night of May 23, then she disappeared sometime between two and three in the morning."

A short pause followed.

"That could fit," said the voice thoughtfully. "The contact materialized just before two, Chinese time."

"And then she immediately takes off." Xin smiled thinly. "Clever kid."

"Where else have you been?"

"In her room. Nothing. No computer. She did a great job of clearing everything up before she disappeared. There's no trace of her at the university either, and it wasn't possible to see her file. I could arrange to do so, but I'd prefer it if you took care of that. I'm sure you can get into the university's database."

"Which university?"

"Shanghai University, Shangda Lu, in the Bao Shan District."

"Kenny, I don't need to remind you how explosive this thing is. So step up the pace! We need this girl's computer. Without fail!"

"You'll get it, *and* the girl," said Xin, ending the call.

He stared back out into the urban desert.

The computer. He had no doubt that Yoyo had it with her. Xin wondered what the reasons for her overhasty departure had been. She must have realized that someone had not only noticed her hacking and started a counterattack on her system, but that they had also downloaded her data, and therefore knew her identity. That was reason enough for concern, but not to flee in panic. Quite a few networks protected themselves by launching a lightning attack to deactivate the computers which had intentionally or unintentionally hacked into theirs and, if possible, they transferred the hacker's data right away. That alone wasn't enough. There must have been something else to make Yoyo think she wasn't safe anymore.

There was only one possible explanation.

Yoyo had read something she wasn't supposed to have read.

Which meant the encoding had temporarily failed. An error in the system. A hole had unexpectedly opened up and provided her access. If that was the case, the consequences really could be terrible! The question was how quickly the hole had closed up again. Not quickly enough, that much was clear; just that brief glimpse had been enough to make the girl take flight.

But how much did she really know?

He needed more than the computer. He had to find Yoyo before she had the chance to pass on what she knew. The only hope so far was

Grand Cherokee Wang. Quite a poor hope, admittedly. But when had hope ever been more than certainty's pitiful sister? In any case, the guy would sell Yoyo, and her computer included, the second she so much as set foot back in the apartment.

Xin frowned. Something in the way he was standing displeased him. He took a step backward until he was positioned exactly between two joists, the tips of his shoes at equal distance from where the floor bordered the window.

There, that was better.

PUDONG

"I've known Yoyo since the day she was born," said Tu. "She was just like any normal teenager while she was growing up, her brain full of romantic ideas. Then she experienced something that changed her. Nothing spectacular, but I think it was one of those crossroads in life when you decide who you're going to be. Have you heard of Mian Mian?"

"The author?"

"Yes, that's the one."

Jericho thought for a moment. "It must be an eternity since I read one of her books. She was a figurehead of the scene, right? Quite popular in Europe. I remember being amazed that she made it past the censorship."

"Oh, her books were banned for a long time! But by now she can do whatever she wants. When Shanghai declared itself to be the nightlife and party capital, she represented the area of conflict between glamour and the gutter, because she knew and could speak convincingly about both. Today, she's a kind of patron saint of the local art scene. In her mid fifties, established, even the Party uses her as a figurehead. In the summer of 2016 she gave a reading from her new novel, in Guan Di in Fuxing Park shortly before it was torn down, and Yoyo went along. Afterward, she had the chance to speak with Mian Mian, and they ended up doing a crawl around the clubs and galleries, which lasted many hours. After that, it was like she was intoxicated. You have to appreciate the symbolic coincidence, you see. Mian Mian started writing when she was sixteen, as an immediate consequence of her best friend committing suicide, and Yoyo had just turned sixteen."

"So she decided to become a writer."

"She decided to change the world. To some extent, it was romantically motivated, but she also had an admirably clear take on reality. At around that time my own star was beginning to rise. I knew Chen Hongbing from the nineties and liked him a great deal. He entrusted his daughter to me because he believed she could learn from me. Yoyo had always been very fond of the virtual world; she practically lived on the Internet. She was particularly interested in the vanishing dividing lines between the actual world and the artificial one. In 2018, I was elected onto the board of Dao IT, and Yoyo was just coming to grips with her studies at the time. Chen supported her as much as he could, but she placed a lot of importance on earning her own money. When she heard I was taking over the department for Virtual Environments, she pestered me to find a job for her there."

"What did she study anyway?"

"Journalism, politics, and psychology. The first to learn how to write, the second to know what to write about, and psychology—"

"To understand her father."

"She wouldn't put it quite like that. The way she sees it, China is like a patient in constant danger of succumbing to insanity. So she looks for diagnoses for our diseased society. And that, of course, is where Chen Hongbing comes into the picture."

"She got her tools from you," ruminated Jericho.

"Tools?"

"Of course. When did you found Tu Technologies?"

"2020."

"And Yoyo was there from the start?"

"Of course." Tu's expression seemed to clear. "Ah, I see."

"She's been looking over your shoulder for years. You develop programs for everything under the sun."

"I already know what role we play in the Guardians, unintentionally of course! But beyond that I can assure you that none of my people would ever dream of technologically arming a dissident."

"Chen mentioned that she had already been arrested several times."

"It was actually only during her studies that she realized the true extent to which the authorities censor the Internet. For someone who views the net as their natural habitat, closed doors can be incredibly frustrating."

"So she encountered the Diamond Shield."

Anyone who tried to accelerate on the Chinese data highway soon found themselves up against virtual roadblocks. At the beginning of the millennium, fearing that the new medium could illuminate explosive topics, the Party had developed a highly armed defense program for net censorship, the Golden Shield, followed in 2020 by the Diamond Shield. With its help, an Internet Police force of over 150,000 rummaged their way through chat rooms, blogs, and forums. While the Golden Shield had been like a tracker dog, snuffling through the most far-flung corners of the web for terms like Tiananmen Massacre, Tibet, student revolts, freedom, and human rights, the Diamond Shield was also able to recognize, to a certain extent, contextual meaning in the texts. This was the Party's reaction to the so-called Bodyguard Programs. Titanium Mouse, for example, had figured out after her release how to put critical texts on the net which didn't contain a single word that could be pounced on by the Golden Shield. To do this, she made use of a Bodyguard Program which rapped her on the knuckles, so to speak, while she was typing—if she used any incriminating terms, the Bodyguard would delete them, thus protecting her from herself. As a result the Diamond Shield paid less attention to keywords and instead assessed whole texts, connecting sayings and observations, inspecting the entries for double meanings and coding, and then raised the alarm if subversion was suspected.

Ironically, it was thanks to this very Cerberus that epoch-making advances had been made in the hacker scene, enabling dissidents to unleash the maximum criticism with the minimum of risk. Of course, the Diamond Shield also blocked search engines and websites of foreign news agencies. The whole world had experienced the assassination of Kim Jong-un and the collapse of North Korea, but in the Chinese net none of it had ever happened. The bloody uprising against the junta in Burma might have taken place on Planet Earth, but not on Planet China. Anyone who tried to bring up the sites of Reuters or CNN could be sure of reprisal. To the same extent that the Wall of China was crumbling, the wall the Diamond Shield had erected around the country became stronger by the day, and yet so did the authorities' fear. It wasn't just the community of Chinese hackers who seemed to have sworn a solemn oath to shatter the Diamond Wall into a thousand pieces, but activists all around the world were working away on it too—some in the offices of European, Indian, and American companies; secret services; and government bases. The world was caught up in a cyber war, and, as the foremost aggressor, China was the key target for attack.

"Compared with what was going on with hackers," explained Tu, "inside China and outside, Yoyo's first steps in the net were kid's stuff. With her big, indignantly wide eyes, she hit out at censorship and signed her name underneath in bold. She pleaded for freedom of opinion and demanded access to the inventories of information provided by Google, Alta Vista, and so on. She entered into dialogue with like-minded people who thought chat rooms could be barricaded against unwanted intruders just as easily as broom closets."

"Was she really that naïve?"

"To start with, yes. It's obvious that she wanted to impress Hongbing. In all seriousness, she really thought she was acting in accordance with his wishes. That he would be proud of his little dissident. But Hongbing was horrified."

"He tried to stop her from doing it."

"Yoyo was completely dumbfounded. She just couldn't understand it. Chen became stubborn, and I tell you, he can be as stubborn as a mule! The more Yoyo pushed him to justify his negative reaction, the more he dug his heels in. She argued. She screamed. She cried. But he still wouldn't talk to her. She realized he was worried for her of course, but it wasn't like she'd called for the government to be overthrown, she'd just grumbled a bit."

"And so she confided in you."

"She said she thought her father was just a coward. I certainly didn't let her get away with that one easily. I explained that I understood Hongbing's motivations better than she did, which made her bitter at first. Naturally, she wanted to know why Hongbing didn't trust his own daughter. I told her that his silence had nothing to do with lack of trust, but was related to something private. Do you have children, Owen?"

"No."

"Well, they're little emperors, Owen!"

Little Emperors. Jericho stiffened. What an idiot! It was only a few hours since he'd stopped being tormented by the images of that cellar in Shenzhen, and now Tu was starting on about little emperors.

"They're just as wonderful as they are demanding," Tu continued. "Yoyo, too. Anyway, I made it clear to her that her father had a right to his own life, and that the mere occasion of her birth didn't give her the right to trespass into the secret palaces of his soul, as it were. Children don't understand that. They think their parents are just there to provide a service, existing only to look after them, useful at first, then dumb and ultimately just embarrassing. She defended herself by saying that Hongbing started all of their arguments, that he was trying to control her life, and in that, unfortunately, she was right. Hongbing should have explained to her what it was that had angered him so much."

"But he didn't. So? Did you?"

"He would never allow me to speak to Yoyo about that. Nor to anyone else, for that matter! So I tried to build a bridge between them. Let her know that her father had once met with a great injustice, and that no one suffered more from his silence than he himself. I asked her to be patient with him. With time, Yoyo began to respect my view, and she became very thoughtful. From that point on she confided in me regularly, which was an honor, although not one I would have actively sought out."

"And Hongbing became jealous."

Tu laughed softly, a strange, sad laugh.

"He would never admit it. The bond between him and me goes deep, Owen. But of course he didn't like it. It was inevitable that it would complicate things. Yoyo decided to intensify her tone on the net, to test the authorities' sensitivity threshold. But then again, she was only writing about everyday things: the scene, music, films, and travel, and she also wrote poems and short stories. I don't think she was that clear about what she wanted to be: a serious journalist, a dissident, or just another Shanghai Baby."

"*Shanghai Baby*—wasn't that a book by—"

"Mian Mian." Tu nodded. "At the beginning of the millennium that's what people called young Shanghai writers. The term has gone out of fashion by now. Well, you've seen Yoyo. She made a name for herself in artists' circles, attracted the interest of the intellectuals, so did that make her an author?" Tu shook his head. "She never wrote one good novel. And yet I would trust her to single-handedly get to the bottom of the death of John F. Kennedy. She's a brilliant researcher, excellent on the offensive. The censors picked up on that a long time ago. And Hongbing knows it too. That's why he's so worried, because Yoyo is someone others follow. She has charisma, she's believable. All dangerous qualities in the eyes of the Party."

"When did she first go on their records?"

"To start with, nothing happened. The authorities bided their time. Yoyo was practically part of the furniture at my company; she showed a strong interest in holography and lent a hand in the development of some really fun programs, and the Party can't cope with fun. They just don't know what to make of it. It unsettles them that the Chinese are starting to value fun for the first time in their cultural development."

"Aristotle wrote a book about laughter," said Jericho. "Did you know that?"

"I know my Confucius better."

"No book ever caused more annoyance to the Church than this one did. They said that he who laughs, laughs also about God, the Pope, and the entire clerical apparatus of power."

"Or the Party. That's true, there are some parallels. On the other hand, anyone who's having fun is less angry and less political. For that reason the Party is on board with fun again, and Yoyo really is a fun-loving character. After a while she shifted her energies to singing and started one of these Mando Prog bands that are springing up everywhere. If Yoyo's not there, there is no party! If you're out and about in the scene, it's very difficult to avoid her. Perhaps back then they thought: The more fun the girl has, the less there'll be to fear from her. I'm sure that, had they left her in peace, it might even have worked."

Tu pulled a once-white handkerchief from the depths of his pants and wiped the sweat from his brow.

"But then suddenly, one morning five years ago, all of her blogs were blocked and all entries of her name erased from the net. She was arrested that same day and taken to a police station, where they left her to stew. They accused her of being a threat to the security of the State and of having goaded the citizens into subversion. She spent a month there before Hongbing even knew where they were holding her. He nearly lost his mind! The whole thing was fatefully reminiscent of the Titanium Mouse case. No charge, no trial, no verdict, nothing. Even Yoyo herself didn't know what she was supposed to have done. She was locked up in a cell with two junkies and a woman who had stabbed her husband. The policemen were friendly to her. In the end they told her why she was there. She was alleged to have shown her support for some rock musician, a friend of hers who was in prison for some impudence or other. It was laughable. According to the Constitution, the State prosecutor has six weeks to decide whether to go to trial or release someone. In the end they dropped the case due to lack of evidence, Yoyo received a warning, and they let her go home."

"I guess it goes without saying that Hongbing forbade her to make any more critical comments on the net," Jericho surmised.

"And achieved exactly the opposite. Which means she acted as innocent as a lamb at first, wrote a few articles for Internet magazines, even for Party organs. After a few weeks she stumbled across a case about the dumping of illegal toxic waste in the West Lake. A chemical company near Hangzhou, at the time still under State ownership, had carted over their waste and buried it in the lake, and as a result local residents lost their hair and even worse. The director of the company—"

"—was a cousin of the Minister for Employment and Social Security," Jericho blurted out. "Of course! Yoyo knew that, and that's why she wrote about it."

Tu stared at him in amazement.

"How do you know that?"

"I've finally remembered where I know Yoyo's name from!" He relished the moment as his brain lifted the blockade and released the memory. "I never saw a picture of her. But I remember the toxic waste scandal. It was all over the net back then, illegal dumping. They told her she was mistaken. Yoyo told them where they could stick it, and was promptly arrested."

"Once Yoyo dug her feet in, it was just a matter of hours before all her entries on the Internet were erased again. The security police turned up at her door that same evening, and she found herself back in the cell. Yet, once again, they couldn't accuse her of anything. Her mistake was getting herself tangled up in the web of corruption. The State prosecution demanded to know what was going on. After all, they'd already investigated her the year before and found nothing, but they were put under pressure and had to charge her against their will."

"I remember. She had to go to prison."

"It could have been worse. Hongbing has a few contacts, and I have even better ones. So I found Yoyo a lawyer who managed to negotiate her sentence down to six months."

"But what did they actually charge her with?"

"Passing on State secrets, the same as always." Tu shrugged and smiled bitterly. "The chemical company had entered into a joint venture with a British company, and Yoyo had gone to persuade one of its employees to collect evidence about the cloak-and-dagger operation. That was enough. But it was also enough to attract the media's attention to the case. China's journalists aren't as easily intimidated now as they were back in 2005, or even 2010. When one of their own is in prison, the dogs start to howl, and the Party is divided when it comes to cases of corruption. The story traveled abroad, Reporters without Borders took up Yoyo's cause; the British Prime Minister made a few comments in passing during bilateral talks in Beijing. Three months later, Yoyo was released."

"And the company director went swimming in the lake, right? I heard he killed himself."

"It was probably more like a case of euthanasia," smirked Tu. "The authorities hadn't reckoned with being put under so much public pressure. They were forced to call an investigation. I imagine a lot of names came under question, but after the villain went swimming in his own sewage they could hardly ask him, so to be on the safe side the acting director and plant manager were dismissed, and the investigations dropped. In 2022, Yoyo resumed her studies. Have you read her name anywhere since then?"

Jericho thought for a moment. "Not that I know of."

"Exactly. She really started to behave herself, at least when her own name was under the texts. She wrote articles on travel and cultural events, tried to spread the new Chinese culture of 'fun.' On the side, though, she acquired a bunch of pseudonyms and started to adopt different styles. She communicated via foreign servers, kicked the system up the backside whenever she could. She was like—" Tu laughed, spread his arms out, and made flapping motions. "—Batgirl! A scene girl on the outside, but secretly embarking on a revenge mission against torture, corruption, the death penalty, legalized crime, environmental sins, the whole shebang. She demanded democracy, but a Chinese form of democracy! Yoyo didn't want to follow the Western path; she wanted the hollow, rotting tooth that called itself the Party to be pulled from the country, so real values would have a chance. So we wouldn't be seen as just an economic giant, but also as the representatives of a new humanity."

"God protect us from missionaries," murmured Jericho.

"She isn't a missionary," said Tu. "She's searching for identity."

"Something her father can't give her."

"It's possible that Hongbing is the main motivation, yes. Perhaps all we're dealing with is a child who wants to be picked up and given a hug. But she's not naïve. Not anymore! When she called the Guardians into existence, she knew exactly what she wanted. A phantom army. She wanted to be a power on the net which put the fear of God into the Party, and for that she had to uncover their machinations and damage their image in order to save China's. She needed a good year to build up the Guardians technologically."

Jericho sucked on his cheek. He knew that the discussion had come to an end. Tu wouldn't give away any more than that.

"I need any records of Yoyo you can give me," he said.

"There are some here." Tu reached down next to him, opened a battered leather case, and took a pair of hologoggles and a holostick from it. The stick was smaller than the current models; the glasses were elegantly designed. "These are prototypes. All the programs for which we used Yoyo as a virtual tour guide are saved on it. You can wander through the clubs with her if you like, visit the Jin Mao Tower and the World Financial Center, roam through the Yu Gardens or go to the MOCA Shanghai." He grinned. "You'll have a good time with her. She wrote the texts herself. The stick also contains her personal files, recordings of conversations, photos, and films. That's everything I have."

"Nice." Jericho rolled the stick between his fingers and looked at the glasses. "I've got some hologoggles already."

"Not like these you haven't. We were convinced the usual suspects would spy on that product development. But you seem to have scared them off with your last mission. Dao IT is still nursing its bruises."

Jericho smirked. Dao IT, Tu's former employer, had been less than pleased to lose its Chief Development Officer for Virtual Environments when he had decided to set up independently. Since then the company had broken into Tu Technologies' systems multiple times to download trade secrets. Each time, the hackers had hidden their tracks so skillfully that Jericho had had to use all the tricks of his trade to convict them. Tu had presented the evidence to the courts, and Dao IT had had to pay millions in fines.

"By the way, they made me an offer," he said casually.

"Who?" Tu sat bolt upright. "Dao?"

"Yes, well, they were impressed. They said if I had managed to track them down, it would be good to have me on their side."

The manager pushed his construction of glasses up. He smacked his lips together noisily and cleared his throat.

"I guess they've got no shame."

"I said no of course," said Jericho slowly. Loyalty was a valuable thing. "I just thought you might be interested to know."

"Of course I would." Tu grinned. Then he laughed and slapped Jericho on the shoulder. "Get to work then, *xiongdi.*"

WORLD FINANCIAL CENTER

Grand Cherokee Wang moved his body to an inaudible beat. His head nodded with every step, as if confirming his own coolness. Bouncing at the knees, playing imaginary instruments, he skipped along the glass corridor, clicking his tongue loudly, allowing himself the hint of a swing at the hips and baring his teeth. Oh, how he loved himself! Grand Cherokee Wang, the King of the World. He liked it best up here at night, when he could see his reflection in the glass surface that looked out over the sea of light that was Shanghai: it was as if he were towering out of it in the flesh, a giant! There wasn't a single shop window on Nanjing Donglu he forgot to pay homage to himself in: his beautifully structured face with the gold applications on his forehead and cheekbones, his shoulder-length blue-black hair, the white PVC jacket, although it was actually too warm for it at this time of year, but never mind. Wang and reflective surfaces were a match made in heaven.

He was right at the top.

At least, he worked right at the top, on the ninety-seventh floor of the World Financial Center, because Wang's parents had made their financing of his studies dependent on his willingness to contribute to it with earnings of his own. And so that's what he did. With such dedication that his father began to seriously wonder whether his otherwise less than delightful offspring actually loved working. In reality, though, it was thanks to the nature of this job in particular that Grand Cherokee Wang was now spending more time in the World Financial Center than in the lecture theater, where his presence was more mandatory. On the other hand, it was clear that for a budding electrical and mechanical engineer, there could hardly be a better field trip than to the ninety-seventh floor of the World Financial Center.

Wang had tried to describe it to his grandmother, who had gone blind at the beginning of the millennium before the building had been completed.

"Can you remember the Jin Mao Tower?"

"Of course I can, I'm not stupid. I may be blind, but my memory still works!"

"Then imagine the bottle opener right behind it. You know, don't you, that people call it the bottle opener because—"

"I know they call it that."

"But do you know why?"

"No. But I doubt I'll be able to stop you from telling me."

Wang's grandmother often said that going blind had brought with it a series of advantages, the most pleasing of which was no longer having to see the members of her family.

"So, listen, it's a narrow building, with beautifully winding façades. Completely smooth, nothing jutting out, just glass. The sky's reflected in it, all around the building, like with the Jin Mao Tower. Unbelievable! Almost 500 meters high, 101 floors. How can I describe the shape? It's a quadratic structure at ground level, like a completely normal tower, but as you go higher the two sides level out so it gets narrower and narrower at the top, and the roof is a long ledge."

"I don't know if I want to know this much detail."

"You do! You have to be able to picture what they've managed to construct up there. Originally they planned for a circular opening under the ledge, 50 meters in diameter, but then the Party said it was a no-go because of the symbolism. If it was round, it would look like Japan's Rising Sun"

"The Japanese devil!"

"Exactly, so they built a square opening, 50 by 50 meters. A hole in the heavens. With the angular opening, the whole tower looks like a huge, upright bottle opener, and once it was finished in 2008, everyone called it that; there was nothing they could do about it. The lower section of the hole is a viewing platform with a glass pathway leading up above it. And where it cuts off above, there's a glass deck, with a glass floor too."

"I'll never go up there!"

"Listen, this is where it really gets good: in 2020 someone came up with the absolutely crazy idea of building the highest roller coaster in the world in the opening, the Silver Dragon. Have you heard of it?"

"No. Yes. I don't know."

"The hole was too small for a complete roller coaster of course. I mean, it's huge, but they had something bigger in mind, so they built the roller-coaster station in the opening and laid the track around the building. You climb into the car from the glass corridor, and off it goes, out ten meters beyond the edge of the building, then in a wide arc around the left-side column around to the back of the tower. You hang there in the air above Pudong, half a kilometer up in the sky!"

"That's crazy!"

"It's awesome! At the back, the track climbs steeply toward the roof, circles around the right column, and then flows into a long horizontal section which goes up onto the roof edge. Isn't that wild? Going for a ride on the roof of the World Financial Center!"

"I'd be dead by the time I got to that bit."

"That's true, most people end up peeing in their pants in the first few meters, but that's nothing yet. On the other side of the edge it

suddenly rushes upward. Into a steep curve! Now the car is really racing! And you know what? It races straight into the hole, into this huge
hole, through under the roof axis, then up again, up, up, up, because
you're in the goddamn looping section, high out over the roof, then
steeply back down again, into the hole, around the right column and
back upright and into the station, and three rounds of that. Oh man!"

Every time Grand Cherokee talked about it, he went hot and cold
with excitement.

"Shouldn't you be studying?"

Should he be? In the glass corridor, hips swinging, watching the line
as it pushed its way forward at the barrier, faces turned toward him—
some derailed between anticipation and the rushing onset of panic,
some frozen in shock, others transfigured with the look of addiction—
Grand Cherokee felt at an irreconcilable distance from the depressive
depths of his studies. The university lay half a kilometer below him.
He was far too special for an existence spent in lecture halls. Only the
knowledge that all the cramming would ultimately enable him to create something even greater than the Silver Dragon kept him at it. He
pushed his way through the line of people to the glass door which separated the corridor from the platform, opened it and grinned around
at them.

"I had to go and pee," he said jovially.

Some of them pushed their way forward. Others took a step back,
as if he had just summoned them for execution. He closed the door
behind him, walked into the neighboring glass-paneled room which
housed the computer console, and awoke the dragon. Screens rekin-
dled and lights flickered as the system loaded up. A number of monitors showed the individual sections of the track. The Silver Dragon
was easy to operate, idiot-proof to be precise, but the people waiting
outside didn't know that. For them, he was the magician in his crystal
chamber. *He* was the Silver Dragon! Without Grand Cherokee, there
was no ride.

He made the conjoined wagons roll back a little to the only section
of the track that was surrounded by bars. They shimmered alluringly
in the sun, barely more than silver surfboards on rails. The passengers were safely and securely buckled into their seats, but the ride was
designed to be open-plan. No railing to give the illusion that there was
anything to hold on to during the loop-the-loop. Nothing to distract
you from looking down into the depths. The dragon knew no mercy.

He opened the glass door. Most held their cell phones or e-tickets
in front of the scanner, others had bought a ticket in the foyer. Once
two dozen adrenaline-junkies had crossed through to the platform,
he closed the door again. A chrome-plated barrier pushed down and

opened the way into the dragon. Grand Cherokee helped the passengers into the seats, tested the supports, and sent looks of reassurance into each pair of eyes. A female tourist, Scandinavian in appearance, smiled at him shyly.

"Scared?" he asked, in English.

"Excited," she whispered.

Oh, she was scared all right! How wonderful! Grand Cherokee leaned over to her.

"When the ride's over, I'll show you the control room," he said. "Would you like to see the control room?"

"Oh, that would be—that would be great."

"But only if you're brave." He grinned, giving her a captivating smile. The blonde woman exhaled and smiled at him gratefully.

"I will be. I promise."

Grand Cherokee Wang! The King of the Dragon.

Pacing quickly, he was back in the chamber again. His fingers whizzed over the computer table. Rail security on, start train. It was that easy. That's how quickly you could send people on an unforgettable ride between heaven and hell. The dragon left its barred cage and pushed out over the platform edge, speeding up and disappearing from view. Grand Cherokee turned around. Through the glass corridor he could see the powerful side columns, positioned far apart from one another, segmented into penthouse-size floors, and above him the glass-floored observatory which rose to dizzying heights. Visitors were moving about in it as if they were on black ice, looking down to the corridor 50 meters below with its roller-coaster station, where the next group of daredevils was already starting to gather. And everyone was staring at the left tower, from behind which the train was now pushing its way slowly forward, to climb to the top of the slope, up to the roof, then disappear from view once more.

Grand Cherokee glanced at the monitor.

The wagons were getting closer to the edge of the roof. Beyond it, the track plummeted. He waited. It was the moment he enjoyed the most whenever he had the opportunity to ride along. The first time was the best. The sensation that the rails just suddenly went into the void. To plunge over the edge without anything to grip on to. Thinking the unthinkable, just before the dragon tipped and your gaze rushed ahead into the steep downward curve, before the boiling adrenaline washed every rational thought out of the convolutions of your brain and your lungs expanded into a scream. Tumbling head over heels toward the station, being thrown upside-down, finding yourself weightless above the roof and, immediately afterward, in the racing climb back up to the top.

The cars came back into view.

Fascinated, Grand Cherokee looked up. Time seemed to stand still.

Then the Silver Dragon plunged into the somersault.

He heard the screams even through the glass.

What a moment! What a demonstration of its power over body and spirit, and, in turn, what a triumph to ride the dragon, to *control* it! A feeling of invulnerability overcame Grand Cherokee. He tried to grab a seat on the ride at least once a day, because he was fearless, free from fear of heights, just as he was free of self-doubt, free of shame and scruples, free of the cantankerous voice of reason.

Free of caution.

While two dozen Dragon riders were experiencing their neurochemical inferno above him, he pulled his cell phone out and dialed a number.

"I've got something," he said, trying to stretch the words out so he sounded bored.

"You know where the girl is?"

"I think so."

"Wonderful! That's really wonderful!" The man's voice sounded relieved and grateful. Grand Cherokee curled the corner of his mouth. The guy could try as hard as he liked to play the dear uncle, but it was obvious he wasn't looking for Yoyo so he could take care of her. He was probably secret service, or the police. It didn't matter. The fact was, he had money, and he was prepared to part with some of it. For that the guy would get information that Grand Cherokee didn't even have, because in actual fact he didn't have the faintest idea where she was, nor where she might be. Nor did he know who or what had caused the girl to go into hiding, or even whether she really had gone into hiding at all or perhaps had just taken off on vacation without telling anyone. His stock of knowledge on the matter was as empty as his bank account.

On the other hand, he wondered what it would sound like if he told the truth:

"Yoyo works in the World Financial Center with Tu Technologies downstairs. I'm in charge of the roller-coaster station at the top, for everyone who wants to pee in their pants up here in zero gravity. That's how I met her. She turned up here because she wanted to ride the Dragon. So I let her have a ride and then afterward I showed her how you steer the Dragon, and she thought it was—well—"

The truth, Grand Cherokee, the truth!

"—she thought it was a damn sight cooler than I was, even though that usually does the trick, I mean, letting them ride for free, then a trip with me, then a drink afterward, see? She was crazy about the Dragon, and was looking for a place to crash because she wasn't getting on well with her old man or something, and Li and I happened to have a room free. Although—Li wasn't too happy about it. He says girls disrupt the chemistry, especially when they look like Yoyo, because if they have sex with you, you end up thinking with your cock instead of your brain and then friendships fall apart, but I insisted, and Yoyo moved in. That was only two weeks ago."

End of story. Or, perhaps just a little more:

"I thought that if Yoyo stayed with us I'd manage to get her into bed, but no such luck. She's a party girl; she sings and likes everything, which I like about her, even though it's incomprehensible."

And then:

"Sometimes I saw her hanging around with guys from the real down-and-out neighborhoods. Biker types. Could be a gang. They have these stickers on their jackets: City Demons, I think. Yeah, City Demons."

This was the only thing he'd said that was worthy of being called information.

But he'd be lucky to get any money for that. So it was time to make something up.

"So where is she now?" the voice on the phone wanted to know.

Cherokee hesitated. "We shouldn't discuss that on the—"

"Where are you? I can come right away."

"No, no, I can't right now. Not today. Let's say first thing tomorrow. Around eleven."

"Eleven isn't first thing." The other man paused. "If I understood you correctly, you want to earn some money, right?"

"You did understand me correctly! And *you* want something from *me*, don't you? So who makes the rules?"

"You, my friend." Was it his imagination, or could he hear the man laughing softly? "But how about ten regardless?"

Grand Cherokee thought for a moment. He had to tend to the roller coaster at ten; it opened at half past. But on the other hand, perhaps it was a good idea to speak to Mister Big Money alone. If money was going to change hands, the fewer onlookers there were the better, and at ten they would be completely alone: him, the man and the dragon.

"That's fine." Besides, by then he would have thought of something. "I'll let you know where you need to come."

"Good."

"And bring a nice bulging wallet with you."

"Don't worry. I won't give you cause to complain."

That sounded good.

Did it sound good? The cars rushed in and braked to a halt. The ride was over. Grand Cherokee looked over at the twenty-four pairs of trembling knees. He mentally prepared himself to provide support to the weakest ones.

Yes, it sounded good all right!

Jericho

Yoyo's shared apartment was on Tibet Lu in a neighborhood of identical-looking concrete towers. Just a few years ago there had been a night market here. Crouched gabled houses had thronged alongside one another in the shadow of the skyscrapers, an island of poverty and decay on just four square kilometers, with insufficient water supply and continual blackouts. Traders used to spread their wares out on the sidewalks, opening shops and doors so their living space took on the function of a stockroom and salesroom in one, or simply transforming their entire house into a street kitchen. Practically everything was for sale: household goods, medicinal herbs, roots to strengthen the libido, extracts to combat evil spirits, and souvenirs for tourists who had stumbled across the market accidentally and couldn't tell the difference between plastic and antique Buddhas. Pots steamed in every corner, a smell of fried fat and broth filled the narrow passageways. In no way unpleasant, as Jericho remembered from having strolled through there shortly after his arrival. Some of the things which had changed hands in exchange for a few coins had tasted incredibly good.

And yet a life was considered wretched if the people living it were forced to share a chronically blocked-up toilet between ten, assuming, that is, that their building even offered the luxury of a toilet. Logically then, when the real estate companies and representatives of the town planning department rushed in with their offers, one might have expected collective joy. There was talk of light and airy apartments, of electronic hobs and showers. But none of the residents' eyes had reflected the sparkle of sanitary promise. There was neither excitement nor resistance. They just signed the contracts, looked at one another, and knew that their time had come. This life would come to an end, but it had still been a life nonetheless. The simple houses had seen better times, back before China's economy had started to accelerate in the early nineties. They were run-down, without a doubt, but with some goodwill they could still be called home.

Months later, Jericho had gone back there. At first he thought there must have been a bomb attack. A troupe of workers had been busy razing the entire quarter to the ground. His initial surprise had turned into disbelief when it dawned on him that a good half of the inhabitants were still living there, going about their usual business as wrecking balls swung all around, walls collapsed and dumper trucks transported off tons of rubble.

He had asked what would happen to the people once the whole quarter had disappeared.

"They'll move," one of the builders enlightened him.

"And where to?"

The man's answer never came. Jericho, filled with consternation, had wandered around as darkness crept in, and the stage was set for an amputated night market, its protagonists seeming to stubbornly deny the destruction taking place around them. Whenever he asked someone about it, they simply assured him, calmly and politely, that it was just the way it was. After a while Jericho became convinced that it couldn't solely be down to the broad Shanghai dialect that he only ever understood that one sentence, and that it must actually be the standardized reaction to every kind of catastrophe and injustice. *Mei you banfa*: There's nothing one can do.

Once night fell, a few people became more talkative. A plump old woman, preparing delicious little dumplings in broth, told Jericho that the compensation from the building authorities wasn't anywhere near enough to buy a new apartment. Nor was it enough to rent one for any considerable length of time. A second woman who came over said that each of the inhabitants had been offered a much higher sum to start with, but that no one had received the amount they had been promised. A young man was considering making a complaint, but the plump woman dismissed that with a subdued flick of her hand. Her son had already complained four times. Every complaint had been rejected, but on the fourth time they had locked him up in a cell for a week, only showing him the door after they had administered a number of kicks.

Jericho ended up leaving as clueless as he had come. Now he had returned for a third time, and there was no indication that there had ever been anything here but towers with air-conditioning in front of the windows. The blocks were numbered, but in the advancing dusk the numbers blurred against the background. Some idiot had clearly thought it would be chic to paint pastel on pastel—in huge numbers, admittedly—but in poor light they were as hard to make out as snow-white mountain hares in a snowstorm. Jericho didn't waste time marching up and down the streets. He pulled out his cell phone, entered in the number and let the GPS figure out his location. A grid-section of the city from satellite perspective appeared on the screen. Jericho projected the map onto the wall of a nearby house. The beam was strong enough to generate a brilliantly clear image measuring 2 by 2 meters. The street he was standing on ran diagonally over the wall, along with a number of side and parallel streets. He zoomed in. One blinking signal pinpointed his current location down to the nearest meter, another marked out Yoyo's address.

"Please walk straight ahead for 32 meters," said the cell phone in a friendly tone. "Then turn right."

He deactivated the voice and set off. He had found out all he needed to know: that Yoyo's building was just around the corner and easily reached.

Within two minutes he was ringing the doorbell.

It was a surprise visit and therefore an investment of sorts. The relative slimness of the chance he'd find someone at home was canceled out by the benefits of the surprise attack. The recipient of the visit, if there was one, had no chance to prepare himself, hide things, or rehearse lies. According to Jericho's research, Yoyo's roommates had never had a criminal record; nor had they ever attracted the attention of the authorities. One of them, Zhang Li, was studying Economics and English, the other was enrolled in Electrical and Mechanical Engineering. As far as the authorities were concerned, he was called Wang Jintao, but called himself Grand Cherokee. That was nothing unusual. In the nineties, young Chinese people had begun to put Western names before their family ones, a practice that wasn't always carried out that tastefully. It wasn't uncommon for men, in ignorance of a word's associations, to name themselves after sanitary towels or dog food; while on the women's side, it wasn't unusual to meet a Pershing Song or White House Liang. Wang, for example, had even selected himself an American four-by-four as a forename.

If Tu was to be believed, neither Wang nor Li were stay-at-home types, which meant he could have made the journey here in vain. But after he'd rung for the second time, something surprising happened. Without anyone bothering to use the intercom, the buzzer sounded and the door was released. Walking into a bare hallway, which stank of cabbage, he took the elevator up to the seventh floor and found himself in a whitewashed hallway where the neon lighting was flickering nervously. A little further along, a door opened up. A young man came out and looked Jericho up and down coolly.

There was no doubt it was him!

His forehead and cheekbones were adorned with metallic applications, highly fashionable right now. Their arrival had ended the era of piercings and tattoos. Anyone who still dared to have a ring through their eyebrow or silver in their tongue was seen as an embarrassment. Even the hairstyle, smooth and long, fitted in with the trend. It was known as Indian style, as currently worn by the majority of young men around the globe, apart from the Indians themselves of course, who rejected all responsibility for it. A spray-on shirt emphasized Wang's muscles, his wet-look leather pants gave the impression that they were on duty both day and night. All things considered, the guy didn't look bad, but he didn't look great either. The war-like appearance was lacking about 10 centimeters in height, and the edgy quality of his features might be quite pleasing, but they were devoid of any proportional elegance.

"And you are?" he asked, suppressing a yawn.

Jericho held his cell phone out under Wang's nose and projected a 3D image of his head, along with his police registration number, onto the folded-up display.

"Owen Jericho, web detective."

Wang squinted.

"So I see," he said, trying to sound ironic.

"Could I have a moment of your time?"

"What's up?"

"This is the apartment of Chen Yuyun, is that correct? Yoyo for short."

"Wrong." The guy seemed to chew the word before spitting it out. "This apartment belongs to me and Li, and the little one just dumped her books and clothes here."

"I thought she lived here?"

"Let's get one thing clear, okay? It's not *her* apartment. *I* let her have the room."

"Then you must be Grand Cherokee."

"Yeah!" The mention of his forename made its owner suddenly switch into friendly mode. "You've heard of me?"

"Only good things," lied Jericho. "Would you be able to tell me where I can find Yoyo?"

"Where you could find—" Grand Cherokee paused. For some unknown reason the question seemed to take him by surprise. "That's—" he murmured. "That's really something!"

"I need to speak to her."

"You can't."

"I know Yoyo has disappeared," Jericho added. "That's why I'm here. Her father's looking for her, and he's very worried. So if you know anything about where she is—"

Grand Cherokee stared at him. Something about the boy, or rather about his attitude, irritated Jericho.

"As I said," he repeated. "if you—"

"Just a moment." Grand Cherokee raised his hand. For a few seconds he paused like that, then his features seemed to smooth out.

"Yoyo." He smiled jovially. "But of course. Don't you want to come in?"

Still confused, Jericho entered the narrow hallway, which branched off into a number of other rooms. Grand Cherokee hurried ahead of him, opened the last door, and nodded inside with his head.

"I can show you her room."

Suddenly, Jericho understood. This much cooperation was bordering on calculation. Slowly, he walked into the room and looked around. It didn't say much. There was hardly anything to suggest who lived here except for a few posters of popular figures from the Mando Prog scene. One of the pictures was of Yoyo herself, posing on the stage. A note fluttered around on a pinboard above a cheap desk. Jericho walked over to it and studied the few symbols.

"Dark sesame oil," he read. "300 grams of chicken breast."

Grand Cherokee cleared his throat discreetly.

"Yes?" Jericho turned around to him.

"I could give you some clues about where Yoyo is."

"Excellent."

"Well." Grand Cherokee spread his fingers meaningfully. "She told me a lot, you know? I mean, the little one likes me. She got quite friendly in the last few days she was here."

"Were you friendly too?"

"Let's just say I had the opportunity to be."

"And?"

"Well, come on, that's confidential, man!" Grand Cherokee was clearly making a great effort to look outraged. "I mean, of course we can discuss everything, but—"

"No, it's fine. If it's confidential." Jericho turned away and left him standing there. A wise guy, just as he'd feared. One after another, he pulled open the drawers of the desk. Then he went over to the narrow wall cabinet next to the door and opened it. Jeans, a pullover, and a pair of sneakers which had seen better days. Two cans of disposable clothing spray. Jericho shook it. Half full. Clearly Yoyo had packed the majority of her things in a great hurry and left the apartment in a rush.

"When was the last time you saw your roommate?"

"The last time?" echoed Grand Cherokee.

"The last time." Jericho looked at him. "That's the time after which you didn't see Yoyo anymore, so when was that?"

"Ah, yes, er—" Grand Cherokee seemed as though he was just emerging from deep water. "On the evening of May 23. We had a little party. Li went off to bed at some point, and Yoyo hung around with me for a while. We chatted and had some drinks, and then she went off to her room. A little later I heard her crashing around and opening draw- ers. Shortly after that the house door slammed in the lock."

"When exactly?"

"Between two and three, I guess."

"You guess?"

"It was before three for sure."

Given that Grand Cherokee seemed to be making no effort to stop him from doing so, Jericho carried on searching through Yoyo's room. Out of the corner of his eye he saw the student skulking around hesi- tantly. Jericho's lack of interest in him seemed to be confusing him.

"I could tell you more," he said after a while. "If you're interested."

"Out with it."

"Tomorrow maybe."

"Why not now?"

"Because I need to make a few calls to—I mean, I already know where Yoyo hangs out, but before that—" He stretched out his arms and turned his palms to face upward. "Let's just say, everything has its price."

That was clear enough.

Jericho finished his search and walked back into the hall.

"As long as it's worth its price," he said. "By the way, where's your roommate?"

"Li? No idea. He doesn't know anything anyway."

"Is it just my imagination, or do you not know anything either?"

"Me? Yes, I do."

"But?"

"No but. I just thought perhaps you might think of how someone might be able to release trapped knowledge?" Grand Cherokee grinned up at him.

"I see." Jericho smiled back. "You'd like to negotiate an advance."

"Let's call it a contribution toward expenses."

"And for what, Grand Cherokee, or whatever you're called? So that you can mess me about with your garbled imagination? You don't know shit!"

He turned around to go. Grand Cherokee seemed filled with consternation. Obviously he had seen the conversation as going a little differently. He held Jericho back by the shoulder and shook his head.

"I'm not trying to rip anyone off, man!"

"Then don't."

"Come on! The kind of course I'm on doesn't pay for itself! I'll find out whatever you want to know."

"Wrong! You have nothing to sell me."

"I—" The student searched for words. "Okay, fine. If I tell you something, right here and now, that helps you to make some progress, will you trust me then? That would be my advance, you see?"

"I'm listening."

"So, there's a biker gang that she hangs out with a lot. She rides a motorcycle too. The City Demons—that's what it says on their jackets at any rate."

"And where can I find them?"

"That *was* my advance."

"Now you listen to me," said Jericho, jabbing a finger at his adversary. "Here and now I'm paying you nothing. Because you have nothing. Nothing at all. If you should happen to get hold of some real information, driven by the goodness of your heart—and I mean real information!—then we may be able to do business. Is that clear?"

"Perfectly."

"So when shall I expect your call?"

"Tomorrow afternoon." Grand Cherokee plucked at the tip of his chin. "No, earlier. Perhaps." He gave Jericho a penetrating look. "But then it's payday, man!"

"Then it's payday." Jericho smacked him on the shoulder. "An appropriate amount. Did you want to say anything else?"

Grand Cherokee shook his head silently.

"Then I'll see you tomorrow."

Then I'll see you tomorrow.

He stood in the hallway as if he were rooted to the spot, even once the detective was already on his way downstairs. As he heard the elevator door rattle lightly in the shaft, his thoughts came thick and fast.

Well, this was incredible!

Deep in thought, he went into the kitchen, grabbed a beer from the fridge, and raised the bottle to his lips. What was going on here? What had Yoyo done to make everyone so interested in her disappearance? First that smart guy and now the detective. And, even more importantly:

How could he profit from it?

It wouldn't be easy, that's for sure. Grand Cherokee was under no illusions: his knowledge of her whereabouts was nonexistent, and the next few hours would do little to change that. On the other hand it would be a real stroke of bad luck if he couldn't come up with a few juicy lies by the next morning. The kind of lies that no one could prove, along the lines of: my information is first-hand, I don't know either, clearly Yoyo got wind of something, it was right under our nose, and so on and so forth.

He would have to push the price right up. Play them off against one another! It was a good thing he hadn't told the detective about Xin's visit. People could say what they wanted about him, but certainly not that he was dumb.

I'm too on the ball for the two of you, he thought.

He was already counting the money in his mind.

MAY 26, 2025
The Satellite

ARRIVAL

As if there hadn't been dozens of pairs of boots marking the surface of the Moon with the imprint of mankind's heroism since 2018, Eugene Cernan—the commander of Apollo 17—was still regarded as the last man to have walked on its surface. The years between 1969 and 1972 were monumental in the landscape of American history: a short but magical epoch of manned missions which were strangely counteracted by Nixon bringing the space program back down to earth with a bump. As a result, Cernan became the last one up there to turn off the light. He was, and remained, the last of his century. The eleventh Apollo astronaut on the Moon, he walked around the Mare Serenitatis and made hundreds of those small steps that Neil Armstrong had declared to be such a giant leap for mankind. His team collected the biggest sample of lunar rocks and completed more moon surface trips than any other before them. The commander himself even managed to cause the first-ever automobile accident on a celestial body, smashing up the rear left wing of his Lunar Rover, before—with a talent for improvisation reminiscent of Robinson Crusoe—patching it back together again. Yet none of this was enough to re-enliven the public's interest. It was the end of an era. Cernan, presented with the opportunity to immortalize himself in encyclopedias and textbooks with a thunderous obituary, instead offered words of remarkable helplessness:

"We spent most of the trip home," he said, "debating the color of the Moon."

Incredible. So that was the grand summary of six expensive landings on a rock hundreds of thousands of kilometers away from Earth? That no one even knew what color it was?

"It looks kind of yellow to me," said Rebecca Hsu, after gazing silently out of the small porthole for a long while. Hardly any of them were venturing over to the row of windows anymore. From there, throughout the two days since their launch, they had watched their home planet get smaller and smaller, a ghostly dwindling of familiarity. It was as if they were dividing their loyalty equally at the midway point between the Earth and Moon before fully succumbing to the fascination of the satellite. From 10,000 kilometers away it could still be seen in its entirety, starkly silhouetted against the blackness of outer space around it. And yet this object of romantic contemplation had billowed to become a sphere with menacing presence, a battlefield, scarred by billions of years of celestial bombardment. In complete silence, unbroken by the soundtrack of civilization, they raced toward this strange, alien world. Only the tinnitus-like hiss of the life-support systems indicated that there was any technological activity on board at all. Beyond that, the silence made their heartbeats thunder like bush drums and the blood swirl in their veins. It roused lively chatter within the body about the state of its chemical processes and pushed their imaginations to the very limit.

Olympiada Rogacheva paddled up, in awe of her weightlessness. They had advanced another 1,000 kilometers toward the satellite, and could now see only three-quarters of it.

"It doesn't look yellow," she murmured. "To me it seems more mouse-gray."

"Metallic gray," Rogachev corrected her coldly.

"I'm not so sure," Evelyn Chambers looked over from the next window. "Metallic. Really?"

"Yes, really. Look. Up there to the right, the big, round patch. Dark, like molten iron."

"You've been in the steel industry for too long, Oleg. You could find something metallic in a chocolate pudding."

"Of course he could—the spoon! Woohoo!" Miranda Winter did a somersault, cheering gleefully. Most of the others had tired of doing zero-gravity acrobatics. But Miranda couldn't get enough of them and was rapidly getting on the others' nerves. She was incapable of holding a conversation without rolling through the air, squealing and cackling, thumping people in the ribs or whacking them on the chin as she did. Evelyn, on the receiving end of a kick in the small of her back, snapped: "You're not a merry-go-round, Miranda. Give it a rest will you!"

"But I feel like one!"

"Then close yourself down for repairs or something. It's too cramped in here for all that."

"Hey, Miranda." O'Keefe looked up from reading his book: "Why don't you try imagining you're a blue whale instead?"

"What? Why?"

"Blue whales wouldn't act like that. They're content to just hang around, more or less motionless, and eat plankton."

"They blow water too," Heidrun commented. "Do you want to see Miranda blow water?"

"Sure, why not?"

"You're all being silly," Miranda concluded. "By the way, I think it's kind of blue. The Moon I mean. It's almost eerie."

"Uhhh," O'Keefe shuddered.

"So what color is it?" Olympiada wanted to know.

"It's every color, and yet none." Julian Orley came through the connecting hatch that separated the living quarters of the Charon from the landing module. "No one knows."

"How come?" Rogachev wrinkled his forehead. "I mean, surely we've had enough time to figure that out?"

"Of course. The problem is that no one has seen it through anything other than toned or filtered windows and visors yet. And on top of that, the Moon doesn't have a particularly high albedo—"

"A what?" asked Miranda, rotating like a pig on a spit.

"Reflectivity. The fraction of solar energy which is reflected back to space. The reflection rate of lunar rock is not especially high, particularly not in the maria—"

"I'm not following a word you say."

"The dry plains on the surface of the Moon," explained Julian patiently. "Collectively, they're called maria. The plural of mare. They appear to be even darker than the mountain rings in the craters."

"So why does the Moon look white when we look at it from Earth?"

"Because it has no atmosphere. Sunlight hits its surface unfiltered, in just the same way it would an astronaut's unprotected retina. The UV rays outside are far more dangerous to our eyes than they would be on Earth, that's why the spaceship's windows are tinted."

"But loads of lunar samples have been brought back to Earth," said Rogachev. "What color are they?"

"Dark gray. But that doesn't necessarily mean that the whole Moon is dark gray. Perhaps some parts of it are brown, or even yellow."

"Exactly," said O'Keefe from behind his book.

"Everyone sees it slightly differently. Everyone has their own moon, one might say." Julian went over to join Evelyn. They were passing over a lone gigantic crater which lay far below them. Molten light seemed to stream from its slopes down to the surface surrounding it. "That's Copernicus by the way. According to popular opinion it's the most spectacular of all the lunar craters and over 800 million years old. It's a good 90 kilometers wide, with slopes that would present a challenge to any mountaineer, but the most impressive thing about it is how deep it is. Do you see that massive shadow inside it? It's almost 4 kilometers down to the very bottom."

"There are mountains right in the middle of it," observed Evelyn.

"How is that possible?" wondered Olympiada. "I mean, in the middle of the point of impact? Shouldn't it all be flat?"

Julian fell silent for a while.

"Imagine it like this," he said. "Picture the surface of the Moon, just as you see it now, but without Copernicus. Okay? Everything is still and peaceful. So far! Then, a boulder 11 kilometers in diameter rushes up from the depths of outer space at a speed of 70 kilometers per second, 200 times the speed of sound. There's no atmosphere, nothing at all that could slow it down. Imagine what kind of impact it would make crashing into the surface. That alone would happen in just a few thousandths of a second. The meteor would penetrate the surface by about a 100 meters—not particularly deep you might say, and an 11-kilometer crater like that wouldn't be such a big deal. But there's a little more to it than that. The complex thing about meteorites is that they transform all their kinetic energy into heat at the moment of impact. In other words, they explode! It's this explosion that can create a hole ten to twenty times bigger than the meteorite itself. Millions of tons of rock are blasted in all directions and, in a flash, a wall forms around the crater. The whole thing happens at such speed, the displaced layers of lunar basalt can't be restructured as quickly, so the surface gives in to the shock pressure and is compressed many kilometers deep. Meanwhile, huge clouds of debris are collecting overhead. The meteorite, of course, is now fully transformed into heat and no longer exists in its previous form, so the ground rebounds, shooting upward to form a massive peak in the center of the crater. The rock clouds continue to spread rapidly and once again the absence of any atmosphere to contain the radius of the cloud makes itself felt. Instead the debris is flung further and further out before descending, hundreds of kilometers away, like billions of missiles. You can still see this ring of fallout today, known as an ejecta blanket, especially when there's a full Moon. It has a different albedo to the darker volcanic rock around it, and seems to glow from within. In actual fact, it's just reflecting a little more sunlight. So, that's how you should picture Copernicus coming about. Victor Hugo, by the way, claimed to see an eye within it that looked back at whoever was looking at the Moon."

"Uh-huh," said Olympiada dejectedly.

Julian smiled knowingly to himself, relishing the awkward silence that followed his account. All around him cosmic bombs were crashing into their thoughts and converting kinetic energy into questions such as, in the event of a similar impact threatening Earth, whether it would be better to seek refuge in the cellar or to go for one last beer.

"I guess our atmosphere wouldn't be of much help?" Rebecca Hsu suggested.

"Well . . ." Julian pursed his lips. "Meteorites are always plummeting down to Earth, around forty tons of them a day in fact. Most of them are the size of a grain of sand or pebble and end up burning themselves out. Now and again one the size of a fist will come along, and occasionally something bigger will crash into tundra or the sea. In 1908, for example, a sixty-meter-wide fragment of a comet exploded over Siberia and devastated an area the size of New York."

"I remember hearing about that," said Rogachev drily. "We lost some forest, a few sheep, and a shepherd."

"You would have lost a lot more if it had hit Moscow. But yes, in the main, the universe is essentially past the worst. Meteorites like the one that caused Copernicus have become few and far between."

"How far between exactly?" drawled Heidrun.

Julian pretended to give it some thought. "The last really significant one came down 65 million years ago in the area that's now known as Yucatán. The shockwaves traveled all around the world, causing several years of continuous winter, which led to the loss of considerable amounts of flora and fauna, and unfortunately, almost all the dinosaurs."

"That doesn't answer my question."

"You really want to know when the next one will hit?"

"Just for my own planning purposes, yes."

"Well, according to statistical data there's a global catastrophe every 26 million years. How catastrophic exactly depends on the size of the impactor. An asteroid 75 meters in diameter has the explosive force of 100 Hiroshima bombs. Anything exceeding 2 kilometers can trigger a global winter and would mean the end of mankind."

"So, according to that we're 40 million years overdue," established O'Keefe. "How big was the dinosaur-killer again?"

"Ten kilometers."

"Thank you, Julian, I'm very glad you've brought us up here away from it all."

"So what can we do about it?" asked Rebecca.

"Very little. The nations with space programs have avoided dealing with the problem for years, preferring instead to devote their energy to building up an expensive battery of mid-range missiles. But what we really need is a functioning meteorite defense system. When the hammer falls it won't matter whether you're a Muslim, Jew, Hindu, or Christian, atheist or fundamentalist, or who you're fighting with, none of that will matter. Crash, and that's it! We don't need weapons against each other. What we really need is one that can save us all."

"So true." Rogachev looked at him, expressionless. Then he glided over, took Julian by the arm and pulled him slightly apart from the others.

"But haven't you had that for ages already?" he added, quietly. "Aren't you in the process of developing weapons against meteorites too?"

"We've created a development team, yes," nodded Julian.

"You're developing weapons on the OSS?"

"Defense systems."

"How reassuring for all of us." The Russian smiled thinly.

"It's a research group, Oleg."

"Well, I hear the Pentagon are very interested in this research group."

"Don't worry." Julian smiled back. "I know the rumors. Both Russia and China are constantly accusing us of producing space weapons for the Americans. But it's all nonsense! The sole purpose of our research is to be able to act if the laws of probability come into their own. I sure as hell want to be able to shoot if something like that's on a collision course."

"Weapons can be used against all kinds of things, Julian. You've secured America a position of power in space. You yourself are striving to rule over the energy supply by controlling the technologies. You're wielding a great deal of power, and you're trying to tell me you're not pursuing your own interests?"

"Look out of the window," said Julian calmly. "Look at that blue-white jewel."

"I see it."

"And? Are you homesick?"

Rogachev hesitated. "I don't really use terms like that."

"You can choose whether to believe me on this or not, Oleg, but once this trip is behind you, you'll be a different person. You'll have realized that our planet is a fragile little Christmas-tree bauble, covered by a wafer-thin layer of breathable air, *so far* at least. No borders or national states, just land, sea, and a few billion people who have to share the bauble because it's the only one they've got. Every decision that's not aimed at keeping our planet together, every aggression for some resource or religious idea will sicken you. Perhaps you'll stand on the peak of some crater and cry, or maybe you'll just ask a few sensible questions, but it *will* change you. There's no way back once you've seen the Earth from space, from the distance of the Moon. There's nothing you can do but fall in love with it.—Do you really think I would allow someone to misuse my technologies?"

Rogachev fell silent for a while.

"I don't believe you would *want* to allow it," he said. "I'm just asking myself whether you have any choice in the matter."

"I do, the more friends I get."

"But you're a world champion in making enemies! I know you have a league of extraordinary gentlemen in mind, a world power of independent investors, but for that you're intruding massively into national interests. How does it fit together? You want my money, Russian money, but on the other hand you don't want anything to do with Moscow."

"So is it Russian money just because you're Russian?"

"Well, I'm sure they'd prefer it there if I invested my fortune in national space travel."

"Good luck. Let me know when you've managed to get your own space elevator."

"You don't think we can?"

"You don't even believe it yourself! I own the patents. But still, I have to admit that I wouldn't have gotten this far without America. We've both invested astronomical sums in space travel. But Russia is broke. Putin founded his Mafia state on oil and gas, and now no one

wants it. You played poker and you lost. Don't forget, Oleg, that Orley
Enterprises is ten times the size of Rogamittel. We're the biggest technology company in the world, but my investors and I still need each
other nonetheless. But no one in Moscow would do you any favors. It
may be a patriotic gesture, sponsoring Russia's ramshackle space travel,
but your money would just drain away. You wouldn't last long enough
to catch up with me, because your State would have sucked the very
last drop out of you before you even had the chance, and without creating any decent results either."

This time Rogachev was silent for even longer. Then he smiled
again.

"Moscow would give you more of a free hand than Washington. Are
you sure you don't want to switch sides?"

"I guessed you'd be obliged to ask me that."

"I was asked to test the waters, see how willing you might be."

"First, we're not in the Cold War anymore. Second, Russia can't
afford my exclusivity. Third, I'm not on anyone's side. Does that answer
your question?"

"Let's put it a different way. With the right conditions, would you be
willing to sell your technologies to Russia *too*?"

"Well, would you be prepared to climb on board with me? I mean,
you're certainly not here because you're afraid of Moscow."

Rogachev stroked his chin.

"You know what?" he said. "I suggest we sleep on it and enjoy a few
days of vacation first."

The Charon was essentially a tube, 7 meters in diameter and 28 meters
long, segmented into three parts and connected to a landing module.
A flying omnibus, divided up into sleeping quarters and command
cockpit, bistro and seating area, whose creator had failed to do it
the honor of making it aerodynamic given that it would never be
required to pass through an atmosphere. The Apollo capsules and
the Orion, originally planned as successor to the space shuttle, hadn't
exactly met the expectations of design-accustomed movie-goers either,
but they had at least been able to offer a chicly rounded little nose, which
began to give off a red glow on entering the thermosphere. Compared
with this, the Charon had all the charm of a household appliance.
A ton of white and gray, smooth here, corrugated there, partly filled
with fuel, partly with astronauts, and adorned with the O of Orley
Enterprises.

"Prepare for braking maneuver," said Peter's voice over the
loudspeaker.

Two and a half days in a space shuttle, even if it was incredibly spacious and decorated in a color scheme developed by psychologists,

still brought thoughts of detention centers to mind. The enchantment
of the unfamiliar lost its luster when confronted with the proximity
and monotony of their surroundings, and came out in debates about
the state of the planet, as well as unexpected chumminess and openly
expressed dislike. Sushma and Mukesh Nair, aided by their charismatic
shyness, rallied like-minded people around them, including Eva Borelius, Karla Kramp, Marc Edwards, and Mimi Parker. They engaged in
relaxed conversation, that is until Mimi initiated a discussion about
Darwinism: wasn't it just some dead end the natural sciences had
ended up in thanks to atheistic arrogance, from which only a creationist worldview could offer the way out? Life, she concluded, was far too
complex to have come about by chance in some ancient ocean, and
especially not four billion years ago. Karla responded that comments
like that questioned the complexity of some of the people present, a
riposte which unleashed a series of heated reactions. Aileen Donoghue
came to Mimi's aid, saying that although she didn't want to tie herself
down to the specifics of a few thousand years more or less, she still
questioned any relationship between the species. It was much more
likely that all living beings had been created by God in one breath.
Karla commented that it was perfectly obvious that Mimi was descen-
dent from apes. Besides which, the first two chapters in the Book of
Moses each dealt with the creation of mankind differently, so even the
Old Testament couldn't offer any unity on the process of creation, in
so far as one could base serious scientific knowledge on one single,
historically questionable book.

Meanwhile, bonds were formed between Rebecca Hsu, Momoka
Omura, Olympiada Rogacheva, and Miranda Winter. Evelyn Chambers got on well with everyone, apart from Chuck Donoghue perhaps,
who had told Mimi in confidence that he thought Evelyn was godless,
a comment which she had immediately passed on to Olympiada and
Amber Orley, who, in turn, had told Evelyn. Locatelli, who had now
recovered from his space sickness, started showing off again with stories of sailing and motor yachts and how he had won the America's
Cup, of his love of running, solar-powered racing cars, and the possibility of extracting enough energy even out of a tick that it could make
its contribution to the protection of the environment.

"Every single body, even the human one, is a machine," he said.
"And machines create warmth. All of you here are nothing more
than machines, mere heaters. I tell you, people, if we collected everyone around the world into one great big machine, we wouldn't need
helium-3."

"And what about the soul?" asked Mimi indignantly.

"Bah, the soul!" Locatelli threw his arms apart, floated away a little
and tapped his finger against his skull. "The soul is software, my dear

lady. Just thinking flesh. But if there were a soul, I would be the first to build a machine out of it. Hahaha!"

"Locatelli was telling us the most amazing things," said Heidrun to Walo later. "Do you know what you are?"

"What am I, my love?"

"An oven. Now come here and warm me up."

Mimi and Karla made their peace with one another, Hanna played guitar—unifying the others at least on a musical level, and winning a fan in Locatelli, who was photographing him constantly—and O'Keefe read screenplays. Each one of them acted as though their noses weren't filled with the steadily intensifying mélange of sweat, intimate odors, flatulence, and hair sebum, against which even the high-tech air synthesizer on board was struggling in vain. Space travel might be fascinating, but one of its disadvantages was definitely not being able to open a window to let some fresh air in. Evelyn wondered how it was supposed to work on long-term missions, with all the smells and increasing tension. Hadn't a Russian cosmonaut once said that all the prerequisites for committing murder were there if two men were shut into a narrow cabin and left alone together for two months? But perhaps they would take different people on a mission like that. No individualists, certainly not a load of crazy super-rich people and celebrities. Peter Black, their pilot, certainly seemed well-balanced, one might even say quite boring. A team player without any flamboyant or alarmist characteristics.

"Start braking maneuver."

From a distance of 220 kilometers away they could still see half of the Moon, revealing magnificent detail. It looked so round, on account of its modest proportions, that there seemed good reason to fear they wouldn't be able to get a grip when landing and would just slide down the side. Nina Hedegaard floated over to help them put on their pressure suits, which also contained bladder bags.

"For later, when we land," she explained with a puzzling smile.

"And who says we'll need to go?" called out Momoka Omura.

"Physics." Nina's dimples deepened. "Your bladder could take the onset of gravity as a reason to empty itself without any advance warning. Do you want to soak your pressure suit?"

Momoka looked down at herself as if she already had.

"This whole venture seems to be somewhat lacking in the elegance stakes," she said, pulling on what she had to wear.

Nina shooed the Moon walkers through the connecting air lock into the landing craft, yet another barrel, this time conically shaped at the top and equipped with four powerful telescopic legs. In comparison with the living module it offered all the movement radius of a sardine can. Most of them let the procedure of being strapped in wash over them with the embalmed facial expression of old hands; after all, it was only two and a half days ago that they had sat alongside one another in just the same way, waiting for the shuttle to catapult them from the docking port of the OSS into outer space with an impressive blast of fire. But contrary to all their expectations, the ship had moved away slowly as if it were trying to disappear unnoticed. It was only once they were at a suitable distance from the space city that Peter had ignited the thruster, accelerating to maximum speed then turning off the engines, after which they had raced silently through space toward their pock-marked destination.

The time for relaxing was over, and everyone was happy about it. It was good to finally arrive.

Once again, they were pressed forcefully back into their seats until, at 70 kilometers above the Moon's surface, Peter braked the spaceship down to a speed of 5,600 kilometers per hour, rotated 180 degrees and stabilized in orbit. Below them, craters, rock formations, and powdery gray plateaus drifted past. Just as in the space elevator, cameras were transmitting all the images from outside onto holographic monitors. They did a two-hour lap of honor around the satellite, during which Nina Hedegaard explained the sights and particularities of this foreign world to them.

"As you already know from your preparatory training, a Moon day lasts quite a bit longer than an Earth one," she hissed in her Scandinavian-tinged English. "Fourteen Earth days, eighteen hours, twenty-two minutes and two seconds to be precise, and the Moon night is just as long. We call the boundary between light and shadow the terminator. It moves at an incredibly slow pace, which means you don't need to be afraid of suddenly being plunged into darkness during a walk. But *when* it gets dark, it really does! The terminator is clear-cut: there's light or shadow, but no dusk. Some of the sights lose their appeal in the dull midday light, so that's why we'll visit the most interesting places in the Moon's morning or evening, when the shadows are long."

Beneath them they noticed another impressive crater, followed by a bizarrely fissured landscape.

"The Lunar Apennines," explained Nina. "The whole area is filled with rimae, groove-like structures. Early astronomers thought they were transport networks made by the Selenites. It's a wonderful land-scape! The broad valley winding upward over there is Rima Hadley; it leads through the Swamp of Laziness, a funny name, because there's neither a swamp there, nor is it lazy. But it's like that all over the Moon, seas which aren't actually seas and so on. Do you see the two mountains to the side of the rima? That's Mons Hadley, and beneath it is Mons Hadley Delta. Both of them are well known from photographs, you often see them with a Moon rover in the foreground. The Apollo 15 landed not far from there. The lunar module's landing gear is still there, along with some other things the astronauts left behind."

"What other things?" asked Nair, his eyes gleaming.

"Shit," muttered Locatelli.

"Why do you always have to be so negative?"

"I'm not. They left their shit behind. Everyone knows that, it would have been crazy not to, right? Believe me, wherever there's landing gear like that there'll be astronaut shit lying around somewhere."

Nair nodded. Even that seemed to fascinate him. The spaceship flew swiftly over more rilles, mountains, and craters, and finally over the shore of the Sea of Tranquility. Nina pointed out a small crater, named after Moltke and known for its sprawling cave system, created by flowing lava eons ago.

"Similar systems have been discovered in the walls and plateaus of the Peary Crater in the northern polar region, where the American moon base was built. We'll visit Moltke at the start of the Moon evening, when the terminator is in the middle of the crater. It's a unique sight! And then there's the museum of course, admittedly a little barren scenically, but an essential visit nonetheless because—"

"Let me guess," called Ögi. "Apollo 11."

"Correct," beamed Nina. "It's essential to know that the Apollo missions were dependent on the narrow equatorial belt. Finding a spectacular landing place wasn't the issue, it was just about setting foot on the Moon at all. Of course, it's the symbolic value of the museum that matters most today. By now you'll be able to find evidence of former visits all over the place, and in far more interesting locations, but Armstrong's footprints—well, you can only find them there."

The flight then took them right across the Mare Crisium, the darkest of the Moon seas, in which, as Nina explained, the highest gravity ever measured on the Moon can be found. For a while they saw nothing but wildly fissured landscapes and ever-increasing shadows, which spilled ominously into the valleys and plateaus, forming vast pools and filling the craters until only the highest edges still lay in sunlight. Evelyn shuddered at the thought of having to stumble around in the shapeless darkness; then the very last of the brightly lit islands disappeared and enigmatic darkness covered the monitors, seeping into the arteries and convolutions of the brain and swallowing any peace of mind.

"*The Dark Side of the Moon*," sighed Walo Ögi. "Anybody remember that? Pink Floyd? It was a classic album."

Lynn, who had felt relatively stable during the journey, was now lost in the darkest depths of her soul. Once again, it seemed as if her courage and vitality had been sucked right out of her. On the far side of the Moon, you couldn't see the Earth, nor, unfortunately, the sun. If there is a hell, she thought, then it wouldn't be hot and fiery, but cold, a nihilistic blackness. It wouldn't need the devil or demons, torture slabs, stakes or boiling cauldrons. The absence of the familiar, the inner and outer world, the end of all feeling; that was hell. It was almost like total blindness. It was the death of all hope, fading into fear.

Take a deep breath, *feel* the body.

She needed to move, she had to get out of here and run, because anyone who ran could make the cold star inside them glimmer again, but she sat there, belted in to her seat as the Charon raced through the darkness. What was Ögi talking about? *The Dark Side of the Moon*. Who was Pink Floyd? Why was Nina blabbering relentless nonsense? Couldn't someone make the stupid goose shut up? Twist her neck, tear out her tongue?

"The far side of the Moon isn't necessarily dark," she whispered. "It's just that the same side of it is always facing the Earth."

Tim, who was sitting next to her, turned his head.

"Did you say something?"

"It's just that the same side of it is always facing the Earth. You don't see the far side, but it's illuminated just as often as the front side." Breathless, she stumbled over her words. "The far side isn't dark. Not necessarily. It's just that the same side of it is—"

"Are you afraid, Lynn?"

Tim's concern. Like a rope thrown out for her to catch.

"Nonsense." She drew air into her lungs. "I've already flown this route three times. There's no need to be afraid. We'll be back in the light again soon."

"—can assure you that you're not missing much," Nina was saying. "The front side is far more interesting. Remarkably, there are practically no maria on the far side, no seas. It's saturated with craters, rather monotonous, but nonetheless the ideal location for building a space telescope."

"Why there?" asked Hanna.

"Because the Earth is to the Moon what the Moon is to the Earth, namely a Chinese lantern that intermittently illuminates its surface. Even when it's midnight on the Moon, the surface area is still partially illuminated by the waning residual light of the Earth. The rear side by contrast is, as you can see, as black at night as the cosmos around it: there's no sunlight, no light from the Earth to outshine the view of the stars. Astronomers would love to set up an observation post here, but for now they have to content themselves with a telescope on the Moon's North Pole. It's a compromise at any rate: the sun is low-lying, and you can look at the starry sky on the far side from there."

Lynn reached for Tim's hand and squeezed it. Her thoughts were circling around murder and destruction.

"I don't know how you're doing," he said softly, "but I'm finding this darkness quite oppressive."

Oh, clever Tim! Playing the ally.

"Me too," she said gratefully.

"I guess that's normal, right?"

"It won't be for long."

"And when will we be back in the light?" asked Miranda at the same moment.

"Just another hour," hissed Nina. *Jusssst*, she said, so affected, so foolish. Julian's stupid little hobby. But feeling Tim's hand pressing against hers, Lynn started to relax, and suddenly remembered that she actually liked the Danish woman. So then why did she react so strongly, so aggressively? What's happening to me, she wondered.

What the hell is happening to me?

Once the surface of the Moon had had nothing to offer for a while, the external cameras began to transmit pictures of the starry sky into the Charon, and O'Keefe felt an unexpected rush of familiarity. Even on the OSS he would have gladly gone back to Earth like a shot. Now he just felt a vague longing. Perhaps because the myriad of lights outside were not unlike the sight of distant, illuminated houses and streets, or because the human being, an aquatic mammal, was by virtue of its own origins a child of the cosmos, built from its elements. The contradictory nature of his emotions confused him, like a child who always wanted to be held by the person who wasn't holding him at that moment. He tried to suppress the thought, but ended up thinking and thinking for an hour, unceasingly, about what he really wanted and where he belonged.

His gaze wandered over to Heidrun. She was two rows in front of him, listening to Ögi tell her something in hushed tones. O'Keefe wrinkled his nose and stared at the monitor. The picture changed. For a moment he couldn't figure out what the light blobs were supposed to be, but then he realized he was looking at sun-illuminated peaks which were rising out of the shadows. A sigh of relief went through the Charon. They were flying in the light again, toward the North Pole.

"We'll detach the landing module now," said Black. "The mother ship stays in orbit until we dock back onto it in a week's time. Nina will help you put your helmets on. It may not feel like it, but we're still flying at five times the speed of sound, so prepare yourselves for the next braking maneuver."

"Hey, Momoka," whispered O'Keefe.

The Japanese woman turned her head around lethargically. "What's up?"

"Everything okay there?"

"Of course."

O'Keefe grinned. "Then don't wet yourself."

Locatelli let out a hoarse laugh. Before Momoka had time to come up with a rebuke, Nina appeared and pushed the helmet over her head. Within minutes, they were all sitting there with heads like identical golf balls. They heard a hiss as the connection hatch between the mother ship and landing module closed, then a hollow clunk. The landing module freed itself and moved slowly away. So far, there was no sign of the slamming of the brakes they'd been warned about. The landscape changed once more. The shadows became longer again, an indication that they were approaching the polar region. Lava plateaus gave way to craters and mountain ridges. O'Keefe thought he glimpsed a dust cloud in the far distance just over the site, and then the pressure kicked in, the now almost familiar abuse of the thorax and lungs, except that this time the engines were roaring considerably louder than they had been two hours ago. Worried, he wondered whether they might be in difficulties, until he realized that until now it had always been the thrusters far back in the living quarters which were ignited. For the first time, the landing module was maneuvering by using the engine directly beneath them.

Black's lighting a fire right under our ass, he thought.

With infernal counterthrust, the landing module reduced its speed again as it rushed quickly, much too quickly, toward the surface of the Moon. A display on the screen counted down the distance kilometer by kilometer. What was happening? If they didn't slow down soon they'd be making their own crater. He thought about Julian's portrayal of the transformation of kinetic energy into heat, felt his rib cage getting tighter, tried to concentrate on the screen. Were his eyeballs shaking? What had they told them in their training? That you weren't cut out to be an astronaut if you couldn't control your eyes, because any shaking in the pupils caused blurriness and double vision. They had to be calmly fixed on the instruments. The *correct* instruments, that's what really mattered! How could you press the right buttons if you were seeing double?

Were Black's eyeballs shaking?

The next moment he felt ashamed, full of scorn at himself. He was such an idiot! The centrifuge at the practice site, the launch of the space elevator, braking in the Moon's orbit; each one had put a lot of pressure on him. Compared with all that, this landing was a walk in the park. He should have been calm personified, but the nerves were reaching out toward him with their electricity-laden fingers, and he had to admit to himself that his inability to breathe properly wasn't due to the pressure, but the sheer fear of smashing into the Moon.

Four kilometers, five.

The second display revealed that they were steadily slowing down, and he breathed out a sigh of relief. All the worry had been in vain.

Three kilometers until touchdown. A mountain ridge came into view, a high plateau, lights which segmented a landing field surrounded by protective barriers. Pipes and domes nestled among the rock like armored wood lice, lying in wait for unsuspecting quarry. Solar fields, masts, and antennae shimmered in the light of the low-lying sun; a barrel-shaped structure crowned a nearby hilltop. Further in the distance, open, hangar-like structures could be seen; huge machines crawled through a kind of open-cast mine. A rail system connected the habitats to the spaceport, led into a platform, then branched away from it in a wide curve. O'Keefe saw flights of stairs, hydraulic ramps and manipulator arms which were pointed toward a loading bay, then something white with tall, wide wheels drove along the road and stopped on a bridge; possibly manned, possibly a robot. The Charon shook and sank toward the ground. For a moment it was possible to make out a skyline of massive towers with large, bulky flying machines in between them, tanks and containers, unidentified objects. Something that looked like a praying mantis on wheels rolled off across the airfield, the sheer extent of which was now clear: the size of three or four soccer pitches. The surrounding land and buildings disappeared behind its dam-like borders, then their spaceship touched down carefully with feather-like elegance, teetered imperceptibly, and came to a standstill.

Something tugged softly at O'Keefe. At first he couldn't place it, but then the realization amazed him all the more because of the simplicity of the explanation. Gravity! For the first time since they had set off from the Isla de las Estrellas, excluding acceleration and braking maneuvers, he was no longer weightless. He had a body weight again, and even if it was only a sixth of his weight on Earth, it was still wonderful to weigh something again, a relief after all the days of just drifting around! *Hasta la vista*, Miranda, he thought, that's an end to the acrobatics. No more somersaults, no more elbow attacks. A gust of noise ebbed away in his ear canals, a synaptic afterglow; the engines had been turned off long before, but he just couldn't believe it.

"Ladies and gentlemen," said Black, a little dramatically, "congratulations! You've done it. Nina and I will now help you put on your life-support systems, show you how to regulate the oxygen, cooling, and pressure, and activate your walkie-talkie systems. After that we'll go through a series of leak tests—you should already be familiar with those from the external expedition on the OSS, and if not, there's no cause for concern. We'll supervise everything. As soon as the checks are done, I'll pump the air out of the cabin, and we'll explain the process of disembarkation. Please don't think I'm being rude if I climb out first, it's only to further the preservation of your heroism, because I'll film you as you leave the Charon and we'll also record your comments for posterity. Does that all make sense? Welcome to the Moon!"

PEARY BASE,
NORTH POLE, THE MOON

Leaving behind footprints was a pioneer's privilege, and one which made life a little easier for those of the custodian type, who were aware of the risks, but without being exposed to them. They were familiar with natural phenomenon, the appetite and armory of the local fauna and flora, knew how to adapt themselves to the defiance of the native inhabitants. Their knowledge was all thanks to the feverish, potentially suicidal curiosity of the discoverer type, who neither could nor wanted to do anything other than spend his life walking the narrow line between victory and death. Even in the days of *Homo erectus*, and the anthroposophists were sure of this, humanity had displayed a tendency to split up into a governing majority alongside a small group which just couldn't stay put. The latter had a special gene, known as the Columbus Gene, Novelty-seeking Gene or just D4DR in the extended version, code for an extraordinary willingness to cross borders and take risks. Naturally, all of these adventurous types were less suited for the cultivation of the conquered regions. They preferred discovering new areas, getting themselves bitten by new species of animals, and fulfilling all the prerequisites so that the more conservative types could make advances. They were the eternal scouts, for whom a footprint on terra incognita meant everything. In turn, it was part of the nature of the custodian to subject lime, mud, sand, gravel, silt, and whatever other kind of amorphous unspoiled state there was to the dictatorship of smoothed-out surfaces, which meant that when Evelyn Chambers, awestruck, walked down the gangway of the Charon and stepped on to the surface of the Moon for the first time, she left no lasting impression behind her, instead finding herself back on solid concrete.

For a second she was disappointed. The others, too, were looking at their feet as if walking on the Moon were inextricably linked with hallmarking the regolith.

"You'll leave your stamp behind soon enough," said Julian's voice, switched on in all their helmets.

Some of them laughed. The moment of unmet expectations passed, giving way to amazement and disbelief. Evelyn took a hesitant step, then another, bounced—and was carried over a meter in the air by the force of her thigh muscles.

Unbelievable! Absolutely unbelievable!

After over five days of zero gravity she felt the familiar burden of her weight, and yet she didn't. It was more as though some ominous comic-book radiation had given her superpowers. All around her, the others were leaping wildly around. Black danced attendance among them with his camera.

"Where's the star-spangled banner?" boomed Donoghue. "I want to ram it into the ground!"

"Then you're fifty-six years too late," laughed Ögi. "The Swiss flag on the other hand—"

"Imperialists," sighed Heidrun.

"No chance," said Julian. "Unless you're planning to *blast* your flags into the ground."

"Hey, look at that," called Rebecca Hsu.

Her ample figure shot past the others' heads, her arms windmilling. If it was Rebecca, that is. It wasn't that easy to tell. You couldn't really make out anyone's face through the mirrored visors; only the printed name on the chest section of the suit betrayed the identity of its wearer.

"Come on then," laughed Julian. "Don't be scared!"

Evelyn took a run-up and did a series of clumsy jumps, then sped upward again and turned on her own axis, drunk on high spirits. Then she lost her balance and sank back down to the ground in a meditative pose. She couldn't help breaking out into silly giggles as she landed softly on her behind. Overcome with delight, she stayed where she was, enjoying the surreal scene that was playing out before her. Within seconds the group of well-established movers and shakers had transformed into a horde of first-graders, playmates going wild. She came back to a standing position without any effort whatsoever.

"Good," praised Julian, "very good. The Bolshoi Ballet look like a load of blundering fools compared with you, but I'm afraid we need to interrupt the physical exercise temporarily. You're off to the hotel now, so please turn your attention back to Nina and Peter again."

It was as though he'd broadcast on the wrong frequency. With the defiance of children who had just been called to the dinner table, they finally trickled over in dribs and drabs to gather around their guides. The image of a bunch of ruffians gave way to one of a secret brotherhood as they stood there, searching for the Holy Grail against the panorama of flying castles. Evelyn let her gaze wander. The base could hardly be seen. Only the station platform loomed imposingly over the landing field, erected on 15-meter-high pylons, as Nina explained. Metal staircases and an open elevator led up to the rail tracks, spherical tanks were piled up all around. Two manipulators squatted at the edge of the platform like Jurassic birds, turned to face lobster-like machines with multiple-jointed claws and large loading surfaces. Evelyn guessed their task was probably to receive cargo from the manipulators or to reach it up to them, according to whether goods were being delivered or placed on the rails.

She tried to regulate her breathing. The confinement of the landing module just then had become unbearable for her. She had dreamed feverishly the night before. Higher powers had opened up the Charon using a gigantic can opener and exposed its inhabitants to the vacuum, which had turned out to be just a bunch of human-like creatures gaping in at them, and she had been stark naked. Admittedly it was all a bit silly, but still! The iridescent blue-green imprints of Miranda Winter's heels had been immortalized in her hips, and she'd had enough. She was even more amazed at how big the landing module actually was when she saw it in the expanse of the airfield. An imposing tower on powerful telescopic legs, practically a small skyscraper. More spaceships were distributed across the field, some with open hatches and yawningly empty insides, clearly intended for receiving freight goods. Several smaller machines spread their spider legs and stared straight ahead with their glassy eyes. Evelyn Chambers couldn't help but think of insect spray.

"You'll have to forgive the inhabitants of the base for not coming out to greet you," said Black. "You only go outside if it's absolutely necessary here. Unlike you, these people spend six months on the Moon. A week's worth of cosmic radiation won't harm you so long as you don't go out in a solar storm without protection. But long-term stays are a different story. So as we won't be looking around the base until the day of our departure, there's no reception committee today."

One of the lobster-like robots started up as if by magic, steered over to the Charon, and took some large white containers from its cargo hold.

"Your luggage," Nina explained, "will be exposed to the vacuum for the first time up here, but don't worry, the containers are pressurized. Otherwise your night cream might turn into a monster and attack your T-shirts. Follow me."

It was like going underwater, but without the ambient pressure. Excitedly, Evelyn realized that she didn't weigh 145 pounds anymore, but just 24 pounds, which meant her normal bodily strength would be multiplied by six. As light as a three-year-old, as strong as Superwoman, and carried along by a surge of child-like happiness, she followed Black to the elevator, hopped into the spacious cage, and watched the habitats of the base come back into view as they traveled out over the top of the barriers and onto the station platform. Several more rail tracks ran up here. A lit, empty train lay waiting for them, not unlike one of the bullet trains on Earth, but a little less streamlined in shape, which made it look curiously old-fashioned. But why would it have needed to be aerodynamic? There was no wind up here. There wasn't even any air.

She looked into the distance.

A barrage of images confronted her. A great deal of the surrounding area could be seen from up here. A highland. Hills and ridges, the silhouette of long shadows. Craters, like bowls filled with black ink. A glowing white, low-lying sun dissolved the contours of the horizon; the landscape stood out like stage scenery against the backdrop of outer space. There was no mist or atmosphere to diffuse the light; regardless of its actual distance everything was sharply contoured, as though it were close enough to touch. At the other side of the landing field, the track for the bullet train led into a valley filled with blackness, held its own against the darkness for a while thanks to the height of its columns, and then, without warning, was swallowed by it.

"We're just 15 kilometers away from the Moon's geographical North Pole here," said Black. "It's on a plateau at the northwestern edge of the Peary Crater, where it borders on its neighbor, Hermite. The area is nicknamed 'Mountains of Eternal Light.' Can anyone guess why?"

"Just explain, Peter," said Julian gently.

"Well, at the beginning of the nineties interest in the Pole really grew after it was established that the edges and peaks of some of the craters were in constant sunlight. The main problem with having a manned moon base had always been energy supply, and they wanted to avoid working with nuclear reactors. There was a great deal of resistance to it, even on Earth, because of the fear that a spaceship with a reactor like that on board could crash and fall onto inhabited areas. Back when the station was in the planning stages, helium-3 was still just a vague option, so they backed solar energy as usual. The only thing is, while solar panels are great, unfortunately they're useless at night. A gap of a few hours can be bridged with batteries, but a Moon night lasts fourteen days, and that's how the Pole came into the running. Admittedly the light yield is somewhat less here than at the equator, because the rays of light fall very obliquely, but on the other hand they're constant. If you look over at the hills you'll see entire fields of collectors which are continually aligning their position to face the sun."

Black paused and let them scan the hills for the collectors.

"And yet even the Poles aren't the ideal position for a base. The rays of sunlight fall obliquely, as I already mentioned, it's quite far away from where the action is up here, and it would have been better to have the lunar telescope on the far side. Some critics also point out that by the time the building work began, the use of helium-3 had become a viable option, so ideally the plans should have been thrown out and the base built in the preferred location, where it could be supplied with energy around the clock by a fusion reactor. It's actually a bit of a paradox that helium-3 wasn't used on the Moon of all places, but they followed the original plans regardless. The Poles also have another advantage: the temperature. By Moon standards it's quite moderate here, a constant 104 to 140 degrees Fahrenheit in the sun; while on the equator it's well over 212 degrees Fahrenheit in the midday heat, but at night the

thermometer plummets to minus 356 degrees Fahrenheit. No building material can handle fluctuations like that on a long-term basis: it
would have to expand and contract like crazy, which means it becomes
brittle and leaks. And there's one more consideration in favor of the
Poles. When the sun creeps in as low over the horizon as it does there,
wouldn't that mean there are also areas which are *never* illuminated by
it? If that's the case, then there's the chance of finding something there
that couldn't actually exist on the Moon: water."

"Why can't it exist here?" asked Miranda. "Not even a river or a
small lake?"

"Because it would immediately evaporate in the sun and escape
into open space. The Moon's gravity isn't enough to hold volatile gases;
that's one of the reasons why the Moon has no atmosphere. The only
possibility was of frozen water existing in eternal darkness, locked in
a molecular bond in moon dust brought here by meteorites. The existence of permanently shadowed chasms like these was quickly proved,
for example, the impact craters at the base of the Peary Crater, right
around the corner from here. And measurements really seemed to confirm the presence of water, which would have enormously favored the
development of a complex infrastructure. The alternative was sending
water up here from Earth, which was sheer madness even just from a
financial perspective."

"And have they found water?" asked Rogachev.

"Not so far. A great number of hydrogen deposits of course, but no
water. The base was built here regardless because transporting water
from Earth turned out to be a lot less complicated and expensive than
expected thanks to the space elevator. Now it makes its way to the
OSS in tanks, and from that point on mass doesn't matter anyway. But
of course people are still searching feverishly for signs of H_2O, and
besides—" Black pointed over to the barrel-shaped objects in the distance. "—they've started building a small helium-3 reactor anyway, as
a reserve for the base's steadily increasing energy needs."

"So, if I'm honest," grumbled Momoka Omura, "I was expecting the
moon base to be a little more impressive."

"I think it's very impressive," said Hanna.

"Me too," called Miranda.

"Absolutely," Nair added, laughing. "I still can't believe that I'm on
the Moon, that people live here! It's incredible."

"Wait until you see the Gaia," said Lynn mysteriously. "You probably won't ever want to leave again."

"If it looks like the pile of junk down there then I'll want to leave
immediately," snorted Momoka.

"Baby," said Locatelli, more sharply than usual. "You're insulting
our hosts."

"How? I only—"

"There are moments when even you should keep your mouth shut, don't you think?"

"I beg your pardon? Shut your own!"

"You'll like the hotel, Momoka," Lynn interrupted hurriedly. "Love it, even! And no, it does *not* look like the moon base."

Evelyn grinned. From a business point of view she enjoyed little spats like these, particularly as Locatelli and his Japanese muse usually joined forces when it came to antagonizing others. She had planned to ask Locatelli onto one of her next shows anyway, for which she was contemplating using the title "War of the World Saviors: How the Demise of the Oil Industry Is Stirring up Power Struggles among Suppliers of Alternative Energy." Perhaps one or two private thoughts might punctuate the conversation.

In the best of moods, she followed Black.

LUNAR EXPRESS

They boarded the train via an air lock and took off their helmets and suits. The air was kept at a constant pleasant temperature and the seats, as Rebecca Hsu said with a heartfelt sigh, were the right size to accommodate even an overweight traveler. The remark was addressed to Amber Orley, who Evelyn had hardly talked to so far. Amber was friendly toward everyone though, and even Julian's son turned out to be a sociable sort despite his initial reticence—if you could get past his air of leaden concern when it came to looking after his sister. She was visibly spoiling his mood, and Amber's, and on top of all this she seemed to be putting a strain on Tim's relationship with his father. None of this had escaped Evelyn's attention. She reckoned that Lynn had been faking that attack of space sickness in the Picard. Something wasn't right about her, and Evelyn was determined to find out what. Mukesh Nair had latched on to Tim and was letting him know how wonderful life was, so she sat down next to Amber.

"Unless of course you'd rather sit next to your husband—"

"No, no, that's fine!" Amber leaned closer. "We're on the Moon, isn't that just amazing?"

"It's mind-blowing!" Evelyn agreed.

"And then there's the hotel," she said, rolling her eyes dramatically.

"You know it then? So far they've made such a huge secret out of it. No pictures, no films—"

"Now and again being in the family has its advantages. Lynn showed us the plans."

"I'm bursting with curiosity! Hey, look, we're on our way."

Imperceptibly, the train had started moving. Ethereal music floated through the cabin, light as a breath, languid, as though the orchestra were on drugs.

"That's so beautiful," said Eva Borelius, sitting behind Evelyn. "What is it?"

"Aram Khachaturian," Rogachev answered. "Adagio for Cello and Strings" from the *Gayaneh Suite*.

"Bravo, Oleg." Julian turned around. "Can you also tell us which recording?"

"I believe it has to be the Leningrad Philharmonic, under Gennady Rozhdestvensky, isn't it?"

"My God, that's connoisseurship." Borelius seemed stunned. "You really know your stuff."

"More than anything else, I know how fond our host is of one particular film," said Rogachev in an uncharacteristically cheerful tone. "Let's just say I was well-prepared."

"I had no idea that you were so interested in classical—"

"No," muttered Olympiada quite audibly, "you wouldn't think so to look at him."

Here we go, thought Evelyn. This is getting better and better.

Lynn took up position in the aisle between the seats.

"You may perhaps have noticed," she said speaking into a small microphone, "that it's always up to me to speak when we're talking about the accommodation and facilities. First of all, everything that you see and do on this voyage is a premiere. You were the first guests in the Stellar Island Hotel, and you'll be the first to set foot inside the Gaia. Obviously, you're also the first to enjoy a ride on the Lunar Express, which will take less than two hours to transport us almost 1,300 kilometers to the hotel. The station we've just set out from actually functions more as a sort of shipping facility. Helium-3 is mined in the Mare Imbrium, to the northwest. The tanks are brought here by rail, then they're loaded onto spaceships and brought to the OSS. The cargo line runs parallel with our rails for a while and then it turns off to the west a little before we reach our destination, so it's entirely possible that we'll meet a freight train on our way."

Outside the windows they could see the landing field receding, with its blast walls rearing up around it. The maglev accelerated, drew out from the base along a long, curving downhill path, and rushed toward the shadowed valley.

"Our scheduled time of arrival at the hotel is 19:15, and there's no need for you to bother about your luggage. The robots will take it up to your rooms, and meanwhile we'll meet in the lobby, get to know the hotel crew, take a look around, and then you'll have a chance afterward to freshen up. Dinner will be a little later than usual today, at 20:30. After which I recommend you get some sleep. The journey was fairly strenuous, and you'll be tired; besides which Neil Armstrong reported having slept exceptionally well in his first night on the Moon. So much for the full Moon keeping you awake.—Anymore questions at the moment?"

"Just one." Donoghue raised a hand. "Can we get a drink?"

"Beer, wine, whisky," said Lynn, beaming. "All alcohol-free."

"I knew it."

"It'll do you good," said Aileen happily, and patted his leg.

Donoghue growled something blasphemous, and as if in punishment, darkness swallowed them up. For a while they could still see the top of the crater walls bathed in harsh sunlight, and then these too were lost to view. Nina Hedegaard brought around some snacks. György Ligeti's *Requiem* came over the speakers, just the right music for the pitch-black outside, and the downward slope steepened perceptibly while the Lunar Express picked up speed. Black explained that they

were in a cleft between Peary and Hermite, then they shot out again
into the sunlight, past jagged rock formations and toward a steep-sided
hollow. It grew dark again while they passed through a smaller crater.
Just a moment ago, Evelyn had been burning to draw out some secrets
of family life from Amber, but now all she wanted to do was stare out
in wonder at this untouched alien landscape, the archaic brutality of
its cliff walls and mountain ridges, the velvet silence that lay over the
dust-filled valleys and plains, the complete absence of color. The cold
sunlight fell on the edges of the impact craters, and time itself melted in
its glare. Nobody felt like talking any more, and even Chucky stopped
short in one of his jokes before the feeble punch line and stared out as
though hypnotized. Outside, a blue-white glittering jewel lifted slowly
above the horizon, gaining height with every kilometer they traveled
south—their home, infinitely far away, and achingly beautiful.

Nina and Black chattered on, informative and enthusiastic. They
mentioned the names of further craters, Byrd, Gioja, Main. The peaks
dwindled away to hills, the chasms gave way to light-filled plains. After
an hour, they reached a long rampart wall, Goldschmidt, its western
edge bitten away by the jaws of Anaxagoras, and Nina told them that
this was an especially recent impact. A few of them looked upward,
thinking that recent might mean just now, rather than 100 million
years ago, and then coughed or laughed nervously. They crossed Goldschmidt and sped across a desert landscape, this one a darker color,
and Julian stood up and congratulated them on crossing their first
lunar sea, the Mare Frigoris.

"And why do they call a dry old desert like this a sea?" Miranda
asked, saving her more educated fellow passengers the embarrassment
of having to ask the same question.

"Because earlier, these dark basaltic plains were thought to be seas,"
said Julian. "The assumption was that the Moon had to be shaped in
much the same way as the Earth was. As a result, people imagined that
they could see seas, lakes, bays, and swamps. What's interesting here
is how they got their names, for instance, why this basin is called the
Sea of Cold. There's the Sea of Tranquility, of course; Mare Tranquillitatis, which has gone down in history thanks to Apollo 11. And by the
way, that's why three tiny little craters near the landing site are called
Armstrong, Aldrin, and Collins; give credit where it's due. Then there's
the Sea of Serenity, the Sea of Happiness, the Sea of Clouds, the Sea of
Rains, the Ocean of Storms, the Foaming Sea, the Sea of Waves, and so
on and so forth."

"That sounds like the weather forecast," said Hanna.

"You've hit the nail on the head there." Julian grinned. "It's all due to
a certain Giovanni Battista Riccioli, a seventeenth-century astronomer
and contemporary of Galileo. He had the idea of naming every crater

and every mountain chain after a great astronomer or mathematician, but then he ran out of astronomers, as luck would have it. Later the Russians and the Americans took over his system. Nowadays you can find writers, psychologists, and polar explorers remembered for all time here on the Moon, and there are lunar Alps, Pyrenees, and Andes as well. Anyway, as far as Riccioli was concerned, the dark plains had to be seas. Plutarch had already believed this, and Galileo declared that if the Moon was another Earth, then the light patches were obviously continents and the dark parts must be bodies of water. Naturally Riccioli also wanted to give these seas of his names as well—and that's when he made his big mistake! He reckoned that his observations showed that weather down on the Earth was influenced by the phases of the Moon. For instance, good weather during the waxing Moon—"

"And crappy weather during the waning Moon."

"That's it! Since then the seas in the eastern hemisphere on the Moon have had peaceful, harmonious names, while over in the west it never rains but it pours. And a sea up by the North Pole, obviously, has to be cold, hence Mare Frigoris, the "Sea of Cold."—Oh, look at that! I do believe there's something coming toward us."

Evelyn craned her neck. At first she saw nothing but the endless plain and the rails curving away into the distance; then it leaped out at her. A tiny point, hurtling closer, that flew toward them over the rails and became something long and low with blazing headlamps. Then the two trains passed at a speed approaching 1,500 kilometers per hour, without the least sound or tremor from where they sat.

"Helium-3," said Julian reverentially. "The future."

And he sat down as though there was nothing further to say.

The Lunar Express flew onward. A little later an enormous mountain range showed on the horizon, becoming taller with amazing speed as though the Mare Frigoris really was a sea and the range was rising from its depths. Evelyn remembered hearing from someone that the effect was due to the Moon's curvature. Black told them that this was the crater Plato, a splendid example with a diameter of more than 100 kilometers and walls 2,500 meters high, another little splinter of information fired into Evelyn's overloaded cerebral cortex that stuck there. The Lunar Express swooped smoothly into the Mare Imbrium, the neighboring desert plain. The freight tracks branched off, as announced, and vanished off to the west, while they went around Plato and left it behind. More mountains reared up on the horizon, the Lunar Alps, harsh-lit and shot through with veins of shadow. The rails reared boldly upward into the mountains, where the pillars that held up the maglev track clasped hold of the steep cliffs like claws. The higher they climbed, the more breathtaking the view: stark peaks 2,000 meters tall, overhangs like Cubist sculpture, sharp saw-toothed ridges. One last look down at the dusty carpet of the Mare Imbrium, then the tracks curved away into the sea's hinterland, between peaks and plateaus and onward to the edge of a lunar Grand Canyon, and then—

Evelyn couldn't believe her eyes.

A sigh of astonishment shuddered through the train. The barely audible hum of the motor joined in with the bass notes of the *Zarathustra* theme, pregnant with mystery, while the Lunar Express slowed and then the first fanfares burst out brightly. Strauss might have been thinking of Nietzsche's new dawn, while Kubrick used it for the transformation of the human race into something newer, higher. But right at this moment Evelyn was thinking of Edgar Allan Poe, a writer whose depths she had plumbed enthusiastically in her youth, and she remembered one sentence from his work, the terrifying ending of *Arthur Gordon Pym*:

But there arose in our pathway a shrouded human figure, very far larger in its proportions than any dweller among men. And the hue of the skin of the figure was of the perfect whiteness of the snow.

She held her breath.

Ten, maybe 12 kilometers away from them, atop a plateau, high above a promontory that jutted out like a terrace beneath it and then fell away into a steep canyon, something sat, gazing up at Earth.

A person.

No, it had the shape of a human form. Not a man's shape, but a woman's, perfectly proportioned. Her head, limbs, and body gleamed gently in front of the endless sea of stars. No expression on that face— no mouth, eyes, or nose— but still there was something soulful, almost yearning in her posture as she sat there with her legs hanging over the edge and her arms out to the side, supporting her, elbows straight, her whole attention focused on that silent, distant planet above her where she would never walk.

She was at least 200 meters tall.

DALLAS, TEXAS, USA

If Loreena Keowa hadn't already been the best-known face of Green-watch, they would have had to invent her.

There was no mistaking her ancestry. She was 100 percent Tlingit, a member of the nation that had inhabited the southeast coast of Alaska since time immemorial and whose ancestral homeland included parts of the Yukon Territory and British Columbia. There were about 8,000 Tlingit left, with their numbers falling. Only a few hundred of the old people still spoke the melodic Na-Dené tongue perfectly, although these days more and more young people like Keowa learned it too, see-ing themselves as the standard-bearers of ethnic self-determination in a newly green America.

Keowa came from a Raven clan in Hoonah, the Village on the Cliffs, a Tlingit settlement on Chichagof Island. Now, if she wasn't spend-ing her time in Vancouver, where Greenwatch was headquartered, she lived 40 miles west of Hoonah in Juneau. Her features were unmis-takably Indian, but at the same time bore the signs of white ancestry, although to the best of her knowledge no white man had ever mar-ried into the clan. Without being good-looking in the classical sense, she had a wild and enticing aura about her that could easily seem romantic. Her long, shining black hair exactly matched what a New York stockbroker might expect Indian hair to look like, whereas her style of dress went dead against all the clichés of the noble savage. As far as she was concerned, you could protect the environment quite as well while dressed in Gucci and Armani. She was clear and factual in her work, and hardly ever launched into polemics. Her reports were known to be well researched, unsparing, but at the same time she man-aged never to damn a culprit irredeemably. Her enemies called her a walking compromise, the ideal solution for milksop Wall Street eco-activists, while her defenders valued the way she brought people and viewpoints together. Whatever the truth of it, nobody could claim that Greenwatch's success wasn't largely down to Loreena Keowa. In the past couple of years it had grown from a small Internet channel to take front place among America's ecologically aware TV stations, and had a remarkably good track record when it came to corrections or retractions—no mean feat, given that the race for a scoop on the Inter-net went hand-in-hand with a worrying lack of research credibility.

It was typical for Greenwatch to feel a crude sort of sympathy for the chief strategist of EMCO, Gerald Palstein, who should really count as their bad guy. But Palstein argued for various green positions, and he'd been the victim of an attack in Calgary when he put an end to something that had always made environmental activists turn purple with rage. At the beginning of the millennium, companies such as ExxonMobil had breathed new life into an area of business that had almost been abandoned, and they had the Bush administration's full, eco-unfriendly support. This was the exploitation of oil sands—a mixture of sand, water, and hydrocarbons—with huge reserves in Canada, among other places. The reserves in Athabasca, Peace River, and Cold Lake alone were estimated at 24 billion tons, catapulting the country up in the list of oil-rich nations to place number two, behind Saudi Arabia. Mind you, it cost three times as much to extract the black gold from the sands as from conventional sources, making it a losing business as long as the price per barrel hovered between 20 and 30 dollars. But in the end, rapidly climbing prices had justified the intensive investment, thanks also to Canada's proximity to the thirsty primary consumer, the United States, grateful for every oil supplier that wasn't an Arab nation. The oil companies pounced on the slumbering reserves with dollar signs in their eyes, and within a very short time this led to the complete destruction of the boreal forest in Alberta, the moorland biotopes, the rivers, and lakes. Additionally, 176 pounds of greenhouse gas were released into the atmosphere for every barrel of this synthetic oil extracted, and four barrels of polluted water flowed out to poison the land.

But the price per barrel collapsed, forever. Open-cast extraction stopped overnight, leaving the companies that had driven the business unable to repair the damaged ecosystems. All that was left were ravaged tracts of land, increased incidence of cancer in the population—and companies such as Imperial Oil, a traditional business headquartered in Calgary, which for almost 150 years had made its money from extracting and refining oil and natural gas, and in the end, increasingly from oil sands. Just as it was at the forefront of the industry, the lights went out, and Palstein, strategic director of the majority shareholder EMCO, which owned about two-thirds of Imperial Oil, had to go to Alberta to tell the management and a stunned workforce that they were being let go.

Perhaps because it was more effective to vent anger on one man than on the oh-so-distant Moon, whose resources had led to the disaster, somebody shot at Palstein in Calgary. The deed of a desperate man, at least so most people saw it.

Loreena Keowa thought that there were good grounds for skepticism.

Not that she had an answer either. But how long could an embittered, unemployed shooter expect to escape justice? The attempted killing had been one month ago. A great many things about the theory of an enraged lone gunman didn't make sense, and since Keowa was working anyway on a feature about the environmental destruction wreaked by the oil companies, *The Trash of the Titans*, it made sense to her that she should look into the case in her own way. Even before helium-3, Palstein had been vocal about the need for his industry to switch direction. He was on record as being no friend of the oil-sands project, and she felt that he had been unfairly treated at the press conference in Anchorage. So she had offered him a TV portrait that would show him in a better light. In exchange, she hoped for some inside information about EMCO, the crumbling giant, and more even than that, she was excited at the thought of being able to help clear up the shooting, in the best tradition of American investigative journalism.

Maybe even solving the case.

Palstein had hesitated a while, and in the end invited her to visit him in Texas, in his house on the shore of Lake Lavon. He was convalescing from his injury here, and recovering from being the bearer of bad news. He made one condition: that for the first conversation, she should turn up without her camera team.

"We'll need pictures though," Keowa had said. "We're a TV channel."

"You'll get some. As long as I feel that I can trust you. But I can only take so many knocks, Loreena. We'll speak to one another out for an hour, and then you can grab your crew. Or maybe not."

Now, in the taxi bringing them downtown from the airport, Keowa went through her material one more time. Her camera crew and sound technician were lolling in the back seat, wrung out by the humid heat that lay across Texas far too early this year. EMCO was headquartered next door in Irving, but Palstein lived on the other side of town. They had a light lunch in the Dallas Sheraton, then Palstein's driver arrived at the agreed time pick up Keowa. They left town and drove through the untouched green belt around, until the glittering surface of the lake became visible through the trees to the left. It had been a bumpy flight, followed by a plunge into the sauna-like Dallas temperatures, and she enjoyed the ride in an air-conditioned electric van. After a while the driver turned off into a smaller road and then onto a private driveway that led along the water to Palstein's house, which looked, she mused, something like what she had been expecting. Palstein would have stuck out like a sore thumb in a ranch with buffalo horns and a pillared veranda. This was an airy arrangement of Cubist buildings around green open spaces, with glass frontages, soaring slender framework, and walls that seemed almost weightless; all this suited his character much better.

The driver let her out. A well-built man in slacks and a T-shirt came toward her and asked politely for some identification. Two more men were patrolling down by the wharf. She handed him her ID card, and he held it to the scanner on his phone. He seemed happy with what the screen told him, gave it back to her with a smile, and beckoned her to follow him. They hurried through a Japanese garden and past a large swimming pool, to a jetty where a boat was tied up.

"Do you feel like a ride?"

Palstein was leaning against a post, waiting for her in front of a trim, snow-white yacht with a tall mast and furled sails. He was wearing jeans and a polo shirt, and looked healthier than the last time they had met in Anchorage. The sling on his arm was gone. Keowa pointed to his shoulder.

"Feeling better?"

"Thanks." He took her hand and shook it briefly. "It tugs a little sometimes. Did you have a good flight, Shax' saani Keek'?"

Keowa laughed, caught out. "You know my Indian name?"

"Why not?"

"Hardly anybody does!"

"Etiquette demands that I keep myself informed. Shax' saani Keek', in Tlingit that means *the younger sister of the girls*, am I right?"

"I'm impressed."

"And I'm probably an old show-off." Palstein smiled. "So, what do you say? I can't offer to take you sailing, that wouldn't work yet with my shoulder, but the outboard works and there are cold drinks on board."

Under other circumstances Keowa would have been suspicious. But what would have seemed manipulative coming from anyone else, was just what it seemed coming from Palstein: an invitation from a man who liked his boat and wanted to share a trip.

"Lovely house," said Keowa, once they had motored out a little way from the shore. The heat stood there like a block over the water, not a whisper of a breeze ruffled the lake surface, but all the same it was more bearable than on land. Palstein looked back and then was silent for a minute, as though considering for the first time whether his homestead could be called beautiful.

"It's based on a design by Mies van der Rohe. Do you know his work?"

Keowa shook her head.

"In my view, he's the most important modern architect there was. A German, a great constructivist and a logical thinker. He aimed to tame the chaotic mess that technological civilization churned out and frame it with order and structure. Mind you, he didn't consider that order necessarily meant drawing lines and boundaries—he wanted to create as much open space as possible, a seamless transition between inside and out."

"And between past and future?"

"Absolutely! His work is timeless, because it gives every age what we need. Van der Rohe will never stop influencing architects."

"You like clear structures."

"I like people who can see the whole picture. By the way, I'm sure you know his most famous motto: 'Less is more.'"

"Oh yes." Keowa nodded. "Of course."

"Do you know what I think? If we could perceive the world the way van der Rohe structured his work, we'd be aware of higher-order connections and we'd reach different conclusions. Clarity through reduction. Recognize what's in front of you by clearing away the clutter. A mathematics of thought." He paused. "But you're not here to hear me talking about the beauty of pure number. What would you like to know?"

"Who shot you?"

Palstein nodded, almost a little disappointed, as though he had been expecting something more original.

"The police are looking for one man, someone frustrated, angry."

"Do you still agree with their profiling?"

"I've said that I do."

"Would you care to tell me what you really think?"

He put his chin in his hands. "Let's put it this way: if you want to solve an equation, you need to know the variables. All the same you'll fail if you fall in love with one of the variables and assign it a value that it might not have, and if I'm right, this is exactly what the police are doing. The stupid thing is, though, that I can't offer any better explanation.—What do you think?"

"Hey, well. There's an industry going down the drain here, and you stalk the land like a gravedigger, telling people that they're going to lose their jobs, you're shutting down plants, you're letting companies go to the wall, even if the truth of the matter is that you're not a gravedigger, you're the trauma surgeon."

"It's all a question of perception."

"Quite. Why couldn't it be some husband and father who just snapped? I'm just surprised that they haven't been able to find someone like that in four weeks. The attack was filmed by several broadcasters; you'd think someone would have seen something. Someone acting suspiciously maybe, drawing a weapon, running away, something like that."

"Did you know that there's a complex of buildings across from the podium, over the other side of the square—"

"—and the police think that this is where the shot was fired from. Also that nobody remembers having seen anyone going in, or coming out after the attack. There were policemen nearby, all over the place. Doesn't that seem odd to you? Doesn't the whole thing look more like a professional operation, something planned out in advance?"

"Lee Harvey Oswald fired from a building as well."

"Wait a moment! He fired from where he worked."

"But not on impulse. He must have planned his action, even if there's nothing to say that he was a professional assassin—whatever millions of conspiracy theorists may prefer to believe."

"Agreed. All the same, I have to ask who the bullet was meant for here."

"You mean whether I was being shot as a private individual, as representing EMCO, or maybe as a symbol for the whole system."

"You're not the symbol for the system, Gerald. Militant environmentalists would look for somebody else, not the only one they can sometimes work with. Perhaps it's the other way about, and you're a thorn in the side of militant *representatives* of the system."

"They'd have taken the chance to snuff me out while there were still decisions to be made at EMCO," Palstein said dismissively. "As you so nicely put it, I'm letting Imperial Oil go to the wall and I'm winding down our involvement in oil sands. If I had done this before helium-3, it might have made sense to get me out of the way so as to be able to keep digging around in the muck, but these days? Every unpopular decision I make, the circumstances make for me."

"Good, then let's consider Palstein the private individual. What about revenge?"

"Personally, against me?"

"Have you been stepping on any toes?"

"Not that I know of."

"Not at all? Bedded someone's wife? Stolen their job?"

"Believe me, right now nobody wants *my* job, and I don't have time to go bedding other men's wives. But even if there were personal motives involved, why would someone take a shot at me in such difficult terrain, out in public? He could have killed me here at the lake. In peace and quiet."

"You're well-guarded."

"Only since Calgary."

"Maybe somebody from your own ranks? Do you stand for something that the power holders at EMCO don't want at any price, no matter what the situation?"

Palstein laced his fingers together. He had switched off the outboard, and the little yacht sat on its reflection in the water as though glued in place. Behind Keowa's head, the cheerful hum of a bumblebee lost itself in the silence.

"Of course there are some at EMCO who think we should just sit out the whole helium-3 business," he said. "They think it's idiotic to buy in with Orley. But that's unrealistic. We're going bankrupt. We can't afford to wait anything out."

"Would your death have changed anything for Imperial Oil, in particular?"

"It wouldn't have changed anything for anyone. I wouldn't have been able to make a few meetings." Palstein shrugged. "Well, as it is, some of them I can't make anyway."

"You were supposed to fly to the Moon with Orley. He invited you."

"Truth be told, I asked him whether I could come along. I would have really liked to have flown." A dreamy look came into Palstein's eyes. "As well as which, there are a lot of interesting people up there, maybe I could have talked up a joint venture or two. Oleg Rogachev, for instance, he's worth $56 billion, the world's biggest steel producer. Plenty of people are trying to close a deal with him. Or Warren Locatelli, he's worth nearly as much."

"EMCO and the world market leader in solar cells," smiled Keowa. "Doesn't it make you angry that your industry used to be so powerful, and now you have to court favor with these kinds of people?"

"It makes me angry that EMCO didn't listen to me at the time. I always wanted to work with Locatelli. We should have bought Light-years when the time was right."

"When you still had something to offer him."

"Yes."

"It's absurd, isn't it? Doesn't it seem like history having the last laugh—the oil bosses dictated what happened in the world for nearly a century, and then in the end, they weren't in a position to turn new developments to their advantage?"

"Every kind of rule ends in decadence. Anyway, I'm sorry I can't help you with any more reasons for trying to kill me. I'm afraid you'll have to keep looking elsewhere."

Keowa said nothing. Perhaps it had been naïve of her to hope that out here, on silent Lake Lavon, Palstein would whisper dreadful secrets in her ear. Then she had an idea.

"EMCO still has money, is that right?"

"Absolutely."

"You see." She smiled triumphantly. "So what you did was, you made a decision, where there would have been an alternative."

"And that would have been?"

"If you're investing in Orley Enterprises, then you must be thinking of considerable amounts of money."

"Of course. But really, there's no alternative there either."

"Depends on who's interested, I would say. It needn't necessarily be about keeping EMCO in business."

"What else?"

"Shutting the place down and taking the money elsewhere. I mean, who might have an interest in actually *speeding up* EMCO's end? Perhaps your rescue plan actually gets in someone's way?"

Palstein looked at her with melancholy in his eyes.

"Interesting question."

"Think about it! There are thousands out of work who would reckon it makes a lot more sense for EMCO to use the money for their welfare bills, at least for as long as it takes them to get new jobs, and then the ship can go down for all they care. Then there are the creditors who don't want to see their money blast off to the Moon. A government that has dropped your lot without batting an eyelash. Why exactly? EMCO has know-how, after all."

"We have no know-how. Not on the Moon."

"But isn't it all resource extraction, even up there?"

Palstein shook his head. "It's space travel more than it's anything else. Then, Earth-based technologies can't just be mapped onto the Moon one to one, especially not in our line of work. The lower gravity, the lack of atmosphere, it all brings its own problems. A couple of guys from coal mining are involved, but otherwise they're developing completely new techniques. If you ask me, there's a completely different reason why the government just dropped us. The State wants to control helium-3 extraction, 100 percent. So Washington has grabbed the opportunity with both hands, and they're aiming not just to get out of the armlock the Middle East had them in, they want to be free of the oil companies as well."

"Stick the knife in the kingmaker's ribs," said Keowa, mockingly.

"But of course," said Palstein, almost cheerfully. "Oil has made presidents, but no president wants to be a puppet for private business unless he's the biggest fish in that pond. It's just in the nature of things that the new-crowned king wants to get rid of the kingmaker first thing, if he can. Just think of what happened in Russia in the nineties, think of Vladimir Putin—ah, heck, you're too young to remember that."

"I've studied Russian history," Keowa said, smiling. "Putin was supposed to be the oligarchs' puppet, but they underestimated him. Characters like that guy with the unpronounceable name—"

"Khodorkovsky."

"Right, one of the robber barons from Yeltsin's day. Putin came onto the scene, and a little bit later Khodorkovsky wakes up in a prison camp in Siberia. It happened to a lot of them."

"In our case, the problem solves itself," Palstein grinned.

"Nevertheless," said Keowa insistently. "During the big crisis sixteen years ago governments all over the world put together packages worth billions to save the banks from sinking. There was talk of pain in the financial markets, as though it were the banks and the board members who were suffering, not the armies of small investors who lost their money and never saw it back from State guarantees. But the states helped the banks. And now they're doing nothing. They're letting the oil giants go to the dogs. It doesn't matter how much they'd like to be free of them, *that* can't be in Washington's interest."

Palstein looked at her as though at an interesting fish that he hadn't expected to catch in this lake.

"You want a story, no matter what it takes, don't you?"

"If there is one."

"So you're comparing chalk and cheese just to get one. It was completely different with the banks. Banks are the very essence of the system called capitalism, they hold it up. Do you really believe that back then it was just about individual financial institutions, or about nasty managers and speculators paying themselves performance-related bonuses for no performance at all? It was about keeping the system going that even makes politics *possible*; it was about the temple of capitalism not crashing down. In the final analysis, it was about government's influence on capital which had been lost over time. Let's not kid ourselves, Loreena, the oil companies never played anything like that kind of a role. Our industry was only ever a symptom of the system, it was never part of its structure. You can do without us very well. Those of us who didn't manage to leap aboard the alternative energies bandwagon in time are in our death throes. Why should the State save us? We've nothing to offer it. Back in the day we paid the politicos, which was a comfortable way for them to live, but now you expect them to prop us up? Nobody's interested in that! The State is digging up the helium-3 because it sees the chance to become an investor in its own right again. America now has the once-in-a-lifetime opportunity to secure its energy supply under State control, and this time it won't let the kingmakers appear in the first place."

"That really sounds like a lot of hogwash," said Keowa dismissively. "You name me one capitalist system where capital and private enterprise aren't the real powerbrokers. The United States is switching from EMCO to Orley Enterprises, that's all. Orley will bring Washington to the Moon, build the reactors so that when the stuff gets down to the Earth it does what it has to. The whole project would never have gotten this far without private sector support. And the new kingmaker is sitting on his patents and laying down the law for his partners. Without him, they'd not be able to build any more elevators, any reactors—"

"Julian Orley isn't a kingmaker in the classic sense. He's an alien, if you like. An out-of-worlder. ExxonMobil, later EMCO, they were Americans; they influenced elections in America and stoked foreign insurrections with their money or by running guns. Orley's not like that. He acts like a state himself; he sees himself as a world power in his own right. That's something that the multinationals always flirted with the idea of doing. Answerable to nobody but himself. Julian Orley would never try to topple an American president he didn't like; he'd even have moral scruples against it. He'd simply break off diplomatic relations with Washington and recall his ambassador."

"He really thinks that he's a—state?"

"Are you surprised? Julian's rise to power was all plotted out while governments were still rubbing their eyes and demanding a greater say in how the banks were run. It was their own idea to privatize everything they could lay their hands on, and now they saw the welfare state slipping between their fingers. So all of a sudden they wanted more State power, but were forced to concede that if you take capital into State ownership, you rob it of the very strengths that make it grow, and they went back to business as usual. People contented themselves with the idea that the depression of 2008 to 2012 was just a system overheating, that there was nothing wrong with the system itself. They squandered the chance to reinvent capitalism, and with it the chance to strengthen State power in the long term."

Palstein was gazing off into the distance. He spoke as though giving a lecture, his voice analytical but without empathy.

"That was the moment when private capital took the scepter from government hands once and for all. Human beings became human resources. The parties in the democratic countries were too busy treading on one another's toes, and the totalitarian powers were wheeling and dealing on their own behalf as always; meanwhile the big companies forced their way into every aspect of social life and set up shop for modern society. They took over the water supply, medicine, the food chain; they privatized education; they built their own universities, hospitals, old folks' homes, and graveyards, and it was all bigger, better, and more beautiful than what the State had to offer. They formed an antiwar movement. They started aid programs for the underprivileged. They took up arms against hunger and thirst; against torture; against global warming, overfishing, and resource depletion; against social division, the gap between the rich and the poor. And as they did so, they were reinforcing divisions by deciding who had access and who didn't. They set up generous research budgets, and made the research serve their goals. Planet Earth had been the heritage of all humanity, but now it became an economic asset. They opened up every corner of the planet, every resource. At the same time they put a price on everything, from sources of fresh water all the way to the human genome. They took the world, which had been common to all, and they drew up a catalogue listing what belonged to which owner, they imposed usage fees and access protocols; if you'll let me coin a rather loaded phrase, they put a turnstile on all Creation. Even free education and drinking water tie people into the commercial ideology once they accept the offer, it's the vision of a brand name."

"Wasn't it always like that?" said Keowa. "That the many are rewarded for following the vision of the few, and if they don't, they can expect to be cast out and punished?"

"You're talking about dictators and all their pomp and show. Tut-ankhamun, Julius Caesar, Napoleon, Hitler, Saddam Hussein."

"There are other forms of dictatorship, gentler ones."

"Ancient Rome was a gentle dictatorship." Palstein smiled. "The Romans reckoned that they were the freest people on earth. That was something quite different, Loreena, I'm talking about rulers seizing power who don't even have a country; their states aren't shown on the map. The fact that the oil companies look like losing this battle doesn't mean that industry's grip on politics is loosening, quite the opposite. It just shows that influence has shifted. Here on Earth, Incorporated, other departments have become more influential, and to that extent, you're absolutely right: Orley takes EMCO's place. It's just that EMCO acted in America's interests, because our people were in government, but Orley doesn't even want to govern. That's what makes him so unpredictable. That's what the governments are afraid of.—And now, please consider the whole long history of State failure, and just ask yourself whether this kind of power transfer is really such a bad thing."

"Excuse me?" Keowa cocked her head. "You can't be serious?"

"I'm not trying to sell you anything. I just want you to look at the situation as though it were an equation, look at all the variables, without fear or favor. Can you do that?"

Keowa considered this. Palstein had drawn her into a strange kind of conversation here. She had set out to interview him, and analyze him, and now the tables were turned.

"I believe so," she said.

"And?"

"There is no ideal state of things. But there are approximations. Some of them have been hard-won. When we abolished slavery, the idea of the free citizen won out, at all levels of society. The citizen of a democratic state is bound by the laws but is fundamentally free, isn't that right?"

"*D'accord.*"

"But if you're a member of a company, you're property. That's the change that's happening all over."

"Also right."

"It seems to me about as difficult to break out of this pattern as it would be to suspend the laws of nature. The freedom of the individual is nothing but an idea by now. We live on a globe, and globes are closed systems, they offer no chance of escape and the globe is all divided up. At this very moment, while we sit here on this beautiful lake talking the whole thing through, the Moon in its orbit is being divided up, way over our heads; that's the next globe. There's no such thing as uncommercialized space anymore."

"That is so."

"Well, excuse me, Gerald, yes, I'm a realist—but I'll fight this to the very end!"

"That's your prerogative. I can understand your position, but please, think about it. You can hate the very thought of being property. Or you can make some kind of compromise with it." Palstein ran a rope through his fingers and laughed. All of a sudden he seemed very relaxed, a Buddha at rest. "And perhaps compromise is the better choice."

GAIA, VALLIS ALPINA, THE MOON

The sun was losing mass.

Every minute, 60 million tons of material in its mantle was lost—protons, electrons, helium atoms, and a few other elements with walk-on roles, the ingredients for that mysterious molecular cloud that supposedly gave birth to all the celestial bodies in our system. The solar wind streamed ceaselessly outward, blowing comets off course, fluorescing in the Earth's atmosphere as the aurorae borealis and australis, sweeping away the accretions of gas in interplanetary space and gusting out, far beyond the orbit of Pluto, to the Oort cloud. Cosmic background radiation joined the mix, weak but omnipresent, a newsfeed at the speed of light, speaking of supernovae, neutron stars, black holes, and the birth of the universe.

Ever since the Earth had collided with a proto-planet named Theia and given birth to the Moon, its satellite had been defenseless against all these influences, exposed. The sun's breath blew constantly over the lunar surface. It had no magnetic field to deflect the high-energy particles, and although they only penetrated a few micrometers deep, the lunar dust was saturated with them, and four and a half billion years of meteorite bombardment had turned the whole surface over and over like a plowed field. Since its creation, the Moon had soaked up so much solar plasma that it held enough to bring mankind up here, hungry for resources, armed with spaceships and mining machinery to rip away the Moon's dowry.

Sometimes there were sunstorms.

Spots formed on the sun's surface, huge arcs of plasma leaped across the raging ocean of fire, hurling umpteen times the usual amount of radiation out into space, and the solar wind became a hurricane, howling through the solar system at twice its usual speed. When this happened, astronauts were well-advised to huddle in their habitation modules and not, if at all possible, to be caught in a traveling spaceship. Each ionized particle that passed through a human cell damaged the genetic material irreparably. Every twelve years the solar hurricanes were more frequent: as recently as 2024 they had stopped shuttle traffic for a while and forced the residents at the moon bases underground. Even machines did not cope well with these particle storms, which damaged their outer skin and wiped the data stored in their microchips, caused short circuits and unwanted chain reactions.

Everyone agreed that sunstorms were the biggest danger of manned space flight.

· · ·

On May 26, 2025, the sun was breathing calmly and evenly.

As usual, its breath streamed out into the heliosphere: passed Mercury; mingled with the carbon dioxide on Venus and Mars, and with the Earth's atmosphere; blew straight through the gaseous shells of Jupiter, Saturn, Uranus, and Neptune; washed up on the shores of all their moons and of course reached the Earth's satellite as well, each particle traveling at 400 kilometers per second. The particles plowed into the regolith, clinging to the gray dust, spread out across the plains and the crater walls, and a few billions also collided with the female colossus at the edge of the Vallis Alpina in the lunar north, without penetrating her skin, at least in the parts reinforced with mooncrete. Gaia sat there on her cliff edge, unmoved by the cosmic hailstorm, her eyeless face turned toward the Earth.

Julian's woman in the Moon.

Lynn's nightmare.

The stranded ocean liner clinging to the volcanic slopes of the Isla de las Estrellas, the OSS Grand, both of these were products of her imagination. Gaia, though, was from a dream that Julian had had, in which he saw his daughter sitting on the Moon, none other, a figure all of light in front of the black brocade of space sewn with its millions of stars. Typically for him, he saw Lynn exaggerated to the scale of a metaphor, an ideal of humanity, journeying onward, wise and pure, and he woke up and called her there and then from bed and told her about his dream. And of course Lynn enthusiastically took up the idea of a hotel shaped like the human form, congratulated her father and promised to draw up preliminary designs right away, while this sublime vision that was supposed to be her actually turned her stomach so much that she couldn't sleep for a week. Her eating disorders reached a whole new anorexic level, and she began to gobble down little green tablets to help her master her fear of failure, but somehow she managed to place the colossus at the edge of the Vallis Alpina, a giant of a woman, named after Mother Earth in ancient Greek myth.

Gaia.

And she had built this woman! The very last of her energy might have burned away in the fury of creation, but in return, she could claim a masterpiece. At least, everybody told her that's what it was. She felt no such certainty. The way Julian saw things, she was supposed to recover by working on Gaia; he thought that the project would be a therapy, a countermeasure for the last symptoms of that fearful illness she had just recovered from. He had barely had a clue what the illness was— about as much as if she'd been abducted by aliens and taken to some far-off planet. It was also typical that Julian had convinced himself she was ill because she was short on challenges, stifled by routine, that too much of the same old thing had made her quick blood sluggish. Lynn had been the perfect leader of Orley Travel, the group's tourism arm, for years now. Perhaps she was yearning for something exciting, something new. Perhaps she was under-stimulated. She made the world run on time, but was the world enough? Back in the late 2010s private suborbital spaceflight had been part of the portfolio of Orley Space, along with tourist trips to the OSS and to the smaller orbital hotels, but strictly speaking, all these things were tourism as well.

And so Julian decided that it was not Orley Space that was to be entrusted with the greatest adventure in the whole history of hotel building, but his daughter.

The whole gigantic project was made rather simpler by engineering freedoms, given that everything on the Moon weighed only one sixth of its weight on Earth. What made it harder, was that nobody had any experience at all in lunar high-rise construction. Large parts of the American moon base were underground; the rest was as low-rise as you could get. China had done away completely with the idea of having a site, and its outposts were housed in modular vehicles, built like tanks, that followed along not far behind the mining vehicles by their extraction site. Down at the lunar South Pole, not far from Aitken Crater, a small German moon base shared its little place in the sun with an equivalent French station, each housing two astronauts, while over in the Oceanus Procellarum a lively little automated gizmo surveyed the ideal spot for a Russian base that would never be built. The Mare Serenitatis was home to an inquisitive Indian robot, and Japan had a forlorn uninhabited zone around the corner. Otherwise there was nothing else on the Moon for architectural sightseers. Nevertheless the elevated maglev rails proved that in lunar gravity it was possible to build vaulting filigree frameworks that would have long ago collapsed under their own weight back on Earth.

And Gaia had to be big. This was no bed-and-breakfast operation but a monument to the glory of mankind—and of course a stopover for up to two hundred of the most solvent members of that species.

Lynn had obediently drummed up designers and engineers, and set the plans in motion under the strictest secrecy. It soon became clear that a standing figure would be too tall. So she sketched Gaia seated as an alternative, which met with Julian's especial approval since that was just the way he had dreamed of his hotel. Since there was no question of a detailed depiction of a human body, the first thing the planning team did was fuse the legs together into one massive complex, as though the woman was wearing a narrow skirt that tailed off into a point. The buttocks and thighs were the horizontal base of the building, then below the knee the legs bent downward into the chasm without touching the wall behind them. The daring ambition of this piece of structural engineering was enough in itself to send Lynn clutching the sides of the toilet bowl, where she threw up, half-digested, most of what little food she had been able to choke down. Her tablet consumption rose to compensate, but Julian was in raptures, and the technical team said it could be done.

No need to emphasize that "it can be done" was Julian's favorite phrase.

Thus the feminine attributes of the building all had to be shown in the torso, basically a high-rise with curved walls rather than straight. It was given a waist, and then lines suggesting a bosom—which was the cause of a great deal of argument. The draftsmen, being men, drew breasts that were far too large. Lynn declared that she was not interested in tackling the engineering aspects of porn-star-sized boobies just so as to be able to accommodate a few more guests, and she brushed them out of the picture. Suddenly she found the whole idea of a putting a woman on the Moon a hideous platitude. Julian threw in a remark that making the upper body too narrow made the building look like a man, and wasn't it about time to let a woman represent mankind? One of the architects hinted that Lynn might be a prude. Lynn was enraged. She was no flat-chested goody-goody herself, she yelled, but what exactly was Gaia supposed to embody here? A monument to mammaries? Bust expansion? All right then, said Julian, we want curves. No, Lynn retorted, we want as boyish a figure as we can create. But nothing androgynous, protested the head of the team responsible for the façade. Nothing top-heavy either, Lynn insisted. All right then, suggested Julian, *decently* curved, which sounded like the best solution, but what exactly did decent mean here?

An intern scooted past, sat herself down at the computer without a word and drew a curve. Everyone watched her, looked at it. Everyone liked what they saw. Boyish, but not androgynous. The curve united them all, and the point was settled.

The shoulders were feminine but not narrow, atop towers that swept down to the ground, narrowing as they went, with a slight bend halfway and the stylized representation of open palms placed flat on the ground below. A slender neck grew up from the torso and, above that, a head in perfect proportion with the body—hairless, faceless, nothing but the noble contour of a shapely domed cranium, tilted backward a little so that Gaia was looking toward the Earth. As the whole ensemble took shape on the computer, Lynn suffered stomach cramps and cold sweats, but she patiently took on the next challenge: how to use as much glass as possible while keeping the best possible protection against radiation. She declared that Gaia's "face" should be transparent, that she wanted to put the bars and restaurants in the head, while the back of the head could be clad and reinforced, where the chefs ruled their roost. There should be glass all over the throat and the curve of the breasts, where the suites were. The showpiece was to be a huge Gothic window in the belly, four levels housing reception, casino, tennis courts, and sauna, then glassed-in shins, and viewing platforms on the outside of the arms. Julian complained that the great window reminded him of having to go to church, back when he couldn't object or resist. Lynn replaced the Gothic point with a Romanesque arch, and the window stayed.

All the rest—back and shoulder, ribs and neck, the top of the thighs and the inside of the arms—was clad with armored cast-concrete slabs made from regolith, reinforced with sheet-glass sandwiches that held water between the panes to absorb particles and minimize heat loss. If the Americans were agreeable, the concrete was to be manufactured in the existing production facilities at the North Pole, made without water just by heating up the moon rock and casting it into construction-ready components at an automated factory. Mooncrete was said to be ten times more robust than ordinary concrete, resisting erosion, cosmic rays, and micrometeorites, and it was also cheap.

Gaia's skeleton took shape. The spine was a massive main column enclosing all the cables and ducts that the building would need, as well as three high-speed elevators. Steel ribs sprouted from the column to bear the individual floors and the outer skin, and the secondary supports were anchored deep in the rock of the plateau. There didn't seem to be any need for cross-bracing until somebody realized that the structure would be subject to much greater stresses than initial sketches suggested, since it was surrounded by vacuum, with no atmospheric resistance to the pressure of the artificial atmosphere within. Several assumptions had to be rejected, all the parameters frantically recalculated, until the experts declared that the problem had been solved. Since then, Lynn had had a new nightmare scenario to add to her visions of the end: a hotel that would at some moment suddenly go pop.

But Gaia shone.

She glowed from within, and she glowed with the help of the powerful floodlights that bathed her flawless snow-white exterior in white light. After years of struggle, Lynn had managed it. She had finished building the woman of Julian's dream, at least for the most part. Some of the lower-end rooms still lacked plumbing, the multi-religious chapel at the bend of Gaia's knees needed redundant life-support systems if it was to comply with all safety standards, and as for the banal detail of a spaceport, perhaps they would build one later to allow direct connections between Gaia and the OSS. On the other hand, the Lunar Express beat any direct approach hands down. It was undeniably more fun to arrive by train, and apart from that, they had a launch field for point-to-point flights on the Moon itself. It was all fine.

Except inside Lynn's skull.

Gaia had collapsed so often in her nightmares that she had come to long for the day when catastrophe would come. A whole office full of certificates and affidavits swore that it would never happen, but she knew better. The thought that there was something she had overlooked had driven her mad, and madness was destructive.

None of you is safe, she thought, and introduced the woman—

"—who will be looking after your comfort and security around the clock, together with her team. My dear friends, I'm delighted to introduce you to our hotel director, or should I say the manager here at Gaia, Dana Lawrence."

The Lunar Express had arrived at the hotel's station on schedule. They had run along the edge of the canyon for a while, so that they could enjoy the astonishing view of the building opposite, then crossed over at the further end and approached Gaia in a long, wide curve. Just in front of the hotel the ground sloped upward, so the builders had chosen not to take the rails straight up but to bring them into a tunnel, with the station itself underground. The track ended 300 meters beyond the gigantic figure, in a bare hall. This time there was no vacuum as they disembarked. They walked along passageways and into a wide pressurized corridor, with conveyor bands on the floor which brought them directly under the hotel, then from there to the elevators and up to the lobby, where islands of seating and elegant writing-desks made up one organic landscape. Fish glided behind aquarium panes. Perky little trees bursting with foliage flanked a curving reception desk, and above it holographic projections of the planets circled a bright central star, a model of the solar system with a sun in the middle spewing plasma from its surface. When the guests looked upward, they could see the great hall vanishing in a nest of crisscrossing glass bridges. Since the reception hall was here in Gaia's glass-fronted belly, with the huge Romanesque window arching in front, there was something cathedral-like about it. They looked out across the canyon to the sunlight on the other side and the pillars of the maglev marching away into the distance. The Earth shone up in the sky, a vision of home.

Dana Lawrence nodded at the group of guests.

She had searching gray-green eyes, an oval face and copper-colored hair worn shoulder-length. Her high cheekbones and perfectly arched brows gave her an air of British reserve, almost of unapproachability. Even the sensual curve of her lips did little to change that. Only when she took the trouble to smile was the impression dispelled, but Dana was not overly generous with her smiles. She knew exactly what impression she made, and she knew that she came across as brisk, efficient, and serious—something that people flying all the way to the Moon appreciated.

"Thank you, Lynn," she said and took a step forward. "I hope you had a pleasant journey. As perhaps you know, in future this hotel will have two hundred guests and a hundred staff. Since you'll have the whole place to yourselves for the coming week, we've taken the liberty of cutting back on staff a little, though you won't feel the lack. Our staff are quite experienced in being able to cater to a guest's wishes before they've even been voiced. Sophie Thiel—"

She turned her head to a group of young people who stood there wreathed in smiles, all dressed in Orley Group colors. A girlish woman with freckles stepped forward.

"—is my right hand; she leads the housekeeping department and makes sure the life-support systems function without a hitch. Ashwini Anand—" a delicate, Indian-looking woman with a proud gaze nodded her head "—is responsible for room service and, together with Sophie, takes care of technology and logistics. In the past, astronauts had to endure all sorts of discomforts, first and foremost in their diet. It's been a long road from tube rations to the five-star meal, but you now have the choice between two excellent restaurants under the direction of our head chef Axel Kokoschka." A thickset, bashful man with a baby face and bald head lifted his right hand, shifting his weight from one foot to the other. "He's assisted by our sous-chef Michio Funaki, who will, among other things, be demonstrating how to make fresh-caught sushi on the Moon."

Funaki, a wiry man with a buzz-cut, bowed with his whole upper body.

"All four are highly qualified and have trained in some of the best hotels and kitchens in the world, on top of which they have had two years' experience on the Orley Space Station, making each of them a seasoned astronaut, and they know Gaia's systems just as thoroughly as they know all the transport options hereabouts. In future Sophie, Ashwini, Axel, and Michio will be the middle management here in Gaia, but for the next few days they are exclusively at your service. The same is true of me. Please don't hesitate to speak to me if you have any concerns. It's an honor to have you here as our guests, and we are extremely pleased to see you."

A smile, almost infinitely diluted.

"If there are no further questions for the moment, I would like to show you the hotel. In one hour, at 20:30, we will expect you for dinner in the Selene."

• • •

Under the lobby was the casino, a ballroom with a stage, a cocktail bar, and gambling tables; one floor below began Gaia's lower belly, and the female shape spread out wider at the hips, so that to everyone's astonishment they found two tennis courts waiting for them.

"There are two more outside," said Dana. "For hard-core players. It's no problem playing in space suits, but the trouble comes with the balls. Here on the Moon they can fly hundreds of meters at a time, so we've fenced those courts in."

"How about golf?" Edwards asked.

"Golf on the Moon," said Mimi, giggling. "You'd never find the ball."

"Oh but you do," said Lynn. "We've tried it with tracking beacons in the balls. Via LPCS. It works."

"LP which?"

"Lunar Positioning and Communication System. There are ten satellites orbiting the Moon, letting us communicate and find our way about up here. The golf course is on the other side of the canyon, Shepard's Green. We also call it the 'satellite links.' "

"And who's it named after?" asked Karla.

"Dear old Alan Shepard," Julian laughed. "A real pioneer, he landed with Apollo 14 on the plateau south of Copernicus. The old rascal had actually brought a couple of golf balls along and a six iron head. He hit it and said it went for miles and miles and miles—"

"I most certainly will *not* be playing golf up here," said Aileen Donoghue, emphatically.

"It's not as bad as all that. He never went looking for his ball, but it can hardly have traveled more than 200 or 400 meters. Lunar golf is fun, but the trick of it is not to put too much into your swing."

"Don't they just sink down into the dust?"

"Too light," said Dana. "Try it sometime. We also have holographic tees here in the hotel. Would you like to see the spa?"

The sauna stretched out below the tennis courts, but most impressive of all was the swimming pool in Gaia's buttocks. It took up almost all the available area. The walls and ceiling simulated the starry sky, a hologram of the Earth glowed with a soft light, while the bottom of the pool and the floor all around were built to look like the lunar regolith, with rugged mountain chains on the horizon. The pool itself was a double crater, as large as a lake and surrounded by recliners. The illusion of bathing on the very surface of the Moon was practically perfect.

Heidrun turned her white face to O'Keefe and smiled. "So, who's a big hero? Ready for a race?"

"Any time."

"Careful! You know that I'm better."

"Just wait and see how things work out in reduced gravity," Ögi chuckled. "Could be I'll leave you both behind."

"All right then, you know we've just *got* to have a swimming race," Miranda announced, spreading her fingers. "I lo-o-o-o-ove being in the water."

"I got it. Huey and Dewey." O'Keefe lowered his eyes reverently. "Lord love a duck."

They visited the floor with the conference rooms, the multi-religious chapel, a meditation center, and a sickbay that gleamed reassuringly like a new pin, then up to Gaia's ribcage. The group all had rooms on floors fourteen to sixteen, in the outer curve of the breasts. The lobby lay almost 50 meters below them. To get to their suites from the elevators, they had to cross the glass bridges. More bridges on the lower floors were set at zigzag angles, obviously placed quite at random. None of them had a railing.

"Anyone suffer from vertigo?" asked Dana. Sushma Nair raised her hand, hesitantly. Some of the others looked disconcerted. This time Dana's smile was a little broader.

"Please understand. When you jump from a 2-meter-high wall on the Earth, you reach the ground 0.6 of a second later. During that time, your body has accelerated to 22 kilometers an hour. On the Moon, the same jump would take three times longer, and your final speed would be less than half. That's to say that you would have to jump from a height of 12 meters to get the same effect as a 2-meter jump on the Earth, or in other words, on the Moon you could happily jump from three floors up in an ordinary high-rise. This means that you really don't need to take the lift every time you want to go downstairs. Just jump from bridge to bridge; they're barely 4 meters apart, which is nothing. Anybody want to try?"

"I will," said Carl Hanna.

She gave him an appraising look. Tall, muscly, deliberate in his movements.

"The real experts can jump back up again," she added meaningfully.

Hanna grinned and walked onto the nearest bridge.

"If it turns out she was lying," he called to the others, "just throw her after me, okay?"

He sprang from the bridge with Donoghue's cackles of laughter following after. He fell, and landed 4 meters below without the slightest jar.

"Like jumping down from the curbstone," he called up.

In the next moment O'Keefe sailed out from the edge, then Heidrun. They both landed as though they had never moved any other way.

"My goodness," said Aileen, "My goodness!" and then looked at each of them in turn, with a "My goodness!" for everyone.

"C'mon, guys," Chucky boomed. "Show us what you're made of! Up you come!"

"You'll have to make room." Hanna shooed them away with a flap of his hands. They scurried backward. He looked thoughtfully up at the ledge. When he raised his arms, he was just about 2.5 meters tall, so there was still a 1.5 meters to make up.

"How tall are you?" O'Keefe asked, disconcerted.

"Six foot three."

"Hmm." The Irishman rubbed his chin. "I'm five foot nine."

"Could be a near thing. Heidrun?"

"One hundred and seventy-eight—five foot ten. Whatever. Whoever doesn't make it has to buy us all a meal."

"Forget it." O'Keefe waved the idea away. "It's all free here anyway."

"Then back on Earth. Hey, in Zurich! All right with that? A round of schnitzels in the Kronenhalle."

"Meaning all of us!" called Julian.

"Good, we'll all jump together," Hanna declared. "Make room, so we don't get in one another's way.—You guys up there, get back! Ready!"

"Yes, sir." Heidrun grinned. "Ready."

"And up we go!"

Hanna sprang powerfully upward. It looked astonishingly easy. As calmly as a superhero, he flew toward the ledge, grabbed hold, boosted himself up again, and landed on his feet. Next to him Heidrun fluttered down, struggling for balance. O'Keefe's hands threatened to slip off the edge of the bridge, then he clambered up, as elegantly as circumstances allowed.

"Sorry about that," he said. "Kronenhalle is cancelled."

"You're all invited anyway," Ögi called out, in the tones of a man who embraces the whole world. "This is the first time ever that a Swiss has taken a standing jump of 4 meters. We'll meet again in Zurich!"

"Optimist," said Lynn, so quietly that only Dana heard.

The hotel director was stunned. She acted as though she hadn't heard that wan little word with its insidious undertones.

What was the matter with Orley's daughter?

"Please bear in mind," she said out loud to the group, "that in reduced gravity your body will be losing muscle mass. There are two guest elevators here in Gaia, the E1 and E2, and a staff elevator, but we nevertheless recommend that you work out a lot and take the shortcut via the bridges as often as you can. Now we'll tell you a little more about the facilities and show you the rooms."

Hanna had Sophie Thiel show him all the secrets of his suite. There was no essential difference between the life-support systems here and those aboard the space station.

"The temperature is set to 68 degrees Fahrenheit, but that's adjustable," Sophie Thiel explained with a widescreen smile, pointing out a button by the door; she brushed so close past Hanna as she did so that it was only just within the limits of professionalism. "Your suite has its own water management system, with wonderfully sterile water—"

"Don't use words like that to the customers," Hanna said, looking around and at the same time feeling her hungry gaze on his back. No two ways about it, this Thiel woman liked muscular men. "It sounds as if you're setting out to poison somebody."

"Well then, let's just call it fresh water. Haha."

He turned to face her. Her eyes were half-moons, their color barely discernible; on the other hand she looked as if she had a double ration of bright white teeth and inexhaustible reserves of laughter. She was not the least bit beautiful, but very pretty for all that. A grown-up version of Pippi Longstocking, or whatever that Swedish minx was called. He had found the film on a Sunday afternoon at a hotel in Germany, while he was waiting for hours on end for to meet somebody who had been floating dead in the Rhine all the while, and he had watched it all the way through, curiously moved. A childish, clunky old three-reeler, but the childhood it showed him was so amazingly different from his own that it was practically science fiction. He found himself unable to change channels. He'd never watched a kids' movie before, or at least never one like this.

And he'd never watched another one.

Thiel showed him how the lighting was controlled, opened up a respectable minibar, and told him the numbers to call if he needed anything. The look in her eyes said, *if only things were different. I've worked in the best hotels in the world. Never with guests.* You could hardly say that she put herself forward. She was friendly and professional; it's just that she was also an open book.

But Hanna wasn't here for fun and games.

"If there's anything else you'd like—"

"No, not at the moment. I'll manage."

"Oh, I almost forgot! You'll find your moon slippers in the bottom of the closet." She wrinkled her nose. "We couldn't think of a better name for them. They have lead plates in the soles, in case you want additional weight."

"Why would I want that?"

"Some people prefer to move on the Moon the way they move on Earth."

"I see! Very farsighted of you."

The look in her eyes said, *unless you take a bit of trouble.*

"Well then—until half past eight, in the Selene."

"Yes. Thank you."

He waited until she'd gone. The suite displayed the same discreet, elegant sense of style as the lobby. Hanna didn't know a great deal about design, nothing in fact, but even he could tell that this was the work of experts. After all, he'd had to learn a little about style and appearances to take on this role. Also, he liked clean lines, simple rooms. Much as he loved India, he had always felt rather hemmed in by the local sense of decor, the way they crowded every surface with knick-knacks.

His gaze swept over to the window that took up the whole wall.

They couldn't have found a better place for the hotel, he thought. The plateau below Gaia could be reached by elevator, and from here he saw it stretching away toward the canyon, its tennis courts lost and lonely. You must have a fantastic view of the hotel from down there, it would look like a floodlit sculpture. Over on the left, where the cliffs dropped back and the canyon closed, a natural-seeming path curved away to the other side.

What was it that Julian Orley had said just now? Over on the other side of the Lunar Express tracks was the golf course.

A golf course on the Moon!

Suddenly Hanna felt a touch of regret that he wasn't actually here as the person everybody thought he was. He crushed the feeling before it could get to work on him, opened his silver suitcase and delved into it for his computer, a touchscreen device of the usual sort, no bigger than a chocolate bar, and his toiletry bag. He took an electric trimmer from the depths of the bag. With a practiced twist, he clicked the trimmer apart and took out a tiny circuit board, which he plugged into the computer. Whistling tunelessly, he booted up and watched as the program uploaded and hooked into the LPCS.

A few seconds later the device alerted him that he had a message.

He opened his mail server. The message was from a friend, reminding him not to forget Dexter and Stacey's wedding. Unimpressed by the pending nuptials of a couple who didn't exist anyway, he filtered out the white noise that made up the rest of the message and came up with a few more lines of text, nothing more than the addresses of several dozen Internet sites. Then he uploaded a symbol—snaking reptilian necks, twisted and knotted together, all growing from a single body—and waited a moment.

Something was happening.

Words and syllables slotted together with lightning speed. The actual message took shape before his eyes. Even while the reconstruction was still under way, he knew there had been trouble. The text was short, but peremptory:

The package has been damaged. It is no longer responding to commands and cannot reach deployment under its own power. This changes your mission. You will repair the package or bring the contents to operational destination yourself. If circumstances permit, you can bring forward insertion. Act swiftly!

Swiftly.

Hanna stared at the display. The implications were quite clear, as present as an unwelcome visitor. Swiftly meant now, or as soon as possible without arousing suspicion. It meant that he would have to leave and then return while everybody was asleep.

Back to Peary Base.

TABLE TALK

Since they had made love free-floating in orbit, Tim had spared Amber any further speculation about the state of Lynn's mental health, and tried to convince himself that he was showing consideration for his wife, since she was so grimly determined to enjoy the trip; in fact it was because he was quite busy enough grappling with his own dilemmas. More and more he found himself enjoying a trip that he had resolved wholeheartedly to hate, considering the way the trip had been arranged and Julian's arrogant and high-handed part in it. And the more he was having fun, the more he felt a creeping adolescent sense of betrayal. He was susceptible, he had been corrupted, and by a ticket! He tried to persuade himself that it was only the overwhelming experiences and impressions that somehow, against all expectation, made him like the old snake-charmer. Hadn't he been dead set on hating Julian, the megalomaniac, who couldn't see that he trampled other people underfoot on his march into the future? Who neglected his nearest and dearest, or put them on pedestals, who couldn't understand that they needed a drop of normality in their lives?

It would have been so wonderfully simple just to hate him.

But the Julian he had gotten to know in the narrow confines of the spaceship unnerved him by *not* being ignorant and egomaniacal, or at least not enough to bear out Tim's sweeping condemnation. Rather, he reminded Tim of his childhood, when he had admired Dad so much. Reminded him of Crystal, who right up to the very moment her sanity had finally crumbled away had insisted that she had never known a more loving man than his father, who had called him her sunbeam, bringing her happiness—all too quickly, before he was gone again. She had praised and admired him, and an hour before she died, he had taken to the skies in a suborbital craft of his own design, slipping away into the thermosphere even though he knew how critical her condition was. He had known it—and had forgotten just long enough to break a record, win a prize, and earn his son's everlasting enmity.

Lynn had forgiven Julian.

Tim had not.

Instead he had been hard at work on demonizing the man. And even now he couldn't forgive Julian, even if, or perhaps even because, he could see the pillars that held up his hatred crumbling away. This hotel couldn't have been built solely out of greed and a ruinous sense of self-aggrandizement. There must be more behind it, a dream too overpowering to be shared with only a few family members. Whether he wanted to or not, secretly he was beginning to understand the old guy, the fever in his blood that made him push back all boundaries, his nomadic nature that let him blaze trails where others only saw dead ends, his passionate attachment to progress, innovation, and he began to grow jealous of Julian's great love, the world. And as this change of mind smoldered away below the surface of all he thought he had believed, he felt uncomfortably aware that perhaps he was overreacting where Lynn was concerned, perhaps—without ever intending to!—he was using her as an excuse to get at Julian, that in fact he cared less about her happiness than about Julian's guilt. He flirted with the idea that perhaps she really did feel as fine as she was always claiming, and that he had no reason to feel ashamed of mellowing toward his dad. And suddenly, over dinner in Gaia's nose, or rather where her nose would be if she had one, with the magnificent view of the canyon before his eyes, he wanted nothing more than just to be allowed to have fun, without the ghosts of his past sitting down at table with him, the ghosts that brought out the worst in him.

"It looks like you're enjoying that," Amber said appreciatively.

They were seated at a long table in Selene, with its black-blue-silver decor, eating red mullet with a saffron risotto. The fish tasted fresh-caught, as though it had just come from the sea.

"Bred in salt water," Axel Kokoschka, the chef, informed them. "We've got great big underground tanks."

"Isn't it rather complicated to re-create ocean conditions up here?" asked Karla Kramp. "I mean, you don't just tip salt into the water?"

Kokoschka considered the question. "Not just that, no."

"Salinity varies from one biotope to the next down on Earth, doesn't it? Doesn't it take a particular chemical composition to make an environment where animal life can thrive? Chloride, sulfate, sodium, traces of calcium, potassium, iodine, and so on."

"Fish has to feel at home, yes, that's right."

"I just want to know what's what. Don't a great many fish need a permanent current, a steady oxygen supply, constant temperature, all of that?"

Kokoschka nodded thoughtfully, rubbed his bald head with a shy smile, scratched industriously at his three-day beard. He said, "Quite," and vanished. Karla watched him go, flummoxed.

"Thanks for the explanation!" she called after him.

"Not exactly a great talker, is he?" grinned Tim.

She speared a piece of mullet and made it vanish between her Modigliani lips.

"If he can make a fish taste like this up here on the Moon, for all I care he can cut his own tongue out."

Two restaurants and two bars took up four floors in Gaia's head, their front walls all of glass. The panes curved right the way around to where the temples would be, so that there were widescreen views all around. Selene and Chang'e, the two restaurants, were in the lower half, with the Luna Bar above them, and right up at the top was the Mama Quilla Club for dancing under the stars. From there a glassed-in air lock led to the topmost point of the whole hotel, a viewing terrace which could only be entered in a space suit, offering a spectacular 360-degree view. Koksochka's shyness aside, he served the group of guests with exemplary attention, as did Ashwini Anand, Michio Funaki, and Sophie Thiel. Lynn was praised from all sides for her hotel. She let her own food go cold as she cheerfully doled out information, answered questions at length, in high spirits and visibly flattered by the attention. For a while there was no other topic of conversation but this strange new world they now walked upon, Gaia, and the quality of the food.

Then the focus of talk shifted.

"Chang'e," said Mukesh Nair thoughtfully over the main course, venison with truffles, served with wafer-thin slices of toast that gleamed as the foie gras melted on them. "Isn't that a term from the Chinese space program?"

"Yes and no." Rogachev took a swig of the low-alcohol Château Palmer. "There were a few probes of that name; the Chinese sent them up to explore the Moon at the beginning of the century. But in fact it's a mythological figure."

"Chang'e, the moon goddess," Lynn nodded.

"Gaia seems to have a head full of myths then," smiled Nair. "Selene was the Greek moon goddess, wasn't she? And Luna was the goddess in ancient Rome—"

"Even I know that," said Miranda gleefully. "Luna, and then Sol the sun god, the jerk. Eternal gods, y'know, up, down, round and round, never stopping. One comes home and the other one leaves, like a married couple working different shifts."

"The sun and Moon. Shift workers." Rogachev twitched his lips in a smile. "That makes sense."

"I am so interested in gods and astrology! The stars tell us our future, you know." She leaned forward, overshadowing the venison scraps on her plate with the great twin stars of her breasts, which she had poured into some shimmering scrap of almost nothing for the evening. "And do you know what? You want to hear something else?" She stabbed the air with her fork. "Some of them, the ones that really had a clue what was going on in ancient Rome, they called her Noctiluca, they lit up a temple all for her, at night on the Palatine, that's one of the hills in the city. I've been there, y'know, Rome's full of hills, not a city up in the hills though, it's a city *on* the hills, if you get me."

"You should tell us more about your travels," Nair said amiably. "What does Noctiluca mean?"

"The one who lights up the night," Miranda said solemnly, and rewarded herself with an uncommonly large gulp of red wine.

"And Mama Quilla?"

"Somebody's mom, I'd guess.—Julian, what's Mama Quilla?"

"Well, we were rather running out of moon goddesses," said Julian with relish, "but then Lynn dug up a few more, Ningal, the wife of Sin, the Assyrian god of the Moon; Annit, she was Babylonian; Kusra from Arabia, Isis from Egypt—"

"But we liked Mama Quilla most of all," Lynn spoke across him. "Mother Moon, an Inca goddess. Even today the heirs of the Inca culture worship her as the protector of married women—"

"Oh really?" Olympiada Rogacheva pricked up her ears. "I think the bar might turn out to be my favorite place."

Rogachev didn't bat an eye.

"I find it surprising that you considered using the Chinese moon goddess," said Nair, picking up the thread again hastily before the embarrassment could spread.

"Why not?" asked Julian artlessly. "Are we prejudiced?"

"Well, you are China's greatest competitor!"

"Not me, Mukesh. You mean the United States."

"Yes, of course. But nevertheless, sitting here at this table I see Americans, Canadians, English and Irish, Germans, Swiss, Russians and Indians, and until a while ago we had the pleasure of our French friends' company. But I don't see a single Chinese person."

"Don't worry, they're here," said Rogachev equably. "Unless I'm much mistaken, they're not 1,000 kilometers from here, southwest, busy digging away at the regolith."

"But they're not *here*."

"No Chinese investor has shown an interest in our project," said Julian. "They want their own elevator."

"Don't we all?" remarked Rogachev,

"Yes, but as you have rightly pointed out, unlike Moscow, Beijing is already mining helium-3."

"Talking of the elevator." Ögi scooped up foie gras onto the dark-red meat. "Is it true that they're just about to make the breakthrough?"

"The Chinese?"

"Mmhmm."

"They make that announcement with admirable regularity." Julian smiled knowingly. "If it were actually the case, Zheng Pang-Wang would not take every opportunity he can find to drink tea with me."

"But—" Mukesh Nair propped himself up on his elbows and massaged his imposingly fleshy nose "—isn't it the case that your American friends would take lasting umbrage if you were to flirt with the Chinese, especially after the Moon crisis last year? I mean to say, are you perhaps not quite so free in your decisions as you would like to be?"

Julian pursed his lips. His face darkened, as always when he set out to explain the extent of his independence of all government power. Then he spread his arms in a fatalistic gesture.

"Just look, what's the reason you're all here? Even though the nation-states all make a big noise about how effective their space programs are, they would leap at the chance to get in line with the Americans if the offer were ever made. Or let's say, they'd try to deal as equal partners, meaning that they would pump money into NASA's budget and then they'd get to stake their claims. But the offer's never made, and there's a very good reason for that.—There's an alternative, though. You can support *me*, and this offer is exclusively reserved for private investors. I'm not selling know-how, but I'm inviting participation. Whoever joins in can earn a great deal of money but can't give away any formulas or blueprints. That's why my partners in Washington are prepared to put up with this little dinner party of ours. They know that none of your countries are going to be building a space elevator in the foreseeable future, let alone developing the infrastructure to extract helium-3. There's no technological basis, there's no budget, in short, there's nothing at all. Evidently, people such as yourselves would only ever lose money by investing in your own national space programs at home. Which is why Washington is ready to believe that we're just talking about shares and investment here.—It's a different matter with China though. Beijing has *built* the infrastructure! They're *mining* the helium-3! They've laid their groundwork, but they are working with old-fashioned technology, which limits them. That's their dilemma. They've already come too far to hitch themselves to another partner, but they simply don't have the blasted elevator! Believe me, under the circumstances there's not one Chinese politician or investor who would put even a single yuan into my hands, unless of course—"

"They could buy you," Evelyn Chambers cut in. She was following several conversations at once. "Which is why Zheng Pang-Wang drinks tea with you."

"If there were a Chinese dinner guest at the table tonight, he certainly wouldn't be here intending to invest. Washington would conclude that I was taking offers for a transfer of know-how."

"Don't they already think that, given that you meet with Zheng?" asked Nair.

"People meet all the time in this industry. At congresses, symposia. So what? Zheng's an entertaining old rogue, I like him."

"But your friends are getting nervous anyway, aren't they?"

"They're always nervous."

"They're right to be. Anybody who gets up here will start digging." Ögi wiped his bristling mustache and threw the napkin down by his plate. "Why don't you do it though, Julian?"

"What? Switch sides?"

"No, no. Nobody's talking about switching sides. I mean, why don't you just sell the space elevator technology to any country that wants to buy, and then you'd be rolling in gold? There'd be healthy competition up here on the Moon, and that would be a real boost to your reactor business. You could secure shares in the extraction side of things worldwide, you could negotiate exclusive contracts for the electricity supply, just as our absent friend Tautou controls fresh water. They sign him over whole aquifers in exchange for treatment plants and supply chain."

"Meaning that you would not switch from one dependent position to another," said Rogachev, taking up the idea, "but everybody would depend on *you*." He raised his glass to Julian, slightly mocking. "A true philanthropist."

"And how is that supposed to work?" Rebecca Hsu broke in.

"Why not?" asked Ögi.

"You want to let China, Japan, Russia, India, Germany, France, and who knows else all have access to the elevator technology?"

"Pay for access," Rogachev corrected her.

"It's a bad plan, Oleg. It wouldn't take long for all of them to be knocking heads up here."

"It's a big moon."

"No, it's a small moon. So small that my neighbors in Red China and your American friend, Julian, have nothing better to do with their time than make for the same place to mine in, am I right? It only needed *two* nations," she said, holding up index finger and middle finger, "to start a squabble which is euphemistically described as the Moon crisis. The world was on the brink of armed superpower confrontation, and that wasn't much fun."

"Why did the two of them go to the same place?" Miranda asked ingenuously. "Accidentally?"

"No." Julian shook his head. "Because measurements suggest that the border region between the Oceanus Procellarum and the Mare Imbrium has unusually high concentrations of helium-3, the type you'd usually find only on the dark side of the Moon. There's a bay, the Sinus Iridum, next door and east of the Montes Jura, which seems to be similarly rich in deposits. So obviously everybody claims the right to mine there."

Rebecca furrowed her brow. "And how's that going to be any different with more nations?"

"It should be. If we can divide the Moon up before the gold rush starts. But you're right of course, Rebecca. You're all right. I have to admit that I applaud the idea that space travel should be the concern of the whole human race."

"Perfectly understandable," smiled Nair. "You will only profit from the good cause."

"And us too, of course," Ögi said emphatically.

"Yes, it's a noble ideal." Rogachev put down his cutlery. "There's only one problem, Julian."

"Which is?"

"How to survive such a shift of opinion."

Hanna

Small chocolate cakes, served lukewarm, released a gush of heavy, dark sauce when cut open, flooding out into the colorful fruit purees surrounding them. At about ten o'clock a leaden tiredness descended over the table. Julian announced that the next morning was free time, after which everybody could enjoy the hotel facilities to their heart's content or take a look around the lunar surface nearby. There would be no longer excursions until the day after. Dana Lawrence inquired as to whether everything was to their satisfaction. They all had words of praise, Hanna included.

"And I still don't think that Cobain would mean anything to the kids today if we hadn't made that film," O'Keefe insisted in the elevator. "Just look where grunge has ended up. On the 'lousy music' shelves. Nobody's interested in guys like him anymore. The kids prefer to listen to the artificial stuff, The Week that Was, Ipanema Party, Overload—"

"You used to play grunge with your own band though," said Hanna.

"Yes, and I gave up. My God, I think I was ten years old when Cobain died. I wonder what the hell he meant to me."

"Don't give me that! You played the guy."

"I could play Napoleon as well, you know, doesn't mean I'm going to try to rule all Europe. It's always been like that, people think that whoever their heroes are at the time, they must be important. *Important!* There are always *important* albums in pop music, then twenty years later not a living soul has heard of them."

"Great music stays alive."

"Bullshit. Who knows Prince these days? Who knows Axl Rose? Keith Richards, the only thing we know about him is that he was a mediocre guitar player for a beer-hall band whose songs all sounded the same. Believe you me, the gods of pop are overrated. All stars are overrated. No two ways. We don't go down in history, we just go down to the grave. Unless of course you commit suicide or get shot."

"And why does everyone these days draw on the works of the seventies and eighties? If what you say is true, then—"

"Okay, it just happens to be in fashion."

"Has been for a while."

"And what does that prove? In ten years' time there'll be another nine days' wonder. Nucleosis, for instance, that kind of thing keeps coming around again, two women and a computer, and the computer composes about half their stuff."

"There's always been computers."

"Not always as the composer though. I'm telling you, day after tomorrow, all the stars will be machines."

"Nonsense. They used to say that twenty-five years ago. What came back? Singer-songwriting. Hand-made music will never die."

"Could be. Could be we're just too old. Good night."

"G'night, Finn."

Hanna crossed the bridge to his suite and went in. He'd dutifully followed all the conversations as the evening went on, without getting caught up in complicated discussions. For a while he'd tried to share Eva Borelius's passion for horses, and then had steered her toward music, only to find himself bogged down in German Romanticism, about which he knew less than nothing. O'Keefe saved him with a few remarks about the comatose condition of Britpop at the end of the nineties, about Mando Prog and psychobilly, just the thing to talk about when your thoughts were elsewhere, and Hanna's thoughts really were. Everyone would go off to sleep soon, that much was clear. Back on board the spaceship they had been warned that there'd be a price to pay for the days in zero gravity, the exertions of landing, their bodies adjusting and the flood of new experiences. The bedroom was clad with a mooncrete slab at bed height, so that in an hour at latest, nobody would be looking outside at all, and the staff lived below ground anyway.

Time to wait.

He lay down on the comically thin mattress that was nevertheless enough to support him comfortably here, weighing only 35 pounds as he did; he put his hands behind his head and shut his eyes for a moment. If he stayed lying here, he'd fall asleep, besides which he still had plenty to do before he set out. Whistling gently, he went back into the living room and stroked his guitar case. He strummed a brief flamenco, then turned his instrument over on his knees, felt around the edges, pressed here and there, removed the clasp where the strap clipped on and lifted up the whole back.

There was a thin sheet of material fixed to it, exactly the shape of the guitar body, covered with a tracery of fine lines. Orley's security team hadn't examined his luggage, as they would have done with regular tourists, but had just asked a few polite questions. Nobody had even dreamed of doubting that his guitar was just a guitar. Julian's guests were above all suspicion, but nevertheless the organization had not wanted to take any risks; however, an X-ray would merely have revealed that the instrument had a thicker back than usual. Only an expert would have recognized even this, and certainly wouldn't have known that it was because it was made of two boards lying on top of one another, and that the inner board was made of a special and extremely resistant material.

With both thumbs, he began to press pieces from the sheet. They popped out with a gentle click and fell to the floor, where they lay scattered like the parts of some kind of intelligence test. Next he took the neck of the guitar off the main body and slid out a pipe, 40 centimeters long, and snapped this into two equal parts. Several narrower sections of pipe fell out and rolled over the carpet. Hanna swept them together into a heap, opened his suitcase and emptied the contents of his toiletry bag in front of him. He put the shower gel, the shampoo, and the kneadable earplugs all within reach, pulled the top off one of his two tubes of moisturizer, squeezed a clear stream of what was inside onto one of the components and then pressed another against it. Right away the moisturizing cream and the plastic panel pieces reacted chemically with one another. Hanna knew that at this stage he couldn't afford the slightest mistake, that there was no way of adjusting what he built. He worked with clarity and concentration, without haste, then unscrewed one of the golf balls, took out tiny electronic components, assembled more parts and slotted them into place. In a few minutes he was holding something flat in his hands, a device with a pipe sticking out from the front like the muzzle of a pistol, which indeed it was. It looked curiously archaic. It had a grip, but instead of a trigger, there was simply a switch. Hanna took the remaining pieces and built an identical device, examined both weapons thoroughly and then went on to the next stage of his work.

Here he took apart various bits of kit from his toiletry bag and then put them back together in a different order until he had made twenty projectiles, each with chambers that had to be filled separately. Working with the utmost care, he put tiny quantities of the shower gel into the left chambers, and shampoo into the right, and then sealed the capsules. He took the short shells from the neck of the guitar and put into each one a piece of earplug and a small gelatin capsule from a pack of indigestion tablets. Last of all, he put a payload into the tip of each shell, loading five into the handle of the first weapon he had built and then five into the second. Then he put the base of the guitar back onto the body, fastening the neck in place with an expert twist. He collected the last scraps left over from the plastic sheet and shoved them under everything else in his suitcase. He packed the tubes and bottles back into the toiletry bag, and then paused as he picked up the aftershave.

Ah yes.

He looked at the bottle thoughtfully. Then he lifted the cap, held it up in front of his throat, and pressed the nozzle briefly, firmly.

The aftershave was aftershave.

Nobody crossed his path as he left the suite.

He was wearing a space suit, harness, and survival pack; his helmet was clamped under his arm. One of the loaded guns was nestled against his thigh, hidden in a pocket of the same material as the space suit so that nobody would notice it. He was also carrying five loose rounds of ammunition. Granted, he hardly expected to need to use the pistol tonight. If everything went as planned, he would never be forced to use it at all, but experience had taught him that errors could creep into the tidiest plan with the persistence of cockroaches. Some time or other the gun could turn out to be very useful indeed. From now on, it would be with him at all times.

With nobody around, Gaia's vast body breathed the atmosphere of a monument that had outlived its builders. Far below lay the deserted lobby. He waited for the doors of E2 to slide apart, entered the cabin and pressed 01. The elevator zoomed down to the underground level. He got out in the basement and followed the signs to the wide corridor they had come along just a few hours before, empty here as well, bathed in cold white light and filled with a monotonous hum. Hanna stepped onto one of the conveyor bands. It started up, passing the air locks that led up to the lunar surface, then the vast hallway that led to the garage—as the hotel's underground landing field was called—then a branch corridor to a narrow tunnel, 2 kilometers long, leading dead straight to the small helium-3 reactor that supplied Gaia's energy during the lunar night. At the end of the corridor, he stepped off the conveyor and looked through a window into the station hall. The Lunar Express was sitting on its tracks, linked to the corridor via passageways. He went inside the train and walked down between the empty seats to the driver's chair. The on-board computer was activated, the display all lit up. Hanna entered a code and waited for authorization. Then he turned around, took a seat in the first row, and stretched out his legs.

He would have been able to do none of this if he had been just a regular guest. But Ebola had got everything ready for him. Ebola made sure that there was nothing Carl Hanna couldn't do here on the Moon, no locked doors, no access forbidden.

Slowly, the Lunar Express drew out.

In his forty-four years of life so far Hanna had grown well used to keeping things clear-cut. In India he had taken part in a whole series of covert operations that would hardly have marked him as a friend of the country if he had been exposed. At the same time he had a circle of local friends and lived with Indian women. He worked against his hosts' interests, undermining the federal democracy's economic and military autonomy, but unlike many of his colleagues he didn't spend his time in cheap bars, seedy joints, or expensive clubs that held a liquor license. He didn't tip toddy, or whisky down his gullet, or make racist remarks about the locals when he thought nobody was listening. Instead he took care to integrate himself; he rented a neat little apartment in the heart of New Delhi and developed a passion for curries and the spice market. He wasn't by nature a man who made friends quickly, but over the years the country's culture and people grew on him, and for a while he even flirted with the idea of settling down on the banks of the Yamuna. His job required a talent to deceive and a steady stream of lies, but if he wasn't actually at work, he tried to live an absolutely normal life out there, following the country's motto *Satyameva Jayate*, "Truth alone shall prevail." He felt no contradiction in such a two-faced existence; rather it helped him, Hanna the citizen, break all connections with Hanna the consummate liar, so that they never got in one another's way.

And now too he was enjoying the ride even with the task ahead of him; he enjoyed the unending vistas of the Mare Imbrium, the play of shadows over Plato, the rugged threat of the polar mountains drawing closer, the train's rapid climb. Once more the darkness of the crater's shadow engulfed him as the train raced along the chasm between Peary and Hermite, toward the American moon base, at 700 kilometers an hour.

Then, without warning, it slowed.

And stopped.

The Lunar Express clung to a lonely mountainside amid the no man's land of the polar craters, less than 50 kilometers from the base. Hanna stood up and went to the middle of the train, where lockers lined the aisle. He rolled up the door of one of these and glanced briefly at the box of kit stored behind it, then studied the assembly plan on the back wall. He heaved down an oval platform with folding telescopic legs and eight little spherical tanks. It had short arms with nozzles that could turn in all directions, and two loaded battery packs. A thick column rising from the platform ended in a crossbar with handgrips, between which a display gleamed. It was simplicity itself to assemble the thing: after all the grasshopper had been designed for emergencies, when the tour guide might be incapacitated and the guests had to cope for themselves. When it was fully built it stood on coiled legs and had enough room for two astronauts, the one in front steering. Hanna walked it over to the air lock, went back to the locker, took out a toolbox and a device with a readout screen, and stored both under a hatch on the grasshopper's floor. Then he put on his helmet and let the suit carry out the usual diagnostics before he started evacuation. A few seconds later the outer bulkhead opened. He climbed onto the grasshopper, took out his computer, clipped it on at the side of the control panel, and opened the outer hatch.

The device with the readout began to sweep and search.

Calmly, he punched coordinates into the grasshopper. The LPCS would help him find the package. He was relieved to see that it was still communicating, for otherwise there would have been no chance of finding it in this wasteland of rifts and chasms. The electronic systems were all working, so the problem must be mechanical. A burst of propulsion, and the grasshopper lifted and accelerated. If he wasn't to lose height he constantly had to create lift, while the nozzles twisted and turned to steer him. A flyer like the grasshopper was by its nature limited to a certain radius, but it was an advantage here that there was no air to provide lift for winged flyers—it meant that there was also no atmospheric pressure to brake the grasshopper once it got started. It had a top speed of 80 kilometers an hour, and the little round tanks could carry it an astonishing distance.

The signal was reaching him from just 6 kilometers away. Here in the shadow of the crater wall he was as good as blind, and totally dependent on the weak cones of light from his headlamps, racing ahead as though trying to lose him. Only the grasshopper's radar system kept him from colliding with cliff edges or overhangs. A good distance away, the sunny expanses of the lowland plain met the sharp black line of the mountain shadow, and high above him blinding sunlight capped the peaks of the crater ridge. The tracks of the Lunar Express had a way back swung off between the cliffs to the next valley and the gentle plain that led up to the heights of Peary. The package should long since have been under way there of its own accord, but its signal called to Hanna from the other direction entirely, deep in the crater base.

He choked back his lift. The grasshopper lost height, its fingers of light showing deeply rutted rock. Huge sharp-edged blocks of stone reared up around him, unnerving indications that an avalanche had thundered down into the valley here not long ago—no, not thundered, had tumbled down in utter silence—then the landscape leveled off and the receiver told him that he had reached his destination. Just a few more meters.

Hanna activated the braking jets and peered around with his headlamps for a place to land. Obviously he hadn't reached the foot of the crater wall here. The surface below was still too rubble-strewn and fissured to set the grasshopper down safely. By the time he had finally found a halfway level stretch, he was forced to hike back, leaping and sliding, a kilometer and a half, constantly at risk of losing his balance and slicing open his space suit on the razor-sharp blocks of stone all around. The beam from his helmet lamp wandered aimlessly over heaps of colorless rubble. Several times he had to fight for balance, raising clouds of the fine powdery moon dust, charged with static that made it cling stubbornly to his legs. Gravel leaped out of his path, uncannily alive, and then the ground below him simply stopped, and the light was drowned in featureless blackness. He halted where he was, switched off the helmet lamp, opened his eyes wide, and waited.

The effect was overwhelming.

A billion points of light in the Milky Way above him. No light pollution from any artificial source. Only the grasshopper far behind, a glowing dot marking its position. Hanna was as alone on the Moon as a human being could ever be. Nothing that he had ever experienced came even close, and for a while he even forgot his mission. That membrane that divides a human being from the experiential universe around him melted away. He became bodiless, at one with the nondual world. All things were Hanna, all things were at rest within him, and he was within all things. He remembered a sadhu, a monk, telling him years ago that if he wished, he could drink the Indian Ocean dry at one gulp, a claim that Hanna had found cryptic at the time. And now he was standing here—was he standing?—drinking in the whole universe.

He waited.

After a while the hoped-for change set in, and the darkness proved less impenetrable than he had feared. There were photons traveling within it, reflected from the sunlit crater wall opposite that lunged upward from the plain. His surroundings took shape like a photograph in a bath of developing fluid, more a matter of intuition than perception, but it was enough to reveal that what he had thought to be a slope at his feet was only a sinkhole, which he could get around with just a few steps. He switched the headlamp back on. The spell was banished. He had come back to his senses and set out, keeping an eye on the computer display screen, so deep in concentration that he only saw the object when he was practically on top of it.

A heavy rod, rearing upward!

Hanna tottered, dropping his toolkit and receiver. What was that? The beacon was at least 300 meters out! The thing had almost shattered his visor. Cursing, he began to work his way around it. A little later he knew that it was no fault of the beacon's. This heap of scrap was irrelevant. It was a four-legged transporter crate, its tanks burned out, lying on its side and partially hidden by rubble. His mission had been to pick up the contents, what the organization called the package, the part of the delivery that was actually sending the signal, and bring it to the pole.

But the package wasn't here.

It had to be further down.

When he finally found it, jammed in between boulders, it was a sorry sight. Parts of the side panel had opened up and legs and nozzles sprouted from within, some of them twisted or snapped. Fuel tanks clung to the underbelly like fat insect eggs. Obviously the package had begun to unfold and come to life as it had been designed to do, in order to make its way to deployment, when something unforeseen had happened.

And suddenly Hanna knew what that had been.

His eyes drifted over to the brightly lit peaks. He had no doubt that right from the start, the landing unit had set down too close to the crater's edge. Not a problem in itself. The designers had built in extra tolerances, including for the event that the carrier and its package crashed in the crater. The mechanical parts were supposed to be protected for as long as it took for the sensors to report that it was in a stable position, or give any other indication that the landing had been successful. After which the package was supposed to separate from the undercarriage, unfold its legs once it was at rest, and scuttle away. Obviously the sensors had made their report, but at the very moment the limbs were unfolding, parts of the uphill slope had slipped, carrying the robot along with it. The onrushing rocks had shattered its extremities, and the package had lost all mobility.

Moonquake?

Possibly. The Moon was nothing like the calm and placid place that had once been thought. Laymen might not believe it, but there were frequent tremors. Enormous variations in temperature built up tensions which discharged themselves in massive quakes, and the gravitational pull of sun and Earth could tug at deep-lying strata of the moon rock, which was why Gaia had been built to withstand quakes topping 5 on the Richter scale. Hanna inspected the damaged axles and nozzles, wanting to leave no possibility untried. After twenty sweaty minutes of wrestling with the wreck, he had to concede that there was no fixing it. The loss of some of the spider legs might have been overcome, but the unwelcome fact was that one of the jet nozzles was partially torn away, and another was nowhere to be seen.

The best-laid plans of mice and men, thought Hanna. First there had been Thorn's accident, and then this. All this should have been his job. He should have taken care of the package a year ago, but Thorn's corpse was drifting out there somewhere in the universe.

Expecting further disappointments, he unbolted the hatch at the back, opened the container, and shone his torch inside, but there at least it all seemed undamaged. Hanna breathed freely again. If the cargo had been lost, that would really have been the end; everything else was mere inconvenience. He took the detector in his hand and checked the seams. Intact. No harm done.

Carefully, he pulled it out.

This simply meant that he would have to take the package across for deployment himself. No problem there. There was enough room on the grasshopper platform. For a moment he considered informing mission control, but time was running short. There was no alternative anyway. He had to act. It was best to be back in the hotel before the others started rubbing the sleep from their eyes.

Best never to have been away.

May 27, 2025
Games

XINTIANDI, SHANGHAI, CHINA

Jericho woke up on his couch next to two bottles and a glass streaked with drying red wine, and two emptied packets of mango chips. For a moment he didn't know where he was. He sat up, a process which needed two attempts and which raised the question of how the hell this sodden, heavy sponge had got inside his skull. Then he remembered his good fortune. At the same time he felt some indefinable sort of loss. There was something missing that had grown as familiar as his own heartbeat over the years.

Noise.

Never again would he wake up to the hammering sound of high-rises being built around him. Never again would six lanes of early-morning traffic rattle his eardrums before the sun had even risen. From now on he was living in Xintiandi, where admittedly there were hordes of tourists, but you could cope perfectly well with them. Generally speaking they never arrived before ten o'clock in the morning and then in the late afternoon they retreated, bathed in sweat and with aching feet, back to their hotels, to gather the strength to go out again in the evening to the restaurants. In the evenings it was mostly Shanghaians in the district's bistros, cafés and clubs, the boutiques and movies. In Jericho's new home, you hardly felt either invasion. That was the advantage of a Shikumen house. Outside someone could be driving herds of dinosaurs through the streets, but inside all was peace and quiet.

He rubbed his eyes. You couldn't quite say that he lived here, not yet. There were still packed crates scattered through every room in the loft. At least he'd got as far as installing the new media system. Tu's customer service team had delivered it the evening before, two cheery and helpful representatives hauling the thing upstairs for him and skillfully fitting it in with the decor so that it was hardly noticeable. Right after that, Jericho had had to set out for his surprise visit to Yoyo. It was only after he got back that he had got around to playing with his new toy, and celebrating his first night in Xintiandi while he did so. He'd gone to town on it, so the two empty bottles told him, though his only company had been Animal Ma Liping and the suffering children in their cages. He wondered whether Joanna would have liked this place, then decided not to even contemplate that.

It was good not to need anyone else.

He went to shower, and switched on his various appliances. Most of all he would have liked to unpack the rest of the boxes, but since yesterday Tu Tian and Chen Hongbing had come to join all the other

ghosts crowding the back of his mind, and they urged him on in his
search for Yoyo. Dutifully, he decided to prioritize the case. He shaved,
picked out a pair of light pants and a shirt jacket, uploaded one of Tu's
programs to the datastick in his new hologoggles, and left the house.
    He would spend the next hour with Yoyo.
    Handily, one of the guided tours went through the French Conces-
sion, a colonial relic of the nineteenth century. It was right next door to
Xintiandi, separated only by three levels of city highway. Once he had
taken the underpass and come back up into the sunlight, he walked
along the busy Fuxing Zhong Lu and activated the program's speech
recognition protocol.
    "Start," he said.
    At first nothing happened. The world on the other side of the lens
looked as it always had. People scurried or strolled about. Business
types communed with their cell phones, their eyes fixed on the displays and wireless earbuds firmly in place as they crossed the street,
somehow managing not to get run over. Elegantly dressed women
came in and out of the chic little boutiques around, chatting to one
another or on their phones, while less well-dressed women thronged
the Japanese or American department stores. Groups of tourists photographed what they imagined were authentic examples of colonial
architecture. Cars, minivans, and limousines filled the roads, and dozens of the identical CODs, cars on demand, squeezed in among them
on the way up to the speedway. Electric scooters and hybrid cruisers
wormed their way into gaps in the traffic that were filled before they
had ever really opened. Bicycles with rattling mudguards raced futur-
istic antigrav skates. City buses and vans crept along the packed roads,
a formation of police skymobiles overflew the Fuxing Zhong Lu, a little further on an ambulance took off, turned in the air and flew west.
Gleaming private cars and sky-bikes shot across the sky, following
aerial guidance beacons. Everything rumbled, squealed, or honked;
music blared; advertising slogans and news headlines splashed across
the omnipresent video screens.
    A quiet day in a calm neighborhood.
    The double T of Tu Technologies appeared in front of Jericho's eyes.
The system's projection technology fooled his retina into thinking that
the logo was floating, three-dimensional, above the ground several
meters away. Then it vanished, and the computer in the arm of the
specs projected Yoyo onto the Fuxing Zhong Lu.
    It was astonishing.
    Jericho had seen plenty of holographic projections in his time. The
specs were one continuous curve of glass fibers, and they worked like
a 3D movie that you could carry around on your nose as you walked.
The whole system had nothing in common with the early, bulky virtual

reality view screens. Rather the computer added objects and people into the actual surroundings just by producing them on the glass lens. You could see someone who was not physically present. These could be real people or synthetic avatars, and the program could bring them closer or further away. In electronic environments, they could hardly be told apart from people who were actually there. The problems began out in the real world, when the computer had to combine the avatars' movements and reactions with real-time events. They looked transparent against complex backdrops or if there was movement going on behind them. The illusion was broken completely if real people walked through the space where the avatar appeared to be. They simply walked straight through them. Your cheery chatty virtual pal paid no attention if, while they were talking, a truck ran them over. If you moved your head quickly, they would trail behind like ghosts. The system had to continuously scan and upload the real surroundings and synchronize them with the program to bring appearance and reality back together, and so far the attempt had seemed doomed to failure.

Yoyo, though, appeared one simulated meter away from Jericho, on the sidewalk, showing none of the telltale phantom characteristics of other avatars. She was wearing a close-fitting raspberry catsuit and discreet appliqués, her hair was plaited into a double ponytail, and she was lightly made up.

"Good morning, Mr. Jericho!" she said smiling.

Pedestrians hurried past behind her. Yoyo blocked them from view. Nothing about her looked transparent, there were no fuzzy edges. She walked in front of him and looked straight into his eyes.

"Shall we have a look at the French Concession?" The arm of the specs played the sound of her voice into Jericho's ear via the temporal bone.

"A little louder," he said.

"Of course," came Yoyo's voice, a touch stronger now. "Shall we have a look at the French Concession? It's perfect weather, not a cloud in the sky."

Was that so? Jericho looked upward. It was so.

"That would be nice."

"My pleasure. My name's Yoyo." She hesitated and gave him a look that mixed coquetry with shyness. "May I call you Owen?"

"No problem."

Fascinating. The program had automatically linked up with his ID code. It has recognized him, realized what time of day to use in saying hello, and taken a look at the weather at the same time. Already the team at Tu Technologies had topped everything that Jericho had seen in the field.

"Come along," Yoyo said cheerfully.

Almost with relief, he realized that she no longer seemed so exquisitely beautiful as she had the day before. In flesh and blood, laughing, talking, gesticulating, the ethereal quality that he had thought he saw on Chen's wobbly video was no longer there. What was left was still quite enough to make a pacemaker skip a beat.

Wait a moment. Flesh and blood?

Bits and bytes!

It really was astounding. The computer even calculated the correct angle for the shadow to fall as Yoyo walked in front of him. He no longer wondered how the program had done it but simply concentrated on her walk, her gestures, her movements. His guide turned left, took a place at his side and looked from him to the street and then back again.

"The Si Nan Lu brings together several distinct architectural styles, including those of France, Germany, and Spain. In 2018 the last of the original buildings were torn down, with a few exceptions, and then rebuilt. Using the original plans of course. Now everything is much more beautiful and even more authentic than it used to be." Yoyo smiled a Mona Lisa smile. "The first residents here included important functionaries of both the Nationalist and the Communist governments. Nobody could resist the quarter's generous charms, everybody wanted to come to the Si Nan Lu. Even Zhou Enlai held court here for a while. This lovely three-story garden villa on the left was his home. The style is generally called French, although in fact there are elements of art deco here as well, with Chinese influences. The villa is one of the very few buildings that has so far escaped the Party's mania for renovation."

Jericho was taken aback. How had that got past the censors?

Then he recalled that Tu had talked about a prototype. Meaning that the text would be modified later. He wondered whose idea this deviation had been. Had Tu thought up the joke, or had Yoyo suggested it to him?

"Can we visit the villa?" he asked.

"We can go and have a look at it from inside," Yoyo confirmed. "The interior is largely untouched. Zhou lived a Spartan sort of life; he felt that it was his duty to the proletariat. Maybe too he simply didn't want the Great Helmsman dropping in to rearrange the furniture."

Jericho couldn't help grinning.

"I'd rather keep walking."

"Right you are, Owen. Let the past alone."

Over the next few minutes Yoyo talked about their surroundings without barbed remarks. A couple of turns off the street, they found themselves in a lively little alleyway full of cafés, galleries, ateliers, and picturesque little shops selling artworks. Jericho came here often. He loved the quarter, with its wooden benches and palm trees, the neatly renovated Shikumen houses with flowerpots in the window.

"Until twenty years ago, Taikang Lu Art Street was an insider tip in the art scene," Yoyo explained. "In 1998 a former sweet factory was converted into the International Artists Factory. Advertising agencies and designers moved in, well-known artists opened their studios here, including big names like Huang Yongzheng, Er Dongqiang, and Chen Yifei. Despite all that, for a long time the area was still overshadowed by Moganshan Lu north of the Suzhou Canal, where the official art scene met the underground and the avant-garde and they all dominated Shanghai's art market together. It was only when the Taikang Art Foundation was built in 2015 that the center of balance shifted. It's the complex up there ahead. Locals call it the Jellyfish."

Yoyo pointed to an enormous glass dome that looked astonishingly delicate and airy despite its massive size. It had been designed to mimic biological structures, along the lines of the larger Medusozoa.

"What was here before?" asked Jericho.

"Originally Taikang Lu Art Street ended in a really lovely fish market. You could buy frogs and snakes here as well."

"And where did that go?"

"The fish market was torn down. The Party has a giant airbrush which it can use to remove history. Now this is the Taikang Art Foundation."

"Can we visit the studios?"

"We can visit the studios. Would you like to?"

Yoyo went ahead of him. Taikang Lu Art Street slowly filled up with tourists. It became crowded, but Yoyo looked real and solid as she wormed her way between passers-by. Truth be told, Jericho thought, she actually looked more real than some of the others.

He was brought up short.

Were his eyes playing tricks on him? He concentrated entirely on Yoyo. A group of Japanese tourists approached, shoulder to shoulder, on a collision course, blind to whoever might be coming the other way. He had noticed that the computer had Yoyo step aside whenever there was the chance, but the group blocked the street on both sides. All she could do was drop back before them, or fight her way past. The Japanese, like the Chinese, didn't shrink from barging their way through if they needed to, so Jericho reckoned that if Yoyo were really here she would be using her elbows. Avatars had no elbows, though. Not the sort that others would feel in their ribs.

He watched curiously to see what would happen. A moment later she had passed the group, without it looking as though she had simply walked through. Rather, one of the Japanese seemed to have melted away for a moment to let her by.

Irked, Jericho took off the specs.

Nothing had changed except that Yoyo had vanished. He put them back on again, fought his way through the groups, and saw Yoyo a little further on. Standing on the street. She looked across at him and waved.

"What are you waiting for? Come on!"

Jericho took a few steps. Yoyo waited until he drew level with her, and then she set off. Incredible! How did the trick work? He would hardly be able to understand it without an explanation, so he concentrated on trying to figure out the program. From a purely factual perspective, the programmers had done good work. The tour was well researched and thoroughly plotted. So far, everything Yoyo had told him was right.

"Yoyo—" he began.

"Yes?" Her glance showed amiable interest.

"How long have you had this job?"

"This route is completely new," she answered evasively.

"Not long, then?"

"No."

"And what are you doing tonight?"

She stopped and gave him a smile, sweet as sugar.

"Is that an offer?"

"I'd like to invite you for a meal."

"Pardon me for refusing, but I only have a virtual stomach."

"Would you like to go dancing with me?"

"I would very much like to."

"Great. Where shall we go?"

"I said I would like to." She winked. "Sadly, I can't."

"May I ask you something else?"

"Go right ahead."

"Will you go to bed with me?"

She hesitated for a moment. The smile gave way to a look of mocking good humor.

"You'd be disappointed."

"Why?"

"Because I don't actually exist."

"Get undressed, Yoyo."

"I could put something else on." The smile came back. "Would you like me to put something else on?"

"I want to sleep with you."

"You'd be disappointed."

"I want to have sex with you."

"You're on your own there, Owen."

Aha.

This was definitely not the official version.

"Can we visit the studios?" he asked, repeating the earlier question.

"We can visit the studios. Would you like to?"

"Who programmed you, Yoyo?"

"I was programmed by Tu Technologies."

"Are you a person?"

"I'm a person."

"I hate you, Yoyo."

"I'm very sorry to hear that." She paused. "Would you like to continue the tour?"

"You're a silly, ugly goose."

"I do my best to please. Your tone is not appropriate."

"Pardon me."

"No need. It was probably my mistake."

"Whore."

"Asshole."

WORLD FINANCIAL CENTER

"Yoyo is pretty much in demand, isn't she?"

Grand Cherokee gave Xin a knowing wink as his fingers swept across the smooth surface of the steering deck. One by one, he let the computer check the Silver Dragon's systems. It promised to be a perfect day for a roller-coaster ride, sunny and clear, so that despite the omnipresent blanket of smog passengers would still be able to see such distant buildings as the Shanghai Regent or the Portman Ritz Carlton. The skyscraper façades reflected the early-morning light. Tiny suns came and went on the bodywork of the skymobiles that swept in graceful curves above the Huangpu. Away from the shore, Shanghai blurred together into the vague suggestion of a city, but on the other side of the river the colonial relics of the Bund stood out all the more clearly in a brightly colored row of palaces.

Grand Cherokee had met Xin in the Sky Lobby and chattered incessantly in the elevator on the way up about what a signal honor it was to be allowed to enter the dragon's lair right at this moment. For all that, he told Xin, the track itself wasn't especially interesting, not considered as a roller coaster as such: it had hardly any upside-down stretches, just one classic vertical loop with a heartline roll on either side; well, that meant that there were three zero-g points all in all, but basically it was nothing special. Rather, he went on as they walked through the empty glass corridor, the thrill of the thing lay in its speed, combined with the fact of zooming about half a kilometer above the ground. As he opened up the control room and they went in, he kept up his monologue: this masterpiece of adrenaline was one of a kind, worldwide; controlling the ride needed good nerves, just like riding in it; you needed to be a strong personality to tame the dragon.

"Interesting," Xin had said. "Show me then. What exactly do you have to do?"

This was when Grand Cherokee stopped for a moment. He was accustomed to seeing reality through the distorting mirror of his own inflated ego, but this last remark got through even to him, and he was suddenly rattled. In fact controlling the ride was perfectly straightforward. Any idiot capable of touching three control boxes on a screen could do it. He stammered out something about irony and hyperbole, and showed Xin the controls, telling him that all he really needed to do was clear the safety checks, which meant knowing the security codes.

"There are three of them," he told Xin. "I just put them in one after another—like that—then number two—three—done. System's ready. So now I activate this field on the top right, which unlocks the carriages, this box below starts the catapult, and the program does the rest. This one underneath is the emergency stop. We've never needed it though."

"And what's this for?" Xin pointed to a menu along the upper edge of the screen.

"That's the check assistant. Before I set the ride in motion, I let the computer run through a set of parameters. Mechanical systems, programs."

"Simple really."

"Simple, but clever."

"Almost a pity that we won't have the chance for a ride, but my time is short. I'd like to—"

"In principle, you could climb in," said Grand Cherokee and began the check. "I'll give you such a ride that you won't know which way to stand up when you climb out. I'd have to register it as an unscheduled ride though."

"Don't bother. Let's talk about Yoyo."

This was the point when Grand Cherokee grinned at his visitor and made the crack about Yoyo being pretty much in demand. He wanted to add something, but stopped. Something had changed in the other man's face. There was curiosity there now, not just about where Yoyo might be but about Grand Cherokee himself.

"Who else is interested in her?" Xin asked.

"No idea." Grand Cherokee shrugged. Should he play his trump card already? He had wanted to use the detective to put a little pressure on Xin, but perhaps it was better to play him on the line for a while. "That's what you said."

"Said what?"

"Yoyo needed protection because someone was after her."

"True." Xin inspected the fingernails on his right hand. Grand Cherokee noticed that they were perfectly manicured, all filed down to exactly the same length, the crescents the color of mother-of-pearl. "And you were going to find things out, Wang. Telephone some people, and so on. Bring me to Yoyo. As I remember it, money changed hands. So what do you have for me?"

Pompous asshole, thought Grand Cherokee. In fact he'd thought up a story the night before. It was all based on a remark that Yoyo had made about the party lifestyle getting on her nerves, that she wanted to go to Hangzhou and the West Lake for a weekend. His grandmother had always spouted clichés and proverbs, and wasn't one of them that Hangzhou was the image of Heaven here on Earth? Grand Cherokee had decided that that was where Yoyo could be found, in some romantic little hotel on the West Lake, and the hotel might be called—

Wait though, he shouldn't be too specific. There were all sorts of places to stay right around the lake shores, for every sort of price. Just to be sure, he had done an Internet search and found several named after trees or flowers. He liked that. Yoyo's retreat would be a hotel with a flowery name! Something with a flower, but sadly his contact (who didn't exist anyway) couldn't quite remember what. He hadn't been able to find out more than that for the money, but it was something, wasn't it? Grand Cherokee had laughed out loud at the thought of Xin travelling 170 kilometers to the West Lake to check out every hotel with a botanical name, especially since he planned to send the detective out to the same place. Those two fools wouldn't notice, but they would constantly be crossing paths. For a bit more money, he could also mention the motorcycle mob, a completely different lead, since after all the City Demons had little or nothing to do with West Lake. On the other hand, a motorcycle trip out to the countryside? Why not?

Xin was lost in contemplation of his fingernails. Grand Cherokee considered. Soon enough he'd be spinning the same line to Jericho, through there he ran the risk that the detective might be less generous.

And there was still a chance.

"You know," he said slowly and as neutrally as he could manage, "I've been thinking about it." He finished the check for the Silver Dragon and looked at Xin. "And I think you could pay a bit more to find out where Yoyo is."

Xin didn't look especially surprised. Instead he looked exhausted, as though he'd been waiting for the penny to drop.

"How much?" he asked.

"Ten times."

Shocked at his own daring, Grand Cherokee felt his heart beat faster. If Xin swallowed *that*—

Wait a moment. It could get even better!

"Ten times," he repeated, "and another meeting."

Xin's expression turned to stone.

"What's this about?"

What's it about? thought Grand Cherokee. Simple enough, you varnished monkey. I'll take the money and run off to Jericho, and give him a choice. Either he tops your offer and gets the exclusive story, or he turns me down, and you get it. But not until I've spoken to Jericho. And if Jericho coughs up twenty times as much, then we'll try you for thirty times.

"Yes or no?" he asked.

The corners of Xin's mouth lifted, almost imperceptibly. "Which movie have you got this from, Wang?"

"I don't need to watch any movies. You're after Yoyo, I couldn't care less why. I find it much more interesting that the cops want something from her as well. Conclusion: you're obviously not a cop. Meaning that

you can't do anything to me. You have to take what you can get, and—"
he bowed, and bared his teeth "—when you can get it."

Xin looked around, his smile frozen. Then he glanced at the control
panel.

"Do you know what I hate?" he asked.

"Me?" said Grand Cherokee, laughing.

"You're vermin, Wang, hatred is too good for you. No, I hate spots.
Those greasy fingers of yours have left nasty smears all over the display."

"So?"

"Clean them up."

"Do what?"

"Clean up those greasy smears."

"Listen here, you designer-suited piece of shit, what exactly do you
think—"

Something odd happened then, something Grand Cherokee had
never experienced before. It was quick as lightning, and when it was
over, he was lying on the floor in front of the control panel, and his nose
felt as though a grenade had exploded in it. Flashes of color sparked in
front of his eyes.

"Your face wouldn't do very well to keep things clean," said Xin, then
reached down and pulled Grand Cherokee to his feet like a puppet. "Oh,
you look dreadful. What happened to your nose? Shall we talk?"

Grand Cherokee staggered and put a hand on the console to steady
himself. He felt his face with the other hand. His forehead appliqué fell
into the palm of his hand. He looked at Xin, nonplussed.

Then he swung at him, enraged.

Xin languidly poked him in the sternum.

It was as though somebody had unhooked all systems in the lower
half of Grand Cherokee's body. He fell to one knee while a surge of
pain shot through his chest. His mouth opened, and he made choking sounds. Xin squatted down and supported him with his right arm
before he could collapse.

"It'll pass soon," he said. "I know, for a while you think you'll never
be able to talk again. Wrong though. Generally speaking, people actually find it easier to talk after they've had that done to them. What did
you want to say?"

Grand Cherokee gasped. His lips formed a word.

"Yoyo?" Xin nodded. "A good start. Try your best, Wang, and above
all," he took him under the arms and heaved him up, "get to your feet."

"Yoyo is—" panted Grand Cherokee.

"Where?"

"In Hangzhou."

"Hangzhou?" Xin raised his eyebrows. "Mercy me. Do you actually
know something? Where in Hangzhou?"

"In—a hotel."

"Name?"

"No idea." Grand Cherokee sucked in greedy lungfuls of air. Xin was right. The pain passed, but he didn't feel in the least bit better for it. "Something with flowers."

"Don't make things so complicated," Xin said mildly. "Something with flowers is about as specific as somewhere in China."

"Might have been something with trees, even," Grand Cherokee yelped. "My informant said flowers."

"In Hangzhou?"

"On the West Lake."

"Where on the West Lake? On the city side?"

"Yes, yes!"

"On the western shore then?"

"That's it."

"Aha! Maybe near the Su dam?"

"The—I think so." Grand Cherokee felt a glimmer of hope. "Probably Yes, that's what he said."

"But the city is on the eastern shore."

"P-perhaps I didn't quite hear." The glimmer died away.

"But near the Su dam? Or the Bai dam?"

Bai dam? Su dam? It was becoming ever more complicated. Where were these dams anyway? Grand Cherokee hadn't thought about it all that much. Who the hell expected all these questions?

"I don't know," he said feebly.

"I thought your informant—"

"I just don't know!"

Xin looked at him reproachfully. Then he jabbed his fingers into Grand Cherokee's kidney region.

The effect was indescribable. Grand Cherokee opened and closed his mouth rapidly like a fish snatched from the water, while his eyes opened wide. Xin held him in an iron grip to stop him from collapsing again. For all that the surveillance cameras could see, they were standing side by side like old friends.

"So?"

"I don't know," Grand Cherokee whimpered, while part of him detachedly observed that pain was orange. "Really, I don't."

"What *do* you know, if anything?"

Grand Cherokee lifted his eyes, trembling. There was no mistaking what he could read in Xin's eyes about what would happen to him if he lied one more time.

"Nothing," he whispered.

Xin laughed contemptuously, shook his head and let go of him.

"Do you want the money back?" Grand Cherokee mumbled, and bent over double with the memory of the pain that had shaken his body.

Xin pursed his lips. He looked out at the city shimmering below.

"I keep remembering something you said," he remarked.

Grand Cherokee gaped at him and waited. The part of him that had floated off detached, pointed out that in fifteen minutes the first visitors would be let in, that it would probably be full because the weather was so exceptionally fine.

"You said that Yoyo is pretty much in demand. I believe those were the words you used, am I right?"

Still fifteen minutes.

"You can make up for lost ground, Wang. Tell the truth this time. Who else was asking about her?"

"A detective," muttered Grand Cherokee.

"Very interesting. When was this?"

"Last night. I showed him Yoyo's room. He asked the same questions as you."

"And you gave the same answers. That you'd find something out, but that it would cost a little."

Grand Cherokee nodded, downcast. If Xin went to Owen Jericho with this information, then he could kiss goodbye to that money. Hurrying to carry out the next order before it was given, he took out Jericho's card and handed it to Xin, who took it with both hands, looked at it curiously and put it away.

"Anything else?"

Of course. He could have told Xin about the motorcycle gang. The one trail that might actually lead to Yoyo. But he wouldn't do this fucker any such favor.

"Fuck you," he said instead.

"Meaning no."

Xin looked thoughtful. He stepped out of the open door to the control room, to the area between the turnstile and the platform. He paid no further attention to Grand Cherokee, as though he no longer existed. Which would probably be the best thing right now. Just stop existing until the bastard had left this floor. Not make a peep, become about as big as a mouse, less than a fingerprint on a computer display. All this was as clear as anything ever had been, to the detached part of Grand Cherokee Wang, and he spoke a well-meaning word of warning which the other Wang, the Wang blinded by hatred, ignored. Instead he shuffled after Xin and thought about how he could recover his dignity, the dignity of the man who guarded the dragon, which right now was in a fairly shabby state. *You vicious asshole?* Xin probably knew that he was vicious, and asshole was too small a word. Grand Cherokee reckoned that insults probably slid straight off Xin anyway.

How could he get at the fucker?

And while the detached part of Grand Cherokee was looking for a mousehole to crawl into, he heard Grand Cherokee the big-mouth say:

"Just don't think you're free and clear, you moron!"

Xin, who was just going through the turnstile, stopped.

"First thing I'll do is call Jericho," yelled Grand Cherokee. "Then the cops, right after that. Who's going to be more interested, huh? You make sure you get away from here, out of Shanghai if you can, out of China. Off to the Moon, perhaps they've got something for you up there, 'cos down here I'm going to put the boot into you, you can count on that!"

Xin turned around slowly.

"You silly fool," he said. It sounded almost sympathetic.

"I'll—" Grand Cherokee gulped, and then it dawned on him that he had probably just made the biggest mistake of his life. Xin walked nonchalantly toward him. He didn't look like someone who planned to do much more talking.

Grand Cherokee scuttled backward.

"This area is under video surveillance," he said, trying to put a warning note in his voice; it slipped into panic halfway through.

"You're right," said Xin, nodding. "I should hurry."

Grand Cherokee's stomach cramped. He jumped backward and tried to get a grip on the situation. His foe was standing between him and the passage through to the glass corridor. There was no way past him, and right behind Grand Cherokee was the edge of the platform with the roller-coaster train resting on its rails on the other side. The area where the passengers got on and off was closed off with a transparent wall that curved around underneath, and to the right and left, the tracks curved off into empty space.

The look in Xin's eyes left no room for misunderstanding.

With one leap, Grand Cherokee was in the middle car. He glanced toward the head of the dragon. Each car was nothing more than a platform with seats mounted on it, the back of each seat looking like a huge scale or a wing, which made the vehicle vaguely resemble a silver reptile. The only extra detail was up at the front: a projection, something like a long, narrow skull. There was a separate steering system up there which could be used to move the whole train a short distance, in emergencies. Not through the loops, but along the straight sections of track.

Where the track passed around the building's side pillars, just before it began to climb, there was a short bridge from the track into the building, one on each side. Inside the pillars was plant and electronics, and storage rooms. The steel bridges led right into the glass façades of the pillars, and if necessary they could be used to evacuate the train if for some reason it couldn't get to the boarding platform. The bridges led to a separate staircase and elevator, not reachable from the glass corridor.

Grand Cherokee ran through all of this in his head as he crouched there, which was his second mistake; he was losing time, instead of acting right away. Xin pounced and landed between him and the dragon's head. There were only two rows of seats between them, and Grand Cherokee realized that he had thrown away his chance of reaching the steering unit. He considered jumping back onto the platform, but it was clear that Xin would be right behind him if he did. Probably he wouldn't even make it as far as the turnstile.

Xin came closer. He clambered through the rows of seating so fast that Grand Cherokee stopped thinking and fled to the end of the train. The glass barrier for the boarding platform ended a little way beyond. Here, the track swung out from the front of the building, curved around a good distance and then about 25 meters on, turned the corner that led behind the pillar.

"Very stupid idea," said Xin, as he approached.

Grand Cherokee stared out at the track, then back to Xin. He had long ago realized that he had gone too far, and the guy meant to kill him. Damn Yoyo! What a dumb bitch, getting him into this kind of trouble.

Wrong, the detached part of Grand Cherokee told him, you're dumb yourself. Ever thought you could climb through thin air? And when big-mouth Wang had no reply, the calm, distant voice added: You do have one great advantage. You don't suffer from vertigo.

Does Xin?

Knowing that the enormous height did nothing to him suddenly freed Grand Cherokee's limbs of their paralysis. His mind made up, he put one foot on the track, took one step, another. Half a kilometer below him he saw the green forecourt in front of the World Financial Center, crisscrossed with footpaths. Cars moved like ants along the two levels of the Shiji Dadao, running from the river to the Pudong hinterland. The sun burned down on him through the enormous hole in the tower as he left the protection of the glassed-in boarding platform and went along the track, one meter at a time. Gusts of warm wind tugged at him. To his left, the glass façade of the tower grew further away with every step, or more exactly, he was getting further away from it. To the right he could see the roof of the Jin Mao Tower. The business high-rises of Pudong grouped themselves around and behind it, with the shimmering curve of Huangpu, and Shanghai stretching all around, unimaginably vast.

His heart beating wildly, he stopped and turned his head. Xin was standing at the end of the train, staring at him.

He wasn't following.

The asshole didn't have the guts!

Grand Cherokee took another step and slipped between two of the spars.

His heart stopped beating. Like a cat falling, he flung out all four limbs, grabbed hold of the rail and for a hideous moment swung there above the abyss before he managed, using all his strength, to heave himself up. Panting like an engine, he tried to stand. He was halfway between the boarding platform and the curve of the corner, and the track was beginning to tilt. The wind fluttered his coat, which was turning out to be the least practical garment imaginable for a stroll at 500 meters.

Gasping, he looked around again.

Xin had vanished.

Onward, he thought. How far to the bridge now? Twenty-five meters, thirty? At the most. Get moving! Make sure that you round that corner. Get to safety. Who cares what Xin is doing.

He took heart and walked on, arms stretched for balance, master of himself once more, when he heard the noise.

The noise.

It was something between a rattle and a hum, following a heavy metallic clunk. It drew away in the other direction. It froze the blood in Grand Cherokee's veins, although it was a noise he knew well, a noise he heard every day he spent up here at work.

Xin had woken the Dragon.

He had started the ride!

A scream of fear broke out of him, that was torn away by the warm gusts and scattered over Pudong. Whimpering, he clambered on as fast as he could. His ears told him that the train had just passed the northern pillar, then he saw it climbing the slope through the great gap. At the moment the dragon was still moving slowly, but once it got to the roof it would pick up speed, and then—

He crawled forward like a mad thing in the shadow of the southern pillar. The tilt on the tracks was becoming more pronounced, so that he had no choice but to move ahead on all fours.

Too slow. Too slow!

The fear will burst your heart, thought the detached part of Grand Cherokee. Try cursing.

It helped.

He screamed hell and damnation into the deep blue sky, his voice cracking, grabbed hold of the warm metal of the track and hopped rather than crept forward. The rails had begun to thrum. Twice he nearly lost his balance and fell off the curve, but each time he caught himself and worked his way stubbornly onward. High above him a hollow whistling sound signaled that the carriages had reached their highest point and were now on the flat stretch up above, and he still had not reached his goal. Trying to catch sight of the Dragon, he saw only himself reflected in the mirrored glass on the pillar façade, somehow looking damn good, like a movie hero. All in all he should have been having the time of his life here, but there was the nagging question of the happy ending, the fact that the Dragon had just passed the catapult.

The rails began to vibrate mightily. Grand Cherokee clambered onward, choking out the word "Please!" over and over like a mantra, "Please, please, please—" in sync with the thrumming of the rail.

"Please—"—*Raddangg*—"Please—"—*Raddangg*—

He came around the pillar. He could see the steel bridge not 10 meters in front of him, leading from the rails to the wall of the building.

The Dragon swept down from the roof.

"Please—"

The train hurtled down, thunderous, deafening, into the depths, then coiled in on itself in the loop and shot upward. The whole structure was moving, shaking. The rails seemed to dance to and fro before Grand Cherokee's eyes. He stood up, managed to leap across several spars at once, and keep his balance despite the tilt.

Five meters. Four.

The Dragon rushed down in the loop.

Three meters.

—shot around the corner—

Two.

—flew toward him.

In the moment that the train crossed the point where the bridge led off, Grand Cherokee did the impossible, a superhuman feat. Howling wildly, he leaped clear, an enormous standing jump. The sharp bow of the front carriage passed below him. He stretched out his arms to grab hold of one of the seats, touched something, lost his grip. His body smashed into the backs of the seats in the next row, was flung high, pirouetted and for a moment seemed to be heading into the deep blue sky, as though he had decided to reach outer space.

Then he fell.

The last thing that went through Grand Cherokee's head was that he had at least tried.

That he hadn't been so bad after all.

Xin craned his head. High above him he could see people going into the glass viewing platform. The corridor would be opened soon as well. Time to get going. He knew how things worked in high-rise surveillance control rooms; he knew that hardly anybody would have glanced at the monitors in the last quarter of an hour. Even if they had, they wouldn't have seen much. Leaving aside the two moments when Wang had suddenly dropped to the control room floor, they had been standing close beside one another most of the time. Two close friends having a chat.

But now he had set the Dragon moving. Before the usual time. That would be noticed. He had to get out of here.

Xin hesitated.

Then he quickly wiped his fingerprints from the display with his sleeve, paused, and also wiped the places where Grand Cherokee had fumbled about with his greasy fingers. Otherwise those blasted smears would haunt his dreams. There were some things that tended to cling to the inside of Xin's skull like leeches. Lastly, he hurried along the corridor and left it the way they had come. In the elevator he peeled the wig from his head, took off his glasses, tore the mustache from his upper lip, and turned his jacket inside out. It had been made especially for him, reversible. The gray jacket became sandy beige, and he stuffed the wig, beard, and glasses inside. He decided to change elevators in the Sky Lobby on the twenty-eighth floor, then went down to the basement, through the shopping mall and out into the bright sunshine. Outside he saw people running toward the south side of the building. Cries went up. Somebody shouted that there had been a suicide.

Suicide? All okay then.

As Xin walked onward, faster, under the trees in the park, he took out the detective's card.

MAY 27, 2025
Phantoms

GAIA, VALLIS ALPINA, THE MOON

Julian set great store by his inventive genius that generated so many extraordinary ideas, and in particular by the fact that he could simply choose to switch the thinking process on and off. If unsolved problems tried to join him under the covers, he chose to sleep, and was wafted away on the wings of slumber as soon as his head touched the pillow. Sleep was a cornerstone of his mental and physical health, and up until now, he had always slept extremely well on the Moon.

Just not tonight.

The discussion at dinner was going round and round in his head, like the horses on a merry-go-round; more precisely, Walo Ögi's remark asking why he didn't simply announce a divorce with Washington and declare that his technologies were up for sale to all comers, offering global access. It was true that there was a difference between taking the *best* offer and taking *every* offer. There was, even, a moral distinction. Playing favorites when it came to the well-being of 10 billion people laid him open to charges of perfidious profiteering, even if not one of these 10 billion people was in a position to build a space elevator in the front garden—charges that were unpalatable to a man who outdid all others in arguing for his autonomy as a businessman, who made speeches about global responsibility and the destructive effects of rivalry.

Tonight Julian lay awake because he saw all his private thoughts and arguments confirmed once more. Especially since, aside from all moral considerations, to make his patents generally available would not only boost economic activity on the Moon, it would also mean better business for him. The Swiss investor had put his finger on it: if another three or four nations had a space elevator, and were mining helium-3, the global switch to aneutronic fusion would be complete within a few years. Orley Enterprises, or more exactly Orley Space, could help the less wealthy countries with finance to build their elevators, which would give Orley Fusion the chance to acquire exclusive concessions for their power network. The reactor business would turn a profit and Orley Energy would become the biggest power provider on the planet. He would just have to deal with the fact that Washington would be less than happy about all this.

But it was a little more complicated than that.

Zheng Pang-Wang had tried several times to woo him for Beijing, which Julian had flatly refused until one occasion when they were having lunch together at Hakkasan, the exclusive Chinese restaurant in London, and Julian realized that he would only be betraying his

American partners if he jumped into bed with *one* other trading partner. If on the other hand he offered his goods to *everybody*, this would
effectively be the same as offering everybody in the world a Toyota or
a Big Mac. Obviously Washington would see things a little differently.
They would argue that they had signed a deal based on mutual advantage, a deal where—to continue the fast food metaphor—he supplied
the burger while the government provided the bun, since neither could
act on their own without the other's support.

In a sudden fit of chattiness, he had shared his thoughts with Zheng.
The old fellow nearly dropped his chopsticks.

"No, no, no, honorable friend! You may have a wife and a concubine. Does the concubine want to change anything about the fact that
you are married? Not at all. She's happy to share this pleasant way of
life with the wife, but she will very quickly lose all taste for this at the
thought you may take other mistresses. China has invested too much.
We observe regretfully but respectfully that you feel obliged to your
lawful partner, but if space elevators were suddenly to sprout up like
beanstalks all over, and everybody were to stake a claim on the Moon,
that would be a problem of a different magnitude. Beijing would be
most concerned."

Most concerned.

*"There's only one problem, Julian. How to stay alive after such a
change of direction."*

Rogachev's remark had irked him since it showed once more how
arrogant governments and their organs were. Useless mob. What kind
of globalization was this where the players didn't even seem to want to
peek at the other guy's hand, where if you tried to give everybody an
equal slice of the pie you ran the risk of being murdered? The longer
he considered the matter, the higher the flood of biochemical stimulants to his thalamus, until at last, a little after five o'clock, he had had
enough of tossing and turning in his bed sheets. He took a shower, and
decided to use this unaccustomed attack of sleeplessness to take a stroll
out in the canyon. In fact, he was dog-tired, physically at least, but
nevertheless he went into the living room, put on shorts and T-shirt,
yawned and shoved his feet into some light slippers.

As he raised his head, he thought he saw a movement at the far left
of the window, something flitting at the edge of his vision.

He stared out at the canyon.

Nothing there.

He hesitated, indecisive, then shrugged and left the suite. Nobody
around. Why would there be? Everybody was exhausted, deep asleep. He
went to the locker with the space suits and began to dress, wriggled into
the narrow, steel-reinforced harness, put on the chestplate and backpack,
held his helmet under his elbow and went down to the basement.

As he went into the corridor, he thought for a moment he was hallucinating.

An astronaut was coming toward him from the train station.

Julian blinked. The other man drew nearer fast, carried along by the conveyor. White light delineated his outlines. Suddenly he had the crazy feeling that he was looking at a mirror-world, that he saw himself there at the other end of the corridor. Then a familiar face came into focus—oval head with hair cropped short, strong chin, dark eyes.

"Carl," he called out, astonished.

Hanna seemed no less surprised.

"What are you doing down here?" He stepped off the belt and walked slowly toward Julian, who lifted his eyebrows, unsettled, and peered about as though more early risers might step out of the walls.

"I could ask you the same question."

"Tchh, well, to be honest—" A furtive look showed in Hanna's eyes, and his smile slipped, becoming foolish. "I—"

"Just don't tell me that you went outside!"

"I didn't." Hanna lifted his hands. "Honestly."

"But you wanted to."

"Hmm."

"Go on, say it."

"Well yes. To take a walk. I wanted to go over to the other side of the canyon, look at Gaia from over there."

"On your own?"

"Of course on my own!" Hanna dropped the schoolboy affectations and put on a grown-up face. "You know me. I'm not the type for eight hours of sleep, could even be I'm not house-trained for group trips like this. At any rate, I was lying there in bed and I suddenly wondered what it would be like to be the only person on the Moon. How it would feel to walk around out there without the others. Imagine there was no one here but me."

"That's a half-baked idea."

"Could be yours, though." Hanna rolled his eyes. "C'mon, don't be like that. I mean, over the next few days we're going to be wandering about in herds, aren't we? And that's fine, really. I like the others, I won't go on a walking tour. But I just wanted to know how it would be."

Julian ran his fingertips through his beard.

"Well, it looks as though I don't really have to worry," he grinned. "You've already gotten lost before you could even set foot outside."

"Yes, that was dumb of me, wasn't it?" Hanna laughed. "I forgot where the darned air locks are! I know, you guys showed us, but—"

"Here. Right up ahead."

Hanna turned his head.

"Well, that's great," he said, downcast. "It says so in big fat letters."

Frank Schätzing

"Some lone wolf you are," Julian said mockingly. "As it happens, I was about to do just the same."

"What, just go out on your own?"

"No, you fool, I have a great deal of practical experience which you don't. This isn't just a morning jog! It's dangerous."

"Sure. Life's dangerous."

"Seriously."

"Give me a break, Julian, I know my way around a space suit! I had an EVA on the OSS, I had one on the flight here, all of that is more dangerous than taking a hike out here on the regolith."

"That's true, but—" But I snuck out the same way you did, thought Julian. "Regulations say that nobody goes out on their own. None of the tourists anyway."

"Fine and dandy," said Hanna cheerfully. "Now there's two of us. Unless of course you'd rather go out alone."

"Nonsense." Julian laughed. He went to the air lock and opened the inner door. "You were found out, so that means you *have* to come along with me, like it or not."

Hanna followed him. The air lock was built to take twenty people, so they were rather dwarfed by its dimensions as they stood there letting their suits run through diagnostics. Bemused, he thought about just how unlikely this meeting was, mathematically speaking. If it were true that a person lives in just one of countless parallel universes where every possible course of events is true somewhere: almost identical worlds, radically different worlds with intelligent dinosaurs or where Hitler had won the war, then why did he have to live in the world where Julian had turned up in the corridor at exactly the same time as him? Why not ten minutes later, giving him the chance to get back to his suite unnoticed? The only consolation was that there were other realities where things had turned out even worse, where Julian had actually seen him arrive on the Lunar Express. At least he seemed not to have noticed that at all.

He would have to be more careful, and pay more attention.

He, and Ebola.

Xintiandi, Shanghai, China

"Interesting, that program of yours," said Jericho.

"Ah!" Tu looked pleased. "I was wondering when you would call. Which one did you try out?"

"French Concession. You're not seriously going to put that on the market, are you?"

"We've drawn its sting." Tu grinned. "As I told you, that was a prototype. Strictly for internal use, so please don't go peddling it. I thought that you would appreciate the jokes, and you also wanted to get to know Yoyo."

"Was that her idea? Taking swipes at the Party."

"The whole script is Yoyo's. They're test recordings, she was mostly improvising. Did you try chatting her up?"

"I did. Chatting her up, and calling her names."

Tu giggled. "It's impressive, isn't it?"

"A few more responses to choose from wouldn't hurt. Otherwise, very successful."

"The market-ready version runs on an artificial intelligence. It can generate any response instantly. We didn't even need to film Yoyo to get them, any more than we needed sound recordings. The synthesizer can simulate her voice, her lip movements, gestures, everything really. Your version is very much simpler, but it means you get unadulterated Yoyo."

"You'll have to explain one thing."

"As long as you don't go selling it to Dao."

Idiot, Jericho thought, but he kept it to himself.

"You know I'd never do something like that," he said instead.

"Just a joke." Tu dug around with a toothpick, produced a small green scrap of something, and flicked it away. Jericho tried not to look. For all that, his eyes were irresistibly drawn to where the scrap, whatever it was, had landed. It was irritating mostly because Tu appeared on his new media screen not just life-size but in perfect perspectival detail, so that it looked as though Jericho's loft apartment had grown an extra room. It wouldn't have surprised him to spot the scrap of food lying on his floorboards somewhere. Seeing Tu in 3D was very much less enjoyable than looking at Naomi Liu.

Now she really did have nice legs.

"Owen?"

Jericho blinked. "I noticed that the Yoyo avatar is remarkably stable in crowds. How do you do that?"

"Trade secret," Tu sang happily.

"Tell me. Otherwise I'll have to go and visit my optician."

"There's nothing wrong with your eyes."

"Clearly not. I mean, the glasses themselves are transparent, just like a window. I'm seeing the real world. Your program can project details in, but it can't change reality."

"Is that what it does?" Tu asked, grinning.

"You know perfectly well what it does. It makes people blink out of existence."

"You never thought that perhaps reality is just a projection as well?"

"Could you say that a little less cryptically?"

"Let's say we could do without the lens on the glasses."

"And Yoyo would still appear?"

"Bingo."

"But what would be the substrate?"

"She'd appear because none of what you see is actual reality. There are tiny cameras hidden in the arms of the glasses and in the frame, feeding data on the real world into the computer so that it knows how and where it should fit Yoyo in. What you might have overlooked was the projectors on the inside edge."

"I know that Yoyo is projected onto the lens glass."

"No, that's just what she's not." Tu quaked with suppressed laughter. "The glass is surplus to requirements. The cameras produce a complete image, which is made up of your surroundings, plus Yoyo. Then this image is projected directly onto your retina."

Jericho stared at Tu.

"You mean none of what I saw—"

"Oh, you definitely saw the real world. Just not first-hand. You see what the cameras film, and the film can be manipulated. In real time, of course. We can make the sky pink, make people disappear or have them grow horns. We turn your eyes into the projection screen."

"Unbelievable."

Tu shrugged. "There are useful applications of virtual reality. Did you know that most cases of blindness are caused by clouding in the lens of the human eye? The retina underneath is healthy and functional, so we project the visible world directly into the retina. We make the blind see again. That's the whole trick."

"I see." Jericho rubbed his chin. "And Yoyo's been working on this."

"Exactly."

"You must trust her a lot."

"She's good. She's full of ideas. A veritable ideas factory."

"She's an intern!"

"That hardly matters."

"To me it does. I have to know who I'm dealing with here, Tian. How clued-in is the girl, in truth? Is she really just a—" Dissident, he had been about to say. Stupid mistake. Diamond Shield would have filtered the word out from their conversation in an instant and put it into his file.

"Yoyo knows what's what," Tu said curtly. "I never said it would be easy to find her."

"No," said Jericho, more to himself than to Tu. "You didn't."

"Chin up. I've remembered something else."

"What?"

"Yoyo seems to have friends in a motorcycle gang. She never introduced me, but I remember that she had City Demons on her jackets. That might bring you further forward."

"I know about that already, thanks. Yoyo didn't happen to mention where they hang out?"

"I think you'll have to find that out on your own."

"All right then. If anything else comes back to you—"

"I'll let you know. Wait." Naomi Liu's voice came from the other side of the projection. Tu stood up and disappeared from Jericho's sight. He heard the two of them talking in low tones, then Tu came back.

"Excuse me, Owen, but it looks as though we've had a suicide." He hesitated. "Or an accident."

"What happened?"

"Something awful. Someone fell to his death. The roller coaster had been set in motion, outside its usual hours. It looks as if whoever it was had been working up there. I'll be back in touch, okay?"

"Okay."

They hung up. Jericho stayed there, sitting thoughtfully in front of the empty screen. Something about Tu's remark unsettled him. He wondered why. People threw themselves from skyscrapers the whole time. China had the highest suicide rate in the world, higher even than Japan, and skyscrapers were also the most cost-efficient and effective way to leave this life.

It wasn't about the suicide.

What then?

He fished out the stick that Tu had given him, put it on top of the console, and let the computer download Yoyo's virtual guided tours, her personnel file, records of conversations and documents. The files also contained her genetic code, voiceprint and eyescan, fingerprints and blood group. He could use the tours to get to know her body language and her gestures, her intonation as well, and the documents and conversation sound files would yield all her frequent turns of phrase, figures of speech, and even syntactical patterns. This gave him a usable personality profile. A dossier that he could work from.

Perhaps though he should start from what he *didn't* have.

He went online and set his computer looking for the City Demons. It served him up an Australian soccer club in New South Wales, another in New Zealand, a basketball team from Dodge City, Kansas, and a Vietnamese Goth band.

No demons in Shanghai.

After he had broadened the search mode and told it to allow for spelling errors, he got a hit. Two members of a biker gang called the City Daemons had gotten into a fight with half a dozen drunken North Koreans in the DKD Club on the Huaihai Zhong Lu; the NKs had been singing an anthem about the murder of their dear departed Supreme Leader. The bikers had gotten away with a police caution, since the Chinese leadership had declared Kim Jong-un *persona non grata*, posthumously, in recognition of the prevailing mood in the reunited Korea. Beijing had several reasons to make sure that they nipped in the bud any cult of nostalgia that might develop around North Korean totalitarianism.

City Daemons. With an "a."

Next the computer found a blog where Shanghai hip-hoppers picked up on the incident in the DKD and dwelt on the bravery of two members of the City Demons (with "e"), who had put their lives on the line to sling the North Koreans out on their ear. A link took Jericho to a biker forum, which he browsed through hoping to find out more about the Demons. This confirmed his suspicion that the Demons themselves had posted up the comments. The forum turned out to be an advertising platform for an e-bike and hybrids workshop called Demon Point, whose owner was probably, pretty nearly definitely, a member of the City Demons.

And that was interesting.

The workshop, he learned, lay on the edge of Quyu: a parallel world where hardly anybody had their own computer or a net connection, but there was the black hole of a Cyber Planet on every street corner, sucking in the local youths and never spitting them out again. It was a world ruled by several Triad subclans, sometimes striking deals, mostly at loggerheads, who only really agreed that no kind of crime was off-limits. A world of complex hierarchies, outside of which its inhabitants counted for nothing. A world which sent out battalions of cheap factory workers and unskilled labor to the better parts of the city every day, and then drew them back in every evening. A world which offered few sights but nevertheless drew the well-heeled toward it with some magic charm, offering them something that couldn't be found anywhere else in the Shanghai of urban renewal: the fascinating, iridescent gleam of human decay.

Quyu, the Zone, the forgotten world. The perfect place if you wanted to disappear without trace.

The little bike workshop wasn't in Quyu proper, but it was close enough to function as a gateway in or out. Jericho sighed. He found himself forced to take a step that he didn't like at all. He often worked with the Shanghai police, as he had done just recently. He had good relations with them. The officers would sometimes help him with his own cases, depending on whether they had their own irons in the fire in the cases of corruption or espionage that Jericho was looking into. For all that, they worked shoulder to shoulder when it came to fighting monsters such as Animal Ma Liping. His reputation among the police force was growing, even before he had rooted out the pedophile. When Jericho went out drinking with members of the force, they let it be known that they would like to pass on information if he needed it, and ever since the nightmare in Shenzhen his friend Patrice Ho, a high-ranking officer, owed him a major favor, and had made it clear that this could be a peek into police databases. Jericho would have been all too pleased to call in the favor now, but if the authorities really were after Yoyo, he couldn't even think about it.

And that meant that he had to hack his way in.

He'd dared to do so twice. He'd succeeded twice.

At the time, he had sworn not to chance it a third time. He knew what he'd be in for if they caught wind of him. After Beijing had hacked into European and American government networks in 2007, the West had gone on a counteroffensive, supported by Russian and Arab hackers working off their own grudges. Since then, there was hardly anything China feared more than cyber-attacks. Accordingly, anybody infiltrating Chinese systems was shown no mercy.

With mixed feelings, he set to work.

A little later he had the access he wanted to various archives. Practically every area of the city was decked out with scanners hidden in the walls of houses, in traffic lights and signposts, in door handles and bell-pushes, in advertising hoardings, labels, mirrors, scaffolding, and household devices. They scanned retinas, stored biometrics, analyzed the way people walked and gestured, recorded voices and sounds. While the phone-tapping system had been brought to the peak of perfection some decades ago, using the American NSA system as a model, retinal analysis was a comparatively new phenomenon. The scanner could recognize individual structures in the human iris from several meters away and thereby identify a person. Microscopically small directional microphones filtered the frequencies out of a noisy street crossing until you could hear one voice speaking quite distinctly. The real art of such surveillance lay in evaluating data. The system recognized wanted individuals by the way they moved; it could recognize a face even obscured by a false beard. If Yoyo glanced just once into one of the omnipresent scanners, this would be enough to identify her retina, which had been data-captured first as she was born, again on her first day of school, and then at university enrolment.

It had also been stored when she was arrested, and when she was released.

Jericho's computer started sifting.

It analyzed every twitch of Yoyo's eyes, dived into the crystalline structures of her iris, measured the angle of her lips when she smiled, set up studies for the way her hair moved in the wind, calibrated the sway of her hips, the spread of her fingers as she swung her arms, the line of her wrist as she pointed, her average length of pace. Yoyo became a creature of equations, an algorithm which Jericho sent out into the phantom world of the police surveillance archive, hoping that it would meet its match there. He narrowed down the search window to the time right after she had vanished, but even so the system reported more than 2,000 hits. He uploaded the stolen data to his hard drive, stored it under Yoyofiles and withdrew as quickly as he could. His presence had not been noticed. Time to begin evaluation.

Hold on, there was one piece of the puzzle missing. Unlikely though it might seem, this student with the grandiose name might actually have some information to offer. What was the guy called anyway? Grand Cherokee Wang.

Grand Cherokee—

At that moment, Jericho was struck by the realization.

He had found out in his investigations that Wang had a part-time job at the World Financial Center where Tu's company was headquartered. He handled the Silver Dragon—

And the Silver Dragon was a roller coaster!

The roller coaster had been set in motion, outside its usual hours. It looks as if whoever it was had been working up there.

Jericho gazed into empty air. His gut feelings told him that the student hadn't jumped of his own accord, and it hadn't been an accident. Wang was dead because he had known something about Yoyo. No, not even that! Because he had *given the impression* that he knew something about Yoyo.

This put the case in a whole new light.

He paced through the enormous loft, went into the kitchen and said, "Tea. Lady Gray. One cup, two sugars, milk as usual."

While the machine attended to his order, he went over what he knew. Perhaps he was seeing ghosts, but his knack for spotting patterns and making connections where others saw only fragments had rarely let him down. It was obvious that there was somebody else after Yoyo, besides himself. This wasn't in itself news. Chen and Tu had both voiced their suspicion that Yoyo was on the run. Both of them had also been doubtful that she was wanted by the police, even if Yoyo herself might believe just that. This time, she hadn't been picked up by police officers as had happened twice before; rather she had vanished at dead of night. Why? The decision seemed to have been made in great haste. Something must have made Yoyo fear a visit, in the next few minutes or hours, from people who did not have her best interests at heart. So what had she done *before* she took flight?

Had she been warned?

Who by? Who *against*? If Wang had been telling the truth, she had been alone at the time, so that meant that she might have had a call: Make sure you get out of there. Or an e-mail. Perhaps nothing of the sort. Perhaps she had discovered something on the net, seen something on the news, that frightened her.

A diffident beeping sound from the kitchen let him know that his tea was ready. Jericho picked up the cup, burned his hand, cursed, and took a little sip. He decided to call customer service to reprogram the machine. Two sugars was too sweet, one not sweet enough. Lost in thought, he went back to his office area. Shanghai police were not squeamish, but they were hardly in the habit of throwing suspects off the roof. More likely, Grand Cherokee Wang would have come around in a police station. The kid had wanted to play a bluff. A schemer, who hadn't actually had anything to sell, and had tried his act with the wrong customer.

Whose toes had Yoyo been treading on, for heaven's sake?

"Breaking news," he said. "Shanghai. World Financial Center."

Headlines and images grouped themselves together on the wall. Jericho blew on his tea and asked the computer to read him the latest reports.

"Today at around 10:50 local time a man fell to his death from the Shanghai World Financial Center in Pudong," said a female voice, pleasantly low-pitched. "Initial reports suggest that he worked in the building, with responsibility for watching and operating the Silver Dragon, the world's highest roller coaster. At the time he fell, the ride was in motion, outside of usual hours. The Public Prosecutor has opened proceedings against the ride's owners. It has been impossible to establish so far whether this was an accident or suicide, but everything seems to point to—"

"Show filmed reports only," said Jericho.

A video window opened. A young Chinese woman was standing in front of the Jin Mao Tower with the camera trained on her so that viewers could see the foot of the World Financial Center. Under a veneer of half-hearted distress she was glowing with joy at the thought that some nitwit had given her a headline in the summer silly season by obligingly dying for her.

"It is still a mystery why the roller-coaster ride was even in motion, without passengers and outside of its usual hours," she was saying, imbuing portent and secrecy into every word. "An eyewitness video which happened to be filming the tracks when the accident happened has shed some light on the matter. If indeed it was an accident. There is no confirmation as yet of the identity of the dead—"

"Eyewitness video," Jericho interrupted. "Identity of victim."

"The video is sadly not available." The computer managed to put a note of real regret into the announcement. Jericho had set the system's affective level to 20 percent. At this setting, the voice didn't sound mechanical, but rather warmly human. The computer also had a personality protocol. "There are two reports on the dead man's identity."

"Read, please."

"Shanghai Satellite writes: The dead man is apparently one Wang Jintao. Wang was a student at—"

"The second."

"Xinhua agency reports: The dead man has been positively identified as Wang Jintao, also known as Grand Cherokee, who studied—"

"Reports on the precise circumstances of death."

There were a great many reports, as it turned out, but nobody wanted to commit to a particular story. Nevertheless, they made up an interesting picture. It was certain that somebody had set the Silver Dragon free ten minutes early, before the paying passengers had arrived. Grand Cherokee's job had been to set the system in motion and look after the morning customers, which basically meant working the cash register and starting the ride. Nobody was supposed to be up there with him at the time of the incident, although there were indications that perhaps somebody had been there after all. Two staff members in the Sky Lobby said that they had seen Wang meet a man and go into an elevator with him. Further clues came from the eyewitness video, it seemed, which apparently showed Wang moving around on the tracks as the ride was already in motion.

What the hell had Wang been doing out there?

A short article in the Shanghai Satellite speculated that he could have set the ride going without meaning to. Suicide seemed the more likely explanation. On the other hand, why would somebody wanting to commit suicide pick his way along the track when he could have simply leaped from the open stretch of the boarding platform? Especially, another article added, since there were increasing indications that Wang hadn't actually jumped but had been run over by the train as it came bearing down on him.

Accident after all? At any rate, nobody was talking about murder, although here and there some commentators speculated about an accident caused by someone other than Wang.

Two minutes later Jericho knew better. Xinhua reported that the surveillance camera footage was now being examined. Wang had apparently been accompanied by a tall man who left the floor right after Wang fell. The two men seemed to have had an argument, Wang had certainly been moving along the track with no safety gear, and the train had run into him level with the southern pillar.

Jericho drank his tea and considered.

Who was the murderer?

"Computer," he said. "Open Yoyofiles."

More than 2,000 hits. Where should he begin? He decided to set a profile match of 95 percent, which left 117 files where the surveillance system thought that it had seen Yoyo.

He ordered the computer to select files with direct eye contact.

There was only one, immediately by the block where Yoyo lived, recorded at 02:47. Jericho wouldn't have been able to say exactly where the scanner was, but he suspected it was in a signpost. Exact coordinates were stored in a separate file. There was no doubt that the woman over there on the other side of the street was Yoyo. She was sitting on an unmarked motorcycle, no license plates, her head tilted down, both hands on a crash helmet. Just before she put it on, she lifted her gaze and looked directly into the scanner, then she put down the mirrored faceplate and sped away.

"Gotcha," muttered Jericho. "Computer, rewind."

Yoyo took the helmet briskly off again.

"Stop."

She looked him straight in the eyes.

"Zoom, 230 percent."

The new technology of the wall could give him a life-size view of Yoyo. The way she sat there on her bike, every detail clear in three-dimensional surroundings, it was as though he had opened a door out onto the night from his loft. He had judged the zoom quite well. Yoyo looked about 3 or 4 centimeters taller now than in real life, and the image was pin-sharp. A system that could recognize the structure of an iris from all the way across the street wasn't nicknamed "the freckle-counter" for nothing. Jericho knew that this would be his last good look at Yoyo for some time, so he tried to read what he could out of it.

You're frightened, thought Jericho. But you hide it well.

Also, your mind is made up.

He stepped back. Yoyo was wearing pale jeans, knee-boots, a printed T-shirt down over her hips, and a short puffy jacket of patent leather that looked as though it might have come from one of the spray cans he had found in her room. Most of the slogan printed on her shirt was in shadow, or under the jacket, and only a little showed where the jacket was open at the front. He would look into that later.

"Find this person in the folder called Yoyofiles," he said. "Ninety percent match."

Straight away he got the answer, 76 hits. He considered having the computer play all the films, but told it instead to plot the recordings' coordinates onto a city map of Shanghai. A moment later the map came up on the wall, showing Yoyo's route, where she had gone on the night she disappeared. The last sighting had been just across from Demon Point, the little e-bike and hybrids workshop. After that, the trail went cold.

She was in the forgotten world.

Yoyo had only remained undiscovered in Quyu because there were hardly any surveillance systems there. Even so, Quyu wasn't a slum in the classic sense, not to be compared with the festering shantytowns that surrounded Calcutta, Mexico City, or Bombay and oozed out into the surrounding countryside. As a global city on a par with New York, Shanghai needed Quyu the way the Big Apple needed the Bronx, meaning that the city left the district in peace. It didn't send in the bulldozers, or the riot police. In the years after the turn of the millennium, the historic inner-city areas and slums in the Shanghai interior had been torn down systematically until those boroughs were free of any sort of authentic history. Where the outer district of Baoshan ran up against this new Shanghai core, Quyu had grown up and been allowed to grow, much as a landowner might allow scrubland to grow in order to save the cost of a gardener. Quyu, north-west of Huangpu, now marked the crossover to swaths of makeshift settlements, vestigial villages, run-down small towns and abandoned industrial estates—a Moloch that grabbed more of the surrounding land each year, guzzling down the last remnants of a region that had once been rural.

Quyu was internally autonomous, and externally it was watched as closely as a prison camp; it was one of the most impressive examples of twenty-first-century urban poverty. The population was made up of people displaced from their original homes in the heart of Shanghai, of those who had lived here even before Quyu absorbed their small towns, of migrants from poor provinces lured to the promised land of the global city and living on temporary residence permits that no one ever checked, of battalions of illegal laborers who didn't officially exist. Everybody in Quyu was poor, though some were less poor than others. Most money was made in drugs or in the leisure sector, largely prostitution. The social structure of Quyu's population was unregulated in every way, with not a hint of health insurance, old age pension, or unemployment benefit.

But it was still more than just a horde of beggars.

After all, most of them had work. They manned the assembly lines and the building sites, they cleaned the parks and streets, drove delivery trucks and cleaned the houses of the better-off. They would turn up like ghosts in the regulated world, do their job, and then vanish again once they were no longer needed. They were poor because everybody living in Quyu could be replaced at twenty-four hours' notice. They stayed poor because, in the words of the wise old sage Bill Gates, they were part of a global society divided into those who were networked and those who weren't. In Quyu, nobody was networked, even if they owned a cell phone or a computer. Being networked meant playing the same high-speed game as the rest of the world, not letting your attention lapse for a second. It meant sifting out the relevant information from the irrelevant, grabbing advantages that lapsed as soon as you logged off. It meant being better, faster, leaner, more innovative, and more flexible than the competition at every moment; it meant moving home when required, switching jobs.

It meant getting a place at the table.

Gates had said that the future belonged to the networked. Logically, nonnetworked society therefore had no future. Individuals outside the network were like spiders who didn't spin threads. Nothing got caught in their web. They would starve.

Officially, nobody had starved to death in Quyu yet. Even if the powers-that-be in China had a blind spot when it came to slums or shantytowns, they wouldn't quite so readily allow anyone to die of hunger on the streets of Shanghai. Less from the milk of human kindness, and more because you just couldn't have that sort of thing happening in a world financial center. On the other hand, official attitudes to Quyu mattered not a jot. What sort of official figures might come out of a district with totally opaque demographics, which was widely seen as ungovernable and uncontrollable, which actually ran its own affairs in some incomprehensible way and where the police hardly dared venture, although they had put a ring of iron around its edge? It was known that there was infrastructure of sorts, houses of sorts, some habitable, others barely more than damp caves. Clean drinking water was scarce, power cuts frequent; there was hardly a flush toilet in the place. There were doctors and ambulances in Quyu, hospitals, schools and kindergartens, snack bars, tea houses, bars, movies, and kiosks and street markets of the sort that had almost completely vanished from the rest of Shanghai. Nobody knew, though, how life went on in Quyu exactly. Crimes committed there were hardly followed up, and this too was part of the tacit agreement that the district should look after itself, and was to be cut loose from the dynamic of social development. Residents were given no support but they were not held to account either, as long as they didn't break the law outside the borders of their tribal reservation. There was no future here, and that meant no past, or at least not a past one could boast of or build on. Without a network, they lived outside of time itself, on the dark fringes of a universe whose shining centers were connected by multi-story freeways and sky trains. Certainly the shortest routes from Shanghai city center out to the luxurious commuter towns ran through districts like Quyu,

but that didn't mean anybody had to pass through the forgotten world
and actually take notice of what went on there. The routes simply ran
right *overhead*, as though the place was a swamp.

For a while the leadership in Beijing had asked themselves whether
this method of running Shanghai might lead to revolt. Nobody
doubted that terrorists and criminals had gone to live there. Nevertheless the necessity of tightening the State's grip in the district was
undermined by skepticism that a rabble of migrant farm workers, factory girls, errand boys, and building laborers would ever be able to
coalesce into anything like a workers' uprising. Large-scale political
violence was expected from the bourgeoisie instead, since they had
access to the information superhighway and to all kinds of hi-tech. On
the other hand, the conventional criminals who haunted Quyu would
feel all the safer there, the less danger they were in from outside. When
had the Mafia ever called the workers to arms? In the end, the opinion
prevailed that every criminal in Quyu was one less outside Xaxu, leading Beijing to issue a clear recommendation:

Forget Quyu.

Yoyo had taken shelter in a world which was one of the blank spaces
on the map of urbanization. Jericho wondered whether anyone in
Quyu had ever thought that it was also a form of discrimination *not* to
be under surveillance.

Probably not.

He had spent the evening looking on the Internet for texts that Yoyo
might have written since she went underground. He used the same
technology for this that Diamond Shield used in its hectic search for
dissidents, or that the American secret services used in the unending
war on terror, the same he had used himself against Animal Ma Liping. The rhythms of keystrokes on a computer keyboard were just as
individual as fingerprints. A suspect could be identified in the very
moment that he began to write his text into a browser. Advances in
Social Network Analysis were even more interesting: choice of vocabulary, favored metaphors, everything left grammatical, and semantic
clues. A computer only needed a few hundred words to identify who
was writing with almost 100 percent accuracy. Most interesting of
all, the system didn't just blindly pile up words; it recognized meaning and context. To a certain extent, it actually understood what the
writer was trying to say. It developed an unconscious intelligence, and
became capable of tracking down whole networks, world-spanning
structures of terrorism or organized crime, where neo-Nazis, bombers,
racists, and hooligans living thousands of miles apart met in a virtual
alliance—though in real life they might well have beaten one another
to pulp.

This had helped to track down pedophiles and uncover industrial
espionage, but it also proved to be a nightmare for dissidents and

human rights activists. It was no surprise that repressive regimes in particular showed great interest in the methods of Social Network Analysis. Nevertheless, Yoyo had always managed to stay one step ahead of the security services' analytical programs, until a few days ago when she had been exposed and identified. If indeed that was what had happened. At least Yoyo must have believed that that was the case, and this explained her headlong flight.

What he still couldn't understand was how she noticed.

Jericho yawned.

He was dog-tired. He had had the computer running after clues all night. Obviously he would not be finding Yoyo any time soon. The Internet Police had spent years snapping at her heels, with no success. She probably knew the analytical programs' algorithms inside out and backward; in such matters, working for Tu Technologies was like sitting in the Jade Temple of Enlightenment. Feeling fairly baffled, he wondered how he could manage something that until just recently not even the government had been able to do; but he had one invaluable advantage.

He knew that Yoyo was one of the Guardians.

While the computer was chasing her virtual shadow, Jericho had unpacked the rest of the boxes and turned the loft into something that pretty well resembled an apartment. When at last the furniture was in place, the pictures were hanging on the walls, and his clothes were in the closet, once everything was tidied away and in its place, and Erik Satie's *Trois Gymnopédies* rippled through the room, he felt happy and at peace for the first time in days, free from those images of Shenzhen, and had even lost all interest in Yoyo for the time being.

Owen Jericho, snug in a cocoon of music.

"Match," announced the computer.

Irksome.

So irksome that he decided there and then to dial up the personality protocol by 30 percent. At least then the computer would sound like someone you could share a coffee or a glass of wine with.

"There's a blog entry that looks like Yoyo," said the warm female voice, almost human. "She posted an entry on Brilliant Shit, a Mando Prog forum. Should I read it out?"

"Are you sure that it's Yoyo?"

"Almost certain. She knows how to cover her tracks. I imagine Yoyo is working with distorters. What do you think?"

Without the personality protocol the remark would have come out as: "84.7 percent match. Probability that distorter is being used, 90.2 percent."

"I think it's very probable that she's working with distorters," Jericho agreed.

Distorters were programs that go over a text and alter the writer's personal style. They were becoming more and more popular. Some of them rewrote texts using the style of great poets and writers, so that you could dash off a message and have it reach the recipient looking as though it had been written by Thomas Mann, Ernest Hemingway, or Jonathan Franzen. Other programs imitated politicians. It became dangerous when malevolent hackers cracked the profiles of other, unsuspecting users and borrowed their style. Many dissidents on the net preferred to use distorters that would rewrite with randomly generated standards, using a variety of styles. The most important thing was that the meaning remain the same.

And that was precisely the weak spot in most programs.

"Elements in the blog post are not stylistically uniform," said the computer. "That confirms your theory, Owen."

A nice touch, using his first name. Polite too to pretend that it had been *his* theory, as though the computer itself hadn't suggested that a distorter was at work. God knows, 50 percent personality protocol was enough. At 80 percent the computer would be crawling up his backside. Jericho hesitated. In fact he was fed up with calling the thing "computer." What would a girl like this be called? Maybe—

He programs her with a name.

"Diane?"

"Yes, Owen?"

Great. He likes Diane. Diane is his new right-hand woman.

"Please read the entry."

"Glad to. *Hi all. Back in our galaxy now, have been for a few days. Was really stressed out these last days, is anybody harshing on me? Couldn't help it, really truly. All happened so fast. Shit. Even so quickly you can be forgotten. Only waiting now for the old demons to visit me once more. Yeah, and, I'm busy writing new songs. If any of the band asks: We'll make an appearance once I've got a few euphonious lyrics on the go. Let's prog!*"

Once again Jericho wonders how the program can identify a writer from such a mishmash, but experience has taught him that even less would be enough. Still, he doesn't have to understand it. He's an end user, not a programmer.

"Give me an analysis," he says. It's really quite cozy by now, with Satie and this velvet-smooth voice.

"Of course, Owen."

That's to say, this "of course" has to go. It reminds him of HAL 6000 from *2001: A Space Odyssey*. Ever since the satnav system was invented, every speaking computer has been doing its best to copy crazy HAL.

"The text is supposed to sound cocky," the computer said. "The style is broken though by the terms *even so quickly* and *euphonious. The old demons to visit me once more* seems rather forced, I don't believe that the distorter was at work here. Everything else is just minor detail, *lyrics on the go* for instance doesn't fit the style of the second and third sentences."

"What do you make of the content?"

"Hard to say. I might have a couple of suggestions for you. First off, *galaxy*. That might just be loosely meant, or it might be a synonym for something."

"For instance?"

"Probably for a locality."

"Go on."

"*Demons*. You've already been looking for demons. I suspect that Yoyo is referring here to the City Demons, or City Daemons."

"I'm with you there. By the way, Daemons was a blind alley. Anything else strike you?"

The computer hesitated. The personality protocol once more.

"I don't know enough about Yoyo. I could give you about 380,000 variant interpretations of the other wording and phrases."

"Put a sock in it," Jericho murmured.

"I'm sorry, I didn't quite catch that."

"Doesn't matter. Please search Shanghai for the word *galaxy* in connection with some place or other."

This time the computer didn't hesitate. "No entries."

"Good. Locate where the text was sent from."

"Of course." The computer gave him the coordinates. Jericho is astonished. He hadn't expected it would be so easy to track back the route the message took. He would have thought that Yoyo laid a few more false trails when communicating.

"Are you sure that you haven't just found an intermediary browser?"

"One hundred percent sure, Owen. The message was sent from there at 06:24 local time on the morning of May 24th."

Jericho nods. That's good. That's very good!

And his hope becomes a certainty.

Forgotten World

As Jericho steered his COD along the Huaihai Donglu toward the elway, he went over his conclusions from last night once more.

Hi all. Back in our galaxy now, have been for a few days.

Which could mean, I've been back in Quyu for a few days. Obvious. Not so clear though why Yoyo would call Quyu a galaxy. More likely that she meant one particular place in Quyu.

Was really stressed out these last days, is anybody harshing on me?

Stress. Well, obviously.

And why would anybody be angry at her? That was also fairly easily told. Yoyo wasn't actually asking a question here, she was giving an explanation. That somebody had tracked her down, that this someone was dangerous, and that she didn't know who she was dealing with.

Couldn't help it, really truly. All happened so fast. Shit.

More difficult. She had taken flight at panic speed. But what did the first part mean? What couldn't she help?

Even so quickly you can be forgotten.

Trivially easy. Quyu, the forgotten world. Almost a platitude. Yoyo must have been in a hurry to get the message out.

Only waiting now for the old demons to visit me once more.

Even easier: City Demons, you know where I am.

Yeah, and, I'm busy writing new songs. If any of the band asks: We'll make an appearance once I've got a few euphonious lyrics on the go. Let's prog!

Which was as much as to say, I'm trying to get the problems under control as fast as I can. Until then, we'll disappear.

And who is *we*?

The Guardians.

The city freeway ran at an angle to Jericho's route. An eight-lane road with enough traffic on it for sixteen, and with several stories of elevated highway soaring above. Cars, buses, and vans crawled through the morning as though through aspic. Hundreds of thousands of commuters flooded into the city from the satellite towns, taxi drivers glowered out at the world around. Not even bikers found a spot where they could squeeze through here. They all wore breathing masks, but nevertheless you expected to see them turn blue and slump from their saddles. Even though there were more fuel-cell cars in use in the metropolises of China than anywhere else in the world, more hydrogen motors and more electric engines, a blanket of smoggy exhaust fumes lay over the city.

A special traffic track ran high above everything else. It was supported by slender telescopic legs, had only been opened for use a few years ago, and was reserved exclusively for CODs. Now COD tracks connected all the most important points in the city and led out to the commuter towns and the coast, some of them at dizzying heights. Jericho threaded his way onto the steep entrance ramp, waited for his vehicle to click into place on the rails and entered his destination coordinates. From now on he didn't need to steer the COD, which would have been impossible anyway. As soon as CODs were in the system, the driver played no further part.

Jericho's COD climbed up the slope in a row of identical machines. Up on the track, he could see countless numbers of the cabin-like vehicles racing away at more than 300 kilometers per hour, gleaming silver in the sun. One story down, any sort of movement had ceased.

He leaned back.

The vehicles approaching in the outside lane braked just enough to leave a precisely measured gap for his vehicle to slip into. Jericho loved the moment of rapid acceleration when the COD took off. He was pressed briefly against the back of his seat, then he had reached cruising speed. His phone told him that he had received a message from the computer. The display scanned his iris. An additional voice-print check wasn't really necessary, but Jericho liked to make assurance doubly sure.

"Owen Jericho," he said.

"Good morning, Owen."

"Hello, Diane."

"I've analyzed the writing on Yoyo's shirt. Would you like to see the result?"

He had given the computer this job before he set off. He linked his phone to the interface on the car dashboard.

"What does it say?"

"It's evidently a symbol."

A large A appeared on the COD monitor. At least, Jericho supposed that it was supposed to be an A. The crossbar was missing, although in its place a ragged ring slanted around the letter instead. Underneath he could read four letters, NDRO.

"Have you looked for similar symbols on the net?"

"Yes. What you see here is the result of image enhancement. It's a reconstruction based on high-probability matches. The symbol doesn't turn up anywhere in the data store. The letters might be an abbreviation, or a word fragment. I've found NDRO as an abbreviation several times, just not in China."

"What word do you reckon it might be?"

"My favorites are androgynous, android, Andromeda."

"Thank you, Diane." Jericho thought for a moment. "Can you see whether I left the bedroom window open?"

"It's open."

"Shut it, please."

"Shall do, Owen."

The COD alerted him that it would leave the track in a few seconds. It had taken only four minutes to travel almost 20 kilometers. Jericho took his phone from the interface. The COD slowed, drew out and threaded into the line of cars that were leaving the network just before Quyu. He made fairly good speed down the turn-off and onto the main road. Even here, far outside the city center, the traffic flowed sluggishly, but at least it was moving. Quyu was separated from the city by several stories of freeway. Streets leading out were bundled together by roadblocks and fed through pinch points, with a police station near every one. There were also army barracks to the east and west. For all that, only a very few people in Quyu could even afford a car or the COD hire fee, so that metro lines and trolley-buses connected the district to the city.

The City Demons workshop was just outside Xaxu in a historic quarter, not two kilometers west of here. It was one of the last of the really old quarters. Earlier it had been a village, or a small country town, and sooner or later it would have to give way to the phalanxes of anonymous modern houses. Now that the downtown had been completely remodeled, the planners were having a go at the periphery.

Only Quyu would stay untouched, as ever.

Fast though he had got here on the COD track, it was painfully slow getting to the part of town he wanted to go. It was a typical old-style neighborhood. Stone buildings, one to three stories high, with black and dark red gables, lined busy streets where many little alleys branched off, and courtyards opened up. There were open storefronts and food sellers lurked under colorful awnings, and clotheslines stretched between the houses. The Demon Point workshop took up the whole ground floor of a rust-streaked house with a gap-toothed wooden balcony around its first floor. Some windowpanes were missing, others were crazed and blind.

Jericho parked the COD in a side street and strolled across to the workshop. Several handsome hybrids and e-bikes were lined up in front of other, less attractive specimens. There was nobody to be seen until a thin boy in shorts and a baggy T-shirt smeared with oil came out from a tiny office and got to work on one of the e-bikes with a rag and a can of polish.

"Hello," said Jericho.

The boy looked up briefly and turned back to his work. Jericho squatted down next to him.

"Very nice bike."

"Mmhm."

"I can see how you're polishing it. Are you one of the ones who cleaned the NKs' clocks as well, in the DKD Club?"

The kid grinned and kept on polishing.

"That was Daxiong."

"Good work he did."

"He told the jerks to shut their traps. Even though there were more of them. Said that he didn't feel like listening to their fascist crap."

"I hope he didn't get any trouble from them."

"Little bit." The boy seemed only now to realize that he'd fallen into conversation with somebody he didn't know at all. He put down his rag and looked at Jericho distrustfully. "Who are you anyway?"

"Ahh, I was just headed for Quyu. Sheer chance that I spotted your workshop here. And given that I'd read that blog post—Well, I thought, since I'm here anyway—"

"Interested in a bike?"

Jericho stood up. He looked where the boy was pointing. Over at the back of the workshop, a burly chopper, an electro, was up on its chocks. The rear wheel was missing.

"Why not?" He walked over to the machine and admired it ostentatiously. "Been thinking for years of getting a chopper. Lithium-aluminum battery?"

"That's right. It'll give you 280."

"Range?"

"Four hundred kilometers. Minimum. Are you from downtown?"

"Mmhm."

"That's hell for cars. You should think about it."

"Shall do." Jericho took out his phone. "I don't know my way around here, sadly. I'm supposed to meet someone, but you know how Quyu is for addresses. Maybe you can help me."

The kid shrugged. Jericho projected the A with the hazy ring around it onto the back wall of the workshop. The boy's eyes gave him away—he knew the place.

"That's where you want to go?"

"Is it far?"

"Not really. You just have to—"

"Shut your mouth," said somebody behind him.

Jericho turned around and stared at a chest that began somewhere in the southeast and ended further along to the northeast. Way up above the chest there had to be something that the brute used to think. He put his head back and made out a shaven skull, with eyes so narrow that it was hard to believe he could see through them. A blue appliqué on his chin looked vaguely like a pharaoh's beard. The leather jacket was open at the front, and beneath it he could see the City Demons logo.

"It's fine." The boy looked upward, uncertain. "He was just asking where—"

"What?"

"Everything's okay." Jericho smiled. "I wanted to know whether—"

"What? What do you want to know?"

The man-mountain made no attempt to bend down to talk to him, which would have made conversation considerably easier. Jericho took a step back and turned his projector to the wall again.

"I'm sorry if I've come at a bad moment. I'm looking for an address."

"An address?" The other man turned his massive head and looked—as far as Jericho could tell—at the projected image.

"I mean, is that even an address at all?" Jericho asked. "I've only got—"

"Who gave you that?"

"Someone who didn't have much time to give me directions. Someone from Quyu. Someone I want to help."

"What with?"

"Social problems."

"Is there anyone in Quyu who doesn't have those?"

"True enough." Jericho decided not to take this treatment any longer. "What now? I don't want to keep this person waiting."

"He's also interested in the chopper!" added the boy, in a tone that suggested he had already talked Jericho into buying the machine for an enormous sum.

The man-mountain pursed his lips.

Then he smiled.

The suspicion melted sheer away from his features, making way for warm friendship. An enormous paw swooped through space and landed with a playful smack on Jericho's shoulder.

"Why didn't you say so right away?"

That had broken the ice. His suddenly hearty manner didn't yield any more information though, but rather a detailed description of all the chopper's supposed virtues, and he reached a genial crescendo as he named an exorbitant price. The ogre even managed to price the missing rear wheel separately.

Jericho nodded and nodded. At the end, he shook his head.

"No?" said the giant, surprised.

"Not at that price."

"Fine. Name your price."

"I'll give you another idea. An A with a frayed ring around it and four mysterious letters beneath. You remember? I go there, I come back. Then we do business."

The giant wrinkled his brow laboriously. He was thinking, Jericho had to assume. Then he described a route which seemed to run the whole length and breadth of Quyu.

What had the kid said just now? Not really far?

"And what do the letters mean?"

"NDRO?" The giant laughed. "This friend of yours must really have been in a hurry. It's Andromeda."

"Ah!"

"It's a live-concert venue."

"Thanks."

"Your knowledge of Quyu seems to rest on the very slightest acquaintance, if you don't mind my saying so."

Jericho had to raise his eyebrows. He would never have expected that a man-mountain like this, with such a tough-looking skull, would produce such a refined turn of phrase.

"It's true, I hardly know the place."

"Then take care of yourself."

"Of course. I'll see you later, umm—May I ask your name?"

A grin spread across the huge face.

"Daxiong. Just Daxiong."

Aha. Six Koreans had come away with injuries. Slowly, the story was becoming clearer.

Jericho had never been in Quyu before. He had no idea what was lying in wait for him when he drove through beneath the freeway. But in fact nothing happened. Quyu didn't begin at any clearly marked spot, at least not in this part. It simply just—began. With rows of low-built houses like the ones he had just left. Hardly any shops as such, but instead street vendors side by side, who had spread out onto their sheets and carpets anything that seemed saleable and couldn't run away. A woman in a rickety rattan chair, dozing in the shadow of a makeshift canopy, with a basket of eggplants in front of her. A shopper took two of these, put money in her apron, and went on without waking her. Old people chatting, some in pajamas, others bare-chested. Jostling crowds on crumbling sidewalks. Criss-crossing the street, overhead, the flapping laundry hung out to dry, blouses and shirts waving their sleeves at one another whenever the wind found its way between the houses. Murmurs, chatting and shouting, melodic, booming, shrill or low, all woven together into a cacophony. Cheap pedal-bikes everywhere, clawing at the nerves, squeaking and rattling, the thud of hammers and the whine of drills, the sounds of running repairs, maintenance of the make-do-and-mend school. Some traders spotted Jericho's head of blond hair, leaped to their feet and yelled "Looka, looka!" across the street, waving handbags, watches, sculptures; he ignored them, concentrating on not running anyone over. In Shanghai, downtown Shanghai, traffic was a state of war. Trucks hunted buses, buses chased cars which chased bikes, and all of them together had sworn death to all pedestrians. In Quyu it was less aggressive, but that made it no better. Rather than attacking one another, road users simply ignored one another. Folk who had just now been haggling over chickens or kitchenware would hop down into the road, or stand there in little groups, debating the weather, the price of groceries, their families' health.

With every street he went down, Jericho saw fewer traders aiming at the tourist market. The goods offered for sale became cheaper. As the number of cars on the street dropped, there were more and more pedestrians and bicycles, and the throng thinned out. More and more often he saw half-demolished houses, their missing walls meagerly patched with cardboard and corrugated iron, all of them inhabited. In between, years and years of rubble. A cluster of gray and dull blue modular blocks appeared at the side of the road as though cast carelessly down like dice, arthritic trees twisted double in front of them, the randomly parked cars dating back to the days when Deng Xiaoping had proclaimed the economic miracle which had never quite taken place in this part of China.

All of a sudden it was dark around him.

The deeper Jericho went into the heart of Quyu, the less clearly structured it became. Every possible style of architecture seemed to have been thrown on the heap here. High-rise blocks abandoned halfway alternated with derelict low-rises and silos several stories high, their hideousness emphasized by the peeling remains of several colors of paint. Jericho was most moved by the pathetic attempts to make the uninhabitable look like a habitation. There was something almost like an architectural vernacular going on here in the tangle of handbuilt shacks, most little more than posts rammed into the ground and covered over with tarpaulin. At least there was life here, while the silos looked like postatomic tombs.

In the midst of a wasteland of garbage he stopped and looked at women and children loading whatever they thought they could use onto barrows. Whole swaths here looked as though once-intact city blocks had been pulverized by bombing raids. He tried to remember what he knew about districts like these. A number that he had noticed somewhere flitted through his mind. In 2025, there were 1.5 billion people living in slums worldwide. Twenty years before it had been 1 billion. Every year,20 or 30 million came to join them. A new arrival in the slums had to fight his way up bizarre hierarchies, where those on the lowest rung collected trash and made from it whatever they could sell or trade. According to Daxiong's description, he would need at least another hour to get to the Andromeda. He drove on, thought of the neighborhood he had wound up living in years ago, shortly before it had been torn down to make room for the development where Yoyo lived. At the time he hadn't been able to understand why the residents were so attached to their ruins. He understood that they had no choice, except that some of them could have taken up the offer of being relocated in relatively luxurious apartments outside Shanghai, with running water, baths and toilets, elevators and electricity.

"Here, we exist," they had answered, smiling. "Outside, we are ghosts."

It was only later that he realized that the measure of human misery is not in the condition of the housing. Scarce drinking water, overflowing gutters, blocked drains, all these had their place in the annals of hell. But while people were living on the streets, at least they could meet. It was where they sold their wares. It was where they cooked for the laborers who never otherwise had a chance to make a meal. Food preparation alone provided a living for millions of families, and fed them in turn, a livelihood that could only be earned down at street level, just as the street provided social cohesion. People stood by their doorways, deep in conversation. Life at ground level, the openness of houses, all this spread warmth and comfort. Nobody dropped in to buy something on the tenth floor of a high-rise, and if you stepped outside the door, all you could see was a wall. The road took him to a hill. From up here, he could see in every direction, as much as he could see anything through the dirty brown blanket of smog. The COD was air-conditioned, but Jericho thought he could feel the sun on his skin. All around him was a sight he had grown used to by now. Shacks, high-rise blocks, all more or less shabby, poles standing drunkenly festooned with dangling power cables, rubble, dirt.

Should he go on?

Baffled, he told his phone to take bearings. It projected him right in the middle of no man's land. Off the maps. It was only when he zoomed out that it deigned to show him a couple of main roads that ran through Quyu, if the data was still up-to-date.

Was Yoyo really hiding in this desolation?

He entered the coordinates from where the blog post had been uploaded to Brilliant Shit. The computer showed him a spot not far from Demon Point, near the freeway.

Back the other way.

Swearing, he turned around, narrowly avoided a barrow which several kids were pushing across the road, garnered a few choice insults and then drove off fast, back where he had come from. He passed by on his left the area he had driven through at first, got lost in a tangle of streets, blundered through a garment district, spotted a through road between street stalls heaped with cloths, and found himself on a wide street with walls on each side and remarkably neat-looking houses behind them. It was seething with people and with vehicles of all kinds. The scene was dominated by food stalls, fast food chains, shops, and booths. He passed several branches of Cyber Planet. The whole thing looked like a run-down version of London's legendary Camden Town when there had still been a subculture there to speak of, thirty years ago now. Prostitutes leaned up in doorways. Groups of men who were definitely not in the peace-and-love business sat around in front of cafés and wok kitchens, or walked about with appraising eyes. Jericho's COD was given many thoughtful looks.

According to the computer his destination was very close, but it seemed there was a curse on him. He kept taking wrong turns. Every attempt to get back to the main road led him deeper into this off-kilter world that was obviously ruled by the triads; this must be where the slumlords lived, the lords of decay. Twice, groups of men stopped him and tried to drag him from the car, for whatever reason. At last he found a shortcut, and the quarter was suddenly behind him. The blocky silhouette of a steelworks showed in the distance. He drove over a bulldozed stretch to a gigantic rust-brown complex with chimneys. A group of bikers overtook him, went past, and vanished on the other side of the walls. Jericho followed them. The road led to a large open yard, obviously some kind of gathering place. There were bikes parked everywhere, young people sitting together smoking and drinking. Music boomed across the factory yard. Pubs and clubs, brothels and sex-shops had been set up in empty workshops. The inevitable Cyber Planet took up one whole side of the yard, surrounded by stalls offering hand-made appliqués; another shop was promoting second-hand musical instruments. A two-story brick building stood across from the Cyber Planet. A van was parked in front of the open doors, and martial-looking figures were carrying gear and electronics inside.

Jericho couldn't believe his eyes.

A huge letter A, twice as tall as a man, leaped out at him from above the doors. Underneath, in large letters, a single word:

ANDROMEDA

Tires squealing, he stopped in front of the van, jumped out and walked back a few paces. All at once he realized what the ragged ring that replaced the crossbar on the A was supposed to be. Diane had done her best with the image that she had, but the whole picture only made sense in the original. The ring was a picture of a galaxy, and Andromeda, or rather the Andromeda nebula, was a spiral galaxy in the Andromeda constellation.

Hi all. Back in our galaxy now, have been for a few days.

Yoyo was here!

Or maybe not. Not anymore. Daxiong had sent him on a wild goose chase so as to give her time to disappear. He swore, and squinted up at the sun. The smog smeared its light into a flat film that hurt his eyes. In a foul mood he locked the COD and entered the twilit world of Andromeda. There was this at least: Chen Hongbing had been afraid that his daughter might be sitting in a police cell somewhere with no official charges. Jericho could disabuse him of that worry. On the other hand, Chen hadn't even hired him for this job, at least not in so many words. He could go home. His job was done.

At least, everything *seemed* to say that he had found Yoyo's trail. And then lost it again.

Irritating, that.

He looked around. A spacious foyer. Later in the evening, this would be where they sold tickets, drinks, cigarettes. The wall across from the cash register was hidden by a flurry of posters, flyers, newsletters, and a bulletin board bristling with announcements. Obviously it was some kind of subculture clearinghouse. Jericho went closer. It was mostly requests for work or for rideshares, for rooms, instruments, and software. Second-hand goods of all sorts were offered for sale, some doubtless stolen, and sexual partners for hire—for a night, for longer, for particular tastes. Sometimes the offers matched what other notices sought. Most of the sheets of paper were handwritten, an uncommon sight. He went into the actual concert venue, a bare hall with high windows looking onto the courtyard. Most of the windowpanes were boarded or painted over, so that little light filtered through despite the harsh sun outside. Here and there a sheet of cardboard stood in for missing glass. The far end of the hall was taken up by a stage that could easily have accommodated two full orchestras. Speaker boxes were piled up each side. Two men on ladders were adjusting spotlights, others carried boxes of equipment past him. A steel stair ran up to a balcony along the long side wall across from the windows.

Jericho thought of Chen Hongbing and the suffering in his eyes.

He owed Tu more than just conjecture.

Two men pushed past him with a huge trunk on wheels. One of them lifted the lid and took microphone stands from inside, putting them up to the stage. The other went back toward the foyer, paused, turned his head and stared at Jericho.

"Can I help?" he asked in a tone of voice that suggested he should shove off.

"Who's playing tonight?"

"The Pink Asses."

"The Andromeda was recommended to me," Jericho said. "Apparently you have some of the best concerts in Shanghai."

"Could be."

"I don't know the Pink Asses. Worth my time?"

The man looked at him derisively. He was well-built, handsome, with regular, almost androgynous features and shoulder-length hair. The orange T-shirt above his shiny leather pants clung to him like a second skin; it could have come from a spray can. He wasn't wearing the usual appliqués found in this subculture, or any other jewelry.

"Depends what you like."

"Anything that's good."

"Mando-prog?"

"For instance."

"You're in the wrong place then." The man grinned. "The music sounds just like the band's name."

"It sounds like pink backsides?"

"It sounds like assholes fucked bloody, you idiot. Both genders. Ass Metal, never heard of it? You still want to come?"

Jericho smiled. "We'll see."

The other man rolled his eyes and went outside.

Jericho felt stymied for a moment. Should he perhaps have asked the guy about Yoyo? It was easy to be paranoid in a place like this. Everybody here seemed part of a shadow army whose mission was to stop folks like him asking anything about Yoyo.

"Bullshit," he muttered. "She's a dissident, not the Queen of Quyu."

Tu had spoken of six activists. Six, not sixty. Yoyo's blog post had suggested that all six were members of the City Demons. Further, she had to have helping hands here in the Andromeda. It was quite certain that most people here had no idea who Yoyo was, nor that she was hiding somewhere in the complex. The real problem was that the locals in a place like Quyu refused on principle to answer questions.

As he watched them putting down cables and lugging instruments up to the stage, he considered his options. Daxiong had warned Yoyo that someone was interested in the Andromeda. He must believe that Jericho was still wandering around in the Quyu hinterland with no clue where he was, out of circulation for the next few hours. Yoyo would think the same.

Time was still on his side.

He glanced all about. The stage was covered over by a kind of alcove, where two windows which used to look out over the factory floor were bricked up. Work went on around him. Nobody was paying him any attention. Unhurried, he climbed the metal steps and went along the balcony. It ended in a door, painted gray. He turned the handle. He had been expecting to find it locked, but it swung silently inward and showed him a twilit hallway. He slipped in, went through a doorway to the right and found himself in a neon-lit room with a single window that overlooked the yard.

He was right over the stage.

Even though it was cold, barely furnished, and unwelcoming, there was something indefinably lived-in about the room, typical of a place vacated just moments before. An energy that lingered on, unconscious memories stored in the molecules, objects that had been moved, recently breathed air. He went to a table with chairs around it, Formica seats on rusty legs, under the table a half-full wastepaper basket. A few open shelves, mattresses on the floor, only one of them in use to judge by the tangled sheets and the pillow. Laptops on the shelves, a printer, stacks of paper, some of it printed. More stacks of comics, magazines, books. The centerpiece was a prehistoric stereo with radio and record player. There were vinyl records arranged along the wall, by the look of them survivals from the time when CDs were still rare. Right now of course CDs were a dying species as well. But you could buy records again, in today's download era, new records from new bands.

A few of them really were old, though, as Jericho found out when he squatted down to look. He flicked through the sleeves and read the names on the covers. There were examples of Chinese pop and avant-garde, such as Top Floor Circus, Shen Yin Sui Pian, SondTOY, and Dead J, but also albums by Genesis, Van der Graaf Generator, King Crimson, Magma, and Jethro Tull. There was scarcely a gap in the collection from the sixties and seventies, the era when progressive rock was invented. In the eighties it had been fighting a losing battle against punk and New Wave, in the nineties it was on its last legs, in the first decade of the new millennium it seemed to be dead, and the genre owed its revival not to Europeans but to Chinese DJs who had begun to mix it in with dance beats around 2020. This glittering new mixture of concert rock, dance floor, and Beijing Opera had been enjoying a boom ever since, with new bands sprouting daily. Popular artists such as Zhong Tong Xi, third-party, IN3, and B6 made whole new worlds of sound from the complex concept albums of the progressive era, and the local superstars Mu Ma and Zuo Xiao Zu Zhou organized all-star projects with grand old men of rock such as Peter Hammill, Robert Fripp, Ian Anderson, and Christian Vander, filling clubs and concert arenas.

Yoyo's music.

An omnipresent hum tickled at Jericho's eardrums. He looked up, spotted a refrigerator at the back of the room, went over, and looked in. It was half full of groceries, mostly untouched fast food. Bottles, full or half full, water, juice, beer, a bottle of Chinese whisky. He breathed in the cold air. The refrigerator made a clicking sound. A breath of air stroked the back of his neck.

Jericho froze.

That click hadn't been from the refrigerator.

The next moment he was flying through the air, to land on one of the mattresses with a dull thud. The impact drove all the air from his lungs. Fast as lightning, he rolled to one side and raised his knees. His attacker lunged for him. Jericho slammed his feet at him. The man leaped back, grabbed an ankle, and twisted him about so that he ended up on his stomach. He tried to get up, felt the other man jump on him, and drove an elbow backward in the blind hope of hitting him somewhere it would hurt.

"Take it easy," said a voice that seemed familiar. "Or this mattress will be the last thing you see in your life."

Jericho wriggled. The other man pushed his face deep into the musty fabric. Suddenly he couldn't breathe. Panic galvanized him. He flailed wildly around, kicked his legs, but the man pressed him mercilessly down into the mattress.

"Do we understand one another?"

"Mmmm," said Jericho.

"Is that a yes?"

"MMMMMM!"

His tormentor took his hand from the back of his head. The next moment, the weight was gone from his shoulders. Gasping for breath, Jericho rolled onto his back. The good-looking type he had spoken to earlier was leaning above him, and gave him a knife-blade smile.

"This isn't where the Pink Asses are playing, idiot."

"I wouldn't advise them to."

"What are you looking for up here?"

Well, at least they were on speaking terms now. Jericho sat up and pointed at the shabby furniture.

"You know, I'm a lover of luxury. I was thinking of spending my vacations—"

"Careful, my friend. I don't want to hear anything that might make me angry."

"Can I show you something?"

"Give it a try."

"It's on my computer." Jericho paused. "That's to say, I'll have to reach into my jacket, and I'm going to produce a device. I don't want you thinking it's a weapon and doing something hasty."

The man stared at him. Then he grinned.

"Whatever I do, I can assure you I'll have the time of my life doing it."

Jericho called up Yoyo's image and projected it onto the wall opposite.

"Have you seen her?"

"What do you want with her?"

"I'll tell you when you've answered my question."

"You've got some nerve, little man."

"My name's Jericho," Jericho said patiently. "Owen Jericho, private detective. I'm five foot eleven, so don't call me that. And drop the mind games, I can't concentrate when someone's trying to kill me. So, do you know the girl or not?"

The man hesitated.

"What do you want from Yoyo?"

"Thank you." Jericho switched off the projection. "Yoyo's father, Chen Hongbing, has hired me. He's worried. Truth to tell, he's worried sick."

"And what makes you think his daughter might be here?"

"Among other things, your friendly and forthcoming manner. Incidentally, who do I have the pleasure of addressing?"

"I ask the questions, friend."

"All right." Jericho raised his hands. "Here's a suggestion. I tell the truth, and you stop the hackneyed dialogue. Can we agree on that?"

"Hmm."

"Your name's Hmm?"

"My name's Bide. Zhao Bide."

"Thank you. Yoyo's living here, right?"

"It would be a bit much to call it living."

"So I see. Look, Chen Hongbing is worried. Yoyo hasn't been in touch for days, she didn't turn up for their meeting, he's a bundle of nerves. My job is to find her."

"And do what?"

"And do nothing." Jericho shrugged. "Well, I'll tell her she really should call her father. Do you work here?"

"In a very loose sense."

"Are you one of the City Demons?"

"One of—" Something like annoyance flickered in Zhao's eyes. "No, what makes you think so?"

"It would make sense, wouldn't you say?"

"Do I look like one?"

"Not a clue."

"That's right. You're clueless."

"Right now I think that Yoyo's closest friends are the City Demons." Zhao looked at him mistrustfully.

"Check my story," Jericho added. "You'll find all you need to know about me on the Internet. I don't mean Yoyo any harm. I'm not from the police. I'm not secret service. I'm nobody she needs to be afraid of."

Zhao scratched behind his ear. He seemed at a loss. Then he grabbed Jericho by the upper arm and propelled him toward the door.

"Let's go and drink something, little Jericho. If I find out that you've been lying to me, I'll bury you here in Quyu. Alive, just so you know."

They sat at a café in the sun across from the venue. Zhao ordered, and a girl with so many appliqués stuck onto her shaven scalp that she could have been mistaken for a cyborg brought two bottles of ice-cold beer.

They drank. For a moment, glorious silence reigned.

"It won't be easy to find Yoyo," Zhao said eventually. He took a long swig at his bottle and belched loudly. "It's not just her father who's lost sight of her. So have we."

"Who's we?"

"Us. Yoyo's friends." Zhao looked at him. "What do you know about the girl? How much did they tell you?"

"I know that she's on the run."

"Do you know why?"

"Why do you ask?" Jericho raised his eyebrows. "Wondering if you can trust me?"

"I don't know."

"And I don't know if I can trust *you*, Zhao. I only know that this isn't getting us anywhere."

Zhao seemed to consider this.

"Your knowledge for mine," he suggested.

"You begin."

"Fine then. Yoyo's a dissident. She's put the Party in a fine old tizzy these last few years."

"True."

"As part of a group calling themselves the Guardians. Criticizing the regime, calling for human rights, the odd act of cyber terrorism. All ideas you can agree with. Until recently, she got away with it."

"Also true."

"Your turn."

"In the night of May 25, Yoyo left her apartment in a hell of a hurry and fled to Quyu." Jericho took a swig, put down his bottle, and wiped his mouth. "I can only speculate as to why, but I should imagine she saw something online that scared her."

"All true so far."

"She was found out. Or at least that's what she thinks. With her previous record, she must be more frightened of being exposed than of anything. She was probably expecting a visit from the police or the secret services that same night."

"Quyu is her fallback position," said Zhao. "It's practically free of surveillance, no scanners, no police. Terra incognita."

"Her first port of call was the City Demons workshop. It's just that it's not safe there for very long. So she came here to the Andromeda, as she has done before."

"How did you find out that she was at the Andromeda?"

"Because she posted a message to her friends from here."

"And you read it?"

"It brought me here."

Zhao narrowed his eyes mistrustfully.

"How did you get hold of the message? Usually only the security services can manage something like that."

"Take it easy, little Zhao." Jericho smiled. "Cryptography is part of my job. I'm a cyber-detective, most of my work has to do with industrial espionage and IP infringement."

"And how did Yoyo's father get hold of you?"

"That's really none of your concern." Jericho tipped cold beer down his throat. "You said that Yoyo has disappeared again."

"Looks like. She was supposed to be here."

"When did she vanish?"

"Sometime during the day. Could be that she's just gone for a walk. Maybe we're worrying unnecessarily, but she usually says if she'll be gone for a while."

Jericho turned the bottle between his finger and thumb once more. He wondered how to proceed. Zhao Bide had confirmed his suspicions. Yoyo had been here, but that wouldn't be enough to set Chen Hongbing's mind at ease. The man needed certainty.

"Maybe we really don't need to worry," he said. "The City Demons let her know I was coming. This time, Yoyo disappeared because of me."

"I understand." Zhao pointed his bottle at Jericho's silver COD, gleaming in the sun in front of the Andromeda. "Especially given that you travel fairly ostentatiously, by our standards. CODs don't come to Quyu often."

"Clearly."

"Could be that Yoyo was running from the other guy, though."

Jericho wrinkled his brow. "What other guy?"

Zhao swept his hand further to the right. Jericho followed the motion and saw another COD parked at the other end of the factory hall. Startled, he tried to remember whether it had already been there as he arrived. He had been distracted by the surprise of reaching the Andromeda, combined with the realization that Daxiong had been leading him by the nose. He stood, and put his hand up to shade his eyes. As far as he could see, there was nobody in the other car.

Coincidence?

"Did somebody follow you?" asked Zhao.

Jericho shook his head.

"I blundered around half of Quyu before I got here. There was no COD behind me."

"Are you sure?"

Jericho fell quiet. He knew all too well that a person could be followed without his knowledge. Whoever had parked that car could have already been on his tail in Xintiandi.

Zhao got up as well. "I'll check you out, Jericho," he said. "But my sense for the pure and good tells me that you're clean. We're obviously both concerned for Yoyo's well-being, so I suggest that we team up for a while." He got out a pen, scribbled something down on a scrap of paper, and passed it to Jericho. "My phone number. You give me yours. We'll try to find Yoyo together."

Jericho nodded. He saved the number and handed over his card in exchange. Zhao was still an unknown quantity, but at the moment his suggestion was the best he had to go on.

"We should make a plan," he said.

"The plan is that we commit to sharing information. As soon as one of us sees or hears something, we let the other guy know."

Jericho hesitated. "Do you mind if I ask you a personal question?"

"Just as long as you don't expect me to answer."

"What's your relationship with Yoyo?"

"She's got friends here. I'm one of them."

"I know that she has friends. What I want to know is what *your* relationship with Yoyo is. You're not a City Demon. You know that she's one of the Guardians, but that doesn't mean that you're one yourself."

Zhao emptied his bottle and belched again.

"In Quyu, we're all in it together," he said equably.

"Come on now, Zhao." Jericho shook his head. "Give me an answer or just drop the thing, but don't try this romance-of-the-slums business on me."

Zhao looked at him.

"Do you know Yoyo in person?"

"No, just from recordings."

"Anybody who's met her in person has two choices. He falls in love, or puts his feelings on ice. Since she doesn't want to fall in love with me, I'm working on the second option, but whatever happens, I'll never leave her in the lurch."

Jericho nodded and asked no more questions. He glanced across to the second car again.

"I'm going to have another look around in the Andromeda," he said.

"What for?"

"Perhaps I'll find something that might help us."

"If you like. If you get into trouble, it wasn't me who said you could." He clapped Jericho on the shoulder and went across the yard to the rusty delivery van. Jericho saw him speaking to one of the roadies, gesticulating. It looked as though they were talking about where the stage lighting should go. Then the two of them heaved another wheeled trunk from the van. Jericho waited a minute and followed them inside. As he entered the main hall, the sound engineer's desk was just being set up. There was nobody on the balcony. He went up the steel steps, slipped through the gray door, pulled on a pair of disposable surgical gloves, and went into Yoyo's shabby den once more. The first thing he did was put a bug under one of the floorboards. Then he quickly scanned the piles of printouts, magazines, and books. Nothing there gave him any clues as to where Yoyo might be. Most of it was about music, fashion, design, hip Shanghai, politics, virtual environments, and robotics. Specialist literature that Yoyo probably read to keep up with work at Tu Technologies. He went to the table and sorted through the wastepaper basket underneath: torn packaging, scrunched up and smeared with leftovers. Jericho smoothed them out. Several were from a place called Wong's World, and bore its rather inept logo, a globe on a dish, covered with sauce and served with what was probably supposed to be vegetables. The globe even had a face, and looked visibly depressed.

Jericho took some photos and left the room.

As he went down the steel steps, Zhao looked up at him briefly and then turned back to the mixing desk. Jericho walked past him without a word and went outside. In the foyer, he spotted a poster for the Pink Asses. Unbelievable. They really did use the tagline Ass Metal, promising that their music went "right up your ass."

He was fairly sure that he didn't want to hear that.

As he unlocked the COD, he scanned his surroundings. The second car was still parked a little way away. Somebody had been on his tail; it would be naïve to imagine otherwise. He was probably being watched right at this moment.

A student who had promised to get some information about Yoyo, and fell to his death when his own roller coaster ran him over. A COD that turned up right after he had arrived at the Andromeda. Yoyo's renewed disappearance. How many coincidences did you have to shrug off before dry fear began to fur your tongue? Yoyo hadn't been jumping at shadows. She had every reason to hide, and there was still no knowing who was after her. The government, or its representatives the police and the secret services, would not shrink from murder if circumstances demanded. But what circumstances could force the Party to go this far? Yoyo might have earned the distinction of being an enemy of the State, but killing her for that wouldn't have been the style of a regime that locked dissidents up these days, rather than killing them as in Mao's times.

Or had Yoyo awoken a quite different sort of monster, one that didn't play by the rules?

It was clear that whoever was hunting her also had Jericho in their sights. Too late to drop the case. He started the COD and dialed a number. It rang three times, and then Zhao's voice spoke.

"I'm getting out of here," Jericho said. "In the meantime, you can make yourself useful in this new partnership of ours."

"What should I do?" asked Zhao.

"Keep an eye on the second COD."

"Right you are. I'll be in touch."

Kenny Xin watched him drive away.

Fate was a fickle mistress. It had led him here, from the lofty aerie atop the World Financial Center to the black crud that accumulated under the fingernails of the world's economic superpower. This was always happening to him. No sooner did he think he had escaped the clutches of that syphilitic whore called humankind, thought that he no longer owed her a glance, would never have to endure her stinking breath again, than she dragged him back to her filthy lair. He'd had to endure the revolting sight of her back in Africa, let her touch him until he feared he was infected all over his body, that he would dissolve into a pool of ichorous pus. Now he had ended up in Quyu, and again the hideous mask of her visage was grinning at him and he couldn't turn away. He felt dizzy, as always when overcome by this disgust. The world seemed to hang askew, so that he was amazed not to see the houses tumbling down and the people lose their footing.

He pressed finger and thumb against the bridge of his nose until he could think clearly again.

The detective had disappeared. It would have been the easiest thing in the world to bug his COD, but Xin had no doubt that Jericho had left Quyu for the time being and would return the car to the grid soon. He didn't need to follow it. Jericho couldn't get away from him. His gaze wandered over the yard, and he got rid of the disgust he felt by shedding waves of it to every side. How he hated the people in Quyu! How he had hated the underfed, chronically ill, dispirited creatures in Africa! Not that he had anything against them personally. They were anonymous, mere demographic statistics. He hated them because they were poor. Xin hated their poverty so much that it hurt him to see them alive.

High time to get out of here.

JERICHO

He was just steering up the slipway onto the high-speed track when he got a call. The display stayed dark.

"The guy who's following you has left the complex," Zhao told him.

Automatically, Jericho glanced into the mirror. Silly idea. There were only CODs up here on the tracks, all the same shape and the same color.

"I haven't seen anyone so far," he said. "At least he can't have followed me directly."

"No, he waited a while."

"Can you describe him?"

"Chinese."

"I see."

"About my height. Well-dressed, elegant. Somebody who pretty clearly didn't belong in Xuyu." Zhao paused. "Even you were less out of place."

Jericho thought that he heard a grin in his voice. The COD accelerated.

"I went through Yoyo's wastepaper basket," he said, without responding to Zhao's jab. "She seems to pick up her food in a place called Wong's World. Heard of it?"

"Maybe. Fast food joint?"

"Could be. Might be a supermarket as well."

"I'll find out. Can I reach you this evening?"

"You can reach me any time."

"Thought so. You don't look like a guy who has someone waiting at home."

"Hey, wait a moment!" Jericho yelped. "What do you mean by—?"

"Talk later."

Idiot!

Jericho stared ahead into a red cloud of rage, but it soon dissipated. In its place came a feeling of impotence, vulnerability. The worst of it was that Zhao was right. He had nobody waiting for him, not for years now. The man might be a roughneck, but he was right. This, even though Jericho's type was much in demand. He was trim and blond, and his eyes were light blue; he was generally taken for a Scandinavian, who were well-liked by Chinese women. He was also well aware that he hardly ever paid attention to the man who looked back at him from the mirror. His clothes were functional, but otherwise nondescript. He groomed himself just enough not to look unkempt. He shaved his chin and cheeks every three days, went to the hairdressers every three months to clear the top growth, as he liked to say. He bought T-shirts by the dozen without wondering whether they suited him. Fundamentally, even Tu Tian, fat and bald though he was, took more pains in his artlessly messy way.

When the high-speed track spat him out again at Xintiandi, his anger had given way to a brackish sort of defeatism. He tried to visualize his new home, but found no comfort there. Xintiandi seemed further away than ever, a good-time town where he didn't belong, because it wasn't in his nature to have a good time and others didn't have a good time with him around.

There it was again, the old stigma.

And he had thought he was over it. If there was one thing that Joanna had taught him, it was that he was no longer the kid from his schooldays, the boy who still looked about fifteen when he was eighteen years old. The boy who had never had a girlfriend because every last girl at school was after some other boy. Even that wasn't *quite* true. They had certainly appreciated having him as an understanding male friend, which he reckoned was just an underhanded way of saying a punching bag. They came to him in floods of tears, torturing him with details of their relationships; in endless therapy sessions which they always concluded by telling Jericho that they loved him like a brother, and that he was, thank God, the only boy on Earth who didn't want anything from him.

Brokenhearted, he patched up their tattered souls and only ever once tried anything more, with a snub-nosed brunette who had just been dumped by her older boyfriend, a notorious love cheater. More precisely, he had invited her for a meal and tried to flirt with her a bit. It worked like a dream for two hours, although only because the girl hadn't realized that he was trying to flirt. Even when he put his hand on hers, she just thought that he was being funny. It was only then that she realized that punching bags had feelings too, and she left the restaurant without a word. Owen Jericho had to turn twenty before a Welsh pub landlord's daughter took pity, and took his virginity. She hadn't been pretty, but she had been through the same sort of hell as he had, and this, along with a few pints of lager, was enough for him.

After that it had gone a little better, or even quite well, and he had his revenge on the pathetic wet blanket who had so stubbornly claimed to be Owen Jericho. With Joanna's help he had buried that boy, although it had been a stupid idea to bury him alive, not suspecting that it would be Joanna too who would bring him back from the grave. The zombie had come back here in Shanghai, where the world was reinventing itself, and taken revenge in turn. The zombie was the boy in his eyes who frightened off the women. He scared them. He scared *himself.*

In a foul mood, he steered his car to the nearest COD point and hooked it back up to the grid. The computer calculated what he had to pay and deducted the amount as he held his phone against the interface. Jericho got out. He had to find out why Grand Cherokee had had to die. He stopped in the middle of the street and called Tu Tian. He only spoke a few words to Naomi Liu. She obviously picked up that he was in a bad mood, smiled encouragingly, and put him through.

"I found the girl," he said without preamble.

Tu raised his eyebrows. "That was fast." There was even something like awe in his voice. Then he noticed Jericho's sour look. "And what's the problem? If there is just one problem."

"She slipped through my fingers."

"Ah." Tu tutted. "Well then. You'll have done your best, little Owen."

"I don't particularly want to talk over the details on the phone. Should we set up a meeting with Chen Hongbing, or would you like to hear about it first?"

"She is his daughter," Tu said diplomatically.

"I know. I'll say it straight. I'd rather speak to you first."

Tu looked reassured, as though that was what he had been hoping for. "I think we'll do that, though it doesn't mean we won't do the other," he said magnanimously. "But it would certainly be wise to let me know what's on your mind. When can you be here?"

"In a quarter of an hour, if the roads aren't jammed. Something else, Tian. The fellow who fell from your roof this morning—"

"Yes, a bad business."

"What do you know about it?"

"The circumstances of his death are somewhat curious, to say the least." Tu's eyes gleamed. He seemed less distraught than fascinated. "The guy went for a walk along the tracks, 500 meters up! I ask you, is that normal behavior for a student who was just looking to earn a few yuan on the side? What was he doing there?"

"I hear there's a video."

"An eyewitness video, that's right. It was on the news."

"Have they released it?"

"Yes, but you can't see very much. Just this what's-his-name, Grand Chevrolet, climbing about like a monkey up there and then trying to jump over the carriages."

"Grand Cherokee. His name's Grand Cherokee Wang." Jericho massaged the bridge of his nose. "Tian, I have to ask you for a favor. In the news it said that the surveillance cameras on the top floor of the World Financial Center showed Wang with a man. Obviously they had an argument. I'd like to have a look at the footage, and—" Jericho hesitated, "—at Wang as well, if possible."

Tu stared at him. "I beg your pardon?"

"Well, more specifically—"

"What are you thinking here, Owen? Have you lost your wits? Should I just call up the morgue and say, hey, how are things, could you just take Mr. Wang from the drawer, a friend of mine's got a thing for splatted corpses?"

"I want to see his effects, Tian. Whatever he had in his pockets. His phone for instance."

"How am I supposed to get hold of his phone?"

"You know half of Shanghai."

"But nobody in the morgue!" Tu snorted and shoved his shabby glasses back up; they had worked their way down the bridge of his nose as they talked. His jowls quivered. "And as for what the surveillance tapes show, don't get your hopes up."

"Why not? The footage must be on the system hard drive."

"I'm not authorized to look at it though. I'm just a tenant here, not the owner. Besides, once the police get involved, that footage will be evidence. You're the one with contacts to the police."

"In this case it might not be very wise to bother them."

"Why not?"

"Tell you later."

"I don't know if I can help you."

"Yes or no?"

"Unbelievable!" Tu snapped. "Is that any way to talk to a Chinaman? We don't do 'yes or no.' We Chinese hate to commit ourselves to anything, you must have learned that by now, Longnose."

"I know, you chaps prefer an unambiguous 'maybe.'"

Tu tried to look outraged. Then he grinned and shook his head. "I must be mad. All right though. I'll do whatever I can. I'm really curious to see what you find so interesting about the jumper."

In the few minutes that the conversation had lasted, the traffic on the Yan'an Donglu nearby had increased dramatically. The Huaihai Donglu, running parallel, was also suffering from clogged arteries. This heart attack seized hold of the city center between Huangpu and Luwan twice daily. It was delusional to take your own car, but when Jericho went back to the COD point, he was left standing watching while someone took the last free car. That was the problem with CODs. On the one hand there were too few of them, on the other hand, every COD that wasn't up on the high-speed track was one car too many on the Shanghai streets.

Jericho's mood plummeted. When he had still lived in Pudong, it had been easier to visit Tu. He walked to Huangpi Nanlu metro station and went down into the brightly lit passages, where hundreds of people were being shoved on board the overcrowded Line 1 by stoical crowd-handlers. Hardly had the carriage doors closed than he was bitterly regretting not having walked the mile to the riverbank to catch a ferry. Obviously he still had to learn a few tricks about life in his new neighborhood. He'd never lived so centrally before. In fact, he couldn't remember ever having taken the metro at this time of day. Even less could he imagine doing it again.

The train picked up speed without any of the passengers even swaying. Almost all the men around were holding their arms up in the air so that their hands were in full view. This habit was based on the fear of being accused of groping. Where twelve people were standing shoulder-to-shoulder on every square meter, it was impossible to say whose hand it was on your crotch. There was sexual molestation every day on the most crowded trains, and often the victims didn't even have the chance to turn around. Once more and more men were also being attacked, women too had got into the habit of raising their hands. A metro trip was a silent agony, and the children suffered most of all in the fug of clothes smell, sweat, and genital odor that swirled around their heads.

Jericho was wedged in place right by the doors. As a result, the pressure of the crowd shoved him out onto the platform first at the next stop. He briefly considered going to Houchezhan, where the maglev ran through, connecting Pudong Airport to the town of Suzhou in the west; it ran right past the World Financial Center and offered an invigoratingly luxurious ride, though the price of a ticket was exorbitant, which was why it mostly ran half-empty. He'd be at his destination within a minute, but the problem was that getting to the maglev station would take just as long as going on with the metro to Pudong. Nothing would be gained. At the same moment, the mass of humanity pushed him onto the conveyor for Line 2, and he let them carry him on, comforted by the certain knowledge that the guy who had snapped up the last COD from under his nose wouldn't have got a 100 meters by now.

When he crept out of the air-conditioned passages at Pudong, it felt as though he'd been slapped in the face with a hot towel. The sun hung amid streaks of high cloud, an unfriendly, glaring dot. Slowly, it clouded over. He looked over to the World Financial Center, standing off to one side behind the Jin Mao Tower. Grand Cherokee had been walking along those tracks, as though on a tightrope? Incredible! Either he'd gone mad, or circumstances had left him no choice. He logged on to the Internet and loaded up the eyewitness footage on his phone. The shot was very shaky, but zoomed in crisp and clear. It showed a tiny figure up on the tracks.

"Diane," he said.

"Hello, Owen. What can I do for you?"

"Enhance the video I have open. Get me everything you can with contrast and depth of field. Freeze every three seconds."

"As you say, Owen."

He walked over to the bottle opener, crossed the shopping mall, and went up to the Sky Lobby.

TU TECHNOLOGIES

Tu's company took up floors 74 through 77, with the hotel above and the viewing platform and roller coaster crowning the lot. A woman smiled warmly at Jericho and wished him good morning. Everyone knew her. Her name was Gong Qing, China's newest female superstar, who had won an Oscar last year and had other things to do with her time than checking who came and went at Tu Technologies. Tu's staff were used to it; they simply returned her greeting and went right on past, while visitors were asked their name and invited to place their palm on the actress's outstretched right hand. Jericho did this too. Briefly, he felt the cool surface of Gong Qing's transparent 3D projection box. The system read his fingerprints and the lines on his hand, scanned his iris and stored his voiceprint. Gong Qing confirmed that he was already stored in the system and didn't bother to ask his name. Instead, a friendly look of recognition flitted across her features.

"Thank you, Mr. Jericho. It's a pleasure to see you again. Who would you like to see, please?"

"I have an appointment with Tu Tian," Jericho said.

"Go up to the seventy-seventh floor. Naomi Liu is waiting for you."

In the elevator, Jericho silently paid tribute to Tu's trick of managing to get a different well-known face for the reception routine every three months. He wondered how much Tu had paid the actress, left the elevator, and stepped into a vast room that took up the whole floor. All four floors of Tu Technologies were modeled this way. There were no little territories of desks and offices, no empty lifeless corridors. The staff roved around a manifold workscape assisted by their luggage-like lavobots, which carried an interfaced computer in their innards along with storage space for whatever material a staffer might need for that day's work. All the staffers had their own personal lavobot, which they would pick up at reception in the morning and which followed them around from desk to workplace and docked there. There were open workspaces, closed cubicles, team spaces for brainstorming, and glassed-in soundproofed offices fitted with adjustably tinted glass. In the middle of every floor was a lounge oasis with sofas, a bar and a kitchen, harking back to the fireplaces which early man had gathered around two millennia ago.

We don't just give our staff work to do, Tu used to say. We give them a home to come to.

Naomi Liu sat at her desk flanked by a curved conical screen, 2 meters high. The screen, like the surface of her desk, was transparent. Documents, diagrams, and film clips ghosted across the surfaces, as

Naomi opened or shut them with her fingertips or gave voice commands. When she spotted Jericho, she bared her pearl-white teeth in
a smile.

"And? Happy with your new holowall?"

"I'm afraid not, Naomi. The holograms don't carry your scent
to me."

"You exaggerate so elegantly."

"Not at all. My senses are rather sharper than other people's. Don't
forget, I'm a detective."

"Then of course you'll be able to tell me what perfume I'm wearing
today."

She looked at him half expectantly, half mocking. Jericho didn't
even try to guess a brand name. All perfumes smelled the same to him,
flowers ground to powder and dissolved in alcohol.

"The best," he said.

"That answer gets you through to see the boss. He's in the mountains."

The "mountains" were a shapeless seating range in the back of the
room, its elements ceaselessly adjusting with a life of their own to the
bodies which climbed or sprawled over it. You could flop down, climb
up, or lounge about. The range was stuffed with nanobots which made
sure that the range itself constantly shifted position, as did the bodies
that had plumped down into it. Experts held that thought came more
easily when the body changed posture more often. Practical results
bore them out. Most of Tu Technologies' trailblazing ideas had been
hatched in the cradling dynamic of the mountains.

Tu was enthroned right at the top, with two project managers, looking like a proud, fat kid up there. When he spotted Jericho, he broke off
the conversation, slid down and got to his feet puffing and grunting,
making futile attempts to smooth his rumpled pants. Jericho watched
patiently. He was sure that the pants had already looked like that first
thing in the morning.

"An iron would work wonders there," he said.

"Why?" Tu shrugged. "These are all right."

"Aren't you a bit old to go climbing about like that?"

"Really?"

"You came down that slope about as elegantly as an avalanche, if
you'll pardon my saying so. You might slip a disc."

"My discs are not up for discussion. Come along."

Tu led Jericho to one of the glassed-in offices and shut the door
behind him. Then he turned a switch so that the glass tinted itself dark
and the ceiling began to glow. In a few seconds, the walls were completely opaque. They took seats at the oval conference table, and Tu
settled an expectant look on his face.

"So, what have you got?"

"I don't believe that the authorities are looking for Yoyo," Jericho said. "At least, not the usual security organs."

"Is she still at large?"

"I imagine so, She's gone underground in Quyu."

To his surprise, Tu nodded, as though he had expected nothing less. Jericho told him everything that had happened since last time they spoke. Afterward, Tu sat there in silence for a while.

"And what are your suspicions regarding this student who died?"

"My guts tell me he was murdered."

"Well, hooray for your guts."

"He lived in Yoyo's apartment, Tian. He wanted to drum some money out of me for information which he probably didn't even have. Maybe he was playing the same game with somebody else, who was less patient with that sort of thing. Or maybe he really did know something, and was gotten out of the way before he could tell anybody."

"You, for instance."

"Me for instance." Jericho gnawed at his lip. "Well, it's a theory. But it sounds plausible to me. Yoyo clears off, her roommate makes gnomic remarks about knowing where she is, he wants money, and then he falls off the roof. It rather raises the question of who helped him do that. The police? Not on your life! They would have put the kid through the wringer, not tossed him overboard. Apart from which, they would only have one reason to go after Yoyo, and that would be if they had exposed her. Has there been even a single policeman up here to see you?"

Tu shook his head.

"They'd have come here, you can bet your life on that," Jericho said. "Yoyo works for you. They'd have been knocking at Chen's door, and squeezing Yoyo's roommates for information. None of that happened. She must have been stepping on somebody else's toes. Somebody less squeamish."

Tu pursed his lips. "Hongbing and I could put a blog entry up on this forum she posted to. We could tell her—"

"Forget it. Yoyo can do without you trying to make contact."

"I don't understand. Why didn't she at least send Hongbing some message?"

"Because she's frightened of dragging him into it. Right at the moment, she's completely concentrated on just how much she can risk without bringing danger down upon herself *and other people*. How is she to know whether or not Chen's under surveillance, or you? So she's playing dead, and trying to get some information. She was safe in Quyu, for a while, but then she got word that I was on my way. Since then she knows that I've been there. And that someone was following me. With that, the Andromeda was done with as a hiding place. She had to leave there as well, leaving no more sign than when she left her apartment."

"This Zhao Bide," Tu said thoughtfully. "What part do you think he plays in all this?"

"No idea. He was helping to set up the concert, so presumably he's something to do with the Andromeda."

"A City Demon?"

"He says no."

"On the other hand, he knows that Yoyo is a Guardian."

"Yes, but I get the impression that he knew nothing about the message she posted up on Brilliant Shit. It's hard to place him. Definitely some of the Guardians are also City Demons. But not all the Demons are Guardians. Then there are people who help Yoyo without belonging to either group. Such as Zhao."

"And you think she trusts him?"

"It looks as though he'd very much like her to. Mind you, she hasn't told him where she ran off this time."

"She didn't tell me or Chen either."

"Also true. That doesn't get us any further though." Jericho looked at Tu reproachfully. "As you well know."

Tu returned his gaze equably.

"What are you getting at?"

"Every time Yoyo has to run, the number of people she can trust with her whereabouts becomes smaller. But there have to be some who know quite well."

"And?"

"And with all due respect, I'm wondering whether there's anything you've been keeping from me."

Tu steepled his fingers.

"You think I know the rest of the Guardians?"

"I think that you're trying to protect Yoyo, and yourself as well. Let's assume that strictly speaking you didn't need my help at all. Nevertheless, you gave me this investigation to carry out so that you didn't have to take action yourself. Nobody's supposed to know that Tu Tian is unduly interested in a dissident's whereabouts. Chen Hongbing on the other hand is Yoyo's father; there's no problem if he hires a detective."

Jericho waited to see whether Tu would say anything about that, but all he did was take his crooked glasses off his nose and start polishing them on a corner of his shirt.

"Let's also assume," Jericho went on, "that you know where Yoyo runs away to when there's trouble. And now Chen Hongbing comes along, knowing nothing whatsoever of all this, and asks you for help. Should you tell him what his daughter gets up to online, and that you know all about it? More than that, that you approve of what she does and you know where she's hiding? He would go crazy, so you point him toward me and you also slip me the vital clue. The City Demons. By the way, Grand Cherokee Wang told me about them as well. That was how you told me where I should look. Your plan was simple enough: I find the girl, you keep a low profile, you don't need to bare all to Chen; the father is reassured as to where his daughter is, and his friend can sleep soundly."

Tu looked up briefly and kept on polishing his glasses, not saying a word.

"For all that, what you didn't know and still don't, is who Yoyo's enemies are, and what this whole thing's about. That unsettled you. Now that Yoyo has left the Andromeda, you're groping around in the dark just like I am. Things have gotten complicated. You're just as clueless and worried as Chen, and on top of that, someone's dead."

Breathe on glasses, polish with shirt.

"Meaning that from now on, you *really* need me." Jericho leaned forward. "And this time it's for a *real* investigation."

Breathe, polish.

"But to do that, I have to be *able* to investigate!"

With a dry snap, the arm of the glasses, patched already with double-sided tape, broke. Tu cursed under his breath, cleared his throat noisily, and tried to put them back on the bridge of his nose, where they balanced like a car about to slip off the edge of a cliff.

"I could recommend you an optician, by the way," Jericho added drily. "But first of all you have to tell me what you've been keeping quiet so far. Otherwise I can't help you."

Otherwise, he found himself thinking, I could fall off a roof myself soon enough.

Tu drummed on the table with the arm of his glasses.

"I knew what I was doing when I hired you. It's just that it wouldn't do you any good if I give you the names of the other five Guardians. They'll have gone to ground as well."

"For one thing, I have a trail to follow. For another, I have an ally."

"Zhao Bide?"

"Even if he's not a City Demon, he'll know their faces. I need names and photos."

"Photos, that will take some time." Tu dug around in his ear. "You'll get the names. Anyway, you know one of them already."

"Really?" Jericho raised his eyebrows. "Who?"

"His nickname's Daxiong—Great Bear."

"The man-mountain with the cannonball head?" He tried to imagine Daxiong being politically aware, armed with an intellect that could put the Party in uproar. "I can hardly believe that. I was convinced that his bike had a higher IQ than him."

"A lot of people think that," Tu commented. "A lot of people think that I'm a fat old coot who doesn't have an optician and eats canned crap. Do you really think that Yoyo got away from you because the Great Bear was that dumb? He sent you off on your tour of the underworld, and you meekly followed his directions."

Jericho had to admit that he was right.

"Anyway, Tian, now you know why I don't want to trouble my contacts," he said. "The police might be somewhat surprised. By now they'll have found out that Wang was Yoyo's roommate. They'll make inquiries and they'll find out that I'm looking for the girl. Then they'll start putting two and two together: a dead student, possibly murdered, a dissident with a record, a detective asking questions about one who's also looking for the other. They shouldn't be able to draw these conclusions; I want to be able to investigate discreetly. I might end up giving them the idea that they should pay more attention to Yoyo."

"I understand." Tu's fingers glided across the tabletop, and the wall across from them became a screen. "Have a look at this, then."

He saw the glass corridor and the door to the roller-coaster boarding platform, from the perspective of two security cameras.

"How did you get the footage so quickly?" asked Jericho, surprised.

"Your wish was my command." Tu giggled. "The police put an electronic lock on it, but something like that's not a problem for us. Our own surveillance network is linked in with the in-house cameras, apart from which we also hacked into some totally different systems. There would only have been trouble if they'd put a high-security block in place."

Jericho considered this. Security blocks were commonplace. The fact that the officers in charge hadn't bothered to install one told him something about how important they considered the case to be. Another indication that the police didn't have Yoyo on their radar at all.

Two men appeared in the glass corridor. The shorter man walking in front had long hair and was fashionably dressed, with appliqués on his forehead and cheekbones. It was clearly Grand Cherokee Wang. A tall, slim man in a well-tailored suit walked behind him. There was something dandyish about his combed-back, greased hair, thin mustache, and tinted glasses. Jericho watched the way he turned his head about as he walked, scanning the whole corridor and resting his eyes for a fraction of a second on the security camera.

"Smart operator," he muttered.

The two of them went to the middle of the corridor and disappeared from the corner of one camera's view. The other showed the two of them entering the glass box of the control room with its console.

"They talk for a while." Tu switched to fast-forward. "Nothing very much happens here."

Jericho watched Grand Cherokee gesticulating with jerky speed, obviously showing the other man how the control unit worked. Then the two of them seemed to converse.

"Now watch this," Tu said.

The film slowed down again to real time. The two men still stood next to one another. Grand Cherokee took a step toward the taller man, who stretched out an arm.

The next moment, the student collapsed, crashed his face into the edge of the console and fell to the ground. The other man took hold of him and pulled him back to his feet. Grand Cherokee staggered. The stranger held him tight. On a cursory examination, it must have looked as though he were holding up a friend who had had a sudden dizzy spell. A few seconds went by, then Grand Cherokee fell to his knees again. The tall man squatted down next to him and talked to him. Grand Cherokee doubled over and then lurched to his feet. A little while later the tall man left the control room, but then stopped and turned back. For the first time since he had stepped into the corridor, he turned his face to the camera.

"Stop," said Jericho. "Can you blow him up?"

"No problem." Tu zoomed the torso and face until they filled the screen. Jericho squinted. The man looked like Ryuichi Sakamoto playing the Japanese occupier in Bertolucci's *The Last Emperor*.

"Does he remind you of anybody?" Tu asked.

Jericho hesitated. The resemblance to the Japanese actor-composer was striking. At the same time he had a creeping feeling that he was barking up the wrong tree. The film was ancient, and Sakamoto was well above seventy.

"Not really. Send the picture over to my computer."

Tu let the clip play on. Grand Cherokee Wang left the control room and then recoiled from the stranger. The two of them were lost to view for a while, then the tall man came back into sight. He went into the control room and started working at the console.

"I'm wondering why the security guards didn't react to that," Tu pronounced.

"To what?" Jericho asked.

"What do you mean, to what?" Tu stared at him. "To what you can see here!"

"What does it look like?"

"Well, the two of them had a fight, didn't they?"

"Did they?" Jericho leaned back. "Aside from the fact that Wang fell to the ground twice, nothing happened at all. Maybe he's doped up, or drunk, or not feeling well. Our oily friend helps him back to his feet, that's all. Also, the guards have a hundred stories to watch here, you know how it works. They don't spend their whole time staring at the screens.—Anyway, is there any exterior footage?"

"Yes, but it's only put through to the Silver Dragon control room."

"Meaning that we can't—"

"That *they* can't," said Tu. "We certainly can."

Just at that moment the tall man left the control room, walked along the corridor, and vanished into the next part of the building. Tu started another clip. The screen split up into eight smaller pictures, which taken together showed the whole course of the Silver Dragon's track. One of the cameras showed Grand Cherokee standing at the end of the last carriage and looking behind himself again and again.

Then he stepped out onto the track.

"Freeze," Jericho called. "I want to see his face."

There was no doubt about it, Grand Cherokee's face was frozen in a mask of panic. Jericho felt a mixture of fascination and horror.

"Where does he want to go?"

"He's put some thought into it," Tu said in a low voice, as though talking out loud would make the terrified man on the tracks fall off. Meanwhile, the Silver Dragon left the platform and passed from one camera view to the next. "There are connections between the track and the building on the way around. With a little luck, he'll reach one."

"He won't though," said Jericho.

Tu shook his head silently. Horrified, they watched Grand Cherokee die. For a while neither said a word, until Jericho cleared his throat.

"The time stamps," he said. "Once you compare them there's no doubt that it was our friend who started the Silver Dragon. And something else strikes me. We only saw his face twice, and it wasn't clear either time. He knew how to keep his back to the camera as well."

"And what conclusions do you draw from that?" Tu asked hoarsely.

Jericho looked at him.

"I'm sorry," he said. "But you and Chen—you'll have to get used to the idea that Yoyo has a professional killer after her."

No, he thought, wrong. Not just Yoyo.

Me too.

Tu Technologies was one of the few companies in Shanghai with its own private fleet of skymobiles. In 2016 the World Financial Center had been retrofitted with a hangar for skycars above the offices on the seventy-eighth floor. It had room for two dozen vehicles, half belonging to the company that owned the building, most of these being huge VTOL craft for evacuation. Since Islamist terrorists had steered two passenger jets into the twin towers of the New York World Trade Center not even a quarter-century ago, there had been growing interest in skymobiles with every passing year, leading to the development of various models. By now nearly every newly built super-high-rise in China had flight decks. Seven of the vehicles belonged to the Hyatt: four elegant shuttles with steerable jets, two skybikes, and a gyrocopter. Tu's fleet consisted of two of the helicopter-like gyros and the Silver Surfer, a gleaming ultra-slim VTOL. Last year Jericho had had the treat of piloting it for a few hours: a reward for a job instead of him billing them. It was a wickedly expensive piece of technology. Now Tu was sitting in the pilot seat. He wanted to visit Chen Hongbing, and then had to meet some people for business in Dongtan City, a satellite city of Shanghai on Chongming Island in the Yangtze, which held the record as the world's most environmentally friendly city. Tu Technologies had developed a virtual canal for the city, which was already threaded with dozens of real canals; their glass tunnel would create the illusion of gliding along through a town in the age of the Three Kingdoms, that beloved cradle of so many stories between the Han and the Jin dynasties.

"We've become the world's number one polluter," Tu explained apropos of Dongtan. "Nobody poisons the planet as chronically as China does, not even the United States of America. On the other hand, you won't find anyone else as thorough in applying alternative sustainable designs. Whatever we do, we seem to do it to the limit. That's what we understand by yin and yang these days: pushing the very boundaries."

The huge hangar was brightly lit. The in-house VTOLs rested one next to the other like stranded whales. As Tu steered his manta-flat vehicle over to the starting strip, the glass doors at the front of the hangar slid aside. He swung the machine's four jets to horizontal and accelerated. A howling roar filled the hall, then the Silver Surfer shot out over the edge of the building and fell down toward the Huangpu. Two hundred meters above ground, Hu lifted the machine's nose and steered it over the river in a wide curve.

"I'll give Hongbing a toned-down version," he said. "I'll tell him that the police aren't after Yoyo, but that she might believe they are. And that she's still in Quyu."

"*If* she's still in Quyu," Jericho threw in.

"Whatever. What will you do next?"

"Sift the net, hoping that Yoyo might have left another message. Take a good close look at a fast food chain called Wong's World."

"Never heard of it."

"Probably only exists in Quyu. Yoyo's wastepaper basket was spilling over with Wong's World wrappers. Thirdly, I need information on the Guardians' current projects. Meaning the full picture," he said with a sideways glance. "No cosmetic alterations, no cards up your sleeve."

Tu looked like a deflated balloon. For the first time since Jericho had known him, he looked helpless. The glasses hung uselessly on his nose.

"I'll tell you what I know," he said penitently.

"That's good." Jericho pointed to the bridge of his nose. "Tell me, can you actually see anything with those things?"

Without a word, Tu opened a box in the middle of the instrument panel, took out a completely identical pair of glasses, put them on, and threw the old ones behind him. Jericho spent a moment wondering whether his eyes had been playing tricks on him. Were there really a dozen more pairs stored there?

"Why do you repair your glasses with double-sided tape if you've got so many you could just throw them away?" he asked.

"Why not? That pair was all right."

"It was a long way from—oh, never mind. As far as Hongbing is concerned, I think that sooner or later he'll have to learn the whole truth. What do you say? In the end, he's Yoyo's father. He has a right to know."

"But not yet." Tu flew over the Bund, brought the Silver Surfer lower, and turned south. "You have to treat Hongbing with kid gloves; be very careful what you say to him. And something else; this business with Grand Rococo's mortal remains, or whatever the guy was called—well, I reckon there's no chance of getting at his effects, but I'll think a little more about it. You're mostly interested in his phone, is that right?"

"I want to know who he telephoned ever since Yoyo disappeared."

"Good, I'll do what I can. Where should I drop you?"

"At home."

Tu bled off some speed and steered toward Luwan Skyport, only a few minutes from Xintiandi on foot. As far as the eye could see, the traffic was jammed solid in the streets, only the cabin cars on the COD track sped along. His fingers manipulated the holographic field with the navigation instruments, and the jets swung down to the vertical. They sank gently down as though in an elevator. Jericho looked through the side window. Two city gyrocopters were parked at the edge of the strip, both painted with the markings that identified them as ambulances. Another was just taking off, lifted terrifyingly close to them and roared off toward Huangpu at full power. Jericho felt something in his hip pocket vibrate, took out his phone and saw that somebody was trying to reach him. He picked up the call.

"Hey, little Jericho."

"Zhao Bide." Jericho clicked his tongue. "My new friend and confidant. What can I do for you?"

"Don't you miss Quyu?"

"Give me a reason to miss the place."

"The crab baozi in Wong's World is excellent."

"You found the shop, then."

"I even knew the place. I'd just forgotten what it was called. It's in what you might call the civilized part of Xaxu. You must have driven this way when you came. It's a sort of covered street market. Great big place."

"Good. I'll have a look at it."

"Not so fast, Mr. Detective. There are two markets. The branches are one block apart."

"There isn't a third?"

"Just these two."

The Silver Surfer settled to a halt. Tu shut down the engines.

"I'll be needed in the Andromeda until seven," Zhao said. "At least until the Pink Asses have made it onstage, which isn't always so straightforward. After that I'm free."

Jericho considered. "Good. Let's take up our posts. One of us watching each branch. Could be that Yoyo and her friends come by."

"And what's that worth to me?"

"But Zhao, little Zhao!" Jericho expostulated. "Are those the words of a worried lover?"

"They're the words of a Quyu lover, you hopeless idealist. What about it? Do you want my help or don't you?"

"How much?"

Zhao named a price. Jericho haggled him down to half that, for form's sake.

"And where shall we meet?" he asked.

"At the Andromeda. Half past seven."

"I hope you understand that this is the most boring job in the world," Jericho said. "Sitting still and keeping your eyes peeled without nodding off to sleep."

"Don't bust my balls about it."

"I absolutely won't. See you later."

Tu gave him a sideways look.

"Are you sure you can trust this guy?" he asked. "Perhaps he's talking himself up. Perhaps he just wants the money."

"Perhaps the Pope's a pagan." Jericho shrugged. "I can't do much wrong with Zhao Bide. All he has to do is keep his eyes open, nothing else."

"You know best. Stay available just in case I can find poor Grand Sheraton's phone. Somewhere between his spleen and his liver."

QUYU

When Jericho traveled back to the forgotten world, the traffic was flowing thick as honey. Pretty brisk by Shanghai standards, then. It meant getting home on time, a hot dinner, and children sleepy but still awake so that Mom and Dad could put them to bed together.

On the other hand, if you came from Europe, and were used to things moving a bit faster, every minute on the streets of Shanghai was among the more irksome experiences that life had to offer. Statisticians claimed that the average car driver spent six months of his urban life sitting at red lights, but that was nothing compared with the amount of life wasted in Shanghai traffic jams. Since CODs had ceased to be appropriate for a visit to Quyu, because they would stand out like there like frogs with wings and arouse Yoyo's suspicions, Jericho had no option but to collect his own car from the underground parking garage. In the afternoon he had sent Diane off in search of Zhao Bide on the net, with no result. There was no one by that name on record. Quyu didn't exist, and neither did its inhabitants.

However, there were the other five Guardians, right there as expected, in the university lists.

Yoyo herself had left no new traces after her piece on Brilliant Shit. Once again Jericho wondered who would send a professional hit man after a dissident who, while she was plainly troublesome, wasn't exactly high risk. Leaving aside the police, State elements were certainly involved. The Party was riddled with secret agents like mold in gorgonzola. No one, probably not even the highest officials, knew the full extent of their interpenetration. Against this background there was a covert operation whose goal lay in preventing the distribution of information that Yoyo should never have been able to get hold of.

Which called for more than killing the girl.

Because if her forbidden knowledge came from the net, it was very probably stored on her computer. A circumstance that didn't do much to improve Yoyo's chances of survival, but made it harder to kill her. As long as the whereabouts of the device was unclear, she couldn't simply be gunned down in the street. The killer had to get hold of the computer, and not only that, he would have to find out who she had passed her knowledge on to. His task was that of an epidemiologist: to curb the virus, bring all the infected parties together, eliminate them and, last of all, eliminate the first carrier.

The question was where the epidemiologist was at that moment.

Jericho had expected to be pursued. That morning the killer had still been traveling in a COD. He could have swapped vehicles by now, as Jericho had done. Zhao's description of the man matched the video recordings from the World Financial Center, but Jericho doubted that the stranger would show himself to him. On the other hand, the guy didn't know that Jericho had seen his face, thought he was undiscovered and was perhaps becoming reckless. Whatever the truth of the matter, he would have to be careful not to be too successful in his search for Yoyo, and deliver her up for the slaughter.

When he was 2 kilometers from Quyu, Tu sent him the promised photographs. Apart from "Daxiong" Guan Guo, they showed two girls called "Maggie" Xiao Meiqi and Yin Ziyi, and the male Guardians Tony Sung and Jin Jia Wei. Along with the video stills that showed Grand Cherokee's killer, they formed the basis of his search. The hologoggles and scanners that he brought with him would constantly be able to draw on the data, and immediately demonstrate any agreement. Unfortunately the stills were of poor quality, and left barely any hope that the computer might recognize the killer in the crowd. But Jericho was firmly determined to pull out all the stops. With the scanners alone, he and Zhao had half a dozen reliable sleuths at their disposal, who would attack as soon as Yoyo or one of her people developed a craving for Wong's World.

He took the turn for Quyu and stopped at the edge of the road to change the color of the car. Within seconds, magnetic fields had altered the nanostructure of the paint particles. He'd shelled out a few yuan for his Toyota to have this chameleon-like ability. As he spoke to a client on the phone, the elegant silvery blue turned into a dingy grayish-brown with matt patches. The front part looked as if it had had a rotten paint job. Dark stains defaced the driver's door and created the illusion of dents, with the paint flaking off at the edges. A jagged scratch appeared above the rear left mudguard. By the time Jericho crossed the border separating the realm of the spirits from the world of the living, his car was in a lamentable state—just right if he didn't want to attract attention in the streets of Xaxu.

Zhao had given him a description of the route to the larger of the Wong markets. When he got there, the place was still operating at peak rate. By now he saw this part of Xaxu with different eyes. The largely intact appearance and the busy activity disguised the fact that a fracture in society ran through here, beyond which anyone not in the network lived under the orders of rival triads, whose leaders controlled the turf. In the shadow of the closed-down steelworks to which the district originally owed its existence, the drug trade flourished, money was laundered, prostitution thrived, people dulled their senses in Cyber Planet with virtual wonder-drugs. On the other hand, the triads barely showed the slightest interest in the vast steppes of misery that Jericho had driven through that morning. So Quyu was most honest where it was poorest, and anyone who tried to be honest stayed poor.

Wong's World covered an area the size of a block, and presented itself as a patchwork of steaming cook shops; piles of preserves on huge walls of shelves; stacked-up cages of clucking, hissing, and whining animals; ramshackle stands and curtained-off booths where you could haggle for acid trips, gambling debts, or STDs. Jericho had no doubt that guns were sold at Wong's as well. It was incredibly cramped in there. Scraps of words and laughter flew in raging swarms above the market, along with the hubbub of Chinese pop music from clapped-out speakers. While he was keeping an eye out for Zhao, the man himself broke away from the crowd and came strolling across the street. Jericho lowered the window and beckoned him over. Zhao wore jeans that had seen better days, and a threadbare windbreaker, but he still somehow managed to look neat and tidy. His hair fell silkily as he threw his head back and drank beer from a can that pearled with condensation. He had a battered backpack hung over his shoulder. Without any great haste, he approached Jericho's car and bent down to him.

"Not really your world, is it?"

"I've been in other hells," Jericho said, nodding toward the interior of the car. "Come on, get in. There's something I want to show you."

Zhao walked around the car, opened the door, and slumped onto the passenger seat. For a moment his profile shone in the light of a sunbeam battling its way through the billowing brew of clouds. Jericho looked at him and wondered why someone with his looks hadn't ended up in fashion or movies long ago. Or *had* he seen Zhao in the fashion world? On television? In a magazine? Suddenly it seemed more than likely. Zhao, an ex-model, washed up and unwanted in Quyu.

The first raindrops exploded on the windshield.

"Everything okay?" Zhao asked.

"You?"

"The guys are on stage. Horrible car you're driving, by the way. Vario-paint?"

Jericho was surprised. "You know your stuff."

"A bit. Don't worry. The illusion is perfect." Zhao bent forward and wiped a fleck from the instrument panel with the ball of his hand. "Anybody would fall for it, as long as they didn't get in and see the gleaming inner life."

"Tell me about the other market."

"Just half the size of this one. No chickens, no chicken heads."

Jericho reached behind him and handed Zhao a set of hologoggles. "Ever worn one of these?"

"Of course." Zhao nodded at the branch of Cyber Planet. "Everyone in there wears one of these. You know what they call those shops around here?"

"The Cyber Planets? No."

"Mortuaries. Once you're in there you're as good as dead. I mean, you're breathing, but your existence is reduced to fundamental bodily functions. Eventually they carry you out because you've actually died. People are always dying in Cyber Planet."

"How many times have you been in there?"

"A few."

"You don't look that dead to me."

Zhao looked at him from under lowered eyelids. "I'm above any kind of addiction, little Jericho. Explain these silly glasses to me."

"They make a biometric comparison. A 180-degree panorama scan. I've loaded photographs of Yoyo and five other Guardians onto the hard drive. If any one of the six comes within range, the goggles turn him red and send you a little beep. Loud enough to wake you up if you've drifted off under the weight of all that responsibility. The control on the left arm of the glasses also makes the outer surface reflective, if you want." Jericho dropped the goggles in Zhao's lap and held one of the scanners up under his nose. "I've synchronized three of these things with your specs. You can take them wherever you like, but if possible try and put them somewhere you can't actually see. Here's the focus button, that's how you activate the capture mechanism. They broadcast direct to your specs, and the scanner recordings appear at the bottom of your field of vision."

"I'm impressed," said Zhao, and looked as if he really was. "And how will we communicate?"

"By cell phone. Do you know where you're going to be positioning yourself?"

"Opposite my branch there's a Cyber Planet. Nice big windows to look out of."

Jericho's eye wandered to the Cyber Planet on the corner.

"Good idea," he murmured.

"Of course. Settle yourself in, pay for twenty-four hours; it's more comfortable than sitting in a car. If you sit with the glasses on your nose by the window, everyone's going to think you're screwing a hooker from Mars with four tits. There are snacks and drinks, only moderately palatable. You should really try these crab baozis, man. The food in Wong's World is good and cheap."

"Do you have relatives in there?" Jericho asked derisively.

"No, but I do have taste buds. Would you mind driving me to my stakeout?"

Jericho started the car and had Zhao direct him to his Wong branch. On the way they passed tea rooms and a Japanese noodle bar, where the men were playing cards and Chinese chess, or gesticulating wildly as they talked at each other, many of them naked to the waist and with their heads close shaven.

"These gentlemen are the Xaxus," Zhao said disparagingly. "They divide the day up between them."

"No ambition to saw a bit off for yourself?"

"What makes you say that?"

"What's left for someone like you after they've divided the day up among themselves?"

"It doesn't matter." Zhao shrugged. "I help stoned idiots onto the stage and back down again. That's a job, too."

"Don't get it."

"What's not to get?"

"I don't understand what someone like you is doing in Quyu. You could live anywhere else."

"You think so?" Zhao shook his head. "No one here can live anywhere else. No one *wants* us to live anywhere else."

"Quyu isn't a prison."

"Quyu is a concept, Jericho. Two-thirds of humanity now lives in cities, the countryside's been depopulated. Eventually all the cities will merge into one. They're like carcinomas: sick, proliferating tissue, only the nuclei are healthy, nestling in deserts of despair. The nuclei are sanctuaries, temples of superior development. Human beings live there, real human beings. Guys like you. The rest are cattle, talking animals. Take a look around you. The people here are vegetating at the level of tree-dwellers; they procreate, demolish the planet's resources, kill each other, or die of various illnesses. They're the rejects of creation. The failed part of the experiment."

"And you're part of it too, aren't you? Or have I misunderstood something?"

"Oh, Jericho." Zhao smiled smugly. "The universe has its brightly lit centers, and why? Because darkness prevails in between. Have you ever heard that we must shed light on the darkness of the universe? It's impossible. Any attempt to provide wealth for humanity as a whole is doomed to failure. It just means that everyone's worse off. The superior can't become like the inferior; it must separate itself off if it is to shine. There is no humanity, Jericho, not in the sense of a homogeneous species. There are winners and losers, the ones in the loop and the ones out of it, some on the bright side and most on the dark. The split is complete. No one wants to integrate the Xaxus of this world, break down their boundaries.—Oh, and you've got to turn left here."

Jericho said nothing. The Toyota clattered along a wide, badly paved road, lined with workshops and dirty brick houses. Where Wong's World and the branch of Cyber Planet stood face to face, it opened up into a dusty square and revealed the grounds of the steelworks behind it. The huge blast furnace loomed up above the building.

"You're a mystery to me, Zhao. Who are you really?"

"What do you think?"

"I haven't a clue." Jericho looked at him. "You seem to have a weakness for Yoyo, but when it comes to finding her, you let me pay you as if you were some kind of pimp. You live here and despise your own people. Somehow you don't fit with Quyu."

"Very comforting," Zhao sneered. "Like telling a hemorrhoid it's doing a power of good to the asshole it's grown in."

"Were you born in Quyu, or did you end up here?"

"The latter."

"Which means you can leave again."

"Where to?"

"Hmm." Jericho thought for a moment. "There are possibilities. Let's see how our short-term partnership develops."

Zhao tilted his head and raised an eyebrow.

"Did I understand you correctly? Are you offering me a job?"

"I don't take on any regular employees, but I put teams together as the job requires. You're definitely intelligent, Zhao. I was very impressed by your surprise attack in the Andromeda, you're in good physical condition. I can't exactly claim that I like you, but we don't have to walk down the aisle together. It could be that I need you from time to time."

Zhao's eyes narrowed.

Then he smiled.

At that moment Jericho had a sudden déjà vu. He saw the familiar in the alien. It spread like a drop of dark ink in a clear liquid, quickly and in all directions, so that a moment later he couldn't have said what the impression related to. Everything around him seemed to be striving for resolution, as in a film he'd once seen, although he couldn't remember the ending. No, not a film, more of a dream, an illusion. A reflection in the water that you destroyed as you tried to capture it.

Quyu. The market. Zhao by his side.

"Everything okay?" Zhao asked again.

"Yes." Jericho rubbed his eyes. "We shouldn't waste any time. Let's get started."

"Why don't you do the job with one of your teams?"

"Because the job consists in protecting a dissident whose identity no one knows, apart from a handful of initiates. The fewer people get involved with Yoyo, the better."

"Does that mean you haven't talked about the girl to anyone but me?"

"No. I've met her roommates."

"And?"

"They don't give much away. Do you know them?"

"I've seen them. Yoyo says they know nothing about her double life. One of them isn't interested in her, the other's pissed off that she isn't interested in him. He's inclined to throw his weight around."

"You mean Grand Cherokee Wang?"

"I think that's what he calls himself. Ludicrous name. Windbag. What have they told you?"

"Nothing. Wang's not in a position to tell anybody anything. He's dead."

"Really?" Zhao frowned. "Last time I saw him he looked very much alive. He was boasting about some kind of roller coaster he owns."

"He didn't own anything." Jericho stared out across the crowded market. "I won't try and fool you, Zhao. What we're doing here can get dangerous. For everyone involved. Yoyo seems to have crossed some people who walk over corpses. That was why Wang had to die. I thought you should know that."

"Hmm. Okay."

"Are you still up for it?"

Zhao let a moment pass. He suddenly looked embarrassed.

"Listen, about the money—"

"It's fine."

"No, I don't want you to get the wrong impression. I'd help you even if there was nothing in it for me. It's just—I need the money, that's all. I mean, you saw those guys at the edge of the street, right?"

"Dividing up the day?"

"It would be easy to join in with that. Something is always coming up. Most people live by licking those guys' boots. You get me?"

"I think so."

"And they don't do any of that for nothing, do they?"

"Listen, Zhao, you don't have to apol—"

"I'm not apologizing. I'm just setting you straight on a few things." Zhao stuffed the glasses and scanner in his backpack. "How long do you plan to keep this stakeout going?"

"As long as necessary. I once spent three weeks outside a single front door."

"What, and she didn't invite you in?" Zhao opened the car door.

"Well, somehow that fits."

"What do you mean?"

Zhao shrugged. "Has anyone ever told you you look like the loneliest man in the world? They haven't? Take care of yourself, first-born!"

A thousand answers collected on the tip of Jericho's tongue, but unfortunately not one that would have made him look as if he was in charge. He watched Zhao strolling unhurriedly across to Wong's World, then turned around and drove back to his branch, where he parked the Toyota so that the scanner below the rearview mirror captured part of the market. Then he got out, walked around the square, and decided on two houses whose positions struck him as right. Each one had plenty of possible locations for the additional scanners. He fixed one under a crumbling window ledge, another in a crack in a wall. The devices, black, gleaming, pea-sized spheres, automatically probed their surroundings, and extended tiny telescopic legs to wedge themselves into the stone.

Wong's World was covered.

A gust of wind ran through the clapped-out canyons of the triad city, tugging at awnings, clothes, and nerves. By now it was unbearably sultry; the sky looked like a shroud. A few single, fat drops fell, harbingers of the deluge announced by the faraway rumble. Canopies flapped. Jericho put on his glasses and stepped into the foyer of Cyber Planet.

In principle all the branches of the chain looked the same. You were welcomed by standardized machines lined up like terraced houses, with slits for cash and electronic interfaces for remote withdrawals. Two guards chatted behind a counter, never glancing at the monitors. A lot of the guests were regulars, or so it seemed. They didn't spend long at the machines, but looked into eye-scanners, waited until the armored glass doors opened, and stepped into the area behind with the hesitant gait of the newly blind.

Inside, game consoles and transparent couches were lined up side by side, each fitted with hologoggles. There was a shelf with room for two dozen full-motion suits, rings 3 meters in diameter, within which you could dangle in a sensor suit, in order to enjoy complete freedom of movement. Far at the back there were lockable cabins, toilets, showers, and sleeping-capsules. The rear wall of the huge space was occupied by a kind of supermarket with a bar. Floor-to-ceiling glass windows gave a view of the street and the market. Apart from the guards in the foyer, there was no staff. Everything was automated. Theoretically, you need never leave the Cyber Planet, as long as you were prepared to be satisfied with fast food and soft drinks for the rest of your life. The chain drew you in with special offers of up to a year in which you had to do nothing other than wander through the virtual world wearing a pair of goggles, whether as a passive onlooker or an active designer. You had dreams and nightmares, lived and died.

Jericho paid for twenty-four hours. About half of the couches were occupied when he entered the room, most of them along the big display window. For impenetrable reasons, most of the visitors wanted to be close to the street, even though they were completely cut off from the outside world by goggles and headphones. Jericho spotted an empty berth from which he had a view of Wong's World and the crossroads near where his car was parked, stretched out, and tapped the arm of his goggles. The outside glass of the lenses turned into a mirror. He jammed the remote receiver of his phone in his ear and got ready for a long night.

Or several.

It was possible that Yoyo was miles away by now, and he and Zhao were sitting like idiots in a nightmare delivery station.

He yawned.

All of a sudden it was as if all the light had been sucked from the streets. The storm front drew over Quyu, releasing streams of pitch-black water. Within seconds garbage was floating down the road, people were running wildly in all directions, shoulders hunched, as if that were any use against being completely drenched. The onslaught of a quick succession of violent thunder crashes edged closer. Jericho looked into a sky split by electricity.

A foretaste of destruction.

After an hour in which the street turned into a miniature version of the Yangtze and banked-up garbage formed a dinky little model of the Three Gorges Dam, it had passed. As quickly as it had come, the storm moved on. The murky broth drained away, leaving a vista of garbage and drowned rats against a theatrical background of rising steam. Another hour later a glowing magenta ball had won its battle with the clouds and wasted its fire on streets that were free of tourists. Wong's World welcomed a throng of pale figures, women peeped from tents and shacks, the stale promise of the night, or positioned themselves, scantily dressed, at the crossroads.

At around eleven o'clock a young man on the couch next to Jericho groaned, pulled the goggles from his eyes, sat up, and vomited a stream of watery puke between his legs. The couch's self-cleaning systems hummed immediately into action, sucked the stuff away and flooded the surface with disinfectant.

Jericho asked if he could do anything.

The boy, who could hardly have been more than sixteen, considered him with a mumbled curse and staggered to the bar. His body was emaciated, his eyes no longer focused on the presence of things. After a while he came back, chewing something, probably barely aware of what exactly it was. Jericho felt compelled to point out that he was dehydrated, and buy him a bottle of water, which the boy would presumably chuck in his face by way of thanks. If anything at all was left in his eyes, it was the smoldering aggression of those who fear the loss of their last illusions.

The scanners were silent.

Montes Alpes, The Moon

Southeast of the basin that marked the start of the Vallis Alpina, a row of striking peaks stretched down to the Promontorium Agassiz, a mountainous cape on the edge of the Mare Imbrium. Overall, the formation looked more like the crusts thrown up by terrestrial subduction zones than the ring range normally found on the Moon. It was only from a great altitude that the weird reality was revealed, that the Mare Imbrium, like all maria, was itself a crater of enormous size, produced in the early days of the satellite more than 3 billion years ago, when its mantle had still been liquid under its hardening surface. Cataclysmic impacts had torn the young crust open. Lava had risen from the interior, flowed into the basins, and created those dark basalt plains which led astronomers like Riccioli to conclude the presence of lunar seas. In reality the complete, 250-kilometer alpine chain marked the tenth part of one of those circular ramparts so colossal that giant craters in the format of a Clavius, Copernicus, or Ptolemy shrank to mere pockmarks in comparison.

The mightiest of all these alpine accumulations was Mons Blanc. At a height of 3,500 meters, it fell short of its terrestrial counterpart, but that did not detract from its titanic nature. Not only could you see the vast expanse of the southwestern Mare Imbrium from its slopes, but once you were up here you felt a bit closer to the stars, almost as if they could suddenly spot you, and greet you appropriately.

And greet you they did. In fact when Julian, in the sudden and inexplicable hope of seeing the glowing trail of a shooting star, raised his eyes to Cassiopeia, billions of indifferent eyes momentarily switched places to unite in cosmic reproach, forming a single, clearly legible word: IDIOT! Subtext: you don't get shooting stars without an atmosphere, if anything just asteroids briefly illuminated by sunlight, so please try and think precisely next time!

Julian paused. Of course the sky formed the word only very briefly, so that it was not noticed by Mimi Parker, Marc Edwards, Eva Borelius, or Karla Kramp; nor by Nina Hedegaard, who was leading her little community of mountain climbers—in so far as the conquest of a few hundred meters of gently sloping terrain justified the term mountain climbing. Resting not far away was the Callisto, which had brought them the 40 kilometers from the hotel to here, just below the peak: a clumsy jet shuttle reminiscent of a vastly inflated bumblebee. Julian knew that generations of future tourists would be disappointed by the design of the moon vehicles. But there was no reason for aerodynamics in a vacuum, unless—

Unless you decided to design them aerodynamically anyway, for purely aesthetic reasons.

The thought was enticing, but Julian wasn't in a mood to be seduced. His thought processes were obstructed by shooting stars, even though he wasn't really interested in the stupid things. What had made him think of them? Had he thought of them, in fact, or had he been thinking about transient light phenomena in general? Darting through his brain, leaping from the constant particle-flow of his thoughts, expression of a more complex whole. He tracked down the image, pursued it back through the course of the day to the early hours of the morning, condensed it, forced it into certain coordinates, gave it a place in space and time: very early morning, just before leaving his suite, a glimpse, a flash—

All of a sudden he remembered.

A flash on the outside left edge of the window that took up the wall of the living room facing the gorge. Something darting from right to left, *like* a shooting star, but perhaps you just had to be very tired and sleep-deprived not to work out what it really was. And God knows, he *had* been tired! But Julian's mind was like a film archive, not a scene went missing. In retrospect he saw that the phenomenon was neither virtual in nature nor a product of his imagination, but was extremely real in origin, which meant that he actually had seen something, on the far side of the valley, level with the magnetic rail tracks, even more or less at the height of the rails, where the tracks curved northward—

He had seen the Lunar Express.

He stopped, dumbfounded.

"—much weirder shapes than we're used to on Earth," Nina Hedegaard was explaining, as she walked toward a basalt structure that looked like a Cubist statue. "The reason is that there is no wind to wear away the rock, so nothing erodes. Consequently what is produced—"

He had seen the train! More of an afterimage, but it couldn't have been anything else, and it had been on the way to Gaia.

To the hotel.

"Interesting, what every culture has seen in the Moon," Eva was saying. "Did you know that many Pacific tribes still worship this great lump of rock as a fertility god?"

"A fertility god?" Hedegaard laughed. "The tiniest protozoon wouldn't survive up here."

"I'd have put my money on the sun," said Mimi Parker. Her tone contained a certain contempt for all native cultures because their representatives hadn't come into the world as respectable Christians. "The sun as a giver of life, I mean."

"In tropical regions it's hard to see it that way," Eva replied. "Or in the desert. The sun beats down ruthlessly upon you, twelve months without a break; it scorches harvests, dries up rivers, kills people and animals. But the moon brings coolness and freshness. The fleeting moisture of the day condenses into dew, you can rest and sleep—"

"With each other," Karla finished her sentence.

"Exactly. Among the Maoris, for example, the man only had the job of holding the woman's vagina open with his penis long enough for the moonbeams to penetrate it. It wasn't the man who got the woman pregnant, it was the Moon."

"Take a look. The old whore."

"My God, Karla, how churlish," Edwards laughed. "I think that's not incompatible with the idea of immaculate conception."

"Oh, please!" Mimi fumed. "Perhaps a primitive version of it."

"Why primitive?" asked Kramp waiting to pounce.

"Don't you think that's primitive?"

"That the Moon gets women pregnant? Yeah. As primitive as the idea that some unholy spirit is poking around on Earth and selling the result as an immaculate conception."

"There's no comparison!"

"Why not?"

"Because—well, because there just isn't. One's a primitive superstition, the other is—"

"I just want to understand."

"With all due respect, are you seriously doubting—?"

Hang on. *The* Lunar Express? Was that the one they'd arrived on? There was a second one, after all, parked at the Pole, which was only to be used if tourist numbers exceeded the capacity of the first. Had somebody arrived on the replacement train, at a quarter past five in the morning?

And why didn't he know anything about it?

Had Hanna seen anything?

"Plato must be behind that somewhere," said Edwards, trying to calm things down. "Is the curvature too big?"

"It's not that," said Nina. "You'd be able to make out the top edge of the crater from here, except that the flank facing us is in shadow at the moment. Black against black. But if you turn around, you can make out the Vallis Alpina to the northeast."

"Oh yes! Fantastic."

"It's pretty long," said Mimi.

"A hundred and thirty-four kilometers. Half a Grand Canyon. Come over this way a bit. Up here. Take a look."

"Where to?"

"Follow my outstretched finger. That bright dot."

"Hey! That couldn't possibly be—?"

"Certainly is," cried Marc. "Our hotel!"

"What? Where?"

"There."

"To be perfectly honest, I can see nothing but sun and shade."

"No, there's something there!"

A babble of words, a confusion of thoughts. It could only have been the second train. On closer reflection, hardly surprising. Lynn and Dana Lawrence were taking care of everything. The hotel was their domain, what did he know? Food, oxygen, and fuel had arrived during the night. He was a guest like all the others, he could consider himself lucky that everything was working so smoothly. Be proud! Be proud of Lynn, whatever dire predictions Tim had been gloomily coming up with. Ridiculous, that boy! Did someone stressed build hotels like Gaia?

Or was Lynn another reflection on his retina, whose true nature escaped him?

Unbelievable! Now he was starting to do the same thing himself.

"Julian?"

"What?"

"I suggested that we fly back." Nina's sweet conspiratorial smile behind her helmet could be heard in every word. "Marc and Mimi want to get back to the tennis court before dinner, and apart from that we'll have plenty of time to freshen up."

Freshen up. Cute code words. His right hand rose mechanically to stroke his beard, and instead rubbed against the bottom edge of his visor.

"Yes, of course. Let's go."

"Maybe you've seen me in more spectacular settings before. And thought they were real, even though your rational mind told you it *couldn't* all be real. But then that's the illusionist's job, tricking your reason. And believe me, modern technology can produce *any* kind of illusion."

Finn O'Keefe spread his arms as he walked slowly on.

"But illusions can't produce emotions of the kind that I'm feeling right now. Because what you're seeing here *isn't* a trick! It's by some way the most exciting place I've ever been, far more spectacular than any film."

He stopped and turned toward the camera, with the radiant Gaia in the background.

"Before, when you wanted to fly to the Moon, you had to sit in a movie seat. Today you can experience what I'm experiencing. You can see the Earth, set in such a wonderful starry sky, as if you were seeing all the way to the edge of the universe. I could spend hours trying to describe my feelings to you, but I," he smiled, "am *only* Perry Rhodan.

So let me express myself in the words of Edgar Mitchell, the sixth man to set foot on the satellite, in February 1971: *Suddenly, from behind the rim of the Moon, in long, slow-motion moments of immense majesty, there emerges a sparkling blue and white jewel, a light, delicate sky-blue sphere laced with slowly swirling veils of white, rising gradually like a small pearl in a thick sea of black mystery. It takes more than a moment to fully realize this is Earth . . . home. A sight that changed me forever."*

"Thanks," Lynn exclaimed. "That was great!"

"I don't know." Finn shook his head. The banal realization dawned on him that shaking your head in a space suit doesn't communicate anything to anybody, because your helmet doesn't shake with it. Peter Black checked the result on the display of his film camera. O'Keefe's face was clearly recognizable through his closed visor. He had taken off the gold metalized UV filter, as the surroundings would otherwise have been reflected in it. In spite of his layered contact lenses he wouldn't be able to walk around in the open for very long. And it certainly wasn't a good idea to look into the sun.

"No, it's great," Black agreed.

"I think the quote's too long," said Finn. "Far too long. A real sermon, I nearly dozed off."

"It's sacred."

"No, it's just too long, that's all."

"We'll cut in shots of the Earth," said Lynn. "But if you like we'll do an alternative shot. There's another quote from James Lovell: *People on Earth don't understand what they have. Maybe because not many of them have the opportunity to leave it and then come back."*

"Lovell won't do," said Black. "He never set foot on the Moon."

"Is that so important?" asked O'Keefe.

"Yes and there's another reason why not. He was the commander of Apollo 13. Anybody remember? *Houston, we have a problem.* Lovell and his people nearly snuffed it."

"Didn't Cernan say something clever?" Lynn asked. "He was a pretty good talker."

"Nothing comes to mind."

"Armstrong?"

"*It's one small step for—*"

"Forget it. Aldrin?"

Black thought for a moment. "Yeah, something short, too. *He who has been to the Moon has no more goals on Earth."*

"That sounds a bit fatalistic," Finn complained.

"What happened to the monkeys?" Heidrun's voice joined in. O'Keefe saw her coming down the hill in front of Shepard's Green. Even faceless and armored her elfin figure was unmistakable.

"What monkeys?" Lynn's laugh was slightly too shrill.

"Didn't you send monkeys up at some point? What did they say?"

"I think they spoke Russian," said Black.

"What are you doing here?" O'Keefe grinned. "Don't you fancy golf?"

"I've never fancied golf," Heidrun announced. "I just wanted to watch Walo falling in the dirt as he took his swing."

"I'll tell him."

"He knows. Didn't you boast about beating me at swimming, big mouth? You'd have the opportunity."

"What, now?"

Instead of answering, she waved to him and skipped away on her gazelle-like legs.

"We've got filming to do," he called after her; it was as superfluous as his headshaking, since radio contact remained constant only while visual contact was maintained.

"Dinner's on me if you win," she whispered, a small, white snake in his ear. "Schnitzel and röstis."

"Hey, Finn?" said Lynn.

"Mmhm?"

"I think that's a wrap." Was he wrong, or did she sound nervous? Throughout the whole shoot she'd had a tense expression on her face. "I think the Mitchell quote is fine."

O'Keefe saw Heidrun setting off along the other side of the gorge.

"Yes," he said thoughtfully. "Me too, as a matter of fact."

Nina Hedegaard was freshening herself up, and freshening Julian up as well. He lay on his back as she guided him like a joystick. He didn't have to do much more than put his arms around her buttocks and contract his own from time to time, to establish counterpressure—at least that was normally how things worked, but at the moment her soft, tanned, golden body weighed only nine and a half kilos, and threatened to bounce away whenever he thrust too enthusiastically. On the Moon, taking possession of strategically crucial millimeters called for basic knowledge of applied mechanics: where exactly to grip, what contribution the muscles had to make—biceps, triceps, pectoralis major—holding the hip bones like a hinge, drawing them to him, pushing them away at a precisely calculated angle, then bringing them back down . . . It was all frustratingly complicated. They managed to crack the problem at one point, but Julian didn't feel entirely comfortable. As Hedegaard slowly writhed her way toward a G-spot tornado measuring 5 on the Fujita scale, he was lost in idiotic thoughts, like the consequences of sex on the Moon if a few meddlesome beams in New Zealand had been enough to make little Maoris. Could they expect decuplets? Would Nina squat like a termite queen in the rocky seclusion of the Gaia Hotel, her abdomen monstrously swollen, popping out a human child every four seconds, or would she simply burst?

He stared at her glimmering, carefully trimmed, downy thicket and saw tiny trains driving through it, glittering reflections on spun gold, while his own Lunar Express valiantly stoked the engine. Hedegaard started moaning in Danish, usually a good sign, except that today it sounded somehow cryptic to his ears, as if he were to be sacrificed on the altar of her desire, to bring a Julian or a Juliana into the world as quickly as possible, a future Master or Miss Orley, and he started feeling uneasy. She was twenty-eight years younger than him. He hadn't asked her for ages what *she* expected from all this, not least because in the few private moments that they enjoyed together he hadn't had time to ask any questions, so quickly had they leaped out of their clothes, but eventually he would have to ask her. Above all he would have to ask *himself*. Which was much worse, because he already knew the answer, and it wasn't that of a sixty-year-old man.

He tried to hold out, then he reached his orgasm.

The climax peaked in a brief erasure of all thoughts, swept clean the convolutions of his brain, and reinforced the certainty that old was still twenty years older than he was. For a moment he felt immersed in the pure, delicious moment. Nina snuggled up to him, and his suspicion immediately welled up again. As if sex were merely the pleasurable preamble to a stack of small print, a magnificent portal leading inevitably to the nursery, the most perfidious kind of ambush. He looked helplessly at the blonde shock of hair on his chest. Not that he wanted rid of her. He actually didn't want her to go. It would have been enough for her simply to turn back into the astronaut whose job it was to entertain his guests without that moist promise in her eyes that she would *never leave him*, that henceforth she would *always* be there for him, for a whole *lifetime*! He ran his pointed fingers through the down on the back of her neck, embarrassed by his own reaction.

"I ought to get back to the control room," he murmured.

His suggestion met with harsh, muted sounds.

"Okay, in ten minutes," he agreed. "Shall we shower?"

In the bathroom the general luxury of the equipment continued. Tropically warm rain sprang from a generously curved showerhead, droplets so light that they floated down rather than falling. Hedegaard insisted on soaping him, and concentrated an excess of foam on a small if expanding area. His concern about her excessive demands made way for fresh arousal; the shower cabin was spacious and resplendent with all kinds of handy grips, Hedegaard pressed herself against him and he into her and—bang!—another thirty minutes had passed.

"I've really got to go now," he said into his fluffy towel.

"Will we meet up again later?" she asked. "After dinner?"

He had towel in his eyes, towel in his ears. He didn't hear her, or at least not loudly enough, and when he was about to ask what she'd said she was on the phone to Peter Black about something technical. He slipped quickly into jeans and T-shirt, kissed her quickly on the cheek, and disappeared before she could end the call.

Seconds later he stepped into the control room and found Lynn in a hushed conversation with Dana Lawrence. Ashwini Anand was planning routes for the coming day on a three-dimensional map. Half the room was dominated by a holographic wall, whose windows showed the public areas of the hotel from the perspective of surveillance cameras. Only the suites were unobserved. In the pool, Heidrun, Finn, and Miranda were having a diving competition, watched by Olympiada Rogacheva, whose husband was having a weight-lifting contest with Evelyn Chambers in the gym. The outside cameras showed Marc Edwards and Mimi Parker playing tennis, or at least Julian assumed that it was Marc and Mimi, while the golf players on the far side of the gorge were just setting off for home.

"Everything okay with you guys?" he asked in a pointedly cheerful voice.

"Great." Lynn smiled. Julian noticed that she looked somehow chalky, as if she were the only person in the room being illuminated by a different light source. "How was your trip?"

"Argumentative. Mimi and Karla were discussing the copulative habits of higher beings. We need a telescope on Mons Blanc."

"So you can spy on them?" Lawrence asked without a hint of amusement.

"Hell no, just to get a better view of the hotel. God! I thought everyone would be so awestruck up here that they'd be falling into each other's arms, and instead they're banging on about the Holy Ghost." His eye wandered to the window that showed the station. "Has the train left again?" he asked casually.

"Which train?"

"The Lunar Express. The LE-2, I mean, the one that came in last night. Has it set off again already?"

Dana stared at him as if he had thrown a pile of syllables at her feet and demanded that she cobble a sentence together.

"The LE-2 hasn't arrived."

"It hasn't?"

Anand turned around and smiled. "No, that was the LE-1, the one you arrived on yesterday."

"I know. And where has it been? In the meantime?"

"In the meantime?"

"What are you actually talking about?" Lynn asked.

"Well, about—" Julian hesitated. The screen really did show only one train. He felt a dark premonition creeping up on him, that it was the same Lunar Express that had brought them here. Which led to the reverse conclusion that—

"A train did pull in this morning," he insisted defiantly.

His daughter and Dana exchanged a swift glance.

"Which one?" asked Dana, as if walking on glass.

"That one there." Julian pointed impatiently at the screen.

Silence.

"Certainly not," Anand tried again. "The LE-1 hasn't left the station since it got here."

"But I've seen it."

"Julian—" Lynn began.

"When I was looking out of the window!"

"Dad, you can't have seen it!"

If she had told him she'd temporarily lent the train to a dozen aliens, he would have been less concerned. Only a few hours ago he would have put it all down to a hallucination. Not anymore.

"It's one thing after another," he sighed. "Today I met Carl Hanna, okay? At half past five in the corridor, and then—"

"I'm sorry, but what were you doing in the corridor at half past five?"

"Neither here nor there! Earlier, anyway—"

Hanna? Exactly, Hanna! He would have to ask Hanna. Perhaps he had seen that ominous train. After all, he had been down there before him, exactly at the same time as—

Just a moment. Hanna had come toward him from the station.

"No," he said to himself. "No, no."

"No?" Lynn tilted her head on one side. "What do you mean, no?"

Mad! Completely absurd. Why would Hanna be taking secret joyrides on the Lunar Express?

"Is it possible that you've been dreaming?" she continued. "Hallucinating?"

"I was wide awake."

"Fine, you were awake. To get back to the question of what you were doing at half past five—"

"Simple insomnia! God almighty, I went for a walk."

His eye scoured the monitor wall. Where was the Canadian? There, in the Mama Quilla Club. Slouching, sipping cocktails, on a sofa, with the Donoghues, Nairs, and Locatellis.

"Maybe Julian's right," Dana Lawrence said thoughtfully. "Maybe we really did miss something."

"Nonsense, Dana, no way." Lynn shook her head. "We both know that no train left. Ashwini knows that too."

"Do we really know?"

"Nothing was delivered, no one went anywhere."

"Easy to check." Dana walked to the monitor wall and opened a menu. "We just have to look at the recording."

"Ridiculous! Absolutely ridiculous!" Lynn was getting tense. "We don't need to look at a recording."

"With the best will in the world, I can't imagine why you're so resistant to the idea," Julian said, amazed. "Let's take a look at it. We should have done that right away."

"Dad, we've got everything under control."

"As you wish," said Lawrence. "As a matter of fact it's *my* job to keep everything here under control, isn't it, Lynn? That's why you employed me in the first place. I'm ultimately responsible for the security of your hotel and the well-being of your guests, and monorails that operate all by themselves are at odds with that."

Lynn shrugged. Dana waited for a moment, then issued instructions with darting fingers. Another window opened, showed the interior of the station hall. The time code said May 27, 2025, 05:00.

Should we go further back?'

"No." Julian shook his head. "It was between five fifteen and five thirty."

Dana nodded and ran quickly through the recording.

Nothing happened. The LE-1 didn't leave the station, and the LE-2 didn't pull in either. God in heaven, Julian thought, Lynn's right. I'm hallucinating. He tried to catch her eye and she avoided his, visibly upset that he hadn't simply believed her.

"Hmm," he murmured. "Hmm, okay. Sorry."

"Nothing to be sorry about," Dana said seriously. "It was entirely possible."

"It wasn't," Lynn snarled. When she looked at him at last, her pupils were flickering with fury. "Are you actually sure that you didn't dream that stupid walk of yours? Maybe you weren't in the corridor at all. Maybe you were just *in bed*."

"As I said, I'm sorry." Taken aback, he wondered why she was so furious with him. He'd just wanted to be doubly sure. "Let's just forget it, I made a mistake."

Instead of answering she stepped up to the monitor wall, tapped in a series of orders, and opened another set of recordings. Dana watched, arms folded, while Ashwini Anand pretended she wasn't even there. Julian recognized the underground corridor, 05:20.

"That really isn't necessary," he hissed.

"It isn't?" Lynn raised her eyebrows. "Why not? You wanted to be doubly sure, after all."

She launched the sequence before he could start protesting again. After a few seconds Carl Hanna appeared and climbed on one of the moving walkways. He approached the end of the corridor, looked through the window into the station concourse, and disappeared into one of the passageways that led to the train, only to reappear, seconds later, and be carried back again. Almost simultaneously, Julian stepped out of the lift.

"Congratulations," Lynn said frostily. "You were telling the truth."

"Lynn—"

She brushed the ash-blonde hair off her forehead and turned to face him. Behind the fury in her eyes he thought he recognized something else. Fear, Julian thought. My God, she's frightened! Then, all of a sudden, his daughter smiled, and her smile seemed to erase her fury as completely as if she knew nothing in life but benevolence and forgiveness. With a swing of her hips she came over to him, gave him a smacking kiss on the cheek, and boxed him in the ribs.

"Let me know when a UFO lands," she grinned, and left headquarters.

Julian stared after her. "I will," he murmured.

And suddenly the ghostly thought came to him that his daughter was an actress.

And yet!

In an act of childish perseverance he went to the Mama Quilla Club, whose dance floor was mysteriously illuminated under the eternal light show of the starry sky. Michio Funaki was mixing cocktails behind the bar. When he saw him, Warren Locatelli shot to his feet and raised his glass to him, waving his other hand wildly.

"Julian! That was the most brilliant day of any vacation I've ever had!"

"Impressive, really." Aileen Donoghue laughed in her tinkling soprano. "Even if we've had to learn golf all over again."

"Golf, bullshit!" Locatelli pressed Julian to his chest and pulled him over to the seated group. "Carl and I went charging around in those moon buggies, it was absolutely crazy! You've got to build a racetrack up here, a real fucking Le Mans de la Lune!"

"And he didn't even win," giggled Momoka Omura. "He almost flattened his buggy."

"More to the point, he nearly flattened *me*," said Rebecca Hsu, placing a single peanut between her lips. "Warren's company is inspiring, particularly when you think about moon burials."

"We had a wonderful day," smiled Sushma Nair. "Do come and join us."

"Right away." Julian smiled. "Just for a little while. Carl, have you got a minute?"

"Of course." Hanna swung his legs off his sofa.

"Just don't go missing on me," Locatelli laughed. Recently he and Hanna had been spending a lot of time together. One chatty, the other taciturn, somehow strange, but plainly a friendship was developing there. They went to the bar, where Julian ordered the most complicated cocktail on the menu, an Alpha Centauri.

"Listen, I feel a bit silly." He waited until Funaki was busy, and low-ered his voice. "But I've got to ask you something. When we met in the corridor this morning, you were coming from the station."

Hanna nodded.

"And?" Julian asked.

"And what?"

"Did you take a look inside?"

"Inside the concourse? Once. Through the window." Hanna thought. "After that I went into one of the passageways. You remember, I was a bit dozy when it came to looking for the exits."

"And did you—did you see anything in the concourse?"

"What are you getting at?"

"I mean, the train, was it there? Did it set off, did it pull in?"

"What, the Lunar Express? No."

"So it was just parked there."

"Exactly."

"And you're a hundred percent sure about that?"

"I didn't see anything else. So why do you feel silly?"

"Because—oh, this really isn't the place." And he just told Hanna the whole story, simply out of a need to get rid of it.

"Maybe it was one of those flashes we all see up here," said Hanna.

Julian knew what he was referring to. High-energy particles, pro-tons and heavy atomic nuclei, occasionally broke through the armor of spaceships and space stations, reacted with atoms in the eye, and caused brief flashes of light that were perceived on the retina, but only if you had your eyes shut. Over time you got used to it, until you barely noticed them. Behind the regolith plating of the bedroom they hardly ever occurred. But in the living room—

Funaki set the cocktail down in front of him. Julian stared at the glass without really seeing it.

"Yes, perhaps."

"You just made a mistake," said Hanna. "If you want my advice, you should apologize to Lynn and forget the whole thing."

But Julian couldn't forget it. Something was wrong, something didn't fit. He *knew without question* that he had seen something, just not the train. Something more subtle was bothering him, a crucial detail that proved he wasn't fantasizing. There was a second inner movie that would explain everything if he could just drag it out of his unconscious and look at it, look at it very precisely to understand what he had already seen and just hadn't understood, whether he liked the explanation or not.

He *had* to remember.

Remember!

Juneau, Alaska, USA

Loreena Keowa was irritated. On the day of the boat trip, Palstein had agreed to let the film crew come along, and had delivered a series of powerful quotes, although without giving her that sense of familiarity that she usually developed with her interviewees. By now she knew that Palstein loved the crystalline aesthetic of numbers, with which he rationalized everything and everyone, himself included, although without losing the emotional dimension in his dealings with people. He esteemed the sound-mathematics of a composer like Johann Sebastian Bach, the fractal Minimalism of Steve Reich, and he was also fascinated by the breakdown of all structures and narrative arcs in the music of György Ligeti. He had a Steinway grand, he played well if a bit mechanically, not classics, as Loreena would have expected, but Beatles, Burt Bacharach, Billy Joel, and Elvis Costello. He owned prints by Mondrian, but also an incredibly intense original by Pollock, which looked as if its creator had screamed at the canvas in paint.

Curious to meet Palstein's wife, Loreena had finally shaken the hand of a gracious creature who commandeered her, dragged her through the Japanese garden she had designed herself for a quarter of an hour, and laughed like a bell every now and again for no perceptible reason. Mrs. Palstein was an architect, she learned, and had laid out most of the grounds herself. Determined to use the currency of her newly acquired training in small talk, Loreena asked her about Mies van der Rohe, receiving a mysterious smile in return. Suddenly Mrs. Palstein was treating her as a co-conspirator. Van der Rohe, oh, yes! Did she want to stay to dinner? While she was considering whether or not to agree, the lady's phone rang, and she went off in a conversation about migraines, forgetting Loreena so completely that she found her own way back to the house and, because Palstein had issued no similar invitation, left without dinner.

Afterward, in Juneau, she had admitted to herself that she liked the oil manager, his kindness, his good manners, his melancholy expression, which made her feel strangely exposed, and at the same time made him seem a little weird—and yet she still found him very alien, for reasons she couldn't quite explain. Instead of devoting herself to her report, she had plunged into research, had flown from Texas to Calgary, Alberta, dropping in unannounced on the police station there. With her Native-American face and her peculiar charm, she managed to get to the office of the police lieutenant, who promised to keep her informed about any progress in investigations. Loreena extended her antennae for undertones, and established that there had been no progress, thanked him, took the next flight back to Juneau and, on the way, told her editorial team she wanted them to collect all available footage about what had happened in Calgary. After she landed, she called an intern to her office and told him what they had to look for.

"I realize," she said, "that the police have viewed and analyzed all the pictures a hundred times. So let's look at them another hundred times. Or two hundred if it helps."

On her desk she spread out a few prints showing the square in front of Imperial Oil headquarters. At the time of the shooting, the complex of buildings opposite had lain empty for months, after the open-cast mining company based there had come to a miserable end.

"The police conclude for a whole host of reasons that the shot was fired from the middle one of the three buildings, which are, incidentally, all interconnected. Probably from one of the upper stories. The complex has entrances to the front, the sides, and the back, so there are several possible ways of getting in and out again."

"You really think we'll discover something that the cops have missed?"

"Be optimistic," said Loreena. "Always look on the bright side."

"I've taken a look at the material, Loreena. Almost all the cameras were trained on the crowd and the podium. It was only after the shooting that some of them were clever enough to swing around to the complex, but you don't see anyone coming out."

"So who says we have to concentrate on the complex? The police are doing that. I want us to concentrate on the crowd in the square."

"You mean the guy who did it went from there into the building?"

"I mean that you're a bit of a male chauvinist. It could have been a girl, couldn't it?"

"A killer chick, huh?" giggled the intern.

"Carry on like that and you'll meet one in person. Look at every individual figure in the square. I want to know if anyone filmed the building before, during, and after the attack."

"Oh, God! This is slave labor!"

"Stop whining. Jump to it. I'll take care of YouTube, Facebook, Smallworld, and so on."

After the intern had started viewing the material, she had set about compiling a list of all significant decisions that Palstein had made or advocated over the past six months. She also recorded his resistance to the interests of others. She logged on to forums and blogs, followed the internet debate about closures, acquiescence on the one hand, helpless rage on the other, along with the desire to give the oilmen a good kicking, ideally to put them up against the wall right away, but none of these entries raised a suspicion that its author was in any way connected with the attack. The people involved in open-cast mining were bitter about it, but glad that it was coming to an end, particularly in the Indian communities. It struck her that the Chinese had been taking a great interest in Canadian oil sand over the past two decades, and had put a lot of money into open-cast mining, which they were now losing, and that regardless of the helium-3 revolution they were still, albeit to a waning degree, dependent on oil and gas. On the other hand there was now so much cheap oil available that anything else seemed more sensible than extracting it in the most unprofitable way imaginable. When, in the early hours of the morning, she finally found no more press information and no more postings, she compiled a file about Orley Enterprises, or more precisely about Palstein's attempts to become involved with Orley Energy and Orley Space.

And suddenly she had an idea.

Dog-tired, she set about backing up her newly fledged theory with arguments. They weren't particularly new: someone was trying to undermine Palstein's involvement with Orley. Except that she suddenly realized, clear as day, that the purpose of the attack had been to keep Palstein from traveling to the Moon.

If that was so—

But why? What would Palstein have had to discuss with Julian Orley on the Moon that they couldn't have sorted out on Earth? Or did it have something to do with other people he was supposed to meet there?

She needed the list of participants.

Her eyes stung. Palstein wasn't supposed to fly to the Moon. The thought stayed with her. It continued in confused dreams, the kind you get when you fall asleep in office chairs, it produced visions in her alarmingly cracked brain, of people in space suits shooting at each other from designer buildings, with her caught in the middle.

"Hey, Loreena."

"Mies is very popular on the Moon," she mumbled.

"Meeces? Love 'em to pieces." Someone laughed. She'd been talking nonsense. Blinking and stiff-limbed, she came to. The intern was leaning on the edge of the desk and looked as pleased as punch.

"Shit," she murmured. "I dozed off."

"Yeah, you look like a slaughtered animal. All that's missing is the knife handle sticking out of your chest. Come on, Pocahontas, get a cup of coffee down you. We've got something! I think we've *really* got something!"

MAY 28, 2025
Enemy Contact

QUYU, SHANGHAI, CHINA

At around one o'clock, Jericho had had his fourth phone conversation with Zhao, who was at that instant watching a mass brawl, and assured him that he was enjoying himself enormously.

Net-junkies came and went. Some made the move to the honeycomb sleeping modules. Almost the entire population of the Cyber Planet was male—women were a vanishingly small minority and most of them were pretty long in the tooth. For Jericho, the only halfway healthy-looking people were the users of the full-motion suits and the treadmills, who were forced to take a bit of exercise as they explored virtual universes. Many of them spent their time in parallel worlds like Second Life and Future Earth, or in the Evolutionarium, where they could pretend to be animals, from dinosaurs all the way down to bacteria. Some of the reclining figures moved their sensor-covered hands, drew cryptic patterns in the empty air, a clue that they were attempting to play an active part in something or other. The overwhelming majority didn't lift a finger. They had reached the terminal stage, reduced to being observers of their own extended agonies.

Strangely, the atmosphere had a cathartic effect on Jericho, in which Zhao's defamations melted away to nothing. The net zombies seemed to stir themselves, letting him know it just took an insignificant effort of will to end the status of his loneliness; they pointed at him with desiccated fingers, accused him of flirting with sadness, of having walled himself up in the past and brought about his own misery; they sent him back to life which, so far, hadn't been *nearly* as bad as he thought. He made a thousand resolutions, soap bubbles on whose surfaces the future iridized. In a strange way the Cyber Planet brought him comfort. Then, as if on cue, Zhao called, claiming he just wanted to know how Jericho was doing.

He was doing just fine, Jericho replied.

And again he waited. Even though he had plenty of experience of staring stoically at a single spot, the coming and going in the market was starting to bore him. People ate and drank, haggled, hung around, hooked up, laughed, or got into arguments. The night belonged to the gangsters; it was here that they brought the day's bounty back into the cycle of greed, albeit quite peacefully. He started to envy Zhao his fighting, decided to rely entirely on the scanners for a while, connected the hologoggles up to his phone, and logged in to Second Life. The market vanished, making way for a boulevard with bistros, shops, and a movie theater. Using his phone's touchscreen, Jericho guided his avatar down the street. In this world he was dark-skinned, he had long, black hair, and he was called Juan Narciso Ucañan, a name he'd read years ago in some disaster novel or other. Three good-looking young women were sitting at a table in the sun, all with transparent wings and filigree antennae above their eyes.

"Hi," he said to one of them.

She looked up and beamed at him. Jericho's avatar was a masterpiece of programming, and even by the high standards of Second Life, unusually attractive.

"My name's Juan," he said. "I'm new here."

"Inara," she said. "Inara Gold."

"You're looking great, Inara. Do you fancy a totally awesome experience?"

The avatar that called itself Inara hesitated. That hesitation was typical of the woman hiding behind it. "I'm here with my girlfriends," she said evasively.

"Well, I'd love to," said one of them.

"Me too," laughed the other one.

"Okay, let's the four of us all do something." Jericho Juan put on a wide smile. "But first I need to discuss something with the most beautiful one. Inara."

"Why me?"

"Because I've got a surprise for you." He pointed to an empty chair. "Can I sit down here?"

She nodded. Her big, golden eyes looked at him steadily. He leaned forward and lowered his voice.

"Could we be undisturbed for a moment, beautiful Inara? Just the two of us?"

"It's not up to me, sweetie."

"We're just going anyway," one of the girlfriends said and got to her feet. The other sent a snake-tongue darting from between her teeth, fished an insect out of the air, swallowed it and gave an offended hiss. They both spread their wings and disappeared behind a puff of pink clouds. Inara struck a pose and stretched her ribcage. The fabric of the tight top she was wearing started to become transparent.

"I love surprises," she purred.

"And this is one—Emma."

Emma Deng was so surprised that she momentarily lost control of her clothes. Her top disappeared completely, revealing perfectly formed breasts. A moment later her torso turned black.

"Don't go, Emma," Jericho said quickly. "It would be a mistake."

"Who are you?" hissed the woman who called herself Inara.

"That doesn't matter." His avatar crossed his legs. "You've embezzled 2 million yuan and passed on company secrets to Microsoft. You can't cope with more problems than that all at once."

"How—how did you find me?"

"It wasn't hard. Your preferences, your semantics—"

"My what?"

"Forget it. My specialty is hunting down people on the net, that's all. You've been transmitting for so long now that it was easy to locate you."

Not true, but Jericho knew that Emma Deng didn't have the knowledge to see through his lie. A refined little girl, who had used the fact of her intimate relationship with the senior partner in the company she worked for in order to cheat it for years on end.

"If I want," Jericho went on, "the cops will be at your door in ten minutes. You can run away, but they'll find you just like I did. We'll get you sooner or later, so I advise you to listen."

The woman froze. Outwardly she had as little in common with the real Emma Deng as Owen Jericho had with Juan Narciso Ucañan. If you examined her psychological profile, it was very likely that Emma would opt for a body like Inara Gold's, almost 100 percent. Jericho was definitely pleased with himself.

"I'm listening," she muttered.

"Okay, the honorable Li Shiling is willing to forgive you. That's the information that I'm supposed to pass on to you."

Emma laughed loudly.

"You're joking."

"Not at all."

"Christ, I might be stupid, but I'm not as stupid as that. Shiling wants me to rot in hell."

"That's not unthinkable."

"Great."

"On the other hand Mr. Li seems to be missing the delights of your company. Particularly in the genital region, he's been finding life a little dull since you left."

Inara Gold's beautiful face reflected unconcealed hatred. Jericho assumed that Emma was sitting in front of a full-body scanner that transferred her gestures and facial expressions to her avatar in real time.

"What else did the old fucker have to say for himself?" she hissed.

"You don't want to hear."

"I do. I want to know what I'm letting myself in for."

"A refreshing dip in the Huangpu, with your feet encased in lead? I mean, he's furious! Your second-best option is that he'll hand you over to the authorities. But according to his own personal testimony what he'd really like is for you to go on giving him blowjobs."

"Shiling's disgusting."

"It doesn't seem to have been that bad."

"He forced me!"

"To do what? Relieve him of two million? Sell building plans to the competition? Come on to him, to win his trust?"

Emma looked askance. "And what does he want?"

"Nothing special. He wants you to marry him."

"Shit."

"Could be," Jericho said casually. "The Huangpu's shit too. The quality of the water has declined dramatically. Mr. Li is waiting for your call at the number you know, and he wants to hear a loud, audibly articulated Yes. What do you think, could you do that? What shall I tell him?"

"Shit. Shit!"

"That's not what he wants to hear."

By now Diane had passed on Emma's location via the relevant server. She was in her apartment in Hong Kong. Far away, but not far enough. Nowhere would be far enough, unless she left the solar system.

"He might buy you an apartment in Hong Kong," he added in a conciliatory tone.

Emma gave up.

"Okay," she squeaked.

"Mr. Li is always available to speak to. I'd like to get a cheerful call from him in an hour at the most, otherwise I'll consider myself forced to blow your cover." Jericho paused. "Don't take it personally, Emma. This is how I make my living."

"Yes," she whispered. "We're all whores."

"You said it."

He logged out of Second Life. The viewing window of the specs brightened. At the market, the last punters were on their feet. Most of the stands had closed. Jericho keyed in the time.

Four in the morning.

"Diane," he said into his phone.

"Hi, Owen. You're still awake?"

Jericho smiled. Sympathy from a computer had something going for it if it spoke with Diane's voice. He looked around. Most of the couches were abandoned. Cleaning systems were operating here and there. Even junkies had a vague sense of the time.

"Wake me at seven, Diane."

"Sure, Owen. Oh, Owen?"

"Yes?"

"I'm just receiving a message for you."

"Can you read it out?"

"Zhao Bide writes: *Don't want to wake you in case you've dozed off under the burden of responsibility. Pleasant dreams. When it's all over, let's go and raise a glass.*"

Jericho smiled.

"Write back and tell him—no, don't write anything. I'm going to hit the hay."

"Can I do anything else for you?"

"No thanks, Diane."

"See you later, Owen. Sleep well."

• • •

See you later, Owen.

Later, Owen.

Owen—

Later and later and later, and she doesn't come back. He lies on his bed and waits. On the bed in the dingy room that he hopes so ardently to be able to leave with her.

But Joanna doesn't come back.

Instead, fat caterpillar-like creatures start creeping up the bedsheets—claws clutching the cotton fibers—the click of segmented legs—alarm-bells—groping feelers brushing the soles of his feet—alarm—alarm—

Wake up, Owen!

Wake up!

"Owen?"

He started awake, his body one big heartbeat.

"Owen?"

The early daylight stung his eyes.

"What time?" he murmured.

"It's only twenty-five past six," said Diane. "Sorry if I woke you prematurely. I have a priority A call for you."

Yoyo, the idea darted through his head.

No, the scanners were working independently of Diane, they could have woken him with an unnerving noise that was impossible to ignore. And he would have seen red. But among the people who were slowly repopulating the market, there wasn't a single Guardian to be seen.

"Put them through," he said bluntly.

"What's up? Are you still asleep?"

Tu's square head grinned at him. Behind him, the Serengeti was springing to life. Or something like it: at any rate giraffes and elephants were walking around the landscape. A glowing orange sky hung over pastel-colored mountains. Jericho pulled himself up. Individual snores rang out through Cyber Planet. Only a young woman sat cross-legged on her stool, with a coffee in her right hand. Plainly not a junkie. Jericho assumed she'd just popped in to see the breakfast news.

"I'm in Quyu," he said, suppressing a yawn.

"I just thought. Because of your receptionist. A pretty voice, but normally you pick up yourself."

"Diane is—"

"You call your computer Diane?" Tu asked, interested.

"I'm short-staffed, Tian. You've got Naomi. There was a TV series a long time ago where an FBI agent was always conferring with his secretary, although you never got to see her in person—"

"And her name was Diane?"

"Mmhm."

"Nice," said Tu. "What's wrong with a real secretary?"

"And where would she stay?"

"If she was pretty, your bed. You've made it now, son. You live in a loft in Xintiandi. It's time for you to arrive in your new life."

"Thanks. I'm there."

"You're dealing with people who don't quite get long-term incomers."

"Anything else, Reverend?" Jericho swung himself off his couch, walked to the bar, and chose a cappuccino. "Don't you want to know how our search is going?"

"You haven't got anything."

"How do you work that out?"

"If you had anything, you'd have been rubbing my nose in it for ages."

"Your call is Priority A. Why's that?"

"So that I can boast about being your best member of staff." Tu giggled. "You wanted to know who what's-his-name Wang phoned before he died."

The coffee gurgled into the cardboard cup.

"You mean—?"

"Yes, I do. I'll send you over his telephone traffic. All the conversations he's had since May 26. You can fall at my feet if you like."

"How did you manage that?"

"Certainly not by rummaging through his remains. As luck would have it, I play golf with the CEOs of two service providers. The guy was registered with one of them. My acquaintance was kind enough to pass the data on to me, no questions asked."

"Christ, Tian!" Jericho blew on his coffee. "Now you owe him all the favors in the world, right?"

"Not at all," Tu said in a bored voice. "He owes *me* something."

"Good. Very good."

"Where do we go from here?"

"Diane is constantly checking the net for suspicious texts, Zhao and I are keeping an eye on the markets. If no one appears in the course of the next few hours, I'll have to consider extending the circle of investigators and showing photographs around. I'd rather avoid that if we can." Jericho paused. "How did your conversation with Chen Hongbing go?"

"So-so. He's worried."

"Isn't he at least reassured that she's at liberty?"

"Hongbing has turned worrying into an art form. But he trusts you."

Behind Tu, a big bird of prey flapped into the air. A giraffe came quite close.

"Tell me, where are you?"

"Where do you think?" Tu grinned. "In my office, of course."

"And where are you pretending to be?"

"In South Africa. Pretty, isn't it? It's from the autumn collection. We're offering twelve environments. The software places your image in the background as soon as you make your call, and adapts you to the environment. Have you noticed that the sun's shining on my bald head?"

"And the other environments?"

"The Moon's really brilliant!" Tu beamed. "In the background the American moon base and spaceships landing. The program gives you a space suit. One can see your face through the visor of the helmet. Your voice is a bit distorted, like in the moon landings last century."

"One giant step for mankind," Jericho teased.

"Let me know if anything new comes up."

"Will do."

Jericho took a sip of his coffee. Thin and bitter. He urgently needed fresh air. As he crossed the foyer, Diane told him she had received a data packet from Tu, and passed it on to him. He stepped out into the street, with his eye on the display. Numbers, days, and times became visible. Wang's phone traffic. Diane compared the relevant data with information they had already. Of course Jericho didn't expect any matches.

But she told him there was one.

He frowned. The evening before his death, Grand Cherokee Wang had dialed a number that also appeared among Jericho's contacts. Diane had correlated names and numbers, so that there was no doubt about who the student had phoned on the afternoon of May 26.

Jericho stared at the name.

Suddenly he realized that he'd made a terrible mistake.

STEELWORKS

He had gone for direct confrontation, which temporarily forced him out of his location. After setting up another scanner near the front door of Cyber Planet, Jericho set off. If the scouts caught one of their target people, he could be back within a few minutes.

The streets were still empty, which meant that he made good headway. He parked the Toyota behind a soot-black building, straightened his hologoggles, and approached Wong's World on foot. The glass façade of this Cyber Planet showed that the market was on the way up. This branch of Wong was decidedly less run down than the other one. As Zhao had described it, it lacked the booths for prostitutes and people running gambling games; everything seemed to be entirely devoted to the preparation of food and the sale of groceries. Vegetables, herbs, and spices were displayed in baskets and containers. For one customer, a woman reached into a basket with a grabber and pulled out a snake that went into violent convulsions when the saleswoman routinely cut open its body and pulled off the skin. Jericho turned away and inhaled the smell of fresh wontons and baozis. The stand was busy. Two young men with damply glistening torsos, swathed in the steam that rose from huge pots, swung their ladles, passed bowls of broth and crunchy crab and pork dumplings over the counter. Jericho walked on, ignoring the protests of his stomach. He could eat later. He crossed the street, stepped into Cyber Planet, and glanced around. There was no sign of Zhao. There were no sleeping pods, but he might have gone to the toilet. Jericho waited for ten minutes, but Zhao didn't appear.

He stepped outside again.

And suddenly he saw them.

There were two of them. They were both strolling toward the wonton stall and inadvertently looked in his direction as they did so. Their outlines glowed red on the glass of the hologoggles. The boy was wearing jeans and a T-shirt, the girl a miniskirt, for which she was a stone too heavy, and a biker's jacket with a massive *City Demons* logo. Laden down with Wong's World paper bags they asked the sweaty wonton cooks to put generous portions of soup in sealable plastic bowls, which they received, chatting and laughing, and put in the bags. Both seemed carefree and generally cheerful. They talked to other customers for a while and walked on.

They bought enough breakfast to feed a whole gang.

Jericho followed them, while the computer supplied him with details taken from Tu's database. The girl's name was Xiao Meiqi, known as Maggie, a computer science student. The boy was called Jin Jia Wei, on an electronic technology course. According to Tu, they were part of Yoyo's inner circle. With Daxiong, that meant that Jericho now knew by sight four of the six dissidents. And those two certainly weren't going to be demolishing the contents of those bags all by themselves.

He pushed his way toward them, while at the same time keeping an eye out for Zhao. Maggie Xiao and Jin Jia Wei had their Thermos flasks filled with tea, they bought cigarettes and little cakes with a paste of nuts, honey and red beans that Yoyo loved—so Jericho recalled—then they crossed the street. As soon as he saw their parked e-bikes on the other side, he knew there was no point going on following them on foot. He turned back to his Toyota, started it up, and steered it between passers-by and cyclists. The street was too wide for washing-lines, there was nothing to obstruct his view, so he could see the looming silhouette of the blast furnace a few kilometers away. Jin and Maggie dashed toward it on their bikes. Seconds later Jericho too had left the commotion of the market behind him, and now saw a dusty patch of waste ground, with the old steelworks stretching beyond. The bikes raised clouds of dust. He avoided following the two of them in a straight line, instead driving the Toyota into the shadow of a row of low Portakabins.

Yoyo was hiding somewhere in those industrial ruins, he was sure of it.

He watched apprehensively as the bikes headed toward the blast furnace which, standing out against the light of dawn, looked like a launch pad for spaceships, as Jules Verne might have imagined it: a barrel-shaped cylinder, tapering toward the top, a good 50 meters high, encased in a steel girder construction that still gave an idea of the smelter. Levels of scaffolding, bridges and walkable platforms, connected by beams and stairways, overflowing with pumps, generators, floodlights, wiring, and other equipment. A conveyor belt ran steeply up from the ground to the filling inlet of the furnace. Above it, a massive pipe stretched into the sky, bent abruptly, and ended up in a kind of oversized cooking pot with three huge, upright tanks. Everything in this world seemed to have grown and tangled together. Everything that might have served the exchange of gases and fluids, cables, pipelines, and tubes, created the impression of hopelessly tangled intestines, as if the innards of a colossal machine had turned inside out.

Right in front of the furnace a tower of girders grew from the ground, about half as high. As if put there by magic, a little house with a gabled roof and windows stood at the top of it, connected to the furnace construction by a platform. Clearly it had once served as a control room. Unlike the other buildings around it, its windows were intact. Jin and Maggie guided their bikes into an adjoining low-rise building, and a few moments later, swinging their Wong bags, reappeared and began climbing the zigzag stairways of the tower. Jericho slowed his pace, stopped, and looked up at the former control room.

Was Yoyo up there?

At that moment he saw something approaching from the market and coming to a standstill on the vacant lot. He turned his head and saw a man sitting on a motorcycle. No, not a motorcycle. It looked more as though a running machine, a narwhal, and a jet engine had been combined into something whose purpose wasn't immediately apparent. Stocky, with a wide saddle, closed side panels and a flattened windshield, and a gaping hole where its front wheel should have been. Silvery spokes flashed inside it, plainly a turbine. Pivoting jets emerged along the handlebars and the pillion. Apparently the thing slid along on its smooth belly and two tapering fins that pointed to the rear. It was only on closer inspection that you noticed that a nosewheel grew from the belly, and the fins ended in enclosed spheres, which gave it a certain roadworthiness in spite of its flat bottom. But the actual purpose of the machine was quite different. Years ago, when the first models were ready for production, Jericho had applied for a permit, before balking at the extortionate purchase price. Those things were expensive. Too expensive for Owen Jericho.

Far too expensive for someone from Quyu.

So what was Zhao doing sitting on that thing?

Zhao Bide, who was staring over at the blast furnace, watching Jin and Maggie climb the steps, without noticing Jericho in the shade of the building. Who hadn't called in, in spite of everything they'd agreed, even though he was hot on the heels of two Guardians who would in all likelihood lead him to Yoyo. Whose number Grand Cherokee Wang had dialed the evening before he died, to talk to him for one minute, as Tu's data revealed.

Wang had called Zhao.

Why?

Uneasy and electrified, Jericho was heading across to confront Zhao, who was leaning over right at that moment, and wiping something from the dashboard—just as he had polished the display in Jericho's car.

It all fit.

Cherokee Wang's murderer, just before he fled from the World Financial Center—in an elegant made-to-measure suit, with tinted glasses, a false mustache and wig, which temporarily transformed his even features into the face of Ryuichi Sakamoto—he leaned forward and wiped the controls of the Silver Dragon. But Jericho hadn't been looking carefully enough, because suddenly he reminds him not of a Japanese pop star or a model, but all the time of—

Zhao Bide.

He's the one who's set the hit man on Yoyo's trail.

Just as he puts his foot down on the accelerator, Zhao starts his airbike. A sound of turbines sweeps across the square. The machine

Frank Schätzing

swivels its jets into the upright position, balances for a moment on the tips of its fins, and shoots steeply upward, and Jericho realizes that there is now hardly a chance of saving Yoyo.

How ridiculously easy everything had been.

And at the same time how excruciating.

Although he had barely been able to conquer his dread over the past few hours when fate had decreed that he go to Quyu, once more having the proof before his eyes that the superiority of the human race was the fevered hallucination of religiously infected Darwinists, a tragic error that called for correction. Sheer revulsion had driven him to speak to Jericho about the failure of creation, the unsuccessful part of the experiment—rashness! What Zhao had by the skin of his teeth managed to turn into sarcasm, now reflected Kenny Xin's genuine outrage. The bulk of his species was a seething parasitic mass, a scandal for any creator, if there had ever been one. Only a few people who felt similarly had taken their insight to its conclusion, like that Roman who had burned his city down, even if he was said to have ruined the moment by singing. But Xin wished he could have seen the purifying fire in which the face of poverty blistered and charred; or even more than that:

He wished he could *be* the fire!

Objectively speaking, an eyesore like Quyu deserved to be reduced to ashes. Worldwide, one and a half billion people lived in slums. One and a half billion upon whom life had been squandered, who breathed in precious air and used up valuable resources, without producing anything but more poverty, still more hunger, still more progeny. One and a half billion who were suffocating the world. Still, Quyu would be a start.

But Xin had learned to rein in his feelings. To declare his independence of the dictates of the emotions. He had furiously set about recreating, immunizing, and cleansing himself. So deeply that he would never again be forced to rub his skin off to rid himself of the dirt, the wire-pulling circumstances of his birth, the damp and sticky leavings of daily assaults, the scabs of despair. He had known that he would inevitably perish if he didn't succeed in cleansing himself, and that his own death, the piss-stench of capitulation, would not bring redemption.

So he had acted.

Sometimes, at night, he experienced the day again, over and over. The tribunal of flames. He felt the heat on his cheeks, witnessed the burial of his own sticky corpse, felt the faint amazement of his wonderful, reborn body, his wild joy at the tremendous power that he would now have at his disposal. He was free. Free to do what he felt like. Free to slip into any skin he wished to, such as Zhao Bide's.

How ridiculously simple it had been to latch on to Jericho, to take the man into his service. Grand Cherokee Wang might have been an idiot, but Xin owed him mute thanks for his detective card. Jericho had taken him to Quyu, to the Andromeda, where Xin had decided to take the game to its extreme. No wig this time, no false noses and beards, just appropriate clothing, based on the standard outfit that he carried with him at all times. Perhaps he hadn't looked scruffy enough, he didn't wear appliqués of any kind, but the roadies hadn't minded, they'd just been grateful for someone to help them with the bulky Portakabins, and within a few minutes they'd given him all the information he needed in order to trick Jericho: Ass Metal. The Pink Asses. What could the detective have done but take Xin for one of their own?

Jericho had been the mouse, he was the cat. He had come up with his own makeshift plan. Assault, ceasefire, two beers, a pact. Provided by Hydra with sufficient knowledge about the girl to impress the detective. There were some answers he hadn't been able to give. Jericho's question, for example, about whether he was in City Demon had been a complete curveball. He had known nothing about any organization by that name. There was so much he hadn't known that the unsuspecting detective had kindly told him, like where Yoyo and her Guardians liked to go shopping. It had taken him a quarter of an hour to find out the location of the Wong markets. Zhao Bide was a loyal partner, he made every effort to help, which also involved alerting Jericho's attention to his pursuer—Zhao himself.

He had spent the afternoon in the Hyatt, where he had had a long and thorough shower to get rid of the stench of Xaxu at least for a few hours. There had been a message to the effect that the experts had arrived, and that three airbikes were ready, just as he had demanded. He had sent the two men on ahead, and had followed them at a leisurely pace, back into the dirt where he was to meet Jericho.

Owen Jericho and he had been a good team.

Meanwhile, since the scanners had revealed the reappearance of Maggie Xiao Meiqi and Jin Jia Wei, it was time to give up that partnership. Jericho might waste away in Cyber Planet. The airbike rose into the air until Xin could see the steelworks in all its massive dereliction. Only a few scattered people were in evidence, homeless people and gangs who had found refuge in the factory halls. A little group of bikers crossed the savannahs of the slag fields, came closer. Meanwhile Xiao Meiqi and Jin Jia Wei had worked their way up the system of steps and climbed the platform on which the former control room of the blast furnace rested. The girl disappeared inside, while Jia Wei turned around and looked out onto the square.

His gaze wandered to the sky.

Xin spoke into the microphone, issued instructions. Then he swiveled the jets of the airbike to horizontal.

• • •

Jin Jia Wei had a reputation for being lazy and truculent, and showed little interest in his studies. On the other hand he was a gifted hacker. No more and no less. He didn't share Yoyo's lofty plans but neither did he challenge them, because they actually didn't interest him. She wanted to improve the world? Fine. More fun, at any rate, than moldering away in lecture halls, and anyway Jia Wei was head over heels in love with her, as was everybody, in fact. As ideologist in chief, Yoyo found nicely idiotic reasons to break into alien networks, preferably those of the Party, and besides, she supplied the equipment too. For Jia Wei she was a magic toyshop owner, with him as the lucky boy who was allowed to try out all the lovely things she brought along. She had the ideas, and he had the ploys up his sleeve. What did you call that kind of relationship? Symbiosis?

Something like that.

On the positive side, it was worth noting that he would never have betrayed Yoyo. Not least out of self-interest—after all, the group stood and fell with her and her box of tricks filled by Tu Technologies. In return he was even prepared to make her problems his own, particularly because he felt a little responsible for the tense situation. After all, *he* had advised her on this surefire, super-refined matter, and in that he had been successful, unfortunately too successful. Now Yoyo was troubled by worries that robbed her of sleep, so Jia Wei had spent the past two days trying to find out what had actually gone wrong on the night in question. And found something, an incredible coincidence of events. Now, enveloped in a cloud of wonton fragrances rising from Wong's bags, as he looked across the square, he decided to talk to Yoyo about it right after breakfast. Maggie's jabbering emerged from the control center that they had been using as their headquarters since Andromeda had ceased to be safe; she was chattering cheerfully away into her phone, rounding up the rest of the group.

"Breakfast," she crowed.

Breakfast, exactly. That was what he needed now.

But all of a sudden his feet felt frozen to the spot. From his elevated observation point he could see all the way to the faraway coke plant, whose quenching tower loomed sadly into the dawn sky. The factory grounds were enormous, and included the old steel complex. He wondered where the new sound was coming from, the one that he hadn't heard around here for ages, a distant hiss, as if the air over Wong's World were burning.

He narrowed his eyes.

To the left of the quenching tower, something was hanging in the sky.

It took Jin Jia Wei a second to work out that it was the source of the hiss. A moment later he recognized *what* it was. And although he had

never heard anyone say that intuition was one of his outstanding qualities, he felt the danger emanating from it as if in waves.

No one in Quyu had an airbike.

He recoiled. Between Wong's World and Cyber Planet, he saw two
more of the beefy machines appearing and gliding along not far from
the ground. At the same time a car came careening out from behind
the surrounding portakabins and stopped by the blast furnace. The airbike seemed to inflate, a sensory illusion caused by the high speed of
its approach.

"Yoyo!" he yelled.

The machine came toward him like a flat flying fish. Reflections
of sunlight darted across the flattened windshield and flashed in the
turbine flywheel as the pilot shifted his weight and forced the bike
into a curve. Jia Wei staggered back inside, clutching the bags, as the
hiss swelled and the mouth of the turbine began to widen as if to suck
him into its rotating shredder teeth. A moment later the airbike came
down, sweeping Maggie and Yoyo's voices away in a surge of noise,
touched the floor of the platform, and he saw something flashing in
the pilot's hand—

Xin fired.

The bullets plowed through the boy and the bags he was holding.
Jia Wei's face exploded, bottles burst, hot soup, cola and coffee, blood,
brain matter, wontons, and splinters of bone splatted wildly in all
directions. While the ruptured body was still tipping backward, Xin
had leaped from the saddle and stepped inside the building.

His glance took in the interior in a fraction of a second, probed,
categorized, separated into worth keeping, superfluous, interesting,
and negligible. Panels with their monitors turned off, covered with
dust, suggested a former control center, equipped with measuring and
regulatory technology designed to monitor the blast furnace plant.
The room's current purpose was equally obvious. In the middle of the
room, tables had been shoved together, with highly modern equipment, transparent displays, computers, and keyboards. Plank beds
pushed up against the back wall showed that the control center was
inhabited, or sometimes used as a place to sleep.

He brandished his gun. The fat girl held her hands up, Xiao Meiqi,
or was her name Maggie? Whatever. Her mouth was wide open, her
eyeballs looked as if they were about to leave their sockets, which made
her look rather ugly. Xin shot her down as casually as the powerful
shake hands with those less important than themselves, swept aside
the bags she had set down on the table with the barrel of his gun, and
aimed it at Yoyo.

Not a sound came from her lips.

He tilted his head curiously to one side and looked at her.

He didn't know what he'd expected. People showed fear and shock in different ways. For example, in the last second of his life Jin Jia Wei had looked as if you could actually wring the fear out of him. Meiqi's fear, on the other hand, had reminded him of Edvard Munch's *The Scream*, a distorted image of herself. There were people who preserved their dignity and attractiveness even when they were in pain. Meiqi hadn't been one of them. Hardly anyone was.

Yoyo, on the other hand, just stared at him.

She must have leaped up just as Jia Wei called her name, which explained her crouching, catlike posture. Her eyes were wide, but her face looked strangely unexpressive, regular—*almost* perfect, had a shadow around the corner of her mouth not made her look slightly ordinary. Even so, she was more beautiful than most of the women that Xin had seen in his life. He wondered how much attention such beauty could put up with. Almost a shame they had no time to find out.

Then he saw Yoyo's hands beginning to tremble.

Her resistance was crumbling.

He drew up a chair, sat down on it, and lowered his gun.

"I have three questions for you," he said.

Yoyo said nothing. Xin let a few seconds pass, waited to see her give in, but apart from the fact that she was trembling nothing in her posture changed. She went on staring at him as before.

"I expect a quick and honest answer to all three questions," he went on. "So no excuses." He smiled the way you smile at women whose favor you are trying to win by being open. They might just as well have been sitting in a smart bar or a cozy restaurant. It struck him that he felt decidedly comfortable in Yoyo's company. Perhaps they did still have a little time left together after all.

"And afterward," he said benignly, "let's go on looking."

Jericho saw nothing but dust, whirled up by his own car, as he screeched to a halt below the tower of scaffolding. He drew his Glock from its shoulder-holster, pushed the door open, and dashed to the steps. They were made of steel, like the rest of the construction, and amplified the sound of his footsteps.

Bonggg, bonggg!

He cursed under his breath. Taking two steps at a time, he tried to walk on tiptoe, slipped, and banged his knee painfully against the stair railings.

Idiot! His only advantage was that Zhao hadn't seen him.

That moment shots rang out above him. Jericho hurried on. The closer he got to the platform, the more penetratingly the hiss of the airbike reached his ear. Zhao had not thought it necessary to turn off the engine. Fine. The bike would drown him out. He turned his head and saw movement on the square below him. Motorcyclists. Without paying them any heed, he took the last few steps, paused, and peered across the stairhead.

The airbike was parked right in front of him. The door to the control center was open. He jumped onto the platform, darted over to the building, and paused beside the doorway, back to the wall, gun at eye level. Zhao's voice could be heard, friendly and encouraging:

"First of all, how much do you know? Secondly, who have you told about it? And the third question's very easy to answer." Pause for effect. "It's the sixty-four-thousand-dollar question, Yoyo. It is: Where—is—your—computer?"

She was alive. Good.

Less good was the fact that he couldn't see the killer and therefore didn't know what direction he was looking in at that moment. He ran his eye along the façade. Just before the corner of the building he spotted a small window. Ducking down, he crept over to it and peered inside.

Yoyo was standing behind a table full of computers. All he could see of Zhao was legs, a hand, and the massive barrel of his gun. He was clearly sitting facing Yoyo, which meant that his back was turned to the door. The window was open a crack, so Jericho could hear Zhao saying, "It can't be that hard, can it?"

Yoyo mutely shook her head.

"So?"

No reaction. Zhao sighed.

"Right, perhaps I forgot to explain the rules. It's like this: I ask, you answer. Or even better, you just hand the thing over to me." The gun barrel came down. "That's all you have to do. Okay? If you fail to reply, I'll blow your left foot off."

Jericho had seen enough. A few leaps and he was at the door. He jumped inside and aimed his gun at the back of Zhao's head.

"Sit right where you are! Hands up. No heroics."

A glance took in the scene. At his feet lay the boy's body, shredded as if bombs had gone off in his head and chest. Maggie crouched a few meters away. She kept her head lowered, mutely contemplating her belly, from which amazing quantities of innards spilled. Floor, chairs, and table were sprayed with red. Disheartened, Jericho wondered what Zhao had fired with.

"Flechettes."

"What?"

"Dart-shaped projectiles," Zhao repeated calmly, as if Jericho had asked his question out loud. "Metal Storm, fifty tiny tungsten carbide arrows per round, 1,500 kilometers per hour. Pierce steel plates. Opinions are divided. On the one hand you create one hell of a mess, on the other—"

"Shut up! Hands in the air."

Painfully slowly, Zhao obliged. Jericho caught his breath. He felt helpless and ridiculous. Yoyo's lower lip trembled, her mask slipped, shock took hold of her. At the same time he became aware of a flicker of hope in her eyes. And something else, as if a plan were brewing in her head—

Her body tensed.

"Don't," Jericho warned, speaking in her direction. "No chaos. First of all we have to bring this bastard under control."

Zhao yelled with laughter.

"And how are you going to accomplish that? The way you did in the Andromeda?"

"Shut up."

"I could have killed you."

"Set the weapon down on the floor."

"You owe me a bit of respect, little Jericho."

"I said, put the gun on the floor!"

"Why don't you just go home and forget the whole thing? I would—"

There was a sharp bang. A few centimeters away from Zhao, Jericho's bullet pierced the tabletop. The hit man sighed. He turned his head slowly so that his profile could be seen. He had a tiny transmitter in his ear.

"Really, Owen, that's too much."

"For the last time!"

"It's fine." Zhao shrugged. "I'll set it down on the ground, okay?"

"No."

"Meaning not yet?"

"*Drop* it."

"But—"

"Just let it slip off your knees. Keep your hands in the air. Then kick it over to me."

"You're making a mistake, Owen."

"I *have* made a mistake. Do it, right now, or I'll shoot *your* left foot off."

Zhao gave a thin smile. The gun clattered to the floor. He pushed it with the tip of his boot, so that it slipped a little way toward Jericho and stopped halfway between them.

"Shoot him," Yoyo said hoarsely.

Jericho looked at her.

"That wouldn't be a—"

"Shoot him!" Tears poured from Yoyo's eyes. Her features distorted with revulsion and fury. "Shoot him, shoo—"

"No!" Jericho violently shook his head. "If we want to find out who he's working for, we'll have to—"

He went on talking, but his voice was lost among the hisses and wails of the airbike.

They had got louder. Why?

Yoyo cried out and recoiled. A dull blow made the floor shake as something landed outside the control center. It wasn't Zhao's bike. It was more bikes.

Zhao grinned.

For a paralyzing moment Jericho didn't know what to do. If he turned around, the killer would get hold of his gun again. But he had to know what was happening outside.

And then he understood.

The transmitter in Zhao's ear! It had been broadcasting his voice all that time. He'd called for reinforcements. Zhao got up from his chair, his fingers clutching its back. Jericho raised the Glock. His adversary paused, crouching like a beast of prey, ready to spring.

"Drop it," said a deep voice behind him.

"I'd do what he says, little Owen."

"I'll shoot you first," said Jericho.

"Then shoot." Zhao's dark eyes rested on him, seemed to suck him in. He slowly started to sit up. "There are two of them, by the way, and it's only thanks to me that you're still alive at all."

Footsteps rang out behind Jericho. A hand reached over his shoulder and grabbed his gun. Jericho unresistingly allowed it to be pulled from his fingers. His eyes sought Yoyo's. She was pressing herself against the old control desk, eyes darting back and forth.

A fist pushed him forward.

Zhao took hold of him, drew back his arm and struck him full in the face with the palm of his hand. His head flew sideways. The next blow hit his solar plexus and forced the air from his ribs. Choking, he fell to his knees. Now he could see the two men, one a thick-set, bearded Asian who had been aiming his gun at Yoyo, the other gaunt, fair, and with a Slavic look. They both carried pistols of the same type as their leader's. Zhao laughed quietly. He brushed the silky, black hair off his forehead and drew himself up to his full height. He started walking around Jericho at a measured pace.

"Gentlemen," he said. "What you are experiencing here is the triumph of the cerebellum over the belly. The primacy of planning. That's the only possible way of explaining how a man who effectively had me in his power is now cowering at our feet. A detective, note. A professional." He spat the last word at Jericho's feet. "And yet I welcome his visit. We now have the opportunity to learn more than before. We can, for example, ask Mr. Jericho what he actually wanted to ask *me.*"

Zhao's right hand darted forward, grabbed Jericho's ponytail, pulled him up and to him, so that he could feel the hit man's hot breath on his face.

"The question of the client. Always interesting. Our guest could hardly have hit on the idea of looking for little Yoyo all on his own.

So who is *your* client? I'm right, Owen, am I not? Someone threw the stick. Fetch the stick, Owen! Find Yoyo! Woof!—Isn't there anyone else I should be taking care of?"

Even though the situation was anything but funny, Jericho laughed. "I'd be careful about wasting your time."

"You're so right." Zhao snorted, shoved him aside, and approached Yoyo, who was no longer trying to hide her fear. Her lower lip trembled, streams of moisture glistened on her cheeks. "So let's devote ourselves to our lovely do-gooder here, and ask her to help us in answering questions that have been asked once already. Where—is—your—computer?"

Yoyo stepped back. Again her features underwent a change, as if she had just made a surprising discovery. Zhao paused, plainly irritated. At that very moment Jericho heard a faint, metallic click.

"You're not going to do anything at all," a voice said.

Zhao spun around. Two young men and a woman in bikers' leathers had stepped into the room, machine guns at the ready, aiming at him and his two assistants, who in turn were aiming at the new arrivals. One of them was a giant with a barrel chest, gorilla arms, the top of his head a shaven hemisphere. The point of his chin was extended by a blue prosthesis into an artificial pharaoh's beard. Jericho's breath froze. Daxiong had misled him really badly, but there was no one else that he would rather have seen at that very moment.

Six Koreans, who had all taken a beating—

Daxiong's narrow eyes turned toward Yoyo.

"Come over here," he roared. "The rest of you stay where—"

His voice faded away. It was only now that the giant seemed to take in what had happened in the control center. His gaze wandered from the shredded corpse of Jia Wei to Maggie's grotesquely bent body. His eyes widened very slightly.

"They've killed them," whimpered the girl by his side. All the color had fled from her face.

"Shit," the other guy said. "Oh, shit!"

Jericho's thoughts went running helter-skelter like a pack of dogs. A thousand possible scenarios flooded his imagination. The hitmen, the City Demons, everyone was aiming at everyone else, while Zhao crouched there, waiting, and Yoyo's eyes wandered from one group to the other. No one dared move for fear of disturbing the fragile equilibrium, which would inevitably have ended in disaster.

It was Yoyo who broke the spell. She walked slowly past Zhao and over to Daxiong. Zhao didn't move. Only his eyes followed her.

"Stop."

He said it quietly, no more than a sibilant murmur, but it still drowned out the hiss of the airbikes, the dog-like wheezing of the others, the hammering in Jericho's head, and Yoyo stopped.

"No, come here," Daxiong yelled. "Don't listen to—"

"You won't survive this," Zhao interrupted. "You can't kill us all, so don't even try. Give us what we want to have, tell us what we want to hear and we'll be off. Nothing will happen to anyone."

"Like nothing happened to Jia Wei?" wept the girl with the gun. "Or Maggie?"

"That was inev—No, not like that!"

She had swung the gun around slightly; the fat Asian had also swung the barrel of his gun and was aiming it at her head. Daxiong and the other City Demon reacted in similar fashion. The blond guy's jaws worked away. Zhao raised a pleading hand.

"Enough blood has been spilled!—Yoyo, listen, you've seen something you shouldn't have seen. An accident, a stupid accident, but we can wipe this problem out. I want your computer, I have to know who you've entrusted it to. No more people must die, I promise. Survival in exchange for silence."

You're lying, Jericho thought. Each of your words is pure deceit.

Yoyo turned doubtfully toward Zhao, looked into the beautiful face of the devil.

"Yes, it's fine, Yoyo, all fine!" He nodded. "I give you my word that nothing will happen to anyone as long as you cooperate."

"Shit!" yelled the young man next to Daxiong. "It's all a great big pile of shit! They're going to shoot us all as soon as—"

"You watch yourself!" roared the blond guy.

"Kenny, that won't do any good." The Mongolian-looking man was quaking with nerves. "We should kill them."

"You fat fuck! First we'll take you and—"

"Shut it!"

"One more word! One word and I'll—"

"Stop it! Stop it all of you!"

Eyes darted back and forth, fingers tightened on triggers. As if the room had filled with an inflammable gas, Jericho thought, and now they were all desperate to click their lighters. But Zhao's authority held them all in check. The explosion hadn't happened. Yet.

"Please—give—me—the computer."

Yoyo wiped her hand over her face, smearing it with tears and snot. "Then will you let us go?"

"Answer my questions and give me your computer."

"I have your word?"

"Yes. Then we'll let you go."

"You promise that nothing will happen to Daxiong and Ziyi—and Tony? And that guy there?"

How thoughtful, thought Jericho.

"Don't listen to him," he said. "Zhao will—"

"I've never broken my word," Zhao cut in, paying him no attention. It sounded friendly and honest. "Look, I'm trained to kill people. Like any cop, any soldier, any agent. National security is a higher good than individual human lives, I'm sure you understand that. But I'll keep my promise."

"If you give him the computer, he'll kill us all," Jericho announced. He said it as soberly as possible. "I'm your friend. Your father sent me."

"He's lying." Zhao's voice sounded wheedling. "You know what? You should be far more afraid of him than you are of me. He's playing a game with you, every word he comes out with is a lie."

"He's going to kill you," said Jericho.

"Just let him try," snorted the boy. So his name was Tony. He jutted his chin belligerently, but his voice and his outstretched weapon trembled slightly. Ziyi, the girl, started to sob uncontrollably.

"Just give him that fucking computer!"

"Don't do it," Jericho insisted. "As long as he doesn't know where your computer is, he *has* to let us live."

"Shut up!" Daxiong yelled at him.

"Just give him the damned computer!" Ziyi shouted.

Yoyo walked to the table. Her fingers floated over a device hardly bigger than a bar of chocolate, connected to the keyboard and the screen.

"You're making a mistake," said Jericho dejectedly. All the strength was oozing from his limbs. "He'll kill you."

Zhao looked at him.

"The way you killed Grand Cherokee Wang, Jericho?"

"The way I—*What?*"

Yoyo paused.

"Bullshit!" Jericho shook his head. "He's lying. He's—"

"Just shut your mouth," yelled the fat guy, pulled his gun around, and aimed it at Jericho, who saw with startling clarity every individual drop of sweat on the killer's forehead, glittering like bubble wrap.

Daxiong aimed at Zhao, whose eyes widened.

"No!" he yelled.

The lighter clicked.

Jericho saw Tony lifting his gun, then there were two shots in quick succession, and the fat guy collapsed. Everything happened at the same time. With a deafening bang the fair-haired man's pistol went off and shot away half of Tony's face. He tipped over and obstructed Daxiong's view, while Ziyi squealed and Yoyo stormed toward the door. Zhao tried to grab her, missed her and fell headlong. Jericho reached for the gun on the floor. He grabbed the barrel, but Zhao was faster, while Ziyi was shooting wildly in all directions, forcing the blond guy to take cover behind the table.

He ducked.

Daxiong dashed forward, slipped in Jia Wei's blood and cracked the back of his head on the floor tiles, dragging Jericho with him. A burst of fire plowed up the floor next to him. Jericho rolled away from the unconscious giant and saw Ziyi stride like a vengeful goddess over Tony's corpse, shouting and firing aimlessly. A moment later a bright red fountain sprouted where her right arm had been. The reports from Zhao's pistol rang out as he ran outside. Ziyi hesitated. Glassy-eyed, she turned around, an expression of mild surprise in her eyes, and sprayed her pumping blood at the blond guy, spurting it into his eyes. The man raised a hand to protect himself, tried to avoid her dying body, lost his balance.

Jericho leaped up. Ziyi's severed arm twitched at his feet, and suddenly he was caught up in the vision of a theatrical performance. He was gratefully aware of something within him stepping aside and something else taking control of his thoughts and his motor abilities. He bent down, fumbled the gun from Ziyi's slack fingers, aimed the muzzle at the stumbling hit man and pulled the trigger.

Empty.

With a yell, the blond guy slung the dead girl away from him, reached for his gun and, still blinded by Ziyi's blood, fired his magazine off into the air. Jericho whirled out of the line of fire and without so much as another glance, he leaped over the prostrate bodies and hurried outside.

Xin briefly imagined how simple things might have been. Tracking down the girl and her computer. Knowing which one it was. Charming information out of her as to who he still had to worry about, which would have taken only a few minutes. Xin was sure that Yoyo was extremely susceptible to pain. She would quickly have told him what he needed to know.

Fast work.

Instead, Owen Jericho had turned up as if pulled out of a hat. Xin hadn't the slightest idea what had sent the detective here. Hadn't his disguise been perfect? Irrelevant for the time being. Dark and massive, the blast furnace loomed above him. Two airbikes were parked down below, between Yoyo and the stairs. In her confusion, she had probably spent a moment too long wondering which way was shorter, and meanwhile Xin had managed to get outside and block her exit route. The tower of girderwork provided no opportunity for escape. So she had fled across the bridge connecting the control center and the blast furnace, to the other side, into the middle of the jungle of walkways, equipment, and pipes that ran riot around the crucible.

He came after her, in no particular hurry. Each level of the furnace's scaffolding was connected to the next by a flight of steps, but the way down was blocked by broken props. By now Yoyo too was aware of her mistake. She looked alternately upward and at Xin, as she pushed her way slowly backward. Once again he was sure that he was going to win. He stopped.

"This isn't what I wanted," he called out.

Yoyo's features blurred. For a moment he thought he was about to see her bursting into tears again.

"I never planned to give you the thing," she cried.

"Yoyo, I'm sorry!"

"Then fuck off!"

"Have *I* broken my word?" He put all the hurt he could muster into his words. "Did I?"

"Kiss my butt!"

"Why don't you trust me?"

"Anyone who trusts you dies!"

"*Your* people started it, Yoyo. Be sensible, I just want to talk to you."

Yoyo looked behind her, looked up, and turned her gaze back to Xin. She had almost reached the steps leading to the next level. He set his pistol down in front of him and showed her the palms of both hands.

"No more violence, Yoyo. No bloodshed. I swear."

She hesitated.

Come on, he thought. You can't get down. You're in a trap, little mouse. Stupid little mouse.

But suddenly the mouse seemed anything but helpless. He uneasily wondered who was actually playing games with whom here. The girl was in shock, sure, but as she approached the stairs she no longer resembled the tear-drenched Yoyo who had been ready to hand him her computer just a minute before. In her catlike agility he recognized his own alertness, practiced over the years, and based on stubbornness, suspicion, deviousness, and a will to survive. Yoyo was stronger than he'd imagined.

As soon as she leaped onto the steps he knew that any further diplomacy was a waste of time. If there had ever been a chance of coaxing the girl down, it was gone.

He picked up his gun.

The wail of a turbine rose up behind him. Xin turned around and saw Jericho sitting on the saddle of one of the airbikes, trying to get the vehicle started. He weighed up his options in a flash, but Yoyo took priority. He ignored the detective and hurried after the escaping girl whose footsteps made the passageway above him tremble, and watched through the bars as her silhouette dashed away. A few leaps and he was up there. He found himself in a ravine of struts and pipes, and caught a glimpse of flying hair as Yoyo disappeared behind a rusty pillar; then her footsteps hammered toward the next floor up.

She was slowly turning into a nuisance. High time to bring this matter to a close.

He chased after her, floor after floor, until she had nowhere left to go. A few meters above her the furnace tapered, ending in an inlet through which coke and ore had been funneled in earlier times. Above it rose an angular, winding structure that culminated in a massive exhaust outlet, making the construction visible even from a distance. Vertical scaffolding-rods led to the highest point, about 70 meters up. Nothing beyond that but open sky. No escape was possible, unless you dared to pick your way about 20 meters along a pipe leading sharply downward, and jump another 10 meters down onto the enormous pot-like tank in which it ended.

He listened. It was surprisingly quiet up here, as if the vague and distant sounds of the city and the background noise of Xaxu were a sea that surged below him. The turbines of large aircraft sang somewhere in the stratosphere.

Xin threw his head back. Yoyo had disappeared.

Then he saw her climbing. She clung to the stanchions like a monkey, pulled herself higher up, and he understood that there probably was a possible escape route. A conveyor belt abutted the inlet. It ran down from the top of the furnace to the ground, steep, but walkable.

The bitch.

Did he actually need her alive? She had reached her hand out to the computer, there was no doubt which one it was. It was still in the control room . . . except he didn't know who she'd talked to about the matter.

Cursing, he began his ascent.

A loud hissing sound came toward him. With one hand clamped to the scaffolding and the other gripping his gun, he turned his head.

The airbike was coming straight at him.

Jericho had stalled the first bike he tried. It was a new model, very different from the ones he was used to. The controls gleamed from a flat user interface, there was nothing mechanical on this one. He slipped from the saddle, jumped onto the second airbike, whose engine was running, and ran his hand over the touchscreen. He was luckier this time. The machine reacted like a goaded bull, bucked and reared and tried to throw him off. His hands gripped the handles. Before, they'd been vertical, now they curved upward and could be twisted in all directions. The bike circled wildly. The display blinked like the lights on a fruit machine. Just by chance Jericho touched two of them, and the carousel ride came to an end, but he was carried instead toward the front of the control room; he shifted his body weight, narrowly avoiding collision, and flew in an extended 180-degree turn. His eyes scoured the surroundings.

No trace of Yoyo or Zhao.

He gradually got the knack of turning. He brought the bike up, but neglected to pivot the jets at the same time, which immediately got him into trouble again, because the bike now soared into the sky like a rocket. He felt himself sliding helplessly out of the saddle, and struggled with darting fingers to correct the mistake, regained control, and took another turn with his eyes on the blast furnace.

There they were!

Yoyo had made it to the inlet, where the conveyor belt began, followed by Zhao, who hung 2 meters below her in the scaffolding. Jericho forced the machine upward, in the hope that it would react as he wished. He saw the hit man give a start and hunch his shoulders. Less than half a meter away from him, Jericho swung the airbike round, turned a circle, and bore down on the furnace once more. On the edge of the conveyor belt, Yoyo was looking charmingly helpless. He understood exactly why as he flew over the belt. Where there should have been rollers and struts, part of the construction had simply broken away. For a long stretch only the side braces remained. Getting down from there would have required the skills of a professional tightrope walker.

Yoyo was trapped.

He cursed himself under his breath. Why hadn't he taken the blond guy's pistol off him? There had been weapons lying around all over the control center. He watched furiously as Zhao's head and shoulders appeared over the rim. With one bound the hit man was on the inlet. Yoyo recoiled, went down on all fours, and gripped the brace of the conveyor belt. She nimbly let herself down on it until her feet touched a rod further below, tried to find a halfway solid footing, began lowering herself down, hand after hand, inch after inch—

Slipped.

Horrified, Jericho saw her fall. A jolt ran through her body. At the last second her fingers had closed on the rod she had just been standing on, but now she was dangling over an abyss a good 70 meters deep.

Zhao stared down at her.

Then he left the cover of the girderwork.

"Bad mistake," Jericho snarled. "Very bad mistake!"

By now his glands were firing considerable salvos of adrenaline, whipping his heartbeat and blood pressure up to heroic levels. With each passing second, he was more in control of the machine. Carried on a wave of rage and euphoria, he sent the airbike shooting forward and took aim at Zhao, who was at that moment crouching, about to climb down to Yoyo.

The hit man saw him coming.

Baffled, he came to a halt. The bike shot over the conveyor belt. Anyone else would have been swept into the depths, but Zhao managed to pirouette himself back onto the edge of the inlet. His gun clattered far below. Jericho turned the bike and saw the blond guy staggering out of the control center and getting onto one of the remaining air-bikes. No time to worry about him too. His fingers twitched in all directions. Where on the display—no, wrong, you did it with the handlebars, right? He just had to bring the right handlebar down a touch—

Too much.

The bike plummeted like a stone. Cursing, he caught it, climbed, put his foot down and then immediately decelerated until he hung, jets hissing, right under the wildly flailing Yoyo.

"Jump!" he shouted.

She looked down at him, her face distorted, as her fingers slipped millimeter by millimeter. Gusts of wind grabbed the bike and carried it away. The girders trembled as Zhao jumped gracefully from the edge of the inlet and landed on the lower part of the scaffolding. The hit man plainly didn't suffer from any kind of vertigo. His right hand came down to clutch her wrist. Jericho corrected his position, and the bike spun back under Yoyo.

"Jump, for God's sake! Jump!"

Her right foot struck his temple, and he couldn't see or hear a thing. Now he was underneath her again, looking up. He saw Zhao's fingers stretching out, touching her ankle.

Yoyo let go.

It was a bit like having a sack of cement dropped on him. If he had imagined she would land elegantly on the pillion, he could think again. Yoyo clutched his jacket, slipped off the bike and dangled from him like a gorilla from a rubber tire. With both hands he pulled her back up, as the bike hurtled toward the ground.

She shouted something. It sounded like *maybe*.

Maybe?

The turbine noise rose to a scream. Yoyo's fingers were everywhere, in his clothes, his hair, his face. The dusty plain rushed up at them, they would be smashed to pieces.

But they weren't smashed, they didn't die. He had clearly done something right, because at the same moment as her hands closed around his shoulders and she pressed her torso against his back, the bike shot straight upward again.

"Maybe—"

The words were shredded by the squall. The blond guy was approaching on the left, his face a mask of dried blood, from which hate-filled eyes stared across at them.

"What?" he shouted.

"Maybe," she yelled back, "next time you'll learn to fly the thing *first*, you fucking idiot!"

• • •

Daxiong floated to the surface.

His first impulse was to ask Maggie for a cappuccino, with plenty of sugar and foam, of course. That was why they were here, after all. To have breakfast together, since Yoyo had appointed Andromeda as her summer residence again, as Daxiong jokingly put it, except that right now it seemed to make more sense to go into hiding in the steelworks for a while.

Maggie only ever brought coffee for him. The others, Tony, Yoyo, Maggie herself, Ziyi, and Jia Wei preferred tea, like good Chinese. And like good Chinese they had wontons and baozis for breakfast, they ate pork belly and noodles in broth, swallowed down half-raw shrimps, the whole deal, while for unfathomable reasons his heart still beat for the Grande Nation and was devoted to the buttery, warm smell of freshly baked croissants. By now he was even toying with the possibility that he might have French genes, which anyone who saw his face would strenuously have denied. Daxiong was as Mongolian as a Mongolian could be, and Yoyo was forever rattling off all the wonders of the fun, authentic China that had no need of imported Western culture. Daxiong let her talk. For him, the day began with a proper milk foam mustache. Maggie had called and croaked "Breakfast!" into the receiver, and Ziyi had yelled and screamed.

Why had she done that?

Oh yes, he'd been dreaming. Something terrible! Why would anyone dream something like that? He, Ziyi, and Tony had driven over to the blast furnace, following Maggie's call, when two of those flying motorcycles, which were too expensive for him ever to have afforded one, had landed on the control center platform, where a third one already stood. Amazing. As he approached, he had tried to get through to Maggie, to ask her what kind of guys these were, but she hadn't replied. So they had decided to take the guns out of their saddlebags, just in case.

A funny dream. They were having a party.

They were all enjoying themselves, but Jia Wei couldn't really join in, because there wasn't much left of him, and Maggie had a sore stomach. Tony was missing half of his face, oh dear, that seemed to be why Ziyi had started screaming, now everything fitted into place, and what on earth kind of people were these?

Daxiong opened his eyes.

Xin exploded with fury.

With simian agility, he leaped back down over the scaffolding, struts, and steps. His airbike was still on the platform, engine running. Far below, the detective was wrestling with the hijacked machine, busy driving himself and Yoyo to their deaths.

Jericho, that thorn in his side!

He's on his way out, Xin thought. I've got the computer, Yoyo. Who can you have spoken to apart from your few friends here, and they're dead. I don't need you anymore.

Then he saw Jericho wresting control of the machine, gaining height, moving away from the blast furnace—

And being forced back down again.

The blond guy!

Xin started waving both arms.

"Kill them all!" he yelled. "Finish them off!"

He didn't know if the blond guy had heard him. He leaped energetically over the edge of the walkway, landed with a thump on the steel of the platform, and ran to his bike. The turbine was running. Had Jericho been fiddling around with it? Before his eyes, the two bikes set off at great speed, and disappeared into the intricate labyrinth of the steelworks. He pivoted the jets to vertical. The machine hissed and vibrated.

"Come on!" he shouted.

The airbike was slowly lifting off, when something whistled past his head so close that he felt the draught. He turned the machine in the air and saw the bald-headed giant from the control center, a gun in each hand, firing from both muzzles. Nosediving, Xin attacked him. The giant threw himself to the ground. With a snort of contempt he pulled the airbike back up and flew after the others.

Daxiong sat bolt upright. His heart was thumping, the sun was beating down on him. Across the shimmering fields of slag the vanishing airbikes quickly gained distance, but one of the bikes was unmistakably hounding the other and trying to force it to land.

One of the hitmen was dead in the control room. So who was that on the fleeing bike?

Yoyo?

While he was still thinking about it, he clattered down the zigzag stairs. Apart from him and possibly Yoyo none of the Guardians had survived the massacre. The remaining City Demons knew nothing about the double life of the six of them, even though they might have guessed at various things. Yoyo and he had originally brought the Demons to life as a disguise. A motorcycle association aroused no suspicion; it wasn't considered intellectual and subversive. They could meet easily, particularly in Quyu. Three more members had joined the previous year. Perhaps, Daxiong thought, as he lowered his full 300 pounds onto his motorcycle, the time had come to initiate them. Strictly speaking, he no longer had that option. Whoever their opponent might have been, it was clear that the Guardians had been busted.

As he drove off he selected a number.

There was a ringing noise. It went on too long, far too long. Then he heard the boy's voice.

"Where were you, damn it?" snorted Daxiong.

Lau Ye yawned and talked at the same time. Then he asked a question.

"Don't ask, Ye," Daxiong snorted into the cell phone. "Get Xiao-Tong and Mak over here. Right now! Go to the blast furnace and clear the control room, everything you find there, computer, displays, all of it."

The boy stammered something which Daxiong took to mean that he didn't know where the others were.

"Then find them!" he shouted. "I'll explain it later.—What?—No, don't take the stuff to Andromeda, and not to the workshop.—Then think of something. Somewhere they won't connect with us. Oh, and Ye—" He swallowed. "You will find corpses. Brace yourselves, you hear?"

He rang off before Ye could ask any questions.

Jericho's machine took a blow when the blond guy's airbike collided with its chassis. Time and again he had tried to steer toward the airspace above the steelworkers' housing estate. Every time the blond guy forced him back, stared wildly over at them, and tried to take aim. The lunar landscape of the slag fields sped along beneath them. Once again Jericho tried to turn off to the left. The blond guy speeded up and forced him in the other direction.

"Where are you actually trying to get to?" Yoyo's voice rang in his ears. "We're outdistancing him!"

"You haven't a hope out in the open! Tempt him into the plant."

The blond guy's airbike shot upward and immediately plummeted back down again. Jericho saw the machine's fish belly right above him and then dived. They wobbled along just above ground level.

"Be careful!" Yoyo snapped.

"I know what I'm doing!" Rage welled up in him, but he was actually by no means sure about what he should do. Right in front of him a huge chimney rose out of the ground.

"To the right!" screeched Yoyo. "The right!"

The blond guy drove them further down. The bike scratched along dried-up slag, started skipping, went into a violent roll, then they were around the chimney, only to find themselves in front of a hangar-sized warehouse. They were too close, far too close. No chance of avoiding it, of turning away, of avoiding a collision.

No! The warehouse door was open a crack.

Just before the threatened impact Jericho pulled the machine to the side and shot through it.

Lau Ye dashed through the gloomy concert hall of the Andromeda. He ran as fast as his lanky legs would carry him.

Don't ask any questions. Just don't ask.

He was used to this from Daxiong, and he had never complained. Lau Ye was a novice in the order of the City Demons: he had been the last to join and he was by far the youngest. He respected Daxiong and Yoyo, Ziyi and Maggie, Tony and Jia Wei. He also respected Ma Mak and Hui Xiao-Tong, even though they had only been admitted to the club subsequently. Subsequently in that the others had set up the association together, with Daxiong as founder and Yoyo in the role of Vice President.

But Ye wasn't blind.

Born on the estate just after the steelworks was closed down, with no school education, but more intimately familiar with Xaxu's peculiar qualities and those of its inhabitants, from the very start he had refused to believe that the Demons were just a bike club. Daxiong was from Quyu, too, but he was seen as operating somewhere between the worlds of the connected and the outsiders. No one doubted that he would wake up on the other side one morning, rub his eyes, drive a smart car to an air-conditioned high-rise skyscraper and pursue some well-paid job there. Yoyo, on the other hand, Maggie, Ziyi, Tony, and Jia Wei belonged to Quyu about as much as a string quartet belonged in Andromeda. In the control room they'd set up a kind of Cyber Planet for the privileged, and Yoyo had packed all the super-expensive computers full of brilliant games, but she was from a different world. She went to college. They all went to college to study something that parents considered sensible.

Yeah. Not his.

Lau Ye's parents didn't pay him much attention. At the age of sixteen he might as well have been living on the Moon. His job in Daxiong's workshop and the City Demons were all he had, and he loved being part of it. And so he didn't ask questions, either. He didn't ask whether the only purpose his humble self, Xiao-Tong, and Mak served was to disguise a conspiratorial little student club as something fit for the slums. He didn't ask what the other six organized at their many meetings in the control center when he, Xiao-Tong, and Mak weren't around. Until a few days before, when Yoyo had turned up at the workshop in a complete state. That time he *had* asked Daxiong.

The answer had been a familiar one.

"Don't ask."

"I just want to know if there's anything I can do."

"Yoyo's got problems. Best you stay in the workshop for the time being and avoid the control center."

"What kind of problems?"

"Don't ask."

Don't ask. Except that three days later that guy with the fair hair and the blue eyes had turned up, the one Daxiong had later said looked like a—what was it? Scanavian? Scandinavian! Ye had talked to the man and learned that he wanted to get into Andromeda.

"Cool," he had said to Daxiong later. "You may have sent him on a wild goose chase. Why would you do that?"

"Don't—"

"No. I'm asking."

Daxiong had rubbed his bald head and his chin, had poked around in his ears, tugged on his fake beard, and finally snarled:

"It could be that we're about to get an unwanted visit. Nasty people."

"Like the other guys that time?"

"Exactly."

"And what do they want from us? I mean, what do they want from *us*? What have you done, you—six?"

Daxiong had looked at him for a long time.

"If I confide something in you, little Ye, you'll keep your trap shut and not tell anyone?"

"Okay."

"Not even Mak or Xiao-Tong?"

"O-okay."

"Do I have your word?"

"Of course. Erm—what's going on?"

"Don't ask."

But even on that odd day the standard rebuff hadn't sounded as desperate and furious as it had just now. It seemed as if the suspicions that Ye had held for a long time were being borne out. The six of them had conspiratorial rituals. His limbs quivered as he crossed the inner room, which was still in a state of complete chaos from the previous night, and barely negotiable for leftover food, bottles, cigarette ends, and drug paraphernalia. Alcohol, stale smoke, and piss launched a general attack on his chemoreceptors. Mak and Xiao-Tong had been together for four weeks, and had been at the same concert as him. After that they'd had one hell of a party. It was only toward morning that Ye had crept, royally zonked, to Yoyo's "summer residence." Even now his head felt like an aquarium that the water sloshed around in every time he moved, but Daxiong trusted him.

You'll find corpses—

Something terrible must have happened. Ye guessed where the other two might be found. Ma Mak slept, with his parents and his brothers and sisters, in the ruin of a half-demolished house on the edge of the estate. The family shared a single room, while Hui Xiao-Tong lived alone in a cave-like shed nearby. That was where he would f ind them.

He staggered out into the harsh light, narrowed his eyes, and ran across the vacant lot to his motorcycle.

• • •

Inside the warehouse it was gloomy, a vast space, the ceiling some-where between 20 and 30 meters high, riveted walls, steel joists. Huge racks suggested that cast steel had been stored here in the past.

Shots rang out behind them. Their echo was thrown back by walls and ceilings, acoustic ricochets.

"Oi, watch where you're flying," shouted Yoyo.

Jericho turned his head and saw the blond-haired guy catching up with him.

"Dive!"

Their pursuer approached. Shots whipped through the hall again. Turbine wailing, they raced between the racks toward the rear wall of the warehouse, another door there, ceiling height, which was fortu-nately open. On the other side yawned a space even darker than this one.

Something that looked like a crane emerged from the darkness.

"Careful!"

"If you don't keep your trap shut—"

"Higher! Higher!"

Jericho obeyed. The airbike skipped away over the crane in a break-neck parabola. Suddenly it was too near the ceiling. At the last minute he swiveled the jets in the opposite direction. The machine turned at an angle, darted downward, and started spinning on its axis at fantastic speed. Circling madly they wheeled into the next hall. Jericho caught a glimpse of their pursuer, saw him just passing under the lintel and going into a controlled nosedive, then the blond guy steered his bike into theirs and rammed them from the side, but what was intended to throw them off course had the opposite effect. As if by a miracle the bike stabilized itself. Suddenly they were flying straight ahead once more, worryingly close to the wall. Jericho narrowed his eyes. This fac-tory space seemed even bigger and higher than the one before. A line of rollers, in their hundreds, ran along the floor, clearly a kind of con-veyor belt leading to a tall, looming structure. Massive and gloomy, it looked like a printing press, except that this one would have been producing books for giants.

A rolling mill, it occurred to Jericho. It was the frame for a roller, to crush iron ingots into sheets. The things you know!

Again the blond guy came down, trying to squash them against the wall. Jericho looked across at him. A triumphant grin flashed in the man's blood-spattered face.

At that he saw red.

"Yoyo?"

"What?"

"Hold on tight!"

As soon as she pressed against him, he threw the handlebars around and gave the attacking bike a mighty thump with the back of his own. Yoyo screamed. Splinters of exploding windshield sprayed in all directions. The hit man's bike was slung aside, his gun disappeared into the darkness. Jericho didn't give him time to breathe, he rammed his bike again, as they hurtled side by side toward the rolling mill.

"And with my very warmest wishes," he yelled, "have a bit of this!"

The third blow rammed the blond guy's rear. His bike somersaulted in the air, whirled toward the rolling mill. Jericho drew past him, saw the hit man struggling for control and balance, arms flailing, and settled into the curve. They flew just past the colossus, but instead of the ugly noise of a bike's fatal impact they heard a sequence of loud gunshots. Somehow the guy had managed to avoid a collision and lower his bike to the floor. Like a stone on the surface of the water, it skipped over the rollers of the conveyor belt, tipped over, and threw its rider off.

The next gaping portal opened up in front of them.

"Yoyo," he called back. "How the hell do we get back out of here?"

"We don't." Her outstretched arm pointed past him into the darkness. "Once you're through there, you go straight to hell."

Xin didn't bother about the individual biker who was helplessly trying to follow them. The guy was ridiculous. Huge, clumsy, a joke. Let him empty his magazine into the air. In time he'd wish he'd never been born.

He kept a lookout for the airbikes.

They'd disappeared.

Perplexed, he wheeled above the plant, but it was as if the sky had swallowed up the two machines. The last he had seen of them was when they flew around a complex of factory buildings behind which a single big chimney loomed.

It was there that he had lost track of them.

The grouchy whine of the bike reached him from below. He toyed with the idea of raining a few grenades down on the giant's bald head. His index finger tapped against a spot to the side of the instrument panel, and a cover immediately slid aside just above his right knee. Behind it lay a considerable arsenal of weapons. Xin inspected the contents of the compartment on the other side. All there, hand grenades, sub-machine gun. Gingerly, almost tenderly, his fingers slipped over the butt of the M-79 launcher with the incendiary rounds. All three airbikes were equipped with the same weapons.

Including Jericho's.

He shoved the thought aside and glanced at the altitude gauge: 188 meters above sea level. He continued his search with reduced thrust. The sky couldn't swallow anyone as quickly as that.

• • •

If part of the roof hadn't been open, it would have been pitch-dark. But as it was, spears of white daylight jabbed in at an angle, carving weird details from the walls, casting lattices over walkways, steps, balconies, terraces, pipes, cables, segmented and riveted armor, massive, open bulkheads.

Jericho slowed his bike in the beam of light. Hissing softly, it hovered in the air, which was impregnated with iron, rust, and the smell of rancid grease.

He threw back his head.

"Forget it," called Yoyo. Her voice bounced across walls and ceilings, and was caught between the constructions. "It's barred up there. We won't get through."

Jericho cursed and looked around. He couldn't really tell whether this room was any bigger than the one they had flown through before, but at any rate it looked monumental, almost Wagnerian in its dimensions, a Nibelheim of the industrial age. Steel joists a meter thick ran along the ceiling; open baskets hung from them, anchored to massive hinges, so big that he could have fitted his Toyota inside any one of them. A pipe about 3 meters in diameter grew from the darkness of the vaulted ceiling, led downward at an angle, and finished halfway up the hall. More of the basket-like formations were distributed across the floor, and containers were stacked along the walls.

Yoyo was right. There was something hellish about the whole thing. A chilly hell. Still startled by his unexpected knowledge of the rolling mill, Jericho tried to remember the purpose of this place. Steel was heated here, in colossal containers called converters. Right in front of them gaped their skewed, round mouths, hatches leading to the heart of the volcano, great maws that would normally have glowed red and yellow with molten ore. Now they lay there, black and mysterious, three in all.

A world extinguished.

The hiss of the other airbike came across from beyond the passageway, changed, grew more distinct. It was getting closer.

"Hey, what's with these things?" Yoyo leaned forward and pointed at one of the gaping entrances to the converter. "He won't be able to find us in there."

Jericho didn't reply. The bike would fit quite easily in one of the converters, with both of them on it. The maw was big enough, the container was bulbous and several meters deep. And yet he didn't like the idea that they might be trapped down there. He brought the machine up, toward the ceiling.

"If only you hadn't brought us in here," Yoyo complained.

"If only you'd brought your computer with you," Jericho snarled back. "Then we wouldn't be making targets of ourselves."

Between two joists, right below the ceiling, there was a platform from which you had a vantage point over most of the hall. The converters yawned far below them, separated from one another by large armored bulkheads. Sunbeams stroked their bike, explored its shape, let it go. With extreme concentration Jericho fiddled with the controls, and the jets produced a small amount of reverse thrust, just enough for the machine to move slowly backward over the edge of the platform.

"He's coming," hissed Yoyo.

A beam of light crept into the hall from the neighboring space. The blond guy had turned on the headlight. Jericho silently settled the airbike on the platform and turned off the engine. The hiss faded to a faint hum. He almost felt something like pride at his navigational abilities. The blond guy wouldn't hear them above the noise of his own machine, and the gloom up here would swallow them up. They clung to the ceiling like a fat, lurking insect.

"And by the way I *did* bring my computer," Yoyo whispered.

Puzzled, Jericho turned around to look at her.

"I thought—"

"That *wasn't* my computer. I just wanted him to think it was. I wear mine on my belt."

He raised his hand and hushed her. Far below their pursuer appeared and hovered slowly along underneath them. His bike hissed quietly, and a powerful finger of cold, white light crept around the building. Jericho leaned forward. The blond guy was craning his head in all directions, looking at the ceiling without seeing them, peering between the containers. His gun lay heavy in his right hand.

Had he lost them?

Jericho hesitated. Highly unlikely that the man had gone looking for his pistol after the crash. The force of the collision had slung it far out into the darkness of the hall where the rolling mills were. There was only one explanation. His bike was fitted with more weapons, and if that was true of all of them, then—

On either side of the tank, he thought. That was the only place where there was room, right in front of his legs.

His fingers ran over the body of the bike.

Yep, no doubt about it, there were chambers there, cavities under the casings. But how did you get them open?

Below them, the hit man curved through the hall. The luminous eye darted between constructions and containers, slid along walkways and balconies. Only now did Jericho notice that their pursuer was creeping toward a tunnel-shaped hatch that opened up to the rear of the arched ceiling. Rails led from it to the inside of the hall. The blond guy stopped his bike and glanced in. He seemed uncertain whether to go inside before scouring the entire hall, then he turned back and climbed higher.

He was coming right toward them.

Jericho thought frantically. In a few seconds the killer would find them in their hiding place. Like a man possessed, he searched the casings and the instrument panel for a way of opening the weapon compartments. The hissing got closer. He felt Yoyo's breath on the back of his neck, craned his head, and ventured to look. The blond guy was two-thirds of the way up the hall.

Less than a meter, and he would see them.

But he got no higher.

Instead, his gaze wandered downward and fixed on the mouths of the converters, that were turned toward him, lips rounded as if to suck him in, and Jericho realized what he was thinking. The bike stood motionless above one of the gaping maws. There was inky blackness within the steel cooking pot, no way of telling if anyone was hiding inside. The blond guy reached into a compartment on his bike, pulled something long from it and threw it down, then accelerated and got out of the danger zone.

A second went by.

Another, and another.

Then came the inferno.

The grenade went off with a deafening boom. A column of fire shot several meters out of the converter as the pressure of the explosion burst from the opening, bathed the hall in glowing red light, whirled smoke in all directions. Jericho grimaced, so painful was the echo in his ears.

The rumble of the explosion spread, escaped through the light-slit in the roof of the converter hall, its panes of glass shattered long since, vibrated the air molecules above, and spread through the sky.

Xin heard the explosion 200 meters higher up.

Something had gone up. Where exactly he couldn't have said, but he was sure that there had been a bang in one of the halls lined up to the west of the blast furnace.

Daxiong, on the other hand, had no doubt that the explosion originated in the converter hall.

He pulled the motorcycle around, spraying up gravel, and at the same moment Xin plunged down from the sky like a hawk.

"Get a move on, damn you!"

Lau Ye was really furious. He was hopping from one leg to the other in Xiao-Tong's shed, watching his friends slowly putting on their shirts and pants, as if the process of getting dressed contained incalculable risks. Ma Mak revealed the stoicism of a zombie, not embarrassed in the slightest that little Ye had found her and Xiao-Tong naked, in a position that left no doubt about the activity they had been engaged in when they fell asleep. Xiao-Tong blinked hard, trying to banish tiny living creatures from the corners of his eyes.

"Come on, now!" Ye clenched his fists, headed nowhere. "I promised Daxiong that we'd hurry."

A duet of grunting was heard, but at least the two of them managed to come shuffling after him. Outside, in the early sunlight, they contorted like vampires.

"I need a cup of tea," murmured Mak.

"I need a fuck," grinned Xiao-Tong and grabbed her backside. She shook him off and struggled onto her motorcycle.

"You've lost it."

"You've both lost it," said Ye, and gave Xiao-Tong a shove that managed to get the guy to swing one leg over the saddle. They didn't have far to go. A few blocks up the street was Wong's World, and behind it, in the early morning mist, stood the silhouette of the blast furnace. Xiao-Tong pointed feebly at the market.

"First couldn't we at least go an'—'"

"No," said Ye. "Pull yourselves together. Party over."

That sounded good and very grown-up, he thought. Could have come from Daxiong, and it seemed at least to make a big impression on Xiao-Tong and Mak. Abandoning all resistance they left their bikes where they were, and followed him up the street. The closer they drew to the blast furnace, the tighter the feeling in Ye's guts became, and a terrible fear took hold of him.

Daxiong had said something about corpses.

He avoided mentioning that to Xiao-Tong and Mak. Not now. For the time being he was just glad to have managed to wake them up at all.

Jericho held his breath.

The blond guy had steered the airbike over the second converter, bringing himself a good bit closer to them. Again he drew out a hand grenade, pulled the pin, slung it into the container, and got out of range. There was a bang; the converter spat fire and smoke.

"Let's get out of here," Yoyo whispered in his ear.

"Then he'll get us," Jericho whispered back. "We won't get away from him another time."

They couldn't escape forever. Eventually they would have to finish off the blond guy, particularly since Jericho had no doubt that they would have to deal with Zhao sooner or later. If that was the man's name. One of the hitmen had called him Kenny.

Kenny Zhao Bide?

His gaze darted around. Right below them gaped the maw of the third converter, wide open as if the steel pot were waiting to be fed. A baby dinosaur, Jericho thought. That was what the pot looked like to him. Little birds crouched in the nest with their beaks wide open, greedily demanding worms and beetles, and what were birds if not miniaturized, feathered dinosaurs? This one was massive. With an appetite for something bigger. For human beings.

A moment later the blond guy's bike approached and obstructed his view of the converter. The machine was hovering right above the smelting pot, so close that Jericho could have touched the killer's head with his outstretched arm. A glance at the ceiling would have been enough for the blond guy to see them, but he seemed to have eyes only for the abyss where he assumed the fugitives were hiding.

He bent forward, reached into his arsenal of weapons and pulled out another hand grenade.

"Hold on tight," Jericho said as quietly as possible. Yoyo pressed his upper arm to indicate that she had understood.

The blond guy pulled the pin from the grenade.

Jericho turned on the engine.

The airbike jumped forward and plunged down at the hit man. For a heartbeat Jericho saw him as if in a flash from a camera, his arm raised to throw the primed grenade, head thrown back, eyes wide with amazement, frozen.

Then they crashed straight into him.

Both turbines screamed to life. Jericho boosted thrust. He relentlessly smashed his opponent's bike against the converter, wrenched the handlebars around, and escaped back into the air. The blond guy's machine plunged still further, somersaulted, crashed against the rim of the opening, was slung up in the air, and clattered, dragging its rider with it, into the stygian abyss of the pot. A hollow clank and rattle followed them as they climbed. Desperately trying to get away from the hell that was about to break out, Jericho put his bike at top speed, sending prayers up to the hall ceiling.

Then came the explosion.

A demon rose from the depths of the cauldron, stretched roaring above it, and fired out incandescent thermal waves. Its hot breath gripped Jericho and Yoyo and slung the bike through the air. They were dragged upward, they turned and plunged. A quick sequence of explosions like booming cannons drowned out their cries as the blond guy's whole arsenal went up, one piece after another. The volcano spat fire in all directions, set half the plant ablaze in an instant, while they hurtled spinning toward the ground and Jericho tugged wildly on the handlebars. The bike looped, scraped along a column, and

crash-landed onto a platform. Jericho was breathless. Yoyo screamed
and almost broke his ribs for fear of being thrown off. Raising sparks,
they dashed along the platform, straight toward a wall. He braked, went
into reverse thrust. The machine careened violently, altered course,
and clanged against a balustrade, where it hung vertical for a moment
as if he had suspended it neatly from a hook, then it gave a groan and
tipped over.

Jericho fell on his back. Yoyo rolled over next to him and hauled
herself up. Her left thigh didn't look great, her pants in shreds, the skin
beneath it torn and bloody. Jericho crept on all fours to the balustrade,
grasped the railings, and got unsteadily to his feet. All around him everything was on fire. A smell of tar billowed to the ceiling and began to fog
the hall.

They had to get out of there.

Yoyo bent double beside him and moaned with pain. He helped
her up, as he stared into the thickening wall of smoke. What was that?
Something was vaguely taking shape in the roiling clouds, they were
brightening. At first he thought it might be another source of fire, but
the light was white, spreading evenly, growing in intensity.

The fish-like rump of an airbike pushed its way out of the smoke.

It was Zhao.

As he set his foot on the bottom step of the zigzag stairs, Ye tried to
control the trembling of his knee. His glance wandered along the tower
of scaffolding to the platform on which the control room rested. All of
a sudden he was afraid of what he might see there, so frightened that
his legs threatened to give way.

He looked round.

A battered old car, a Toyota, was parked crookedly just below the
girderwork, and two motorcycles a little further along. That surprised
him. Normally they rode the machines into the adjacent empty building, before going up.

He couldn't take his eyes off the bikes.

One of them was Tony's. And the other? He wasn't sure, but he
thought it might be Ziyi's.

Tony—Ziyi—

What were they to expect up there?

Mak was trotting upstairs like a shadow in Xiao-Tong's wake. Ye
cleared his throat.

"Wait, I've got to—"

"Let's not hang around," she growled. "You've got us out of bed
now—"

"Terrible time of day," Xiao-Tong complained.

"—so you can damn well come too."

Ye wrung his hands. He didn't know what to do. It was time to tell them Daxiong had mentioned corpses. That something terrible had happened in the control center. But his tongue clung to his palate, his throat hurt as he swallowed. He opened his lips, and a croak issued from them.

"I'm coming."

Daxiong hadn't come via the old rolling mill. There was a shortcut, at least he hoped it was still possible to get through it. Trains had once crisscrossed the grounds of the plant, shunting-engines with torpedo-shaped wagons that were filled with liquid pig iron after the blast furnace was tapped. From there they had driven their 1,400-degree cargo to the converter hall, where the iron was poured into huge pans and from there into the steel smelting pots.

Daxiong followed the tracks. They led at least 2 kilometers across the open field and disappeared into a tunnel, more of a covered passageway, really, that opened right into the converter hall. Shots were ringing out from there now. He put his foot right down, caught his front wheel in one of the tracks, slipped. The motorcycle threw him off. He skidded along on the seat of his pants, dumbfounded by his own stupidity, jumped to his feet, cursed. He had got off lightly, but the accident had cost him time.

His eyes scoured the sky.

No trace of an airbike. He righted his toppled motorcycle and tried to start it. After several attempts and encouraging words, the most frequent of which was *Merde!*, the machine finally sprang to life, and Daxiong plunged into the darkness of the passageway. What he saw was less than encouraging. A shunting-engine rested, broad and sedate, on one of the two parallel tracks; another was coupled to two torpedo cars. He wouldn't be able to get by on either side, only the space between the trains was wide enough—but there was something blocking it.

He should have gone through the rolling mill!

Forced to stop, he got off his bike and walked over to the obstruction, which turned out to be a twisted metal frame. Bracing his 300-pound bulk against it, he tried to shift it from its position. Further ahead he could see the dim opening beyond which the hall lay. It couldn't have been more than 20 meters away.

He had to get there.

At that moment there was a third explosion, a salvo this time, much louder than the others. The passageway lit up, something burning flew into it and crashed to the ground. Further explosions followed. As if possessed, Daxiong rattled at the metal frame until at last, with a great creak, it started to give. The thing wasn't heavy, just hopelessly stuck. He tensed his muscles. All hell must have broken loose through there, flames were blazing. Daxiong panted, pulled and tugged, pushed and shoved, and all of a sudden the metal frame yielded and twisted a little to the side.

Still. Just enough of a gap for him to squeeze through.

Xin held a hand in front of his mouth and nose as he rode his air-bike through the billows. Acrid smoke brought tears to his eyes. What in hell's name had the blond guy been up to? Hopefully it had been worth it at least. Beyond the deep blackness he saw flames flickering. His right hand reached for the butt of the submachine gun in its holster and let go of it again.

First he had to find a way out.

The smoke cleared, giving him a view of the hall. The whole place was in flames. Not a soul in sight, just a toppled airbike hanging from the balustrade of a gallery, dented and blackened. The windshield was missing. Xin steered toward it, as a great roll of thunder set the hall trembling. Immediately behind him a column of fire shot into the air, the wave of pressure sending heavy vibrations through his bike. He climbed, then glimpsed a movement at the far end of the hall.

Something came roaring out of the wall. The motorcycle rider. The bald giant.

Xin drew the gun from the holster.

A greasy black cloud billowed over and enveloped him, hot and suf-focating. He held his breath, brought the bike further up, but the cloud wouldn't let go of him. Of course it wouldn't! Smoke drifted upward. What sort of an idiot was he? Blinded and disorientated, he brought the bike back down again. He couldn't even see the lights on the instru-ment panel now. He steered haphazardly to the right and collided with something, then dragged the handlebars around.

Further down. He had to get down there.

Small fires crackled around him, immersing his airbike in a flick-ering red glow. He thought he could hear voices coming from some-where, headed straight ahead to avoid any further collisions, and managed to get out of the cloud. Between flickering flames and plumes of smoke he saw the motorcycle.

Yoyo was sitting on its pillion.

Xin bellowed with fury. The motorcycle disappeared into the wide, low passageway from which it had emerged. With hissing jets he shot after the two of them and followed them into the tunnel. The motor-cycle dashed between two trains. He tried to estimate the amount of room he had: airbikes were a bit broader than motorcycles, but if he was careful he would fit through.

When he was just about to shoot the girl in the back, he saw some-thing blocking the way.

Iron bars. Bent, wedged.

Beside himself with fury, he was forced to look as Yoyo and the giant ducked their heads and managed by a hair to get under the twisted metal. He himself would have been skewered. Not a chance. His bike was too wide, too high. He pivoted the jets and braked, but his momentum carried him on toward the metal poles. For a moment Xin was filled with a paralyzing sense of complete helplessness; he pulled the bike around sideways-on, scraping along against the trains, and metal crunched against metal as he managed to reduce his speed.

He held his breath.

The airbike stopped, just centimeters away from the metal frame.

Seething with rage, he stared through it. Daylight entered at the end of the passageway. The motorcycle engine seemed to give him an insolent growl as it disappeared from view. Close to losing his self-control, Xin wrenched the airbike around, flew back into the hall, plunged into the smoke, sped through the rolling mill and the warehouse and back outside. Above the slagheap, he turned in a great circle, grateful for the fresh air, opened the cover of the second weapon chamber and reached inside. When his hand came back out, it was holding something long and heavy. Then, at great speed, he bore down on the blast furnace.

Jericho spat and coughed. The smoke billowed into every corner. He wouldn't survive another fight in this inferno. If he didn't get out of here right away, it would all be too late. Another few minutes, and he might as well just settle down and fill his lungs with tar until they were the color of licorice.

He hoped devoutly that Yoyo had made it. Everything had happened at impossible speed. Their escape over the platform, Zhao's bike. Then, all of a sudden, Daxiong. The hit man must have seen him, but something had kept him from reacting right away, fire, perhaps, welling smoke. They had had time to get to Daxiong, who stopped his bike all of a sudden and paused with the engine running. There had been a flicker of puzzlement in the giant's narrow eyes, as he wondered how he would get them both on his narrow pillion.

"Go, Yoyo," Jericho had said.

"I can't—"

"Go, damn it! No speeches, just fuck off! I'll be fine."

She had looked at him, soot-blackened, unkempt, and plainly shocked, with a mixture of fury and defiance in her eyes. And all of a sudden he had seen that strange sadness in her, which he knew from Chen's photographs. Then Yoyo had jumped on Daxiong's pillion. At that moment Zhao had spotted them both.

Jericho clung to the hope that they'd got away from the hit man. Visibility was getting worse and worse. With his sleeve pressed to his mouth and nose, he edged his way up to the gallery and inspected the airbike. In poor shape, but the damage seemed to be more cosmetic in nature. Hoping the handlebars weren't damaged, he bent down and hoisted the machine upright.

His eye fell on something small.

It lay on the ground next to the airbike, something flat, silvery, gleaming. He picked it up, surprised, looked at it, turned it around in his hand—

Yoyo's computer!

She must have lost it here. When she fell off the bike.

He'd found Yoyo's computer!

He quickly slipped the device into his jacket, swung onto his saddle, and started the bike. The familiar hiss.

He had to get out of there.

It had been worse than he had feared. Ma Mak had suddenly thrown up, Xiao-Tong alternately yelled curses and the names of their dead friends, and looked as if he would never recover.

Ye was crying.

He knew he would never be able to get these images out of his head. Never in his life.

Don't ask any questions.

"We've got to pack all the stuff up," he sniffed.

"I can't," wailed Mak.

"We promised Daxiong. Something to do with all this stuff. It's all got to go." He started unplugging computers and disconnecting displays. Xiao-Tong stared at him numbly.

"What on earth's happened here?" he whispered.

"Dunno."

"Where's Yoyo?"

"No idea. Are you going to help me now?"

Mak wiped her mouth, picked up a keyboard, and pulled it from the computer. Eventually Xiao-Tong joined in as well. They stuffed the equipment into cardboard boxes and dragged them outside. They didn't touch the corpses, they tried not to look at them or, even worse, to walk through the still damp pools of blood. Everything was covered with blood, the room, the table, the screens, everything. Mak put her arms around a cardboard box, lifted it and set it down again. Ye saw her shoulders twitching. Her head swung back and forth like clockwork, unable to accept what she saw. He stroked her back, took the box from her hands, and pulled it through Tony's blood—or was it Jia Wei's, or Ziyi's—and outside.

He paused for a moment, snorted, and looked up at the sky.

What was that?

Something was approaching from out of the air beyond the halls. It was quick, and coming closer. A high-pitched hiss heralded its arrival. A flying device. Like a motorcycle, but without wheels. Someone was sitting in the saddle steering the thing, steering it straight at the control room—

Ye blinked, screened his eyes against the sun with his hand.

Daxiong?

He was gradually able to make out details. Not who was driving the machine, but that the driver or pilot or whatever you called him was holding something long that flashed for a second in the sun—

"Hey," he called out. "Come and take a look at th—"

Something detached itself from the flying motorcycle and came hurtling at him with the speed of a rocket.

It *was* a rocket.

"—is," he whispered.

His last thought was that he must be dreaming. That it wasn't happening, because it couldn't possibly happen.

Don't ask any questions.

Xin sped away.

The little house resting on the scaffolding seemed to inflate for a second, as if taking a deep breath. Then the front part blew apart in a fiery cloud, slinging rubble in all directions, crashing against the main structure of the blast furnace, the façades of the adjacent buildings, the forecourt. Xin curved around and fired further rockets at the rear façade. What remained of the side walls exploded, and the roof collapsed. The struts of the girderwork tower supporting the blazing ruin snapped. The control room began to topple, raining down flaming fragments, broke apart in the middle, and sent a flurry of sparks through the tower.

Xin felt a sudden twinge of satisfaction as he spotted Jericho's Toyota in the midst of the avalanche of rubble. A moment later there was nothing more to be seen of the car. The detritus of the old control center spilled over the ground until all that remained upright was what was left of the scaffolding, a pyre, testimony to the cathartic power of heavy explosives.

Jericho's heart felt cold and clammy as he left the darkness of the warehouse. He saw people running shouting across the slagheaps, drawn by the roar of the fire, whose black column of smoke, scattered with flying sparks, rose far above the furnace and reached toward the pale, early sun.

Had Yoyo been in the building? Had she and Daxiong gone back there? Had Zhao caught them there in the end?

No, Zhao, Kenny, or whatever his name was must have destroyed the building for some other reason. Because Yoyo had left him thinking that the computer was still there. He had wiped out most of the Guardians and now he'd destroyed their meeting-point, too, with all the electronics it contained, decapitated the organization, killed anyone Yoyo might have confided in.

He devoutly hoped that her head start had been enough to let her get away from Zhao.

He flew closer. The airbike was harder to steer now than it had been before the crash in the converter hall. It was possible one of the jets had been twisted and could no longer be precisely adjusted anymore. Trying to tilt the bike out of its crooked angle, he didn't immediately understand what it was that he actually saw. The memory of his car came sketchily to mind, parked below the tower of scaffolding. It was only when he was so close to the fire that the heat forced him to turn away that he knew for sure that his Toyota was burning at the bottom of the column of flames.

Fear, exhaustion, everything was swept away by a wave of ungovernable fury. He searched feverishly for the mechanism that would open the side compartments, to shoot Zhao from the sky with his own weapons. But nothing opened, and Zhao was nowhere to be seen.

The forecourt filled with people. They came from all directions, on foot, on bicycles, and on motorcycles. The whole of Wong's World was pouring toward the blast furnace, even Cyber Planet opened its doors, releasing pale and baffled figures, unable to believe what they saw.

Nothing helped. Under such circumstances even the police might have been expected to remember that forgotten world. Jericho climbed. He saw various people pointing at him, thrust his engine, and passed over the industrial estate.

Xin saw the airbike getting smaller.

A good way away from the scene, he perched on the top of a chimney like a buzzard. For a moment he had considered finishing Jericho off with a well-aimed bullet as well, but the detective might still prove useful. Xin let him go. Yoyo was more important. She couldn't have got far, and yet he would have to get used to the idea of having lost the girl for the time being. He decided to stay here and keep watch for her at least until the forces of law and order arrived.

In spite of his defeat, he had a clear image of the universe at that moment. Existences that came into being and then exploded, a surging froth of birth and death, while Xin remained immortal, the center, the point where all lines crossed. The idea reassured him. He had sown chaos and destruction, but he had done it for a higher good. The remains of the girderwork joined the burning ruins on the ground; in the west the flames rose high from the converter hall. Lesser men than he would have called it destruction, but Xin saw nothing but harmony. The cleansing fire spread, healing the world of the infectious afflictions of poverty, cauterizing the pus from the organism of the megalopolis.

At the same time, with conscientious precision, he recapitulated his commission, translated into the language of money. Because Xin had learned to navigate safely on the ocean of his thoughts. Without the slightest doubt, he was insane, as his family had always maintained, except that he understood his insanity. Of all the things he liked about himself, this one filled him with special pride, being a self-analyst, able to establish quite objectively: he was a perfect example of a psychopath. What terrible power that realization contained! Knowing who he was. At one and the same second, being able to be *everything* all at the same time—artist, sadist, empath, higher being, ordinary Joe. Right now it was the careerist who had assumed control of his various personalities, the conventional one who liked to attend to business and then relax in a villa by the sea, surrounded by helpful staff, feeling like the center of the universe. It was that down-to-earth, predictable Xin who restrained his crazed, pyromaniac alter ego in his place and taught him efficiency.

He was so many people. So many things.

High up on his chimney Xin, the planner, started wondering what he had to do to make Yoyo come to him of her own accord.

JERICHO

For a while, Owen Jericho rode his bike under the elevated highway that separated Quyu from the real world. Below him, the traffic headed noisily westward, counterpointed by the boom and roar of the CODs on the freeway above him. He was trapped in a sandwich of noise. When two police skymobiles came chasing over with their sirens wailing, he took refuge between the sand-colored skyscrapers that typified the urban desert around the central district of Shanghai, and followed the course of the main road to Hongkou. As he did so, he tried to stay as low as possible in the canyon of buildings. He assumed that he was flying below the permitted altitude, but he didn't feel at ease on the battered airbike. And he didn't want to experience a sudden engine failure high above the rooftops. Trying to compensate for the leftward tilt of the vehicle, he wound his way between façades, pillars, traffic-light poles, electric wires, and elevated road signs, looking alternately straight ahead, into the rearview mirror, and toward the sky as he waited for Zhao. It was only when he had crossed Hongkou and flown the bike out toward the river that he started to think he might have shaken him off. If Zhao had even *wanted* to follow him. He plunged into the busy shopping streets behind the colonial façade of the Bund, landed to the west of Huaihai Park, and dragged the airbike to the Xintiandi underground parking garage. The left rear wheel got stuck and scraped noisily over the asphalt. For a moment he wondered where to park it, until he remembered what had happened to his car.

At least he had a parking space for this thing now.

The scraping of the damaged wheel echoed angrily against the ramp walls as he steered the airbike toward the space reserved for him. He tried to forget his fury over the loss of his car, and grant priority to Yoyo's well-being. In a mood of selflessness he extended his concern to Daxiong, as he hurried through the parking garage, hoping no one would see him with his soot-blackened face, but there wasn't even anyone in the elevator. There was a uniform light on the walls, the unit hummed gently. By the time he finally slammed the door of his loft behind him, he was certain no one had caught sight of him.

He sighed with relief and ran his hands over his face and through his hair.

He closed his eyes.

Immediately he saw the corpses, the boy with his face shot away, the dying, spinning girl with bright red fountains shooting from her shredded shoulder artery, her severed arm, saw himself freeing the gun from her clawed fingers—what was up, what was going wrong? Hadn't he wanted to lead a peaceful life? And now this. Within a few days. Abused children, mutilated young people, he himself more dead than alive. Reality? A dream, a film?

A film, exactly. And popcorn and something nice and cold. Lean back. What was on next? *Quyu II, the Return?*

Impressions came chasing after him like rabid dogs. He mustn't let it all get to him. He would never be able to get rid of it again; from now on the images would visit him on sleepless nights, but for now he had to think. Stack up his thoughts like building blocks. Make a plan.

Scattering T-shirt and pants carelessly around the sitting room, he went to the bathroom, turned on the shower, washed soot and blood from his skin, and took stock. Yoyo and Daxiong had gotten away. A hypothesis, admittedly, temporarily elevated to the status of fact, but then he had to have *something* to go on. Secondly, Yoyo had been able to save her computer, which was now in his possession. Of course Zhao wouldn't be so naïve as to believe that all the data were on the hard drive of a single, small device. The control room hadn't been destroyed on a whim, it had served the purpose of annihilating the group's infrastructure and possibly all the other devices that Yoyo had transferred the data onto. On the other hand Yoyo's bluff might have achieved the desired effect when she suggested to Zhao that she'd left her computer at the control center. Zhao must have believed he'd solved that problem at least.

What would he do next?

The answer was obvious. He would of course ask himself the question that had been troubling him ceaselessly for days: Who had Yoyo told about her discovery, and who out of them was still alive?

I know about it, he thought, as the hot streams of water massaged the back of his neck. No, wrong! I know that she's found something out, but I don't know what. Zhao, on the other hand, knows that I know precisely nothing. Nice and Socratic. I'm not really an accessory, I'm only a witness to a few regrettable incidents.

Only? Quite enough to get him second place on Zhao's hit list.

On the other hand, what were the chances that Zhao planned to kill him as well? Very high, looking at it realistically, but first he might hope that Jericho, the dewy-eyed idiot, would lead him to Yoyo a second time.

Jericho paused, his hair a foam sculpture.

Then why hadn't Zhao followed him here?

Very simple. Because Yoyo had actually been able to get away! Zhao assumed she was still in Quyu. He had preferred to continue with the chase. And in any case he didn't need to follow Jericho, since he knew exactly where he would find him.

Still. He'd gained some time.

How much?

He rinsed his hair. Black trickles ran down his chest and arms, as if new dirt were constantly emerging from his pores. A stinging pain testified to some of the grazes he'd got when he crashed in the converter hall. He wondered how Yoyo was at that moment. Probably traumatized, although her big mouth hadn't seemed to be in a state of shock. She'd still been capable of producing a reliable torrent of insults, suggesting a certain mental balance and, at the very least, a degree of resilience. The girl, he guessed, was as tough as sharkskin.

He turned off the tap.

Zhao would show up sooner or later. It was quite possible that he was already on his way. He reached for a towel, ran, still drying himself, through the sunlit expanse of his loft, which he would have to leave again almost as soon as he'd moved in, slipped into fresh clothes, tidied his hair very slightly. Next on the agenda was the flight of Owen Jericho, Inc.—which consisted of Jericho himself, Diane, and all his technical equipment. He disconnected the hard drive, a portable unit the size of a shoe box, and stuffed it in a backpack along with the keyboard, a foldable touchscreen surface, and a transparent 20-inch display. Along with that he packed his ID card, money, his spare cell phone, a small hard drive for backups, Yoyo's computer, headphones, and Tu's hologoggles. He stuffed underwear and T-shirts in with it, a spare pair of pants, slippers, shaving materials, some pens, and paper. The only things left in the loft were his control console and large screen, a few bits of hardware, and various built-in drives, all of which were, without Diane, as useless as prosthetic limbs without anyone to wear them. No one who managed to get in here would find a bit or a byte, they wouldn't be able to reconstruct Jericho's work. The apartment was more or less data-free.

Without turning around again, he went outside.

In the underground parking garage he strapped the backpack onto the pillion seat of the airbike and examined the bent jet. With both hands he forced it back into its position. The result didn't look very convincing, but at least it could be adjusted now. Then he fiddled around with the tailfin, drove the bike up the ramp and, with a certain satisfaction, noticed that the sound of scraping had gone. The ball wheel was turning again. He had swapped the car for an airbike, not voluntarily, but it was still a swap.

Outside the sun poured its light down like phosphorescent milk. Jericho narrowed his eyes, but Zhao was nowhere to be seen.

Where to now?

He wouldn't have to go far. In a city like Shanghai the best hiding place was always right around the corner. Instead of heading for the notoriously jammed Huaihai Donglu, he took less frequented alleyways that connected Xintiandi with the Yu Gardens, to the Liuhekou

Lu, known for a long time as an authentic residue of Shanghai that had stirred the imaginations of incorrigible colonial romantics. But what, over the passing centuries, did authenticity consist of? Only what existed, the Party taught. There had been a covered market here, scattered with flower stalls, echoing with the scolding of all kinds of animals, chickens jerking their heads back and forth to demonstrate their edible freshness, crickets tapping away against the walls of jam jars and bringing consolation to their owners, whose lives were not all that different in the end. Then, three years ago, the market had made way for a handsome Shikumen complex, full of bistros, Internet cafés, boutiques, and galleries. Diagonally opposite, a few last market stalls were asserting themselves with the defiance of old gentlemen stopping in the middle of the street and threatening approaching cars with sticks until friendly fellow citizens walked them to the other side and assured them of the utter pointlessness of their actions. They too were still a piece of "authentic" Shanghai. Tomorrow they would have disappeared, to make way for a new "authenticity."

Jericho parked the bike two floors down in the underground parking garage of the complex and withdrew into the back corner of a bistro, where he ordered coffee. Although he wasn't even slightly hungry, he also asked for a cheese baguette, bit into it, scattered crumbs on his T-shirt and pants, and noted with some satisfaction that it didn't all come right back up again.

How far would Zhao go?

This temporary equilibrium was much more bitter than the coffee that he was gulping down. No car. No loft, because it was uninhabitable for the time being. In the sights of a hit man, with his back to the wall. No option but to run away. Forced to act, except that he didn't think he was capable of action. There was no way back into normality, except by getting to the bottom of things. Understanding how the whole drama played out. Find out who had commissioned Zhao.

Jericho stared straight ahead.

Hang on, though! He wasn't entirely incapable of action. Zhao might have forced him onto the defensive, but he had something the hit man didn't know about. His secret weapon, the key to everything.

Yoyo's computer.

He had to find out what she had found out.

Then he would track her down again, to take her back to her father. Chen Hongbing. Was it a good idea to call him? Tu Tian had established the contact, but in point of fact Chen was his client. The man had a right to be informed, but what would he say to him? All fine, Yoyo's in great shape . . . No, honorable Chen, it isn't the police who are after her, just a hardened hit man with a weakness for explosive devices, but hey, don't worry, she's still got both arms and legs and her whole face, haha! Where is she? Well, she's on the run! Me too, see you soon.

What *could* he say, if he didn't want the man to die of a heart attack?

And what if he did get the police involved? Of course he would have to give them a bit of background, not least concerning Yoyo. Which risked drawing attention to the girl. They would ask what part she'd played in the massacre, look at her data, establish that she was on file, even that she had a criminal record. Impossible. The police were out of the question, even though Zhao wasn't a cop, regardless of what he might have told Yoyo in the control center:

I'm trained to kill people. Like all policemen, like all soldiers, all agents.

All agents?

National security is a higher good than individual human lives.

The secret service, on the other hand, had already blown plenty of other things sky high, particularly when they got involved in matters of national security. Zhao could have been bluffing, but what if he actually had the blessing of the authorities?

But what about calling Tu?

That looked pretty pointless too. Jericho forced himself to think clearly. First switch on Diane. He looked around. The bistro was two-thirds full, but the tables around him were free. Here and there young people were writing on their laptops or making phone calls. He set keyboard and screen in front of him and connected both to the hard drive in the backpack. Then he jammed in the headset earbud and linked the system to Yoyo's computer. A symbol appeared, a crouching wolf threateningly showing its fangs. Below it appeared some text:

I'm inviting you to dinner.

Okay, then, thought Jericho.

"Hi Diane," he said quietly.

"Hi, Owen." Diane's velvety timbre. The consolation of the machine. "How did things go?"

"Fucking awful."

"Sorry to hear that." How honest that sounded. Okay, then, it wasn't *dis*honest. "Can I help?"

You could be made of flesh and blood, thought Jericho.

"Please open the file 'I'm inviting you to dinner.' You'll find access data in Yoyofiles."

Silence fell for two seconds. Then Diane said:

"The file is locked four times. I've been able to use three of the tools successfully. I haven't got the fourth access authorization."

"Which tools worked?"

"Iris, voice, and fingerprint. All assigned to Chen Yuyun."

"Which one's missing?"

"A password, by the look of it. Shall I decipher?"

"Do that. Have you any idea how long the decoding's going to take you?"

"Afraid not. At the moment I can only speculate that the coding includes several words. Or one unusually long one. Is there anything else I can do for you?"

"Go online," said Jericho. "That's it. See you later, Diane."

"See you later, Owen."

He logged on to Brilliant Shit. If his assumption was correct, the Guardians' blog was being used as a dead letter drop, and regularly checked.

Jericho to Demon, he wrote. *I've got your computer.* He added a phone number and an e-mail address, stayed logged in, and stored the blog as an icon. As soon as someone saved a message in it, Diane would let him know right away. By now he felt a little better. He bit into his baguette, topped up his coffee, and decided to contact Tu.

A call came in for him.

Jericho stared at the display. No picture, no number.

Yoyo? So quickly?

"Hi, Owen," said a very familiar voice.

"Zhao." Everything inside Jericho shrank to a tiny lump. He paused for a moment and tried to sound relaxed. "Or should I say Kenny?"

"Kenny?"

"Don't pretend to be more stupid than you are! Didn't that fat ass-hole call you that before he kicked the bucket?"

"Oh, right." The other man laughed quietly. "As you wish, then—Kenny."

"Kenny who? Kenny Zhao Bide?"

"Kenny's just fine."

"Okay, Kenny." Jericho took a deep breath. "Then wash your ears out. Yoyo's slipped through your fingers. I got away from you. You won't get any further as long as one of us has a reason to feel threatened by you."

A sigh of resignation came through the receiver.

"I'm not threatening anybody."

"Yes you are. You're shooting people and blowing up buildings."

"You've got to look the facts in the face, Owen. You put up a decent fight, you and the girl. Admirable, but not especially clever, I'm afraid to say. If Yoyo had cooperated, everyone might still be alive."

"Ridiculous."

"It was your people who started all the shooting."

"Not at all. They only started shooting because you'd killed Xiao Meiqi and Jin Jia Wei."

"That was unavoidable."

"Really?"

"Yoyo would hardly have talked to me otherwise. Later I did everything in my power to avert any further bloodshed."

"What do you want, Kenny?"

"What do you think I want? Yoyo, of course."

"To do what?"

"To ask her what she knows and who she's told."

"You—"

"Don't worry!" Kenny cut in. "I'm not planning on killing even more people. But I'm under a certain amount of pressure, you know? Pressure to succeed. These are the times we're living in, everyone constantly wants to see results, so what would you do in my place? Come away empty-handed?"

"You've got your hands pretty full. You've destroyed Yoyo's computer, and the complete infrastructure of the Guardians. Do you really think any of them wants to mess with you again?"

"Owen," said Kenny in the voice of a teacher who needs to explain everything three times. "I don't know anything. I don't know whether I destroyed Yoyo's infrastructure, how many computers she transferred the data to, whether everyone she confided in died in the control center. What about that huge bike-riding baby? What about you? Didn't she tell you anything?"

"We won't get any further like this. Where are you anyway?"

Kenny paused for a moment.

"Nice apartment. Looks like you've done some house-clearing."

Jericho gave a sour smile. He felt a kind of satisfaction in being proved right and having got out in good time.

"You'll find a cold beer in the fridge," he said. "Take it and go."

"I can't do that, Owen."

"Why not?"

"Haven't you had jobs to do, like I do? Aren't you used to taking things to their conclusion?"

"I'll tell you once more—"

"Imagine the inferno if the flames should take hold of other parts of the building."

Jericho's mouth dried up all of a sudden.

"What flames?"

"The ones from your apartment." Kenny's voice had dropped to a whisper, and he suddenly reminded Jericho of a snake. A huge, talking snake, stuffed into the body of a human being. "I'm thinking of the people, and also of you. I mean, everything here looks new and expensive, you've probably put all your savings into it. Wouldn't it be terrible to lose all that in one go, just for a matter of principle, out of solidarity with some pig-headed girl?"

Jericho said nothing.

"Can you imagine my situation any better now?"

A host of insults collected on the tip of Jericho's tongue. Instead he said as quietly as possible:

"Yes, I think so."

"That's a weight off my mind. Really! I mean, we weren't a bad team, Owen. Our interests are marginally different, but basically we want the same thing in the end."

"And now?"

"Just tell me where Yoyo is."

"I don't know."

Kenny seemed to think about it.

"Good. I believe you. So you'll have to track her down for me."

Track her down—

Good God! What sort of idiot was he? He didn't know what tricks the hit man had up his sleeve, but doubtless everything he said was designed to drag the conversation out. Kenny was trying to track *him* down. To locate him.

Without hesitation, Jericho hung up.

Less than a minute later his phone lit up again.

"I give you two hours," hissed Kenny. "Not a minute longer. Then I want to hear something that will put my mind at rest, otherwise I'll consider myself forced to undertake a radical restructuring of the building."

Two hours.

What was Jericho supposed to do in two hours?

He hastily bundled the display and the keyboard back into his backpack, put some money on the table, and left the bistro without a backward glance. He strode toward the elevator, took it down to the underground garage, climbed onto his bike, and brought it out onto Liuhekou Lu, where he started the engine and flew toward the river. During the short flight a bulky ambulance hovered below him, big enough for him to land on. In the distance he saw an armada of unmanned fire engines making for the hinterland of Pudong. Private skymobiles crossed his path, pleasure blimps bobbed above the Huangpu. For a moment he considered flying to the WFC and looking up Tu, but it was too early for that. He would need peace to carry out his plan, and he had to have somewhere to stay, for as long as Kenny robbed him of the warmth and security of Xintiadi.

And he knew where.

Looming over the grand buildings of the Bund was one of the most peculiar hotels in Shanghai. Like a huge lotus blossom, China's symbol of growth and affluence, the roof of the Westin Shanghai Bund Center opened itself up to the sky. It made some people think of an agave, others of an outsize octopus extending its tentacles to filter birds and skymobiles out of the air. Jericho saw it only as a refuge whose manager played in the same golf club as himself and Tu Tian. A casual acquaintance without the bonus of familiarity, but Tu liked the man, and tended to use the hotel as accommodation for business partners too lowly for the WFC and the Jin Mao Tower. Jericho was also granted the indulgence of special conditions, a favor that he had so far never called on. Now, since he felt little desire to wander nomadically from bistro to bistro, he decided to make use of it. After he had landed his bike by the front entrance, he stepped into the lobby and asked for a single room. The cameras set into the wall scanned him and passed the relevant information on to the receptionist. She smilingly greeted him by name, a sign that he was already on their files, and asked him to set his phone down on the touchscreen. The hotel computer compared Jericho's ID with the database, authorized the reservation, and uploaded the access code to Jericho's hard drive.

"Would you like us to take your car to the underground parking garage?" the woman asked, and performed the trick of speaking with a smile even though her lips never met.

"I've come on an airbike," said Jericho.

"We've got a landing bay, as I'm sure you know," said the smile fixed to the corners of the receptionist's mouth. "Do you want us to park your bike there for you?"

"No, I'll do that myself." He grinned. "Quite honestly, I need every hour of flying time I can get."

"Oh, I understand." The smile switched from routine politeness to routine cordiality. "Safe journey up there. Don't forget, the hotel façade can take more knocks than you can."

"I'll bear it in mind."

He left the lobby and flew his bike up along the glazed outside wall, constantly accompanied by his reflection. For the first time he became aware that he wasn't wearing a helmet, as the regulations for airbikes demanded. Another reason to keep away from the police. If they found out that the bike wasn't registered to him, it was going to be a tough thing to explain.

The landing pad was open and almost empty, aside from the hotel's own shuttles. Nearly all twentieth-century visions of the future had assumed some form of private urban air traffic powered by lightbeams, taking it for granted that aerial traffic would shape the face of cities. In fact, the number of such skymobiles was tiny, and they were restricted to State and city institutions, a few exclusive taxi companies and millionaires like Tu Tian. In purely infrastructural terms, of course, there were good reasons for lightening ground traffic by exploiting the airborne variety, except that all these considerations faced a great Godzilla of a counterargument: fuel consumption. To counteract the force of gravity you needed powerful turbines and a whole load of energy. The economical alternative, the gyrocopter, spiraled its way into the air by rotor power like a helicopter, but had the disadvantage of excessively massive rotor blades. Financially, the expense of making cars fly was entirely disproportionate to the effect, and airbikes, even though they were more economical and affordable, weren't really an exception to that. They were still expensive enough to make Jericho wonder who could afford to supply a hit man with three—especially customized models. The police, chronically underfunded? Hardly. Secret services? More likely. The army?

Was Kenny a soldier? Was the army behind all this?

With his backpack over his shoulder, Jericho took the elevator to his floor and held his phone up to the infrared port beside the door to his room. It swung open, revealing a view of the room behind it. Fussy and staid, was his first impression. All in great condition, but stylistically nowhere. Jericho didn't care. Within a few minutes he had freed Diane from her backpack and connected her up. That made this room his new investigation agency.

Would Kenny set the loft on fire?

Jericho rubbed his temples. He wouldn't be surprised, but on the other hand he doubted that the hit man would wait in Xintiandi until he called. Kenny would try to arrest Yoyo on his own initiative, probably aware that Jericho wasn't automatically prepared for collaboration just because he was waving a box of matches around.

"Diane?"

"I'm here, Owen."

"How's the search for the password going?"

It was a stupid question. As long as Diane registered no success, he didn't need to worry about where things went from here. But talking to the computer made him feel as if he was in charge of a little team that was doing everything in its power.

"You'll be the first to know," said Diane.

Jericho gave a start. Was that humor? Not bad. He lay down on the huge bed with its gaudy yellow cover and felt terribly tired and useless. Owen Jericho, cyber-detective. Hilarious. He had been supposed to find Yoyo, and instead he'd put a psychopath on her trail. How in God's name would he explain that to Tu, let alone to Chen Hongbing?

"Owen?"

"Diane?"

"Someone's uploading a post to Brilliant Shit."

Jericho jolted upright.

"Read it to me."

At first he was disappointed. It was a list of coordinates, with no sender or any kind of accompanying text. Time, input code, nothing else.

An address in Second Life.

Did it come from Yoyo?

With leaden head and arms, he pulled himself upright, walked over to the little desk where he'd put his screen and keyboard, and took a look at the short text. At length he found a single letter that he'd probably overlooked: a D.

Demon.

Jericho took a look at his watch. Just after eleven. At twelve o'clock Yoyo was waiting for him in the virtual world. As long as the message really did come from her and wasn't another attempt by Kenny to locate him. Had he given away the address of the blog to the hit man? Not as far as he remembered. Kenny couldn't be so cunning as to turn up all of a sudden in Brilliant Shit as well, but caution was plainly advised. Jericho decided not to take a risk. From now on he would put any online communication through the anonymizer.

He lay back on the bed and stared at the ceiling.

There was nothing he could do.

After a few minutes the turbulent sea of his nerves was calm once more. He dozed off, but he didn't sink into a relaxing sleep. Just below the surface of his consciousness, he was haunted by images of creeping torsos that weren't human beings, but failed designs of human beings, grotesquely distorted and incomplete, covered with blood and mucus like newborn babies. He saw legless creatures, their faces nothing but smooth, gleaming surfaces, split down the middle by obscenely twitching pink openings. Half-charred lumps teetered toward him like spiders on a thousand legs or more. Eyes and mouths suddenly opened up in a scab of shapeless tissue. Something blind stretched toward him, darting a gnarled tongue between fanged jaws, and yet Jericho felt no fear, just a weary sadness, since he knew that in another life all these monstrosities had been as human as he was himself.

Then he fell, and found himself back on a bed, but it was a different bed from the one on which he had lain down. Dark and damp, lit by feeble moonlight that fell through a dirty window and outlined the bleak, bare room where he had ended up, it seemed to exert a curious power over him. Lucidly dreaming, he realized that he must be in his comfortable, boringly furnished room, but he couldn't sit up and open his eyes. He was bound to this rotting mattress as if by magnetic force, swathed in weird, dry silence.

And in the midst of that silence he suddenly heard the click of chitin-armored legs.

Jagged feet scratched at the edges of the bedsheets, snagged in the fabric and drew fat, segmented bodies up to him. A wave of anxiety washed over him. His horror was due less to the question of what the armored creatures wanted to do to him, than to the most terrible of all realizations, that a perfidious dream had slung him back into the past, to a phase of his life that he thought he had long since overcome.

His rise through society in Shanghai, the peace that he had made with Joanna, his arrival in Xintiandi, it was all revealed as a fantasy, the real dream, from which the invisible insects were now waking him with their rustles and clicks.

Close beside him, someone had begun to whimper, in high, singing tones. Everything sank back into darkness, because the fact that his eyes were closed was starting to defeat the vision of that terrifying room. His mind found its way back to reality, except that nobody seemed to have told his body. It didn't respond, it wouldn't move. He was starting to fight against that weird rigidity by emitting those whimpers, real sounds that anyone who had been in the room could have heard as clearly as he did himself, and finally, by summoning all his powers, he managed to move the little finger of his left hand. He was wide awake by now. He remembered stories about people who—having apparently passed away—had been carried to the grave, while they actually saw every moment with crystal clarity, and without the slightest chance of being able to attract anyone's attention, and he whimpered still louder in his panic and despair.

It was Diane who rescued him.

"Owen, I've cracked Yoyo's password."

A twitch ran through his paralyzed body. Jericho sat up. The computer's voice had broken the spell, dream images gurgled away down the drain of oblivion. He took a few deep breaths before asking:

"What was it?"

"*Eat me and I'll eat you alive.*"

My God, Yoyo, he thought. How overdramatic. At the same time he was grateful that she had clearly chosen the access code in a fit of rebellious romanticism, rather than opting for the more secure variation of a random sequence of letters and digits, which would have been much harder to decode.

"Download the content," he said.

"I've done it."

"Save it in Yoyofiles."

"With pleasure."

Jericho sighed. How was he going to wean Diane off her habit of saying *With pleasure*? Much as he liked her voice, her tone, the words bothered him more each time. There was something servile about it that he found repulsive. He rubbed his eyes and squatted on the edge of the desk chair, his eyes fixed on the monitor.

"Diane?"

"Yes, Owen?"

"Can you—I mean, would it be possible for you to delete the phrase *With pleasure* from your vocabulary?"

"What do you mean exactly? *With pleasure*? Or *the phrase with pleasure*?"

"With pleasure."

"I can offer to suppress the phrase for you."

"Great idea. Do that!"

He almost expected the computer to grant his wish with another *With pleasure*, but Diane just said silkily:

"Done."

And how amazingly simple. Why hadn't he thought of it years ago? "Show me all the downloads in Yoyofiles from May of this year, sorted by time of day."

A short list appeared on the screen, totaling about two dozen entries. Jericho skimmed them and concentrated his attention on the time leading up to Yoyo's escape.

There was something.

His weariness fled instantly. About half an hour before Yoyo left her apartment, data had been transferred to her computer, two files in different formats. He asked Diane to open one of them. It was a shimmering symbol of intertwined lines. It pulsed as if it were breathing. Jericho took a closer look.

Snakes?

It actually did look like a nest of snakes. Snakes twining into a kind of reptilian eye. It seemed to rest in the center of a body, from which the snake bodies emerged: a single, surreal-looking creature that somehow reminded Jericho of school visits.

Where did snakes go creeping around all over the place in mythology?

He looked at the second file.

friends-of-iceland.com
en-medio-de-la-suiza-es
Brainlab.de/Quantengravitationstheorie/Planck/uni-kassel/32241/html
instead of
Vanessacraig.com
Hoteconomics.com
Littlewonder.at

Jericho rubbed his chin.

You didn't have to be particularly intelligent to understand what it meant. Three websites were to be exchanged. He wondered how Yoyo had got hold of the data. He asked Diane to open the three pages at the top, one by one, all of which were innocuous and generally accessible pages. *friends-of-iceland* was a blog. In it, Scottish immigrants to Iceland swapped experiences, provided useful tips to new arrivals and those who were thinking of emigrating, and put photographs on the net. *en-medio-de-la-suiza* was also devoted to the charms of living abroad. Produced in Spain, the page provided a great deal of visual material about

Switzerland, in the form of 3D films. Jericho looked at some of them. They had been filmed from a plane or helicopter. At a low altitude he flew over Zürich, landscapes of the canton of Uri and picturesque collections of houses and barns that lay scattered along a winding river.

Brainlab.de/Quantengravitationstheorie/Planck/uni-kassel/32241 /html, finally, came from Germany and consisted of closely typed lines of text, examining over twelve pages a phenomenon that physics described as "quantum foam." It described what happened if you applied quantum theory and the General Theory of Relativity to the so-called Planck length, which gave you foaming space-time bubbles and at the same time a scientific dilemma, because those bubbles overrode the calculations of General Relativity. The text was remarkable for its lack of paragraphs, and was plainly written for people whose notion of ecstasy involved a blackboard scribbled all over with formulas.

Scotland, Spain, Germany. The joys of Iceland. The beauty of Switzerland. Quantum physics.

Hardly designed to provoke fear and horror.

Curious, he called up the websites that were supposed to be swapped. Vanessa Craig was revealed as a student of agricultural science from Dallas, Texas, who was spending a few months on an exchange program in Russia. In her online diary she wrote quite unexcitingly about her little university town near Moscow. She was homesick and lovesick and complained of the low temperatures responsible for the innate melancholy of the Russian soul. Behind *Hoteconomics,* an American website offering up-to-the-minute economy news, was *Littlewonder,* an Austrian portal for handmade toys, specializing in the needs of preschool children.

What was all this? What did travel reports, toys, quantum physics, the global economy, and the notes of a shivering American have in common?

Nothing.

And that was precisely the quality required by dead letter drops. You walked by, looked at them without suspecting for a moment that they might contain something other than what they actually contained. Yoyo must have found their common properties. Something you couldn't see, but was still there. Again Jericho opened the Spanish address with the film clips from Switzerland, clicked on the snake symbol, and moved it aside.

Nothing happened. As if pulled by elastic bands, it darted back into the empty space of the display.

"Weird," Jericho murmured. "I could have sworn—"

That it's a mask.

A mask to reveal hidden content in the apparently harmless context of the pages. A decoding program. Again he dragged it onto the Spanish website, and again it slipped away.

"Okay then, friends of Iceland. Let's see what you have to offer."

And this time it happened.

The moment he dragged the snake symbol to the blog, an extra window opened. It contained a few apparently unconnected words, but his instinct hadn't failed him.

> Jan in business address: Oranienburger Strasse 50, continues a that he statement coup Donner be There are

"I knew it! I knew it!"

Jericho clenched his fists. Excited now, he went to work. The snake icon was a key. Anyone who had concealed messages in the pages was using a special algorithm, and the parameters for that algorithm lay in the mask. He opened the page with the essay about quantum foam and repeated the procedure. Further words were added to the fragment:

> Jan in Andre runs business address: Oranienburger Strasse 50, 10117 Berlin. continues a grave that he knows all about One way or another statement coup Chinese government implemented of timing and Donner be liquidated. There are

There are? Whatever there were. This stuff here was far more likely to alarm somebody who was the focus of State surveillance! What looked at first glance like sheer Dadaism was really part of a larger message, the text of which had been sent to an unknown number of mailboxes.

Dead letter drops existed wherever states and institutions spied on one another and agents had to avoid being seen together, Jericho thought. During the Cold War they had been the most common form of message transmission. Almost anything at all could be used: garbage containers, holes in trees, cracks in masonry, public phone books, magazines in waiting rooms, vases and sugar bowls in restaurants, the cisterns in public bathrooms. The drop was a place accessible to anyone, where you left something that anybody might see, but which only the initiated recognized as a message. Transmitter and receiver agreed on a period of time, the transmitter deposited what he wanted to pass on—documents, microfilms, demands for cash, journalistically controversial material—left a sign at an agreed place that something was waiting in the drop, and disappeared. A little later the receiver came along, picked up the transmission, left a sign of his own that it had been collected, and also went on his way. The system worked as long as the physical exchange of hardware was involved. Since encrypted messages were now passed on via the Internet, they had fallen out of fashion, and were reserved for cases where the information to be passed on could not, with the best will in the world, be transmitted down a fiber-optic cable.

At least that was what people said.

In fact the drop was celebrating an unparalleled renaissance, particularly where electronic encryption was forbidden or if there was a risk that the net police had been given a spare key. The new drops were harmless files and websites that anyone could access. What they contained was unremarkable as long as the content was suited to the transmission of the message. A sentence consisting of twelve words could be broken down into twelve parts and distributed across twelve websites. Word one, *The*, could appear in the second line of a travel piece, word two in the sixth line of the third paragraph of a specialist scientific article, and where it was absolutely imperative that a word should not appear, it was broken down into individual letters that could be found anywhere.

However, no one could do anything with the files while they weren't in possession of a key that separated the words or letters from their contexts and combined them to form a new, secret meaning, a mask, like the kind used in former times, when the Bible or the works of Tolstoy were made to reveal the most incredible content simply by placing a sheet of variously perforated cardboard over a particular page. The matter that appeared in the holes produced the message. In the world of the World Wide Web that mask was a program. Parts of such a program had clearly made their way onto Yoyo's computer, along with an indication that three drops had been replaced by three different ones. Jericho had no idea how many drops were involved overall. It could be dozens, hundreds. Clearly, other addresses were needed for the meaning of the message to be revealed, but Jericho was beginning to understand why Yoyo must have become convinced that she had kicked a hornets' nest.

Jan in Andre runs business address: Oranienburger Strasse 50, 10117 Berlin.

Who could that be? Someone called Jan or Andre, perhaps even a woman—*Jan in*: Janine? Could you run a business address? Unfortunate choice of words. Something was missing, although the address seemed to be complete.

continues a grave that he knows all about One way or another

Something was continuing, and someone knew about it.

that he knows all about

He? Not a woman, then? *Jan in Andre*. Was that one continuous name? Now the controversial bit:

statement coup Chinese government

Here Yoyo's eyes must have popped out of her head. The Chinese government, mentioned in the same breath as the idea of a coup. A person who had *knowledge* of it, possibly to the cost of the people undertaking the coup. Who or what was to be overthrown? The government in Beijing? Were there plans for a coup in parliament, among the military, abroad? Hard to imagine. It was more likely that the statement referred to a coup in another country, and that the Chinese government was involved in it. A coup that had succeeded or failed, or else was still to come.

Was there anyone who could have blown the cover on Beijing's role?

implemented of timing and Donner be liquidated

Gobbledygook apart from one word: liquidated. Liquidate Donner? Donner and Blitzen? Donner kebab? Hardly. As everywhere throughout the fragment, crucial passages were missing here too. The text might have been completed with a few words, but it might equally have been hundreds of pages long, and everything that Jericho thought he was reading into it might prove to be erroneous. But if that wasn't the case, a murder was being reported, announced, or at least recommended here.

He studied the text once more.

timing. This was about a sequence of events. A sequence of events that was under threat? Yoyo must have assembled the puzzle just as he had, reached similar conclusions, and immediately gone into hiding as if the devil were on her tail. And it was perfectly possible to see the Chinese State security service in that light. And yet her escape didn't really make sense. She had been working with controversial material for years. The fragment should surely have aroused her curiosity, stirred her enthusiasm, and instead it had thrown her into a panic.

Had it? Or had she hurried enthusiastically to Quyu, to round up the Guardians and start doing background research in the shelter of the control center?

No, that would have been absurd. She wouldn't have left her father without a word. There could have been only one reason, that she was worried about putting him and herself in danger by making too close contact. Because she assumed that she was under surveillance. More than that! That night she must have had cause to worry that her enemies would be outside the door in a few minutes, because she had broken into their secret information channels and been noticed.

They had detected Yoyo.

Jericho called to mind her piece on Brilliant Shit, had Diane load the text, and read it again:

"Hi all. Back in our galaxy now, have been for a few days. Was really stressed out these last days, is anybody harshing on me? Couldn't help it, really truly. All happened so fast. Shit. Even so quickly you can be forgotten. Only waiting now for the old demons to visit me once more. Yeah, and, I'm busy writing new songs. If any of the band asks: We'll make an appearance once I've got a few euphonious lyrics on the go. Let's prog!"

No one victorious would write like that. It was a cry for help from someone losing control. When she was uploading the web addresses and the mask, she must have realized that she'd been located. That was why she had left so quickly.

He studied the fragment again.
"Diane, find 50 Oranienburger Strasse, 10117 Berlin."
The reply came in an instant. Jericho looked at his watch. Two minutes to twelve. He connected the hologoggles to the computer, logged on, and chose the coordinates entered by Yoyo.

THE SECOND WORLD

Since the middle of the last decade, when Second Life had been restructured after its predictable collapse, there was no longer a central hub, any more than the space-time continuum had a real center, just an infinite number of observation points, each of which created the *illusion* of being the center, the way an earth-dweller felt that his location was fixed and the whole cosmos was something spinning around him, moving away from him or toward him. An astronaut on the Moon and every creature in the universe felt exactly the same, wherever they happened to be. In the real universe, the totality of all particles was interlinked, which meant that every particle was able to occupy its relative center.

Similarly, Second Life had turned into a peer-to-peer network, an almost infinite, decentralized, and self-organizing system in which every server—like a planet—formed a hub, which was connected by a random number of interfaces with every other hub. Each participant was automatically a host and a user of the worlds of others. How many planets Second Life comprised, who inhabited or controlled them, was unknown. Of course there were lists, cybernetic maps, well-known travel routes and records that made it possible to realize oneself in the virtual world in the first place, just as the outside universe was subject to physical boundary conditions. Within these standards, avatars traveled to all the places on the web that were known to them, and to which they were granted access. But there was no longer anyone who was familiar with *everything*.

Jericho would have expected to land at such an unknown place, but Yoyo's coordinates led to a public hub. Almost every metropolis in the real world had been virtually copied by now, so he traveled from Shanghai to Shanghai, to find himself back in the People's Square, or at any rate in a nearly identical copy of it. Unlike the real Shanghai, there were no traffic jams and beyond the city boundaries no districts like Quyu. On the other hand new edifices were constantly going up, staying for a while, changing or disappearing with the speed of a mouse click.

The builder and owner of Cyber-Shanghai was the Chinese government, and it was financed by both Chinese and foreign companies. The Party also maintained a second Beijing, a second Hong Kong and a virtual Chongqing. Like all net cities based on real models, the charm of the depiction lay in the relationship between authenticity and idealism. It could hardly come as a surprise that more Americans lived in Cyber-Shanghai than Chinese, and that most Chinese-looking avatars were bots, machines disguised as living creatures. In turn, some Chinese had second homes in Cyber-New York, in virtual Paris, or Berlin.

French and Spanish people tended to live in Marrakech, Istanbul, and Baghdad. Germans and the Irish liked Rome. The British were drawn to New Delhi and Cape Town, and Indians to London. Anyone who dreamed of living in New York and couldn't afford it found an afford-able and entirely authentic Big Apple on the net, only wilder, more progressive, and even a bit more interesting than the original. People doing business in virtual Paris didn't seek seclusion, but were interested in as many interfaces with the real world as possible. BMW, Mercedes Benz, and other car manufacturers didn't sell fantasy constructs in the cyber-cities, but prototypes of what they actually planned to build.

Basically net cities were nothing but colossal experimental labs in which no one thought twice of traveling by spaceship rather than by ship, as long as the Statue of Liberty stood where it belonged. The own-ers, meaning the countries in question, were opening another chapter in globalization here, but above all they were remodeling the world of human beings in a peculiar way. Crime and terrorism did exist in the virtual New York; buildings were destroyed by data attack, avatars were sexually molested. There were muggings, break-ins, grievous bodily harm, and rape; you could be imprisoned or exiled. There was only one thing that didn't exist:

Poverty.

What was produced on the net was by no means an illustration of society. You could fall ill here. Hackers planted cyber-plagues and scat-tered viruses. You could have an accident or simply not feel so great, or become addicted to something. In times of ultra-thin sensor skins that you slipped into in order to feel the illusion of perfect graphics on your body as well, cybersex was a great source of income and expenditure. Compulsive gaming flourished, avatars suffered from morbid fears like claustrophobia, agoraphobia, and arachnophobia. But far and wide there was no hint of overpopulation. The poor as a source of all evil had been identified and removed from human perception. Networked people could afford a Mumbai or a Rio de Janeiro that was constantly growing, with no impoverishment involved, because bits and bytes were an abundant resource. Even natural disasters had haunted the cyber-cities—anyone who lived in Tokyo expected an authentic little earthquake from time to time.

But there were no slums.

The representation of the world as it could be became the world itself, with all the light and shade of real existence—and demonstrated who was responsible for global abuse. Not capitalism, not the industrial societies that supposedly didn't want to share. With empirical ruth-lessness the virtual experiment identified the guilty as those who had the least. The army of the poor in Quyu, in the Brazilian favelas, the Turkish gecekondular, the megaslums of Mumbai and Nairobi, billions of people who lived on less than a dollar a day—in cyberspace they weren't isolated and locked away, not exploited in the class war, not the object of Third World summits, development aid, pangs of conscience and denial, they weren't even hate objects.

They simply didn't exist.

And suddenly everything worked smoothly. So where did the problem lie? Who was responsible for the lack of space, overexploitation, environmental pollution, since the virtual universe worked so wonderfully well without poverty? It was the poor. No point stressing the impossibility of comparing the two systems, the carbon-based and the hard-drive-based. With the naïve cynicism of the philosopher who sees overpopulation as the root of all human evil, and stops listening as soon as consequences are discussed, representatives of the net community pointed out that there were no poor here. Not because someone had cut funds, knocked down slums, or even killed millions. They had simply never appeared. Second Life showed what the world looked like without them, and it certainly looked considerably better, *honi soit qui mal y pense.*

Of course there were other things that didn't exist in virtual Shanghai. There was no smog, for example, which always unsettled Jericho. Precisely because simulation took human visual habits into account, the lack of the permanent haze completely altered the overall impression.

He looked around and waited.

Avatars and bots of all kinds were on the move, many flying or floating along above the ground. Hardly anyone was walking. Walking in Second Life enjoyed a certain popularity, but more on short journeys. It was only in rurally programmed worlds that you encountered hikers, who could walk for hours. There was swiftly flowing traffic even above the highest buildings. Here too, the programmed Shanghai differed from the real one. On the net the vision of an air-propelled infrastructure had become reality.

Noisy and gesticulating, a group of extraterrestrial immigrants was heading toward Shanghai Art Museum. Recently reptiloids from Canis Major had been turning up in increasing numbers. No one really had much idea who was in charge of them. They were considered mysterious and uncouth, but they did successful business with new technologies for heightening sensitivity. Cyber-Shanghai was entirely controlled by State security which, with a great deal of trouble and the use of a number of bots, kept the huge cyber-cities under control. Possibly the reptiloids were just a few tolerated hackers, but they might equally have been disguised officers from Cypol. By now extraterrestrials were staggering around all the net metropolises, which hugely extended the possibilities of trade. As a general rule, software companies lay behind these, taking into account the fact that virtual universes had to offer constantly new attractions. The astral light-forms from Aldebaran, for example, with which you could temporarily merge in order to enjoy unimagined sound experiences, had by now been unmasked as representatives of IBM.

Jericho wondered what form Yoyo would appear in.

After a minute or so he glimpsed an elegant, French-looking woman with big dark eyes and a black pageboy cut crossing the square toward him. She was wearing an emerald green pantsuit and stilettos. To Jericho she looked like a character out of a Hollywood film from the sixties in which Frenchwomen looked the way American directors imagined them. Jericho, who had several identities in Second Life, had appeared as himself, so that the woman recognized him right away. She stopped right in front of him, looked at him seriously, and held out her open right hand.

"Yoyo?" he asked.

She put her finger to her lips, took his hand, and pulled him after her. She stopped by one of the flower stalls near the entrance to the subway, let go of his hand, and opened a tiny handkerchief. The head of a lizard, the same emerald green as her outfit, peeped out from it. The creature's golden eyes fastened on Jericho. Then the slender body darted upward, landed on the ground at their feet, and wriggled along the floral carpet, where it paused and looked around at them, as if to check that they were following it.

A moment later a transparent sphere about 3 meters in diameter was floating closely above her. The lizard turned around and darted a forked tongue.

"Just a moment," he said. "Before we—"

The woman drew him to her and gave him a shove. The impetus propelled him straight into the inside of the sphere. He sank into a chair that hadn't been there a moment before, as far as he remembered, or at least the sphere had looked completely empty from outside. She jumped after him, sat down beside him, and crossed her legs. Jericho saw the lizard looking up at them through the transparent floor.

Then it had disappeared. In its place an illuminated and apparently bottomless shaft had opened up.

"'ave you a strong estomac?" The woman smiled. She sounded so French that a real French person would have been horrified.

Jericho shrugged. "Depends what—"

"Good."

The sphere plunged down the shaft like a stone.

The illusion was so real that all of Jericho's skin, muscle, and brain vessels suddenly contracted and adrenaline pumped violently into his bloodstream. His pulse and heartbeat quickened. For a moment he was actually glad not to have burdened his stomach with a generous breakfast.

"Juste shut you' eyes if you don't bear it," twittered his companion, as if he had complained about something. Jericho looked at her. She was still smiling, a mischievous smile, he thought.

"Thanks, I like it."

The surprise effect had fled. From now on he could choose which standpoint to emphasize. That of sitting in a hotel room watching a well-made film, or actually experiencing all this. Had he been wearing a sensor skin the choice would have been difficult, almost impossible. The skins erased all distance from the artificial world, while he was wearing only glasses and gloves. The rest of his equipment had stayed in Xintiandi.

"Some people 'ave an injection," the Frenchwoman said calmly. "'ave you been once in a tank?"

Jericho nodded. In the bigger branches of Cyber Planet, which were visited by the more affluent customers, there were tanks filled with cooking salt solution, in which you floated weightlessly, dressed in a sensor skin. Your eyes were protected by 3D glasses, you breathed through tiny tubes that you were barely aware of. Conditions in which you experienced virtuality in such a way that reality afterward seemed shabby, artificial, and irritating.

"A tiny little injection," the woman continued, "into the corners of your eyes. It paralyze the lids. The eyes are moistened, but you cannot anymore close them. You have to watch everything. *C'est pour les masochistes.*"

It's far worse having to *listen* to everything, Jericho thought. For instance, your ridiculous accent. He wondered how he knew the woman. She must have come from some film or other.

"Where are we actually going, Yoyo?" he asked, even though he had guessed. This connection was a wormhole: it led out of the monitored world of cybernetic Shanghai into a region that was probably unknown to the Internet Police. Lights darted past, a crazy flickering. The sphere started to turn. Jericho looked between his feet through the transparent floor and saw an end to the shaft, except that it seemed to be widening.

"Yo Yo?" She laughed a tinkling laugh. "I am not Yo Yo. *Le violà!*"

A moment later they were floating under a pulsating starry sky. Rotating slowly before their eyes was a shimmering structure that looked like a spiral galaxy and yet could have been something completely different. It looked to Jericho like something alive. He leaned forward, but they spent only a few seconds in this majestic continuum before shooting into the middle of a conduit of light.

And floated again.

This time he knew they had reached their goal.

"Impressed?" asked the woman.

Jericho said nothing. Miles below them stretched a boundless, blue-green ocean. Tiny clouds drifted close above the surface, their backs sprinkled with pink and orange. The sphere sank toward something big that drifted high above the clouds, something with a mountain and wooded slopes, waterfalls, meadows, and beaches. Jericho glimpsed swarms of flying creatures. Colossal beasts grazed on the banks of a glittering river, which snaked around the volcanic peak and flowed into the sea—

No, not flowed.

Fell!

In a great banner of foam the water plunged over the edge of the flying island and scattered into the bluish green of the ocean. The closer they came, the more it looked to Jericho like a gigantic UFO. He threw his head back and saw two suns shining in the sky, one emitting a white light, the other bathed in a strange, turquoise aura. Their vehicle fell faster, braked, and followed the course of the river. Jericho caught a swift glimpse of the enormous animals—they weren't like anything he had ever seen before. Then they darted off over gently undulating fields, beyond which the terrain fell to a snow-white beach.

"You will be picked up once more," said the Frenchwoman, with a little wave. The sphere disappeared, as did she, and Jericho found himself squatting in the sand.

"I'm here," said Yoyo.

He raised his head and saw her coming toward him, barefoot, her slender body swathed in a short, shiny tunic. Her avatar was the perfect depiction of her, which somehow relieved him. After that fanciful copy of Irma La Douce he'd worried—

That was it! The Frenchwoman had reminded him of a character in a film, and now he knew at last who it was. She was the perfect recreation of Shirley McLaine in her role as Irma La Douce. An ancient flick, sixty or seventy years old. That Jericho knew it at all was down to his passion for twentieth-century cinema.

Yoyo looked at him in silence for a while. Then she said, "Is it true about Grand Cherokee?"

"What?"

"That you killed him."

Jericho shook his head.

"It's only true that he's dead. Kenny killed him."

"Kenny?"

"The man who murdered your friends too."

"I don't know if I can trust you."

She came up to him and fixed him with her dark eyes. "You saved me in the steelworks, but that doesn't necessarily mean anything, or does it?"

"No," he admitted. "Not necessarily."

She nodded. "Let's walk for a while."

Jericho looked around. He didn't know what to make of it all. Filigree creatures were landing a little way off, neither birds nor insects. They reminded him of flying plants, if anything. He tore his eyes away and together they strolled along the beach.

"We came across the ocean when we were looking around the net for safe hiding places," Yoyo explained. "Pure chance. Perhaps we should have moved here with the control center right away, but I wasn't entirely sure if we'd really be undisturbed here."

"So you didn't program this world?" asked Jericho.

"The island, yes. Everything else was here. Ocean, sky and clouds, weird animals in the water, which sometimes come right close to the surface. The two suns go up and down, slightly out of sync. There's also land. So far we've only seen some in the distance."

"Someone must have made all this."

"You think so?"

"There's a server with the data stored on it."

"We haven't been able to identify it so far. I'm inclined to think there's a whole network involved."

"Possibly a government network," Jericho speculated.

"Hardly."

"How can you be sure of that? I mean, what's going on here? In whose interest is it to create a world like this? For what purpose?"

"An end in itself, perhaps?" She shrugged. "Nobody today is capable of grasping Second Life as a whole. Over the past few years tools have been produced in vast numbers, and they're constantly being modified. Everyone builds his own world. Most of it's garbage, some of it's incredibly brilliant. You can get in here, not there. In general they adhere to the rule that everyone can see what other people see, but I'm not sure even that's true. In some regions they have completely alien algorithms."

Jericho had stepped close to the edge. Where water should have played on the beach, the strand fell vertiginously away. Far below them the light of the suns scattered on the rippled surface of the ocean.

"You mean, this world was made by bots?"

"I'm not the sort of idiot who makes a new religion out of disk space." Yoyo stepped up next to him. "But what I think is that artificial intelligence is starting to penetrate the web in a way that its creators couldn't have imagined. Computers are creating computers. Second Life has reached a stage whereby it's developing out of its own impulses. Adaptation and selection, you understand? No one can say when that started, and no one has any idea where it's going to end. What's happening is the consistent continuation of evolution with other means. Cybernetic Darwinism."

"How did you get here?"

"What I said. Chance. We were looking for a bugproof corner. I thought it was hopelessly old-fashioned, squatting like migrant workers in the Andromeda or the steelworks, where Cypol could walk through the door at any time. Okay, they can kick in your door on the net as well. If you encrypt, you're finished, you might as well just invite them to arrest you. We communicated via blogs, with data distortion and anonymization. But even that didn't do it. So I thought, let's move to Second Life. There they can go searching for you like mad, but they don't know what they're looking for. All their ontologies and taxonomies don't work here."

Jericho nodded. Second Life was an ideal hiding place, if you wanted to escape State surveillance. Virtual worlds were far more complicated in their construction and more difficult to control than simple blogs or chat rooms. There was a difference between putting textual building blocks in a suspicious context and drawing conclusions about conspiracies and dodgy attitudes from the gestures, facial expressions, appearance, and environments of virtual people. In Second Life everything and everyone can be code, whether friend or foe.

It was only logical that no single organization in China had as many staff as the State internet surveillance authority. Cypol tried to penetrate every area of the virtual cosmos, and it was no more able to do that than the regular police were able to infiltrate the population in the real world. In spite of their massive apparatus they lacked the human staff required to keep countless millions of users under observation. Cypol relied on destabilization. Not everyone in Second Life was a government agent by any means, but they could be: the sharp businesswoman, the friendly banker, the stripper, the willing sex partner, the alien and the winged dragon, the robot and the DJ, even a tree, a guitar, or a whole building. As an additional consequence of chronic staff shortage, the government worked with great armies of bots, avatars that were guided not by human beings, but by machines pretending to be human beings.

By now there were highly refined bot programs. Every now and again, in the course of his Second Life missions, Jericho allowed Diane to take virtual form, and she appeared as a tiny, fluttering elf, white, androgynous, with insect-like, black eyes, and transparent dragonfly wings. She might equally well have appeared as a seductive woman and turned the heads of real guys who didn't notice that they were flirting with a computer. At moments like that Diane became a bot that you could only track down using the Turing test, a procedure that no machine was capable of performing, even in 2025. Anyone could carry out the test. It involved engaging a machine in dialogue long enough for it to reveal its cognitive limitations and out itself as a refined but ultimately stupid program.

And herein lay the problem of bot agents. Without genuine intelligence and capacity for abstraction, they were hardly capable of unmasking the behavior and appearance of virtual people as codes. Small wonder, then, that Yoyo and her Guardians had focused their attention on Second Life: since the decentralized structure of the peer-to-peer network was ideally suited to the creation of hidden spaces, it was extremely hard to identify senders and receivers of data, and the number of worlds tended toward infinity. In fact, only the itineraries of the data between the servers could be reconstructed.

Servers themselves worked with many electronic doorkeepers. Anyone who visited a server and was allowed in was subject to the control of the webmaster in question, while visitors to the server couldn't check one another if they didn't have the requisite authorization.

The webmaster of Cyber-Shanghai was Beijing. If Jericho had had an investigation center in the virtual metropolis, he would have been a tenant of the Chinese government, which meant that the authorities would be able to knock at his door and turn his electronic office on its head with a search warrant (although to do that they would have needed judicial permission, which the Chinese were reluctant to grant). That was the only reason Jericho had never considered moving his office there.

He looked out at the bluish-green expanse.

Was it possible that this world had actually been created by a bot network? If computers developed something like aesthetic aspirations, they were copied from those of human beings, while at the same time being unsettlingly alien.

"And is the island safe?"

Yoyo nodded. "We've drilled into cyberspace at every available point to build our own planets, in such a way that not everyone can get there. Jia Wei—" She hesitated. "—has calculated millions of simultaneous possibilities. That included modifying the protocol. Not significantly, just in such a way that the uninitiated end up in a jumble of data if they don't have the right key. No idea how many variations we tried out, we generated them at random because we thought it was a new idea. Instead we ended up here."

"And the protocol is—"

"A little green lizard."

Yoyo smiled. It was the same sad smile that he knew from Chen Hongbing's photograph.

"Of course Cyber-Shanghai's server records the intervention, but it doesn't raise the alarm. It doesn't register the momentary opening of an electronic wormhole, through which you escape into a kind of parallel universe. As far as it's concerned, all that happens is that someone opens a door and closes it again."

"I figured it was something like that." Jericho nodded. "So who's Irma La Douce?"

"Hey!" Yoyo raised her eyebrows. "You know Irma La Douce?"

"Of course."

"Heavens! I hadn't the slightest idea who she was when Daxiong turned up with her."

"A film. A lovely film."

"A film about a French *poule*."

"Perhaps it doesn't necessarily represent the glorious Chinese culture," said Jericho mildly. "But there's something else, think about it. The avatar is, incidentally, a perfect copy of Shirley McLaine."

"She—erm—was an actress, right? A French one."

"American."

Yoyo seemed to think for a second. Then she suddenly laughed out loud.

"Oh, that's going to nettle Daxiong. He thinks he knows everything there is to know."

"About films?"

"Not at all. Daxiong has this thing about France. As if we didn't have enough culture of our own. He could bang on at you all day about—Oh, it doesn't matter."

She turned away and ran her hand over her eyes. Jericho left her in peace. When she turned back to face him he saw the smeared remains of a tear on her cheek.

"You've got my computer," she said. "So, what do you want? What do you want from me?"

"Nothing," said Jericho.

"But?"

"Your father sent me. He's terribly worried about you."

"Don't think I don't care," she said belligerently.

"I don't." He shook his head. "I know you don't want to worry him. You thought your communications were being monitored, and that if you sent him an e-mail they'd pounce on him and give him a going-over. Am I right?"

She stared gloomily ahead.

"Hongbing doesn't know about blogs and virtual worlds," Jericho went on. "He's happy to be able to use an antediluvian cell phone. And he's consoling himself with the idea that his daughter has learned her lesson. He doesn't know what you're doing. Or let's say, he guesses what you're up to and doesn't know. I'm sure he hasn't the faintest idea that Tu Tian is protecting you."

"Tian!" cried Yoyo. "He commissioned you, right?"

"He referred your father to me."

"Sure, because Hongbing never—But why didn't he—?"

"Why didn't he send a message for you to the Andromeda? Even though he knew where you'd holed up? I mean, you never told him anything about the blast furnace, so in the end he got nervous—"

"How do you know Tian?"

"He's a friend of mine. And, I should think, a kind of unofficial member of the Guardians. At least he supported you as best he could. The stuff in the control center came from him, didn't it? Tian was just as much of a dissident as you are now."

"As we were."

Oh, right, thought Jericho. What a miserable subject. Whatever they were talking about, that was where they would always end up.

"Tian didn't need to send me a message," said Yoyo. "He knew it wouldn't change a thing."

"Exactly. But it changed something when Hongbing hit on the idea of having a search made for you. A risky enterprise. Your father might prefer to act ignorant, but he knew he couldn't get the police involved. I guess he secretly knew that you were going through the Party's garbage containers out the back. So he asked Tu Tian, the way you ask somebody with connections like that, and also because he accepted through gritted teeth that Tian might have been closer to you than your own—"

"That's not true," Yoyo rounded on him. "You're talking nonsense!"

"But that's how it looks to—"

"That has nothing to do with you! Nothing at all, okay? Keep out of my private life."

Jericho tilted his head.

"Okay, princess. As far as I can. So what was Tian supposed to do? Slap Hongbing on the shoulder and say, no need to worry? I know something you don't know. But all right, your private life is sacred to me, even if it's cost me my car and possibly my apartment, which could go up in flames at any moment. You're causing a lot of stress, Yoyo."

A wrinkle of fury appeared between her eyebrows. She opened her mouth, but Jericho interrupted: "Save it for later."

"But—"

"We can't go on wasting time on your island forever. Let's see how we're going to get ourselves out of this mess."

"We?"

"You're not listening, are you?" Jericho showed his teeth. "I'm in this too, so take a good hard look, young lady! You've lost your friends. Why do you think all this happened? Because you stirred up a bit of dust? The Party is used to stepping in dissident shit. They might send you to jail for it, but they're never going to send someone like Kenny."

Her eyes filled with tears.

"I couldn't—"

Jericho bit his lip. He was about to make a mistake. Blaming Yoyo for the deaths of the others was as unfair as it was stupid.

"I'm sorry," he said hastily.

She sniffed, took a step in one direction, then another, and then sliced the air with her trembling hands.

"Maybe I should have—I should have—"

"No, it's okay. There's nothing you can do about it."

"If only I hadn't come up with that stupid idea!"

"Tell me about it. What did you do?"

"Nothing would have happened. It's my fault, I—"

"It isn't."

"It is!"

"No, Yoyo, there's nothing you can do about it. Tell me what you've done. What happened during the night?"

"I didn't want any of that." Her lips trembled. "It's my fault they're dead. They're all dead."

"Yoyo—"

She threw her hands to her face. Jericho walked over, gently took her wrists, and tried to draw them down. She pulled back and staggered away from him.

He heard a deep, throaty growl behind him.

What was it this time? He slowly turned around and looked into the golden eyes of an enormous bear.

Very impressive, he thought.

"Daxiong."

The bear showed its teeth. Jericho didn't move. The beast was pretty much as big as a middle-sized pony. Of course the simulation didn't put him in any danger, but he didn't know what impulses were emitted by the gloves. They produced haptic sensations, meaning that they stimulated the nerves. Would they also emit pain if the monster decided to start chewing his fingers?

"It's okay." Yoyo had joined him. She stroked the huge animal's fur, then looked at Jericho. Her voice was calm again, almost expressionless.

"We tried something out that night," she said. "A way of sending messages."

"Via e-mail?"

"Yes. The whole thing was my idea. Jia Wei supplied the method."

She tapped the bear on the nose. It lowered its head and a moment later it was gone.

"We're in touch with a lot of activists," she went on. "We wouldn't be able to get hold of the relevant information without them. Of course we can't openly ask Washington what dirty tricks China's up to, and I'm registered as a dissident, okay?"

"Okay."

"So, Second Life is one way of tricking Cypol. It always involves a lot of effort. Good for a meeting like ours, but I wanted something quick and uncomplicated, just to send through a photograph or a few lines." Yoyo stared at the spot where the bear had stood. "And there's a constant traffic of mails. Boring, unsuspicious mails containing nothing that would scare the Politburo. So we've tried to hop other people's freight trains."

"Parasite mails?"

"Piggybacks, parasites, stowaways—whatever you want to call it. Jia Wei and I wrote a protocol that lets you encode messages in white noise and decode them again; we used it between Daxiong and me and decided to do a test."

Jericho was gradually working out what had happened that night. The basic idea was designed to trick even the cleverest surveillance experts. It was based on the fundamental principle of e-mail traffic, which was that mails were primarily a collection of data, little travelers that wanted to be helped on their way. So they were crammed into packets of data like passengers into railway cars, and like those cars the packets had a standard length. If one car was full, the next one turned up, until there was room for the whole message and it could be sent, with the receiver's web address up at the front as the locomotive.

But the difference in the quantities of data usually meant that the last compartment was only partly occupied. The phrase *end of message* defined where the message ended, but because a packet could only be sent as a whole, there was usually some data-free space left over, what was known as white noise. As it arrived, the receiving computer selected the official data of the message, cut the rest off, and threw it away. It didn't occur to anyone to look through the white noise for further content, because there was nothing to be found there.

That was where the idea began. Whoever had it first, it was and remained brilliant. A secret message was coded in such a way that it looked like white noise, was immediately switched for the real white noise and sent on its way like a stowaway. There was only one problem that needed to be solved. You had to send the message yourself, or have access to the sender's computer. There was no reason not to let stowaways travel on their own trains. But once you'd attracted attention, your e-mail traffic would be under constant surveillance. Organizations like Cypol might be overstretched, but they weren't stupid, so it was to be feared that they would also check up on white noise.

But there was a solution, which was to use other people's e-mail traffic. Two dissidents who wanted to pass a conspiratorial message one to the other each needed a router or illegal railway station to stop passing data-trains, and of course they had to agree on the same train. It might be birthday greetings from Mr. Huang in Shenzen to his nephew Yi living in Beijing, both reputable citizens with nothing bad to be said about them as far as the State was concerned. So Mr. Huang sent off his birthday greetings without guessing for a moment that his train was about to make an unscheduled stop with Dissident One, who took charge of the white noise, swapped it for the disguised message, and sent the train on its way again. But before it reached Yi, it was stopped again, this time by Dissident Two, who received the message, decoded it, replaced it with real white noise, and now at last it went on to the nephew in Beijing, who was assured of Mr. Huang's esteem, while neither of them knew what purpose they had served. The whole thing suggested innocent tourists who had drugs secretly smuggled into their luggage at the airport and then taken out again at the other end, with the significant difference that the drugs didn't assume the appearance and consistency of their underwear.

"Of course we weren't so naïve as to assume that we'd invented the trick," said Yoyo. "But it's really not that likely that you're going to come across an e-mail that already has a stowaway."

"And whose official mail did you intercept?"

"It came from some government authority or other." Yoyo shrugged. "The Ministry of Energy or something."

"Where exactly?"

"Wait, it was—it was—" She frowned and looked defiant. "Okay, don't know."

"I'm sorry?" Jericho looked at her in disbelief. "You don't know who—?"

"For the love of heaven! It was only a test! Just to see if I could get into it!"

"And what did you write?"

"Just something."

"Come on! What was it?"

"I—" She seemed to chew the sentence a number of times before spitting it out at Jericho's feet: "*Catch me if you can.*"

"*Catch me if you can?*"

"Am I talking Mongolian? Yesss!"

"Why that?"

"*Why that?*" she said, copying him. "Doesn't matter. Because I thought it was cool, that's why."

"Very cool. In a test—"

"Oh, son-of-a-turtle!" She rolled her eyes. "No—one—was—supposed—to—read—it!"

Jericho sighed and shook his head.

"All right. Go on?"

"The protocol was set to real time. Stop mail, take out noise, put in own message, encode, pass on, all at the same time. So, I write, and at the same time I notice there's something in it already! That I haven't taken out any white noise at all, but some kind of mysterious stuff."

"Because someone else was trying to do the same thing as you were."

"Yes."

Jericho nodded. In fairness, he had to admit that Yoyo couldn't have anticipated this development.

"But by then the e-mail was already on its way again," he said. "To the person that the mysterious stuff was meant for. Except that it never got there, because you'd taken it out and swapped it."

"Unwittingly."

"Doesn't matter. Imagine this. They're waiting for some complex, secret information. Instead they read: *Catch me if you can.*" Jericho couldn't help it. He raised his hands in the air and applauded. "Bravo, Yoyo. Lovely little provocation. My congratulations."

"Oh, fuck you! Of course they immediately worked out that someone had broken in."

"And they were prepared."

"Yes, unlike me." She pulled a sour face. "I mean, I don't know if they'd expected something like that *exactly*, but their defenses work, you'd have to give them that. Some kind of watchdog program immediately started barking: woof! An extra hub has appeared in the predetermined route, it shouldn't be there. Grrr, where are our data?"

"And traced you back?"

"Traced me back?" Yoyo gave a short, sharp laugh. "They attacked me! They attacked my computer, I don't know how. It was absolutely terrifying! While I'm still gawping at what I've pulled out of the water, I see them starting to download my data. I couldn't get online quickly enough as they went through my stuff. They knew exactly who I was—and *where* I was!"

"Does that mean you don't have an anonymizer—"

"I'm not stupid," she hissed. "Of course I use an anonymizer. But if you're implementing something completely new and playing around with it, you're forced to open up your system for a moment. Otherwise the protection tools downstairs would get in your way, that's what they're there for."

"So you turned various things off."

"I had to take that risk." Her eyes flashed with fury. "I had to be sure we could work like that."

"Well, now you know."

"Lovely, Mister Brain Box." She folded her arms. "What would you have done?"

"One bit at a time," said Jericho. "First take out the attachment and check it for land mines. Then put my own thing in there. Leave myself the option of cancelling everything before I send it off. And most importantly, don't put any smug little phrases in there, even if you've encoded it as noise a thousand times over."

"What's the point of data transfer that doesn't make sense?"

"We're talking about a test. As long as you don't know for sure whether your data transfer is safe or not, you've got to sound like a communication error. They might have wondered where their message ended up, but it wouldn't immediately have occurred to them that someone was tapping off their communication."

She looked at him as if she was thinking of tearing his throat out. Then she spread her arms and let them fall back helplessly by her side.

"Okay, it was a mistake!"

"A big mistake."

"Could I have guessed, out of all the billions and billions of mails I would hit on one that had already been infiltrated?"

Jericho looked at her. His rage had flared up for a moment, less about the mistake than about the fact that someone with Yoyo's experience could have made it. With her complacency, she hadn't just put her own life on the line. Almost the whole of her group had been killed, and Jericho didn't feel exactly safe. Then his fury evaporated. He saw the mixture of fear and dismay on her face and shook his head.

"No. You couldn't."

"So who's on my case?"

"Our case, Yoyo, if you'll forgive me. If I might just remind you about me and my problems."

She averted her head, looked out at the sea, and back at him.

"Okay. Ours."

"Doubtless someone with power. People with money and influence, technically advanced. To be quite honest I doubt that their communication is still at the experimental stage. You've tried something out. They've been doing it for ages. Just by chance you're using the same protocol, which allowed each of you to read the other's data. From that point it gets speculative, but I also believe that they're influential enough not to be dependent on other people's e-mails."

"You mean—"

"Let's assume they're sending mails from their own servers. Quite officially. They're based in public institutions, they can check incoming and outgoing traffic, and pack anything in there as they see fit."

"They sound like senior officials."

"You think it's the Party?"

"Who else? All the Guardians' operations are—were—directed against the Party. And we have no illusions about it, the Guardians are—were—"

"—another word for Yoyo."

"I was the head. Along with Daxiong."

"I know. You mouthed off, which got State security on your back. Since then you've tried to find ways of protecting yourself. Second Life, parasite e-mails. And in the process, without meaning to, you break into a secret data transfer, and your worst fears become reality. There's something about 'coup' and 'liquidating' in connection with the Chinese government, and a minute later they've tracked you down."

"What would you have done in my place?"

"What indeed?" Jericho laughed mirthlessly. "I'd have got the hell out, just like you did."

"That's comforting." She hesitated. "So did you—were you on my computer?"

"Yes."

Jericho expected another blaze of fury, but she just sighed and looked out at the ocean.

"Don't worry," he said. "I haven't been snooping. I've just tried to introduce some clarity into the whole business."

"Did you get anywhere with the third website?"

"The Swiss films?"

"Mmhm."

"Not so far. But there must be something on there. Either you need a separate mask or there's something we've overlooked. At the moment I think it's about a coup in which the Chinese government was—or will be—involved, and that someone knows too much and that his liquidation is being considered."

"Someone called Jan or Andre."

"More likely Andre. Did you research the address in Berlin?"

"Yes."

"Interesting, isn't it? *Donner be liquidated.* Somebody called Andre Donner runs a restaurant specializing in African delicacies at that address."

"The Muntu. I'd got that far."

"But what does that tell us?" Jericho reflected. "Is Andre Donner in danger of being liquidated? I mean, what does a Berlin chef know about Beijing's involvement in some sort of planned coup? And what about the second man?"

"Jan?"

"Yes. Is he the killer?"

Or, is Jan the same as Kenny? Jericho thought, but kept the thought to himself. His imagination was fizzing. Basically the fragment of text was too mutilated to provide any useful conclusions.

"It's an African restaurant," Yoyo said thoughtfully. "And it hasn't been around for very long."

Jericho looked at her in amazement.

"Okay, I've had more time to look into it," she added. "There are reviews on the net. Donner opened Muntu in December 2024—"

"Only six months ago?"

"Exactly. You can hardly find any information about the man himself. A Dutchman who lived in Cape Town for a while, perhaps was even born there. That's it. But the African connection is interesting in that—"

"—in that Africa's familiar with coups." Jericho nodded. "That means we need to take a closer look at the more recent chronology of any dubious or violent government takeovers. An interesting approach. Except that South Africa is ruled out. They've been stable for a long time."

They fell silent for a while.

"You wanted to know who we were dealing with," he said at last. "To engineer coups you need money and influence, both political and economic. But above all you need to have a capable executive, and one that's willing to engage in violence. So these people have managed to set an expert with reinforcements on your trail. Equipped like an army. So let's assume that certain government circles are behind this. Then I think I can put your mind at rest in one respect."

Yoyo raised her eyebrows.

"They're not interested in dissidents," Jericho said finally. "They don't give a damn about what you're up to. They would have hunted down anyone who got in their way . . ."

"Very reassuring," Yoyo sneered. "And instead they have hordes of cops who will, when time's up, give me the pleasant feeling that it's not because of my dissident activities that they're going to kill me. Thanks Jericho. I can sleep again at last."

He gazed along the beach. Shimmering in the double sunlight, it looked oddly vivid. Patterns formed spontaneously in the sand and immediately blurred again. Some of the flower-like creatures spread their wings, transparent and veined as leaves. Clouds of golden dust puffed up among them, and were carried over the edge of the island, where they scattered in the wind. Yoyo and Daxiong had programmed a world of unsettling beauty.

"Okay," he said. "I have a few suggestions. First of all I need your permission to upload your data onto my computer. As far as I can tell, all your backup systems have been destroyed."

"Apart from one."

"I know. Can I ask what computer you're connected to at the moment?"

She chewed her lip and looked around, as if there were someone there to advise her.

"It's at Daxiong's," she said reluctantly.

"Where? In the workshop?"

"Yes. He lives there."

"And you'll get away straight after the meeting."

"Daxiong's cellar is safe, we—"

"Kenny fires rockets," Jericho interrupted her gruffly, "which means that nothing is safe. The workshop is registered as Demon Point, under the name City Demons. It's only a matter of time until Kenny turns up there or sends someone. Does Daxiong have a complete copy of your data?"

"No."

"Then let me download it."

"Okay."

Jericho thought for a moment and counted the points up on his fingers. "Secondly, we'll follow the African trail. Thirdly, we'll try to crack the Spanish website with the films of Switzerland. Both down to me. Diane has the relevant programs, she—"

"Diane?"

"My—my—" Suddenly he felt embarrassed. "Doesn't matter. Fourthly, what do all six pages, valid and invalid, have in common?"

"That's obvious." Yoyo looked at him uncomprehendingly. "They contain, or contained—"

"And following on from that?"

"Hey! Can you stop sounding like a bloody headmaster?"

"Someone will have to check them," Jericho continued, unfazed, "to make sure that the mask—the decoder program—always fits. In terms of content there doesn't seem to be a connection, all the pages are publicly accessible and registered in various countries. But who initiated them? If we can find a common initiator, we might be able to find out which other pages he controls. The more pages we find that fit our mask, the more we will decode."

"I don't know how to do that. And neither does Tian."

"But I do." Jericho took a deep breath. For a moment he imagined it was the clear air of the ocean planet flowing through his capillaries, but he was only breathing whatever the air-conditioning was blowing into his room. With every word he uttered he felt strength and resolution returning. The certainty that he hadn't been handed over defenseless to Kenny and the people behind him flooded his consciousness like a physical glow. "Fifth, we assume that Andre Donner is on the hit list same as we are. And that immediately gives us two reasons to get in contact with him. To find out more about our own case, and to warn him."

"If he needs a warning."

"So we have nothing to lose. Do we?"

"No."

"Okay then." He hesitated. "Yoyo, I don't want to keep coming back to it, but who else have you told about your discovery? I mean, which of them—"

"Which of them is still alive?" she asked bitterly.

Jericho said nothing.

"Only Daxiong," she said. "And you."

She crouched down and let nacreous sand slip through her fingers. The thin streams formed mysterious patterns on the ground before vanishing in a shimmer of light. Then she raised her head.

"I want to call my father."

Jericho nodded. "That would have been my next suggestion."

He wondered if it mightn't have been more sensible to make contact with Tu first. But that decision was entirely up to the girl at his feet, who was now slowly standing up and looking at him with beautiful, sad eyes.

"Shall I leave you alone?" he asked.

"No." She gave an unladylike sniff, and turned her back on him. "Maybe it's better if you're here."

The fingers of her right hand moved through the void, etching something into it. A moment later a dark field appeared in the clear air. An old-fashioned dial tone was heard, absurdly mundane and out of place in this strange world.

"He hasn't activated picture mode," she said, as if apologizing for Hongbing's backwardness.

"I know, his old phone. You gave it to him."

"I'm amazed he's still using it," she snorted. It went on ringing. "He should really be at the car dealership. If he doesn't pick up, I'll call th—"

The dial tone stopped. There was a quiet rustling sound, along with other background noises. No one spoke.

Yoyo looked uncertainly at Jericho.

"Father?" she whispered.

The answer came quietly. It crept up ominously, a fat, weary snake rearing up to take a closer look at its next victim.

"I'm not your father, Yoyo."

Jericho didn't know what was going to happen. Yoyo was stricken, her friends were dead. She had to deal with the sort of images that are only bearable in nightmares, whose horror subsides in the morning light. But there was no awaking from this nightmare—Kenny's voice seeped like poison into the island idyll. But when Yoyo spoke, there was nothing but suppressed rage in her words.

"Where is my father?"

Kenny took his time, a long time, before answering. Yoyo in turn said nothing, waiting frostily, so both of them remained silent, a mute test of strength.

"I've given him the day off," he said at last. He crowned the remark with a smug, quiet chuckle.

"That doesn't answer my question."

"No one told you to ask questions."

"Is he well?"

"Very well. He's taking a rest."

The way Kenny said "very well" was designed to suggest the precise opposite. Yoyo clenched her fists.

"Listen, you sick fuck. I want to talk to my father right away, you hear? After that you can make your demands, but first give me a sign of life, or else you can go on talking to yourself. Did you get any of that?"

Kenny let the rustling noise continue down the line for a while.

"Yoyo, my jade girl," he sighed. "Clearly your worldview is based on a series of misunderstandings. In stories like this the roles are assigned in a different way. Every one of your words that doesn't meet with my absolute approval will cause pain to Hongbing. I'll let you off with the 'sick fuck.'" He giggled. "You could even be right."

Vain as a peacock, thought Jericho. Kenny might be a pretty exotic specimen of a contract killer, but he seemed much closer to the profile of a psychopathic serial killer. Narcissistic, in love with his own words, flirting affectionately with his own obnoxiousness.

"A sign of life," Yoyo insisted.

All of a sudden the black rectangle changed. Kenny's face filled it almost completely. He hovered above the pearly beach like a spirit in a bottle. Then he vanished from the camera's perspective, and a room became visible, with a wall of windows at the back, bright daylight falling through them. The outlines of some items of furniture could be seen, a chair with someone sitting on it. In front of it, something black, massive, and three-legged.

"Father," whispered Yoyo.

"Please say something, honorable Chen," said Kenny's voice.

Chen Hongbing sat as motionless on his chair as if he had become a part of it. With the light behind him, it was almost impossible to make out his face. When he spoke he sounded as if someone was walking on dry leaves.

"Yoyo. Are you okay?"

"Father," she cried. "It's all fine, everything's going to be fine!"

"It—I'm so sorry."

"No, I'm the one who's sorry. I really am!" A moment later her eyes filled with tears. With a visible effort of will she forced herself to calm down. Kenny appeared in the picture again.

"Terrible quality, this phone," he said. "I'm afraid your father could hardly hear you. Perhaps you could come and see him, what do you think?"

"If you do anything—" Yoyo began unsteadily.

"What I do is entirely up to you," Kenny replied coolly. "He's quite comfortable at the moment, except that his mobility is a little restricted. He is sitting in the sights of an automatic rifle. He can speak and blink. If he suddenly feels like jumping in the air or just raising his arm, the gun will go off. Unfortunately it will also do that if he tries to scratch himself. Not quite so cozy, perhaps."

"Please don't hurt him," sobbed Yoyo.

"I'm not interested in hurting anyone, believe it or not. So come here, and come quickly." Kenny paused. When he went on talking, the snakelike tone had left his voice. Suddenly he sounded friendly again, almost matey, the way Zhao Bide had spoken. "Your father has my word that nothing will happen as long as you cooperate. That involves telling me the names of everyone who knows about the intercepted message, or even what was in it. And you are to give me every, really *every* drive with a download of the message on it."

"You destroyed my computer," said Yoyo.

"I destroyed something, yes. But did I destroy *everything*?"

"Don't contradict him," Jericho whispered to Yoyo.

She said nothing.

"You see." Kenny smiled as if his assumption had been confirmed. "Don't worry, I'll keep my word. And bring that shaven-headed giant with you, you remember the one. You will both come in through the front door, it's open." He paused. Something seemed to go through his head, then he asked, "By the way, has this guy Owen Jericho been in touch with you?"

"Jericho?" Yoyo echoed.

"The detective?"

Jericho had been keeping out of view of the phone, so that he saw the scene in Chen's apartment, but couldn't be seen by Kenny. He gave Yoyo a sign and shook his head violently.

"I have no idea where that idiot is," she said contemptuously.

"Why so harsh?" Kenny raised his eyebrows in amazement. "He saved you."

"He wants to jerk me around the same as you do, doesn't he? You said he killed Grand Cherokee."

A flicker of amusement played around Kenny's lips.

"Yes. Of course. So, when can you get here?"

"As quick as I can," sniffed Yoyo. "Depends on the traffic. Quarter of an hour? Is that okay?"

"Completely okay. You and Daxiong. Unarmed. I see a gun, Chen dies. Anyone else comes through the door, he dies. Anyone tries to disarm the automatic rifle, off it goes. As soon as everything's sorted out, we'll leave the house together. Oh, yes—if reinforcements are waiting outside or anyone tries to play the hero, Chen dies too. He can only leave his chair when I've deactivated the mechanism."

The line went dead.

The weird calls of big animals reached them from the distance. A breeze rustled the bushes that lined the beach to the meadow, and set clusters of blossom bobbing up and down.

"That bastard," groaned Yoyo. "That damned—"

"Whatever he is, he's not omnipotent."

"He isn't?" she yelled at him. "You saw what's going on! Do you really think he'll let him live? Or me?"

"Yoyo—"

"So what am I supposed to do?" She shrank back. Her lower lip was trembling. She shook her head, as tears ran down her cheeks. "What on earth am I supposed to do? What should I do?"

"Hey," he said. "We'll get him out of there. I promise you. No one's going to die, you hear?"

"And how are you going to achieve that?"

Jericho started walking up and down. He didn't really know either, yet. Bit by bit, a plan was starting to form in his head. A crazy undertaking that depended on a whole series of very different factors. The glass façade behind Chen Hongbing played a part in it, as did the captured airbike. He needed to talk to Tu Tian as well.

"Forget it," said Yoyo breathlessly. "Let's go."

"Wait."

"But I can't wait! I have to get to my father. Let's get out of here." She held her right hand out to him.

"Hang on, Yoyo—"

"Now!"

"Just one minute. I—" He chewed on his bottom lip. "I know how we're going to do this. I know!"

HONGKOU

The house on Siping Lu, number 1276, had retained the monotonous pastel of some of the apartment complexes built in the Shanghai district of Hongkou at the turn of the millennium. When the weather was gloomy it seemed to disappear into the sky. As if to counteract this, emphatically green-tinted panes of glass broke up the façade, another stylistic device of an era that made even skyscrapers look like cheap toys.

Unlike the high-rises a street further on, number 1276 contented itself with six floors, had generously sized balconies, and also flaunted what looked a bit like a pagoda roof. On either side of the balconies, the dirty white boxes of the air-conditioning system clung to the plaster. Listlessly flapping in the wind was a tattered banner, on which the inhabitants of the building demanded the immediate suspension of building work on the Maglev, another elevated highway that would lead right past their front door, and whose pillars already loomed high above the street. Aside from this pitiful gesture toward revolt, the building was no different from number 1274 or 1278.

The apartment, covering an area of 38 square meters, comprised a living room with a wall unit, dining area, and sofa bed; a separate bedroom; a tiny bathroom; and a kitchen, only slightly bigger, that opened onto the dining table. There was no hall, and instead a screen at the side masked off the front door, creating a small amount of intimacy.

Until recently at any rate.

Now it leaned folded against the wall, so that the whole of the area around the front door was visible. Xin had made himself comfortable on the sofa bed, a little way away from the chair on whose edge Chen Hongbing sat as if lost in contemplation, tall, angular, bolt upright. His temples glistened in the light that fell through the glass façade to the rear and dissolved into tiny droplets of sweat that covered his taut skin. Xin weighed the remote control for the automatic rifle in his hand, a flat, feather-light screen. He had told the old man that any sudden movement would lead to his death. But the mechanism had not been activated. Xin didn't want to risk the old man bringing about his own demise through sheer nervousness.

"Maybe you should take me hostage," Chen said into the silence.

Xin yawned. "Haven't I done that already?"

"I mean, I—I could put myself at your mercy for longer, until you no longer saw Yoyo as a threat."

"And where would that get you?"

"My daughter would live," Chen replied hoarsely. It looked odd, the way he uttered words without any gestures, struggling to keep even the movements of his lips to the barest minimum.

Xin pretended to think for a moment.

"No, she will survive as long as she convinces me."

"I'm asking you only for my daughter's life." Chen's breathing was shallow. "I don't care about anything else."

"That honors you," said Xin. "It brings you close to the martyrs."

Suddenly he thought he saw the old man smiling. It was barely noticeable, but Xin had an eye for such small things.

"What's cheered you up?"

"The fact that you've misunderstood the situation. You think you can kill me, but there isn't much left to kill. You're too late. I've died already."

Xin began to answer, then looked at the man with fresh interest. As a rule he didn't set much store by other people's private affairs, particularly when they were eking out their final minutes. But suddenly he craved to know what Chen had meant. He got up and stood behind the tripod on which the rifle stood, so that it looked as if it were actually growing from his belly. "You'll have to explain that to me."

"I don't think it will interest you," said Chen. He looked up and his eyes were like two wounds. All of a sudden Xin had the feeling of being able to see inside that thin body, and glimpse the black mirror of a sea below a moonless sky. In its depths he sensed old suffering, self-hatred and repulsion, he heard screams and pleas, doors rattling and slamming shut. Groans of resignation, echoing faintly down endless, windowless corridors. They had tried to break Chen, for four whole years. Xin knew that, without knowing it. He effortlessly identified the focus point, he could touch the spots where people were most vulnerable, just as a single glance into the detective's eyes had been enough to spot his loneliness.

"You were in jail," he said.

"Not directly."

Xin hesitated. Might he have been mistaken?

"At any rate you were robbed of your freedom."

"Freedom?" Chen made a noise between a croak and a sigh. "What's that? Are you freer than me right now, when I'm sitting on this chair and you're standing in front of me? Does that thing you're pointing at me give you freedom? Do you lose your freedom if you're locked up?"

Xin pursed his lips. "You explain it to me."

"No one needs to explain it to you," Chen croaked. "You know better than anyone."

"What?"

"That anyone who threatens anyone else is frightened. Anyone who points a gun at anyone is frightened."

"So *I'm* frightened?" Xin laughed.

"Yes," Chen replied succinctly. "Repression is always based on fear. Fear of dissident opinions. Fear of being unmasked. Fear of losing power, of rejection, of insignificance. The more weapons you deploy, the higher the walls you build, the more ingenious your forms of torture, the more you are only demonstrating your own impotence. You remember Tiananmen? What happened in the Square of Heavenly Peace?"

"The student unrest?"

"I don't know how old you are. You were probably still a child when that happened. Young people demonstrating for something that had already been fought for by many others: freedom. And lined up against them a State almost paralyzed, shaken to its foundations, so much so that it finally sent in the tanks and everything sank into chaos. Who do you think was more frightened then? The students? Or the Party?"

"I was five years old," said Xin, amazed to find himself talking to a hostage as though they were sitting together in a tea house. "How the hell should I know?"

"You know. You're pointing a gun at me right now."

"True. So I would guess that you're the one who should be shit scared right now, old man!"

"You'd think so, wouldn't you?" Again a ghostly smile distorted Chen's features. "And yet I fear only for the life of my daughter. And the other thing that frightens me is that I might have got everything wrong. Stayed silent when I should have talked. That's all. Your gun there can't scare me. My inner demons are more than a match for your ridiculous gun. But you're frightened. You're frightened about what might be left if you were robbed of your weapons and other attributes of power. You're afraid of backsliding."

Xin stared at the old man.

"There's no backsliding, haven't you worked that out? There's only striding ahead in time. Just a permanent Now. The past is cold ashes."

"I agree with you there. Apart from one thing. The cold ashes are what destroys people. The consequences of destruction, on the other hand, remain."

"You can even cleanse yourself of those."

"Cleanse?" Bafflement flickered in Chen's eyes. "Of what?"

"Of what was. When you consign it to the flames. When you *burn* it! The fire purifies your soul, do you understand? So that you are born a second time."

Chen's wounded gaze drilled into his own.

"Are you talking about revenge?"

"Revenge?" Xin bared his teeth. "Revenge only makes an adversary bigger, it gives him meaning. I'm talking about complete extinction! About overcoming your own history. What tormented you, your—demons!"

"You mean you can burn those demons?"

"Of course you can!" How stupid did you have to be to deny that fundamental certainty? The whole universe, all being, all becoming, was based on transience.

"But what," Chen said after thinking for a while, "if you discover that there are no spirits? No demons. That the past has only shaped you like an image and the spirits are part of yourself. Don't you then try to extinguish yourself? In that case, is your cleansing not self-mutilation?"

Xin lowered his eyelids. The conversation was taking a turn that fascinated him.

"What have *you* burned?" asked Chen.

He wondered how to explain it to Chen, so that he would understand Xin's greatness. But suddenly he heard something. Footsteps in the corridor.

"Another time, honorable Chen," he whispered.

He walked quickly back to the sofa and turned on the automatic trigger. Now it was happening. One false move from Chen, and his body would be shredded. The footsteps came closer.

Then the door swung open and—

Yoyo saw her father sitting on the chair, facing the muzzle of the rifle. He didn't move, only his eyeballs turned slowly toward her. She sensed the tension in Daxiong's massive body beside her and stepped inside, clutching the little computer in her right hand. In the background the hit man rose from the edge of the sofa. He too held something in his hand, gleaming and flat.

"Hello, Yoyo," he hissed. "How lovely to see you again."

"Father," she said, ignoring him. "Are you okay?"

Chen Hongbing attempted a crooked smile. "In the circumstances, I would say so."

"He's fine as long as you stick to our agreement," Kenny said. "The automatic trigger has been activated. Any movement by Chen will kill him." He held the remote control in the air. "Of course I can operate the trigger, too. So whatever you were planning, forget it."

"And where do we go from here?" growled Daxiong.

"First shut the door behind you."

Daxiong gave the door a shove. It fell silently shut.

"And now?"

Kenny turned his back on them and glanced out of the glass façade at the back. He didn't seem to be in any particular hurry. Yoyo shivered and held up the computer.

"You wanted this," she said.

The hit man looked outside again for a moment. Then he turned toward them.

"Let's say yes for the time being."

"Yes or no?"

Yoyo was gradually getting nervous, but she tried not to show it. Something must have gone wrong. Why was it taking so long? Where was Jericho?

"Well?" Kenny nodded encouragingly at her. "I'm listening."

"No. I've got a few things to clear up first."

"I think I remember that we discussed everything clearly."

She shook her head. "Nothing's clear yet. What guarantee do we have that you'll let us live?"

Kenny smiled like someone experiencing an anticipated disappointment "Spare us this, Yoyo. We're not here to negotiate."

"True," snorted Daxiong. "Do you know what I think? As soon as you have what you want, you'll waste us."

"Exactly," nodded Yoyo. "So why should we tell you anything if you're going to kill us anyway? Maybe we'll take a few secrets with us to the grave."

"I gave you my word," Kenny said very quietly. "That should be enough for you."

"Your word wasn't worth much this morning."

"But we can play the game another way too," he went on, ignoring her remark. "No one has to die right away. Look at your father, Yoyo. He's a brave man, who isn't afraid of death. I can't help admiring him. I wonder how much pain he can bear."

Hongbing uttered a croaking laugh. "You'd be amazed," he said.

The hit man grinned.

"Boot up your computer. Get the encrypted file up on the screen and throw it over to me. You have no options left, Yoyo. Just your faith."

Damn Jericho, she thought. What's going on? We can't keep this bastard hanging on much longer.

Where are you?

Jericho cursed.

Until a moment ago it had gone smoothly. Almost too smoothly. While Yoyo and Daxiong were on their way to Chen, he had spoken to Tu and managed to break open the weapon chambers of the air-bike. He had chosen a high-velocity rapid fire automatic laser rifle that lay heavy and secure in the hand, started the engine, and flown the machine unimpeded to the agreed meeting point.

They had met not far from number 1276 for a quick briefing.

"It's the eighth building along." Yoyo had pointed down the street. "The backyards are all the same, with lawns and trees and a path connecting them. It's the left window side, fourth floor."

"Good," Jericho nodded.

"Have you brought my computer?"

"Yes. Daxiong too?"

"Here." The giant had handed him a rather ancient-looking computer. Jericho transferred the fragment of encrypted text to it.

"Can I have mine back now?" asked Yoyo.

"Of course." Jericho had put her computer back in his pocket. "When all this is over. It'll be safer with me until then. Kenny mustn't get the chance to take it from you."

She said nothing, which he took as a sign of assent. He had looked from her to Daxiong and back again.

"All okay?"

"So far, yes."

"You go into the apartment in five minutes exactly."

"Okay."

"And I'll be there straight after, and get his back to the wall. Any more questions?"

They both mutely shook their heads.

"Good."

In five minutes.

That was now! And he was still standing on the corner of the street, because the airbike had suddenly started behaving like a diva who refused to go on stage, however much you cajoled her.

"Come on," he snapped.

This part of Hongkou was entirely residential, and Siping Lu was a feeder road, several lanes wide. There were hardly any shops, or restaurants either. The sidewalks were correspondingly empty, since the Chinese, even forty years after Deng Xiaoping's legendary opening up to the West, showed no real liking for strolling as the French, Germans, and Italians did. The traffic flowed quickly along, spanned by pedestrian bridges at regular intervals. Because most commuters had been at their desks since the early hours of the morning, the volume of vehicles remained relatively small. From the central strip separating the lanes the massive pillars of the future Maglev elevated highway rose and threw long, menacing shadows. A small park with a lawn, a pond, and a little wood occupied the opposite side of the road, where old people, divorced from time, practiced Qi Gong. It was like watching two films running at different speeds. Against the backdrop of the slow-motion ballet, the cars looked as though they were traveling faster than they really were.

No one paid Jericho any attention in his audible dispute with the airbike, in which he spoke and the machine remained stubbornly silent.

The seconds flew by.

At last he interrupted his monologue and dealt the vehicle a kick in the side, which the plastic casing absorbed so silently that it amounted to an insult. He feverishly ran through the alternatives. As he did so, he went on mechanically trying to start the airbike, so that he was still brooding when the rotors of the turbine suddenly began to turn and the familiar hiss climbed the scale of frequencies, higher and higher, until it finally invited him to fly as if there had never been a problem.

"Fine," said Yoyo. "You've won."

She crouched down and slid the little computer along the floor toward Kenny. When she stood up again, her eyes met Hongbing's. He seemed to be asking her forgiveness for the fact that he could contribute nothing more toward solving her problems than to sit there frozen. In fact, Kenny's perfidious arrangement even kept him from throwing himself at the man who was threatening his daughter. He wouldn't make the first meter. Nothing would have been gained.

"There's nothing you can do," she said. And then, trusting that Jericho was still on his way, she added, "Whatever happens, Father, don't move from the spot, you hear? Not an inch."

"Touching." Kenny smiled. "I could puke."

He lifted the computer and glanced at the screen for a moment. Then he gave Yoyo a contemptuous look.

"Pretty ancient model, isn't it?"

She shrugged.

"Are you sure you've given me the right one?"

"It's the one for backups."

"Okay, part two. Who else knows about your little outing to forbidden climes?"

"Daxiong," said Yoyo, pointing at him. "And Shi Wanxing."

Daxiong gave her a quick look of surprise. It wasn't just Kenny who would be wondering who Shi Wanxing was. In fact she'd spontaneously invented the name in the hope that Daxiong might understand her bluff and play along. Now that the hit man had taken her computer, or what he thought was her computer, they were effectively dead. She had to try to keep him at arm's length.

"Wanxing?" Kenny's eyes narrowed. "Who is that?"

"He—" began Yoyo.

"Shut up." Kenny nodded to Daxiong. "I asked him."

Daxiong let a moment's silence pass, a moment that seemed to stretch into eternity. Then, jutting his pharaoh beard, he said, "Shi Wanxing is, apart from us, the last person you haven't killed. The last surviving Guardian. I didn't know Yoyo had confided in him."

Kenny frowned suspiciously. "Even she doesn't seem to have known that until a minute ago."

"We don't agree on the subject of Wanxing," growled Daxiong. "Yoyo thinks a lot of him, for some reason. I didn't want to have him in the group at all. He talks too much."

"Wanxing is an outstanding crypto-analyst," Yoyo replied scornfully.

"That's why you shouldn't have transferred all your data to him right away," Daxiong complained.

"Why not? He was supposed to decode the page with the Switzerland films on it."

"And? Did he?"

"No idea."

"He did absolutely fuck all, is what he did!"

"Hey, Daxiong!" Yoyo railed at him. "What's really at issue here? Just the fact that you can't stand him."

"He's a loudmouth."

"I trust him."

"But you can't trust him."

"Wanxing is no loudmouth."

"Frogshit!" said Daxiong, getting angry. "It's all he fucking is!"

Kenny tilted his head. He didn't really seem to know what to make of the argument.

"If Wanxing talked to anyone at all about it, it was because he needed extra tools," Yoyo roared. "After *you* completely failed!"

"That's exactly what I'm saying."

"What?"

"That Sara and Zheiying are in possession of this fucking message."

"What? Why them?"

"Why? Are you blind? Because he likes Sara."

"So do you!"

"Hey," said Kenny.

"You're out of your mind," Daxiong snapped. "Shall we talk about your relationship with Zheiying? The way you make him look like an idiot just because h—"

"Hey!" Kenny yelled, throwing his computer at Daxiong's feet. "What the hell's going on? Are you mocking me? Who's Wanxing, who are these other people? Who all knows about this? Say something, somebody, or I'll blow the old guy to pieces!"

Yoyo opened her mouth and closed it again. She couldn't take her eyes off the hit man, who seemed to have worked something out. That they were bluffing, keeping him at arm's length. That they were actually staring past him, at the source of the hissing noise that Kenny hadn't noticed because he had allowed himself to be distracted by the staged argument. Kenny, the bomb that had to be defused, like in the old films. Just another few seconds. The countdown approaching zero, half a dozen wires, all the same color, but only one that you could cut through.

"You're in the crosshairs," she said quietly.

• • •

Xin looked at his display. It showed him what the scanner of the automatic rifle saw: Chen Hongbing, pressed into his seat. Part of the rear glass façade. A dark outline at the edge of the picture.

Something had appeared behind Chen.

"If my father dies, you're dead," said Yoyo. "Same if you attack us or try to escape. So listen. One of your airbikes is hovering outside the window right now. Owen Jericho is sitting on it, and he's pointing something at you. I'm not familiar with these things, but judging by the size of it, I'd say that he could blow *you* to pieces with it, so try to keep your temper under control."

Xin put his thoughts and feelings in order like an accountant. He'd get annoyed later. He had no doubt that Yoyo was telling the truth. If Chen died that second, he would die too. The girl and her enormous friend were unarmed, while he had a gun tucked into the top of his pants—not much of an advantage really, because before he had drawn the gun he would be dead too.

"What should I do?" he asked calmly.

"Turn off the trigger. That gun. I want my father to get up and come over to us."

"Right. To do that I'll have to turn off automatic activation. I'll have to touch it, okay?"

"If this is one of your tricks—" roared Daxiong.

"I'm not about to commit suicide. It's just a remote control."

"Go on," nodded Yoyo.

Xin tapped on the touchscreen and switched off the automatic trigger. The gun was no longer programmed to respond to Chen Hongbing's movements. It was entirely under his control again.

"Just a moment." He quickly keyed in swivel angle, rotation speed and fire frequency. "All done. Stand up, honorable Chen. Go to your daughter."

Chen Hongbing seemed to hesitate.

Then he hurried from his chair and to the side.

Xin fell to the ground and pressed *Start.*

Cave dwellers, savannah runners, they'd experienced everything by the twenty-first century. They saw the rustling of the grass, heard what the wind carried to them, were astonishingly able simultaneously to respond to and intuitively assess a variety of stimuli. Some people drew more from their ancient inheritance than others, and some had preserved their instincts, developed over six million years of human history, to an extraordinary degree.

Owen Jericho was one of those.

He had driven the bike right up to the glass façade, clutching his rapid fire rifle, held so that the red laser dot was resting on Kenny's back. He hung there like a dragonfly, well aware that the hit man must have heard the hissing of the jets long before, but Kenny had shown no sign of turning round. He wasn't prepared for an attack from that direction. They had him over a barrel.

Yoyo said something and pointed at her father.

The laser dot quivered between Kenny's shoulder blades.

Chen's thin, lanky body tensed, the hit man bent his arms. It was possible that he was holding something in his left hand, which he was using with his right.

Then it happened—and Jericho's ancient legacy took hold. His perception speeded up so quickly that the world seemed to be heading for a standstill and all sounds dropped to sub-audible levels. There was nothing but a dull background hum. As if he had become weightless, Chen slowly rose from the chair, moved away from the seat, centimeter by centimeter, left leg braced against the floor, right leg bent as he tipped to the side. It was a preparation for a leap, and even before it had really begun, Kenny showed that he was about to throw himself to the floor. Jericho registered all of this, Chen's escape and Kenny's leap, intuitively made connections between them and centered his attention on the remote-controlled gun. Even before it began to turn on its tripod, he knew exactly what was about to happen. Chen was able to escape because the gun was no longer aimed at him. The hit man wasn't running away from Jericho's gun, he was fleeing his own, which he was at that very moment directing to fire at the windows.

The same evolutionary calculation that had saved leaping hunters millions of years before taught Jericho to climb a second before the barrel spat its first bullets. He had changed position by the time they left the muzzle.

Then things speeded up.

The gun on the tripod swung around and rattled off its rounds, then turned further on its axis. All the windows exploded. The burst took in Jericho's bike, but he had managed to climb high enough to avoid being hit himself. Two of the bullets struck the rotating wheels of the engine. There was a sound like a cracking bell. The airbike took a terrible blow.

It dropped.

"Down!" yelled Daxiong and threw himself sideways. Three hundred pounds had to get moving, but almost all of Daxiong's colossal body was muscles, so he managed to shove Yoyo and reach Chen Hongbing with a few leaps, the gun following after him. Bullets drilled into the wall and ceiling. Wood, glass, and plaster sprayed from gaping holes. Daxiong saw Yoyo fall. At a frequency of eight rounds per second, the gun shredded the door they had been standing outside just a moment before, kept on turning, pursuing him as he breathlessly tried to flee. He collided with Hongbing and pulled him to the floor.

The wall exploded above their heads.

Jericho fell.

Apparently unconnected factors combined unexpectedly, including the principles of construction of flying machines, the effects of heavy ballistics, and the ambitions of the city parks commission. Tokyo, for example, symbolized a people that had always lived in a state of extreme self-confinement, which was why you hardly ever saw a tree there. Shanghai, on the other hand, was bursting with parks and tree-lined streets, which enormously enhanced the quality of life, and was also ideal when it came to considerably softening the fall of an airbike plummeting from about 12 meters in the air. Encouraged by the humid climate, the birch trees in the hinterland of Siping Lu had grown luxuriously rampant. The bike crashed into the dense foliage of a treetop and threw Jericho off. He fell into the branches, which grew denser as he fell; he flailed around, fell further, whipped by twigs and thrashed by thickening boughs until at last he managed to cling on to one and dangled from it, legs flailing, 4 to 5 meters above the courtyard.

Too high to jump.

Where was the airbike?

A crunching and splintering announced that he had overtaken the machine on his way down. It was raging high above him. He threw his head back and saw something flying at him, tried to get out of its way, too late. A branch crashed against his forehead.

When his eyesight had cleared, the airbike was coming straight at him.

Xin rolled over.

Dense clouds of plaster dust formed in front of his eyes. Near the shattered door he saw Yoyo creeping over to her father on her elbows. By now the spinning rifle had completed its first circuit, and was moving on, still spitting fire, to its second.

"Yoyo, get out!" he heard Daxiong shouting. "Get out of here!"

"Father!"

Xin waited until the bullets had passed by him, then jumped up and slipped his index finger over the touchscreen of the remote control, stopped the weapon, pulled his finger down and to the right, and the gun followed his movements, and spat a burst of fire at the very spot where Chen and the giant were just getting back to their feet. The bullets missed them by millimeters. Still crouching, they staggered into the next room. Xin fired into the wall, but the masonry had already survived the first shots.

Whatever. In there they were trapped.

He calmly swung the gun around to the left. In a fierce staccato the gun hammered its rounds into the concrete, plowed through a half-shattered shelf, and brought it crashing down completely. A series of craters appeared in quick succession, tracing a line that continued all the way to the girl on the floor.

Yoyo stared at it. Panicking, she tried to get to her feet, but she was ridiculously slow. Her eyes widened when she realized that she was about to die.

"Bye bye, Yoyo," he hissed.

Turbine mouth downward, the airbike crashed through the branches as if to kill Jericho and swallow him up at the same time.

He *had* to jump!

The splintering and crashing came to a stop. The machine's rump had jammed less than half a meter above him and come to a juddering standstill.

Bark, leaves, and twigs rattled down on him. He looked into the shattered rotors of the turbine, swung toward the trunk and spotted a branch below him that might support his weight.

Worryingly thin, on closer inspection.

Too thin.

The rain of twigs resumed.

He had no choice, dropped, climbed back up, felt the wood yielding under his weight, and wrapped his arms around the trunk.

Xin heard the scream, which had come not from Yoyo but from the giant, who stormed in from the next room, hurled himself like a demolition ball against the tripod, and brought it crashing down. The rifle pointed at the ceiling now, bringing down lumps of brick the size of fists. Xin pressed *Stop* and drew his handgun. He saw Hongbing running over to Yoyo, who leaped to her feet and pulled open what was left of the splintered door to the apartment.

As Xin took aim at her, Daxiong pulled his legs away.

Xin collapsed onto his back and nimbly rolled sideways. Daxiong crashed to the floor. Xin raised his pistol, but the giant pushed himself up with amazing dexterity and knocked it from his hand. Xin gave him a kick at the spot where his wardrobe-sized chest met his chin, which must therefore have been something like an Adam's apple. Daxiong's pharaoh beard splintered. The giant staggered backward and uttered a choking croak. With a racing dive Xin was on the pistol, grabbed hold of its butt, felt himself being grabbed and held aloft like a child. Kicking out in all directions, he struggled in vain to free himself from the man's grasp. Daxiong's huge paws gripped him like vices as he carried him to the glass façade.

His plan was obvious.

Xin reached back and fired haphazardly. A muffled groan led him to assume that he had hit his target, although it didn't keep Daxiong from hoisting him higher and violently hurling him through one of the windows. There wasn't much glass left in the frame. Under other circumstances the impact would have meant certain death, but the injury had cost the giant some of his strength. Xin spread his arms and legs like a cat, tried to find something to hold on to, and caught hold of a strut that hadn't been shattered in the hail of gunfire. His body swung outside. For a moment he looked down at the green sea of leaves below him, tensed his muscles to get back inside, saw Daxiong's fist flying at him, and slipped away.

He fell.

A little way.

In an instant he spotted and grabbed the bulky box of the air-conditioning system. A jolt ran through his body, his hands clawed around the box, which scraped sideways. Far below him there was crashing, splintering, and rattling as if a huge animal were raging in the treetops.

Jericho? That was exactly the spot where the detective had fallen.

No matter. He had to get back into the apartment. Using all his strength he pulled himself up, braced his feet against the masonry, and started climbing.

Jericho clung desperately to the tree trunk. His feet slipped. No bark to claw on to. Just 3 meters above the ground he decided to let go, pushed himself away, landed on both feet, lost his balance, fell on his back, and saw the airbike plunging down on top of him.

Airbike falls from tree and kills detective.

There were headlines that you didn't want to imagine in print.

With all his strength he catapulted himself sideways. The airbike struck the ground beside him with such force that he was afraid the arsenal of weapons would go up, but he was spared that disaster at least. The bike lay on its side; two jets and part of the casing had come off. As a result it had ceased to function as a flying machine. He looked up, but the treetops obscured the view of Chen's apartment. When he staggered to the house wall he thought he saw a foot disappearing over the window ledge and narrowed his eyes.

The foot was gone.

He looked around, discovered a back door, pressed the handle, and found it was open. Behind it, the corridor lay in darkness. Cool air drifted toward him. He slipped inside and took a moment to find his bearings, saw a turn in the corridor, and followed its course. After a short flight of steps he found himself beside the elevator shaft. Ahead of him, the hall stretched to the front door. A series of loud thumps came from the stairwell. Someone was charging down the stairs like an elephant. Jericho jerked backward, hid behind the elevator shaft, and waited to see who would appear in the hall.

It was Daxiong. The giant staggered and rested his arm against the wall. His jacket was torn and bloodstained over his right shoulder. A few quick steps and Jericho was beside him.

"What's going on? Where are Yoyo and Chen?"

Daxiong spun around, fist ready to strike. Then he recognized Jericho, turned, and stumbled toward the front door.

"Outside," he snorted.

"And Kenny?"

"Outside too."

His knees gave. Jericho grabbed him under the arms.

"Stand up," he panted.

"I'm too heavy."

"Nonsense. I've rocked bigger babies than you before. What do you mean outside?"

Daxiong clawed one of his great hands into Jericho's shoulder and shifted his weight to him. Of course he was too heavy. Far too heavy. Almost like dragging a medium-sized dinosaur around with you. Jericho pulled the door open, and they staggered together into the sunlight.

"I threw him out," wheezed Daxiong. "Out of the window. The bastard."

"I think the bastard's crept back in again." Jericho quickly scanned the surroundings. A car and a bike were both on the move, some way apart.

"They must be here somewhere—there!"

Between the vehicles Yoyo waved at them from the other side of the road. She was on the saddle of one of the two motorcycles on which she and Daxiong had arrived. Beside her, Chen Hongbing shifted nervously from one foot to the other. Yoyo pointed to the second motorcycle and shouted something.

"Exactly," growled Daxiong. He took his hand off Jericho's shoulder and stomped unsteadily off. "Let's get out of here."

The pagoda-like roof of the building flattened in the middle section, by the shaft of the stairwell. Xin had parked his airbike next to it when he'd gone down to the fourth floor, and now he charged back into the open, gun at the ready, safety catch released in haste, bleeding from a thousand cuts. He ran to the edge of the roof. The pagoda sloped gently below him and hid most of the street, but he could still make out the struts for the new elevated highway and the park on the other side.

He saw Yoyo and her father standing next to a footbridge.

He took aim and realized that his magazine was empty. With a howl of rage he threw the gun away, ran to his airbike, sat on it, started the engine, and climbed until he had a wider view of the whole road. Jericho and Daxiong were running along it. They had crossed the central reservation and were now halfway over the bridge. The traffic surged along below them. From the air they looked like mice in a lab run. One of them limping.

The giant. He *had* hit him.

Xin reached down into the weapon chamber and brought out a submachine gun. Jets wailing, he plunged.

Jericho saw him coming. He grabbed Daxiong—running in front of him, bent almost double—by the sleeve of his jacket and pointed into the air.

"Shit," gasped Daxiong. He raised both arms to alert the others to the bike, and groaned. His face was contorted with pain. But Yoyo had also realized the danger she was in. She jumped from her motorcycle and started running as fast as she could toward the park, with Hongbing hot on her heels.

"Daxiong," yelled Jericho. "We've got to get back."

"No!"

"We'll never make it."

He gave the giant a shove and pushed him to the point where the walkway crossed the central reservation, next to one of the massive pillar constructions on which the rails of the Maglev were going to run. Prongs jutted out from it at regular intervals. Jericho swung himself over the parapet and started climbing down. He hoped Daxiong would be able to summon the strength to follow him. There was no way he could carry the guy down there.

The airbike shot across the footbridge. Shots rang out loudly. Daxiong lost his grip and landed heavily in the grass of the central reservation. Jericho ran to the fallen man, who sat up and uttered a roar that easily drowned out the sound of the cars. To Jericho's relief Daxiong wasn't shouting with pain, but bawled a cascade of curses all of which concerned Kenny's slow and painful demise.

"Up with you," Jericho shouted at him.

"I can't!"

"Yes you can. I'm not particularly responsive to stranded whales."

Daxiong turned his narrow gaze on him.

"I'll tear his stomach out," he shouted. "And his guts! First his large intestine, then the small one—"

"As you wish. On your feet now!"

Xin came around in a circle and took aim at Yoyo.

A moment later they had disappeared under the lush foliage of the trees that surrounded the park. He brought the bike down and swept over the field toward the Qi Gong group. Heads high, shoulders lowered, upper and lower body in harmony, the old people stretched their arms out, turned their palms, and brought them slowly upward, stretched their limbs, craned their arms until it looked as if they were keeping the sky from plummeting down on Siping Lu. He saw the fugitives appear between plane trees and weeping willows and fired, tearing gaping holes in the wood. The front members of the group fell out of sync with the rest. They forgot to clasp their fingers, missed the slow exhalation, turned their heads.

A moment later they scattered, as the airbike swept through them.

Xin slowed the bike and headed toward the little wood into which Yoyo and her father had disappeared. No sign of them. He pulled up the nose of the airbike and quickly gained height. Maybe they wanted to seize the right moment and run out on the other side, to get to their motorcycles. Jets hissing, he aimed for the two machines. Being powered by electricity, they wouldn't explode, but after an intensive bombardment they would no longer be usable.

He saw a movement in the central reservation. Ah! Jericho and the colossus who'd tried to throw him out of the window.

So much the better.

"Here he comes!"

Daxiong nodded feebly. They waited until the last moment, then fled between the pillars as the first shots plowed through the grass and struck the concrete. The airbike dashed past them and then performed a quick turn.

"To the other side."

They took cover again, hoping to keep Kenny at bay. They could always take shelter behind one of the columns. At least that was what Jericho hoped.

Daxiong leaned next to him, drenched in sweat, breath rattling. His face was now worryingly pale.

"I'm not going to be able to keep this up for much longer," he panted.

"You won't need to," said Jericho, but he was starting to worry that for some reason the last part of his plan mightn't work quite as well as he had hoped. His eyes swept the sky. Vehicles roared past on either side at irregular intervals. The hiss of the turbine moved away. For a moment he allowed himself to believe that the hit man had given up. If he was high enough, the pillar wouldn't be much use to them. They could circle the thing like rabbits, but sooner or later they would be hit.

"—and his appendix, if he's still got one," croaked Daxiong. "I'll drag that out of him too. Or first the appendix and then—"

Grass and soil sprayed up at their feet. Jericho circled the pillar. Daxiong came staggering after him, barely capable of keeping on his feet.

"Are you okay?" asked Jericho.

"That son of a bitch hit me somewhere in the back," Daxiong murmured. He coughed and collapsed. "I think I'm going to—"

"Daxiong! For God's sake! You can't give in now. Do you hear me? Don't faint!"

"I'm—I'm trying—I—"

"There! Look!"

Something had appeared in the sky in the distance, flat and silvery. It dived and came very quickly toward them.

"Daxiong," yelled Jericho. "We're saved!"

The giant smiled. "That's nice," he said dreamily and tipped sideways.

Xin had briefly shifted his attention to the little wood, so he didn't see the shimmering flatfish until it was almost too late. Within a few seconds it grew menacingly large, but the pilot showed no sign of veering away from him. He gave a start, then realized that the new arrival planned to ram him into the ground. Startled, he raised his arm and fired off a few rounds that the vehicle elegantly dodged, before immediately heading straight back toward him again.

Whoever was steering the skymobile was a master of navigation.

He let the airbike drop like a stone and caught it again right above the traffic. The silver discus went into a nosedive. Xin turned, passed over the woods and the artificial lake, twisted and dodged, and still couldn't shake off his pursuer. The silver discus chased him across the park and back to the road, then suddenly turned off and rose steeply into the sky. Xin watched after him in confusion, slowed his bike down, and held it hovering above the flow of traffic.

The strange machine disappeared.

Cursing, he remembered what he had to do. It was humiliating! Yoyo and old Chen were hiding somewhere in the bushes watching everything, an idea that made him boil with fury. He would use the grenade launcher and set the woods ablaze—but first Jericho and Daxiong had to go. No police had turned up yet. Gun at the ready, he was heading toward the pillar with the two idiots hiding behind it, when he saw the silver discus coming back and heading straight for him.

He hid his gun. Below him, antediluvian cars impregnated the air with exhaust and street dust. He was seething with rage. He wouldn't allow himself to be hunted again. He would bring that guy down from the sky. His fingers closed around the butt of the rocket launcher, but it was stuck. He rattled at it frantically, looked down, and lost his concentration for a moment.

There was a loud honking noise.

Louder, closer.

Irritated, Xin raised his head.

The façade of a roaring heavy goods vehicle, growing, vast. The airbike had dropped while he was battling with the launcher. With horror,
he saw the driver shouting and gesticulating behind the windshield,
pulled the bike back up, and missed the roof of the driver's cabin by
inches, only to see the discus shooting away above him, so close that
its shock wave gripped the airbike and whirled it around like a leaf. He
flew from the saddle in a high arc and landed on his back. The impact
left him breathless. He instinctively reached his arms up, but nothing
drove over him. He was lying on something that was solid yet yielding. Battling for breath, he pulled himself upright and saw rusty planks
supporting the pile of whatever he was rolling in.

No. Not planks. Body-work. Xin reached into the mass and let it
trickle through his fingers.

Sand.

He had fallen into a heap of sand.

With a cry of rage he got to his feet, saw houses, masts, and traffic
lights drifting past him, lost his balance, and landed back in the sand
as the huge truck he was lying on turned off, accelerated, and drove
him out of Hongkou, away from Daxiong, Jericho, Yoyo, Chen, and
Siping Lu.

On the inside of the four westbound lanes, the traffic started to back
up. The airbike had fallen on the central reservation, scattering parts
of its shell over the street and forcing some drivers into bold braking
maneuvers. If there were no collisions, this was due only to the compulsory introduction of presafe sensors, which even old models had
had to adopt. Radar systems with CMOS cameras constantly analyzed
distance and automatically braked the car if the driver in front came
to an abrupt standstill. Only flying objects obviously created problems
for the sensors.

Meanwhile the Silver Surfer had landed in the park. Jericho peered
between the cars and saw the vehicle's side doors lifting and a familiar,
fleshy figure climbing out. Then he saw someone else, and his heart
thumped with joy.

Yoyo and Chen came running out of the wood.

"Daxiong!" He bent down to the giant and patted his cheek. "Get
up. Come on."

Daxiong murmured something unfriendly. Jericho brought his
hand back and gave him two loud slaps, and jumped backward just in
case he had underestimated the giant's reflexes. But Daxiong just sat
up, sighed, and looked as if he were about to sink back again. Jericho
took his arm and gripped it tightly for a few seconds, before the massive body slipped away from him.

"Damn it, Daxiong!"

He couldn't let the wounded man fall into a coma. Not here. Further slaps were needed. This time he was more successful.

"Have you lost your mind?" Daxiong yelled.

Jericho pointed at the prongs in the pillar that led up to the footbridge. "You can go to sleep in a minute. First we've got to get up there."

Daxiong tried to support himself on his left arm, collapsed, tried again, and got to his feet. Jericho felt terribly sorry for him. In the movies people with bullet wounds went on charging around the place doing heroic things, but the reality was very different. The wound on Daxiong's back might just have been a graze, but the very shock of it, caused by the velocity of the dart bullets, was enough to send a person out of his mind. Daxiong had lost a lot of blood, and the wound must have been very painful.

His gaze wandered up the ladder. By now his face was ashen.

"I won't get up there, Owen," he whispered.

Jericho breathed out. Daxiong was right. He didn't even feel all that steady on his feet himself. He estimated the width of the central reservation—just wide enough, he thought, and took out his cell phone. Two beeps later he had Tu on the line. Jericho could see him over in the park, while Yoyo and Chen were climbing into the skymobile.

"Tian?"

His voice was suddenly trembling. All of him, and everything around him, had suddenly started trembling.

"My God, Owen!" trumpeted Tu. "What's up? We're waiting for you."

"Sorry." He gulped. "You were great, but I'm afraid the big challenge still lies ahead of you."

"What? Which one do you mean?"

"Precision landing. Central reservation. See you soon, old friend."

Tu's Silver Surfer had been designed as a two-seater with an ejector seat. Under the combined weight of five people, two of them massively obese, it shed some of its agility. It also became horribly cramped. They shifted Daxiong to the passenger seat and squashed in together behind him. Hopelessly overladen, the Silver Surfer took off with all the elegance of an arthritic duck. Jericho was surprised it could fly at all. Tu guided the machine over the uniform red-brown roofs of the residential complexes of Hongkou, crossed the Huangpu, and headed for the northern shore of the financial district. Within view of the Yangpu Bridge lay the park-like gardens of the Pudong International Medical Center, a collection of weightless-looking glass cocoons, nestling in spruce gardens with artificial lakes, bamboo glades, and secret pavilions. The renowned private clinic had been built only a few years previously. It represented the new, "natural" Shanghai, based on plans which demonstrated that if you built something shaped like the neck of a brachiosaurus it might provide lovely views, but otherwise it created nothing but problems. (The ultimate example of architectural phallic delusion, the Nakheel Tower, also loomed half-finished above the now bankrupt city of Dubai, as if to confirm the platitude that the biggest guy isn't the one with the longest. The monster had been planned to reach a height of 1,400 meters. After just over a kilometer the work had been suspended; the architects, in their bid to climb to heaven, had been defeated by the banality of their concept; the *casa erecta* was ripe for inclusion in the book of heroic failures.) Structures like the interlocking cells of the Pudong International Medical Center came much closer to the demands of a metropolis that saw itself as a gigantic urban protozoon; its metabolism was based on neuronal interconnections rather than unfeasibly vast dimensions.

"I know someone here."

As ever when anything new happened in Shanghai, Tu was on intimate terms with people at the top, in this instance the head of surgery. After they had handed over Daxiong, the men had had a quiet chat. It ended with the assurance that Daxiong's injury would be treated, with no questions asked. The giant had to be stitched up, and would have to get used to the idea of a nice smart scar. And he would be in pain for a while.

"But there are things you can do about that," the surgeon said as he left, smiling reassuringly at everyone. "There are things you can do about everything these days."

In private clinics, his expression added.

Jericho would have liked to ask what he planned to do about Yoyo's pain over the loss of her friends, about Chen Hongbing's emotional torment, and his own inner movies, but instead he just shook Daxiong's hand and wished him all the best. The giant looked at him expressionlessly. Then he let go of his hand, stretched out his right arm, and drew him to him. Jericho groaned. If Daxiong could hug you with a gaping wound in his back, he preferred not to know what declarations of love he was capable of in a state of perfect physical health.

"You're not so bad," said Daxiong.

"My pleasure," Jericho grinned. "Be nice to the nurses."

"And you look after Yoyo until I'm out."

"Will do."

"So, see you tonight."

Jericho thought he had misheard. Daxiong turned his head to one side as if any further discussion about the time of his release were a simple waste of time.

"Leave it," said Yoyo as she left. "I'm just glad he didn't want to come with us right away."

"And now?" asked Chen Hongbing as they trotted back to the Silver Surfer. It was the first time he had said anything at all since they had left the park. His blank face, whatever hell had caused it, made him seem strangely uninvolved, almost uninterested.

"I think there are some things I should explain to you." Yoyo lowered her head. "Except—perhaps not right now."

Chen raised his hands in a helpless gesture.

"I don't understand all this." His gaze wandered to Jericho. "But you'd—"

"I found her," Jericho nodded. "Just like you wanted."

"Yesss," Chen said slowly. He seemed to be wondering whether this was really what he had wanted.

"I'm sorry about what happened."

"No, no. I'm the one who should be thanking you!"

That sounded exactly like the man who, two days ago—had it really only been two days ago?—had come into his office, conspicuous for his excessive formality. But lurking in the background there was also the question of how someone might seriously expect thanks for having set off on a simple missing-person job and come back with the Horsemen of the Apocalypse in hot pursuit.

Jericho said nothing. Chen said nothing back. Yoyo had discovered something fascinating in the sky. Tu paced about for a while among ferns, bamboo, and black pines, and issued a stream of instructions into his phone.

"So," he announced when he came back.

"So what?" asked Jericho.

"So someone's going to the Westin to collect your computer and the rest of your stuff and bring them to my place, where you'll be living for the next little while."

"Oh. Fine."

"And I've organized two people to keep an eye on your loft in Xintiandi. Two more are on their way to Siping Lu. To clean up and stand watch." He cleared his throat and put his arm around Chen's shoulders. "Of course we'll have to ask ourselves, my dear Hongbing, what we will tell the police when they come to examine the state of your sitting room."

"That means we're flying to your place?" Yoyo concluded.

Tu looked at them all. "Does anyone have a better idea."

Silence.

"Anyone rather spend the night at home? No? Then excuse me."

With a quiet hum, the Silver Surfer lifted its wing doors.

"The highest are the wise," Jericho whispered as he climbed into the back seat.

Tu glared at him.

"Those who are *born* wise," he said. "Get Confucius out of your head. I can do it better than you. Longnose!"

Without Daxiong, who counted as two, the flying machine swiftly gained altitude. Tu lived in a villa in a gated area, a fortress-like guarded compound in the hinterland of Pudong, surrounded by park-like areas of green. They landed right in front of the main building, peeled themselves from their upholstered seats, and climbed a flight of steps leading to a porch with double doors.

One of the doors opened. An attractive Chinese woman with red-dyed hair appeared in the doorway. She was the complete opposite of Yoyo. Less beautiful, but more elegant in her appearance and, strangely, more sensual. A person with no gaps in her CV, who was used to having the world rotate around her. Tu greeted her with a hug and marched inside. Jericho followed him. The woman smiled and kissed him fleetingly on both cheeks.

"Hi, Owen," she said in a sonorous voice.

Jericho returned her smile.

"Hi, Joanna."

PUDONG

Tu had instructed Joanna to focus all her care and attention on Chen as soon as they got back. What he really wanted was for her to distract him for a while, a task which Joanna dedicated herself to fully. Steering the confused Chen into her palatial kitchen with the same uncompromising attitude as someone pushing a shopping cart in front of them, she demanded to know what tea he preferred, asked whether he would like a sauna, a bath, or a hot shower, where it hurt, what had happened, whether he would like some cold chicken from the fridge. He didn't know how it had all ended up like that, the guy just suddenly appeared in the room with the gun, and oh God, how did he even get in, and oh, you've got scratches all over you, they could get inflamed, hold still, don't argue, and so on and so forth. She didn't have a clue what was going on, of course. But Joanna wouldn't have been Joanna if that had been a problem. She exuded the bountiful aromas of her optimism, bathing Chen in confidence until he was ready to believe that everything would be okay, purely because she said so. Jericho had never met any other person with such powers of conviction that things would turn out fine, without having the faintest idea *how*. Joanna bluffed for all she was worth. In her world, the tail wagged the dog. Presumably Chen was convinced that he was having a conversation, or even that he had started it. Joanna had a way of driving a man in front of her in such a manner that he would swear it was *her* following *him*.

"So what should we do?" hissed Tu.

"Notify the police," said Jericho tersely. "Before they turn up of their own accord."

"You want to go on the offensive?"

"What other option do we have? That maniac set half the steelworks on fire. It won't take them long to find the bodies and then some witnesses in Quyu. It looks as if a bomb just went off on Siping Lu—doesn't it, Yoyo—?"

"Yes."

"—and there's a crashed airbike decomposing in the courtyard, chock full with heavy-duty weapons. And one that brought the traffic to a standstill. They'll be able to piece together some of the puzzle from all that."

"But how much of it?"

"I'm telling you, it will only be a few hours before they start asking what your friend Hongbing had to do with the massacre in Quyu. They'll think of Yoyo in no time at all. I mean, the thing in the steel factory looks like some campaign of destruction against the City Demons, don't you think? And Yoyo's part of the group."

"And what about you?" asked Yoyo. "Do you reckon they'll think of you too?"

"How would they? My car was incinerated in Quyu."

"But they'll be able to identify it." Tu pursed his lips. "And besides, Siping Lu has security cameras. Which means they'll have recordings of all of you meeting up, of Yoyo and Daxiong going into the building, of how that—that—"

"Kenny."

"—Kenny guy herded the two of you in front of him—"

"Not just us," said Jericho. "Think about it. You were just as easily visible, in your state of heavenly wrath. And who is it that works in your company to finance her studies?"

"Yoyo, the girl who just can't keep her mouth shut," snorted Yoyo.

"Yes, my dear, you really do have a sparkling reputation," commented Tu, scratching his bald head. With his new glasses on, he looked almost civilized. "So what are we going to tell them? That Yoyo happened to overhear Kenny, completely by chance, while—"

"Forget it," Yoyo interrupted him. "You want me to tell the police that I'm in possession of secret information? With my record? If that asshole is from the government I might as well lock myself up and throw away the key. Or better still, just shoot myself!"

"I don't think the police are in on this," said Jericho.

"Yes, but you don't know what might happen if they get their hands on me."

"Hold on a second." Tu was shaking his head energetically. "Let's be realistic. We're assuming the Shanghai police force has the same powers of deduction as a quantum computer. They're not going to put all the pieces together *that* quickly."

"Well, either way, we still need to notify them," said Jericho.

"But perhaps not right away."

"Yes, *right away*. If someone trashes your apartment and you don't report it, that looks odd. Not to mention that Yoyo, Daxiong, and I turned up just beforehand, and that I have a flying machine just like Kenny's."

"Okay fine, then how about this: someone holds up a motorcycle club in Quyu and causes a bloodbath. He has accomplices, all of them on flying machines. What they don't realize is that Yoyo had a family friend visiting, Owen, and he ends up creating a hell of a problem for them, right? Both Yoyo and Owen get hold of one of the airbikes and are able to flee. Not long after, Yoyo receives a call from Hongbing, telling her that someone's trying to break into his apartment."

"No way!" Yoyo shook her head. "You don't call your daughter if someone's trying to break into your place."

"Fine, then—"

"I know. Kenny threatened to kill all the members of your family," Jericho suggested. "So you call your father. He doesn't answer, so you go to see him, enlisting the help of Hongbing's best friend, Tian."

"And we have no idea what the guys want?" asked Yoyo skeptically. "You expect them to believe that?"

"That's the plan."

"God, what an absurd story."

"The most important thing is to keep you out of it," said Tu. "No dissident background, no Guardians." He gave Yoyo a reproachful look. "On that note, you could have told me you were all hanging out in a blast furnace. I only knew about the Andromeda."

"I'm sorry. You weren't supposed to get dragged that far into it."

"How do you figure that out? I provided the infrastructure for you and your troop of pests. You can't get much deeper involved than that." Tu sighed. "But fine. Point two on the agenda. What do we tell Hongbing?"

Yoyo hesitated. "The same story?"

"*What?*" barked Jericho.

"Well, I just thought—"

"You want to have your father believing this was all the act of some nut job?" Suddenly he was furious with her. He pictured Hongbing, filled with all that sorrow. And now they wanted to pull the wool over his eyes yet again?

"Owen." Yoyo raised her hand. "It's great, everything you've done for us, but this really has nothing to do with you."

"Your father deserves an explanation!"

"I'm not sure if he really wants one."

"Exactly. You're not *sure*. My God, he was taken hostage, held at gunpoint, his daughter was threatened, his apartment destroyed. You *have* to tell him the truth! Anything else is pure cowardice."

"Stay out of it!"

"Yoyo," said Tu softly but firmly, as if commanding a dog to come to heel.

"What?" she snapped. "What is it? It has nothing to do with him! You said yourself that it would be a mistake to burden my father with it."

"The circumstances have changed. Owen's right."

"Oh yes, I forgot." Yoyo contorted her face mockingly. "He's a family friend now."

"No. He's just right—pure and simple."

"But why? What does Owen know about my father?"

"Well, what do you know about him?" asked Jericho, antagonized.

Frank Schätzing

Yoyo glared at him. Clearly he'd hit a sore spot.

"Hongbing is embittered, set in his ways, introverted," said Tu. "But I know him! I'm waiting for the day when he'll break out of that bitter shell, and I don't know whether I should long for it or dread it. He's had to spend years of his life feeling utterly, terribly helpless. Up until now there was no reason to rub his nose in the fact that you're China's most-wanted dissident, but that just changed. After this morning he knows full bloody well that you have some explaining to do."

Yoyo shook her head unhappily.

"He'll hate me."

"He's more likely to hate me for having helped you, but I don't genu-inely believe that either. You can't carry on lying to him, Yoyo. For him, the worst possible thing would be you not confiding in him. You'd be taking away his—" Tu seemed to be struggling to find the words, "his purpose as a father."

"His purpose as a father?" echoed Yoyo, as if she'd misheard.

"Yes. Everybody needs to feel significant in some way or another. Hongbing tried to do something too, a long time ago, and he was pun-ished for it. His purpose was taken away from him."

"And now he's punishing me."

"Punishing you is the last thing he wants to do."

Yoyo stared at him.

"But he's never spoken to me about his life, Tian! Never! He's never confided in me! And you don't think that's a punishment? In what way have I been significant to him? Okay, he worries about me from morn-ing to night, and I'm sure he'd rather lock me in out of sheer worry, but what's the point? What does he want from me if he won't even talk to me?"

"He's ashamed," said Tu softly.

"Of what? I'm the one suffering. I have a—a zombie for a father!"

"You can't talk like that."

"Can't I? What about *him* explaining something to *me* for a change?"

"He'll probably have to," nodded Tu.

"Oh, great! When?"

"It's your turn first."

"Why me *again*?" exploded Yoyo. "Why not him?"

"Because you're the one in the position to reach out to him."

"Don't come to me with your emotional guilt trip," she shouted. "My friends are dead, and my father was nearly killed too. I'm the one who's had the most to deal with here."

"We've all had a lot to deal with," Jericho interrupted. He had heard enough. "So solve your problems, but solve them somewhere else. Tian, when do you think my computer will be here?"

"In a few minutes," said Tian, grateful for the change of subject.

"Good. I'll get to work on the Swiss films again. Can I use your office?"

"Of course." Tu hesitated, then shrugged his shoulders submissively. "So I'll notify the police then. Agreed?"

"Yes, do it."

"Are we all available for questioning?"

"There's no point hiding, otherwise they'll just pay us personal visits." Jericho furrowed his brow. "They may have already started. The first victim in Kenny's dirty game was Grand Cherokee Wang." He looked at Yoyo. "Your roommate. They're going to be all over you like a pack of hungry wolves."

"They can go ahead," said Yoyo grimly. "Let's see them try and eat me."

"Eat me, and I'll eat you alive."

"Well remembered," snorted Yoyo, turning around and walking off to the kitchen.

Jericho was ecstatic to have Diane back again. Without holding out any great hopes, he checked the three websites which were supposed to be interchanged according to the report, and was disappointed. The mask hadn't unearthed anything. It seemed they really had been taken out of circulation.

So that just left him with the Swiss films and a hunch.

He gave Diane a series of directions. With programmed courtesy, she informed him that the analysis would take some time, which meant it could just as easily take five years as five minutes. The computer had no plan on this front. He might as well have asked Alexander Fleming how long he would need to discover penicillin. As the films were three-dimensional, Diane had to go through data cubes rather than data surfaces, which threatened to drag the process out for a long time.

Joanna came in, bringing him some tea and English biscuits.

It was four years now since they had broken up, but Jericho still didn't know how to act around the woman who had lured him to Shanghai and then left him out of the blue. At least, that's how it had seemed to him: that Joanna had ditched him in order to marry someone who was hitting the big time in the Chinese boom, someone who didn't conform in the slightest to what one might assume to be her ideal partner. But it was this very man who had become Jericho's closest friend: a friendship, initiated by Joanna, which had started out within the cocoon of a business relationship, and developed in such a way that neither Tu nor Jericho had really realized it was even happening. It had come down to Joanna to alert them to the fact they had become more deeply attached, at the same time hoping to make Jericho realize it was about time he stopped seeing himself as indebted to everyone.

"I don't," he had retorted with a baffled expression, as if she had just suggested he shouldn't walk to work on all fours anymore.

But Jericho knew exactly what she meant. She had exaggerated a bit of course, which was in her nature, because Joanna went to the other extreme: she hardly ever felt guilt. This might lead to accusations of self-righteousness, but her behavior was far from amoral. She just lacked the guilt that all children were born into. From the day you first come into the world, you find yourself being constantly admonished, lectured, caught in the act, always in the wrong, subjected to judgment and constant corrections, all of which are intended to make an imperfect human being into a better one. The extent of the improvement is measured by how much you live up to others' expectations, an experiment doomed to failure. It normally leads to failure for all involved. Accompanied by good wishes and silent reproaches, you ultimately end up taking your own path and forget to grant the child within you absolution, a child accustomed to being scolded for running off alone. Rushing through the crossroads of "I can't, I shouldn't, I'm not allowed," you always find yourself back in the same place you set out from a long time ago, regardless of how old you may have become in the process. Your whole life long, you see yourself through the eyes of others, measure yourself by their standards, judge yourself by their canon of values, condemn yourself with their indignation, and you are never enough.

You are never enough for yourself.

That was what Joanna had meant. She had developed a remarkable talent for freeing herself from the entanglements of her childhood. Her way of looking at things was genuine, as sharp as a knife, her behavior consistent. She had considered herself fully within her rights to break up with Jericho. She knew that the breakdown of their relationship would cause him pain, but in Joanna's world, this kind of pain was no more the result of culpable behavior than toothache. She hadn't robbed him, hadn't publicly humiliated him, hadn't continually deceived him. She paid no attention to what others felt she should have done or not done. The only person whose gaze she wanted to be able to meet was the one right opposite her in the mirror.

"How are you?" asked Jericho.

"Well, how do you think?" Joanna sank down into one of the cantilever chairs scattered around Tu's office. "Very agitated."

She didn't look particularly agitated. She looked intrigued, and a little concerned. Jericho drank his tea.

"Did Tian tell you what happened?"

"He gave me an overview in passing, so now I know *his* version." Joanna took a biscuit and nibbled at it thoughtfully. "And I've heard Hongbing's too of course. It sounds dreadful. I wanted to speak to Yoyo, but she's in the middle of battling out her tiresome father-daughter conflict."

Jericho hesitated. "Do you actually know what that's about?"

"I'm not stupid." She jerked her thumb in the direction of the door. "I also know that Tian is involved."

"And that's not a problem for you?"

"It's his business. He must know what's he's doing. I'm too shamefully lacking in ambition myself, as you know. I wouldn't make a very convincing dissident. But I understand. His motivations seem clear to me, so he has my unconditional support."

Jericho was silent. It was obvious that Chen Hongbing wasn't the only one who had eaten bitterness at some point in his past. Tu's professional status implied all manner of things, but not collaboration with a group of dissidents. There must be something from way back that was influencing his behavior.

"Maybe he'll tell you about it someday," Joanna added, eating another biscuit. "In any case, you've all been hunting, and now I'm coming to gather. And as Yoyo is otherwise engaged, I'm starting with you."

Jericho briefly explained what had taken place since Chen's visit to Xintiandi. Joanna didn't interrupt him; that is if you didn't count the occasional Ahhs, Mmhms, and Ohhs, which were ritually expressed in China as a form of courtesy to assure the other person of your attentiveness. During his report, she also devoured all of the biscuits and drank most of the tea. That was fine by Jericho. He still didn't have even the slightest appetite. After he finished talking, they both fell silent for a while.

"It sounds like you've all got a long-term problem," she said finally.

"Yes."

"Tian too?" It sounded like *Me too?* Jericho was just about to tell her that her own well-being should be the least of her worries, but stopped himself; perhaps he was reading too much into her question.

"You can work that out for yourself," he said. "In any case, even Kenny will have to acknowledge the fact that he's fucked things up. By now we could have confided in anyone under the sun. He missed his opportunity to eliminate everyone who knew about it."

"You mean he won't keep trying to get Yoyo?"

Jericho pressed his fingers against the bridge of his nose. He could feel a headache coming on.

"It's hard to tell," he said.

"In what way?"

"Believe me, I've met psychopaths who are bad to the core, ones who tortured their victims, filleted them, canned them, let them die of thirst, cut off this or that, things you wouldn't believe. Their type are motivated purely by obsession. And then there are the professional killers."

"Who combine business with pleasure."

"The main thing is that they see it as a job. It brings them money. They don't develop any emotional connection to their victims, they just do their job. Kenny botched his up. Aggravating for him, but usually you'd expect him to leave us in peace from now on and turn his attention to other jobs."

"But you don't think that's the case?"

"He's a professional *and* a psycho." Jericho circled his index finger over his temple. "And those guys are a little harder to classify."

"Which means?"

"Someone like Kenny could feel offended that we've not all been eliminated as planned. He might think we shouldn't have put up a fight. It's possible that he'll do nothing. But it's just as possible that he'll set my loft on fire, or your house, or lie in wait for us and shoot us down, and all just because he's angry."

"I see you're full of optimism as usual."

Jericho glowered at her. "I thought that was *your* job."

He knew his retort was unfair, but she had provoked him. It was a shabby, mean little comment with sharp teeth and threadbare fur, which had scurried up in a surprise attack, sank its teeth in, and then died with a cackle.

"Jerk."

"Sorry," he said.

"Don't be." She stood up and ruffled his hair. Strangely, Jericho felt both comforted and humiliated by her gesture. A display lit up on Tu's computer console. The guard reported that the police had arrived and wished to question Tu as well as the others present on the incidents in Quyu and Hongkou.

The questioning went as questioning tended to go with citizens of a higher social standing. An investigating civil servant with assistants in tow showed great courtesy, assuring all of those present of her sympathy and describing the incidents in quick succession as "horrifying" and "abhorrent," Mr. Tu as an "outstanding member of society," Chen and Yoyo as "heroic" and, Jericho as a "valued friend of the authorities." In between all that, she flung questions around like circus knives. It was clear she didn't believe the story in the very parts where it wasn't true, for example when it came to Kenny's motive. Her gaze resembled that of a butcher, talking encouragingly to a pig as he carved it in his mind's eye.

Chen looked even more hollow-cheeked than normal. Tu's face had a purple tinge to it, while Yoyo's was filled with bitter pride. Clearly the arrival of the police had torn them from a heated discussion. Jericho realized that the inspector had gauged the emotional climate down to the exact degree, but she wasn't commenting on it for the time being. It was only in the course of the individual interrogations that she became more explicit. She was a middle-aged woman with smoothly brushed hair and intelligent eyes, behind what looked like old-fashioned glasses with small lenses and thick frames. But Jericho knew better. It was actually a MindReader, a portable computer which filmed the person opposite, ran their expression through an amplifier, and projected the result in real time onto the lenses of the glasses. In this way, the merest hint of a smug smile could become perfectly clear to the wearer. A nervous blink would mimic an earthquake. Tell-tale signals in facial expressions that wouldn't normally be noticed became readable. Jericho guessed that she had also linked an Interpreter to it, which dramatized the tone, accentuation, and flow of his voice. The effect was uncanny. If you combined the forces of MindReader and Interpreter, the people being questioned suddenly sounded like bad actors, turning into grimacing, crude robots, despite fully believing they had their reactions under control.

Jericho himself had already worked with both programs. Only very experienced investigators used them. It took years of practice to correctly read the discrepancies between the expression, intonation, and content of a statement. He showed no sign of having recognized the device, told his version of the incident stoically, and fended off question after question.

"And you're really just a friend of the family?"

"And there was no particular reason why you happened to be in the steel factory today of all days?"

"Those guys arrived at the factory at exactly the same time as you, and you expect me to believe that that's pure coincidence?"

"Did you perhaps have a commission in Quyu?"

"Don't you find it strange that Grand Cherokee Wang was murdered one day after you went looking for him?"

"Did you know that Chen Yuyun was once imprisoned for political agitation and passing on State secrets?"

"Did you also know that Tu Tian has not always behaved in the best interests of the Chinese State and our justified concerns for its internal stability?"

"What do you know about Chen Hongbing's past?"

"Am I really supposed to believe that not one of you—although the actions indicate an act which was planned long in advance!—had the faintest clue who this Kenny is and what he wants?"

"I'll ask you once more: What commission did you have that led you to Quyu?"

And so on and so forth.

Eventually she gave up, leaned back, and took the glasses off. She smiled, but her gaze continued to saw away at him, hacking off tiny pieces.

"You've been in Shanghai for four and a half years," she stated. "According to what I hear, you have an excellent reputation as an investigator."

"Thank you, it's an honor to hear that."

"So how is business going?"

"I can't complain."

"I'm pleased to hear it." She put the tips of her fingers together. "Rest assured that you are highly valued in my field. You have successfully collaborated with us a number of times and each time you have displayed a high level of willingness to cooperate. This is one of the reasons why we would like to extend your work permit—" here, her right hand made a waving motion, illustrating some vague future "—and then to extend it again and again. Precisely because our relationship is based on reciprocity. Do you understand what I mean?"

"You've expressed it very clearly."

"Good. Now that that's clear, I'd like to ask you an informal question."

"If I'm able to answer it, I will."

"I'm sure you can." She leaned over and sank her voice conspiratorially. "I would like to know what you would make of all this if you were in my seat. You have experience, intuition, you have a good nose. What would you be thinking?"

Jericho resolved not to get taken in by her.

"I would exert more pressure."

"Oh?" She looked surprised, as if he had just invited her to torture him with burning cigarettes.

"Pressure on my team," he added. "To make sure they put all their energy into getting their hands on the man who is responsible for the attacks, and into investigating his background, instead of getting taken in by the crude idea of making victims into perpetrators and threatening them with deportation. Does my answer suffice?"

"I'll make a note of it."

As far as Jericho could tell, she didn't seem in the slightest bit taken aback. It was clear that she doubted the substance of his statement, but she knew equally well that she had nothing on him. He was more worried about the others. Practically everyone besides him seemed to have come into conflict with the law in one way or another, which put them at the mercy of the police.

"I would like to express my sympathy once again," she said, in a different tone now. "You went through a great deal. We will do everything we can to bring those responsible to justice."

Jericho nodded. "Let me know if I can be of any assistance."

She stood up and held out her hand.

"Rest assured I will."

• • •

"So?"

Tu had come into the room. It was late afternoon by now; the skies were overcast and light drizzle was falling on Pudong. The investigators had retreated.

"Nothing new." Jericho stretched. "Diane is keeping herself busy with the Swiss films. We're also trying to trace the six websites back to a common source. So far there's nothing to indicate that there is one, but that doesn't necessarily mean anything."

"That's not what I meant." Tu pulled a chair over and sank down into it, panting. Jericho noticed that his shirt sleeves were pushed up to different heights. "How did the questioning go?"

"How do you think it went? She didn't believe a word I said."

"She didn't believe me either." For some unknown reason this seemed to fill Tu with satisfaction. "Nor Yoyo. Hongbing was the only one she seemed to handle with kid gloves."

"Of course," murmured Jericho.

From the very moment Chen had first come into his office in Xintiandi, he had noticed something about him that was hard to define, something in his eyes, in his tautly stretched face, something which gave the impression that his soul had been peeled away. Now he realized what he had seen, and the investigator must have seen it too. The idea that this man could lie was inconceivable. Nothing in Chen's features was capable of even hosting a lie. This left him completely at the mercy of his surroundings. He couldn't bear dishonesty, neither from himself nor from others.

"Tian—" he said, hesitantly.

"Mmhm?"

"There may be a problem with regard to how we proceed from here. Don't get me wrong, it's not—" He searched for the words.

"What is it? Out with it."

"I know too little about you."

Tu was silent.

"Too little about you and Chen Hongbing. I know it has nothing to do with me. It's just—in order to judge what danger you're in regarding the authorities, I would need to—well—I would need an idea, but—"

Tu pursed his lips. "I understand."

"No, I don't think you do," said Jericho. "You think I'm being nosy. You're wrong. I couldn't care less. Well no, that's not it. I mean that I respect your silence. Whatever has happened in your or Chen's past has nothing to do with me. But in that case *you* have to be the one to say where we go from here. You're better placed to judge—"

"It's fine," mumbled Tu.

"It's your business. I respect—"

"No, you're right."

"Under no circumstances do I want to be inconsiderate of—"

"Enough, *xiongdi*." Tu clapped him on the shoulder. "Consideration is the very foundation of your being; you don't need to explain yourself. In any case, I've often thought about strengthening our friendship by confessing a little of my past to you." His gaze wandered over to the door. Somewhere in the great expanse of the house, Yoyo and her father were wrestling with the past and future. "It's just that I fear I have to get back in the ring."

"To mediate?"

"To take some of the heat. Yoyo and I have decided to clear the air. By the end of the day Hongbing will know the whole truth."

"And how is he taking it so far?"

"I'm sure he's not exactly over the moon." Tu belched. "But I'm not seriously concerned. The more pressing question is how long he proposes to brood in his anger. Sooner or later he has to see that you can't earn trust by denying your child long-overdue answers. He'll have to tell Yoyo his truth too." Tu sighed. "What happens then, I really don't know. It's not that Hongbing seriously believes a part of his life didn't happen. He just can't bring himself to tell someone he loves about it. Because he's ashamed. He's just an old crab really. And try telling a crab it should cast off its shell."

"Well, if he did he would be the first crab to be able to do without it."

"Oh, they shed them a lot when they're young in order to grow. It's a dangerous undertaking though, because the new shell is very soft for the first few hours. They're very vulnerable for that time, easy targets, without any protection. But if they didn't shed them, there wouldn't be enough space for them to live." Tu stood up. "And as I said, Hongbing is a pretty old crab, but his shell has definitely got too small for him. I think he needs to shed it again so he doesn't end up shattering into a thousand pieces from the pressure."

Tu laid his right hand on Jericho's shoulder for a moment. Then he left the room.

Dusk stole in, stuffy and damp.

Diane was still processing.

Jericho wandered through the house and went to see Joanna in her studio, a glass pagoda temple backing onto the artificial lake which formed the center of the property. He wasn't surprised to find her working on one of her large-format portraits. Joanna wasn't the type to wander through the house wringing her hands if they could be put to better use. She had turned on bright lamps and was giving depth and contour to two beautiful socialites who were pictured arm in arm in front of a mirror, looking as if they had danced through three days and nights straight.

After Chen had emerged, flushed with anger, and disappeared into the guest rooms on the first floor, Tu had intensified the security around his villa and fled to his office. Yoyo had crossed Jericho's path as he walked through the entrance hall. She looked as though she had been crying, and had waved her hands around as if trying to signal that he shouldn't ask any questions. Just when she was about to climb the stairs, her father had appeared on the landing, heading stormily for the bathroom, which was enough for Yoyo to hastily change direction and wander off into the garden, where Jericho had just been coming in from.

All at once, he had felt terribly out of place.

Tu's butler saw him standing around and rushed to attend to his needs. Jericho turned down hot lavender baths and Thai massages, ordered some tea, and unexpectedly felt a craving for the kind of biscuits Joanna had brought him just hours before, only to scoff them all under his nose. The butler offered to make up the salon for him. For want of a better idea, Jericho nodded, paced around in a circle twice, and noticed that the feeling of being out of place was accompanied by the quicksand-like sensation of helplessness.

Something had to happen.

And it did.

"Owen? This is Diane."

He felt a *frisson* of excitement, pulled out his phone, and spoke into it breathlessly. "Yes, Diane? What is it?"

"I've found something in the films that will interest you. A watermark. There's a film within a film."

Oh, Diane! thought Jericho. I could kiss you. If you looked only half as good as you sound I would even marry you, but you're just a damn computer. But never mind. Make me happy!

"Wait there," he called, as if there were some risk she might decide otherwise and leave the house. "I'm coming."

Yoyo would have liked to convince herself she was past the worst, but she felt the worst still lay before her, and three times as intense. Hongbing had screamed and shouted. They had argued for over an hour. As a result, her eyes were sore and filled with salty tears, as if she had seen nothing but misery and hardship her whole life. She felt guilty about everything. About the massacre in the steelworks, the destruction of the apartment, her father's despair, and finally about the fact that Hongbing didn't love her. Almost as soon as it had appeared, this last thought entered into sinister alliances with all possible forms of self-loathing and gave birth to a new guilt, namely, having done Hongbing an injustice. Of course he had loved her, how could he not have? How low did you have to sink to assume anything else but love from your own father? But now just that thought alone made her undeserving of love, and Hongbing had taken the only logical step and stopped loving her. So what was she complaining about? She was to blame for the fact that his mask of a face had not melted, but shattered.

She had disappointed everyone.

For a while she hung around silently in Joanna's studio, watching as Tian's beautiful wife conjured up a feverish sparkle in the eyes of the exhausted teenagers, that last glimmer of energy moments before all systems shut down. On the monstrous two-and-a-half-by-four-meter canvas, she portrayed carefree natures through pigments: two ornamental fish in the shallow waters of their sensitivities, whose only worry in life was how not to die from boredom before the next party kicked off. Realizing that the worst massacres in the lives of the two beauties were probably the ones they had caused in the hearts of pubescent boys, Yoyo cried a little more.

She was probably doing these girls an injustice too. Was she really any better? She had certainly been no stranger to excess in the last few years. She was more than familiar with the moment when one faded out like a dwindling, bright red dot in the blackness of a charred wick. She had sung incessantly against Hongbing's sadness, danced against it, smoked and fucked against it, without once flagging with a sooth-ing emptiness in her gaze like the princesses of the night on Joanna's canvas. Each time, her last thought had been that the excesses weren't worth dying for, that she would have much rather been sitting at home listening to what her father had to tell her about the time before she was born. But Hongbing hadn't told her one single thing.

Joanna created eyelashes with a flourish, pressed in smatterings of mascara and distributed makeup in the corner of the eyes and onto cheekbones. Yoyo watched, overcome with melancholy. She liked Joanna's flirtation with society, the way she wore its colorful plumage. There was no canvas big enough to depict the way China entertained itself, Joanna always said. After all, China was a big country, and so she explained to her feathered friends, whenever they came to sharpen their beaks and sip at champagne, that lack of content couldn't be portrayed on a small scale. It was a witty and catchy comment, but really incom-prehensible in an artistic sense. She pompously celebrated the beauty of emptiness and the emptiness of beauty, sold her fans something they could look at, and neglected to tell them it was actually a mirror.

"Don't forget," she always said with her most charming Joanna smile. "I'm in the picture too. In every single one. Including yours."

Yoyo envied Joanna. She envied the egoism with which she sailed through life, and without picking up any bruises along the way. She envied her ability to be uninterested, and her lack of concern in show-ing it. Yoyo, on the other hand, was interested in everything, and compulsively so. Could that ever end well? Sure, the Guardians had accomplished quite a lot of things. Under their pressure, imprisoned journalists had been released, corrupt civil servants stripped of office, and environmental scandals solved. While Joanna's hands were being manicured, Yoyo had been busy dirtying hers by delving them into painful subjects, never tiring in demanding China's right to its own culture of fun. This had given her the reputation of being a nationalist from time to time. Just as well. She was a hedonistic preacher, a liberal nationalist who got fired up by the injustice in the world. Wonderful! And yet there were so many other things she could do. She was sure she could find something, as long as it meant not having to be Chen Yuyun.

Joanna painted, and was simply Joanna. Self-involved, carefree, and rich. Everything that repulsed Yoyo from the bottom of her heart, and yet she yearned for it too. Someone who offered security. Someone who wouldn't step aside, because it was something they never did.

She was crying again.

After a while, Yoyo's supply of tears was exhausted. Joanna cleaned her brushes in turpentine. Over the glass surfaces of the pagoda roof, the sky was working its way through every shade of gray in preparation for the evening.

"So how did it go? Well?"

Yoyo sniffed and shook her head.

"It must have gone well," Joanna decided. "You screamed at each other, and you cried. That's good."

"You think?"

Joanna turned to her and smiled.

"Well, it's certainly better than him swallowing his own tongue and talking to the walls at night."

"I shouldn't have lied to him like that," said Yoyo and coughed, her airways blocked from all the crying. "I hurt him. You should have seen him."

"Nonsense, sweetheart. You didn't hurt him. You told him the truth."

"Yes, that's what I mean."

"No, you're getting confused. You're acting as though speaking frankly were some huge moral issue. If you tell the truth, you're one of the good guys. How it's received is a different matter, but that's what psychiatrists are for. There's nothing more you can do to help your father bite the bullet."

"To be honest, I've got no idea what I'm supposed to do now."

"I do." Joanna stretched out her slim fingers, one after another. "Run yourself a bath, go a few rounds with the punching bag, go shopping. Spend money. Lots of money."

Yoyo rubbed her elbows. "I'm not you, Joanna."

"No one suggested you take off and buy a Rolls-Royce. I want you to understand the principles of cause and effect. The truth is a good thing, even if it can be unpleasant at times. And if it is unpleasant, it strengthens the body's defenses."

"And did it strengthen Owen's defenses?"

Joanna held a thick paintbrush up to the light and fanned the bristles out with her fingernail.

"Tian told me that you were together," Yoyo added quickly. "Before you got married."

"Yes, we were together."

"Okay. We don't have to talk about it if you don't want to."

"It's fine." She put the paintbrush down and gave her a beaming smile. "We had a great time."

"So why did you break up? I mean, he's a really nice guy."

Yoyo was surprised by her own words. Did she think Owen Jericho was nice? So far he had only come up in connection with firearms, death, and severe bodily harm. On the other hand, he had saved her life. Do you automatically think someone is nice because they save your life?

"Relationships are contracts that can be terminated at any time, my dear," said Joanna, picking up the second brush. "Without notice. You don't quit sexual relations six weeks before the end of the quarter. If it's not working anymore, you have to go."

"And what wasn't working?"

"Everything. The Owen who came with me to Shanghai bore no resemblance to the one I had met in London."

"You were in London?"

"Is this an interview?" Joanna raised her eyebrows. "If it is I'd like to see the article for authorization later."

"No, I'm genuinely interested. I mean, we haven't known each other for that long, right? You and Tian, you've been together now for—how many years?"

"Four."

"Exactly. And we haven't had much of a chance to talk."

"Woman to woman, you mean?"

"No, not all that garbage, it's just, I've known Tian forever, my whole life, but you—"

"You don't know anything about me." Joanna smirked mockingly. "And now you're worried about good old Tian, because you can't imagine what a beautiful and spoilt woman would want from a bald-headed, sloppy, overweight old sack who, despite having money coming out of his ears, still fixes his glasses with double-sided tape and wears the seat of his pants around the backs of his knees."

"I didn't say that," replied Yoyo angrily.

"But you thought it. And so did Owen. Fine, I'll tell you a story. It's a lesson about the economics of love. It begins in London, where I moved in 2017 to study English Literature, Western Art, and Painting; something for which you need to be either crazy, an idealist, or from a rich background. My father was Pan Zemin—"

"The Environment Minister?"

"Deputy Environment Minister."

"Hey," cried Yoyo, "we always admired your father."

"He'd have liked that."

"He publicly addressed a number of problems." Warming enthusiasm flooded through Yoyo. "He was really brave. And the way he pushed to put more money into solar research, to increase the energy yield—"

"Yes, generally speaking he was pretty salubrious," said Joanna drily, "but it didn't hurt that one of the companies which made the breakthrough belonged to him. As I said, crazy, idealistic, or from a rich background. In London, the Chinese community had long since outgrown Gerrard Street by then. There were a lot of good clubs in Soho that were popular with Chinese and Europeans. I met Owen in one of them. That was 2019, and I liked him. Oh, I liked him a lot!"

"Yes, well, he's very good-looking."

"He's easy on the eye, let's say. But the great thing about him wasn't the way he looked, but the fact that he wasn't afraid of me. It was awful, how all the men were instantly afraid of me: such losers; I used to eat them for breakfast." She smiled maliciously and twirled another brush through the turpentine. "But Owen seemed determined not to let himself be influenced by my undeniably dazzling looks or my financial independence, and for two whole hours he managed not to look at my tits. That spoke volumes. He also respected my intelligence; I could tell by the way he contradicted me. He was a cyber-cop at Scotland Yard, where they don't exactly shower you in gold, but then I wasn't interested in money. Owen could have slept under London Bridge and I would have lain down next to him." She paused. "Well, let's say I would have bought it and then lain down. We were very much in love."

"So how could that go wrong?"

"Yes, how?" Joanna gave a melodious little sigh. "In 2020, my father suffered a stroke and was considerate enough not to wake up again. He left behind a respectable fortune, a wife whose patience had been tested and who endured his passing as unquestioningly as she had endured him, and also three children, of whom I am the eldest. Mom was often lonely, and with the unhoped-for inheritance I'd just received, I felt there was no need for me to keep clogging up the lecture halls in London. So I decided to go back. I asked Owen what he thought of us moving to Shanghai, and he said, without giving it much thought: Sure, let's move to Shanghai. And you know, that was strange in itself."

"Why? That was exactly what you wanted."

"Of course, but he didn't have even the slightest objection. And we'd only been together for half a year. But that's the problem. If men do what you tell them to, they're suspect, and if they oppose us we think they're ridiculous. Back then I thought, well, it's because he loves me so much, which was a good thing in itself, because as long as he loved me, he would only betray himself and not me. But back then I was already beginning to ask myself which one of us loved the other more."

"And he loved you too much."

"No, he loved himself too little. But I only realized that after we arrived in Shanghai. To start with, everything was great. He knew his way around, liked the city, and had been there numerous times during bilateral investigations. At New Scotland Yard he was a kind of in-house Sinologist, and I should mention that Owen doesn't learn languages laboriously like other people do; he simply swallows them down and then brings them back up in well-worded formulations. I suggested he take a job with the Shanghai Department for Cybercrime, because they already knew and valued him there—"

"Cypol," snorted Yoyo.

"Yes, your good friends. We moved into an apartment in Pudong and planned a lifetime of happiness. And that's when it started. Little things. His gaze started to waver when he spoke to me. He started to suck up to me. Sure, we were living in *my* country, meeting *my* people, including politicians, intellectuals, and all kinds of representatives of society, every one of whom sucked up to me. In my circle, greatness is the result of the degradation of others, but Owen's knees became weaker and weaker. His wonderful self-confidence melted like butter in the sun, he seemed to degenerate, get pimples again, and after a while he asked me, full of timidity, if I loved him. I was totally taken aback! It was like he'd just asked me, right in front of a bright blue sky, if the sun was shining."

"Perhaps he sensed you didn't love him as much as you had before."

"It's the other way around, sweetheart. The doubts came with the doubter. Owen didn't have the slightest reason to mistrust me, even though he probably thought he did. He had stopped trusting *himself*; that was the problem! You can only fall in love when you're on an equal standing, but if your partner is bowed over in front of you, you have no choice but to look down on him."

"Did he get jealous?"

"Jealousy's such an ugly addiction. Nothing makes you smaller or less attractive." Joanna walked over to an open store cupboard, in which dozens of tubes lay next to one another. "Yes, he did. He was possessed by some old insecurity. Our relationship lost its equilibrium. I'm a positive person, sweetie, and I don't know how to be any other way, which meant that next to me Owen looked increasingly like a pot plant someone had forgotten to water. My optimism left him to wither. The worse he felt, the more I enjoyed my life, or that's what he thought anyway. That was complete nonsense of course! I had always enjoyed life, but before that we used to enjoy it together." She took out a tube of vermilion and squeezed a small splodge of it onto a palette. "I left him so that he could finally find himself."

"How considerate of you," scoffed Yoyo.

"I know how you see it." Joanna paused for a second. "But you're wrong. I could have grown old with him. But Owen had lost his faith. The world is an illusion; everything is an illusion, love intrinsically so. If you stop believing in it, it disappears. If you stop feeling, the sun becomes just a blob and flowers become brambles. That's the whole story."

Yoyo padded over to a footstool and sank down onto it.

"You know what?" she said. "I feel sorry for him."

"Who?"

"Owen, of course."

"*Tsk, tsk*." Joanna shook her head disapprovingly. "How rude. I thought you would grant him a little more respect. Owen is talented, intelligent, charming, attractive. He could be anything he wants to be; everyone knows that. Everyone except him."

"He probably believed it for a while. Back in London."

"Yes, because of the sheer surprise that things were working out with us he temporarily forgot to be a pathetic little jerk."

Yoyo stared at her. "Tell me, are you really this heartless, or are you just pretending to be?"

"I'm honest and I try not to be corny. What do you want? Sentimentality? Then go to the movies."

"Fine. So what happened next?"

"He moved out right away of course. I offered to support him, but he turned it down. After a few months he left his job, purely because *I* had got it for him."

"Why didn't he go back to England?"

"You'd have to ask him that yourself."

"You never spoke about it?"

"We kept in touch, sure. There were just a few weeks when we didn't talk, a time during which I fell in love with Tian, whom I had already met at a number of parties. When Owen found out we were seeing each other his entire worldview collapsed." Joanna looked at Yoyo. "And yet I don't care how old, fat, or bald a man is. None of that matters. Tian is genuine, honest, and straightforward, and I sure as hell value that! A fighter, a rock. Quick-witted, educated, liberal—"

"Rich," completed Yoyo.

"I was rich already. Of course I liked the fact that Tian was looking for a challenge, that he was achieving success after success. But

when it comes down to it there's nothing he can do that Owen wouldn't
be able to do too. Except that Tian's existence is shaped by an almost
unshakable belief in himself. He thinks he's beautiful and that makes
him beautiful. That's why I love him."

Joanna's story had begun to have a pleasantly numbing effect on
Yoyo. She suddenly realized that she could breathe more easily when
other people's problems were the topic of conversation. At the very
least it was good to know that other people *had* problems. Even if they
could have done with being just a little bit bigger to fully distract her
from the morning's events.

"And what happened with Owen after that?" she asked.

Joanna turned her attentions to the oily strand on her palette and
stirred it into a crème with a pointed paintbrush.

"Ask him," she said, without looking up. "I've told my story. I'm not
responsible for his."

Yoyo slid indecisively back and forth in her seat. She didn't like
Joanna's unexpected uncommunicativeness. She decided to press her,
but just at that moment Tu came into the studio.

"There you are!" he said to Yoyo, as if she were obliged to let him
know where she was.

"Has something happened?" she asked.

"Yes. Owen's been working hard. Come with me to the office, it
looks like he's found out a whole load of stuff."

Yoyo got up and looked over to Joanna. "Are you coming?"

Joanna smiled. Vermilion dripped down from the tip of her paintbrush like old, noble blood.

"No, sweetheart, you go ahead. I'd only ask stupid questions."

At 19:20 hours, Tu, Jericho, and Yoyo immersed themselves in the beauty
of the Swiss Alps. A 3D film was playing in large format on Tu's multimedia wall. It showed a cable car rising up from a picturesque little town
and heading toward a neat alpine pasture, over ravines and forests of fir
trees. A low, classic-looking building came into view. The Spanish commentator lauded it as one of the first designer hotels in the Alps, praising
the rooms for their comfort and the kitchen for its dumplings, before
heading off to accompany a group of hikers across a meadow. Cows
plodded over curiously. A pretty city girl watched them approach with
skepticism, started walking quickly, then broke into a run toward the
valley, where two donkeys came shuffling out of their hutch, gray and
tired, and herded her back toward the cows. Some of the hikers laughed.
The next scene showed a farmer kicking one of the cows up the backside.

"Up here, traditions are still quite coarse and primordial," explained
the Spanish commentator in the tone of some behavioral scientist who
has just discovered that chimpanzees aren't that intelligent after all.

"Well, this is great," said Yoyo.

Neither she nor Tu spoke Spanish, but that didn't matter. Jericho stubbornly let the film play on, champing at the bit for his big moment.

"I don't need to explain to either of you how a film like this is developed," he said. "And you both know about watermarks too. So—"

"Excuse me," said someone from the door.

They turned around. Chen Hongbing had come in. He paused, hesitantly took a step toward them, and straightened himself up.

"I don't want to interrupt. I just wanted to—"

"Hongbing," Tu hurried over to his friend and put his arm around his shoulder. "How lovely that you're here."

"Well." Hongbing cleared his throat. "I thought, we should make them smart, shouldn't we? Not for my sake, but—" He went over to Yoyo, looked at her and then away again, looked around at the others, massaged the tip of his chin, and waved his hands around indecisively. Yoyo stared up at him, confused. "So, the thing is, I'm afraid I don't know."

"You don't know what, may I ask?" Jericho asked cautiously. Chen gestured vaguely toward the film playing on the screen.

"How something like that is developed. A, erm—watermark." He cleared his throat again. "But I don't want to hold you up, don't worry. I just wanted to be here too."

"You're not holding us up, Father," said Yoyo softly.

Chen snuffled, let out a whole cascade of throat-clearing noises, and mumbled something incomprehensible. Then he took Yoyo's hand, gave it a brief, firm squeeze, and let it go again.

Yoyo's eyes started to shine.

"No problem, honorable Chen," said Jericho. "Have the others brought you up to date with what we know?"

"Chen, just call me Chen. Yes, I know about the—the garbled report."

"Good. We didn't have much more than that until just now. Just a hunch that there must be something else in the films." He wondered how he could make all of this comprehensible to Chen. When it came to technology, the man was endearingly clueless. "You see, it's like this: every data stream is made up of data packages. Try imagining a swarm of bees, several million bees of different colors, who keep rearranging themselves in new ways so that your eyes see moving pictures. And now imagine that some of these bees are encoded. In a way that isn't visible to the viewer. But if you have a special algorithm—"

"Algorithm?"

"A mask, a decoding process. It lets you block out all of the non-encoded bees. Only the encoded ones stay. And suddenly you realize that they represent something too. You see a film within a film. That's called an electronic watermark. It's not a new process: at the beginning

of the millennium it was used to encode films and songs when the entertainment industry was fighting against pirate copiers. It was enough to
make just a small adjustment in the frequency spectrum of a song. The
human ear can't tell the difference, but it enabled the computer to investigate the origin of the CD." He paused. "Today, the difference is this: the
old Internet mapped the data streams two-dimensionally, whereas nowadays the Internet is construed for three-dimensional content. These
kind of data streams have to be pictured cubically, which offers much
better opportunities for hosting complex watermarks. Although, admittedly, decoding has become equally complex." ·

"And you've decoded one of these watermarks?" asked Chen,
awestruck.

"Yes. That is, Diane—erm, my computer—found a way to make it
visible."

By now, the group of hikers had valiantly climbed to a high plateau.
The pretty city girl was approaching a sheep. The sheep didn't budge,
and stared at the woman, who took this as encouragement to circle
around giving it a wide berth.

"Don't keep us in suspense," said Yoyo.

"Okay." Jericho looked back at the wall. "Diane, start the film again.
Decoded and compressed, high resolution."

The alpine world disappeared. In its place appeared a recording of
a car journey, filmed from inside the vehicle. It made its way along a
bumpy street. Hilly farmland stretched out on both sides, broken up
now and then by bushes and the occasional tree. There were a few huts
here and there, most of them very run-down. The sky was swollen with
rain clouds. As the landscape steepened and became more densely
populated with trees, the gray cross-hatchings of downpours stopped.

A truck was being driven a fair way ahead of the car, whirling up
dust. There were a number of black men sitting in the back, most clad
only in shorts. They looked lethargic, at least as far as you could tell
from this distance and through the dirt from the road. Then the camera swung around to the driver, a man with ash-blond hair, a mustache, and a strong jawline, wearing sunglasses.

The person holding the camera said something incomprehensible.
The blond man glanced over and grinned.

"Of course," he said in Spanish. "Praise the President."

They both laughed.

The picture changed. The same man was shown sitting at a long
table in the company of men in uniform, this time dressed in a khaki
shirt and light jacket, and without sunglasses. The camera zoomed in
on him. His eyebrows and lashes were as pale as the hair on his head,
his eyes watery blue, one of them with a fixed gaze, possibly a glass eye.
Then the camera panned out and captured the table in its entirety. Two

Chinese men in suits and ties were presenting some charts. The target audience of their report seemed to be a brawny figure at the head of the table, bald, bull-necked, and as black as polished ebony. He was wearing a plain coat. The uniforms of the other participants, who were also black, seemed more formal, dark with red-gold epaulettes and all kinds of decorations, but the bullish one was clearly the nucleus of the whole meeting, while the blond seemed to be taking on the role of spectator.

This conversation was taking place in Spanish too. The Chinese spokesman was fluent, but had an appalling accent. The topic of discussion was clearly the building of a gas to liquid plant, which was eliciting approving nods from the bullish man. The Chinese man asked his colleague for some files, with a light Beijing accent.

The camera zoomed in on the blond man again. He was making notes and following the presentation attentively.

Lines and whirling shapes suddenly flashed across the multimedia wall. Someone was trying to focus the picture. A street came into view, an inner-city landscape, full of cars. Someone was coming out of a glass building on the other side of the street, where holographic advertisement films were hovering over the façade like ghosts. The camera zoomed in on the person, going hazy many times in the process, then captured the head and upper body. Tall, clean-shaven and with his hair dyed dark, at first glance the blond was hardly recognizable. He looked around then walked off down the street. The camera flickered again, then came back into focus to show him sitting in the sun, flicking through a magazine. Now and then he sipped at a cup, then he looked up and the film ended abruptly.

"That's all there is," said Jericho.

For a while, they were all silent. Then Yoyo said:

"It's to do with Chinese interests in Africa, right? I mean, that conference, it was obvious."

"Could be. Did any of them look familiar to you?"

Yoyo hesitated. "I've seen the bull-necked guy before."

"And the Chinese men?"

"They look like corporate types. What was it about again? Gas to liquid plants? Oil managers, I'd say. Sinopec or Petrochina."

"But you don't know them?"

"No."

"Any other thoughts, anyone?"

He looked around. Tu seemed to want to say something, but shook his head.

"Okay. I haven't had a chance to analyze the film yet, but I can tell you a few things. In my opinion the recordings are purely and simply about the blond guy. Twice we see him in an African country, where he seems to hold a public position, then later, with his appearance changed, in a city somewhere in the world. He's dyed his hair darker and shaved off the mustache. Conclusions?"

"Two," said Yoyo. "Either he's on a secret mission, or he had to go underground."

"Very good. So let's ask ourselves—"

"Owen." Tu gave him a lenient smile. "Could you not come straight to the point?"

"Sorry." Jericho shrugged apologetically. "So, I instructed Diane to scour the Internet in search of the man, and she found him." He added a dramatic pause, not caring whether Tu liked it or not. "Our friend's name is Jan Kees Vogelaar."

Yoyo stared at him. "There's a Jan in the text fragment!"

"Exactly. So we've got two men who are connected with the incidents of the last few days. One of them being Andre Donner, about whom all we know is that he's running an African restaurant in Berlin, but nonetheless. And Jan Kees Vogelaar, top mercenary and personal security adviser to a certain Juan Alfonso Nguema Mayé, if that rings any bells with any of you."

"Mayé," echoed Tu. "Wait, where have I—?"

"In the news. From 2017 to 2024 Juan Mayé was the president and sole dictator of Equatorial Guinea." Jericho paused. "Until he was violently removed from office."

"That's right," murmured Tu. "Look—we may have our coup."

"Possibly. So let's assume it's not about plans to overthrow the Communist Party after all, nor some other crazy conspiracy story. That means the coup being discussed in the text fragment would have taken place a long time ago. Last July, to be precise. And with the *involvement* of the Chinese government no less!"

Chen raised his hand. "Where is Equatorial Guinea anyway?"

"In West Africa," Yoyo explained. "A horrid little coastal state with a hell of a lot of oil. And the guy with the bull-neck—"

"—is Mayé," confirmed Jericho. "Or rather, *was*. His ambitions to stay in power didn't do him any good. They blew him and his whole clique up. No one survived. It was all over the news in 2024."

"I remember. We were planning to do some research about Equatorial Guinea back then. When we were still interested in foreign politics."

"Why aren't you now?"

Yoyo shrugged. "What else can you do when the garbage is piling up in front of your own door? You walk through the streets and see the migrant workers sleeping on the building sites the way they always have, the same place where they fuck, breed, and kick the bucket. You see the illegal immigrants without papers, without work permits, without health insurance. The filth in Quyu. The lines in front of the appeal offices, the government-hired thugs who turn up at night and beat

them black and blue until they've forgotten what they wanted to complain about. And all the while Reporters Without Borders announce
that freedom of opinion has demonstrably improved in China. I know
it sounds cynical, but after a while the problems of exploited Africans
don't even register on your radar."

Chen lowered his gaze, painfully moved.

"Let's stick with Vogelaar for now," decided Tu. "What else can you
tell us about him?"

Jericho projected a chart onto the wall. "I've investigated him as
much as I could. Born in South Africa in 1962 as the son of a Dutch
immigrant, he did military service, studied at the military academy,
and then in 1983, aged twenty-one, he signed up as an NCO with the
notorious Koevoet."

"I've never heard of them," said Yoyo.

"Koevoet was a paramilitary unit of the South African police
formed to combat SWAPO, a guerrilla troop fighting for the independence of South West Africa, now Namibia. Back then, the South African Union refused to retreat from the area despite a UN resolution,
and instead built up Koevoet, which, by the way, is the Dutch word
for crowbar. Quite a rough bunch. Predominantly native tribal war-
riors and trackers. Exclusively white officers. They hunted down the
SWAPO rebels in armored cars and killed many thousands of people.
They were said to have tortured and raped too. Vogelaar even became
an officer, but by the end of the eighties the group had come to an end
and was disbanded."

"How do you know all that?" asked Tu in amazement.

"I looked it up. I just wanted to know who we're dealing with here.
And it's very interesting by the way. Koevoet is one of the causes of
the South African mercenary problem: at any rate, the troop included
three thousand men who found themselves unemployed after the end
of apartheid. Most of them, including Vogelaar, found jobs with private mercenary firms. After the suppression of Koevoet at the end of
the eighties, he got into the arms trade, working as a military adviser
in conflict areas. Then, in 1995, he went to Executive Outcomes, a privately run security company and meeting place for a large proportion
of the former military elite. By the time Vogelaar joined, the outfit was
already playing a leading role in the worldwide mercenary trade, after
initially being content with infiltrating the ANC. By the mid nineties,
Executive Outcomes had built up perfect connections. A network of
military service companies, oil and mining firms: one which headed
lucrative contract wars and was very happy to profit from the petroleum industry. They ended the civil war in Somalia in the interest of
American oil companies, and in Sierra Leone they recaptured diamond mines which had fallen into the hands of the rebels. Vogelaar

built up excellent contacts there. Four years later he transferred to Outcomes' offshoot Sandline International, but it drew unwanted attention
through botched operations and ended up abandoning all activities
in 2004. He eventually founded Mamba, his own security company,
which operated predominantly in Nigeria and Kenya. And Kenya is
where we lose all trace of him, sometime during the unrest after the
2007 elections." Jericho looked at them apologetically. "Or, let's say
that's where I lose trace of him. In any case, he appears again in 2017, at
Mayé's side, whose security apparatus he led from then on."

"A gap of ten years," commented Tu.

"Didn't Mayé take power by military coup himself?" asked Yoyo.
"Vogelaar may have helped him with that."

"It's possible." Tu grimaced. "Africa and its regicides. Stabbing
everyone in the back. After a while you lose perspective. It just surprises me that they still have a clue what's going on."

Chen cleared his throat. "May I, erm, contribute something?"

"Hongbing, of course! We're all ears. Go ahead."

"Well." Chen looked at Jericho. "You said that the whole clique of
this Mayé guy got killed in the coup, right?"

"Correct."

"And I'm translating clique in the broadest sense of the word as
government."

"Also correct."

"Well, a coup without any fatalities at all would be unusual, to say
the least." Suddenly, Chen seemed jovial and analytical. "Or, let's say,
when weapons come into play, collateral damage is par for the course.
But if the entire government clique was killed—then it can hardly be
described as collateral damage, can it?"

"What are you getting at?"

"That the coup wasn't so much about forcing Mayé and his people
out of office, but more about exterminating them. Every single one of
them. It was planned that way from the start, or that's how it looks to
me at any rate. It wasn't just a coup. It was planned mass murder."

"Oh, Father," sighed Yoyo softly. "What a Guardian you would have
made."

"Hongbing is right," said Tu quickly, before Chen could splutter
at Yoyo's observation. "And as we're clearly not afraid to poke around
in the dark, we may as well jump straight to assuming the worst. The
dragon has already feasted. Our country brought about this atrocity,
or at least helped with it." He sank his double chin down onto his right
palm, where it rested plumply. "On the other hand, what reason would
Beijing have for annihilating an entire West African kleptocracy?"

Yoyo opened her eyes wide in disbelief.

"You don't think they're capable of it? Hey, what's wrong with you?"

"Calm down, child, I think they're capable of anything. I'd just like to know *why.*"

"This—" Chen's right hand made vague grasping motions. "What was he called again, the mercenary?"

"Vogelaar. Jan Kees Vogelaar."

"Well, he would know."

"That's true, he—"

They all looked at one another.

And suddenly it dawned on Jericho.

Of course! If Chen was right and the Mayé government really had been the victim of an assassination, then there could only be two reasons. One, public anger had boiled over. It wouldn't be the first time an enraged mob had lynched its former tormentors, but something like that usually happened spontaneously, and moreover used different methods of execution: dismembering by machete, a burning car tire around the neck, clubbing to death. In the short time available, Jericho hadn't been able to find out much about relationships in the crisis-torn West African state, but Mayé's fall still seemed like the result of a perfectly planned, simultaneously realized operation. Within just a few hours, all the members of the close circle around the dictator were dead. As if the plan had been to silence the entire setup. Mayé and six of his ministers had died in an explosion caused by a long-range missile, while a further ten ministers and generals had been shot.

But one of them had got away. Jan Kees Vogelaar.

Why? Had Vogelaar been playing both sides? A coup of this caliber was only possible with connections on the inside. Was Mayé's security boss a traitor? Assuming that this was true, then—

"—Andre Donner is a witness," murmured Jericho.

"Sorry?" asked Tu.

Jericho was staring into space.

—Donner be liquidated—

"Could you perhaps let us in on your thoughts?" Yoyo suggested.

"*Donner be liquidated,*" said Jericho. He looked at them each in turn. "I know it's bold to try to read so much into a few scraps of text. But this part seems clear to me. I've no idea who Donner is, but let's assume he knows the true background to the coup. That he knows who's pulling the strings. Then—"

—continues a grave—

A grave what? Risk? A risk that Donner, after having gone underground, might divulge what he knew?

—that he knows all about—

—statement coup Chinese government—

"Then what?" repeated Yoyo.

"Pay attention!" shouted Jericho, worked up. "Let's assume Donner knows the Chinese government were involved in the coup. And that he also knows why. He could flee. He's probably not even called Donner yet in Equatorial Guinea, he's somewhere in the—in the government? Yes, in the government! Or he's high up in the military, a general or something. But whatever he is, he needs a new identity. So he becomes Donner, Andre Donner. If we had photos of those formerly in power and one of him, we'd be able to recognize him! He goes to Berlin, far away, and builds up a new existence, a new life. New papers, new background."

"Opens a restaurant," says Tu. "And then he gets tracked down."

"Yes. Vogelaar is given the commission of coordinating the simultaneous liquidation of the Mayé clan. One of them slips through his fingers, someone who could ruin everything. Think of the fuss they made trying to eliminate Yoyo just because she intercepted some cryptic material. Vogelaar's backers are worried. As long as Donner is still alive he could decide to bust the whole thing open."

"The fact that a foreign regime brought the coup about, for example."

"Which wouldn't be anything new," said Jericho. "Just look at all the places where the CIA has played a part: 1962, attempted coup in Cuba. Early seventies, Chile. 2018, the collapse in North Korea. No one had any doubt that they were involved in the assassination of Kim Jong-un. There are also some who claim China helped in Saudi Arabia in 2015, so why not in West Africa too?"

"I see. And now Vogelaar has arrived in Berlin to eliminate the miraculously rediscovered Donner." Tu gave his neck a thorough scratch. "That really is bold."

"But conceivable." Chen gave a slight cough. "It's perfectly clear to me anyway."

"So there you go," whispered Yoyo.

"What?" asked Jericho.

"Well what do you think?" she snapped. "Like I said! It's the government. I have the Party at my throat!"

"Yes," said Jericho wearily. "It looks that way."

She put her face in her hands. "We need to know more about this country. More about Vogelaar, more about Donner. The more we know, the better equipped we'll be to defend ourselves. Failing that I'll just have to pack my bags. And so will all of you. I'm sorry."

Tu studied his fingernails.

"Good idea," he said.

Yoyo lifted her face from the grave-like shape formed by her hands. "What?"

"To pack your things, leave the country. It's a good idea. That's exactly what we'll do."

"I don't understand."

"What is there to understand? We'll look for this Donner guy. He's in grave danger. We'll warn him, and in return he'll tell us what we need to know."

"You want to—" Jericho thought he'd misheard. "Tian, the man lives in Berlin. That's in Germany!"

"If they even let us out at all," said Yoyo.

"One at a time." Tu raised his hands. "You lot have more reservations than a porcupine about to engage in sexual activity. As if I were suggesting fleeing headlong over the border. Think about it for a second, the police were just here in this very house. Do you seriously believe we would still be sitting here if they had wanted to grab us? No, we'll just go on a little trip, all official and above board. In my private jet, if you'll allow me to extend the invitation."

"And when do you want to set off?"

"Sometime after midnight."

Jericho stared at him, then Yoyo, then Chen.

"Shouldn't we perhaps—"

"That's the soonest we can do it," said Tu apologetically. "I've still got a dinner that I can't put off, not for love nor money. It's in an hour's time."

"Shouldn't we try calling Donner first? How do you even know for sure that he's still in Berlin? Perhaps he's gone away somewhere. Gone underground."

"You want to warn him we're coming?"

"I just think—"

"That's a lousy idea, Owen. Let's say he answers the phone and believes you. Then we've lost him. You won't have time to catch your breath and ask questions in the time it would take him to disappear. And besides, what else are you going to do? If you sit around here in Pudong you're just going to be making a dent in all my sofa cushions."

"So you expect us to go to Berlin," croaked Hongbing. "In the middle of the night?"

"I have beds on board."

"But—"

"You're not coming anyway. Just the rapid response team: Owen, Yoyo, and I."

"Why not me?" asked Chen, suddenly outraged.

"It would be too tiring for you. No, no arguments! A small, agile troop is just right for this kind of thing. Nimble and agile. In the meantime, I'm sure Joanna can drown you in tea and give you foot massages."

Jericho tried to picture Tu as agile and nimble.

"And if we don't find Donner?" he asked.

"Then we'll wait for him."

"What if he doesn't come?"

"Then we'll just fly back."

"And who," he asked, fueled by a dark suspicion, "might the pilot be?"

Tu raised his eyebrows. "Who do you think? Me."

A few kilometers away and several meters higher up, Xin looked down on the city at night.

After a traffic jam had finally slowed the blasted dump truck down to a walking pace, he had jumped off, caught the subway to Pudong—given that there was no free COD in sight—put the last few hundred meters to the Jin Mao Tower behind him at a running pace, and then crossed the lobby as if he had taken leave of his senses. He was on a mission to satiate his hunger for something sweet, and there was a chocolate boutique in the foyer boasting pralines for the price of haute couture. Xin had purchased a pack of them, half of which he plundered just during the journey upward. Chocolate, he had realized, helped him to think. After arriving in his suite he had thrown off his clothes, rushed into the huge marble bathroom, turned the shower on, and almost rubbed his skin away in his attempt to cleanse himself of the filth of Xaxu and the stain of his defeat.

Yoyo had got away from him yet again, and this time he didn't have the faintest idea where she might be. The answer machine was on at Jericho's place. Fueled by a surge of hate, Xin contemplated blowing up the detective agency. Then he discarded the thought. He couldn't afford to be vindictive in his current situation, and besides, after the disaster in Hongkou he didn't have the appropriate weapons. What's more, it was clear to him that there was no real reason to punish someone purely because they had made use of their God-given right to defend themselves.

Cleansed, enveloped in a cocoon of toweling and at an agreeable distance from the city, Xin tried to impose some order on the hornet swarm of his thoughts. First, he picked up the clothes lying all around him and dumped them in the washing basket. Then he glanced over at the ravaged box of pralines. Accustomed to subjecting his consumption of any kind of food to a master plan, and one which was intended to maintain the symmetry of what was on offer for as long as possible, Xin shuddered at what he had done. He normally ate from the outside, working his way in. There should be no excessive decimation, and the relationship of the components to one another had to remain constant. Just devouring everything on one side of the packaging was an unthinkable act! But that was exactly what he had done. He'd pounced on it like an animal, like one of those degenerate creatures in Quyu.

He sank down into the sprawling armchair in front of the floor-to-ceiling window and watched as dusk enveloped Shanghai. The city was sprinkled with multicolored lights, an impressive spectacle despite the lousy weather, but all Xin could see was the betrayal of his aesthetic principles. Jericho, Yoyo, Yoyo, Jericho. The transgressions in the box needed to be corrected. Where was Yoyo? Where was the detective? Who had been driving the silver flying machine? The box, the box! Unless he created order there he would drift right into insanity. He began to rearrange the remaining pralines according to the Rorschach style, starting from scratch again and again until an axis ran through the box, a stable, regulatory element, on either side of which the remaining pralines mirrored each other. After that he felt better, and he began to take stock of things. There was no longer any point in following Yoyo and the detective. In just a few days everything would be over anyway, and then they could talk all they wanted. They were no longer important. The operation was the priority now, and there was only one person who could still endanger the plan. Xin wondered what conclusions Jericho had drawn from the fragments of the message that he, Kenny Xin, had sent to the heads of Hydra after tracking down the Berlin restaurant of a certain Andre Donner, recommending his immediate liquidation. Unfortunately he had attached a modified decoding program to the mail, an improved, quicker version. Every few months, the codes were exchanged for new ones. The fact that Yoyo had intercepted this very e-mail had been the worst possible luck.

And there was nothing that could be done about it.

Andre Donner. Nice name, nice try.

He dialed a number on his cell phone.

"Hydra," he said.

"Have you eliminated the problem?"

As always, their conversation was transmitted in code. In just a few words, Xin reported on what had happened. His conversation partner fell silent for a while. Then he said:

"That's a mess, Kenny. You've done nothing you can be proud of."

"Those that live in glass houses shouldn't throw stones," responded Xin ill-temperedly. "If you'd implemented a safe algorithm, we wouldn't even be in this situation."

"It *is* safe. And that's not the issue here."

"The issue is whatever I consider worthy of being the issue."

"You've got some nerve."

"Oh really?" Xin roared with laughter. "You're my contact man, or had you already forgotten that? Just a glorified Dictaphone. If I want to hear a lecture, I'll call him."

The other man cleared his throat indignantly. "So what are you suggesting?"

"The same thing I've already suggested. Our friend in Berlin has to be got rid of. Anything less would be irresponsible. And besides, the address of the restaurant is in the goddamn e-mail. If Jericho comes up with the idea of getting in touch with him, then we really have a problem!"

"You want to go to Berlin?"

"As soon as possible. I'm not leaving that to anyone else."

"Wait." The line went dead for a moment. Then the voice came back. "We'll book a night flight for you."

"What about backup?"

"Already on its way. The specialist is setting off in advance as requested. Try to be more careful with the personnel and equipment this time."

Xin curled his lip contemptuously. "Don't worry."

"No, after all, I'm just the Dictaphone," said the voice icily. "But he's worried. So make sure you *finish* the job this time."

CALGARY, ALBERTA, CANADA

On April 21, Sid Bruford and two of his friends made a pilgrimage to an event in Calgary, where EMCO had proposed to outline a future that no longer existed. No one harbored any illusions that Gerald Palstein would announce anything other than the end of oil-sand mining in Alberta, which meant that all hopes were now focused on strategies for redevelopment, consolidation, or at the very least a social security plan. It was in hope of this that they were standing there, aside from the fact that it was only right and proper to be present at your own burial.

The plaza, a square park in front of the company headquarters, was filling slowly but steadily with people. As if mocking their misery, a bright yellow sun shone down on the crowd from a steel blue sky, creating a climate of new beginnings and confidence. Bruford, unwilling to abandon himself to the general bitterness, had decided to make the best of the situation. It was part of the dance of death to make fatalism look like self-confidence, to stock up on the required quota of beer and to avoid violence wherever possible. They talked about baseball for a while and stayed toward the back of the crowd, where the air was less saturated with sweat. Bruford held up his cell phone and circled, trying to capture the atmosphere around them. Two pleasingly scantily clad girls came into sight, noticed him, and then started to pose, giggling. A complex of empty buildings stretched out behind them, the headquarters of a now-bankrupt firm for drilling technology, if he remembered rightly. The girls liked him—that was as sure a bet as the closure of Imperial Oil. He had handsome, almost Italian-looking features, and the sculpture of his body was his incentive for wearing little more than shorts and a muscle shirt, even in frosty temperatures. He lingered on them with the phone's camera and laughed. The girls teased. After a few minutes he turned back to his friends for a second, then when he looked around at the girls again, he realized that they were now filming him. Flattered, he began to play the fool, pulling faces, swaggering around, and even his friends felt encouraged to join in. None of them was behaving particularly maturely, or like people who had just had their sole source of income taken from them. The girls began, amid fits of laughter, to enact scenes from Hollywood films, prompting the boys to respond to their pantomime repertoire, calling out the solutions to one another boisterously. The day was shaping up to be more fun than expected. Besides, whenever Bruford examined his reflection in the mirror he always thought he would be better placed in the film industry than the Cold Lake open-cast mine. Perhaps he would even be grateful to EMCO one day. His mood soared up to the April sun on the wings of Icarus, with the result that he almost missed the small, bald-headed oil manager climbing up onto the platform.

Someone tapped him on the shoulder. It was time. Bruford turned his head just in time to see Palstein stumble. The man steadied himself, wobbled, and then collapsed. Security personnel rushed past, forming a wall against the chanting crowd. Bruford craned his neck. Was it a heart attack, a circulatory collapse, a stroke? He pushed forward, holding his cell phone up above the heads of the agitated crowd. It was an assassination attempt, it was obvious! Hadn't people seen enough of that kind of thing in films! The stumble, a mishap. But something had jerked the manager around before he had fallen to the floor. A shot, what else? Someone must have shot at Palstein—that had to be it!

What Bruford didn't know was that twenty minutes before the incident, while he was filming the girls, one of the security cameras had captured him for just a few seconds, albeit blurred and out of focus. When the police came to analyze the transmitted material, they simply overlooked him.

But the people from Greenwatch didn't.

He could still hardly believe they had managed to track him down from just that snippet of film, on the snowball principle, as Loreena Keowa, the high-cheekboned, not particularly pretty and yet somehow sweat-inducingly arousing native Indian girl had explained to him. Greenwatch had quickly come to the conclusion that the men next to him, who were easier to make out on the film, must be his friends, and then one of them had said something to an old man in the row in front of them. It was Jack "pain-in-the-ass" Becker of course, he could still remember that, because Becker had wound him up to no end with his sentimentality. Unlike the others, Becker, who had worn his Imperial Oil coat that day, had been captured sharply on the film, and Keowa clearly had contacts in the human resources department of the company. She had identified him, called him, and showed him the recording, upon which "what's-in-it-for-me" Becker had named both Bruford's friends and Bruford himself.

And now he was sitting here. It was a scary world! Anyone could be tracked down. On the other hand, there were worse things than sitting next to Loreena in her rented Dodge, fifty Canadian dollars richer, watching her as she loaded his blurry videos onto her computer. Loreena in her chic clothes, which didn't seem quite right for an eco-girl. A number of things were going through his head. Whether he should have asked for more money. What Greenwatch intended to do with the films. Why native Indian hair was always so shiny, and what he would need to do to make his that shiny for his career in Hollywood.

"Shouldn't we go to the police?" he heard himself suggest. A sensible question, he thought. Loreena stared at the display, concentrating on the transfer process.

"Rest assured, we will," she murmured.

"Yes, but when?"

"It doesn't matter when," grumbled Loreena's companion from the back seat.

"I don't know." He shook his head and made an expression of genuine concern, proof of his acting talents; he'd always known it, it was what he'd been born to do. "I don't want to get dragged into anything. We're obligated to tell them really, aren't we?"

"So why didn't you do it?"

"I didn't think of it. But now that we're talking about it—"

"Yes, you're right of course, we should reconsider the deal." Loreena turned her head toward him. "Do we know whether the material is worth fifty dollars? Perhaps there's not even anything on there."

Bruford hesitated. "But that would be your problem."

"But then perhaps it's worth a hundred dollars, you see?" She raised an eyebrow. "Don't you think, Sid? On the condition that a certain someone stops asking questions and worrying about the police?"

Bruford suppressed a grin. That was exactly what he had wanted her to say.

"Sure," he said thoughtfully. "I think that could be the case."

She reached into her jacket and brought out another fifty, as if she had reckoned on this development. Bruford took it and put it with the other one.

"There seems to be quite a nest in your jacket," he said.

"No, Sid, there were only two. And perhaps they'll have to go back in if I come to the conclusion that you can't be trusted."

"Then I'll just take something else." Now he couldn't help but grin. "You have other good things inside your jacket that come in twos."

Loreena glanced at her companion, who looked willing to resort to violence.

"Okay," he muttered. "I'm sorry."

"No problem. It was a pleasure meeting you."

He understood. With a shrug of his shoulders he opened the passenger door.

"Oh, and one more thing, Sid, just in case you do decide to call the police in a sudden passion of loyalty to the law: the money in your pocket constitutes withholding evidence for the purpose of your own personal gain. That's an offense, do you understand?"

Bruford stopped short. He suddenly felt deeply offended. With one leg already on the sidewalk, he leaned back in toward her.

"Are you trying to threaten me?"

"Now you listen up, Sid—"

"No, *you* listen up! My job has gone down the crapper. I'm trying to get what I can, but a deal is a deal! Is that clear? I may have a loose tongue, but that doesn't mean I shit all over people. So kiss my ass and look after your own business."

"What a snitch," said the intern contemptuously as Bruford set off down the street without looking back at them. "For another hundred dollars he'd have flogged his own grandmother."

Loreena watched him go.

"No, he was right. We insulted him. If anyone behaved dubiously then it's us."

"While we're on the subject—*shouldn't* we hand this footage over to the cops?"

Loreena hesitated. She hated the idea of doing something illegal, but she was a journalist, and journalists thrived on having a head start. Without giving an answer, she connected her computer to the in-car system. The Dodge she had rented at the airport had a large display.

"Come up front," she said. "Let's have a look at what good old Sid has to offer first."

"It's a bit of a blind bargain."

"Sometimes you have to take risks."

They saw a blurred panning shot, a crowd of people, food stalls, the headquarters of Imperial Oil, a podium. Then Bruford's friends, grinning broadly into the camera. Bruford had been filming straight ahead initially, then he started to swivel around. Two young women came into the shot, noticed that they were being filmed, and started fooling around.

"They're having fun," laughed the intern. "Pretty hot, too. Especially the blonde."

"Hey, you're supposed to be paying attention to the background."

"I can do both."

"Oh, sure. Men and multitasking."

They fell silent. Bruford had used up a lot of memory space on the two backwater beauties' performance, in the course of which several people walked into the shot, three policemen appeared, two of them took off again, and one took up his post in the shadow of the building. The girls contorted themselves into a clumsy performance, the significance of which Loreena couldn't decipher at first, until the intern whistled through his teeth.

"Not bad at all! Do you recognize it?"

"No."

"That's from *Alien Speedmaster 7*!"

"From what?"

"You don't know *Alien Speedmaster 7*?" His amazement seemed to know no bounds. "Don't you ever go to the movies?"

"Yes, but it sounds as though I see different films from you."

"Well, there's a gap in your education there. Look what they're doing now! I think they're reenacting the scene from *Death Chat*, you know the one, where those small, intelligent creatures go for the woman with the artificial arm and—"

"No, I don't know."

The girls doubled up with laughter. This was disheartening. They had already looked at half of the material without seeing anything more than pubescent nonsense.

"What are they doing now?" puzzled the intern.

"Would you just keep your eyes on the building?"

"It looks like—"

"*Please!*"

"No, wait! I think that's from the slushy love film that was hyped up so much last year. A bit cheesy if you ask me. That guy's in it, that horny old man—you know the one. God, what's his name? Tell me!"

"Absolutely no idea."

"Yeah, the old bastard who recently got an honorary Oscar for his life's work!"

"Richard Gere?"

"Yes, exactly! Gere! He plays the grandfather of—"

"Ssh!" Loreena silenced him with a hand motion. "Look."

From the side exit of the central building, two athletic-looking men in casual clothes came out, strolled over to the patrolling policeman, and started speaking to him. Both were wearing sunglasses.

"They don't look like oil workers."

"No." Loreena leaned forward, wondering why she had a feeling of déjà vu. She played the section back again and again, zooming in on their faces. A moment later, a slim woman dressed in a pantsuit walked out of the building and positioned herself next to the entrance. The policeman pointed to something, the men looked in the direction of his outstretched hand, one of them holding something under his nose, which might have been a map of the city, and the conversation continued. In the background, a pot-bellied man with long black hair approached, wound his way toward the unguarded side entrance, and shuffled inside.

"Look at that," whispered Loreena.

A few moments later, the athletic-looking men shook the policeman's hand and headed off. The woman in the pantsuit leaned against a tree, her arms folded, and then Bruford's recording jumped. Sequences followed in which the girls continued to get up to mischief, without anything happening in the immediate vicinity of the building, then the crowd of people and the podium came into view. Both uniformed officials and civilians were pushing their way forward, everything was hectic. Images that had clearly been filmed right after the assassination attempt.

"The guy that disappeared into the house—" said the intern.

"Could be anyone. The janitor, the engineer, some tramp." Loreena paused for breath. "But if not—"

"Then we just saw the killer."

"Yes, the man who shot Gerald Palstein."

They exchanged glances like two scientists who had just discovered an unknown, probably fatal virus and could see a Nobel Prize glimmering against the abyss of horror. Loreena isolated a freeze-frame of the fat man, enlarged it, connected her computer with the base station in Juneau, and loaded the Magnifier, a program that could do wonders with even the grainiest of material. Within seconds, the blurred features became more contoured, strands of greasy hair separated from white skin, a straggly mustache corresponded with sparse chin stubble.

"He looks Asian," said the intern.

Chinese, Loreena thought suddenly. China was involved in the Canadian oil-sand trade. Hadn't they even acquired licenses? On the other hand, what would the death of an EMCO manager change about the fact that Alberta was lost? Or was Imperial Oil in Chinese hands? But then EMCO would have belonged to them too. No, it didn't make sense. And killing Palstein certainly didn't. As he himself had said: *Every unpopular decision I make reduces my popularity, but I'm really only the strategic leader.*

She stroked her chin.

The sequence with the fat man alone was enough to justify a report, even if the guy turned out to be harmless. Yet it would make the police look like a laughing stock. Greenwatch would have used up all its ammunition at once. A brief triumph that would cost them their decisive head start in the investigations. The chance of solving the case by themselves would be blown.

Perhaps, thought Loreena, you should be content with what you have.

Indecisive, she rewound the film to the moment when the men with the sunglasses engaged the policeman in conversation. She zoomed in on them and let the Magnifier do its work, extracting details from the blurred image which, with all likelihood, came very close to their actual appearance. But even after that the policeman still looked unidentifiable, just an average policeman. The taller of the two men, however, looked familiar to her. Very familiar in fact.

The computer informed her that the editorial office in Vancouver wanted to speak to her. The face of Sina, editor for Society and Miscellaneous, appeared on the display.

"You wanted to know whether any other managerial figures from the oil trade have been injured since the beginning of the year."

"Yes, that's right."

"Bingo. Three, one of them being Umar a-Hamid."

"The OPEC Foreign Minister?"

"Correct. He fell off his horse in January and broke his leg. He's recovered now. The nag was suspected of having connections in the Islamist camp. No, I'm just kidding. The next, Prokofi Pavlovich Kiselyev—"

"Who in God's name is that?"

"The former Project Manager of Gazprom in West Siberia. He died in March, a car accident, reported to be his own fault. The man was ninety-four years old and half blind. That's it for this year."

"You said there were three."

"I took the liberty of going further back. Which brings it to three. There's always someone of course, one gets sick, another dies, a suicide here and there, nothing unusual. Until you look at the case of Alejandro Ruiz, the strategic second in command of Repsol."

"Repsol? Weren't they taken over by ENI in 2022?"

"It was discussed, but it never actually happened. In any case, Ruiz was, or is, quite an important figure in strategic management."

"And now? Which is it: *was* or *is*?"

"That's the problem. We're not sure if he can still be counted as being alive. He disappeared three years ago on an inspection trip to Peru."

"Just like that?"

"Overnight. He vanished. Lost without a trace in Lima."

"What else do you know about him?"

"Not much, but if you like I can change that."

"Please do. And thank you."

Alejandro Ruiz—

Repsol was a Spanish-Argentine company, trailing at the bottom of the field's top ten. There weren't all that many points of contact between the Spanish and EMCO. Was she risking wasting her time? Did the disappearance of a Spanish oil strategist in Lima in 2022 have anything to do with this?

Palstein was a strategist too.

Her thoughts oscillated between this new information and Bruford's film recordings, trying to make some kind of sense out of them, knotting the ropes of logic together.

And, suddenly, she knew who the man in the sunglasses was.

"Really! I swear to you!"

They were sitting in a small café on the Fifth Avenue Southwest, just a few blocks away from the Imperial Oil Limited headquarters. Loreena was drinking her third cappuccino, and the intern was sucking at a Diet Cola and devouring an awe-inspiring breakfast, composed of porridge, fried potatoes, scrambled eggs, bacon, pancakes, and much, much more. Loreena's analytical mind couldn't help wondering why someone would drink Diet Cola in the face of neutron-star-like calorie compression. Fascinated, she watched as he led a spoon of warm gruel, saturated in maple syrup, toward his mouth for processing.

"The Magnifier can't perform miracles," said the intern. "The picture isn't that sharp."

"But I saw the guy just two days ago, and he was *this* close to me." She held her hand in front of her face. Through the gaps between her fingers, she saw a sausage disappear. "*This close!*"

"Which makes me a little concerned that you may have kissed him."

"Don't be silly. He wanted to see my ID card. As if Palstein's house were the Pentagon or something."

The intern put his spoon down and wrinkled his forehead.

"There's nothing unusual about his security people keeping a check on things."

"And did they? Did they check up on things? What had they lost in the house anyway?"

"As I said." He picked his spoon back up. "They were keeping a check that—"

"All that cholesterol has blocked up your synapses!" she said angrily. "It's obvious that he would have security personnel around him, and police too, I mean, he didn't exactly come bearing Christmas presents. But would you send your private bodyguard into an empty house opposite? After all, Palstein isn't Kennedy. How likely is it that someone would shoot at him from there?"

His answer got lost amid a struggle with an oversized piece of pancake.

"Let's assume the Asian guy was harmless," she continued. "He may have just been looking for a bathroom. That would either mean that Palstein's people overlooked him, or that they weren't interested in the fact that he went in. Both are unlikely."

"The two guys were talking to the policeman. They couldn't even see him."

"And the woman?"

"Are you sure she was one of them?"

"She came out immediately after them. And besides, those security types all look the same. So, suppose that the Chinese guy is our killer."

"What makes you think he's Chinese?"

"Asian. It doesn't matter." She leaned over. "Just think, will you, three security people! One standing close to the entrance. Two others chatting with a policeman, just a few meters away. And none of them notices the grotesquely overweight apparition entering a building they were supposed to be guarding?"

"Perhaps the Chinese—the Asian guy was security too. Didn't Palstein tell you that he only started using a security team after Calgary? I find that much more surprising."

"No, he didn't." She rolled her cup around, mixing the espresso with foam. "Just that they've been guarding *his house* since Calgary."

"Well, it would have been better to take on someone else."

Loreena stared at the foam and espresso mixture.

Would have been better—

"Damn, you're right."

"Of course I am," said the intern, scraping together the remains of the porridge. "About what?"

"He can't trust them."

"Because they're a dead loss. Too dumb to—"

"No, they're not." Unbelievable! Why had she only thought of it now? The security people let the killer pass! In full knowledge of who he was! More than that, they distracted the policeman and kept their eyes on the surroundings to make sure no one stopped him from entering the house.

"Good God," she whispered.

Dallas, Texas, USA

"It's not long ago that the ability to secure the necessary fossil fuel resources was crucial to the geopolitical role of a nation state. It was under this premise that we foresaw China leading the economic nations in the medium term, knocking the USA down to a distant second, followed by India."

Gerald Palstein's guest lectureship at UT Dallas, a state university in the suburb of Richardson, had brought around six hundred students into the lecture hall, most of them budding managers, economists, and information scientists. It was very popular, which was as much down to Palstein's media savvy as to the fact that he was depicting a wide-screen panorama of failure, in which a *Titanic* of an energy industry rammed right into an iceberg called helium-3.

"Russia's role at this time was one of a major power as far as oil and gas were concerned. Gazprom was also referred to as a weapon. And no one used this weapon in the battle for Russia's geostrategic role as ably as the country's former president Vladimir Putin. Does anyone here still remember his nickname?"

"Gasputin," called a young woman from the front row. There was laughter. Palstein raised his eyebrows approvingly.

"Very good. At the time, the Americans looked on with concern as China openly flirted with Russia regarding its energy requirements, and also strengthened its contacts to OPEC. The latter was pleased of course. They hadn't been courted like that in a long time and were hoping for a renaissance of their former status. And so the oil nations in the Gulf started to invest their money in the accounts of the Industrial and Commercial Bank of China, in Turkey and India instead of in American institutions, and China began to settle the bill for its oil supplies from Iran in euros instead of dollars. The balance of power shifted, along with the motivation for America's efforts to free itself from dependence on Eastern oil supplies. In 2006, representatives from Saudi Arabia traveled to Beijing to sign a number of treaties. Even Kuwait was wooing China, because it was afraid of losing ground to Russia. China knew how to exploit all of that. Although I wouldn't want to encourage any hate-filled stereotypes, one might picture the energy-hungry China of the first decade of our millennium as an octopus whose arms were silently unfurling, largely unnoticed, in the traditional mining regions of the Western oil multinationals. In the White House, they developed scenarios in which radical forces toppled the Saudi ruling dynasties, all based on the expectation that China would be involved and would ultimately station Chinese nuclear missiles in the Saudi desert. This fear was, as we now know, not completely unfounded. The fall of the house of Saud most definitely took place with concealed Chinese participation. And it's certain that if the recent conflict between Islamist and monarchist forces had grown to epic proportions and caused a public clash between China and America, then the dawning potential of helium-3 would not have led Washington's interest in another direction."

Palstein dabbed sweat from his brow. It was hot in the lecture hall. He wished he were on board a ship on a lake somewhere or, even better, out on the open sea with invigorating winds all around him.

"We can assume the following: if gas and oil had continued to play the dominant role, the world would look a little different today. China might have overtaken the USA, instead of just catching up with them. The Chinese, Russian, and Gulf states would have made an energy pact. Iran, relatively recently in possession of nuclear devices, would have more power internally than is the case today, despite its nuclear armament, and would probably have exercised more pressure on New Delhi, who, back in 2006, already had its sights on a pipeline project in partnership with Tehran, through which Caspian oil would flow to India. This pipeline was supposed to end at the Red Sea, but then the oil wouldn't have been able to flow to Israel, so for that reason the United States was against it. Not an easy situation for India. A collaboration with Iran ran the risk of angering America, while concessions to Washington would have aggravated Iran. In order to escape this Catch-22, the Indians looked to a third power, to help integrate the existing two, having good contacts with both China and Iran. And so the Russians came back into play in the form of Gazprom, taking every opportunity they had to strengthen their nation, for example by turning off the gas taps to their neighboring states and blackmailing them. Do you recognize the formation of blocs that this heralded? Russia, China, India, OPEC—that couldn't have been in Washington's interest. Faced with this situation, George W. Bush's successor, Barack Obama, turned to diplomacy. He tried to improve relations with Russia and to take the wind out of Iran's sails, a clever strategy that worked in part. But of course even Obama would have been forced to secure the USA's energy requirements by force if he had to, if the technological advancement which Washington achieved through its collaboration with Orley Enterprises hadn't opened up completely new possibilities to the Americans—"

A staff member of the UTD office came into the lecture hall, paced briskly toward him, and pressed a note into his hand. Palstein smiled out into the auditorium.

"Please excuse me for a moment. What is it?" he asked softly.

"Someone wants to speak to you on the telephone, a Miss—"

"Can't it wait twenty minutes? I'm in the middle of a lecture."

"She said it was urgent. *Very* urgent!"

"What was her name again?"

"Keowa. Loreena Keowa, a journalist. I wanted to put her off until later, but . . ."

Palstein thought for a moment. "No, it's fine. Thank you."

He excused himself once again, left the auditorium, walked out into the hallway, and dialed Loreena's number.

"Shax' saani Keek," he said, as her face appeared on the display of his cell phone. "How are you?"

"I know I'm interrupting."

"To be honest, yes. I've got one minute, then I've got to get back to educating the future elite. What can I do for you?"

"I'm hoping it's me that can do something for *you*, Gerald. But for that I need a few more minutes of your time."

"It's a bit awkward right now."

"It's in *your* interest."

"Hmm." He looked out through the window across the sunlit campus. "Okay, fine. Give me a quarter of an hour to finish my talk. I'll call you immediately afterward."

"Make sure no one's listening in."

Twenty minutes later, he called her from an isolated bench in the shadow of a chestnut tree, with a view out over the university grounds. Two of his security people were patrolling within sight. All around, students were hurrying toward unknown futures.

"You sure know how to worry a man," he said.

"Do we have an agreement on reciprocity?"

"What do you mean?"

"We help one another," said Loreena. "I get information, you get protection."

"Sorry?"

"Are we in agreement?"

"Hmm." Now he was really curious. "Fine, yes, we are."

"Good. I'm sending you a few photos on your cell phone. Open them while we talk."

His cell phone confirmed the arrival of a multimedia message. One after another, he loaded the pictures. They showed two men in sunglasses, and a woman.

"Which of them do you know?"

"All of them," he said. "They work for me. Security staff. You must have met one of them, out on Lavon Lake. Lars Gudmundsson. He has the internal power of command."

"That's right, I met him. Did you order the three of them to guard the building that you were presumably shot at from on April 21?"

"Well, that would be a bit of an exaggeration." Palstein hesitated. "They were just supposed to keep an eye on the surrounding area. To be honest, I wasn't even sure if I should bring them. Having private security makes you seem like you're putting on airs, like you think you're so incredibly important. But there had been a few threats against EMCO, and against me too—"

"Threats?"

"Oh, stupid things. Nothing that we needed to take seriously. Just resentful people with existential angst."

"Gerald, are the Chinese involved in any way with EMCO?"

"The Chinese?"

"Yes."

"Not really. I mean, there were many attempts to take over our subsidiaries. EMCO itself is—was—too tough a nut for them to crack. And of course they had a good old poach in our coalmines."

"Canadian oil sand?"

"That too."

"Okay. I'm sending you another photo."

This time an Asian face appeared on the display. Long, unkempt hair, a straggly beard.

"No" he said.

"You haven't seen him before?"

"Not that I know of. If you could let me in on—"

"Of course. Listen, Gerald, this man entered the empty building just before you took to the podium. Your security team was in the building too. In our view there's very little doubt that Gudmundsson's people not only let the Asian man pass, but also made sure that he *could*."

Palstein stared at the photo in silence.

"Are you completely sure that you've never seen him before?" pressed Loreena.

"Not consciously, at any rate. I would remember someone like him."

"Could he be one of your people?"

"My people?"

"I mean, do you know all your bodyguards personally, or does Gudmundsson—"

"Of course I know every single one of them, what do you expect? And besides, there aren't that many. Five in total."

"Whom you trust."

"Of course. They are paid by us, and besides, a respected agency for personal security provided them, EMCO has been working with them for years."

"Then you may have a problem. If this Asian guy really is the man who shot at you, then there's good reason to believe that your own people are in on it. I need to ask you one more question—please excuse my abruptness."

"No, it's fine."

"Does the name Alejandro Ruiz mean anything to you?"

"Ruiz?" Palstein was silent for a few seconds. "Wait a moment—that does ring a bell."

"I'll help you. Repsol. Strategic management."

"Repsol—yes, I think—yes, for sure, Ruiz. We were on the same flight once. It was a while ago."

"What do you know about him?"

"Practically nothing. My God, Loreena, we're not talking about some close-knit family here, the oil trade is huge, there are a zillion people working in it. Even now, by the way."

"It seems Ruiz was an important man."

"Was?"

"He disappeared, three years ago in Lima."

"Under what circumstances?"

"During a business trip. You see, I'm interested to find out whether the attack in Calgary has any precedents. Whether it was perhaps less about you personally and more about what you represent. So I put Ruiz's files together. Happily married, two healthy children, no debts. But he does have opponents in his own field for whom he was too liberal, too environmentally aware; he was a moralist—nicknamed Ruiz El Verde. For example, he spoke out against oil-sand exploitation and pushed for more exploration of the deep sea. Now, I don't need to tell you that the companies always shied away from cost-intensive exploration proposals when oil prices were low, and three years ago the demise was already well under way. Ruiz urged Repsol to strengthen their involvement with alternative energies. Does that remind you of anyone? Yourself perhaps?"

Incredible, thought Palstein.

"It could all be a coincidence," Loreena continued. "Ruiz's disappearance. China's engagement in the oil-sand trade. Even the Asian man your people allowed into the house. Perhaps he's just harmless and I'm seeing ghosts, but my gut instinct and common sense are telling me that we're on the right track."

"And what do you think I should do now?"

"Don't trust Gudmundsson and his people. If it should all turn out to be a mistake, I'll be the first one to eat humble pie. Until then: rack your brains! About Ruiz. About critical overlaps with China. About pitfalls in your own business; and another thing too—think about who might have had a vested interest in you *not* going along on the Moon flight. You can call me, or we can meet up, at any time. Try to find out who the Asian in the photo is, perhaps he might be on EMCO's internal database. Invest in personal security, throw Gudmundsson and his team out on their asses as far as I'm concerned, but don't go to the police. That's the only thing I'm asking of you."

"Then you're asking a lot!"

"Just not for the moment."

"This could all be evidence."

"Gerald," said Loreena insistently. "I promise you, I won't do anything that puts you in danger, nor keep things from the police. It's just for the moment. I need a head start to be able to get an exclusive on the story."

"Do you realize what you're telling me here? What you're asking of me?"

"We have a deal, Gerald. I may have found your would-be assassin, and that's more than the police managed in four weeks. Give me time. We're working on it under extreme pressure. I'll serve those pigs up to you on a silver platter."

Palstein fell silent. Then he sighed. "Fine," he said. "Do whatever you think is right."

MAY 29, 2025
The Mercenary

Night Flight

There was one good thing you could say about Teodoro Obiang Nguema Mbasogo: after he'd come to power in August 1979, the human rights situation in Equatorial Guinea had visibly improved. From that point on, there were no more mass crucifixions along the highway to the airport, and the skulls of the opposition were no longer impaled on stakes for all to see.

"A true philanthropist," scoffed Yoyo.

"But not the first," said Jericho. "Have you heard of Fernão do Pó?"

Heading toward Berlin at twice the speed of sound, they traveled backward in time, from the Shanghai dawn to the Berlin night, from the year 2025 to the beginnings of a continent in which it seemed everything that could go wrong, always did. Africa, the unloved cradle of humanity, characterized by dead-straight borders which severed its ancient tendons and nerves, creating countries of bizarre geometry, the smallest of which lay patchwork-like on the western fringes, its history reading like a chronicle of continual rape.

"Fernão do Pó? Who on earth is he?"

"Another philanthropist. After a fashion."

As Tu had insisted on flying his company jet himself, Jericho and Yoyo had the luxurious, twelve-seater passenger cabin to themselves. They were using two monitors, supported by Diane, to familiarize themselves with Equatorial Guinea in the hope of finding answers to the questions of the last two days. The picture only became more and more confusing with each piece of information the computer provided, and the only thing that had become clear was that the events in Equatorial Guinea could only be understood if one looked at their development from the very beginning. And that beginning started with:

Fernão do Pó.

A stagnant lake. Dead calm. Curtains of rain billow out over the coastline.

Sweat and rainwater mix on skin, making it look as though it's been boiled in steam. Orchestrated by the cries of small seabirds, the boats are lowered into the water. The oarsman pulling, a man upright in the bow. The shore comes closer, vegetation takes shape against the deepening gray. The man walks onto the shore, looks around. Once again, an area's transformation into a state-like zone starts with a Portuguese man.

In 1469, do Pó's caravels anchor beneath the elbow of Africa, right where the continent tapers off dramatically. The discoverer, the legitimate successor of Henry the Navigator, lands on an island and calls it Formosa on account of its beauty. Bantus live here, the small Bubi tribe. They welcome the visitors in a friendly manner, unaware that their kingdom has just changed hands. From the very moment when do Pó left his bootprints in the sand, they are now subjects of his majesty Alfonso V of Portugal, to whom Pope Nicholas had handed over the entire African island, along with monopoly on trade and sole maritime law, a few years before. At least, the Pope believed that Africa was an island, sharing that misconception with Western Christianity. Do Pó provided proof to the contrary. It was discovered that Africa was in actual fact a continent, and one with a long and fertile coastline, inhabited by dark-skinned people who seemed to have very little to do and who were in dire need of Christianization. This, in turn, corresponded perfectly with the crux of the papal bull, which decreed that non-believers were to be steamrollered into slavery—a recommendation with which Alfonso and his seafarers were happy to comply.

The day that do Pó arrived changed everything. And yet, ultimately, nothing. If he hadn't come, then sooner or later someone else would have. Many followed in his footsteps, and the slave trade thrived for three hundred years. Then the Portuguese crown exchanged its ownership of African territory for colonies in Brazil, and the Bantu changed masters. Spain was the new owner. The British, French, and Germans began to get involved, all of them fighting for the areas from Cape Santa Clara right up to the Niger Delta—

"And then they tried to oppress the natives, a task which was made easier by the discord among the Bantu, or to be more precise, the growing rivalry between the Bubi and Fang."

"Fang?" grinned Yoyo. "Fang Bubi?"

"It's no laughing matter," said Jericho. "This is Africa's traumatic past."

"Yes, I know. The colonialists thought about everything, just not about ethnic roots. Look at Rwanda, Hutu and Tutsi—"

"Okay." Jericho massaged the back of his neck. "On the other hand let's not pretend that it's a purely African invention."

"No, you Europeans of all people should keep quiet on that matter."

"Why?"

Yoyo's eyes widened. "Oh, come on! Look at Serbia and Kosovo. There's still no peace even seventeen years after independence! Then the Basques, the Scottish and the Welsh. Northern Ireland."

Jericho listened, his arms crossed.

"Taiwan," he said. "Tibet."

"That's—"

"Different? Just because you lot don't want to discuss it?"

"Nonsense," said Yoyo, irritated. "Taiwan belongs to mainland China, that's why it's different."

"Well, you lot are the only ones who believe that. And no one is overly pleased that you're threatening the Taiwanese with nuclear missiles."

"Fine, smart-ass." Yoyo leaned forward. "So what would happen if, all of a sudden, let's say Texas, the Cowboys . . . if they suddenly declared their independence?"

"Now that really is different," sighed Jericho.

"Oh sure. Completely different."

"Yes. And as far as Tibet is concerned—"

"Tibet today, Xinjiang tomorrow, then inner Mongolia, Guanxi, Hong Kong—why can't you Europeans grasp the fact that a One China policy is best for security? Our huge kingdom will fall into chaos if we allow it to fall apart. We *have* to keep China together!"

"With force."

"No, force is the wrong way. We didn't do our homework there."

"You can say that again!" Jericho shook his head. "Somehow I just can't figure you out. After all, you're the one who's so passionate about human rights. That's what I thought, anyway."

"And it's true."

"But?"

"No but. I'm a nationalist."

"Hmm."

"That doesn't compute with you, right? That the two can coexist. Human rights and nationalism."

Jericho spread his hands out acquiescently. "I'm happy to learn."

"Then learn. I'm not a fascist, not a racist, nothing of the kind. But I am absolutely convinced that China is a great country with a great culture—"

"Which you yourselves have trampled all over."

"Listen, Owen, let's get one basic thing straight. Give it a rest with all the *you, you lot, your people*! When the Red Guards were hanging teachers from trees, I wasn't even a twinkle in my father's eye. I'd rather you tell me how the whole thing with Bubi Fang carries on, if that's even relevant."

"Fang," Jericho corrected her patiently. "The Bubi lived on the island. They didn't care two figs about the coast until Spain united the mainland and islands into the Republic of Equatorial Guinea. And the Fang dominated on the mainland: another Bantu tribe, who greatly outnumbered the Bubi and were less than pleased at being thrown in a pot with them overnight. In 1964, Spain gave the country full autonomy, which in practice meant that they fenced two groups who couldn't stand each other inside a state border and left them to their own devices. Something that could only end in disaster."

Yoyo looked at him with her dark eyes. And suddenly, she smiled. So unexpected and untimely a smile that he could do little else but stare back at her, confused.

"By the way, I wanted to thank you," she said.

"Thank me?"

"You saved my life."

Jericho hesitated. The whole time, while he had swum so bravely through the hot water that Yoyo had got herself into, he had contented himself with his own sense of reward. Now he felt taken by surprise.

"No need," he said feebly. "It's just the way things turned out."

"Owen—"

"I didn't have any choice. If I had known—"

"No, Owen, don't." She shook her head. "Say something nice."

"Something nice? After all the trouble that you've—"

"Hey." She reached out. Her slender fingers clasped around his hand and squeezed firmly. "Say something nice to me. Right now!"

She moved closer to him, and something changed. So far he had only seen Yoyo's beauty, and the small flaws in it. Now, waves of unsettling intensity washed over him. Unlike Joanna, who controlled and regulated her erotic potential like the volume dial on a radio, Yoyo could do nothing else but burn seductively, relentless, a bright, hot star. And suddenly he realized that he would do everything in his power to make sure that this star never burned out. He wanted to see her laugh.

"Well." He cleared his throat. "Any time."

"Any time what?"

"I'd do it again, any time. If you ever need saving, let me know. I'll be there." More throat-clearing. "And now—"

"Thank you, Owen. Thank you."

"—let's carry on with Mayé. When does it get interesting for us?"

She let his hand go and sank back in her seat.

"Difficult to say. I'd say that in order to understand the relations in the country, we need to go back to independence. With the change to—"

Papa Macías.

In October 1968, the same damp and humid climate reigned in the Gulf of Guinea as on any other day of the year. Sometimes it rained, then the land, islands, and sea would brood in sunshine that made the beaches glisten and brought all activity to a standstill. The capital city, located on the island and little more than a collection of mildewed colonial buildings with huts gathered around them, was seeing the advent of the first State President of the independent republic of Equatorial Guinea, chosen by the people in a memorable election campaign. Francisco Macías Nguema of the Fang tribe promises justice and Socialism, and forces the remaining Spanish troops to retreat, an action which had already been agreed in any case, although they had imagined a slightly more conciliatory end. But "Papa," as the president named himself out of his love for his people, is accustomed to having a good and hearty breakfast. The defeated colonialists were horrified to discover that he was a cannibal, with a tendency to eat the brains and testicles of his enemies. You couldn't expect a teary good-bye from someone like that.

And yet that's exactly what happened.

A sea of tears, a sea of blood.

The young republic was defiled almost as soon as it was born. No one there was prepared for something as exotic as market economy, but at least they enjoyed a flourishing trade in cocoa and tropical woods. Macías, however, enflamed with glowing admiration for Marxist-Leninist supported despotism, was interested in other things. The last units of the Guardia Civil had barely cleared their posts before it became clear what was to be expected from testicle-eating Papa and his Partido Unico Nacional. The army reinforced Macías's claim to god-like absolute dictatorship with clubs, firearms, and machetes, prompting the remaining European civilians to flee the country in terror. Numerous posts were taken by members of his Esangui clan, a sub-tribe of the Fang. The fact that the island, the most attractive part of the country, seat of the government and economic center, was Bubi territory had been a thorn in the side of the numerically superior Fang for a long time. Macías fanned the flames of this hate. At least he had had the decency to annul the constitution before breaking it.

From that point on, the Bubi felt the full force of his paternal care.

More than fifty thousand people were slaughtered, incarcerated, tortured to death, including all members of the opposition. Anyone who was able to fled abroad. And because Papa didn't trust anyone, not even his own family, even the Fang became a target for the president. Over a third of the population were forced into exile or disappeared in camps, while hundreds of Cuban military advisers were given free rein to prowl around the country; after all, Moscow was a reliable friend. By the mid seventies, Papa had managed to annihilate the local economy so thoroughly that he needed to bring Nigerian workers into the country. But they too soon take to their heels and flee. Without further ado, the country's father enforces compulsory work for all, thereby unleashing a further mass exodus. Numerous schools are closed, something that doesn't stop Papa from calling himself the Grand Master of the People's Education, Knowledge, and Traditional Culture. In his delusion of divinity, he also bolts up and barricades all the churches, proclaims atheism, and devotes himself to the reinvigoration of magic rituals. The continent is now experiencing the heyday of dictatorship. Macías is referred to in the same breath as Jean-Bedel Bokassa, who also had himself crowned and was utterly convinced he was Jesus's thirteenth apostle; he is likened to Idi Amin and the Cambodian Pol Pot.

• • •

"At the end of the day, he was an even bigger criminal than Mayé," said Yoyo. "But no one cared. Papa didn't have anything that would have been worth caring about. As a good patriot, he renamed everything that didn't yet have an African name, and since then the mainland has been called Mbini, the island Bioko, and the capital city Malabo. By the way, I also looked into Mayé's native background. He's from the Fang tribe."

"And what happened to this splendid Papa?"

Yoyo made a snipping motion with her fingers. "He was got rid of. A coup."

"With support from abroad?"

"It seems not. Papa's family values got out of hand; he even started to execute his close relatives. His own wife fled over the border in the dead of night. No one from his clan was safe anymore, and in the end it became too much for one of them."

In 1979, there was singing and dancing in Equatorial Guinea.

A man in a plain uniform stands in the entrance of a vault, where glowing ghosts dart over the walls and ceiling, generated by the crackling fire in the middle of the room. He is inconspicuousness personified. From time to time, he gives instructions under his breath, prompting the guards to give the dancers, who have been hopping around the fire and singing Papa's praises in grotesque liveliness for hours, a helping hand with red-hot pokers. It smells of decadence and burnt flesh. Mosquitoes buzz around. In the gloomy corners and along the walls, the scene is mirrored in the eyes of rats. Anyone who tips over the brink into exhaustion is dragged up, beaten until they bleed, and hauled outside. Almost all of them, apart from the uniformed men, are undernourished and dehydrated, many show signs of mistreatment, and others have yellow fever and malaria written on their gaunt faces.

Black Beach Party: just a normal day in Black Beach Prison, the infamous jail in Malabo that makes America's Devil Island look like a relaxing spa resort.

The man watches for a while longer, then leaves the dance of death, his face filled with worry. His name is Teodoro Obiang Nguema Mbasogo, nephew of the president, Commander of the National Guard and Director of the Black Beach Institution. He is responsible for scenes like these, so highly valued by Papa—just as the president enjoys spending his birthdays shooting prisoners in the Malabo stadium with "Those Were The Days, My Friend" blasting out at full volume. But Obiang's concern wasn't for the prisoners, most of whom would never get out of this shabby, parking garage-like fortress alive. It was his own life he feared for, and he had every reason to do so. These days, everyone in

Papa's clan had to confront the possibility of suddenly falling victim to the president's paranoia and being sent off into the eternal rainforests to a soundtrack of Mary Hopkin.

So even Obiang was afraid.

And yet his own family values weren't that different from those of his cutthroat uncle. Macías's fear of clans was part of his blood; a fear of the preferential politics which saw clans give their sons and daughters to other clans in order to stay in power. Papa himself felt the full force of it when Obiang staged a coup and chased The Unique Wonder out of office. Papa, deprived of his power, fled headlong into the jungle, but not before first burning the remaining local currency. Over one hundred million dollars go up in flames in his villa, literally the very last of the State money. By the time Obiang's henchmen tracked down the weakened Macías among the huge ferns and piles of ape shit, Equatorial Guinea was as bare as a bone. They drive the man to Malabo, play him "Those Were The Days," and bullet by bullet deliver him to the ghosts of his forefathers, a task taken care of by Moroccan soldiers—his own people are too afraid of the cannibal's dark magic.

And so the highest military council takes command of government business. Like all newly enthroned leaders, Obiang makes well-meaning promises to the people, proclaims a parliamentary democracy and, at the end of the eighties, even allows elections. Numerous candidates are suggested: but by him. Obiang wins, primarily because his Partido Democrático de Guinea Ecuatorial runs without competition, the representatives of which celebrate with a big party in Black Beach Prison. The government regrows like a lizard's tail: the same blood, the same genes. Esangui-Fang even. It's a family business. Anyone who criticizes it will soon be dancing and singing around the fire, the only thing that's changed is the wording. Obiang's temper isn't anywhere near as bad as Papa's; he's much more preoccupied with reestablishing trust abroad, making tentative links with the enduringly snubbed Spain, and informing the Soviets that they are no longer friends. Equatorial Guinea begins to look more like a state again, and less like a subtropical Dachau. Money flows into the country. Annabon, Bioko's sister island, is large and beautiful, ideal for the disposal of nuclear waste, something for which the First World is prepared to pay a pretty penny. The only problem is that Annabon is inhabited, but it won't be for much longer. Illegal fishing, arms smuggling, the drug trade, and child labor: Obiang pulls out all the stops and transforms the green patch in the Gulf of Guinea into a lovely little gangster's paradise.

Foreign creditors put the pressure on. Democracy is a necessity. Obiang reluctantly accepts opposition parties, but despite using all his criminal talents, he is still 250 million dollars in the red. Then something inexplicable happens, something which gives the future a completely new shine overnight. First near Bioko, and then off the mainland coast. Something which makes the president round his lips reverently, as round as one needs to shape them in order to articulate a certain word.

"Oil."

"Exactly," said Jericho. "The first sites were detected at the beginning of the nineties, and after that the race was on. There's a constant stream of companies interested in the Gulf. Not one of them makes any more references to human rights. All of a sudden, mining licenses are more popular topics of conversation."

"And Obiang cashes in."

"And cleans up, because of the low prices." Jericho pointed at his screen. "If you want to see the list of people who were imprisoned or murdered—"

"Show me."

"Spain was the exception, I should add. Madrid clearly does get worked up about human rights infringements."

"Respect to them."

"No, it was motivated by frustration. Some opposition forces had found shelter in Spain and railed against Obiang's clan, so he was a little reluctant to grant licenses to Spanish companies. The Spanish government reacted bitterly and suspended foreign aid in protest. Heart-warming really, because Mobil opens up another oilfield near Malabo just a little later, and Equatorial Guinea's economic growth shoots up by forty percent. Then it's one after another: there are discoveries near Bioko, near Mbini, a building boom in Malabo; oil towns such as Luba and Bata spring up. Obiang has no more political opponents; he is the oil prince. His reelection in the mid-nineties turns into a farce. The only competitor who can be taken seriously, Severo Moto from the Progressive Party, is sentenced to a hundred years' imprisonment for high treason and escapes to Spain by the skin of his teeth."

"Interesting." Yoyo looked at him thoughtfully. "And who held the most licenses?"

"America."

"What about China?"

"Not at the time." Jericho shook his head. "The US companies took the lead. They were the quickest and forced outrageous treaties on Obiang; he had very little understanding of the trade and signed everything they put in front of him. The ethnic shambles between the Fang and Bubi reached a new peak. There were very few Bubi on the mainland, but they're in the majority on Bioko, where the coastline was suddenly spluttering with oil. They all used to be poor, and in theory this should have made them all rich, but Obiang only lined his own pockets. The protests started in 1998. The Bubi founded a movement, fighting for the independence of Bioko, and there's no way Obiang would allow that."

"Soviet troops have hauled the tanks out of the garage for far lesser reasons than that."

"Chinese troops—"

"—too." Yoyo rolled her eyes. "Yes, I know. So how did Obiang react?"

"He didn't. He refused to enter into discussion. Radical Bubi mount attacks on police stations and military bases. They're in despair, made to feel like second-class citizens every day. Which isn't to say that the Fang are having a better time of it, but it hits the Bubi the hardest. And yet there's technically enough money around for each person to build themselves a villa in the jungle. On the other hand—"

"—there's a hell in every heaven," as the people of Malabo said back at the beginning of the millennium, and by that they meant that heaven stands out against hell like a gold ingot swimming in a sea of shit.

Right before the boom, Equatorial Guinea topped the list of poorest countries. The coffee export industry collapsed in Bioko, and a number of coffee plantations along the coast disappeared under the chummy presence of all manner of weeds. Precious wood species are said to be profitable, so they start to fell obeche and bongossi trees and then just stare at the fallen trunks, because there are no machines to take them away, not to mention transport routes. Malaria, the mistress of the jungle, conspires with the miserable healthcare to reduce the average life expectancy to forty-nine years, backed up by an up-and-coming epidemic called AIDS. All across the land, the only thing flourishing besides fame, orchids, and bromeliads is corruption.

Four years later, the sweaty region in Africa's armpit registers a yearly GDP growth of twenty-four percent. The oil and dollars flow, but there is little change to the living conditions. Obiang suspects that he was taken to the cleaners during the negotiations for the license contracts. Not even the sentencing of popular Bubi leaders to imprisonment and death improves his mood. It's not that the president is struggling financially; after all, he gets rich while black Africa perishes of AIDS, signs a trade agreement with Nigeria for collaboration in oil mining and launches an attack on the exploitation of natural gas resources. It's just that other dictators have made more lucrative deals. In 2002, a year before the elections, dozens of alleged rebels were arrested, including numerous opposition leaders, which has a wondrous influence on poll attendance. No one of clear mind had any doubt that Obiang would be reelected—but the fact that he won one hundred and three percent of the votes amazed even the most hard-boiled analysts. Strengthened by experience and referendum, Obiang assigns licenses under stricter conditions, and the coffers are finally rewarded. Teodorin, his eldest son and Forestry Minister, is able to jet around between Hollywood, Manhattan, and Paris, buy Bentleys, Lamborghinis, and luxury villas by the dozen and spend his time at champagne parties, dreaming of the day when his father will lose the battle against his prostate and hand the presidency over to him.

In the meantime, his father is given a helping hand by a bank in Washington, which discreetly reallocates thirty-five million dollars from the State account to private ones. When the whole thing gets blown open, the president acts offended, although not particularly bothered. You can have a good life with a ruined reputation in "Africa's Kuwait," as Equatorial Guinea has become known by then. The country is among the most significant oil producers in Africa and records the biggest economic growth in the world. The dictator nurtures his reputation for taking after his uncle in culinary matters, playing up to rumors of not being averse to the crisply fried liver of an opponent if the right wine has been selected to accompany it. It's all play-acting of course, but the impact is considerable. Human rights organizations are outraged, dedicating articles to him, and at home no one dares to pick an argument with Obiang. The idea of being tenderized and then devoured in Black Beach is not appealing.

Elsewhere, people are not so sickened. George W. Bush, usually less than fond of Africa on account of it being full of epidemics, of fly-covered, starved faces and poisonous creatures, starts to change his mind. Profoundly upset by the attacks of 9/11, he is striving for independence from the oil of the Middle East, and over a hundred billion barrels of the best petroleum are alleged to be stored in West Africa alone. Bush plans to cover twenty-five percent of America's needs from there by 2015. While Amnesty International gets overwhelmed, drowning in horrendous reports, Bush invites Obiang and other African kleptocrats to a coy breakfast in the White House. Meanwhile, Condoleezza Rice gives a press conference and publicly expresses solidarity: Obiang is described as "a good friend," whose engagement for human rights is valued. The good friend smiles modestly, and Ms. Rice smiles along with him. The other side of the cameras, the managers of Exxon, Amerada Hess, and other oil companies are smiling too. By 2004, Equatorial Guinea's oil mining is entirely in US hands; the companies transfer seven hundred million dollars directly to Obiang's accounts in Washington each year.

Which is rather odd.

Because no one visiting Malabo will see any sign of this wealth. The four-lane Carretera del Aeropuerto which leads from the airport right into its colonial center is still the only tarmacked road in the country. The old town, partly renovated, partly disintegrated, is ridden with brothels and drinking holes. Extravagant cross-country vehicles are parked in front of the air-conditioned and ugly government palace. The only hotel exudes all the charm of an emergency accommodation building. There's no school anywhere that would have been worthy of the name. There are no daily papers, no smiles on the faces, no public voice. Here and there, scaffolding leans against scaffolding like drunk men huddling together, but only on constructions carried out for the Obiangs; apart from the villas of the kleptocracy, hardly any building work gets finished. Those are the only new structures: monuments of monstrous tastelessness, just like the warehouses and quarters for foreign oil workers which spring out of the ground overnight. As if embarrassed to be there, the American embassy cowers between the surrounding houses, while a little further on, the other side of the cordoned-off Exxon grounds, the Chinese embassy flaunts itself brazenly.

"So they did start to court Obiang," said Yoyo. "Even though almost everything was owned by the Americans."

"They tried, anyway," said Jericho. "But they weren't that successful to begin with. After all, Obiang's new circle of friends didn't just include the Bush dynasty. Even the EU Commission was eagerly rolling out the red carpet for him, especially the French. What did a ban on religion or torture matter? The fact that the only human rights organization in the country was controlled by the government, along with the radio and television; they couldn't care less. The fact that two-thirds of the population were living on less than two dollars a day; *mei you banfa*, there was nothing that could be done. The region was of vital interest, anyone who comes too late loses out, and the Chinese were just too slow."

"And how did the locals react to the oil workers being there?"

"They didn't. The workers were flown straight into sealed-off company grounds. Marathon built their own town not far from Malabo, around a gas to liquid plant, and at times there were more than four thousand people living there. A highly secured Green Zone with its own energy grid, water supply, restaurants, shops, and movie theaters. Do you know what the workers called it? Pleasantville."

"How sweet."

"Indeed. When a dictator gives you permission to plunder his mineral resources while his own people are butchering monkeys out of sheer hunger, you don't exactly want to let those people catch sight of you. And *they* certainly don't want to see you. But they aren't even put in that awkward situation, because the companies are self-sufficient. The local private economy doesn't benefit in the slightest from the fact that several thousand Americans are squatting just a few kilometers away. Most of the oil workers spent months in ghettos like those or on their rig, fucking AIDS-free girls from Cameroon, gobbling down piles of malaria tablets, and making sure they arrived back home without having made any contact with the country. No one wanted contact. The main thing was that Obiang was firmly in the saddle, and, therefore, the American oil industry too."

"But something must have gone wrong. For the Yanks, I mean. By Mayé's time they were practically out of the game."

"It did go wrong," nodded Jericho. "The decline began in 2004. But that was actually down to an Englishman. I'd hazard a guess that our story and the mess we've got mixed up in really started after the Wonga Coup."

"After what?"

"After the—"

Wonga Coup. A Bantu term. Wonga meaning money, dosh, dough, moolah. A flippant way of describing one of the most ridiculous attempted coups of all time.

In March 2004, a rattling Boeing of prehistoric design lands in Harare airport in Zimbabwe, packed full of mercenaries from South Africa, Angola, and Namibia. The plan is to take weapons and ammunition on board, fly on to Malabo, and meet up with a little group of fighters smuggled in ahead of them. Together, they then plan to overthrow the government in a surprise attack, shoot down Obiang or throw him into his own prison, the main priority being a change of power. The day before, and as if by magic, the leader of the oppositional progressive party Severo Moto arrives in nearby Mali from his Madrid exile, thereby enabling him to get to Malabo within the hour to have his feet kissed by the grateful hordes.

But it didn't quite turn out like that. The South African secret services—on the alert against the now unemployed henchmen of apartheid—got wind of the plan and warned Obiang. Simultaneously, the Zimbabwe government were informed of the arrival of a bunch of dreamers convinced they could rewrite history by letting rip with some decommissioned Kalashnikovs. The trap snaps down on both sides: they were all arrested and given immediate prison sentences, and that was that.

Or that *would have been* that.

Because unfortunately—for those behind the coup—the people questioned betrayed their confidentiality vows in the hope of lighter sentences. And so the full force of the law makes itself felt. One of the ringleaders of the unlucky commandos was a former British officer and long-time leader of a private mercenary firm, which had links with a certain Jan Kees Vogelaar. The officer, imprisoned in Zimbabwe, is able to tell them that a dodgy oil manager with a British passport is behind the whole thing, and above all a relative of a former British prime minister, who is alleged to have put up considerable sums of money for the operation. Just this information alone is enough to elicit statements from Obiang hinting at handing over certain parts of the perpetrators' anatomy to his cook, if they ever get their hands on them. This and the prospect of dance lessons in Black Beach—and worse—contribute immensely to the loosening of the mercenary leader's tongue. Then the truth comes out.

The real financiers are the blue blood oil companies, the crème of the trade, who were disgruntled at the sputtering wealth being divided up between American companies and the impossibility of getting a foot in the door with Obiang. No offense intended, but they wanted to change a few things. Severo Moto had been chosen to undertake the distribution of the cake. A puppet president who, among other things, had promised to favor Spanish oil companies too.

And then the mercenary drops the real bomb:

They all knew about it!

The CIA. British MI6. The Spanish secret service. They all knew—and they all helped. It was even said Spanish warships had been en route to Equatorial Guinea, an infinite loop of colonialism. Obiang was outraged. Even his brunch buddy from Washington stabbed him in the back. No longer willing to stabilize him, Bush was prepared to divide up shares among the English and the Spanish in the interest of a puppet government, and to negotiate more favorable mining conditions in turn. Obiang rages against the whole sorry lot of them—and decides to help put their plan into action: he really does redistribute the mining rights. Just in a completely different way from how the global strategists imagined. American companies get the boot, and in their place the South Africans get the lot. Relations with José María Aznar, Severo Moto's friend and host to forty thousand Equatorial Guinea residents in exile, are suspended. France, on the other hand, is alleged to have helped to prevent the coup, and so Obiang looks favorably on the Grande Nation.

And wasn't there a country on the starting blocks, waiting for America to go it alone?

"China comes into play."

"Yes, although treading delicately. Obiang seems prepared to forgive and forget at first. Aznar has been voted out by then, making Spain approachable again, so he launches into a charm offensive. By the same token, Washington tries its hand with diplomatic reparations. Smiling competitions with Condoleezza Rice, new contracts, all of that. By 2008, the companies are pumping half a million barrels a year from the sea off Obiang's *own country*, the country that records the highest income per capita in the whole of Africa. Analysts estimate that there is more oil stored in Equatorial Guinea than in Kuwait. The bulk of it flows into the USA, a little to France, Italy, and Spain, but the real winner—"

"—is China."

"Exactly! They caught up with America. Slyly and quietly."

"I get it." Yoyo looked at him, her eyelids drooping. Jericho felt strangely spaced out too. The lack of sleep and the gliding jet at twice the speed of sound were starting to have a narcotic effect. "And Obiang?"

"Still angry. Furious! He realizes of course, that high-ranking members of his government must have known about the plans to overthrow him. You can only arrange a coup like that with support from the inside. So heads roll, and from then on he doesn't trust anyone. He gets himself a Moroccan bodyguard out of fear of his own people. At the same time, though, he demands to be courted in a bizarre way. When the Exxon bosses arrive, they have to address his ministers and generals as *Excelentissimo*. Former slaves encounter former slave traders, everyone detests everyone else. The board members of the oil firms hate having to sit at a table with the jungle chiefs, but they do it regardless because both sides stand to make a huge profit."

"And the country is still on its knees."

"There are some benefits for the Fang, but generally speaking the economy is corrupt. Sure, there are a few more nice cars parked in the slums, but running water and electricity are still in short supply. The country is paying for the curse of having natural resources. Who would still want to work or educate themselves if money were flowing into their accounts of its own accord? The wealth transforms some into predators and others into zombies. Bush states that he plans to pump the sea floor near Malabo empty by 2030, and promises Obiang he'll leave him in peace with regard to human rights and coup plans, as well as reward him appropriately."

"That sounds like a good deal. For Obiang, I mean."

"Yes, he could have contented himself with that. But he didn't. Because good old Obiang—"

—is an elephant: unforgiving, mistrustful. As elephants tend to be. He just can't forget that Bush, the Brits, and the Spanish wanted to do the dirty on him. The pistons of his lubricated power machine rise and fall cheerfully, everything running like clockwork, including his sparkling reelection in 2009. There's such immense wealth that lesser quantities finally spill over to the middle and lower classes too, enough to anaesthetize any revolutionary ideas for the time being. But Obiang still plots his revenge.

Ironically, of all things it's the change of government in Washington that heralds the new era. In a way, it was possible to rely on Bush, who lacked the same amount of morals as he endeavored to fake in his speeches. Barack Obama, on the other hand, the high priest of Change, dreaded the thought of tucking into hard-boiled eggs in the company of reputed cannibals behind closed doors. Eagerly attempting to reestablish America's worse for wear image around the world, he hauled terms like democracy and human rights out of the sewers of Bush's vocabulary, listened courteously to the UN when sanctions against rogue regimes were the topic of debate, and aggravated Obiang with his humanitarian demands.

In the fanfare of changed American rhetoric, Obiang is probably the only one to notice that two heavily armed US military bases have sprung up in São Tomé and Príncipe overnight, right in front of his nose. Oil is suspected around this small island state too. By now, China and the USA are engaged in a real race in the resources market. The treasures of the earth seem solely destined to be divided up between the two economic giants. Officially, the two bases are supposed to secure trouble-free transport of gas and oil in the Gulf of Guinea, but Obiang senses betrayal. His fall would make things a great deal easier for the Americans. And they will force his fall, as long as he continues to go to bed with each and every whore instead of marrying just one of them.

Obiang looks to the East.

In 2010, Beijing ascended to become Africa's biggest financial backer, ahead of even the World Bank. The president figures out two geostrategic equations. The first is that China is least likely to carry out a coup against him, so long as he favors them in commodities poker. The second is that Beijing is most likely to overthrow him if he doesn't, so he gives more licenses to China. The alarm bells start to ring in Washington. Just like before, they still try to maintain close relations with states that have something they want. US representatives travel to corrupt meetings under the soaking skies of Malabo. An unblemished cosmopolitan on the surface, Obiang assures his American friends of his undiminished appreciation while, behind their backs, he puts an end to contracts, redistributes mining rights at will, commences license fees, and stirs up public opinion against the Western "exploiters." These actions result in infringements on US institutions, imprisonments, and the deportation of American workers. Washington considers it necessary to threaten Obiang with sanctions and isolation, and the climate rapidly deteriorates.

Then, drunk on power, Obiang crosses the line. Peeved at the extension of the American military bases, he has Marathon's oil town "Pleasantville" attacked in the dead of night. This culminates in a real battle at Punta Europa, with casualties on both sides. As always, the president denies any part in it, expresses deep consternation and promises that he, like his uncle before him, plans to nail the guilty parties to stakes along the side of the highway. But in doing so, he makes the mistake of casting the blame onto the Bubi, a spark that triggers an explosion. Distracted by geostrategy, Obiang failed to notice that the ethnic conflict had long since overstepped the border of controllability. The Bubi defend themselves against the accusations, attack Fangs of the Esangui clan, and are riddled with bullets by Obiang's paramilitaries, but this time his intimidation tactics don't have the usual impact. Marathon people identify the corpse of a fallen attacker as an officer of the Equatorial Guinea army, a Fang who was loyal to the party line, and one who was also related by marriage to Obiang. Washington doesn't rule out taking military action. Obiang pointedly has Americans arrested and accuses Obama of trying to engineer his overthrow, a statement which encourages Bubi politicians to send signals to Washington. Severo Moto, the unlucky almost-president, who has little else to do but chew on the bones of failure in Spanish exile, conveys the details: if Malabo, the capital city, can be successfully brought under control, then—and only then!—can a coup have any chance of success. The hearts of the Bubi beat for America. And so a new equation is made: America plus Bubi equals coup equals China out and America in. Officially, the Americans turn down a coup, of course, but the trenches are dug.

Obiang gets nervous.

He tries to unite the Fang to support him, but their belated rage at his failings puts paid to that. Most Fang had no better a time of it under his regime than the Bubi. By now, they are discontented and disunited. The ruling clan in particular shows itself to be a stronghold of Shakespearean plotting. Barricaded behind his puppet guard, the president fails to notice that America has begun to buy Fang and Bubi leaders off in secret, urging them to shake hands and make peace. China makes a bid too. The Equatorial Guinea parliament is up for auction, a Sotheby's full of corruption. The scattered Bubi parties at home and abroad find themselves in shaky alliances. Obiang responds with terror; civil-war-like conditions shake the country and draw the attention of the foreign media. The USA finally drops the oil prince. He is ordered to call a reelection or, preferably, to step down immediately. Beside himself with rage, Obiang threatens the Bubi with genocide and expresses his desire to eat a whole lot of fried liver. But by now the resistance can no longer be contained.

To add to the confusion, Fang clans from the less than wealthy hinterlands unexpectedly join the Bubi side. Obiang shouts for military helicopters, Beijing hesitates. The hands-off principle, the most important cornerstone of Chinese foreign policy, won't tolerate military intervention. At the same time, the UN assembly strives for resolutions against Equatorial Guinea. China exercises its veto, the EU demands Obiang's resignation. Cameroon wants to mediate, but both sides of the Atlantic are in agreement: Obiang's time is up. The guy has to go. One way or another.

In 2015, a year before his time in office is up, weakened by both politics and his prostate, the dictator finally buckles. A tired old man is shown on State TV describing the carcass of his health, citing it as the reason why he is no longer able to serve his beloved people in the reliable way they have become accustomed to. Ergo, for the good of Equatorial Guinea, he is now handing over his power to younger hands, and in particular to—to—to—

According to the script, Obiang's eldest son Teodorin was supposed to rush out from behind the curtain in full presidential regalia, but he had planned ahead, making himself scarce in the Bermuda triangle of the jet set. In any case, the majority of his uncles and cousins wanted to see Obiang's second-born in power instead: Gabriel, who managed the oil trade. The USA—a bitter opponent of Teodorin since he had boasted years ago of wanting to renegotiate all the oil treaties to America's disadvantage—spread rumors that Teodorin was planning Gabriel's murder. Suddenly, no one seemed to want to take the reins anymore. Obiang, disgusted by the whiff of cowardice, decides without further ado to nominate an interim candidate, one who will lead government business for the duration of his office and then organize fair elections with the inclusion of all parties and candidates. The chosen one is the commander in chief of the armed forces, a cousin of Obiang's, whose chest is covered with medals for loyal service, including the prevention of numerous assassination and coup attempts as well as the imprisonment and torture of innumerable Bubi and Fang. He is—

Brigadier General Juan Alfonso Nguema Mayé. Huge and bald-headed, with a broad, captivating smile. Mayé, running a store for oil tankers in Berlin and devouring Yoyo's eyeballs with relish, while Jan Kees Vogelaar—

"Owen."

Mayé transforms into Kenny, comes closer, black against a wall of flames, raises his arm, and Jericho sees that he's waving Yoyo's eyeless skull.

Give me your computer, he says.

Give me—

"Owen, wake up."

Someone is shaking him by the shoulder. Yoyo's voice snuggles into his ear. He breathes in her scent and opens his eyes. Tu is standing behind her, grinning down at him.

"What's going on?" Jericho gestures toward the cockpit with his thumb. "Shouldn't you be sitting up front?"

"Autopilot, *xiongdi*," said Tu. "A wonderful invention. I had to stand in for you temporarily. Do you want to hear how the Mayé story continues?"

"Erm—"

"That might have been a yes," whispered Yoyo, turned toward Tu. "What do you reckon, did he say yes?"

"It sounds more like he wants coffee. Would you like a coffee, Owen?"

"Hmm?"

"Would you like a coffee?"

"I—No, no coffee."

"He's in another world, our innterrrrimm candidaaaa," whispered Yoyo conspiratorially.

Tu chortled. "Innterrrrimm candidaaaa," he repeated, against a backdrop of Yoyo's melodic giggling. Both were highly amused, and Owen was clearly the source of their merriment. Disgruntled, he looked out of the window into the night and then back again.

"How long was I out for?"

"Oh, a good hour."

"I'm sorry, I didn't mean to—"

Yoyo stared at him. She tried to keep a straight face, then she and Tu burst out laughing. They cackled idiotically at the tops of their voices, nervous and breathless.

"Hey! What's so funny?"

"Nothing." They were still panting and laughing.

"There's clearly something."

"No, nothing, Owen, it's nothing. It's just that—"

"What?"

Altitude sickness, he thought. The beginnings of hysteria. You hear of people who start laughing after traumatic events and then just can't stop. Astonishingly, even though he didn't have the faintest clue what it was about, he felt a painful longing to laugh along, whatever it was. That's not good, he thought. We're all going crazy.

"So?"

"Well." Yoyo blew her nose and wiped the corners of her eyes. "Oh, it's silly really, Owen. I lost you in the middle of a sentence. Your last word was—"

"What?"

"I guess it was meant to be interim candidate. You said, Obiang had an inteeeeriiim—"

Tu was making bleating noises.

"Candidaaaaaa—"

"You've both lost your minds."

"Come on Owen. It's funny," grunted Tu. "It's really funny!"

"Why, for God's sake?"

"You fell asleep in the middle of the sentence," giggled Yoyo. "Your head fell forward in a funny way, your lower jaw dropped down, like—"

Jericho waited patiently until her reenactment of his degradation had reached its drooling conclusion. Tu dabbed the sweat from his bald head. In moments like these, the English and Chinese senses of humor seemed to be galaxies apart, but Jericho suddenly realized he was laughing too. For some reason it felt good. As if someone had put the furniture inside his mind in order and let some fresh air in.

"Right then." Tu patted him on the shoulder. "I'm going up front again. Yoyo will tell you the rest. Then we can draw our conclusions."

"Where did we get to?" asked Jericho.

"To interiiiiiim—" chirruped Yoyo.

"Enough now."

"No, I'm being serious. To General Mayé."

She was right, that was where they had left off. Obiang had named his highest commander in chief as his successor. Mayé was supposed to use the time the outgoing president had left in office to prepare for democratic elections, and yet . . .

No one trusted the brigadier general. Mayé was seen as a hard-liner and as Obiang's puppet. There was no doubt that the elections would result in either Mayé himself or one of the president's sons seizing power. Definitely not the kind of result anyone would like.

Apart from Beijing, that is.

What happened next was so surprising, both for Obiang and Mayé, that even weeks later they were still convinced it was a bad dream. On the day when office was to be handed over, a boldly soldered-together alliance of Bubi and Fang, including members of the armed forces, simultaneously stormed numerous police stations in Malabo as well as the seat of government, taking the dictator and his designated successor prisoner. They drove them to the Cameroon border and threw them out of the country without any further ado. America's investment had paid off: practically every key position in government circles had been bought. This even turned out to be to Obiang's advantage, because America refused to tolerate any cases of lynch justice for the logistic and strategic support of the coup.

For the next few hours, the country seemed to have no leader.

Then Severo Moto's successor emerged from an airplane, a university-educated economist by the name of Juan Aristide Ndongo, from the Bubi clan. He had once been forced to reside in Black Beach for a number of years for his criticism of the regime, and for that reason had gained the trust of a large proportion of the population. Ndongo was known to be clever, friendly and weak, the ideal Manchurian candidate. The Fang and Bubi agreed on him in advance with the USA, Great Britain, and Spain, expecting to be able to spoon-feed good old Ndongo to their heart's desire, but he surprised them by having his own plans. The speedy dissolution of parliament is followed by the equally speedy formation of a new government, in which the Bubi and Fang are equally represented. Ndongo promises to create the long overdue infrastructure, a pulsing educational system, to reinvigorate the economy and to provide healthcare and prosperity for everyone. But, above all, he rails against China's bloodsucking vampire capitalism, which he sees as having destroyed Equatorial Guinea in collaboration with Obiang's recklessness. He also puts a stop to Beijing's license treaties and puts the American ones back in force, without forgetting—with wise foresight—the Spanish, British, French, and Germans.

But reality catches up with Ndongo like a pack of hungry dogs. His attempts to put his plans into action aggravate the Fang elite, who hadn't reckoned with his political survival instinct. He puts oil income into trust funds instead of transferring it to private accounts, and by doing so keeps the money out of the reach of corruption. He keeps to his promise and builds streets and hospitals, kick-starts the wood trade, and relaxes censorship. In doing so, he provokes the hate of the Obiang clique who, they now realize, let themselves be bought without taking into consideration that the preaching Bubi politician intended to take the lead. Within the first year after the coup, the hard-liners move over to the opposition. Ndongo's successes just feed their hatred, so they try to sabotage him wherever possible, denouncing his inability to rid the world of ethnic resentment and stirring it up in the process. They claim that Ndongo is just another Obiang, a puppet of the USA, and that he will discriminate against the Fang. Many bravely initiated projects grind to a halt. AIDS grows rampant, crime is rife, and Ndongo's parliament proves itself to be just as corrupt as his predecessor's, while the president, hobbling around defiantly on the crutches of legality, begins to lose touch.

In the second year under Ndongo's rule, radical Esangui-Fang launch attacks on American and European oil institutions. Bubi and Fang go for each other's necks as they have since time immemorial, terrorist cells thwart every attempt at political stabilization, and Ndongo's idea of a better world collapses with a crash. He has gone too far for his opponents, but not far enough for his friends. In a painful act of self-denial, Ndongo takes a harsher stance, carries out mass arrests and loses what was once his only capital overnight: integrity.

Meanwhile, Mayé is warming up on the sidelines in Cameroon.

"From the outside," said Yoyo, "it looked like this: Obiang, sick and bitter, hangs around in the neighboring country and pressures Mayé to force Ndongo out of office at the next available opportunity. But the old man doesn't want Mayé himself to rule, but rather to prepare the ground for Teodorin and Gabriel, who have sunk sobbing into one another's arms at the mere thought of Ndongo. Rivalry is no longer the issue. The country is destabilized and Ndongo is for it. All Mayé would really need to do is travel in and say Boo! Aside from the fact that he can't enter the country of course."

"But because putschists don't need a visa—"

"—he agrees and sets off. It's common knowledge by then that Mayé has already made contact with a private mercenary firm, African Protection Services, APS for short. And they—" Yoyo paused for a short, dramatic moment "—are of interest to us!"

"Let me guess. This is where Vogelaar comes back into the picture."

Yoyo smiled smugly. "I've found the missing years. Does the name ArmorGroup ring any bells with you?"

"It does. It's a London security giant."

"In 2008 ArmorGroup took on a mandate in Kenya. Around that time, a smaller company, Armed African Services, went through a demerger. Vogelaar's Mamba was operating in the same crisis area. They crossed paths, perhaps one of them approached the other and borrowed some ammunition or something, but to cut a long story short they took a liking to one another and formed APS in 2010, with Vogelaar at management level. Do you see?"

"I do. So Mayé overthrew Ndongo with the help of APS. But who paid APS?"

"That's exactly the point. Mayé was incredibly friendly with China."

"You mean—"

"I mean that we assumed the whole time that the coup attempt discussed in the text fragment was the one from last year. But Beijing would have had far more reason to pull the strings in 2017."

Jericho thought for a moment. He tried to remember who was in power in Malabo back then. The longer he thought about it, the more convinced he was that Ndongo had taken up his old seat again.

"And how did Mayé's coup go?"

"Without a hitch. As a precaution, Ndongo was out of the country. But no one seemed particularly surprised by it. No resistance, no fatalities. The only one who was shocked was Obiang. Mayé had numerous opposition members imprisoned, including Obiang's closest confidants, Teodorin supporters, Gabrielists—"

"Because he had no intention of stepping down."

"Bingo."

"And Vogelaar became his security boss."

"Yep."

"Is there proof that China was tied up in it?"

"Owen, what's wrong with you?" Yoyo reprimanded him. "There's never proof, you know that. But on the other hand you would have to be a zombie to overlook the fact that Exxon, Marathon, and Co. got the chop immediately after the putsch, whereas the Chinese company Sinopec was suddenly swimming in oil from Equatorial Guinea. Then there's Mayé's speeches: they owed the Chinese their gratitude, China had always been a brother, blah blah blah. When it came down to it, he wholeheartedly agreed to his country being sold out to China."

Jericho nodded. It was obvious that Yoyo was right: Mayé had taken power with the help of the Chinese and, as agreed, hadn't forgotten to reward them. But then why did they later want to kill him?'

"And if it wasn't the Chinese . . ." said Yoyo, as if she had read his thoughts. "Last year, I mean."

"Then who?"

"Is it that hard to guess? Mayé doesn't miss a single opportunity to snub the Americans. He has their representatives imprisoned, breaks all contracts, aids and abets terrorist attacks on American institutions, even though he denies it outright in diplomatic circles. In any case, it was enough that Washington was threatening him with sanctions and invasion."

"It sounds like saber-rattling."

"That's precisely the question."

"So what then? The guy ruled for seven years. What happened in that time?"

"He held his hand out. Finished the economy off. Made opposition members disappear, had them tortured, beheaded, who knows what else. Before long, Obiang looked like a philanthropist compared with Mayé, but now they had him by the neck. Mayé didn't get involved with cannibalism, witchcraft and the whole black magic scene, but he was certainly developing considerable delusions of grandeur. He built skyscrapers that no one moved into, but he didn't care, the important thing was how the skyline looked. He planned Equatorial Guinea's own version of Las Vegas and wanted to set up an opera house in the sea. The final straw was when he announced that Equatorial Guinea was promoting itself to become a Space nation, to which end, and in all seriousness, he had a launching pad built in the middle of the jungle."

"Wait a second—" It slowly dawned on Jericho that he had read something about it at the time. An African dictator who had built a space-rocket launch base and bragged to the rest of the world that his country would be sending astronauts to the Moon. "Wasn't that—?"

"In 2022," said Yoyo. "Two years before he was overthrown."

"And what happened?"

"Well, do you see any Africans in space?"

"No."

"Exactly. He did send one thing up though. A news satellite."

"And what on earth did Mayé need a news satellite for?"

Yoyo circled her finger over her temple. "Because he wasn't all there, Owen. Why do men get penis extensions? They're nothing but space-rocket launch bases on a smaller scale. But the whole thing became a mockery because the satellite broke down just a few weeks after the launch."

"But it *was* launched."

"Yes, without a hitch."

"Then what happened?"

"Nothing really. Two years later, Mayé was liquidated, and Ndongo came back." Yoyo leaned back. Her entire posture said she was ready to call it a day and unwind. "You probably know more about that than I do. That was the part you researched."

"But I don't know much about Ndongo."

"Oh well," Yoyo shrugged. "If you want to find out who footed the bill this time then you'll need to take a close look at Ndongo's oil politics. I've got no idea whether he has been as loyally devoted to China as Mayé was."

"Definitely not."

"How do you know?"

"You said yourself that he would have attacked China pretty heftily. I don't think there's any doubt about that. Ndongo was put in there by the USA and taken out by China."

"So who took Mayé out?"

Jericho gnawed on his lower lip.

statement coup Chinese government

"Something in this story doesn't make sense," he said. "In the text fragment it's about a coup that China is tied up in, but they can't mean the coup of 2017. For one thing, that's eight years ago. And in any case, everyone suspects Beijing was involved in it anyway, so why would they be hunting us down because of that? And another thing, it was explicitly about Donner and Vogelaar. But Vogelaar only comes up in connection with Mayé."

"Or was placed there by Beijing back then. Maybe as a kind of guard for Mayé. A spy."

"And Donner?"

"Think back, it wasn't just a coup last year. It was an execution. A concerted effort to get rid of witnesses. Mayé must have known something, or rather, he and his staff must have. Something so explosive that someone was prepared to kill him for it."

"Something about China."

"Why else would China have cleared someone out of the way that they themselves put in power? Perhaps Mayé became a liability. And Donner was one of his staff."

"And Vogelaar was the one who had contact with Beijing. As security chief, he was closest to Mayé. So he recommends decapitating Mayé's regime."

"And they do. Apart from Donner."

"He gets away."

"And now Vogelaar is supposed to find him and give him the same send-off he gave Mayé. That's why they're after us. Because we know that Donner's cover has been blown. Because we could beat Vogelaar to it. Because we could warn Donner."

"And Kenny?"

"He might be Vogelaar's Chinese contact."

Jericho's brain was throbbing. If the yarn they were spinning was actually true, then Donner's life was hanging by a silk thread.

No, there had to be more to it. It wasn't just about them preventing Donner from being killed. That was part of it, certainly, but the real reason for the brutal hunt of the last twenty-four hours was something else. Someone was worried that they could find out what Donner *knew*.

He stared out into the night and hoped they weren't too late.

BERLIN, GERMANY

A glowing circuit board. A mildewed spider's web against a black background. Colonies of endlessly interwoven deep-sea organisms, the neuron landscape of an endlessly sprawling brain, a cosmos slipping away. At night, and seen from a great height, the world looks like anything but a globe illuminated only by streetlamps, neon signs, cars, and house lights, by exhausted taxi drivers and shift workers, by the perpetual search for diversion and by worries which find their expression in sleeplessness and apartments lit up into the early hours. What—in the eyes of an extraterrestrial observer—might look like a coded message, actually means: Yes, we *are* alone in the universe, everyone for themselves and all for one, and we're here in the dark wilderness too, except that we're underdeveloped, poor, and cut off from everything.

Jericho stared indecisively out of the window. Yoyo had dozed off in her seat, the jet was preparing for landing. Tu didn't like engaging in conversation while he was at the controls. Left to his own devices, Jericho had tried for a while to wring information about Ndongo's current time in office out of the Internet, but the media interest in Equatorial Guinea seemed to have vanished with Mayé's departure. He suddenly felt his motivation ebbing away. Yoyo's light, melodic snoring had the air of a soliloquy to it. Her chest rose and sank, then she gave a start and her eyes rolled under her eyelids. Jericho watched her. It was almost as though the confusing moment of intimacy they had shared had never happened.

He turned his head and let his gaze wander out over the ghost of light as it become steadily denser. At a height of 10 kilometers, he had felt a gnawing loneliness, too far from the Earth, not close enough to the skies. He was grateful for every meter that the plane sank closer to the ground, allowing the strange pattern to form familiar pictures again. Buildings, streets, and squares created the illusion of familiarity. Jericho had been in Berlin a number of times. He spoke German well, not perfectly, because he had never made the effort to learn it, but what he could say was accent-free. As soon as he put his mind to boning up on a language he mastered it in a matter of weeks, and, in any case, just listening was enough to be able to understand.

He fervently hoped that they would find Andre Donner still alive.

At 04:14, they landed in Berlin Brandenburg airport. Tu set off to arrange a rental car. When he came back he was morosely waving an Audi stick.

"I would have preferred another make," he moaned as they crossed the neon wasteland of the parking lot in search of their vehicle. Jericho trotted behind him with his backpack slung over his shoulder, accompanied by a shuffling and sedated-looking Yoyo, whom they had barely managed to wake. Apart from Diane and some hardware, he had nothing else with him. Tu had refused to take him to Xintiandi before their departure so he could pack a few essentials. Not even Yoyo had been permitted to go back to her apartment, although she had been bold enough to protest, making Tu see red.

"No discussion!" he had scolded her. "Kenny and his mob could be lying in wait. They'd either finish you off right on the spot or follow you to me."

"Then just send one of your people instead."

"They'd still follow them."

"Or just let me—"

"Forget it!"

"For God's sake! I can't just run around in the same smelly clothes for days on end! And nor can Owen, right? Or can you, Owen?"

"Don't try ganging up on me. I said no! Berlin is a civilized city; I hear they have socks, underwear, running water, and even electricity there."

There was electricity; that much was true. But beyond that a hot shower or the scent of fresh laundry seemed light years away in that deserted, car-packed hangar. Tu hurried past dozens of identical-looking metal and synthetic-fiber bodies, swinging his full-to-bursting travel bag, chivvied the others along, and finally spotted the dark, discreet limousine.

"The car's not bad at all," Jericho dared to comment.

"I would have preferred a Chinese make."

"What are you talking about? You don't drive a Chinese car. Not even when you're in China."

"Funny," said Tu, as the car read the data from the stick and obediently opened its doors. "Such a talented investigator, but in some respects you're from the Stone Age. I drive a Jaguar, and Jaguar is a Chinese make."

"Since when?"

"Since three years ago. We bought it from the Indians, just like we bought Bentley from the Germans. I would just as happily have taken a Bentley of course."

"Why not a Rolls?"

"Under no circumstances! Rolls-Royce is Indian."

"You two are nuts," yawned Yoyo and lay down across the back seat.

"Listen," said Jericho, as he slid onto the passenger seat. "They don't automatically become Chinese models just because you buy them. They're English. People buy them because they like English cars, and that's precisely why you buy them too."

"But they belong—"

"—to the Chinese, I know. Sometimes the entire globalization process just seems like one big misunderstanding."

"Oh, come on, Owen! Really!"

"I'm serious."

"Comments like that didn't have any punch even twenty years ago."

Tu steered the car in slalom through the aisles, whose uniformity was only outdone by the fact that they seemed so infinite in number. "I'd rather you told me whether you've found out anything else that might be of interest to us."

Jericho gave him a brief overview of Ndongo's unsuccessful attempt to reform the country and do business with the United States again, and of Mayé's subsequent coup, Beijing's obvious implication in it, and Mayé's China politics. He also mentioned the dictator's growing delusions of grandeur, his failed space program, and his violent removal from power.

"The official story is that Mayé and his clique fell victim to a Bubi revolt which was supported by influential Fang groups," he said. "Which would be plausible. But Obiang certainly wasn't behind it. Since his expulsion to Cameroon he's become quite a hermit and, according to rumor, is fighting his final battle against cancer."

"And it wouldn't have been the sons either?"

"No."

"Well," Tu clicked his tongue. "There's surprisingly little information about what's been happening there over the last year, don't you think?"

Jericho gave him an appraising look. "Is it just my imagination, or do you know something that I should know?"

"*Oída ouk eidós*," said Tu innocently.

"That's not Confucius."

"I know, are you impressed? It's Plato, Socrates's apologia: I know that I know not."

"Show-off."

"Not at all. It's perfectly fitting for what I'm trying to say. I do know that there's an explanation for the diminished interest in Equatorial Guinea, but I just can't work out what it is. I know it's something obvious though. Something that's right in front of our noses."

"Does it also explain why there was hardly any public speculation about involvement from abroad?"

"Ask me after I've figured out what it is."

Jericho listened to the navigation system for a while.

"Look, the problem is that the coup wouldn't have been possible without outside help," he said. "It's clear that Mayé was installed there by the Chinese, so one would assume that America did it. But our text fragment says something different, that China had its finger in the pie too. If that's correct, then the submissive servant wasn't submissive enough when it really came down to it."

"You mean he was no longer willing to comply with Beijing's wishes?"

"Yoyo and I are leaning toward the view that he and his inner circle could even have become dangerous for China."

"Which would explain why the Chinese build him up first and then kill him," concluded Tu.

"And accept the considerable disadvantages too."

"How do you mean?"

"Oil. Gas. Ndongo had never been Beijing's friend."

Tu opened his mouth. For a moment he looked as though he had grasped something which had far-reaching implications. The he clapped his lower jaw back up. Jericho raised an eyebrow.

"You wanted to say something?"

"Later."

They fell silent. Yoyo had fallen asleep on the back seat again. Once they were finally on the autobahn, dawn began to break and the traffic became busier. The navigation system issued muted directions. They approached Berlin Mitte, were directed toward Potsdamer Platz and, by 05:30 a.m., had secured spacious rooms in the newly renovated Hyatt. An hour later, they sat down to breakfast. The choice was more than ample. Yoyo had overcome her tiredness and was shoveling immense quantities of scrambled eggs and bacon into her mouth. Tu, much less picky, instead made his way diagonally through what was on offer, managing to combine smoked fish and chocolate spread in such a repulsive way that Jericho had to avert his gaze. As usual, Tu didn't even seem to register what he was eating. He noisily watered down the mélange with green tea and started to talk:

"You can't still be tired, you slept enough in Shanghai, so—"

"I didn't even get a wink of sleep," groaned Yoyo. "Only just then on the plane."

"The same with me," admitted Jericho. "Every time I thought I was dropping off it felt as if I was falling into an electrical field."

"God, that's it!" Yoyo opened her eyes wide and touched his hand, as though in reflex. "That's exactly what it feels like. As if someone's running a bolt of electricity through you."

"Yes, you jump—"

"And then you're awake again! The whole night through."

"Interesting." Tu looked at them each in turn and shook his head. "I mean, I went through the little Depression of 2010, the Yuan Crisis of 2018, the recession two years ago—and I didn't let any of it rob me of my sleep."

"Oh no?" drawled Yoyo. "Did someone slaughter your friends in front of your eyes too, and then almost hound you to death afterward?"

Tu cocked his head to one side.

"So you think you're the only person who's seen others die?"

"I have no idea."

"Exactly."

"I mean, I have no idea what *you've* seen."

"If you don't have any idea—"

"No, I don't!" hissed Yoyo. "And do you know why not? Because you and my father brood about your miserable pasts by yourselves! I don't care what you've both been through. Maggie, Tony, Jia Wei, and Ziyi were shot into shreds in front of my eyes. Xiao-Tong, Mak, and Ye are dead too. I don't even want to start on Grand Cherokee; and the fact that my father, Daxiong, and Owen are still alive is bordering on a miracle. So I've allowed myself to lose a little sleep over it. Do you have any other clever comments?"

"You should keep your outbreaks of emotion—"

"No, *you* should!" Yoyo waved her hands around wildly in the air. "Hongbing, tell your child the truth, you have to trust her, you can't keep up this silence any longer, blah blah blah. God, you're the master of blah blah blah, Tian, you're sooo understanding and constructive! But when it comes to you, you keep things under wraps, right?"

"If I could just—" interjected Jericho.

"You're no better than Hongbing, do you know that?"

"Hey!" Jericho leaned over. "I've no idea why you guys came to Berlin, but I want to find Andre Donner, is that clear? So sort your issues out somewhere else."

"Tell *him* that."

Tu kneaded his hands morosely. He slurped tea, took a bite of a sausage, shoved the rest in after it, scrunched up his serviette, and threw it carelessly onto the plate. Clearly he wasn't anywhere near as untouchable as he liked to imply. For a while, hurt silence reigned.

"Fine. As far as I'm concerned you can have a nap. But at some point in the course of the morning it would be advisable for you to stock up on the essentials, underwear, T-shirts, cosmetics, whatever. Perhaps we'll be back home again by this time tomorrow, but perhaps we won't. There's a shopping mall just opposite the hotel. Go and get what you need. After that we'll pay Muntu a visit. Is the place open at midday?"

"From twelve until two. According to the website."

"Good."

"I'm not sure." Jericho tore a croissant to pieces indecisively. "We shouldn't just all rock up there at once."

"Why not?"

"We want to warn Donner, not make him take flight. A European-looking guy, a Chinese girl, fine. In the city we'd just look like a normal couple. But add another Chinese guy and Donner could get suspicious."

"You think? Berlin is full of Chinese people."

"Do they go to African restaurants?"

"Please! We're the most culturally open people in the world."

"You're as open as a vacuum cleaner," said Jericho. "You suck up everything that isn't screwed on and riveted, but gastronomically you're all ignorant."

"You're confusing us with the Japanese."

"Not at all. The Japanese are culinary fascists. You lot, on the other hand, are just ignorant."

"I'm sure things would look different at McDonald's."

"Oh, come on!" Jericho couldn't help but laugh. Discussing food with Tu was almost as absurd as explaining the benefits of vegetarianism to a shark. "When you guys are abroad you always go to Chinese restaurants, right? All I'm saying is that the man who now goes by the name of Donner has had bad experiences with Chinese people, if our theories are correct. He's being hunted. The organization that Vogelaar and Kenny belong to want to kill him."

"Hmm." Tu pursed his lips. "Perhaps you're right."

"Of course he's right," said Yoyo to her plate.

"Fine then, you two go to Muntu. I'll hold the fort here."

"You could amuse yourself with Diane in the meantime," suggested Jericho. "Try to find out more about how Mayé was overthrown. And more about Ndongo. What drives him, what are his interests, who's supporting him? And why has there not been any more news from Equatorial Guinea?"

"I think I already know."

Jericho stopped. Even Yoyo seemed to have overcome her hurt pride and was looking at him expectantly. Tu stretched out his fingers and massaged the globe of his belly.

"And?"

"Later." Tu got up. "You have things to do, I have things to do. Have a good sleep. After that you can go and exhaust my credit cards."

Jericho would have preferred to track down Donner as soon as they landed and, if need be, turn up on his doorstep and get him out of bed, but there was no private address on record for him anywhere. He instructed the hotel computer to wake him at 10 a.m. He feared he'd relive the nightmare of the previous night, interspersed with phases of just staring at his eyelids from the inside, but instead he slept a deep and dreamless sleep for two hours and awoke in a much better mood and full of purpose. Yoyo seemed more cheerful too. They made their way through the mall, purchased underwear, shirts, and toothbrushes, and commented on the everyday life going on around them. Yoyo bought several bottles of spray-on clothing. It was hot and sunny in Berlin, so they didn't need more than just a few things. Jericho avoided asking her about her private life. He didn't really know how to act around the girl in this relatively normal setting; for a change there wasn't anything to research, nor was there anything to run from. Yoyo displayed an almost dismissive lack of concern by skipping around in front of him in the tiniest of tops, touching him every few minutes, pulling him here and there and getting so close to him that the only possible explanation for her actions seemed to be her complete lack of sexual interest in him.

That's exactly what it is, concurred the pimply boy hiding in the shade at the corner of the playground, seeking comfort from Radiohead, Keane, and Oasis. That's what women are like; you're just a thing to them, not someone who can express desire or intentions. A conglomerate of cells only spat into life to be a friend to them. They would rather be seduced by their teddy bears than acknowledge the possibility that you could fall in love with them.

Bite me, Jericho told him. Pussy.

After that, the pus-filled, pubescent-stubble-covered ghost retreated, and Yoyo's company really began to grow on him. Nonetheless, he was still relieved when it got closer to twelve and it was time to drive to Oranienburger Strasse. Muntu was on the ground floor of a beautifully renovated old building just a few hundred meters from the banks of the Spree, where Museum Island divided the water like a stranded whale. They almost walked right past it—the tiny restaurant was crammed furtively between a Christian bookstore and a branch of the Bank of Beijing, as if it wanted to make a surprise attack on passers-by. Over the door and windows was a cracked wooden panel with MUNTU in archaic-looking lettering, and underneath, *The Charm of West African Cuisine.*

"It's cute," said Yoyo as they stepped inside.

Jericho looked around. Ochre and banana-yellow colored walls, offset with blue on the skirting boards. Batik-patterned tablecloths, above which paper lamps hung down like huge, glimmering turnips. Wooden pillars and ceiling beams were painted and decorated with carvings. The end wall of the square room was dominated by a bar of rustic design, and to the left of that swing doors covered with mythical images led through into the kitchen. There was no trace here of the battle sculptures, spears, shields, and masks commonly found in similar establishments, an agreeable omission which suggested authenticity.

Only a few of the tables were occupied. Yoyo headed toward a table near the bar. A figure broke away from the half shadow behind it and came over to them. The woman might have been in her early forties, possibly older. Wrinkles came late to African women, which made guessing their age a challenge. Her slim-fitting dress was hued with powerful, earthy colors, and a matching headdress unfurled from an explosion of Rasta locks. She was very dark and quite attractive, and had a laugh that didn't seem acquainted with the compromise of a smile.

"My name is Nyela," she said in guttural German. "Would you like a drink?"

Yoyo looked at Jericho, confused. He mimed bringing a glass to his lips.

"Ah, okay," said Yoyo. "Cola."

"How boring." Nyela switched to English instantly. "Have you ever tried palm wine? It's fermented palm juice made from flower bulbs."

Without waiting for an answer, she disappeared behind the bar, came back with two beakers of a milky-looking drink, and laid out English menus in front of them.

"We're out of ostrich steak. I'll be back in a moment."

Jericho took a sip. The wine tasted good, cool and a little sharp. Yoyo's gaze followed Nyela to the neighboring table.

"What now?"

"We order something."

"Why aren't you asking to see Donner? I thought it was urgent."

"It is." Jericho leaned over. "I just don't think it's a good idea if we blurt it out just like that. In his position I would be a bit mistrustful if someone asked for me for no reason."

"But we're not asking for no reason."

"And what do you want her to tell him? That he's going to be killed? Then he'll slip through our fingers."

"We'll have to ask for him at some point."

"And we will."

"Okay, fine, you're the boss." Yoyo opened her menu. "So what do you feel like today, boss? Ragout of Kudu-antelope perhaps? Monkey penis with skinned-alive frogs?"

"Don't be silly." Jericho let his gaze wander over the starters and main courses. "It all sounds really good. Jolof rice for example, I had that back in London."

"Never had it."

"All it takes is a little courage," Jericho teased her. "Think of how we Europeans have to suffer in Sichuan."

"No, I'm not so sure. Adalu, Akara, Dodo." Her eyes flitted back and forth. "Look at the crazy names these things have. How about some Nunu, Owen? Some nice Nunu."

Jericho paused. "You're on the menu too."

"Eh?"

"Efo-Yoyo Stew!" He laughed loudly. "Well, we know what you're having then."

"Are you insane? What on earth is it?" She wrinkled her brow and read: "Spinach sauce with crabs and chicken and—ishu? What the heck is ishu?"

"Yam dumplings." The black woman had come back over to their table. "No party without yams."

"What are yams?"

"It's a root. The queen of all roots! The women cook them and then pound them with a pestle and mortar. It really builds the muscles." Nyela gave a deep and melodic laugh and showed them a well-sculpted biceps. "Men are too lazy for it. Probably too dumb too, no offense my friend." Her hand clasped Jericho's shoulder in a familiar way. A spicy scent came off her, a raw seduction.

"You know what?" said Jericho cheerfully. "Just put something together for us."

"He's no fool," said Nyela, winking at Yoyo. "Letting the women decide."

She disappeared into the kitchen. Not even ten minutes later, she came back bearing two trays groaning with dishes.

"*Paradise is here*," she sang.

Yoyo, her face full of mistrust, watched as Nyela put down little plates and bowls in front of them.

"Ceesbaar, pancakes made from plantain. Akara, deep-fried dumplings with shrimps. Samosas, pastry parcels with minced beef. Those are Moyinmoyin, bean cakes with crabs and turkey meat. Next to that is Efo-Egusi, spinach with melon seeds, beef, and dried cod. Here, Nunu, made from millet and yogurt. Then Adalu, bean and banana stew with fish. Brochettes, little fish skewers. Dodo, roasted in peanut oil, and—tapioca pudding!"

"Ah," said Yoyo.

Jericho stretched out his finger and sampled the Akara, Samosas, and Moyinmoyin in quick succession.

"Delicious," he cried, before Nyela could get away again. "How is it possible that I'd never heard of this place before?"

Nyela hesitated. Catching sight of a raised hand at the neighboring table, she excused herself, took their order, delivered it to the kitchen and then came back.

"That's easy," she said. "We only opened six months ago."

Jericho was stuffing his mouth full of Nunu while Yoyo nibbled timidly at one of the fish skewers. "And where were you before that?"

"Africa. Cameroon."

"You speak excellent English."

"I can get by. German is much harder. It's a strange language."

"Isn't Cameroon French-speaking?" asked Yoyo.

"African," said Nyela, with a facial expression that implied Yoyo had just cracked a good joke. "Cameroon *was* once French. A large part of it at any rate. Many languages are spoken there: Bantu, Kotoko and Shuwa, French, English, Camfranglais."

"And you're the one who cooked all these wonderful things?" asked Jericho.

"Most of them."

"Nyela, you're a goddess."

Nyela laughed, so loudly that the paper lamps shook.

"Is he always this charming?" she wanted to know. "Such a charming liar?"

Yoyo didn't answer, coughing instead. She seemed to have just realized that the spiciness of the pancakes struck with a malicious delay. Jericho took a slug of palm wine.

"Nyela, we've been play-acting a little. Muntu was actually recommended to us. So we're not here completely by chance. We would like to include you in a food guide. Would you be interested?"

"What kind of guide?"

"A virtual city guide," said Yoyo, who had got a grip of herself again and, her eyes sparkling, picked up on Jericho's idea. "People could get a three-dimensional experience of your restaurant in it by putting on hologlasses. Are you familiar with holographics?"

Nyela shook her head, visibly amused. "My specialty is the law, my child. I studied law in Jaunde."

"Picture it like this. We produce a walk-in image of the restaurant as a computer program. With the necessary equipment, people can even take a peek into the cooking pots. But there is also a simpler version, just an entry online."

"I can't say I fully understand, but it sounds good."

"Are you in?"

"Of course."

"Then we just need to take care of the formalities," said Jericho. "If I've been correctly informed, you're not the owner?"

"Muntu belongs to my husband."

"Andre Donner?"

"Yes."

"Oh, you're Mrs. Donner?" He raised his eyebrows, feigning sudden realization. "May I ask—your husband—I mean, Donner isn't an African name—"

"Boer. Andre is from South Africa."

"No, what a love story!" cried Yoyo in delight. "South Africa and Cameroon."

"And you two?" grinned Nyela. "What's your story?"

Jericho was just about to reply when Yoyo's fingers flew nimbly across like a squirrel and covered his.

"Shanghai and London," she whispered happily.

"Not bad either," said Nyela cheerfully. "I'll tell you what, my girl. Love is a language that everyone can understand. It's the only one you'll ever need."

"We—" said Jericho.

"—are in love, and we work together," smiled Yoyo. "Just like you and your husband. It's so wonderful!"

Jericho could almost hear the string section warming up. He didn't know how to pull his hand back without making it look suspicious. Nyela looked at them both, visibly moved.

"And where did you meet?"

"In Shanghai." Yoyo giggled. "I was his tour guide. To be more specific, he had the glasses on, the holo things. Owen fell in love with my hologram, isn't that sweet? After that he did everything he could to get to know me. I didn't want to at first, but—"

"Amazing."

"Yes, and you? Where did you meet your husband? South Africa? Or was it in Equatoria—"

"Sorry to interrupt," interjected Jericho. "But we still have a lot of things to do. So, Nyela, in order to prepare the entry we need to speak to your husband. We need his signature. Perhaps he's here now?"

Nyela looked at him thoughtfully with her shining white eyes. Then she pointed at the tapioca pudding.

"Have you tried it yet?"

"Not yet."

"Then you're not going anywhere, not for the time being at least." Her grin lit up the room. "Not until you've eaten everything up."

"No problem," purred Yoyo. "Owen loves African food. Don't you, poppet?"

Jericho thought he must be hearing things.

"I sometimes call him poppet," Yoyo confided in Nyela, who seemed interested and not at all embarrassed. "When we're by ourselves."

"Like now?"

"Yes, like now. What do you think, poppet, shall we stay a little longer?"

Jericho stared at her. "Of course, you old bag. Whatever you say."

Yoyo's smile frosted over. Her fingers made their retreat. Jericho felt a mixture of regret and relief.

"Andre isn't here right now, by the way," said Nyela. "How long will you be in Berlin?"

"Not long. We've got an early flight." Jericho scratched the back of his head. "There isn't any chance that we could meet him at short notice is there? This evening perhaps?"

"We're actually closed this evening. Although—" Nyela put a finger to her lips. "Okay, wait a moment. I'll be back shortly."

She disappeared through the swing doors.

"Did you really call me an old bag?" asked Yoyo under her breath.

"I did. And I meant it."

"Oh. Thanks."

"You're welcome, poppet."

"But why?" she protested. "What I said was nice! I said something nice, and you—"

"Consider yourself lucky I didn't say something worse."

"Owen, what's all this about?" A steep fold was building up between Yoyo's brows. "I thought you knew how to joke around."

"You nearly let the cat out of the bag, you idiot! You were about to say Equatorial Guinea."

"I wasn't."

"I heard it!"

"But she didn't." Yoyo rolled her eyes. "Okay, I'm sorry, calm down. At the very most she would have thought I said the equator. And that makes sense, right? Cameroon is on the equator."

"*Gabon* is on the equator."

"Daft know-all."

"Toad."

"Jerk!"

"Are we having a relationship crisis?" mocked Jericho. "We shouldn't push it, darling, or we might as well leave right now."

"So I'm the one that's pushed it too far? Because I was nice to you?"

"No, not because of that. Because you weren't being careful."

He knew he was reacting too harshly, but he was boiling over with rage. Yoyo looked away, morosely. They were still silent when Nyela came back to the table.

"What a shame," she said. "Andre is obviously on the move. And can't be reached. But he should be giving me a call sometime in the next few hours. Can you give me your cell phone number? I'll call you."

"Of course." Jericho wrote his number on a paper serviette. "I'll make sure my phone's turned on."

"We'd like to be in this guide of yours." Nyela laughed her throaty, African laugh. "Even though I don't have a clue what hologoggles are."

"We'll put you in," smiled Jericho. "With or without the goggles."

"Wow, a restaurant guide. What a great idea!"

Yoyo fidgeted along behind him resentfully as they left Muntu. The midday light was crystal clear, a hot early summer Berlin day, the sky an upside-down, sparkling blue swimming-pool. But Jericho didn't stop to take it all in. He crossed the street, marched into the shade of the row of buildings opposite, and halted so suddenly that Yoyo almost ran into him. He turned around and stared at the restaurant.

"She didn't notice anything," Yoyo assured him. "I'm sure she didn't."

Jericho didn't answer. He gazed thoughtfully over at Muntu. Yoyo paced on the spot, planted herself in front of him, and then waved her hand around in front of his eyes.

"Everything okay, Owen? Is there anyone at home?"

He rubbed the bridge of his nose. Then he looked at his watch.

"Fine, you don't have to speak to me," she warbled. "We can write to each other. Yes, that's a good idea! You can write everything down on a little piece of paper and give it to someone to give to me. And I—"

"You can make yourself useful."

"Oh, you do have a voice!" Yoyo bowed in front of an imaginary audience. "Ladies and gentlemen, the moment you've all been waiting for. The man has spoken. It is with great pride that we present to you—"

"You can shadow Nyela."

"Excuse me?"

"I've no idea whether she noticed your slip or not, but there's one thing I don't buy: her claim that Donner couldn't be reached."

"Why?"

"She was in the kitchen too long."

"You mean that Donner would be suspicious if someone wanted to include his restaurant in a guide?"

"You said it yourself—a great idea," Jericho flashed back at her. "Your irony was clear enough."

"Could you stop being mad at me for just a minute?"

"There are two possibilities. Either she bought it. Which doesn't necessarily mean that he did. But it doesn't really matter what story we dished up. Donner will be suspicious by nature, toward everyone and everything. The second possibility is that she didn't believe a word we said. Either way, he needs to find out who we are, what we want from him, and what we have to tell him. He needs to make quite certain. I'd hazard a guess that they've already spoken on the phone. If Nyela leaves the restaurant it could be that she's going to meet him.—Either that or he'll turn up here."

"What for?"

"To get here before someone can surprise him on his own premises. Or maybe just because he has garlic to chop. Things to do, whatever."

"Which means you'll watch the restaurant?"

Jericho nodded. "Did you notice the camera?" he asked, trying to make the tone of his voice more gentle now.

"What camera?"

"There was one installed above the bar. It didn't look like one, but I'm familiar with them. Muntu is under surveillance. Perhaps Donner will want to look at the recording before he agrees to a meeting."

"And what if none of that's right? What if you're wrong?"

"Then we wait until Nyela calls us. Or until she leads you to Donner's private residence."

"I mean, if he's not suspicious at all. If he really does want to meet us about the food guide, just not until this evening. Aren't we frittering away the chance to warn him *in time*? Shouldn't we tell Nyela the truth?"

"And have him take off? We didn't come here to save his life, but to find something out from him. And to do that we need to *meet* him!"

"I know that," retorted Yoyo irritably. "But if he's already dead he can't tell us anything anyway."

"Yoyo, for God's sake, I know that! But what are we supposed to do? We have to take a risk. And, believe me, he *is* mistrustful! He may even mistrust Nyela."

"His own wife?"

"Yes, his wife. Do you trust her?"

"Okay, fine," murmured Yoyo. "So I'll shadow Nyela then."

"Do that. Call me if you notice anything."

"I might need the car."

Jericho looked around and spotted a Starbucks. They had parked the Audi a few meters further down, in full sight of Muntu.

"No problem. We'll sit over there, have a coffee, and keep our eyes on the restaurant. If she goes anywhere, you follow her. On foot, by car, whatever's necessary. I'll hold the fort here."

"We don't even know what Donner looks like."

"White, I guess. It's a Boer name, South African—"

"Great," said Yoyo. "That narrows it down considerably."

"I could easily widen it again. Donner might be from a mixed marriage. He wouldn't be the first black person on the Cape to have a white surname."

"You sure know how to look on the bright side, don't you?"

"I'm renowned for it."

Jericho had committed the faces of the other guests in the restaurant to memory. After he and Yoyo left, three more couples had gone in, as well as a lone old man accompanied by his incessantly yapping alter ego. In the time that followed, they watched as Muntu emptied person by person. The man and dog were the last to leave, and after that Jericho was convinced there were no guests left inside. More time passed. Yoyo drank tea by the bucket load. Shortly after three, a dark-skinned man came out onto the street, unchained a bicycle, and pedaled off. Clearly one of the kitchen staff, perhaps Nyela's sous-chef.

"So this is what you do?" she asked, somehow managing not to sound scornful. "Spy on people for hours on end?"

"Most of the time I'm online."

"Uh-huh. And what do you do there?"

"Spy on people."

"It's so *dull*." She pulled a dripping teabag from her cup. "One big, long, boring wait."

"I don't entirely agree with you. There are a lot of fun aspects and it's certainly lively. From time to time someone sets a steelworks on fire. There are lovely little chases, you get to save people and fly half-way across the world at the drop of a hat. Is your life so much more exciting?"

Expecting her to protest, he stared back out of the window, but Yoyo seemed to be giving it serious thought.

"No," she said, "it's not. But it is more social."

"But society can do your head in," said Jericho, then brought up his hand to silence her. Nyela was just leaving Muntu. She had swapped the colorful folklore of her dress for jeans and a T-shirt.

"Time for your mission," he said.

Yoyo dropped her teabag, gathered up the car keys and her cell phone, and ran outside. Jericho watched as she started the car. Nyela paced away in lengthy strides and disappeared around the corner of a house. The car followed her slowly. Jericho hoped Yoyo wouldn't be too obvious. He had tried to give her a brief overview of the basic rules of a subtle observation, which included not ramming your bumper right into the behind of the person you were observing.

She phoned just ten minutes later. "There's a parking lot two streets down. Nyela just left it."

"What's she driving?"

"A Nissan OneOne. SolarHybrid."

The small, nimble town car, designed for heavy traffic, could reduce its floor space by shortening the wheelbase. Against that, the Audi was a cumbersome monstrosity, only superior on highways.

"Stay close to her," he said. "Let me know if anything happens."

After that he rang Tu and brought him up to date.

"And how's it going there?"

"I'm having fun with Diane," said Tu. "A lovely program. Not top of the range anymore, mind you, but we're having a good time nonetheless."

"The program is completely new," protested Jericho.

"New is something that hasn't been built yet," Tu advised him.

"Get to the point."

"So, with regard to Ndongo: he seems to be striving for more balance than during his first time in office, and is resisting influence from the Chinese, but this time without snubbing Beijing. His sympathies clearly lie with Washington and the EU. On the other hand, he made it known at the beginning of the year that he wants to consider the interests of all countries equally, as long as they don't show tendencies toward economic annexation. He also pushed a few scraps over to Sinopec. Other than that, he's trying to clean up the pigsty that Mayé left behind."

"He sounds like less of a puppet than before."

"That's right. And do you know why? We all know! They've got oil and gas down there. And by the ton. The answer to questions that no one's asking anymore. That's where the problem lies, and it seems it became Mayé's problem too. Do you see?"

"Helium-3?"

"What else?"

Of course! Everyone knew it. It was just that they also quickly forgot who was affected by the shift in circumstances brought about by the Moon business.

"At the start of 2020 it was clear that helium-3 would supersede fossil fuels," said Tu. "The United States put all their eggs in one basket. Into the development of the space elevator, the extension of the infrastructure on the Moon, the commercial backing of helium-3, Julian Orley. He, in turn, worked feverishly on his fusion reactors. Orley and the USA created an immense bubble back then. It could have all gone horribly wrong if it had burst. The biggest company of all time would have exploded like a cluster bomb, the USA would have suffered painful losses in fossil poker with their unilateral arrangement on the Moon, millions and millions of people would have lost their money. Africa would have been able to continue swimming in wealth, financing the never-ending civil wars from oil income and dictating conditions to the rich nations. Think back to the barrel price in 2019."

"It was still up then."

"For the last time. Because we know it worked! Orley and the USA built their elevator, and the first one ever at that! I've researched it in detail, Owen. On August 1, 2022, the moon base was put into operation, and a few days later, so was the American mining station. Two weeks later the mining of helium-3 officially began. A month and a half later, on October 5, the first Orley reactor went onto the network and fulfilled all expectations. The fusion age had begun; helium-3 became the energy source of the future. In December, the barrel price was a hundred and twenty dollars, the following February it sank to seventy-six dollars, and in March China followed suit and sent its first helium-3 deliveries to Earth, albeit with conventional rocket technology and in minute quantities. Nonetheless, the two most commodity-hungry nations were on the Moon. Others panted along behind them: India, Japan, the Europeans, all obsessed with staking their claim. It's not that oil didn't play a part anymore, but the dependence on it was dwindling. The summer of 2023, fifty-five dollars a barrel. Autumn, forty-two dollars. Even that was fairly high, but it kept going down. People expected brisk trade, that it would never be that cheap again, but they were wrong. The important consumer nations had stocked up their supplies in good time. No one sees the need for more depots, and in the car sector electricity becomes a serious option. The countries that export fossil fuels, which have relied exclusively on their income from the oil and gas trade and therefore neglected their native economy, feel the full impact of the resource curse, particularly in Africa. Potentates like Obiang or Mayé see the end dawning. Now they have to pay the price for milking their countries to death. They don't make the rules anymore. Their pals from overseas, who they played off so wonderfully against each other for decades on end, have had enough of being messed around and having very little to show for it, and now, to top it all off, they aren't interested in oil any more either! That, my friend, is the reason why Washington's indignation over Mayé sounded more and more scripted as time went on. For China it's a done deal, catching up with America and freeing itself from the fossil fetters. So what does the crazed man go and do?"

"You're not seriously suggesting that Mayé started his idiotic space program in order to land on the Moon and develop helium-3?"

"Yes. Precisely that."

"Tian, please. He was a madman. The torturer of a country where the greatest technological achievement was the painstaking maintenance of a functioning power network."

"Of course. But he said it."

"That he wanted to go to the Moon? Mayé?"

"That's what he said. Diane found quotations. He was clearly an idiot. On the other hand, experts attested to the launch pad being in good working order. He sent a news satellite into orbit with it, at any rate."

"Which broke down."

"Regardless. The launch was successful."

"How did he finance even the launch pad?"

"I guess he used the national budget. Shut down hospitals, I don't know. The interesting thing is that Mayé's overthrow definitely wasn't the result of other countries' interest in his oil. So what worried Beijing so much that they felt it necessary to get rid of the ruling clique of a tiny little country which had become entirely uninteresting, both economically and politically—and right down to the very last man? With this question in mind, I kept looking—and I found something."

"Tell me."

"On June 28, 2024, a month before his death, Mayé publicly chastised the exploitative nature of the First World on national television and directed explicit accusations at Beijing. He claimed that China had dropped Africa like a hot potato, the money promised to them had never materialized, and above all, that they were responsible for the entire continent withering away."

"Who did he think he was, Africa's lawyer?"

"Yes, it's laughable, isn't it? But then, while he was saying all this, he let something slip that he shouldn't have. He said that if Beijing didn't fulfill its obligations, he would be forced to hawk information about that would incriminate China all over the world. He publicly threatened the Party." Tu paused. "And a month later he was no longer able to talk."

"And he made no indication of what that information was?"

"Indirectly, yes. He said that his country wouldn't let anyone bring it down. And, in particular, that the space program would be extended and another satellite launched, and that certain contemporaries would be well advised to offer their full support unless they wanted a rude awakening."

Jericho paused. "What did China have to do with Mayé's space program?"

"Officially, nothing. But even the dumbest person can figure out that no one in Equatorial Guinea was in the position to build something like that. I mean, physically speaking maybe, but not to make the whole thing a reality. The only thing Mayé came up with was the idea. He waved his millions, and they came from all around: engineers, constructors, physicists. French, German, Russian, American, Indian, from all over the world. But if you look a little closer, one name in particular stands out—Zheng Pang-Wang."

"The Zheng Group?" Jericho blurted out, amazed.

"That's the one. Large parts of the construction were in Zheng's hands."

"As far as I know, Zheng is closely connected with the Chinese space travel program."

"Space travel and reactor technologies. Zheng Pang-Wang isn't just one of the ten richest men in the world, and one with an enormous influence on Chinese politics at that—he also seems to have decided to become Julian Orley's Chinese counterpart. The cadre are resting their biggest hopes on him. They expect that, sooner or later, he'll build them their own space elevator and a functioning fusion reactor. So far, though, he hasn't delivered either of them. There's a rumor that he's putting much more energy into infiltrating and spying on Orley Enterprises. In official circles he's trying to get Orley to collaborate. There's even talk that Orley and Zheng like each other, but that doesn't necessarily mean anything."

Jericho thought for a moment.

"Mayé's assassins acted fast, don't you think?"

"Suspiciously so, if you ask me."

"Conjuring Ndongo up out of nowhere, and then the logistics of the attack. You can't plan something like that in four weeks."

"I agree with you. The coup was prepared just in case Mayé said the wrong thing."

"Which he did—"

"Excuse me, Owen," said Diane's voice. "May I interrupt you?"

"What's up, Diane?"

"I have a Priority A call for you. Yoyo Chen Yuyun."

"No problem," said Tu. "I've told you everything I needed to anyway. Keep me posted, okay?"

"I will. Put her through, Diane."

"Owen?" Yoyo's voice came through, embedded in street sounds. "Nyela got out of the car in the city center. I followed her for a bit; she was looking in the shop windows and speaking on the phone. She didn't look particularly worked up or concerned. Two minutes ago she met a man, and now they're both sitting in the sun in front of a café."

"Doing what?"

"Chatting, having a drink. The guy is dark, but not black, perhaps mixed race. Around fifty years old. You saw the photos of Mayé and his staff. Did any of them look like that?"

"There aren't that many photos. And none of them show all of his staff. There's always someone or other next to him, but you could try searching for the list of his ministers that died during the attack." Jericho tried to remember the pictures. "None of them had that skin-color, I think."

"What should I do?"

"Keep at it. How are they acting around each other?"

"Friendly. A little kiss when they met, a hug. Nothing extreme."

"Do you have a rough idea where you are?"

"We drove over that river twice—the Sprii, Spraa, Spree—one crossing right after the other. The café is in an old railway station, one built in brick with round arches, but nicely renovated. Wait a moment."

Yoyo marched along the brick façade and looked out for any markings, street signs, or the name of the station. Hordes of people were streaming down from the steps of the subway station. Owing to the beautiful weather, the forecourt looked as if it were under siege: young people and tourists were pushing the turnover in the numerous pubs, bars, bistros, and restaurants sky-high. Clearly Nyela had led her into one of the hip quarters of the city. Yoyo liked it here. It reminded her a little of Xintiandi.

"Don't worry," said Jericho. "I think I know where you are. You must have driven over Museum Island."

"I'll be able to tell you in a second."

"Okay."

Yoyo spotted a white S on a green background. Next to it, something was written in light green lettering. She opened her lips and hesitated. How did one pronounce *s*, *c* and *h* one behind the other?

"Hacke—s—cher—Mar—"

"Hackescher Markt?"

"Yes. It could be that."

"Okay. Keep your eye on both of them. If nothing happens here I'll come and join you."

"Okay."

She ended the call and turned around. The station was excreting an even bigger contingent of travelers, most of whom seemed to be trying to catch up on the time they had lost. The rest, chattering away, spread out among the folding chairs and tables of the outdoor eateries, on the hunt for free seats. Suddenly, Yoyo found herself staring at a battery of backs. She stuck her elbows out and pushed her way forward. A waiter circled over like a fighter jet and made a move to run her down. With a dart, she managed to escape behind a little green and yellow tree. Scribble-covered boards were obstructing her view. She ran out past the tables into the square, and approached the café with the blue and white striped awning, under which Nyela and the light-skinned black man were sitting.

Were *supposed* to be sitting.

Yoyo's heart skipped a beat. She ran inside. No one. Back out again. No Nyela, no companion.

"Shit," she mumbled. "Shit, shit, shit!"

But cursing wouldn't bring them back again, so she rushed back out onto the main street, to where Nyela had succeeded in securing a parking place in rush hour and where she herself had parked the car beneath a strict "No Parking" sign.

The Nissan was gone. Breaking down both physically and mentally, she ran on, issuing pleading looks in all directions, up and down the street, begging fate for mercy, just to curse it the very next moment, and then finally gave up, out of breath and with sharp pains in her sides. None of it helped. She had fucked it up. All because of a lousy sign. Just because she had insisted on being able to tell Jericho where she was.

How was she supposed to tell him *this*?

A lighter-skinned black man around fifty years old. Jericho tried to imagine him. He could fit in with Nyela in terms of age.

Andre Donner?

Indecisive, he looked over at Muntu. It was all quiet. The lights were out, as far as he could tell through the mirrored glass anyway. After a few minutes he pulled out his cell phone, logged into Diane's database, and loaded the photos of Mayé they had found on the Internet.

Almost all of them came from online articles about the coup. The whole thing had made waves only in the West African media, where sumptuously illustrated biographies of the dead dictator had appeared as a result of the putsch: Mayé on a visit to a waterworks, Mayé inspecting a military parade, Mayé orating, patting children's heads, flanked by oil workers on a platform. A man who, even in the pictures, oozed physical presence and narcissism. Anyone who managed to make it into a picture with him seemed strangely out of focus, insignificant, overshadowed, irrelevant. Aided by the captions, Jericho identified ministers and generals who had died in the coup. The others pictured remained nameless. What united them was their dark or very dark skin color, typical of the equatorial regions.

Jericho loaded the film which showed Mayé with Vogelaar, various ministers, representatives from the army and the two Chinese managers at the conference table. He zoomed in on the faces and studied the background. A uniformed man sat two seats behind Vogelaar, following the Chinese presentation with an arrogantly bored expression; he might have passed for lighter-skinned, but then again it could just have been down to the effect of the overhead lighting.

Was one of them Donner?

He looked up and stopped short.

The entrance door to Muntu was open.

No, it had just swung shut! Behind the glass, a tall shadow became visible and disappeared into the reflections of the building opposite. Jericho suppressed a curse. While he had turned his attention to the idiotic task of trying to recognize a man he had never seen among a group of complete strangers, someone had gone in over there. If he really had gone in, that is, and not opened the door from the inside. Hastily, he pushed his chair back, tucked away his cell phone, and walked outside.

Was it Donner he'd seen?

He crossed the street, cupped his hands around his eyes, and peered in through the small window. The restaurant lay in darkness. No one to be seen. The only thing of note was a blue flicker from a defective emergency light, behind the small windows in the swing doors that led to the kitchen.

Had his senses been playing tricks on him?

No, there was no chance of that.

He pushed against the door. Cool, stagnant restaurant air wafted toward him. He glanced quickly around at the tautly pulled tablecloths, the motionless ferns, and the bar. From the other side of the swing doors he heard a machine start up, possibly an air-conditioner. He froze and listened. No more sounds. Nothing to suggest that anyone was here apart from him.

But where could the man have disappeared to?

Automatically, his right hand grazed the hilt of his Glock. It was resting in its usual place, narrow and discreet. Even though he had come to warn Donner, there was no way of predicting how the man would respond to his visit. He paced lightly over to the bar and looked behind the ornate counter. No one. Behind the swing doors, the gleam of light flickered icily. He went back into the middle of the room and turned his head toward the bead curtain in front of the toilets. Thinking that he saw some of the cords swinging softly, he looked more closely. Like naughty children caught in the act, they froze into motionlessness.

He blinked.

Nothing was moving. Nothing at all. Nonetheless, he went closer and peeped through the bead lattice into a short, gloomy corridor.

"Andre Donner?"

He didn't expect any answer, nor did he get one. The door on the left led, as far as he could tell, to the men's toilets, and opposite them was their female counterpart. At the end of the corridor was another door, marked "Private." He pushed his hand between the cords, awakening them to a lively murmur, then pulled them further apart. He hesitated. Maybe he should put off the inspection of the toilets and the private room until later. His gaze wandered back to the swing doors, and at that moment the hum of the generator stopped. He could now clearly hear—

Nothing.

He had preferred the sounds of the machine.

"Andre Donner?"

He was answered by dry stillness. Even the noises from the street seemed to be cut off here. Slowly, he walked over to the swing doors and peered through one of the tiny windows. There wasn't much to see. A little world of its own, made up of chrome and white tiles, chopped up in a strobe effect by the defective fluorescent lamp. The archaic body of a gas cooker with dark attachments, covered by a tarnished cooker hood. The corner of a workbench. Roasting pans and pots were piled up in a cupboard.

He walked in.

The kitchen wasn't that small after all. It was surprisingly spacious for a restaurant like Muntu. Three walls were taken up with shelves, cupboards, refrigerators, a sink unit, oven, and microwave. Along the fourth wall were storage surfaces and struts, draped with casserole dishes, pans, soup ladles, and splatter screens. A longish work table took up the center of the room, occupied at the stove end by two huge pans, bowls of finely chopped vegetables under cling film and closed polystyrene boxes. As if to balance it out, a huge slicing machine was enthroned at the opposite end. The kitchen smelled of stock, congealed frying fat, disinfectant, and the cold sweetness of thawing meat. The latter was resting half-covered on a baking tray, pale brown in the pulsing light and coated with iridescent skin, its bones protruding. It looked like the hind leg of some huge animal. Kudu-antelope, thought Jericho. He couldn't picture the breed, but he was sure he was staring at the leg of an antelope. He suddenly pictured the whitish tendons and ligaments under the fur of a living creature, a masterpiece of evolution which enabled the animal to take such stupendous leaps. A highly developed flight mechanism, but ultimately useless against the smallest and quickest of all predators, the rifle barrel. Cautiously, he went closer to the stove. The bluish flicker was increasingly reminiscent of an insecticide device, every flicker a record of death. Smeared wings and little legs, compound eyes, staring unfazed before they boiled in the electronic heat and exploded. In the crystal silence, he could now hear the humming of the lights too, their stumbling clicking when they sprang on and then died again, like some strange code. His gaze fell on a casserole dish on the stove. The contents gripped his attention. He looked in. Something was wriggling in it, something that seemed to be alive and squirming in the pulse of the lights, a headless, rolled-up snake.

Jericho stared at it.

He suddenly felt the temperature fall by several degrees. Pressure exerted itself on his chest as fingers encircled his heart, trying to bring it to a standstill. The hairs on the back of his neck stood up. He felt someone breathing behind him and knew that he was no longer alone in the kitchen. The other person had stalked in without a sound, appeared from nowhere, a professional, a master of disguise.

Jericho turned around.

The man was considerably taller than him, dark-haired, with a strong jawline and light, penetrating eyes. In an earlier life he had had a beard and been ash-blond, something which was only detectable from his light eyelashes and brows, but Jericho recognized him at once. He was familiar with the faces of this man; he had seen them again just a few minutes ago, on the display of his cell phone.

Jan Kees Vogelaar.

Alarmed thoughts came in a rush: Vogelaar was waiting for Donner in order to kill him. Had already killed him. A body in the freezer cabinet. And he was in the worst possible position, much too close to his opponent. Unbelievable stupidity on his part, to have gone into the kitchen. The ghostly effect of the flickering neon light. The weapon in Vogelaar's hand, pointing at his abdomen. Talk or fight? The failure of rational thinking.

Reflexes.

He ducked and aimed a blow at Vogelaar's wrist. A shot freed itself from the weapon, echoing into the base of the cooker. Springing back up, he rammed his skull against the man's chin, saw him stagger, grabbed the saucepan, and hurled it toward him. A twitching alien whipped out, the skinned body of the snake. It smacked Vogelaar in the face, the casserole dish scraped his forehead. With all his strength, Jericho kicked out at the hand holding the gun, which clattered to the floor and slid under the workbench. He reached for his Glock, grasped the hilt, and tumbled backward as if he'd just been hit by a ram. Vogelaar had got a grip of himself, turned on his own axis as quick as lightning, flung up his right leg, and given him a kick in the chest.

All the air drained from his lungs. Helpless, he crashed into the cooker. Vogelaar whirled up to him like a dervish. The next kick got him in the shoulder, another, his knee. He fell to the floor with a cry. The huge man leaned over, grabbed his lower arm and rammed it hard against the edge of the cooker, again and again. Jericho's fingers twitched, opened out. Somehow he managed to maintain his grip on the Glock and sink his left hand into Vogelaar's solar plexus, but it had zero impact. His opponent hit his lower arm again. A sharp pain flooded through him. This time, the pistol flew out of his hand in a wide arc. He punched Vogelaar's ribs repeatedly with his free hand, around his kidneys, then felt the grip around his arm loosen. Released, he crawled sideways.

Where was the Glock?

There! Not even half a meter away.

He threw himself forward. Vogelaar was quicker, pulling Jericho up and hurling him toward one of the huge pans. Instinctively, he tried to get a grip on it, buckled over as Vogelaar kicked him in the back of his knees, and ripped the pan down with him as he fell. A torrent of greasy broth gushed down over him, hailing bones, vegetables, and meat. Filthy and wet, he writhed around on the kitchen floor, then saw the other man leaning over him, saw his fist coming down toward him, grabbed the empty pan with both hands and rammed it as hard as he could against Vogelaar's shins.

The South African tried to suppress a cry of pain and stumbled. Like an amphibian, Jericho glided through the pool of liquid, grabbed a bowl of finely chopped tomato, and threw it at Vogelaar, then another, fruit salad relieved of gravity: mango, pineapple, and kiwi in free fall. For a few seconds, his adversary was busy with dodging maneuvers, giving him enough time to gain a meter of distance before the giant attacked again. Jericho fled around the workbench, grabbed the struts of a high cabinet, bringing pots, cans, bowls and sifters, pans, casserole dishes, and cutlery drawers crashing down to the floor. Vogelaar sprang back, away from the avalanche. In no time, half of the kitchen was blocked. There was only one route left out, along the opposite side of the workbench.

But Vogelaar was closer to the swing doors.

You idiot, Jericho cursed to himself. You've backed yourself right into the trap.

The South African bared his teeth sneeringly. He seemed to be thinking exactly the same thing, except that Jericho's predicament was visibly cheering him. Eyeing each other, they paused, each clasping their end of the workbench. In the flicker of the neon light Jericho had the opportunity to get a good look at the man for the first time. His short-term memory simultaneously unearthed the birth date of the former mercenary, and he suddenly realized that his opponent was long past sixty. A fighting machine of pensionable age, against which the privilege of youth withered away, a farce. Vogelaar didn't seem in the slightest bit tired, while he was puffing like a steam engine. He saw the man's eyes light up, reflecting the flicker of the neon light. Then, without any warning, it went dark.

The light had given up the ghost. Vogelaar faded into a silhouette, a black mass emitting a low, triumphant laugh. Jericho narrowed his eyes. The only light still coming in was through the gaps in the swing doors, just enough to see the only remaining escape route. Like a crab, he shuffled out from the protection of his cover. As if mirroring his movements, the silhouette of the South African set itself in motion too. An illusion. He wouldn't get to the doors fast enough. Perhaps a little conversation was advisable.

"Hey, let's cut the crap, shall we?"

Silence.

"We won't achieve anything like this. We should talk."

The disheartened tremolo in his voice wasn't good at all. Jericho took a deep breath and tried again.

"This is a misunderstanding." That was better. "I'm not your enemy."

"How stupid do you think I am?"

An answer, at least, albeit croaky and threatening and not exactly emanating a desire for understanding. The silhouette came closer. Jericho backed off, grappled behind him, got hold of something jagged and heavy, and closed his fingers around it in the hope that it was suitable as a weapon.

With a dry bang, the lights sprang back on.

Vogelaar stormed over, swinging a worryingly long kitchen knife, and Jericho was paralyzed by a déjà vu. Shenzhen. Ma Liping, the Paradise of the Little Emperors. At the very last second, he pulled up what he was holding in his hand. The knife sliced the radish in two, whizzed through the air, and missed him by a hair. Jericho stumbled backward. The giant chased him around the table toward the upturned cabinet. On a wing and a prayer, he reached into the pile of kitchen utensils that had poured out from it, grabbed hold of a baking sheet, and held it in front of him like a shield. Clanging steel screeched over aluminum. He wouldn't be able to fend off Vogelaar's enraged attacks for long, so he grabbed the tray with both hands and went into the attack, swinging it around wildly and landing an audible hit. Vogelaar swayed. Jericho threw the tray at his head, fell to the floor, rolled under the table through to the other side, sprang to his feet, and started to run. Vogelaar would have to go around the table—

Vogelaar went *over* the table.

Just centimeters before the door he felt himself get grabbed and pulled back with such force that he lost his footing. Effortlessly, Vogelaar spun him around and knocked him down. He crashed against something hard, making him lose his hearing and sight, then realized that the South African was holding his head against the meat slicing machine. The next moment, the blade began to rotate. Jericho wriggled, trying to break free. Vogelaar turned his arm behind his back until it made a cracking sound. The blade sped up.

"Who are you?"

"Owen Jericho," he wheezed, his heart in his throat. "Restaurant critic."

"And what do you want here?"

"Nothing, nothing at all. Donner, to speak to Donner—"

"Andre Donner?"

"Yes. Yes!"

"About a restaurant review?"

"Yes, damn it!"

"With a gun?"

"I—"

"Wrong answer." The South African pressed his head against the metal and pushed it toward the racing blade. "And a wrong answer costs an ear."

"No!"

Jericho gave a howl. Burning pain shot through his outer ear. In fear and panic, he kicked his feet out and heard a muffled blow. The pressure on his shoulder suddenly gave way. Vogelaar slumped over him. He pulled himself to his feet, saw his torturer stagger and rammed his elbow into his face. The other man sank his fingers into his belt, then toppled over. Jericho held onto the edge of the table to avoid being dragged down with him. Something big and dark landed on the back of Vogelaar's head. The man collapsed and didn't move again.

Yoyo was staring at him, both hands clasped around the bones of the frozen antelope leg.

"My God, Owen! Who is this asshole?"

Dazed, Jericho felt behind his ear and touched raw, ripped-open flesh. When he looked at his finger, it was red with blood.

"Jan Kees Vogelaar," he mumbled.

"Damn it! And Donner?"

"No idea." He drew air into his lungs. Then he crouched down next to the motionless body. "Quick, we have to turn him over."

Without asking any more questions, Yoyo threw the antelope leg aside and helped him. With combined effort, they managed to roll Vogelaar onto his back.

"You're bleeding," she said, casually.

"I know." He opened Vogelaar's belt buckle and pulled it out of the loops. "Is there any of my ear left?"

"Hard to say. It doesn't really look like an ear anymore."

"That's what I was afraid of. Back on his stomach."

The same sweat-inducing process. He bent Vogelaar's lower arms behind him and tied them tightly together. The unconscious man breathed heavily and groaned. His fingers twitched.

"Clobber him again if necessary," said Jericho, looking around. "We'll maneuver him over to the fridge over there. The one next to the microwave."

Together, they gripped the heavy body under the arms, dragged it across the tiles, and lifted it up. Vogelaar weighed around a hundred kilos, but his groaning and blinking suggested that he wasn't far from regaining consciousness. Hastily, Jericho whipped his own belt off and tied him to the fridge door handle with it. Sitting upright and with his head dangling down, the South African now had a martyred look about him. The flickering of the neon light became a constant, sterile brightness. Yoyo had found the light switch. Jericho crept over the kitchen floor, spotted his Glock and his opponent's pistol, and seized both.

"Bastard," spluttered Vogelaar, as if he were spitting snot into the gutter.

Jericho handed Yoyo the pistol and fixed his gaze on the restrained man.

"You should choose your words more carefully. I might be offended. I could, for example, think about the fact that my ear hurts, and who I have to thank for that."

The South African stared at him, with a look full of hate. Suddenly, he began to tear at his shackles like mad. The fridge moved forward a centimeter. Jericho released the safety catch on the Glock and pressed it against Vogelaar's nose.

"Wrong reaction," he said.

"Kiss my ass!"

"And a wrong reaction will cost you the tip of your nose. Do you want to go through life without a nose, Vogelaar? Do you want to look like an idiot?"

Vogelaar ground his jaw, but stopped his attempts to free himself. Clearly the idea of a noseless existence bothered him more than the threat of losing his life.

"Why all the fuss?" he asked sullenly. "I mean, you're going to shoot me anyway."

"Why do you think that?"

"Why?" Vogelaar laughed with disbelief. "Man, don't bother messing around."

His healthy eye wandered over to Yoyo. The glass eye stared straight ahead. "What's with you guys anyway? I thought Kenny would insist on finishing off the job himself."

Inside Jericho's brain, cogs interlocked, circuits loaded up, and the Department for Astonishing Developments and Incomprehensible Activities started its working day.

"You know Kenny?"

Vogelaar blinked, confused. "Of course I know him."

"Now listen here," said Jericho, crouching down. "We have a document, only fragmentary admittedly, but I'd have to be a real idiot not to realize that you're here to kill Andre Donner. So, first things first. Let's start with Donner, okay? Where is he?"

Something in Vogelaar's gaze changed. His rage gave way to pure, complete confusion.

"You're wrong," he said. "You'd have to be a complete idiot to believe that I'm here to do that."

"Where in God's name is Andre Donner?"

"Are you completely stupid, or what? I'm—"

"For the last time!" screamed Jericho. "Where is he?"

"Look!" the man tied to the fridge screamed back at him. "Open your eyes."

Well, said the manager of the Department for Astonishing Developments and Incomprehensible Activities, it looks like we'll miss out on the award for lateral thinking again.

"I don't understand—"

"He's sitting in front of you! I—am—Andre—Donner!"

MERCENARY

The wars of the modern age, explicitly the First and Second World Wars, are regarded as international conflicts, established on the basis of the laws of war and executed by state-owned forces. In many parts of the world, this has led to the mistaken notion that soldiers have in actual fact always been armed civil servants, who earn money even when there is no one to attack and nothing to defend. It's unimaginable that divisions of the US Army, the Royal Air Force, the *forces armées*, or the Bundeswehr would rampage through their own country, plundering and raping. The introduction of compulsory military service actually seemed to herald the end of the forces which had decisively shaped warfare until then. King David's Kerethites and Pelethites, the Greek hoplites in Persia's army, the marauding hordes of late medieval Brabants and Armagnacs, mercenaries in the Thirty Years' War, and private armies in colonialist Africa: they all served whoever happened to be the most generous master at the time. They were paid for fighting, not for sitting around in barracks.

In the twentieth century, the retreat of the colonial powers lured many mercenaries into the turmoil of postindependence Africa, where persecution and expulsion, coups and genocide were the order of the day under the new, ethnically disunited rulers. Ordered not to intervene, the West began to secure its interests with the help of private troops rather than on an official level—for example their efforts to oppose the establishment of Communism on African soil. The Communists' approach was no different. States like South Africa also got themselves paramilitary task forces like Koevoet, and procured lucrative long-term positions for the contract soldiers. The old-style mercenary seemed to have found his niche in among the dictators and rebels.

Then everything changed.

With a sigh from history, the Soviet empire collapsed; without a whimper, banal and irretrievable. East Germany ceased to exist. London's U-turn called the IRA into question, apartheid came to an end on the Cape, the Cold War was declared over, Great Britain and the USA reduced their troops, and political change in South America discredited thousands in the armed forces. All over the world, soldiers, policemen, secret service workers, resistance fighters, and terrorists lost their jobs and their raison d'être. That was nothing new. Years before, unemployed Vietnam War veterans had founded private military and security services in the USA, ones that ventured where Washington didn't dare get caught. Serving the CIA, these firms hunted unpleasant rulers out of power, trafficked weapons and drugs and, incidentally, also relieved the strain on the defense budget. Now, though, the market was collapsing under a surplus of trained fighters fighting each other for the last crisis zones in the era of Nelson Mandela and Russian-American chumminess. The remaining despots could only do so much to encroach on human rights; there simply wasn't enough for everyone. And then the curtain rose on a new act.

The new players were Saddam Hussein, arrogant and voracious, and Slobodan Milošević, delirious with nationalism. Perfect antagonists of an otherwise peace-loving humanity, one which yet again speedily agrees to permit war as a continuation of politics, but this time with other means. Foolishly, a few soldiers too many had been laid off in the frenzy of reconciliation. The mercenaries were on the march again. Authorized by the United Nations, they polish up their tarnished image by helping to conquer the lunatic in the Gulf and the monster of the Balkans, and secure peace. Then, one day, two passenger jets fly into the Twin Towers and send the final remains of the pacifist mindset up in flames. Determined to bring the axis of evil to its knees, George W. Bush, otherwise known as the biggest political bankruptcy in American history, bestows on the USA thousands of dead GIs and a fiscal hole the size of a lunar crater. Practically all its allies are forced to learn how terribly expensive war is and how much more expensive it is to win peace, especially with the employment of regular armies. But on the other hand, given that the way war is led is no longer up for debate, commission after commission goes to the efficient and discreet private security firms.

Fittingly, Africa uses its raw materials to enter the playing field of globalization. Wounds that were long believed healed burst open, petrodollars split whole nations, and the gravitational forces of East and West pull at everything. Somalia becomes synonymous with blood and tears. Millions of people die during the civil war in the Democratic Republic of Congo. Barely recovered from the wrangling between the government and liberation armies, the Sudan staggers into the Darfur conflict, the pull of which grips the whole of central Africa. With France as a silent partner, Chad's dictator invests trillions of oil money in arms purchases and destabilizes the region in his own special way. The parties of the North and South are smashing each other's heads in on the Ivory Coast, while violence is rampant in oil-rich South Nigeria. Senegal, Congo-Brazzaville, Burundi, and Uganda top the scale of inhumane acts. Even supposedly stable nations like Kenya sink into chaos in just a short time. Almost everything that was supposed to improve just gets worse.

The only people things improve for are the likes of Jan Kees Vogelaar. At the beginning of the millennium, his Mamba supports the peace troop of the African Union in Darfur, reduces the popularity of the

Arabic Sudanese in the guerrilla camps, and takes on lucrative man-
dates in Kenya and Nigeria. After the foundation of African Protection
Services, Vogelaar is able to expand his activities to more crisis areas.
APS develops for Africa in a similar manner to how Blackwater developed for Iraq. By 2016, the group of companies makes a name for itself
in the safeguarding of oil plants and transport routes for raw materials,
the conduct of negotiations with hostage-takers, and the exploration
of exotic locations for Western, Asian, and multinational companies,
which are increasingly acquiring a taste for hiring private armies.

But it remains a painstaking business, and Vogelaar gets tired of
changing sides again and again. After years of instability on all fronts
he begins to long for something more lasting and solid, for that one,
ultimate commission.

And then it comes.

"In the form of Kenny Xin," said Vogelaar. "Or rather Kenny's company, which practically handed me the future on a silver platter."

"Xin," echoed Yoyo. "The name doesn't exactly suit him." Jericho
knew what she meant. Xin was the Chinese word for heart.

"And who's behind the company?" he asked.

"Back then, it was the Chinese secret service." The South African
rubbed his wrists, which were marked by the welts of the belt. "But as
time went on I started to have my doubts about that."

The revelation of Donner's identity had thrown everything off kilter.
Adjusting to the new situation Jericho had first seized the opportunity
to take a quick look at his ear in the toilet mirror. It looked awful,
drenched in scarlet; the blood had run down his neck in streaks and
into the neckline of his T-shirt, where it had congealed and was now
encrusted. Bleeding, drenched with fish stock and covered in the
remains of squashed root vegetables, he was a wretched sight. After he'd
washed the blood away, though, things looked a little better. Instead of
finding himself faced with a problem of van Gogh proportions, he discovered he had actually only lost a carpaccio-thin slice of ear muscle.
Yoyo, directed by Vogelaar to the kitchen's first aid box, had bandaged
him up. It had felt as if her touch was much more tender than the task
required; if he were a dog, one might have referred to it as petting, but
he wasn't a dog, and Yoyo was probably just doing her job. Vogelaar
had watched them, suddenly looking very tired, as if he had years of
sleep to catch up on.

"If you're not here to kill me, then what in God's name are you here
for?"

"To warn you, you stupid bastard," explained Yoyo in a friendly
tone.

"About who?"

"About the people who are planning to kill you!"

Jerico pulled his cell phone out and silently projected the text fragment and then the film onto the wall, the clip which showed Vogelaar in Africa.

"Where did you get that from?"

"We don't know. We stumbled across it on the Internet, but ever since then your friend Kenny has been trying to kill us."

"My friend Kenny." A sound somewhere between a laugh and a grunt came from Vogelaar. "Let's be frank now, there's no way you came here because you were seriously concerned about my survival."

"Of course not. Especially not after the meat-slicer incident."

"Well, how was I supposed to know who you were?"

"You could have asked."

"Asked? Are you right in the head? You forced your way into my kitchen and attacked me!"

"Well, after you—"

"Good God, what was I supposed to do? What would you have done in my position? Nyela phoned and told me that two clowns were sitting in my restaurant pretending to be restaurant critics."

"See!" said Yoyo, triumphantly. "I told you—"

"*That* wasn't the problem, little one! You were the problem. Your little slip of the tongue. No one here knows anything about our time in Equatorial Guinea. Nyela is from Cameroon and I'm a South African Boer. The Donners were never in Equatorial Guinea."

Yoyo looked embarrassed.

"Did you watch the films from the security camera?" Jericho wanted to know.

"Aha, so you noticed the camera?"

"I'm a detective."

"Of course I looked at them. I'm prepared for everything, boy. I had actually hoped to live out the rest of my life in peace here. New identity, new home. But Kenny doesn't give up. The bastard has never given up yet."

"Do you think the text came from him?"

"What I think is that you should untie me right away, or you can figure the rest of it out by yourself."

And so, with an uneasy feeling, he had untied Vogelaar while Yoyo covered him with the gun. But the only thing the South African did was go next door and put palm wine, rum, and coke on the table. He then proceeded to listen to their story as he led one cigarillo after another to its cremation.

"What kind of deal did Kenny offer you?" asked Jericho as he gulped down a glass of rum he felt was more than well earned.

"A kind of second Wonga coup."

"Not exactly a good omen."

"Yes, but the circumstances had changed. Ndongo wasn't Obiang, and he certainly wasn't as closely guarded. Practically all the key positions in his government had been bought by the USA and Great Britain. It's just that money doesn't make a good building block, not in the long term, anyway. You have to constantly replaster it, otherwise the place will collapse above your head. And besides, Ndongo was a Bubi. The Fang only got involved with him because they'd been having just as bad a time of it, and things threatened to be even worse under Mayé. Back then, the APS operated along the entire west coast of Africa. In Cameroon, we were protecting oil plants against the resistance. It was in Jaunde that I met Nyela, by the way, the first woman who inspired me to bring some kind of order into my life."

"Is she really called Nyela?" asked Yoyo.

"Are you crazy?" snorted Vogelaar. "No one uses their real name if their life is at stake. In any case, one beautiful day I arrive in my office, and there sits Kenny, waiting to explain the Chinese interests to me." Vogelaar puffed away, veiling himself in smoke. "He had this strange way of switching terminology when it came to his clients. Sometimes he spoke about the Communist Party, sometimes about the secret service, and at others it sounded like he was there in the service of the State oil trade. When I demanded a little more clarity, he wanted to hear my thoughts on the difference between governments and companies. I thought about it and realized there wasn't one. Strictly speaking, I haven't found one in over forty years."

"And Kenny suggested a coup."

"The Chinese were quite bitter about the American presence in the Gulf of Guinea. Remember that we're talking about the time before helium-3; the area was like pure gold back then. Besides that, they felt they were entitled to something that Washington had helped itself to since time immemorial. I tried to make Kenny realize that there was a difference between *protecting* governments from guerrillas and actually overthrowing them. I told him about the Wonga Coup, about the mercenary, how he was rotting in Black Beach because of it, and how a Briton had come out looking like a complete fool. He responded by sharing information about the overthrow of the Saudi royal family the year before, and I almost passed out. It had been obvious to all of us, of course, that China had supported the Saudi Islamists, but if what Kenny told me is true, then Beijing did more than just provide a little assistance. Believe me, I can smell bullshit from ten miles away upwind. Kenny wasn't bullshitting. He was telling the truth, and so I decided to carry on listening to him."

"I guess he was on excellent terms with Mayé."

"They were certainly in contact. In 2016, Kenny was still in second rank, but I knew right away that the guy would soon pop up in a more exposed position." Vogelaar laughed softly. "If you meet him, he actually seems like a nice guy. But he's not. He's at his most dangerous when he's pretending to be nice."

"Can anyone be nice in this business?" asked Yoyo.

"Of course. Why not?"

"Well, take mercenaries for example." She shrugged. "I mean, aren't they all more or less—erm—racists?"

Good God, Yoyo, thought Jericho, what are you playing at? Vogelaar slowly turned his head to face her and let smoke billow out of the corner of his mouth. He looked like a huge, steaming animal.

"Don't be shy, speak your mind."

"Koevoet. Apartheid. Do I need to go on?"

"I was a professional racist, my girl, if you're directing that at me. Give me money, and I hate the blacks. Give me money, and I hate the whites. It's real racists who screw up the fun. By the way, there are racists in the army too."

"But you're for sale. As opposed to regular—"

"We're for sale, sure, but we don't betray anyone. And do you know why? Because we're not on anyone's side. Our only loyalty is to the contract."

"But if you—"

"We're *unable* to commit any kind of betrayal."

"Well, I see it differently."

Jericho was fidgeting uneasily on his chair. What was Yoyo thinking, impaling Vogelaar on the stake of her indignation, and now of all moments? He was just opening his mouth to interrupt when a trace of realization flitted across her face. With sudden humility, she slurped on her cola and asked:

"So who made contact with whom? Mayé with the Chinese? Or the other way around?"

Vogelaar looked at her, debating his answer. Then he shrugged his shoulders and poured an almost overflowing glass of rum down his throat.

"Your people approached Mayé, as far as I know."

"You mean the Chinese," Yoyo corrected him.

"*Your* people," Vogelaar repeated mercilessly. "They came and knocked the doors down, doors that were already wide open. After all, the point was that Obiang had dramatically misjudged things with Mayé. He wanted someone he could direct from behind the scenes, but he picked the wrong guy. Without helium-3, Mayé would probably still be in Malabo."

"But he did end up being a puppet just recently."

"Sure, but for the Chinese, the buffoon of a ranking world power. That's different from letting yourself be spoon-fed by a terminally ill ex-dictator. When Kenny turned up at my place, he had already done his research and decided that we were the best match. So I listened to him calmly—and then refused."

"Why?" wondered Jericho.

"So he would come down from his high horse. He was disappointed of course. And uneasy too, because he had opened up and made himself vulnerable. Then I told him that perhaps there was a chance after all. But for that he would have to throw more on the scales than the commission for a coup. I made it clear to him that I was tired of the trench warfare, this constant haggling for jobs, but that, on the other hand, I would bore myself to death if I went off to live in some villa somewhere. I was nearing some sort of retirement, but I didn't want it to be of a retiring nature."

"So you asked for a position in Mayé's government. That's quite an unusual request for a mercenary."

"Kenny understood. A few days later we met with Mayé, who banged on at me for two long hours about his lousy family, and Kenny had to make all kinds of promises to him. There was no way there was a position in it for me too! He kept me in suspense for hours on end, then he switched sides, to cuddly old Uncle Mayé, and pulled the rabbit out of the hat."

"And offered you the position of security manager."

"The funny thing is that it was Kenny's idea. But he buttered the old guy up so much he thought it was his own. So the deal was done. The rest was child's play. I took care of the logistics, put commandos together, organized the weapons and helicopter, the usual rigmarole. You know the rest. The Chinese were adamant that the whole thing had to go off without any bloodshed and that Ndongo had to leave the country unscathed, and we managed all of that."

"Beijing didn't seem to have that many concerns last year."

"There was much more to play for last year. In 2017 it was just about an adjustment to the power relationships."

"*Just*, sure."

"Oh, come on! Everyone knew that clever journalists would write clever articles sooner or later. Beijing's role was clear just from the redistribution of the mining licenses. And so what? People are used to 'arranged' changes in government. But they're less used to killings. Especially when you're trying to clean up your image. The Party hadn't forgotten the Olympic gauntlet-running of 2008. That's also why the House of Saud got off so lightly in 2015 when the Islamists captured Riyadh. It was Beijing's condition for financing the fun. Anyway, we advanced into Malabo, Mayé squeezed his fat ass into the seat of

Frank Schätzing

government, I built up EcuaSec, the Equatorial Guinea secret service, had the entire opposition imprisoned, and that was that."

"And that didn't make you sick?" asked Yoyo.

"Sick?" Vogelaar put the glass to his lips. "I only got sick once in my life. From rotten tuna."

Jericho shot Yoyo a look like daggers. "And then what?"

"As expected, Kenny landed on his feet shortly after we heaved Mayé into power and ended up with more authority. Equatorial Guinea became a playground to him. Every few weeks he would relax in the lobby of the Paraíso, a hotel for oil workers, where he treated himself to hookers and waited for my reports. We had agreed in Cameroon that I would keep an eye on Mayé—"

"So that was the deal."

"Of course. As I said, it was Kenny's idea. No one got as close to Mayé as I did. He accepted me as a close confidant."

"A confidant who also happened to be spying on him."

"Just in case the fatty escaped our leash. I was being watched too of course. That's Kenny's principle, how he builds up his clique: everyone keeps an eye on everyone else. But I always had one more pair of eyes than the others."

"Yes, made of glass," scoffed Yoyo.

"I see more with one healthy one than you do with two," retorted Vogelaar. "I quickly found out who the moles were that Kenny had set on me. Half of EcuaSec was infiltrated. I didn't let on that I knew of course. Instead, I began to watch Kenny myself; I wanted to find out more about him and his men."

"All I know is that he's completely insane."

"Let's just say he loves extremes. I found out that he lived in London for three years, assigned to the Chinese military attaché, and spent two years in Washington, specializing in conspiracy. Officially, he belonged to Zhong Chan Er Bu, the military news service, the second department of the General Staff of the People's Liberation Army. Unfortunately my contacts there turned out to be scarce, but I did know a few people who had worked with Kenny in the past in the fifth office of the Guojia Anquan Bu, the ministry for state security. According to them he had outstanding analytical abilities and an instinct for how people's minds work. They also commented that when it came to sabotage and contract killing, he handled things with quite a—well, uncompromising attitude."

"In other words, our friend was a killer."

"Which in itself isn't any cause for alarm. But there was something else too."

Vogelaar paused to light another cigar. He did it slowly and elaborately, switching from the spoken word to smoke signals and immersing himself in his own thoughts for a while.

"They thought there was something monstrous about him," he continued. "Which my gut instinct had told me too, although I couldn't really say why. So I tried to delve deeper into Kenny's past. I found the usual military service, his studies, pilot training, arms certificate, all the normal stuff. I was just about to give up when I stumbled on a special unit with the beautiful name of Yü Shen—"

"Lovely," said Yoyo sarcastically.

"Yü Shen?" Jericho wrinkled his forehead. "That rings a bell. It has something to do with eternal damnation, doesn't it?"

"Yü Shen is the Hell God," Yoyo explained to him. "A Taoist figure based on the old Chinese belief that hell is divided up into ten empires, deep inside the earth, each of which is ruled by a Hell King. The Hell God is the highest power. The dead have to answer to him and the judges of hell."

"So that means everyone goes to hell?"

"To start with, yes. And everyone appears before a special court, according to his or her actions. The good ones are sent back to the surface and are reborn in a higher incarnation. The bad ones are reborn too, after they've served their time in hell, but as animals."

Jericho looked at Vogelaar.

"So what was Kenny Xin reborn as?"

"Good question. A beast in human form?"

"And what was he before?"

Vogelaar sucked at his cigar.

"I tried to collect information about Yü Shen. It was a difficult task. Officially, the department doesn't exist, and it's actually very similar to the hell court. It recruits its members from prisons, psychiatric institutions, and clinics for brain research. You might say they search for evil. For highly gifted people whose psychic defect is so far over the inhibition threshold that they would normally be locked away. But, with Yü Shen, they get a second chance. Not that they want to make them into better people there, mind you, it's more about how to *use* their evil. They carry out tests. All kinds of tests, the type you wouldn't even want to hear about. After a year, they decide whether you'll be reborn in freedom, for example in the military or secret service, or whether you'll live out your life in the hell of the institution."

"It sounds like an army of butchers," said Yoyo, disgusted.

"Not necessarily. Some Yü Shen graduates have gone on to have incredible careers."

"And Kenny?"

"When Yü Shen tracked him down, he had just turned fifteen and was in an institution for mentally disturbed young offenders. Most of what happened before that remained in darkness. It seems he grew up in bitter poverty, in the corner of a settlement where not even tramps dare to go. A father, mother, and two siblings. I don't know much more detail than that. Just that one night, when he was ten years old, he poured two canisters of gasoline onto his family's corrugated iron shack while they were all sleeping. Then he blocked up all the escape routes with barricades he had spent weeks making out of garbage, hooked them all up so that no one could get out, and set the whole thing on fire."

Yoyo stared at him.

"And his—?"

"Burnt to death."

"The whole family?"

"Every one of them. It was pure chance that some shrink got wind of it and took the boy away with him. He declared that Kenny possessed outstanding intelligence and well-developed clarity of thought. The boy didn't deny anything, didn't utter a single word in attempt to explain why he had done it. For four years he was passed around circles of experts, each of them trying to get to the bottom of his behavior, until ultimately Yü Shen became aware of his existence."

"And they let him loose on humanity!"

"He was declared to be healthy."

"Healthy?"

"In the sense that he was in control of himself. They didn't find anything. No mental illness that features in the textbooks at any rate. Just a bizarre compulsion for order, a fascination with symmetry. Classical symptoms of compulsive behavior, but overall nothing that could brand him as being insane. He was just—evil."

For a while, there was an uneasy silence. Jericho thought back over what he knew about Xin. His love of directing the action, the eerie ability he had of reading people's minds. Vogelaar was right. Kenny *was* evil. And yet he had the feeling that wasn't all there was to it. It was as if some dark code underlay his behavior, one that he followed and felt bound to.

"Now, in the meantime I had no reason to mistrust Kenny. Everything was running like a well-oiled machine. Beijing kept to its promise not to get involved, Mayé was enjoying the status of an autonomous ruler. Oil flowed in return for money. Then the decline came. The whole world was talking about helium-3, everyone wanted to go to the Moon. Interest in fossil resources kept falling, and Mayé couldn't do a thing about it. Nothing at all. Neither executions nor fits of madness could help." Vogelaar flicked ashes from his cigar. "So, on April 30, 2022, he called me to his office. As I walked in, he was sitting there with a number of men and women, who he introduced to us as representatives of the Chinese Air and Space Travel Ministry."

"I know what they wanted!" Yoyo waved her hand eagerly as if she were in a classroom. "They suggested building a launching pad."

"So it wasn't Mayé's idea at all," Jericho said.

"No, it wasn't. He wanted to know what it was for of course. They said it was to shoot a satellite into space. He asked what kind of satellite. They said: 'Just a satellite, it doesn't matter what kind. Do you want a satellite? Your own, Equatorial Guinea news satellite? You can have it. The only important thing to us is the launch, and that no one finds out who's behind it.'"

"But why?" asked Jericho, dumbfounded. "What did they have to gain from shooting Chinese satellites up from African soil?"

"That's what we wanted to know too, naturally. They told us there was a space treaty agreed upon in the sixties at the initiative of the United Nations, then signed and ratified by the majority of member states. It's about who outer space belongs to, what they can or can't do, and who can permit or forbid things. Part of the treaty is a liability clause, later put in concrete terms in a special agreement, which regulates all the claims regarding accidents with artificial celestial bodies. For example: if a meteorite falls into your garden and kills your chickens, you can't do a thing. But if it's not a meteorite but a satellite with a nuclear reactor, and it doesn't fall on your chickens but right smack bang in central Berlin, then that would cause damage of astronomic proportions, not to mention the dead and wounded and the soaring cancer rate. So who would be liable for that?"

"Whoever caused it?"

"Correct. The state that sent it up, and the treaty dictates that the liability has no limits. If Germany can prove it was a Chinese satellite, then China has to cough up. The decisive factor is always whose territory something was launched from. So the more a nation launches, the higher the risk they run of having to pay up at some point. That's why, according to the delegates, they were now negotiating with states who were willing to allow China to build launch pads on their territory and pass them off to the world as being their own."

"But that would make those states liable!"

"Guys like Mayé don't have any issues with driving their own people into ruin. He had long since piled the millions from the oil trade into private bunkers, just like Obiang did before him. The only thing he cared about was what was in it for him. So Kenny named a figure. It was exorbitantly high. Mayé tried to stay calm, while all the while he was pissing himself with joy under his tropical wood desk."

"Didn't the whole thing seem completely absurd to him?"

"The delegation claimed that Beijing was concluding deals like these for minimization of risk. That the danger of a satellite falling was becoming less and less, and that it wasn't to do with military operations, it was merely about the testing of a new, experimental initiative. The only thing Mayé had to do was strut about as the father of Equatorial Guinea space travel and pledge his lifelong silence about who was really behind it. And for that, they were prepared to pay for his satellite."

"What an idiot," commented Yoyo.

"Well, think about it. Equatorial Guinea, the first African country with its own space program."

"But didn't anyone notice that loads of Chinese people were running around when they were building the launching pad?" asked Jericho.

"It wasn't like that. There was an official announcement. Mayé informed the world that he wanted to get in on the space travel scene, invited specialists over to Equatorial Guinea, and of course the Chinese came too. The whole thing was organized perfectly. In the end, Russians, Koreans, French, and Germans all ended up working on the launch pad too, without noticing whose tune they were dancing to."

"And the Zheng Group?"

"Ah!" Vogelaar raised his eyebrows admiringly. "You've done your research. That's right, a large part of the construction was developed by Zheng. They had a team on site the whole time. They started in December and a year later the thing was up. On April 15, 2024, Mayé's first and only news satellite was shot into space in a festive ceremony."

"He must have practically burst with pride."

"Mayé was obsessed with the thing. There was a model of it hanging in his office, it rode along the ceiling on a rail and then circled around him at his desk, the sun of Equatorial Guinea."

"But not for very long."

"Not even three weeks. First a temporary failure, then radio silence. The news spread of course. Mayé became the subject of ridicule and malice. It wasn't that he really needed a satellite; after all, he had coped perfectly well without one before. But he had taken his place in international circles, he wanted to be part of it all and now he had to contend with this major fall. He made a regular fool of himself, and even the Bubi in Black Beach were rolling around in their cells with laughter. Mayé was frothing with rage, screaming for Kenny, who informed him that there were more pressing concerns. And there were. The Chinese and Americans were threatening each other with military action, each of them accusing the other of having stationed weapons on the Moon. I advised Mayé to hold back, but he kept on and on. Eventually, at the beginning of June, when the Moon crisis was just starting to defuse, Kenny traveled to Malabo for talks. Mayé refused to restrain himself, demanding a new satellite immediately. But then he made a mistake. He mentioned his suspicion that there was more behind the launch than the testing of some experimental initiative."

Jericho leaned forward. "What did he mean by that?"

Vogelaar blew smoke, in memory of bygone times.

"It was something he'd heard from me. Something I had found out. About the whole project."

"So you had the whole thing investigated?"

"Of course. I kept a closer eye on the building of the ramp and the launch than Kenny would have liked, but in such a way that he didn't notice. In the process, I stumbled upon inconsistencies. I told Mayé about it and impressed upon him the need to keep it to himself, but the idiot had nothing better to do than threaten Kenny."

"How did Kenny react to it?"

"In a nice manner. And that was what concerned me. He said that Mayé didn't need to worry, that there would be some way of agreeing on things."

"That sounds like a preannounced execution."

"That's exactly what I thought. A lot of fuss had been caused by that point. So the only option was to find out the whole truth, to increase the pressure on Kenny so much that he couldn't simply get rid of us. And I did find out. When Kenny next turned up, Mayé received him in the company of his most important ministers and military staff. We confronted him with the facts. He was silent. For a long time. A very long time. Then he asked us if we realized we were playing with our lives."

"The beginning of the end."

"Not necessarily. It showed that he was taking us seriously. That he wanted to negotiate." Vogelaar laughed joylessly. "But Mayé messed the whole thing up again by demanding horrendous sums, practically a genuflection. Kenny couldn't give him what he wanted. He seemed to be making things easy for Mayé, though, and I genuinely got the impression that he didn't want things to escalate, but Mayé, in his arrogance, was unstoppable. By the end he was screaming that the whole world would find out about it all. Kenny stood up, hesitated. Then he gave a broad grin and said, okay, I give in. You'll have what you desire, Mr. Dictator, give me two weeks. He said that and then left."

Vogelaar watched the smoke from his cigar float away.

"At that moment I knew that Mayé had just condemned us all to death. He may have been basking in the belief of being the victor, but he was already dead. I didn't waste any time convincing him otherwise, and just went home. My wife and I packed our bags. I always have a few identities up my sleeve, an escape plan or something. The following morning we disappeared from Equatorial Guinea. We left all of our possessions behind, everything apart from a suitcase full of money and a pile of false papers. Kenny's henchmen were on our heels right away, but my plan was perfect. It wasn't the first time I'd had to go underground. We dodged them again and again until we had thrown them off. Once we got to Berlin, we became Andre and Nyela Donner, a

South African agricultural engineer and a qualified lawyer from Cameroon with a gastronomic background, and looked for some premises. The day we opened, Ndongo was filling his pants in Malabo, and Mayé was dead. Everyone who knew about it was dead."

"Apart from one person."

"Yes."

"So what was the space program really about?"

Vogelaar stretched out a finger and pushed a half-full glass over the tablecloth. The rum sparkled in the light of the paper lamp, a frenzy of movement and reflection.

"Come on, don't make me keep asking. Why did it all happen?"

The mercenary propped his chin in his hands meditatively.

"It should be me asking who's coming after the two of you."

"Oh, sure!" Yoyo glared at him angrily. "What do you think we've been doing the whole day?"

"Obviously I'm asking myself the same thing."

"Probably Zhong Chan Er Bu," conjectured Jericho. "The Chinese secret service. After everything you've told us."

"I'm not so sure any more. I've since started to believe that Kenny's strange delegation represented neither the Chinese government nor the Chinese space travel authorities. Both of them are probably still none the wiser that they were used as a pretext."

Jericho stared at him in amazement.

"They were very convincing, Jericho."

"But the Party must have realized what was happening in their name. Mayé must have mentioned it on official state visits."

"Nonsense, think about it! There were no Chinese government visits to Equatorial Guinea, just as Mayé was never invited to the Forbidden City. No one wanted to be seen with him. A little minister of the energy authorities might pop up coyly here and there, but otherwise Chinese oil people kept their heads down. Beijing had always emphasized the fact that its only relationship with Equatorial Guinea was strictly trade-related."

"But they didn't have any problems with being photographed with dictators in Mugabe's era."

"They didn't overthrow Mugabe. After a coup, it's not the done thing for the initiators to draw attention to themselves. The Chinese are more careful nowadays."

"But what about Zheng?"

"What about him?"

"The Zheng Group works for the Chinese space travel authority. Scrub that, they *are* the space travel authority, and they did construction work for Mayé too. It must have come out then that official positions had been used as a pretext."

"Who says Zheng was consulted? Inside an authority, there are those that know and those that don't. His company accepted a commission on the free market. And so what?"

"The Party allowed their most important construction company to build a foreign launch pad."

"You can't control companies like Zheng or Orley; not even the Party can do that, nor do they want to. The Chinese prime minister has shares in Zheng, so that would have meant keeping an eye on himself too. On the contrary, Beijing welcomed the fact that Zheng responded to the invitation to tender, because it made espionage there easier."

"So why did you become suspicious?"

Vogelaar smiled thinly.

"Because I'm always suspicious. That's how I found out that Kenny left Zhong Chan Er Bu in 2022. He now works purely on a freelance basis for the military secret service."

"Just a second," said Yoyo. "The coup that brought Mayé to power—"

"Was financed by Chinese oil companies, ratified by Beijing and executed by the Chinese secret service, with our help."

"And the launching pad?"

"That had nothing to do with it. The launching pad just brought new protagonists onto the scene. Beijing was only ever concerned with commodities. The people that talked us into the launching pad had other interests."

"So Kenny changed camps?"

"I'm not sure whether he did or not. Perhaps he just broadened his circle of activity. I don't think he explicitly contravened Beijing's interests, rather that he saw someone else's interests as being more important."

"And the Mayé coup?"

"The launching pad people were to blame for that. It's possible that the Party approved of it. But they were certainly never asked."

"Is that what you believe or what you *know*?"

"What I believe."

"Vogelaar," said Yoyo insistently. "You have to tell us what you found out about the launching pad, do you hear?"

Vogelaar put his fingertips together. He fixed his gaze on his thumbs, brought them toward the tip of his nose, and then looked at the ceiling. Then, slowly, he nodded.

"Okay. Agreed."

"Tell us."

"For a quarter of a million euros."

"What?" Jericho fought for air. "Have you gone insane?"

"For that you'll get a dossier, everything's in it."

"You're crazy!"

"Not in the slightest. Nyela and I have to go underground, and right away. A large part of my fortune is frozen in Equatorial Guinea. What I was able to take with me is tied up in Muntu and the apartment upstairs. By tomorrow I'll have sold whatever I can, but Nyela and I will have to start again from scratch."

"Damn it, Vogelaar!" exploded Yoyo. "You really are the most filthy, ungrateful—"

"One hundred thousand," said Jericho. "Not a cent more."

Vogelaar shook his head. "I'm not negotiating."

"Because you're not in a position to. Think properly now. It's a hundred thousand or nothing."

"You need the dossier."

"And you need the money."

Yoyo looked as though she wanted to drag Vogelaar straight off to the slicing machine. Jericho kept an eye on her. If it came to it he was prepared to give the South African a good going over with the Glock, but he doubted that Vogelaar would let it go that far again. They had to reach an agreement with him somehow.

He waited.

After what felt like an eternity, Vogelaar breathed out, long and slow, and for the first time Jericho sensed the big man's fear.

"One hundred thousand. In cash, to be clear! Money in exchange for the dossier."

"Here?"

"Not here. Somewhere busy." With a nod of his head, he gestured outside. "Tomorrow at midday in the Pergamon Museum. That's right around the corner. Take Monbijou Strasse down to the Spree, then go over the river to Museum Island and to the James Simon Gallery. That's where the stream of tourists divides between the museums. We'll meet at the Ishtar Gate opposite the Processional Way. Nyela and I will leave immediately afterward, so make sure you're on time."

"And where do you plan to go?"

Vogelaar stared at him for a long time.

"You really don't need to know that," he said.

"Fantastic! So where are you going to get a hundred thousand euros from?" Yoyo asked as they crossed the street to where the Audi was parked.

"How should I know?" Jericho shrugged. "It's still better than a quarter of a million."

"Oh, much better."

"Okay." He stopped abruptly. "So what do you think I ought to have done? Tortured the truth out of him?"

"Exactly that. We should have beaten it out of him!"

"Great idea." Jericho felt his ear where it had been bandaged up. It was thick and puffy. He felt like a plush toy rabbit. "I can just imagine the scene. I hold him down while you beat him to a pulp with an antelope haunch."

"Good of you to mention it. I—"

"And Vogelaar would have just let us do that to him."

"But I *did* beat him to a pulp with the antelope haunch!"

"So you did." Jericho walked on, and opened the car door. "How did you get here anyway? Weren't you supposed to be keeping an eye on Nyela?"

"That just about beats everything." Yoyo flung open the passenger door, flopped down in her seat, and twisted her arms into a knot. "You'd have ended up as cold cuts if I hadn't come along, you asshole."

Jericho kept quiet.

Had he just made a mistake?

"I don't know where we're going to get the money either," he conceded. "And I don't want to count on Tu's help, not automatically."

Yoyo grumbled something he didn't catch.

"Well then," Jericho said. "Let's go to the hotel, shall we?"

No answer.

He sighed, and started the car.

"I'll ask Tu, in any case," he said. "He can lend it to me. Or give it as an advance."

"Whver."

"Maybe he's got some news for us. He's been playing about with Diane since this morning."

Silence.

"I called him before I went into Muntu. Very interesting stuff he's found out. Confirms everything that Vogelaar said. Should I tell you what Tu told me?"

"'f y'wnt."

He couldn't get anything else out of her. All the way to the Hyatt, all she would do was spit out knotty strings of consonants. Jericho reported his conversation with Tu, in the cheery tones of a man pushing water uphill, until in the end he couldn't keep up the pretense that nothing was wrong. In the Hyatt's underground garage, he finally gave up.

"Okay," he said. "You're right."

Arms folded, she stared dead ahead.

"I behaved very badly. I should have thanked you."

"N'wrries." On the other hand, at least she wasn't jumping out of the car.

"Without you, Vogelaar would have killed me. You saved my life." He cleared his throat. "So, umm—thank you, okay? I mean that, really. I'll never forget it. It was extremely brave of you."

She turned her head and looked at him, her brows drawn down like thunder.

"Why exactly are you such a halfwit?"

"No idea." Jericho stared at the steering wheel. "Maybe I just never learned."

"Learned what?"

"How to be considerate."

"I think that you can be, though. Very considerate." Her arms, folded tight, relaxed a little. They even slipped apart a bit. "Do you know what else I think?"

Jericho raised his eyebrows.

"I think that you're least considerate toward people you actually care about."

He caught his breath. Not stupid, this one.

"And who helped you with that little insight?" he asked, nursing a suspicion.

"What do you mean?"

"I was just thinking it's the kind of thing that Joanna might have said."

"I don't need Joanna for that."

"You didn't happen to talk to her about me, then?"

"Of course I did," she admitted right away. "She told me that the two of you were an item."

"And what else?"

"That *you* fucked it up."

"Ah."

"She said it was because you didn't like yourself—you're never nice to yourself—*not at all nice to yourself.*"

Jericho pursed his lips. He lined up some counterarguments, and each looked more threadbare than the next. He held them back. God knows they had better things to do here than rummage through their emotional baggage, but somehow he suddenly felt as if he'd been caught with his pants down. As if Joanna had stripped him bare and was marching him about by the ring in his nose. Yoyo shook her head.

"No, Owen, she didn't say anything bad about you."

"Hmm. I'll think about it."

"Do that." She grinned. The way he surrendered seemed to have smoothed her ruffled feathers. "We mustn't rule out the possibility that we'll have to save one another's lives a few more times."

"As I believe I've already said—any time!" He hesitated. "About Nyela—"

"My fault. After I screwed it up, I thought the best thing to do would be to come back quickly."

Jericho felt his ear. "To be honest," he said, "I'm glad you did screw it up."

CALGARY, ALBERTA, CANADA

Pounding the streets of Calgary and showing people the photograph of a possible gunman was more or less like knocking down an anthill and looking for one particular ant. Just a moment ago one and a half million people had been hard at work here, busy making more goods for the shelves and building more blocks on the streets of Canada's fastest-growing city, industrious citizens flooding the streets, but now they seemed to have lost all sense of direction in an instant. Loreena welcomed the switch to helium-3 in the energy industry, but for all that she couldn't bear the grim spectacle of mass unemployment, the decline of whole cities and provinces, the impending bankruptcy of countries which had made their money almost entirely from oil and gas. Ecologists had always had an idealistic vision of a smooth and manageable transition, with Mr. Fossilosaurus given a gold watch and sent packing to a nice quiet retirement home, where he would then draw his last breath after a dignified decline, while ten billion people cheerily got their electricity from helium-3 generators. But transition had never gone smoothly, never in history. Not in the Cambrian epoch, not in the Ordovician, the Devonian, not at the end of the Permian, Triassic, or Cretaceous, and not in the Upper Pleistocene either. That was when a new species called mankind appeared, a self-aware creature who added war and economic crisis to the catalogue of boundary events that already included volcanic eruption, meteorites, ice ages, and epidemics. So the brave new world of clean fusion came hand in hand with a full-blown global economic crisis, whether the heralds of the new dawn liked it or not.

She put fruit, yogurt, and bread rolls onto her tray and took it over to the table, where the intern was already piling into his second stack of pancakes.

"Yesterday was a disappointment then," he said.

Loreena shrugged. The Westin Calgary had the advantage of being near the Imperial Oil building on 4th Avenue Southwest, so after she had telephoned Palstein she had decided to take rooms for the night there for herself and the kid. After that they retraced the mysterious fat man's steps. It was a dispiriting business. On Bruford's video, he came in from the north. Most hotels were to the south, west, or east though. He could have been staying in any one of them, *if* he had been staying in a hotel at all. Perhaps he even lived in the city. There was a clear Asian presence here. Just a walk away from the Bow River, the third largest Chinatown in Canada after Vancouver and Toronto stretched down Calgary's lively Center Street. In the Sheraton, not far from Prince's Park Island, the staff thought that they remembered a tall, shabby-looking Asian man with a paunch on him, but he hadn't been a guest. They had showed his picture around shops and restaurants, and had even paid a visit to Calgary International Airport, all to no avail. The only good news this morning for Keowa was her breakfast, a filling but not fattening tray of pineapple, sunflower seed rolls, and low-fat yogurt.

Just as she was pouring a cup of herbal tea, Sina called, from the Vancouver desk for high society and other gossip.

"Alejandro Ruiz, fifty-two years old. Last heard of as a member of the strategic board for Repsol, or more exactly Repsol YPF to give it its full name, incorporated in Madrid—"

"I know all that already."

"Wait though! They're market leaders in Spain and Argentina, for a long while they were the biggest energy corporation in private hands, they're focused on exploration, production, and refineries; they're also world number three in LNG. They've never held any stake in alternative energies. Just to make up for it, the Mapuche Indians in Argentina have been bringing lawsuits against them like clockwork for the past twenty years, accusing them of polluting the groundwater."

It was news to Loreena that this tribe was so litigious.

"Are there even any Mapuche left?"

"Oh yes! They're in Argentina and Chile. Even if the Chilean government stubbornly denies that there's *ever* been any such thing as the Mapuche. Makes you laugh, eh? Anyway, Repsol's one of those companies where the lights are going out floor by floor. And Ruiz wasn't just vice-president for strategy, which is what I thought yesterday, he was also directly responsible for petrochemical activities in twenty-nine countries, as of July 2022."

"That's odd," said Loreena.

"Why?"

"I mean, given the way the company's set up. Why would they make somebody strategic director who demands they diversify into solar power, and uses funny words like ethics?"

"Most of the time they just put him on the payroll as their ecological conscience so they wouldn't look dumb in public. He was a second-ranker in the corporate hierarchy, so he could bark but he couldn't bite. But by 2022 the tanker was well and truly headed for the rocks. In a situation like that, you could have appointed an Andalusian donkey to the top job. Once it was obvious that Repsol was going to be one of the big losers, they needed a scapegoat at the helm, that's all."

"By 2022 Ruiz had no chance of preventing catastrophe."

"I know. Still, he tried pretty much everything he could. He even tried striking a deal with Orley Enterprises."

"Say what?" said Loreena, taken aback.

"I watched a couple of videos. He gives a good impression, this guy. His wife and daughter in Madrid are distraught over whether he'll ever turn up again. I'll send you contact details for them, and for some of his colleagues at Repsol. Best of luck."

"You're gonna call Ruiz's old lady?" the intern asked once she had finished speaking to Vancouver.

Loreena got up. "Any reason why not?"

"The time. Also, you can't speak Spanish."

"It's half past five in the afternoon in Madrid."

"Hey, really?" He licked grease off his fingers. "I thought it was always night in Europe when it's day here."

Loreena opened her mouth to answer, stopped, shook her head, and went up to her room. She was pleased to get through on her first attempt. Señora Ruiz looked distracted, and tried to rebuff her at first but in the end was very helpful; above all, she spoke excellent English, as Loreena had secretly been hoping, since indeed she didn't speak Spanish. They talked for about ten minutes, then she called one of the strategic team at Repsol, who had also been a friend of Ruiz out of the office. Sina had hunted down numbers for some more of his colleagues, but they were all newly unemployed.

She was interested by what she found out.

She looked out of the window. A gray sky brooded over the city, warning that all things must pass. Drizzling curtains of rain blurred the lines of the Calgary Tower, 190 meters tall, built by the oil companies Marathon and Husky Oil back in the day. There was something skeletal about the high-rises. A once-prosperous city was shedding weight fast, devouring its own reserves of stored fat. After thinking things over for a while, she called Vancouver again.

"Can you reconstruct the last few days before Ruiz disappeared?"

"Depends what you want to know."

"I've just been speaking with his wife, and one of his colleagues. Ruiz's last stop before he flew on to Lima was in Beijing."

"Beijing?" asked Sina, surprised. "What was Ruiz doing in Beijing?"

"Yes indeed. What?"

"Repsol has no stake in China."

"Not quite true. There was definitely a joint venture with Sinopec, it had been planned for a while. Some kind of exploration deal. They spent a week bashing it into shape. I'm more interested in what he did on the last day, right before he left China. On September 1, 2022, to be exact. Apparently he was taking part in some conference that his colleague I spoke to knew next to nothing about. All he knew was that it took place outside Beijing. He reckoned there had to be some papers about it lying around somewhere, and he'll have a look."

"Nobody knows what the conference was about?"

"Ruiz was Strategic Director. Autonomous. He didn't have to sit up and beg for every little thing. Señora Ruiz tells me that her Alejandro was a very warm-hearted, easygoing person—"

"Sobs."

"I'm getting somewhere. He wasn't the type to get upset over nothing. They had spoken on the phone just before the conference, and he was all smiles and sunshine. He had helped get the joint venture on its feet, he was in a good mood, he was cracking jokes and looking forward to Peru. But when he called from the plane to Lima, he seemed fairly downcast."

"This was the day after the mysterious conference?"

"Exactly."

"And did she ask him why?"

"She supposed that something must have gone wrong in Beijing, something that really got to him, but he didn't want to talk about it, she tells me. All in all he seemed like a different person, he was in a very uncharacteristic mood, upset and nervous. Then he called her one last time from Lima. He sounded desperate. Almost scared."

"This was just before he disappeared?"

"The same night, yes. It was the last she heard from him."

"And what am I to do now?"

"Dig around, as usual. I want to know what kind of meeting he was attending in China. Where it happened, what it was all about, who was there."

"Hmm. I'll do what I can, okay?"

"But?"

Sina hesitated. "Susan wants another word with you."

Loreena frowned. Susan Hudsucker was the Greenwatch number one. She had an idea what was coming, and come indeed it did, just as she expected: when, Susan asked, did Loreena expect to be done with her documentary about the oil companies' environmental sins? If at all possible, they wanted to broadcast *Trash of the Titans* while there were still titans around, and didn't she think she might be barking up the wrong tree with Palstein?

Loreena said she was trying to solve an attempted murder.

Susan said that Greenwatch wasn't the FBI.

But it could be that the shooting had a lot to do with the subject of her documentary.

Susan was skeptical, although on the other hand Loreena wasn't someone that even she could push around.

"Maybe you should bear in mind that what you're doing could be dangerous," she said.

"When has our work ever not been dangerous?" snorted Loreena. "Investigative work is always dangerous."

"Loreena, this is about an attempted *murder!*"

"Listen, Susan." She paced up and down the hotel room like a tiger in a cage. "I can't give you all the details right now. We'll take the first plane to Vancouver tomorrow morning and call an editorial conference. Then you'll all see that this is an *extremely* hot story, and that we've already got a whole lot further than the darn police. I mean, we'd be fools not to stick with this one!"

"I don't want to stand in your way. It's just that we have an awful lot else to do as well. *Trash of the Titans* needs to be finished, I can't take you off that task."

"Don't worry about that."

"But I do worry."

"Apart from all that, I did a deal with Palstein. If we solve this case, he'll give us the deep dirt on EMCO."

Susan sighed. "Tomorrow we'll decide what happens next, okay?"

"But by then Sina has to—"

"Tomorrow, Loreena."

"Susan—"

"Please! We'll do everything you want, but first we have to talk about it."

"Oh, shit, Susan!"

"Sid will come get you. Let him know in good time when you're landing."

Gritting her teeth, Loreena paced the room, thumped her clenched fist on the wall several times, and then went back down to the restaurant, where the intern was digging into a huge portion of chocolate mousse.

"Why do you stuff your face like that all the time?" she snarled at him.

"I'm having a growth spurt." He raised his eyes, sluggishly. "That doesn't seem to have been a particularly good call to Señora Ruiz."

"No, that was fine." She slumped down sulkily into her chair, looked into the empty cup, and rattled the empty teapot. "The not particularly good call was with Susan. She thinks we should be concentrating on *Trash of the Titans.*"

"Oops," said the intern. "That's not good."

"All the same. We fly to Vancouver first thing tomorrow and we'll figure it out. I'm not going to let it slip through my fingers now!"

"So we're still working on *Trash of the—*"

"No, no!" She leaned down. "*I* will be working on *Trash of the Titans.* You take a good look at Lars Gudmundsson."

"Palstein's bodyguard?"

"That's the guy. Him, and his team. I found out that he worked for an outfit in Dallas called Eagle Eye, cute name, huh? Personal protections,

Frank Schätzing

mercenaries. Check Gudmundsson out, tell me his shoe size and his favorite food. I want to know everything there is to know about the guy."

The intern looked uncertain. "What if he notices something? Catches us sniffing around after him."

Loreena gave him a thin smile. "If he notices anything, we've made a mistake. And do we make mistakes?"

"I do, sure."

"I don't. So eat up before I get sick from watching you. We've work to do."

GRAND HYATT

They were sitting in the lobby by the fireplace. Tu listened to their report as he guzzled down nuts by the handful. He was scooping them from the little bowl by his vodka martini faster than he could gulp them down, so that his cheeks filled out like a squirrel in the autumn.

"One hundred thousand," he said thoughtfully.

"And that's his final price." Jericho fished around in the bowl. A single remaining peanut sought to escape his clutches. "Vogelaar won't be beaten down."

"Then we'll pay him."

"Just so we're all on the same page here," said Yoyo, smiling sweetly, "*I* don't have a hundred thousand."

"So what? Do you really think that I flew the whole way here just to give up because of a measly hundred thousand? You'll have the money tomorrow morning."

"Tian, I—" Jericho managed to catch the nut between finger and thumb, and popped it into his mouth, where it rattled around on his tongue, lonely. "I wouldn't like to see you shell out the money."

"Why not? I'm the client."

"Well, as to that."

"Am I somehow not your client?"

"Actually that's Chen, and he doesn't have a—"

"No, *actually*, it's me, and I'll pick up the tab," Tu said emphatically. "The main thing is that your friend hands over the dossier."

"Well that's very—noble of you."

"Don't fall on my neck weeping. This is what we call expenses." Tu dismissed the topic. "As for myself, I can report that after some hours spent in the pleasant but somewhat sexless company of your Diane, we've identified the provider who hosted those dead letter boxes."

"You decoded the message?" Yoyo yelped.

"Shhh." Tu twinkled merrily at the waiter, who had come to exchange the empty bowl for another, brimming with nuts. He chomped away and waited until the man was out of earshot. "First of all I tracked down the central router. Very sophisticated system, that. The web pages were bounced from server to server until they appeared to be hosted in several different countries. If you track them all back though, you end up at one single, common server. And that—marvelous to report!—is in Beijing."

"Incredible," Yoyo exclaimed, "who's the host?"

"Hard to say. Mind you, I'm afraid that this server might turn out not to be the last link in the chain either."

"If we had some way of tracking each and every page routed out from there—"

"There's no list, if that's what you mean. Anyway, Diane is working with the latest miraculous software from Tu Technologies, so she found some more dead letter boxes in the web which respond to the same mask." A reverential look passed over Tu's features. He looked at each of them in turn. "The text is now a little longer."

> *Jan Kees Vogelaar is living in Berlin under the name Andre Donner, where he runs an African private and business address: Oranienburger Strasse 50, 10117 Berlin. What should we continues to represent a grave risk to the operation not doubt that he knows all about the. knows at least about the but some doubt as to whether. One way or another any statement lasting Admittedly, since his no public comment about the facts behind the coup. Nevertheless Ndongo's that the Chinese government planned and implemented regime change. Vogelaar has little about the nature of Operation of timing Furthermore, Orley Enterprises and have no reason to suspect disruption. Nobody there suspects everything. I count because I know, Nevertheless urgently recommend that Donner be liquidated. There are good reasons to*

"Orley Enterprises." Yoyo frowned quizzically.

"Interesting, isn't it?" Tu grinned slyly. "The world's biggest technology corporation. We were just talking about them! If you ask me, that throws a whole new light on the matter. It seems to have less to do with some violent handover of power in Equatorial Guinea and much more to do with who's top dog—"

"—out in space." Jericho felt his ear. Right now he felt as though he'd been slogging and stumbling along a rutted country road for hours, and had just found out that the main road was running alongside. According to Vogelaar, their problems had begun in 2022 when a delegation paid a visit, supposedly from the Chinese aerospace ministry; Mayé had seen all his hopes dashed and was ready to take any deal. He signed a contract which could hardly have been more absurd, but Kenny stood for Beijing, and so Mayé had believed that he was dealing with an official delegation.

"Good." He steepled his fingers. "Let's forget Mayé for a moment. Yoyo, do you remember what Vogelaar said about the launching pad? Who built it?"

"The Zheng Group."

"Exactly, Zheng. And who is Zheng's biggest competitor?"

"America." Yoyo frowned again. "No. Orley Enterprises."

"Which more or less amounts to the same thing, if I'm not mistaken. Orley helped the Americans toward lunar supremacy, and he's always just ahead of Zheng, any way you look at it. So Zheng turns to espionage—"

"Or to sabotage."

"I see that you've got it." Tu scrabbled around in the Brazil nuts and pistachios. "They're talking about an *operation*, and the fact that Vogelaar *continues to represent a grave risk* because he *knows all about* something. But what kind of operation could this be where people have to die in droves to keep it secret?"

Yoyo's face clouded over.

"An operation that's not been carried out yet," she said slowly.

"I think so too," Jericho said, nodding. "Vogelaar doesn't seem to know anything about the *nature* or its *timing*, but he could send the whole thing sky-high if he made a *public comment about the facts behind the coup*. The whole world still believes that Ndongo got the presidency back under his own steam, or with Beijing's help—"

"Quite, and just for once we're not going to fall into the usual trap," said Tu. "Then there's more. *Furthermore, Orley Enterprises*—blah blah— *have no reason to suspect disruption*. And—"

"*Nobody there suspects everything.*"

"So they suspect something." Yoyo looked from one to the other. "Isn't that right? I mean, that's what you'd say if they know *something*."

"We can't assume that the second phrase is actually complete, just because it looks it," Jericho said. "What's quite clear is that Orley Enterprises is part of the picture somehow. Then Zheng stands on the other side. The disaster in Equatorial Guinea is all down to some faked-up space program that he got onto its feet. Zheng represents Beijing, although he could be acting on his own account. Julian Orley stands for Washington, he's the savior of the American space program and Zheng's natural enemy—"

"That's only true to a limited extent," Tu butted in. "Julian Orley is English himself, if I'm not mistaken, and he only plays that game with the Americans because they're useful to him. Even he's just acting on his own account."

"So what's going on here? A proxy war?"

"Possibly. We've known since last year if not before that the Moon's got the potential to cause a crisis."

"Vogelaar sees things differently," Yoyo threw in. "He reckons that Beijing was just a bluff on the part of whoever was actually behind the Equatorial Guinea satellite program."

"Call it Beijing or call it Zheng." Tu shrugged. "Do we really want to rule out the possibility that if a global corporation planned an attack on a rival, its government would give tacit approval?"

"Do dogs get in dogfights?"

"Wait a moment." Jericho put his fingers to his lips. "Orley Enterprises, haven't they just been in the news? There was a report about the
Moon crisis a few days ago, and—"

"Orley is always in the news."

"Yes, but this time there really was something new."

"Of course!" A spark of recognition lit up in Yoyo's eyes. "Gaia!"

"What?"

"The hotel! The hotel on the Moon! Gaia!"

"That's right," Jericho said pensively. "They're planning a hotel up
there."

"I think they've even built it by now," Tu said, frowning in thought.
"It was supposed to be ready last year, and then there were delays
thanks to the helium-3 flare-up. Nobody knows what it looks like.
Orley's big secret."

"You can find all kinds of speculation on the net," said Yoyo. "And
you're right, it *is* ready. Sometime around about now there's even supposed to be—Hmm."

"What?"

"I think there's supposed to be an inaugural trip. Some gang of
filthy rich guests are flying up there. Maybe even Orley himself. Utterly
exclusive."

Jericho stared at her. "Are you saying that the operation might have
to do with this hotel?"

"Interesting." Tu ran his fingers through the sparse growth at the
sides of his head. "We should get to work right away. We'll have to learn
all the latest about Orley Enterprises. What's up right now? What's
planned in the near future? Then we'll have a look at the Zheng Group.
Once we have Vogelaar's dossier on top of all that, we'll probably be one
giant leap further.—When were you going to meet this guy, anyway?"

"Tomorrow, noon," said Jericho. "At the Pergamon Museum."

"Never heard of it."

"Of course you haven't. Three thousand years of Chinese civilization puts everything else just that little bit out of focus." Jericho rubbed
his jaw and looked at Yoyo. "By the way, I don't think it's a good idea if
we both turn up there."

"Now wait a moment!" she protested. "So far we've been through
everything together."

"I know. Nevertheless."

"I see!" She tightened her lips into a hostile line. "You're still pissed
off because of Nyela."

"No, not in the least. Really, I'm not."

"Do you think that Vogelaar will try to shove you into the meat-
slicer again?"

"He's unpredictable."

"He wants money, Owen! He chose to meet in a public place. What's going to happen there?"

"Owen's right," Tu put in. "Do we know whether Vogelaar even has this dossier?"

Yoyo frowned. "What do you mean?"

"Just what I say. He *told* you about a dossier. Did he actually show you one?"

"Of course not, he wants us to give him the—"

"So he could have been bluffing," Tu interrupted her. "Precisely *because* he wants the money. He could try to get the drop on Owen in the museum and make off with the hundred thousand."

"Get the drop on him how?"

"Like this." Jericho stretched out an index finger and put it to his temple. "It works, even in crowds."

"Well great!" Yoyo squirmed in her seat from rage and frustration. "So that's why you want to go into the museum on your own?"

"Believe me, it's safer."

"It would be safer with me and my haunch of antelope."

"I'm faster and more adaptable on my own. I don't have to watch out for anyone but myself."

"Like you can look after yourself, bunnikins."

"I can look out well enough to save your skin twice."

"Oh, so that's what it's about," Yoyo huffed, turning red. "You're worried you'd have to save my skin a third time. You think I'm a nitwit."

"You're anything but a nitwit."

"So what am I?"

"Could it perhaps be that you're trouble?"

"I should hope so!"

"Yoyo," Tu said gently but firmly. "I think the decision's been made."

Yoyo had got herself worked up into a storm of indignation, and now came the cloudburst. Fat tears like raindrops gathered in the corners of her eyes, brimmed over her eyelids.

"I don't want to just sit around!" she said in a ragged voice. "I got all of us into this mess. Don't you understand that I want to do something?"

"Of course we do. You'll be doing something if you help me with the research."

The waiter appeared and checked their table. Tu plunged his hand into the bowl, as though afraid that he hadn't been giving due attention to the nuts.

"We'll haff to fime oup emryfing abou' Orley," he muttered indistinctly. "On fop of all vat—" he swallowed, "—I want to know more about Zheng's solo projects. After all, he's the only Chinese entrepreneur who could go building a satellite launch pad anywhere on Earth without prior state approval. You see, my dear Yoyo, even if Owen were to beg me on bended knee to let him take you with him, I'd still refuse."

Yoyo glowered at him. "You eat like a pig, just so you know."

"Are you going to help me or are you not?"

"Have you two alpha males even considered letting Orley Enterprises know?"

"I have," Tu said. "All the same, I don't know exactly what we could tell them."

"That something is going to happen, at some point in time, though we don't know what it is or what's the target, but that they are possibly the victim."

"All admirably specific. Shall we also tell them that Zheng is behind the whole thing?"

"Or Beijing. Or the Chinese secret service." Yoyo was visibly calming down. For the time being, it seemed that the dams would not burst. "We don't know when the attack is going to take place—if indeed it *is* an attack. Mayé was deposed right around the time of the Moon crisis, it could even be that the crisis *was* the operation, but our text tells us something quite different. It's still to come. But when? How much time do we have? We zoomed over to Berlin at Mach 2 to warn Vogelaar. We should send word to Orley Enterprises at the speed of light, even if our message is very vague."

"Excellent strategic argumentation," Jericho put in.

Yoyo leaned back. She looked only halfway mollified. Jericho knew what she was going through, the rage, the shame, and the helplessness of a child who isn't even allowed to clear up the mess she's made; he knew that her father's reproachful silence loomed up somewhere inside her. Like so many children, she had learned early enough that she wasn't up to some unspoken standards.

There was a pimply boy who knew all about such things.

Like the goddess Kali, the Orley conglomerate had many arms growing from its torso, so many that at some point Tu got fed up with following links and flowcharts. The company presented some excellent targets for attack. The hotel project was nominally part of Orley Space, which was responsible for the space program and ancillary technologies, but then again it wasn't, because private travel to the Space Station and the Moon came under Orley Travel. For helium-3 mining and freight, NASA and the U.S. Treasury were the people to talk to, but then again so were Orley Space and Orley Energy, whose main business was building fusion reactors. The further they delved into the labyrinthine structures of the company, the less they felt they knew about where the "operation" might be aimed. Orley Entertainment produced films such as *Perry Rhodan*, which had made the Irish actor Finn O'Keefe one of the top earners in the movie world; it was also experimenting with the next generation of 3D movies, and had built an Orley Sphere in several cities around the globe, each a huge spherical arena for grandiose concerts and events, seating thirty thousand visitors. Currently a concert on the OSS was in the planning stages, to be given by David Bowie— almost eighty years old—and this of course was Orley Entertainment's brief, but Orley Space and Orley Travel were also part of the project. There was a division for marketing and communication, Orley Media, as well as an innovation incubator where young researchers tweaked tomorrow's world into shape—this was Orley Origin. Once you got to the Internet, the conglomerate grew and ramified like a spiral galaxy. When Diane tried the simple keyword *news*, it came up with a complete agenda for the twenty-first century. Everything was new, and everything really did mean *everything*, since there was hardly a field of human endeavor where Orley Enterprises wasn't trying to plant their flag, all of course with fervent belief and noble intent. There seemed no end to their search by the time they found OneWorld, an initiative which Julian Orley had founded to prevent global collapse; it poured forth projects for prevention and adaptation as reliably as the gushing geysers of Iceland, constantly testing new fuels and reagents, new kinds of engine, new this that and the other, all the way up to the meteorite shields which were being developed aboard the OSS in collaboration with Orley Space and Orley Origin.

And all of this under the aegis of Julian Orley, icon, philanthropist, and eccentric, more like a rock star than a business mogul, smiling youthfully, the promise of endless adventure on his lips; he was America's ally and at the same time nobody's partner, a concerned citizen, generous patron, unpredictable genius, a master of time and space, the high priest of what-if, a man who seemed to hold the patent on planet Earth and interplanetary space around, even on the future itself.

Diane also informed them that Gaia, the hotel on the Moon, was now open for a select group of guests led by Julian and Lynn Orley. The trip was organized by—

"That's enough for me," Tu declared, and called company headquarters in London, asking to be put through to Central Security. Jennifer Shaw, the chief of security, was in a meeting, and her deputy Andrew Norrington was traveling. In the end Tu spoke to a woman called Edda Hoff, number three in the hierarchy, who wore her hair in a pageboy cut like a crash helmet. She had all the personality and approachability of an electronic voice menu: if you want to report a terrorist attack, please say "one." For bribery, corruption, and espionage, say "two." If you wish to attack us yourself, please say "three." She spoke as though Orley Enterprises spent the whole day fielding calls from people warning of dark deeds or announcing their own.

Tu sent her the text fragment. She read it carefully, without a flicker of expression passing across her mask-like face. She listened calmly to his explanations. It was only when Tu started talking about the hotel that her features came to life, and she raised her eyebrows so that they almost met her black fringe.

"And what makes you so sure that the attack is going to target Gaia?"

"I heard that it was open for business," Tu explained.

"Not officially. The first group of visitors arrived there a few days ago, Julian Orley's personal guests. He himself—" She stopped speaking.

"Is up there?" Tu completed the sentence for her. "*That* would make me nervous!"

"There's nothing in the document about the timing of the operation," she said somewhat pedantically. "It's all rather vague."

"What's not so vague is that innocent people have lost their lives because of this document," Tu said, almost cheerfully. "They're dead, dead as doornails, definitely dead, nothing vague about it, if you see what I mean. As for ourselves, we've also risked our lives so that you can read it."

Hoff seemed to consider. "How can I reach you?"

Tu gave her his phone number, and Jericho's.

"Do you plan to do anything about it?" he asked. "And if so, when?"

"We'll let Gaia know. Within the next couple of hours." The corners of her mouth lifted slightly, giving the illusion of a smile. "Thank you for letting us know. We'll call you."

The screen went dark.

"Was that a woman?" Yoyo wondered out loud. "Or a robot?"

Tu snorted with laughter. "Diane?"

"Good evening, Mister Tu."

"Just call me Tian."

"I shall do so."

"How are you, Diane?"

"Thank you, Tian, I'm very well," Diane said in her warm alto voice. "What can I do for you?"

Tu turned back to the others. "I've no idea who or what Edda Hoff is," he whispered. "But compared with her, Diane is *definitely* a woman. Owen, I owe you an apology. I'm beginning to understand you."

GAIA, VALLIS ALPINA, THE MOON

"Is there someone close to you whom you can trust unreservedly?"

Lynn thought about this. Her first instinct was to say Julian's name, but suddenly she felt uncertain about this. She loved her father and admired him, and of course he trusted *her*. But whenever she saw herself through his eyes she was terrified by the image of the woman with sea-blue eyes, the woman Julian called his daughter, and the worst of it was that she could only ever see herself through his eyes, that even as a child she had yearned for his approval as a plant turns toward the sun. But she wasn't that woman. So how could she trust *him*, since clearly he knew nothing at all of how she felt, didn't know that she was just a puppet on strings, a shape-shifting monster, a mimic, a tumor, a thing?

"Who are you thinking of at the moment?" asked ISLAND-II.

"Of my father. Julian Orley."

"Julian Orley is your father?" the program asked, just to be sure.

"Yes."

"He's not the person you trust, though."

It wasn't a question, it was a statement of fact. The man sitting across from her leaned forward. Lynn breathed heavily, and the sensors in her T-shirt dutifully registered her breathing and stored it in the database. The polygraph measured her body temperature, pulse, heartbeat, and even her neuronal activity; the program scanned her voice frequencies as she spoke, measured her gestures, the way her pupils expanded or contracted, every movement of her eye muscles, each drop of sweat that formed. With every passing second of measurement, Lynn supplied more information for ISLAND-II, giving the program more to work with when it made statements about her.

The man seemed to stop and think for a moment. Then he smiled encouragingly. He was strongly built, completely bald, with friendly, thoughtful eyes. He seemed to be able to look through every veil that Lynn had wrapped around herself, her diorama of concealment, to pierce every layer with his glance but without that cool invasive gaze that psychologists so often used to put their patients under the microscope.

"Good, Lynn. Let's stick with the people around you right now. Tell me the names of the people you feel close to right now.—And please leave a couple of seconds between every name."

She looked at her fingernails. Talking to ISLAND-II was like walking a tightrope in the darkness to an unknown goal—along a torch-beam. The trick of it was to think of yourself as just as unreal as the program. The best thing was that there was no way of making a fool of yourself. For instance, Lynn had no idea at all whether there had ever been a real person who had served as the model for the bald man; the only thing she knew for sure was that it was impossible for him to feel contempt for her concerns. ISLAND-II—the *Integrated System for Listening and Analysis of Neurological Data*—was only as human as the therapists had programmed it to be.

"Julian Orley," Lynn repeated—although the program had already struck him from the list of people she trusted—and she obediently included a brief pause. "Tim Orley—Amber Orley—Evelyn Chambers—that's all of them, I think."

Evelyn? Did she really trust America's most powerful talk-show queen? On the other hand, why not? Evelyn was a friend, even if they hadn't spoken much since the trip began. But the question had been about people she felt close to. What did "close" have to do with trusting a person?

The man looked at her.

"I've learned a great deal about you in the past quarter of an hour," he said. "You're afraid. Less because of any actual concrete threats than because you have thoughts which make you horribly afraid. For as long as you do that, you can't feel anything else. And then because you've lost that ability to feel, you lurch into a depression, this makes you more afraid, and most of all you're afraid of fear itself. Unfortunately, when you're in this frame of mind, every one of your thoughts grows to monstrous size, so you make the mistake of imagining that there's some substance to what you're thinking and that's to blame for your condition. So you try to get rid of them at the level of substance, and you end up doing entirely the opposite. They only look like monsters, but the more seriously you take them, the bigger and stronger they grow."

He paused to let his words sink in.

"But in point of fact the substance is practically interchangeable. It's not the substance of your thoughts that makes them frightening. Fear is a physical phenomenon. It's the fear that creates the substance. Your heartbeat speeds up, your chest tightens, you tense up, stiffen, you become rigid. Your inward horizons shrink down and now you feel helpless and no longer free. You rage against it, like an animal in a cage. All these physical symptoms taken together make you give your thoughts such weight, Lynn, that's why they have such horrible power over you. It's important that you learn to see through the mechanism. It's nothing more than that, you see. As soon as you manage to relax you'll be able to break the spiral. The more intensely you feel yourself, the less power your thoughts have to torture you. That's why any sort of therapy will have to begin with physical exercise. Sport, lots of sport. Exercise, feel the burn, make your muscles ache. Sharpen up your senses. Hearing, sight, taste, smell, touch. Leave all these projections behind and get out into the real world. Breathe deeply, feel your body.—Do you have any questions?"

"No. Actually, yes." Lynn wrung her hands. "I understand what you mean, but—but—it's just that these really are very specific fears. I mean, I'm not just making this up! What I've done here, what I've let myself in for. My thoughts only ever have to do with—destruction, disaster—death. Other people, dying. Killing, torturing them, destroying them!—I am so horribly afraid of turning into something, suddenly slipping my leash, that I'll leap on the others, tear them to shreds, people I love! Something eating away at me from inside, until there's nothing left of me but a shell, and inside that shell something awful, something strange, and—I don't know who I am any longer. I don't know how much longer I can take all the pressure—"

Suddenly there were tears in her eyes, drops of sheer despair. Her chin trembled. There seemed to be fluids spouting from everywhere, from her nose, the corners of her mouth, spilling over her lower lip. The man leaned backward and looked at her from under lowered eyelids, maybe expecting that she would add something, but she couldn't say any more, she could only gasp for air. She wished she could vanish from this world, back to the womb, not to Crystal's though—the woman had never been able to offer her safety or warmth, all she had done was pass on her melancholy poison, the bad code written in her genes. She wished she had a father who would tell her that it had just been a bad dream, but not Julian—he would take her in his arms and comfort her, yes, but he wouldn't have the least idea of what her problem was, any more than he had been able to understand Crystal's depression and her later mental illness. That didn't mean though that Julian despised weakness, he just couldn't *understand* it! Lynn wanted to be back in the loving arms of parents who had never existed.

"I have very high expectations of myself," she said, straining to sound businesslike. "And then—I feel sure that they're too high, and I hate myself for falling short—for failing."

She felt herself become transparent, and clutched her arms tightly around herself though it did nothing to make the feeling go away. She was talking to a computer, but she had rarely felt so exposed.

"I'll just suggest another way you could look at it," ISLAND-II said after a while. "These aren't *your* expectations. They are other people's expectations, but you've bought into them so completely that you *think* that they are yours. So you try to bring your actions into line with these expectations. You don't place any value on who you truly are, but rather on how other people would like you to be. But you can't deny your real self forever, you can't spend forever running yourself down. Do you understand what I mean?"

"Yes," she whispered. "I think I do."

The man looked at her for a while, friendly, analytical.

"How do you feel right now?"

"Don't know."

"The person you really are knows. Try to feel that feeling."

"I can't," she whimpered. "I can't do something like that. I can't get—close to myself."

"You don't have to conceal anything here, Lynn." The man smiled. "Not from me. Don't forget, I'm just a program. Albeit a very intelligent one."

Conceal? Oh yes, she was the queen of concealment, had been since her childhood, when she had spent hours in front of the mirror, herself and her reflection practicing concealment together, until she was able to project any possible expression onto her pretty face: confidence, when she was about to fall to pieces, easygoing calm when the winds of stress were screaming all around her, bluffing with an empty hand. And how quickly she had learned what such tactics could achieve, when the man she most wanted to please disapproved of the very idea of such concealment. But he couldn't see through her mimicry, and in the end even she couldn't see through it. In the hectic attempt to keep up with the pace he set, she developed a deep-seated aversion to finer feelings, her own included. She began to despise her fellow man's maudlin moods and public passions. Souls stripped bare, suffering on display, the clingy confidentialities of unearned intimacy. Letting the whole world know what side of bed you'd got out that morning, letting them all peer in at the bubbling chemistry of your mind—all this was repulsive. How much she preferred her own clean, hygienic concealment. Until that day five years ago when everything changed—

"What you're feeling is rage," ISLAND-II said calmly.

"Rage?"

"Yes. Unfettered rage. There's a Lynn Orley trapped inside who wants to break out at last, and be loved, wants herself to love her. This Lynn has to tear down a great many walls, she has to free herself of a great many expectations. Are you surprised that she wants to maim and kill?"

"But I don't want to maim and kill," she sobbed. "But I can't—can't do anything to stop—"

"Of course you don't want to. Not physically. You don't want to do anything to anyone, Lynn, have no fear on that front. You're only torturing one person, yourself. There's no monster inside you."

"But these thoughts just won't leave me alone!"

"It's the other way around, Lynn. You won't leave them alone."

"But I'm trying. I'm trying everything I can!"

"They'll become weaker the stronger the real Lynn grows. What you think is some monstrous transformation is really just a new birth, a beginning. We also call it liberation. You kick and bite, you want to get out. And of course as you do that, something else dies, your old self, the identity that was forced upon you. Do you know what the three childhood neuroses are?"

Lynn shook her head.

"They're as follows: I have to. I mustn't. I ought to. Please repeat."

"I—have to, mustn't—ought to—"

"How does it sound?"

"All fucked up."

"From today, they don't count for you any longer. You aren't that child any longer. From now on, all that counts is: I am."

"*I am what I am—*" Lynn sang in a wavering voice. "And who am I?"

"You're the one who knows what you think and what you're doing. You are what's left when you have shucked away all those people you think are you, until all that's left is pure awareness. Have you ever had the feeling of watching yourself think? That you can see the thoughts rising up and then vanishing again?"

Lynn nodded weakly.

"And that's a very important truth as well, Lynn. You are not your thoughts. Do you understand? You are *not* your thoughts. You are not the same as what you *imagine* the world to be."

"No, I don't understand."

"An example. Are you aware right now that you can see the holographic image of a man?"

"Yes."

"What else can you see?"

"Furniture. The chair I'm sitting on. A few gadgets, technology. Walls, floor, ceiling."

"Where are you, exactly?"

"I'm sitting on a chair."

"And what are you doing?"

"Nothing.—listening. Talking."

"When?"

"What do you mean, when?"

"Tell me when this is happening."

"Well, now."

"And that's all we need. You are well aware of the world that's really there, around you, you can cut through to the world as it is. To the here and now. Then after that there's another now, and another now, and now, now, now, and so on and so forth. Lynn, everything else is just projections, fantasy, speculation.—Do you find the here and now threatening?"

"We're on the Moon. Anything could go wrong, and then—"

"Stop. You're slipping away into hypotheticals again. Stay with what really is."

"Well then," said Lynn, unwillingly. "No. Nothing threatening."

"You see? Reality is not threatening. When you leave this room, you'll meet other people, you'll do other things, you'll experience a new now, then another now, and then another. You can look at each moment as it comes, and ask if it's threatening, but there's only one thought not allowed here—*What if?* The question is—*What is?* And then you'll find, nearly all the time, that the only threat is in your imaginings."

"*I'm* dangerous," Lynn whispered.

"No. You *think* that you're dangerous, so much so that it frightens you. But that's just a thought. It pops up and goes boo, and then you fall for it. Eighty-five percent of everything that goes through our heads is garbage. Most of it we don't even register. Sometimes, though, a thought comes along and goes boo, and we jump with fright. But *we are not* these thoughts. You needn't be afraid."

"O-okay."

The man was quiet for a while.

"Do you want to tell me any more about yourself?"

"Yes. No, another time. I'll have to end the session—for now."

"Good. One more thing. Earlier I asked you whom you trust."

"Yes."

"I assessed your physiological responses as you named each name. I recommend that you confide in one of these people. Talk to Tim Orley."

Confide in a *person.*

"Thank you," Lynn said mechanically, without even thinking whether ISLAND-II cared for the common courtesies. The bald man smiled.

"Come again whenever you like."

She switched him off, removed the sensors from her forehead, took off the T-shirt, and put on one of her own. She stared at the empty glass plate for a while, unable to stand up, even though standing up was easier here on the fucking Moon than anywhere else.

Had it been wise to come here? To sweat and strain in front of a mirror that she really didn't want to look into? Famously, ISLAND-II could deliver some astonishing results. Since it had come along, manned spaceflight without regular psychotherapy was unimaginable. During the 1970s, of course, the age of hero worship, people would have been more likely to believe that Uncle Scrooge McDuck was real than they'd have believed that astronauts could suffer from depression, but now, in the era of the long-haul mission, everything depended on the mysteries of the human mind. Nobody wanted to screw up grotesquely expensive undertakings such as the planned missions to Mars just because of neurotic compulsions. The greatest danger didn't come from meteorites or technical failure, but rather from panic, phobias, rivalry displays, and the good old sex drive, all of which urgently demanded a psychologist on board ship. Simulations had been tried, which yielded much food for thought. In two cases out of five, the psychologist lost his mind before anyone else, and began to drive the other crew members mad with his analytical skills. But even when he managed to keep it together, his presence didn't have the desired effect. It became clear that the other astronauts would rather swallow their own tongues than confide their troubles to a living, breathing fellow crew member, who could pass judgment on them. There were tragically obvious reasons for such self-censorship: men were worried for their careers, and women were scared of judgment and scorn.

Which was how virtual therapists had joined the game. At first, simple programs ran through questionnaires and gave advice straight out of the self-help shelves, then later came scripted exchanges, then finally software capable of complex dialogues. There was nothing here that could replace a video-link and a chat with friends and family, but what could be done on Mars, where it was virtually impossible to get a connection? In the end, prize-winning cybertherapists had developed a program which combined advanced dialogue capacity with simultaneous evaluation of the most extensive corpus of knowledge that any artificial intelligence had ever had access to. Skeptics proclaimed that every individual human being had their own specific needs, that only another human being could ever understand, but results seemed to show quite the opposite. There might be many doors to the labyrinth of the human soul, but once you'd wandered around in there for a while you always reached familiar ground. There weren't millions of different psychological profiles, just a few basic patterns repeated a millionfold. In the end, you always hit the same old neuroses, complexes, and traumas, and most of them were acute in nature, such as squabbles over who had eaten whose last pot of chocolate pudding. Since then, ISLAND-I had been used in space stations, remote research installations, and corporate headquarters all around the globe, while the incomparably more advanced ISLAND-II was so far only installed in Gaia's meditation centers and therapy rooms. Even its programmers didn't quite understand this pseudo-personality, a creature with no Promethean spark but able to learn astonishingly fast and reach remarkable conclusions.

After a while Lynn summoned up the energy to leave the therapy center. As she walked to the lobby, her body language shifted to exude good cheer and brisk confidence. Guests walked past, euphoric, fidgeting restlessly, eyes as wide as children's, back from their excursions to the lava caves in Moltke Crater, the peak of Mons Blanc, or the depths of the Vallis Alpina. They chattered away about mankind's civilizing mission in the universe (specifically through tennis and golf), about the thrill of water sports in the pool here, about shuttle flights, grass-hopper trips, moon-buggy rides, and of course, over and over again, about the view they had of Earth. Quarrels and disagreements seemed buried in the regolith by now. They were all talking to one another. Momoka Omura actually used words like *creation, humility*; Chuck Donoghue said that Evelyn Chambers was a real lady; Mimi Parker giggled as she agreed to take a sauna with Karla Kramp. Good cheer hung like a miasma over any honest, straightforward resentments they might have harbored. They were all hugs and smiles, even Oleg Rogachev, who forced each and every one of his fellow guests into a round of judo and sent them flying through the air for meters at a time with a naga waza, grinning like a fox, *and of course nobody got hurt*! It was enough to make her throw up, but Lynn the chameleon listened to all the stories as though she were learning the secret of life, accepted compliments as a whore accepts payment, smiled as she suffered, suffered as she smiled. Quarter to eight, time to look forward to dinner. In her mind's eye she saw the first course served and devoured, saw a fish-bone stick in Aileen's throat, saw Rogachev spitting blood, Heidrun choking, saw Gaia's faceplate burst open and the whole merry gang of bastards sucked outside, defenseless in the vacuum, popping open, boiling, freezing.

Well, you didn't go pop right away.

But their own mothers wouldn't have recognized the corpses.

Dana Lawrence looked up as Lynn came into the control room. She glanced at the clock. There were a few minutes yet before feeding time, and she had to go down to the basement for a routine check. Normally Ashwini Anand would take over in the control room while she was away, but she was just now looking into why the robot had failed to change the sheets in the Nairs' suite.

"Everything all right?" Lynn asked.

"So far, yes. There's been a tech failure up on level twenty-seven, nothing important."

Lynn's eyes flickered. It was enough to trigger Dana's analytical turn of mind. She wondered what was wrong with Julian's daughter. More and more, she was showing signs of uncertainty, irritability. Why had she so vehemently refused to show Julian the footage two days ago? She looked at Lynn searchingly, but the woman had pulled herself together by now.

"Can you manage, Dana?"

"No problem. Look, since you happen to be here, could I ask you for a favor? I have to go downstairs for ten minutes. There'll be nobody in the control room during that time, and—"

"Just route it all through your phone."

"I do, usually. It's just I'd like to keep an eye on everything when it all gets going in the restaurant. Could you take over for a while?"

"Of course." Lynn smiled. "Go on then, never fear."

You're acting, Dana thought. What are you hiding? What's your problem?

"Thank you," she said. "See you soon."

The control room. Little Olympus.

There were so many buttons you could press here, systems you could reprogram, settings and parameters you could shift. Increase the oxygen level until everything burst into flame. Mix in a lethal level of carbon dioxide. Shut all the bulkheads and lock away the restaurant party until they all went mad, one after another. Pump the sludge into the drinking water so that everyone fell ill. Stop the elevators. Unplug the reactor. Increase the internal air pressure and then shunt it all out in one go. All kinds of fun you could have. There were no limits to creativity here.

I am dangerous.

Lynn's eyes drifted across the wall of monitors, all the areas under surveillance.

No. You are not your thoughts!

"*I am what I am*," she sang softly.

Another tune joined in. A call from London, Orley headquarters, Central Security. Lynn frowned. Her hand hovered indecisively over the touchscreen, then she took the call, feeling queasy. Edda Hoff's face appeared on the screen, with her pageboy cut. Her mask-like features gave no clue as to whether she had good news or bad to report.

"Hallo, Lynn," she said in a flat voice. "How are you?"

"Couldn't be better! The trip's a complete success. And down there? Body count? Armageddon?"

Hoff took worryingly long to reply.

"To be honest, I don't know."

"You don't know?"

"A few hours ago someone got in touch with us. A certain Tu Tian, a Chinese businessman, currently in Berlin. He had a rather convoluted story to tell us. Apparently he and some friends of his have ended up in possession of restricted information, and since then they've been on somebody's hit list."

"And what does that have to do with us?"

"The text that caused all this kerfuffle is very broken up. There are only fragments, but from the little that they've been able to send us it doesn't read much like a bedtime story."

"What is it, exactly?"

"I'll send it over to you."

A few lines of text appeared on a separate screen. Lynn read the text, read it again, then once more, hoping that the name Orley might perhaps vanish, but it just seemed to grow bigger every time she read it. She stared at the document, paralyzed, and felt a black wave of panic roll toward her as though the conversation with ISLAND-II had never taken place.

Nobody there suspects everything.

"And?" Hoff urged her. "What do you think?"

"It's a fragment, as you say." Just don't show any uncertainty! "A puzzle. As long as we don't have the full text, we may perhaps be reading more into it than is really there."

"Tu is worried that there will be an attack on Gaia."

"That's going a bit far, don't you think?"

"Depends how you look at it."

"There's nothing here to tell us when this operation is even going to take place."

"That's what I told him. On the other hand, we can't simply ignore what's going on."

"What is going on though, Edda? To decide whether or not you're going to ignore something, you need to know what it is, don't you? But we just don't know. Orley has interests worldwide: if there really is something planned against us, it doesn't necessarily have to be aimed at Gaia. How did this Chinese gentleman get that idea?"

"Because the reports are in all the newspapers."

"I see." Her thoughts raced. The edges of the room seemed to be blurring and fading. "Well, that's true, the hotel is certainly most in the news, but that doesn't automatically mean that it's most at risk. At any rate, we really can't afford any upset up here at the moment, you do understand that, don't you Edda? Not with *these* guests! There's no way we can risk scaring away potential investors with this sort of thing."

"I don't want to scare anyone away," Hoff said, somewhat indignantly. "I'm doing my job."

"Of course."

"Apart from which, I didn't want to bother you about it, I thought I would speak to Dana Lawrence, but you just happened to pick up. And I'm not daft, Lynn. I know that you've got a crowd of investors up there, all very important people, ultra-rich, famous faces. But isn't that exactly what might suggest that the hotel is in some sort of danger?"

Lynn kept quiet.

"Be all that as it may," she said in the end. "You did the right thing telling us so quickly. We'll keep our eyes open up here, and you should do the same. Stay alert. Have you already talked to Norrington and Jennifer Shaw?"

"No. First of all I checked out this character Tu."

"And?"

"A self-made millionaire from the first wave. Extremely successful. He runs a high-tech holography and virtual environments outfit in Shanghai. I found a few interviews and articles about him. Definitely not a nutcase."

"Good. Stick with it. Tell me if there are any developments, and—Edda?"

"Yes?"

"Speak to *me* first if anything happens."

"I'll have to tell Norrington and Jennifer as well of course—"

"Certainly you shall. Until then, Edda."

Lynn ended the call and stared dead ahead. A few minutes later Dana came up from the basement levels. She got up, smiled, and wished the director good evening, without breathing a word about the call. She left the control room at a steady pace, took the elevator up to Gaia's curved bosom, squirmed into her suite as soon as the door slid open, and dashed into the bathroom. She tore open the packet of green tablets and gulped down three of them, and even as she choked them down she was wrestling with a dark glass jar full of little capsules the size and shape of maggots.

It slipped through her fingers. Fell.

She snatched and caught it. Two little maggots crept out into the palm of her violently quivering hand. She shoved them hurriedly between her lips and washed them down with water. When she raised her head there was a Gorgon staring at her, a fearsome face with serpent hair; she wouldn't have felt surprised if she'd turned to stone on the spot. She was gripped tight by the feeling that she was falling, and that the fall would never end. The stuff wasn't working, not fast enough, she was rushing onward, headlong into madness, she would go mad if it didn't work, mad, mad—

Sobbing, she ran into the living room, forgot the lesser gravity for a moment, slammed straight into the wall, and fell on her back. Helpfully, she ended up where she had wanted to be anyway, even if not quite like this, but what the hell. There it was, the minibar, right in front of her nose. Cola, water, juice, everything out, there had to be a bottle of red wine here somewhere, or even better the whisky, the little emergency ration that she had smuggled in, even though you weren't supposed to drink alcohol up on the Moon, blah blah blah, get it down, neck it—

The bourbon burned her throat as it went down. She crept back to the bathroom on all fours as her ribcage quivered from the coming eruption. She just made it to the toilet, clutched the sides of the bowl, and spewed out a jet of whisky, tablets, and whatever else was in her stomach. The vomit splattered against the ceramic in front of her, and some of it splashed back onto her face. Where were the tablets? A sour stench assailed her nose, brought tears to her eyes. She couldn't see anything. She retched again, although there was nothing left to bring up, until at last she could wrench herself away from the toilet bowl and collapse beside it. Whimpering, motionless, she lay there bathed in sweat and vomit, staring at the ceiling—and all at once she could breathe again.

Tim. ISLAND-II had said that she should talk to Tim. Where was he? At dinner? Had they already started? It's twenty past eight, you silly cow, of course they've started, a quick hello from the kitchen staff, fripperies of foam and essence and whatever damn thing those fools served up; anything she ate would come straight up again, but she had to go there, she couldn't stay lying here forever could she, somebody would come and break the door down.

Fear is a physical phenomenon.

Oh how true, you clever-clogs machine, you Socrates!

All these physical symptoms together make you give your thoughts such weight, Lynn, that's why they have such horrible power over you.

She sat up carefully. Something buzzed and boomed inside her skull. She felt as though she had lain in the baking Sahara sun for a year, but she could still think straight, and her nerves slowly settled back down from the hideous shock that had set them thrumming. She climbed to her feet like an old woman, and looked at herself in the mirror.

"God, you look like shit," she murmured.

As soon as you manage to relax you'll be able to break the spiral. The more intensely you feel yourself, the less power your thoughts have to torture you.

Well then. They'd just have to eat the first course without her. What she saw in the mirror there couldn't be fixed with just a bit of blush. She would have to retouch, for sure, but she'd be able to do that too. Then she would turn up in the Selene just in time for the main course, glowing and beautiful, the queen of concealment.

A succubus dressed as an angel.

BERLIN, GERMANY

Tu insisted on an evening's entertainment once he had shot off messages to all and sundry, hoping to get some inside information about the Zheng Group. Some of the people he wrote to were already lying in their beds in Shanghai or Beijing at this time of day, while others were in America—these he either spoke with, or he left a message asking them to call him back. He quipped that at the end of the day, any information he could get about Zheng from America was going to be better than anything from China.

"Why's that?" Jericho asked, as they were served their Wienerschnitzel in the legendary Borchardt restaurant.

"Why?" Tu raised his eyebrows. "America is our best friend!"

"That's right," Yoyo said. "Whenever we Chinese want to know anything about China, we ask America."

"Fine friends you have," Jericho remarked. "That friendship of yours makes the rest of the world quake in their boots."

"Oh, Owen, come on now. Really."

"Seriously! Didn't you say yourself that the Moon crisis was as bad as the Cuban crisis?"

Tu lifted up his schnitzel with his knife where it spilled over the edge of the plate, and peered doubtfully underneath, as though perhaps he might find something there to explain why Europeans didn't cut their meat up into bite-sized morsels like civilized folk. He would rather have gone to a Chinese restaurant, but he had given way in the face of a dual chorus of "You cannot be serious!"

"Quite so," he said. "And I was as worried sick about it as you were. But you just have to remember that China and America simply *can't* go to war. They are the twin giants of the global economy, and they might be at odds but they're joined at the hip. Traditionally, archenemies have always done the best deals, there are advantages to not actually liking the guy you're doing business with. If you like your trading partner, deals are guaranteed to go wobbly, but antipathy puts you on your guard. That's why China does so extraordinarily well when it trades with the nations it likes least of all, meaning the USA and Japan. Of course, if I wanted to know something about America, naturally I would get in touch with the Zhong Chan Er Bu."

"That's all a heap of platitudes." Jericho began to eat. "The idea that the citizens of totalitarian regimes can find out most about themselves if they ask the people whose job it is to spy on them. We're talking about something else. Even the Americans can't peer into Zheng Pang-Wang's mind."

"True. It's still worth asking the CIA and the NSA though, if you want to know something about him. Or for my money you could ask the Bundesnachrichtendienst, the SIS, or the Sluzhba Vneshney Razvedki, or Mossad, or the Indian secret service. You're a detective, Owen, you believe in infiltration. So do they. Anyway, experience has shown by now that it's easier to infiltrate a government than a company." Tu squeezed some lemon onto his schnitzel, though from the look on his face he seemed worried it might jump from the plate and run out of the door. "You said earlier that Orley Enterprises and the USA are the same thing in the end. They are. But only to the extent that Orley can set the conditions for American space flight. Of course, they don't like that. They hate the idea, but the truth is that the USA is *totally dependent* on Orley. Their space program and their whole energy plan is drip-fed from the world's biggest tech company, it's plugged in to Julian Orley's money and his techs' know-how. To that extent, Orley might be the same thing as American spaceflight, but Washington's a long way from being the same as Orley. Even if you knew everything about what the American government was planning, you still wouldn't have much idea about Orley Enterprises. That corporation's a fortress. It's a parallel universe. It's a state in its own right. Extraterritorial."

"And Zheng?"

"Well that's different. American presidents may have been in hock to the oil lobby, or the steel barons, or the military-industrial complex, but they were never totally identical. Even if that's just because the big corporations are by definition private in democratic countries. It's different in China—historically, they're rooted in the State, but they do what they like."

"Are you telling me that the Party has lost power to the corporations?" Jericho asked. "I'd be surprised to hear that."

"Bullshit." Yoyo shook her head. "Losing power implies that somebody has shoved you aside and now rules in your place. But you're still there, for all that maybe you're sitting in opposition. But nobody shoved anybody aside in China, it was more like a one-hundred-percent transformation, a metamorphosis. Every old Communist who kicked the bucket made room for some bright young thing with a Party membership book in his pocket and a chair on the board of a profit-making company."

"It's not much different in America."

"But it is. Washington has lost power to Orley Enterprises, and that probably makes the government stare out of the window cursing on rainy days, but at least there's somebody to stare and curse. There are no State institutions left in China where that could happen. The whole shooting match might still call itself Communism, but it's really just a self-appointed government by corporate consortium."

"You can look at it the other way around though," said Tu, as though the two of them were moderating a political talk show. "China is governed by managers who have a second job in politics. The Western world still has a few heads of state who'll say No when private enterprise is saying Yes. Maybe the great big No dwindles away to a hopeless little bleating No, but at least there's still something or someone defending a position. In China you just have to imagine what No looks like when it's made up of a whole load of Yeses. When Deng Xiaoping decided to allow some experiments in privatization, lots of people wondered how much privatization would be allowed in the future. Well, the question's obsolete by now, since in the end Communism itself was privatized." He put down his knife and fork, picked the schnitzel up in his fingers, and bit into it. "And that, Owen, is why it's simpler to get information about a Chinese company from abroad than it is in China. If you want internal details about Zheng, all you have to do is tap into the flow of intelligence in all the nations spying on Beijing. And as it happens, I know some people in the intelligence services."

Jericho fell silent. He had no idea who Tu knew, or when he had crossed paths with the secret services in his busy lifetime, but he knew that he had rarely been given such a clear picture of a world where either the governments had been taken over by the corporations, or the corporations had lifted themselves clear of all governmental control.

Who was their enemy?

Around ten o'clock he felt tired, drained, while Yoyo was suggesting that they check out the local night life and see what trouble they could get into. She was in frantic high spirits. Tu demanded a look at the Kurfürstendamm. Jericho logged into Diane and teased out a list of the hot clubs and karaoke bars. Then he said he'd go back to the hotel, using the excuse that he had to work, which even happened to be true. He had been neglecting some of his clients dreadfully these past two days.

Yoyo protested. He had to come along!

Jericho hesitated. He had basically made up his mind to go back to the hotel, but all of a sudden he felt like giving in. When she protested, some previously undiscovered reserve battery had flooded his system with extra energy. It felt like extra oil in his tank, a warm feeling around the ribcage.

"Well, to be honest I really ought to—" he said, for form's sake.

"Okay. See you later then."

The battery spluttered and died. The world snapped back into the unending winter of his teenage years, when he had only ever been invited to parties so that people could say afterward that they hadn't forgotten him. It flashed through his mind that Yoyo would have plenty of fun without him, just as everybody else had been able to have plenty of fun without him back then.

How he had hated his youth.

"Well?" she asked, her eyes cold.

"Have fun," he said. "See you later."

Later turned out to mean after he had done absolutely none of the things that he had gone back to the hotel to do. He lay there wondering where he had taken that wrong turn in life, why he always ended up where he least wanted to be, as one did in a nightmare. He was like a traveler standing at the luggage carousel waiting for a lost suitcase, while it was probably being auctioned off somewhere at the other end of the world; he waited and waited, and the certainty crept over him that maybe all he would ever do in life would be to wait.

About two o'clock he was half-watching a botched 3D remake of Tarantino's classic *Kill Bill* when there was a shy knock at his door. He climbed to his feet, opened the door, and saw Yoyo standing in the hallway.

"Can I come in?" she asked.

Automatically, he looked at the digital clock on his video wall.

"Thanks." She shoved past him and came into his room, not quite steady on her feet. "I know how late it is."

Her eyes were as sad as a dog's. A cigarette between her fingers sent up its curls of smoke, and she'd evidently had a good deal to drink. By the look of her, they'd even run into a minor tornado somewhere on their adventures, which had left her rumpled. Jericho rather doubted that she'd had fun that evening after all.

"What are you doing right now?" she asked inquisitively. "Got a lot of work done?"

"Not bad."

Jericho stood there. There would have been no point telling her that he had spent the last few hours wrestling with his inner eighteen-year-old. "And you? Had a good time?"

"Oh, fantastic!" She spread out her arms and spun about, so that Jericho suddenly felt he should hurry to catch her. "We ended up in some karaoke bar that was playing pure shit, but Tu and I managed to liven up the joint all the same."

He sat down on the edge of the bed. "You sang?"

"And how." Yoyo giggled. "Tian doesn't know even one line of lyrics, and I know them all backward. A couple of guys hanging around there told us we should come along to a gig in a club. Some band called Tokyo Hotel. I thought they'd be Japanese! But they were German, old guys, dinosaurs of rock."

"Sounds good."

"Yes, but I had to go and pee after half an hour, and I couldn't find the bathroom anywhere. So we had to go in the bushes, and then on to the next bar that was still open. No idea where that was."

She fell quiet all of a sudden, and slumped down onto the edge of the bed next to him.

"And?" he asked.

"Hmm. Tian told me something.—Do you want to know what?"

Suddenly he was seized by the idiotic notion of kissing her and finding out what Tu had said that way, simply sucking the knowledge out of her. Drunk and disheveled as she was, pasty and drawn, she seemed lovelier than ever. He felt it briefly in his loins and then right away felt the pain of knowing that Yoyo had come here to *talk*.

He stared at Diane, sitting there cool and sexless. Yoyo looked down and sucked the last life from her cigarette.

"I'd like to tell you, you know."

"Okaaay," Jericho said, drawing out the word. He was turning her down flat and there was no way she couldn't know it.

"Well only if you're not—" She hesitated.

"What?"

"Maybe it is a bit late though. Is it?"

No, it's just the right moment, the adult man in his head shouted, but he was on autopilot now, frustration and misery had taken charge and were consummately giving Yoyo the cold shoulder. They looked at one another across an emotional Grand Canyon.

"Well then—I probably ought to go."

"Sleep tight," he heard himself say.

She got to her feet. Jericho was baffled by his own behavior, but did nothing to stop her going. She paused for a moment, drifted indecisively over to the computer, and then back again.

"We might hate it now but someday we'll look back on this time of life and we'll love it," she said, suddenly speaking clearly. "Someday we'll have to make peace, or we'll go mad."

"You're twenty-five years old," Jericho said, tired. "You can make peace with whoever you please."

"What the hell do you know?" she muttered and ran from the room.

CALGARY, ALBERTA, CANADA

She felt like a Dobermann chained up in front of a butcher's shop. Loreena Keowa couldn't think of any other way to describe it; her instinct had taken her straight to Beijing, to the conference which had led to Alejandro Ruiz vanishing so completely. She had caught the scent, she was just about to bite, she could sink her teeth into it, and now Susan wanted to *talk*. Why? What about? Sina couldn't give her any more help for now, because Susan Hudsucker had reservations. What a pointless waste of time and of opportunity! Loreena didn't doubt for a second that the reason for Ruiz's disappearance would become clear as day if only she knew what the conference had been about, and that the mystery of the attempt on Palstein's life would be solved at the same time. She was *so* close!

And now Susan wanted to *talk*.

Listlessly, she typed a couple of sentences into the *Trash of the Titans* script on her laptop. Strictly speaking, she didn't even need Sina's help. Sitting here in Calgary, she could access the databases at Vancouver headquarters just as easily as she could reach her own computer back home in Juneau. If she wanted, she could *be* headquarters. She could have searched the network off her own bat. All that was keeping her playing by the rules was respect, and the fact that so far Susan Hudsucker had always covered her back when it came to it. So she was planning to bring the chief a good, well-researched treatment—for *Trash of the Titans, part 1: The Beginnings*—to sweeten her up before she wooed her over to her cause, setting out the facts that would force her to make Palstein a priority.

Loreena shut her laptop. She caught the eye of the Chinese waiter killing time behind the bar polishing glasses, and held up her empty glass to let him know that she wanted another Labatt Blue. It was oppressively empty here in the Keg Steakhouse and Bar at the Calgary Westin hotel. She was looking forward to a grilled salmon and a Caesar salad, and impatient for the intern to arrive. She was more and more cautious about eating with him, mind you, since she was afraid he could well explode, showering her with the vast quantities of sausage, steak, and scrambled eggs she had seen him shovel down in the past few days. On the other hand, the kid was good at what he did. He'd certainly have some information for her, when he did turn up.

The waiter brought her beer. Loreena was just about to take a sip when her phone rang.

"Good evening, Shax' saani Keek," said Gerald Palstein.

"Oh, Gerald," she replied, pleased. "How are you? Quite a coincidence you should call, we're just busy right now with your friend Gudmundsson. Have you slung him out yet?"

"Loreena—"

"Maybe we should keep an eye on him for a while first."

"Loreena, he's disappeared."

It took Loreena a moment to realize what Palstein had just said. She stood up, took her beer, left the bar, and found a private spot in the lobby.

"Gudmundsson has disappeared?" she asked, keeping her voice down.

"Him, and all his team," said Palstein, looking worried. "Since noon today. Nobody knows where. Eagle Eye can't reach him at any of his numbers, but I learned that one of your people had called them and had been asking about him."

Loreena hesitated. "If I'm going to find out who shot you, there's no getting past Gudmundsson."

"I'm not sure we still have a deal."

"One moment!" she yelped. "Just because—"

"No, you listen to me a moment, will you? You're not a professional investigator, Loreena. Don't get me wrong, I'm deeply indebted to you. I'd never have known otherwise that Gudmundsson was working against me! Believe me, I'll do everything I can to support your ecological reporting, that's one promise I will keep, but from now on you should leave all this detective work to the police."

"Gerald—"

"No." Palstein shook his head. "They've got you in their sights. Get out of their cross-hairs, Loreena, these are people who kill to get what they want."

"Gerald, have you ever wondered why you're still alive?"

"I was stupidly lucky, that's all."

"No, I mean why you're *still* alive. Perhaps it was never even about killing you. Perhaps you'd be alive now even if you *hadn't* stumbled on the podium like that."

"Do you mean—"

"Or perhaps they couldn't care either way. Think about it! Gudmundsson could have taken potshots at you a thousand times over by now, but instead you're running around without a care. I'm sure that the attack was simply intended to get you out of the way for a while."

"Hmm."

"All right, one small correction," she added. "If you hadn't stumbled, that bullet would have hit you in the head. But everything else is right, it *has* to be. Somebody wanted to stop you from doing something. My guess is stop you from flying to the Moon with Orley. And that worked, so why should they kill you now? Could be that Alejandro Ruiz wasn't so lucky—"

"Ruiz?"

"Strategic Director at Repsol."

"Slow down, my head's spinning. I really can't see any connection between myself and Ruiz."

"I can though," she breathed, looking around to see whether anyone was within earshot. "My God, Gerald! You're the Strategic Director of a company that has spent pretty nearly its whole existence doing exactly what you didn't want it to do. It was only when everything was far too late and it was all going downhill that they gave you the power to do anything, and there's hardly anything you can do. This is exactly how it was with Ruiz! He was a voice of conscience, he fouled their nest and got on their nerves. He kept up the pressure on Repsol to get into solar power, he wanted a partnership with Orley Enterprises just like you did! He was talking to a brick wall there. And all of a sudden, when the ship's already sinking, they make him Strategic Director. You and Ruiz both spent years arguing for a stake in alternative energy, you're ignored and then put on the throne, one of you gets shot, the other one disappears in Lima, and you don't see a connection?"

Palstein didn't answer.

"On September 1, 2022," Loreena went on, "the day before he flew to Lima, Ruiz took part in a mysterious conference somewhere near Beijing. Something must have happened there. Something that shook him so badly that his own wife barely recognized his voice. Does that ring any bells?"

"Yes. Warning bells."

"And what does that tell you?"

"That you're in danger. When you tell me all this, I actually think your suspicions are right. We can't ignore parallels like this."

"There you have it."

"And that's exactly why I'm worried." Palstein shook his head. "Please, Loreena. I don't want you to come to any harm because of me—"

"I'll be careful."

"*You'll* be careful?" He laughed harshly. "I was duped by my own bodyguard, and believe me, *I* was careful! Are you going to leave the detective work to the—"

"No, Gerald," she pleaded. "Twenty-four hours, give me twenty-four hours, every good thriller gives the detective twenty-four hours! I'm flying to Vancouver first thing tomorrow morning, then the whole thing goes up to boardroom level. All of Greenwatch will be working on the story. Tomorrow night I'll know what the conference was about, who Gudmundsson is really working for, and if I don't, I swear to you we'll bring the police on board. That's *my* promise to you, but *give me that much time.*"

Palstein looked at her with his sad eyes, and sighed.

"All right then. How many people have you shown those photographs to, of Gudmundsson and the Asian guy?"

"A few. Nobody recognizes Fatty."

"And this business with Ruiz?"

"Three, maybe four people know about it. I'm the only one who knows everything."

"Then do at least this much for me. Keep it that way until you land in Vancouver. In the meantime, don't go lifting up any more rocks."

"Hmm. Okay."

"Promise?" he asked, doubtful.

"Honest Injun. You know what that means, for me."

"Of course." He smiled. "Shax' saani Keek.'"

"Take care of yourself, Gerald."

"And call me when you get to Vancouver."

"I will do. First thing."

She hung up. The picture of Palstein faded out. Somewhat surprised, Loreena discovered that she found him oddly attractive, even if he was melancholic, in love with mathematics in that abstract way of his, a man who listened to weird music by dead avant-garde composers. On top of all which, he was shorter than her, a trim little man, almost skinny, losing his hair, the exact opposite of the broad-shouldered masculine type she usually went for. He had regular features, but they weren't especially striking; there was just something reassuring in his dark velvet eyes. She was back in the bar, still looking thoughtfully at the blank screen, when the chair across from her scraped noisily back.

"I'm dying of hunger here," said the intern. "Where's the menu?"

She put her phone away. "I hope you've been busy. Steaks for information. One to one."

"Should be enough here for two pounds of T-bone." He spread out a dozen sheets of paper in front of himself. "All right, watch this. I called Eagle Eye, the security company that provided Palstein's bodyguard. Dished them up a story about a journalist in peril, working on a sensitive story, needs protection, told them you'd just recently met Gudmundsson, Palstein had told you a lot of good things about him, yadda yadda yadda. They told me that Gudmundsson's a freelancer and fairly busy keeping an eye on the oilman, so they'd have to see whether he still had any spare capacity, if not, they could put together a tailor-made team for you. By the way, they knew about you."

Loreena raised her eyebrows. "Oh yes?"

"From the web. Your reportage. They were pretty taken with the idea of protecting Loreena Keowa."

"Flattering. Do they use a lot of freelancers?"

"Almost exclusively. Half of them are ex-police, the others are a mix of Navy SEALs, Army Rangers, and Green Berets, some of them were mercenaries, active right around the world. Then they use ex-secret service agents for logistics and information operations, they prefer CIA, Mossad, or the Germans. They tell me that the Bundesnachrichtendienst have excellent contacts, and the Israelis of course, but sometimes they even get guys from the KGB wandering into Eagle Eye, even Chinese or Koreans. If you ask, they'll give you the CV of any of their agents. They don't keep these things secret, quite the opposite! The career histories are part of their reputation."

"And Gudmundsson?"

"He's half Icelandic, hence the name. Grew up in Washington. Ex-Navy SEAL, trained as a sniper, he's got his hands dirty, you could say. When he was twenty-five he joined a mercenary army, Mamba."

"Never heard of them."

"They were operating in Kenya and Nigeria at the beginning of the century. Then he went on to a similar operation in West Africa called African Protection Services, APS for short."

"Hmm. Africa."

"Yes, but he's been back in the States for five years now. He offers his expertise to private security companies, Eagle Eye and others, usually as project manager."

Loreena thought it over. Africa? Was it important where Gudmundsson had worked before? What was certain was that he had betrayed one of his employer's clients. She couldn't rule out that Eagle Eye was involved there, but nor could she assume that that was the case. It was a well-respected company and their services were used by a lot of well-known figures. Interesting that Eagle Eye was already employing Gudmundsson at the time Ruiz disappeared. So what had Gudmundsson been doing on the night of the second to the third of September 2022? Where had he been the night Ruiz went missing? In Peru, perhaps?

"Was that all?" she asked. "Nothing else?"

"Hey, come on there, that's not bad."

"Might be enough for a roast potato." She grinned. "Okay, okay! And a couple of spare ribs."

May 30, 2025
Memory Crystal

BERLIN, GERMANY

Exobiologists had come up with scenarios for extraterrestrial life where you would least expect it. Weird forms of life thrived in volcanic vents, braved oceans of sulfur and ammonia, sprouted under the icy crust of frozen moons or glided with splendid lethargy through the banded skies of Jupiter, giant creatures with wings like manta rays, buoyed up by hydrogen in their body cavities that kept them from crashing down to the gas giant's metallic core.

At 06:30, one such creature was approaching Berlin.

Its skin shone in the cold, hard light of dawn as it curved slowly about and lost height. Its wingspan was almost 100 meters. Its body and wings flowed seamlessly together, ending in a tiny vestige of a head that seemed to point to only rudimentary intelligence, compared with the size of the whole thing. But appearances were deceptive. In fact, this head brought together the whole calculating capacity of four autonomous computer systems which kept the monstrous body aloft, all under the supervision of pilot and co-pilot.

It was an Air China flying wing, coming in to land at Berlin. There was room on board for around one thousand passengers. The engineers who had built it were fed up with screwing their lifting surfaces onto canisters, and instead had created a low, hollow, symmetrical craft packed with seating all the way to its wingtips, an aerodynamic miracle. The giant's engines were embedded in the stern. Because of the phenomenally large surface area, it generated thrust even at low engine speeds, while at the same time the ray-shaped wings made for increased lift and kept turbulence to a minimum. This reduced fuel consumption and kept engine noise to a socially acceptable sixty-three decibels. The designers had even done without windows for the sake of the aerodynamics. Instead, tiny cameras along the midline filmed the world outside and broadcast their pictures to 3D screens which simulated glass panes. Flying here was a feast for the senses. All the same, airsickness could strike those who had the cheap seats out in the wingtips, which could hop as much as 25 meters up and down when the aircraft banked, and bore the brunt of the turbulence.

By contrast, the man walking back to his seat from the on-board massage parlor with a spring in his step was enjoying the luxury of the Platinum Lounge. Here, the simulation showed him nothing less than the view from the cockpit, a fascinating panorama with perfect depth of field. He sank back into the cushions and shut his eyes. His seat was precisely on the aircraft's axis, which was a stroke of luck considering how late he had booked. For all that, the people who had booked the flight for him knew his preferences. Accordingly, they had made sure they made their own luck. They knew that rather than take a seat just next to the axis, he would prefer to travel in a wingtip—or in the basket of a hot-air balloon, be dangled from a Zeppelin's bag, or clutched in the claws of the roc bird. A middle seat was a middle seat, and not up for negotiation. The closer a thing was to perfection, the less he could bear falling short of that ideal, and something inside him pushed him to set things right right away.

He looked out at Berlin below him in the sunlight, surrounded by green spaces, rivers, sparkling lakes. Then the city itself, a jewel box containing many different epochs. Long shadows fell in the morning light. The flying wing banked in a one-hundred-eighty-degree curve, then fell to earth, speeding over the tower blocks, the public parks and avenues, dropping quickly. For a moment it looked from his exposed vantage point as though they were headed straight into the runway, then the pilot lifted the nose and they landed, almost imperceptibly.

The mood inside the aircraft changed subtly. For the last few hours the future had been in abeyance, a matter of aerodynamics and good will. Now it came rushing back to them with all its demands. Conversation broke out, newspapers and books were hastily put away, the aircraft came to rest. Huge hatched gateways opened to let the passengers flood out to all corners of the airport. The man picked up his hand luggage, and was one of the first to leave the plane. His data were already stored in the airport security system here. Air China had sent his files across to the German authorities not twenty minutes after takeoff in Pudong, and right now the footage from the on-board cameras was also being transmitted. As he neared the gates, the German computer already knew what he had eaten and drunk on board, which films he had watched, which stewardess he had flirted with and which he had complained to, and how often he had gone to the toilet. The system had his digital photograph, his voiceprint, his fingerprints, iris scan, and of course it knew his first stop in Berlin, the Hotel Adlon.

He put his phone and then the palm of his right hand onto the scanner plate, said his name, and looked into the camera at the automated gate while the computer read his RFID coordinates. The system compared the data, identified him, and let him through. Through the gates, the manned counters were lined up in a row. Two policewomen passed his luggage through the X-ray and asked him about the purpose of his visit. He answered in a cordial but somewhat distracted manner, as though his thoughts were elsewhere, at the next meeting. They wanted to know if this was his first time in Berlin. He said yes—and indeed he had never visited the city before. It was only when they handed back his phone that he let genuine warmth enter his voice, saying good-bye to them both and telling them he hoped they didn't have to spend their whole day standing behind this counter. As he spoke, he looked the younger policewoman straight in the eyes, wordlessly telling her that for his part, he wouldn't at all mind spending this lovely sunny Berlin morning with her.

A tiny, conspiratorial smile shot back at him, the most she would allow herself. You're a good-looking guy and no mistake, it said, and your suit is wonderfully well cut, we both know what we're after, thank you for the flowers, and now get lost. Meanwhile she said out loud, "Welcome to Berlin, Zhao *xiansheng*. Enjoy your visit."

He walked on, pleased that in this country they knew the proper forms of address. Ever since Chinese had become compulsory at most schools in Europe, travelers could at least be sure that traditional Chinese first names and family names wouldn't get mixed up, and that the family name would be followed by the right honorific. At the exit a pale, bald man with eyes like a St. Bernard and hangdog jowls was waiting for him. He was tall, strongly built, and wore his leather jacket fastened all the way to the neck.

"*Fáilte*, Kenny," he said softly.

"Mickey." Xin gave him a hearty clap on the shoulder in greeting without breaking stride. "How's the last remnants of the IRA?"

"Couple of them dead." The bald man fell in step beside him. "I hardly have contact with them these days. Which name did you fly in with?"

"Zhao Bide. Is everything organized?"

"All in place. Had a hell of a delay in Dublin, mind you. Didn't get in here until after midnight, what a shitty flight. Well, that's life, I suppose."

"And the guns?"

"Got them ready."

"Where?"

"In the car. Do you want to go to the hotel first? Or should we go straight to Muntu? It's still dark there, mind. So's the upstairs apartment. Probably still asleep."

Xin considered. Already, a week ago, once his people had cracked Vogelaar's new identity, Mickey Reardon had dropped by Muntu to check the place out for possible entrances. Alarm systems had been his specialty back in Northern Ireland. Since the IRA had fallen apart he, like many former members, was at work on the open market, and from time to time did jobs for foreign intelligence agencies as well, such as the Zhong Chan Er Bu. Ordinarily Xin liked to work with younger partners, but Mickey was in good shape even if he was in his late fifties; he knew his way around a gun and could navigate any electronic security system blindfolded. Xin had worked with him several times before, and in the end had recommended him to Hydra. Since then

Frank Schätzing

he'd been on Kenny's team. He might not be a towering intellect, but he didn't ask questions either.

"Off to the hotel quickly," Xin decided. "Then we'll get it over and done with." He squinted up into the sunlight and swept the long hair from his brow. "They say Berlin's very nice. Maybe it is. I still want to be out of here this evening at the latest, though."

But Jan Kees Vogelaar wasn't asleep.

He hadn't shut an eye all night, which was only partly to do with the headache left behind by Yoyo clouting him with a joint of meat. It was much more to do with talking to Nyela and agreeing on a plan to flee to France for the time being, where he had contacts with some retired Foreign Legionnaires. While Nyela began to pack, he organized their new identities. That evening Luc and Nadine Bombard, descended from French colonists out in Cameroon, would arrive in Paris.

At half past seven he called Leto, a friend of theirs, half Gabonese, who had come to Berlin a few years ago to help his white father fight his cancer. Nyela had met him the day before on the city's grand avenue, Unter den Linden. Leto had been in Mamba before the company joined the newly founded African Protection Services, and had helped them open Muntu. He was the only one in Germany they could trust, even if he didn't know all the details of why Vogelaar had had to get out of Equatorial Guinea. As far as he knew, Mayé had been toppled by Ndongo, financed by who knew which foreign powers. Vogelaar had avoided setting him right on the matter.

"We'll have to disappear," he said brusquely.

Leto had obviously just got out of bed to answer the call, but was so surprised he forgot to yawn.

"What do you mean, disappear?"

"Leave the country. They're onto us."

"Shit!"

"Yes, shit. Listen, can you do me a favor?"

"Of course."

"When the banks open in two hours' time I'm going to empty our accounts, and then I'll have a few things to take care of. Meanwhile Nyela will go downstairs to Muntu and pack whatever we can take from there. It would be good if you could keep her company there. Just to be on the safe side, until I'm back."

"Sure."

"Best thing is if you meet her up in the apartment."

"I'll do that. When do you want to leave?"

"Right after noon."

Leto fell silent for a moment.

"I don't understand it," he said. "Why don't they just leave you in peace? Ndongo's been back in power for a year now. You're hardly any threat to him any longer."

"He's probably still not got over me putsching him out of office back then," Vogelaar lied.

"That's ridiculous," Leto snorted. "It was Mayé. You simply got paid for it, it wasn't anything personal."

"All I need to know is that the goons have turned up here. Can you be with Nyela by half past eight?"

"Of course. No problem."

An hour and a half later Vogelaar flung himself into the stream of rush-hour traffic. The traffic lights took so long to change they seemed to be doing it out of spite. He crossed Französische Strasse, made it as far as Taubenstrasse, squeezed his Nissan into a tiny parking spot, and went into the foyer of his bank. The temple of capitalism was full to the brim. There was a huge crush in front of the self-service computers and the staffed windows, as though half of Berlin had decided to flee the city together with himself and Nyela. His personal banker was dealing with a red-faced old woman who kept pounding the flat of her hand against the counter in front of the window to punctuate her harangue; Vogelaar caught his eye, and gave him a signal to let him know he'd wait next door. He hurried over to the lounge, collapsed into one of the elegant leather armchairs, and fumed.

He'd wasted his time. Why hadn't he withdrawn the money the afternoon before?

Then he realized that by the time Jericho and his Chinese girlfriend had left, the banks were probably closed. Which didn't make him any less angry. Really, it was archaic that he had to hang around here like this. Banks were computerized businesses, it was only because he wanted to carry the money from his account home as cash that he needed to be physically present. Glowering, he ordered a cappuccino. He had hoped that his banker would call him in the next couple of minutes and ask him to come back to the foyer, but this hope was dashed to pieces under the red-faced woman's avalanche of words. All the other counters had lines snaking around them as well, mostly old people, very old some of them. The graying of Berlin seemed in full swing now; even in the moneyed boulevards a tide of worry backed up like stagnant water, the worry about old age and its insecurities.

To his surprise his telephone did ring, just as he raised the coffee to his lips. He got up, balancing the cup so that he could take it across with him, glanced at the display and saw that the call wasn't from the bank foyer at all. It was Nyela's number. He sat down again, picked up the call and spoke, expecting to see her face.

Instead, Leto was staring at him.

Right away he realized that something wasn't right. Leto seemed distraught about something. Not quite that. Rather, he looked as though he had got over whatever had upset him, and had decided to keep that look on his face to the end of his days. Then Vogelaar realized that the end had already come.

Leto was dead.

"Nyela? What's up? What's happened?"

Whoever was holding Nyela's phone stepped back, so that he could see all of Leto's upper body. He was leaning, slumped over the bar. A thin trickle of blood ran down his neck, as though embarrassed to be there.

"Don't worry, Jan. We killed him quite quietly. Don't want you getting into trouble with the neighbors."

The man who had spoken turned the phone toward himself.

"Kenny," Vogelaar whispered.

"Happy to see me?" Xin smirked at him. "You see, I was missing you. I spent a whole year wondering how the hell you managed to slip through my fingers."

"Where's Nyela?" Vogelaar heard himself ask, his voice dwindling and dropping.

"Wait, I'll hand you over. No, I'll show you her."

The picture lurched again and showed the restaurant. Nyela was sitting on a chair, a sculpture of sheer fear, her eyes open wide with terror. A pale, bald man clamped her tight to the chair, his arm stretched across her. He was holding a scalpel in his other hand. The tip of the blade hung motionless in the air, not a centimeter from Nyela's left eye.

"That's how things are," Xin's voice said.

Vogelaar heard himself make a choking noise. He couldn't remember ever having made a sound like that before.

"Don't do anything to her," he gasped. "Leave her alone."

"I wouldn't read too much into the situation," Xin said. "Mickey's very professional, he has a steady hand. He only gets twitchy if I do."

"What do I have to do? Tell me what I have to do."

"Take me seriously."

"I do, I take you seriously."

"Of course you do." Xin's voice suddenly changed, dark, hissing. "On the other hand, I know what you're capable of, Jan. You can't help yourself. Right now there's a thousand plans racing through your head, you're thinking how you could trick me.—But I don't want you to trick me. I don't want you even to try."

"I won't try."

"Now that would surprise me."

"You have my word."

"No. You won't really understand why you shouldn't even try until you've grasped the basic importance of saving your wife's sight."

The camera zoomed in closer. Nyela's face filled the screen, twisted with fear.

"Jan," she whimpered.

"Kenny, listen to me," Vogelaar whispered hoarsely. "I told you that you have my word! Stop all that, I—"

"One eye is quite enough for anyone to see with."

"Kenny—"

"So if you could grasp the importance of saving what *remains* of her sight, then—"

"Kenny, no!"

"Sorry, Jan. I'm getting twitchy."

Nyela's scream as the scalpel struck was a mere chirrup from the phone's speakers. But Vogelaar's yell split the air.

GRAND HYATT

Jericho blinked.

Something had woken him up. He turned on his side and glanced at the clock display. Almost ten! He hadn't intended to sleep this long. He leaped out of bed, heard the room's phone ringing, and picked up.

"I've got your money," Tu said. "One hundred thousand euros, just as our dog of war demands, not too many small-denomination notes, you'll be able to get through the museum door."

"Good," said Jericho.

"Are you coming down to breakfast?"

"Yes, I—Think I will."

"Come on then. Yoyo's making a spectacle of herself with the scrambled eggs. I'll keep some warm for you before she eats it all."

Yoyo.

Jericho hung up, went into the bathroom, and looked into the mirror. The blond man with the three-day beard who stared back at him was a fearless crime fighter who put his life on the line, but didn't know how to use a razor or even a comb. Who didn't even, come to think of it, have the decency to say No loud and clear, not even when he really wanted to say Yes. He had a nagging feeling that last night he had screwed everything up again, whatever "everything" meant here. Yoyo had come along to his room, drunk as a skunk but in a chatty mood, she could hardly have found her way there by accident, and she'd wanted to *talk*. The pimply kid inside him hated that idea. But what was talking, except a little ritual that might lead who knows where? It was person-to-person, it was open-ended. Anything could have happened, but he had taken umbrage and had let her scurry off, then stubbornly watched the remake of *Kill Bill* right to the end. It had been about as abysmally bad as he deserved. This arrested adolescence was like lying on a bed of nails, but at last he had fallen comatose into a restless sleep and dreamed of missing one train after another at shadowy stations, and running through a dreary Berlin no-man's-land where huge insects lurked in cavernous houses, chirruping like monstrous crickets. Antennae waved at him from every doorway and corner, chitinous limbs scuttled hastily back into the cracks in the wall in a game of half-hearted hide-and-seek.

Trains. What heavy-handed symbolism. How could he be having such ploddingly obvious dreams? He looked the blond man in the eyes, and imagined him simply turning away and walking off into the mirror, leaving him alone there in the bathroom, sick and tired of his inadequacies, the inadequacies of that pimply kid.

He had to get rid of the kid somehow. Anyhow. Enough was enough!

VOGELAAR

His shout burst through the lounge like a nuclear blast, tearing to shreds all conversation, all thought. Sleepy jazz muzak tinkled away in the sudden silence. On the low glass table in front of him, an abstract composition in coffee and foamed milk surrounded a jagged heap of shattered porcelain.

He stared at the display.

"Do you understand me?" Xin asked.

His knees gave way. Nyela's muffled sobs sounded in his ear as he sank back into the leather chair. Nothing had happened. The scalpel had not plunged into her eye, had not sliced through pupil and iris. It had simply twitched, and then stopped dead still once more.

"Yes," Vogelaar whispered. "I understand."

"Good. If you play by my rules, nothing will happen to her. As for what will happen to *you* though—"

"I understand." Vogelaar coughed. "Why all the extra effort?"

"Extra?"

"You could have killed me by now. As I left the building, on my drive across town, even here in the bank—"

The picture vanished, and then he saw Xin again.

"Quite simple," he said, back to his chatty old self. "Because you've never worked without a safety net and an escape hatch. You believe in life after death, or at least you believe in lawyers opening deposit boxes and releasing their contents to the press. You've made arrangements in case you die suddenly."

"Do you need help?"

Vogelaar looked up. One of the lounge staff, with a startled look on his face, a hint of disapproval. No screaming and shouting in banks. At most, they were places where you could contemplate a dignified suicide. Vogelaar shook his head.

"No, I—it's just that I've had some bad news."

"If there's anything that we can do—"

"It's a private matter."

The man smiled with relief. It wasn't about money. Someone had died, or had an accident.

"As I say, if—"

"Thank you."

The staffer left. Vogelaar watched him go, then got up and left the lounge hurriedly.

"Go on," he said into the phone.

"Your sort of insurance rather depends on the idea that if anyone's out to cause you harm, they'll go after *you*," Xin continued. "So you can warn them to keep their hands off. If I don't turn up to take afternoon tea tomorrow at such and such a time and place, with all my bits and pieces intact, the bomb goes off somewhere. It's a lone wolf strategy, because for most of your life you were a lone wolf.—But you're not any longer. Perhaps you should have changed your plans."

"I have."

"You haven't. That bomb will only be detonated if it's your life at stake."

"My life, and my wife's."

"Not exactly. You've changed your mind but you haven't changed your habits. Earlier you'd have said, get the hell back on the next plane out, Kenny, there's nothing you can do. Or, kill me and see what happens. But now you're telling me, leave Nyela alone or I'll make things hot for you."

"You can be sure of that!"

"Meaning that you could still set off the bomb." Xin paused. "But then what would we do with your poor innocent wife? Or to put it another way, how long would we do it to her for?"

Vogelaar had crossed the foyer, and went out into the crowds on Friedrichstrasse.

"That's enough, Kenny. I see what you mean."

"Really? Back when Vogelaar only cared about Vogelaar, life was hard for people like me. Back then you'd have said, go on, kill the woman, torture her to death, see where it gets you. We'd have played a little poker, and in the end you'd have won."

"I'm warning you. If you harm even a hair on Nyela's head—"

"Would you die for her?"

"Just come out with it and tell me what you want."

"I want an answer."

Vogelaar felt his mind soar, saw his whole life spread out beneath his wings. What he saw was a bug, biting, pinching, stinging, playing dead, or scuttling lightning-fast into a crack. A drone, a programmed thing, but one whose armor had been corroded these past few years by regular doses of empathy. His instincts had been ruined once he realized that there was in fact a purpose to life, that there could even be a purpose to dying so that others might live. Xin was right. His plans were out of date. This bug was sick and tired of creeping into cracks, but right now the future held nothing else.

"Yes," he said. "I would die for Nyela."

"Why?"

"To save her."

"No, Jan. You'd die because altruism is an egotist's crowning glory, and you're a deeply egotistical man. Nothing appeals more to a man's self-importance than martyrdom, and you've always had a very high sense of your own importance."

"Don't speechify, Kenny."

"You have to know that you won't save anyone with your death, not if you try to cheat. You'd be leaving Nyela on her own. There'd be no end to her suffering. You'd have achieved nothing."

"I understand."

"So what's your escape hatch this time?"

"A dossier."

"This is what Mayé wanted to blackmail us with?"

"Yes."

"Where?"

"In the Crystal Brain. It's on a memory crystal."

"Who knows about it?"

"Only my lawyer, and my wife."

"Nyela knows what's in the dossier?"

"Yes."

"And your lawyer?"

"He doesn't know a thing. He just has instructions to retrieve the crystal if I should die a violent death, and upload the contents to a distributor feed."

"Why didn't you tell him what was in the dossier?"

"Because it's got nothing to do with him," Vogelaar snorted, growing angry. "The dossier only exists to protect Nyela's life, and mine."

"That means that as soon as I have this crystal—Good, go get it. How long do you need?"

"An hour at most."

"Is there anyone coming by here before then we should know about? Cleaner, kitchen porter, postman?"

"No one."

"Off you go then, old friend. Don't dawdle now."

Vogelaar was no tree hugger. He drove a solar-powered Nissan because Nyela was concerned about the environment. He realized of course that more small cars meant less traffic in the city, but something in his genes cried out for a jeep. But now that he was crawling painfully through the government quarter, he cursed aloud every vehicle bigger than his own, and felt a sweeping rage against all the damned ignorant drivers hereabouts.

And in fact Germany was the country with the most innovative car technologies that had ever been left to slumber in a drawer. Hardly any market worldwide was fonder of gasoline motors and speedsters. While in Asia and the USA the number of hybrid cars on the roads had been steadily dropping in favor of ever more sustainable designs, in Germany the hybrid itself had never even made a dent. Nowhere else were hydrogen, fuel cells, and electric cars condemned to such a miserable waking death. And nowhere else in the world did men set such store by having a big, *imposing* car, and by driving it themselves— despite the availability of sophisticated and totally safe autopilots. It was as though whenever the Germanic national character set out to find itself, it always ended up, with tiresome predictability, behind the steering wheel. The only thing less popular hereabouts than the compact car was the future itself.

All of which explained why the Nissan crept along so slowly. Vogelaar swore, and slapped the wheel. When he finally turned into the parking garage at the Crystal Brain, he was bathed in sweat. He leaped from the cabin and strode hurriedly across to the main entrance.

Einstein looked him square in the face, briefly.

The building had been put up in 2020, not far from the government quarter, but it still looked as though it had just landed. It was a cubist glass UFO with dozens of perfectly faceted surfaces where the logo, *Crystal Brain*, came and went, glowing like a passing thought. Worlds showed like ghosts in the façade as you approached, different from every angle: raptors loping across the Jurassic savannah, stone-age hunters hurling their spears at mammoths, Assyrian kings holding court. He saw Greek hoplites, Roman emperors, Napoleon on horseback, and Egyptian princesses, pyramids and Gothic cathedrals, the *Kon-Tiki* and the *Titanic*, satellites, space stations, moon bases, the stern face of Abraham Lincoln, Shakespeare's bald head and smiling face, Bismarck, Niels Bohr, Werner Heisenberg, Konrad Adenauer, Marilyn Monroe, John Lennon, Mahatma Gandhi, Neil Armstrong, Nelson Mandela, Helmut Kohl, Bill Gates, the Dalai Lama, Thomas Reiter, Julian Orley, geocentric, heliocentric, and modern representations of the universe, abstract diagrams of quantum worlds on the Planck scale, molecules, atoms, quarks, and superstrings like model building blocks, the invention of the wheel, of printing, of curried sausage. All this and infinitely more was there, holographically embedded in the huge walls; it came to life, breathed, pulsated; the figures turned their heads, winked, smiled, shook hands, walked, flew, swam, and vanished again as the viewer moved around them. The exterior alone was a masterpiece, a wonder of the modern world, and yet it represented barely a fraction of what was hidden within.

When Vogelaar stepped inside the Crystal Brain, he was entering the world's largest concentration of knowledge in the smallest space.

He walked through the foyer's shimmering dome. Elevators rose and fell to either side of him, seemingly unsupported, a sophisticated optical illusion. They were a fractal representation of the building itself, just as everything in the Crystal Brain was built using the principle of self-similarity. The smallest component, the memory crystal, resembled the largest, the building itself. A crystal in a crystal in a crystal.

The world's memory.

The tales that mankind had to tell about the world could fit either in one single book, or into so many that even a whole extra planet full of libraries would not be enough to hold them. The Bible, the Qur'an, and the Torah knew nothing of evolution, or of the tangled chains of causality, or of Schrödinger's cat, nothing of the uncertainty principle or standard deviation, nothing of non-linear equations and black holes, nothing of the multiverse, of extra-dimensional space or of how time's arrow could be made to point backward. These books were sturdy, impregnable vehicles of faith driving down a one-way street to the absolute truth; they made vast claims, but they were compact.

Look beyond these, though, and the planet was bursting with information.

History alone was a vast academic discipline: millions and millions of works dedicated to deciphering the past, like a cloud chamber filled with the trails of fleeting elementary particles. It was almost impossible to determine their speed and direction, regardless whether they had to do with the color of Charlemagne's hair or with whether he had ever even existed. There was huge variety in the fields of physics, philosophy, futurology. The dizzying number of all articles published to date, all the essays, novellas, novels, poems, song lyrics, the works of Bob Dylan alone and then all the commentary about them! The verbiage of assembly instructions for stainless-steel barbecue grills, the meteorological data that had heaped up since records began, the collected speeches of the Dalai Lama, the totality of every menu from every Chinese restaurant from Cape Horn to the Bosphorus, the avaricious words from every one of Uncle Scrooge McDuck's speech balloons, the angry, exasperated replies that his hapless nephews quack in turn, the careful record of every leaflet from every packet sold of hemorrhoid cream or antidepressives . . .

There was definitely a storage problem.

The book was definitely not the answer.

But CD-ROMs, DVDs, and hard drives had also run up against the limits of their capacity, helpless in the face of the exponential growth of information. They were threatened by digital oblivion. Given how long chiseled stone slabs could last, Christianity could take comfort in the thought that the Ten Commandments still existed somewhere. Books could only last about two hundred years, unless they were printed with iron-free ink on acid-free paper, in which case their life expectancy was triple that. Celluloid film was estimated to last about four hundred years, CDs and DVDs maybe one hundred, while floppy discs lasted maybe a decade. Even so, floppies were still in theory better than USB sticks, which showed signs of amnesia after only three years, but then again there were no floppy disc drives any longer. There were thus three principal obstacles to a permanently accessible and truly compact global memory: limited storage capacity, rapid storage decay, rapid hardware obsolescence.

Holographics had solved all three problems in one blow.

The eight stories of the Crystal Brain housed racks of crystals and laser reading desks, roomy lounges for historical sightseers; it was an El Dorado for an alien who might happen along one day far in the future, clearing away the rampant vegetation in search of human artifacts. Vogelaar, though, blind to the glories around him, made for one of the elevators and rode it down to the second sub-basement, where storage space could be rented for private data. He authorized himself— eye scan, handprint, all the usual—and was let through to an atrium glowing with diffuse light.

"Number 17-44-27-15," he said.

The system asked him if he wanted a place at the lasers. Vogelaar declined, saying that he would take his data away with him.

"Aisle 17, section B-2," the system said. "Do you know your way around, or would you like directions?"

"I know my way."

"Please retrieve your crystal within five minutes."

A glass door slid back at the end of the atrium. Behind it, aisles branched off to either side, their walls apparently smooth and featureless. Lines ran along the floor, marked with aisle and section numbers. Vogelaar went to his aisle, stopped after a few steps, and turned his head to the left. Only the closest examination revealed that the mirror-smooth wall was in fact divided up into tiny squares.

"17-44-27-15 is being prepared for delivery," the system said.

A faint mechanical click sounded from the mirror. Then a thin, rectangular rod slid out. The transparent object inside was about the size of half a sugar cube. One of millions of crystals that made up the totality of the Crystal Brain, high-efficiency optical storage media with integrated data processing and encryption. They had no moving parts and were practically indestructible. Memory crystals had a storage capacity of one to five terabytes, and were readable at several gigabytes per second. Access time was well under a millisecond. The storage was written in by lasers, etching electronically readable data patterns into the layers of the crystal. A single layer could hold millions of bits; one crystal could hold thousands of pages. Vogelaar's dossier took up only a tiny fraction of that.

"Please remove your crystal."

Vogelaar looked at the tiny object and felt his mood plunge. Suddenly he was overcome by despair. He sank down against the wall opposite, unable to pick up the little cube.

How could it all have gone so horribly wrong?

It had all been in vain.

No, it hadn't. There was still a chance.

He considered just how far he could trust Xin. In fact, incredible though it might sound, he *could* trust the killer, to a certain extent, at least within Xin's own strictly defined limits of madness and self-control. Vogelaar didn't doubt for a moment that, in the final analysis, Kenny managed to keep his madness at bay with his manic penchant for numbers and symmetry, his constant search for oases of order and his highly personal code of honor. Xin knew perfectly well that he was mad. On the surface, he seemed eloquent, convivial and cultured. But Vogelaar had some idea of just how hard Xin found it to hold an ordinary conversation, and how hard he tried regardless. There must be some final scrap of humanity left alive inside him, a yearning that he could not admit even to himself, a need to be something other than what he was. Something that prevented him from simply gunning down anybody in his way, from setting the world on fire, from becoming the final all-engulfing flame. If he gave Xin this crystal, he would have to make a deal with him for Nyela's life and his own, although perhaps it would only be Nyela. One way or another, he'd have to decide whether he was going to give the killer everything, this dossier—

And the *copy* of the dossier.

"Please remove your crystal within the next sixty seconds."

He shrugged himself away from the wall, took the little cube between his finger and thumb, and held it up to the light. He could see tiny faultlines inside, history in miniature. He put it in his pocket. He left the basement as quickly as he had arrived, took the elevator upstairs, quickened his pace as he came out onto the parking garage, and started the Nissan. By some miracle the traffic had ebbed away, so that he was able to park in front of the restaurant before his time ran out. This time he didn't allow himself a moment's delay but got out and walked to the entrance with his hands raised, palms outward. He saw the bald man through the glass pane of the door, a silenced pistol in his right hand. Slowly, he opened the door and peered into the gloom. Leto's feet were sticking out from behind the bar.

"Where's Nyela?"

"Went in there with Kenny," said the bald man, in a thick Irish accent. He motioned with his gun toward the swing doors. Vogelaar didn't spare him a glance as he walked through the dining area and into the kitchen. The gunman followed.

"Jan!"

Nyela wanted to go to him. Xin held her back, a hand on her shoulder.

"Let her go," said Vogelaar.

"You can say hello later. What happened, Jan? Your kitchen looks like it was hit by a herd of elephants."

"I know." Vogelaar looked at the chaos left behind by his fight with Jericho, his face expressionless. "Do you want to clean up, Kenny? Put everything back? You'll find all you need under the sink: scourers, cleaning spray—I know that you can't bear to look at a mess."

"That's in my own world. This is yours. Where's the crystal?"

Vogelaar reached into his jacket pocket and put the memory crystal on a clear spot on the worktable. Xin picked it up in his fingertips and turned it this way and that.

"And you're sure that this is the right one?"

"Dead sure."

"I want to go to my husband," Nyela said, softly but emphatically. Her eyes looked sore from weeping, but she seemed to be keeping it together.

"Of course," Xin murmured. "Go to him."

He was gazing at the crystal as though under a spell. Vogelaar knew why. Crystals were one of those forms that Xin loved. Their structure and purity fascinated him.

"You've got what you wanted," he said. "I kept my promise."

Xin looked up. "And I never even gave one."

"What did you do then?"

"I was just talking through the options. It's really too risky to let the two of you live."

"That's not true."

"Jan, you disappoint me!"

"You promised to spare Nyela's life."

"Either he lets us both live or neither." She hugged herself close to Vogelaar's chest. "If he kills you, he can shoot me right away as well."

"No, Nyela." Vogelaar shook his head. "I won't let that—"

"Do you really believe that I'd just watch this bastard shoot you?" she hissed, her voice dripping with hate. "He's a monster. How many years he came and went at our home, accepted our drinks, put his feet up on our terrace. Hey, Kenny, do you want a drink? I'll mix you a drink that will make the flames shoot out of your eyes."

"Nyela—"

"You leave my husband alone, do you hear me?" Nyela screamed. "Don't touch him, or I'll come back from the dead to have my revenge, you miserable wretch, you—"

Xin's face clouded with resignation. He turned away, shaking his head, tired.

"Why does nobody listen to me?"

"What?"

"As if I had ever minced my words. As if the rules hadn't been clear from the start."

"We aren't here to follow your shitty rules!"

"They're not shitty," Xin sighed. "They're just—rules. A game. You played too. You made wrong moves. You lost. You have to know how to leave the game."

Vogelaar looked at him.

"You'll keep your promise," he said quietly.

"One more time, Jan, I never gave you a—"

"I mean the promise you're about to give."

"That I'm—about to?"

"Yes. You see, there's still something you want, Kenny. Something I can give you."

"What are you talking about?"

"I'm talking about Owen Jericho."

Xin spun about. "You know where Jericho is?"

"His life for Nyela's," Vogelaar said. "And spare me the rest of your threats. If we die, we die without a word.—Unless—"

"Unless what?"

"You promise to spare Nyela. Then I'll serve you up Jericho on a silver tray."

"No, Jan!" Nyela looked at him, pleading. "Without you I couldn't—"

"You wouldn't have to," Vogelaar said calmly. "The second promise concerns myself."

"Your life against whose?" Xin asked threateningly.

"A girl called Yoyo."

Xin stared at him. Then he began to laugh. Softly, almost silently. Then louder. Holding his sides, throwing back his head, hammering his fists against the tall fridge, quivering with hilarity as though he was having a fit.

"Incredible!" he gasped out. "Unbelievable."

"Is everything all right, Kenny?" The bald man furrowed his brow. "Are you okay?"

"All right?" spluttered Xin. "That girl, Mickey, that detective, the two of them should get a medal! What an achievement! They took those few scraps of text and—incredible, it's just incredible! They tracked you down, Jan, they—" He stopped. His eyes opened wide, even more astonished. "Did they actually come to *warn* you?"

"Yes, Kenny," Vogelaar said calmly. "They warned me."

"And you're betraying them?"

Vogelaar was silent.

"You try to find fault with my morals, you reproach me with some promise I've supposedly made, and then you rat out the people who came to save your life." Xin nodded as though he had just learned a valuable lesson. "Look at that, just look at that. Unredeemed man. What did you tell the two of them about our adventure in Africa?"

"Nothing."

"You're lying."

"I'd like to be," Vogelaar snarled. "In fact I offered them a deal. The dossier, for money. We were just about to make the exchange."

"That's priceless," chuckled Xin.

"And? What now?"

"Sorry, old friend." Xin wiped a tear of laughter from the corner of his eye. "Life doesn't offer all that many surprises, but this—and do you know what's the best thing about it? I even *considered* that they might come and find you! Just as you consider the possibility that *perhaps* next week you'll be hit by a meteorite, that *perhaps* there's a God. I fly off to Berlin in a tearing hurry to prevent something that I never really—never!—thought would actually happen, but life—Jan, my dear Jan! Life is just too wonderful. Too wonderful!"

"Get to the point, Kenny."

Xin threw his hands in the air in a gesture that said, let's all have a drink. A baron among his minions.

"Good!" he guffawed. "Why the hell not!"

"What does that mean?"

"It's a promise. It means you have my promise! If everything runs on rails, no hiccups, no tricks from you, not even *thinking* about tricks, not even a wrinkle in the skin—*then* the two of you can live." He came closer and narrowed his eyes. His voice took on that hissing note again. "But if, contrary to my expectations, *anything* from that dossier becomes public, then I promise that Nyela will die by inches, you can't even begin to imagine how! And you'll be allowed to watch. You'll see how I pull her teeth out one by one, see me cut off her fingers and toes, gouge out her eyes, I'll flay the skin from her back in strips, and all that while Mickey here rapes her over and over again until there's nothing left for him to fuck but a whimpering lump of bloody meat, and by then she's still *a long way* from dead, Jan, a *long* way, I promise you that; and I'll keep every one of *these* promises."

Vogelaar felt Xin's breath on his face, looked into those cold eyes, dark as night, felt Nyela tremble in his arms, heard his heartbeat in the sudden silence. He believed every word that Xin said.

With a dry crack, the faulty neon tube gave up the ghost.

"Sounds good," he said. "It's a deal."

Museum Island

In satellite images of Berlin, the Museum Island in the river Spree stuck out like a wedge, a kilometer and a half long, driven slapdash into the neatly laid parquetry of the city's boulevards. An ensemble of imposing buildings, linked by broad paths and walkways, housing exhibits from over six thousand years of world history. Visitors could pass from huge halls the size of cathedrals, through quiet cloisters, to great courtyards flooded with light, could get lost in the megalomaniac grandeur of ancient architecture or lose track of time in silent galleries full of more human-scale artworks. At the northern end of the island, the Bode Museum towered above the water like some baroque ocean liner, its columned prow crowned with a great dome, while at the southern end of the whole complex a Classicist façade churned out crowds of visitors in its wake. Most imposing of all was the Pergamon Museum, a vast building like something glimpsed in a dream—if a bewhiskered German patriot of the nineteenth century had nodded off dreaming over a book of Greek myth. A huge, glowering central hall was flanked by two identical wings to either side, colossal rows of pillars marching off to end in Doric temple façades. The ground plan had originally been a U-shape, but in 2015 a fourth wing had been added, glassed-in, that made the building into a square. Here, as in no other museum on Earth, visitors could walk through millennia of human history, Egyptian, Islamic, Near Eastern, and Roman.

Jericho had often crossed the island during trips to Berlin, taking one of the many bridges that moored it to the city, without ever having set foot in one of the museums. There had never been time. Now, as he hurried along the banks of the Spree, the thought that the time had finally come was not a cheering one. His jacket bulged with all the packets of money which made up Vogelaar's payment. His Glock was in its holster, invisible to all. He looked like any other tourist, but he felt like the proverbial goose, off to meet the fox for dinner. As long as Vogelaar actually had the dossier, the two of them would make the exchange quite quietly and calmly, cash for information, and be on their way. If he didn't, there would be trouble in store. The mercenary would want the money by hook or by crook, and he would certainly not rely on a smile and a kind word to get it.

Jericho felt his ear and slowed his pace.

The Pergamon Museum's temple façade seemed to stare at him, each window a watchful eye. In the fourth wing, crowds of culture vultures jostled along the glass hallway, among the last surviving traces of lost empires. He walked on, glancing at his watch. Quarter past eleven.

They had agreed on twelve o'clock, but Jericho wanted to get to know the museum first. On his right, a long, modern building abutted the rest, its lower story modeled after the older architecture while the top was a tall, airy colonnade: the James Simon Gallery, entrance to the museum island's web of walkways. Visitors bustled across to the island in a chattering, sweating throng. Jericho joined the crowd crossing this arm of the Spree and was carried along up a grandiose stairway to the top floor of the gallery. He bought his ticket in a spacious hall lined with terraces and cafés, and followed the signs for the Pergamon Museum.

His first impression as he entered the southern wing of the museum was that he had walked into nirvana. The only feature in the room which tied it to earthly time and space was the Romanesque arched window toward the river. The exhibits were lifted clean out of any historical context, displayed in a space so huge it could almost be hyperspace, and looked splendid yet lonely at one and the same time, a chilly, hypothetical view of history. Jericho turned right and walked along a kind of street, with walls on either side, its frieze and battlements glowing with rich color, reading the explanatory captions as he went. The animals in the frieze represented the Babylonian gods, with stately lions for Ishtar, goddess of love and protector of armies, serpentine dragons for Marduk, god of fertility and eternal life, patron of the city of Babylon, and wild bulls for Adad, lord of storms. Nebuchadnezzar II had ordered an inscription for the walls, reading "May ye walk in joy upon this Processional Way, oh ye gods." He could never have dreamed that the moment would come when groups of Japanese and Korean tourists would mill about in confusion here, losing their bearings amid the grandeur of the past, hurrying to catch up with the wrong tour guide, confused by identical tabards. There was a model of Babylon in a glass cube, with a truncated pyramid in the middle soaring heavenward; this was the ziggurat, the temple of Marduk. So that was where the God of the Old Testament had poured out his wrath, onto this surprisingly low tower, where he had confounded their language. Right then. This street had originally led to the ziggurat from the Ishtar Gate, which dominated the next hall, blue and yellow, glorious, shining like the sun, covered like the walls of the Way with the gods' totem animals. The mass of visitors crowding the Way gave some idea of what it must have been like here at the time of the great processions.

Rush hour in Babylon.

Jericho went through the gate of Babylon and emerged 660 years later from a Roman gate that took up the whole wall of the next hall: the Market Gate of Miletus, two stories high, a showpiece of transitional architecture, halfway between Hellenistic and Roman. He kept a constant lookout for exit routes. So far, it was easy to keep his bearings in the museum. The only thing that might slow him down was the density

of the crowd of visitors, moving only at glacial speeds. Next to him, a
Korean man was gesticulating furiously, telling his tour guide that he
had lost his wife to the Japanese, only to learn that *he* had ended up with
the Japanese. This was the modern equivalent of the Tower of Babel, with
languages mixing in confusion: the tourist group huddled into a knot.
Jericho edged his way around them and escaped to the next hall.

He knew where he was at once.

This was where Vogelaar had chosen for the meeting. The room was
the size of a hangar, but more than half of it was taken up by the front
of a colossal Roman temple. Even the stairway leading up to the colon-
nades had to be a good 20 meters wide. All around the base of the temple ran a comic strip in marble, twice the height of a man, which the
museum signs announced as the famous frieze of the Gigantomachy,
showing the story of the Greek gods' battle against the giants. It was the
tale of an attempted coup, making it the perfect place to meet Vogelaar: Zeus had slighted Gaia by imprisoning her monstrous children,
the Titans, in Tartarus—a sort of primordial Black Beach Prison. Gaia
was determined to free them from the underworld and get rid of the
hated father of the gods and all his corrupt crew, so she roused up to
rebellion her children who were still at liberty. These were the giants,
and Gaia knew that they could not be killed at the hands of a god.
The giants were well-known ruffians, and just to make them scarier,
they had giant snakes for legs. They leaped at the chance to protect their
mother's honor, and this gave Zeus the pretext to indulge in yet another
of his many dalliances with human women—*this is just a strategic move,
Hera, it's not how it looks!*—and to father Hercules, a mortal, who would
be able to sort the giants out. The giants put up a fight, chucking around
hilltops and tree trunks, so Athena rose to the challenge—*Anything
you can do, I can do better!*—and flung whole islands at them, burying
one of the ringleaders, Enkelados, under nothing less than Sicily; from
that moment on, the giant blew his fiery breath up through Etna, while
another, Mimas, was trapped beneath Vesuvius, and Poseidon scored a
square hit on a third giant with the island of Kos. Most of them, though,
succumbed to Hercules's poisoned arrows, until the whole serpent-
legged brood was exterminated. The frieze told the same old story, of a
struggle for power, with the same old weapons. Who were the Fang, who
were the Bubi, and who were the colonialists? Who bankrolled whom,
and why? Had there been a dossier back then as well, containing the
whole story, something like "The Truth about the Gigantomachy" or
"The Olympus Files"? A dossier like the one that the last surviving giant
from Equatorial Guinea claimed to have?

Jericho's gaze turned to the stairway.

There were three entrances to the pillared central hall, where the
altar had once stood. Vogelaar had said he'd be waiting there. He

climbed the gleaming marble steps, went through the columns, and found himself in a large, rectangular space, brightly lit, with another, smaller frieze running around its walls. From up here there was a good view of everything happening down at the bottom of the stairs, as long as you didn't mind being seen in turn. Further back in the room, and you were safely out of sight.

Jericho looked at his watch.

Half past eleven. Time to explore the rest of the museum.

He left the temple hall the other way and went into the north wing, where he found other examples of Hellenistic architecture. And what if Vogelaar *didn't* have a dossier? He paced along the façade of the Mshatta palace, a desert castle from the eighth century. He was increasingly worried that the whole thing might be a trap. Romanesque windows marked the end of the north wing, but he couldn't have said what he had seen in this part of the museum. As a scouting trip to learn the lie of the land, this was a wash-out. Stone faces stared down at him. He turned left. The way through to the fourth wing of the museum, the glass wing, led between rams and sphinxes, past pharaohs, through the temple gate from Kalabsha and beneath artifacts from the pyramid temple of Sahuré. Suddenly Jericho felt reminded of another glass corridor, the one where the ill-fated Grand Cherokee Wang had met Kenny Xin. An omen? With a grating sound, arms lifted, spear tips raised, granite fingers closed on the hilts of swords carved from stone. He went on, the daylight flooding in on him. To his right he could look through the windows that covered the whole wall, down to one of the bridges over this arm of the Spree, while to his left the inner courtyard of the museum stretched away. In front of him was an obelisk showing priest-kings gesturing strangely from the backs of glaring beasts, and in the corner was a statue of the weather god Hadad. Here the glass corridor joined the museum's south wing and completed the circuit, leading back to the Babylonian Processional Way.

Twenty to twelve.

He went into the Pergamon hall for the second time, and found it besieged by art students who had parked themselves on the landing with sketch pads and were beginning to turn the glories of antiquity into rough sketches for their own future careers. He started up the steps with a feeling of foreboding. In the inner courtyard with the Telephos frieze, visitors were shuffling from one marble fragment to the next, seeking history's secrets in the missing arms and noses. Jericho's head pounded as he paced among the crippled heroes, eavesdropping on a father who was lecturing his offspring in muffled tones, stifling whatever faint glimmer of interest they might ever have had in ancient sculpture. With every date he mentioned, the kids' frowns grew deeper. The look in their eyes spoke of honest bafflement—why were grown-ups so keen on broken statuary? How could anyone get through life without arms? Why not just fix the things? Their voices were older than their years as they feigned enthusiasm for smashed thighs, stone stumps, and the fragmentary face of a king, without hope of escape.

Without hope of escape—

That was it. Up here, he was trapped.

Pessimist, he scolded himself. They had saved Vogelaar's life, and furthermore the Telephos hall wasn't the kitchen at Muntu. The exchange would take place, swift and silent. The worst that could happen would be that the documents didn't contain what the seller claimed. He tried to relax, but his shoulders had frozen solid with tension. The father was doing his best to enthuse his children for the beauty of a right breast, floating free, which must, he explained, have been part of the lovely goddess Isis. Their eyes darted about, wondering what was lovely or beautiful here. Jericho turned away, glad all over again that he was no longer young.

VOGELAAR

His thoughts were a whirl. He was caught up on a merry-go-round of ifs and buts as his feet carried him mechanically along the Processional Way. *If* Jericho and the girl got there at the time agreed, *if* Xin kept to the arrangement, *if* he could actually trust the Chinese assassin— but what if he couldn't? Here and now, he was in danger of letting the last chance to free Nyela slip through his fingers, but she was in the clutches of a madman who quite possibly never even intended to let her, or him, live. He had decades of experience in finding his way out of tight spots, but it was no use. He was unarmed, he didn't even have a phone, in the middle of a crowded museum, and his chances of putting one over Xin were slim—but it wasn't impossible. Could he really afford not to use any tricks? Just how dangerous was this Mickey who was currently watching over Nyela? The Irishman gave the impression of being just another hapless career criminal, but if he worked for Xin, he had to be dangerous. Nevertheless Vogelaar reckoned he could get rid of the guy, but first of all he had to deal with Xin.

An attack then. Or not? In the next couple of minutes, before he reached the Pergamon hall. Unarmed and with no plan.

Not a glimmer!

No, he *couldn't* attack. The only way to get one over that madman was blind luck, but what if Xin actually intended to keep his promise? What if Vogelaar failed in his attempt to put one past him, and in failing, actually *caused* Nyela's death, not to mention his own?

Trick him? Trust him? Trick him?

Five minutes earlier, in the James Simon Gallery.

"I understand you," Xin says gently. "I wouldn't trust me either." He's close behind Vogelaar, the flechette pistol hidden under his jacket.

"And?" Vogelaar asks. "Would you be right?"

Xin considers for a moment.

"Have you ever got to grips with astrophysics?"

"There were other things in my life," Vogelaar snarls. "Coups, armed conflict—"

"A pity. You would understand me better. Physicists are concerned, among other things, with the parameters of a stable universe. Or indeed of any universe which could come into existence at all, as such. There's a long list of facts to deal with, but it all comes down to two different points of view. One of them says that the universe is infinitely stable, that it never even had any choice but to develop in the form in which we know it. If things had been different, perhaps no life would

Frank Schätzing

have been able to arise. Pondering such matters though is as pointless as wondering what your life might have been like if you'd been born a woman."

"Sounds fatalistic, boring."

"Philosophically speaking, I quite agree. Which is why the other camp likes to speak of the infinite fragility of the universe, of the fact that even the smallest variation in initial parameters could lead to fundamental changes. A tiny little bit more mass. Just a very few less of this or that elementary particle. The first camp say that all sounds too contingent, and they're right. But the second viewpoint does come closer to the way we imagine existence to be. What if . . . ? For myself, I prefer a vision of order and predictability, grounded in binding, non-negotiable parameters. And that's the spirit in which we made our agreement, you and I."

"Meaning that you can always come up with some reason you needn't keep your promise."

"You have a petty mind, if I may be so bold as to say so."

Vogelaar turns around and stares at him.

"Oh, I already see what you mean! I understand how you see yourself. Might the problem perhaps be that your—" he waved his hand in the air in a circle "—idea of universal order doesn't hold true for your fellow mortals?"

"What's up all of a sudden, Jan? You were calmer just a moment ago."

"I couldn't give a damn what you think about that! I want to hear you say that Nyela will be safe if I keep my side of the bargain."

"She's my guarantee that you'll keep it."

"And then?"

"As I have said before—"

"Say it again!"

"My goodness me, Jan! Truth doesn't become any more true just from being repeated." Xin sighs and looks up at the ceiling. "If you like, though. As long as Mickey's with her, Nyela's fine, she's safe. If everything else goes according to our agreement, nothing will happen to either of you. That's the deal. Are you content?"

"Partly. The devil never does anything without his reasons."

"I appreciate the flattery. Now do me a favor and move your ass."

The Market Gate of Miletus.

Xin's words in his ear. What if he turned around, right now, this moment? Ran through the museum full tilt, tried to reach the restaurant before him? That would definitely change the parameters! But to do that he would have to know exactly where Xin was. He had stayed behind as they went into the south wing. Vogelaar had turned around once to try to spot him, but hadn't been able to see him among the hordes of tour groups. He didn't doubt that the killer was watching his every step, but he also knew that from now on in, Xin would stay invisible until the time was ripe. Jericho and the girl were sitting in a trap in the Telephos hall. He would show up as though out of thin air, shoot twice—

Or would it be three times?

Trust him? Trick him?

Xin wasn't sane. He didn't live in the real world, he lived in some *abstraction* of reality. Which was actually a reason to trust him. His madness forced him to cling to order. Perhaps Xin wasn't even *able* to break a promise, as long as all the parameters were observed.

He shrugged his way through the crowds and approached the entrance to the Pergamon hall, a smaller gate in the Hellenistic façade, which was just now being cleaned and restored. To leave a clear view of the architecture, the museum had clad it with glass walls rather than shrouds. The glass reflected the spotlights from the ceiling, and the statues and the columns all around, the visitors, himself—

And someone else.

Vogelaar stared.

For the length of a heartbeat he was helpless against rising panic. Iron bands clamped his ribcage, and an electric field paralyzed his legs. Rage, hate, grief, and fear pooled like a thrombosis in his feet, which became numb, refused to take one more step. Instead of horror at all the things that could happen to Nyela, he felt the searing certainty of what had most probably already happened.

As long as Mickey's with her, Nyela's fine—

Then why was Mickey in the museum?

Because Nyela was no longer alive.

It could only be that. Would Xin have allowed her to stay in the restaurant unguarded? Vogelaar walked on as though drunk. He had failed. He had surrendered to the childish hope that the madman might keep his promises. Instead, Xin had ordered the Irishman to come along to the museum to share the work of killing. That was all. Just as Nyela had never had a chance, right from the start, he too would die along with Yoyo and Jericho, in the little room at the top of the temple, if not before.

The thought acted like an acid, dissolving his fears in a trice. Ice-cold rage flooded in instead. One by one, his survival mechanisms clicked into place, and he felt the metamorphosis, felt himself become once more the bug he had been for most of his life. He marched onward, chitin-clad, through the gate and into the Pergamon hall next door. Watchful, he waved his antennae, saw all the hall through faceted eyes: over there, at the opposite end of the great hall, another gate that was the partner of the one he had come through, tiny, almost ashamed to be so small but nevertheless bravely doing its work, one narrow little bypass in the flow of bodies through the museum, pumping tirelessly. To his left, isolated parts of the frieze standing alone on pillars and pedestals, to his right the temple with the stairway, up above the colonnade, leading through to the Telephos hall where Jericho and the girl would be, waiting for a dossier that they would never see now, that they would never need. It would have all been so simple, so quickly over and done with. He would have been a hundred thousand euros richer, and he would have handed them the second dossier. The duplicate that apart from him only Nyela had known about—

Had known?

How could he be *sure* that she was dead?

Because she was.

Wishful thinking. No part of a bug's existence.

Vogelaar's jaw worked back and forth. Platoons of tourists thronged the stairway to the colonnade, many sitting on the steps as though planning to have lunch there. Vogelaar spotted a younger group all armed with sketch pads and pencils, their faces fixed in concentration, rapt in their struggle with immortal art. A few curious passers-by were peering over their shoulders. He swept his eyes across the students, one by one, and stopped at a pale girl with a sharp nose who had gathered no admirers around her. He walked up to her, unhurried. On the white sheet of paper, Zeus fought the giant Porphyrion, and the two of them together fought the girl's artistic ineptitude, her inability to breathe life into the scene. She must have had a good twenty pencils in the case next to her, and the number was obviously inversely proportional to her talent. Clearly every euro of tip money from the evening job waiting tables went on her art supplies. She was throwing money away in the deluded belief that in art, having the right kit is half the struggle.

He leaned down to her and said in his friendliest voice, "Could you perhaps—excuse me!—lend me one of your pencils?"

She blinked up at him, startled.

"Just for a moment," he added quickly. "I want to jot something down. Forgot my pen, as always."

"Hmm, ye-e-es," she said, slowly, obviously upset at the thought that pencils might be used for writing as well. In the next moment she seemed to have come to terms with the idea. "Yes, of course! Pick any one."

"That's very kind of you."

He chose a long, neatly sharpened pencil which looked sturdier than the rest, and straightened up. Xin was watching him at this moment, he had no doubt. Xin saw everything and would draw his own conclusions from whatever Vogelaar did, meaning that he only had seconds.

He turned around, lightning-fast.

Mickey was only a few steps behind him, and stared at him like a surprised mastiff, then half-heartedly tried to hide behind a group of

Spanish-speaking pensioners. Vogelaar was at his side with just a few brisk paces. The Irishman fumbled at his hip with his right hand. Obviously Xin had never given him instructions against the event anything like this should happen, since he seemed absolutely flummoxed. His jowls wobbled with fury, his eyes darted hectically to and fro, sweat broke out on his pate.

Vogelaar put a hand to the back of his head, pulled him toward himself, and rammed the pencil into his right eye.

The Irishman gave a blood-curdling scream. He twitched, and blood spouted from the entry wound. Vogelaar pushed the flat of his hand more firmly against the end of the pencil, drove it deeper into the eye socket, felt the tip break through bone and enter the brain. Mickey slumped, his bowels and bladder emptying. Vogelaar felt for the killer's gun and tore it from the holster.

"Jericho!" he yelled.

STAMPEDE

Jericho had chosen to wait for the South African on the other side of the temple, hidden behind a phalanx of free-standing sculpture exhibits, uncomfortably aware that Vogelaar could get the drop on him. He was even more frightened by what he saw now. It was worse than any of the scenarios his overheated imagination had dreamed up over the past couple of hours, since it meant that the handover had failed. No doubt about it.

Everything was going horribly wrong. With his Glock in his right hand, he broke cover. Shock waves of horror and revulsion were spreading out from the scene of the attack; he could hear screams, shrieks, groans, noises that defied description. The immediate eyewitnesses had reeled back to form a kind of small arena, with Vogelaar and the bald man in the middle, like a pair of modern-day gladiators. Others had frozen with terror as though struck by a Gorgon's gaze, as motionless as the gods and giants all around. Pencils dropped from the art students' nerveless fingers. The girl with the sharp nose leaped up, bouncing on the balls of her feet like a rubber ball, and held her hands in front of her mouth as though trying to stop herself squeaking. Little yelps of fear slipped through her half-open lips, as regular as an alarm. Everywhere heads turned, eyes went wide with shock, people walked faster, groups broke apart. The fight-or-flight response was beginning to set in.

All structures were breaking down. And in the midst of it all, Jericho saw the angel of death.

He was running toward Vogelaar, who was buckling under his victim's weight. The dying man fell to the ground, dragging the South African with him. The angel was closing in from the northern wing, white-haired, ferociously mustached, his eyes hidden by tinted glasses, but the way he moved left no doubt as to his identity. Nor did the pistol that seemed to leap into his hand as he ran.

Vogelaar saw him coming as well.

Yelling, he managed to heave the bald man back up. The next moment the leather jacket covering his torso exploded, as the shots that had been meant for Vogelaar smacked into him. Jericho threw himself to the ground. Vogelaar struggled to shove the dead man aside and opened fire in turn on Xin, who took cover among the screaming, running crowd. A woman was hit in the shoulder and dropped to the ground.

"No point!" Jericho yelled. "Get out of here."

The South African kicked at the corpse, trying to get free. Jericho dragged him to his feet. With a sound like meat slapping down onto a butcher's block, Vogelaar's upper thigh burst open. He collapsed against Jericho and clutched him tight.

"Get to the restaurant," he gasped. "Nyela—"

Jericho grabbed him under the arms without letting go of the Glock. He was heavy, much too heavy. All hell was breaking loose around them.

"Pull yourself together," he grunted. "You've got to—"

Vogelaar stared at him. He sank slowly to the ground, and Jericho realized that Xin had shot him again. Panic swept over him. He scanned the crowd for the killer, spotted his shock of white hair. He only had moments before Xin would have another clear line of sight.

"Get up," he screamed. "Get going!"

Vogelaar slipped from his grasp. His face was going waxen, mask-like, horribly fast. He fell on his back, and a surge of bright red blood gushed from his mouth.

"Nyela—don't know if—probably dead, but—perhaps—"

"No," Jericho whispered. "You can't die on me—"

A few meters away, a man was lifted up and flung forward as though by a giant fist. He flew through the air and then crashed to the ground, spread-eagled.

Xin was clearing his way through.

Vogelaar, Jericho thought desperately, you can't just croak on me now, where's the dossier, you're our last hope, get up, for goodness' sake. Get up.—Get up!

Then he turned and ran as fast as he could.

Vogelaar stared into the light.

He had never been a religious man, and even now he found that the promise of heaven sounded tawdry and hollow. Why should every fool who'd ever drawn breath find their way to the Other Side? Religion was just one of those cracks this bug had never scuttled into. He couldn't understand a character like Cyrano de Bergerac, who had spent a lifetime scoffing at religion and then felt a pang of fear at the last moment, humbly seeking forgiveness on his deathbed in case there was a God after all. Life ended. Why waste what time was left to him believing in some paradise? This was only the neon, streaming white light down onto him from the ceiling, the artificial daylight of the museum hall. The white light that people spoke of after near-death experiences. The Hereafter, supposedly. In truth it was nothing but hallucinogenic tryptamine alkaloids flooding the brain.

How stupid of him not to have given Jericho the dossier! Done with now. Dead and gone. He felt a faint flicker of hope that he had been wrong about Nyela. Hope that she was still alive, that the detective could do something for her—if he got out alive. Otherwise, the situation was beyond his control, beyond his concern—but it wasn't the worst way to die, his last thoughts with the only person he had loved more than himself.

Now he was freed from his armor, his bug's shell. Free at last?

Xin came into view.

Gasping and grunting, Vogelaar lifted his gun, or rather strained every muscle to do so. He might just as well have been trying to fling a dumbbell at Xin. The pistol lay in his hand, heavy as lead. He only just had strength enough left to shoot daggers from his eyes.

The killer curled his lips contemptuously.

"Parameters, you idiot!" he said.

Xin shot Vogelaar in the chest and stalked on past without giving the dead man a second glance. Did he have any cause to reproach himself? Had it been a mistake to order Mickey along to the museum at the last moment, so that nothing went wrong this time? Vogelaar had spotted the Irishman, had drawn the wrong conclusion—and all this time Nyela was hanging from two pairs of handcuffs in the cellar at Muntu. Unharmed, as Xin had promised.

Hadn't he *said* that he'd let her live?

He'd done that, damn it!

Yes, he would have let them *both* live! He'd have been *happy* to let them live! Vogelaar hadn't understood anything, the stupid ape. Now it was all past help, the laws cried out for vengeance. Now he *had* to kill the woman. He'd promised *that*, too.

Xin began to run, driving the crowd before him like lowing cattle, dumb animals all trying to crush through the narrow gate at the same time. A girl in front of him stumbled and fell to the ground. He trampled her underfoot, flung another to the side, cracked the pistol grip against the side of an old man's head, fought his way through, charged like a battering ram at the ruck of fleeing tourists and plunged out the other side, his gaze fixed on the Market Gate of Miletus, where Jericho had just vanished through into the next wing. He squeezed off a burst of fire, sending splinters flying from two-thousand-year-old stone. People screamed, ran, flung themselves to the ground, the same old tiresome spectacle. Swinging his pistol like a club, he followed Jericho, saw him melt into the crowd of visitors thronging the Processional Way, and then in his place two uniformed figures ran out from a corridor off to the side, their weapons at the ready but without the first idea of who their enemy really was. He mowed them down without breaking stride. A bow wave of panic washed before him, all the way to Babylon.

Where was that blasted detective?

• • •

Jericho ran along the Processional Way.

How absurd it was to be running away with a loaded gun in his hand, instead of using it. But if he stopped, Xin would shoot him before he could even turn around and aim. The killer was trained to hit small targets and to use any window that presented itself. He swung his Glock like Moses swinging his staff, shouting "Get out of the way!," parting the sea of people, and ran to the black statue of Hadad, past grinning sculptures of crouching lions. The beasts looked as though they had poodles or mastiffs somewhere in their bloodline. Had the cultures of the ancient world ever even seen lions, or had they only existed in the limited imaginations of sculptors working to order? Perhaps they'd just been bad sculptors. Not everything that found its way into museums necessarily had to be any good. And what the hell was he thinking about, at a moment like this!

A family scattered to all sides in front of him.

Beyond Hadad, a row of tall, slender columns marched away meaninglessly, no longer supporting whatever it was they had once held up. Following an inner impulse, he flung himself to the right, heard the dull crack of a pistol being fired, and heard the shot thud into the storm god, ran toward the glassed fourth wing—

And stopped.

Stepping into that glass corridor meant that he would be trapped in the museum, running around the square all over again. He could get to the James Simon Gallery by going left here, and right now, just for a moment, he was out of Xin's sight—

He dropped to all fours like a dog, scuttled behind the pillars, seeking cover, then crept back the other way, and from the corner of his eye he saw Xin running into the glass hall. Jericho stuffed the Glock back into his pocket. From now on he was just one of many, trying like all the rest of them to avoid becoming a statistic on the evening news report. A tsunami of rumor and consternation swept through the museum entrance hall, so that nobody paid him any attention as he hurried outside, running rather than walking down the steps to the river. He crossed the bridge back where he had come this morning.

Nyela. The dossier.

He had to get to Muntu.

Things were calmer in the glass hall. Xin scanned the crowd for Jericho's blond hair. His pistol cast a spell of fearful silence on all around, but something was wrong. If Jericho had come through here before him, armed, shouting, running, people would be a lot less relaxed. Obviously they thought that he was a policeman of some kind, on patrol. He glanced along the corridor, its western wall glowing with noon sunlight. In front of him an obelisk from Sahuré's temple, the pharaohs on their plinths, the glowering temple gate of Kalabsha—he couldn't rule out that Jericho might have the nerve to be hiding behind any of these. He'd had ten seconds' head start, maximum, but enough to get behind one of the pharaohs.

And if he'd gone north—

No. Xin had seen him run in *here*.

Cautiously, he pushed on, taking shelter among the museum visitors—who were growing visibly more nervous. He aimed his gun behind plinths, pillars, façades, statues. Jericho had to be *somewhere* in this hall, but there were no shots, nobody broke cover to dash away, there was no headlong frontal assault. Meanwhile the tension was building up to open terror, worry tipped over into the fear that perhaps this man was a terrorist after all. Armed men would be turning up shortly, he was sure of that. If he didn't find the detective in a hurry, he'd have to disappear himself, leaving the job unfinished.

"Jericho!" he yelled.

His voice fell unheeded on the glass walls.

"Come on out. We'll talk."

No answer.

"I promise that we'll *talk*, do you hear me?"

Talk, then shoot, he thought, but all was silent. Obviously he hadn't expected Jericho to step out from the shadows with a look of cheery relief on his face, but what really enraged him was the total lack of any reaction—except, that is, that everyone around him was suddenly in a hurry to leave the wing. Seething, he stalked onward, saw a movement in among the pillars of the Kalabsha Gate, and fired. A Japanese tourist staggered out of the shadows, hands clutching her camera and a look of mild astonishment on her face. She took one last picture as if by reflex and then fell headlong. Panic spread, unleashing a stampede. Xin took advantage of the confusion, ran to the end of the hall, and looked wildly around to all sides.

"Jericho!" he shouted.

He ran back, stared down through the glass at the inner courtyard, turned his head. He could hear heavy boots approaching from the passage to the James Simon Gallery. His eye fell on the bridge leading away from the Pergamon Museum, swept along the pavement by the riverside—

There! Blond hair, Scandinavian almost, a good way off by now. Jericho was running as though there were devils after him, and Xin realized that the detective had tricked him. There was a crowd forming now between the statues of the pharaohs. Security personnel were trying to get through the rush of visitors coming the other way—and these guards had sub-machine guns. He had wasted too much time, shed too much blood to expect these new arrivals not to shoot first and ask questions later. He needed a hostage.

A girl slipped on the gallery's smooth polished floor.

With one leap, he was behind her, catching hold, hauling her up, and he pressed the muzzle of his pistol to her temple. The child froze and then began to cry. A young woman gave a piercing scream, stretched out her hands, but was knocked aside by others running to escape, and her husband grabbed hold of her, held her back from rushing to certain death. The next moment, uniformed figures took up positions on either side of the parents, calling out something in German. Xin didn't understand but he had a pretty shrewd idea of what they wanted. Without taking his eyes off them, he dragged the girl over to the tall windows and looked down to the bridge over the Spree, where by now a few gawkers had gathered.

He leaned down to the little girl.

"It'll all be all right," he said softly into her ear. "I promise." She didn't understand a word of Mandarin of course, but the sibilant syllables had their effect. Her little body relaxed as though hypnotized. She became calmer, breathing in short, shallow gasps like a rabbit.

"That's good," he whispered. "Don't be afraid."

"Marian!" Her mother screamed, raw misery in her voice. "Marian!"

"Marian," Xin repeated amiably. "That's a very pretty name."

He pulled the trigger.

Cries and shouts went up as the windowpane burst apart under the impact of dozens of flechette rounds. He had swung the pistol away at the last moment, lightning-fast. Splinters of glass flew around their ears. He shielded the girl from the shrapnel with his torso, then shoved her away, crossed his arms in front of his head and chest, and leaped out. While the officers were still trying to work out what had happened, he had landed catlike among the onlookers three meters below, and he began to run.

JERICHO

Muntu was closed. Hardly pausing, Jericho fired two shots into the lock and then kicked in the door. It slammed back against the wall inside. He rushed headlong into the dining area, looked behind the bar, and then jumped back: but the man staring at him with puzzlement in his eyes, a light-skinned African, was clearly dead. Yesterday's chaos reigned unchallenged in the kitchen. Nobody had cleaned up since his fight with Vogelaar.

There was no sign of Nyela.

Frantically, he charged through the beaded curtain, flung open both toilet doors, then tugged uselessly at the handle of a third door—*Private*, it said, and it was locked. He shot out this lock as well. Worn stairs led down into the darkness. A smell of mold, and disinfectants. The chalky smell of damp plaster. Memories of Shenzhen, the steps leading down to Hell. He hesitated. His hand fumbled for the light switch, found it. At the bottom of the stairs a light bulb glowed in its cage. Whitewashed plaster, a stained concrete floor, a spider scuttling away. He went down a step at a time, his Glock at the ready, his skin crawling, overcome by nausea. Kenny Xin. Animal Ma Liping. Who or what was awaiting him down below? What kind of creatures would leap out at him now, what images would burn their way into his brain?

He stepped off the last stair. He looked around. A short corridor, piled high with crates and barrels. A steel door, half open.

He went through, his gaze darting, gun ready.

Nyela!

She was squatting down on the floor with her arms behind her back, her mouth covered with tape. Her eyes glowed in the half-light. He hurried across to her, holstered his Glock, tore the tape away, and put his fingers to his lips. Not yet. First he had to get her out of the cuffs. Her jailers had locked her to the pipework, and he didn't imagine that the key would be lying about somewhere as a reward for keen-eyed detectives.

"I'll be right back," he whispered.

Back in the kitchen, he pulled open drawers, rummaged through the tools, steel, copper, chrome, looked around all the tabletops and finally found what he was looking for: a cleaver. He hurried back down to the cellar.

"Lean forward," he ordered. "I need some room."

Nyela nodded and turned away from him so that he had a good view of her hands. The pipe was worryingly short. Just a few centimeters from her wrists, it turned into the wall and vanished into the crumbling mortar. He took a deep breath, concentrated, and brought the blade down. The whole radiator sang like a struck bell. He frowned. There was a dent in the pipe, but otherwise nothing had changed. He struck again, and a third time, a fourth, until the pipe burst open, so that he could pry it apart with the handle of the cleaver. The chain of the cuffs scraped through the gap.

"Where—" Nyela began to ask.

"Over there." Jericho motioned with his chin, ordering her over to a metal worktable. "Back to the tabletop, palms down, as flat as you can. Pull the chain tight."

Nyela's features clouded over with a premonition of the dreadful news she knew she was about to receive. She did as he said, turning her hands about.

"Don't move," Jericho said. "Stay still, quite still."

She looked down at the floor. He fixed his eyes on the middle of the chain, and struck. One blow broke the chain.

"Now let's get out of here."

"No." She stood in his way. "Where's Jan? What happened?"

Jericho felt his tongue go numb.

"He's dead," he said.

Nyela looked at him. Whatever he had expected, bewilderment, shock, tears, didn't happen. Just a quiet grief, her love for the man who now lay dead in the museum, and at the same time a curious nonchalance, as though to say, there it is then, so it goes, it had to happen sometime. He hesitated, then hugged Nyela tight for a moment. She responded, a gentle embrace.

"I'll get you out of here," he promised.

"Yes," she said, tired, nodding. "I hear that a lot."

There was nobody upstairs, just the dead man staring out from behind the bar as though waiting for an explanation of what had happened to him. Jericho hurried to the closed door of the restaurant and peered outside.

"We'll have to run for it."

"Why?"

"My car's a few streets away."

"Mine isn't." Nyela leaned across the bar, opened a drawer, and took out a datastick. "Jan was using it earlier today. He must have parked it in front of Muntu."

Yoyo had spoken of a Nissan OneOne. There was just such a car, parked a few steps away, its legs drawn up. The cabin was egg-shaped, its design rather like a friendly little whale. The legs on either side were thick at the base, tapering toward the wheels. When the legs were stretched out flat, the cabin hung low to the ground, but if the driver drew in his wheels, the legs drew inward and upward, lifting the cabin. The low, aerodynamic profile, like a sports car, changed to become a compact, taller car. Jericho stepped out of the door and scanned the street. Shapes and colors seemed overexposed in the noonday sun. There was a smell of pollen, and of baking tarmac. There were hardly any pedestrians to be seen, but the traffic had picked up. He put his head back and looked up at a cigar-shaped tourist zeppelin that bumbled cheerfully into view, its engines droning.

"All clear," he called back inside. "Come on out."

The car roof reflected the sky, the clouds, and the buildings around, curving them into an Einsteinian space. Nyela unlocked the car, and the roof lifted like a hatch. The interior was surprisingly roomy, with a long bench right across it and extra folding seats.

"Where to?" she asked.

"The Grand Hyatt."

"Got you." She swung herself inside, and Jericho slid in next to her. He saw that the Nissan's steering column was adjustable. The whole thing could be swung across from the driver's side to the passenger's. The tinted glass filtered the harsher wavelengths out of the noonday light and created a cocoon-like atmosphere. The electric motor sprang to life, humming gently.

"Nyela, I—" Jericho massaged the bridge of his nose. "I have to ask you something."

She looked at him, the life draining from her eyes.

"What?"

"Your husband was going to give me a dossier."

"A—My God!" She pressed her hand to her mouth. "You don't have it? He couldn't even get the dossier to you?"

Jericho shook his head, silent.

"We could have blown the bastard's game for good and all!"

"He had it with him?"

"Not the one from the Crystal Brain, Kenny has that one, but—"

Of course he does, Jericho thought, tired.

"But the duplicate—"

"One moment!" Jericho grabbed her arm. "There's a duplicate?"

"He wanted to give it to you." She looked at him, pleading. "Believe me, Jan had no choice, he had to sacrifice you and the girl! That wasn't in his nature, he wouldn't have double-crossed you. He always—"

"*Where is it*, Nyela?"

"I thought he'd have told you."

"Told me what?" Jericho felt he was going mad. "Nyela, damn it all, where did he have—"

"Have, have!" She shook her head furiously, spread out her fingers. "You're asking the wrong questions. He *is* the duplicate!"

Jericho stared at her.

"What do you m—"

Her throat opened out in a red fan. Something warm sprayed out at him. He flung himself down onto Nyela's lap. Above him, the Nissan's cabin exploded, the foam seat stuffing splattered about his ears. Still bent down, he grabbed hold of the steering wheel, tugged it toward himself, revved up, and sped away. A salvo stitched through the car's carbon-fiber hull with a dry staccato. Jericho raised his head just far enough to see over the dashboard, then felt Nyela slump heavily against his shoulder, and he lost control. The car careened down the street, lurched into the opposite lane, and climbed the pavement, leaving the squeal of brakes and blare of horns in its wake. Pedestrians scattered. At the last moment, he wrenched the wheel to the left to come back across to his side of the street, almost colliding with a van. As the van swerved aside and rammed several parked cars, he bumped up onto the curb this side and steered for the Spree.

There, tall, white-haired, he saw the angel of death.

Xin fired as he ran, coming directly toward him. Jericho nudged the wheel again. The Nissan threatened to tip over, the cabin was too high up on its legs, the wheels too close together for maneuvers like this. He scanned the dashboard desperately. Xin had stopped to take aim. With a loud crack, part of the wrecked roof broke away. The Nissan raced toward Xin, and Jericho braced himself for an impact.

Xin leaped aside.

The car sped past him like a giant runaway pram. Xin fired after it, heard brakes squealing, dodged out of the path of a limousine by a hair's breadth, and stumbled across to the other lane, forcing a motor-cyclist to veer crazily. The bike skidded and slanted. Xin dodged away again, felt something brush against him, and he flew through the air; he slammed full length against the pavement, on his front. A compact car had struck him, and now the driver was roaring away. Other cars stopped, people climbed out. He rolled onto his back, moved his arms and legs, saw the motorcyclist running toward him, and fumbled for his pistol.

"Good God!" The man leaned over him. "What happened?" he asked in English. "Are you all right?"

Xin grabbed his gun and shoved it under the man's nose.

"Couldn't be better," he said.

The motorcyclist turned pale and scuttled backward. Xin leaped to his feet. A few steps took him to the bike, and he swung himself into the saddle and thrashed off toward the Spree, where he drew up, tires squealing, and looked about in all directions.

There! The Nissan. It ran a red light, vanished southward.

• • •

Jericho looked about and saw him coming.

He had gone the wrong way. The Audi was somewhere else entirely. He could have changed cars by now, got out of this wrecked Nissan and away from the dead woman. The corpse was flung about this way and that, and kept thumping against him. He looked all over the dashboard for the control that would let the legs down. Pretty nearly everything was controlled via the touchscreen, there must be some symbol somewhere there, but he couldn't concentrate. He kept having to dodge, swerve, brake, accelerate.

Xin was catching up.

Jericho rumbled along the promenade by the river, across the cobblestones, cut off a truck and emerged onto a majestic boulevard fringed with grand Prussian buildings. He tried to remember how to get to the hotel from here. Up on its stilts, the Nissan lurched from side to side, always threatening to tip over. All of a sudden he realized that he had no plan. Not a glimmer! He was racing through central Berlin in a wrecked compact car with a dead woman at his side, and Xin was after him, growing inexorably closer.

The traffic ground to a halt ahead. Jericho changed lanes. Another jam. Change again. A gap, a jam, a gap. Bumping from lane to lane like a pinball, he drove toward a huge equestrian statue which marked the beginning of a central island, planted with trees right down its length, a broad green lane dividing the traffic flows. He wrenched the wheel to the right, smashed into the curb, and climbed it. All of a sudden he was surrounded by pedestrians. He jammed the flat of his hand against the horn, veered about, frantically trying not to run anyone over, then the jam was past, and he slalomed back down onto the road. He was going too fast, and the wheels had no grip on the road surface. The car skidded across the crosswalk toward the central reservation, lost contact with the tarmac. On two wheels, he was racing toward the line of trees, and he threw his weight to the side. Something slammed. The car shuddered, leaped violently, bark scraped, huge clouds of dust billowed up. The central island stretching away in front of him was almost empty of people, flanked by linden trees and by benches. To either side the traffic blurred behind the thick green foliage, an impressionist smear of cars, buses, bicycle rickshaws, color, light, movement.

He glanced backward.

Xin's motorcycle was thrashing on under the low-hanging branches, hunting him like a beast of prey.

Jericho accelerated. More people suddenly. A café, shady, romantic, jutting out into the tree-lined walk. Yelled curses, shaken fists, scurrying backward. A kiosk with tall tables standing around, people playing pétanque. He was racing toward a crossroads, saw the traffic lights changing through a gap in the leaves, yellow, red, and then he was cutting under the noses of dozens of cars ready to move, and was on the next stretch of the central strip. The chorus of blaring horns died away behind him. Glance back, no sign of Xin. Jericho yelled hoarsely. Lost him! He'd shaken Xin off, at least for the moment. He'd won some time, valuable seconds, every second worth an eternity.

Suddenly, he also got his bearings back.

A snack bar blocked his way, but the traffic was thinner on both sides. Jericho steered the Nissan out of the shadow of the trees, back down onto the road, and saw it on the skyline ahead of him, the Brandenburg Gate, still some way off. Not for the first time, he felt surprised at how grand it looked in photographs and how small it really was. The Prussian-era courtyards and palaces were giving way now to modern architecture, the bistros and shops were ending, there were fewer pedestrians about. Soon enough the boulevard would end at Pariser Platz, with the Academy of Arts, the French Embassy, the American, and he hoped he could turn off there. North or south, and then—

Jericho squinted.

Something was going on up ahead. To his left, the trees had ended, so that he could see the whole width of the boulevard. Horrified, he saw that he was coming to a roadblock. Whole sections of the road were barricaded off. A monstrous robot was stretching out its cantilevered arm, lowering some huge, long object down to the road surface, and he could see Xin's motorcycle tearing toward him in his only remaining rearview mirror.

Jericho cursed. Whatever was being built up ahead had turned it into a blind alley for him. The construction robot was swinging an enormous steel girder slant-wise across the sidewalk and the road, while building workers waved away whatever cars had ended up here despite the road signs. There must have been announcements for the diversion, but of course he hadn't seen them because he'd been tearing down the central reservation, and now there was nowhere to turn aside to, the girder was sinking lower, Xin was coming closer, he was readying his gun—

Where was the control for the legs?

The first of the workers had turned around and spotted him, jumped aside. Shots slammed into the rear of the Nissan. If he braked now, Xin would blow his head off, and if he didn't, the girder would knock it clean off, nor could he turn around, he was going too fast, much too fast, and he couldn't find the icon on the touchscreen—

There! Not an icon at all, but a switch! A plain and simple, old-fashioned switch.

In a trice the Nissan had stretched out its wheels, becoming a low-slung, wide vehicle. The girder grew larger in front of Jericho's eyes, much too fast, dark, threatening, less than a meter and a half off the ground, a thick gray line, an end point. In a ridiculous reflex he lifted his arm up in front of his face as the cabin of his car sank further downward, then there was a splintering, crunching sound as the edge of the steel swept away what was left of the roof. He pressed himself down into his seat. As flat as a flounder, the car shot through beneath the girder; it was briefly night, then clear blue day again. The crossroads, a bus, an inevitable collision. As though a film had jumped frames, all of a sudden the Nissan was 2 meters further to the right, began to turn, skated across Pariser Platz, cyclists, pedestrians, the whole world running from him. Scrabbling to get the car back under control, he screeched toward the Brandenburg Gate. A police gyrocopter came into view above the bronze statue atop the Gate, an ultralight helicopter, half open, a loudspeaker voice booming down at him. His plan to speed through the Doric columns of the Gate and get away the other side was thwarted by a row of low posts that blocked any such attempt. He braked. The Nissan fishtailed, slid, crashed against the posts, and came to a stop. Next to him, Nyela seemed to want to say something. She straightened up, then her body was flung forward and back again into her seat, as though she had had second thoughts.

Jericho leaped clear of the wreckage.

The gyrocopter sank toward him. He ran for his life, under the Gate and through to the other side, where the boulevard continued, becoming a main road several lanes wide. Far off he could see a tall, slim column, and the road forked here just in front of the Gate. Without even looking at the traffic lights or signs, he hurried over a crosswalk. Brakes screamed, and there was a crash as somebody shunted the car in front. Weird. Were there really cars still on the road without proximity pilots? A superannuated convertible zipped under his nose, missing running over his feet by a hair's breadth, and he heard furious yelling. He started back, then sprinted, reaching the other side by dashing past a truck's radiator grille, and ran into a cool green passageway. This was the Tiergarten, the green park at the heart of Berlin. Sand, gravel, quiet pathways. In front of him was the statue of a lion. More trees, opening out into lawns, paths branching out in all directions. He raced down one, running, running, running until he could be sure that there was nobody following him, no Xin and no gyrocopter. He only stopped when he got to a small lake, and bent down with his hands on his knees, his sides aching, a sour taste on his tongue. He fought for breath. Gasped, spat, coughed. His heart was pounding like a battering ram. As though it wanted to break out of his ribcage.

An elderly lady looked across at him briefly, then turned her attention back to her little grandson, who was doing his best not to fall off his bike.

XIN

At last he had cleared the girder, but he had lost valuable time. He saw the Nissan racing away from him ahead, and he rode around the bus, leaning into the curve, taking aim. It looked as though the detective had lost control of the car. Good. Xin squeezed off a salvo just as a gyrocopter appeared above the Gate. To his astonishment, the police seemed to be paying more attention to his motorcycle than to Jericho, who at that moment jumped out of his car and ran away. The police dropped lower, faced the copter directly toward him; he heard shouted commands. He assessed the situation, thinking lightning-fast. The gyrocopter was still perhaps a meter above the ground. It was impossible to get past, and if he shot at the copter, the police would have no qualms about opening fire in return. He yanked his bike around and roared off along the street that crossed the boulevard.

The gyrocopter gave chase right away. As he sped over the next crossroads, something splattered onto the tarmac in front of him, swelled up, and set solid. They were firing foam cannons at him! One round of that in his spokes, and his ride would come to a sudden end. The stuff set lightning-fast and hard as rock. Xin swerved, saw how the road in front of him led up over a bridge, turned right instead, and found that he was back on the riverbank, on the Spree. If he hadn't lost his bearings, this should lead back to the Museum Island. Not a good idea to pop up there again, it must be crawling with police by now. He heard the dry clattering of the copter behind him, then above him, then ahead. The gyrocopter set down, forcing him to brake to a stop. He wheeled about, a breakneck turn, and raced off the other way, only to spot another police flyer hanging, apparently motionless, over the dome of the parliament building, the Reichstag. It shot toward him.

They had him trapped.

Xin thrashed his bike onward, headed for the Reichstag, the river to his right. Tourists were thronging up the grand stairway outside, and the promenade opened out. There was government architecture all along the river here, steel and glass dotted here and there with petite little trees, elegant topiary. Sightseeing boats chugged along the Spree, took a curve further along the river, and went under a filigree bridge.

And above everything, the two copters.

Xin aimed for the bridge. A group of young people scattered in front of his eyes. He revved hard, sat up on his back wheel, gunned the engine for all it was worth, and shot over the edge. For a moment the motorcycle hung above the water; the river below him was a sculpture of glass, the gyrocopters hung in the sky as though nailed there. Xin felt a pleasant

breeze on his skin, an intimation of what it would be like to live a completely different life, but there was no other that he could live.

He took his hands from the handlebars.

The surface splintered into kaleidoscopes, water thumped in his
ears. He tried to get away from the sinking bike as fast as he could. The
front wheel caught him a blow across the hip. He ignored the pain,
surfaced, pumped his lungs full of air, and dived again, deep enough
not to be seen from the air. With powerful strokes, he made for mid-
stream, one of the tourist boats thrumming above him. He had been
trained to stay underwater for a long while, but he would have to surface sooner or later, and he had two copters to deal with. They would
split up, one of them looking for him upstream, one downstream. His
reflexes racing, he saw the dark bulk of the sightseeing boat moving
away above him, and kicked his way up. He surfaced with his head
just by the stern of the boat, which sat low enough in the water that he
could grab one of the stanchions down by the windows. He slipped,
grabbed hold again, clung tight, and peered up into the sky, partly
obscured by the boat's deck and viewing platforms.

One of the gyrocopters was circling over the spot where he had
gone under. He could hear the other one, but not see it. In the next
moment it appeared, directly over the ship, and Xin slipped underwater again without letting go of the stanchion. He held his breath for as
long as he could. When he risked another look, they were just passing
under a bridge.

The copter was moving away.

He let the boat carry him along for a little while longer, then pushed
away, swam to the bank, and hauled himself up. There was a concrete
embankment in front of him, with a busy road running beyond it. As
far as he could see, the police were still searching on the other side of
the bridge. He felt for his wig, but it was on the bottom of the Spree
by now. He quickly tore off the false beard, peeled off his jacket, left
everything there in the water, and crept ashore, dripping wet. He had
lost his gun as well, but had been able to keep hold of his phone, which
was waterproof, thank God. He felt the reassuring grip of the money
belt around his waist that held credit cards and the memory crystal.
Xin made a point of carrying credit cards around with him, even if
they were reckoned to be old-fashioned and everybody made purchases using the ID codes in their phones. He didn't like to show up on
records when he went clothes shopping though.

Not far away was an express railway, up on its viaduct. He glanced
up and down the street. It curved away to a building with a glass dome
and gleaming blocks clustered about it, which had to be Berlin's main
railway station. He rolled up his shirtsleeves, swept back his smooth,
dark hair, and walked along the street, quickly but without haste.

Traffic streamed past him. He saw another gyrocopter a little way off, but since by now he hardly matched the description of the man the police were looking for, he felt fairly safe. He resisted the impulse to quicken his pace. In ten minutes he had reached the station concourse, and took cash from an ATM with one of his cards. He found a leisurewear store and bought jeans, sneakers, and a T-shirt. The salesgirl, studded with appliqués, looked at him in astonishment. He dressed in the clothes that he had bought and asked the salesgirl for a plastic bag. He paid cash, stuffed his wet clothes into the bag, and then dropped it into a sidewalk garbage container outside, and went back to the Hotel Adlon by taxi.

JERICHO

As far as he remembered, the Hyatt was south of the Tiergarten Park, but then he lost his bearings among all the forked paths and duck ponds, and wandered from one idyllic glade to the next. He could hear traffic sounds some indefinable way off. The sun shone down on him, unnaturally bright. He was overcome by nausea, stitches yanked at his ribs, there was a pain spreading down from his shoulder to his left arm. The sky, the trees, the people around were all sucked into a red tunnel. Was this what a heart attack felt like? He stumbled across to a bush, his knees weak as wax, and threw up. After that he felt better, and he made it as far as the main road. At a crossroads he recognized several of the buildings, saw a Keith Haring sculpture and realized that the Grand Hyatt was just around the corner. He could have sworn that he'd been in the park for hours, but when he looked at his watch, he saw that not even fifteen minutes had passed since he had crashed at the Brandenburg Gate. It was just before half past twelve.

He called Tu.

"We're upstairs in your room. Yoyo and I—"

"Stay there. I'm coming up."

Since Diane was in Jericho's room they had made it their command center, so as to be able to research further and keep trying to decrypt more messages. In the elevator, his thoughts shifted gear, becoming inordinately clear, self-aware. He hadn't often been so completely at a loss. So incapable of acting. Nyela had been as good as safe, and he had still lost her.

"What happened?" Tu jumped to his feet and came toward him. "Is everything—"

"No." Jericho reached into his jacket, fished out the packages of money and threw them onto the bed. "Here's your money back. That's all the good news there is."

Tu picked up one of the packages and shook his head.

"That's not good news."

"It's not." In curt sentences, he described how events had unfolded. Striving to remain objective, he only managed to make the whole story sound more dreadful. Yoyo grew paler with every word.

"Nyela," she whispered. "Whatever have we done?"

"Nothing." He rubbed his hands over his face, tired, dispirited. "It would have happened one way or another all the same. All we did was keep her alive a couple of minutes longer."

"No dossier." Her face clouded over. "All for nothing."

"According to Nyela, he must have been carrying it around with him!" Jericho walked over to the window and stared out, seeing nothing. "Vogelaar had sold us out to Xin, but he was trying to turn the tables one more time. At the last moment, whatever it was that moved him to do so. He *wanted* me to have that dossier."

"Curses and maledictions." Tu punched a fist into the palm of his other hand. "And Nyela's quite sure—"

"*Was* sure, Tian. She was sure."

"—that he had it with him? She specifically said—"

"She said that Kenny had got hold of the original."

"The memory crystal."

"Yes. But apparently there was a duplicate."

"Which Vogelaar was going to bring into the museum."

"Wait a moment." Yoyo frowned. "That means that he still has it on him?"

"Irrelevant." Jericho pressed two fingers against his brow. Now they really were at a dead end. "The police will have taken it as evidence. But good, that means we have nothing more to decide. From now on, we aren't working on our own anymore. I imagine we can trust the local authorities here, so that means—"

He stopped.

He heard Tu speaking as though through cotton balls, heard him saying something about surveillance cameras that would have got his picture in the museum, that they would have put his picture out on the wanted list by now, that you couldn't trust the authorities anywhere in this world. But more clearly, more meaningfully now, he heard again the last words that Nyela had ever spoken:

You're asking the wrong questions. He is the duplicate!

He *is* the duplicate?

"My God, how simple," he whispered.

"What's simple?" Tu asked, baffled.

He turned around. Both of them stared at him. There it was again, his assurance, that he thought he had lost.

"I think I know where Vogelaar hid his dossier."

ADLON

Xin took out the memory crystal, turned it between his fingers, and smiled. Useless knowledge. All in all, he could rest content. Paying no attention to the grand interior, he strode across the hotel lobby, went up to his suite, and tried his phone before anything else. The manufacturer's guarantee said that it was waterproof up to 20 meters, and indeed it was working as well as ever. Looking at the display, he saw that his contact had been trying to reach him, just before he had got his sights on Vogelaar.

"Hydra," he said.

His voice was recorded, checked, ID'd.

"Orley have received a warning," his contact announced.

"What?" Xin exploded. "When?"

"Yesterday, late afternoon."

"Details?"

"Someone named Tu sent across a document. It was obviously a fragment of your message." The other man drew a deep breath. "Kenny, they must have been able to decipher more as well! How could that happen, I thought—"

"What do you mean?" Xin began to pace up and down the room. "What sort of fragment?"

"I don't know yet."

"Then I'm telling you this: you'll take all of our pages down from the web."

"If we do that, our whole e-mail communication breaks down."

"You've tried that argument on me before."

"And I was right."

"Yes, and look where it got you." Xin tried to calm down. He opened the minibar's fridge and mechanically began to shift the bottles until they were exactly the same distance apart. "The e-mail idea was good for exchanging complex information and for using the global server; phones are enough for everything else. The die is cast. We can't change anything now anyway. The only thing that could still go wrong would be if my message were cracked completely, so take the pages down from the web!" He paused. "Have you already told *him*?"

"He knows."

"And?"

The other man sighed. "He agrees with you. He thinks we should block the pages too, so I'll do what's needed. Your turn now. What's happening with Vogelaar?"

"He's been dealt with."

"No more danger?"

"He had created a dossier. Memory crystal. I've got the thing now. His wife was the only one who knew all about it, she's dead too."

"Good news there for a change, Kenny."

"I wish I could say the same about yours," Xin snapped. "Why am I just hearing about this warning now?"

"Because I only learned about it myself this morning."

"How did the company react?"

"They called Gaia."

"What?" Xin practically dropped the telephone. "They've told Gaia?"

"Calm down. Probably because it's in the news just now. As far as I know everything's running to plan, they haven't cancelled any of the trips, nobody wants to leave early."

"And who took the call at Gaia?"

"I'm expecting more details any moment."

Xin stared into the fridge.

"Well fine," he said. "Find out something for me in the meantime, and fast. Find Yoyo and Jericho in Berlin."

"What? They're in *Berlin*?"

"They must be staying somewhere. Hack into the hotel booking systems, the immigration databases, I don't care how you do it but find them."

"Dear God," the other man groaned.

"What's up?" Xin asked threateningly. "Are you losing your nerve?"

"No, that's no problem. Okay then. I'll do what I can."

"No," Xin snarled. "You'll do more than that."

HYATT

Just before Xin shot her, Nyela had spread her fingers as though to emphasize what she was saying. He had thought that it was only a gesture of exasperation, but in fact she'd been doing something different. She had been pointing to her face, and at that moment, it was supposed to be Vogelaar's face. She had been pointing to her eyes.

He is the duplicate!

Vogelaar's glass eye was a memory crystal. He carried the duplicate around with him, in his eye-socket.

"What a sly fox," Yoyo said, half admiring, half disgusted.

Tu snorted with laughter. "He could hardly have found a better place for it. An eye for the facts."

"So that they come to light once he dies." Yoyo had more color in her face now. Jericho remembered last night. Not ten hours had passed since she had left his room with sunken, hollow eyes, looking dissolute, flushed, blotchy, stinking of cigarette smoke and red wine. She had gone pale again now—after all, life was playing them one dirty trick after another—but other than that, the night's excesses hadn't left a mark on her. Yoyo looked fresh, smooth-skinned and perky, practically rejuvenated. Jericho was depressed by what this said about youth and intoxicants. For himself, when he'd been drinking the night away, the enzymes only ever worked fitfully, at best, at patching him up again.

"You know this sort of thing, Owen," Tu said. "What happens during a forensic autopsy? Will they look at the glass eye as well?"

"They'll certainly remove it while they work."

"And a memory crystal would stand out?"

"Anybody with medical training would certainly notice," Yoyo said. "Assuming that Owen's right, then the police will have our dossier in their hands in the next few hours."

Jericho rubbed his chin. He didn't much like the idea of tangling with the German police. They'd be interrogated for hours, treated with suspicion, quite likely they'd never get a look at Vogelaar's data. Their own investigation would slow down to a crawl.

Tu handed him a printout.

"Perhaps you should have a look at what we found out while you were away. We've bolded everything that's new."

Jan Kees Vogelaar is living in Berlin under the name Andre Donner, where he runs an African private and business address: Oranienburger Strasse 50, 10117 Berlin. What should we continues to represent a grave risk to the operation not doubt that he knows all about the **payload** *rockets. knows at least about the but some doubt as to whether. One way or another any statement lasting Admittedly, since his **Vogelaar has made** no public comment about the facts behind the coup. Nevertheless Ndongo's that the Chinese government planned and implemented regime change. Vogelaar has little about the nature of Operation **insight** of timing Furthermore, Orley Enterprises and have no reason to suspect disruption. Nobody there suspects **and by then** everything **is underway**. I count because I know, Nevertheless urgently recommend that Donner be liquidated. There are good reasons to*

"Payload rockets." Jericho looked up. "That's another thing that supports what Vogelaar said. That satellite launch was about more than just an experimental rocket."

"A payload rocket has to be delivering something," Tu said. "How did Mayé's satellite get up into orbit?"

"Payload rocket," Jericho suggested. "They're called carrier rockets as well, I think."

"But there's nothing here about a satellite."

"No. Looks like it has nothing to do with the satellite. It's about some other payload."

Tu nodded. "I took the opportunity to talk to some people who my people have helped out in the past. I couldn't get any definite information, but they gave me some well-founded supposition. Apparently, the Chinese government has never launched its own space projects from foreign soil. That story about wanting to avoid the insurance treaties is as threadbare as Chairman Mao's shroud. The whole thing must have been dreamed up for Mayé's benefit; at any rate it doesn't accord with current practice to shuffle the risk onto other states like that."

"So it could have been something that Zheng was doing on his own account?"

"There's no record of the Zheng Group having been active in Africa anywhere but in Equatorial Guinea, that one time. It looks doubtful that they were acting for Beijing. My informants don't think so. So did the Chinese government have anything to do with the Equatorial Guinea space program, or with the coup against Mayé? Yes, if you are working on the premise that people like Zheng Pang-Wang *are* the government. Not if we're talking about the government as such."

"Which proves again that the Party is just a pretext, a phantom," Yoyo said contemptuously. "There's no dividing line between politics and business any longer. The State can't be trusted to act in State interests. China's oilmen putsched Mayé into power, the Zhong Chan Er Bu helped them, and the whole Party knows it. Could be that Zheng putsched him out again afterward. He's our biggest industrialist, a power in his own right."

"And the Party wouldn't have known about that."

"Quite so." Yoyo tapped the page. "And then further down: *Nobody there suspects*—what? Something or other. The *everything* turns out to go with the next bit of the sentence. *Everything is underway.* They sit there and debate whether it's even worthwhile getting rid of Vogelaar at this stage. I don't know about you, but to me that sounds as though the balloon's about to go up."

"Any ideas about the bit before that?"

"Vogelaar didn't know about the timing any more than the nature of the operation." Tu shrugged. "I don't think any of it gets us anywhere."

"Well that's great," Jericho said. "We're stuck."

Yoyo toppled backward onto the bed, her arms spread wide. Then she sat up suddenly.

"How does that work with Vogelaar, exactly?"

"What do you mean?" Jericho blinked, confused. "How does what work?"

"Well, right now." She pursed her lips. "Or let's go back an hour. Twelve o'clock. Blam. Blam! Vogelaar's shot, he's lying dead in the museum. What happens next?"

"A specialist police team arrives. The scene of the crime is secured, then forensics get to work."

"What happens to the corpse?"

"Right now, it'll still be there. Forensics work takes time. Then it'll be on the autopsy table at, say, two o'clock at the latest, then they'll cut him open, snip snap."

"And the eye?"

"Depends. The forensic surgeon isn't an investigating officer himself, it's a bit different from how you might have seen it at the movies. He just makes a note of everything worth handing over to the investigating team. Assuming that he notices anything odd about the eye, he'll put it in his report. Maybe he'll put it back into the socket, maybe he'll put it aside as evidence."

"How long does an autopsy take?"

"Depends on the case. There'll be no doubt here about the cause of death, Vogelaar was shot, so it'll be quick. They'll be done in two or three hours."

"And then?"

"The forensic surgeon will sign the corpse over." Jericho gave a wry grin. "You can pick it up, if you bring a hearse."

"Good. We'll go get it."

"Great plan." Tu stared at her. "Where are you going to get a hearse?"

"No idea. Since when have we been scared of a challenge?"

"We're not, but—"

"Why do we even need a *hearse*?" Yoyo sat up straight now, all vim and vigor. "Why not go and get him in an ordinary car? What if we were next of kin?"

"Well, sure," Tu said mockingly. "You could easily be his sister. The hair, the eyes—"

"Hold on!" Jericho raised a hand. "First off, we wouldn't get anywhere without a hearse. Secondly, if they've taken the eye, Vogelaar's corpse will be no use to you at all."

Yoyo's burst of energy melted away. She folded her arms and frowned despondently.

"Thirdly," Jericho said, "that's still a good idea you had there."

Tu narrowed his eyes. "What are you thinking of doing?"

"Me?" Jericho shrugged. "Nothing. Probably I daren't even show my face any more in Berlin, they'll pick me up on the spot. My hands are tied." He smiled grimly. "Yours aren't though."

Charité Hospital, Institute
of Forensic Pathology

Around three o'clock, Jan Kees Vogelaar was looking fairly good. Granted, his face was waxy and he was dead as a doornail, but he wore a proud sneer on his face that seemed to say, kiss my ass. A few hours ago he had been lying in a pool of his own blood, his eyes wide open, his limbs twisted, looking more like the Ides of March. Fallen like Caesar beneath a Roman temple. A death that may sound romantic in the textbooks, but in fact it was a bloody mess. The bald man lying next to him, likewise dead, did little to make the picture any prettier.

Once he had been photographed from all angles, and the dead man next to him with the pencil jutting from his eye, they zipped him up into a plastic bag and drove him across to the Institute of Forensic Pathology at the Charité Hospital. Here he was weighed and measured, his identifying features noted down, and he was put into cold storage. He didn't stay there for long, however, but was taken out and X-rayed several times. This showed where the flechettes had lodged or broken apart in his body, as well as revealing old bone breakages, mended now, and a titanium knee. It also showed that his left eye was artificial. He was wheeled into the autopsy theater, along with the bald man, where they were just about to slice him open when Nyela was brought in as well. This meant that three of the five dissection tables were occupied by as yet unidentified corpses. The surgeons removed Vogelaar's organs, examined them, weighed them, drained off bodily fluids and measured the volumes, noted down all their procedures and findings. Meanwhile a case team was hastily assembled, and the investigating officers compared photographs of the corpses with pictures from the city police files. It was soon established that the female corpse had been found in a car registered in the name of Andre Donner, resident in Berlin since a year ago. He was a restaurant owner, married to Nyela Donner, and a photograph from her records left no doubt as to the dead woman's identity.

The bald man's name, though, was not so easily established.

Just as Donner (alias Vogelaar) was being sewn back up, the pathology lab got a phone call from the German Foreign Office, saying that Donner's murder had caught the attention of the Chinese authorities. Chinese and German police working together, so the civil servant on the phone said, had been investigating a gang of technology smugglers for some time. Perhaps the restaurant owner's death had something to do with a failed handover, and Donner might well not be Donner at all, but somebody else entirely, an alias. The Berlin government was very keen to do what they could to help the Chinese investigators, and two of them would be arriving in a few minutes to take a quick look at the body. Could the autopsy team please treat them as guests of the government?

The trainee doctor who took the call said that she would have to make inquiries. The civil servant gave his name and a telephone number, asked her to move as quickly as she could, and hung up. Next, the trainee spoke to the head of the Institute, who told her to check with the Foreign Office that it was all above board, and to bring the Chinese investigators through to the theater as soon as they arrived.

4-9-3-0—she dialed—

—and was put through. It really was the Foreign Office number, but the extension number was a little special. It didn't actually exist. Thus she wasn't actually put through where she thought she would be when she heard a recorded voice saying:

"This is the Foreign Office. Currently all our lines are busy. You will be put through to the next free line. This is the Foreign Office. Currently—" Then a woman's voice, gentle, melodious: "Foreign Office, good afternoon, my name is Regina Schilling."

"Institute of Forensic Pathology, Charité. Could you put me through please to—erm—" The woman on the line paused, probably looking at her notes. "Mr. Helge Malchow."

"One moment," said Diane.

Jericho grinned. He had picked a first name and family name quite at random out of the Berlin telephone book, and had programmed a few sentences into Diane. The whole little show would certainly dispel any doubts the caller might have that she was speaking to the Foreign Office—and not, for instance, to a computer in a hotel room. Diane's German was perfect, of course.

"Mr. Malchow's line is busy at the moment," Diane told the trainee. "Would you like to hold?"

"Will it take long?"

Jericho pointed to the right answer.

"Just a moment," Diane said, and then cheerfully, "Ah, I see that he's just hung up. I'll put you through. Have a pleasant day."

"Thank you."

"Helge Malchow," Jericho said.

"Charité Hospital. You called about the Chinese police delegation."

"That's right." His own German wasn't bad at all. Maybe a bit rusty. "Have they arrived yet?"

"No, but they're quite welcome. They should drive to Building O."

"Splendid."

"Perhaps you could tell me their names?"

"Superintendent Tu Tian is leading the investigation, Inspector Chen Yuyun will be with him. The two of them are working undercover, so perhaps you could be so good as to let them see what they need as quickly as you can, not too much red tape." It was a ludicrous claim, but it sounded halfway plausible. "By the way, you'll find that they only speak English."

"That's fine. We'll keep the red tape to a mini—"

"Thank you very much indeed." Jericho hung up, and dialed Tu's number.

"All systems go," he said.

Tu put his phone down and looked at Yoyo. She could see it in his eyes that he absolutely loathed what they were about to do.

"I never wanted to see another corpse in my life," he said. "Corpses in tiled rooms. Never again."

"Sometime or other we'll all be corpses in tiled rooms."

"At least I won't have to see that for myself, when it's me."

"You don't know that. They say that you see yourself when you die. See yourself lying there, and you couldn't care less."

"I could care."

Yoyo hesitated, then reached out and squeezed Tu's hand. Her slim white fingers against his soft, liver-spotted flesh. A child seeking to reassure a giant. She thought of the evening before and the story Tu had told her during the course of the night, of people locked away in prison for so long that in the end the prison was in them. For years now she had been carrying around her own burden of self-reproach, certain that in some obscure way she was responsible for the grownups' pain; and now that burden was taken from her shoulders and replaced instead with the truth, which was so much worse, so much more depressing. She had smoked, drank, cried, and felt helpless, useless, the way children feel when they see their parents' moods, so complex, so painful, moods that they can't understand and think must be something to do with them. Every argument Tu used to make her feel better about it just deepened the pain. His story freed her from the accumulated years of self-pity, but now she felt a vast pity for Hongbing instead, and wondered if she wanted a father she had to pity. Now she was ashamed of even having had the thought, and again she felt guilty.

"Nobody wants to pity his parents," Tu had said. "We want them to protect us for a while, and then at some point we want to leave them alone. The most we can achieve is to understand what they do, and forgive the child we used to be."

For all that, Tu deserved pity as well, but he seemed not to need it, unlike her father. She suspected that it had been far worse for him than it had been for Tu. But unlike the bitterness that Hongbing had eaten, Tu's fate seemed to her—

"Not so bad?" Tu had laughed. "Of course. I'm not even your uncle. I'm an old fart with a young wife. When you look at me, you see who I am, not who I was. There's no history to chain us together."

"But we're—friends?"

"Yes, we're friends, and if you were a bit more interested in my bank balance and had fewer scruples, we could be lovers. But you can only see Hongbing in one particular way, that's genetics for you. No place for pity there. It just doesn't feature. We each have our own genetic destiny, and when we've played that role to the fullest, then perhaps we can see our parents for what they really are, understand them, accept them, respect them, maybe even love them. For what they always were: just people."

Oh God, and then dropping in on Jericho late at night. What an embarrassment! She'd been carried away by the intoxicating notion of storming his room, and then she'd crept out without achieving anything, like a silly drunk. It had been a whim, of course, and like all such whims it only made her feel stupidly ashamed. In retrospect, she didn't even know what she had wanted there.

Or did she?

"Let's get this over with," said Tu.

They'd picked up the Audi a quarter of an hour ago from the street by the Spree, and now they were parked across from the Institute of Forensic Pathology, Charité Hospital. Tu started the engine and drove up to the barrier at the front gate. He waved his ID out of the window at the guard, told him that the Foreign Office had approved their visit, and asked the way to Building O. They drove along past grand red-brick façades. Splendid green lawns beneath spreading leafy boughs called out to them to stop and linger with a loaf of bread, some cheese, a bottle of Chianti, to make the most of every minute before the die was cast and they had to enter Building O. They felt that same yearning for peace and quiet that even the liveliest extrovert feels in a graveyard.

After driving straight ahead for a long while, then turning twice, they stopped in front of a light, airy, somewhat sterile building with all the charm of a provincial clinic. There were only three police cars parked in the forecourt, with the green Berlin livery and marked *Forensics*. All this understated modesty unsettled Yoyo, gave her the odd feeling that they weren't where they needed to be, that the corpses must be somewhere else. She had imagined that in a megalopolis like Berlin, where people died every minute of every day, the Institute of Forensic Pathology had to be a vast hangar-like edifice, but this little low building hardly suggested doctors arguing, inspectors, profilers, all the scenes she knew from the movies. They went up three steps, rang the bell by a glass door, and were let through by two women in white coats, one tall, young and rather pretty, the other short and wiry, in her late forties, apple-cheeked and with a no-nonsense haircut. The older woman introduced herself as Dr. Marika Voss, and her young companion as Svenja Maas. Tu and Yoyo held out their IDs. Dr. Voss glanced at the characters and nodded as though she dealt with Chinese documentation every working day.

"Yes, you have been announced to us," she said, in stiffly formal English. "Miss Chen Yuyun?"

Yoyo shook her hand. The doctor looked thoughtful for a moment. Clearly she was doing her best to reconcile Yoyo's appearance with what she imagined an undercover homicide squad must look like. She glanced across to Svenja Maas and then back again, as though remembering with an effort that there were good-looking people in all walks of life.

"And you are mister—"

"Superintendent Tu Tian. This is very good of you," Tu said amiably. "We don't want to take up too much of your time. Have you already completed the autopsy?"

"You are interested in Andre Donner?"

"Yes."

"We just finished with him a few minutes ago, but not yet with Nyela Donner. She is being examined two tables further on. Do you need to look at her as well?"

"No."

"Or at the second dead man from the museum? We don't have his identity yet."

Tu frowned.

"Perhaps. Yes, I think so."

"Good. Please come."

Dr. Voss looked into a scanner. Another door opened. They entered a corridor, and here for the first time Yoyo smelled that sharp, sweet smell that the people on television always ward off with a bit of balm rubbed under their noses. It was bacterial decay; the smell thickened, from a mere hint to a miasma, as they went downstairs to the autopsy section, and from a miasma to a brackish pool as they entered the lobby to the theater. A young man with an Arabic look about him was uploading children's portrait photos to a monitor screen. Yoyo didn't even want to think about children, here. Nor did she need to, since Dr. Voss had just pressed something into her hand. She looked at the little tube, utterly at a loss, and felt her ignorance open up beneath her like a trapdoor.

"For our visitors," the doctor said. "You know, of course."

No, she didn't know.

"For rubbing under your nose." Dr. Voss raised her eyebrows in surprise. "I thought that you would—"

"This is Miss Chen's first case involving forensic pathology," Tu said, taking the tube from Yoyo's fingers. As though he had done it all his life, he squeezed out two pea-sized blobs of the paste it contained and smeared them under his nostrils. "She's here to get some experience."

Dr. Voss nodded understandingly.

"You've not been paying attention in theory class, Inspector," Tu teased her in Chinese, passing Yoyo the tube. She rolled her eyes at him and rubbed a squeeze of the stuff on her upper lip, only to find out the next moment that it was, quite definitely, too much. A minty bomb exploded into her nasal passages, swept through her brain, and blasted the smell of decay aside. Svenja Maas watched her with conspiratorial interest, the fellow-feeling of two beautiful people who meet in the company of the less well favored.

"You get used to it at some point," she declared, the voice of experience.

Yoyo smiled faintly.

They followed the doctor into the theater, tiled red and white with frosted glass windows and boxy ceiling lights. Five autopsy tables were lined up next to one another. The first two were empty, but two surgeons were bent over the table in the middle, one of them just lifting the lungs from a yawning gap in the ribcage of the black woman they were working on, while the other said something into a microphone. The lungs went onto a scale. Dr. Voss led the group past the fourth table, where a large corpse lay under a white sheet, and she stopped at the last. Here too the corpse was covered, but she turned the sheet back and they saw Jan Kees Vogelaar, alias Andre Donner.

Yoyo looked at him.

She hadn't particularly liked the man, but now that she saw him lying there, a Y-shaped incision freshly sewn up on his torso, she felt sorry. Just as she had felt sorry for Jack Nicholson in One Flew Over the Cuckoo's Nest, for Robert de Niro in Heat, Kevin Costner in A Perfect World, Chris Pine in Neighborhood, Emma Watson in Pale Days. All those who had so very nearly made it, but who always failed at the last moment no matter how often you watched the film.

"If you don't need me," Dr. Voss said, "I'll leave you with Frau Maas. She assisted in the Donner autopsy and should be able to answer any questions you have."

"Well then," said Tu, switching to Chinese. "Let's get started, Comrade."

They leaned down to look at his face, waxy, already tinged with blue. Yoyo tried to remember which side Vogelaar had his glass eye on. Jericho had insisted it was the right side. She wasn't so sure herself. She could readily have sworn that it was the left. It was a magnificently well made eye, and under Vogelaar's closed lids there was no telling which it might be.

"Not sure?" Tu frowned.

"No, and that's Owen's fault." Yoyo looked askance at Svenja Maas, who had stepped back. "Let our friend there show you the fellow on the next table."

"Fine, I'll keep her off your back."

"It'll be all right." Yoyo gave a sour smile. "There are only two possibilities."

She wasn't getting used to the sight of corpses, or to the idea that people she had barely got to know dropped like flies. But even as she veered between fascination and disgust, an unexpected sense of calm took hold of her, deep and clear, like a mountain lake. Tu turned to Svenja Maas and pointed to the body on table four, still under its sheet.

"Could you please uncover this man for us?"

Stupid. The trainee doctor stepped around the wrong side of the table. From where she was, she still had a good view of Yoyo. Tu shifted position to block her view.

"Great Heavens above," he cried out. "What happened to his eye?"

"He was attacked with a pencil," the trainee doctor said, not without some admiration in her voice. "Straight through the bone and into the brain."

"And how exactly did that happen?"

Yoyo put two fingers onto Vogelaar's right eyelid and lifted it. It seemed to have no particular temperature, neither cold nor warm. While Svenja Maas was explaining about angle of entry and pressure, she pressed her middle finger and thumb into the corner of the eye. The eyeball seemed to sit much too firmly in the eye socket, more like a glass marble than soft and slippery, so that for a moment she wasn't sure that Jericho hadn't been right after all, and she shoved her fingers deeper into the socket.

Resistance. Were those muscles? The eye wasn't coming out, rather it tugged backward, leaking some kind of fluid, like a cornered animal.

That wasn't a glass eye, not on her life.

"The shaft splintered," Maas said, walking over to the organ table between the corpse and the washbasin, where something lay in a transparent plastic bag on a tray. Quickly, Yoyo pulled her fingers out of the socket, just before Maas happened to glance over at her. She thought she heard a squelching sound as she did so, reproachful, tell-tale. Tu hurried to block the sightlines again. Yoyo shuddered. Could the woman have heard something? Had there been anything to hear, or had she just imagined it, expecting an eye socket to squelch as you take your fingers out?

The surface of the calm lake inside her began to ruffle. There was something sticky on her fingers. Jericho had been wrong! While Tu twinkled at Svenja Maas, asking interested questions about her work, she plunged her fingers into Vogelaar's left eye socket. Right away she could feel that this was different. The surface was harder, definitely artificial. She pushed further, flexed her middle finger and thumb. All the while, Tu was asking learned questions about the improvised use of drawing equipment as weapons. Maas pronounced that everything could be a weapon, and stepped to the left. Tu declared that she was absolutely right, and stepped to the right. The pathologists at the middle table were busy with Nyela.

Yoyo took a deep breath, high on mint rub.

Now!

The glass eye popped out, almost trustingly, and nestled into the palm of her hand. She slipped it into her jacket, closed Vogelaar's sunken eyelid as best she could, and saw that she had caused lasting disfigurement. Too late. She quickly pulled the sheet back up over his face and took two steps to Tu's side.

"There is no doubt any longer about Andre Donner," she said in English.

Tu stopped in the middle of a question.

"Oh, good," he said. "Very good. I think we can go."

"When will you want my report, Superintendent?"

"What kind of question is that, Inspector! As soon as possible. The director of prosecutions is breathing down our neck."

Curtain, applause, Yoyo thought.

"Are you done?" Svenja Maas looked from one to the other, disgruntled to be so abruptly ignored.

"Yes, we don't want to discommode you any further."

"You are not—erm—discommoding me."

"No, you are right of course, it was a pleasure. Good-bye, and best wishes to Dr. Voss."

Svenja Maas shrugged and led them out to the lobby, where they said good-bye. Tu marched ahead, sped up on the stairs, and practically raced along the corridor. Yoyo scurried after him. The last of her calm was gone. They didn't need any authorization to leave. They went out into the parking garage and headed for the Audi, when suddenly a commanding voice rang out from the building.

"Mr. Tu, Miss Chen!"

Yoyo froze. Slowly she turned, and saw Dr. Marika Voss standing on the steps, her chin raised.

They've noticed, Yoyo thought. We were too slow.

"Please forgive our hasty departure." Tu raised his arms apologetically. "We wanted to say good-bye, but we couldn't find you."

"Was everything as you had hoped?"

"You were extremely helpful!"

"I'm glad of that." She smiled suddenly. "Well then, I hope that you make progress with your investigations."

"Thanks to your help, we shall make great strides."

"Good day to you."

Dr. Voss marched back inside, and Yoyo felt as though she had turned to butter in the sunshine. She slid into the Audi, and melted onto the seat.

"Do you have it?" Tu asked.

"I have it," she replied, with the last of her strength.

Svenja Maas wasn't exactly offended, but she was rather peeved. As she went back into the autopsy theater she felt a nagging suspicion that the Chinese policeman hadn't really been interested in her, just in keeping up some Asiatic notion of etiquette. She went to the furthest tables and noticed that his young inspector had put the sheet back up over Donner's corpse, though not very neatly. She tugged at it irritably, and found that the whole thing was crooked. She turned the sheet down.

She saw right away that something was wrong. Vogelaar's right eye wasn't looking good, but the left eye was horrible.

With a dark presentiment, she lifted the lid.

The glass eye was missing.

For a moment she flushed hot and cold at the thought that she would be blamed. She had left the eye in its socket, but only because she wanted to take it out later and show it to a prosthetics expert. They had noticed something odd about it. It looked as though it had something inside, maybe some sort of mechanism with which Vogelaar could see, perhaps something else. They hadn't really considered it significant.

Obviously they had been wrong.

Electrified, she ran from the theater and up the stairs. She found Dr. Marika Voss in the corridor.

"Are the Chinese police still here?" she asked breathlessly.

"The Chinese?" Dr. Voss raised her eyebrows. "No, they just left. Why?"

"Shit! Shit! Shit!"

"What's up?" the older woman demanded.

"They took something with them," Maas stammered. Bastards, landing her in it like this!

"With them?" Voss echoed.

"The eye. The glass eye."

The doctor hadn't been in the team who had examined Donner. She knew nothing about the eye, but she understood all the same that they would be in trouble.

"I'll call the guards at the gate," she said.

• • •

The car glided along the main road on the hospital campus, past the stern red-brick buildings, the peaceful lawns and paths, the shady trees.

"Hey," Yoyo said, frowning. "What's going on up ahead?"

Somebody came running out of the guards' cabin, a man in uniform. He raised his hands as though directing an airplane on the runway. At the same time, the barrier began to drop. Obviously the fuss was about them.

"I should imagine we've been found out."

"Great. Now what?"

"All down to you." Tu looked across at her. "How do you like Berlin? Do you want to stay?"

"Not at any cost."

"Thought not," he said, accelerated, and shot under the barrier, so close that Yoyo was surprised not to hear it scrape across the roof. Behind them, the guard's yells drifted like pollen on the summer air.

ADLON

The symbol shimmering on the display showed many twisting reptilian necks, all springing from a single body. Nine heads. The symbol of Hydra.

Xin clapped the phone to his ear.

"We've sent you data from several major Berlin hotels," said the caller. "No luck with the smaller ones. There's a hell of a lot of them, all Berlin seems to be nothing but hotels. The problem was that working so fast, we couldn't get into every single computer—"

"Understood. And?"

"No hits."

"They *must* be staying somewhere," Xin insisted.

"They're not in any of the international chains. No Chen Yuyun and no Owen Jericho. However, I can give you more details of the warning that reached London yesterday. I'll send you the text, do you want to hear it first?"

"Spit it out."

Xin listened to the fragmentary sentences that he already knew so well. He considered just how dangerous this fire might be that Yoyo and Jericho had started. It was hardly a fragment by now. They had decrypted almost ninety percent of the message. All the same, the really important parts, the decisive information, was still missing. And it hadn't been Jericho, or the girl, who had called Edda Hoff, but a man called Tu. Hoff was number three in the Orley security chain of command, and Xin knew very little about her, other than that she was quite unimaginative and accordingly would never exaggerate, or downplay, a threat.

"Hoff made the decision on her own account, and she told the whole corporation that there may perhaps be an attack, without pretending that she had any real information," the caller said. "Gaia was informed as well, just like every other link in the corporate network, but they saw no reason to change the program up on the Moon. Hoff seems to have let all the right people know." The caller didn't dare name names over the telephone, even though it was practically impossible that anyone might be listening in on this connection. On the other hand, they had never expected that the encrypted messages piggybacking on harmless e-mail attachments could be cracked.

"Tu," said Xin thoughtfully.

"That's the name he gave. I'll send you over his cell phone number. We don't know where he was calling from."

Unlike the astonishing diversity of given names, the number of Chinese family names was limited indeed. The vast majority of Chinese

people shared just a few dozen clan names, mostly monosyllables—the
so-called Old Hundred Names. It was not uncommon for an entire
village to be called Zheng, Wang, Han, Ma, Hu, or Tu. Nevertheless
Xin couldn't shake off the feeling that he had heard the name Tu quite
recently, and in connection with Yoyo.

"Have you taken those pages down from the web?" he asked, since
inspiration failed to strike.

"That channel of communication has been closed."

Xin knew what the decision entailed, so he understood why his
caller was so sullen. The man at the other end of the line had himself suggested the piggyback encryption, and had written the code. It
had served them well for three years. Hydra's heads had been able to
exchange messages in real time, functioning as one great brain.

"We'll get over it," he said, trying to sound friendly. "The net served
its purpose for us, and more, and it's all down to you! Everybody
respects your contribution. Just as everybody will understand why we
decided to break off simultaneous communication so close to our goal.
The time has come when there's nothing more to say. All we can do is
await developments."

Xin hung up, stared down at his feet, and shifted them to a parallel position, ankles and instep exactly the same distance apart, not
touching. Slowly, he drew his knees inward. How he hated the tangled
web of accident and circumstance! As soon as he felt the hairs on his
calves begin to brush against one another, he adjusted his feet, shifted
his thighs, his arms, his hands, his shoulders, positioning them symmetrically along the line of an imaginary axis, until he sat there as an
exact mirror image, one side of his body the perfect reflection of the
other. This usually helped him to get his thoughts in order, but this
time the technique failed. He felt dizzy with self-doubt, blindsided by
the thought that perhaps he'd done everything wrong, that hunting
Yoyo down had only made things worse.

Thoughts and afterthoughts.

Losing control.

His heart hammered like a piston. Only one last nudge, he felt, and
he would burst apart into a thousand pieces. No, not him. His shell.
The human cloak called Kenny Xin. He felt like a host body for his own
larval self, felt like a cocoon, a pupa, the mid-stage of some metamorphosis, and he was horribly afraid of whatever it was that was eating
him from the inside. Sometimes it grew, flexed itself, and choked the
breath in his throat, and he couldn't tame it, couldn't take the strain
any longer; at these moments he had to give the beast something to
calm it, just as he had allowed it to burn the hut where his torturers
had kept him. Unredeemed, sick and poverty-stricken as they were,
he had given them to the flames, and in that moment had felt himself

made free, cleansed of all suffering, his mind clear and unclouded. Since then he had often wondered whether he had gone mad that day, or been cured of madness. He could hardly remember the time before. At most, he remembered his disgust at living in this world. His hatred toward his parents for having given him birth, even if at such a tender age he knew little of just how he had been thrust into this world. He only felt certain that his family was responsible for his life, which was already enough to make him hate them, and that they were making it a living hell.

That there was no sense to his existence.

It was only after the fire that the sense of it all became clear. Could he be mad when suddenly, everything made sense? How many so-called sane people spent their days in the most senseless activities? How much of accepted morality was based on ritual and dogma, with not the least shred of sense to it? The fire had broadened his horizons, so that all at once he recognized the plan, creation's twisting labyrinthine paths, its abstract beauty. There was no way back from here. He had moved up to a higher level which some might call madness, but which was simply an insight of such all-illuming power that he had to struggle to encompass it. Any attempt to share it with others was mere vanity. How could he explain to others that everything he did flowed from a higher insight? It was the price that he paid, by making other people pay.

No. He hadn't made things worse.

He had had to make sure!

Xin imagined his own brain. A Rorschach universe. The purity of symmetry, predictability, control. Slowly, he felt his calm return. He stood up, plugged the phone into the room's computer console, and uploaded the hotel reservation lists. He went through them one by one. Naturally he didn't expect to see Chen Yuyun or Owen Jericho turn up in the lists. Hydra's hackers had gone through the lists several times over once they had broken into the hotel systems. He didn't exactly know what he expected to find, he only knew that he felt he would find *something*.

And what a find.

It fell into place like the last piece of a puzzle, neatly explaining everything that had happened in the museum and answering half a dozen other questions besides. Three rooms in the Grand Hyatt on Marlene-Dietrich-Platz had been booked to a company called Tu Technologies, registered in Shanghai. They had been booked by the director of the company, who had signed for them in person. Tu Tian.

The outfit that Yoyo worked for.

That was where he knew the name from!

He loaded the company homepage and found a portrait of the owner. A plump man, almost bald, with a pate like a billiard ball. All in all, so ugly that he came out the other side as rather appealing. His thick lips could make a frog turn green with envy, but they were somehow sensual at the same time. His eyes, peering out from behind a tiny pair of glasses, glowed with humor and pitiless intelligence. He radiated a Buddha-like calm and iron determination, all at once. Xin could tell at first sight that Tu Tian was a street fighter, a jackal in jester's clothing. Somebody he could ill afford to underestimate. If he was helping Yoyo and Jericho, that meant that they were mobile, that they could leave Berlin as quickly as they had shown up.

The Vogelaars were dead. Which meant that they *would* be leaving Berlin.

Very soon. Now.

Xin strapped on his gun. He chose a long red wig and a face mask with a matching beard, then stuck appliqués to his forehead and cheekbones. He pulled on an emerald-green duster coat, put on a slim pair of mirrored holospecs, and stopped in front of the mirror for a few seconds to check the effect. He looked like a pop star. Like a typical mando-progger, who had made more money than he'd ever had good taste.

He hurried from the hotel, flagged down a taxi, and ordered it to the Grand Hyatt.

HYATT

Tu's face showed up on the screen. Jericho was hardly surprised to hear him say:

"Get Diane packed. We're leaving."

"What about the glass eye?"

Yoyo's fingers appeared onscreen. Vogelaar's false eye stared at him. Denuded of its eyelids, it looked somehow surprised, even a little indignant.

"There's no doubt that it's a memory crystal," he heard her say. "I had a look at it, it's the usual pattern. Hurry up. The cops will be with you shortly."

"Where are you now?"

"On our way to you," Tu said. "They've got the car's license plate. In other words, they know that it's a rental car, they know who rented it, they know where he lives, and so on and so forth. I should guess that they'll make the connection with this morning's unhappy events."

"And with your jet," said Jericho.

"With my—"

"*Fuck!*" said Yoyo's voice. "He's right!"

"As soon as they find out that you rented the car at the airport, they'll figure it out," said Jericho. "They'll arrest us even before we check the car back."

"How much time do we have?"

"Hard to say. The first thing they'll do is go through the passenger lists of all the flights that landed before you went to the rental desk. That will take a while. They won't find anything, but since you must have got here somehow or other, they'll check the private flights."

"It'll take us at least half an hour to get to the airport in the Audi."

"That could be too late."

"Forget the fucking Audi," Yoyo called out. "If we're to have any chance at all, we need a skycab."

"I could order one," Jericho suggested.

"Do that," Tu agreed. "We'll be at the hotel in ten minutes."

"Your wish is my command."

Jericho hung up and ran out to the corridor. As he dashed toward the elevators, he could see with his mind's eye how the efficient German police would be unraveling the puzzle of their arrival, dauntless, dutiful, and assuming the worst. He went up to the roof and found the skyport empty. A liveried hotel employee beamed at him from over the edge of his terminal. Jericho's arrival seemed to give him a new purpose in life, stranded up here as he was on the lonely expanse of the roof.

"Would you like to order an aircab?" he asked.

"Yes, that's it."

"One moment please." He slid his fingers busily across the console. "I could have one here for you in ten to fifteen minutes."

"As quick as you can!"

"While you're waiting, would you like any help with your lugg—"

The sentence probably ended with—*age*, but Jericho was back in the elevator. He hurried to his room and shoved Diane into his back-pack with all the hardware. He packed whatever clothing lay around on top, checked and holstered his Glock, ran along the corridor, and left a note for Tu:

I'm on the flight deck.

Charité Hospital, Institute
of Forensic Pathology

"No, he's not," said the voice on the telephone.

Dr. Marika Voss hopped from one foot to another, while Svenja Maas stood next to her, pale and wringing her hands.

"Malchow," she repeated stubbornly. "Hel—ge Mal—chow."

"As I've already said—"

"My colleague called him."

"That may well be, but—"

"First she was held in a queue, then one of your switchboard staff put her through. To Malchow. To Hel—"

"There's no such person."

"But—"

"Listen," said the voice, growing audibly less patient as the conversation went around and around in circles. "I would very much like to help you, but we have nobody of that name in the whole Foreign Office! And the extension number that you gave me doesn't exist either!"

Dr. Voss pressed her lips together indignantly. She'd known as much, ever since the automated dialing system had told her that there was no such number. Despite all this, she saw no reason to back down.

"But the woman on the switchboard—"

"Ah yes, the switchboard." A short pause, a sigh. "And what was the woman called?"

"What was she called?" Dr. Voss hissed.

"Something like Schill or Schall," Maas whispered, hunched over, miserable.

"Schill or Schall, my colleague says."

"No."

"No?"

"We do have a Scholl. Miss Scholl."

"Scholl?" asked Dr. Voss.

Maas shook her head. "It was Schill."

"It was Schill."

"I'm sorry. No Schill, no Schall, no Malchow. I really do advise you to call the police. Clearly you've been the butt of a very nasty joke."

Dr. Voss gave in. She thanked the civil servant in an icy tone, then called the number for the police. At her side, Svenja Maas wilted.

Within five minutes the case officers had tracked down the license plate. Within seconds, they knew the name of the rental firm's client.

They compared that information with the records from immigration, and learned that Tu Tian had touched down in Berlin early the day before, giving the Grand Hyatt on Marlene-Dietrich-Platz as his address.

Two minutes after that, a team was dispatched to visit the hotel.

HYATT

Thanks to Tu's dauntless driving, they reached the hotel sooner than they had expected, and with even more reason to get away again as quickly as they could—he must have chalked up dozens of traffic offenses between the hospital at Turmstrasse and the hotel on Marlene-Dietrich-Platz. He got out, threw the keys to the concierge, and asked him to take the car down to the underground parking garage.

"Shall we go to the bar?" Yoyo asked, loudly enough that the man couldn't help but overhear it. Tu winked, understanding her plan, and picked up the charade.

"To tell you the truth, I feel like something sweet."

"There's a Starbucks in the Sony Center. Up the street."

"Great. See you there. I'll just go tell Owen."

It was vaudeville stuff of course, but it might buy them some time. They crossed the lobby as fast as they could without arousing suspicion, went up to the seventh floor, and headed for their rooms.

"Leave everything there that you don't need," Tu called to her. "Bring only the bare essentials."

"Easy enough," Yoyo snorted. "I don't have anything! You look after yourself, don't waste time fussing with your suitcase."

"I don't care about fashion, me."

"True enough, we'll have to work on that. See you on the flight deck in two minutes."

Seven floors below, Xin jumped out of the taxi. By now he knew what floor they were on, what room numbers, the only thing he didn't know was who had which room. All the rooms were booked to Tu Technologies, and neither Yoyo nor Jericho were mentioned by name. He walked into the lobby in his full battledress. Hyatt staff and guests would certainly remember who had walked in at 15:30: a tall man, a striking figure with a flowing mane of red hair and a Genghis Khan mustache, probably some sort of artsy type. Holospecs hid the Asiatic cast of his eyes. He could easily be taken for European. The best disguise was to make yourself noticed.

He walked into an elevator and pressed for the seventh floor.

Nothing happened.

Xin frowned, then spotted the thumbscan plate. Of course. The elevator worked on authorization only, as in most international hotels. He trotted obediently back into the lobby, where a contingent of his fellow countrymen was just making their way to the reception desk. There was a sudden throng. The staff at the desk steeled themselves for the task of making sense of the new arrivals' broken English, riddling out what they meant from what they said, and adding to the rich confusion with their own small store of Chinese words. Xin headed purposefully to the only receptionist who was busy with other tasks, in this case the telephone. He drew himself up to his full height and then wondered what on earth he could ask her.

How do I get up to the seventh floor?

Would you like to check in?—No, I have some friends staying here and I wanted to drop in on them.—I can authorize you and then call them for you, to let them know you're coming.—Ahh, you know how it is, actually I wanted to surprise them.—I understand! If you wait just a moment, I'll ride up with you. It's all a bit busy at the moment, as you see, but in a few minutes' time . . . —Can't we be a bit quicker?—Well, you see, I'm not really supposed to—it's really just guests who can—

Xin turned away. The whole thing was too complicated. He didn't want to leave his thumbprint in the Hyatt's system, any more than he wanted to risk Tu, Jericho, or Yoyo being warned. He mingled in with the other Chinese.

Jericho saw the skycab lift over the Tiergarten Park and make for the Hyatt, a muscular-looking VTOL with four turbines. It came in fast, dipped its jets with a hissing snarl, and sank slowly down onto the landing pad.

"Your taxi's here," the hotel employee said smiling, the joy in his voice announcing how wonderful it was that air transport was so widely available these days, and what a pleasure it was to see people use it.

In the next moment Yoyo hurried from the terminal, a crumpled shopping bag under her arm and Tu trotting in her wake. He was pulling his suitcase along behind him as though it were a recalcitrant child.

The taxi settled.

"Just what the doctor ordered," Tu beamed.

"Just what the *detective* ordered," Jericho reminded him amiably.

"Enough strutting and preening, you two." Yoyo headed for the boarding hatch. "Is your jet cleared for take off?"

It was as though her question had slammed on the brakes in Tu's stride. He stopped, fumbled at the bare expanse of his scalp, and tried to twist his fingers into the tiny short hairs there.

"What is it?"

"I forgot something," he said.

"Say it's not so." Yoyo stared at him.

"It is. My phone. I just now thought, all I need to do is call the airport from the taxi, and then I realized—"

"You have to go back to your room?"

"Erm—yes." Tu left his suitcase where it was, turned around, and hurried back to the elevator. "I'll be right back. Right back."

. . .

When Xin heard that the elderly Chinese couple in front of him intended to book one of the Grand Hyatt's finest and most expensive suites, he felt a warm glow of pleasure. Not because of any sudden spasm of altruism, but because the suite was on the seventh floor. Right where he wanted to be.

The husband put his thumb on the scanplate. A young receptionist offered to show the couple up to their room, and they strolled across to the elevator together. Xin fell in behind them. As they stood there waiting for the elevator, the wife turned to look at him, her curiosity as strong as an elastic band tugging her head around. She looked in bemusement at the tumble of hair over his shoulders, and in bafflement at his holospecs. She eyed the toes of his snakeskin boots dubiously, visibly nervous at the thought of having to share a hotel with the likes of him. Her husband stuck to her side, short and stocky, and stared at the gap where the elevator doors met until they opened. They went into the elevator together. Nobody asked whether he was with the group. The young receptionist smiled warmly at him, and he smiled back, just as warmly.

"Seventh floor as well?" she asked, in English just to be on the safe side.

"Yes, please," he said.

Next to him, the Chinese woman stiffened, horribly sure now that he was living on the same floor.

Tu tore back the bed sheets but his phone wasn't there, any more than it had been on the desk or on either of the nightstands. He rummaged through sheets, flung pillows aside, grabbed fistfuls of linen and damask, slid his fingers in between the mattress and the frame.

Nothing.

Who had he called last? Who had he been meaning to call?

The airport. At least, he had wanted to, but then he had decided to call later. He had even had the thing in his hand.

And he'd put it down.

He swept his eyes over the desk again, the chairs, armchair, carpeting. Incredible, he was getting old! What had he been doing just before? He saw himself standing there, his phone in his right hand, while there was something in his left hand too, something just below waist height—

Aha, of course!

Seventh floor.

The Chinese wife pushed herself brusquely past the young receptionist to get out of the elevator, as though she feared that Xin might bite her at the last moment. Her husband, though, had a sudden access of Western etiquette, and took a step back to let the young woman go first, smiling broadly at her. Xin waited until the group was out of sight. The hotel corridors stretched around a sunny atrium space, four arms of a square, with the guest rooms along the front edges. He looked at the wall map. He was glad to see the receptionist and the Chinese couple had set off in the opposite direction from the rooms which Tu had taken.

He was alone.

The carpet muffled his steps. He passed a club lounge, turned into the next corridor, stopped, recalled Tu's room numbers.

712, 717, 727.

712 was to his left. He walked on quickly, counting up. 717, also locked. His coat swung out around him as he stopped still, dead in the middle of the corridor. 727 was ajar.

Tu? Jericho? Yoyo?

One of the three of them would soon regret not having locked up.

Yoyo saw the gyrocopter first.

"Where?" Jericho yelped.

"I think it's headed this way." She ran to the edge of the skyport and stood there, hopping from one leg to the other. "Oh, shit! The cops. It's the cops!"

Jericho had been chatting with the skycab pilot, but now he shaded his eyes with his hand. Yoyo was right. It was a police gyrocopter, coming closer, like the one he had seen above the Brandenburg Gate a few hours ago.

"They could be here for any one of a thousand reasons."

Yoyo hared across to him. "Tian will screw it all up."

"Nothing's screwed up yet." Jericho nodded toward the skycab. "We'll get in. That way at least they won't see you leaping about up here."

"Ha!" Tu called out.

He'd gone to have a pee, of course! And while he'd been peeing, guiding the stream with his left hand and holding the phone in his right, he'd had a momentary brain fart and had almost shaken the last drop off his phone and talked to his dick. Mankind at the mercy of communication technology.

So he had put the thing to one side, the phone that is, and had attended to the call of nature. The bathroom was inside the main suite, like a room within a room, with two doors, opposite one another. You could go into it from the bedroom, and from the front lobby. Tu slid back the glass door by the bed and looked first at the toilet. The phone was lying there on top of the cistern.

Little bastard, he thought. Now to get out of here.

• • •

Xin went into the open room and looked about. A short front lobby led into a brightly lit larger room, obviously the suite. Directly to his right was a frosted glass door, closed. He could hear steps from behind it, and tuneless whistling. There was someone in the bathroom.

His hand slid under his emerald-green coat.

The gyrocopter settled down.

Yoyo squirmed back into her seat as though she wanted to melt into the upholstery. Jericho risked a glance outside. Two uniformed officers got out of the ultralight craft, went to the hotel clerk at the terminal, and talked to him.

"What are they after this time?" grumbled the pilot, in German-accented English, and craned his neck inquisitively. "Even up in the air they don't leave you alone."

"It's good that they keep an eye on things though," Yoyo trilled cheerfully.

Jericho looked askance at her. He expected the hotel clerk to point across at them at any moment. If the patrol had brought photos with them, then they were sunk. The man gesticulated, pointed inside the terminal to the elevators.

Jericho held his breath.

He saw the policemen exchange a few words, then one of them looked across at the skycab. For a moment it seemed that he was looking straight at Jericho. Then he glanced away, and the two of them vanished beneath the terminal roof.

"Let's just hope that Tu doesn't walk right into them," Yoyo hissed.

The steps came closer. He heard something clatter. A silhouette appeared behind the frosted glass and stopped there, right in front of the bathroom door.

Xin readied his weapon.

He yanked the door open and grabbed the man behind it, shoving him against the wall at the back, then pulled the door closed behind him and pressed the muzzle of the gun against the man's temple.

"Don't make a sound," he said.

"What did you say?" one of the policemen asked.

The other pointed forward. "I think 727 is open."

"So it is."

"I reckon we needn't think much more about which room to start with, wouldn't you say?"

They had taken the elevator down from the flight deck to the seventh floor and set out in search of the rooms which the Chinese mogul had taken. His picture had been stored in the airport databases, and was on their phones now, so they had a pretty good idea of what he looked like. On the other hand, they had no idea which of the three rooms he might be in.

"We should have shown that guy on the roof Tu's picture."

"What makes you think so?" his colleague whispered back.

"Just because."

The other officer gnawed at his lip. They had only asked where the rooms were.

"I don't know. What can the guy on rooftop duty tell us?"

They could see a little way through the open door of 727, and into the hallway.

"Whatever," the other man whispered. "It's too late anyway."

Xin listened.

His left hand was over the fat man's mouth—he could feel sweat pearling under his fingers—and his gun was still pressed against his forehead. He would have liked the chance to ask a few questions, but now the situation had changed. Men just in front of the door to the room, at least two of them, trying to keep their voices down. They were doomed to failure there—Xin had ears like a beast of prey. As far as he was concerned, the two of them were not whispering but bellowing like drunks at a summer barbecue.

Right at this moment, they were very interested in room 727.

A muffled sound broke free from the man in front of him, a grunt from somewhere deep in the ribcage. Xin shook his head, a warning, and . . .

Tu held his breath. He stood there frozen like a statue, his eyes wide. The slightest mistake and things would be over for him, that much was clear.

Over and done with.

The police officers looked at one another. They readied their weapons, then one of them pointed to the door of the room and nodded.

In we go, he said wordlessly.

Xin ran through his options.

He could warn his victim: say one word, and you're dead! Then he'd hide in the small toilet cabin next to the shower, and hope that the man was scared enough not to betray his presence. This was risky. It would be even riskier to take him hostage. How would he get a hostage out of the Grand Hyatt? He didn't know who those men out there were. Since they were trying not to make any noise, they were probably security, maybe police.

Or maybe Jericho?

There were two doors to this bathroom. Both were drawn shut. All he could do was hope that the men would look first at the bedroom behind, and then come into the bathroom through that door. This would give him the chance to slip away unnoticed through the door to the hallway. But in order to do that—

Lightning-fast, without letting go of his gun, he placed his hands on either side of the fat man's head, and with a practiced movement broke his neck. The man's body slumped. Xin caught him as he dropped, and slid him silently down to the floor.

The policemen crept along the short corridor. A mirror to their left cast their reflections back at them for company. On the right hand they saw a frosted glass door, which must lead to the bathroom. One of the two stopped, and looked at his colleague questioningly.

The other man hesitated, shook his head, and pointed forward.

Slowly, they paced on.

Tu could breathe again.

When he had left his room and seen two uniformed officers in the corridor, his heart had sunk in his chest, right down to the thread-bare seat of his pants. Without even daring to shut the door behind himself, he had watched the policemen slow their stride at room 727, where they stopped and talked, too quiet for him to hear. They had their backs to him the whole time—although it was certainly him they were after, and there he stood, not 10 meters from them, rooted to the spot as though paralyzed, so that all they would have needed to do was turn around and scoop him up in their net.

But they hadn't turned around.

For some reason, all their attention was on Yoyo's room. And suddenly Tu knew why. The door was ajar. He understood it at the moment when the two policemen went inside, and he realized how outrageously lucky he had been.

Why had Yoyo left her door open? Hurry? Bad habits?

Who cared.

Quietly, he shut 717, tiptoed down the corridor past the lounge on the left, and found the elevators. He pressed his thumb to the scanplate and looked up at the display.

All the elevators were downstairs.

Xin strained his senses, following the men. There were two of them, just as he had conjectured, and right now they were going into the bedroom, where their footsteps parted ways.

He glanced down at the dead body in hotel livery, its head at an unnatural angle on the broken neck. The man's right hand still held the little bottle of shampoo that he had been about to put under the mirror.

At the same moment, Xin remembered that he had seen a room service trolley in the corridor. Not making a sound, he slid open the bathroom door to the front hall, slipped out, and pulled it closed behind him. He spotted a uniformed arm and shoulder in the room, hoped that they had not left another officer in front of the door, and slipped out of the room, quiet as a cat.

Tu hopped from toe to toe, snorting, peering about. He spread his fingers out, then clenched his fists.

Come along, come along, he thought. Blasted elevator! Just bring me up to the damn roof.

The levels were ticking by painfully slowly on the display. Two cabins were headed up. One was stopped on five, the other on six, right below him. For a moment Tu felt murderous rage at the people getting in and out of the elevators down there. They were taking up his time. He hated them with all his heart.

Come on there, he thought. Come on!

Room 727.

The policemen approached the glass door that led straight from the double bed to the bathroom. For a moment, they paused there, listening for noises from inside, but all was quiet.

At last one of them plucked up his nerve.

They must be finding the body about now.

Pacing with care, Xin approached the turn in the corridor that led on to the elevators. He stayed calm. The police had not seen him going out. He had shut the glass door behind himself, ever attentive to detail. There was nothing to show that whoever had murdered the hotel employee had been in the bathroom just a few seconds before.

No need to hurry.

Seven!

Tu could have sworn that the elevator had crept up those last few meters. Finally the gleaming steel doors swept apart, letting out a horde of young folk, expensively dressed. He shoved his way brusquely through them, put his thumb to the scanplate, and pressed *Skyport*. The doors slid shut.

Xin rounded the corner. Hotel guests came toward him the other way. He saw one of the elevators just closing, headed for the next one, pressed the sensor, and waited.

Seconds later he was on his way down to the lobby.

• • •

"There you are at last!" Yoyo called.

Tu rushed from the terminal, leaning forward as he ran as though trying to outrun his own legs. He tumbled into the cabin, slumped down into the seat across from them, and signaled to the pilot.

"You look as though you've seen a ghost," Jericho observed, while the cab swung its jets downward.

"Two." Tu held up his index and middle finger to make the point, then realized he had just made a V for victory and grinned. "They didn't see me though."

"Idiot," Yoyo spat at him, softly.

"Well, do please excuse me."

"Don't do anything like that again! Owen and I were sweating bullets."

They lifted off. The police gyrocopter dwindled away behind them on the landing platform, then the pilot accelerated and left Potsdamer Platz behind. Tu looked out of the window, indignant.

"Feel free to keep sweating," he said. "We're not out of the woods yet."

"What were the cops doing down there?"

"They went into your room. Speaking of which, you left it open."

"I did not."

"That's odd." Tu shrugged. "Well, maybe it was room service."

"Whatever. They won't find anything there. I didn't leave anything behind."

"Didn't forget anything?"

"Forget?" Yoyo stared at him. "Is this really you, asking me, whether *I* forgot anything?"

Tu cleared his throat several times in a row, took out his phone, and called the airport. Of course you forgot something, Jericho thought to himself. Same as we all forgot something. Fingerprints, hair, DNA. While his friend was on the phone, he wondered whether it might not have been smarter after all to let the local authorities know what was going on. Tu seemed to share Yoyo's antipathy to the police, but Germany was not China. So far Germany had no obvious interests at stake in this drama that they were all living through. In the meantime, they had begun to act more and more like the outlaws. Although they weren't the ones who had committed the crimes, it must seem that they were up to their necks in guilt.

Tu snapped his phone shut and looked at Jericho for an age, while the skycab raced toward the airport.

"Forget it," he said.

"Forget what?"

"You're wondering whether we shouldn't just give ourselves up."

"I don't know," Jericho sighed.

"I do, though. Until we know what's in this dossier, and we've spoken to the delightful Edda Hoff one more time, we won't trust any intelligence agency in the world." Tu pointed to his own temple, twirling his finger meaningfully. "Except this one."

The massacre in the Pergamon Museum had thrown police headquarters into an uproar that made a hornets' nest look quiet. And now this as well—a dead Indonesian room service worker, a man with no record of misbehavior, who spoke hardly any German, whose whole job was to dole out soap, toilet paper, and bedtime sweets. The risks of such a job were grumbling guests or messy rooms, not a broken neck when the body lotion began to run out.

Setting aside the two dead police from the museum for a moment, several people had some obscure connection with this new death. A murdered restaurateur from South Africa, who had taken another man with him as he died, killing the mystery man with a pencil—suggesting that he had skills mostly lacking in the restaurant business. Then his black wife, who had been shot in her car and then driven halfway across town. There was the driver to consider as well, a white man, blond, who had clearly been trying to help Donner in the museum but who had become a target in turn, drawing fire from Donner's killer, another mystery man, tall with white hair, a bristling mustache, wearing a suit and spectacles. Then there was a Chinese industrialist, head of a Shanghai technology enterprise, who had himself claimed to be a policeman and had stolen Donner's glass eye, helped by a young Chinese woman. Then last of all the Indonesian man, whose role in life had been to make sure that guests were never left lacking in the bathroom and that they always found a little treat on their pillow at bedtime.

Puzzling, all very puzzling!

Sensibly, the investigating team didn't attempt to solve all the puzzles at once, even though there were some obvious conclusions to be drawn. Whoever else he was, the white-haired man was clearly a professional killer; the glass eye held some secret around which the whole business probably revolved; and the Indonesian victim had just been at the wrong place at the wrong time. For the moment, however, the Chinese business mogul would be at the center of the investigation—less because they wanted to understand his motives than because they simply wanted to pick him up as soon as possible. The three rooms that he had taken in the Grand Hyatt didn't look as though the guests would be returning any time soon. All that was known for sure was that Tu and the woman had driven back from the Institute of Forensic Pathology to the hotel at full tilt, had told the concierge to put the Audi down in the parking garage, and then had vanished into the lobby, chatting.

What had they been chatting about?

The concierge remembered quite clearly. They had been planning to meet some third person in the Sony Center, because the fat man had said that he wanted "something sweet." Oh, and the woman had been very, *very* pretty! The police officers pressed the concierge on whether he understood Chinese, and he said he didn't, that the two of them had been speaking English. This made the head of the inquiry team suspicious—Dr. Marika Voss had reported that they had spoken Chinese to one another in the autopsy theater. Just to be on the safe side, he had sent two men over to the Sony Center, not expecting that they would find anyone there, and set his team to digging up exactly how Tu had arrived.

The longer he thought about it, the more certain he felt that Tu and the blond man were in it together.

The skycab had needed only a trifling eight minutes to get to the airport, but it seemed like an eternity to Jericho. In his thoughts, he was imagining what the case team would be doing. What would they prioritize? Who would their inquiries focus on? He had been at the scene of the shooting himself, and witnesses had seen him running toward the Tiergarten. They would want to know more about him. It certainly counted against him that he had been carrying a gun in the museum, although ballistics would show that he hadn't shot Nyela. As for Yoyo and Tu, they had impersonated police officers and then maltreated a corpse, on top of which Tu had driven a hole through the highway code, but the police had several leads to follow. In a way, that was good, since it meant that they would be that much slower making progress. They would have to check identities, draw up timelines, take statements, look for motives. They would get bogged down in speculation.

On the other hand, they had been notably efficient so far. They had turned up at the Grand Hyatt impressively fast, meaning that they already had Tu in their sights. It wasn't clear yet whether they knew about his jet, or indeed whether they had made the assumption that he would be leaving Berlin at short notice.

The skycab circled above the private airport.

They lost height, banking about in a broad curve. They could see Tu's Aerion Supersonic from here. Its stubby wings, set far back on the fuselage, made it look like a seabird, craning its neck curiously, as eager to be gone as they were. The pilot tilted the jets, let the machine sink down, and landed with a gentle rocking motion not far from the plane. Tu handed him a banknote.

"Keep the change," he said in English.

The size of the tip made the pilot leap to attention and offer his help in loading the jet. Since they didn't even have luggage to unload from his cab, apart from Tu's small suitcase, he asked whether there was anything else he could do for them. Tu thought for a moment.

"Just wait here until we take off," he said. "And don't say a word to anyone until we do."

The chief case officer was just on his way to the police skyport when his phone rang. Before he could take the call, he saw an officer running across the flight pad toward him.

"We've got Baldy," he heard her shout.

He hesitated. The call was from one of the men he had detailed to find out more about what Tu was up to in Berlin. Meanwhile the policewoman had stopped in front of him, breathlessly holding her phone out under his nose. It showed a picture of the man who was, right now, lying on the dissection table with splinters of pencil in his frontal lobe.

"I'll call back," he said into the telephone. "Two minutes."

"Mickey Reardon," the policewoman told him. "An old fossil from the Irish underground, a specialist in alarms systems. He's been freelancing for every secret service you could mention ever since the IRA decommissioned their weapons twenty years ago, and he's worked for a lot of outfits that are half political, half organized crime."

"An Irishman? God help us all."

He couldn't have liked it any worse if Reardon had turned out to be ex-North Korean People's Army. Whenever a regular army or a resistance movement lost its raison d'être, it would spit out creatures like Reardon, who would often make deals with international secret services if they weren't working for organized crime outright.

"Who did he work for?"

"We only know some names. He was with the US secret service a lot, then for Mossad, Zhong Chan Er Bu, our own guys. Quite the multi-talent, very clever at shutting down security systems but also at installing them. He was wanted for a number of instances of grievous bodily harm, and suspected of murder as well."

"Reardon was armed," said the inspector thoughtfully. "Meaning he was on a mission. Donner gets rid of him, then he's shot. By our white-haired gentleman. Is this a secret service operation? Reardon and Mr. White on one side, Donner and Mr. Blond on the other side, Blondie tries to help Donner—"

He had almost forgotten that he was on his way to the Grand Hyatt.

"We need to get moving," his sergeant said.

So it was only once they were in the air that he remembered he had been going to call someone back.

• • •

The jet taxied onto the runway. Tu choked back his engines and waited for permission to take off. He was far more nervous than he was letting on. Strictly speaking, Jericho was right. What they were doing here flew in the face of reason. They were picking a fight with the German police for no reason at all. Indeed, the police might even have been able to help them.

They might not have, though.

Tu had his own bitter experience of the arbitrariness of state power, which had certainly left him with scars, though he tried hard not to jump at shadows. Admittedly, his paranoia was rooted in events that lay twenty-eight years back. Here he was, though, holding the others hostage to his own mistrust, especially Yoyo, who was most receptive to such paranoid behaviors for reasons of her own. There was no doubt that he was manipulating them. He tried to persuade himself that he was doing the right thing, and perhaps he was even right about that, but it wasn't about that, hadn't been for a long time now. As he had walked the streets of Berlin at night with Yoyo, he had realized that the only difference between Hongbing's paranoia and his own was that he was more cheerful about it. His old friend wandered the vaults of his memory forlornly, while he strode through them, whistling cheerfully. Compared with Hongbing, he was fighting fit, but he couldn't fight hard enough to cope with all that life had to throw at him, not on his own.

So he had told her something of the past, and all he had achieved was to make her more confused and depressed. None of it was any help. He would have to tell her the rest as well, tell her what he had never told anybody else except Joanna, tell her the whole story. He would assume Hongbing's tacit approval, and he would cut the whole miserable tangle just as soon as the opportunity presented itself. He would have much preferred it if Hongbing himself had told Yoyo the truth, but this way was good as well. Anything was better than silence.

We have to close the door on our past, he thought. Not run away from it, not escape into success or into depression.

The voice in his earphones gave him permission.

Tu brought the jet engines up to speed and engaged thrust. The acceleration pushed him back into his seat, and they took off.

Only a few minutes later the chief case officer learned that Tu had arrived by private plane, an Aerion Supersonic. The rooms in the Hyatt were abandoned; the Chinese mogul and his companions had obviously left. Perhaps they were still in Berlin, since they hadn't checked out, and the Audi that Tu had hired at the airport was still in the Grand Hyatt's underground parking garage. This was the car whose registration number had set the case team onto his trail.

On the other hand, there was a corpse in one of the rooms. The inspector ordered his team to secure the mogul's jet, just in case. Then a few minutes after that, he learned that he had lost the decisive moment by paying attention instead to Mickey Reardon's identification. He let rip with a string of curses so ripely inventive that the case officers all around him froze in their tracks, but it was no use.

Tu Tian had left Berlin, destination unknown.

AERION SUPERSONIC

"*Of course* she can read memory crystals," Jericho yelled into the cockpit, as if Tu had asked him whether he washed every day.

"A thousand apologies," Tu shouted back. "I'd forgotten she was a sort of surrogate wife."

Jericho lifted Diane's compact body from his backpack, connected it to the ports of the on-board electronics, and set up the monitor on its seat bracket. The Pratt & Whitney turbines wrapped the Aerion in a cocoon of noise. The trapezoid-winged craft was still climbing. Sitting next to him, Yoyo was working on Vogelaar's glass eye, screwing it apart and taking from it a glittering structure the size of a sugar lump. Tu circled the plane. Berlin tilted toward them through the side windows, while at the same time the sky on the other side turned a deep, dark blue.

"Hi, Diane."

"Hi, Owen," said the soft, familiar voice. "How are you?"

"Could be better."

"What can I do to make you *well*?"

"Plenty," Yoyo said in a quietly mocking voice. "One day you'll have to tell me if she's a good kisser."

Jericho grimaced. "Open the Crystal Reader, Diane."

A little rod slid from the front of the computer, sheathed in a transparent frame. The jet swung back to the horizontal and went on gaining height. Below them the massive scab of urban development made way for green-brown-yellow arable land, patchworked with small wooded areas, roads, and villages. As if daubed on, rivers and lakes shimmered in the afternoon sunlight.

"Shame. I'll be really pissed off if that huge mess in the Charité wasn't worth it," growled Yoyo. She leaned across to Jericho and set the cube in the surround, and the tiny drawer slid shut again.

"Everyone made sacrifices," he said wearily, while Diane uploaded the data. "After all, Tian was prepared to chuck a hundred thousand euros to the four winds."

"Not to mention your ear." Yoyo looked at him. "Or at least the snippet of your ear. The atomic layer of your—"

"The *serious* injury to my ear. There."

The screen filled with symbols. Jericho held his breath. The dossier was much bigger than he had thought. He immediately felt that ambivalent dread that you feel just before you enter the monster's lair to see it in all its terrifying hideousness and ascertain its true nature once and for all. In a few minutes they would know the reason for the hunt that had claimed so many victims, almost including themselves, and he knew they weren't going to like what they saw. Even Yoyo seemed hesitant. She put a finger to her lips and paused.

"If I'd been him," she said, "I'd have provided a short version. Wouldn't you?"

"Yes," Jericho nodded. "But where?"

"Here." Her finger wandered across to a symbol marked *JKV Intro*.

"JKV?" He narrowed his eyes.

"Jan Kees Vogelaar."

"Sounds good. Let's try it. Diane?"

"Yes, Owen."

"Open JKV Intro."

There sat Vogelaar, in shirt and shorts, on a veranda, under a roughly hewn wooden roof, and with a drink beside him. In the background, hilly scrubland fell away to the coast. Here and there palms were sticking up from low mixed vegetation. It was plainly drizzling. A sky of indeterminate color hung over the scene and softened the horizon of a far-off sea.

"The likelihood that I am no longer alive at this second," Vogelaar said without preamble, "is relatively high, so listen very carefully now, whoever you are. You won't be having any more information from me in person."

Jericho leaned forward. It was spooky, looking Vogelaar in the eyes. More precisely, they were looking at him *through* one of his eyes. Unlike in Berlin, he was ash-blond again, with a bushy mustache, light-colored eyebrows and eyelashes.

"There are no bugs here. You wouldn't think intimacy was a problem in a country that consists almost entirely of swamp and rain forest, but Mayé is infected with the same paranoia as almost all potentates of his stamp. I think even Ndongo would have been interested in going on listening to the parrots. But as they've appointed me head of security, the task of snooping on the good people of Equatorial Guinea, particularly the ruling family and our valued foreign guests, has fallen to me. My task is to protect Mayé. He trusts me, and I don't plan to abuse that trust."

Vogelaar spread his arms in a gesture that took in the hinterland. "As you see, we live in paradise. The apples drop into your mouth, and as you would expect of any decent paradise, a snake is creeping around the place, and it wants to know that everything is under control. Kenny Xin doesn't trust anyone. Not even me, although he describes himself as my friend and he was the one who got me this extremely remunerative job in the first place. Hi there, Kenny, by the way. You see, your suspicion was justified." He laughed. "I doubt very much that you know the guy, but he's the reason why I'm presenting this file. Some of the attached documents deal with him, so let's just say that in 2017, on the instructions of the Chinese oil companies and with the approval of Beijing, he organized the coup against Juan Aristide Ndongo and, with my help, or more precisely with the help of African Protection Services, carried it out and enthroned Mayé. The dossier records a chronicle of coups, internal information about Beijing's role in Africa, and much else besides, but at its heart there lies a quite different subject."

He crossed his legs and wearily waved away a flying insect the size of a human fist.

"Perhaps someone remembers the launch pad that Mayé had built on Bioko. International companies were involved, under the aegis of the Zheng Group, which allows us to assume that China had a hand in this as well. Personally I don't believe that. Nor is it true, even though we've repeatedly sold the idea in public, that our space program was an initiative one hundred percent down to Mayé. In fact it was initiated by a group of *possibly* Chinese investors which, in my opinion—and contrary to their own account—is not identical with Beijing and was represented by Kenny Xin at the time. The fact is that this organization wanted to fire an information satellite from our soil into space, supposedly as an investigation into new kinds of rocket propulsion. Mayé was supposed to be able to use the satellite for civilian purposes, with the proviso that the whole space project was presented as his own idea. I've attached the blueprints for the launch pad, along with a list of all the companies which helped to build it."

"He's still mocking us," Yoyo hissed.

"Hardly." Jericho shook his head. "He can't mock us anymore."

"But that's exactly what he did in Muntu—"

"Wait." Jericho raised his hand. "Listen!"

"—the launch was scheduled for two days later. This meant that the preparations should actually have been completed, and only the satellite had still to be put on the tip of the rocket. That same night a convoy of armored cars arrived on the grounds of the launch pad. Something was brought into the construction hangar and coupled with the satellite: a container the size of a very big suitcase or a small cupboard, fitted with landing equipment, jets, and spherical tanks. The whole thing could be collapsed so that it didn't take up much room. Only close contacts of Xin dealt with the delivery and assembly of the craft, no foreign constructors were present, not even anyone from the Zheng Group. Neither Mayé nor his people knew at this point that anything but the said satellite was to be fired into space. I'm not a specialist in space travel, by the way, but I assume that the container held a small, automatic spaceship, a kind of landing unit. My people photographed the arrival of the convoy and the container; you will find the pictures in the files KON_PICS and SAT_PICS." Vogelaar grinned. "Are you still watching, Kenny? While you deludedly thought you were observing me, did it never occur to you that *we* were observing *you*?"

"So." Tu came out of the cockpit and joined them in the corridor. "We're flying on autopilot. We're on course for London via Amsterdam, so let's have a dr—"

"Shhh!" hissed Yoyo.

"—was of course interested in what was in that container," Vogelaar went on. "So I had to reconstruct the route it had taken—I should perhaps mention that the people who delivered it at dead of night were almost all Chinese. Anyway, we managed to trace the route of the plane that had brought it to Africa back through a series of intermediate landings. For obvious reasons I had expected that the plane had originally started off in China, but to my surprise it came from Korea, or more precisely from a remote airport in North Korea, near the border."

In the background it had started raining heavily. A rising rustle mingled with Vogelaar's words, a changing gray blurred the sky, scrubland, and sea.

"I've built up extensive contacts over the years. Not least with Southeast Asia. Someone who still owed me something set about working out what had been loaded on at the airport. You must know, the whole area is extremely unsafe. There's a lot of piracy in the surrounding waters, a high level of criminality, unemployment, and frustration. The South has been paying for the North's reconstruction since 2015, but the money is disappearing in a vast bubble of speculation. Both sides feel they've been tricked, and they aren't happy about it. Corruption and black market dealings are flourishing as a result, and one of the most lucrative markets is the trade in Kim Jong-un's former arsenal of weapons, particularly the warheads. Especially popular are the mini-nukes, small atom bombs with considerable destructive power. The Soviets certainly experimented with them, in fact all the nuclear powers did. Kim had a few too, hundreds even. Except nobody knows where they ended up. After the collapse of the North Korean regime, the death of Kim, and reunification they had suddenly disappeared, and since they aren't particularly big—"

The soldier measured out a length of about a meter with his hands.

"—and not much thicker than a shoe box, they won't be all that easy to find. A mini-nuke has the advantage of fitting into the smallest hiding place, whatever infernal power it's capable of unleashing." He smiled. "For example a small, automatic spaceship fired into space piggy-backing on a satellite."

Jericho stared at the monitor. Behind Vogelaar the skies had opened.

"I wanted to know if anyone had been doing any sort of shopping on the black market not long ago. My contact confirmed this. Just two years before, in the no-man's-land between North and South, Korean nuclear material had switched owners in a private transaction. I'm always suspicious these days, and as everybody knows you should treat hearsay with caution—but there are lots of signs that I knew the buyer very well."

"I don't believe it," Tu said. "They fired an atom bomb into space?"

Vogelaar leaned forward.

"Our old friend Kenny Xin had bought the thing. And I knew already why he had hit on the idea of building the launching pad in our quiet little jungle paradise. The whole thing was illegal in the extreme! It wouldn't have been possible to plant an atom bomb unnoticed on a state space agency. Kenny's employers *had* to find a neutral country, ideally a banana republic, whose ruling clique wasn't above any kind of deal. Some unloved patch of soil where no one was watching your every move. And the ideal launching pads for rockets are distributed in the area around the equator. Which was proof for me that China's Communist Party, at least at the highest levels of government, wasn't involved in this one, or else they could simply have launched the phony satellite from their official launch pads in Xichang, Taiyuan, Hainan, or Mongolia, and not a soul would ever have guessed what it was carrying. So in my opinion we're dealing with a non-state, criminal or terrorist association. Which doesn't mean that *individual* state organizations aren't involved. Let's not forget, China's secret services have been developing a grotesque life of their own in the meantime, and Washington doesn't always know what the CIA's getting up to. But it could also be that there's a big company behind it. Or else good old Dr. Mabuse, if anyone still remembers him."

"And the bomb's target—" whispered Yoyo.

Vogelaar leaned back, took a swig from his drink, and stroked his mustache.

"This file was actually conceived as life insurance," he said. "For me and for my wife, whom you may have met as Nyela. Clearly it hasn't been able to save us, so now it will serve to bring down the men behind the organization. Kenny would definitely be of crucial importance, because he has contact with the head of the gang and might know his identity. I've attached his eye scans, fingerprints, and voice samples, under KXIN_PERS, but he definitely isn't the instigator. So who is? Certainly not Korea, they're just selling off their Great Leader's belongings. The Communist Party, secretly arming space? As I've said, they wouldn't have needed a launch pad in Equatorial Guinea to do that. Zheng-style forces close to the government? Possibly. Perhaps the answer lies in the race to the Moon. China has made it clear more than once that it condemns America's rush into space, and Beijing is also projecting its dissatisfaction on to Orley Enterprises, Zheng's successful competitor. Or else somebody's trying to use China, because it's doing so well against the backdrop of the scramble for helium-3 and so on. With a strategically deployed atom bomb you could set the superpowers against one another, but what would be the point? They would both emerge weakened from an armed conflict. But perhaps that's exactly what they want to achieve, so who could profit from their weakness?"

The jet sped along in a straight line. UFOs could have been flying ahead of them and they wouldn't even have noticed. Their attention was focused on the monitor.

"Now we get to the question of where the bomb is at the moment. Still in the satellite? Or was it dropped as the launch vehicle was carrying it into space? There was no nuclear explosion on Earth, but okay, it needn't have exploded. On the other hand it would be idiotic to send a bomb first into orbit and from there back to Earth. Now, I think I can give a partial answer. Because even in the control room we were able to look over Kenny's people's shoulders. Under DISCONNECT_SAT you'll find film material that not only shows the satellite maintaining its position in orbit, but also something breaking away and flying off on an independent course. There's no doubt about what it is, but *where* did the mini-nuke go after decoupling? That's easy to answer too. Somewhere that an atom bomb couldn't have been sent by official channels. And what for? To destroy something that can't be easily destroyed from Earth. The target lies in space."

Vogelaar put his fingers together.

"I'll give you one last mystery for the road. It concerns the fact that I am speaking to you in the year 2024. I don't want to bore you with personal stories, but our cute little state is bankrupt, no one is fighting over our oil anymore, Mayé is starting to go around the bend, and to be honest I'd somehow imagined my government job would be more one of supporting the interests of the state. But no matter. Just bear in mind that construction of the launch pad began two years ago, and I'm sure the planning of the enterprise goes back even further than that. So the deployment of the bomb was planned a long time ago. Now it's up there. When's it going to go off? What is certain is that the target must have existed years ago, or else people knew that it *would* exist at the time of the launch of the satellite. As I said, I'm not a space expert, there are a few potential targets around the Earth and on the Moon, but to my knowledge only one has been completed and opened, probably this year. A hotel, planned for ages, location the Moon, building contractor Orley Enterprises. Does that tell us anything? Of course it does! Julian Orley, Zheng's great adversary, responsible for the permanent disadvantage of the Chinese."

Vogelaar raised his glass in a toast to them. Behind him, Equatorial Guinea drowned in tropical torrents.

"So have fun with your investigation. I haven't been able to assemble anything more than this. You'll have to find out the rest for yourselves. And come and see me, if you know where my grave is. Nyela and I would be delighted."

The recording ended. The only sound was the even humming of the turbines. Slowly, as if in a trance, Yoyo turned her head and looked first at Jericho and then at Tu. Her lips formed two words.

"Edda Hoff."

"Yes." Tu nodded grimly. "And fast!"

MAY 30, 2025
The Warning

Aristarchus Plateau, The Moon

The space shuttle Ganymede was a Hornet-model flying machine, with ion propulsion and pivotable jets to achieve thrust in any desired direction. In outward appearance, it resembled a grotesquely swollen transport helicopter, Eurocopter HTH class without rotors, but sitting on short, fat legs; inside it offered the comfort of a private jet. All thirty-six seats could be turned into couches at the press of a button, each seat had its own multimedia console. There was a tiny, extravagantly equipped galley which lacked only alcohol, in line with the regulation that crews must not dull their senses in the course of the day.

At present Gaia had two Hornet shuttles, the Ganymede and the Callisto. That afternoon they were both hurtling through the vacuum, more than 1,400 kilometers apart: Callisto heading toward Rupes Recta, a colossal fault in the middle of the Mare Nubium, 250 meters high and so long that you had a sense that it circled the whole of the Moon; Ganymede flying straight toward the Aristarchus Plateau, an archipelago of craters in the middle of the Ocean of Storms. A few hours previously the Callisto, flown by Nina Hedegaard and carrying the Ögis, Nairs, Donoghues, and Finn, had visited the Descartes Highlands, where the landing stage of Apollo 16 dozed in the sun and a derelict moon car exuded a nostalgic charm, while Ganymede had borne down upon the crater of Copernicus. From the lofty heights of its outer ring, the travelers had admired its rough central range, they had penetrated its capacious interior and shuddered to think what sort of giant must have fallen from the sky here 800 million years ago.

The world was nothing but stone, and yet it was so much more.

The soft, undulating structure of its plains led you to forget that the maria were not true seas, nor the crater bottoms lakes. Curious structures suggested former habitation, as if H. G. Wells's space-traveling heroes had actually encountered insectoid selenites and herds of moon cows here, before being abducted into the machine world of the lunar underground. They had seen a lot that day, Carl Hanna, Marc Edwards and Mimi Parker, Amber and the Locatellis, Evelyn Chambers and Oleg Rogachev, whose wife lay grimly by the moon pool, but Julian insisted that the highlight was still to come. The first spurs of the high plateau appeared in the northwest. Peter Black made the shuttle climb high above the Aristarchus Crater, which looked as if it was cast out of light.

"The Arena of the Spirits," Julian whispered with an air of mystery, a youthful grin playing around the corners of his mouth. "An observation point for sinister light phenomena. Some people are convinced that Aristarchus is inhabited by demons."

"Interesting," said Evelyn Chambers. "Perhaps we should leave Momoka here for a while."

"That would be the end of any sinister phenomena," Momoka observed drily. "After only an hour in my company the last demon would have emigrated to Mars."

Locatelli raised his eyebrows, full of admiration at how coquettishly his wife was twisting and turning in the mirror of her own self-criticism.

"And can you tell us something about the cause?" Rogachev asked.

"Yeah, well, there are a lot of arguments about that. For decades light phenomena have been witnessed in Aristarchus and other craters, but until a few years ago ultra-orthodox astronomers refused even to acknowledge the existence of such 'Lunar Transient Phenomena.'"

"Perhaps volcanoes?" Hanna suggested.

"Wilhelm Herschel, an astronomer of the late eighteenth century, was convinced of that. Very popular in his day. He was one of the first to spot red dots in the lunar night, some of them around here. Herschel supposed they were glowing lava. Later his sightings were confirmed; other observers reported a violet haze, menacingly dark clouds, lightning, flames, and sparks, all extremely mysterious."

"To spit lava, the Moon would have to have a liquid core," said Amber. "Does it?"

"You see, that's the rub." Julian smiled. "It's generally assumed that it does, but so deep underground that volcanic eruptions are ruled out as an explanation."

Momoka peered suspiciously out of the side windows into Aristarchus's gaping mouth.

"You can stop trying to make things so exciting," Evelyn said after a while.

"Wouldn't you rather believe in demons?"

"I don't see demons as romantic," said Parker. "It would mean the Devil living on the Moon."

"So?" Locatelli shrugged. "Sooner here than in California."

"So the Devil is someone you make jokes about."

"Fine." Julian raised his hands. "There is a bit of volcanic activity up here. No lava streams, admittedly, but it's been noted that the phenomena always occur when the Moon is closest to the Earth, so when gravity is tugging at it particularly hard. The consequences are lunar quakes. When that happens, pores and cracks appear, hot gases emerge from the deeper regions to the surface, bursting out at high pressure, regolith is fired out, albedo accumulates at the exit point, and already you have a glowing cloud."

"I get it," said Momoka. "It needs to fart."

"You should stop giving away all the tricks," Amber said with a sideways glance at Parker. "I thought the demons were more exciting."

"And what's that thing there?" Edwards narrowed his eyes and pointed outside. Something massive was twisting its way northwest of the crater, across the plateau with all its furrows and potholes. It looked like a huge snake, or rather like the cast for a snake, a beast of mythical proportions. The funnel-shaped head joined a twisting body that narrowed until it opened up, thin and pointed, in the next plain along. The whole thing looked as if it had once been the resting place of Ananden, the ancient Indian world snake that carried the Earth and the Universe, the scaly, breathing throne of the god Vishnu.

"That," said Julian, "is Schröter's Valley."

Black soared above the formation at great height, so that they could admire its vast dimensions, the whole of the great Moon valley, as Julian explained, four billion years old; and other people had in fact been struck by its serpentine nature. The head crater, 6 kilometers across, was called Cobra's Head, a cobra that twisted 168 kilometers to the shore of the Oceanus Procellarum. On a plateau that overlooked Cobra's Head from the northeast, a leveled area came into view, lined with hangars and collectors. A radio mast gleamed in the sunlight. Black brought the vehicle down toward the landing field and set Ganymede down gently on its beetle legs.

"Schröter space station," he said, and grinned conspiratorially at Julian. "Welcome to the Realm of the Spirits. The chances of us seeing any are slight, and yet, ladies and gentlemen, stay away from suspicious-looking holes and cracks. Helmets and armor on. Five in the air lock at any one time, like this morning. Julian, Amber, Carl, Oleg and Evelyn first, followed by Marc, Mimi, Warren, Momoka and me. If I may ask you."

Unlike the landing module of the Charon, in a Hornet shuttle you didn't have to suck out all the air in the cabin, but left it via a lift that doubled as an air lock. Black extended the shaft. They took their chest armor from the shelf and helped each other into their tightly fitting suits, while Julian tried to banish the shadow that stripped his mood of its usual radiant power. Lynn was starting to change, he couldn't deny it. She was showing signs of inner seclusion, had developed unattractive rings around her eyes, and was treating him with growing and unmotivated aggression. In his puzzlement he had confided in Hanna, a mistake, perhaps, although he couldn't say exactly why. The Canadian was fine, in fact. And yet he had recently started feeling slightly shy around Hanna, as if he would only have to look a bit more closely, and unsettling trigonometric connections would appear between him, Lynn, and the ghostly train. The longer he brooded about it, the more certain he was that the solution was right before his eyes. He saw the truth without recognizing it. A detail of banal validity, but as long as his inner projectionist slept the sleep of the just, he couldn't reach it.

Along with the others, he entered the air lock and put his helmet on. Through the viewing windows he could see the interior of the shuttle, while the air was being sucked out of the air lock. He saw Locatelli delivering speeches, Momoka helping Parker into the survival backpack, then the elevator cabin plummeted, emerged from the belly of the Ganymede, and traveled down the shaft to just above the asphalt of the landing field. A ramp emerged from the floor of the cabin, and they stepped outside along it. It had not been planned for shuttles to land on anything but solid surfaces, but if such a landing were necessary, any contact between the cabin and the fine dust of the regolith was to be kept to a minimum, because otherwise—

Julian hesitated.

All of a sudden it was as if the projectionist had rubbed his eyes. Yawning, he pulled himself together to climb down into the archive and look for the missing roll of film.

He had just seen it again: the truth.

And again he hadn't understood it.

He watched with irritation as the second group left the air lock. Black waved them over to one of the cylindrical hangars. Three open rovers were parked in it, surprisingly like historical moon cars, but with three axles, bigger wheels, and room for six people in each. The improved design of the rover, Black explained, made it faster than in the early years of lunar car manufacture, and also fit to drive on extremely uneven ground. Each of the wheel mountings could swing if necessary to a ninety-degree vertical, which was enough to let it simply drive over large boulders.

"But not on the path that we're about to take," he added. "We're following the northern stretch of the valley until the first turning of the cobra's body. A rocky outcrop there, the spur of the Rupes-Toscanelli scarp, runs right up to the edge of the gorge, Snake Hill. I'll tell you no more than that for the time being."

"And how far are we going?" Locatelli wanted to know.

"Not far. Just 8 kilometers, but the journey is spectacular, right along the edge of the Vallis."

"Can I drive?" Locatelli was jumping around with excitement. "I really want to drive that thing!"

"Of course." Black laughed. "The steering is easy, it's the same as the buggies. You shouldn't drive straight at the biggest obstacles, if you don't want to go flying out of your seat, but otherwise—"

"Of course not," said Locatelli, already imagining his foot on the accelerator.

"Will we let him have his fun?" Julian said to Momoka.

"Of course. As long as you let me have the fun of driving in the other rover."

"Good. Warren is driving rover number two, and promises to bring Carl, Mimi, and Marc safely to their destination, the rest of us will take the first one. Who's the chauffeur?"

When everyone said they wanted to be the chauffeur, the choice fell on Amber. She was told how the various functions worked, took a test drive, and got everything right right away.

"I want one of these when we're back down there," she cried.

"You don't," Julian grinned. "It's six times as heavy down there. It would fall to bits in the garage."

The convoy set off. Black let Amber drive ahead to keep Locatelli from breaking speed records, so that they had been driving for ten minutes when the valley dropped away on their left in a wide curve. A narrow path led to a high ridge, from which you could enjoy an incomparable view of the Vallis Schröteri. You could see almost the whole course of it from there, but something else was holding everyone's attention. It was a crane, mounted on a platform that loomed into the gorge. As they approached they made out a winch at ground level. A steel cable ran through the cantilever and led to a capacious double seat. There was no need to explain how the crane worked. Once you had taken your seat, the cantilever swung over the gorge, and you floated, legs dangling, above the abyss.

"Brilliant! Absolutely brilliant!" Marc Edwards's extreme-sport soul was boiling over. He jumped from the parked rover, stepped to the edge of the platform, and looked down. "What's the drop here? How far could we abseil down?"

"Right to the bottom," Peter Black explained, as if he had dug the gorge with his own hands. "One thousand meters."

"To hell with the Grand Canyon," Locatelli observed with familiar sophistication. "It's a trickle of piss compared to this one."

"Does that thing work?" Edwards asked.

"Of course," said Julian. "Once the factory's up and running, we'll build a few more."

"I absolutely have to try it out!"

"*We* absolutely have to try it out," Mimi Parker corrected him.

"Me too." Julian thought he could see Rogachev smiling. "Perhaps Evelyn would keep me company?"

"Oh, Oleg," laughed Evelyn. "You want to die with me?"

"No one will die as long as I'm working the winch," Black promised. "Okay, Mimi and Marc will go down first—"

"I'm going with Carl," said Amber. "If he has the guts."

"I do. With you I always do."

"So then Amber with Carl after that, and then Oleg and Evelyn. Momoka?"

"No way."

"Then Momoka will come with us," Julian suggested. "The rest of us will climb Snake Hill in the meantime. Oleg, Evelyn, you too. It'll take a while before Peter has lowered those four down and hoisted them back up again."

"I've thought about it a bit," said Amber. "I'd rather go up the mountain with you. What's up with you, Carl?"

"Hey! Are you wussing out?"

"Don't get your hopes up."

"Then see you later. Take care. I'll take a look and see what lies ahead."

Hanna watched the others start their climb. The path led gently upward, curved around, and disappeared into a ravine. It reappeared a considerable stretch further up, ran along the flank for about 100 meters, a steep climb now, and then vanished from view once more. Clearly you had to circle the slope to reach the high plateau. Hanna would have loved to go with them, but he was more fascinated by the gorge, a kilometer deep, with vertical walls on all sides. Perhaps he could climb the high plain later on, with Mimi and Marc. He would have preferred to take the trip on his own, but wherever he went, someone would be talking to him on his headset. At least you could turn individual participants on or off, only the guides were transmitting at all times, and had a right of access to everyone's auditory canal.

He watched with interest as Black released the winch, opened the faceplate of the console, and activated the controls by pressing on one of five fist-sized buttons. Primitive lunar technology, one might have thought, built for the clumsy extremities of aliens—and wasn't that exactly what they were on this strange satellite, aliens, extraterrestrials, their fingers forced into hard shells? Black pressed a second button. The cantilever was set in motion and began to swing in. Parker and Edwards jostled each other impatiently on the edge of the platform.

"What are the other buttons for?" Hanna asked.

"The blue one swings the crane back out again," said Black. "The one below it turns the winch on."

"So the black one's there to bring the lift back up again?"

"You've got it. Child's play. Like most things on the Moon, in fact, so that not everything depends on the expert."

"If he's dead, for example." Edwards stepped back from the edge to make room for the incoming elevator.

"Don't say things like that," Parker protested.

"Don't worry." Black opened the safety guard of the seats. "I'd consider it quite irresponsible of me to die while you're hanging there. If some unexpected local demons swallow me up unexpectedly, you'll still have Carl. He'll winch you back up again. Ready? Off we go!"

• • •

"Shit!" said Locatelli.

They had passed the ink-black shadow of the ravine, climbed the slope, and had just reached the spot where the flank curved around, when he noticed. He looked irritably down into the valley. The gorge gaped far below them, 4 kilometers wide, so that the platform stuck to the edge of the rock like a toy, populated by tiny, springy figures, hopping up and down. Peter was just helping the Californian into the seat, while Hanna studied the winch.

"What's up?" Momoka turned around.

"I forgot my camera."

"Idiot."

"Really?" Locatelli took a sharp breath. "And who's the other idiot? Think about it."

"Hey, no need to fight," Amber cut in. "We'll just take my cam—"

"Are you talking about me?" Momoka snapped.

"Who else? You could have thought about it too."

"Shut the hell up, Warren. What would I want to do with your stupid camera?"

"Lots, my lotus flower! Who wants to be filmed from dawn until dusk, as if the crap that you produce for the movies wasn't enough?"

"I wouldn't pose in front of your camera if you paid me!"

"That is so funny! You really mean that? You start pissing yourself as soon as you *see* a camera."

"Nicely put, asshole. Go and get it, then."

"You bet I well," snapped Locatelli and turned on his heel.

"Hey, Warren," called Evelyn, quietly rapt. "You're not going all the way back just for—"

"Yep."

"Wait!" shouted Julian. "Take Amber's camera, she's right. You can film Momoka with it until she pleads for mercy."

"No! I'm going to get the damned thing!"

He stamped defiantly back in the direction of the ravine.

"I know he doesn't have an easy life with me," he heard Momoka saying quietly to the others, as if he couldn't hear every single word. "But Warren's only happy when something's getting on his nerves."

"Quite honestly, you both seem to need that," Amber remarked.

"Ah, yes." Momoka sighed. "I love it when he hits back. That's when I love him most."

Julian, advancing with the pace of a natural leader, had almost reached the plateau when he heard Sophie's voice in his helmet. Parked some way off, he could just see the rovers via which he was connected to the Ganymede, and via it with Gaia.

"What is it, Sophie?"

"I'm sorry, sir, call from Earth. I've got Jennifer Shaw on the line for you. Please switch to O-SEC."

O-SEC. Bug-proof connection. It meant that he had to sever his contact with the group. No one would be able to hear what his company's security adviser had to tell him.

"Fine." He obliged. "We're on our own."

"Julian!" Jennifer's voice, urgent. "I won't trouble you with an endless preamble. Lynn will have told you about the warning we received yesterday. We've just—"

"Lynn?" Julian interrupted her, surprised. He turned to the others and gestured to them to stop. "No. Lynn didn't tell me anything about a warning."

"She didn't?" Jennifer said, puzzled.

"When's that supposed to have been?"

"Last night. Edda Hoff talked to your daughter. Lynn wanted to be kept informed about the matter. Of course I assumed that she—"

"What *matter* are we talking about, Jennifer? I don't understand a word."

Jennifer fell silent for a moment. The delay between Earth and Moon lasted only a second, but it was enough to create irritating little pauses.

"Two days ago we received a warning from a Chinese businessman," she said. "He happened to come into possession of a garbled text document, and since then he's been on the run. The text suggests—or seems to suggest—that one of the company's plants is threatened with attack."

"What's that you say? Hoff said *that* to my daughter?"

"Yes."

"Lynn? Lynn, are you there?"

"I'm here, Dad."

"What's going on? What's all this about?"

"I—I didn't want to bother you with it." Her voice sounded quavery and upset. "Of course I—"

"Lynn, Julian, I'm sorry," Jennifer cut in. "But there's no time for all this. The Chinese guy called me again a short time ago, or one of his people did. They're coming straight to us. This morning they tried to find out more about the background to the document, and it ended in disaster. There were casualties, but they've got some new information."

"What kind of information? Jennifer, who—"

"Wait, Julian. We're in contact with the Chinese jet. I'll put you through."

A second passed, then a strange man's voice was heard, amid an atmospheric hiss:

"Mr. Orley? My name is Owen Jericho. I know you have a thousand questions, but I've got to ask you to listen to me now. By completing the document we've been able to discover that an information satellite was fired into the Earth's orbit from African soil. The operator was the former government of Equatorial Guinea, General Juan Mayé, who took over in a coup."

"Yes, I know," said Julian. "Mayé and his satellite. He made a laughing stock of himself with that thing."

"What you may not know is that Mayé was a straw man for Chinese lobbyists. It's possible that he was put in power at the instigation of Beijing, but it was certainly done with their connivance. By now other people are in power in Equatorial Guinea, but during his time in office the Chinese sponsored his space program. Does the name Zheng mean anything to you?"

"The Zheng Group? Of course!"

"Zheng made lots of their technology available to him at the time, and provided know-how and hardware. But the satellite was just a pretext to fire something else into orbit from Mayé's state territory. Something that no official site would have allowed through."

"What was that?"

"A bomb. A Korean atom bomb."

Julian froze. He feared what this man Jericho was getting at. He watched uneasily as the others scattered and gesticulated on the path.

"The Koreans?" he echoed. "What on earth do I have to do with—"

"Not the Koreans, Mr. Orley, but what Kim Jong-un's abandoned ghost train left behind. We're talking about the black market mafia. In other words, China, or somebody who's hiding behind China, has bought a handy little atom bomb from Korean stock, a so-called mini-nuke. We're sure that this bomb left the satellite just as it entered its orbit—so a year ago—then traveled on from there to an unknown destination. And in our opinion that destination is *not* on Earth."

"Just a moment." *Not on Earth.* "You mean—"

"We mean it's meant to destroy one of your space installations, yes. Probably Gaia. The Moon hotel."

"And what makes you suspect that?" Julian heard himself saying in a remarkably calm voice.

"The time delay. Of course there are a few variations. But none of them really explains why the thing has been up there for a year without being set off. Unless something got in the way." Jericho paused for a miserably long time. "Wasn't Gaia originally supposed to have opened in 2024? And that was postponed because of the Moon crisis?"

Julian said nothing, as something was set in motion, slowly but inexorably, inside his head. The projectionist slipped by, put in the reel of film and—

"Carl," he whispered.

"Sorry?" asked Jericho.

"In the morning, two days ago," cried Julian. "My God! I saw it and didn't understand. Carl Hanna, one of our guests. I ran into him in the corridor, he said he'd been looking for the exit and hadn't found it, but he was lying to us! He was outside."

"Julian." Dana Lawrence joined in the conversation. "I'm afraid you're wrong. You've seen the recordings. Carl definitely didn't go outside."

"He did, Dana. He did! And idiot that I am, I even saw it. Down in the corridor, even though I didn't understand it. Someone faked the recordings, reedited the shots. He steps onto the passageway to the Lunar Express—"

"And reappears a few seconds later."

"No, he was outside! He steps on it wearing a very clean suit, Dana, clean as a whistle! And when he comes out again, there are traces of moon dust on his legs. That was what I was looking for the whole time, that subliminal certainty that something was wrong."

"Just a moment," Dana said sharply. "I'll get the recordings up on screen."

Clever Julian, thought Hanna.

He stood there motionlessly while the cantilever swung over the gorge, Mimi and Marc hung laughing over the abyss, and Black set the winch in motion, and he heard something that he shouldn't have heard. But he was switched in. This time, once again, Ebola ensured that he was able to function, even though his room to maneuver was dramatically shrinking. He would never have expected to get busted, his identity was airtight. Not even when Vic Thorn had died had the operation been as precarious as it was right now. All of a sudden the planned course of action was out the window; he had to act, carry out his mission prematurely, use the seconds, minutes at most, that Ebola had gained for him to create the maximum possible confusion and take to his heels.

"Have the hotel searched right now," Owen Jericho was saying. "This guy Carl, perhaps he's been outside to hide the bomb in Gaia. Ask him—"

"I will ask him," hissed Julian. "Oh, I'll ask him!"

Yeah, right, thought Hanna.

The elevator sank slowly into the gorge. Black stood by the winch, waving at the Californians. Wanted to know what it felt like being just a kilometer above the ground.

"Amazing!" raved Parker. "Better than parachute jumping. Better than anything."

Hanna got moving, stretched his arms out.

"Can you speed the pace up a bit?" asked Edwards. "Speed it up. Let us fly!"

"Sure, I—"

With both hands Hanna grabbed Black by the backpack, pulled him away from the console, lifted him in the air, and carried him to the edge.

"Hey!" The pilot reached behind him. "Carl, is that you?"

Hanna said nothing, walked quickly on. His victim turned, kicked his legs, tried to get a hold of his assailant.

"Carl, what's going on? Have you gone mad?—No!"

He hurled Black over the edge of the platform. For a moment the pilot seemed to find purchase in the void, then he fell, comparatively slowly at first, getting faster and faster. His shrill scream mingled with Mimi Parker's.

Nothing, not even a sixth of terrestrial gravity, could save a person falling into an abyss from a height of 1,000 meters.

GAIA, VALLIS ALPINA, THE MOON

"Julian?" called Sophie. "Miss Shaw?"

"What's going on?" snapped Dana.

"Radio silence. Both gone." She tried in turn to reestablish connection with headquarters in London and with Julian, but all communication had been interrupted, immediately after the start of the video showing the miraculous sullying of Hanna's trouser legs in the sterile surroundings of a passageway. The Canadian, small and cheerful, went for a walk on the corridor conveyor belt, unnoticed by anyone.

"Julian? Please come in!"

"Try to reach the Earth in the conventional manner," said Dana. "Oh, don't worry, let me do it."

She pushed Sophie aside, pulled up a menu, switched from LPCS on direct aerial connection to the terrestrial Tracking and Data Relay Satellite System, targeted ground stations, which was just possible within view of Earth, but Gaia seemed to have been deprived of her sensory organs. Lynn stared, her hand in front of her mouth, at the monitor wall, while Sophie shifted nervously from one leg to the other.

"I was carrying on the conversation quite normally when—"

"Don't apologize before I start blaming you," Dana yelled at her. "Keep on trying. Perform an analysis. I want to know where the problem lies. Lynn?"

Lynn turned her head as if in a trance.

"Can I speak to you for a minute?"

"What?"

Rigid with fury Dana left the control center. Lynn followed her into the hall like a robot.

"I think—"

"Sorry!" Dana flashed her inquisitorial, gray-green eyes. "You're my boss, Lynn, and that means I have to be respectful. But now I have to ask you very clearly what yesterday's warning was about."

Lynn looked as if she had been recalled to life after a long period of unconsciousness. She raised a hand and studied its palm as if it contained something very attractive.

"It was all pretty vague."

"What was vague?"

"Edda Hoff called and said a few people were planning some sort of attack on an Orley plant. It sounded—well, vague. Not like anything to worry about."

"Why didn't you tell me about it right away?"

"I didn't think it was necessary."

"I'm the manager *and* the security officer of this hotel, and you didn't think it was necessary?"

Lynn stopped studying the palm of her hand and stared furiously back.

"As you have already observed, Dana, I am your boss and, no, I *didn't* think it was necessary to inform you. According to Hoff it was an *extremely vague* suspicion that *somewhere* in the world at *some* point an attack on *one* of our plants was planned, which was why she wanted to talk to me or Julian and not to *you*, and Julian had enough on his plate, so *I* asked to be kept informed. Does that answer your question?"

Dana took a step nearer. As if the prospect of disaster were not hovering above the hotel, Lynn found herself immersed in fascinated thoughts about the mysteries of the Dana physiognomy. How could such a sensually full mouth look so hard? Was the pallor of the face, framed by coppery red, due to the light, to a genetic predisposition, or merely to Dana's bitterness? How was it possible to seethe with rage and yet reveal such mask-like indifference?

"Maybe you missed a few things back there," the manager said quietly. "But there was talk of this hotel being blown up by an atom bomb. One of your guests seems to be involved in it. We've lost contact with your father and with Earth. You should at any rate have talked to me about it."

"You know what?" said Lynn. "You should get on with your work."

She left Dana standing and went back to the control center. The video of Hanna was still flickering on the monitor wall. The manager followed her slowly.

"I'd love to," she said icily. "Are you overworked, Lynn? Are you up to this? A moment ago you looked as if you'd been paralyzed."

Sophie looked up and away again, not liking what she saw.

"I'm afraid we've had a satellite failure," she said. "I can't reach Earth or Ganymede or Callisto. Shall I try Peary Base?"

"Later. First we'll have to talk through the next few steps. If what we've just heard is true, we're threatened with catastrophe."

"What kind of catastrophe?" asked Tim.

Aristarchus Plateau, The Moon

Locatelli caught his breath.

He saw Black disappearing just as he stepped from the shadow of the ravine and back into the sunlight. He stared at the scene as if nailed to the spot. It wasn't easy to tell who had pushed whom into the gorge, and he had switched the gang down there to mute, but there was no doubt that it had been deliberate.

It had been no accident. That was murder!

Warren Locatelli was accused of lots of dubious qualities: uncouthness, recklessness, narcissism, and much besides, but cowardice wasn't among them. His Italian-Algerian temperament broke through, flooded his thoughts. As he started running he saw the murderer pull something from his thigh.

And Edwards saw it too.

Below them, Black's flailing figure became smaller and smaller. He knew enough about gravitational physics to be aware that the pilot would not survive the fall, despite the reduction in gravitational pull. The rate of his fall might be slower than on Earth, 12 meters might be the equivalent of two, but there was no air resistance to counteract it. Black's body would be accelerated in a linear fashion, determined entirely by mass attraction. With each second his speed would increase by 1.63 meters per second until he landed at the bottom like a meteorite.

And he and Mimi would—

He was filled with fresh horror. He looked to the edge of the platform and saw the astronaut who had pushed Black into the depths, holding something long and flat in his right hand.

"Carl?" he wheezed.

The astronaut didn't reply. In the same moment Edwards worked out that they too were in extreme danger. He started tugging like mad on his safety guard, bent it to the side, and rose from his seat. They had to get out of here. Climb up the rope, back over the cantilever to solid ground, their only chance.

"What are you doing?" screamed Mimi.

Edwards was about to reply, but the answer stuck in his throat. The astronaut raised the long object, aimed it at the seat contraption and fired. Instead of gunpowder the little piece of plasticene detonated in the shell. The liquid from the jelly capsule evaporated, swelled to many times its volume, and produced sufficient pressure to fire the projectile at him at high speed. It pierced Parker's helmet, at which point the shower gel and shampoo combined to form what they really were, namely explosives, and the chairlift flew apart along with its occupants, flinging steel, fiberglass, electronics, and body parts in all directions.

Hanna reholstered his weapon and strode toward the parked rovers.

Locatelli was faster. He jumped, scrabbled, slipped down the path, but he had a longer distance to travel. So he looked on as the fleeing astronaut reached the front of a rover and swung himself onto the driver's seat. Now once more within view of Julian's group, he heard a Babel of voices breaking out in his helmet, provoked by something that Amber had said. A moment later the murderer drove away at great speed.

"Shit," wheezed Locatelli. "Stop, you bastard!"

"Warren, what's going on?" said Momoka. "Answer please."

"I'm here."

"Amber said you'd made contact with Black and heard screams. She says—"

Locatelli stumbled. His leaps were too high, too risky. He missed the path, spread his arms out, landed on a steep bank of gravel and turned a somersault.

"Warren! For Christ's sake, what's going on?"

Up and down switched places. He hurtled downward at high speed, toward the edge of the gorge. His body, light as a child's, took off every few meters, and soared briefly before landing again, so that he could no longer see or hear; dust, nothing but dust, but his suit didn't seem to have been damaged. Otherwise I'd be dead, he thought, that doesn't take long out here, you're dead before you've even noticed.

"Warren!"

"A minute," he yelled. "Ow! Ouch! A minute!"

"Where are—"

The connection went dead. He slid along the plain on his belly, pushed himself up and landed on his feet, hurried to the second rover. With one spring he was behind the wheel. By now he was being yelled at from all directions, but he'd stopped paying the slightest attention. He didn't doubt for a moment what the guy was planning, namely to leave them here and clear off on Ganymede.

Was the bastard listening?

It was better to turn off all his connections. The other guy should learn as late as possible that someone was following him. He quickly pressed the central switch, silenced the voices in his head, put his foot on the accelerator, and dashed after the fleeing man.

Gaia, Vallis Alpina, The Moon

Tim had just appeared in the control center when Dana gave a warning about some sort of catastrophe. The atmospheric barometer was clearly below freezing, with the hotel manager as cooling element, it seemed to him, while Sophie's features were helpless and Lynn's desolate. She looked to Tim like a drowning woman whose fear did battle with the fury of not having learned to swim in time.

"What's up?" he asked.

Dana looked at him thoughtfully. Then she delivered her report. Concise, to the point, toneless, without euphemism or downplaying of any kind. Within a minute Tim knew that someone was trying to blow Gaia to atoms, that the Chinese might be behind it, but that in all likelihood it was Carl Hanna, nice, guitar-playing Carl, in whose company Amber was currently out and about.

"For heaven's sake," he said. "How certain is it that there's a bomb?"

"Nothing's certain. Speculations, but as long as they haven't been refuted we should give them the status of facts." Her eyes emitted a freezing beam toward Lynn. "Miss Orley, any ideas, in your capacity as boss?"

Lynn gasped for air.

"There isn't the slightest reason to blow up Gaia! It must be a mistake."

"Thanks, that's a great help to us. Give me a directive, or allow me to make some suggestions of my own. We could order an evacuation, for example."

Lynn clenched her fists. She looked as if she wanted to tear out Dana's voice box.

"*If* there really was a bomb in the hotel, why didn't it go off ages ago? I mean, who or what was it being aimed at? The construction site? Anyone in particular?"

"We're all in danger," said Tim. "Who's going to bring an atom bomb to the Moon with a view to sparing human lives?"

"Exactly." Lynn looked at them in turn. "And so far we've all gathered together every night, so why hasn't anything happened? Perhaps because there is no bomb? Because someone's just trying to scare us?"

"Hmm," said Sophie hesitantly. "As this guy Jericho's already said, Hanna's task might have been to get the bomb here. If it reached the Moon a year ago—"

"Did Gaia even exist a year ago?" asked Tim.

"In its raw state," Lynn nodded.

"That means it could have been here since then."

"An atom bomb?" Dana's face expressed skepticism. "Sorry, but even I don't believe *that*. I don't know much about mini-nukes, I have no idea about atomic weapons, but I think I know they give off radiation. Wouldn't this bomb do that too? How long could you ignore something like that?"

"Perhaps Hanna only brought it up here the day before yesterday," Sophie concluded. "On his nighttime—"

"That's all so speculative!" Lynn flung her hand in the air with exasperation. "Just because he had some dust on his pants. And even if he did, why didn't he set it off ages ago?"

"Perhaps he was waiting for the right moment," Tim suggested.

"And when would that be?"

"No idea." Sophie shook her head. Her curls flew around as if having a party, in spite of the drama of the situation. "Certainly not now. Apart from Miss Orley and Tim there are only comparatively unimportant people here."

"Fine!" said Lynn triumphantly. "Then that means that we don't have to evacuate after all."

"I'm not keen on an evacuation, if that's what you mean," Dana replied calmly. "But I'll do it if it strikes me as advisable. For the time being I agree with Sophie. Things will probably only get critical when the shuttles come back, which should be happening at about seven o'clock. At the moment it's—" she looked at the electronic display "—16:20. More than two and a half hours to look for the thing."

"Excuse me?" Lynn rolled her eyes. "We're supposed to comb the hotel?"

"Yes. In teams."

"We'd be looking for a needle in a haystack!"

"And finding it if there is one. Sophie, get the rest of them together. We'll concentrate on places where a thing like that could be hidden."

"How big is a mini-nuke?" Sophie asked helplessly.

"The size of a briefcase?" Dana shrugged. "Does anyone know?"

Shaking of heads. Sophie opened several windows with schemagrams and tables full of numbers.

"At any rate, we're not registering any unusual radiation levels," she said. "No increased radioactivity, no additional sources of heat."

"Because there's no bomb here," sulked Lynn.

"And the sensors cover every area?" asked Tim.

"Every accessible area, yes."

"We should address another issue before we set off on our search," said Dana. "In my view we're not just dealing with a bomb."

"What else, then?"

"With a traitor."

"Oh Christ!" Lynn shook her head. "I thought Carl was the bad guy."

"Carl is *a* bad guy. But who reedited the video? Who helped him leave Gaia on the Lunar Express?" she added with a sidelong glance at Lynn. "Your father seems to have a very keen faculty of observation."

"You think one of us is working for Carl?" asked Tim.

"You don't?"

"I don't know enough about it."

"You know exactly as much as the rest of us do. How is Hanna going to cope up here all by himself? Acting and blurring his traces at the same time? Why did the satellites fail when his name was mentioned? How much can we put down to chance?"

"But who would it be?" Sophie's girlish face was filled with horror. "Nobody on the staff. And certainly not one of the guests."

"Hanna came here as a guest. A guest personally chosen by Julian Orley. How could he win so much trust?" Dana studied Lynn. Her gaze wandered on to Sophie, and settled on Tim. "So, the other one, who is he? Or is it a she? Someone in this room?"

"Utter nonsense," snapped Lynn.

"Could be. But that's one reason for us to search in teams." Dana smiled thinly. "So that we can keep an eye on each other."

Aristarchus Plateau, The Moon

Hanna only registered that he was being chased after quite a long time. The last thing he had heard amid the chaos in his helmet was that there was no longer any connection between Gaia and headquarters in London, or the Chinese jet. Hydra had discussed a few possible ways of paralyzing communication from the Moon or the Earth if the situation required. Clearly Ebola had been active. Now they were only connected by the radio in their suits, or by the aerials of the rovers and the shuttle, although that required visible contact. The last voice he had heard was Locatelli's, which had clearly been closer to him than the others.

Was *he* charging after him?

Hanna swerved around a small crater. The rover's top speed was 80 kilometers an hour, which was almost impossible to reach. The vehicle was light, particularly when under-occupied, and kept lifting off the ground, leaving clouds of dust behind. Somewhere in the washed-out gray the other vehicle had suddenly appeared, and it was quickly approaching. Either the driver had underestimated the particular qualities of gravity up here, or he was working from professional experience.

Locatelli was a racing driver.

It *had* to be him!

Hanna briefly considered stopping and blowing him up, but the swirl of dust wouldn't exactly help his aim, and he would also lose time. Better to increase his distance. Once he had reached the shuttle it didn't matter what became of Locatelli and the others. It wasn't likely they'd manage to leave the Aristarchus Plateau, but even if they did, they wouldn't be able to stop him. He had more than enough time left to carry out the operation and settle in the OSS. From there he could—

The right front wheel sped up. The rover performed a leap, landed crookedly, skidded along, and wrapped Hanna in gray clouds. For a moment he lost his bearings. Uncertain in which direction to turn, he set off again, found himself facing the gaping depths of the Schröter Valley, and at the very last second quickly whipped the wheel around and saved himself as best he could. Clearly, the only weapon that could be used against Locatelli was speed.

Dust. The monster that swallowed everything up.

Locatelli cursed. The bastard in front of him was whirling up so much of it that he had to hold back to keep from getting too close to him and dashing blindly to his death. Then, all of a sudden, it looked as if the murderer himself were driving into the abyss. He was just short of the edge when he regained control over his vehicle and whipped it on, whirling up clouds of tiny particles that glittered in their billions in the sunlight, as if the regolith were filled with glass. Darkness fell around Locatelli, then the clouds lifted. A moment later he saw the rover right in front of him with astonishing clarity. The subfloor had changed, asphalted terrain now, only a few hundred meters still to go to the Ganymede. Dark and massive it rested on its beetle legs—

What had the guy actually fired at him? A tiny island of pensiveness appeared in the whipped-up ocean of his fury, a place of quiet contemplation. What in hell's name was he doing here? What could he do to someone who was carrying deadly weapons and had no discernible qualms about using them? A moment later new waves of fury thundered through him, blowing away all his reservations. The murderer didn't even seem to find him worth a bullet. He hurtled like mad toward the shuttle, brought the rover to a standstill under the tail, jumped from his seat, and hurried to the air lock shaft that protruded from the Ganymede's abdomen like a monstrous birth canal. Only at the last second, with one leg in the cabin, did he pause and turn his reflective visor toward Locatelli.

"You miserable creep!" cried Locatelli, trying to wrest from the electric motor a performance that it had never managed before. "Wait, just wait!"

The astronaut put his hand to his thigh and drew the long, flat thing.

His inner Oceanus Procellarum was becalmed. His Algerian and Italian legacy fled, leaving a genuine, rationally thinking American who finally realized what an unfavorable position his recklessness had placed him in. He saw himself through the eyes of his enemy, the crosshairs practically painted on his helmet, one big invitation to pull the trigger—

"Shit," he whispered.

He let go of the wheel as if it were made of red-hot steel, jumped from the rover, turned a somersault, and skidded away across the smooth asphalt, as the vehicle dashed on with no one to stop it, straight toward Ganymede and the astronaut. A bright flash outshone the cold, white sun in the sky. The rover was hurled upward, stood upright, and spat parts of its frame, splinters of chassis, scraps of gold foil, and electronic components in all directions. Locatelli instinctively threw his arms together over his helmet. Beside him, debris plowed grooves into the asphalt. He quickly rolled onto his back, then as he sat up he saw one of the wheels wobbling wildly toward him; he catapulted himself out of the way and got to his feet.

No! *Not on my watch!*

Crouching and expecting the worst, he ran across the landing field, but his adversary had vanished. He saw the illuminated cabin climbing the air lock shaft. A few minutes more. He couldn't let the murderer steal the Ganymede and leave them in the desert. Heedless of the injuries he had dealt himself in his stunt, he ran under the body of the shuttle to the air lock shaft. The elevator cabin was gone, but the display showed a red light, and while it was red, Black had explained to them, the shaft couldn't be retracted. The astronaut must still be in the air lock shaft, which was probably being filled with air at that very minute. Good, very good.

Locatelli panted, waited.

Green!

He struck the call button with the flat of his hand.

Hanna wasted no time taking off his helmet after leaving the air lock shaft. He hurried between the rows of seats to the cockpit. Had he killed Locatelli? Probably not. The man had jumped off, Hanna had seen his body flying through the vacuum, before the projectile had struck the rover. The wreck might have crashed on top of him, or he might have been hit by some of the flying debris. Without looking behind him, he slipped into the pilot's seat and ran an eye over the display. He knew what the devices were for, he had had an opportunity to familiarize himself with the workings of all lunar vehicles some months ago. Thanks to Hydra's perfect preparatory work he even knew enough to drive the spaceship back into orbit, and from there to the OSS, and he wasn't alone on board as long as Ebola found a way of contacting him after communication had been blocked. Something he probably didn't need to worry about. Ebola would make sure he got there, and appeared in the right place at the right time.

His fingers slid over the controls.

He hesitated.

What was that? The shaft wouldn't move. The display was red, which meant that the cabin was currently being drained, or filled with air—or on its way!

He quickly turned around.

No, it was there, the space evenly lit behind the narrow windows, and deserted. Hanna narrowed his eyes. He paused. A sudden urge impelled him to get up and check, but he couldn't afford any further delays, and the light had just switched from red to green.

Ganymede was ready to go.

"There. There!"

Amber pointed excitedly into the sky. A long way off something was climbing steeply into the sky, something long that glinted in the sun.

"The Ganymede!"

They had come hurrying down the path, mindless, breathless, in clumsy kangaroo leaps, back to the crane platform, only to discover that both rovers had disappeared. Not a soul far and wide. Black's cries still echoed in Amber's ears. He had started screaming at the very moment when she had switched him on to ask him what was going on down there:

Carl, what's going on? Have you gone m—No!

Carl?

She had run anxiously out onto the platform and seen what was left of the gondola in which Mimi and Marc should have been sitting. More precisely, there was no gondola. Just the useless back of a chair, twisted steel, the contorted scrap of a safety guard and behind it, wedged in, something white, something numbingly familiar—

A single leg.

Only an extreme effort of will had kept her from throwing up in her helmet, while the others had stared down into the gorge and kept a lookout for the missing man. But large parts of the valley were in shadow, so they couldn't see anything at all.

"They're dead," Rogachev had stated at last.

"How can you claim that they're dead?" Evelyn said excitedly.

"That *is* a corpse." Rogachev pointed to the amputated leg in the ruined gondola.

"No, that's—that's—"

None of them had managed to speak its name. What an unbearable idea, that the fate of that shredded individual would only be fulfilled when it gave that limb an identity and thus retrospectively supplied the facts.

"We have to look for her," said Evelyn.

"Later." Julian stared at the place where the vehicles had just been standing. "We have worse things to worry about right now."

"Don't you think that's bad enough?" snapped Momoka.

"I think it's terrible. But first we have to find the rovers."

"Warren?" Momoka resumed her mantra-like calls to her husband. "Warren, where are you?"

"Assuming they managed it—" Evelyn tried again.

"*They're dead,*" Rogachev cut her off in a voice of ice. "Five people are missing. At least two of those are alive, otherwise both vehicles couldn't have disappeared, but the others are down there. Do you want to abseil down there and poke about in the dark?"

"How do you know it isn't—it isn't Carl down there?"

"Because Carl's alive," Amber had said wearily, to keep things short. "I think he has Peter and the others on his conscience."

"What makes you so sure about that?"

"Amber's right," Julian had said. "Carl's a traitor, I realized that a few minutes ago. Believe me, we do have a bigger problem than that here! We urgently have to think about how we—"

At that moment Amber had seen the shuttle rising on the horizon. For a moment it seemed to stand still above Cobra's Head, then it came toward them and suddenly got bigger.

It's flying this way, she thought.

The armored body was gaining form and outline, but also, worryingly, altitude. Whoever was flying the Ganymede plainly didn't plan to land and pick them up. The machine moved silently overhead, accelerated, turned in a northerly direction, shrank to a dot, and disappeared.

"Julian, call Gaia," urged Evelyn. "They've got to pick us up from here."

"It's not going to happen." Julian sighed. "The connection's been broken."

"Broken?" cried Momoka, horrified. "How come it's broken?"

"No idea. I did say we had a bigger problem."

BERLIN, GERMANY

Xin's transformation back from a lion-maned Mando-Progger to a perfectly normal contract killer was as good as complete when his contact called.

On the way back from the Grand Hyatt he had constantly asked what the two policemen had been doing there. No doubt about it, they had been after Tu—Jericho and the girl as well—but to what end? Jericho wasn't mentioned by name in Berlin, so the investigators had their sights set on Tu. Why him, of all people?

On the other hand he didn't care. Admittedly he had had to disappear without having achieved anything, but his intuition told him he had arrived too late anyway. The group had cleared out. So what? What were they going to do? Vogelaar and his wife were dead, the crystal was in his possession. While he put his wigs and fake beards away, he took the call.

"Kenny, damn it, how could that happen?"

No *Hydra*, no other greeting. Just anxious whispering. Xin hesitated. His contact was beside himself.

"How could what happen?" he asked warily.

"It's all going down the tubes! This guy Tu and this guy Jericho and the girl, all the contraband is on its way to us, and they *know*! They know everything! About the package, about the *attack*! They've even had a chance to talk to Julian Orley. *Our cover's being blown!*"

Xin froze. The Mando-Progger's Tartar beard lay in his hand like a small, dead animal.

"That's impossible," he whispered.

"Impossible? Well, then perhaps you could come *here*! Right now the company's being hit by a devastating earthquake."

"But I've got the dossier."

"So have they!"

A volley of oaths rained down on Xin, taking in, among other hardships, the unmasking of Hanna and the activation of the communication block. The latter had been planned as an emergency measure in case details of the attack were to seep through prematurely to the Moon. Something no one at Hydra had seriously reckoned with, but that was exactly what had happened.

"When was the net jammed?" asked Xin.

"During the linkup." The other man breathed sharply into the receiver. "Over the next twenty-four hours the Moon will be cut off from everything, but we can't keep the block going forever. I just hope Hanna gets the situation under control. Not to mention Ebola."

Ebola. Hanna's right hand was a specialist when it came to infecting supposedly independent systems and weakening them from within. That Ebola had managed to interrupt the fatal linkup could be seen as a brilliant maneuver, a skillful turnaround in the adverse wind of circumstances, but unfortunately on a leaking boat.

Vogelaar had outwitted him.

No! Xin forced himself to calm down. They weren't leaking yet. He had chosen Hanna and Ebola because they knew how to improvise and would keep the upper hand, regardless of how inauspicious the circumstances might be. He planned not to waste a second brooding on the possibility that the undertaking might go wrong.

"And how are you going to force this Tu and his rat pack to see sense?" the other man raged. "You've lost Mickey Reardon, two of your people died in Shanghai, you can't count on Gudmundsson and his team at the moment, they're otherwise engaged, so how do you think—"

"Not at all," Xin cut in.

Puzzled, his contact fell silent.

"There's no longer any point in eliminating Tu's group," Xin explained to him. "The facts of the situation have become common knowledge, the dissemination of the dossier can no longer be stopped. Everything else is decided on the Moon."

"Damn it, Kenny. We've been busted!"

"No. My task right now is to protect Hydra from being unmasked. Does *he* know about it yet?"

"I told him five minutes ago. He'd be glad of a personal call from you, otherwise I've got to sign off now; such a fucking mess! What happens if they track me down? What am I supposed to do then?"

"Nobody's going to get busted."

"But they're bringing the dossier with them! I don't know what's in it. Perhaps it would be better—"

"Just chill." The tearful whining at the other end was starting to make Xin feel ill. "I'll come to London as quickly as possible. I'll be near you, and if things get tight I'll get you out."

"My God, Kenny! How on earth could this happen?"

"Pull yourself together," Xin snapped. "The only risk is that you lose your nerve. Go back to the others and act as if nothing's wrong."

"I hope Hanna knows what he's doing."

"That's why I chose him."

Xin finished the conversation, swapped his phone from one hand to the other, and inspected the room. As might have been expected, he noticed thousands of things that weren't right, things that were asymmetrical, things that were out of proportion, strange excrescences in the design, an irritating bouquet of flowers. The florist hadn't been skilled enough to make the number of petals a multiple of the number of the flowers, thus giving the sorry effort some kind of mathematical meaning. For want of a self-contained idea, the supposedly aesthetic function failing to correspond to a structural one, the arrangement had something menacingly haphazard about it—a nightmare for Xin. The mere idea of being unable to produce a rationale for one's actions was totally horrifying! He reluctantly dialed another number, held his cell phone in his left hand, while the fingers of his right gripped the flowers and tried to correct the arrangement.

"Hydra," he said.

"How big is the dossier?" asked the voice.

"I haven't had a chance to read it yet." Xin pinched at a lily. "I'm sorry about what happened. Of course I'll assume full responsibility, but we could do nothing more than threaten Vogelaar with torture and death. He must have passed on a copy of the dossier to Jericho."

"You're not guilty," said the voice. "What's crucial is that the block still stands. What do you have in mind?"

"Change of tack. Take the heat off Jericho, Tu, and Yoyo. Their death is no longer a priority, and we can't influence what's happening on the Moon. I remain convinced that the operation will be a complete success. The important thing now is to preserve Hydra's anonymity."

"Do we agree on the weak points?"

"From my point of view there's only the one we've already discussed."

"That's exactly how I see it."

Xin considered the flower arrangement. Not really any better, still without any semiotic content. "I'll take the next plane to London."

"Are you well enough equipped there?"

"Airbike and everything. If necessary I can summon reinforcements."

"Gudmundsson is busy, you know that."

"My net stretches wide. I could set legions marching, but that won't be necessary. I keep myself constantly at the ready, that should do it."

"Tell me about the basic information in the dossier. Now that we've shelved e-mail communication, unfortunately you can't send it to me anymore."

"But it was still right to take the pages off the net."

"Keep me posted."

Xin paused.

Then he threw his phone on the bed and turned his mounting rage on orchids, lilies, and crocuses. He had to leave Berlin as soon as possible, but he couldn't even leave this room as long as the arrangement was subject to an unsatisfactory structure. The world was not random. Not haphazard. Everything had to yield a meaning. Where the meaning ended, madness began.

The head of a lily broke off.

Bobbing with fury, Kenny Xin tore the whole arrangement out of its bowl and shoved it in the garbage.

GAIA, VALLIS ALPINA, THE MOON

Lynn had decided to search the subterranean areas of Gaia along with Sophie. Tim sensed the reason for that. She dreaded arguments with him, because she knew very well that she would no longer be able to keep up her pretense. She was still able to lie to herself. Her attitude alternated between moments of complete clarity, subjectivity, and erupting fury. That abysmal, night-black fear dwelt once more in her every glance, the fear that might easily have killed her years before, and Tim thought he noticed something else in it, something vaguely insidious that frightened him to the core. As he poked through the casino with Axel Kokoschka, the chef, his concern swung from her to Amber, who was traveling with a suspected terrorist. Julian had received the information on a protected frequency, but how had he reacted? Peter Black was with him. Had they caught Carl?

What was happening right now on the Aristarchus Plateau?

Amber, he thought, come in! Please!

Gaia's underground floors, by Dana's estimation, deserved particular attention, because it was from there that a bomb would release its greatest destructive force. Michio Funaki and Ashwini Anand had been assigned to the staff accommodation areas, Lynn and Sophie to the underground greenhouses, aquaria, and storage units. Gaia's mirror world stretched down deep—but then staff plans for 2026 allowed for one employee per guest.

"In the meantime I will try to reach Peary Base," Dana had said before they went off in different directions.

"How, without a satellite?" Tim had asked.

"Via the dedicated line. There's a direct laser connection between Gaia and the base. We send the data back and forth via a system of mirrors."

"What do you mean, mirrors? Ordinary, common-or-garden mirrors?"

"The first one is on the far side of the gorge. A thin, very high mast. You can see it from your suite."

"And how many are there?"

"Not all that many. A dozen to the Pole. Arranged in such a way that the light-beam passes around crater rims and mountains. To reach shuttles, spaceships, or even the Earth, of course you need satellites, but for interlunar communication between two fixed points there's nothing better. No atmosphere to scatter the light, no rain—so I'll set out our situation to them in the hope that they aren't having any problems with their satellites there, but my optimism is muted."

And then, after Lynn had disappeared with Sophie into the elevator, Dana had taken him aside.

"Tim, this is awkward for me. You know I don't tend to beat around the bush, but in this case—"

He sighed, troubled by dark forebodings. "Is it about Lynn?"

"Yes. What's up with her?"

Tim looked at the floor, at the walls, wherever you looked to keep from returning the other person's gaze.

"Look, Lynn and I never had personal contact," Dana went on. "But she supported my appointment at the time, and trained me up, in the camp, on the Moon, confidently and competently, entirely admirable. Now she strikes me as irresponsible, erratic, belligerent. She's changed completely."

"I—" Tim hemmed and hawed for a moment. "I'll talk to her."

"I didn't ask you to."

Her quizzical eyes fastened on his. Suddenly it occurred to Tim that Dana Lawrence wasn't blinking. He hadn't seen her blink once for ages. He remembered a film, *Alien*, a quite old but still excellent flick that Julian loved, and in which one of the crew members was unexpectedly revealed as an android.

"I don't know how I should answer that," he said.

"No, you do, you know very well." She lowered her voice. "Lynn is your sister, Tim. I want to know if we can trust her. Has she got herself under control?"

The clouds began to clear in Tim's head. He looked at the manager, illuminated by the realization of what she actually meant.

"Are you suggesting Lynn is Carl's accomplice?" he asked, almost lost for words.

"I just want to hear what you think."

"You're crazy."

"All of this is crazy. Come on, we're running out of time. It would be a great weight off my mind if I was wrong, but three days ago Lynn tried with all her might to persuade her father that he was imagining things. She wanted to withhold the surveillance camera videos from him, she left me in the dark about Edda Hoff's warning, although she really *should* have talked to me. All in all she's behaving as if we had dreamed up the events of the past thirty minutes, even though she herself has been involved from the very start."

That's not true, Tim wanted to say, and in fact Dana was wrong about one thing. Lynn hadn't been there from the start. Sophie had taken the call while his sister had been sitting in the Selene with the manager and the cooks, talking about the possibility of a picnic at the bottom of the Vallis Alpina. Jennifer Shaw had wanted to talk to Lynn or her father, so Sophie had immediately sent a message to the Selene and the security advisers had immediately put it through to Julian on the Aristarchus Plateau. By the time Lynn and Dana had reached head-quarters, the conversation was already well under way.

But what difference did that make?

"As you said before, Lynn is my sister." He straightened up and shifted away a little. "I'd walk through hot coals for her."

"That's not enough for me."

"Well it'll have to be."

"Tim." Dana sighed. "I just want to make sure that we're not about to face problems from somewhere we least expect it. Tell me what's up. I'll treat our conversation with complete confidentiality; no one will find out about it if you don't want them to. Not Julian, and certainly not Lynn."

"Dana, really—"

"I've *got* to be able to do my job!"

Tim said nothing for a moment.

"She had a breakdown," he said flatly. "A few years ago. Exhausted, depressed. It came and went, but since then I can't stop worrying that it might repeat itself."

"Burnout?"

"No, more of an—" The word wouldn't leave his lips.

"Illness?" Dana completed his sentence.

"Lynn played it down, but—yes. A morbid disposition. Her—our mother was depressive, in the end she—"

He fell silent. Dana waited to see if he was going to add anything, but he thought he'd said enough.

"Thanks," she said seriously. "Please keep an eye on your sister."

He nodded unhappily, joined Kokoschka, and they set off, equipped with portable detectors, while he felt like a miserable bloody collabo-rator. At the same time he was tormented by Dana's suspicion. Not because he saw Lynn as being exposed to unjustified suspicions, but because uncertainty was gnawing at him. Could he really walk through hot coals for Lynn? He would give his life for her, that much he knew, regardless of what she did.

But he just wasn't *completely sure*.

GANYMEDE

Locatelli lay in a fetal position, legs bent, on the floor of the air lock just by the bulkheads. Almost two-thirds of the cabin was glazed, but as long as he stayed down low, shielded by the screen, no one would be able to see him from the passenger space or the cockpit. He feverishly developed and rejected one plan after another. Every time he turned his head, he could just make out the indicators on the inside wall of the air lock, showing pressure, air and ambient temperature. The cabin was pressurized, but he didn't dare take off his helmet. He was too worried that the pilot might, at that precise moment, get the idea of subjecting the air lock to an inspection, just as he was busying himself with his damned helmet. He had squeezed his way in between the bulkheads as soon as they had slid apart, pressed the up button, and dropped to the floor, without wasting a fragment of a second. And yet it couldn't have escaped the guy that the cabin had gone back down again.

He cautiously raised himself up a little and peered around for anything that might serve as a weapon, but there was nothing inside the air lock that could be used to slash or stab. The Ganymede was still accelerating. He guessed that there must be an autopilot, but as long as the shuttle hadn't reached its final speed, whoever-was-sitting-up-at-the-front couldn't take his eyes off the controls. Later it might be too late to shed his armor and his helmet. Perhaps he really *should* do it now.

At that moment an idea came to him.

He quickly released the catches of the helmet and took it off, set it down next to him, and started frantically working away at his chest armor. The acceleration pressure eased off. He hastily fiddled around with the valves and fasteners, peeled himself out of his survival backpack, and pushed everything a little way away. Now he was more mobile, and he also had something that could be used as a weapon in a surprise attack. Every muscle tensed, he lay there and waited. The shuttle flew in a bend, and went on gaining altitude. His head roared with the certainty that this was his only chance. If he didn't catch and whack Peter or Carl, whichever of them was flying the Ganymede, at the first opportunity, he might as well say good-bye to the world.

Don't complain, asshole, he thought, this was what you wanted. And strangely—or not—his inner voice, in all its condescension, and down to peculiarities of its modulation, including the rolled, Asian R, sounded exactly like Momoka's.

GAIA, VALLIS ALPINA, THE MOON

Dana walked to her desk and paused.

Depressive. That explained a few things. But how did depressive states develop? Into apathy? Aggression? Would Lynn freak out? What was Julian's daughter likely to do?

She established the laser connection with Peary Base. After a few seconds the face of Deputy Commander Tommy Wachowski appeared on the screen. There wasn't much in the way of regular exchange between hotel and base, which meant that it was ages since she had last spoken to him. Wachowski looked tense and relieved at the same time, as if she had taken a weight off his mind with her call. Dana thought she knew the reason. A moment later Wachowski confirmed her suspicion.

"Am I happy to see you," he growled. "I thought we'd never get through to anyone ever again."

"Have you been having problems with the satellites?" she asked.

His eyes widened. "How do you know that?"

"Because we have too. We were in contact with Earth when the connection went down. We haven't been able to get through since then, not even to our shuttles."

"We've been having pretty much the same thing. Completely cut off. The problem is that we're in the shadow of the libration. Alternative channels are out. We're relying on LPCS; do you have any idea what's going on?"

"No." Dana shook her head. "At the moment we haven't a clue. Not a clue. You?"

ARISTARCHUS PLATEAU, THE MOON

The Moon was quite definitely more suited to route marches than the Earth, because of its lower gravitation. Space suits quite definitely weren't. Even though the exosuits provided a high level of comfort and mobility, you were, regardless of the air-conditioning, in an incubator. The more energy you expended, the more you sweated, and 8 kilometers, even performing leaps that would have done credit to a kangaroo, remained 8 kilometers.

Assailed by questions, Julian had divulged various things: he had talked about his nocturnal observation of the Lunar Express, about Hanna's lies and dodges, and had told them something was under way against Orley Enterprises somewhere in the world. But the idea that terrorists might try to blow up his hotel with an atom bomb he kept to himself, just as he refrained from mentioning Lynn's inexcusable derelictions of duty. He was terribly worried about her, but there was a great gulf of understanding in the mountain range of his concern, in which a horrible black worm of anxiety wriggled. Who had actually reedited the video; who had hooked up Hanna? Because there was no doubt that the Canadian had been listening in earlier: he had gone into action even while that man Jericho had been setting out his suspicions! And finally, who had deactivated the satellites in perfect synchronization with Hanna's flight? The worm turned, glistened, quivered, and gave birth to the idea of an assistant, an accomplice in the hotel, male or female. Someone who had inexplicably refused to let him see the manipulated video, and whose attitude was becoming more mysterious with each passing hour.

"And how are we going to get out of here?" Evelyn wanted to know. "Back to the hotel, without a shuttle or radio contact?"

"I'm just wondering where Carl's trying to get to," Rogachev mused.

"Like that matters right now," snorted Momoka.

"Why was he in such a rush to get away? Nothing could have been pinned on him. Well, there's the fact that he doesn't stick too closely to the truth, but okay. Why the hurry?"

"Maybe he's planning something," said Amber. "Something he has to get done in time, now that his cover's been blown."

In time. That was it! How did the accomplice in the hotel manage to get away—if he existed at all? How likely was the danger of a bomb going off in Gaia within the next hour? Wouldn't Hanna's journey have had to take him back to Gaia, to set it off? Or was the bomb already ticking? In which case—

Lynn! He must have been crazy to suspect her! But even if she had some macabre, incomprehensible part in the drama, did she realize what she'd let herself in for? Did she have even the tiniest idea what was going on? Could Hanna have roped her in for his purposes, on some pretext or other; could he have exploited her mental state, somehow hoodwinked her into doing things for him the significance of which she completely misunderstood?

Perhaps he should have listened more closely to Tim.

Should have! The grammar of missed opportunities.

"Julian?"

"What?"

"How are we going to get out of here?" Evelyn asked again.

He hesitated. "Peter knows—he *knew* that Schröter spaceport better than I did. I don't think there are any flying machines there, but there's definitely a third moonmobile. So we'll get away in any event."

"But where to?" asked Rogachev. "Crossing the Mare Imbrium in a moon car isn't exactly an encouraging prospect."

"How far are we from the hotel, anyway?" asked Amber.

"About 1,300 kilometers."

"And how long will our oxygen hold out?"

"Forget it," wheezed Momoka. "Certainly not long enough to get to the Vallis Alpina by car. What do you say, Julian? How long would it take to do cover 1,300 kilometers at eighty max?"

"Sixteen hours," said Julian. "But realistically we'll hardly be able to go at eighty."

"Sixty?"

"Maybe fifty."

"Oh, brilliant!" laughed Momoka. "Then we can take bets on who packs up first. Us or the car."

"Stop it," said Amber.

"My bet's on us."

"This is pointless, Momoka. Why don't we—"

"Then the car will keep going for a while with your corpses inside, until eventually—"

"Momoka!" yelled Amber. "Shut. The. Fuck. Up!"

"Right, that's enough!" Julian stopped and raised both hands. "I know we have a stack of terrible things to work out. Nothing makes any sense, practically no information is confirmed. At the moment the only thing we can do is think in a straight line, *from one step to the next*, and the next step will be an examination of the Schröter spaceport. We've got enough oxygen to do that." He paused. "Now that Peter's dead—"

"If he really is," said Evelyn.

"As Peter is *probably* dead, I'll take his place. Okay? Responsibility for the group lies with me now, and from this moment I only want to hear constructive comments."

"I've got a constructive comment," said Rogachev.

"Great stuff, Oleg," sneered Momoka. "Constructive comments are at a premium right now."

Rogachev ignored her. "Aren't the helium-3 mines a bit closer to the Aristarchus Plateau than the hotel?"

"That's right," said Julian. "Not half as far."

"So if we could get there—"

"The mines are automatic," Momoka objected. "Peter told me. It's all robots."

"Okay," said Evelyn thoughtfully. "Even so, they must have some sort of infrastructure, don't they? Accommodation for maintenance staff. Some means of transport."

"There's definitely a survival depot," said Julian. "Good idea, Oleg. So let's go!"

The fact that their oxygen wouldn't get them to the mining zone he left unspoken.

GANYMEDE

Hanna hurried toward his goal on the hypothetical line of fifty degrees longitude, pulling the shadow of the Ganymede at a rate of 1,200 kilometers an hour across the velvet monotony of the northern Oceanus Procellarum. His gaze rested on the controls. He couldn't get any more speed out of the shuttle. He still had another hour and a quarter to go, but given the pitiful possibilities at Julian's group's disposal that was hardly cause for concern. Even if they managed to leave the Plateau, he still had a luxurious amount of time to finish his task and leave the Moon. But whether Ebola would get there in time, now that everything was in chaos, was anybody's guess. Admittedly he planned to wait as long as possible. But he would have to fly off sooner or later; alone if necessary. Those were the rules. Alliances served a purpose.

On his right there began a plain covered with tiny craters, which separated the northern Mare Imbrium from the Oceanus Procellarum. Behind it the helium-3 mining zone stretched into the bay Sinus Iridum, the area in which the Americans and the Chinese had got into such arguments the previous year. Kenny Xin had told him loads about that. Mad he might be, yet it was worth listening to him.

He looked wearily around.

The air lock was bathed in a diffuse light. There was nothing to suggest that Locatelli had made it to the shuttle. And anyway, the noise of the bulkhead would give him away as soon as it opened. He turned his attention back to the controls and looked out of the window. A larger crater came into view, Mairan, as the holographic map on the console told him. The Ganymede had been traveling for a good twenty minutes now, and he was almost starting to feel something like boredom.

Okay then.

He stood up, grabbed his weapon with the non-explosive rounds, and walked between the seats to the air lock. The closer he got, the deeper he could see into the cabin, but at the moment it was actually empty. It was only when he was a couple of steps away that something massive and white entered his field of vision, something on the floor, and he stopped.

A survival backpack. At least that was what it looked like.

Did that mean Locatelli had actually done it?

He stepped slowly closer. Other details became visible: the shoulder of a piece of chest armor, a bent leg. It was only when he was standing so close to the glass that his breath condensed on it into a film of tiny droplets that he was also able to make out part of the face, a lifelessly staring eye, a half-open mouth. Locatelli seemed to be resting his back against the bulkhead, and he didn't look particularly well, in fact he looked a bit dead.

Hanna's fingers clutched the weapon. He rested his free hand on the sensor field, raised the bulkhead, and took a step back.

Locatelli slumped out from the cabin like a sack and stared at the ceiling. His left arm weakly struck the floor, his fingers open as if he were begging for a final pittance. His right hand, still in the air lock, was wrapped around the lower edge of his helmet. There was no outward sign of injury, and in any case he had been able to take off his armor before he collapsed.

Hanna frowned, leaned forward, and paused.

At that moment he realized that something was wrong. The unusually healthy color of the man's face might have been just about compatible with his being a corpse—but Warren Locatelli was definitely the first dead person he'd ever seen sweating.

So, Hanna.

Locatelli cried out. With all his might he swung the helmet, hit Hanna's arm, saw the weapon flying away, leaped up.

Hanna staggered.

That the Canadian would see through his bluff and shoot him a moment later had been Locatelli's worst-case expectation. So, two seconds after the attack, what surprised him most of all was that he was still alive. Countless times during the sequence of eternities that had passed since the shuttle lifted off, he had tried to imagine the situation and calculate his chances. Now here they were, and there was no longer any time to think, not even to wonder or catch his breath. Trusting, in the Celtic manner, to the effects of a good shout, loud and inarticulate like an attacking horde, he thrashed away at his opponent with his helmet, again and again, without a pause, without giving him the slightest opportunity to retreat, saw his knees bending, aimed at the top of his shaven head, and struck again, as hard as he could. The Canadian made a grab for him. Locatelli dealt him a kick to the shoulder. God knew, he had fought quite enough in his life, both often and enthusiastically, but never with a professional hit man, as Hanna plainly was when you looked at things with a lucid eye, so for the sake of certainty he brought the helmet down on his head once more, even though the man hadn't moved a muscle for ages, grabbed for the curious weapon, staggered a few steps back and took aim.

Spurts of blood from the back of Hanna's head, on the floor.

Locatelli's hand was shaking.

After a while, quivering with fear, he risked stepping forward again, crouched down, and held the barrel to Hanna's temple. No reaction. The Canadian's eyes were shut and his breathing was heavy. Locatelli blinked, felt his heartbeat gradually slowing down. Waited. Nothing happened. Went on waiting.

Nothing. Nothing at all.

Gradually he was starting to believe that the man really was unconscious.

Where should he put him? He thought frantically. Perhaps he should chuck him in the air lock and simply get rid of him on the flight. But that would have been murder, and even at his most reckless Locatelli was no murderer. And he wanted to know why Peter, Mimi, and Marc had had to die; what Hanna's crappy aims had been. He needed information, and anyway, Momoka, Julian, and the others, were stuck on the Aristarchus Plateau! He had to get back and pick them up; that had absolute priority.

And how, smart-ass?

His gaze wandered to the cockpit. He knew how to drive a racing car, how to sail a yacht into the wind. But he hadn't the faintest idea about Hornets, or about where the Ganymede was headed, how high and how fast it flew. Nothing on board was designed to lift his spirits. Here the Canadian, who would eventually come around, there the unfamiliar world of the cockpit. He hadn't the first clue. He would have to learn, and fast.

No. First of all he had to put Hanna somewhere.

Because nothing occurred to him even after he had gone on thinking for a few minutes longer, he dragged the motionless body toward the cockpit, dumped it behind the co-pilot's seat, and looked around for something to tie it up with.

There didn't seem to be anything like that on board, either.

Right. At least no one could say things were getting boring.

London, Great Britain

One of the last works of the venerable Sir Norman Foster stood on the Isle of Dogs, a droplet-shaped peninsula in London's East End. Bent into a U at this point, the Thames flowed around an area of business districts, elegantly restored docks, exclusive apartments, and preserved remainders of social housing, whose traditional inhabitants were reduced to the status of extras in this affluent architectural idyll. As early as the 1990s, well-to-do Londoners had discovered the hidden charms of the area for themselves; artists, galleries, medium-sized companies had moved here to bear down on the crumbling working-class estates like so many pest controllers. After over two decades of violent social tensions, the last stretches of estate streets had now been lovingly restored, as if by museum curators, and the families living there had been made protected species, which meant turning them, with financial support, into the kind of happy social case that stressed managers were able to envy without drawing suspicions of cynicism.

In 2025 there was no one left on the Isle of Dogs who was still really poor. Certainly not in the shadow of the Big O.

The construction of the new headquarters of Orley Enterprises had begun even in Jericho's day, the year before the fear of losing Joanna had sent him to Shanghai. In the south-east of the Isle of Dogs, in the former Island Gardens, resting on a low plinth—if you could call a twelve-story complex low—was an O 250 meters in diameter, circled parabolically by an artificial orange moon which contained several conference rooms and was reached via airy bridges. More than 5,000 staff swarmed around the light-flooded atriums, gardens, and open-plan offices of the big glass torus, busy as termites. A flight pad had been worked into the roof area so skillfully that the curve of the O was preserved from every perspective. Only as you approached it from the air did you notice that the zenith of the building was not arched but flat, a surface with two dozen helicopters and skymobiles arranged around it.

Tu's jet had landed in Heathrow at a quarter past four. While it was still on the runway, the company's security forces had welcomed them and brought them to the firm's helicopter, which flew them straight to the Isle of Dogs. Further north stretched the skyscrapers of Canary Wharf, vainly straining to be a match for the Big O, which towered over everything else. Private boats, tiny and white, moved about on the waters of the renovated docks. Jericho saw two men stepping onto the landing pad. The helicopter turned in the air, settled on the pad, and opened its side door. The men's steps quickened. One, with black, wiry

hair and a monobrow, held his right hand out to Jericho, then recon-
sidered and held it out to Yoyo.

"Andrew Norrington," he said. "Deputy head of security. Chen
Yuyun, I assume."

"Just Yoyo." She shook his outstretched hand. "The honorable Tu
Tian, Owen Jericho. Also *very* honorable."

The other man coughed, wiped his palms on his pantlegs and nodded at everyone.

"Tom Merrick, information services."

Jericho studied him. He was young, prematurely bald, and clearly
afflicted with inhibitions that kept him from looking anyone in the eye
for longer than two seconds.

"Tom is our specialist in all kinds of communication and information transmission," said Norrington. "Did you bring the dossier?"

Instead of replying, Jericho held the tiny cube into the light.

"Very good!" Norrington nodded. "Come."

The path led them inside the roof onto a grassy track and across a
bridge, beyond which there stretched a bank of glass elevators. The eye
fell into the open interior of the Big O, crisscrossed by further bridges.
People hurried busily back and forth on them. A good 150 meters below
him, Jericho saw elevator-like cabins traveling along the loop of the hollow; then they stepped into one of the high-speed elevators, plunged
toward the ground and through it, and stopped on sub-level 4. Norrington marched ahead of them. Without slowing his pace, he made for
a reflective wall that opened silently, and they plunged into the world of
high security, dominated by computer desks and monitor walls. Men
and women spoke into headsets. Video conferences were under way. Tu
straightened his glasses on the bridge of his nose, made some contented
noises, and craned his neck, transfixed by so much technology.

"Our communications center," Norrington explained. "From here
we stay in contact with Orley facilities everywhere in the world. We
work according to the specifications of our subcontractors, which
means that there are no continental heads, only security advisers to
the individual subsidiaries, who report to London. All company data
come together here."

"How far under the ground are we?" asked Yoyo.

"Not *that* far. Fifteen meters. We had a lot of problems with groundwater at first, but things are sorted out now. For understandable reasons we had to protect Central Security, avoid any kind of attacks from
the air, for example, and if necessary the underground of the Big O
serves as a nuclear bunker."

"That means that if England falls—"

"—Orley will still be standing."

"The King is dead, long live the King."

"Don't worry." Norrington smiled. "England isn't going to fall. Our country is changing; we had to accept the disappearance of the red telephone boxes and the red buses, but the Royal Family is non-negotiable. If it comes to the crunch, we still have room for the King down here."

He led them into a conference room with holographic screens running all the way around it. Two women stood in hushed conversation. Jericho recognized one of them right away. The deep black pageboy cut over the pale face belonged to Edda Hoff. The other woman was plump, with appealing if grumpy features, blue-gray eyes, and short, white hair.

"Jennifer Shaw," she said.

In charge of Central Security, Jericho completed in his head. Guard dog number one in the global Orley empire. Hands were shaken again.

"Coffee?" asked Jennifer. "Water? Tea?"

"Something." Tu had spotted a memory crystal reading device, and was making resolutely toward it. "Anything."

"Red wine," said Yoyo.

Jennifer raised an eyebrow. "Medium-bodied? Full-bodied? Barrel-aged?"

"Something along the lines of a narcotic, if possible."

"Narcotic and anything," nodded Edda Hoff, who then went outside for a moment and came back in as the others were taking their seats. Tu put the crystal in the reader and nodded to everyone.

"With your permission we'll let an old rascal speak first," he said. "It is to him that you owe your glimpse into the sick brain of your enemies, and in any case I should like to sweep away any remaining doubts about our credibility."

"Where is the man now?" Jennifer leaned back.

"Dead," said Jericho. "He was murdered right in front of my eyes. They were trying to stop him passing on his knowledge."

"Plainly without success," said Jennifer. "How did you come into possession of the crystal?"

"I stole his eye," said Yoyo. "His left one."

Jennifer thought for a second.

"Yes, you should balk at nothing. Let your dead friend take the floor."

"The whole thing, erm, seems to be some sort of satellite breakdown," said Tom Merrick, the IT Security supervisor, after Vogelaar had evoked Armageddon under West Africa's streaming sky. "At least that's what it looks like."

"What else could it be?" asked Jericho.

"Right, that's a bit complicated. First of all satellites aren't things that you can click on and off as you feel like it. You have to know their codes if you want to control them." Merrick's gaze slipped away. "Okay, you can find out that kind of thing through espionage. You can knock out a communications satellite with directed data streams, for a few hours or a day; you can also destroy it with radiation, but what we have here is a total breakdown, you understand? We can't contact either Gaia or Peary Base."

"Peary Base?" echoed Tu. "The American moon base, right?"

"Exactly. For that one all you'd need to do is black the LPCS, the lunar satellites, because of the libration, but—"

"Libration?" Yoyo looked blank.

"The Moon seems to stand still," Norrington cut in before Merrick could reply. "But that's an illusion. It does in fact rotate. Within one Earth rotation, it turns once on its own axis, with the effect that we always see the same side. That's a thing called bound rotation, typical, by the way, of most of the moons in the solar system. However—"

"Yes, yes!" Merrick nodded impatiently. "You have to explain to them that the angular velocity with which the Moon circles a larger body, in terms of its own rotation—"

"I think our guests would like you to keep it simpler, Tom. Basically the Moon, because of its rotation behavior, wobbles slightly. As a result, we get to see more than half of the Moon's surface, in fact it's almost sixty percent. Conversely, the marginal regions disappear at times."

"And they disappear from radio range," Merrick broke in. "Conventional radio requires visual contact, unless you have an atmosphere that reflects radio waves, but there isn't one on the Moon. And at the moment the North Pole and Peary Base are in the libration shadow, so they can't be reached directly from the Earth via radio waves. So the Moon has been equipped with ten satellites of its own, the Lunar Positioning and Communication System, LPCS for short, which circle one another within range of the base. We're in constant contact with at least five of them, so we should be able to contact Peary, regardless of libration."

"And what's to say that somebody hasn't taken control of precisely those ten satellites?"

"Nothing. That is to say, everything! You know how many satellites you would have to knock out to cut off the whole of the Moon from the Earth? Gaia doesn't actually have a libration problem. It's in visual range, so it can be reached at any time by TDRS satellites, even without LPCS. Except we no longer have a connection with Gaia either."

"So someone must be blocking—"

"—terrestrial satellites too, yes, that's one hell of a lot of codes, but yes, I think so. It's just not a lot of use to them in the long term. They could attack TDRS headquarters in White Sands and paralyze all the Tracking and Data Relay Satellites at a stroke, but then we'd just switch to ground stations or civilian stations like Artemis, which are equipped with S-band transponders and pivotable antennae. How would anyone interfere with all of those?"

"That's precisely the problem," said Edda Hoff. "We're in touch with every available ground station in the world. There's no contact up there."

"After the breakdown of the conference system we immediately informed NASA and Orley Space in Washington," said Jennifer. "And of course the Mission Control Center in Houston and our own control centers on the Isla de las Estrellas and in Perth. Nothing but radio silence."

"And what could be the reason for that?" Jericho rubbed the tip of his chin. "If not interference with the satellites?"

Merrick studied the lines in his right palm.

"I don't know yet."

"Are Peary Base and Gaia cut off from one another as well?"

"Not necessarily." Norrington shook his head. "There's a non-satellite laser connection between them."

"So if you got through to the Base—"

"Our message could be passed on to Gaia."

Jennifer leaned forward. "Listen, Owen, I won't deny that until a moment ago I had some doubts about whether the evidence you have points convincingly to a threat to Gaia. You three could have been a gang of hysterical fantasists."

"And what's your opinion now?" asked Tu.

"I'm inclined to believe you. According to your file, the bomb has been dormant up there since April of last year. The opening of Gaia was actually planned for 2024, but the Moon crisis thwarted that one. So it would make sense to detonate the bomb now that it's finished. As soon as we get a warning through to the hotel, someone sabotages our communication, another clue that it *is* going to happen, but above all that someone's got their eye on us, during these very seconds. And that's extremely worrying. On the one hand because it suggests that we have a mole in our ranks, on the other because it means that someone up there will try to get the bomb into Gaia and set it off, if they haven't done so already."

"Listening to Vogelaar," Norrington said, "you'd see the Chinese everywhere."

"Not impossible." She paused. "But Julian already suspected someone before the connection was severed. A guest. In fact *the* guest, the last to join the group. The perpetrator might be known to us."

"Carl Hanna," said Norrington.

"Carl Hanna." Jennifer nodded. "So please be so kind as to get hold of his papers for me. Screen the guy. I want to know what he had for breakfast! Edda, put me through to NASA and issue orders to the OSS. Our people or theirs need to send a shuttle to Gaia."

Hoff hesitated. "If the OSS has capacity at the moment."

"I don't care whether they have capacity. I just care that they do it. And *right away*."

Aristarchus Plateau, The Moon

The rover Julian had mentioned was parked in the dugout, but the second was stranded on the runway, scorched as if it had got in the way of a shuttle jet. All that remained of the third one, however, was a pile of junk. Debris lay scattered all around the place, so Momoka immediately set off in search of Locatelli's remains. She scoured the area in grim silence. After that it was agreed that Locatelli wasn't here, and nor was any part of him.

They all knew what that meant. Locatelli must have managed to get on board the shuttle.

They listlessly trawled through the hangars. Clearly the Schröter spaceport was still in the finishing stages. Everything suggested that air locks and pressurized habitats were planned, so that people would be able to survive here for a while, but nowhere was there a sign of a life-support system. A cold room, for the preparation of foodstuffs, lay abandoned. The section of the hangar in which the moonmobile was parked was identified by inscriptions stating that grasshoppers should have been stored there, but there was no sign of one far or wide.

"Well," Evelyn observed caustically, after glances into steel containers that should have contained space suits revealed nothing but a yawning void. "Theoretically, at least, we're in safety. The whole thing should just have happened four weeks later."

"Is the stupid moonmobile really all we've got?" groaned Momoka.

"No, we've got more than that," said Julian's voice. He was walking through the next room with Amber and Rogachev. "You should come over here."

"Nothing that flies," he went on. "But a few things that drive. That burnt rover out there hasn't got any prettier, but it does work. So along with the one in the hangar we've got two. And look what Amber has found: charged replacement batteries for both vehicles; and in the trunk of the undamaged rover enough extra oxygen for two people."

"There are five of us," said Momoka. "Can we connect the tanks to our suits in alternation?"

"Yeah, that's fine. The supplies wouldn't get you to Gaia, and the rovers would be worthless in the Alps. But whatever happens, our supplies will be enough to take us to the mining station."

"And does anyone know the way?"

Amber waved a stack of slides around. "These guys do."

"What, *maps*?"

"They were in the rover."

"Oh great!" Momoka snorted. "Like Vasco da Gama! What sort of crap technology is that, when you can't even program in your journey?"

"The technology of a civilization that increasingly confuses its achievements with magic," Rogachev coolly. "Or might it have escaped you that the satellite communication has gone down? No guidance system without LPCS."

"It hasn't escaped me," said Momoka sulkily. "And incidentally, I've got a constructive remark as well."

"Let's hear it."

"We can't really make ourselves comfortable in this mining station, can we? I think we've got to make contact with the hotel, and that doesn't seem to be happening at the moment because of the satellite strike. So how are we going to get to the hotel under our own power?"

"What are you getting at?"

"Are there any flying machines in the mining station?"

"Maybe some grasshoppers."

"Yeah, those'll get you around the Moon just fine, but at a snail's pace. Except if I remember correctly, the helium tanks are taken to the Pole by magnetic rail. Right? That means there's a station there, and a train goes from there to Peary Base. And from Peary Base—"

Julian said nothing.

Of course, he thought. That might work. How obvious! Hard to believe, but just for a change Momoka really had come up with something constructive.

GANYMEDE

Locatelli stared at the control displays.

He had worked out by now that Hanna was taking his bearings from the holographic map, a kind of substitute LPCS. The outside cameras synched a real-time image of the visible area of the landscape with a 3D model in the computer into which you'd programmed your destination and route. That meant you could hold a steady course, practically on autopilot, because the system continually corrected itself, although that called for a high altitude. Locatelli guessed that Hanna had programmed in a destination that the controls were unable to tell him anything about. He would have bet that the Canadian was flying back to the hotel, but they were too far west for that. To get to Gaia he would have had to take a northeasterly course, and instead it looked as if he was stubbornly heading due north at fifty degrees longitude.

Was Hanna trying to get to the Pole?

Questions accumulated. Why did Hanna not use LPCS? How did you land a thing like that? How did you slow down? They were hurtling along at 1,200 kilometers an hour, 10 kilometers up, extremely worrying. How long would their fuel hold out if the jets had to constantly generate thrust in order to keep Ganymede at this altitude, and accelerate at the same time?

He picked up his helmet and tried to make contact with Momoka via his suit connection. When he received no answer, he tried to get through to Julian and switched to conference reception. Nothing, just atmospheric hiss. Perhaps the suit systems didn't work at such distances; after all, they had been flying northward for half an hour. He scanned the map and reached the conclusion that there must by now be over 500 kilometers between the shuttle and the Aristarchus Plateau. On the right, a considerable way off, a crater stood out in the middle of a plateau: Mairan, the map told him. Another, Louville, appeared over the edge of the horizon to the north. It was time to get to know the cockpit. It must at least be possible to contact the hotel from the Ganymede.

His eye fell on a diagram above the windshield, which he hadn't noticed until then. A simple set of instructions, but enough to get him to the main menu, and suddenly everything was much easier than he'd thought. Admittedly he still didn't know how to fly the thing, but at least he knew how to work the radio. His disappointment was all the greater, then, when he still heard nothing but silence. At first he thought the radio mustn't be working, but then at last he worked out that the satellites were out of operation.

So that was why Hanna had switched to map navigation.

At the same moment he understood why he couldn't get through to anybody on conventional channels. Traditional radio meant that the partners had to be within visible range of each other, so that there was nothing between the transmitter and the receiver to absorb the radio waves, and in the case of the Moon the strong curvature quickly absorbed all contact. That was why his connection with Momoka and the others had been severed earlier on as well, because they had been on the other side of Snake Hill when the chase was taking place. Which was how he now knew the exact time of the satellite failure.

It coincided with Hanna's escape.

Coincidence? Never in a million years! There was something bigger going on here.

Behind him, Hanna groaned quietly. Locatelli turned his head. After a long search he had finally found a few straps for holding down cargo, and tied him to the front row of seats. You couldn't exactly have claimed that he was wrapped up like a package, but Hanna wouldn't be able to free himself quickly enough to stop Locatelli from shooting him in the leg with his own gun. He studied the murderer's pale face for a moment, but the Canadian kept his eyes closed.

He turned back to the control panel. After a while he thought he had worked out various things, such as how to regulate the altitude of Ganymede, to make it climb or descend by—

That was it. Of course!

Locatelli was suddenly very excited. The Moon had no atmosphere, so in fact flight altitude couldn't have anything to do with it, although of course it meant you were eating into your fuel supplies. It didn't alter the general conditions; a vacuum was a vacuum. But the higher he climbed, the less noticeable the curvature became, until it was entirely irrelevant. As far as he remembered, only the Rupes-Toscanelli Plateau stretched northeast of the Schröter Valley, with Snake Hill. If they weren't cowering under the spurs of rock right now, but had fought their way through to the space station, he *had* to get through to them!

His fingers darted over the controls. The shuttle had a frightening number of jets, he established, some pointing stiffly downward, others backward, others still were on a pivot. He decided to ignore the pivotable ones, and switch thrust entirely to the vertical. He entered a value at random—

Suddenly the air was squeezed from his lungs.

Damn it! Too much, much too much! What sort of stupid idiot was he! Why hadn't he started with less? The idea of a calm flight was out the window, the Ganymede shot upward like mad, rattled, vibrated, and bucked as if trying to shake him out of its innards. He quickly reduced the thrust, worked out that not all jets were firing evenly, hence the vibrations, corrected, regulated, balanced, and the shuttle calmed down and continued climbing, now at a more moderate speed.

Good, Warren. Very good!

"Locatelli to Orley," he shouted. "Momoka. Julian. Come in please."

All kinds of white noise emerged from the speakers, but nothing that even slightly resembled human articulation. The Ganymede was approaching the thirteen-kilometer mark. After its initial bickering, it allowed itself to be ridden like the most placid of ponies, and climbed constantly higher, while Locatelli shouted Julian and Momoka's names in turn.

Fourteen kilometers.

The landscape stretched below him. Again there was rattling and trembling, as the irritable automatic controls registered deviations from the longitudinal bearings and roughly compensated for them.

"Locatelli to Orley. Julian! Momoka! Oleg, Evelyn. Can anybody hear me? Come in! Locatelli to—"

14.6-14.7-14.8

He gradually started to feel queasy, even though the rational part of his brain quickly reassured him that he could theoretically fly into outer space. All just a matter of fuel.

"Momoka! Julian!"

15.4-15.5-15.6

Nothing.

"Warren Locatelli to Orley. Come in please."

Hiss. Crackle.

"Locatelli to Orley. Julian! Momoka!"

"Warren!"

ARISTARCHUS PLATEAU, THE MOON

"Warren! Warren! I've got Warren on the line!"

Momoka started to do a kind of St. Vitus' dance around the charred rover, whose bed they had started to load with batteries. They paused, all listening. His voice rang out with promising volume in their helmets, clear and distinct, as if he were standing right next to them.

"Warren, darling, sweetie!" cried Momoka. "Where are you? Sweetheart, oh my sweetheart! Are you okay?"

"All fine. You?"

"A few of us are missing, we don't know exactly what happened. Peter, Mimi, Marc—"

"Dead," said Locatelli.

Not that any confirmation was required. But the word fell like a blade and guillotined the unregenerate little optimist who had, until that moment, been tirelessly coming out with all kinds of murmured ifs and could-bes. There was a moment of hurt silence.

"Where are you now?" asked Julian, audibly chastened.

"In the shuttle. Carl, the bastard, slung Peter into the gorge and then blew up Mimi and Marc, and then he hijacked the shuttle, but I managed to get on board."

"And where's Carl?"

"He's unconscious. I knocked him out and tied him to the seats."

"You're a hero," cried Momoka, delighted. "You know that? You're a goddamn hero!"

"Of course, what else? I'm a hero in a spaceship that's going incredibly fast, with no idea of how to fly the stupid thing. That is, I'm getting the hang of it now. Turning around, getting down, and landing, not so sure about."

"Can you get through to the hotel?" asked Julian.

"Don't think so. Too far away, too many mountains. I'm over 15 kilometers up, to be quite honest I'm starting to feel something like vertigo. And I don't know how much gas I've got left."

"Fine, no problem. I'll help. Just stay up there for the time being, because of the radio connection."

"The LPCS has failed, right?"

"Sabotage, if you ask me. Did Carl actually say anything to you?"

"I didn't give him much of a chance to say anything."

"Oh, my hero!"

"Do you know your position?"

"Fifty degrees west, forty-six degrees north. On the right there's a crater plateau, with mountains attached to it."

"Give me some kind of name."

"Wait a second: Montes Jura."

"Very good. Listen, Warren, you've got to—"

GANYMEDE

Locatelli listened carefully to Julian's instructions. As he did so, he found himself suspecting that his friend didn't know what needed to be done down to the last detail either, but definitely had more of a notion about how to fly a Hornet shuttle than he did himself. For example, he knew how to take a turn. Locatelli would have adjusted the jets individually, and plunged to his death as a result. Whereas in fact it was relatively simple, if you bore in mind simple things like turning off the automatic course programming and switched to manual.

"Keep to the right, fly east, toward the Montes Jura, and then make a big 180-degree turn and head south again."

"I'm with you."

"Not even nearly. Don't make any tight turns, okay? Make sure they're wide. You're going at 1,200 kilometers an hour!"

Locatelli did as he was told. Perhaps he was an excessively obedient pupil, because the bend turned into an extended sightseeing tour of the landscape. When he had turned the Ganymede, he found himself to the west of forty degrees longitude, with the jagged agglomeration of the Jurassic mountains below him, arranged in a circle around a vast bay. The bay was called Sinus Iridum and adjoined the Mare Ibrium, and somehow the name struck him as familiar. Then he remembered. Sinus Iridum was the apple of discord that sparked the Moon crisis in 2024. From the windows of the cockpit he had a breathtaking view. Hardly anywhere else was the illusion of land and sea so perfect; all that was missing was a blue glow on the velvet basalt base of the Mare Ibrium. It looked particularly velvety here, most of all where it abutted the southwestern foothills of the mountains.

"Where are you?" asked Julian.

"Southern half of Sinus Iridum. There's a spit of land ahead of me. Cape Heraclides. Shall I go lower? Then I won't have such a long journey down later on."

"Do that. We'll just check how long the connection lasts."

"Fine. When it goes, I'll climb again."

"It'll get more stable the closer you get, anyway."

Locatelli hesitated. Going lower, fine. Perhaps it would be even better to cut back the speed a bit. Not much, just enough to take it below 1,000 kilometers an hour. What he was doing wasn't even slightly comparable to a flight through the Earth's atmosphere, where you had to battle with air levels and turbulence, but hours upon hours in airplanes had got him used to lengthy landings, so he decelerated and began to drop.

The Ganymede plummeted like a stone toward the ground. What had he done?

The shuttle settled at an angle. Noise flooded the interior, the tortured wails of overextended technology.

"Julian," he cried. "I've fucked up!"

"What's wrong?"

"I'm crashing!"

"What have you done? Tell me what you've done!"

Locatelli's hands fluttered over the controls, uncertain about which fields they should press, which switches they should use.

"I think I've got speed and altitude regulation mixed up."

"Okay. But don't lose your head!"

"I'm not losing my head!" yelled Locatelli, about to lose his head.

"Do the following. Just go—"

The line went dead. Shit, shit, shit! Fingers clawed, he crouched over the console. He didn't know what to do, but to do nothing would mean certain death, so he had to do *something*, but *what*?

He tried to balance out his crooked angle with a counterthrust.

The shuttle roared like a giant wounded animal, started reeling violently, and tilted to the other side. A moment later it lurched so hard that Locatelli was afraid it would break into a thousand pieces. He looked helplessly in all directions, turned his head instinctively—

Carl Hanna was staring at him.

Hanna, whose fault it all was. Under any other circumstances Locatelli would have got up, smacked him one, and given him valuable advice about how to treat your vacation acquaintances, but that was out of the question right now. He saw that the Canadian was starting to tug like mad on his fetters, ignored him, and bent over the console again. The shuttle was rapidly losing velocity, and tilting still further. Locatelli decided not to worry about the plunge for the time being, and instead to concentrate on stabilizing his position, but the only result of his efforts was that he suddenly had no power over the controls.

"Warren, you—"

Hanna shouted something.

"—you've gone into automatic! You've got to—"

Why didn't that idiot just keep his trap shut?

"—you're out of manual! Warren, damn it to hell! Untie me."

"Fuck off."

"We're both going to die!"

Locatelli poked stubbornly around in the main menu. The altitude meter was counting down worryingly quickly, 5.0-4.8-4.6, they were hurtling toward the lunar ground like a meteor. A few moments before, in his excitement, he must have pressed something, he must have activated some function that had effectively disempowered him and stripped him of access to any kind of navigation. Now it looked as if he could do whatever he liked, and it would have not had the slightest influence on the behavior of the Ganymede.

"Warren!"

Who was that this time?

Try and remember, do what you did before. What worked so well under Julian's instructions. Turn off automatic pilot, switch to manual.

But how? How?

"Release me, Warren!"

Why wasn't it working this time? Fucking touchscreen! What kind of a crappy cockpit was it; nothing but virtual fields, unfamiliar electronic landscapes, cryptic symbols instead of solid rocker switches with sensible inscriptions like HELLO, WARREN, TURN ME THE OTHER WAY AND IT'LL ALL BE FINE.

"We're going to die, Warren! That won't do anybody any good. You *can't* want that!"

"Forget it, asshole."

"I won't hurt you, you hear me? Just set me free!"

The ground, skewed at a forty-five-degree angle, was menacingly gaining presence; the range on his right-hand side stretched its peaks over the shuttle's flight path. As it grew closer, Sinus Iridum looked as if it were undergoing a weird and inexplicable transformation. In places the basalt plain seemed to be frozen in a process of decomposition, more mist than solid surface, with dark and mysterious phenomena in it. Little more than one kilometer separated the shuttle from the place where it was bound to crash. A vague blur turned into the line of the magnetic rail, and domes, antennae, and scaffolding loomed out of it. Locatelli caught a quick glimpse of a collection of insectoid formations on an incline, and then they too were past, and they went on falling to their doom.

"Warren, you stubborn idiot!"

The worst thing was, Hanna was right.

"Fine!"

Cursing, he staggered from his seat, practically weightless, given the insane speed of their descent. Everything around him was rattling, vibrating, and roaring. The floor was at an extreme angle, it was hardly possible to stand on it except that he was floating anyway. Grabbing his gun, he made his way hand over hand toward the Canadian, crawled behind him, and tugged at his bonds with his free hand.

Nothing. As if they were welded together.

Good work, Warren. Well done!

He would need both his hands. Such a fucking mess! Where should he put the gun? Wedge it under his arm, and quick! Don't panic, now. Disentangle the knots, loosen them, untie them carefully. The straps slid down. Hanna stretched his arms, leaped up, grabbed the arm of the pilot's seat and pulled himself into it. His eye fell on the console.

"Thought so," Locatelli heard him say.

With some effort he heaved himself into the co-pilot's seat. The Canadian ignored him. He worked with great concentration, gave a series of instructions, and the Ganymede righted itself. Below them drifted an endless sea of dust, blurred fingers poked from it, reaching for them, stirred up by something vast and insect-like, creeping slowly across the plain. Locatelli held his breath. In the formless gray, huge, glistening beetles seemed to be moving around, then all of a sudden he felt as if his brain were being pushed out through his ears. Hanna violently braked the shuttle. Swaths of smoke whirled in front of the glass. They thundered along blindly, far too fast! A moment ago he had been ready to smash Hanna to a pulp, now he felt a powerful desire to see him at work, as the master of the situation. Sweat ran down Hanna's face, the muscles of his jaw protruded. From the rear part of the Ganymede came a great bang that sounded like an explosion, even louder roaring, the nose of the shuttle rose—

Contact with the ground.

In a flash the landing struts broke away. Locatelli was slung from his seat as if a giant had kicked the Ganymede in the belly; he performed a somersault and slid unimpeded to the rear. All the bones in his body seemed to want to switch places with each other. Jets hissing, the shuttle plowed through the regolith, bounced, crashed down again, hurtled on, bucked and lurched, but the tail stayed firm. Locatelli reached desperately around for something he could hold onto. His hand closed on a stanchion. Muscles tensed, he drew himself up, lost his balance, and was flying forward when the hurtling wreck collided with something, reared up, and scraped its way up a hill. Just as the machine came to rest in an avalanche of debris, he landed heavily between the seats, was carried on by the momentum of his own acceleration, and bumped his head.

Everything around him turned red.

Then black.

Aristarchus Plateau, The Moon

The brief moment of euphoria at the sound of Locatelli's voice had made way for greater anxiety. Julian was uninterruptedly trying to get through to the Ganymede, but apart from a hiss nothing issued from the speakers.

"Crashed," Momoka whispered, over and over again.

"That needn't mean anything," Evelyn said, trying to console her. "Nothing at all. He must have got the thing under control, Momoka. He's done it before."

"But he's not in contact."

"Because he's flying too low. He *can't* get in contact."

"We'll know in half an hour," said Rogachev calmly. "He should have arrived by then."

"That's true." Amber sat down on the floor. "Let's wait."

"It's not as simple as that," said Julian. "If we wait too long we'll use up too much oxygen. Then we won't even get to the production sites."

"You mean we're *that* low?"

"Depends how you look at it. We could spare half an hour. But nothing must go wrong after that! And we don't know whether the rovers will get through. We may find points where they can't go on; we'll have to factor in detours."

"Julian's right," said Evelyn. "It's too risky. We've just got one chance."

"But if Warren comes and we're gone," Momoka wailed. "How's he supposed to find us?"

"Maybe we could leave something behind," Rogachev said after a brief, stumped pause.

"A message?"

"A sign," Amber suggested. "We could form an arrow out of the debris from the wrecked rover. So that he knows in which direction we've gone."

"Wait." Julian was thinking. "That's not such a bad idea. And it occurs to me that our routes should actually cross. His last position was Cape Heraclides—that was the direction he was headed. And that's exactly where we've got to get to. If we stay switched to receive, sooner or later he'll make radio contact with us."

"You mean he—" Momoka gulped. "He's alive?"

"Warren?" Julian laughed. "Please! No one's going to break him, no one knows that better than you. And anyway, those things aren't that hard to fly."

"What if he had to do a crash landing?"

"We'll meet him on the way."

They loaded up the rovers with the spare batteries and oxygen supplies, carried debris, empty shelves, and containers out of the shacks and arranged them all into an arrow pointing north. On the right they formed an H and a 3 out of rocks.

"Excellent," said Evelyn contentedly.

"That's what you call a detailed location," Amber agreed. A tiny hope was gradually forming. "At least it'll help him find us."

"Yes, you're right." All the arrogance had fled from Momoka's voice. Now she only sounded terribly concerned and a tiny bit grateful. "That's unmistakable."

"Then we should get going," urged Rogachev. "Suggestions about who should take which rover?"

"Let Julian decide. He's the boss."

"And the boss drives ahead," said Julian. "Along with Amber. We're polite, too, and we're going to let you guys have the nicer car."

"Hmm, then—"

It was strange. Even though they couldn't survive here, each one of them felt the same ludicrous unease at leaving the spaceport. Perhaps because it looked like safety, even though it offered none. Now they would be heading for the desert. To no-man's-land.

They stared at each other, without actually being able to see anyone's face.

"Come on," Julian decided at last. "Let's get going."

London, Great Britain

It was doubtless very sensible of Jennifer Shaw to have brought in people from Scotland Yard who, when the talk turned to Korean nuclear material, immediately informed the SIS. Since Orley Enterprises was based on British soil, and a non-British facility seemed to be involved, MI5 and MI6 were both let loose on the company. Jericho, on the other hand, felt as if they were running on the spot. Not because he missed Xin and the witch hunt he had unleashed, but because all initiative seemed suddenly to have been taken out of his, Yoyo's, and Tu's hands. The Big O swarmed with nothing but investigators that late afternoon. Jennifer insisted on having them there for every conversation, with the result that they droned out the same endless answers to the same endless questions, until Tu, red-faced with fury, under questioning from one of Her Majesty's agents, demanded the return of his suitcase.

"What's up?" Yoyo asked irritably.

"Didn't you hear the question?" Tu pointed a fleshy finger at the officer, who impassively wrote something down in his tiny book.

"Yes, I did," she said cautiously.

"And?"

"He really only—"

"He's insulting me! That guy insulted me!"

"I only asked you why you dodged the German authorities," the agent said very calmly.

"I *didn't* dodge them!" Tu snapped at him. "I never dodge anybody! But I do know which people I can trust, and police officers are rarely among them, *very* rarely."

"That doesn't necessarily speak in your favor."

"It doesn't?"

Edda Hoff's waxy face showed signs of life.

"Perhaps you should bear in mind that it is to Mr. Tu and his companions that we owe evidence that your authorities for a long time failed to provide," she said in that special toneless voice of hers.

The man snapped the book shut.

"Nonetheless, it would have been better for everyone if you'd only cooperated with our German colleagues from the start," he said. "Or did you have reasons for not wanting to?"

Tu jumped up and brought both fists down on the table.

"What are you insinuating?"

"Nothing, just—"

"Who are you, in fact? The damned Gestapo?"

"Hey." Jericho took Tu by the shoulders and tried to pull him back into his chair, which was like trying to shift a parking meter. "No one's insinuating anything. They *have* to check us out. Why don't you just tell him—"

"What, then, what?" Tu stared at him. "That guy? Am I supposed to tell him how the police threw me about for six months of my life, so I still wake up drenched in sweat? So that I'm afraid to go to sleep because it might all start up again in my dreams?"

"No, it's just—" Jericho paused. What had his friend just said?

"Tian." Yoyo rested a hand on Tu's fist.

"No, I've had enough." Tu shook her off, escaped Jericho's clutches, and stomped away. "I want to go to a hotel. Right now! I want a break, I just want to be left in peace for an hour."

"You don't need to go to a hotel," said Edda. "We have guest rooms in the Big O. I could have one prepared for you."

"Do that."

The MI6 man set the book down on the table in front of him, and twisted around toward Tu as he headed for the door. "The questioning isn't over yet. You can't just—"

"Yes I can," Tu said as he left. "If you really need an asshole to put under general suspicion, use your own."

Jericho would have liked to ask Tu, otherwise so relaxed and controlled, and to whose house the Chinese police had paid regular visits only a few days before, what had provoked his rage to such an extent, but the nature of the investigations hurled him from one conversation into the next. His friend disappeared with a remarkably solicitous Edda Hoff; the MI6 investigator went on his way. For the few seconds that elapsed before the arrival of Jennifer Shaw, he felt a festering unease, particularly since Yoyo, the guardian of dark secrets, was staring ostentatiously into the distance, joining in with Tu's misery.

"And once again you know more than I do," he said.

She nodded mutely.

"And it's none of my business."

"It's something *I* can't tell you." Yoyo turned her head toward him. Her eyes glistened as if Tu's outburst had caused new cracks in the dam of her self-control. It was slowly starting to seem to Jericho that the whole Chen family, along with their wealthy mentor, were on the edge of a nervous breakdown, in constant danger of exploding under the pressure of traumatic bulges. Whatever it was that troubled them, it was starting to get on his nerves.

"I understand," he growled.

And he actually did understand. The phenomenon of being tongue-tied even when you *wanted* to speak was one that he was all too familiar with. He silently looked at his fingers, which were cracked, the nails jagged, the cuticles ragged. They were not attractive. He was clean, but not well looked after. Joanna had said that. For a long time he hadn't been able to tell the difference, but at that moment he wouldn't have been able to shake hands with himself. He neglected himself. Yoyo didn't love herself, the same went for Chen, and, to a startling extent, for Tu, the rock on which all egocentricity was founded. Were there any heads left in which the past wasn't moldering away?

Jennifer came into the room.

"I heard you don't feel like talking anymore."

"Wrong." Yoyo rubbed her eyes. "We just don't like people who don't know our history sticking their big fat noses into it."

"SIS has finished stocktaking." Jennifer handed out thin piles of paper. "You're credible, all three of you."

"Oh, thanks."

"Actually you could join your friend Tian. I'm very grateful to you, seriously!" Her blue-green eyes said precisely that, and a tiny bit more.

"But?"

"I'd be even more grateful to you if you'd go on supporting our investigation."

"We're happy to if you'll let us," said Jericho.

"Then I assume that's resolved to our mutual satisfaction." Jennifer sat down. "You're familiar with the coded message, you have been able to speculate in greater detail than we have about its missing parts, you have had contact with Kenny Xin, you know about Beijing's involvement in African coups d'état, Korean mini-nukes, a conspiracy operating past all state institutions—would you like to hear something you don't already know, for a change? Does the name Gerald Palstein mean anything to you?"

"Palstein." Jericho scoured his memory. "Never heard of him."

"A chess piece. A rook, more of a queen, moved by circumstances. Palstein is the Strategic Planner for EMCO."

"EMCO the oil giant?"

"The collapsing oil giant. Formerly number one among the companies following conservative paths that are currently perishing from an overdose of helium-3. Palstein's task was supposed to be to save EMCO, and instead he has little more to do than cancel plans for exploration, close down one subsidiary after another, and consign whole tribes to unemployment. In political terms not much is happening. It's all the more remarkable that Palstein won't admit defeat. In opposition to the senior board members, he took an interest in alternative energies years ago, and particularly in us. He would have liked to join us, but at the time EMCO thought we were working on things like time travel and teleporting. They didn't take the whole business, helium-3, the space elevator and so on, seriously, and when the reality of what we were doing finally kicked in no one took *them* seriously. But Palstein seems quite determined to win the battle."

"Sounds like Don Quixote?"

"That would be to underestimate him. He isn't one to tilt at windmills. Palstein knows that helium-3 is unbeatable, so he wants into the business. The only possible way is through us, and EMCO isn't exactly broke yet. But a lot of people would rather see the remaining millions being put into protection for the workers. Palstein, on the other hand, maintains that the best protection is the continuing existence of the company, and says the money should be put into maintenance projects. Maybe that's what earned him the rifle bullet."

"Just a moment." Jericho paused. "There was something about this on the web. An assassination attempt on an oil manager, that's right! Last month in Canada. Nearly got him."

"It *did* get him, but fortunately only in the shoulder. A few days prior he and Julian negotiated EMCO participation in Orley Space. By that time it was already fixed that Palstein should go to the Moon for the unofficial opening of Gaia. He'd secured himself a place years ago, but with a gunshot wound, with your arm in a sling, you don't fly to the Moon."

"I get it. Carl Hanna went instead. The guy that Orley suspects. The one you set Norrington on."

Jennifer's fingers slid over the tabletop. A man's face appeared on the screen, angular, with heavy eyebrows, his beard and hair shorn almost to the skin.

"Carl Hanna. A Canadian investor. At least that's what he claims to be. Of course Norrington checked him out when they were assembling the group. Now you don't need to put people like Mukesh Nair and Oleg Rogachev under the microscope—"

"Rogachev," Yoyo echoed.

Jennifer Shaw looked at the stack of printed pages. "I've put together a list for you, of the guests that Julian's traveling with. You might be more familiar with some of the others. Finn O'Keefe, for example—"

"The actor?" Yoyo's eyes sparkled. "Of course."

"Or Evelyn Chambers. Everybody knows America's talk-show queen. Miranda Winter, always involved in some kind of scandal, darling of the tabloids; but the real money is with the investors. Most of them are well-known figures, but Hanna seemed like a blank page. A diplomat's son, born in New Delhi, moved to Canada, studied Economics in Vancouver, Bachelor of Arts and Science. Entered the stock market and investment business, repeated stays in India. Worth an estimated fifteen billion dollars, after he inherited a lot of money and invested the money cleverly, in oil and gas, by the way, before switching to alternative energies at the right time. Remains involved in Warren Locatelli's Light-years, Marc Edwards's Quantime Inc., and a number of other companies. By his own account he considered investing in helium-3 before, but he thought it was too much of a fly-by-night proposition at first."

"Although that's changed, as we know."

"As have the indicators for an investment. A year and a half ago, at a sailing tournament organized by Locatelli, he met Julian and Lynn, Julian's daughter. They liked each other, but what was crucial was that Hanna thought out loud about sponsoring India's space program because of his old associations with the place. The bait, you might say, that landed Julian like a big fat cod. The group going to the Moon had already been decided, so Julian offered him a trip for the following year." Jennifer paused. "You're an experienced investigator, Owen. How much of Carl Hanna's CV could be faked?"

"All of it," said Jericho.

"His business interests have been confirmed."

"Since when?"

"Hanna joined Light-years two years ago."

"Two years is nothing. Long periods abroad, possibly born abroad, standard spy stuff. In the emerging countries all our investigations trickle away; nobody's surprised when birth certificates disappear. Sloppy work by local authorities is the order of the day. Second, investor. A disguise par excellence. Money has no personality, leaves no lasting impression. No one can prove who's really invested or since when. With a bit of preparation you could pull something out of a hat and everyone will swear it's a rabbit. Do you know him personally?"

"Yep. Pleasant enough. Attentive, friendly, not exactly chatty. Bit of a loner."

"Hobbies? Bound to be something solitary."

"He dives."

"Diving. Mountain climbing. Typical interests of private investigators and secret agents. You hardly need witnesses for either."

"Plays guitar."

"That fits. An instrument evokes the appearance of authenticity and creates sympathy." Jericho rested his chin on his hands. "And now you think Palstein had to be sacrificed to make room for Hanna."

"I'm convinced of it."

"I'm not," Yoyo objected. "Couldn't Hanna have been picked for your tour group if he'd just begged nicely? I mean, one more or less, you're not going to shoot somebody for it."

Jennifer shook her head.

"It's different with space travel. Where you're going there are no natural resources, either to move you around or keep you alive. Every breath you take, every bite you eat, every sip of water is factored in. Every extra pound on board a shuttle is reflected in fuel. Even the space elevator is no exception. Once it's full it's full. In a vehicle that accelerates to twelve times the speed of sound, you don't really want any standing room."

"What does Norrington have to say so far?"

"Hmm. The CV looks airtight. He's working on it."

"And you're quite sure Hanna's our man?"

Jennifer said nothing for a while.

"Look, your late friend Vogelaar spouted a whole lot of hints. About China, the Zheng Group above all. The Russians used to be the bad guys, now it's the Chinese. Should we be bothered that Hanna's about as Chinese as a St. Bernard dog? If Beijing really is behind the attack, they couldn't do anything better than send up a European, everything signed and sealed, in our elevator and with an invitation from Gaia. Someone who can move about freely up there. But, Owen, I'm sure that Hanna's our man. Julian himself gave us confirmation of that before he got cut off."

Yoyo glanced at the guest list and set it down again. "That means, the more we know about the attack on Palstein, the better we understand what's happening on the Moon. So where is this guy based? Where is EMCO based? In America?"

"In Dallas," said Jennifer. "Texas."

"Great. Seven—no, six hours behind. Our friend Palstein's having lunch. Give him a call."

Jennifer smiled. "That's what I was just going to do."

DALLAS, TEXAS, USA

Palstein's office was on the seventeenth floor of EMCO headquarters, close to several conference rooms which, like inadequately insulated basements, filled again every hour with the brackish water of bad news, every time it seemed just to have been emptied. The meeting in which he had now been stuck for over two hours was no exception. An exploratory project off the coast of Ecuador, at a depth of 3,000 meters, launched as a blue-chip enterprise but now nothing but a rusting legacy. Two platforms, giving rise to the question whether they should be dragged to land or sunk, which hadn't been that easy to answer in the wake of the legendary Brent Spar debacle.

His secretary came into the room.

"Would it be possible for you to come to the phone for a moment?"

"Is it important?" Palstein asked with barely concealed gratitude at being temporarily removed from the ranks of the dead.

"Orley Enterprises." She looked around with an encouraging smile. "Coffee, anyone? Espresso? Doughnuts?"

"Subsidies," said an elderly man in a croaking voice. No one laughed. Palstein got to his feet.

"Have you heard anything yet from Loreena Keowa?" he asked as he left the room.

"No."

"Right." He looked at his watch. "I guess she'll be on the plane already."

"Shall I try her cell phone?"

"No, I think Loreena was going to take a later flight. She said something about getting in around twelve."

"Where?"

"Vancouver."

"Thanks for that. You've just reinforced my certainty that I will keep my job for another while yet."

He stared at her.

"Twelve o'clock in Vancouver is two o'clock in Texas," she said.

"I see!" He laughed. "My goodness. What would I do without you?"

"Exactly. Small conference room, video link."

A tense-looking group appeared on the wall monitor. Jennifer Shaw, the security chief of Orley Enterprises, was sitting with a fair-haired, stubbly man and a remarkably pretty Asian girl at a battered-looking table.

"Sorry to bother you, Gerald," she said.

"Not sorry you did." He smiled and leaned, arms folded, against the edge of the desk. "Good to see you, Jennifer. I'm afraid I haven't got much time at the moment."

"I know. We dragged you out of a meeting. Can I introduce you? Chen Yuyun—"

"Yoyo," said Yoyo.

"And Owen Jericho. Unfortunately the reason for my call is anything but welcome. However, it may illuminate some questions that you may have been asking yourself every day since Calgary."

"Calgary?" Palstein frowned. "Let's hear it."

Jennifer told him about the chance of a nuclear attack on Gaia, and that someone had probably wanted him out of the way to make room for a terrorist in Julian's tour group. Palstein's thoughts wandered to Loreena.

Someone wanted to stop you doing something. It seems to me it was going to the Moon with Orley.

"My God," he whispered. "That's terrible."

"We need your help, Gerald." Jennifer leaned forward, grumpy, plump, a monument of mistrust. "We need all the picture evidence that the American and Canadian authorities hold about the attack on you, and any other information you might have, texts, state of the investigation. Of course we could take the official route, but you know the people involved in the investigation personally. It would be nice if you could speed up the process. Texas has a busy afternoon ahead, full of hard-working officials who might still be able to give us something today."

"Have you called in the British police?"

"Special Branch, the Secret Intelligence Service. Of course we'll immediately pass on the material to the State authorities, but as you can imagine my job description doesn't just involve passing things on."

"I'll do what I can." Palstein shook his head, visibly agitated. "Sorry, but this is all a big nightmare. The attempt on my life, and now this. It's less than a week since I wished Julian a pleasant journey. We were going to sign contracts as soon as he got back."

"I know. Still no reason not to."

"Why would anyone want to destroy Gaia?"

"That's what we're trying to find out, Gerald. And possibly, at the same time, who it was that shot you."

"Mr. Palstein." The fair-haired man spoke for the first time. "I know you've been asked this a thousand times, but do you suspect anyone yourself?"

"Well." Palstein sighed and rubbed his eyes. "Until a few days ago I would have sworn that someone was just venting his disappointment, Mr.—"

"Jericho."

"Mr. Jericho." Palstein was already standing with one foot in the adjacent conference room. "We've had to fire an awful lot of people recently. Close down firms. You know what's going on. But there are people who assume the same as you do. That the purpose of the attack was to keep me from flying to the Moon. Except that nobody's been able to tell me why."

"Things are clearer now."

"Distinctly so. But these people—or one person, to be more precise—they don't rule out Chinese interests being involved."

Jennifer, Jericho, and the girl exchanged glances.

"And what leads these people to make their assumption?"

Palstein hesitated. "Listen, Jennifer, I've got to go back in, hard as it is. First I'll make sure that you get hold of the material as quickly as possible. But there's one area in which I'll have to ask you to be patient."

"Which is that?"

"There's a film that *possibly* shows the man who shot me."

"What?" Chen Yuyun sat bolt upright. "But that's exactly what—"

"And you'll get it." Palstein raised both hands in a conciliatory manner. "Except that I've promised the person who found the film that I'd keep it under wraps for the time being. In a few hours I will call that person and ask them to release the video, and until then I ask for your understanding."

The pretty Chinese girl stared at him.

"We've been through quite a lot," she said quietly.

"Me too." Palstein pointed at his shoulder. "But fairness dictates that sequence of events."

"Fine." Jennifer smiled. "Of course we'll respect your decision."

"One last question," said Jericho.

"Fire away."

"The man the person thinks is the murderer—can you make him out clearly?"

"Pretty clearly, yes."

"And is he Chinese?"

"Asian." Palstein fell silent for a moment. "Possibly Chinese. Yes. He's *probably* Chinese."

CAPE HERACLIDES,
MONTES JURA, THE MOON

Locatelli was amazed. He had reached a great insight, namely that his head was the Moon, his scalp the Moon's surface, with the maria and the craters pulled over the concave bulge of the bone. From this he learned two things: one, why so much moon dust had trickled into his brain, and two, that the whole trip as he remembered it had never happened at all, but had sprung entirely from his imagination, particularly the regrettable last chapter. He would open his eyes, trusting to the comforting certainty that no one could reproach him for anything, and even the impression of constantly whirling gray would find a natural explanation. The only thing that still puzzled him was the part the universe played in the whole thing. That it was pressing against the right side of his face amazed and confused him, but since he only had to open his eyes—

It wasn't the universe. It was the ground he was lying on.

Click, click.

He raised his head and gave a start. A circular saw of torment was running through his head. Shapes, colors, a blur. All bathed in a diffuse light, at once dazzling and crepuscular, so that he had to shut his eyelids tight. A constant clicking sound reached him. He tried to raise a hand, without success. It was busy somewhere with the other one, they were both off behind his back and refused to be parted.

Click, click.

His vision cleared. A little way off he saw ungainly boots and something long that swung gently back and forth and bumped with the regularity of a Chinese water torture against the edge of the pilot's seat, on which the owner of the boots was crouching. Locatelli twisted his head and saw Carl Hanna, who was looking at him thoughtfully, his gun in his right hand, as if he had been sitting there for an eternity. He was rhythmically tapping the barrel against the seat.

Click, click.

Locatelli coughed.

"Did we crash?" he croaked.

Hanna went on looking at him and said nothing. Images merged to form memories. No, they had landed. A crash landing. They'd gone hurtling across the regolith and collided with something. From that point onward he could remember only that they must have switched roles in the meantime, because he was now the one who was tied up. Seething shame welled up in him. He'd messed up.

Click, click.

"Can you stop tapping that fucking thing against the chair?" he groaned. "It's really annoying."

To his surprise Hanna actually did stop. He set the gun aside and rubbed the point of his chin.

"And what will I do with you now?" he asked.

It didn't sound as if he really expected a constructive suggestion. Instead, there were undertones of resignation in his words, a hint of quiet regret that frightened Locatelli more than if Hanna had shouted at him.

"Why don't you just let me go?" he suggested hoarsely.

The Canadian shook his head. "I can't do that."

"Why not? What would be the alternative?"

"Not to let you go."

"Shoot me down, then."

"I don't know, Warren." Hanna shrugged. "Why do you have to act the hero on top of everything?"

"I understand." Locatelli gulped. "So why didn't you do that a long time ago? Or do you have some sort of quota? No more than three in a single day? You bastard!" All of a sudden he saw the horses galloping away, with him running after them to catch them, because it probably wasn't the best idea to annoy Hanna even more, but in the meltdown of his fury all his clear thoughts had vanished. He heaved himself up, managed to get into a seated position, and glared with hatred at Hanna. "Do you actually enjoy this? Do you get off on killing people? What sort of a perverse piece of shit are you, Carl? You revolt me! What the hell are you doing here? What do you want from us?"

"I'm doing my job."

"Your job? Was it your fucking job to push Peter into the gorge? To blow up Marc and Mimi? Is *that* your fucking job, you stupid idiot?"

Stop, Warren!

"You fucker! You piece of shit!"

Stop it!

"You fucking douche! Wait until I get my hands free."

Oh, Warren. Stupid, too stupid! Why had he said that? Why hadn't he just *thought* it? Hanna frowned, but it looked as if he hadn't really been listening. His gaze wandered to the air lock, then suddenly he bent forward.

"Now be careful, Warren. What I do has more to do with logging trees and drying marshes. You understand? Killing can be necessary, but my job consists not in destroying something, but in preserving or building something else. A house, an idea, a system: whatever you like."

"So what crappy system is legitimized through killing?"

"All of them."

"You sick fuck. And for what system did you kill Mimi, Marc, and Peter?"

"Stop it, Warren. You're not seriously trying to force a guilt complex on me?"

"Are you working for some fucking government or other?"

"In the end we're all working for some fucking government or other." Hanna sat back with a sigh of forbearance. "Okay, I'll tell you something. You remember the global economic crisis sixteen years ago? The whole world was gnashing its teeth. Including India. But there, the crisis also provoked a spike of activity! People invested in environmental protection, high tech, education and agriculture, relaxed the caste system, exported services and innovations, halved poverty. A billion and a half of predominantly young, extremely motivated architects of globalization pushed their way to third place in the global economy."

Locatelli nodded, puzzled. He hadn't the faintest notion why Hanna was telling him this, but it was better than being shot for want of conversational material.

"Of course Washington wondered how to respond. For example they were troubled by the idea that a stronger India, if it got closer to Beijing, might forget about good old Uncle Sam. What bloc would crystallize out of that? India and the USA? Or India, China, and Russia? Washington had always seen the Indians as important allies, and would have loved to use them against China, for example, but New Delhi was insisting on autonomy, and didn't want to be talked around, let alone used, by anybody."

"What does all this have to do with us?"

"In this phase, Warren, people like me were sent to the Subcontinent to make sure all the spin was going in the right direction. We were instructed to support the Indian miracle with all our might, but when the Chinese ambassador was blown up in 2014 by LeMGI, the League for a Muslim Greater India, Indo-Chinese relations darkened just at the right moment, favoring the finalization of certain important Indo-American agreements."

"You are—hang on a second!" Locatelli flashed his teeth. "You're not trying to tell me—"

"Yep. It's thanks to some of these agreements, for example, that your solar collectors make such a huge profit on the Indian market."

"You're a fucking CIA agent!"

Hanna gave a mildly complacent smile. "LeMGI was my idea. One of a huge number of tricks to offset the possibility of Chinese-Indian-Russian bloc formation. Some of those tricks worked, occasionally at the cost of human lives, our own, in fact. With all due respect for your genius, Warren, people like you get rich and influential under certain conditions that had to be put in place by other people, if necessary the government. Can you rule out the possibility that your market leader-ship on the other side of the planet might have been bought with a few human lives?"

"What?" Locatelli exploded. "Are you out of your mind?"

"Can you rule it out?"

"I'm not the damned government! Of course I can—"

"But you're a beneficiary. You think I'm a bastard. But you only looked on while I did something that everybody does, and from which you profit every day without a thought. The paradigm shift in energy supply, aneutronic, clean fusion; that sounds good, really good, and the improved yield of your solar cells has revolutionized the market in solar panels. Congratulations. But when has anyone ever risen to the top without others falling? Sometimes you need a bit of help, and we're the ones who provide it."

Locatelli looked into Hanna's eyes for the twitch that betrays the presence of lunacy, tics, traumas, and inner demons. But there was nothing but cold, dark calm.

"And what does the CIA want from us?" he asked.

"The CIA? Nothing, as far as I know. I'm no longer part of the fam-ily. Until seven years ago I was paid by the State, but one day you realize that you can get the same job from the same people for three times the pay. All you have to do is go independent on the free market, and call your boss not Mr. President, but Mr. CEO. Of course you've always known that you were actually working for the Vatican, the Mafia, the banks, the energy cartels, the arms producers, the environmental lobby, the Rockefellers, Warren Buffets, Zheng Pang-Wangs, and Julian Orleys of this world; so from now on you're just working directly for them. It may of course happen that you go on representing the inter-ests of some government or other. You just have to extend the concept of government appropriately: to groups like Orley Enterprises, which have accrued so much power that they *are* the government. The world is governed by companies and cartels, crossing all national boundaries. The overlaps with elected parliamentary governments are anywhere between random and complete. You never really know exactly who you're working for, so you stop asking, because it doesn't make any difference anyway."

"I'm sorry?" Locatelli's eyes threatened to pop from his head. "You don't even know *who* you're doing this for?"

"I couldn't tell you unequivocally, at any rate."

"But you've killed three people!" Locatelli yelled. "You stupid ass-hole, with your secret-agent attitude, you don't do something like that just because it's a *job!*"

Hanna opened his mouth, shut it again, and ran his hand over his eyes as if to wipe away something ugly that he'd just seen.

"Okay, it was a mistake. I shouldn't have told you all that, I should be cleverer! It always ends up exactly the same, with somebody saying asshole. Not that I'm insulted, it's just all that wasted time. Annihilated capital."

He got to his feet, grew to menacing, primeval height, 2 meters of muscle encased in steel-reinforced synthetic fiber, crowned by the cold intelligence of an analyst who has just lost his patience. Locatelli feverishly wondered how this ridiculous conversation could be held in check.

"There was no need to kill Mimi and Marc," he said hastily. "You did *that* out of pure pleasure at least."

Hanna shook his head thoughtfully.

"You don't understand, Warren. You know people like me from the movies, and you think we're all psychopaths. But killing isn't a pleasure or a burden. It's an act of depersonalization. You can't see a person and a goal at the same time. Back in the Schröter Valley, those three were too close, even Mimi and Marc. Marc, for example, would have been able to climb back along the cantilever and follow me in the second rover, not to mention Peter. I couldn't take any kind of risk."

"In that case why didn't you just kill all of—"

"Because I thought the rest of you were up on Snake Hill, and therefore too far away to be dangerous to me. Whether you believe me or not, Warren, I'm trying to *spare* lives."

"How comforting," Locatelli murmured.

"But I hadn't reckoned with you. Why were you suddenly there?"

"I'd gone back."

"Why? You didn't want to see the lovely view?"

"Forgot my camera." His voice sounded awkward to his own ears, embarrassed and hurt. Hanna smiled sympathetically.

"The most trivial things can change the course of your life," he said. "That's how things are."

Locatelli pursed his lips, stared at the tips of his boots, and fought down an attack of hysterical laughter. There he sat, worrying about whether his confession of forgetfulness would be posthumously weighed against his actions, reducing his heroic status. Would it? At least there would be some kind of obituary! A stirring speech. A toast, a bit of music: *Oh Danny Boy*—

He looked up.

"Why am I still alive, Carl? Aren't you in a hurry? What's all this game-playing about?"

Hanna looked at him from dark, unfathomable eyes.

"I'm not playing games, Warren. I'm not treacherous enough for that. You were unconscious for over an hour. While you were out, I analyzed our situation. Doesn't look so great."

"Mine certainly doesn't."

"Nor mine. I couldn't understand why I wasn't able to get the thing off the ground at the last minute. We should really have been able to avoid the crash landing with vertical counterthrust. But the jets failed above the ground, when we were flying through those clouds of dust, perhaps they got blocked. Unfortunately, when we came down it knocked away our ground struts, so the Ganymede is lying on its belly, dug a fair way into the ground. I probably don't need to tell you what that means."

Locatelli threw his head back and closed his eyes.

"We can't get out," he said. "The air lock shaft won't extend."

"A bit of a design flaw, if you ask my opinion. Installing the only portal on the underside."

"No emergency exit?"

"Oh, there is: the freight room in the tail. It can be vacuumed out and flooded with air, so in principle it's an air lock too. The rear hatch can be lowered and extended into a ramp—but as I said, the Ganymede has plowed several kilometers through the regolith, before clattering its way into a rock face over the last few meters. There are boulders lying around all over the place, as far as you can see. I think some of them are blocking the hatch. It won't open more than half a meter."

Locatelli thought about it. It was funny, in fact. Really funny.

"Why are you surprised?" he laughed hoarsely. "You're in jail, Carl. Right where you belong."

"But so are you."

"So? Does it make any kind of difference whether you finish me off here or out there?"

"Warren—"

"It doesn't matter. It couldn't matter less! Welcome to prison."

"If I'd wanted to finish you off, you would never have come round. You understand? I don't plan to finish you off."

Locatelli hesitated. His laughter died away.

"You really mean that?"

"At the moment you aren't any sort of threat to me. You're not going to dupe me again like you did in the air lock. So you have the choice of being obstructive or cooperating."

"And what," Locatelli said slowly, "would my outlook be like if I chose to cooperate?"

"Your temporary survival."

"But temporary isn't enough."

"All I can offer. Or let's say, if you play along, at least you won't face any danger from me. I can promise you that much."

Locatelli fell silent for a second.

"Fine, then. I'm listening."

ROVER

Over the past half hour Amber had given up all hope of ever reaching the production plant. Seen from a high altitude, the Aristarchus Plateau looked like a softly undulating picture book landscape for lunar drivers, particularly along the Schröter Valley, where the terrain appeared to be entirely smooth, almost as if planed. But at ground level you got an idea of the day-to-day life of an ant. Everything grew into an obstacle. As effortlessly as the rovers were able to drive over smaller bumps and boulders in their path, thanks to their flexible axles, they proved more susceptible to the tiny craters, potholes, and cracks that opened up in front of them, forcing them to navigate from one hindrance to the next at between 20 and 30 kilometers an hour. It was only once they were past a collection of bigger craters on the way toward the Oceanus Procellarum that the ground evened out, and their progress became faster.

Since then, Amber had looked into the sky more and more often, in the hope of seeing the Ganymede appearing on the horizon, while her hope made way for the horrible certainty that Locatelli hadn't made it. Momoka, who was driving the second rover, had lapsed into silence. No one was particularly talkative. Only after quite a long time did Amber speak to her father-in-law on a special frequency so that the others couldn't listen in on the conversation.

"You kept a few things to yourself back then."

"How do you work that out?"

"Just a gut feeling." She scanned the horizon. "A little thing that tells women when men are lying or not telling the whole truth."

"That's enough of your intuition."

"No, really. It's just that women are more gifted at lying. We've perfected the repertoire of dissimulation; that's why we can see the truth gleaming through as if through fine silk, when you lie. You talked about the possibility of an attack. On some Orley facility somewhere or other. Carl runs amok, communication fails, and in retrospect it becomes clear that he went behind your back two days ago, and took a night-time joyride on the Lunar Express."

"And none of it makes any sense."

"No, it does. It makes sense if Carl's the guy who's supposed to carry out the attack."

"Here on the Moon?"

"Don't act like I'm retarded. Here on the Moon! Which would mean that it isn't just *some facility or other*, but one in particular."

They scooted on across the dark, monotonous basalt of the Oceanus Procellarum, already within the vicinity of the Mare Imbrium. For the first time they were able to take the rover up to its top speed, albeit at the cost of a very bumpy ride, as the chassis seesawed up and down and the vehicle kept lifting off the ground. In the distance, hills became visible, the Gruithuisen region, a chain of craters, mountains, and extinct volcanic domes that stretched all the way to Cape Heraclides.

"One more thing," said Julian. "Can I talk to you about Lynn?"

"As long as it leads to an answer to my question, whenever you like."

"How does she seem to you?"

"She's got a problem."

"Tim's always saying that."

"Given that he's *always* saying it, you really don't listen to him very often."

"Because he's always going on at me! You know that. It's impossible to say a sensible word about the girl to him!"

"Perhaps because good sense hasn't much to do with her condition."

"Then *you* tell me what her problem is."

"Her imagination, I would say."

"Oh, brilliant!" snorted Julian. "If that were the case, I'd be inundated with problems."

"When the imagination overpowers reason, it's always a kind of madness," Amber observed sententiously. "You're a bit mad too, but you're a special case. You distribute your madness to everybody with both hands, you cultivate it, people applaud you for it. You love your madness, and that's why it loves you and enables you to save the world. Have you ever been troubled by the idea that you might have overstretched yourself?"

"I worry about making wrong decisions."

"That's not the same thing. I mean, do you ever feel anything like anxiety?"

"Everyone gets frightened."

"Hang on there. Fear. Slight difference! Fear is the result of your startled reason, my dear Julian; it's real, because it's object-related and because it's explained by concrete factors. We're afraid of dogs, drunk Arsenal fans, and possible changes to tax legislation. I'm talking about anxiety. The vague fog in which anything at all might be lurking. The anxiety that you might fail, that you might fall short, you might have misjudged yourself, that you might cause some sort of disaster, paralyzing anxiety, the fear of yourself, in the end. Ever have that?"

"Hmm." Julian fell silent for a moment. "Should I?"

"No, what would be the point? You are who you are. But Lynn isn't like that."

"She's never said anything about anxiety."

"Wrong. You weren't listening, because your ears were always full of adrenaline. Do you at least know what happened five years ago?"

"I know she had a huge amount to do. My fault, perhaps. But I said, take a rest, didn't I? And she did. And after that she built the Stellar

Island Hotel, the OSS Grand, Gaia, she was more efficient than ever. So if it's exhaustion that you're all making such a fuss about, then—"

"We're not making a fuss," Amber said, annoyed now. "And by the way, I was always the one who defended you to Tim, so much so that he's been asking me if I get money for it. And every time I say, blessed are the ignorant. Believe me, Julian, I'm on your side. I've always had a heart for slow-witted people. I can even see some lovable aspects in *your* boneheadedness; maybe that's a product of social work. So I actually love you for not understanding the slightest thing, but that doesn't mean it has to stay that way, does it? And you still haven't worked out what's going on."

"That's enough."

"Just to remind you, it was *you* who wanted to talk to me about Lynn rather than answering my question."

"So explain to me what's wrong with her."

"You want me to explain your daughter's psyche to you, here in the middle of the Oceanus Procellarum?"

"I'd be grateful for any attempt to do so."

"Oh my good God." She thought for a second. "Okay, then, the headlines: do you believe Lynn was suffering from exhaustion back then?"

"Yes."

"Would you be surprised if I told you that overwork was the least of Lynn's problems? Otherwise she could never have run Orley Travel or built your hotels. No, her problem is that as soon as she closes her eyes, mini-Lynns of every age start crowding in on her. Baby Lynns, child Lynns, teenager Lynns, daughter Lynns, daddy's-little-girl Lynns, who think they can only earn your recognition by becoming an even tougher cookie than you are. Lynn is absolutely terrified of this army from the past, which controls her day and night. She thinks control is everything. But she's even more afraid of losing control, because she's worried that something terrible might come to light, a Lynn who can't exist, or perhaps even no Lynn at all, because the end of control would also mean the end of her existence. Do you understand?"

"I'm not entirely sure," said Julian, like someone moving through a forest dotted with mantraps.

"For Lynn, the idea of not having herself under control is more than frightening. For her, the loss of control basically means madness. She's afraid of ending up like Crystal."

"You mean—" He hesitated. "She's afraid of going *mad*?"

"Tim thinks that's the case. He's spent more time with her, he's bound to know better, but I think, yes, that's it exactly. Or it was five years ago."

"*That's* what she's afraid of?"

"Afraid of failing, afraid of losing control and losing her mind. But what frightened her most were the terrible things she might be capable of in order to stay in control.—By the way, did you know that suicide is also an act of control?"

"Why are you talking about suicide now, for heaven's sake?"

"Come on, Julian." Amber sighed. "Because it's all part of it. It doesn't have to be physical suicide. I mean any act of self-destruction, destruction of your health, your existence, as soon as the fear of being exposed to destruction by outside forces becomes unbearable. You'd rather destroy yourself than let someone else do it. The ultimate act of control."

"And—" Julian hesitated, "—is it true that Lynn's showing signs again, of—of this—"

"At first I thought Tim was exaggerating. Now I think he's right."

"But why don't *I* see it? Why doesn't something like that get through *to me*? Lynn has never shown me any weakness."

"So do you do that? Show weakness?"

"I don't know, Amber. I don't think about things like that."

"Exactly. You don't think. But nothing does any good, Julian. She doesn't need time off to recover. She needs treatment. A long, very long course of treatment. At the end of that she may take over Orley Enterprises completely. But she might just paint flower paintings or grow hemp in Sri Lanka. Who knows who your daughter really is. She doesn't know, in any event."

Julian slowly breathed out.

"Amber," he said. "There's a chance that someone's trying to blow Gaia up with an atom bomb. And that Lynn's somehow involved."

The revelation struck her with such force that she was momentarily lost for words. Her eyes drifted hopefully toward the sky, although she knew that Ganymede wouldn't be coming.

"How certain is it?" she asked.

"Pure speculation on the part of some people I don't even know. And I don't know anything more than that, I swear. But what happened today shows that there must be something in it. You're right. Carl's task might be to carry out the attack. And I fear—okay, there's some evidence that someone on the Moon is helping him, and—"

"You think it's Lynn?"

"I don't *want* to believe that, but—"

"Why, in God's name? It's *her* hotel. Why should she be involved in an attack on her *own* hotel?"

"Perhaps she doesn't know what's really going on, but she didn't want to show me the surveillance videos from the corridor which would have proved that Hanna was outside, traveling on the Lunar Express. She has access to all the systems in the hotel, Amber, she could interfere with the communication if she wanted, and she's aggressive and strange, a mystery—"

"And Tim's in Gaia," whispered Amber.

CAPE HERACLIDES, THE MOON

"Right, listen to me. I've got to get out of here as quickly as possible."

"Fine."

"I've found a grasshopper in the storeroom, and a buggy. As to the hopper, I'm worried that the steering unit was damaged in the impact, but the buggy seems intact. That means we've got to get the rear hatch open."

"What happens if we can't get out?"

"We can get out. It won't be entirely without danger, but if we put on our space suits and hold on tight at the right moment, I can get us out of the Ganymede. Then you'll help me to shift the debris and drive the buggy out. Then we'll see how it goes."

Locatelli blinked suspiciously. "If you're trying to trick me, Carl, then you can do your shit on your own—"

"If *you're* trying to trick *me*, Warren, I *will* do my shit on my own—is that clear?"

"Yes it is." Locatelli nodded respectfully.

Hanna stuck the gun in a holster on his thigh, where it disappeared completely, knelt down behind him, and quickly untied him. Locatelli stretched his arms. He was careful not to make any quick movements, extended his fingers, rubbed his wrists. It was only now that he noticed the slight angle of the shuttle. He still felt dazed. He hesitantly made his way to the cockpit and looked outside. Rising terrain stretched before his eyes. There was a fine haze in the air.

Air—what was he thinking of? It was dust, lousy, omnipresent moon dust, which hung like an optical illusion over the slope and settled, a dirty gray, on the glass. It wasn't being held up by air molecules, so what was keeping the stuff up there?

"Electrostatics," he mused.

"The dust?" Hanna joined him. "I wondered about that too. We're very close to the production site; tons of regolith are dug up here. Still, it's amazing that it doesn't sink to the ground."

"No, I think it does," Locatelli guessed. "Most of it, anyway. Remember, when we were driving the buggy we stirred up loads of it, and it all fell back right away, apart from the really fine stuff, the microscopic particles."

"Never mind. Come on."

They put on their helmets and body armor, and established radio contact. Hanna directed Warren to the rear of the vehicle behind the last row of seats, and pointed to the line of backrests.

"Set your back against them," he said. "To protect you. The panes in the cockpit must be made of armored glass, so I'll aim at one of the struts. The explosive power should be enough to crack them. Otherwise, we'll have to expect a considerable amount of flying splinters. If we're successful there's going to be a hell of a draught, so stay in the cover of the seats and hold on tight."

"What about the oxygen? Won't it go up in flames?"

"No, the concentration's the same as it is on Earth. Ready?"

Locatelli crouched behind the row of seats. In other circumstances he would have been splendidly amused, but even as it was he couldn't complain about a lack of adrenaline release.

"Ready," he said.

Hanna pushed in beside him, brought an almost identical looking gun out of a holster on his other thigh, leaned into the central aisle, and pointed the barrel into the cockpit. Locatelli thought he heard a high-frequency hiss, and then came a detonation, so short that the explosion seemed to swallow itself just as it was produced—

Then came the suction.

Objects, splinters, and shards came flying from all directions, whirled wildly around, past him and toward the cockpit. Anything that wasn't screwed or welded down was dragged outside. The escaping air pulled on his arms and legs, and pressed him against the seat backs. Something struck his visor, indefinable things hit his shoulders and hips, a bat swarm of brochures and books came flying aggressively at them, covers flapping frantically. A volume suddenly clung to his chest armor, slid reluctantly along it, pages fluttering, broke away and disappeared down the aisle. Everything happened in complete silence.

Then it was over.

Was it really? Locatelli waited another few seconds. He slowly pulled himself up along the back of the seat and looked toward the cockpit. Where the front panes had been, a huge hole now gaped.

"My goodness." He gasped for breath. "What is that thing you're firing there?"

"Homemade, secret." Hanna got up and stepped into the aisle. "Come on, we've got to get back to the storeroom."

The storeroom looked less chaotic than Locatelli had expected. The individual parts of a grasshopper lay strewn over the floor. He picked them up, one by one. The steering unit had been partly destroyed, but the buggy—a small two-seater vehicle with a flatbed for cargo—was undamaged in its mountings. Additional mountings indicated that if need be, six such vehicles could be transported. He quickly helped Hanna unfasten the buggy. The loading hatch, which was also the back wall of the storeroom, was slightly open, as if it had been dented in the impact. A hands' length of starry sky gleamed in at them. Hanna walked over to a rolling wall, opened it, took out batteries and two survival backpacks, and stuffed everything on the bed of the buggy. They left the cargo area, and helped each other out of the hole in the cockpit. The ground lay some meters below them. Locatelli jumped nimbly down, rounded the nose of the beached Ganymede and, holding his breath, looked out across the plain.

It was a ghostly sight.

As far as the eye could see, areas of swirled-up regolith stretched across the Sinus Iridum to form the swirling shape of a bell. Where the dust became more permeable, the velvety nature of the background seemed to have made way for a darker consistency. A swath of destruction led from the clouds of dust to the beach of the rising rocky terrain on which they stood, continued there as a jagged gap, described an upward curve and ended at the shuttle which, as Locatelli recognized now, had collided with an overhang and produced an avalanche. Boulders of all sizes had piled up around the tail of the Ganymede; some had rattled down the hill, but one of the biggest bits of rubble blocked the lower third of the rear hatch. The craggy ridge of the Jura Mountains ran to the northwest.

"Not all that much," Hanna observed. "I was afraid the rubble would reach all the way up."

"No, it's not much," Locatelli confirmed sourly. "It's just that they're fucking enormous. That one there must weigh several tons."

"Divided by six. Let's get to work."

Gaia, Vallis Alpina, The Moon

At half past six, Dana called the search parties back to headquarters. Lynn and Sophie had scoured most of the staff accommodation and part of the suites in the thorax, Michio Funaki and Ashwini Anand had crept like cockroaches through the greenhouses, and had turned every scrap of green and every tomato upside down before devoting themselves to the meditation center and the multi-religious church. The third team, last of all, was able to report that the pool, the health center, and the casino were, as Kokoschka put it, clean, stressing the word like Philip Marlowe after patting down a suspect.

"And that's exactly where the problem lies," said Dana. "In appearance. Have we had a chance to look inside the walls and floors? In the life-support systems?"

Kokoschka waved his detector tellingly. "Didn't even click."

"Yes, of course, but we don't know enough about mini-nukes."

"It was your idea to search the hotel," Lynn said furiously. "So don't start telling us it was pointless. And besides, Sophie and I *did* look in the life-support systems, anywhere there might be room for such a thing."

"So?" Dana stared at her with X-ray eyes. "How do you know how much room a mini-nuke takes up?"

"That's not fair, Dana," said Tim quietly.

"I'm not being unfair in the slightest," she replied, without looking at him. "I'm concerned with minimizing risks, and the search contributed to that. We've looked in the important places, I was in the head, even though I'm still of the view that there might be a bomb at some deeper, more central point."

"Or not," mused Anand. "It's an atom bomb. The explosive force would be huge, so that it might not matter where you put it."

"It might not." Dana nodded slowly. "At any rate what I've heard doesn't put my mind at rest. At least I was able to have a conversation with Peary Base. As I suspected, they've got the same problem; they've lost contact with the Earth and our shuttles, and they're also in the libration shadow. After I told the deputy commander a short version of—"

"What?" Lynn exploded. "You told him what's going on here?"

"Calm down. I was—"

"You told him about the bomb?" Lynn jumped to her feet. "You're not going to do that, do you hear me? We can't afford that!"

"—told the deputy commander—"

"Not without my authorization!"

"—about the satellite failure," Dana said, very slightly louder, but with a voice that sounded as if she were sawing through a bone.

"And told him we couldn't get through to our guests. That was what we agreed, correct, Miss Orley? After that I wanted to know if he'd received any unusual news from Earth before the satellites failed. But he didn't know anything."

"So you *did* tell him—"

"No, I was just putting out feelers. And he didn't have anything to say. The base is an American facility. If Jennifer Shaw had decided to tell Houston about the bomb in the meantime, she got there too late. At least too late to tell the base crew before the satellites went down. They don't know anything about our problems over there, but I did take the opportunity to tell them of my concerns for the fate of the Ganymede. Against a background of a possible accident."

Lynn's gaze darted around the room and fixed itself on Tim.

"We can't run the risk of this getting out."

"If the Ganymede doesn't reply soon, it *will* get out," said Dana. "Then we'll have to ask the base to send a shuttle to the Aristarchus Plateau to take a look."

"No way! We mustn't worry Julian's guests."

Oh, Lynn! Disastrous, disastrous. Tim resisted the impulse to rest his hand on her forearm like a nurse.

"So what would you do?" he asked quickly.

"Perhaps—" She kneaded her fingers, struggled for clarity. "First keep looking."

"The guests will be back in half an hour," said Funaki. "They'll want their drinks."

"Let Axel take care of that. No, you, Michio. You're the face of the bar. The rest of us will have to take our time. Stay calm. We'll have to plan the next few steps *calmly*."

"I'm calm," said Dana blankly.

"I'll take another look at the surveillance videos," Sophie suggested. "From the night Hanna disappeared and the ones from the day after."

"What for?" asked Kokoschka. Only now did Tim notice that the chef was staring steadily at the freckled German girl from his hungry St. Bernard's eyes, as if testing the quality of her cuts, loins, rump and breasts, and that his eyes darted furtively away every time she looked back. Aha, he thought, the cook's in love.

"Right." Sophie shrugged. "Whoever reedited the recordings would have had to turn up in the control center, right? I mean, he must have been captured on some camera or other. So if we can reconstruct—"

"Good idea!" Lynn cried exuberantly. "Very good! Carl and this— this second person. We'll have to pump them."

"Pump them," echoed Dana.

"Have you got a better suggestion?" Lynn sneered.

"But Hanna isn't here."

"So? Julian will be here soon, and he'll bring him with him. Why should we drive ourselves nuts until then? Let's ask him, and besides—" her eyes gleamed "—nothing can happen to us here as long as we keep Carl in Gaia! He's hardly going to atomize himself."

"Course not," Kokoschka addressed his paunch. "Suicide bomber. Never heard of it."

"What do you mean?" Lynn snapped. "Are you trying to provoke me?"

"What?" The chef recoiled and ran his hand nervously over his bald head. "No, I—sorry, I didn't mean to—"

"Does Carl Hanna look like an Islamist or something?"

"No, sorry. Really."

"Then stop talking such garbage!"

"We—our nerves are all a bit on edge."

"Didn't you say the Chinese were behind it?" Anand asked uncertainly.

"This guy Jericho said that," Sophie replied.

"How many Chinese Islamists are there," Funaki pondered.

"Interesting question."

"Oh, nonsense!" Dana raised her hands. "Enough. Christians have taken the shortcut to heaven too. Such garbage! In my view Lynn's just produced an argument that gives us a bit of time, as long as we can really lay our hands on this ominous second person. I think we should do as you suggested—Anand and Kokoschka will look behind the walls and floors, Sophie will watch the videos, Funaki will go down to the service section, Lynn and I—"

"Gaia, please come in!"

Dana paused. They stared at each other. The system put through a wireless message. Seven pairs of eyes were filled with hope that the call might have come through via satellite. Sophie leaped to her feet and glanced at the display.

"Callisto, this is Gaia," she replied breathlessly.

"Hungry crowd on the way!" crowed Nina. "Do you see us? If there's nothing on the table in five minutes, we're going over to the Chinese."

"Fuck," whispered Dana. "They're in range."

Through the panorama window of the abdomen they saw the gleaming, sunlit shuttle in the sky. The Callisto had approached the hotel from behind, and was flying in a final, athletic parabola. Every trip ritually ended with a fly-over above Gaia.

"You couldn't eat as much as we've cooked," Sophie twittered with frantic exuberance. "How was your day?"

"Great! And we didn't care *a damn* that you haven't spoken to us for hours."

"We didn't feel like talking to you."

"Seriously, what's up?"

"Satellite failure," said Sophie.

"That's what I was afraid of. We couldn't get through to Julian either. Do you know what's up?"

"Not yet."

"Weird. How could all the satellites fail at the same time?"

"You've probably rammed them accidentally. Stop chatting now, Nina, and bring your starvelings down."

"*Oui, mon général!*"

"Then we'd have them back," said Anand, looking around.

"Yes." Dana watched after the Callisto until it disappeared beyond the window. "Plus the likelihood that one of them's playing a dirty game with us. What do you think, Lynn? Shall we give them a welcome party?"

With some relief Tim registered that Dana had switched back to first names. A peace offering? Or just a tactic to lull Lynn into a false sense of security? He didn't doubt that the hotel manager still suspected his sister of conspiracy, but Lynn visibly relaxed.

"Not a word to the guests," she said.

"Okay," Dana nodded. "For the time being. But once everyone's there we'll have to make a real job of it. Either Hanna and his gang give it to us straight, or we inform the base and evacuate the hotel."

"We'll see."

"Let's give the Ganymede another hour."

"What makes you think the Ganymede needs another hour?"

Lynn's really lost touch with reality, thought Tim. Or else *she's* playing the dirty game.

Error! Unauthorized thought.

"Whatever," said Dana. "Let's go."

CALGARY TO VANCOUVER, CANADA

"Believe me, I've really scoured the net," said the intern. "I can't offer you anything more than I did last night."

The Westjet Airlines Boeing 737 plummeted in an air pocket. A hundred milliliters of orange juice sluiced from the cup as Loreena took off the tinfoil lid, spraying over her jacket and drenching her croissant.

"Shit!" she cursed.

"Gudmundsson's time at APS—"

"Shit! Fucking shit!" Juice dripped from the tray into her lap. "Who was APS again?"

"African Protection Services."

"Oh, right."

"So, before Gudmundsson's time at APS, there was this period with Mamba, the other security company that was in operation in Kenya and Nigeria at the start of the millennium, which merged with a similar kind of crowd called Armed African Services to form the APS in 2010. Gudmundsson led various teams—"

"You told me that yesterday," said Loreena, trying to use her tiny paper napkin economically.

"—and was involved in operations in Gabon and Equatorial Guinea. Are you going to eat that?"

"What?"

"The croissant. It looks pretty awful, if you ask me."

Loreena glanced at the dripping pastry. Previously it had just been floppy, now it was floppy and wet.

"No way."

The intern lunged across and stuck half of it in his mouth.

"Here and there we find clues that APS helped some bush dictator or other to force his way into power," he said, chewing. "The APS always denied it, but there seems to be something in it. So Gudmundsson might have been involved in a coup before he left the company to go freelance. The APS was now run by a guy called Jan Kees Vogelaar, who was also a high-up in Mamba. Incidentally, Vogelaar then became a member of the government in Equatorial Guinea, that's where the coup took pl—"

"Forget it."

"You wanted me to look into Gudmundsson's background," the intern said, insulted.

"Yes, his, not some guy called Fogelhair or whatever his name is." She dabbed orange juice from her pantlegs. "Is there nothing about what he did three years ago, whether he was in Peru or somewhere? I thought they were all pretty forthcoming at Eagle Eye."

"Patience, Pocahontas. I'm working on it."

Loreena looked out of the window. Their flight was taking them over the Rocky Mountains. Short but turbulent. The Boeing shook. She drank the rest of the juice down and said, "I want to give Susan as many facts as I can, you understand? She's got to work out that we can't get out of this one. We're in it up to our necks."

"Hmyeah." The second half of the croissant joined the first. "*Supposing* Ruiz really does have something to do with Palstein. All you've got at the moment is a suspicion."

"I have my instinct."

"Indian bullshit."

"Just wait. And could you stop chattering until you've swallowed? That thing doesn't look any prettier in your oral cavity."

"Oh, God," sighed the intern. "You've really got problems."

Loreena looked outside again. The jagged ridges of the Rockies were passing far below her. The intern had meant something quite different, but what he said reminded her of Palstein's worried glance from the previous day. That she was smilingly preparing her own downfall. That she would have problems if she went on lifting up stones with creatures like Lars Gudmundsson lurking underneath them. And? Had Woodward and Bernstein been intimidated by the creepy-crawlies that Nixon threw at them? Palstein's anxiety was valid; Susan's worries irritated her. Was that a reason to throw away their chance to solve *their own* Watergate conspiracy?

Good intentions are useless, she thought. Courage can't be bought. Mine certainly can't.

After a while she dictated the facts of her research so far into her cell phone, let the software turn her spoken words into writing, attached Bruford's film material, and sent the dossier to both their e-mail addresses.

Better safe than sorry.

They passed through the turbulence.

Three-quarters of an hour later the plane came down toward the foothills of the Coast Mountains and began its descent toward Vancouver International Airport. The weather was fine. Little white clouds drifted inland, sunlight glittered on the Strait of Georgia. The dark wooded body of Vancouver Island evoked Indian myths and the scent of arborvitae and Douglas firs. As they came down, Loreena's mood lifted, because they had actually found out a hell of a lot over the previous few days. Perhaps they should settle for what they knew about Gudmundsson, and instead concentrate all their resources on researching the background to the ominous conference in Beijing. As the Boeing taxied to a standstill, she drew up a strategically sensible procedure for the imminent editorial conference, whereby she would act at first as if Palstein's name had never been mentioned. Put up a smoke screen around Susan. Enthusiastically address the topic of *Trash of the Titans*, show them her treatment, prove that they were taking their homework seriously. Then deliver their royal flush with the photograph of the fat Asian guy. Well, maybe not a royal flush. But she was perfectly willing to call what they had a full house.

"I just hope Sid's on time," said the intern as they walked through the terminal with the woodcuts of the First Nations. "Actually he's never on time."

"Then we'll just wait a few minutes," she hummed cheerfully.

"But I'm hungry. Can't we go to McDonald's first?"

"Tell your stomach—"

"Fine."

But Sid Holland, Greenwatch's political history editor, was unusually right on time. He had an ancient, souped-up Thunderbird, in the four-seater open-top version, and loved the car so much that he would gladly have driven half the editorial team through the district just to have a ride in it.

"Susan's looking forward to it," he said. "She hopes you've got something about *Trash of the Titans* in your bag."

"Is there any breakfast?" asked the intern.

"Dude, it's half past eleven!"

"Lunch?"

Loreena looked into the azure-blue sky as the intern climbed into the back seat, and thought of her Pulitzer Prize. Sid drove the car from the airport island across the Arthur Laing Bridge and in a northwesterly direction through the neighborhoods of Marpole, Kerrisdale, and Dunbar Southlands. Past the end of the built-up areas the Pacific Spirit Regional Park began. Southwest Marine Drive, the four-lane feeder road, ran along the coast through dense vegetation toward the grounds of the university at Point Gray, far more than a classical campus, almost a small unincorporated city with a smart adjacent district of extremely Canadian-looking houses and well-tended villas. Thanks to the power of viewing figures, Greenwatch was able to live in one of the villas. Studios and editing suites were decentralized, most of the staff scattered around Canada and Alaska, so that all that remained in Point Gray were the offices of the supreme command and some stylish conference rooms. It was down to Loreena's influence that good conscience was able to unfold in elegant surroundings.

Things would go even better for Greenwatch.

The traffic was moderate, there weren't many cars about on Marine Drive. On their left the forest opened up, providing a view of a still sea and far-off, pastel-colored mountain ranges. Hundreds of tree trunks made into rafts rested in the shallow water, evidence that the timber industry was still flourishing in spite of massive deforestation. Loreena closed her eyes and enjoyed the airstream. When she opened her eyes again, she glanced into the side mirror.

An SUV was driving close behind them, a massive, gray off-road vehicle with darkened windows.

Suddenly she was overcome by a feeling of unease.

She wondered how often she had looked into her side mirror over the past quarter of an hour. Probably all the time, without being aware of it. Loreena was a super-alert passenger, and her constant shouts of "Red!" and "When's it going to turn green!" and "Watch where you're driving!" got on some people's nerves. Nothing escaped her. Not even who was driving behind them.

Frowning, she turned her head.

The feeling condensed into certainty. Now she was completely sure that the SUV had been tailgating them ever since the airport. The windshield reflected the sky, so that the two occupants could only be made out very vaguely. She looked thoughtfully ahead again. The road ran evenly through luxuriant green, divided along the middle by a yellowing strip of grass on which bushes and low trees were planted at irregular intervals. Another off-road vehicle was coming toward them, equally dark, a different one.

Was she going mad? Was she developing a peculiar little paranoid fantasy? How many dark SUVs were there in Vancouver? Hundreds, certainly. Thousands. To western Canadians off-road vehicles were something like seashells to hermit crabs.

Stop thinking this stuff, she thought.

On the other hand it couldn't hurt if she jotted down the license plate number of the car. She took out her cell phone as the SUV suddenly switched lanes and pulled up even with them so that she couldn't see the number plate anymore. Loreena knitted her brows. Fool, she thought. Couldn't you wait another few seconds? I was about to give you my—

The SUV came closer.

"Hey!" Sid honked his horn and gesticulated toward the other vehicle. "Keep your eye on the road, you idiot!"

Still closer.

"What's up with him?" barked Sid. "Is he drunk?"

No, thought Loreena, filled with sudden unease; no one's drunk around here. Someone knows exactly what he's doing.

Sid accelerated. So did the SUV.

"What a stupid idiot!" he raged. "That guy ought to—"

"Careful!" yelled the intern.

Loreena saw the huge car coming, settled into her seatbelt, tried to put some distance between herself and the door, then the SUV collided with the side of the Thunderbird and forced it into the central reservation. Sid cursed and pulled the wheel around, frantically trying not to end up in the opposite lane. Veering wildly they plowed through soil, brushed past low bushes, just missed a tree. The engine of the sports car wailed. Sid put his foot down. The SUV drew up and rammed them again, harder this time. Loreena lurched about in her seat. The metal screech of punished metal echoed in her aural passages, and suddenly they were in the opposite lane, they heard furious honking, swerved at the last moment.

"My car!" wailed Sid. "My lovely car!"

Grim-faced, he steered the Thunderbird back onto the strip of green, but in that section someone had placed greater emphasis on bushes. They plunged noisily into a hedge. Branches flew off in all directions as the sports car crashed through several different varieties of shrub. On the right-hand side the SUV dashed along and blocked their way back onto the street. Sid braked abruptly and tried to get behind the SUV, which thwarted his intention by also decelerating.

At that very moment he hurtled forward again.

This time Sid was quicker. Neatly avoiding a collision, he crossed the two opposite lanes and only just managed to dodge a motorcycle and turn into Old Marine Drive, a narrow, potholed street that led a few kilometers along the woods to the university grounds, where it opened back into the main road. There was no one to be seen for miles around; dense, dark green proliferated on both sides. Loreena registered that her seatbelt had been torn from its moorings, and clutched the edge of the windshield.

My God, she thought. What do they want from us?

Oddly, it didn't occur to her that the attack might have anything to do with Palstein, Ruiz, and the whole story. She thought instead of juvenile delinquents, carjackers, or someone who did that kind of thing just for fun, who must be completely insane. She looked behind her. Potholes, woods, nothing else. For a moment she was surviving on the tender shoot of hope that Sid might have shaken off his pursuer with his maneuver, when he appeared behind them and came relentlessly closer.

A scraping noise emerged from the Thunderbird's engine compartment. The car stuttered.

"Faster!" she screamed.

"I'm driving as fast as I can," Sid yelled back. Instead they were losing speed, growing steadily slower.

"You *must* be able to go faster!"

"I don't know what's going on." Sid let go of the wheel and waved his hands around in the air. "Something's fucked, no idea what."

"Hands on the wheel!"

"Oh God almighty," groaned the intern and ducked his head. The massive, dark front of the SUV roared up and crashed into them from behind. The Thunderbird gave a leap. Loreena was slung forward and bumped her head.

"Come on!" Sid pleaded with the car. "Come on!"

Once again the SUV hammered into their rear. The Thunderbird made unhealthy noises, then their attacker was suddenly beside them, pushing them easily aside. Sid cursed, steered like crazy in the opposite direction, put his foot down, braked—

Lost control.

The moment of liftoff had the entirely curious effect that at the same moment every sound—not only that of the tires on the gravel of the street, but also the sounds of the engine, of the SUV—seemed to die away, apart from the single, bubbling call of a bird. They turned over and over in peaceful silence, the trees grew momentarily down from the sky toward them, bushy clouds sprinkled an endless blue sea of unfathomable depth, then there was a change of perspective, the wood was at an angle, a roaring and scraping, and everything was back, the whole terrifying cacophony of the crash. Loreena was hurled from her seat. Arms flailing, she sailed through the air, while below her the Thunderbird skidded down the embankment, undercarriage toward her, tires spinning, an animal devouring bushes and foliage. Still flying, she became aware of the wreck abruptly reaching a standstill and coming to rest, then a piece of meadow came rushing toward her at breakneck speed.

She had no idea what exactly she broke as she landed, but judging by the pain the damage must have been considerable. Her body was slung around several times, onto her back, onto her belly, onto her side. What wasn't broken broke now. At last, after what seemed like an eternity, she lay there, limbs outstretched, blood in her eyes, blood in her mouth.

Her first thought was that she was still alive.

Her second, that her phone was flashing in the sun not very far away. It sparkled on a flat stone like an exhibition piece, right in the middle, as if lovingly placed there. Further down lay the shattered Thunderbird in the trellis of broken trees, scattered with twigs, bark, and leaves, and in the car, in fact more out than in, Sid dangled, his head half torn from his shoulders, staring at her.

Tires approached across gravel and grass.

"Loreena?"

The cry reached her, thin and plaintive. She raised her eyes and saw the intern lying in the shadow of a fir tree. He tried to prop himself up, collapsed, tried again. The car stopped. Someone came down the embankment with long, not particularly hurried steps. A man, tall, dark pants, white shirt, sunglasses. He casually held a long-barreled pistol in his right hand.

"I'll be right with you," he said. "Just a moment."

Silencer, the thought ran through her head.

He smiled in a rather businesslike manner as he walked past her, stepped up to the intern and fired three shots at him, until the boy stopped moving. It went pop, pop, pop. Loreena opened her mouth because she wanted to scream, to wail, to call for help, but only an ebbing sigh escaped her chest. Every breath was torture. She struggled forward, propped her elbows in the grass, and crawled toward the stone with the phone on it.

The man came back, picked it up and put it in his pocket.

She gave up. Rolled onto her back, blinked into the sun, and thought how right Palstein had been. How close they had been, how *bloody* close! Lars Gudmundsson's head and torso entered her field of vision, the muzzle of his pistol.

"You're very clever," he said. "A very clever woman."

"I know," groaned Loreena.

"I'm sorry."

"It's all—it's all on the net," she murmured. "It's all—"

"We'll check that," he said in a friendly voice and pulled the trigger.

GAIA, VALLIS ALPINA, THE MOON

Nina Hedegaard tried to catch a thousand birds as she sweated away in the Finnish sauna, in a state of mounting frustration. Everywhere she saw the peacock plumage of affluence, heard a twittering exchange about nests and young, and imagined that carefree daydreaming that was only possible in Julian's world. A thousand wonderful, wildly fluttering thoughts. But Julian wasn't there, and the birds refused to be lured into the pen of her life plans. Whenever she thought she was holding at least a sparrow, after Julian had murmured something that sounded halfway authoritative in her ear, even that little hope escaped, and joined all the other ideas, enticingly close and at the same time unattainably far off, of her inflamed imagination. By now she had serious doubts about Julian's honesty. As if he didn't know *full well* that she had hopes. Why couldn't he confess openly to her? Did he have an act of adultery to conceal, social ostracism to fight against? Not a bit of it. He was single, just as she was single, good-looking and lovable single, not rich, perhaps, but then he was rich himself, so what was the problem?

Her frustration seeped like dew from every pore, collected on her forearms, breasts, and belly. She furiously distributed layer after layer of warm sweat, let her hands circle around her inner thighs, her fingers working their way slowly to the middle, settling in her crotch, twitching, untamable, abject, pleasure-seeking digits. Shocking! Along with her fury, she was seized with a furious desire to make the absent figure present in her mind, and—but that was impossible, absolutely out of the question.

To cut a long story short, Julian just wanted to fuck her. That was it. He felt nothing; he didn't love. He just wanted to fuck a nice little Danish astronaut if he felt like it. Just as he fucked the whole world when he felt like it.

Stupid idiot!

She violently pulled her hands away, pressed them to the edge of the wooden bench beside her hips, and looked out at the wonder of the gorge with its pastel-colored surfaces and uncompromising shadows. Thousands upon thousands of bright, frozen stars suddenly seemed more attainable than the life that she would have liked to live by his side. She wasn't concerned with his money, or rather it wasn't *really* about the money, even though she didn't necessarily scorn it. No, she wanted a place in that vision-filled brain, capable of dreaming up space elevators; she wanted to be Julian's personal stroke of genius, his most brilliant idea, and to be seen as such by the world, as the woman he desired. She hadn't just fucked her way to that, she'd *earned* it!

Telling him things like that was the reason she was sitting here. Without wanting to put any pressure on him, of course. Just a bit of homeo-
pathically prescribed planning for the future, allied to what she saw as
the dazzlingly attractive option of an act of love in the sauna, as soon as
the Ganymede landed. That was what they had agreed, and Julian had
promised to join her right away, but now it was a quarter to eight, and
on demand she would have to listen to an unconvincing-sounding Lynn
as she served up the fairy tale that the group, enchanted by the Schröter
Valley, had forgotten time and would be an hour or two late.

How could Lynn have known that without a satellite connection?

Okay, she didn't know. Even in the morning, Julian had talked about
an extended excursion into the hinterland of Snake Hill, and predicted
a late return. No cause for concern. Everything was bound to be fine.

Fine. Ha, ha.

Nina stared dully ahead. Perhaps it was fine to fuck the guests around,
but not her, thank you very much. She should never have got involved
with the richest old codger in the world. It was as simple as that. High
time to take an ice-cold shower and do a few lengths in the pool.

"No, there's something solemn about it," Ögi said. "Only if you tran-
scend it, of course."

"If you what?" smiled Winter.

"If you reduce the immediately perceptible to its significance, my
dear," Ögi explained. "The most difficult exercise these days. Some
people call it religion."

"A tilted flag? An old landing module?"

"An old landing module and the essentially rather unexciting leftovers of two men in a boring-looking area of the Moon—but they were
the first men who ever set foot on it! Do you understand? It gives the
whole of the Mare Tranquillitatis a—a—"

Ögi struggled for words.

"Sacred dignity?" Aileen Donoghue suggested, with gleaming eyes
and a churchgoing tone.

"Exactly!"

"Aha," said Winter.

"Do you have to believe in God to feel that?" Rebecca Hsu fished
a glacé cherry out of her drink, pursed her lips, and sucked it into her
mouth. A quiet slurp and it was gone. "I just found it significant, but
sacred—"

"Because you have no sacred tradition," Chucky said to her. "Your
people, I mean. Your nation. The Chinese don't hold with the sacred."

"Thanks for reminding me. At least now I know why I liked the
Rupes Recta better."

They had assembled for communicative relaxation exercises in the
Mama Quilla Club, and were trying to quell their anxiety about the

continued absence of the Ganymede by vociferously going through the day's events. In the western Mare Tranquillitatis they had admired the landing console of the very first lunar module, with which Neil Armstrong and Buzz Aldrin had landed on the satellite in 1969. The area was considered a culturally protected area, along with three little craters, named after the pioneers and the third man, Michael Collins, who had had to stay in the spaceship. Even during their approach, from a great height, the museum, as the region was generally known, had revealed the full banality of man's arrival. Small and parasitic, like a fly on the hide of an elephant, the console stuck to the regolith, and Armstrong's famous boot print lay in splendor under a glass case. A place for pilgrims. Doubtless there were more magnificent cathedrals, and yet Ögi was right when he felt there was something in it that bestowed significance and greatness on the human race. It was the certainty that they wouldn't have been able to stand there if those men hadn't taken the journey through the airless wastes and performed the miracle of the first moon landing. So what they felt was respect, in the end. Later that afternoon, in the view of the infinite-looking wall of Rupes Recta, which looked as if the whole Moon continued on a level 200 meters higher up, they had succumbed to the sublimity of the cosmic architecture, deeply impressed, admittedly, but without feeling the curiously touching power emanated by the pitiful memorabilia of human presence in the Mare Tranquillitatis. At that moment most of them had understood that they were not pioneers. No one said Hello to a pioneer. He was greeted not by shabby metal frames, not by boot prints, but only by loneliness, the unknown.

Lynn Orley and Dana Lawrence made a great effort to keep the cheerful chitchat going until Olympiada Rogacheva set down her glass and said, "I'd like to talk to my husband now."

The others fell silent. Clammy consternation settled on the gathering. She had just broken an unspoken covenant that they should not worry, but somehow everyone seemed happy about it, particularly Chuck, who had already had to tell three miserable jokes just to drown out the sound of his menacingly grumbling belly.

"Come on, Dana," he blustered. "What's going on? What are you not telling us?"

"A satellite breakdown is nothing serious, Mr. Donoghue."

"Chuck."

"Chuck. For example a mini-meteorite the size of a grain of sand can temporarily paralyze a satellite, and the LPCS—"

"But you don't need the LPCS. Armstrong's gang didn't have an LPCS."

"I can assure you that the technical defect will soon be repaired. That will take a while, but soon we'll be in contact with the Earth exactly as we were before."

"It's odd, though, having no sign of them," said Aileen.

"Not at all." Lynn gave a strained smile. "You know Julian. He's orga-nized a huge schedule. He said even this morning that they'd probably be late.—And by the way, have you seen the system of grooves between the Mare Tranquillitatis and the Sinus Medii? You must have, when you flew to Rupes Recta."

"Yes, they look like streets," said Hsu, and the whistling in the forest resumed.

Olympiada stared straight ahead. Winter noticed her catatonia, stopped licking at the sugar rim of her strawberry daiquiri, edged closer, and put a tanned arm around her narrow, drooping shoulders.

"Don't worry, sweetie. You'll have him back soon enough."

"I feel so shabby," Olympiada replied quietly.

"Why shabby?"

"So miserable. So useless. When you really want to talk to some-body you despise, just because there's no one else there. It's pitiful."

"But you've got us!" Winter murmured, and kissed her on the tem-ple, a seal of sisterhood. Only then did she seem to understand what Olympiada had just said. "So what do you mean, despise? Not Oleg, surely?"

"Who else?"

"Hmph! You despise Oleg?"

"We despise each other."

Winter considered those words. She tried out, one at a time, a col-lection of suitable-seeming facial expressions: amazement, reflection, sympathy, puzzlement; she studied the outward appearance of the Rus-sian woman as if seeing her for the very first time. Olympiada's evening wear, a catsuit, one of Mimi Parker's, that changed color according to the wearer's state of mind, hung on her as if it had been thrown over the back of a chair, eyeliner and jewelry competed to remove the traces of years of neglect and marital suffering. She could have looked so much better. A bit of botox in her cheeks and forehead, hyaluron to smooth the wrinkles around her mouth, a little implant here and there to firm up her confidence and her connective tissues. At that moment she decided to have the implants in her own bottom changed as soon as they got back. There was something wrong with them, if you sat on them for too long.

"Why don't you just leave him?" she asked.

"Why doesn't a doormat leave the front door that it lies outside?" Olympiada mused.

Oh, God almighty! Winter was puzzled. Of course she found her-self irresistible in all her firm glory, but did you really have to look like a gym-ripped Valkyrie to be spared the sort of thoughts that Olym-piada wallowed in?

"Listen," she said. "I think you're making a mistake. A big fat error of reasoning."

"Really?"

"Really. You think you're shabby because you think no one wants you, so you allow yourself to be shabbily treated, just to be treated at all."

"Hmm."

"But the truth is that no one wants you because you feel shabby. You understand? The other way around. Casuality, causality or whatever it's called, that thing with cause and effect, I'm not that educated, but I know that's how it works. You *think* other people think you're crap, so you feel crap and look crap, and in the end what everyone sees is crap, so it comes full circle, am I making myself understood? A kind of inner—prejudgment. Because in fact you're your own biggest, erm— enemy. And because at some level you enjoy it. You *want* to suffer."

Wow, that sounded awesome! As if she'd been to college.

"You think?" Olympiada asked, and looked at Winter from the gloomy November puddles that were her eyes.

"Of course!" She liked this, it was getting really psychological. She ought to do this kind of thing more often. "And you know why you want to suffer? Because you're looking for confirmation! Because you think you're, as we've seen, you think you're—" Vocabulary, Miranda, vocabulary! Not just crap, what's another word? "Shit. You think you're shit, nothing else, but being shit is still better than being nothing at all, and if someone else thinks you're shit too, you understand, then that's a crystal clear confirmation of what you think."

"Heavens above."

"Misery is reliable, believe me."

"I don't know."

"No, it is, feeling shit gives you something to depend on. What do people say when they go to church? God, I am sinful, worthless, I've done terrible things, even before I was born, I'm a miserable piece of filth, forgive me, and if you can't that's okay too, you're right, I'm just an ant, an original ant—"

"Original ant?"

"Yes, original something or other!" She gesticulated wildly, as if intoxicated. "There's something like that in Christian stuff, where you're the lowest of the low from the get-go. That's exactly how you feel. You think suffering is home. Wrong. Suffering is shit."

"You never suffer?"

"Of course I do, like a dog! You know that. I was an alcoholic, I was described as the worst actress ever; I was in jail, in court. Wow!" She laughed, in love with the disaster of her own biography. "That was out of order."

"But why does none of that matter to you?"

"It does, it does! Bad luck really matters to me."

"But you don't think that from the outset you're, erm—"

"No." Winter shook her head. "Just briefly, when I was drinking. Otherwise I wouldn't know what I was talking about here. But not fundamentally."

Olympiada smiled for the first time that evening, carefully, as if she wasn't sure that her face was made for it.

"Will you tell me a secret, Miranda?"

"Anything, darling."

"How do you become like you?"

"No idea." Winter reflected, thought seriously about the question. "I think you need a certain lack of—imagination."

"Lack of *imagination*?"

"Yes." She laughed a whinnying laugh. "Just imagine, I have no imagination. Not a scrap. I can't see myself the way others do. I mean, I can see that they think I'm cool, that they undress me with their eyes, fine. But otherwise I see myself only through my own eyes, and if I don't like something I change it. I just can't imagine how other people want me to be, so I don't try to be that way." She paused and indicated to Funaki that her glass was empty. "And now you stop seeing yourself through Oleg's eyes, okay? You're nice, really nice! Oh, my God, you're a member of the Russian—what is it again?"

"Parliament."

"And rich and everything! And where your appearance is concerned, okay, fine, I'll be honest with you, but give me four weeks and I'll make a femme fatale out of you! You don't need any of that, Olympiada. You certainly don't need to miss Oleg."

"Hmm."

"You know what?" She gripped Olympiada's upper arm and lowered her voice. "Now I'll tell you a real secret: men only make women feel they're shit because they feel shit themselves. You get it? They try to break our confidence, they try to steal it from us because they have none themselves. Don't do that! Don't let them do that to you! You have to fly your own flag, honey. You're not what he wants you to be." Complicated sentence structure, but it worked. She was getting better and better.

"He might never come back," Olympiada murmured, apparently spotting a path opening up into sunnier climes.

"Exactly. Fuck him."

Olympiada sighed. "Okay."

"Michio, my darling," Winter crowed, and waved her empty glass. "One of these for my friend!"

Sophie Thiel was stumbling around in betrayal and deception when Tim came into the control center. A dozen windows on the big multimedia wall reanimated the past.

"Totally fake," said Sophie listlessly.

He watched people crossing the lobby, entering the control center, going about their work, leaving it. Then the rooms lay there again, gloomy and desperate, lit only by the harsh reflection of the sunlight on the edge of the gorge and the controls of the tireless machinery that kept the hotel alive. Sophie pointed to one of the shots. The camera angle was arranged in such a way that you could make out the far side of the Vallis Alpina, with mountains and monorail through the panorama window.

"The control center, deserted. That night when Hanna went out on the Lunar Express."

Tim narrowed his eyes and leaned forward.

"Don't try just yet, you won't get to see him. Your sister would say it's because no one went anywhere. In fact, someone's playing us with the oldest trick in the book. You see that thing blinking on the right-hand edge of the video wall?"

"Yes."

"At almost exactly the same time something lights up down here, and there, a bit further on, an indicator light comes on. You see? Trivial things that no one would normally notice, but I've taken the trouble to look for matches. Take a look at the time code."

05:53, Tim read.

"You'll find exactly the same sequence at ten past five."

"Coincidence?"

"Not if close analysis reveals a tiny jump in the shadow on the Moon's surface. The sequence was copied and added to hide an event that lasted just two minutes."

"The arrival of the Lunar Express," whispered Tim.

"Yes, and that's exactly how it goes on. Hanna in the corridor, edited out, just like your father said. The control center, apparently empty. But there was someone there. Someone who sat here and changed these videos; he's just cut himself out. Perfectly done, the whole thing. The lobby, a different perspective that would show you Mr. X coming into the control center, but also faked, unfortunately."

"Someone must have spent an endless amount of time over it," Tim said, amazed.

"No, it's pretty fast if you know what needs to be done."

"Astounding!"

"Frustrating above all, because it doesn't get us anywhere. Now we know *that* it was done. But not *who* did it."

Tim pursed his lips. Suddenly he had an idea.

"Sophie, if we can trace back *when* the work on the videos was done—if we could take a look at the records—I mean, can you manipulate the records as well?"

She frowned. "Only if you take a lot of trouble."

"But it could be done?"

"Basically it couldn't. The intervention would be recorded as well.— Hmm. I see."

"If we knew the exact times of the interventions, we could match them with the presence and absence of the guests and the staff. Who was where at the time in question? Who saw who? Our mystery person can't possibly have changed *all* the data in the hotel system in the time available to him. So as soon as we see the records—"

"We'll have him." Sophie nodded. "But to do that we'd need an authorization program."

"I've got one."

"What?" She looked at him in surprise. "An authorization program for this system?"

"No, a common or garden little mole that I downloaded from the net last winter to look at a colleague's data. With his permission," he added quickly. "His system took a screenshot every sixty seconds, and I had to get at those shots, but I didn't have authorization. So I resorted to the knowledge of some of my students. One of them recommended Gravedigger, an, erm, a not entirely legal reconstruction program, but one that's quite easy to get hold of and compatible with almost every system. I kept it. It's on my computer, and my computer—"

"—is here in Gaia."

"Bingo." Tim grinned. "In my room."

Sophie smiled broadly. "Right, Mr. Orley, so if you don't mind—"

"I'm on my way."

It was only when he was on the way to the suite that it occurred to him that there might be another reason why Sophie found nothing but manipulated videos:

She herself had recut the material.

Mukesh Nair pulled himself snorting out of the crater pool. A little further off Sushma was toweling herself dry, in conversation with Eva Borelius and Karla Kramp, while Heidrun Ögi and Finn O'Keefe played childish competitions, to see who could stay underwater longest. The Earth shone in through the panorama window, like a reliable old friend. Nair picked a towel off the pile and rubbed the water out of his hair.

"Do you feel like this?" he said. "When I see our home, it's curious: it looks entirely unimpressed."

"Unimpressed by what?" asked Karla and disappeared into her dressing gown.

"By us." Mukesh Nair lowered the towel and looked up to the sky. "By the consequences of our actions. It's got hotter everywhere. Previously inhabited areas are underwater, others are turning into deserts. Whole tribes of people are on the move, hungry, thirsty, unemployed, homeless; we're seeing the biggest migrations in centuries, but there's no sign of it at all. Not from this distance."

"Looking at the old lady from this distance, you wouldn't know if we were bombing each other flat," said Karla. "Means nothing."

Nair shook his head, fascinated.

"The deserts must have got bigger, don't you think? Whole coastlines have changed. But if you're far enough away—it doesn't change her beauty in the slightest."

"If you're far enough away," Sushma smiled, "even I'm beautiful."

"Oh, Sushma!" The Indian tilted his head and laughed, showing perfectly restored teeth. "You will always be the most beautiful woman in the world to me, near or far. You're my most beautiful vegetable of all!"

"There's a compliment," said Heidrun to Finn, water in one ear, Nair's flattering baritone in the other. "Why do I never get to hear things like that?"

"Because I'm not Walo."

"Lousy explanation."

"Comparing people to foodstuffs is his department."

"Is it just me, or have you stopped making much of an effort lately?"

"Vegetables don't spring to mind when I look at you. Asparagus, perhaps."

"Finn, I really have to say, that's going to get you nowhere." She hurried to the edge of the pool, straightened, and sent a great spray of water in Nair's direction. "Hey! What are you talking about?"

"The beauty of the Earth," smiled Sushma Nair. "And a bit about the beauty of women."

"Same thing," said Heidrun. "The Earth is female."

Eva tied the belt of her kimono. "You see beauty out there?"

"Of course," Nair nodded enthusiastically. "Beauty and simplicity."

"Shall I tell you what I see?" Eva Borelius said after thinking for a moment. "A misunderstanding."

"How so?"

"Complete disproportion. The Earth out there has nothing to do with our familiar perception of it."

"That's true," said Heidrun. "For example, Switzerland normally seems the size of Africa to a Swiss person. On the other hand, in the emotional reality of a Swiss person, Africa shrinks to a hot, damp island full of poor people, mosquitoes, snakes, and diseases."

"That's exactly what I'm talking about." Eva nodded. "I see a beautiful planet, but not one that we share. A world which, in terms of what some have and others don't, should look completely different."

"Bravo." Finn O'Keefe bobbed over and applauded.

"Enough, Finn," hissed Heidrun. "Do you even know what we're talking about?"

"Of course," he yawned. "About how Eva Borelius had to fly to the Moon to discover the bleedin' obvious."

"No." Eva laughed drily and started picking up her swimming things. "I've always known what the planet looks like, Finn, but it's still different seeing it like this. It reminds me who we're actually researching for."

"You're researching for the guy who's paying you. Have you only just realized?"

"That free research is going down the toilet? No."

"Not that you personally have any reason to complain," Karla joined in maliciously.

"Hey, hang on." Eva, caught in a pincer movement, raised her eyebrows. "Am I complaining?"

Karla looked innocently back. "I just wanted to say."

"Of course, stem cell research brings in money, so she gets some too. It cost a lot of money to take the isolation and investigation of adult cells and develop it into the production of artificial tissue. Now we've decoded the protein blueprints of our body cells, we work successfully with molecular prosthetics, we have replacements for destroyed nerves and burnt skin, we can produce new cardiac muscle cells, we can cure cancer, because not even the wealthiest people in the world are spared heart attacks, cancer, and burn injuries." She paused. "But they are spared malaria. And cholera. Those are diseases for poor people. If we were to apportion budgets purely on the quantitative occurrence of such diseases, the greatest amount of research money would flow to the Third World. Instead, the majority of all malaria patents, even the most promising, are put on ice, because you can't earn any money with them."

Nair went on looking at the far-away Earth, still smiling, but more thoughtfully.

"I come from an unimaginably big country," he said. "And at the same time from a graspable cosmos. I've never had the impression that there's just one world, not least because we see it from all perspectives at the same time. No one sees it as a whole, no one sees the whole truth. But if we see the world as a multiplicity of small, interlocking worlds, each determined by its own rules, you can try to improve some of them. And that helps you to understand the whole. If my job had been to improve *the* world, I would definitely have failed."

"So what have you improved?" asked Karla.

"A few of those little worlds." He beamed at them. "At least I hope so."

"You've carpeted India with air-conditioned shopping centers, connected whole villages to the Internet, provided God knows how many thousands of Indian farmers with a basic living. But haven't you also opened the door to multinational companies, by offering them the chance to get involved?"

"Of course."

"And haven't some of them gratefully taken up your model, rented Indian land, and replaced the farmers with machines and cheap laborers?"

Nair's smile froze on his face. "Any idea can be corrupted."

"I'd just like to understand."

"Certainly, such things happen. We can't allow that."

"Look, I don't entirely agree with your romanticization of inequality. Small, autonomous worlds. You do a lot of good things, Mukesh, but you're globalization personified. Which I think is fine, as long as the tiny little worlds aren't swallowed up by the big companies—"

"Shouldn't we be getting back to our rooms?" said Eva.

"Yes, of course." Karla shrugged. "Let's go. Typical of you, always going on about how annoyed you are, and then getting all ashamed when I mention some concrete examples."

"Where have the others got to, by the way?" Sushma shook her head uneasily. "They should have been back ages ago."

"When we came down here they were still on their way."

"And they still are, by the look of it," said Nair. Then he rested a friendly hand on Karla's shoulder. "And you're completely right, Karla. We should talk about this kind of thing more often. And not spare each other's feelings."

"Shall I tell you how I see it?" asked Finn.

They all looked at him.

"I see two dozen of the richest people on this much-discussed planet Earth feeling trapped between malaria and champagne and, in line with the disproportion that you mentioned, Eva, escaping to the Moon, where they reach remarkable insights in the most expensive hotel in the solar system.—You know what? I'm going for another couple of laps."

Sophie had installed Tim's program and asked him casually whether it hadn't occurred to him that she might be the traitor. He had looked baffled for a moment, before exploding with laughter.

"Is it that obvious?"

"You bet."

"Well—"

"I'm not," she said. "Happy now?"

He laughed again. "If people got out of jail by saying that, we could convert our prisons into hen houses."

"You're a teacher, right?"

"Yes."

"How many times do you hear that every day?"

"What? It's not me, it wasn't me?" He shrugged. "No idea. I usually lose track at about midday. But okay, it wasn't you. Do you suspect anybody?"

She lowered her head over the keyboard, so that her blonde curls hid her facial expression.

"Not directly."

"You're thinking about my sister, aren't you?" He sighed. "Come on, Sophie, it's not a problem, I'm not mad at you. You're not the only person who feels that way. Dana has completely homed in on Lynn."

"I know." Sophie looked up. "But I don't believe for a second that your sister has anything to do with it. Lynn built this hotel. It would be completely idiotic. And what's more, it's only just now occurred to me, but when she refused to let your father see the corridor video—why would she have done that? I mean, why, if she had actually recut it herself? In her place I'd have proudly rubbed his nose in it."

Tim looked grateful and curiously glum at the same time. It was immediately clear to her that he was more inclined toward Dana's opinion than her own, and that he was bothered by the fact.

"Quite honestly," she smiled shyly, "I was wondering before whether you yourself mightn't—"

"Ah!" he grinned. "No, it wasn't me."

"More hen houses." She smiled back. "Would you like to keep me company while I reconstruct the records?"

"No, I'd just like to see where Lynn's got to. But call me if you think of anything." He smiled. "You're very brave, Sophie. Will you manage?"

"Somehow."

"Not a bit scared?"

She shrugged. "Oddly, the thing I'm least worried about is the idea of being blown up. It's too unreal. If it does happen, we'll all go in a flash, but we're not going to know all that much about it."

"I feel the same."

"So what are *you* afraid of?"

"Right now? I'm worried about Amber. Very worried. About my wife, about my father—"

"About your sister—"

"Yes. About Lynn, too. See you later, Sophie."

"That wasn't nice," Heidrun mocked, after the others had fled the pool area. Only she and Finn were still drifting in the black water of the crater, somewhere between idyll and apocalypse.

"But true," said Finn, launching into a crawl away from her.

She pushed her wet hair behind her ears. Below the surface of the water her body was compressed into a bony caricature of itself, as if the waves were starting to dissolve her. Finn cut a swath through the water like a motorboat, sending watery chaos in all directions, great surges that a swimmer could never have produced in terrestrial waters. An amusement factor reserved only for moon travelers. You could catapult yourself out of the water like a dolphin and, when you splashed back in again, set small tsunamis on their way. You were operating in arrogant opposition to the laws of gravity, but Finn's mood was closer to the gray of the surrounding landscape. Heidrun stretched, dived, slipped after him and past him, and burst through the surface. Finn saw that the way to the opposite edge of the crater was blocked, and balanced himself in the water.

"What's up?" she asked. "Bad mood?"

"No idea." He shrugged. "Aren't you supposed to be going up?"

"And what about you?"

"I haven't made any dates with anybody."

Heidrun thought for a moment. Had she made any dates? With Walo, of course, but could you really describe the day-to-day magnetism of marriage as a date?

"So you've no idea what your mood is."

"I don't know."

It was true, she guessed, Finn probably just had no idea why his mood had so suddenly soured. He had been in great form all day, he had made her laugh with his laconic sarcasm, a gift that Heidrun valued above all others. She liked men whose wit sprang from easy understatement, which gave them the ultimate accolade of cool. In her opinion there was hardly anything more erotic than laughter, sadly an attitude fraught with difficulties, because the majority of the male sex tended to try to produce it intellectually. The result was usually tiresome and discouraging. In their constant bid to score points with hilarious thigh-slappers, these suitors lost what remained of their natural machismo, and there was much worse to come. For her part, Heidrun derived intense and noisy pleasure from sex, and had ended up in paroxysms of laughter during so many orgasms that the gentlemen in question, convinced that they were the object of her laughter, were thrown spontaneously off their stroke. The drop in pleasure pressure was always followed by the same embarrassment; she always felt guilty, but what was she supposed to do? She loved laughing. Ögi was the first to understand. Heidrun's natural responses neither inhibited his erections nor slowed him down in any way. Walo Ögi with his chiseled Zürich physiognomy, which could break out into ringing laughter at any time, took sex no more seriously than she did, with the result that they both enjoyed it a great deal more.

Finn, on the other hand. Viewed objectively, in so far as the objectification of beauty was ever justified, he was far better looking than

Walo, in terms of classical proportion at any rate: he was perfectly built and a good sixteen years younger. Apart from that, he had the appearance of an uncommunicative and sometimes sulky melancholic. He concealed his stroppiness behind insecurity, his shyness behind indifference, but he was enough of an actor to flirt professionally with all of these qualities. As a result he was surrounded by the aura of mystery that turned millions of emancipated female individuals into spineless mush. Supposedly shy, he cultivated the pose of the eternal outsider in a world whose cofounder and original inhabitant he was; he acted the part of the lout, as if Marlon Brando, James Dean, and Johnny Depp hadn't already taken the idea to ludicrous extremes, and exuded a sweaty rebellious appeal. He couldn't, with the best will in the world, ever have been described as the life and soul. And yet behind the forbidding façade Heidrun sensed an inclination to excess, to anarchic fun, to wild parties, as long as the right people were invited. She had no doubt that one could fool about with him, and have laughing sex until libido and diaphragm both gave in, after hours.

"They're getting on your nerves, aren't they?" she surmised. "Our lovely fellow travelers."

Finn rubbed water out of his eyes.

"I get on my own nerves," he said. "Because I think it's my problem."

"What is?"

"Not rising like a spiritual soufflé up here. It seems almost unavoidable. Everyone is constantly coming out with the loveliest philosophical observations. There isn't anyone who hasn't a clever thing to say. Some of them burst into tears at the very sight of the Earth, others wallow in self-mortification at the thought of their earthly striving. Eva sees injustice and Mukesh Nair sees miracles and wonder in every grain of moon dust. A complete social elite seem determined to relativize their previous lives, just because they're sitting on a lump of stone so far from the Earth that you can see the whole thing. And what occurs to me? Just a stupid old saying from the Pre-Cambrian era of space travel."

"Let's hear it."

"Astronauts are men who don't have to bring their wives anything back from their travels."

"Pretty dumb."

"You see? Everyone seems to *find himself* up here. And I don't even know what I'm supposed to be *looking* for."

"So? Let them."

"I did say it isn't their problem. It's mine."

"You're complaining on quite a high level, my dearest Finn."

"No, I'm not." He glared at her angrily. "It hasn't the slightest thing to do with self-pity. I just feel *empty*, crippled. I'd love to feel that same powerful emotion, vaporize with reverence and get back to Earth inside out, to preach the word of enlightenment, but I don't feel any of it. I can't think of anything to say about this trip except that it's nice, it's a bit different. But it is, and remains, the bloody Moon, damn it all! No higher level of existence, no understanding or comprehension of anything at all. It doesn't spiritualize me, it stirs nothing in me, and that's *got* to be my problem! *There must be more!* I feel as if I've withered away."

Doggy-Paddling, they drifted toward one another. And while Heidrun was still wondering what she could reply to this outburst without sounding like a maiden aunt, she was suddenly close to him. His lines and wrinkles revealed a life of clueless carousal. She recognized Finn's inability to make his brilliant talent chime with the banal realization that in spite of his special gift he was not a special person, simply alive and, like everyone else, damned, on the highway that they were all hurtling along, one day to crash into the wall without ever having come close to the meaning of everything. Not a trace of apotheosis. Just someone who had had too much of everything without ever feeling sated by it, and who now, in his total cluelessness, reacted more honestly to the impressions of the journey than the rest of the group put together.

A moment later she sensed him.

She felt his hands on her hips, her backside. She felt them exploring her waist and back, his lips strangely cool on hers, wrapped both legs around him and pulled him so tightly to her that his sex pressed against hers, ambushed by the brazenness of his approach and even more by her own simmering readiness for a fling. She knew she was about to do something incredibly stupid that she would bitterly regret afterward, but the whole catechism of marital fidelity was consumed in the heat of that moment, and if men thought with their dicks, as was so often rightly said, then her will and intelligence had just irrevocably faded away in her cunt, and that too was something so terrifyingly banal that all she could do was erupt with laughter.

Finn joined in.

It was the worst thing he could have done. Even an irritated twitch of his eyebrows would have saved her, a hint of incomprehension, but he just laughed and started rubbing her between the legs until she was terrified, even as her fingers clawed at the hem of his trunks and pulled them down, to liberate the engorged beast behind them.

Water monkeys, she thought. We're water monkeys!

Uh! Uh!

"I'd leave it if I were you," she heard Nina Hedegaard saying, just before the water started splashing. "He'll bring you nothing but frustration and a whole host of problems."

As if struck by lightning they parted. Finn reached irritably for his trunks. Heidrun dipped her head beneath the surface, breathed in crater water, came back up, and coughed her lungs up. Scooping water like a paddle steamer, Nina passed them on her back.

"Sorry, I didn't want to spoil your fun. But you should really think about it."

And that was that.

Heidrun lacked the genetic prerequisites for blushing, but at that moment she could have sworn she turned *beetroot*, a beacon of embarrassment. She stared at Finn. To her infinite relief nothing in his expression suggested that the past few minutes had been embarrassing to him, only regret and a vague understanding that it was over. He plainly still wanted her, and she wanted him a bit less, but at the same time she felt an urgent longing for Walo, and the desire to kiss Nina for her intervention.

"Yeah, we—" Finn grinned crookedly, "—were just about to go upstairs."

"So I saw," Nina said sullenly. She swam powerfully over to them and stood up in the water. "I'll keep my mouth shut, don't worry. The rest is your business. They're starting to get worried up there. Julian's group still isn't back, and neither are the satellites."

"Didn't Julian say anything?" Heidrun asked, her whole body still one big heartbeat. "This morning, I mean."

"No, he said they'd be showing up later. Too busy a schedule. Says Lynn."

"Then that's how it is."

"Seems odd to me."

"Julian would definitely have tried to get through, to you first of all," said O'Keefe.

"Yeah, great, and what would you do, Finn, if you didn't get through? You'd be on time! So as not to worry the others. And I'm not stupid. There's more to it than that. There's something they aren't telling me."

"Who's they?"

"Dana Lawrence, the cold fish. Lynn. Who knows. Dinner's now been arranged for nine, by the way."

Heidrun could tell by the tip of Finn's nose that he was thinking exactly the same as she was, whether they shouldn't make use of that time in his suite. But it was a pale, threadbare thought, less than a thought, in fact, since it came not from the head, not from the heart, but from the abdomen, whose coup had just been permanently thwarted. Finn slipped over and gave her a quick kiss. There was something conciliatory, something final about it.

"Come on," he said. "Let's go up and join the others."

London, Great Britain

After the conversation with Palstein, Jericho had taken a trip around the highly armed world of the information center and introduced Jennifer to the contents of his backpack.

"Diane," he said. "The fourth member of the alliance."

"Diane?" an eyebrow rose in her grumpy face.

"Mmhm. Diane."

"I see. Your daughter or your wife?"

Since then Diane had been alternately connected to the public internet and the internal, hacker-protected intranet of the Big O, a system locked against the outside world, with no way in, but no way out either. Jennifer had summarily authorized him to access parts of the company's own database, equipped with a password that allowed him to trace the global network of the company, its history, and its staff structure. At the same time, thanks to Diane, he was working on familiar ground. Without the company of Tu or of Yoyo, who had wanted to visit the fat guy for a few minutes and had been overdue since then, he felt miserably alone, just a messenger, good enough to lay his head on the line for others, but not to be taken into anybody's friendly confidence.

Pah, friends! Let the two of them wallow in misery. At last he was warmed again by Diane's soft, dark computer voice, untroubled by any kind of sensitivity.

He asked her to go through the net for arrangements of terms: *Palstein, attempted murder, assassination, assassin, Orley, China, investigations, discoveries, results,* etc. On the oil manager's initiative, the Canadian authorities had sent a large supply of pictures and film material which he, Edda Hoff, a member of the IT security department, and a woman from MI6 were now assessing together. If only Palstein had been willing to hand over the video that supposedly showed his attacker, they could presumably have spared themselves all that wretched work. Diane brought him things she'd found about the Calgary shooting the way a cat brings in half-dead mice, but where the rest of the decoding of the text fragment was concerned she was poking around in the dark. Clearly the hurricane murmur of the dark network had fallen silent. In contrast, pictures, reports, assessments, and conspiracy theories about Calgary were flooding in, but without shedding light on anything.

He went to see Jennifer Shaw.

"Good to see you." Jennifer was in a video conference with representatives of MI6, and waved him in. "If you've got anything new—"

"When was Gaia originally supposed to open?" Jericho asked, pulling up a chair.

"You know that. Last year."

"When exactly?"

"Okay, it had been planned for late summer, but projects like that are never as ready as you hope they're going to be. It could have been autumn or winter."

"And because of the Moon crisis—"

"No, not just because of that." Norrington came into the room. "You're in the temple of truth here, Owen. We're happy to admit that there were technical delays. The unofficial opening was scheduled for August 2024, but even without a crisis we'd hardly have managed it before 2025."

"So the completion date wasn't foreseeable at the time?"

"Why do you ask?" one of the MI6 people wanted to know.

"Because I'm wondering whether the mini-nuke was put up there only in order to destroy Gaia. Something people knew *would* be finished, but didn't know *when*. But when the satellite was started, it wasn't finished."

"You're right," the MI6 man said thoughtfully. "They could have waited for the launch, in fact they should have done."

"Why should they have done?" asked another one.

"Because every atom bomb gives off radiation. You can't store a thing like that on the Moon indefinitely, where there's no convection to carry away the heat. There's a danger of the bomb overheating and going off prematurely."

"So it was definitely supposed to detonate in 2024," Jennifer surmised.

"That's exactly what I mean," said Jericho. "Was it or is it meant only for Gaia? How much explosive do you need to blow up a hotel?"

"Lots," said Norrington.

"But not an atom bomb?"

"Not unless you want to contaminate the whole site, the wider surroundings," said the MI6 man.

Jericho nodded. "So what's up with it?"

"With the Vallis Alpina?" Jennifer thought for a minute. "Nothing, as far as I know. But that needn't mean anything."

"What are you getting at?" asked Norrington.

"Very simple," Jericho said. "If we agree that the bomb was to be detonated in 2024, regardless of whether Gaia had been completed or not, the question arises of why it didn't happen."

"Because something got in the way," Jennifer reflected.

Jericho smiled. "Because something got in *someone's* way. Because *someone* was prevented from setting the thing off, one way or another. That means we should stop wondering about the where and the when, and concentrate on that person who *possibly*, in fact *probably* isn't called Carl Hanna. So who was on the Moon or on the way to the Moon last year, who could have detonated the bomb? What happened to make sure that it didn't go off?"

And meanwhile he was thinking: who am I telling all this to? Jennifer had mentioned the possibility of a mole, a traitor who drew his information from the inner security circle. Who was the mole? Edda Hoff, opaque and brittle? One of the divisional directors? Tom Merrick, that bundle of nerves responsible for communication security; could he have been responsible for the block that he was pretending to investigate? And apart from Andrew Norrington, was there someone listening to his hypotheses who shouldn't have known about them? Always allowing that Jennifer hadn't mentioned moles to distract attention from herself.

How safe were they really in the Big O?

Gaia, Vallis Alpina, The Moon

The chronological recording was swiftly reconstructed. True to its name, the Gravedigger burrowed its way into the depths of the system and drew up a complete list, but because this encompassed activities carried out over several days, it looked like something that would keep you occupied for three rainy weekends.

"Shit," whispered Sophie.

But if you cut down the periods of time in question, the work went faster than you might have expected. And the faker's trail ran like a pattern through the recordings, because after every action he erased his traces. The video of Hanna's nighttime trip, for example, had been recut while the Canadian had been exploring Gaia's surroundings with Julian, or more precisely between a quarter past six and half past on the morning in question. Unambiguous proof that Hanna himself hadn't set about erasing his traces.

Where had *she* been at that point? In bed. Hadn't got up until seven. Until then the lobby and the control center had been populated only by machines. In a simultaneous projection, she screened all the recordings of the period during which the phantom had done his work, but no one left his room, no one crouched in a hidden corner operating the system from somewhere else.

Impossible!

Someone must surely have been wandering about the hotel at that time.

Had these videos been manipulated too?

She studied the recordings more precisely, and had the computer examine all the films for subsequently introduced cuts.

Sure enough.

Sophie stared at the monitor wall. This thing was getting increasingly weird. Everything she saw here, or rather didn't see, was evidence of unsettling professionalism and strength of nerve. If it went on like this, in the end she would have to go through every single order in the vague hope that the faker might give himself away by some tiny blunder. Just as it had soared a moment before, her mood now plummeted. It was pointless. The stranger had used his time and opportunities to the full; he was ahead of her.

Maybe she should approach the business the other way around, she thought. Start with the *last* significant event, the satellite failure. Perhaps the phantom hadn't had time to clean up after himself when that happened.

She isolated the passage from the conference call until it suddenly broke off, and had the computer play through the whole sequence again. Her own actions were visible in the reconstruction: her taking the call, informing Dana and Lynn in the Selene, and putting it through to Julian Orley. After that—

A shadow settled over her. She gave a start, threw her head back, and sat bolt upright.

"Erm—thought you might be hungry."

"Axel!"

Kokoschka's monolithic appearance darkened her desktop. He held a plate in his right hand. The bony claw of a rack of lamb protruded from it, a nutty smell of courgettes wafted toward her.

"God, Axel!" she panted. "You frightened the life out of me!"

"I'm sorry, I—"

"Don't worry. Phew! Shouldn't you be tearing up walls and floors?"

"Cerberus took us off the job," he grinned. "Hungry? East Friesian saltmarsh lamb."

He looked at her, to the side, at the floor, then dared to make eye contact again. Christ, no. She'd guessed it. German boy loves German girl. Kokoschka had fallen for her.

"That's really sweet of you," she said, glancing at the plate.

His grin widened and he set the dish down on a free corner of the desktop, next to her, along with a napkin and cutlery. Suddenly she realized that over the course of the past hour hunger had crept up on her and was devouring her from within. She greedily inhaled the aromas. Kokoschka had separated out the cutlets for her. She took one of the fragile ribs between her fingers and gnawed the butter-soft flesh from the bone, as she turned once again to the screens.

"Whatcha doin'?" asked Kokoschka.

"Checking the recordings from the afternoon," she said with her mouth full. "To see if I can find something out about the satellite failure."

"Do you think we've really got a bomb?"

"Not the faintest, Axel."

"Hmm. Weird. Doesn't really bother me, to be honest." His forehead was covered with sweat. In visible contradiction to his words, he seemed nervous and twitchy, stepped from one leg to the other, sniffed. "So you're trying to find out where the bomb is?"

"No, I want to know who Hanna's accomplice—"

She stared at him.

Kokoschka held her eye for a few seconds, then his eyes drifted down to the video wall. He was perspiring more heavily now. His bald head was drenched, a vein throbbed in his temple. Sophie stopped chewing, and paused with her chin thrust out and her cheek bulging.

"Okay, you've probably known for ages," Kokoschka said wearily into the room.

She gulped, and recoiled. "What?"
He looked at her.

"Could we have a quick chat?" Dana nodded to Lynn to follow her to the stairs that led from the Mama Quilla Club to the Luna Bar below it, and from there to the Selene and Change. At that moment everyone's attention was focused on Chuck, who stood there with a sly grin on his face, holding both hands, palms up and all ten fingers pointing upward, stretched out in front of him.

"What does the Pope mean when he does this?"

"No idea," said Olympiada gloomily. Winter, unfamiliar with the habits of the Pontifex and clerical matters in general, shook her head in hopeful expectation that she might possibly get the punchline, while a chill gust of outrage blew all the benevolence from Aileen's features. Rebecca Hsu sat next to her like a circus lion on a bar stool, and spoke into her hand computer in a hushed voice. Walo Ögi had absconded to his suite to read.

"Chuck, please don't."

"Oh, come on, Aileen."

"Don't tell this one!"

"What does the Pope mean?" Winter giggled.

"Chuck, no!"

"Very simple." Donoghue snapped nine fingers back, so that only the middle finger of his right hand was still pointing upward. "The same as *this*, but in ten languages."

Winter went on giggling, Hsu laughed, Olympiada grimaced. Aileen looked around at everyone, hoping for forgiveness, with a tortured, powerless smile on her face. Lynn processed none of this as she would usually have done. Whatever she saw and heard looked like a sequence of rattling, stroboscopic flashes. Aileen accused Chuck of violating a joke-free zone called the church, about which *everyone had agreed*, mercilessly wielding her falsetto scalpel, while Winter tee-heed inanely, a source of relentless torment.

"We must assume that something has happened on the Aristarchus Plateau," Dana Lawrence said abruptly. "Something unpleasant."

Lynn's fingers bent and stretched.

"Okay, we'll send Nina out in the shuttle."

"We should do that," Dana nodded. "And evacuate Gaia."

"Hang on! We said we were going to wait."

"What for?"

"For Julian."

Dana glanced quickly at the seated group. Miranda Winter was chortling, "That's great. Why in ten languages?" while Chuck eyed them suspiciously.

"Don't you listen?" she hissed. "I mentioned that Julian's team might be having difficulties. We have no idea whether they're going to turn up here, and we have a bomb threat. There are guests in the hotel now. We *have* to evacuate."

"But we've laid nine places for dinner."

"That doesn't matter now."

"It does."

"It doesn't, Lynn. I've had enough. I'll call everyone together. Meet at half past eight in the Mama Quilla Club, give it to them straight. Then we'll send out a radio flare for Julian, Nina will go in search of them, the rest of us will take the Lunar Express to—"

"Nonsense. You're talking nonsense!"

"*I'm* talking nonsense?"

Chuck got to his feet and smoothed his pantlegs.

"I really thought you knew," Kokoschka said, embarrassed.

Sophie shook her head in mute horror.

"Hmm." He wiped the sweat from his brow. "Doesn't really matter anyway. Bad moment, I guess."

"What for?"

"I've fallen—I've sort of fallen—oh, forget it. I just wanted to say that I really—erm—"

Sophie melted with relief. Her hand strayed to the plate, but her belly hadn't yet accepted the fact that Kokoschka had only wanted to declare his love, and it categorically refused to take in any more food.

"I like you too," she said, trying to make sure that the *like* really meant *like* and nothing more.

Kokoschka rubbed his fingers over his spanking clean chef's jacket.

"I can't wait to see if you find something," he said, looking at the display.

"Me too, you can be sure of that." Switch of topic, thank heavens. She looked at the picture details, the list of recordings, the data flow. "The whole thing is very mysterious. We—"

She took a closer look.

"What's *that*?" she whispered.

Kokoschka pushed in closer. "What?"

Sophie paused the reconstruction program. There was something. Something weird that she couldn't quite place. A kind of menu, but a sort she'd never seen before. Simple, compact, connected to a rat's tail of data, bundles of commands that had been sent only seconds before the breakdown of communication from Gaia. She understood a bit of computer language. She could read a lot of it, but this cryptic sequence of commands would have been meaningless in her eyes, if some of the codes hadn't seemed familiar.

Codes for satellites.

The command to freeze communications had come from Gaia. She could see when and from where it had happened.

She knew *who* had done it.

"Oh, my Christ," she whispered.

Fear, terrible, long-suppressed fear flooded all her cells, all her thoughts. Her fingers started trembling. Kokoschka leaned down to her.

"What's up?" he asked

All sign of shyness had fled. The German's eyes peered from his angular head. She spun around in her chair, opened a drawer, reached for a piece of paper, a pen, as she now no longer trusted the computer system. She hastily scribbled a few words on the paper, folded it together, and pressed the little paper packet into his hand.

"Take this to Tim Orley," she whispered. "Right away."

"What is it?"

She hesitated. Should she tell him what she had found? Why not? But Kokoschka, with his childish temperament, was unpredictable, strong as a bear, capable of running off and thumping the person in question, which might prove to be a mistake.

"Just take it to Tim," she said quietly. "Wherever he is. Tell him to come here right away. Please, Axel, be quick. Don't waste any time."

Kokoschka turned the packet over in his fingers and stared at it for a second. Then he nodded, turned around, and disappeared without another word.

"We *can't* evacuate," Lynn insisted feverishly. Her fingers became claws, her perfectly filed nails pressed into the flesh of her palms. "We can't gamble with the trust of our guests."

"With the greatest respect, have you gone mad?" whispered Dana. "This place could go up at any minute, and you're talking about abusing the trust of your guests?"

Lynn stared at her and shook her head. Chuck strode resolutely forward.

"Enough of this nonsense," he said. "I demand to know right now what's actually going on here."

"Nothing," said Dana. "We're just considering sending Nina Hedegaard to the Artistarchus Plateau on the Callisto, in case there really is something—"

"Listen, girly, I may be old, but I'm not stupid." Chuck leaned down to Dana, and brought his great leonine head level with her eyes. "So don't underestimate me, okay? I run the best hotels in the world, I've built more of the things than you will ever set foot in, so stop trying to bullshit me."

"No one's bullshitting you, Chuck, we've just—"

"Lynn." Donoghue spread his arms in a conciliatory gesture. "Please tell her to drop it! I know this conniving expression, this whispering. Obviously there's a crisis, but can you please *tell me what's happening here?*"

Chuck had stopped being Chuck. He'd turned into a battering ram; he was trying to get inside her, to overwhelm her, but she wouldn't let him in, wouldn't let anyone in, she had to resist!—Julian. Where was Julian? Far away! Just as he always had been, throughout her life. When she was born. When she needed him. When Crystal died. When, when, when. Julian? Far away! All the responsibility rested on her shoulders.

"Lynn?"

Don't lose control. Not now. Hold off the breakdown that was clearly coming with the inevitability of a supernova, long enough to act. Hold off Dana, her enemy. And everyone else who knew. Each one of them was her enemy. She was completely alone. She could only rely on herself.

"Please excuse me."

She had to act. Bumble, hum, buzz, bzzzz. A swarm of hornets, she ran down the stairs to the elevator.

Chuck watched her open-mouthed.

"What's up with her?"

"No idea," said Dana.

"I didn't mean to insult her," he stammered. "I really didn't. I just wanted to—"

"Do me a favor, okay? Go and join the others."

Chuck rubbed his chin.

"Please, Chuck," she said. "It's all okay. I'll keep you posted, I promise."

She left him standing there and went after Lynn.

It wasn't that Axel Kokoschka thought he was overweight, or not *really*. On the other hand his art represented the compatibility of genuine gourmet cuisine with the requirements of a fitness society fixated on the burning of calories. And in those terms he *was* overweight. Firmly resolved to reduce the fifteen kilos that he weighed up here at least to fourteen, he hardly ever used the elevators. Here again he leaped from bridge to bridge, forcing his burly body up one floor after another, and then took the flight of stairs to the neck. The area between Gaia's shoulders and head was little more than a mezzanine where the passenger elevators stopped, and only the freight elevators and the staff elevator continued to the kitchen. Where the side neck muscles would have been in a human being, stairs led to the suite wing below, swinging into the head with its restaurants and bars. The neck was also a storage area for spherical tanks of liquid oxygen to make up for any leakage.

The tanks were hidden behind the walls and took up a considerable amount of room, so that only Gaia's throat was glazed. A number of oxygen candles hung in wall holders.

Kokoschka snorted. Without resorting to the scales, he knew he had in fact put on some weight over the past few days. No wonder Sophie had been a bit standoffish with him. He would have to work out more often, go to the gym, on the treadmill, or else his fleshly contact would be restricted to fillets, schnitzels, and mince.

There was no one in Chang'e. Selene, a floor up, was also contenting itself with its own company, and so was the Luna Bar. To judge by the voices, the gang was right up at the top. Strangely, Kokoschka barely felt frightened, in spite of the possible risk of death. He couldn't imagine an atom bomb, or an atom bomb exploding. And besides, they hadn't found anything, and wouldn't such a thing give off radiation? He was far more concerned about Sophie. Something had startled her. All of a sudden she had seemed absolutely terrified, and then there was that scribbled note that she had given him to give to Tim.

But Tim Orley wasn't there. Only the Donoghues, Rebecca Hsu, Miranda Winter, and the Russian's sad wife sat hunched over their drinks, looking dazed. Funaki said Tim had been there just before he arrived, and had asked after Lynn, while as for her, she had lost her head a few moments before.

"And I hadn't done anything," Donoghue mumbled to nobody in particular. "I really hadn't."

"Yeah." Aileen looked sagely around. "She's looked stressed lately, don't you think?"

"Lynn's okay."

"Well that's how it seemed to me. Not you? Even in the space station."

"Lynn's okay," Chuck repeated. "It's this hotel manager I can't stand."

"Why not?" Rebecca raised her eyebrows. "She's just doing her job."

"She's hiding something."

"Yes, then—" Kokoschka made as if to leave the Mama Quilla Club. "Then—"

"My experience tells me so!" Chuck slammed his hand down on the table. "And my prostate. Where experience fails, my prostate knows. I'm telling you, she's shitting all of us. I wouldn't be surprised if we found out that she was pulling the wool over all our eyes."

"Then I need to—"

"And what are you going to surprise us with this evening, young man?" Aileen asked in a saccharine voice.

Kokoschka ran his hand over his bald head. Amazing, just a few millimeters of scalp. How it kept producing more sweat. Layer after layer, as if he were sweating out his brain.

"Ossobucco with risotto milanese," he murmured.

"Oooh!" said Winter. "I love risotto!"

"I make it the Venetian way," Aileen told Kokoschka. "You know you constantly have to keep stirring? Never stop stirring."

"He's a chef, darling," said Chuck.

"I know that. May I ask where you learned your craft?"

"Erm . . ." Kokoschka squirmed, like a fly on flypaper. "Sylt—among other places."

"Oh, Sylt, wait, that's, that's, don't tell me, it's that city in northern Norway, right? Up at the top."

"No."

"It isn't?"

"No." He had to get away, find Tim. "An island."

"And *who* did you learn from, Alex?" Aileen twinkled intimately at him. "I can say Alex, can't I?"

"Axel. From Johannes King. Sorry, I've really got to—"

"Do you use beef marrow in your risotto?"

Kokoschka looked nervously at the stairs, a fox in a trap, a fish in a net.

"Come on, tell us your secrets," Aileen smiled. "Sit down, Alex, Axel, sit down."

The deeper Sophie Thiel dug into the recordings, the stranger it all seemed. Via cleverly disguised cross-connections, you reached lists of unofficial hot keys, some of them cryptic, others designed to control the hotel's communication system. Among other things, they also blocked the laser connection between Gaia and the Moon Base, or more precisely they directed the signal to a cell phone connection. By now she also thought she knew what the mysterious menu was for. It wasn't the LPCS itself that was coming under attack, it was more that an impulse was sent to the Earth, and as far as she could tell that impulse had prompted a block that didn't just affect lunar satellites. A lot of work had been done here; the Moon had been completely cut off from the Earth.

And suddenly she doubted that all that effort had been devoted only to the purpose of destroying the hotel.

Who *were* they?

Tim! She desperately hoped Tim would appear at last. Hadn't Axel found him? She didn't know enough to lift the block, particularly since she didn't know what it had actually unleashed. On the other hand she was confident that she could undo the interference with the laser connection to Peary Base. She would make contact with the astronauts there and ask for help, even if it might put her life in danger, because somebody might be listening in on her, but in that case she would just lock herself away somewhere.

Lock herself away, what nonsense! Childish idea. Where are you going to lock yourself away when the bomb goes off?

She had to get out of here! They all had to get out of here!

Her fingers darted over the touchscreen, barely touching the smooth, cool surface. After a few seconds she heard footsteps, and the familiar shadow settled on her again. The lamb cutlets were going cold beside her, in silent reproach.

"Did you find him?" she asked, without looking up, as she corrected a command. She had to rewrite that one sequence, but perhaps it wasn't even Axel, it was Tim.

No reply.

Sophie looked up.

As she leaped up and recoiled, sending her chair flying, she realized that she had made a crucial blunder. She should have stayed calm. She shouldn't have turned a hair. Instead her eyes were wide with horror, revealing all her deadly knowledge.

"You," Sophie whispered. "It's you."

Again, no answer. At least not in words.

Heidrun felt a little awkward as she stepped into the suite, in dressing gown and flipflops. Unusually, but in pointed contrast to Finn, she had opted against the familiar rock-climbing match up the bridges, and instead primly pressed the elevator button, as if it was the last thing that the pitiful remains of her arrogance could still manage. Aghast at what she had just surrendered, when Walo had never been unsatisfactory in that regard, she had the elevator cabin carry her up to Gaia's ribcage, away from the pool of temptation, stiff as a board, no false moves, just carefully sniffing her fingers for traces of lust. She felt as if her whole body exuded betrayal. The air in the elevator struck her as heavy with clues, thick with vaginal aromas and the ozone stench of alien sperm, even though nothing had happened, at least not *really*, and yet—

Walo, her heart thumped. Walo, oh Walo!

She found him reading, gave him a kiss, that familiar, scratchy mustachioed kiss. He smiled.

"Have fun?"

"Lots," she said and fled to the bathroom. "And you? Not in the bar?"

"I was, darling. It was only moderately bearable. Chuck's jokes are starting to offend Aileen's Christian sensibilities. A while ago he asked what a healthy dog and a shortsighted gynecologist have in common."

"Let me guess. A wet nose?"

"So I thought I might as well read."

She looked at herself in the mirror, her white, violet-eyed elfin face, just as she had seen Finn's face down below, in the merciless light of the realization that people aged, they aged inexorably, that their once immaculate skin began to wrinkle, that she was a depressing forty-six, and had something in common with many men who tried to recapture their lost youth, something that women generally said they would never undergo: a real mid-life crisis.

If you want to grow old with someone, she thought, you shouldn't need anyone else to make you feel younger.

And she loved Walo, she loved him so much!

Naked, she walked back into the living room, lay down on the carpet in front of him, folded her hands behind her head, stretched out a foot and tapped his left knee.

"What are you reading there?"

He lowered the book and studied her outstretched body with a smile.

"Whatever it was," he said, "I've just forgotten it."

Tim pressed the door buzzer again.

"Lynn? Please let me in. Let's talk."

No reaction. What if he was mistaken? He'd just missed her in the Mama Quilla Club, and had assumed that she had gone to her suite. But perhaps she was doing other things. What frightened him more than any bomb was the idea that she might actually be losing her mind, that she had already lost it. Crystal, too, hadn't just been depressive, she'd increasingly lost touch with reality.

"Lynn? If you're there, open up."

After a while he gave in and jumped along the bridges to the lobby, deeply concerned. He wondered what Sophie was up to. Whether the Gravedigger had uncovered the footage. At the same time his thoughts revolved around himself: Amber, Julian, bomb, Lynn, Hanna, accomplices, satellite failure, bomb, Amber, Lynn, worries that devoured one another, a madhouse.

The control center was empty, Sophie was nowhere to be seen.

"Sophie?"

He looked helplessly around. A bulkhead led to a back room, but when he put his finger on the sensor field, he found it was locked. He saw Dana running toward him through the lobby. She entered the control center, and looked around with a frown.

"Have you seen Sophie?"

"No."

"Is everything spiraling out of control?" Her face darkened. "She was supposed to be here. Someone has to be in the control center. I guess you haven't bumped into Kokoschka?"

"No." Tim scratched the back of his head. "Weird. Sophie was working on something very interesting."

"Which was?"

He told Dana about the authorization program and what they'd hoped to find with it. The manager's face was expressionless. When he had finished, she did what he too had done when he came in, and studied the monitor wall.

"Forget it," said Tim. "There's nothing there."

"No, she doesn't seem to have got very far. Did she even install the program?"

"I was there when she did."

Dana walked in silence to the touchscreen, keyed in the call-codes of Ashwini Anand, Axel Kokoschka, Michio Funaki, and Sophie Thiel and put all of them on a single channel. Only Ashwini and Michio replied.

"Can anyone tell me where Sophie and Axel are?"

"Not here," said Michio. Chuck's booming bass voice could be heard in the background.

"Not with me either," said Ashwini. "Isn't Sophie in the control center?"

"No. Tell them to check in as soon as possible if you meet them. Point number two, we're evacuating."

"What?" cried Tim.

She told him to keep his voice down.

"In five minutes I'm going to put out a message and ask our guests to make their way to the Mama Quilla Club at half past eight. You are to be there too. We'll tell them exactly what's going on, and then leave the hotel together."

"What's happening to the Ganymede?" Anand asked.

"I don't know." She glanced at the time. "We're going to put out a radio flare for the Ganymede, which will reach it as soon as it's within range of Gaia. They aren't to land, but to fly on immediately to Peary Base. Not a word to the guests before eight thirty."

"Got it."

"Okay," said Funaki.

"I'm not surprised about Axel Kokoschka," said Dana, and rang off. "You can never get hold of him, he's always forgetting his phone. A great chef, a hopeless knucklehead in every other respect. If he and Sophie haven't appeared by eight-thirty, put out a call for them."

"Are we really going to clear this place?" asked Tim.

"What would you do in my place?"

"I don't know."

"You see? I do, though. Let's not fool ourselves, your father's been overdue for an hour and a half now, and even though we haven't found a bomb, it doesn't necessarily mean that it isn't ticking away somewhere even so." She put a finger to her lips. "Hmm. Do atom bombs tick?"

"No idea."

"No matter. We'll send Nina Hedegaard to the Aristarchus Plateau and take the Lunar Express to the base."

"End of a pleasure trip," said Tim, and suddenly he became aware that his bottom lip was beginning to tremble. Amber! He fought against it and stared at his shoes. Dana let a smile play around her lips.

"We will find Ganymede," she said. "Hey, Tim, chin up."

"It's okay."

"I need you with a clear head right now. Go back to the bar, tell a joke, lighten the mood a bit."

Tim gulped. "Chuck's the guy in charge of jokes."

"Tell *better ones.*"

"Mr. Orley? Er—Tim?"

The fitness area was huge. Quite how huge, you discovered when you set about trying to find someone there, and Kokoschka looked conscientiously. After escaping Aileen's suffocating curiosity, he had to face fatherly advice from Chuck. He should look for Julian's son where men who valued high life expectation and firm abdominal muscles tended to go, and where Tim had been going every evening.

But the gyms were deserted, the tennis courts abandoned. In the steam bath, a mist of droplets mixed with tinkling far-eastern music. Tim wasn't in the Finnish sauna, he wasn't pounding along a treadmill or punishing an exercise bike, in fact he seemed instead to have put all his energy into running away from Kokoschka. A moment of optimism when he heard sounds from the pool, but it made for disappointment when he discovered that only Nina Hedegaard was there, swimming lonely lengths in the crater. Tim wasn't there, and he hadn't been there, and what was going on, where was the Ganymede, and were the satellites still sleeping?

Kokoschka concluded that Nina knew nothing about the bomb. Perhaps because in all the excitement they'd forgotten to tell her. He was tempted for a moment to put her in the picture, but tough girl Dana might have reasons for restricting the number of initiates. He was a chef, not a corrector of higher decisions, so he mumbled a word of thanks and decided to give Sophie Thiel at least an interim report.

As soon as Tim appeared in Gaia's forehead again, the announcement came through:

"As you will already have established, ladies and gentlemen, our schedule is rather disrupted, not least because Ganymede is late and we are unfortunately having problems with satellite communication." Dana's voice sounded apathetic and toneless. "There is no need to worry, but I ask all of Gaia's guests and staff members to make their way to the Mama Quilla Club at eight thirty p.m., where we will inform you about the latest state of development. Please be on time."

"That's in ten minutes," Rebecca said in a thick voice.

"Doesn't sound good," muttered Chuck.

"How come?" Unimpressed, Miranda emptied down a bowl of cheese puffs. "She said there was no need to worry."

"Sure, that's her job." Chuck slipped angrily back and forth, fists clenched, drumming arhythmically on the seat of his chair. "I'm telling you, she's messing with us. I've been saying that all along!"

"At least we're going to be informed now," Aileen reassured him.

"No, Chuck's right," Olympiada observed listlessly. "The most reliable clue for an impending catastrophe is when higher authorities deny them."

"Garbage," said Miranda.

"No, we've got to assume the worst," Donoghue said to Olympiada. Miranda plundered another bowl.

"You guys are all so negative. Bad karma."

"Remember my words."

"Silly nonsense."

"I know this from my parliamentary work," Olympiada explained to her half-empty glass. "For example when we say we aren't going to raise taxes, it means we are. And when—"

"But we're not in parliament," Tim replied, more sharply than he had meant to. "So far everything in this hotel has been organized very professionally, hasn't it?"

She looked at him. "My husband is on Ganymede."

"So's my wife."

"Okay, you all can wait." Chuck jumped up and hurried to the stairs. "I'm going down there!"

"Where's Sophie?"

"*Mister* Kokoschka!" Dana glared at him. "How about being contactable for a change?"

Kokoschka flinched. He rubbed his big paws on his jacket and glanced around the control center.

"Sorry. I know we're supposed to be meeting in the Mama Quilla—"

"Get used to carrying your phone around with you. The question comes back to you. Where is Sophie?"

"Sophie?" Kokoschka started poking around in his left ear. "I thought she was here. Don't know. Shall I start on the dinner? I've got to—" He hesitated. The note seemed to be burning a hole in his jacket pocket. "You wouldn't happen to know where Tim Orley is?"

"What is this?" A wrinkle appeared between Dana's eyebrows. "A quiz show? Are we playing hide and seek?"

"I'm just asking."

"Tim Orley should be in the bar. He went up there a few minutes ago."

"Okay, then—" Kokoschka took a step back.

"Stay where you are," Dana said severely. "Tell me again exactly where you looked this afternoon. Did you check the sauna, too?"

"Yep." He fidgeted around in the doorway, suddenly very worried about Sophie. What was going on?

"Calm down," said Dana. "We'll go up there together in a few minutes."

The bar was filling up. Karla Kramp and Eva Borelius appeared on the stairs, followed by the Nairs and Finn, and blocked Chuck's way as he came charging down pursued by the four horsemen of the Apocalypse.

"Do you know anything?" He flashed his eyes at them.

"No more than you do, I should think." Eva shrugged. "They want to tell us something."

"I hope it's nothing bad," said Sushma anxiously.

"It'll be more than the time of day, I can promise you that," blustered Donoghue. "Something's happened."

"You think?"

"Friends, why all this speculation?" Nair smiled. "In a few minutes we will know more."

"In a few minutes we'll hear a load of prepared blarney," Chuck bellowed. "I could tell by looking at Lynn and all those plaster saints. You can't fool Chucky."

"Who says they're trying to fool you?" asked Finn.

"My experience," snapped Donoghue. "My prostate!"

"Have you had the golden finger?"

"Now listen, young man—"

"What are you getting worked up about? That they're hiding something from us? They aren't, you know."

"They aren't?" Chuck narrowed his eyes. "And how do you know that?"

"*My* prostate!" Finn grinned. "Claptrap, Chucky, if they wanted to keep something from us, they'd hardly have called a meeting."

"But I don't want to know what just *anyone* gets to hear." Chuck struck his chest with his fist. "I want the *whole* truth, you understand?" He pushed past them. "And first, I'm telling you now, I'm not letting that stupid skank of a hotel manager go up there, just so as you know!"

"Tsk, tsk." Karla watched after him. "For a hotelier, he really sounds like a grumpy guest."

"We've got to get up there," said Heidrun.

She was half lying on top of Ögi, half beside him, with his hairy arm under her back. As if infected by the virus of infidelity, she had forced him to make love, to receive the antidote to her own lust, and it was at the sound of Dana's voice that she had experienced an exorbitant neuronal firework, as if it had been sparked by the hotel manager's monotonous voice. Whatever the reason for the disturbance, Heidrun was so furious with Dana that she chose to ignore the announcement, and proceeded to do just that for a whole six minutes, with Ögi's fingers stroking the back of her neck.

"What time is it?" he asked.

She rolled reluctantly onto her back and glanced at the digital display above the door.

"Four minutes before half past eight. We *could* still try to be on time."

"What, are you crazy?"

"It's what people generally expect of the Swiss."

"Time to demolish some clichés, perhaps?" Ögi picked up a strand of her hair. Unpigmented keratin, but in it he saw white moonlight melting between his fingers. "Okay, perhaps you're right, we shouldn't dawdle. People will be getting worried."

"About Ganymede?"

"About whatever. It isn't very comforting to be invited to this kind of meeting."

"Motormouth told us not to worry."

"And you couldn't really say we had, could you?" He grinned and sat up. "Come on, *mein Schatz*. Let's get into social contract mode."

With silent, sweating Kokoschka by her side, Dana was going up. The elevator stopped at the fifteenth floor. Lynn joined them. She looked dreadful, as if she'd aged several years, hardly able to focus, her eyes darting unsteadily around. A curiously distant, sly looking smile played around the corners of her mouth.

"What's all this?" she said to Dana without looking at her. She ignored Kokoschka completely.

"What's all what?"

"What's the meeting for?"

The elevator doors closed.

"We're evacuating," Dana said bluntly. "Where have you been, Lynn? Have you seen Sophie?"

"Sophie?" Lynn looked at her as if she'd never heard the name before, but thought it was very interesting.

"Yes. You remember Sophie Thiel."

"We can't evacuate," Lynn said, almost cheerfully. "Julian wouldn't want that."

"Your father isn't here."

"Call it off."

"Excuse me, but I think it's exactly what he would want."

"No! No, no, no, no, no."

"Yes, Lynn."

"You're messing up the whole trip."

Kokoschka hunched his shoulders and stuck his hand in his pocket. Dana noticed and gave a start. Was he holding something in his hand?

"You stupid bitch," Lynn said brightly, and the elevator doors opened again.

Chuck Donoghue was waiting in the neck. He was quivering with rage. Aileen came hurrying down the stairs wearing a concerned expression. Dana came out of the elevator, with Lynn and Kokoschka hot on her heels.

"What can I do for you, Chuck?"

"You're taking us for idiots, aren't you?"

"I'm here to inform you about the state of developments." Dana faked a smile. "So could we go upstairs, please?"

"No, we couldn't."

"Please, Chucky." Aileen fiddled with Donoghue's sleeve. The elevator doors slid shut. "Listen to what she has to say."

"I'll listen to it *here*."

"There's nothing to say," Lynn twittered. "Everything's hunky dory. Shall we go and eat?"

"I want to know what's going on right now," snapped Donoghue. He came closer, entered her personal space. "Where's Julian? Where are the others? You've known what's happening for ages, why can't we talk to anybody? You've known all along."

"Are you threatening me, Chuck?"

"Come on. Say it."

Dana Lawrence didn't budge from the spot. She stared calmly into the big man's eyes. To do so, she had to throw her head back, but inside it was as if she was looking down at Donoghue.

"*When* I've told you, shall we go up?"

Donoghue clearly hadn't expected her to give in so easily. He took a step back.

"Of course," Aileen hurried to reassure her in his place.

"Yes, of course," Donoghue added lamely.

"No!" screamed Lynn.

Tim heard her in the Mama Quilla Club, even though the Chang'e, the Selene, and the Luna Bar were in between. He heard her fear, her rage, her madness. All at once he leaped to his feet and dived down the stairs taking four at a time. Dana's authoritarian alto joined in, counterpointed by arpeggios of high, frightened, Aileen wails, over Donoghue's rumbling bass. He plunged down into Gaia's throat.

Strange. His sister had pulled one of the oxygen candles from its mounting and was swinging the steel cylinder like a club, while Dana, Chuck, Aileen, and Kokoschka circled her like a pack of wolves.

Tim pushed his way between the Donoghues, saw Lynn stepping back and roared, "What's going on? What are you doing to her?"

"Why don't you ask *her* what she's doing to us," growled Chuck.

"Lynn—"

"Leave me alone! Don't get too close!"

Tim held his hand out to her. She recoiled still further, raised the candle, and stared at him, eyes darting from side to side.

"Tell me what's going on."

"She wants to evacuate Gaia," Lynn panted. "That's what's going on. The bitch wants to evacuate Gaia."

Kokoschka was so confused that he didn't even try to understand what was going on. Clearly the business manager of Orley Travel was going mad. His thoughts had turned entirely to Tim and the end of his personal odyssey. He drew Sophie's note from his pocket. "Mr. Orley, I've got—"

Tim ignored him. "Lynn, come to your senses."

"She wants to evacuate the hotel." The woman's voice was reduced to a whisper. "But I won't let her, under any circumstances."

"Of course, we've got to talk about it. But first give me the candle."

"Evacuate?" Chuck echoed, eyes rolling.

"You should listen to your brother." Dana pointed at Lynn's makeshift club. "You're putting us all in danger."

Tim knew what she meant. The cylinder contained large quantities of compressed oxygen, and Lynn's fingers were dangerously close to the detonator. As soon as she set the exothermic reaction in motion, the contents would spread slowly into the environment, a pointless waste, along with the danger that the partial pressure of the oxygen would exceed permitted levels. The cartridges were meant for emergencies, when breathable air was in short supply.

"Mr. Orley!" Kokoschka was waving a piece of paper.

"*What do you mean evacuate?*" Donoghue snapped.

"Dana's right," said Tim. "Please, Lynn. Give me the candle."

"Julian doesn't want us to evacuate," Lynn explained dreamily to an imaginary audience. For a second she seemed completely absent, then her gaze settled on her brother. "You know that, don't you? We mustn't frighten Daddy's guests, so we'll all stay here like good boys and girls."

"That would suit you, wouldn't it?" Dana snorted.

Lynn's dreamy expression made way for seething fury. She swung the cartridge again.

"Tim, tell her to shut up!"

"Oh, so I'm supposed to shut up, am I?" Dana took a step forward. "What about, Lynn? Everybody here has known for ages."

Tim looked at her in confusion. "What are you talking about?"

"About how your sister manipulated the tapes. That she's been used by Hanna. That she's losing her marbles. Isn't that true, Miss Orley?"

Lynn ducked down. A sly spark appeared in her eyes, then she suddenly jumped forward and swung a blow at Dana, who effortlessly dodged it.

"*You* were the one who let Hanna take his trip on the Lunar Express. Why, Lynn? Was he supposed to bring something back? To us in the hotel?"

"Stop!"

"You blocked the satellites. You're paranoid, Lynn. You're in cahoots with a criminal."

"*What do you mean, evacuate?*" roared Chuck. He gripped Dana roughly by the shoulder. "*I said, what do you mean, evacuate?*"

The manager whirled around and knocked his hand away.

"You shut your mouth!"

Donoghue's massive head turned crimson. "You—you jumped-up chambermaid, I'll—"

"Chuck, no!" pleaded Aileen.

"*Miss Orley*—" Dana repeated.

With a tormented expression on her face, Lynn shook her head. Tears were collecting on her eyelids.

"What have you done with Sophie Thiel, Lynn?" Dana insisted. "*You* were in the control center not long ago."

"That's not true. I've been—"

"Of course you were there!"

"Dana, that's enough," hissed Tim.

"You bet." Dana glared at him. "*I've* had enough. I've had enough of this circus. Give up, Lynn. Tell us the truth about this bomb."

"*Bomb?*" roared Chuck. He charged forward like a water buffalo, pushed Lynn against the wall, stretched out his big hands, and pulled the cartridge from her fingers. "Has everybody here gone mad?"

Lynn's fingers bent into claws. She lashed out and drew a bloody trail across Donoghue's cheek. Before Chuck could recover from his amazement, she was at the stairs, jumped down, and disappeared into the floor below.

"Lynn!" cried Tim.

"No, wait! Please wait!"

Kokoschka watched in horror as young Orley dashed after his crazed sister. Stay here, he thought, not again, I've got to give you—

"Sophie told me to give you—"

Too late. Run after him? But the general madness required its tribute, so that he had to look on helplessly as Chuck raged at the hotel manager and stormed after her, holding the oxygen candle menacingly aloft. Storms raged inside his head, downdraughts, plunging temperatures, tornadoes, accumulated fear. Something terrible would happen.

His thoughts danced around like faded leaves, blown in all directions by gusts of confusion. Every time he tried to catch them, they whirled away, while he impotently turned and turned. What was he to do? At last he caught one of those leaves, it flapped and fluttered, trying desperately to escape: that whatever Sophie had written on that piece of paper would explain the escalation that was going on in front of his eyes, that the piece of paper would tell him what he needed to do, that perhaps, seeing as how he hadn't managed to carry out his mission, he ought to read it.

Fingers trembling, he unfolded the piece of paper.

At that moment, Dana sensed the change. Her whole body reacted. All the hairs on her forearms registered the disaster. Voices reached her from the restaurant. The tumult must have reached the upper floors, and some people were coming down to see what had happened, while Axel's statue-like face sent out waves of disbelief and fury.

Dana slowly turned her head toward him.

The chef stared at her, a piece of paper in his left hand. His right hand slowly rose, an index finger raised in accusation. Dana took the paper from him and glanced at the words scribbled on it.

"Bullshit," she said.

"No." Kokoschka came closer. "No, not bullshit. She found out. *She found out!*"

"Who found out what?" barked Donoghue.

"Sophie." Kokoschka's finger twitched; an eyeless, sniffing creature, it swung around and rested on Dana. "*She's the one.* Not Lynn. It's her!"

"You've been spending too much time at the oven." Dana stepped back. "Your brain's overcooked, you big idiot."

"No." Kokoschka's massive form started moving, a Frankenstein's monster taking its first steps. "She paralyzed the communications. She wants to blow us all up! *She's the one! Dana Lawrence!*"

"You're mad!"

"Oh, really?" Donoghue's eyes narrowed to slits. "I think we can find that one out pretty quickly." He picked up the oxygen cartridge and approached her from the other side. "I remember this great joke where—"

Dana reached into her hip pocket, drew her gun, and pointed it at Donoghue's head.

"Here comes the punchline," she said, and squeezed the trigger.

Donoghue stopped dead. Brain matter spilled from the hole in his forehead, a trickle of blood ran between his eyebrows and along the bridge of his nose. The candle slipped from his hands. Aileen's mouth gaped, and an unearthly wail issued from it. Dana was just swinging the gun around, when the doors of E2 opened and Ashwini Anand stepped out, impelled into the lion's den by her fear of being late. The bullet struck the Indian woman before she had a chance to grasp the situation. She slumped to the ground and blocked the elevator door, but her unexpected arrival had lost Dana valuable seconds, which Kokoschka exploited to go on the attack. She took aim at him and at the same moment she was attacked by Aileen, who leaped at her, grabbed her hair, and pulled her head back. Aileen was still uninterruptedly wailing, a ghostly funeral lament. Dana reached behind her, trying to shake Aileen off and Kokoschka grabbed her wrist and she managed to knee him in the testicles, before firing off two shots. The chef bent double, but he managed to knock the gun from Dana's fingers. She struck him in the throat with the edge of her hand, and shook the Fury from her back with a roll of her shoulders. Almost gracefully, Aileen sailed against her husband, who was still standing, and dragged him down with her. Kokoschka was crawling along the floor on all fours. Dana kicked him in the chest, just as she heard a metallic hiss that didn't bode well.

The bulkheads were closing.

She stared at the holes in the wall, where the two stray bullets had struck.

The tanks! They must have hit one of the hidden tanks. Compressed oxygen was bursting out, raising the partial pressure and causing the sensors to close off access to the levels above and below. It wasn't impossible that the external cooling pipe had been hit, releasing toxic, inflammable ammonia.

She was in a bomb.

She had to get out of here!

The invisible gas settled on the wildly flailing Aileen, on Chuck's corpse, streamed into the open elevator, whose doors were blocked by Anand's dead body. Kokoschka's eyes widened. Gurgling, he got to his feet and stretched out both arms toward Dana. She paid him no attention and ran off. The doors were closing at worrying speed. With one bound she reached the entrance to the suites, jumped, and just managed to get past the bulkhead from Gaia's neck, then somersaulted down the stairs and landed on her back.

Kokoschka came after her. Properly trained, he knew the potentially disastrous effect of an uncontrolled release of oxygen. Desperate to get out in time, he followed Dana to the bulkhead, but didn't get all the way through. He was trapped.

"No, no, no, no, no . . ." he whimpered.

Now he could hear the faint hiss of the escaping oxygen. Terrified, he tried to brace himself against the approaching metal plate. His breath was forced out of him, his organs crushed. He heard one of his lower ribs breaking, saw Aileen kneeling over Chuck's corpse and burying her face in the crook of his neck. A metallic taste spread through his mouth, and his eyes bulged. He tried to shout, but all he managed was a dying croak.

"Chuck," Aileen whimpered.

There was a not especially loud, puffing sound as the oxygen went up. Two glowing spears of fire suddenly thrust from the wall where the bullets had hit, striking Aileen, Chuck's corpse, and Ashwini Anand's bent body, the walls and the floor. The flames quickly swept along the elevator doors, forced their way into the open cabin of the staff elevator, like living creatures, fire spirits in orgiastic exuberance. A moment later half of the mezzanine was alight. Kokoschka had never seen a fire raging like that. People said that fires spread more slowly in reduced gravity, but this—

He spewed a stream of blood. The bulkhead pressed relentlessly against his tortured body, and as if the fire had only just noticed him, it reared up to new height and seemed to pause uncertainly for a moment.

Then it leaped at him hungrily.

Miranda Winter had, with Sushma Nair, set off for the lower floors, once it could no longer be ignored that there were noisy arguments going on down there. On the stairs from Selene to Chang'e, they heard two muffled bangs in quick succession, which anyone who had ever been to the movies would have recognized as pistol shots from a silenced weapon, followed by Aileen's bloodcurdling howl, then some bell-like chimes, as if a hammer were being struck against metal. Sushma's expression turned to one of naked fear; Winter, however was made of sterner stuff, so she beckoned Sushma to wait and approached the passageway through the neck.

What the—?

"The bulkhead is closing," she cried. "Hey, they're locking us in!"

Baffled, she stepped closer to get a glimpse through the crack of what lay below.

A figure of flame came flying at her. The demon hissed and roared at her, reached for her with sparks flying from its finger, singed her eyelids, brows, and hair. She stumbled, fell, and pushed herself up as she tried to get away from the raging flames.

"Oh, shit!" she cried. "Get out, Sushma, get out!"

The demon tumbled and licked its way around, multiplied, giving birth to new, twitching creatures that darted around gleefully setting ablaze anything that stood in their way. With uncanny speed they covered the glass façade, found little of interest there, and concentrated their campaign on the floor, the pillars, and the furniture. Miranda leaped to her feet, hurried up the stairs, driving the distraught Sushma

ahead of her with a series of loud shrieks. The bulkheads to Selene
were closing right above them. A wall of heat was surging at them from
behind. Sushma stumbled. Miranda slapped her on the backside, and
Sushma pushed her way past the bulkhead to the next floor up.

Close! Christ, that was close!

Like a gymnast, she grabbed the edge of the bulkhead and pulled
herself up on it. For a moment she was afraid her ankle would get stuck
in the lock, but then, by a hair, she got into Selene, and the bulkhead
closed with a dull thud and saved them from the wave of fire.

"The others," she panted. "God alive! The others!"

Dana was lying on her back, Kokoschka's legs pedaling wildly above
her, hammering the steps of the spiral staircase. The roar of the fire
reached her from the neck, followed by the flames themselves, greedily
creeping up Kokoschka's jacket and pants. They looked as if they were
feeling, searching for something. They flowed in waves over the ceiling, the structure and its coverings in its quest for food.

Dana leaped to her feet.

She had to dislodge Kokoschka's body so that the bulkhead could
close. Oxygen fires were uncontrollable, hotter and more destructive
than any conventional kind of fire. Even though the gas as such didn't
burn, it fatally encouraged the destruction of all kinds of material,
and it was heavier than air. The blaze would spill like lava from Gaia's
throat, and engulf the entire suite section. One leap and she was at
the manual control panel, crouched down to get as far as she could
from the heat, and activated the mechanism that operated the bulkhead. It opened, and Kokoschka was free. He dashed down the steps
and leaped onto the gallery, kicking instinctively around. Tentacles of
flame shot from the gap, as if to drag back the prey that had just been
snatched from them. But the bulkhead closed on them, cutting off the
blaze and isolating Gaia's neck from its shoulders.

The chef was a human torch. A fog of chemical extinguishing agents
forced its way out of the ventilation system, but it wasn't nearly enough.
In a few moments, the plants, the walls, the floor would all be ablaze.
Dana pulled a portable CO_2 fire extinguisher from the wall, emptied
it on the body now lying motionless, and then pointed what was left
at the ceiling. In the inferno above her, the extinguisher system had
probably given up long ago. By now the temperatures up there must
be unimaginable. Sooty smoke entered her airways and blinded her
eyes. Her chest began to hurt. If she didn't get fresh air in a minute, she
would die of smoke poisoning. Kokoschka, the stairs, and parts of the
ceiling were still smoldering away, little fires still flared here and there,
but instead of trying to quell them, she staggered along the gallery,
eyes streaming, unable to breathe, the creak and clatter of the bulkhead

in her ears, now sealing off Gaia's shoulder. Where the gallery ended in the figure's right arm, there was an emergency storeroom which contained, alongside the inevitable candles, some oxygen masks. She quickly put one of the masks on, greedily sucked in the oxygen and watched as access to the arm was sealed off.

She hadn't been fast enough.

She was trapped.

Tim managed to catch up with his sister in the hall. She'd been trying to escape across the glass bridges, leaping like a satyr but with her knees trembling, so that he was terrified he was about to watch her slip to her doom, but nothing could stop her attempt to escape. It was only at the last jump that she faltered, fell, and crept away on all fours. Tim jumped down immediately behind her and grabbed her ankle. Lynn's elbows bent. She slipped away on her belly, trying to escape him. He held her firmly, turned her on her back, and received a smack in the face. Lynn panted, grunted, tried to scratch him. He gripped her wrists and forced her down.

"No!" he cried. "Stop! It's me!"

She raged and snapped at him. It was like fighting a rabid animal. Now that her hands had been immobilized, she struck out with her legs, threw herself back and forth, then suddenly rolled her eyes and lay slack. Her breathing was fitful. For a moment he was afraid he was going to lose her to unconsciousness, then he saw her eyelids flutter. Her eyes cleared. "It's fine," he said. "I'm with you."

"I'm sorry," she whimpered. "I'm so sorry!"

She started sobbing. He let go of her wrists, took her in his arms, and started rocking her like a baby.

"Help me, Tim. Please help me."

"I'm here. It's fine. Everything's fine."

"No, it isn't." She pressed herself against him, clawed her fingers into the fabric of his jacket. "I'm going mad. I'm losing my mind. I—"

The rest was drowned by fresh sobbing, and Tim felt as unprepared as a schoolboy, even though it was the terrifying specter of this situation that had prompted him to come on Julian's idiotic pleasure trip in the first place. But now his brain threatened to go on strike on grounds of continuous overload, and abandon him to naked terror. He threw back his head and looked at the phantom of smoke in the dome of the atrium, menacingly spreading its wings. Something grew from the balconies, metal plates, enormous bulkheads, and he started to sense that something terrible was going on up there.

Cape Heraclides, Montes Jura, The Moon

For the first few minutes they had made quick progress, until it turned out that the bigger boulders supported one another, and developed a curious dynamism of their own as soon as you removed one of them. Several times he and Hanna were nearly crushed by a rolling rock. Whenever Locatelli jumped out of the way at the last second, his mind came up with bold scenarios of cause and effect in which debris—guided in precise trajectories—would crush Hanna as flat as a pancake. The Achilles' heel of all these plans was that nothing in the field of debris around Ganymede lent itself to precise calculation, so he resigned himself to cooperation. They carried the rubble down, alert, watching out for each other's safety; they pushed, pulled, dragged and lifted, and after two hours of backbreaking work they reached their physical limits. Several of the colossal boulders showed some movement, to be sure, but refused to be shifted. Breathless, Locatelli leaned against one of the rocks and was amazed not to hear Hanna panting like a dog as well.

Clearly the Canadian was in better shape.

"What now?" he asked.

"What indeed. We've got to get the hatch open."

"Oh really, smartass? Shame it's impossible."

Hanna leaned down and studied the blockage. Locatelli could hear the gears whirring in his head.

"Why don't you chuck one of your bombs in?" he suggested. "Let's blow these damn things up."

"No, the energy would disperse outside. Although—" Hanna hesitated, stepped over, and crouched down to a spot where two of the rocks touched. His hand dug into the crack in the ground and brought out some gravel. "Perhaps you're right."

"Of course I'm right," panted Locatelli. "I'm generally right. The bane and blessing of my existence. The deeper your blasted shot goes in, the more it can do."

"Even so, I'm not sure the explosive will be enough. The stones are enormous."

"But porous! This stuff's basalt, volcanic rock. With a bit of luck bits of it will come flying off, and you'll destabilize the whole pile."

"Fine," Hanna agreed. "Let's try that."

They began deepening and widening the channel. After an interval the Canadian disappeared inside the ship, brought out the console struts of the grasshopper, and they went on digging with that make-shift tool; they scraped and scrabbled until Hanna thought the channel was deep enough. At an appropriate distance from the Ganymede, at a slightly elevated position, they piled the smaller stones from the surroundings into a wall, lay down flat behind it, and Hanna took aim.

"Heads down!"

Like a newborn cosmos, a gray cloud expanded among the rocks. Warren Locatelli crouched lower. Bits of rock were hitting the basalt to right and left of the wall. When he raised his head above the parapet, it looked at first as if nothing had happened. Then he saw the huge boulder at the front shifting incredibly slowly and then spinning on its own axis. The one next to it dislodged as well, pushed its neighbor aside, and immediately collapsed, sending fragments scattering down the slope.

"Yeah!" cried Locatelli. "My idea. My idea!"

The big boulder was still spinning, and when it was jostled by a third that toppled into the gap, it finally leaned over, rolled heavily a few more meters, and produced a chain reaction of tumbling debris that rattled cheerfully down the hill.

"Yeah! Yeah!"

He jumped to his feet. They leaped from their improvised trench, and shoved the remaining rubble aside. Drunk on dopamine and thrilled by their joint success, Locatelli forgot the circumstances of their enmity, as if the disputes of the past few hours had been based on a script error, in which Hanna, the good friend, had been unjustly demonized, and was now, once again, someone you could run races and blow up moon mountains with. They freed the hatch of the Ganymede, and Hanna gave him a friendly slap on the shoulder.

"Well done, Warren. Very good!"

That contact, even though he barely felt it through his thick armor, brought Warren to his senses with a start. He couldn't get so drunk on his body's stimulants that he would actually let Hanna touch him. He had always liked the Canadian, with his moderate machismo, his monosyllabic manner, and now he thought he could discern something vaguely friendly about him, which made things even worse.

"Let's get it over with," he said roughly. "You open the hatch, I drive the buggy out and—"

"No, you can take a break," Hanna said equably. "I'll drive it out myself."

"Why? Do you think I'll try and get away?"

"Yes, that's exactly what I think."

And you're right, you fucker, thought Locatelli. He had flirted with the idea. Now he had conflicted feelings. He watched Hanna as he ran up the slope, climbed the nose of the Ganymede, and disappeared from view. Suddenly he was aware that the hit man didn't need him anymore. Feeling uneasy, he took a step back, as the hatch swung open and started to lower. He could see the inside of the freight space. A ramp emerged from the tipping hatch, and there was Hanna, already standing next to the buggy. He sat down in the driver's seat, checked the controls, and started. The ramp came down toward the ground, and Locatelli spotted that its rim wasn't going to make contact. The furrow that the shuttle had made had piled the debris up too far. It stopped a good meter above the regolith. For a moment the little vehicle looked like an animal about to spring, then it came to a standstill just beyond the edge of the ramp.

Locatelli hesitated. He didn't really know what to hope for, or what to fear. For a moment he had been worried that Hanna might simply drive on and leave him here, in the shadow of a broken-down spaceship that could no longer even be flooded with breathable air. Now, when he saw the Canadian climbing out, the source of his unease shifted to the possibility that the Canadian would proceed to make short work of him before driving off. Nervously, he took a step toward the ramp.

"What's up?" asked Hanna. "Aren't you coming?"

"Coming?" echoed Locatelli.

"You can still be useful to me."

Useful. Aha.

"And for how long," Locatelli asked, "will I be useful?"

"Until we've reached the American extraction station." Hanna pointed outside at the dusty plain. "When you were unconscious, I did a rough calculation of our position. What I see from here tells me that we're stranded precisely at the tip of Cape Heraclides. That means that the station is to the northeast, in the middle of the basalt lake, where the Sinus Iridum and the Mare Imbrium meet. About 100 kilometers from here."

"And why do you want to go there?"

"The station's automated," said Hanna. "But inspectors are always going there. A terminal was set up for them. Pressurized. A normal little base, where you could live for several months. We'll have to rely on our own sense of direction to get there, since all the satellites are out."

"Turn them back on, then."

"What makes you think I can do that?"

"What makes you think I've got shit for brains?" barked Locatelli. "They all failed when you set off on your crazy little journey. Are you trying to tell me that was coincidence?"

Hanna said nothing for a few moments.

"Of course not," he said. "But it's not in my power to correct that. We had to interrupt communication after I'd been busted, and now stop bugging me, okay? Help me to navigate and I'll leave you at the extraction station. If you want to live—"

Hanna went on talking, but Locatelli wasn't listening. He stared past the ramp. Something to the side of the Ganymede had attracted his attention.

"—rid of me," Hanna was saying. "You've just got to—"

Why was dust swirling up where the body of the shuttle was in the regolith? Little clouds puffing up along its flank, like an approaching steam train. What was happening? The outlines of the spaceship blurred, its steel fuselage quivered. The edge of the ramp barely rose above the debris, but more dust was pouring out. The ground was trembling too.

"—then we'll—"

"The shuttle's slipping!" yelled Locatelli.

Hanna jerked around. The Ganymede reared up, no longer stabilized by the boulders that they had blown away. A moment later it started moving again and slipped backward, spraying up sand and gravel. Locatelli saw Hanna dash up and jump onto the ramp that was now hurtling toward them, which swept the buggy up and away; he tried to leap to safety, stumbled, and fell. He was back on his feet in a moment, pushed himself away, dived to the side—

Another half meter and he would have done it.

The moment the rim cut into his belly, he saw with crystal clarity the image of Carl Hanna who, a universe further off, had done the right thing and sought refuge in altitude. Then a searing pain erased all other thoughts. He instinctively gripped the steel, a torero impaled on the bull's horns, shaken to the core by the downhill race of the Ganymede, which dropped one last time, pitched, and slung him away in a high arc. He landed on his back several meters away, became aware that the shuttle had stopped sliding just as suddenly as it had started, wedged on a ledge of rock, saw the buggy somersaulting and Hanna leaping along the loading bed and jumping into the rubble.

He pressed both hands to his belly, as hard as he could.

Hanna came running across and bent over him. Locatelli tried to say something, but all that came out was groaning and retching. He didn't need to look down at himself—which he couldn't have done anyway—to know that his suit had a tiny tear in it. If he was still alive, it was only because bio-suits didn't immediately burst like balloons, losing all their air all at once.

Perhaps if he kept his hands pressed against the wound—

"You're bleeding," said Hanna.

"Sh-shit," he managed to gasp. "Can you—?"

"Idiot!" How strange. The Canadian seemed to be angry. "What were you doing? I spared you, for God's sake! I could have brought you to safety!"

"I'm—I'm s—"

What? Sorry? Was he apologizing to Hanna for allowing himself to be rammed in the body by the Ganymede? Whose fault was that, then, damn it? But right now he felt terribly cold, and he understood that apart from Hanna he had no one now.

"Please—don't—let—me—"

"You're going to die," Hanna said soberly.

"N-no."

"There's nothing to be done, Warren. The vacuum will suck you empty as soon as you take your hands away."

Locatelli's lips moved. Connect me to something, he wanted to say, repair the suit, but all that came out was gurgles and coughing.

"Every second that we drag things out, you will suffer."

Suffer? He shook his head weakly. Stupid idea, he thought as he did so. No one can see you anyway. Each saw himself reflected in the helmet of the other. Searing hooks tore at his guts. He groaned.

"Warren?" Hanna's hands approached his helmet. "Do you hear me?"

"Shhhh—"

"Look at the stars. Look at the starry sky."

"Carl—" he whispered. The pain was almost unbearable.

"I'm with you. Look at the stars."

The stars. They circled above Locatelli, sending out messages that he didn't understand. Not yet. Oh, Christ, he thought, as Hanna busied himself with his helmet, who ever died with such an image before his eyes? How fantastic, in fact.

"Sh—it," he gasped once more, still his favorite word.

His helmet was taken off.

Gaia, Vallis Alpina, The Moon

However many heads Hydra had, at that moment they all had cause for the greatest concern.

And there had been problems on the horizon. The disaster of 2024 cast its long shadow, since Vic Thorn, the bacillus that they had been cultivating at such expense, had vanished into the expanses of interstellar space. More than a year of dread, month by month, during which the package frayed her nerves, as no one was able to say whether it would be able to survive that long in the lonely bleakness of the crater. Admittedly mini-nukes were almost impossible to find, as Dana Lawrence knew very well, although of course she hadn't told the assiduous afternoon search party. The little nuclear weapons got their energy from uranium-235. They didn't give off gamma rays like their beloved cousins, but instead produced alpha waves; even a sheet of paper was enough to dupe detectors. Nonetheless, in a stored state they gave off thermal energy, that had to be dispersed somewhere or other, a process performed on Earth by the atmosphere. On the Moon, on the other hand, there were no busily circulating molecules to pick up the little packets of heat and carry them off. To counteract the overheating of an atom bomb in an airless space, you needed big radiators, which the little bomb did not possess, because it was designed to be hidden for three months after the landing of Thorn, who would have been just around the corner from it on the moon base. If everything had gone to plan, Thorn would have positioned the bomb, set the timer, headed for Earth on the pretext of sudden illness, and the rest would have been available to read in the chronicles of noteworthy disasters.

Dana looked with revulsion at Kokoschka's charred and smoking body. At last she had managed to put out the remaining fires. She couldn't imagine what kind of inferno was currently raging in Gaia's sealed-off neck, but there too the flames must already have consumed much of the oxygen that had been there at the outset. The life-saving mask filled her lungs with oxygen, and a visual barrier protected her eyes against the stinging smoke, but the real problem was that she wasn't going to get out of here very quickly.

And all because of Julian's crazy daughter!

What the hell was up with Lynn? Never, not during her interviews for the job, and not afterward, either, had she ever given the impression of being mad. Controlling, certainly. Almost pathological in her striving for perfection, but she also *seemed* to be more or less perfect. But even until a few days previously, Dana wouldn't have been able to say anything else about Lynn Orley, except that she was the legitimate

architect of three extraordinary hotels, and completely capable of running a global company.

Then, as a complete surprise, the first symptoms of paranoia had
appeared and, initially uneasy, Dana had seen a certain potential in
them, because the change in Lynn's nature predestined Lynn for the
role of scapegoat. She hadn't let an opportunity pass to discredit Julian's
daughter and feed suspicions of her dishonesty. But back in the Mama
Quilla Club, with Donoghue bellowing in her ear, she had suddenly
been filled with the worry that Lynn might spoil everything. For the
sake of caution, she had followed her, but Lynn had only withdrawn
to her suite, so she had gone on to the control center, to find Sophie
Thiel, incapable of any kind of dissemblance, eating from the Tree
of Knowledge. Weak nerves, that one, although she deserved to be
admired for her meticulous detective work. Dana's only mistake had
promptly become an albatross—not immediately manipulating the
recordings after she'd sent the search parties off on their wild goose
chase. With a single glance, Sophie had worked out that her boss had
started the communications block during the conference call between
Earth and Moon, on the pretext of loading the video of the corridor.
Clever, Sophie, really clever. Aware that digital messengers were terribly indiscreet, Sophie had relied on pen, paper, and Kokoschka, and
given the infatuated lunkhead the task of looking for Tim, to tell him
who the real enemy was. It was only chance that she had ended up in
the control center at the right time, otherwise she might have been
unmasked even sooner.

Now the recordings had been corrected, although that probably
didn't matter anymore. The opportunity to lock both guests and staff
away in Gaia's head on the pretext of a meeting, and turn their air off,
so that she could head for Peary Base, had been irrevocably missed.
She was trapped.

Dana breathed deeply into her mask.

The circulators hummed around her. They did battle with the sooty
remains of the flames, sucked up the toxic components, and pumped
fresh oxygen into the wing. More in a spirit of sportsmanship than
anything else, Dana got to work on the bulkhead beyond which escala-
tors led down Gaia's arm into the lower levels, turned on the automatic
settings, tried muscle power, with no success. And how could it have
worked? In the hermetically sealed area, the partial destruction of the
oxygen had produced a slight but serious reduction in pressure. Until
it was resolved, the armor plating wasn't going to budge an inch. She
could safely ignore the bulkhead opposite, behind which Gaia's uncon-
taminated half lay. It would take at least two hours until pressure was
restored. Time enough to wonder about how that damn detective had
managed to penetrate Hydra's data banks. Any other setbacks could

have been coped with, for example the bomb sustaining damage when it fell into the crater, or Julian's unexpected appearance in the corridor when Hanna had come back from his nighttime excursion. Dana had manipulated the data, and skillfully blurred all the traces. No reason for panic.

But then everything had spun out of control.

At the same time, Hydra seemed to have emerged strengthened from its setback with Thorn, and they had agreed to give it a second try, with a team this time. No one was being recruited from NASA now. Thorn had been a lucky break: a generally popular bastard, yet in spite of his ostentatious joviality he was nobody's friend, and was free of any moral principles whatsoever. Years ago, Hydra had sensed his corruptibility; when he had still been training in simulators on Earth, they had observed him and finally made him an offer that he, by now elevated to the rank of moon base commander, had turned down without a flicker of an eyelash, but also with a request for double the money. When this turned out not to be a problem, everything else had gone like clockwork. In the jungle of Equatorial Guinea, work was coming to an end, Hydra's buyers had been successful in the black market of international terrorism. A masterpiece of criminal logistics was taking shape, conceived by a phantom that Dana had never met, but whose master of ceremonies she knew very well.

Kenny Xin, the crazed prince of darkness.

Even though he was the very model of a psychopath, and she found him in many respects unappealing, Dana could not conceal a certain admiration for him. For the architecture of the conspiracy of which she had been a part for years, crossing continental and cosmic bridges, Hydra couldn't have wished for a better stress analyst. Immediately after Thorn's death, Xin, more familiar than anyone else with the pandemonium of freelance spies, ex-secret service men, and contract killers, had engaged in a conversation with Dana—a former Mossad agent, specializing in the infiltration of luxury hotels, which meant that she was particularly qualified for Gaia—and had also come up with the ideal cover of a Canadian investor to win Julian's trust.

But judging by events, the prince of darkness had lost control of the situation.

Dana wondered if there was anyone still alive in the hotel. The area that she was trapped in looked deserted, but she didn't know who had been in Gaia's head when the oxygen had gone up. If luck had been on her side, they would all have been there. Not that she had any particular predilection for mass murder, but the group's fate had been sealed the minute Carl Hanna's cover had been blown. Dana was sure that the man would reach the moon base, but she couldn't know when and whether she would be able to contact him. By blocking communications, she

had tried to allow him a little time; however, if Jennifer Shaw and that
detective managed to contact Peary Base via NASA, it would be a real
disaster. Hanna had a better chance of carrying out his mission if there
was no one waiting at the North Pole to stop him.

The idea of the communication block had also been a well-aimed
and timely arrow from Kenny Xin's inexhaustible quiver of farsighted
ideas. Sending the guests off in search of the bomb had been a cinch.
Like listening in on Tommy Wachowski, the deputy commander of
the base, although of course not asking him for help in the search for
the Ganymede. To her great relief, they had known nothing at the Pole
about a planned attack, a clear indication that neither Jennifer Shaw
nor NASA had been able to get a warning to them before communications had broken down. Then she had manipulated the laser connection so that calls from the base were received only on her phone. Now
she just had to wait until Hanna called, and leave the hotel for good.

But first she would have to get rid of the guests. With the best will
in the world, she couldn't send that crowd to the Pole and risk them
getting there before Hanna and telling stories about atom bombs. No
one from the group must reach the base.

Who had survived?

Lynn, she thought. And Tim. Those two at least. They were somewhere in the hotel, possibly in the control center.

Time to make contact.

CAPE HERACLIDES,
MONTES JURA, THE MOON

The behavior of bodies in a vacuum has always inspired vivid speculation. Some of these stories correspond to fact. Objects of soft consistency with air pockets, for example, stretch apart like dough as the
gas forces its way out. This isn't caused by the vacuum sucking it out,
but by the atmosphere exerting pressure. Some things deform, others explode. Frothy, chocolate-coated marshmallows balloon up to
four times their volume. If the original ambient pressure were then
to be reinstated, they would transform into shapeless grease, indicating profound structural dilapidation. A knotted condom, however,
would regain its original form after a temporary existence as a balloon.
Of course, it certainly wouldn't be advisable to use it for its originally
intended purpose. A cow's lung would collapse into shreds, while holey
cheese and eggplants would show no visible change, and nor would
chickens' eggs. Beer foams up like crazy, pommes frites secrete fat and
solidify, and ketchup packets buckle.

When it comes to human beings, the rumor stubbornly persists that
we would explode if exposed to a vacuum. After all, we're more like
marshmallows than condoms in consistency: soft, porous, and interwoven with gases and fluids. And yet, something much more complex
happened when Warren Locatelli's helmet came off. Pressurized water
in deep-sea trenches on Earth doesn't start to boil until it reaches 200
to 300 degrees Celsius, whereas in the rarefied air of Mount Everest
it would start to boil at 70 degrees; on the same principle, the liquid
components in Locatelli's skull boiled within a fraction of a second of
being exposed to a complete lack of pressure, then immediately cooled
again due to the induced loss of energy. Anything that vaporizes in
a vacuum creates evaporative cooling, so the now liquefied Locatelli
froze as soon as he had boiled. His skull didn't explode, but his physiognomy went through rapid changes and left behind a mask-like grimace, coated with a thin layer of ice. As he was in the shadow of a rock
overhang, the ice would stay until the beams of light stretched across
and evaporated it. Lastly, Locatelli would suffer terrible sunburn, but
luckily he wouldn't feel a thing. He died so suddenly that the last thing
he noticed was the beauty of the starlit sky.

Hanna sat up straight.

It was just as he had said. The act of killing was neither a burden
nor a source of pleasure. His victims never came back to haunt him
in his sleep. If he had been convinced that Locatelli posed a danger

Frank Schätzing

to him, he would have shot him. But at some point in the course of the last two hours, he had become convinced that he didn't need to. Locatelli's bravery had won his respect, and even though the guy had been a pompous, arrogant jerk, Hanna had developed something akin to a fondness for him, accompanied by the desire to protect him. The prospect of saving Locatelli's life had, in some indefinable way, done him good.

At least he had saved him from suffering.

He turned away and erased the dead man from his memory. He had to finish the job.

The buggy lay on its side, having been pushed against the rock face by the Ganymede. Hanna heaved the vehicle back upright and inspected it. He immediately noticed that one of the axles had been so badly damaged that the question was not *whether* it would break, but *when*. He could only hope that the buggy would hold out until he reached the mining station.

Without giving Locatelli or the shuttle another glance, he drove off.

GAIA, VALLIS ALPINA, THE MOON

It was unbelievable, thought Finn O'Keefe, how deathly pale Mukesh suddenly looked. Incomprehensible that someone whose natural pigmentation resembled that of Italian espresso could ever look so pale. His blood-drained face was as empty as the words he used in a vain attempt to raise their morale.

"They'll come for us, Sushma, don't worry."

"Who's 'they'?"

"You know, our friend Funaki—"

"No, Mukesh, there's no one left, he can't get hold of anyone!" Sushma began to sob. "No one's answering at the control center, and it's on fire, everything's in flames down there!"

How strange. O'Keefe couldn't stop staring at Mukesh. Particularly his nose. It was as though it had gone numb, a pale radish stuck onto Mr. Tomato's face. The subject of his interest laid his arm protectively around Sushma's shoulders.

"He'll get in touch with someone, my love. I'm sure of it."

"Has it got a little warmer already?" Rebecca Hsu's brow was wrinkled with alarm. "By a few degrees?"

"No," said Eva Borelius.

"Well, I think it has."

"*You've* probably got warmer, Rebecca." Karla Kramp went over to the landing and looked down. "A side effect of stress hormones, increased blood pressure. It's completely normal at your age."

O'Keefe followed her. Two stories below, the spiral staircase ended at a steel barrier.

"Perhaps we should try to open the bulkheads," he suggested.

Funaki looked over at them and shook his head.

"As long as the indicators on the control panel are still lit red, we'd better leave it alone. There's a risk of fatality."

"But why?" Miranda fished a strawberry out of her Daiquiri and sucked the fruit pulp from its little green star. "The automatic system has shut down, so it should be okay for us to take a look, shouldn't it?" Her skin was reminiscent of cooked lobster; her face and cleavage glowing. Her chemical-saturated hair had been badly singed above the forehead, and even her eyebrows were damaged. Regardless of all that, she exuded the kind of confidence found only in people who are either especially superior or especially simple.

"It's not that easy," said Funaki.

"Nonsense." She licked strawberry juices from the corner of her mouth. "Just a quick look. If it's still burning, we'll close up again quickly."

"You wouldn't even be able to get the bulkheads open."

"Finn has strong muscles, and Mukesh—"

"It has nothing to do with body strength. Not when the partial pressure of the oxygen has dropped."

"I see." Miranda raised what remained of her eyebrows in interest. "Wasn't he one of the Arthurian knights?"

"Sorry?"

"Partial."

"Percival," said Olympiada Rogacheva wearily.

"Oh, that's right. So what does he have to do with our oxygen?"

"Michio, you old Samurai," O'Keefe turned around. "Please be so kind as to talk in a way that the billionairess can understand you. I think you meant to say that there's now a vacuum on the other side, right? Which means we need to think of another way of getting out of here."

"But how?" Eva looked at him helplessly. "Without the elevator."

They had climbed down to Selene in order to inspect the staff elevator, the only one of the three elevators that went through into the restaurant area, but Funaki had energetically intervened:

"Not until the system or control center signal that it's safe! We don't know what's happening in the elevator shaft. If you don't want to be hit by a wall of flames, then don't even think about opening those doors."

But the control center still hadn't been in touch.

"If we need to we can climb down through the ventilation shaft," he had added. "It's not the most comfortable of methods, but it's safe."

A while had passed since then. Karla looked back down into the worm casing of the spiral staircase.

"Well, I'm certainly not going to let myself get roasted up here," she decided.

"Roasted?" Hsu's eyes widened in horror. "Why? Do you mean that—"

"Karla," whispered Eva. "Do you have to?"

"What?" Karla whispered back in German. "There's nothing but stars above us. We can't get to the viewing platform without space suits, and everything's burning down below. Fire has a tendency to rise, you know. If Funaki doesn't make contact with the control center soon, we'll all meet our maker up here, mark my words. I want to get out of here."

"We all want to get out of here, but—"

"Michio!" A distorted voice came out of the intercom in the bar. "Michio, can you hear me? It's Tim. Tim Orley!"

Maybe he'd got his priorities wrong. He should have ignored Lynn's misery and made contact with the others without delay, but in the face of her suffering that had seemed an unbearable prospect. The level of her sobbing seemed to indicate that the medication she had taken was helping a little. He had got the elevator at once, calling it down from the very top in order to go to her suite on the thirteenth floor with her. At first, only his subconscious registered the fact that it was unusually warm in the cabin. It was only once they reached the glass bridge that he had remembered the worrying noises from the neck of Gaia, the phantom of smoke in the dome of the atrium and how the architecture seemed, bizarrely, to be in motion. Then he had looked up at the ceiling.

A massive armor shield was stretched out above him.

Perplexed, he wondered where the steel panels and bulkheads had come from all of a sudden. They must have been stored between the floors, hidden from view.

What on earth had happened up there?

By the time they got to the bathroom, Lynn was shaking so much that he had to lay the green tablets and white capsules she asked for on her tongue, one after another, and hold the glass for her as she drank, panting, like a little child. The resulting coughing fit gave reason to fear that she might bring up the cocktail of medicine again in a projectile arc, but then it had begun to take effect. A quarter of an hour later, she had got a grip of herself; at least enough to allow them to leave the suite. They immediately ran into Heidrun and Walo Ögi.

"What's wrong?" asked the Swiss man in a concerned voice as he looked around. "Where are the others?"

"Up there," whispered Lynn. Based on the color of her skin, she could have passed for Heidrun's sister.

"We've been up there," said Ögi. "We wanted to go to the meeting, but everything's locked up and barricaded."

"Barricaded?"

"I think you'd better come with us," said Heidrun.

It was only as they went further up that Tim realized just how extensive the armor plating really was. A solid steel wall without even the slightest hint of a gap had descended down diagonally over the gallery. The doors of E2, one of the two guest elevators, had disappeared behind it, as had the left-hand side entrance to the neck. The one accessible spiral staircase ended in a closed bulkhead. It was only now that he realized his vision was imperceptibly impaired, as if some wafer-thin film had been pulled over his retina. Here and there, black bits of fluff were spinning through the air. He reached out to catch some and they crumbled into grease between his fingers.

"Soot," he said.

"Do you smell that?" Ögi was snuffling all around, his mustache twitching. "Like something's burnt."

Horror crept over him. If the bulkheads were closed, then that could only mean it was *still* burning! Filled with dread, they rode down and could already hear Funaki's urgent calls by the time they reached the lobby. Lynn shuffled over to the controls, activated the speech function, waved her brother over wearily, and sank down into one of the rolling chairs.

"Michio!" called Tim breathlessly. "Michio, can you hear me? Tim here! Tim Orley!"

"Mr. Orley!" Funaki's relief was palpable. "We thought no one would ever answer. I've been trying to reach someone for half an hour."

"I'm sorry, we had to—we had a few problems to solve."

"Where's Miss Dana?"

"Not here."

"Sophie?"

"She's not here either, none of the staff are. Just the Ögis, my sister, and I."

Funaki fell silent for a moment. "Then I fear you'll have even more problems to solve, Tim. We're stuck up here."

"What happened—"

"Control center!" Dana's voice. "Please respond."

"Excuse me a moment, Michio." Wrinkling his brow, he tried to orientate between the two flashing indicators. "I'll be back in just a moment—I have Dana Lawrence—just a moment, for God's sake, how do I switch over?"

His sister heaved herself up from the chair with a blank expression, pushed him aside, and tapped a flashing section of the controls.

"Dana? It's Lynn here."

"Lynn! Finally. I've been trying for half an hour—"

"You can save the speech, Funaki already did it. Where are you?"

"Locked in. In the right shoulder."

"Fine, we'll be in touch. Stand by."

"But I have to—"

"Shut your mouth, Dana. Just wait until someone's ready to play with you."

"What did you say?" Dana exploded.

"Oh yes, and you're fired. Michio?" Lynn put the enraged hotel director on hold. "This is Lynn Orley. Can you tell me your location?"

"Okay, yes. The Mama Quilla Club, the Luna Bar, and the Selene are accessible, but the Chang'e is sealed off. According to the computer the conditions beneath are life-threatening. A fire in the neck of the automatic system must have caused the area to be sealed off. Miss Miranda saw a jet of flame—"

"*Saw* one?" They heard Miranda's penetrating voice in the background. "I was practically barbecued by it."

"—and only just managed to get away."

Lynn leaned heavily against the control console. To Tim, she looked like a zombie trying to do something its body was no longer capable of. "Who was in the neck when the fire broke out?" she asked, her voice flat.

"We're not entirely sure. It seems like there was an argument there. The Donoghues left the bar to find out, and we heard Miss Dana's voice, and—" He hesitated. "And yours, Miss Orley. *Sumimasen*, but you probably know better yourself who was there."

Lynn fell silent for a few seconds.

"Yes, I know," she said softly. "At least for the time before I—left. Your observations are correct. Just after Tim and I left, it must have—" She cleared her throat. "Who's with you right now?"

Funaki said nine names and assured her that, apart from Miranda's minor burns, they were all uninjured. Tim shuddered at the thought of the neck, now completely sealed off. He didn't dare imagine what fate had befallen Chuck, Aileen, and the chef.

"Thanks, Michio." Lynn's fingers wandered over the touchscreen, altering controls, changing parameters.

"What are you doing?" asked Tim.

"I'm stopping the convection in the elevator section and in the ventilation shafts."

"Convection?" echoed Ögi.

"The air circulation. There could be massive amounts of smoke forming up there. We have to stop the ventilators from distributing it and encouraging the fire to spread. Dana?"

"Lynn, damn it! You can't do this to me, I—"

"Are you alone?"

"Yes."

"What happened?"

"I—listen, I'm sorry if I accused you of being in the wrong, but *everything* indicated that *you* were the one we were looking for. I'm responsible for the safety of the hotel, so that's why—"

"You *were*."

"I had no other choice. And you have to admit that your recent behavior hasn't exactly been normal." Dana hesitated. As she continued, her voice suddenly sounded sympathetic, as if there should be a leather psychologist's chair and a diploma on the wall. "No one is angry with you. Anyone can stumble now and then, but maybe you're ill, Lynn. Maybe you need help. Are you sure you still have things under control? Would *you* have trusted you?"

For a moment, the incapacitating tone seemed to be taking effect. Lynn sank her head and breathed deeply. Then she stiffened and jutted her chin out.

"The only thing I need to know is that I have you under control, you scheming little bitch."

"No, Lynn, you don't understand, I—"

"You won't do this to me twice, do you hear?"

"I just want to—"

"Shut it. What happened in the neck?"

"But that's what I've been trying to tell you the whole time."

"What then?"

"Kokoschka. He betrayed you! It was him."

"Ko-Kokoschka?"

"Yes! He was Hanna's accomplice."

"Dana!" Tim walked over. "It's me. Are you sure about that? I think he wanted to give me something."

"No idea what, but that's right, yes. He got really angry when you didn't pay attention to him, it seemed things didn't go as he had imagined. Then—right after you and Lyn left the neck, Anand appeared. I don't know exactly what she had found out and how, but she said straight to Kokoschka's face that he was the agent, and Kokoschka, my God . . . he just snapped. He pulled out a gun and shot her, then Chuck and Aileen too, everything happened so horribly quickly. I tried to knock the gun out of his hand, and it went off, then one of the oxygen tanks suddenly started spitting out fire and—I just ran, just got out, before the bulkheads closed. He came after me, but he didn't make it. He burned. The gallery burned, everything. I—" Dana's voice ebbed away. As she continued, her attempt to control her emotions was audible. "I managed to get him out and close the bulkhead, to extinguish the flames, but—"

"What is it? Are *you* okay?"

"Yes, thank you, Tim." There was a muffled cough. "I've probably inhaled a little too much CO_2 into my lungs, but I'm okay. I'll keep myself going with oxygen masks until the pressure comes back and the bulkheads open."

"And—Kokoschka?"

"Dead. I couldn't get anything else out of him. Unfortunately."

Silent horror and complete incomprehension descended over Heidrun and Walo's faces. Lynn stepped away from the console, swayed a little, staggered, and then crashed down into the chair.

"It's my fault," she whispered. "All of this is my fault."

Nina Hedegaard had long suspected that Julian might be a reincarnation of the Comte de Saint-Germain: the alchemist and adventurer regarded as "immortal and all-knowing," as Voltaire once wrote to Frederick the Great, and whose mysterious elixirs and essences he had wanted to use in order to unleash the lasting strength and stamina of a thirty-year-old. During her two semesters of studying history—which she passed inadvertently due to the blossoming of a brief liaison with a historian—the mysterious count had been Nina's favorite figure. An ingenious gambler, companion to Casanova, and teacher to Cagliostro, even the pompadours hung on his every word, because he claimed to be in possession of an *Aqua benedetta*, a potion which stopped the ageing process. Born sometime in the early eighteenth century, official date of death 1784; biographers constantly claimed that they still found traces of him in the nineteenth century. Rich, eloquent, charming and—behind the façade of wanting to make the world a better place—thoroughly unscrupulous; it could only be Julian! The twenty-first-century Comte de Saint-Germain had created a space station and hotel on the Moon, making gold out of earth just as he had since time began, this time by transforming his alchemical genius helium-3 into energy, creating carbon tubes instead of diamonds, making a fool of the world and breaking the heart of a petite Danish pilot.

Exhausted from self-pity and six consecutive nights of sex, unproductive conversations about a future together, more sex, brooding wakefulness, and a mere three hours of sleep, she felt so close to fainting that she had finally been tempted away from the pool and into the chill-out room. She didn't feel the slightest desire to have another opulent dinner in Selene, play-acting the sweet travel guide. She'd had enough. Either Julian went public about their relationship while they were still on the Moon, or he could rot alone on the Aristarchus Plateau. Her bad mood swelled into a reservoir of rage. So they couldn't make contact? There was no response from Ganymede? The last sighting of the count was in 2025? Well, so what! It wasn't her responsibility to keep checking up and searching. She was completely worn out, and now she didn't even want Julian to find her—if he ever turned up again. In reality, she wanted nothing more than for him to find her, but just not right now. She wanted him to go out of his mind with worry first. To beat his fists into the empty pillow beside him. Miss her. Simmer in his guilt. Yes, that's what he should do!

Similar to the design of the pool, the chill-out area was modeled on the surface of the Moon, full of little craters and secluded corners. Her bathrobe slung around her, she selected a discreetly located lounge chair, perfectly suited to not being found, stretched out on it, and fell into a deep, dreamless sleep in just a matter of minutes. Breathing evenly, away from the gaze of possible search parties, she rested at the very base of all consciousness. Removed from time and reality, lured into the waiting room of death, she snored softly and felt nothing but heavenly peace, and then not even that.

• • •

Four stories above her, hell was bubbling away.

Even though Gaia in its intact state resembled a youthful, perfectly functioning organism, whose life-support systems predestined it for heroic acts, gold medals, and immortality, a few stray projectiles from a handgun had been enough to turn all the advantages of its systems and sub-systems against it in the blink of an eye. The hidden tanks, designed to offset shortages in the bioregenerative circulation by pumping the most accurately gauged quantities of oxygen into the atmosphere, had revealed themselves to be a fatal weakness. Twenty minutes after the catastrophe had struck, the affected tank was already burnt out, while other systems, originally intended to be life-saving, gave the hellfire new nourishment. By this point, the sealed-off area had temperatures of over 1000 degrees Celsius. The casing on the oxygen candles had melted and liberated their contents, burning coolants had caused the pipelines to explode, and supposedly inflammable wall casings were flowing down like glowing slurry. Unlike in the Earth's gravitational pull, the blaze didn't flare up high, but instead drifted curiously around, creeping into every corner, including the cabin of E2, the guest elevator, the doors of which hadn't managed to shut in time because Anand's collapsed body was blocking them. Only tarry clumps and bones remained of the three corpses; everything else had been swallowed up by the flame monster. Human tissue, synthetic materials, plants, and still its hunger was far from satiated. While the prisoners in the Mama Quilla Club were planning their escape with Lynn and Tim, while Dana Lawrence was foaming with rage, hammering against the closed bulkhead, and while Nina Hedegaard was sleeping through the destruction, the flames raged against a second tank, until eventually its sealing couldn't hold out anymore and a further twenty liters of compressed oxygen unleashed the next phase of the inferno. In the absence of other materials, the monster began to gnaw at the security glass of the window and at the steel brace which held Gaia's neck upright, weakening its structural solidarity.

At a quarter past nine, the first load-bearing constructions slowly began to give way.

"No, it was absolutely right not to use the elevator," they heard Lynn say through the intercom system. She sounded tired and drained, robbed of all her strength. "The problem is that we can only make assumptions from down here. The sensors in the neck have failed; it's possible that it's still burning down there. The fire-extinguishing system was clearly able to make some progress in Change, but there's still contamination and considerable vacuum pressure. Almost all the oxygen has gone to blazes. I imagine the ventilators will balance that out in the course of the next two hours, just like in the shoulder area."

"But we can't wait two hours," said Funaki, with a sideways glance at Rebecca Hsu. "And it's getting hotter in here too."

"Okay, then—"

"What about the ventilator shafts? We could climb down over the staircase."

"The data for that is contradictory. There seems to have been a slight loss of pressure in the eastern shaft, but that might just be because a little bit of smoke forced its way in. The western shaft looks okay. As far as the guest elevators are concerned, E2 has broken down, its cabin is stuck in the neck, and the staff elevator is in the cellar. E1 is in the lobby, near us. We've used it several times without any problems."

"E1 won't be of much help to us," said Funaki. "It stops in the neck. If we're going to use anything it can only be the staff elevator, that's the only one that goes through to Selene."

"Just a moment."

Muffled voices could be heard in the control center. First Tim's, then Walo Ögi's.

"I'd like to remind you that E1 and E2 are a good distance apart," Funaki added. "If E2 has been compromised, that doesn't affect E1. The staff elevator, on the other hand, travels between the two, and would get very close to E2."

"Lynn?" O'Keefe leaned over the intercom. "Could the fire spread to the other elevator shafts?"

"In principle, no." She hesitated. "The likelihood is very slim. The shaft system is connected via passageways, but structured in such a way that flames and smoke can't spread that quickly. And besides, the shaft itself is inflammable."

"What does 'that quickly' mean exactly?" asked Eva Borelius.

"It means that we should test it," said Lynn with a steady voice. "We'll send the staff elevator up to you. If the system considers it to be safe, its doors would open in Selene. After that we'll call it back, look inside, and if there's nothing to suggest otherwise, we'll send it up again. Then you should be able to actually use it."

O'Keefe exchanged glances with Funaki and tried to make eye contact with the others. Sushma was frozen in a state of fear, Olympiada was gnawing at her lower lip, and Karla and Eva were signaling their agreement.

"Sounds sensible," said Mukesh.

"Yes." A nervous laugh escaped from Karla. "Better than smoke-filled ventilation shafts."

"Okay," decided Funaki. "So let's do it."

"Nothing can shock me now anyway," warbled Miranda.

The reenlivening effect of having a plan seeped into the bloodstream of the small group and motivated them to climb down to Selene, where the temperatures were significantly higher. Funaki threw a precaution-ary glance at the bulkheads on the floor. There was nothing to suggest that smoke or flames were making their way upward.

They waited. After a short while they heard the elevator approach-ing. For what felt like an eternity, the doors remained closed, then finally glided silently apart.

The cabin looked the same as it always did.

Funaki took a step inside and looked around.

"It looks good. Very good even."

"Mukesh." Sushma grabbed her husband's upper arm and looked at him pleadingly. "Did you hear what he said? We could go now—"

"No, no." Funaki, with one leg still in the cabin, turned around hur-riedly and shook his head. "We're supposed to send it down empty. Just like Miss Orley said."

"But it's fine." Sushma's shoulders were quivering with tension. "It's intact, isn't it? Every time we send it back and forth, it could only get more dangerous. I want to go down now, *please*, Mukesh."

"Oh, honey, I don't know." Mukesh looked at Funaki uncertainly. "If Michio says—"

"It's *my* decision!"

The Japanese man grimaced and scratched himself behind the ear.

"I'm in," said Karla. "I agree."

"What, you want to go down now?" asked Eva. "Do you think that's a good idea?"

"What is there to debate? The cabin made it up, so it will make it back down again too. Sushma's right."

"I'm coming in any case," said Hsu. "Finn?"

O'Keefe shook his head.

"I'm staying here."

"Me too," said Olympiada.

Funaki looked helplessly at Miranda Winter. She ran her hands through the singed tips of her hair and pinched her nose.

"So, the thing is, I believe in voices," she said, rolling her eyes toward the ceiling. "Voices from the universe, you know, sometimes you have to listen really closely, then the universe speaks to you and tells you what you have to do."

"Uh-huh," said Karla.

"You have to listen with your whole body of course."

O'Keefe gave her a friendly nod. "And what does it say, the cosmos?"

"To wait. I mean, that *I* should wait!" she hurried to confirm. "It can only speak for me after all."

"Of course."

"We're losing time," urged Funaki. "They've already called the ele-vator back down again. The light's flashing."

Mukesh grasped Sushma's hand.

"Come on" he said.

They walked past Funaki into the cabin, followed by Hsu, Karla and Eva, who peered in skeptically.

"You're coming too?" asked Karla, surprised.

"Do you think I'm going to let you go down by yourselves?"

"It's best if you stay in Selene." Mukesh called out to those staying behind. "We'll send the elevator back right away."

The doors closed.

Am I too cautious, wondered O'Keefe? When all is said and done, am I just a coward?

Suddenly, the disquieting feeling crept over him that he'd just thrown away his last chance of getting out of here alive.

"It's awful," said Eva softly. "When I think of how Aileen and Chuck—"

"Don't think about it then," said Karla, staring straight ahead.

The cabin set itself in motion.

"It's moving," commented Hsu.

"I just hope it will a second time too," said Sushma, concerned. "The others should have come with us."

"Don't worry," Mukesh reassured her. "It *will*."

The familiar feeling of weight loss set in. The elevator sped up, past—

—the cabin of E2, the interior of which was shimmering with red-yellow embers as the oxygen tank incessantly spat flames out into the wasteland of the neck. Inside the elevator it was getting hotter and hotter. In spite of their density, the panes of the glazed section at the front were straining to brace themselves against the fire, but in vain, as the pressure began to shift to the inside and forced the components of the cabin slowly but steadily apart. The elevator shafts were separated from one another by thin, longitudinal walls, that were pierced by passageways a meter square. Contrary to their outer appearance, they were incredibly robust, made of mooncrete and designed to stand up to even heavy loads.

Not as heavy as this, though, admittedly.

For over three-quarters of an hour, ferrostatic tension had been building up inside the cabin. Now that the tolerable maximum had been exceeded, it exploded with such destructive force that one of the side casings split off with a deafening noise, smashed the shaft wall into pieces, and spread out like shrapnel into the neighboring shaft, making the staff elevator come to a jolting standstill.

• • •

It stopped so abruptly that its passengers were torn off their feet, shot up weightlessly, banged their heads together and tumbled down wildly. In the next moment, something crashed down onto the roof, making the cabin shake heftily.

"What was that?" Sushma sat up and looked around, her eyes wide. "What happened?"

"We're stuck!"

"Mukesh?" Panic rippled through her voice. "I want to get out. I want to get out *immediately.*"

"Calm down, my love, I'm sure everything is—"

"I want to get out. *I want to get out!*"

He took her arm and spoke to her insistently, quickly, and under his breath. One after another, they clambered to their feet, their faces pale and anxious.

"Did you hear that crash?" Hsu stared up at the roof of the cabin.

"But we were already past it," Karla said to herself, as if wanting to make the obvious impossible. "We were already below the gallery."

"Something stopped us." Eva glanced at the controls. The lights had gone dark. She pressed the button for the intercom system. "Hello? Can anyone hear us?"

No answer.

"What a mess," cursed Hsu.

"I want to get out," pleaded Sushma. "Please, I want—"

"Don't start!" Hsu barked at her. "You were the one that talked us into getting in this thing. It's because of you that we're stuck."

"You didn't have to come too!" Mukesh replied, furiously. "Leave her be."

"Oh, shut it, Mukesh."

"Hey!" Eva interrupted. "Don't argue, we—"

Something made a crunching noise above them. A hollow, grinding noise joined it, followed by deathly silence.

The cabin jolted.

Then it fell.

"You did what?"

Lynn stared at the monitor and Funaki's baffled face.

"They wanted to get in at all costs, Miss Orley," the Japanese man groaned. He gazed downward. His head jerked forward and backward in quick succession, gestures of submission. "What was I supposed to do? I'm not an army general, people have their own free will."

"But it didn't work! And we can't make contact with them anymore."

"Did they—get stuck?"

Lynn glanced at the controls. They had seen the cabin stop suddenly under the gallery, but after that the icon had disappeared.

No one said a word. Walo Ögi was pacing through the room, while Heidrun and Tim stared at the controls as if they could conjure up the icon again just by gazing at it.

There was a state of emergency in Lynn's mind.

The drugs had unleashed their narcotic effect while the acute drama lashed away at her, pushing her beyond her limits. She felt confused, drunk almost, but at the same time acutely aware of every detail of her surroundings; a strange, unsettling clarity. There was no before and after, no more primary and secondary perception. Everything bombarded her at once, while less and less was making its way out. Different levels of reality layered on top of one another, broke apart, forced their way back together again, splintered, and created surreal background scenery for the performance of incomprehensible plays. The blood rushed in her ears. For the hundredth, thousandth, zillionth time, she asked herself how on earth she could have let herself in for this, building space stations and moon hotels, instead of finally standing up to Julian and making it clear to him that she wasn't perfect, wasn't a superhuman, wasn't even a healthy human for that matter. She should have told him that the task would destroy her, that you may well need a lunatic to create something brilliant and crazy, but certainly not to maintain it or even promote it. Because that, *precisely that*, was a task for the healthy ones, the mentally clear and stable, those who flirted with lunacy, flirted with it without a care in the world, not having the slightest idea what it really felt like.

How long would she be able to keep going?

Her head was ringing. She closed her eyes, pressing the tips of her fingers against her temples. She had to stay upright. She couldn't allow the dam holding the flood of blackness to break. She was the only one that knew the hotel like the back of her hand. She had built it.

It was all down to her.

Filled with fear, she opened her eyes.

The symbol was back.

"Help! Help! Can anyone hear us?"

Eva hammered furiously on the intercom button, shouting and shouting, while Sushma threw herself against the closed internal doors and tried to force them apart with her bare hands. Mukesh pulled her back by her shoulders and held her close to him.

"I want to get out of here," she whimpered. "Please."

The elevator had only dropped a meter, but the blood had rushed from all five faces and collected in their feet. As white as chalk, they looked at one another, like a group of ghosts suddenly realizing they have already been dead for a long time.

"Okay." Eva abandoned the intercom, raised her hand, and tried to sound practical, which she was remarkably successful in doing. "The most important thing now is that we stay calm. That means you too, Sushma. Sushma? Okay?"

Sushma nodded, her lower lip trembling, her face wet with tears.

"Good. We don't know what's wrong, and we can't get through to anyone, so we have to find out."

"It can't be all that bad," said Hsu. "I mean, there's only a sixth of the—"

"Twelve meters on the Moon are like two on Earth, you know that," retorted Karla. "And I guess we're about 120 meters up."

"Sshh! Listen."

A rising and falling roaring sound filled their ears. A tormented howling mixed in with it, like a material under intense strain. Eva looked up to the ceiling. There was a bulkhead in clear view in the middle. She saw the operator control next to the display. She hesitated for a moment, then activated the mechanism. For a number of seconds, nothing happened, giving rise to the fear that this function had been damaged too. How were they supposed to get outside if the bulkhead had failed? But even while she was still pondering the alternatives, it stirred into motion and slowly rose. A flickering orange-red glow made its way in, the roaring intensified. She crouched down, pushing off from her knees, got a grip on the edge of the hatch, pulled herself up with a powerful swinging movement, and clambered onto the roof.

"My God," she whispered.

On the right-hand side, a large section of the dividing wall had been torn away, which meant she could see through to the neighboring shaft. Five, perhaps 6 meters above her, was the smoldering, half-destroyed cabin of E2. The side casing was completely gone, exposing its inside, the source of the roaring sound, which was now even louder. Red apparitions darted across the floor of the burning elevator, streaks of rust were collecting further up in the shaft. There was debris wherever she looked. A bizarrely distorted, glowing and pulsing piece of metal was directly in front of her feet. She took a step back. At first she thought the brake shoes of the staff elevator had gripped and surrounded the guide rails, but on closer inspection two of them seemed to be blocked by splinters or possibly damaged. The heat was making thick beads of sweat build up over her forehead and upper lip.

Then, suddenly, the floor collapsed from under her feet.

A collective scream forced its way up to her as the cabin dropped another meter. Eva staggered, caught her balance, and saw that one of the brake shoes had opened up. No, worse than that, it had broken! In panic, she looked for a way out. Right in front of her eyes was the lower edge of the doors which led to the gallery. She wedged her finger between the gap, making a useless attempt to open them, but of course they didn't move a single millimeter. Why would they? These weren't normal elevator doors, but completely sealed-off bulkheads. As long as the system didn't decide to open them, or unless someone activated them from the outside, she was only making a fool of herself and wasting valuable time.

"Eva!" She heard Sushma sniveling. "What's happening?"

It was hard for her to ignore the poor woman, but she didn't have time to tend to the others' sensitivities as well. Feverishly, she searched for a solution. The still intact wall, she now noticed, revealed a passage through to the E1 shaft, around a square meter in size. Several meters above, she spotted another passage, too high to reach, and the glowing and smoky fragments of the blasted away cabin casing were splayed out in it. Feeling an unpleasant pressure on her chest, Eva turned to the other side to get a look at the E2 shaft. The entire upper section of the dividing wall had disappeared, replaced by a huge, gaping hole, the jagged edge of which was level with her forehead. She had to hoist herself up a bit to look over it. Vertical guide rails stretched down into the depths of the unknown. There were crossbars positioned at intervals in between, wide enough to be able to get a grip and a foothold on them, and on the other side of the shaft she saw—

A passageway.

A rectangular hole leading into a short, horizontal tunnel. It lay there buried in the wall, dark and mysterious, but Eva was pretty sure she knew where it led, and it was big enough for two people to crawl along it at once. With a little dexterity, they'd be able to get across to it.

The cabin creaked in its rails beneath her, metal scraping over metal. Mukesh Nair hoisted himself up through the hatch, raised his head and stared, aghast, at the glowing wreckage of E2.

"Good God! What happened here—?"

"Everyone out," said Eva. She pushed past him and called down to the others. "Out, quickly! And be careful, there's burning debris everywhere."

"What's the plan?" asked Mukesh.

"Help me."

The elevator groaned and dropped a little more, while sparks rained down on her from above. In pain, Eva felt the dot-sized burns on her hands and upper arms. She had picked out a simple, sleeveless top for the evening, and now she was cursing herself for it. Hurrying, she helped Karla, Sushma, and the alarmingly stiff Rebecca Hsu clamber out, until they were all standing on the roof.

"Take your clothes off," said Eva, untucking her top from her pants and pulling it over her head. "T-shirts, blouses, shirts, anything you can wrap around your hands."

Sushma's head jerked back and forth.

"Why?"

"Because we'll burn our mitts if we don't protect them." She gestured her head toward the gaping opening. "We need to get over there. Once you get to the other side, stay right up against the wall. There's strutting between the elevator rails that you can grip onto to make your way along. Don't look down, or up, just keep going. There's a passageway on the other side, and I suspect it leads into the ventilator shaft."

"I'll never make it," said Sushma in an anxious whisper.

"Yes, you will," said Hsu decisively. "We'll all make it, including you. And I'm sorry about before."

Sushma smiled, her lips twitching. Without hesitation, Eva ripped the thin fabric of her top. It had been sinfully expensive, but that was irrelevant now. She wrapped the scraps around her hands and wrists and helped Karla deconstruct her own T-shirt while Mukesh assisted his wife. Hsu cursed as she stripped down to her underwear, despairing at the misappropriation of her cocktail dress. Mukesh handed her strips of his shirt.

"Good" said Eva. "I'll go first."

The cabin of the staff elevator shook. Eva clasped the edge of the destroyed dividing wall, pulled herself up, and swung a leg onto the other side.

Not look down?

Eva, Eva. It was easier said than done. She suddenly felt queasy, and her courage disintegrated. The distant bottom of the shaft disappeared into the ominous darkness, and even the bars suddenly seemed disconcertingly narrow. Forcing herself not to look up at the demolished remains of cabin E2, she reached out, grabbed one of the bars, and felt the heat penetrate the material wrapped around her hand. With her teeth clenched, she clambered right over to the other side and rested her feet on the hot steel.

Well, it wasn't exactly a boulevard. But she was standing.

Resolved, she dared to take a step sideways and groped her way forward until she reached the front-facing shaft wall. She bridged the corner with her leg and sent the tip of her foot searching for something to grip on to. Her upper body leaned backward, the material of her improvised bandage slipped off against the steel of the brace. For a moment she feared losing her grip and clung on with her heart beating wildly. She couldn't stop herself from craning her head back and staring at the underside of the glowing cabin. E2 was now directly above her, black and threatening, its edges fiery.

If the thing falls now, she thought to herself, at least I won't have to worry about whether they still have the blouse at Louis Vuitton. Then she realized that Rebecca Hsu had bought Louis Vuitton, years ago even.

Rebecca will just have to sort something out for me then, she thought grimly.

She tightened her grip. With one more courageous step, she reached the bars on the front wall. Quickly now! The heat was starting to get painful through the bandages, burn blisters were inevitable. They wouldn't be able to last all that long in here, and to top it all off she had a sneaking suspicion that the smoke was making its way downward now too. Arching her feet like a ballerina, she pushed her way past the lower edge of the elevator doors, then conquered the second corner as well. The opening was to her right, barely a meter away. Cautiously, she turned her head and saw Karla at the height of the doors, closely followed by Sushma, who had her face turned toward the wall and was obediently refusing to look up or down. Mukesh, who had just made it to the other side, secured himself with his right hand and helped Hsu heave her ample body across the ledge.

"Take care of Sushma," said Hsu, ignoring Mukesh's outstretched hand. "I can make it by myse—"

Her words were drowned out by metallic screeching. She hurriedly swung herself over the ledge. A crash and clatter sounded out, disappearing quickly into the depths as the staff elevator fell.

"Everything okay?" Mukesh's voice echoed off the walls and was swallowed by the abyss.

Hsu nodded, trembling on one of the bars. "God that's hot!"

"Wait, I'm coming."

"No, I'm fine. Go. Go!"

Eva took a deep breath and pushed herself forward to just below the passageway. It was higher up than she had thought and she could only just peer over the ledge, but there were two narrow rungs built into the wall. With a chin-up, she managed to get inside. She crawled forward and, almost immediately, her hands came up against a metal plate which sealed off the back of the passageway. To the side of it was a small control panel. Taking a chance, she pressed her finger on it, and at the same moment icy horror rushed through her.

Vacuum pressure! What if the fire and smoke had already annihilated too much of the oxygen in the elevator shaft?

To her incredible relief, the panel glided to the side and revealed an evenly lit, two-meter-square shaft. There was a ladder on the left-hand side. She contorted herself to turn around, crept back, and stretched both hands out toward Karla.

"In here," she called, her voice reverberating. "The ventilation shaft is behind here."

Karla slithered into the passage next to her.

"Climb down the ladder," said Eva. "At some point there should be a way of getting out."

"What about you?"

"I'm helping the others."

"Okay."

Sushma turned her face toward her. In it, hope and deathly fear were grappling for supremacy.

"Everything's okay, Sushma." Eva smiled. "Everything's fine now."

There was a loud creak above her, then a metallic crash, and sparks rained down in dense showers.

Eva looked up. A fiery glow was gleaming through a crack in the cabin. Had that been there before? It looked as though the floor of the burning cabin was beginning to break away from the rest of it.

No, she thought. Not yet. Please!

Hsu looked toward the ceiling in alarm as she battled to overcome the second corner. Her knees were shaking violently.

Sushma started to cry. Hastily, Eva pulled the Indian woman into the shaft, helped by Mukesh, who pushed from below and then hesitated, unsure as to whether he should follow his wife or help Hsu, who was edging her way along centimeter by centimeter.

"Get in!" ordered Eva. "I'll take care of Rebecca. Come on!"

Mukesh obeyed, squeezed past her, and disappeared into the ventilation shaft. Another creak came from above. The glowing rain became denser. Hsu screamed as sparks landed on her naked shoulders. She pressed herself against the wall, unable to carry on, frozen with fear.

"Rebecca!" Eva stretched her upper body out.

"I can't," groaned Hsu.

"You're almost there." She stretched her long arms out to the Chinese woman, trying to get a hold on her.

"My legs aren't doing what I tell them."

"Just a little further! Hold on to me."

Volley-like blows droned through the shaft. The cabin floor of E2 bulged out, then exploded into pieces.

No, pleaded Eva. Not now. Not yet. Please not yet!

She reached out as far as she could. Fiery reflections darted over the walls of the shaft. The Chinese woman overcame both her rigidity and the corner, managed to take an utterly fearless step, came closer, made her way to right beneath her, grasped her outstretched right hand, lifted her gaze to Eva—

And then up to the ceiling.

Time stood still.

With a crash, the floor plate broke free. Hsu's features contorted, reflecting the realization that she had lost, and froze. For the duration of a heartbeat, her gaze rested on Eva.

"No!" screamed Eva. "No!"

The Chinese woman pulled her hands away. As if wanting to welcome her end with open arms, she spread them out, let herself fall and tipped backward into the shaft. Eva reacted instinctively. In a flash, she pulled back, protected her head, and buried her face in her elbows. Centimeters away from her, the cabin floor thundered past, spitting out fountains of embers. It singed her lower arms, hands, and hair, but she didn't feel a thing. The elevator shaft filled with the sounds of crashing and banging. In distraught disbelief, she pulled herself over the edge and watched as the fiery cloud became smaller and paler, until it seemed to implode into the depths as the cabin floor fell deeper and deeper.

Rebecca's coffin lid.

"No," she whispered.

Tongues of fire lashed down from above. Eva pulled herself back into the ventilation shaft. Her feet found the ladder of their own accord. There was an identical control panel to the one in the passageway. On autopilot now, she touched it, and the trapdoor glided shut without a sound. Below her, she heard voices, the echo of feet on metallic ladder rungs. She had lost all concept of an imaginable future. Listlessly, she hung there in the heat of the shaft. The heat was unbearable here too, but she was shaking all over, freezing, as if her heart were pumping icy water, and couldn't get a grip of her thoughts, not even when the tears began to stream over her bony cheeks.

"Eva?" It was Karla, from deep below her. "Eva, are you there?"

Silently, she made her way down. To wherever that might be.

"Hey!" Heidrun pointed at the wall monitor showing the plan of the elevators. Through a channel to the left of E2, glowing dots were moving, disappearing for a short while, then appearing again, constantly changing their position. "What's that?"

"The ventilation shaft!" Lynn pushed her sweat-soaked hair off her forehead. "They're in the ventilation shaft."

By now, the staff elevator had disappeared from the screen. The computer reported it as having fallen, but had no information about E2 at all.

"Can they get out of there by themselves?" asked Ögi.

"It depends. If the fire has spread to the elevator shaft, then the loss of pressure could mean the exits are blocked."

"If there were a fire in the ventilation shaft they would be dead by now."

"The E2 shaft is on fire too, but they still made it through and across to the other side." Lynn massaged her temples. "Someone has to go to the lobby, quickly!"

"I'll go," said Heidrun.

"Good. To the left of E2 there's a wall casing made of bamboo—"

"I know it."

"The trough is on rails; just push it to the side. Behind it, you'll see a bulkhead with a control panel."

Heidrun nodded and set off.

"It leads into a short passageway," Lynn called after her. "Very short, not even 2 meters long, then there's another bulkhead. From there—"

"—it leads into the ventilation shaft. I've got it."

In long, bouncing strides, she hurried through the lobby, under the circulating model of the solar system and through to the elevators, of which only one was still usable at most. She turned her attention to the bamboo trough, rolled it aside, then hesitated. Mid-motion, she suddenly felt paralyzed. Millimeters over the sensor, the tips of her fingers froze, while a chill crept down her spine at the thought of what might lie behind the bulkhead. Would flames lash out at her? Was this her last conscious moment, would it be her last memory of a life of physical freedom, free from injury?

The fear subsided. Resolved now, she tapped the field. The bulkhead swung open and cool air came out. She walked into the passageway, opened the second bulkhead, put her head through, and looked up. It was a surreal sight. Walls, ladders, and emergency lights stretched out toward a murky vanishing point. High above her, she caught sight of people on the rungs.

"Down here!" she cried. "Here!"

Miranda Winter had lost her composure.

"Rebecca?" she sobbed.

Feeling distanced from the situation for a moment, O'Keefe reflected that she was one of the few people who still looked attractive while they were in tears. Many with well-formed physiognomy took on frog-like features in a state of tormented suffering, while others looked as if they actually wanted to laugh and weren't really sure how. Eyebrows slid up to the hairline, usually pretty noses swelled up to become oozing boils. He had seen every conceivable deformation in his time, but Miranda's despair harbored erotic charm, accentuated by her streaky, running black makeup.

Why was something like that going through his mind? He was tired of his thoughts. They were all just diversionary tactics to prevent him from feeling. And for what? Because grief created intimacy with others who were grieving, and because he took care to keep his distance from all kinds of intimacy? Was it really so much better to stumble out of Madigan's Pub on Talbot Street, utterly alone and completely pissed, all just to keep his distance?

"So we'll use the ventilation shafts," resumed Funaki, struggling to stay composed.

"Not the western shaft," said Lynn's image on the monitor. "It's too close to E2, and besides, the sensors there are reporting increasing smoke development. Try the other side, everything seems to be okay there."

"And what—" Funaki swallowed. "What about the others? Are they at least—"

Lynn fell silent. She looked away. O'Keefe noticed how awful she looked, just a Lynn-like shell with something staring out from it. Something he had no desire to get to know.

"They're fine," she said tonelessly.

Funaki nodded in self-reproach. "Then we'll open up the eastern shaft now."

"See you in the lobby, Michio. You know the way out."

As it happened, there was nothing left that could be burned.

The second oxygen tank had been drained to the last dregs, and all that remained of the three corpses was caked ashes. Whatever could have gone up in flames was already consumed, but it still continued to flicker and glow. After the partial fall of E2, the smoke in the shaft of the staff elevator had risen and become trapped, prevented from circulating by the shutdown of the ventilators, which would have distributed it everywhere. The temperature difference had created its own circulation system, however, and more and more clouds of smoke were emerging from the deformed materials. This meant that the elevator shaft which Eva and the others had crossed through barely fifteen minutes before now didn't even offer a breath of air or a centimeter of vision. At the height of the cabin's smoldering remains, the sealed trapdoors had melted to the west ventilation shaft, and this too was now full of smoke, although the shields of the east shaft were holding out for the time being. In the neck of Gaia, the temperature still resembled that of a solar furnace, dramatically increasing the viscosity of the steel beam which was supporting the head of the figure. Once again, Gaia's chin tilted a little, and this time—

—it was noticeable.

"The floor just moved," whispered Olympiada Rogacheva, grabbing on to Miranda, whose flood of tears ran dry at that very moment.

"I'm sure it's built to be elastic," she sniffed, patting Olympiada's hand. "Don't worry, sweetheart. Skyscrapers on Earth shake too, you know, when there's an earthquake."

"*You* may well be built elastically." O'Keefe stared outside, his mouth dry. "But Gaia certainly isn't."

"How would you know? Hey, Michio, what—"

"There's no time!" Funaki stood on the landing, waving wildly with both arms. "Come on. Quickly!"

"Maybe we're just suffering from mass hysteria," said Miranda to the distraught Olympiada as she followed Funaki into the Luna Bar and from there down into Selene. Again, the floor gave way beneath them.

"*Chikusho!*" hissed Funaki.

O'Keefe's knowledge of Japanese was practically non-existent, but after several days in the company of Momoka Omura he had become sufficiently familiar with swearwords.

"That bad?" he asked.

"Very. We can't afford to lose a single second." Funaki opened a cabinet, took out four oxygen masks, and hurried to one of the two free-standing columns, which O'Keefe had until now assumed to be decorative, clad with holographs of constellations. Now, as the Japanese man pushed one of their surfaces to the side, a man-size bulkhead came into view behind it.

"The ventilation shaft!"

"Yes." Funaki nodded. "It starts up here. Let's all cross our fingers. The control center said it's smoke-free inside, no loss of pressure." He handed out the masks. "But regardless. Let's put them on until we know for sure. Just slip them on so they're snug and the eyes are protected behind the visor.—No, the other way around, Miss Olympiada, the other way around!" His hands flapped around. "Miss Miranda, could you help her? Thank you. Mr. O'Keefe, may I see? Yes, just like that. Very good."

In no time at all, he had pulled his own mask on, checked it, and carried on talking, his voice muffled now. "As soon as the bulkhead is open, I'll go in. Wait until I give you the signal, then follow me one after the other, first Miss Olympiada, then Miss Miranda, then Mr. O'Keefe bringing up the rear. The ladder leads directly into the lobby. Stay close to me. Any questions?"

The women shook their heads.

"No," said Finn.

Funaki tapped the sensor, stepped back, and waited. The bulkhead swung open and warm air came out. O'Keefe stepped next to the Japanese man and looked down. They peered into a dimly lit shaft which dropped down into the depths.

"Visibility seems clear."

Funaki nodded. "Wait until I give the green light."

He climbed in, put both feet on the rungs, put his hands on the side struts and began to clamber down. His chest, shoulders, and head disappeared beneath the ledge. O'Keefe peered in after him. Funaki looked around and gazed appraisingly down below. After about 5 meters, he stopped his descent and tipped his face up toward them.

"Everything's okay so far. Come on."

"Olympiada, darling!" Miranda took the Russian woman in her arms, held her close, and kissed her on the forehead. "We're almost there, my sweet." She sank her voice to a whisper: "And after that you leave him. Do you hear me? You have to. Leave him. No woman has to put up with that."

• • •

The molecular bonds were starting to break.

It would have taken higher temperatures to melt the steel like butter, but the heat was still enough to transform some of the braces into a kind of glutinous rubber, which slowly deformed under the pressure of the tons of weight they bore. Gaia's head visibly compacted the weakened materials together and, in the process, created tensions which the stressed glass façade and mooncrete plates weren't able to stand up to. The water between the panes of the double glazing, evaporating, forced the structures apart—and, suddenly, one of the concrete modules simply broke right across, the full width of it.

Gaia's lower jaw dropped heavily onto the glass façade.

One after another, the inner and outer panes shattered. Splinters and water vapor swirled into the vacuum; rendered unstable, structural elements, tattered components of the life-support systems, and ashes were carried away in a chain reaction. The artificial atmosphere spread out around Gaia's neck like a cloud and evaporated in the heat of the sun's rays. But the major part was in the shade, with the result that the air crystallized as the coldness of outer space forced its way inside, extinguishing all flames in a second and cooling down the glowing steel so quickly that it wasn't able to solidify slowly, but instead froze in brittle fragility.

The support beams held out for a few more seconds.

Then they gave way.

This time, Gaia's head sank forward much more, held only by the main cord of the massive steel spine, which so far had not been so badly affected. The last remains of the neck front splintered, the chin tilted further, the layers of insulation above the shoulders cracked, the concrete modules ruptured, and a gaping hole opened up in the ventilation shaft.

O'Keefe stumbled backward over a table. Olympiada, who was just about to clamber into the shaft, was hurled against Miranda, knocking her down to the floor.

We're falling, he thought. The head is falling!

Full of horror, he pulled himself up, trying to get a grip of something. His right hand grasped hold of the edge of the air lock.

"Into the shaft," he cried out. "Quickly!"

He looked inside.

Into the shaft?

Maybe not! Funaki was staring up at him with his eyes wide, trying to climb back up again, but something was stopping him, pulling at him with all its might. He screamed something and stretched out his arm. O'Keefe leaned over to grasp his outstretched hand, when he suddenly had the eerie sensation that he was looking into the gullet of a living thing. His hair, his clothes, everything began to flap wildly. A powerful suction seized him, and in a flash he realized what was happening.

The air was being sucked out of Gaia's head. There must be a leak somewhere in the shaft.

The vacuum was threatening to swallow them up.

He braced himself against the frame, trying to reach Funaki's hand. The Japanese man tried with all his might to reach the next rung of the ladder. Out of the corner of his eye, O'Keefe saw the bulkhead starting to move, making its way up, the goddamn automatic mechanism, but it was just doing its job; the shaft had to close so they wouldn't all be sucked into it, but Funaki, he couldn't leave Funaki! Hands clung to his clothing; Miranda and Olympiada were screaming, preventing him from being sucked in. The bulkhead came closer. He stretched out his arm as far as he could, felt his fingertips touch the other man's for a second—then Funaki was torn from the rungs and disappeared into the abyss with a shrill scream.

The women pulled him away. The bulkhead slammed shut in front of his eyes. Breathless, they helped one another up, struggling to balance on the uneven floor of the restaurant. Eerie creaks and groans forced their way up to them from Gaia's depths, harbingers of even worse disaster.

Dana heard the same noises directly above her. A powerful blow had ripped her off her feet, followed by an immense roar, which had died away as abruptly as it came. But the gallery still seemed to be echoing from the explosion-like crash which had come before the roar. The entire building had swung like a tuning fork, then finally settled, and all at once there was deathly silence. Apart from the wails and squeaks in the roof, which sounded like cats roaming through the night in search of mates.

She ran to the bulkhead and hit her hands against the mechanism. It stayed shut.

"Lynn," she screamed.

No answer.

"Lynn! What's going on? Lynn!"

No one in the control center responded.

"Come on, talk to me! Something huge has broken up there. I don't want to die in here."

She looked around. By now, visibility in the gallery was pretty much clear again; the ventilators had done a good job. The pressure would soon be restored, but if what had happened up there was what she feared, then this area was in danger of being buried under the weight of the head sooner or later too.

She had to get out of here! She had to take control again.

"Lynn!"

"Dana." Lynn sounded like a robot. "There have been a number of incidents. Wait your turn."

Dana sank down with her back to the wall, exhausted. That damn bitch! She couldn't blame her of course, she had every reason to be angry, but pure hatred for Julian's daughter was burning up within Dana. In a way that was completely contrary to her nature, she began to take it personally. Lynn had brought this disaster on her. Just you wait, she thought.

CAPE HERACLIDES,
MONTES JURA, THE MOON

At about eleven o'clock, Momoka suddenly stopped.

"If he fell anywhere, then it would have been here," she said.

Julian, who was driving ahead of her, stopped too. They parked behind one another on the sunlit expanse of the Mare Imbrium. To their left, Cape Heraclides and the southern foothills of the Montes Jura towered out from the basalt sea, the steep outposts of the Sinus Iridum, the Rainbow Bay. It wasn't difficult to imagine that, instead of sitting in rovers, they were in expedition boats, looking at the land across the calm sea; the only thing missing was perhaps a little color and the picturesque appearance of a lighthouse on the rocky cliffs. As if to complete the illusion, satellite images were displaying the widely dispersed, flat waves in which the frozen flood of the Mare fell into the Rainbow Bay. They were, however, old images, as the weather conditions over Sinus Iridum had changed since the beginning of helium-3 mining. A broad bank of fog had now swallowed the waves and seemed to be drawing in landward. From where they had stopped, they could just make out the clouds in the distance, a shapeless gray weighing down on the stony sea.

"Could he have flown another route?" asked Evelyn.

"It's possible." Julian looked up at the sky, as if Locatelli had left some sign behind for them in it.

"Probable even," said Rogachev. "He had problems regaining control of the shuttle. If he succeeded, he could have drifted off course a fair bit."

"Where exactly is the mining station again?" asked Amber.

"In the mining zone." Julian pointed his outstretched arm toward the dust barrier. "Just 100 kilometers from here on the axis between Cape Heraclides and Cape Laplace in the north."

"By the way, how's our oxygen looking?"

"Good, considering the circumstances. The problem is that we can't rely on the maps anymore."

Amber lowered her map. Until now, she had had the advantage of clear visibility. Every crater, every hill marked on the lunar maps had reliably appeared on the horizon at some point, clarifying their position precisely, but in the sea of dust their sense of orientation would be incredibly reduced.

"So we should try our best not to get lost," Evelyn put in with matter-of-fact firmness.

"And Warren?" asked Momoka insistently. "What about Warren?"

"Well," Julian hesitated. "If only we knew that."

"What a helpful response, thank you!" She snorted. "Why don't we look for him?"

"We can't risk that, Momoka."

"Why not? We have to go to the foot of the Cape anyway."

"And from there directly on to the station."

"We don't even know if he really fell," Evelyn reflected. "Maybe—"

"Of course he did!" exploded Momoka. "Don't kid yourself! Do you really want to drive happily on while he's stuck in a wreck together with that asshole Carl?"

"There's no question of us doing it happily," protested Evelyn. "But the zone is huge. He could be anywhere."

"But—"

"We're not looking for him," said Julian decisively. "I can't be responsible for that."

"You really are unbelievable!"

"No, but it would be unbelievable to not get to the mining station because of you," said Evelyn, her tone audibly cooler. "It's not that we don't care about Warren, but we can't search the entire Mare Imbrium until we run out of oxygen."

"I have a suggestion." Oleg cleared his throat. "In a way, Momoka is right. We have to go over to the Cape anyway, so why don't we just drive along a little and keep our eyes open? Not an organized search, just 3 or 4 kilometers, and then on toward the mining station."

"Sounds sensible," said Evelyn.

Julian pondered the suggestion for a moment. So far they hadn't needed to touch the oxygen reserves.

"Okay, I think we can do that," he said reluctantly.

They veered off, headed for the landmass, and steered into the bay a little, the ascending mountain range to their left. A few minutes later, they reached a shallow ditch which stretched out diagonally across the ground, seeming to emerge right out of the fog.

Julian slowed down the rover.

"That's not a ditch," said Oleg.

They were staring at a broadly carved-out path. It had been torn into the regolith like a wound, its edges forced up.

"It's fresh," said Amber.

Momoka stood up from her seat and stared into the distant cloud, then turned to the other side.

"There," she whispered.

Something was lying at an angle on the slope where the strand of the Cape swung up to the mountain range. It was reflecting the sunlight: a small, elongated, and alarmingly familiar shape.

It also marked the end of the path.

Without saying a word, Julian accelerated. He drove at top speed, and yet Momoka still managed to overtake him. The terrain was only gently inclined, bearable for the rovers, which thanks to the flexible wheel suspension were able to work their way swiftly up the path. By now there was no longer any doubt that they were looking at the wreck of the Ganymede. Its legs gone, it rested in the middle of the rockfall on the slope, wedged tightly between larger chunks of rock. Its rear hatch was wide open. Not far from the ramp lay a body, its head and shoulders in the shadow of the rock. While Julian was still figuring out how he could hold Momoka back, she had already jumped down from the driver's seat and was rushing up the hill. He heard her wheezing on the speakers in his helmet, saw her fall to her knees. Her upper body was swallowed by the shadow, then a short, ghostly cry resounded out.

"Evelyn," said Julian on a separate frequency to Evelyn. "I think you would be the best one to . . ."

"Okay," said Evelyn unhappily. "I'll look after her."

SINUS IRIDUM, THE MOON

Considering all the setbacks he had faced so far, Hanna had been amazed to make it to the mining station without problem. He was all too familiar with the nature of escalation. The damaged axle of the buggy was *bound* to break apart prematurely, and that's exactly what it did, the dramaturgy of failure obliging 15 kilometers too soon. It wasn't a pothole or geological fault that finished it off, however. It broke in two with banal finality on even ground, bringing the vehicle to an abrupt halt, forcing it into a spin, and that was that.

Hanna sprang down into the debris. The basic rule of survival was to think positive. The fact that the old banger had even made it that long, for example. And the fact that he had an extraordinary sense of orientation, which had enabled him to find his way without fail so far. Regardless of the miserable visibility, he had held his course, of that he was certain. As long as he just kept going in a straight line, he should reach the mining station within about an hour. But he would have to really watch out from now on. The dust concealed dangers that weren't so easy to get away from on foot as in the buggy. He would have to keep his distance. Admittedly the beetles were quite slow, but the filigree, nimble spiders had a tendency to make unpleasant surprise appearances.

Hanna let his gaze wander. Some distance away, he saw a ghostly silhouette hurrying along toward him. He walked over to the buggy's cargo bed, grabbed a survival pack in each hand, and marched off.

Cape Heraclides,
Montes Jura, The Moon

While Evelyn attended to her emotional support duties, Julian, Amber, and Oleg feverishly searched the inside of the wreck and the nearby area, but there was nothing to suggest that Hanna was still around.

"How did he get away?" Amber wondered.

"The Ganymede had a buggy on board," said Julian, as he trudged around the nose of the shuttle. "And it's disappeared."

"Yes, and I know where," Oleg's voice rang out from the opposite end of the ship. "Maybe you should come over here."

Seconds later, they were all standing in the path. So far they had only noticed the devastation the shuttle had inflicted on the regolith when making its emergency landing, the brutality with which it had dug into the surface, but something different now captured their attention: a story about someone who had set off into the far-away dust, a story told by—

"Tire tracks," said Julian.

"Your buggy," confirmed Oleg. "Hanna has driven down along the path and out onto the plain. I don't know how well he knows the area, but what else could he be interested in other than the place we also want to get to?"

"So the bastard just fucked off!" Momoka came over with Evelyn, down from the hill where Warren Locatelli lay.

"Momoka," began Julian. "I'm so terribly—"

"There's no need. No outpourings of sympathy, please. The only thing I'm interested in is killing him."

"We'll give Warren a proper burial."

"There's no time for that." Her voice had lost all modulation. Auto-pilot driven by rage. "I looked at Warren's face, Julian. And do you know what? He spoke to me. Not some jabbering from the other side, not that old shit. He would speak to you too, if you took the effort to go over there to him. You just have to look him in the face. He doesn't look the same as he did before, but you can hear him say loudly and clearly that humans have no business being up here. None at all! Not us, and not you either," she added in a hostile tone.

"Momoka, I—"

"He said we should never have accepted your invitation!"

But you did, thought Julian, even though he didn't say a word.

"Carl has driven to the mining zone," said Amber.

"Very well." Momoka marched over to the rovers. "We have to go there anyway, right?"

"No, wait," said Julian.

"For what?" She stopped. "You seemed to be in a hurry just now."

"I've found some additional oxygen reserves in the storage space of the shuttle. Really, Momoka, we have time to give him a decent—"

"That's very sensitive of you, but Warren is already buried. Carl slit open his stomach and took off his helmet. I don't see any reason to stone him too."

There was icy silence for a second.

"So?" she asked. "Shall we go?"

"I'll drive," said Evelyn.

"I'm happy to as well—" Oleg offered.

"None of you will drive," decided Momoka. "If any of us has reason to drive, then it's me. To follow him."

"Are you sure?" asked Amber cautiously.

"I've never been so sure," said Momoka, and her voice made her visor steam up.

"Fine." Julian looked out over the plain. "Seeing as we don't have any satellite connection, I'll link the four of us on one frequency. From now on, no one will be able to hear us, not even Carl, should we get close to him. It might help."

GAIA, VALLIS ALPINA, THE MOON

"There must be a way!"

Tim had lost all sense of time. Seconds seemed to drag out endlessly, but at the same time an hour dwindled into a disheartening nothing, brief enough to feel useless. Although the deaths had had the relative advantage of distracting them from the bomb, it took on a new, tyrannical presence now that they had alerted the prisoners to the threatening cataclysm. Strangely, Lynn seemed to gain more strength the more confused the situation became. It wasn't that she was really doing any better, but catastrophes, *real* catastrophes, seemed to have an exorcising effect on the demons in her head—even her perception of Tim was gradually becoming closer to his true nature. They were nothing other than the monsters of hypothesis, creatures from the family of what-ifs, the genus of could-bes, all equipped with the torture devices of paths left untaken.

He felt deeply sorry for his sister.

The fear that her work could turn out to be vulnerable and faulty must have cost her every last rational thought. Tim was now convinced that his uneasiness, fed by Dana Lawrence's suspicions, had proved to be a tragic misunderstanding. Lynn wasn't the one trying to cause damage to her own creation and its inhabitants. Her mind might be struggling against disintegration, but for the moment there was probably nothing better than for her to be forced to react by her nightmares being realized. After all, she was even explaining the latest developments to Dana, her newly elected arch enemy, and taking a huge, humbling leap by asking the fired director for her advice.

"We've looked at the images from the external camera," she said. "The flames have clearly led to a partial breakdown in the steel skeleton within Gaia's neck. So the fire should have been extinguished, but now the structure is damaged. There are a number of gaping leaks up there."

Dana was silent. She seemed to be thinking.

"Come on, Dana," pressed Lynn. "I need your assessment of the situation."

"Well, what's yours?"

"That there's only one way out for Miranda, Olympiada, and Finn, and it's not downward."

"Over the viewing terrace you mean?"

"Yes. Out through the air lock in the Mama Quilla Club."

"We'd have to overcome two problems with that," said Dana. "First, you can't climb up over the outside of the head."

"Yes you can. We planned for a roll-out ladder in case of emergency."

"But it wasn't installed."

"Why not? According to the safety regulations—"

"For optical reasons. On your instructions, by the way," added Dana, with audible satisfaction. "We could carry out the installation of course, but it would be dreadfully complicated under the prevailing conditions and it would also take a considerable amount of time."

"The second problem is harder to solve," interjected O'Keefe, who was switched on to their frequency. So the fiber optic connection still seemed to be intact at least. "We don't have any space suits up here. So the terrace won't be much help to us."

"Couldn't we bring some up?" asked Ögi. He was relentlessly pacing the room, taking equally long, precisely measured steps, or so it seemed to Tim. He was the only one who had stayed behind in the control center. The others were seated in the lobby, trying to get a grip on things with Heidrun's help. "El still seems to be functioning."

"But El only goes to the neck," said Tim.

"Forget it." Lynn shook her head. "The shaft is completely sealed off to protect us from the vacuum. After the structural changes up there the doors wouldn't open up again anyway. There's only one option."

"Through the air lock," said Dana.

"Yes." Lynn dug her teeth into her lower lip. "From the outside. We have to get the suits inside through the air lock of the viewing platform."

"But for that you'll have to bring them *up* first?" said Finn. "And it won't stop creaking up here so it has to be quick! I don't know how much longer the head will hold."

"Callisto," said Dana. "Bring them up on the Callisto."

"Where is Nina anyway?" asked Tim.

Lynn looked at him in surprise. In the heat of the moment she had completely forgotten the Danish pilot.

"Wasn't she with you in the bar?" asked Lynn.

"Who, Nina?" O'Keefe shook his head. "No."

"And has someone down here—" Lynn paused. "Oh shit! In order to bring up the Callisto, we need someone who can carry out precision maneuvers in a large craft." The last trace of color drained from her face. "We have to find Nina!"

"We can't wait that long," urged Finn.

"Then—" She tried to catch her breath in an effort to fight off a panic attack. "We could—we have ten grasshoppers in the garage! Almost all of you have already flown a craft like that."

"Sure, close to the ground," said Dana. "But do you think you could manage this? Climb up more than 150 meters with a grasshopper and carry out a precision landing on the terrace?"

"The precision landing isn't a problem," said Tim. "But the height—"

"Technically speaking the height is the least of our worries; theoretically they can be used to fly in open space." Lynn brushed her hands over her eyes. "But Dana's right. *I* don't trust myself. Not in my condition. I'd lose my nerve."

It was the first time she had publicly dropped her guard. Tim had never known her to do that. He took it as a good sign.

"Okay, fine," he said. "How many of the things do we need? Each hopper can take one additional person, so three all together, right? Three pilots. I'll do it. Walo?"

"I've never been up that high with one, but if Lynn thinks it will work—"

Tim ran into the lobby and clapped his hands.

"Someone!" he called. "We need one person for the third hopper."

"Me" said Heidrun, without knowing what it was even about.

"Are you sure? You have to land the thing on Gaia's head. Do you think you can do it?"

"Generally speaking, I think I'm capable of doing anything . . ."

"No fear of heights?"

". . . but whether I manage it or not is a different matter."

"No, it's not." Tim shook his head. "You *have* to manage it. You have to know *now* whether you can or not, otherwise—"

She stood up and brushed her white hair behind her ears.

"No, no 'otherwise.' I'll manage it."

There were spares of all the space suits concealed behind a wall in the lobby, which meant they didn't have to go up over the bridges to the lockers. They helped each other into the suits, put the gear for Olympiada Rogacheva, Miranda, and Finn together and packed it into boxes.

"Are there problems in the corridor?" asked Tim.

"No, the sensors are registering steady values." Lynn went ahead of them, led them to a passageway on the other side of the elevators, and opened a large bulkhead. Behind it was a spacious stairway with steep steps.

"You'll get down below this way. I'll open the garage from the control center."

Tim reflected that she should perhaps have built a route like this upstairs too, but bit back the observation.

"Good luck," said Lynn.

Tim hesitated. Then he put both arms around his sister and pulled her close. "I know what you're going through," he said softly. "And I'm unbelievably proud of you. I have no idea how you're coping with all this."

"Nor do I," she whispered.

"Everything's going to be fine," he said.

"What's left?" She pulled away from his embrace and grasped his hands. "Tim, you have to believe me, I have nothing to do with Carl, no matter what Dana says. It's myself I'm destroying, not anything else."

"This isn't *your* fault, Lynn. There's nothing you can do!"

"Now go." The corner of her mouth twitched. "Quickly!"

• • •

There was something inherently calming about the empty, coolly lit corridor, designed to reinstate and strengthen trust in technological advancement. Its rationality made it seem immune to corruption from recklessly caused catastrophes, but Tim reminded himself that, in a way, it had all started here, with the appearance of Carl Hanna rousing Julian's mistrust. He wondered whether the bomb was hidden below them. A few hours hadn't been enough to search every nook and cranny. How small was a mini-nuke? Was it under the conveyor belt that stretched out alongside them? Under one of the floor tiles? Behind the wall, in the ceiling?

They had suggested that Sushma, Mukesh, Eva, and Karla take the Lunar Express to the foot of the Montes Alpes and wait there at a safe distance until they had either freed the prisoners or been blown to smithereens with the hotel. But they had all insisted on staying, even Sushma, who had bravely tried to suppress her fear. In order to give their battered morale a boost, Lynn had ended up sending the women to look for Nina Hedegaard, since this would at least keep them occupied. Tim hoped fervently that his sister wouldn't crack up back at the control center, but was reassured to a certain extent by the fact that Mukesh had stayed with her. They reached the garage and saw the rafters of the retractable roof disappear into their cases. The starry sky was twinkling above them. A dozen buggies stood there waiting for a party that would never take place.

The shapeless Callisto rested opposite them with clumsy assertiveness, as if suggesting it was capable of flying to Mars. *Ugly but reliable*, as poor Chuck had joked just the day before. Compared with the shuttle, the laughable grasshoppers looked like toys.

"Who's flying in front?" asked Heidrun.

"Tim," said Ögi decisively as he stowed the box containing Olympiada's suit into the small cargo hold. "Then you, then me, to make sure I don't lose you."

"Lynn," said Tim over his helmet radio. "We're setting off."

He still couldn't get used to the lack of engine noise. The hopper rose without a sound, exited the garage, and started its ascent. From behind, Gaia looked just the same as it always had: superior and indestructible. The camera in his helmet sent images back to the control center. He flew in an arc, as agreed with Lynn beforehand, so she could get an idea of how the front section looked. He intensified the thrust, let the force carry him toward the shoulder of the huge figure, then held his breath.

"Good God." Walo's voice piped up in his helmet.

It had been obvious even from the side view that something wasn't right. Parts of the façade were missing or lay in ruins, and in places the naked steel of the support framework was exposed. Now, as they flew directly toward it, the full extent of the destruction was revealed. The contourless face was no longer focused on the Earth, but just beneath it. Where the neck had once been, there was now a gaping, black, collapsed hole. The complete front section was broken away, and Gaia's chin was sunk so far that only the lower half of the elevator doors were still peeping out.

Tim steered the hopper closer. The colossal skull seemed to be hanging by a thread at the neck. E2 stood open, its insides just a gullet corroded by flames. Steel columns, grotesquely deformed, faced toward him. His stomach filled with dread, he dared to look down one more time. There was debris distributed all over the figure's upper thigh, albeit not much. And it looked as if Gaia were nodding to him. Finn was right: they had come not a moment too soon.

On the ascent, he saw the sealed-off Chang'e, and was convinced he could make out smoke and rust inside it, burnt furnishings, but the dark windows with their gold filtering concealed what lay beyond, leaving any detail to the imagination. Out of the blue, he was overcome by an attack of vertigo. The hopper's platform had no railings, and any flying carpet would have seemed like a spacious dance floor in comparison. Quickly reassuring himself that Heidrun and Walo were behind him, he passed Selene and the Luna Bar and followed the arch of the forehead around to the viewing platform. Figures started to move beneath him: O'Keefe, Olympiada, and Miranda were making their way toward the air lock. He swiveled the jets, reduced his speed, overshot the terrace a little, turned, and came to a standstill right next to the railing. Not the most elegant of landings. Alongside him, at an appropriate distance, Heidrun landed as if she had been flying hoppers her whole life. Meanwhile, Ögi flew a lap of honor amid a great deal of cursing, then finally forced the hopper down, clattering one of the telescopic legs along the railing in the process.

"I'm actually a gliding and ballooning enthusiast," he said apologetically, before unloading his box and carrying it to the air lock, a double bulkhead in the floor which measured several meters in diameter. "But Switzerland is a little more spacious."

Tim jumped off his hopper.

"Finn, we're above you," he said. Lynn had connected their helmet radios with the Gaia's internal network so that everyone could communicate at once. A few seconds passed, then O'Keefe chimed in.

"Okay, Tim. What should we do?"

"Nothing just yet. We'll call up the air lock elevator, send the boxes with the space suits down to you and—"

He stopped.

Was it his imagination, or had the floor begun to shake under his feet?

"Hurry up!" called O'Keefe. "It's starting again!"

Where was the control console for the air lock? There. His fingers darted as he entered the command, and the air was sucked out at an agonizingly slow speed. The shaking intensified and became like an earthquake, then the whole thing stopped as abruptly as it had begun.

"The elevator's on its way up," Ögi gasped breathlessly.

The air lock doors opened on the floor beneath them. A glass cabin pushed its way out, spacious enough to hold a dozen people, and opened at the front. They quickly piled the boxes inside.

"I'll go down with them," said Heidrun.

"What?" Ögi looked alarmed. "Why?"

"To help them. With the suits, so it's quicker." Before he could protest, she had disappeared into the cabin and pressed the downward switch. The elevator closed.

"My darling," whispered Ögi.

"Don't worry, Commander. We'll all be back in five minutes."

Finn O'Keefe saw the elevator approaching, with someone in it whose slim legs were familiar to him even through centimeter-thick, steel-fiber-strengthened artificial fibers. He waited impatiently until the internal pressure was restored and the front bulkhead had glided to the side.

"Here we go!" said Heidrun, throwing the first of the boxes toward him.

Olympiada, as white as chalk, handed the second box on to Miranda, then began to empty her own.

"Thank you," she said earnestly. "I'll never forget this."

In immense hurry, they slipped into their gear: helping one another, closing hinges, fastening clamps, heaving packs onto their backs, and putting their helmets on.

"Would it be asking too much to want to get out of the hotel right away?" asked Miranda. "It's just, you know, I don't want to get blown into the sky, and I've emptied the mini-bar already, so—"

"You can count on it," said Lynn's voice.

"Oh, don't get me wrong," Miranda hurried to assure her. "There's nothing wrong with your hotel."

"Yes there is. It's a piece of shit," said Lynn coldly.

Miranda giggled.

At that very moment, the floor gave way.

For one strange moment, Tim thought the entire opposite side of the ravine was being lifted up by elemental forces. Then, as he watched the grasshoppers hopping across the terrace and Ögi whooshing toward the railings with his arms flailing about, he lost his balance, landed on his stomach, and slid behind the flying machines.

Gaia was bowing her head in face of the inevitable.

Chaos roared in his helmet. Anyone who had a voice was screaming in competition with all the others. He rolled onto his back, got back on his feet, and stretched out, which was a mistake, because he lost his balance again right away. He was pulled forcefully against the railing, tumbled right over it, and smacked down onto the smooth, sloping glass surface.

And slid down.

No, he thought. No!

In fear and panic, he tried to get a grip on the reflective surface, but there was nothing there to get hold of. He slipped further, away from the protective enclosure of the terrace. One of the hoppers sailed down behind him and crashed onto the glass. Tim reached out for it and grasped the steering handle just as he saw another flying device disappear into the depths. It suddenly felt as if he were hovering in the air; he couldn't get a grip anymore and hung over the abyss, his legs flailing around. With his hand clamped onto the machine's handle, he screamed "Stop!"—and as if his plea, his wretched wish to survive, had been acknowledged somewhere out there among the cold gaze of the myriad stars, the movement of the huge skull came to an abrupt halt.

"Tim! Tim!"

"Everything's okay, Lynn," he panted. "Everything's—"

Okay? Nothing was okay. With both arms—thank God he wasn't heavy—he pulled himself up on the flying device, noticing with relief that one of its telescopic legs had got wedged in the railings, then realizing, with horror, that it was slowly slipping out.

A jolt went through the hopper.

Dismayed, Tim dangled in open air, unable to decide whether he should resume his ascent and thereby rip the hopper out of its anchorage once and for all, or not move at all, which would only delay his death by a few seconds. At the next moment, a figure appeared behind the terrace railing, climbed over it, and slid carefully downward, both hands bent around the rails.

"Climb up onto me," panted Ögi. "Come on!"

Ögi's feet were now level with Tim's helmet, right next to him. Tim gasped for air, reached his arm out—

The hopper came loose.

Swinging back and forth, he hung on to Ögi's ankles, grasped his shin guards, clung to his knees, climbed up him like a ladder and over the railing, then helped his rescuer to get back to safety. In front of them, tilted to about forty-five degrees, the floor of the terrace rose up into the heights like a smooth slide.

He had survived.
But they'd now lost all three grasshoppers.

"No! I'm flying up there."
Lynn pushed herself away from the control panel, crumpled over, and fell against Mukesh. Horrified, the Indian stared at the wall monitor, watching the terrible images being transmitted by Tim's camera and the external cameras on the opposite side of the ravine. The glass-fiber connection to the Mama Quilla Club had been broken, but they could now hear the voices of those trapped via the helmet radio.
"It's stopped." Miranda, out of breath. "What do we do now?"
"Olympiada?" O'Keefe.
"I'm here." Olympiada spoke, sounding haggard.
"Where?"
"Behind the bar, I'm . . . behind the bar."
"My darling?" Ögi, distraught. "Where on earth—"
"I don't know." Heidrun, sucking in air through her teeth. "Somewhere. Hit my head."
"Everyone out!" Tim. "You can't stay there. See whether the air lock is working."
Lynn's temples were throbbing with hypnotic rhythm. Colorful smog began to whirl around. Having to watch Gaia's skull tilt so suddenly that the chin was now almost resting on the chest had made her heart stop, and now it was pumping all the harder to make up for it. Gaia looked as though she were sleeping. Her head must truly now be hanging on to the shoulders by a thread.
"Everything's at an angle," said O'Keefe. "We're tumbling all over each other like skittles; I don't know if we'll even get into the air lock."
Head. Head. Head. How much longer would *her* head stay on her shoulders?
"We'll come and get you," she said. "We still have seven grasshoppers. I'll fly."
"Me too," said Mukesh.
"We need a third. Quickly! Get Karla, she's in the best state out of all of us."
Mukesh hurried out. Lynn followed him and plundered the depot with the substitute space suits. Several were missing, including hers. Suddenly remembering that not all the suits were stored in the lobby, she ran back into the control center and to the closed bulkhead on the rear wall. Behind it lay a small storeroom for spare equipment, including fire extinguishers, suits, and air masks. She waited until the steel door had glided to the side, walked in, and was surprised to find the light on. Her gaze fell on the locker with the equipment, on the piles of boxes, on the dead faces of the air masks neatly lined up in their cabinets, and

on the dead face of Sophie Thiel, who was leaning upright against the wall. Her eyes were open, and her pretty face had been divided in two by a streak of dried blood originating from a hole in her forehead.

Lynn didn't move.

She just stood there, staring at the corpse. Strangely—and *thankfully*, in the face of everything—it didn't unleash any emotions in her. None at all. Maybe it was just the fact that its appearance was too much and too late, or the pushiness with which it demanded its moment in the limelight amid an inferno of Dante-like proportions, as if they didn't have other problems. So after a few seconds, she ignored Sophie and started carrying out the boxes containing the bio-suits.

"Hello, Lynn."

She looked up, confused.

Dana Lawrence was standing in the doorway.

Heidrun and O'Keefe made their way hand over hand over table and chair legs, supporting, pulling and pushing Olympiada up toward the air lock. Contrary to what she had thought, the Russian woman had not fallen behind the bar, but behind the DJ booth. Meanwhile, Miranda hung on to the side of the air lock like a monkey on a pole, her hand laid across the sensor field to keep it open.

"Can you guys make it? Shall I help?"

"I can get up there by myself," groaned Olympiada defiantly.

"No, you can't," said Heidrun. "Your leg is injured; you can hardly stand on it."

The main problem resulting from the change to their spatial surroundings was not so much the tilting of the floor, as that of the air lock. The front section was now turned toward Gaia's glass face and pointing downward. And it wasn't just that it was incredibly difficult to get into it in this way; if they didn't watch out up there, they would fall outside faster than they intended.

"You'll have to try to get behind the elevator as soon as you get to the terrace," said Tim. "It will give you something to grip. Oh, and bring something long and sharp with you, like a knife."

"What for?" groaned O'Keefe, as he steered Olympiada toward Miranda Winter's outstretched hand.

"To block the cabin so it doesn't go down again."

"I said I could manage." Olympiada wrapped her hands around the cabin railing and pulled herself into the elevator with a grimly determined expression. "Go and look for your knife, Finn."

They grasped the railing tightly and waited. O'Keefe was only gone for a minute. When he came back, carrying an ice pick, he had a wad of material flung over his shoulder. Miranda let the bulkheads close and pump the air out.

The cabin shuddered.

"Not again," groaned Olympiada.

"Don't worry," Miranda reassured her. "It'll stop in a second."

"What are you planning to do?" asked Dana.

The bulkheads had finally opened and the armored plating had crept back into the hidden cavities. Freed from her prison, Dana had jumped down from the gallery over the bridge into the lobby, all the while thinking through her next steps: to break off the rescue mission, capture the Callisto, and get the hell out of here. In the course of the past one and a half hours, she had been forced to win back trust by making like she sympathized with Lynn, but that was over now. Julian's hated daughter was alone in the control center. She was no serious opponent; the loss of her weapon wouldn't make the task easy, but she could make do with her hands.

"I'm flying up there," said Lynn, her face devoid of any expression, then went back into the room and hauled out two large boxes containing space suits. Dana cocked her head. Had she not seen Sophie? No, there was no way she hadn't seen her, but why did she seem so unaffected? Surely such a sight would have thrown her off track, but Lynn looked indifferent, as if she were on autopilot. Her gaze empty, she took off her jacket and began to unbutton her blouse.

"Come on, Dana, get yourself a suit too."

"What for?"

"You're flying one of the hoppers. The more of us there are, the quicker—" Suddenly, she stopped and stared at Dana with her red-rimmed eyes. "Hey, you've piloted the Callisto before, right?"

Dana came slowly closer, bent over, and readied her own bodily murder weapons.

"Yes," she said slowly.

"Good, then we'll do it like that. No hoppers."

Incoherent conversation came out of the loudspeakers, hastily uttered sentences. Silently, Dana walked around the console.

"Hey, Dana!" Lynn wrinkled her forehead. "Are you listening to me?"

She moved faster. Lynn craned her head back, looked her up and down from beneath her half-closed eyelids, and took a step back. Her expression came back to life. A hardly perceptible flicker betrayed her suspicion.

"You'll fly the Callisto, do you hear me?"

Sure, thought Dana, but without you.

"No, that won't be necessary!"

As if she'd been hit by lightning, Dana stopped and turned around. Nina had come into the control center, accompanied by Karla. She was dressed in her space suit, carrying her helmet under her arm, and looked thoroughly contrite.

"I'm sorry, Lynn, Miss Lawrence, I'm very sorry indeed: I wasn't at my post. I fell asleep in the rest area. Karla walked past me three times, but then she managed to find me after all and told me everything. I'll fly the shuttle."

Dana forced a smile. She would have been confident enough of taking on Lynn and Karla, but Nina Hedegaard was incredibly fit and had quick reflexes. At that moment, Mukesh Nair stormed in, bathed in sweat, and the bubble of Dana's quick getaway burst.

"Karla," he called, exhausted. "There you are. And Nina! Miss Lawrence, thank heavens."

"Our plan has changed," said Lynn. "Nina's flying up with the shuttle." She walked over to the console and spoke into the microphone: "Sushma, Eva, back to the control center. Right away!"

Dana folded her arms behind her back. Nina was by far the better pilot; any objections on her part would have been futile.

"You have a lot to make up for," she said strictly. "I'm sure you realize that."

"I'm sorry, really I am!" Nina lowered her gaze. "I'll get them out of there."

"I'll come too. You'll need help."

Without waiting for an answer, Dana walked across the control center, went into the room containing Sophie's corpse, and jumped back. Feigning rage and horror, she spun around toward Lynn.

"Damn it! Why didn't you tell me about *that*?"

"Because it's not important," answered Lynn calmly.

"Not important? Again something that's not important? Are you completely insa—"

In a flash, Lynn stormed over, grabbed Dana by the neck and threw her against the doorframe, making her head jerk back and crash against it painfully.

"Just you dare," she hissed.

"You *are* insane."

"If you suggest one more time that I'm insane, you'll get a very tangible impression of what insanity really is. Mukesh, put your suit on, the box with the XL label! Karla, box S!"

Dana stared at her with unconcealed rage. Her entire body was trembling. She could have killed Julian's daughter with a few unspectacular hand movements, right this very second. Without breaking eye contact, she put one finger after another around Lynn's wrist and wrenched it from her throat.

"Now, now Lynn," she whispered. "Not in front of the guests! How would that look?"

• • •

After Gaia's last nod, the air lock was jutting out from the viewing platform at such an angle that it was now pointing at the faraway Earth
like a cannon. They held on to the railing, and each other, as the cabin
bulkheads glided to the side.

"Oh, wonderful," said Miranda sarcastically. The view over the terrace couldn't have been more worrying.

The world had tipped by forty-five degrees; millions of tons of rock
seemed to be eager to topple toward them from the ravine opposite.
Where the terrace ended, Tim and Ögi were huddled against the railing to prevent whichever one of them might lose their grip from falling
into the depths. Miranda reached out for the frame of the open air lock,
grasped hold of it, and pulled herself outside. The boots of her bio-suit
were equipped with powerful treads to prevent them from slipping.
Her fingers found a grip in an indentation. With her legs spread and
the unrolled wad of material—several tablecloths from Selene knotted
together—slung around her hips, she worked her way up the slope. The
makeshift rope had been O'Keefe's brilliant idea; the other end of it was
fastened to Olympiada's chest guard.

"Okay. Pass her toward me."

Heidrun steered the Russian woman out of the air lock, waited until
she had a firm grasp on the railing, then let her go. Olympiada immediately crumpled over and slipped down the slope, but instead of falling she
hung on the end of Miranda's umbilical cord. Miranda climbed further
up along the shaft of the cabin until she was able to crawl under it. With
her feet wedged against the wall of the shaft, she heaved Olympiada up,
unknotted the cloth, and let it back down. Heidrun then hurried swiftly
upward, followed by O'Keefe, who had rammed the ice pick into the air
lock door to prevent it from shutting and sending the shaft back down.

"Everything okay there?" called Ögi.

"More than okay!" said Heidrun.

"Good. We're coming up to you."

It was relatively easy to pull themselves up over the railing, but once
they got there it was still a fair distance to the air lock. Miranda threw
the rope to them. After two attempts, Tim finally got hold of it, knotted
it around the bars of the railing, and they made their way across hand
over hand. It was incredibly tight behind the cabin with six of them, but
at least they had a stable wall at their backs to prevent them from sliding down. They clung on alongside one another, hardly daring to move
through fear that too much movement could tip Gaia's head clean off.

"Lynn, everyone's outside now," said Tim.

The glass wall shook. Heidrun reached for Ögi's hand.

"Lynn?"

No answer.

"Strange," sighed Miranda. "I never thought I'd end up regretting it."

"Regretting what?" asked Olympiada hoarsely.

"The swimming accident."

"Before Miami?" She cleared her throat. "The one you went to court for?"

"Yes, exactly. My poor Louis."

"What exactly do you regret?" asked O'Keefe, tired. "The fact that he died, or that you helped?"

"I was found innocent," said Miranda, in an almost cheerful tone. "They couldn't prove anything."

A new quake ran through Gaia's skull and refused to let up. Olympiada groaned and fastened her grip to O'Keefe's thigh.

"Lynn!" screamed Tim. "What's going on there?"

"Tim?" It was Lynn. Finally! "Hold on, I'm on my way. We're coming to get you."

Lynn had insisted on their all leaving the Gaia together. In the maelstrom of her disintegrating sanity, the realization still won through that Dana was playing dirty somehow, and that it wouldn't have been a good idea to let her fly alone with Nina. Resolving both evacuation and rescue at the same time seemed to be the most efficient plan, and had a sense of well-ordered finality. She graciously acknowledged Dana's laboriously concealed rage and ferocious hate and felt herself become strangely calm. Yet at the same time she was overwhelmed by the desire to roar with laughter. It was just that, if she started, she probably wouldn't ever be able to stop.

They went into the sweltering body of the Callisto. Nina opened the rear hatch and ignited the jets. They rose vertically up into the star-sprinkled circus dome, below which they had once had the best seats in the house for viewing magic tricks and clownery, and where they now had to pull off the murderous acrobatics of saving lives.

"Hey, you guys," said Nina. "Are you still there?"

"Not for much longer," prophesied Heidrun.

"We can forget the shuttle air lock. It's too near to the engines, and I have to maintain the counterthrust in order not to slip. I'll approach in reverse with the rear hatch open, okay? I'll have to avoid touching the head, so get ready to do some chin-ups."

"Chin-ups, somersaults, we'll do whatever you want."

They ascended further. First Gaia's back was visible from the cockpit of the shuttle, then the neck with its exposed steel backbone came into full view. Lynn couldn't help thinking about what Gaia embodied in Julian's eyes: her own image, to excess. And they really were becoming more and more alike. Two queens about to lose their heads.

The Callisto rose up slowly over the curve of the skull.

O'Keefe helped the others onto their feet. Pressed between the air lock wall and the terrace floor, they gripped on to one another and waved at the helmeted silhouette behind the cockpit window. The shuttle began to turn on its axis, first turning its side toward them, then the open rear with the lowered tailboard.

"Nearer!" shouted Tim.

A jolt went through the head. Ögi lost his grip and was caught by Heidrun. The Callisto swiveled two of its jets. With absolute precision, Nina Hedegaard steered the huge craft backward. The tailboard came closer, closer still, too close—

"Stop!"

The shuttle stopped, motionless in open space.

"Can you make it?" asked Nina.

O'Keefe raised both hands, grabbed the edge, and pulled himself up onto the tailboard with a powerful swinging motion. He turned around right away, lay down on his stomach, and stretched his arms out below.

"Nina? Can you lower the machine a little further?"

"I'll try."

His right hand brushed Heidrun's fingertips. The Callisto sank another meter, now hovering at helmet height across from the others.

"That's as far as I can go," said Nina. "I'm afraid of touching the head."

"That'll do." Heidrun clambered up to O'Keefe on the hatch. To the right of her, Ögi pulled himself up, crouched down, and grasped Olympiada, who was handed up to him from below, steadying herself on his shoulder. Hands stretched out toward Miranda and Tim, helping them up.

"We made it," whispered Olympiada, then crumpled over, as the damaged bone in her shin finally broke. With a scream, she rolled over the edge of the hatch and tumbled back into the tiny gap between the terrace and the air lock.

"Olympiada!"

Miranda, who was almost all the way up, dropped back down next to the Russian woman and grabbed her under the arms.

"No—don't—"

"Are you crazy? Up you go—as if I would leave you lying here."

"I'm useless," whimpered Olympiada.

"No, you're wonderful, you just don't know it yet."

Miranda effortlessly lifted the petite woman up and toward O'Keefe, who pulled her back on to the tailboard and handed her over to Tim.

"Yeah!" called Miranda. "See, there was nothing to it!"

She laughed and stretched her arms out. O'Keefe went to grab her, but her hands were suddenly out of reach. Confused, he leaned his upper body further forward. She was moving away from him at an ever greater speed, and for a moment he thought Nina had flown away without her. Then he realized the shuttle hadn't moved an inch.

Gaia's head was breaking off!

"Miranda!" he screamed.

He could hear her choking gasps in his helmet as if she were right there next to him, while her tottering form dwindled before his eyes. She was waving her arms wildly, which in some gruesome way could have been mistaken for a gesture of exuberance, the way they knew her to be, always in a good mood, always pushing herself to the very limit, but as she called O'Keefe's name, her voice expressed the absolute despair of a person who knew that nothing and no one would be able to save them.

"Finn! Finn!—Finn!"

"Miranda!"

Then she fell.

Her body tipped over the cabin shaft, flashed in the sunlight, and then disappeared behind the head of Gaia, which did a half turn, seemed to stand still for a moment, then fell completely from the shoulders, crashing into the immense Romanesque window of the abdominal wall.

"Inside, everyone inside!" shouted O'Keefe, his voice cracking. "Nina!"

"What's wrong, Finn, we—"

"She fell!" He jumped into the cargo hold. "Miranda fell overboard; you have to go around to the front section."

"Is everyone else in?"

His eyes darted around. Next to him, Tim stumbled across, a groaning Olympiada in his arms, and collapsed down to the floor of the hold.

"Yes! Quickly, for heaven's sake, go quickly!"

Not waiting until the hatch was closed, he ran like crazy to the connecting bulkhead and pushed himself through while there was still barely a crack's width open. Stumbling along the central passageway, he was hurled against a seat, the revving of the engines in his ears as Nina steered the Callisto backward over the figure's tattered stump of a neck. Then he struggled to his feet again and rushed into the cockpit.

And looked down.

The abdominal cavity was destroyed. Fireballs appeared which extinguished as soon as they were ignited. Rubble rained down as the ribcage containing the suites collapsed floor by floor. Then, Gaia's immense, queen-like skull, the glazing on the face surprisingly still intact, rolled over the gentle inclination of the upper thigh toward the valley, passed the knee almost hesitantly, and shattered 200 meters below on the plateau.

"Go down! Down!"

The shuttle sank downward, but Miranda was nowhere to be seen, neither on the upper surface of the thigh, now covered in debris, nor on the moon surface around it.

"To the plateau! She was torn down with it! You have to—"

"Finn—"

"No! Look! Look for her!"

Without arguing, Nina turned the shuttle around, descended further, and flew in a curve directly over and around the widely scattered remains of the head. By now, the others were gathering together in the space behind the cockpit.

"She can't have disappeared!" screamed O'Keefe.

"Finn."

He felt the soft pressure of a hand on his upper arm and turned around. Heidrun had taken her helmet off and was looking at him with red eyes.

"She can't have just disappeared," he repeated softly.

"She's dead, Finn. Miranda's dead."

He stared at her.

Then he started to cry. Blinded by tears, he sank to the floor in front of Heidrun. He couldn't remember ever having cried.

Lynn sat in the first row of seats, distancing herself from the group, completely expressionless. She had beamed her former light for the last time, had unified the group in the glow of the dying star that she was, had illuminated them, blinded and driven back Dana, her enemy, but the fuel of her life's energy was used up now, her collapse unavoidable. Everything inside her skull was rushing around with maximum kinetic energy: impressions, facts, probability of occurrences. Dependable knowledge pulverized into hypotheses. The unending condensing of impressions caused them to be fractured into the smallest, the very smallest thought particles, to which no time, no perceptual level, no history could be assigned. Increasingly brief thought phases, thought particles whirling at the speed of light, a collapsing spirit, unceasingly crashing without the opposing pressure of will, falling short of the event horizon. No transmission, only reception now, ongoing compromise, the end of all processes, of all contour, all form, just situation, and even the pitiful remains of what had once been Lynn Orley would corrode and evaporate under their own pressure, leaving nothing behind but an abandoned, imaginary space.

Someone had died. So many had died.

Her memory was empty.

LONDON, GREAT BRITAIN

Yoyo, presumed missing, had arrived at the stroke of 22:00 just as Diane was carrying out the electronic exhumation of a person presumed dead. Presumed, because no one had been able to get even a fleeting glance of the corpse. Because it was still undiscovered, as all objects moving in unknown or unpredictable orbits tend to be.

"Victor Thorn, known as Vic," Jericho said, without deigning to ask Yoyo why five minutes had turned into three hours and what Tu was up to in his state of rage.

"I'm sorry, I . . ." Yoyo fidgeted hesitantly. She had a frog in her throat and it had to come out. "I know I was planning to be back much sooner—"

"Commander of the first moon base occupation. A NASA man. In 2021, he ran the show for six months."

"—Tian isn't really like that. I mean, you know him."

"It seems that Thorn did a good job. So good, that in 2024 they entrusted him with another six-month mission."

"To be honest, we haven't spoken that much," said Yoyo, a little shrilly. The frog was croaking on her tongue. "He was just terribly angry. We ended up watching a film, pretending everything was normal, you know. It was probably the worst conceivable moment, but you shouldn't believe—"

"Yoyo." Jericho sighed and shrugged his shoulders. "It's your business. It has nothing to do with me."

"Of course it has something to do with you!"

The frog was on the move.

"No, it doesn't." To his amazement, he meant it. The old, unconquered hurt which had lingered on him so long, like a bad odor on clothes, gave way to the insight that neither Tu nor Yoyo was responsible for his bad mood. However well they were doing, it really had nothing to do with him. "It's your lives, your story. You don't have to tell me anything."

Yoyo stared at the monitor unhappily. Their surroundings left a little to be desired in terms of intimacy. The space in the communications center had been screened in a makeshift way; people were working all around them, like microorganisms in the abdominal cavity of the Big O, digesting and processing information, then expelling it.

"And if I *want* to tell you something?"

"Then now is definitely not a good time."

"Fine." She sighed. "So what's this about Thorn?"

"Well, assuming that the explosion of the mini-nuke was planned for 2024 *without fail*—then someone must have been up there at the time: to hide, position, and ignite the bomb. Either that or someone else was supposed to travel on after it and do that."

"Sounds logical."

"But no explosion was registered, and the people from MI6 think that storing a mini-nuke in a vacuum for too long could pose the risk of a premature decay. So why wasn't it ignited?"

Yoyo looked at him, a small, steep line of thoughtfulness between her eyes.

"Because the person in question wasn't able to carry out the ignition as planned. Because something happened."

"Correct. So I sent Diane on the hunt. There's information on the internet about all the space missions in the last year, and I stumbled across Thorn. A fatal accident during an external mission on the OSS, on August 2, 2024. It was completely unexpected and happened before he could take up his position on Peary Base, but the most significant thing is that it was almost three months to the day after Mayé's satellite was launched."

Yoyo gnawed at her lower lip.

"And the Chinese? Have you checked?"

"You can't 'check' the Chinese," said Jericho. "The best you can find is their own statements, and according to them there was no loss of personnel in 2024."

"Apart from the Moon crisis. The commander of the Chinese base was imprisoned by the Americans."

"Oh, come on! First they shoot an atomic bomb up to the Moon as part of some unbelievably elaborate and sophisticated camouflage maneuver, then a few taikonauts stumble into American mining territory like a couple of idiots and get themselves caught?"

"Hmm." Yoyo wrinkled her forehead. "So someone took the elevator. But to do that they would either have had to plant someone in an authorized team—"

"Or bribe someone who was already in it."

"And Thorn *was* in the team."

"On his mission to the Moon, all official and aboveboard." Jericho nodded. "In the role of a commander, with almost unlimited access. And above all, he knew his way around up there like the back of his hand. He'd been there before."

"Have you told Shaw and Norrington about this?" Yoyo's eyes were gleaming. Suddenly she was a Guardian again, infected by curiosity.

"No." Jericho stood up. "But I think we should remedy that right away."

Shaw and Norrington were wandering around somewhere in the Big O with delegates from MI5, but Edda Hoff gobbled up the fillet steak of their investigations hungrily. She knew about Thorn's case of course, but so far no one had come up with the idea that the respected two-time commander of Peary Base might have been the chosen one for blowing Gaia to smithereens. She promised to put together some information about Thorn and fill her superiors in on Jericho's theory. Then Tu Tian reappeared, looking perfectly composed, as if nothing had happened. He told a joke and listened to the latest news before retreating into the guest area.

"Business," he said, with an apologetic gesture. "The day's just getting started in China. Armies of hard-working competitors are sharpening their knives; I can't act as if I don't have a company to run. So if you don't need me to save the world—"

"No, not right this moment, Tian."

"Excellent. *Fenshou!*"

Shaw and Norrington came back in, but Hoff was tied up in a video conversation with NASA. Jericho was just about to speak to Shaw about Vic Thorn when Tom Merrick announced that, in all probability, he had found the reason for the communication blockade but was unable to lift it.

"Knowing why it doesn't work is still progress," said Shaw as they gathered in the large conference room.

"As I already mentioned—" Merrick's gaze flitted from one face to the next "—to be able to cut the Moon off from all communication, you'd need to interfere with so many satellites and ground control stations that it would be practically impossible. So my guess is that it's something else: IOF."

"IO what?" said Shaw.

Merrick looked at her as if he found it incomprehensible that people didn't talk exclusively in abbreviations.

"Information Overflow."

"Paralysis of the terminal device by botnet mass mails," said Yoyo. "Data congestion."

One of the MI6 people present looked confused.

"Imagine there's someone sitting in a room, and you want to silence them," she explained. "And you don't want them to be able to hear either. Assuming that you succeed in getting your hands on all the keys, you'll try to bolt all the doors in order to cut them off from the world. The doors are the satellites and ground control stations, but you can't stop more and more doors being built in, not to mention the fact that you won't be able to get all the keys anyway. The alternative is incredibly simple. You just go into the room, put a gag in their mouth and cotton balls in their ears."

"So, as far as I understand it, that man is Gaia's computer."

"Two men," said Merrick. "Gaia's computer and the Peary Base system."

"Don't they have any mirror systems?" asked Jericho.

"Okay, four men then." Merrick waved his hand impatiently. "Or even more, as it's possible the shuttles' satellite receivers were gagged too. In any case, the procedure is much more efficient because you only interfere with the terminal device, that is the IP addresses of the people you want to target. Everything is fine with the satellites, you can have a million of them flying around and it won't change anything, quite the contrary. Nowadays, satellites and ground control stations function increasingly as knots in an IP network, like an internet in space! The botnet can jump from one knot to another in order to fight its way through."

Jericho realized immediately that Merrick was right. In essence, botnets were old hat. Hackers gained control over as many computers as possible by implanting special software. Generally speaking, the users didn't know that it would make their computers turn into bots, soldiers of an automated army. Theoretically, the illegal software could lie dormant in the infiltrated computers indefinitely, until it awakened at a preprogrammed time and prompted its host computer to ceaselessly send e-mails to a defined target: totally legal inquiries, but in torrential proportions. On the black market for cyberterrorism, networks with up to 100,000 bots had been exposed. When the botnet struck, it simultaneously fired billions of e-mails and flooded the target with data, until the attacked computer was no longer able to cope with the volume and perished under IOF, Information Overflow.

"What are your thoughts, Tom?" asked Shaw. "How long can they keep their attacks up for?"

"It's difficult to say. Botnets are usually unstoppable. You tell the software in advance how long it should keep at it for, then smuggle it in. After that, there's no way of getting to it."

"But can't you also program into the software when it should stop?"

"Sure, you can do anything. But my suspicion is that the one we're dealing with is a little different. The attack came as a direct reaction to our attempt to warn Julian and the Gaia, so someone *must* have started the bots individually."

"Which means they must have directed a query at this someone after the software was installed," said Yoyo. "And that question was: Shall I attack? So the person in question must have said yes at some stage."

"And while they were attacking the Gaia and Peary Base, they directed another query at Mister Unknown," nodded Merrick. "This time: Shall I stop?"

"So if we only knew who started it—" said the MI6 man.

"Then we could make him stop it."

"Where could the person be?" asked Shaw.

Merrick stared at her. "How should I know? There could be a number of people involved. The person who set the attacks in motion could be on the Moon. If he smuggled control software into the Gaia's computer, then it would have been no problem for him to start the bots from there, although admittedly he would have crippled himself in the process. So I suspect the jerk who can stop all this madness is somewhere on Earth. For heaven's sake, Jennifer!" His arms flailed around wildly. "He could be anywhere. He could be *here*. In the Big O. In this very room!"

Not long after, they heard from Gerald Palstein. The face staring at them through the monitor window from Texas looked dejected, and Jericho couldn't help being reminded of Shaw's words, about the unpleasant decisions EMCO's chief strategist was responsible for on a daily basis. Then he looked closer.

No, it was something else. Palstein looked like someone who had just been given devastating news.

"I can supply you with the film now," he said wearily.

"You were able to speak to your contact?" Shaw's voice sneaked up, cautious and tentative.

"No." Palstein rubbed his eyes. "Something happened."

For a moment, his forehead appeared in disproportion to the rest of his body as he leaned forward and pressed something underneath the transmission camera. Then the image changed, and they saw a news report from CNN.

"An incomprehensible tragedy took place today in Vancouver in Canada," said Christine Roberts, the smartly dressed frontwoman of *Breaking News*. "In an act of unprecedented violence, practically the entire leadership of the internet portal Greenwatch has been wiped out. The ecologically orientated station, known for its engaged and critical reportage, has contributed again and again to the resolution of environmental scandals in recent years, as well as bringing multiple suits against companies and politicians. They were known to be balanced and fair. Our correspondent in Vancouver can now speak to us. Rick Lester, are there any indications yet as to who could be behind the bloodbath which may mean the end of Greenwatch?"

The picture changed. Early evening light. A man in front of a Canadian villa-style property, crime scene tape fluttering all around him, along with police vehicles and uniformed officers.

"No, Christine, and that's exactly what makes the whole thing so eerie: so far there are no clues at all as to who is responsible for these murders, or rather executions, and above all, why." Rick Lester spoke in an emphasized staccato, pausing after every half sentence. "Greenwatch were working, as we now know, on an extensive report about the destruction of the boreal forest in Canada and other parts of the world, so that would make the oil industry a prime suspect, but the report was more looking back at what damage has been caused over the years, that can't be undone, and at first glance there's nothing there which could serve as an explanation for a massacre like this."

"There's now talk of ten fatalities, Rick. What exactly happened, and what names are among the victims?"

"So, I should add that this is probably a concerted action, because it not only affected the headquarters of Greenwatch, where seven people have been found dead—" he turned slightly to indicate the scene behind him, "—but a quarter of an hour before there was also a wild pursuit on Marine Drive, a coastal road that leads out to Point Gray, and witnesses claim to have seen a large 4x4 repeatedly ram into a Thunderbird containing three Greenwatch staff, and then intentionally cause an accident. It seems that two of the people in the car initially survived the crash, but were then immediately shot. One of the victims is, incidentally, the chief reporter of Greenwatch, Loreena Keowa. So the murderers may have driven on to the Greenwatch headquarters, here at Point Gray, gained access, and created this bloodbath within a matter of minutes."

"A bloodbath which—according to the latest reports—also cost the director, Susan Hudsucker, her life?"

"Yes, that has been confirmed."

"It's terrible, Rick, really unbelievable, but it's not just the murders which are giving the investigators clues, but some things which seem to have disappeared—"

"That's right, Christine, and this shines a particular light on the incident. Because there is not one single computer to be found in the whole building; all of Greenwatch's data has been stolen, as well as handwritten notes, so pretty much the station's entire memory."

"Rick, doesn't that imply that someone here was trying to prevent the publication of potentially controversial information?"

Lester nodded. "Someone was undoubtedly trying to *delay* its publication, and we've just heard that contact has been made with freelance workers to find out more about the current projects, but Greenwatch always took great pains to keep hot information and stories within the inner circle right up to the last moment, so it could mean those final projects will never be reconstructed."

"An immense tragedy indeed. So, that's all from Vancouver for now, thank you, Rick Lester. And now—"

The recording came to an end. Palstein reappeared, alone in front of the polished mahogany table in his conference room in Dallas.

"Was that your contact person?" asked Shaw. "The woman in the car?"

"Yes" nodded Palstein. "Loreena Keowa."

"And you think the events are directly connected to the assassination attempt in Calgary?"

"I don't know." Palstein sighed. "A film clip turned up showing a man. He could be the assassin, but does that justify a massacre like this? I mean, I'm in possession of the pictures too, and Loreena said she showed them to a number of people. We were planning to talk on the phone right after her landing in Vancouver, I asked her to call me without fail—"

"Because you were worried."

"Yes, of course." Palstein shook his head. "It was like she was obsessed with the case. I was very worried."

"Mr. Palstein," said Jericho. "How quickly could we get hold of the film? Every second—"

"No problem. I can show you the extract right away."

The picture changed once again. This time, they saw the entrance hall of a building. Jericho thought he recognized the run-down façade: the empty business complex opposite the Imperial Oil HQ in Calgary, from which the shot at Palstein was alleged to have been fired. People were walking around aimlessly. Two men and a woman came out of the building into the sunlight. The men joined a policeman and engaged him in conversation, while the woman positioned herself to the side. A figure crept up from the left, a fat, bulky man with long black hair.

Jericho leaned forward. A still image appeared on the monitor, just a head and shoulders. He was clearly an Asian man. A corpulent, unkempt appearance, greasy hair, his beard thin and disheveled; but what couldn't be accomplished with a bit of latex, foam and makeup?

Even Yoyo was staring at the Asian man.

"Almost unrecognizable," she whispered.

Shaw looked at her keenly. "You know him?"

"Absolutely." Jericho nodded. He couldn't help but laugh. "Unbelievable, but it's him!"

The disguise was worthy of an Oscar, but the circumstances under which they had met him meant they couldn't be misled. Jericho had already fallen for it once, but wouldn't let it happen again, even if the bastard covered himself in fur and went down on all fours.

"That," he said, "is without a doubt the Calgary assassin."

Shaw raised her eyebrows. "And do you have a name?"

"Yes, but it won't help you much. The guy is as volatile as gas. His name is Xin. Kenny Xin."

SINUS IRIDUM, THE MOON

The Land of Mist.

It was only after getting to the Moon that Evelyn had learned the astronauts' name for the mining zone, and to her the term seemed corny and inapplicable. According to her school education, mist was a meteorological phenomenon, an aerosol, and there was certainly no droplet formation on the Moon. She had asked around as to whether the name resulted from some pretentious need to pay homage to Riccioli and his historical misinterpretations, but didn't receive any adequate answers. In general, the zone was hardly ever discussed. Julian had scheduled in a presentation of a documentary for the last day of their stay; so there were no plans to visit the mining zone at all.

But now that she had ended up here after all, one glance was enough to make her see why prosaic minds had named the stretch of land between Sinus Iridum and Mare Imbrium the Land of Mist. A flat, iridescent barrier stretched out from horizon to horizon, over a kilometer high and not in the slightest bit suited to lifting Chambers's mood. It weighed down on the land desolately, hopelessness which had turned into dust. No one in their right mind would feel the desire to cross it.

But Hanna's wheel tracks led right into it.

He had driven down the path for several hundred meters, then veered off in a north-easterly direction. According to Julian, he was traveling along the imaginary line that linked Cape Heraclides to Cape Laplace. Giving in to the conflicting hope that their opponent might be a survival expert, and possibly the better pathfinder, they followed in his tracks. Amber continued to study her maps, but as good as their services had been so far, here they proved to be useless. Everywhere they looked, visibility was cut short by mist, sometimes after 100 meters, but mostly after just 10 meters. There was no horizon now, no hills, no mountain ranges, only Hanna's solitary tracks on his way into the unknown. Something that fed on life itself crept up out of the dust, weighed heavily on Chambers's rib cage, and unleashed in her the childlike longing to cry. The Moon was dead matter, and yet until now she had seen it as strangely alive, like an old and wise human being, a wonderful Methuselah, whose wrinkles preserved the history of creation. Here, though, history seemed to have been erased. The familiar powdery consistency of the regolith, its gentle slopes and miniature craters, had given way to crumbly uniformity, as if something had glided over and subjected it to an eerie transformation. For a moment, she thought she could make out the edge of a small crater, but it vanished into dust before her eyes, a mere hallucination.

"There's nothing left here to get your bearings from," said Julian to Amber. "The beetles have changed the landscape permanently."

Beetles? Evelyn stopped. She couldn't recall ever having heard of beetles being on the Moon. But whatever they were up to, in her eyes it amounted to desecration. All around them, it looked as though someone had inflicted grievous bodily harm on the satellite. This crumbly stuff was the ashes of the dead. It was racked up in parallel, shallow ramparts, like powerful furrows, as if something had been plowing the ground.

"Julian, it looks awful here," she said.

"I know. Not exactly the dream destination for tourists. People only ever come here if there are problems the maintenance robots can't cope with."

"And what in God's name are the beetles?"

"Look over there." Julian raised his arm and pointed ahead. "That's one."

She squinted. At first she just saw the sunlight flickering on the dust particles. Then, amid enigmatic gray tones, a silhouette came into view at an indefinable distance from them, a thing of primeval appearance. It slowly pushed its hunched, strangely weightless looking body forward, making bizarre details visible: a rotating jaw system beneath a low, oblate head, which rummaged industriously through the regolith, insectoid legs spread out wide. Unrelentingly, it kept adding to the dust across the plateau, causing it to whirl around as it continued to eat and move forward. The microscopic suspended matter enshrouded its bulky body, surrounding its legs like a cocoon. By now, Evelyn was pretty sure she knew what she was looking at, except all her perceptions were stunted by the impression of just how inconceivably powerful the beetle was. The nearer they got to it, the more monstrous it looked, stretching out its humpback, which was covered in enormous, glinting, shell-like mirrors, a mythical monster, as tall as a high-rise building.

Julian bore down on it.

"Momoka, stay behind me," he ordered. "We have to stick together. If we want to stay on course, we can't avoid getting close to these machines. They're sluggish, but sluggishness is relative when you consider their size."

The visibility got worse. By the time the velvet-like regolith was under their wheels again just before they reached the beetle, its torso was outlined, dark and threatening, against the clouded sky. For its enormous height, it was astonishingly narrow.

It disappeared behind plumes of whirling dust. As the giant lifted one of its powerful, many-jointed legs and took a step forward, it seemed to Evelyn as if it was ever so slowly swiveling its stooped skull around to look at them. The rover shook softly. She put it down to Momoka driving over a bump on the ground, but an inner certainty told her it had happened at the very moment when the beetle rammed its foot into the regolith.

"A mining machine!" Rogachev turned around to stare at the vanishing silhouette. "Fantastic! How could you have kept that from me for so long?"

"We call them beetles," said Julian. "On account of their shape and the way they move. And yes, they are fantastic. But there are far too few of them."

"Do they turn the regolith into this—stuff?" asked Evelyn, thinking of the crumbly wasteland.

Julian hesitated. "As I said, they transform the landscape."

"I was just wondering, I mean, I wasn't really sure how the mining takes place. I thought, I mean, I expected to see something along the lines of drilling rigs."

As soon as the words had left her mouth, she felt ashamed for discussing mining techniques with Julian so casually, as if forgetting that Momoka had been confronted with Locatelli's deformed corpse just half an hour before. Since their departure from the Cape, the Japanese woman had not uttered a single word, but then she was certainly driving the rover with care. She had retreated within herself, in an eerie, ghostly way. The creature behind the reflective visor pane steering the vehicle could easily have been mistaken for a robot.

"Helium-3 can't be produced in the same way as oil, gas, or coal," said Julian. "The isotope is atomically bound into the moon dust. Around three nanograms per gram of regolith, evenly distributed."

"Nanogram, wait a moment," pondered Evelyn. "That's a billionth of a gram, right?"

"So little?" Rogachev was stunned.

"Not *that* little," said Julian. "Just think, the stuff was stored up over billions of years by solar wind. Far over half a billion tons in total, ten times as much as all the coal, oil, and gas reserves on Earth! That's a hell of a lot! It's just that, in order to get to it, you have to process the moon surface too."

So that's what you call it, thought Evelyn. Processing. And out of that comes a wasteland of crumb-like debris. Feeling uneasy, she stared off into the glistening distance. Far behind them, a second beetle was creeping through the dust, and suddenly the terrain became ugly and crumbly again.

"And yet it's an astonishingly low concentration," Rogachev persisted. "It sounds to me as though *vast* amounts of lunar soil would need to be processed. How deep do those things burrow down into the ground?"

"Two to 3 meters. Helium-3 can still be found even 5 meters down, but they get most of it from above that."

"And that's enough?"

"It depends what for."

"I mean, is it enough to supply the world with helium-3?"

"Well, it was enough to make the fossil energy market collapse on Earth."

"It collapsed prematurely. How many machines are in use at the moment?"

"Thirty. Believe me, Oleg, helium-3 represents a lasting solution to our energy problems, and the Moon can provide it. But you're right of course. We need a lot more machines to be able to graze all the terrain."

"Graze," echoed Amber. "That sounds more like a cow than a beetle."

"Yes." Julian's laughter was a little forced. "They really do move across the land like herds. Like a herd of cows."

"Impressive," said Rogachev, but Evelyn thought she could detect a hint of skepticism in his words. The silhouette of a third beetle came into sight in the hazy distance. It seemed to be standing still. Evelyn's attention was drawn to something agile, something smaller, that was approaching the machine from behind, at first glance a flying machine, until the suspicion took hold that the thing was hurrying over on high, intricate legs, and she couldn't help thinking of a spider. The apparition paused underneath the monstrous abdomen, ducked down, and seemed to temporarily merge with the beetle. Evelyn stared at it curiously. She wanted to ask Julian, but Momoka's silence weighed heavily over the group like a stormy sky, so she held her tongue, deeply unsettled. This insectarium was not at all to her liking. Not that she had anything against technology: she conscientiously drove her environmentally friendly electric car, had converted her home to Locatelli's solar technology, and always separated her trash—though she certainly couldn't claim a devoutly green mindset. Phenomena like robotics, nanotechnology, and space travel were just as interesting to her as waterfalls, giant sequoia trees, and the endangered tufted-ear marmosets, whose continued existence couldn't necessarily be regarded as essential to the Earth's ecological foundations. New technologies fascinated her, but something about this realm of the dead exuded a horror that even Rogachev's less-than-squeamish industrial nature seemed to be developing antibodies against.

Hanna's tracks veered off in a wide arc. The huge imprints suggested that he had been forced to dodge one of the mining machines. The crater-like tracks were joined by some of lesser diameter, and less deep too. Evelyn looked behind and saw a beetle shimmering in its cocoon of dust like a mirage. She couldn't make out the spider-like creature anymore. She closed her eyes, and the image of the colossal machine left a ghostly afterglow on her retinas.

The beetle was eating.

It worked its way unceasingly through the undergrowth with its shovel-like jaw, loosening the rocks, sieving out the indigestible fragments, and guiding the fine-grained matter that remained into its glowing insides. Meanwhile, huge reflectors atop its hunchback followed the course of the sun, bundled photons, and sent them off to smaller parabolic reflectors. From there, the light made its way into the cybernetic organism and created a burning hell of 1000 degrees Celsius, not enough to melt the regolith, but enough to divest it of its bound elements. Hydrogen, carbon and nitrogen, and minute quantities of helium-3 rose in gas form into the solar oven, and from there made their way into the highly compressed counter world of its abdomen. At minus 260 degrees Celsius and under enormous pressure, the obtained gases condensed into liquid and were then transmitted to batteries of spherical tanks, separated according to their elementary affiliation: minute amounts of helium-3, every drop a carefully protected treasure, and everything else in huge quantities. Despite the potential value of the hydrogen for fuel production, the nitrogen for the enrichment of air supplies, and the carbon for building materials, vast as the beetle was it still had to release most of these liquefied elements back into the vacuum, where they instantly evaporated, forming a fleeting, cyclically renewed atmosphere around the machine. In this way the beetles altered everything around them: the lunar soil, which they regurgitated in the form of baked crumbs, and the vacuum, which was constantly enriched with the noble gases that the machine constantly expelled.

As a result of the gas emissions, the dust around the machine became even denser. Strictly speaking, given that there were no air molecules to hold the floating pieces of rock in suspension, they should have been incapable of forming the kilometer-high barrier. But it was the very lack of atmospheric pressure, as well as the scant gravity and electrostatic phenomena, that caused their extremely long and high flight paths, from which they sank down, as if reluctantly, hours later. So, over time, a permanent haze had descended over the mining zone. The clouds produced by the beetle under high pressure formed additional dust in such large quantities that the chewing apparatus and insect legs completely disappeared behind it at times. In addition to this, there was an iridescent gleam on the crystalline structure of the suspended matter, almost like aurora, which made it even harder to see.

This was exactly what happened to Hanna on his solitary trek; the reason why he only became aware of the proximity of one of the mining machines crossing his path once its shovel had practically swallowed him up and passed him through the sieve—only a jump of possibly record-breaking proportions had saved him from being industrially processed. He hastily put some distance between himself and the beetle, aghast that he'd overlooked something so colossal that it could make the ground shake. The machine had towered above him, but it was a well-known fact that small creatures tended to be blinded when they got too close to large ones. He aligned his course to the path of the machine and carried on. From the inexhaustible information provided as part of the conspiracy, he knew that the beetles plowed the regolith in rectangular paths on the imaginary line between Cape Heraclides and Cape Laplace, and that you couldn't miss the station as long as you kept at a ninety-degree angle to the pasture routes—the only orientation device in a world where, due to the lack of a magnetic field, even compasses didn't work. He had been on the go for well over an hour now since the buggy had served its last, and his long, springing steps had necessitated his breaking into his first oxygen reserves. But he still didn't feel any sign of fatigue. As long as nothing unexpected happened, the mining station should appear before him in the next fifteen to twenty minutes. If not, he would be in serious trouble, and there would be plenty of time to worry then.

Totally unexpectedly, they met a spider.

It emerged from the shadow of a beetle and crossed their path with such speed that Julian had to whip the steering wheel around to stop them from colliding with it. For a moment, Evelyn was reminded of H. G. Wells's tripods, the machines from Mars in *War of the Worlds* which attacked entire cities using heat rays, burning them to cinders. But this thing had eight legs instead of three, daddy-long-legs-thin and several meters long, making it look as if its body were hovering in space. There were dozens of spherical tanks lined up right behind its pincers. Another thing that set the spider apart from its Martian colleagues was its complete lack of interest in human presence. Without Julian's quick-wittedness, Evelyn suspected it would simply have run right over the vehicle.

"What in God's name was that brute of a thing?" shrieked Momoka.

She was communicating again now, although admittedly in a way which was provoking wistful memories of her silence. Any trace of grief seemed to have been promptly transformed into rage. Evelyn suddenly wondered whether Momoka's joyless personality was less shaped by arrogance than by pent-up aggression, hoarded over many years, and she became less and less happy about her driving the rover. Her heart racing, she stared after the robot as it hurried away. In front of them, Julian slowly began to drive forward again.

"A spider," he said, as if there had been any doubt on the matter. "Loading and unloading robots. They receive the full tanks from the beetles, exchange them for empty ones, bring the loot to the station, and load them up to be transported on."

"I don't exactly feel welcome here," observed Rogachev.

"They won't hurt you," murmured Amber. "They just want to play."

"Is the area under surveillance?"

"Yes and no."

"Which means?"

"The CCTV only switches on if there's an error message. As I said, the mining is automated. Distributed intelligence in a real-time network. The robots only react to each other; we don't exist in their internal image."

"Pieces of shit!" snarled Momoka. "Your goddamn Moon is starting to really get on my tits."

"Maybe it would be worth enriching their internal image with some additional data," Evelyn suggested. "I mean, if a spider has room in its reality cosmos for something as space-consuming as a beetle, surely it can't be that complicated to squeeze in *Homo sapiens* too."

"Humans aren't supposed be in the mining zone," said Julian, a little on edge. "The zone is a self-enclosed technosphere."

"And how big is this technosphere?"

"At the moment, 100 square kilometers. On the American side. The Chinese occupy a smaller zone."

"And you're sure that those are American machines?"

"The Chinese use caterpillar tracks."

"Well," said Evelyn. "At least we won't get trampled by the enemy."

From that point on, they paid even more attention to what was lurking in the shadows, and—because it was impossible to hear anything in a vacuum—also strained their eyes until they hurt. That's how Amber noticed the buggy, even from a distance.

"What's going on?" asked Momoka as she saw Julian stop.

"Carl might be up ahead."

"Oh, that's good." She laughed drily. "Very good! For me, not for him." She tried to overtake Julian but Rogachev put his hand on her forearm.

"Wait."

"What for, for God's sake?"

"I said, wait."

His unusually authoritative tone made Momoka stop. Rogachev pulled himself up. There were no spiders nor beetles as far as the eye could see. The baked regolith was the only indication that the mining machines had already processed this part of the Sinus Iridum. Amid the bleak landscape, Hanna's buggy looked like the remains of a long lost battle.

"I can't see him anywhere," said Amber after a while.

"No." Rogachev turned his upper body around and back. "It really doesn't look like he's there."

"How could you tell in all this fucking dust?" growled Momoka. "He could be anywhere."

"I don't know, Momoka. All I know is that—so far—we haven't been shot at."

There was expectant silence for a while.

"Okay," Julian decided. "Let's go over there."

Within a few minutes it became clear that Hanna wasn't lying in wait for them somewhere. His buggy had succumbed to an axle fracture. Bootprints led off in a straight line away from it.

"He set off on foot," commented Amber.

"Will he be able to make it?" asked Evelyn.

"Sure, as long as he has enough air." Julian bent over the cargo area. "He hasn't left anything behind in any case, and I know for sure that he took oxygen reserves from the Ganymede with him."

"Shouldn't we be there soon?" Evelyn stared into the distance. "I mean, we've been on the move for over an hour now."

"According to the rover it's another 15 kilometers to the station."

"A piece of cake then, really."

"For us, but not so much for him." Julian straightened up. "He'll need one to two hours from here. That means he's still out there somewhere. There's no way he's already reached the station."

"So we'll run into him."

"And soon, I think."

"And what will we do with him when we do?"

"The question's more what he'll do with us" snorted Amber.

"Well I know what *I'm* going to do with him," hissed Momoka. "I'm going to—"

"No, you won't," Julian interrupted her. "Don't get me wrong, Momoka. We're grieving with you, but—"

"Oh, spare me that shit!"

"But we have to find out what Carl is planning. I want to know what this is all about. We need him alive!"

"That won't be easy," said Rogachev. "He's armed."

"Do you have any ideas?"

"Well." Rogachev was silent for a moment. "We've got the advantage in some ways. We have the rovers. And we're approaching him from behind. If he doesn't happen to turn around right at the decisive moment, then we could drive right up without him even realizing."

"And do you want to risk him shooting at us as soon as he does realize?" Amber turned around. "Driving right up close is all well and good. But what then?"

"We could surround him," Julian mused. "Approach from both sides."

"Then he'd definitely see us," said Rogachev.

"How about a friendly ramming?" Evelyn suggested.

"Hmm, not bad." Julian thought for a moment. "Let's say we drive next to one another, nice and slow. Then one of us can run him down from behind, and then, before he has time to react, the ones in the other rover can jump down and grab his weapons, and so on."

"And so on. So who's doing the ramming?"

"Julian," said Rogachev. "And we'll form the attack commando unit."

"And who's driving?"

"Well." Rogachev turned around to Momoka, who was standing there motionless as if waiting for someone to activate her vital functions. "Momoka is very emotionally charged right now."

"Don't you worry about me," said Momoka tonelessly.

"But I do," said Rogachev coolly. "I don't know whether we can let you drive. You'll mess things up."

"And?" Momoka broke out of her frozen state and climbed back into the driver's seat. "What's the alternative, Oleg? If you let me jump on him you'll be risking much more. For example, the fact that I'll smash in his visor with the nearest available rock."

"We need him alive," Julian repeated insistently. "Under no circumstances will we—"

"I got it!" she snapped.

"No vigilantes, Momoka!"

"I'll play by the rules. We'll do it the way you just said."

"Sure?"

Momoka sighed. When she spoke, her voice trembled as if she was holding back tears. "Yes, I'm sure. I promise."

"I don't trust you," said Rogachev after a while.

"You don't?"

"No. I think you'll put us all in danger. But it's your decision, Julian. If you want to let her drive—then go ahead."

Hanna saw the mining machine approaching from the left. Dust billowed out around its legs and shovel wheels, while freezing clouds forced their way out of its sides and mixed with the suspended matter to form a hazy camouflage. He tried to estimate whether he could safely cross in front of it. It was pretty close already, but if he stepped up his pace he should be able to manage it.

On Earth, he thought to himself, that thing would create a hell of a racket. Here, it approached with malicious silence. The only thing he could hear was the whoosh of the air-conditioning system in his suit and his own, disciplined breathing. He knew that silence nourished foolishness, and that—especially in the glistening haze—correct estimations of distance were hardly possible, but on the other hand he didn't feel the slightest inclination to wait until the monstrous thing had crawled by. The mining station had to be really close by now. He'd had enough now, he just wanted to get there.

Clasping the last of the survival backpacks tightly under his arm, he sprinted off.

• • •

"I see him!"

The Canadian's blurred silhouette had appeared on the horizon. He was sprinting over the plain with long springing jumps, while the colossal body of a mining machine was approaching from the left. Julian waved Momoka's rover over next to his and waited until they were alongside each other.

"He's taking quite a risk there," whispered Amber.

"And rather an inconvenient one, for us," grumbled Rogachev. "The beetle is already quite close. Should we really risk it?"

"I don't know." Julian hesitated. "If we let the machine pass it could take ages."

"We could drive around it," suggested Evelyn.

"And then what?"

"Approach him from the other side."

"No, then he'll see us. Our only chance of taking him by surprise is if we stay behind."

"Then let's go," hissed Momoka. "If *he* can get through ahead of the beetle, then so can *we*."

"The machine really is very close, Momoka," said Rogachev insistently. "Shouldn't we wait? I mean, it's not like Carl can give us the slip."

"Unless he's seen us," Evelyn pondered.

"Then he would have shot at us."

"Perhaps he's trying to throw us off."

"Not Carl. He's a professional. I know people like him; none of them would think twice about shooting in his situation." Rogachev paused. "Nor would I, for that matter."

The rovers were approaching the fleeing figure at a steady speed. At the same time, the beetle was getting closer and closer to Hanna, who was now running even faster. The stomping choreography of the six powerful insect legs was only vaguely outlined in the dust. The Canadian looked like vermin in front of the monstrosity, but he seemed to have estimated his chances accurately.

"He's going to get through," whispered Momoka.

"And then some," said Amber. "Oleg's right, he can't slip through our fingers. We should wait."

"Nonsense! We'll make it."

"But why would we take a risk, and especially now? We have his footprints."

"The beetle will erase them."

"So far we've found them again every time."

"Momoka," said Rogachev in a dangerously quiet tone. "You promised—"

"End of discussion," decided Julian. "We'll wait."

"No!"

Momoka's rover jerked as she pressed down on the pedal. Regolith sprayed up on all sides. Rogachev, who had almost straightened himself up, lost his grip, was hurled out of the vehicle, and landed in the dust. The vehicle swerved for a moment, then thrashed forward.

"You piece of shit!" she screamed. "You miserable—"

"Momoka, no!"

"Come back!"

Paying no attention to their cries, Momoka sped the rover forward and after the running figure. Evelyn held tightly to the back seat but was thrown backward, hearing Rogachev utter a string of sonorous Russian swearwords. They shot off toward Hanna at top speed. In a matter of seconds he would be killed by the force of the collision.

"Momoka, stop! We need him—"

At that moment, the Canadian turned around.

Hanna believed neither in intuition nor in some higher inspiration. As far as he remembered, none of his colleagues who had trusted their gut, so to speak, had survived that long. The regulatory authority of the intellect commanded the use of careful thought to compensate for the lack of eyes in the back of one's head; anything else was pure chance, although looking behind him at that one, decisive moment turned out to be pretty useful too.

He saw the rover shooting toward him.

Assessment of the situation: a design he was familiar with from the Schröter space station, so they had clearly made it from Aristarchus to here. He and the vehicle, tangential to the marching direction of the beetle. Time until the mining machine arrives: unknown. Time until the collision with the rover: three seconds. Pulling out weapon and firing: pointless. Two seconds. One second—

He threw himself to the side.

Rolling away, he got back onto his feet and found himself dangerously close to the beetle. Tons of regolith were spraying up high in front of his eyes. Behind it gaped the cloud-covered, jagged mouth of a gigantic shovel, filled to the brim and rising up from the ground, followed by another, another, another. The mining wheel was turning at an incredible speed, hovering from left to right in the process, transporting more and more masses of lunar rock into the sieve and onto the conveyor belt. The beetle took a step forward, stomping powerfully, making the ground shake.

Where was the rover?

Hanna whipped around. He saw his spare backpack lying on the ground a short distance away; it had slipped from him when he fell. He needed the oxygen reserves, but the vehicle had already turned in a fountain of dust and was speeding over to him again, and now there was a second rover too, approaching from the opposite side. His hand moved up to his thigh, tearing the weapon with the explosive bullets from its case.

"I knew it!" cursed Rogachev. "I knew it!"

He had clambered onto the seat behind Julian as Hanna flew through the air, had seen him thud down and get back up again. The Canadian produced a long and thin object, clearly undecided as to which of the two vehicles he should target. The second of hesitation sealed his fate. Momoka's rover caught him on the shoulder with one of its man-size wheels. He flew a considerable distance, landed on his side, and rolled over toward the walking factory, directly toward the rotating shovel, which was approaching at a worryingly fast pace.

"Enough, Momoka," screamed Julian. "Let *us* get the bastard."

But it seemed the Japanese woman was suffering from sudden deafness. Even while Hanna was still pulling himself up, visibly dazed, she jerked the steering wheel around once again, forced the vehicle into too sharp a turn, and lost control. This time, everything went wrong. The vehicle became airborne, overturned several times in a row, and plowed through the spraying rocks toward the beetle. Momoka was hurled out and slid through the rubble with her arms and legs spreadeagled, screaming like a banshee. She jumped up and rushed on, seemingly uninjured, and went straight for Hanna. Horrified, Amber watched as the rover came to a halt with its wheels still in the air, a blanket of dust sinking down on it.

"My God, Evelyn," she groaned. "Evelyn!"

Evelyn's only thought was to grip on to the strutting of the seat as tightly as she could. Unable to scream, she tried to picture the vehicle as a beetle, within which she would be protected as long as she managed not to lose her grip. Momoka had disappeared. There was no up or down anymore, only bumps and dust and more bumps, smashing the chassis to pieces. Finally, she did let go. She fell to the ground and stared up at a wheel wobbling above her.

The rover had come to a halt, and she was alive. So far.

She immediately tried to free herself from the wreck, but she was stuck. But where? Her arms were free. She kicked her legs forcefully, and she could move them too, but the pile of junk still didn't want to let her go. The ground shuddered as something colossal rammed into the regolith, right next to her, and with icy clarity she realized what it was.

"Evelyn!" Amber. "Evelyn!"

"I'm stuck," she screamed. "I'm stuck!"

The ground trembled again.

The robots only react to one another; we're not present in their internal image.

She had to get out of here! As fast as she could!

She began to pull wildly at the frame, scared out of her wits, but it was as if she were rooted to it, as if her back were soldered to the rover. She began to howl like a wolf in a trap, because she knew she would die.

Julian brought his rover to a standstill right next to the wreckage. He didn't care in the slightest what Hanna and Momoka were doing. The two of them had disappeared on the other side of the mining machine, away from the gluttonous shoveling.

They had to get Evelyn out of there.

Rogachev and Amber jumped from their seats and hurried over to the wrecked vehicle. Evelyn stretched her arm out toward them. It wasn't hard to see that her backpack had wedged itself into the grotesquely twisted strutting and was alarmingly stuck. Julian, overcome with worry, dared to glance up. The colossal body of the machine was making its way unrelentingly forward, darkening the sky, bathing the plain, people and vehicles in its ravine-like shadow. The strutting of its armored plates was only visible in silhouette: rivets, seams, and bolts, the trichinae mechanism of the pipes. The insectoid-like curve of the skull with its chewing apparatus, sieves and mining belts swayed slowly back and forth, as if the thing were picking up their scent. Conically formed hip joints sprang out from angled legs, each around 10 meters high, multiple-jointed and as thick as the crossbeams of a building crane.

The crashed rover lay directly in its path.

At that moment, in a way that was more perceptible than it was visible, the leg right at the front of its body lethargically began to rise up.

Hanna struggled to get his bearings.

He had hit the back of his head on the inner casing of his helmet, something which should have been practically impossible, because the head covering was supposed to be large enough to prevent such accidents. His skull and neck hurt, and his shoulder too had seen better days, but at least the armor seemed to have absorbed some of the collision. He could move his arms still, but the weapon with the explosive bullets had fallen from his hand.

He couldn't lose his weapon!

Red and yellow circles were rotating in front of his eyes, trying to suck away his consciousness. Half blinded, he stumbled a few steps forward, fell on his knees, then shook his head and fought against a strong wave of nausea.

Momoka was just a few steps behind him.

She rushed along, fueled by hate. Like Medea, Electra, Nemesis, she was the incarnation of vengeance, unchecked by any reason, without fear, without any plan. All thought processes were brought to a standstill; her thoughts were ruled purely by the idea of killing Hanna, and she didn't care how.

Something on the ground caught her gaze.

Something long and light in color. It reminded her of a gun, but there was no trigger, just some buttons.

It *was* a gun.

Hanna's gun!

"Try to push the strap down."

"Which strap, dammit?"

"There, that one! Strap, bar, whatever it is!"

Whatever it *was*, thought Amber, before the rover had been transformed into a pile of debris. A piece of the shaft? The mount from a radio receiver? She pushed against it with all her might while Rogachev pulled at the back of Chambers's seat. A part of it had wedged itself between the backpack and her suit and was refusing to budge.

"Hurry!" shouted Julian.

Rogachev kicked against the backrest with his boot. It gave way a little, but the real problem was the twisted bar. Amber looked up and saw the mining machine's foot rising higher and higher, like something out of a nightmare.

"Again, Oleg," she pleaded. "Kick it again."

The foot was now hovering above their heads. Wheelbarrow-sized loads of dust and small stones hailed down on them. Rogachev cursed again in Russian, which Amber interpreted as a bad sign. She pushed herself against the strap once more, burrowing the tips of her boots into the ground, tensing her muscles, and suddenly the entire thing broke right through the middle. Rogachev grabbed it, pulled the released backrest out from under the backpack, and hurled it away.

"I'll make it by myself from here!"

In a flash, Evelyn pulled herself out of the rubble and jumped up. They ran away just as the beetle's leg was making its descent, throwing themselves onto the back seat of Julian's rover. At the very moment when he drove away, the monstrous foot crashed down onto the wreck and crunched it with such force that their getaway car was jolted into the air for a second.

"Where to now?" called Julian.

Amber pointed into the dust. "The other side. They must be on the other side of the machine!"

What a discovery! Momoka bent over, clasped the unexpected instrument of her vengeance, and went after Hanna, who had pulled himself to his feet and was staggering away like a drunkard. It had become significantly darker and a hazy shadow had descended on them, but

Momoka paid no attention to it. She made a leap and kicked out at the Canadian, knocking him off his feet once again.

Hanna rolled onto his stomach.

No, don't shoot yet, she told herself. She wanted him to be watching her as she did it. To look at her as he died! Breathless, she waited until he had rolled over, then pointed the weapon at his helmet.

"You piece of shit!"

She pressed one of the buttons. Then another.

"Do you see this? Do you see it, you piece of shit?"

Nothing. How did you shoot this thing? Oh, it must be here, a safety measure: the detonator was protected by a shield, so she just had to push it up with her thumb, and then—

Hanna crawled backward, staring at the armored, faceless figure in disbelief. It could only be her. He would have credited Rogachev with the same fighting spirit, but this person was small and petite, unmistakably Momoka Omura, and she was ready to make him pay for Warren Locatelli's death. She had discovered the safety shield. She was pushing it up. He had no chance of grabbing the weapon in time. He had to get away, put distance between himself and the Japanese woman. Was she screaming at him? Momoka was locked on to a different frequency, but he was certain she was screaming at him, and suddenly he felt unfairly treated. I didn't kill your husband, he wanted to say, as if that would have changed anything, but he *hadn't* killed him, instead he had wanted to spare him and make his death less painful, and now he was going to be punished for that?

His gaze wandered to a point high above her.

Oh God!

Distance! He had to get away!

"Through the legs," called Amber.

"Are you crazy?" Julian was driving alongside the mining machine at high speed. "Was that not enough for you just now?"

She leaned back and stared up at the giant. Julian was right. It was too dangerous. It was only now, right next to it, that she realized how huge the beetle really was. A walking mountain. Each one of its six legs could end her existence with just one blow. The highest concentration of dust was beneath the torso, visibility was non-existent, and to top it all off, extensive white clouds were breaking out of openings along the torso seam and spreading out rapidly. They made it past the machine and drove around its rear end, from which avalanches of baked regolith were hailing out. They dodged the rain of debris and drove back along the other side.

Back to the monster's head.

Momoka wanted to relish the moment as long as she could, so she didn't press immediately, but instead watched as Hanna crawled away, as if there were still the ghost of a chance he could get away from her. Ha! As if there were even the slightest cause to hope that she would change her mind.

"Scared?" she hissed.

He should be scared. Just like Warren had been scared. We need him alive, she heard Julian bleating in her mind, that shitty, stupid asshole who had lured them here, to the fucking Moon, her and Warren. Alive? Fuck you, Julian! *She needed him dead!* And she would kill him, now, as he pulled himself to his feet. *Sayonara*, Carl Hanna. A good moment.

She could barely see.

It was darkening rapidly. What was happening? She leaned back and looked up. Unbelievable! Fucking Moon! This Moon was really starting to get on her—

"Tits," she whispered.

A huge black stomper of a foot hung in the air above her.

Then it came down.

The beetle ended Momoka's life without giving her the opportunity for inner reflection; something that wouldn't have suited her character anyway. Instead, in honor of her temperament and her belief that people should die as they lived, she exploded one last time: in the course of her physical compression, Hanna's weapon smashed against the breastplate of her space suit and one of the bullets broke in half. A chemical union occurred between shower gel and shampoo. The projectile flew apart, and the nine remaining ones blew up with it, blasting the beetle's foot clean away.

This time, an error message was sent to the control center of the moon base. It informed the crew about material damage to the front left walking apparatus of BUG-24, signifying that the machine was in danger of failure and had to shut itself down, which it did that very moment. It stopped all activity directly after the explosion, but that was of no help. The beetle's amputation was complete. Overloaded by the loss of the front leg, the middle one buckled too, and the colossal machine began to tilt.

Tits. That was the last word they had heard from Momoka.

"I can't see her," said Amber.

And how could we, in all this dust, thought Evelyn. Her entire body was still shaking. She was reliving the moment in her mind again and again; the moment when she had almost been trampled, a true groundhog day of a thought, splintering off into an eerie alternate reality crowned by the notion that she would wake up the next moment and find she had only dreamed her escape, and the steel foot would—

Steel foot?

Evelyn looked more closely. Something about the beetle was nagging at her. Was she hallucinating? Had they got closer to the machine, or had the machine got closer to them?

Then she saw that one of the beetle's legs was breaking away.

"It's tipping over," she stammered.

"What?"

"It's tipping over!" Evelyn began to shout. "It's tipping over! The machine's tipping over. It's tipping over!"

In a second, they were all shouting over one another. The powerful body had unmistakably lost its balance and was indeed beginning to tip over. Fatally, it was tipping in the wrong direction.

In their direction.

Julian changed course, trying to get power out of the rover that it just didn't possess. On their way from Aristarchus, 80 kilometers per hour had often seemed unreasonably fast to them, when the vehicle, despite being restricted by its weight and lack of traction, had completed the most adventurous leaps and jumps. Now Evelyn felt they were crawling along at a snail's pace. She looked behind them and saw the machine struggling to balance. For one blessed moment it seemed as if the giant had stabilized again, but it was beyond hope. Although the rear leg held up to the weight at first, it soon started to sway back and forth.

Then it collapsed.

The monster's torso crashed down into the regolith in a spring tide of dust, and the immense abdomen tilted toward them.

"What's *that*?" screamed Amber at the same moment.

It took Evelyn a moment to realize that her agitation wasn't caused by the machine, but by something else that was rushing toward them from the opposite direction.

"Swerve! Swerve!"

"I can't swerve!"

While the beetle continued to fall at an ever greater speed, they found themselves confronted with a spider that had appeared out of nowhere, whose internal world clearly failed to recognize not only humans, but falling mining machines too. The loading robot hurried purposefully toward the collapsing giant, seemingly intent on cutting off their path. Julian jerked the steering wheel to the left, and the robot changed its course too.

"Right! Right!"

The ground shook. A shock wave gripped the rover and submerged the world in cold gray. The vehicle skidded then began to turn on its own axis, knocking one of the spider's filigree legs off. The spider began to stagger. Traveling backward, Evelyn saw the mining machine go down, a collapsing mountain in a hurricane of whirling regolith. The rover took a hit, came to an abrupt halt, and tipped over. High above them, the spider went into a frenzy, teetering around aimlessly on its long legs.

"Get out!" screamed Rogachev.

They jumped out of their seats, fell, stumbled, and ran for their lives. New clouds shot over and wrapped around them, carrying them off. A huge parabolic reflector spun toward Evelyn, rotating like the blade of an oversized buzz saw. It hacked into the ground not even an arm's length away from her and disappeared, rolling into the pyroclastic grayness. The beetle had gone down completely, missing her by a hair's breadth and catching the injured spider instead. With its pincers flailing wildly, it went into an arabesque, lost its grip, and collapsed feebly, directly above the rover. Its torso crashed into the steering wheel and seats, then bounced up one more time, rotated, and released helium-3 tanks in all directions, aggressive, hopping spherical things which began to hunt down the fleeing people.

Evelyn ran.

And so did Hanna.

At the moment when the beetle's leg came down on Momoka, he knew what catastrophe was about to unfold. The mining machine's motion apparatus looked incredibly stable, but ten simultaneously fired detonating caps were designed to rip even the most stable of structures to shreds. Hanna had no intention of waiting to see whether the remaining legs would compensate for the loss. He hadn't gone far by the time the collision shook the ground and gave him his answer. All around him, a layer of the finest powder flew up. He ran on without stopping. It was only after a while that he forced himself to stop, wheezing, with a painful head and throbbing shoulder. He gave himself a shake and looked back at the scene of the disaster. Gray clouds were forming some distance away. He should have still been able to see the bold silhouette of the machine from here. He took its disappearance as an indication that it really had crashed down. With any luck it had caused havoc among his pursuers, a vague prospect, he had to admit.

What else could go wrong? What in God's name was he doing wrong?

He wasn't doing anything wrong. The circumstances were what they were. He had learned a long time ago how it felt to be in the pinball machine of circumstance. To be relentlessly pinged around in it, however clever one saw oneself to be. It was so much harder to gain control over oneself than it was to take it away from others. Plans were constructs, well thought out, straight lines. On the drawing board, they functioned excellently. In practice, though, it was about not going off course along the winding road of chance. He knew all of that, so why was he getting worked up?

Fine, so the worst possible scenario was that, apart from Momoka, they had all made it through. He thought he remembered having seen her rover crash, but supposing they had managed to heave it onto its wheels again, they still had two vehicles. He, on the other hand, was on foot and robbed of his explosives. Status: critical!

He moved his arm cautiously, stretching it out and bending it. Nothing was broken, nothing dislocated. It was possible that he was concussed. Apart from that, though, he was fine, and he still had the two pistols with conventional bullets, which admittedly made smaller holes, but were just as deadly.

Which direction had he run in? His head-over-heels flight had brought him into uncharted territory. That was bad. Without the beetle tracks, he could end up missing the station. His own tracks were sure to be visible over the not-yet-processed ground, but then the rover hadn't turned up yet. They might be looking for Momoka, but could they risk letting him get away for her sake? If they really did still have both the rovers, then wouldn't one of them have started hunting him down by now?

Maybe things weren't that bad after all. Strengthened by confidence, he turned his attention to working out where he was.

They struggled up one by one, clumsy, dazed, their white space suits dirty, as though they were clambering out of their own graves. All around them, it looked like the scene after a bomb attack or a natural catastrophe. The hunchback of the mining machine, still towering up into the skies, now a massif in the regolith. The snapped spider limbs of the loading robot. Their smashed rover. And over everything, a ghost of swirling dust.

"Momoka?"

They called her name unrelentingly, wandering around in search, but received no answer, nor did they find any trace of her. Momoka seemed to have been swallowed up by the dust, and suddenly Evelyn couldn't even see the others anymore. She stopped. Shuddered as something cold touched her deep within. The dust around her billowed out, forming a kind of tunnel. On the other side it seemed different in nature, darker, more threatening, and at the same time more inviting; and all of a sudden it seemed to Evelyn that she was seeing herself disappear in the tunnel, and with every step that she took away from herself, her silhouette swirled beyond recognition, until she lost herself. An indefinable amount of time later, she found the others on the other side.

"Where were you?" asked Julian, concerned. "We were calling you the whole time."

Where had she been? At a border, a border to forgetting. She had glanced momentarily into the shadows; that's how it had seemed to her at least, as if something were tugging and sucking at her, using its dark temptations to try to make her surrender. She knew about the irrationality of perception. Borderline experiences had been the subject of esoteric debate on her programs more than once, without she herself having any perception of the other side, but in the moment when Amber, Oleg, and Julian turned up by her side again, she had known that Momoka Omura was dead. The silence that met their calls was the silence of death. The only thing they found were tracks, which led away from the head of the beetle and which could only be Hanna's.

But Momoka had disappeared without a trace.

In the moments that followed, Evelyn didn't say a word about her unusual experience. After a short time, they gave up the search and went back to the rover. It was no longer functional, but at least they managed to salvage their oxygen supplies. For the first time since they had been on Hanna's trail, it looked as though his tracks were going to lead them the wrong way.

They weighed up their options.

In the end, they decided to keep following him.

May 31, 2025

Mini-nuke

CALLISTO

Finn O'Keefe closed his eyes. He was no coward. And the absence of other human beings certainly didn't scare him. He had discovered years ago how calm and agreeable his own company could be, and had experienced many wonderful moments of solitude with nothing above him but the sky and the cries of seagulls riding the salty west winds, scanning the sea for telltale signs of glistening backs. The only time he ever experienced loneliness, solitude's desperate sister, was in crowded places. For this reason, the Moon was completely to his taste, despite having so far failed to have any spiritual effect on him. It was easy to be alone here: all you had to do was go behind a hill, switch yourself off from the radio wave chatter and pretend the others didn't even exist.

Now, on the flight to Peary Base, his self-deception was revealed. It was laughable to think that you could turn your back on the world in the certainty that it was still there, to assume that you could opt back into its incredibly noisy civilization at any moment. Even in the expanse of the Mojave Desert, in the mountain range of the Himalayas, or in the perpetual ice, you would still be sharing the planet with thinking beings, a thought which gave solitude a comfortable foundation.

But the Moon was *lonely*.

Banished from Gaia's protective body, cut off from all communication and from the whole of humanity, it had become clear to him during the two hours they had been en route that Luna placed no value on *Homo sapiens*. Never before had he felt so ignored and devoid of importance. The hotel, gone to ruin. Peary Base, no longer a certainty. The plateaus and mountain ranges all around them suddenly seemed hostile—no, not even that, because hostility would mean they were acknowledged here. But in the context of what religious people defined as Creation, the human race clearly had less significance than a microbe under a skirting board. If one took Luna to be exemplary of the trillions of galaxies in the visible cosmos, it became clear that all of this had *not* been made for humans—if it had been *made* at all.

He suddenly found comfort in the group and was thankful for every word that was spoken. And even though he hadn't known Miranda Winter that well, her death felt like a personal tragedy, because just a few centimeters would have been enough to prevent it. She might have driven her beloved Louis insane, named her breasts, and believed any old nonsense that dried-up old Hollywood divas like Olinda Brannigan deduced from tarot cards and tea leaves; but the way she saw herself, her resolutely cheerful determination not to let anything or anyone destroy her good mood, the sublime in the ridiculous, he had admired all of that about her, and possibly even loved it a little too. He wondered whether he had ever been as honest in his arrogance as Miranda Winter had been in her simplicity.

His gaze wandered over to Lynn Orley.

What had happened to *her*?

The living dead. It was as though she had been erased. Nina had mentioned some kind of shock to Wachowski, but it she seemed to be working her way through some kind of self-destruction program; she hadn't spoken a single word since Miranda's death. There was hardly anything to indicate that she was even aware of her surroundings. Everything—

—had vanished into the event horizon; nothing could make its way out.

She had become a black hole.

And yet, sitting in the depths of the black hole, she found herself capable of following the echoes of her thoughts. This was unusual for a Hawking-like black hole. Something wasn't right. If she really had fallen into her collapsed core and ended up as a singularity, this would also have meant the end of all cognition. Instead, she had made her way to *somewhere*. There was certainly no other way to explain the fact that she was still thinking and making speculations, although she had to admit she would probably be doing better if certain green tablets hadn't been burned when—

—with the destruction of the hotel, any hope of a message from Hanna had been erased. If he was still able to send out messages, that was.

By now, with the chaotic evening on her mind, Dana was having doubts about this. Was a little pessimism advisable? After all, anything could have happened on Aristarchus. Maybe—although of course without writing Hanna off right away—she should confront the possibility of taking things into her own hands. Her cover hadn't been blown yet, and her avowed opponent didn't seem aware of anything, not even herself. All the others trusted her. Even Tim, who—

—was in increasing despair about how to fairly distribute his worries. Worries for Amber, for Julian (more than he would like to admit), for Lynn and all the rest in the shuttle, and the others wherever they were at that moment; worries as to the limit of his own capacity for suffering, one endless round of anxiety. After flying for more than two hours they had to be nearing the Base by now, but they still hadn't been able to establish contact. Dana had put it down to the tiresome satellite problem, and said they would have a connection as soon as they came into the transmission area. Tim's list of concerns expanded to include the horror of a deserted and somehow destroyed base. The time crept by, or was it racing? The Moon offered no reference points for human perceptions of the passing of time; his species' timekeeping had absurd continuance only within the enclave of the Callisto, while all around them there was no time, and they would never arrive anywhere ever again.

And as the horror of the vision, fed by his torturously brooding imagination, threatened to overpower him—

—three words and a yawn provided the solution.

"Tommy Wachowski. Peary Base."

"Peary Base, this is Callisto. We're coming in for landing. Request permission to land in around ten minutes."

"A social visit?" Wachowski asked sleepily. "Heavens. Do you know how late it is? I just hope we've cleaned up and cleared away the bottles."

"This is no time for jokes," said Nina.

"Just a moment." Wachowski's tone changed in a flash. "Landing field 7. Do you need assistance?"

"We're okay. One injured, not life-threatening, and one person in shock."

"Why aren't you flying to Gaia?"

"We've come from there. There was a fire. Gaia has been destroyed, but there are other reasons why we can't go back to Vallis Alpina."

"God! What's happened?"

"Tommy," Dana tuned in. "We'll tell you the details later, okay? We have a lot to report and a great deal more to process. But right now we're just happy to be able to land."

Wachowski fell silent for a moment.

"Okay," he said. "We'll get everything ready here. See you soon."

American Mining Station,
Sinus Iridum, The Moon

The dust cleared after just a quarter of an hour, restoring the views over to the distant Mare Imbrium, to the mountain range of Montes Jura—and to the mining station.

Hanna allowed himself a moment of rest, stretching out and tilting his head back. Despite veering too far northwest, he had nearly made it. As long as he kept up the pace he would be there very soon. His hunch that the others were either dead or severely limited in their transport capabilities had turned into a certainty. They could have caught up with him in no time with a rover, but no one had appeared.

His head felt as though it were stuffed with cotton balls, and he was struggling against light dizziness and nausea. He started to walk again. Within a quarter of an hour, he reached the station. Unlike Peary Base, its design was entirely celestial: a large, regolith-covered igloo, connected to cylindrical, pressurized insectoids, a U-formation of spherical tank depots and hangars framing a landing field, bordered by the railhead with its main and siding tracks. Steps and elevators led up to the tracks, freight trains—basic flat-bed wagons coupled together—dozed ahead of their next journey. To the side of the landing field, two dozen spiders, frozen and motionless, waited for the command to deployment. Two more had taken up position right next to the rail track and were loading one of the trains with spherical tanks, while a third, fully laden, was on the approach. The plant seemed to be undergoing some development, and Hanna noticed that the hangars, depots, and the igloo-shaped habitat were resting on caterpillar tracks. As soon as the zone had been fully processed, the entire station would move on. The visibility was much better here, even though a thin veil of dust hung over everything. Harsh, bright sunlight was reflected back by the crystalline facets of the suspended particles, creating an oppressive, post-nuclear-disaster mood. A world of machines.

Hanna searched through the hangars and, alongside various maintenance robots, managed to find four robust grasshoppers with larger cargo holds and higher stilts than the ones used in Gaia. There was no trace of anything quicker, like a shuttle. There were no conventionally driven vehicles here at all; in the mining zone everything was on legs, thereby reducing the amount of dust stirred up and providing better protection for the mechanical components. The beetles' maintenance interfaces were located in the head and the hunchback, which made the design of the grasshoppers logical. They could get above the blanket of dust and, from there, execute precision landings on the vast bodies; the robots took care of the rest. Hanna had no doubt that one of the hoppers would get him to his destination—they hardly used any fuel—but they were terribly slow. He would be en route for almost two days with one of those things, the cargo hold filled up with oxygen reserves—always supposing he found something of the kind in the station. His suit would provide him with drinking water, but he wouldn't be able to have a bite to eat. Still, he was prepared to put up with that, but not with the time delay.

He *had* to act within the next two hours.

He paced through the air lock of the habitat and went into a disinfection room, where cleaning fluids were sprayed on him at high pressure to cleanse his suit of moon dust. Then he was finally able to take his helmet off and search the quarters. It was spacious and comfortable enough that you could tolerate several days here, with sanitary facilities, a kitchen, a generous amount of food supplies, working and sleeping quarters, a communal room, even a small fitness center. Hanna paid a visit to the toilet, ate two wholegrain bars covered in chocolate, drank as much water as he could manage, washed his face, and looked for headache tablets. The station pharmacy was excellently equipped. After that, he inspected one of the insectoid transporters connected to the station, but that too proved to be unsuitable for his needs, because it was even slower than the hoppers. He at least managed to find additional oxygen reserves which would assure his survival out there for some days. But on the question of how to finish the job in the near future, he was still at a loss.

He put his helmet back on and hauled all the oxygen reserves he could find out to the landing field.

His gaze wandered over to the spiders. The last one in the row was just heaving its tanks onto the freight train, that was loaded almost to capacity, then securing them in place with the rib-like clamps which extended from the sides. From the looks of things, the train would soon be setting off toward the moon base.

At 700 kilometers an hour!

His thoughts came tumbling thick and fast. There were still around a dozen tanks to be loaded. He had maybe ten minutes. Too little to destroy the hoppers as he had planned, but he could still take the oxygen reserves with him. Running now, he brought them to the elevator and threw them in. The barred cabin set off at an annoyingly slow pace. He could see the spider's legs through the crossbars, its body, the industrious pincers. Three tanks to go. He rushed out onto the railway platform and squeezed the reserves between the piled-up globes on a freight wagon. The penultimate tank was passed over by the praying-mantis-like extremities and stowed away. Where would be the best place to sit? Nonsense, there was no ideal location; this wasn't the Lunar Express, it was a cargo train. Certainly one whose acceleration a human could survive without harm. Beyond that, it didn't matter how quickly the train went. In the moon vacuum it was no different to being in free fall, where you could leave the vessel at 40,000 kilometers an hour and take a casual look around.

The last tank was just being secured.

In front of the tanks! That was the best place.

He pulled himself up onto the wagon bed, then went hand over hand along the metal globes and under the spider's pincers to the front, until he found a place which seemed good to him, an empty passage between two traction elements. He squeezed himself in, crouched down, wedged in his feet, and leaned his back against the tanks.

And waited.

Minutes passed by, and he started to have doubts. Had he been wrong? The fact that the train was fully loaded didn't necessarily mean it was setting off now. But while he was still brooding over it, there was a slight jolt. Turning his head, he saw the spider disappear from his field of vision. Then the pressure of acceleration followed as the train got faster and faster. The plane flew past him, the dust saturation around him gradually gave way. For the first time since his cover had been blown, Hanna didn't feel trapped in a nightmare of someone else's making.

"Lousy grasshoppers!" cursed Julian.

They had made it to the mining station with the very last of their strength. Oleg Rogachev, trained to stay standing for so long that his opponent would fall over from exhaustion, was the only one to show no sign of fatigue. He had rediscovered his gentle, controlled way of speaking and was emitting the freshness of an air-conditioned room. Amber, however, could have sworn that her space suit had developed a life of its own, maliciously intent on obstructing her movements and exposing her to the unfamiliar experience of claustrophobia. Soaking wet, she slumped in her gear, bathed in bad odors. Evelyn was faring similarly, traumatized from almost being trampled to death and still a little unsure on her feet. Even Julian seemed to be discovering, with surprise, that he really was sixty years old. Never before had they heard Peter Pan snort so loudly.

It didn't take them long to discover that there wasn't a single oxygen reserve in the entire station.

"We could get some air from the life-support systems," Evelyn suggested.

"We could, but it's not that easy." They were sitting in the living quarters, helmets off, drinking tea. Julian's face was flushed and his beard unkempt, as if he'd been burrowing around in it for hours on end on the hunt for solutions. "We need *compressed* oxygen. For that we'd need to make various conversions, and to be honest—"

"Don't beat around the bush, Julian. Just come out with it."

"—at the moment I'm not sure how that works. I mean, I know roughly. But that won't solve our problem. We would only be able fill up our own tanks. All the reserve tanks have disappeared."

"Carl," said Rogachev tonelessly.

Amber stared straight ahead. Of course. Hanna had been in the living quarters. They had searched the station in constant expectation of being attacked by him, but he had disappeared without a trace. Which raised the question of how, as it seemed no hoppers were missing—until Julian discovered the transport and operation schedules and found out that a helium-3 transport had set off to Peary Base immediately before they had arrived.

"So he's on his way there."

"Yes. And from the Pole back to the hotel."

"Right, let's follow him then! When does the next train leave?"

"Hmm, let me see . . . oh, the day after tomorrow."

"*The day after tomorrow?*"

"Guys, the Americans aren't pumping streams of helium-3 on an hourly basis here! It's just small quantities. At some stage in the future there'll be more trains, but right now—"

"The day after tomorrow. Dammit! That's two days of sitting around."

Even the satellites were still refusing to offer them any concessions. Amber crouched in front of her now cold cup of tea, as if by pulling her shoulders up she could stop her head falling down to her feet. Some governing authority seemed to have taken up residence inside her skull. She was afraid of cracking up over her fear for Tim, Lynn, and the others. But at the same time she felt as though she were looking at the mountainous skyline of a desk weighed down with the demands of her own survival. No one came to help. Applications for grief and sadness lay around unprocessed, the empathy department had all gone for a coffee break, and the answering machine was on in the Department of Examination for Post-Traumatic Stress Disorder, announcing only the hours of business. Every other service desk had closed due to dismissals. She wanted to cry, or at least whimper a little, but tears required a request form that couldn't be located, and the Dissociation Department was putting in overtime. Escape plans were checked, considered, and discarded as her shocked self sat there in the company of five dead people, waiting for one of the neurotransmitters hurrying by to declare themselves responsible.

"And how far will we get with the grasshoppers?" she asked.

"Theoretically, to the hotel." Julian gnawed at his lower lip. "But that would take two days. And we don't have enough oxygen for that."

"Could we perhaps reprogram the control system for the trains?" asked Oleg Rogachev. "There are some parked outside after all. If we could manage to start one of them—"

"*I* certainly can't do anything like that. Can you?"

"Okay, let's take a different approach," said Evelyn. "How much longer will our reserves last?"

"Three to four hours each, I guess."

"Right, so that means we can forget all forms of transport that take longer than that."

"Well we won't get to the hotel with that much, that's for sure. Here, on the other hand, our ability to survive is practically unlimited."

"So you want to rot in here while everything else gets destroyed?" cried Amber angrily. "What about the insectoids? Those strange crawling vehicles. They're equipped with life-support systems, right?"

"Yes, and they're even slower than the hoppers. With them it would take three or four days to get even to the foot of the Alps. And climbing after that would take longer than our reserves will last."

"The oxygen again," said Evelyn bitterly.

"It's not just that, Evelyn. Even if we had enough of it, we're still running out of time."

Oleg looked at Julian intently. "What do you mean by that?"

"What?"

"That we're running out of time."

Julian held the Russian's gaze. He tried to get the words out several times, then turned his head toward Amber in a silent plea for help. She nodded imperceptibly. Julian opened up the dungeons of discretion and finally told Evelyn and Rogachev the whole truth.

Rogachev's face was expressionless. Evelyn was looking at the tip of her fingers, stupefied. Her lips moved as if she were uttering inaudible prayers.

"And that's everything?" she said finally.

"Far from it." Julian shook his head gloomily. "But that's all I know. Honestly! I would never have brought you all here if I had had the slightest suspicion that—"

"No one is accusing you of thoughtlessness," said Oleg coolly. "On the other hand, it is your hotel. So, *think*. Do you have any idea why someone would blow up Gaia, and with an atomic bomb at that?"

"I've been racking my brains for hours trying to work that one out."

"And?"

"I don't have a clue."

"Exactly." Oleg nodded. "It doesn't make any sense. Unless there's something about the hotel that you yourself don't know."

Or about its *architect*, thought Amber. Julian's suspicion came to her mind. She dismissed the thought as nonsense, but the uneasy feeling remained.

"Why the Gaia?" brooded Oleg. "Why a nuclear bomb? I mean, that's completely over the top."

"Unless it's not just about the hotel."

"Don't mini-nukes have less explosive force than normal nuclear bombs?" asked Amber.

"Yes, that's true." Oleg nodded. "On the scale of the largest possible disaster. Which means you could contaminate half of the Vallis Alpina even with a mini-nuke. So what's there? What's the deal with the alpine valley, Julian?"

"Again: not the faintest idea!"

"Maybe it's nothing," said Evelyn. "I mean, all we have to go on is this detective's theory."

"You're wrong." Julian shook his head. "We have five dead people and a killer flushed out of hiding. Everything that Carl's done in the last hours amounts to an admission of guilt."

Oleg put his fingertips together.

"Maybe we should stop wishing for the impossible."

"Well, there's an idea."

"Patience." Oleg uttered a humorless laugh. "If we can't get to the hotel via the direct route, then we should think about making a detour. Do you know what?" He looked at them each in turn. "I'm going to tell you a joke."

"A joke." Evelyn stared at him distrustfully. "Should I be worried?"

"The joke of my life. My father often told it. A little story he believed led people toward ideas—"

"Well, given that Chucky's not here—"

Julian propped his chin in his hands. "Go on then."

"So, two Chukchi are walking through the Serengeti when a lion suddenly jumps out at them from behind the bushes. Both of them are scared out of their wits. The lion growls and is clearly very hungry, so one of the Chukchi runs away as quickly as he can. But the other one pulls his backpack from his shoulder, opens it in a leisurely fashion, takes a pair of running shoes out and puts them on. Are you crazy, shouts the fleeing Chukchi; do you seriously think those shoes will make you faster than the lion? No, says his friend, they won't." Oleg smiled broadly. "But they'll make me faster than you."

Julian looked at the Russian. His shoulders shook, then he started to giggle. Evelyn joined in, a little hesitantly. Amber inspected the contents in a bureaucratic manner then decided to laugh too.

"So we need running shoes," she said. "Great, Oleg. Let's just run home."

Julian's expression froze. "Hang on!"

"What is it?"

"We *have* running shoes!"

"What?"

"I'm such an idiot." He looked at them, his eyes wide in amazement that he hadn't thought of it sooner. "The Chinese are our running shoes."

"The Chinese?"

"The Chinese mining station. Of course! It's inhabited. We could get there within an hour with the grasshoppers, without our oxygen reserves running out; there are shuttles there, they have their own satellites—"

"And they could be behind the attack!" cried Amber. "Isn't that what that Jericho guy suspected?"

"Yes, but the people we have to thank for warning us are Chinese too." Suddenly, decisiveness was shining in Julian's gaze again. "I mean, what do we have to lose? If there really is a Chinese conspiracy against Orley Enterprises, then bad luck. We can hardly make things any worse. But if not, or if these Chinese people in particular aren't behind it—then all we can do is win."

They looked at one another, letting the thought sink in.

"You should tell jokes more often," said Evelyn to Oleg.

The Russian shrugged his shoulders. "Do I look like I know any more?"

"No." Julian laughed. "Come on. Let's pack our stuff."

LONDON, GREAT BRITAIN

The China theory.

Ever since they had recognized Kenny Xin in the fat Asian from Calgary, the term had been in frequent use in the Big O and at SIS. The never entirely believed and yet the most logical of all explanations, that a Chinese causative agent was causing havoc in Orley's bloodstream, was experiencing a renaissance. And why? Because of a Chinese assassination attempt.

Jericho was more at a loss than ever.

After the initial moment of triumph at having exposed Kenny Xin, joining the small streams of realization into a river, he had begun to doubt the paradox of the obvious more and more. At first glance, the China theory made sense. Xin had turned out to be the nucleus of atrocious activity all over the world, and all of his actions served the implementation of the planned attack. Admittedly, he could hardly be held responsible for the massacre in Vancouver: although a jet could have taken him from Berlin to Canada in time to murder ten people there, Jericho doubted he had left Europe. It was more likely that he had followed them to London and was observing the goings on from somewhere close by, like a fly on the wall. He could have delegated Vancouver, and it was obvious he had helpers, Chinese for sure. Maye's launching pad, the purchase and installation of the mini-nuke, all of it was in Chinese hands. China was said to be the provocateur of the Moon crisis, Beijing resented the USA, Zheng was trying to both fight Orley *and* get on his side. In short, the China theory conformed perfectly to secret-service thought processes. In Jericho's view there was only one thing to say against it: when it came down to it, it just didn't add up.

"Damn, you're good." Norrington sounded appalled. "It was Xin who shot at Palstein; that must give you food for thought."

"It does," said Jericho.

"The guy isn't just someone's weapon, but I don't need to tell you that! He's right at the top of the organization, and he's a *goddamn Chinese secret service man*. It would be negligent to rule out China being behind all this."

Yoyo indicated she'd had enough of sitting around in a cellar, however nicely furnished it might be.

"I asked Jennifer. She said the atomic obliteration of London wouldn't take place before tomorrow morning, so we might as well go to one of the large offices up in the roof with Diane."

In its simplicity, it was the best idea for a long while.

The two of them went up. London at two o'clock in the morning was a sea of lights, and it was London: perhaps not the most modern, but for Jericho the most beautiful and charming city in the world. The O_2 Arena was gleaming on the opposite bank of the Thames, and the Hungerford Bridge lay to the west, held up by glistening spider's webs and towered over by the wheel of the London Eye. The orange luminescent moon circled mysteriously in the gravitational field of the Big O. Yoyo leaned back on the floor-to-ceiling window, unleashing in Jericho the spontaneous impulse to grab her in his arms and hold her tight.

"Doesn't the thing in Vancouver remind you of Quyu?"

The paleness of defeat had retreated from their features, red wine and fighting spirit were conjuring up fresh sparkle in their eyes.

"I don't think that was Xin," he said.

"But the process is similar. The Guardians, Greenwatch, and in both cases information was spread virulently through the net. Containing that spread is practically impossible. So you don't attempt a surgically precise operation, but instead immediately destroy the entire infrastructure and kill everyone that comes into question as a knowledge carrier. And even that doesn't give you any guarantees, but you can delay the spread. That's exactly what Kenny's doing. I'm telling you, he'd blow up this very building if he could be sure that it would buy him some time."

"Because the operation is about to take place."

"And we can't do a damn thing about it." Yoyo slammed her fist into the palm of her other hand. "Time's working against us. He's going to win, Owen; that piece of shit is going to win."

Jericho walked up next to her and looked out into the London night.

"We have to find out who's pulling the strings. *Before* they can carry out the attack."

"But how?" snorted Yoyo. "We only ever find Xin."

"And MI6 have homed in on the Chinese. The MI5, Norrington, Shaw—"

"Well." She shrugged. "We thought it was them almost the whole time too, right?"

Jericho sighed. She was right, of course. They were the ones who had ignited the China theory smoke bomb.

"On the other hand, as you've already said: the Moon crisis doesn't fit. Why would China unleash an argument over mining zones at a time when the last thing it needs is international attention?"

"Norrington thinks it's a distraction tactic."

"Great distraction tactic. It led to Beijing being accused of putting weapons on the Moon! Not exactly trust-inspiring if a bomb does end up going off. And besides, Owen, why didn't they just send a Chinese assassin up in a Chinese rocket?"

"Because, according to Norrington, a member of the tour group had better access to the Gaia."

"Nonsense, what kind of access? To set off an atomic bomb? You don't need access for that, you just chuck it down outside the door, make a run for it, and blow the thing sky high. Remember what Vogelaar said. It was Zheng he didn't trust, not Beijing."

"And what would Zheng get from killing Orley and destroying his hotel? Would that help him to build better space elevators? Better fusion reactors?"

"Hmm." Yoyo sucked on her index finger. "Unless Orley's death would turn the balance of power in the company upside down to Zheng's advantage."

"Vogelaar had another theory."

"That someone's trying to turn the Moon powers against one another?"

"Well, it wouldn't have to go to extremes right away. They wouldn't unleash world war that quickly. But a few things would change."

"One of them would be weakened—"

"And the third party strengthened, secretly laughing all the while." Jericho hit the palm of his hand against the window pane. "Do you see, that's what strikes me about the whole thing. It's all so obvious! It seems so—staged!"

"Okay, fine, let's leave China aside for a moment. Who else would benefit from Orley's downfall?"

"A bullet would be enough for just him. You don't need a nuclear bomb for that." Jericho turned away. "You know what, before we drive ourselves crazy going over it all, we should ask Aunt Jennifer."

"MI6 loves the China theory," said Shaw a few minutes later. "And so does MI5. Andrew Norrington even wants to call in the Chinese ambassador."

"And you?"

"I'm torn. The theory doesn't seem to make sense to me, but then it doesn't necessarily make much sense to a dog when his master puts the dog food on the top shelf. We *have* to put China as the focus of our mistrust. And as far as Julian is concerned, there are whole armies who would rather see him dead than alive."

"There's a rumor that he wants to make his patent accessible to the world."

"That's possible," Shaw conceded.

"Could that be in Zheng's interest?"

"It definitely wouldn't be in America's. A change at the top of our organization would be very useful to Washington right now. The chemistry is a little off at the moment, as you know."

Jericho hesitated. The branch of a new thought was appearing in his mind and developing lively side shoots.

"Are there individuals in the Orley enterprise who don't agree with Julian?" he asked. "Who represent Washington's position?"

Shaw smiled grimly.

"What do you think? That we hold hands? Just the fact that Julian is *considering* freeing himself from American monogamy is considered by many to be tantamount to sacrilege. Except, as long as the boss has the say, they just grumble over their beers and keep their traps shut. You would like Julian, Owen, he's the kind of man you can have fun with. Meanwhile you quickly forget that he'll fight to get what he wants with despotic energy, if that's what it takes. Creatives and strategists have all the freedom they want with him, as long as they sing from his hymn sheet. Palace revolutionaries should just be happy that the guillotine was done away with."

"Isn't his daughter the second in command in the company? What does she think about the patent thing?"

"Exactly the same as her father. I know what you're getting at. You can't corrode Orley Enterprises from the inside."

"Unless—"

"Over Julian's dead body."

"There you go," said Yoyo, unmoved. "There may be forces in the company that want him dead, but can't do anything by themselves. Who would they collaborate with?"

"The CIA," said Shaw, without hesitation.

"Oh."

"I know that for a fact. The CIA are developing scenarios of what form a partnership without Julian might take. They're thinking about everything. The Americans are worried about their national security."

"It's a known fact that the State can withdraw patents if national security is at risk" said Jericho.

"Yes, but Julian is British, not American. And the Brits have no issues with him, quite the opposite in fact. With the taxes he pays, the prime minister himself would personally take a bullet for him. And besides, it's about economy, not war. Julian isn't endangering anyone's national security, just their profits."

"The only way of controlling the company from the outside would be to get rid of him."

"Correct."

"Could Zheng Pang-Wang—?"

"No. After all, Zheng's hopes rest entirely on Julian, and the possibility that he may at least talk him into a joint venture one day. As soon as other people are running Orley, Zheng would be completely out of the picture. That reminds me, Edda put together the data you asked for."

"Yes, it's about—"

"Vic Thorn, I know. Interesting idea. Excuse me, Owen, I'm just getting a call from our control center in the Isla de las Estrellas. We'll put the data on your computer."

"The CIA," ruminated Yoyo. "That's a new one."

"Yet another theory." Jericho rested his head in his hands. It suddenly felt as heavy as lead. "Getting rid of their own business partner and putting the blame on the Chinese."

"Plausible?"

"Of course it is!"

They sat there silently for a while. An icon had appeared on Diane's monitor, VICTHORN, but Jericho was overcome by the paralysis of mental overload. He needed a jump start to get going. Some insignificant little victory.

"Listen," he said. "We're going to do something now that we should have done a lot sooner."

He pulled the icon of the intertwined snake bodies onto the screen and named it UNKNOWN.

"Diane."

"Yes, Owen?"

"Look in the net for equivalents of UNKNOWN. What is it about? Show me the corresponding data and deliver contextual background."

"One moment, Owen."

Yoyo came and sat next to him, crossed her arms on the table, and laid her chin in the crook of an elbow. "Her voice is very lovely, I grant you," she said. "If she looked as—"

The screen filled with images.

"Would you like to hear a summary, Owen?"

"Yes, please, Diane."

"It's very likely that the graphics show a Hydra. A nine-headed, snake-like monster from Greek mythology, which lived in the swamps of the Argolid and prowled through the surrounding lands, killing cattle and humans and destroying harvests. Even though the Hydra's middle head was immortal, she was defeated by Heracles, a son of Zeus. Would you like to hear more about Heracles?"

"Tell me how Heracles defeated the Hydra."

"The snake's distinguishing characteristic was that it grew two new heads for every one that was chopped off, with the result that it became increasingly dangerous as the fight went on. It was only when Heracles began to *burn* off the neck stumps with the help of his nephew Ioalaus that the new heads were no longer able to grow. Eventually, Heracles succeeded in striking off Hydra's immortal head too. He dismembered the body and immersed a stake in its blood, which from then on could create incurable wounds. Would you like to hear more details?"

"Not right now, Diane, thank you."

"A Greek monster," said Yoyo, her eyes wide. "In the picture it looks more Asian."

"An organization with lots of heads."

"That grow back when you knock them off."

"But would Chinese conspirators really make a creature from Greek mythology into their symbol?"

Yoyo stared at the monitor. Diane had found around two dozen images of the Hydra, various depictions, in artifacts spread across two millennia, all of which showed a scaly snake body with nine tongued heads.

"No, not a chance in hell," she said.

PEARY BASE,
NORTH POLE, THE MOON

They felt a little like the survivors from a wagon train of white set-
tlers, the ones who had made it to the fort in the nick of time, even
though there were no equivalents of Indians to be seen anywhere. But
at the moment when the Callisto descended over the base's space station, O'Keefe couldn't help but picture US cavalry stationed at the Pole,
a troop of riders who came tearing over the plateau to protect them,
hats and flashing epaulettes, fanfares, shots fired in the air, the familiar
tropes: *Are you safe, Sergeant?—Aye, sir! A hell of a journey. I didn't
think we'd make it.—I see the Donoghues aren't here.—Dead, sir.—Blast!
And the staff?—Dead, sir, all dead.—My God! And Winter?—Didn't
make it, sir. We lost Hsu too.—Terrible!—Yes, sir, horrible.*
    How strange. Even something as exotic as space travel only seemed
to function through the cultivation of earthly myths, by imposing
elements of the familiar onto the unfamiliar. Something designed to
expand the mind ended up being subjected to musty familiarity and
forced into narrow spectrums of association. Perhaps people couldn't
help it. Perhaps making the unusual seem banal prevented them from
perishing of their own banality, even if it meant their subconscious
calling on the services of the Western, a genre whose task had been to
put a chaotic world back to order with the assistance of sharp ammunition and sublime landscapes. *A lot of bad things have happened,
Sergeant.—Aye, sir.—So many have died.—Aye.—But look at the land,
Sergeant! Is it not worth every man lost?—I wouldn't miss it, sir!—What
a wonderful country! Our hearts beat for it, our blood flows for it. We
may die, but the land remains.—I love this country.—By God, me too!
Let's ride!*
    My ass!
    As soon as Nina landed the Callisto at the Pole, all eyes were
directed toward the Charon. To the southern end of the landing field,
surrounded by the base's spaceships, the landing module rested like a
small, impregnable castle on stilt legs. O'Keefe recalled their first leaps
and steps, filled with that conquistador-like feeling of having conquered something, unsuspecting that they would come back just a few
days later, depleted and demoralized. The monochrome landscape and
mother-of-pearl sea of stars had lost none of their beauty, even after the
disaster in Gaia, but their gazes had now turned inward. The adventure was over. The desire to escape had extinguished the pioneering
spirit.

Frank Schätzing

"Well, I don't know." Leland Palmer, a small, Irish-looking man and commander of the base, looked around at them skeptically. "None of it seems to make sense to me."

"Well, then a lot of people had to die for something that makes no sense," said O'Keefe.

A robot bus had brought them from the landing field to Igloo 2, one of the two domed living quarters which formed the center of the base. Igloo 1 contained the headquarters and scientific working area, while its neighboring counterpart was for leisure activities and medical care. In a lounge which oscillated between comfort and functionality, they had told the residents their story, while Karla, Eva, and the Nairs were examined for signs of smoke poisoning and Olympiada Rogacheva, in a state of self-reproach, had her leg put in splints. Lynn had sat among them silently for a while, until Tim, his face contorted with worry, had taken her hand and told her she should lie down, sleep and forget, a suggestion that she had followed apathetically.

"I mean there's no sense to the *expense*," said Palmer. "I mean, just look at what a simple oxygen fire can do! What would someone need a *nuclear bomb* for?"

"Unless you factor in the location," Dana suggested.

"You mean you think the bomb isn't for the Gaia at all?"

"Not exclusively, I would say."

"That's true," said Ögi. "A few hand grenades, correctly positioned, would have done the job, no problem. I happen to know a thing or two about mini-nukes—"

"You do?" said Heidrun, amazed.

"From the television, my dear. And one thing I know is that you shouldn't let yourself be fooled by the cute terminology, you know, Mini Rock, Mini Mouse, Mini Nuke. Every one of the mini-nukes which disappeared from the holdings of the former Soviet Union in the early nineties was capable of obliterating Manhattan."

"So what are they trying to destroy, then?" asked Wachowski.

"Gaia is at the edge of a basin," said Tim, his head resting in his hands. "Where the Vallis Alpina rounds out."

"What would happen if someone set off a nuclear bomb in a basin like that?" asked O'Keefe.

"Well." Wachowski shrugged. "It would contaminate it."

"More than that," said Palmer. "There's no air here to spread radioactive material, no atmospheric fallout. But on the other hand nor is there anything to slow down the explosion's energy. The direct destruction itself would be enormous, a bit like the impact of a meteorite. The pressure would blast away the edges of the basin, the heat would turn its walls to glass, vast quantities of rock would be catapulted into the air, but above all, the detonation would be tunneled."

"Which means?" asked Heidrun.

"That there's only one direction, apart from upward, that the pressure can be released."

"Into the valley."

"Yes. The waves of pressure would graze along the entire Vallis Alpina, accelerated by the steep walls. I'd estimate that the whole area would be lost."

"But to what purpose? What's so special about the valley, apart from the fact that it's beautiful?"

Tim crossed his fingers and shook his head. "I'm more concerned with wondering why the bomb hasn't gone off yet."

"Well, up to three and a half hours ago it hadn't gone off yet," O'Keefe corrected him. "By now it could have blown sky high."

"And we wouldn't have a clue here!" growled Wachowski. "What a mess! What the hell is wrong with the satellites?"

I could tell you all a thing or two, thought Dana. "Either way," she said, "we won't solve the problem here and now, and to be honest I'm not interested right at this moment. I want to know what has happened on Aristarchus."

"The shuttles should be fueled up soon," promised Wachowski.

"Hmm, Carl." Heidrun wrinkled her forehead. "I wonder what he'll do?"

"That depends. Is he alive? Are the others alive? Was he able to flee? My bet is that he still has something he needs to do in the hotel," Dana said.

"And what would that be?" asked Tim.

"Priming the bomb." She looked at him. "What else?"

"He needs to prime it?"

"Possibly," nodded Wachowski. "How else would you ignite the thing?"

"Remote control."

"In order to ignite it via remote control you'd need a very large antenna, which you would have seen when you were searching the Gaia. Otherwise, he'll need to do the ignition himself."

"Which explains why we're still alive," said Ögi. "Carl didn't have a chance to set up a timed fuse. His plans were turned upside down."

"Do we care about that?" O'Keefe looked around at them all. "I wouldn't waste a minute looking for him. Let's concentrate on the Ganymede."

"I totally agree with you," Dana said, "but it could come down to the same thing. If we find the Ganymede, we may stumble upon Hanna."

"That's fine by me," growled O'Keefe. "More than fine."

Nina came into the lounge.

"We're ready!"

"Good." Dana and Palmer had agreed to send two search teams off right away. Nina was to fly the Callisto to the Plato crater, follow the Montes Jura along the mining zones, and then head for Aristarchus. The Io, a shuttle belonging to Peary Base, would set off fifteen minutes later, keep a southerly course by Plato, and then, 500 kilometers on, swing over the plain of the Mare Imbrium toward Callisto. Dana got up. "Let's put the teams together."

"You can fly with me."

"Thank you, but I think my presence is more needed here. Someone has to look after the others. How many people can you spare, Leland?"

Palmer rubbed his chin. "Kyra Gore is our head pilot. She can fly the Io with Annie Jagellovsk, our astronomer—"

"My apologies," Dana cut him off mid sentence. "I didn't express myself correctly. How many people have to stay in the base in order to ensure everything can function?"

"One. Well, let's say two."

"I want you to be clear about how dangerous this man is. It's possible that the search teams will be forced to attack Hanna. They may have to free the group from under his control. Each shuttle should be occupied by four, or preferably five people."

"But there're only eight of us."

"I'll come too," said O'Keefe.

"Me too," said Tim.

"Heidrun and I—" Ögi started to say.

"I'm sorry, Walo, but you're not the ideal person." Dana made the effort to smile. "You're certainly courageous enough, but we need younger, fitter people. So, Tim and Finn will fly with Nina, plus two more people from the base. The Io will fly with five men from the base—"

"Just a minute." Palmer was trying to rein in the galloping horse. "That would be an extraordinary mission."

"Well, we have an extraordinary problem," replied Dana ungraciously. "In case you haven't noticed."

"Six out of eight people. I'd need to consult—"

"Consult who?"

"Well—"

"You won't reach anyone."

"Okay, but—it's not that simple, Dana. That's three-quarters of my team. And the shuttles will have no contact to base for most of the time."

"View *me* as a reinforcement here," said Dana. "My responsibility is the safety of Julian Orley and his guests. And, to be honest, Leland, I would be less than understanding if the rescue mission were to fail due to lack of—"

"Fine." Palmer exchanged a look with Wachowski. "I think it's doable. Tommy, you stay here and—hmm, Minnie DeLucas."

"Who's that?" asked Dana.

"Our specialist for life-support systems."

"Wouldn't it be better if Jan stayed?" wondered Wachowski.

"And who's *that*?"

"Jan Crippen. Our technical director."

"Not necessarily," said Palmer. "Minnie can take on his duties, and besides, we won't be gone for all that long."

"I don't care how long you're gone," said Dana. "As long as you find Julian Orley."

More importantly, as long as you're all out of the picture for the next few hours, she thought. Carl and I can handle Wachowski and this woman DeLucas.

If Hanna was still coming, that was.

At around 02:40 that morning, the shuttle bus finally took the search teams over to the landing field.

O'Keefe sat on the bench of the open vehicle and let his gaze wander. On their second evening on the Moon, in an effort not to expose himself to too much conversation, he had retreated to the Gaia's multimedia center before the meal was over, and had watched a film about Peary Base. So he knew that it covered over 10 square kilometers and that the landing field alone took up three times the space of a football field. The silo-like towers on the western wall were spaceships left behind by the teams who had first ventured to the North Pole. Originally converted into living quarters, they now served as emergency accommodation, themselves dwarfed by a telescope currently under construction, while the domes in the center, Igloos 1 and 2, formed the heart of the base. Both had been brought to the Pole as collapsible structures, and had then been blown up to house size and coated with a layer of regolith several meters thick, in order to protect the inhabitants from solar storms and meteorites. Air locks had been cut into the walls, the ground leveled off all around them, and vehicles and equipment had been stored in hangars, those halved tubes which Momoka had referred to in her usual defeatist manner as junk, and which were actually burnt-out fuel tanks from the Space Shuttle era.

Over the years, the station had grown, expanding to include streets, annex buildings, and a vast open-cast mine. In the distance, against a backdrop of automated factories in which the regolith was processed into building components, the framework of huge, open assembly facilities towered up. Manipulators ran on rails along the bodies of mining machines in the making: welding, riveting, and adjusting parts, while humanoid robots carried out precise mechanical work. Cable cars and railway trucks were carrying material from the factories to the building yards. Wherever you looked, machines were hard at work. Lifelessness in its most vivid form.

O'Keefe looked toward the east as the bus made its way toward the landing field, 2 kilometers away from the main site. Fields of solar collectors, their panels directed at the wandering, never-setting sun, covered low, undulating hills. The craters were interspersed with canals of lava. Thanks to them, Peary Base had a widely ramified system of natural catacombs, the majority of which hadn't yet been explored. Just one feature betrayed what the ground was concealing: a crack, or rather a chasm. It gaped at its full width in the high plateau, spread out to the west, and opened into a steeply descending valley, the bottom of which wasn't touched by a single ray of sunlight. Bridges crossed over what seemed like the remains of a severe earthquake, although it was actually a caved-in lava canal, through which liquid stone had flowed billions of years ago. As O'Keefe knew from the documentary, some of the cave branches led into the chasm, which made him wonder whether the underground of the base was accessible from there.

They drove through the gate in the screens surrounding the landing field. There was moderate activity taking place all around them. One of the grasshopper-like forklifts was corresponding soundlessly with a manipulator, whose segmented arm rose in their direction like a final greeting, then froze. So far as could be seen, the tracks on the rail station gallery lay there abandoned. Beneath the harsh, uneven light, the lonely route wound off into the valley. The activity of the machines had a ritualistic quality to it; one could even say postapocalyptic mindlessness, an image of strange self-contentment.

What would they find at Aristarchus? Suddenly, he was overcome by the desire to go to sleep and wake up in the timelessness of a Dublin pub of somewhat ill repute, where the customers were more concerned with the accurate proportion of foam to black stout than all the wonders of the Milky Way put together, and often sighed in remembrance of allegedly better times as they raised the glasses to their lips.

LONDON, GREAT BRITAIN

The night crawled by.

Yoyo was off somewhere on the phone to Chen Hongbing, Tu was discussing the possibility of a joint venture with Dao IT, his still furious, abhorrent competitor, and Jericho was struggling to keep his eyes open. Three hundred meters above London, his brain had turned into a swamp, gurgling and mumbling with decaying theories, all paths either reaching a dead-end or getting lost in the unknown. He was finding it harder and harder to concentrate. Vic Thorn on his journey into eternity. Kenny Xin, slinking toward Palstein's planned assassination. The nine heads of Hydra. Carl Hanna, on whom Norrington hadn't yet managed to find even the smallest blemish. Diane with her ever increasing messages about Calgary and the massacre in Vancouver. Sinister representatives of the CIA, living up to the cliché. From a great height, he could see himself running around in a circle so big it felt like he was going in a straight line, but he always ended up back in the same place.

He was absolutely shattered.

Yoyo came back from her phone conversation just as he was about to stretch out on the floor and close his eyes for a moment. But then he might have gone to sleep, and his overtaxed brain would have conjured up dreams of hunting and being hunted. He was actually pleased that Yoyo was keeping him awake, even though her mercurial vitality was increasingly getting on his nerves. Since their arrival in the Big O, she had single-handedly polished off a bottle of Brunello di Montalcino, had the ruby-red tones of Sangiovese Grosso in her cheeks, and the never-tiring look of youth, and all without showing any sign of drunkenness. For every cigarette she smoked, two new ones seemed to grow out of her fingers. She was even more unpredictable than the Welsh weather: gloomy and glowering one moment, bright the next.

"How's your father doing?" he yawned.

"As can be expected." Yoyo sank down into a swivel chair then jumped right up again. "Really well actually. I didn't tell him everything, of course. Like what happened at the Pergamon Museum; he doesn't need to know that, right? Just so you know, in case you speak to him."

"I can't see any reason why I should."

"Hongbing is your client." She went over to the coffee machine. "Have you forgotten that already?"

Jericho blinked. He suspected that, if he looked in the mirror, he would find his eyes had been replaced by computer monitors. He forced himself to look up from the screen.

"I brought you back to him," he said. "So the honorable Chen is no longer my client."

"Oh great." Yoyo studied the selection on the machine. "There's a thousand varieties of coffee, but no tea."

"Look more closely. The English are tea drinkers."

"Where is it then?"

"Bottom right. Hot water. The box of teabags is next to it. So what did you tell him?"

"Hongbing?" Yoyo rummaged through the box. "I told him that we had a heartfelt conversation with Vogelaar and that he filled us in on what was going on, and that Donner turned out to be a cover." She put her cup under the nozzle, dropped in a bag of Oolong, and ran boiling water over it.

"So in other words you said we were having a lovely vacation," mocked Jericho. "And have we been to Madame Tussaud's and shopping on the King's Road?"

"So should I have told him about the experience of pressing the eyeballs out of a dead man?"

"Fine, enough said. A mocha, please."

"A what?"

"Coffee with chocolate. Left row, third button from the top. So how far did you get with Thorn?"

They had divided up their tasks, which meant that Yoyo was evaluating the data relayed by Edda Hoff and completing it with information she found online.

"I'll be finished in a few minutes," she said, watching as the machine spat out a mixture of cappuccino and chocolate. "Would I be correct in assuming that you're tired?"

Jericho was just about to answer when he realized that Diane was simultaneously uploading 112 new reports about Calgary and Vancouver. He sank into a depressed silence. Yoyo put the steaming cup in front of him and began to slurp down her tea in front of her monitor. He listlessly decided to have one final look at the message that had set everything off, then to go and sleep.

Just as the text appeared on his screen, Yoyo whistled lightly through her teeth.

"Do you want to know who was project leader for the Peary missions from 2020 to the end of 2024?"

"From the way you say it I take it that I do want to know."

"Andrew Norrington."

"Norrington?" Jericho's slumped shoulders tightened up. "Shaw's deputy?"

"Wait." She wrinkled her brow. "There were a number of project leaders, but Norrington was definitely in the team. It doesn't say to what extent or how direct his contact with Thorn was."

"And you're sure it's the same Norrington?"

"Andrew Norrington," she read. "Responsible for personnel and security, transferred in November 2024 to Orley Enterprises as deputy head of security."

"Strange." Jericho wrinkled his forehead. "So it should have rung a bell with Hoff when I spoke to her about Thorn."

"She's Norrington's subordinate. Why would she be concerned with the details of his past career?"

"But Norrington didn't say anything either."

"Did you speak to him about Thorn?"

"Not directly. Shaw and he were in a meeting. I came over and said that some unexpected event must have stopped the mini-nuke being ignited the year before."

"Mind you, Shaw already knew about your Vic Thorn theory."

"That's true, probably from Hoff. Hmm. She must have noticed that Norrington was with NASA at the same time as Thorn. Sure, she had a hell of a lot on her plate—but Norrington—"

"You mean, he should have thought of Thorn himself?"

"Maybe that's asking too much." Jericho rested his chin in his hands. "But do you know what? I'm going to go and ask him."

"Victor Thorn—"

Norrington was sitting in his surprisingly small office, one of the few rooms that weren't open-plan. Jericho had turned up unannounced, as if he were just passing.

"Yes, Thorn," he nodded. "He could be our man, don't you think?"

Norrington gazed at an imaginary point in the room.

"Hmm," he said distinctly, very distinctly. A clearly audible *H*, followed by a time-winning *mmm*. "Interesting thought."

"He died three months after the launch of the satellite. It would fit time-wise."

"You're right. Why didn't I think of that myself?"

"People often overlook the things that are right in front of them." Jericho smiled. "Did you have close contact with him?"

"No." Norrington shook his head slowly. "I'm sure I wouldn't have been so slow on the uptake if I had."

"No contact at all?"

"My role was related to the general project security. Sure, we crossed each other's path now and then, but other people were responsible for personnel issues."

"And what was Thorn like?"

"As I said, we had nothing to do with one another. Rumor was that he was a playboy, which may have been an exaggeration. I think he just enjoyed life, but on the other hand he was enormously disciplined. A good—a *very* good astronaut. People don't normally get put forward for a second Peary mission that quickly."

"Think back, Andrew," asked Jericho. "Any information would be helpful."

"Of course. Although I fear that I won't be able to offer anything that enlightening. Is Jennifer already in the picture on this?"

"Hoff seems to have mentioned it to her. She knew about my suspicion."

"She didn't tell *me*." Norrington sighed. "But you can see what it's like here: we rush from one meeting to the next, everything so chaotic. Hanna is driving me insane. I can't find anything dodgy in his background, and God knows it's not the first time I've looked."

"You were responsible for the tour group?"

"Yes. We didn't know much about Hanna, but Julian was adamant about taking him along. Believe you me, I X-rayed the guy thoroughly. And nothing: he was clean."

"Anything new from Merrick?"

"No. He's trying to make contact. His botnet theory is probably correct." Norrington hesitated. "Owen, I don't mean to suggest I don't trust your instincts, but we have to look at other Orley organizations too. We can't be certain that we're not dealing with a concerted action. Give me a bit of time with Thorn. I'll be in touch as soon as I can."

"He's lying," said Yoyo, when Jericho came back and filled her in on the conversation. "Norrington knew Thorn."

"He didn't say he didn't *know* him."

"No, I mean he *really* knew him." Yoyo pointed at her monitor. "Thorn attracted a lot of interest from the media, because of Peary, but also because he was good-looking and talkative. There are dozens of interviews with him, but I found the best one while you were away. A special report about the Peary crew of 2024, plus a human-interest piece. Vic Thorn, sought-after bachelor, on the Moon for the second time, blah blah blah. They took a film crew to his house and were given access while he threw a birthday party, and guess who was on the guest list?"

She started the video. An open-plan kitchen, a relaxed atmosphere. About two dozen people gathered around platters of finger food. Light jazz breezing over a sea of chatter, classics from the Rat Pack era. People dancing in the background, and a lot of dedicated drinking. Thorn laughs into the camera and says something about how wonderful friendship is, then can be seen in animated discussion with a man who slaps him familiarly on the shoulder a few frames later.

"Is that what people who don't have any contact with one another look like?"

Jericho shook his head.

"Most definitely not."

"That some of these men will soon spend six months on another celestial body," said the female commentator, "seems strangely unreal on an evening like this, where—"

"It could be coincidence," Yoyo conceded. "We can't necessarily assume that Norrington is our mole, or even that Thorn had something to do with it. It's pure speculation."

"Nonetheless, I want to know more about his time with NASA. What exactly he was responsible for, how close the contact really was. We know one thing for sure: he lied when he denied knowing Thorn well."

"—already his second mission in the Mountains of Eternal Light," the commentator was saying. "So called because the sun never sets at the lunar Pole. Originally, this played a decisive role for the energy supply to Peary Base, but since then the construction of a fusion reactor has—"

"Mountains of Eternal Light," whispered Jericho.

Yoyo looked up at him, confused.

"Yes, that's what the Polar regions are called. You know that."

The cogs were turning in Jericho's mind. As if in a trance, he went over to his desk and stared at the text of the fragmentary message:

> Jan Kees Vogelaar is living in Berlin under the name Andre Donner, where he runs an African private and business address: Oranienburger Strasse 50, 10117 Berlin. What should we continues to represent a grave risk to the operation not doubt that he knows all about the payload rockets. knows at least about the but some doubt as to whether. One way or another any statement lasting Admittedly, since his Vogelaar has made no public comment about the facts behind the coup. Nevertheless Ndongo's that the Chinese government planned and implemented regime change. Vogelaar has little about the nature of Operation MoonLight of timing Furthermore, Orley Enterprises and have no reason to suspect disruption. Nobody there suspects and by then everything is underway. I count because I know, Nevertheless urgently recommend that Donner be liquidated. There are good reasons to

There was very little of the text that still puzzled him. In essence, just one single word, added before the dark network went silent, and only because it occupied the space between *Operation* and *of timing* in such an odd way, as if it didn't belong there.

insight

That's what he'd assumed it said, at any rate.

"Diane. Fragment analysis. Attribute the origin data to the text building stones."

"Color recognition?"

"Yes please."

A moment later, words like *payload rocket, knowledge,* and *Enterprises* were transformed into colorful chains of alphabet letters. *Ent erpr ises* was, for example, assembled from three sections of data, and *k now led ge* appeared in even more colors. Other terms, on the other hand, like *Operation* and *implemented,* came from a single data section.

Two fragments created *insight.*

"Oh God," whispered Jericho.

"What's wrong?" Yoyo jumped up, came over, and leaned over his shoulder.

"I think we've made a mistake."

"A mistake?"

"A huge mistake." How could he have missed it? It was right in front of him. "We may have put them on the wrong track. The bomb isn't supposed to go off in Gaia—"

"Not in Gaia? But—"

"There would be no point if it did, and we knew that the whole time. Idiot! I'm such a stupid, blind idiot!"

Operation Mo o n Light

Operation Mountains of Eternal Light.

CHINESE MINING STATION, SINUS IRIDUM, THE MOON

Jia Keqiang was no politician. He was a taikonaut, a geologist, and a major, in that order, or possibly the other way around depending on his mood, but he was no politician, that was for sure. In his experience, the only difference between Chinese and American spacemen, or indeed Russian, Indian, German, and French, was the ideology behind them, and whether they were called astronauts, cosmonauts, or taikonauts. What they all had in common though was a way of looking at the big picture which politicians, in his experience, never had, except of course for those few statesmen who had been in space themselves. Hua Liwei, his predecessor up on the Moon, had been an American captive for a while and still took every official appearance as an opportunity to accuse the Americans of hair-raising breaches of the lunar peace, but this couldn't shake Jia's opinion that spacemen were easygoing, unpolitical people. It was just that each and every one of them followed their script faithfully. Even Hua Liwei, once he had a drink or two inside him in private, would happily admit that he liked the Yanks, that they had treated him very well and that, as it happened, they had some excellent Scotch tucked away in the catacombs at Peary Base.

Mind you, Hua also reckoned that the Americans were to blame for the whole farcical episode, and Jia agreed with him there. Nevertheless, he had done his best during the Moon crisis to argue for de-escalation and understanding all around, using what influence he had. The Party held him in high esteem as a bright young hope of the Chinese space program; he was a highly decorated officer in the Air Force, and had trained as a taikonaut under the watchful eye of the legendary Zhai Zhigang. On top of all this, he also had a doctorate in geology, specializing in exogeology, qualifying him to work on the helium-3 mining operation. Zhai had passed on to Jia his love of ballroom dancing, and he was also inordinately fond of naval history, spending hours on end researching the brief flowering of Chinese seamanship in the fifteenth century and the fabled nine-masted ships of the time; he had painstakingly built a three-meter-long scale model of Admiral Zhang He's flagship. When he wasn't up in space, he loved to sail with his wife and sons, to read books on maritime history, and to cook, which he did as a sort of meditation. He was proud that his country had become the first after the USA to make it to the Moon, he was irked that Zheng Pang-Wang hadn't made any progress on the space elevator, he was worried about America's dominance in space, and he was slow to make

Frank Schätzing

predictions about the future. He was a perfect public face for China: friendly, media-savvy, patriotic, and always careful to keep to himself his own personal opinion that politicians both sides of the Great Wall were not the brightest bulbs in the shop. "Frankly," as the Americans would say, he thought that politicians were idiots.

But right now he had to think about politics, if he didn't want to lose control of the story he'd suddenly found himself caught up in.

Julian Orley was sitting across from him.

The very fact that he was here was remarkable enough, but what Orley had to tell him was even more startling. Twenty minutes ago he had appeared from the dustbowl of the mining camp, along with his daughter-in-law, the American talk-show queen Evelyn Chambers, and some Russian Jia knew nothing at all about, all riding on grass-hoppers like a squad of defeated Jedi fleeing the field, and they had asked for shelter and for help. Everyone in the base had been asleep, of course, since it was half past three in the morning, though Orley seemed surprised when Jia pointed this out to him. They had hur-ried to take care of their unexpected guests, fussed around them, and made hot tea, but even so the commander found himself in a tricky situation, since—

"—without wishing to offend, Mr. Orley, last time the Americans entered our territory, there was some trouble."

They had tried talking Chinese for a while, but Orley's laborious, broken Mandarin was no match for Jia's fluent English. Jia's crew, Zhou Jinping and Na Mou, were in the next room, looking after the others. Evelyn Chambers in particular was in a bad state, showing signs of an imminent nervous breakdown.

"Your territory?" Orley raised an eyebrow. "Wasn't it the other way around?"

"We are of course aware that America takes, let us say, a different view of the matter," Jia said. "That is, regarding who intruded into whose territory. Perception is such a subjective thing."

"It certainly is." The Englishman nodded. "But you see, Com-mander, I couldn't give two hoots about any of that. I'm not answerable for the local mining operation, or for Washington's territorial issues. I've built an elevator, a space station, and a hotel."

"If you will permit me an observation, that list is not quite com-plete. You benefit from the mining, because you're the one who can build the reactors."

"Still, I do it as a private businessman."

"NASA's technologies would be inconceivable without Orley Enter-prises, and vice versa. In China's view, that makes you more than just a private businessman."

Orley smiled. "So why does Zheng Pang-Wang constantly remind me that that's just what I am?"

"Perhaps to reassure you that you have a free choice in the matter?" Jia smiled back. "Please don't misunderstand me. I would not presume to question the honorable Zheng's motives, but he is no more a private businessman than you are. You have more influence over world politics than many a politician. More tea?"

"Please."

"You see, I am concerned that you should understand my situation, Mr. Orley—"

"Julian."

Jia was silent for a moment, uncomfortable, then poured the tea. He had never understood what made the English and the Americans so keen to get onto first-name terms at every conceivable opportunity.

"The extended agreements signed in November 2024 commit us to helping one another here on the Moon," he said. "We are taikonauts, you are astronauts, we are all of us humanity's ambassadors to the stars. We should stand shoulder to shoulder. Speaking personally, I would allow you to use our shuttle the moment you ask for it, but the very fact that it is *you* asking gives the whole thing a very political aspect. On top of all which, there might be nuclear bombs involved."

"It wouldn't be the first time we've had Chinese help in the matter. Without that, we'd probably know nothing at all about the bomb, and we'd be hiking happily around the lunar hills with Hanna until the whole place blew up."

"Hmm, well—"

"On the other hand—" Orley steepled his fingers. "I'll put my cards on the table. The people who warned us can't rule out that China might actually have a hand in the planned attack—"

"Preposterous!" Jia snorted. "What interest would my country have in destroying your hotel?"

"You think it's ridiculous?"

"Quite ridiculous!"

Julian looked thoughtfully at the man sitting across from him. Jia was a pleasant enough guy, but he was a Beijing company man through and through. If the plot against Orley Enterprises really had been hatched in China, then Jia might well have some part in it. In which case, he was speaking to his enemy right now, which was one more reason to speak openly; he would have to make the man understand that the puppet masters were about to be unmasked, and that it might be a good move to spill the beans. If Jericho and his friends were wrong, then every secret and suspicion he aired was just one step closer to winning Jia's trust. He leaned forward.

"The bomb was put into orbit in 2024," he said.

"Okay, so?"

"That was when we had that crisis you mentioned."

"We did everything that we could to ensure a peaceful resolution."

"There's no arguing, though, that at the time, Beijing wasn't very well inclined toward Washington. This being so, you may be interested to learn that the bomb was bought from Korean stockpiles, on the black market, and that the buyers were Chinese."

Jia looked at him in astonishment. Then he passed his hand over his eyes, as though he had just walked head-on into a cobweb.

"We're a nuclear power," he said. "Why would the Party buy nuclear weapons on the black market?"

"I never said that it was the Party who bought it."

"Hmm. Go on."

"It's also worth noting that although the bomb was launched from African soil, the president of Equatorial Guinea at the time was just a puppet, and one that *your* government had installed. From what I understand, the technology for the Equatorial Guinea space program all came from Zheng—"

"Hold on!" Jia expostulated. "What are you saying? That Zheng wanted to destroy your hotel, with an atom bomb?"

"Please persuade me otherwise."

"Why would he do that?"

"I have no idea. Because we're commercial rivals?"

"But you're not! You're not competing for the same markets. You're competing for know-how. So you spy on one another, pay bribes, argue your corner, try to form alliances—but you don't start hurling nuclear bombs about."

"The gloves are off now."

"But an attack like that would be of absolutely no benefit to Zheng, or to my country! What would destroying your hotel do to change the balance of power, even if you died as well?"

"Quite so. What?"

For a long moment Jia said nothing at all, but kneaded at the bridge of his nose and kept his lids shut tight. When he opened them again, the question in his eyes was easy to read.

"No," Julian answered.

"No?"

"My visit here isn't part of some double-cross, honorable Jia, it's not a plan or an operation. I truly have no wish to harm you or your country. There's a lot I could have left unmentioned if I had wanted to steer your decision making."

"And what do you expect me to do now?"

"I can tell you what I need."

"You want me to take you and your friends back to the hotel with our shuttle?"

"As fast as you can! My son and daughter are in Gaia, as well as the guests and staff. We have reason to fear that Hanna is making his own way back there.—I also need the use of your satellites."

"My satellites?"

"Yes. Have you had any trouble with them in the last few hours?"

"Not that I know of."

"Ours have failed completely, as I told you at the beginning. Yours seem to be working. I need two connections. One to my headquarters in London, and another to Gaia." Julian paused. "I have put my trust in you completely, Commander, even at the risk of your refusing my request. I can do no more. The rest is up to you."

The taikonaut fell silent again, then said slowly, "You would of course be in China's debt if I were to help you."

"Of course."

Julian could see the wheels going around in Jia's head. Right at this moment, the commander was worrying about whether his visitor might actually be right, and his government had plotted some dirty trick that he knew nothing about. And whether, perhaps, he was in danger of committing high treason if he offered unconditional help to the man who had put America where it was today.

Julian cleared his throat.

"Perhaps you might bear in mind that somebody is trying to make a cat's paw of your country," he said. "I wouldn't take too kindly to that, if I were you."

Jia glowered at him.

"Entry-level Psychology."

"Ah, well." Julian shrugged and smiled. "Something of the sort."

"Go next door and join your friends," Jia said. "Wait."

Chambers couldn't stop the loop from playing. Over and over again she saw the beetle's foot coming down to crush her, and suddenly she began to twitch epileptically. She slid down the wall of the hab module like a wet rag. Amber and Oleg were in there with her. It was cramped in the station, horribly cramped, quite unlike the American living quarters. Na Mou, the taikonaut, was fussing over them with tea and spicy crab cakes. While Julian was softening up the commander, Chambers had been telling the Chinese woman about the events of the last few hours. Perhaps Na understood more English than she spoke, but Chambers herself was so horrified by her own story that the words stuck in her throat.

"You lie down," Na said, kindly. She was a Mongolian-looking woman with broad cheekbones and strongly slanted eyes, with something of the past about her, a suggestion of marching parades and collective farms.

"It keeps on coming," Chambers whispered. "It keeps on and on."

"Yes. Legs up."

"Whether I shut my eyes or keep them open, it never stops." She grabbed Na's wrist, and felt ice-cold sweat start up on her own upper lip and forehead. "I'll be squashed any moment. By a beetle. Isn't that crazy? People squash beetles, not the other way around. But I can't stop seeing it."

"You *can* stop." Amber turned away from Zhou Jinping, the third crew member at the base, who had been questioning her eagerly. She sat down next to Chambers. "You've had a shock, that's all."

"No, I—"

"It's okay, Evy. I'm pretty close to collapsing myself."

"No, there was something there." Chambers rolled her eyes, rather like a voodoo priestess in her trance, a mambo. "Death was there."

"I know."

"No, I was over on the other side, do you understand? I was really there. And Momoka was there, and—I mean, I knew that she was dead, but—"

Two dams broke, grief and shock, and tears spilled down over Chambers's beautiful Latin features. She gesticulated as though trying to ward off some spell, then let her hands drop, exhausted, and began to cry. Amber put an arm around her shoulder and drew her in close, gently.

"Too much," Na Mou said, nodding wisely.

"It'll all be all right, Evy."

"I wanted to ask her what happens to us next," Chambers sobbed. "It was so cold in her world. I think she laid a curse on me, she makes me see this terrible sight over and over, she must have seen something just as awful before she died, and—"

"Evy," Amber said quietly but firmly. "You're not clairvoyant. Your nerves are shot, that's all."

"I didn't even like her very much."

"None of us liked her very much." Amber sighed. "Apart from Warren, I suppose."

"But that's awful!" Chambers clung tightly to her, racked by sobs. "And now she's gone, we couldn't even—couldn't even say something nice—"

Do we have to? Amber thought. Do you have to say nice things to someone who's clearly a bitch, just on the off-chance that she'll kick the bucket in the near future?

"I don't think she really saw it like that," she said.

"Really?"

"Really. Momoka had her own ideas about what's nice or not."

Chambers buried her face in Amber's shoulder. The most powerful woman in American media, the voice who made presidents, cried for a few more minutes until she fell asleep from sheer exhaustion. Na Mou and Zhou Jinping had fallen quiet, respecting her sorrow. Rogachev was lying on one of the narrow beds, his legs crossed, and scribbling away on a piece of paper they had found for him.

"What are you doing there?" Amber asked, tired.

The Russian twiddled the pen in his fingers without looking at her.

"I'm doing my sums."

Jia Keqiang was wrestling with himself. It was a tough fight.

Plentiful experience told him what a long and stony path lay ahead if he took the matter through official channels, just as he knew that the Chinese space agency was largely staffed by paranoiacs. On the other hand, all he needed to do was make one telephone call, and he'd be free of all responsibility. He'd be out of danger of making any mistake, whereas if he spoke up for Orley on his own initiative he would be doomed to mistakes. All he had to do was pass the buck to one of the Party paper-shufflers, and if Orley's hotel actually was destroyed, it would be no fault of his. Then Beijing would have to face accusations of failing to live up to their treaty obligations and provide adequate help, while he could make loud noises about how he had wanted to help and hadn't been allowed. He could sleep easy in his bed, and not worry about his career.

If he *could* sleep easy.

On the other hand—what if Orley was right, and Beijing really was pulling the strings?

He turned his teacup thoughtfully between his fingers, staring down into the green tea. What then? He would dutifully call his superiors and tell them of Orley's suspicions, only to find himself up to the neck in state secrets. *Real* state secrets, which were no concern at all of his, because nobody had brought him into the circle. Obviously, he'd be classed as a national security risk right away. Flying Julian Orley over to Gaia in the shuttle was the least of his problems. It was hostile territory up here, and in case of doubt, they just didn't fly. Similarly, it would need permission and approvals in triplicate to let the Englishman use Chinese satellites to communicate. Before the Moon crisis, Jia would have been able to make a decision like that on his own, but that option was off the table now.

He would *have* to call.

So what would he tell them?

He pushed his teacup from right to left, left to right.

And all of a sudden he knew.

There was still a risk, but it could work. He stood up, went to the control panel, put a call through to Earth, and had two short conversations.

• • •

"I'll sum it up," Jia said, after he had asked Julian back into the narrow control room to join him. "You invite some friends for a private trip. Quite unexpectedly, one of your guests turns out to be a killer, he mows down five people and leaves you stranded on the Aristarchus Plateau."

"That's right."

"All this in response to his overhearing a conversation between yourself, Gaia, and company headquarters in London, which was about how terrorists may have smuggled a nuclear bomb onto the Moon to destroy an American or Chinese moon base."

"A Chi—" Julian blinked, bewildered. Then he understood. "Yes. That's right. That's just how it was."

"And you have no idea who might be behind it."

"Now that you put it that way, Commander, I haven't the foggiest idea. All I know is that Chinese or American citizens may be in danger."

"Mmhm." Jia nodded earnestly. "I understand. That makes it all very clear. By which I mean to say that it is in the interests of our national security to look into the matter together with you. I have explained precisely these facts to my superiors, and I have been given permission to prepare the satellite for your use, and then to fly you on to Vallis Alpina afterward."

Julian looked at the taikonaut.

"Thank you," he said softly.

"I'm pleased to be able to help."

"You do know, however, that the conversation I am about to conduct may lead to some unjustifiable accusations against China."

Jia shrugged.

"All that matters is that I don't know right now."

Shaw stood by the table of the conference room. She looked unkempt, as though she had been running about the whole day. Andrew Norrington and Edda Hoff were with her. Behind them, a rather rumpled-looking blond man leaned in the doorway.

"Julian!" she called aloud. "My God, are you all right? We've been trying to reach you for hours."

"Have you been able to make contact with Gaia?"

"No."

"Why not? You should be able to reach Gaia by the normal radio chann—"

"We've tried that. Nobody is responding."

Julian felt his heart skip a beat.

"Before you ask, there hasn't been an explosion at Vallis Alpina," Shaw said hurriedly. "At least that much is good news."

"And the base? Have you been able to talk to the moon base?"

"No response."

"Erm, Julian," Norrington broke in. "Our theory is that somebody is using the satellites to disrupt communication by unleashing a huge botnet on the Moon. The comms equipment up there is completely clogged up, so to speak. The truth is, we're half blind and completely deaf, we need information from you."

"How could anybody clog up our comms?" Julian snapped.

"Quite simple. You need an inside man."

Inside man. Inside woman. Great God, why couldn't he shake the idea that Lynn had something to do with it.

"We're just going over Hanna's background," Hoff said. "There's not a great deal we can say about him for sure, though his whole life story turns out not to be worth the paper it's printed on. We are however agreed that he can't be operating on his own up there."

"Once again, *where are you?*" Norrington urged him.

Julian sighed. He gave a brief account of what had happened in the hours since communications had collapsed. Shaw's face turned paler with every death he recounted.

"Jia Keqiang has been kind enough to agree to fly us to the hotel," he finished up. "We'll try to reach Gaia through the Chinese satellite first, to—"

"Mr. Orley." The blond man straightened up from the doorway and took a step forward. "You shouldn't fly back to Gaia."

Julian looked at the man, frowning in confusion. Then all of a sudden he realized.

"You're Owen Jericho."

"Yes."

"I beg your pardon." He spread his hands. "I should have thanked you long ago, but—"

"Some other time. Does the name Hydra mean anything to you?"

Julian stared.

"Greek mythology," he ventured. "Monster with nine heads."

"Nothing else spring to mind?"

"No."

"It looks as though an organization called Hydra is responsible for all this. Heads that grow back when you cut them off. A great many heads. Invincible, worldwide. For a while we thought that the people pulling the strings were in Chinese high finance or politics, but whichever way you look at it, that doesn't make any sense. By the way, a friend of yours was on Hydra's hit list."

"What? Who was that, for Heaven's sake?"

"Gerald Palstein."

"What? Why would they want to get Gerald?"

"That's the easiest question to answer," Norrington chipped in. "When Palstein was shot, that meant that he had to pull out of the moon trip at short notice and make room for Hanna."

"But how—"

"Later." Jericho came closer. "The most important thing for you to know right now is that the attack isn't aimed at Gaia."

"It's not?" Julian asked. "But you said—"

"I know. It looks like we made a mistake. In the meantime we've been able to decode more of the message, and it seems that the bomb isn't there to destroy your hotel."

"But what, then?"

There was silence for a moment, as though everyone in the room was waiting for someone else to spill the beans.

"Peary Base," Shaw said.

Julian stared at her, his mouth open. Jia looked as though the ground had opened up under his feet.

"Beijing would never plan—" he began.

"We're not certain that Beijing's behind it," Shaw interrupted. "At least, not Chinese government circles. But that's irrelevant right now. Hydra want to contaminate Peary Crater, the Mountains of Eternal Light, the whole region! They don't want anything from us, they just used us to get up to the Moon. Contact the base right away, however you do it! They've got to search the place with a fine-toothed comb, and evacuate if need be."

"Good God," Julian whispered. "Who are Hydra?"

"No idea. But whoever they are—they want to wipe America off the face of the Moon."

"And Carl's headed there right now." In an instant, it all became clear. He leaped to his feet and stared at Jia. "He's going to arm the bomb. He'll arm it, and then clear out!"

They couldn't reach Peary Base with the Chinese satellite either, which made Orley even more frantic. They tried to reach Gaia, with no luck. Then the base again. Then Gaia again. Shortly after four o'clock, they gave up.

"It can't be anything to do with our satellite," Jia argued. "We could talk to London no problem."

Orley looked at him. "Are you thinking what I'm thinking?"

"That the bomb has already exploded, and that's why we can't reach anybody?" Jia rubbed his eyes. "I'll admit, I had considered it."

"It's horrific," Orley whispered.

"But we heard that the satellites aren't the problem. It's the communications equipment. Peary Base and Gaia have been attacked, we haven't. Which means that we can communicate, just not with the hotel, and not with the Pole. Besides, a nuclear explosion—" Jia hesitated. "Don't you think we'd have been told? My country keeps a very close eye on the Moon. I think your hotel must still be in one piece."

"But the base is in the libration shadow, which means that your country can watch until they go blue in the face, they won't see anything!"

"Please be assured that China has nothing to do with it."

"I don't understand." Orley paced around the small control room. "I simply don't understand. What's all this in aid of?"

Jia turned his head. "When do you want to set off?"

"Now. I'll tell the others." Orley paused. "I am really very grateful, Commander. Very."

"Keqiang," Jia heard himself say.

Really? For a moment, he felt an urge to withdraw the offer, but he liked this easygoing, long-haired Englishman. Had he been too harsh in judging the relaxed Western ways? Maybe being on first-name terms was a step toward harmony among the nations.

"One thing's for sure, Keqiang," Orley said with a sour grimace. "There'd have been no Moon crisis if it had been down to us two."

At that moment, they heard his name.

It droned from the loudspeakers, part of a looped message, an automatic broadcast signal.

"Callisto to Ganymede. Callisto to Julian Orley. Please come in. Julian Orley, Ganymede, please come in. Callisto to—"

Jia leaped up and raced to the console.

"Callisto? This is Jia Keqiang, commander of the Chinese mining operations. Where are you?"

For a second there was only crackling from the loudspeakers, then Nina Hedegaard's face appeared on the screen.

"We're flying over the Montes Jura," she said. "How come—"

"We're keeping our ears open. Are you looking for Julian Orley?"

"Yes," she said emphatically, "*yes!*"

Julian shoved into view. "Nina! Where are you?"

"Julian!" Suddenly Tim's face appeared next to hers. "At last! Is everybody all right?"

"I'm afraid not."

"But—" Tim was visibly distraught.

"That's to say, Amber's fine," Julian reassured him hurriedly. "What happened to Lynn? And Gaia? Tim, what's going on here?"

"We don't know. Lynn's—we're alive."

"You're *alive*?"

"Gaia was destroyed."

Julian stared at the screen, lost for words.

"There was a fire, several people died. We had to evacuate anyway, because of the bomb."

The bomb—

"No, Tim." He shook his head, and clenched his fists.

"Don't worry, we're safe. At the moon base. That's where we just flew from. There are two search parties out to—"

"Are you in touch with the base?"

"No, they're cut off from the outside world."

"Tim—"

"Julian, I'm coming in to land," Nina said. "We'll be back at the Pole in an hour. Then we can—"

"Too late, that's too late!" he yelled. "The bomb's not in Gaia. Do you hear? Gaia has nothing to do with all that. The bomb's stored at the Pole, it's meant for the moon base. Where's Lynn, Tim? *Where's Lynn?*"

Tim froze. His lips formed three silent words:

At the Pole.

"Don't tell me that!" Julian wrung his hands and looked about frantically. "You have to get her out some—"

"Julian," Nina said. "The second search party set out after us; they're circling over the Mare Imbrium. As soon as we've picked you up, we'll climb until we can make contact and we'll send them straight back to the base. They're closer than we are."

"Hurry! Carl's on his way to Peary. He's going to arm it!"

"We're on our way."

Peary Base,
North Pole, The Moon

Dana Lawrence sat in the half-dark of the command center in Igloo 1, breathing in pure oxygen through a mask, staring dead ahead. She'd had enough oxygen back in Gaia to see to the smoke inhalation, but a couple more breaths couldn't hurt.

"Don't you want to go get some sleep?" Wachowski asked sympathetically. The lights from the control panels and screens bathed his face in an anemic blue-white glow. "I'll wake you if anything happens."

"Thanks, I'm fine."

In fact she didn't feel tired at all. For as long as she could remember, all her strength had been focused on not falling asleep. In the sickbay, Kramp, Eva, and the Nairs were lying comatose, exhausted. They were all under sedation, and tended by DeLucas, the station medic and life-support specialist. Even DeLucas, though, had no idea what Lynn needed. A young geologist called Jean-Jacques Laurie had suggested leaving her in the care of ISLAND-I, an older model than ISLAND-II. The programmed psychologist had diagnosed shock, to nobody's astonishment, along with a possible case of late-onset psychosomatic mutism. Since then, Julian's daughter had been either lying wide-eyed in the dark, or wandering about like a zombie, a prisoner in her own body. The Ögis were the only ones who were healthy and in full possession of their wits, and they had taken a room in one of the western towers. The base was short-staffed, all the survivors were out of action, the search parties had set off on their fools' errand, and Hanna would be trying to get back to the hotel. God knows she had done everything she could to make things easy for him, but Hanna wasn't coming. By now it was past four o'clock, and any confidence she had had that he would turn up was gone. The plan had been that they would carry out the operation together, but in this trade, you fought side by side with your comrade until circumstances demanded you sacrifice him. In two to three hours, the search parties would be back. By then, one of them *had* to have done the deed.

She got up.

"I'm going to stretch my legs. It'll help me stay awake."

"We brew a pretty good coffee up here as well," Wachowski said.

"I know. I've had four cups already."

"I'll put on some more."

"I've had enough smoke inside me to poison my system, thanks, I won't risk a caffeine overdose. I'll be next door in the fitness room if anything happens."

"Dana?" Wachowski smiled, embarrassed.

"Yes?"

"I can call you Dana, can't I?"

Dana raised an eyebrow. "Of course—Tommy."

"Respect."

"Oh." She smiled again. "Thank you."

"I really mean it. You're keeping it all together! After everything that happened, Orley can be glad he has you. You're keeping a cool head."

"Well, I try to."

"His daughter's pretty much in a world of her own."

"Hmm. ISLAND-I says she's suffering from shock."

"Pretty severe shock. What's up with her? You know her better, Dana, what's her problem?"

Dana was silent for a moment.

"The same problem we all have," she said as she left the room. "She has her demons."

HANNA

The freight train with the helium-3 tanks shot up the valley bed to Peary launch field at more than 700 kilometers per hour, but Hanna's thoughts were moving faster.

He had to arm the bomb, but before he did that, it would be best to make contact with Dana. He hadn't the first idea what might have happened at the hotel. All he knew for sure was that with his cover blown, they had a lot less room to maneuver. If he waited for her at the Pole, they could escape together, but he'd find himself an officially wanted man, by the time they boarded the OSS at the latest, and he could forget taking the elevator back down to Earth. The whole screwup called for quick action. Set the fuse timer, then get out of there on the Charon. Xin's finely crafted plan could still work. Not exactly in all details, perhaps, but with the same results. It would be best if Dana were still safely tucked away in the Vallis Alpina, putting on a show of concern, and hoping that the Chinese could put her through to Earth under their treaty obligations for mutual assistance.

The high plain drew closer. He could see the blast walls around the spaceport, the hangars, antennae, the neat lines of human presence. He was pressed against the tank in front of him as the maglev slowed, much more sharply than the Lunar Express. For a moment he was afraid that he had misjudged things, that he would be crushed in the murderous deceleration, then the train slid around the last curve as gently as a Sunday excursion and drew to a halt at the station. Hanna jumped onto the platform before a manipulator arm could mistake him for a helium-3 tank, taking care to stay out of sight of the surveillance cameras. All around him the machinery awoke to life, forklifts rolled up, the arms began to unload. He scurried to the further edge of the platform and leaped the 15 meters to the ground in a single bound. Two kilometers of rough ground stretched away ahead of him, broken only by the road from the spaceport to the igloos. They showed starkly against the hills beyond and the factory buildings around, flanked on either side by the towers of the residential quarters, and in among them, a seemingly random assortment of warehouses and huts. Some distance away, a vast structure reared out of the stony surge of a hillside, the shell of the helium-3 power station, under construction.

Hanna loped off at an even, unhurried pace, keeping off the road and in the shelter of the slopes for as long as he could see the base to his right. Soon enough there'd be another sun shining here, only briefly but so blazing bright, and it would change everything. The landscape around. The course of history.

LAWRENCE

She went up to the top level of Igloo 1 in the elevator, then took the connecting walkway between the two domes. Beneath her the road ran off to the factories behind. There were a few small windows here, with views out to the edge of the crater, the industrial plant, and the spaceport. The sun cast a panorama of shadow like a painting by Giorgio de Chirico, but Dana had no eyes for the surreal beauty of the landscape under the billions of stars. Intent on her task, she crossed to Igloo 2, took the elevator down to the lounge, where she put on the armored plates and backpack of her space suit. She picked up her helmet and then took the elevator on down, past the fitness studios and the sickbay, through a layer of rock into the winding labyrinthine caves and pathways of the underground level. She had memorized every detail of Peary Base from Thorn's maps and descriptions, so that without ever having been here before, she knew what lay ahead of her, knew which way to turn once the elevator doors glided apart.

She stepped out onto a seabed.

At least that was how it looked. The glass walls of fishtanks stretched up, meters high, all around her. Flickering pools of light chased one another like will-o-the-wisps across the floor, reflected from the water when the ruffled surface was stirred up by salmon and trout and perch as they darted about, by the schools of fish flitting back and forth. A little while later the cave divided, most branches leading off into the darkness, only a few passages shimmering with blue-green or white light, and beyond them the greenhouses, the genetic laboratories, and production facilities which kept the moon base stocked with fruit and vegetables. She crossed a passageway, walked along a short corridor, and emerged into a vast, almost round stone hall. She could have taken an elevator down here directly from Igloo 1, but Wachowski had to believe that she was in the fitness studio. Her eyes swept around the place, looking for cameras. There hadn't been any here back in Thorn's day, nor could she see any now. Even if there was any such thing down here, Wachowski would have enough on his hands—short-staffed as the moon base was—watching the external cameras. The fishtanks and kitchen gardens were the last thing that he would be looking at.

Several passageways led off from the hall, leading to the laboratories, storehouses, and residential blocks. Only one passage had an air lock, which led onto hundreds of kilometers of unexplored caves, unused, branching endlessly in the vacuum. Most of the lava tubes petered out in the cliff-like rim of Peary Crater, while others burrowed downward, some of them opening out into the canyon fault that ran through the whole site. She put on her helmet, stepped into the air lock, and pumped out the air. After a minute, the outer door opened. She switched on her helmet lamp and went into an unhewn rocky passageway which led her onward into the darkness, black as night. The torchbeam skittered nervously over vitrified basalt. After about 100 meters, she saw a gap open up in the wall to her left, just as Hanna had said. It was narrow, unnervingly so. She squirmed through, pulled her shoulders in, got down on all fours when the roof suddenly dipped down toward her, and crawled through the last part of the cleft on her belly. It had almost become too narrow to bear when the walls suddenly swept apart and she could see a pile of rubble that had obviously been heaped up by the hand of man; she stretched out both hands and moved the rocks aside.

She could see something low, flat, and shimmering. Something with a blinking display, and an arming panel.

Hanna had positioned it neatly, she had to admit.

All of a sudden she realized that her cloud had a silver lining here. If all had gone according to plan, the package would have reached the base of the canyon under its own power, and lain there undisturbed until the last day of the trip. Only then, during the official visit to the base just before they all returned to the OSS, would Hanna have left the group, retrieved the contents, and taken the bomb up into the caves. Charon would have left the Moon that same evening, and then the payload would have blown twenty-four hours later. But the package's mechanisms had failed, so Hanna had had to take the contents up to the base ahead of schedule, to hide the mini-nuke here in the bowels of the caves. In hindsight, since his cover had been blown and everything thrown into disarray, it was a blessing that he had been forced to do that.

She opened the catch, lifted the cover to the keypad, and hesitated.

When should she set the detonator for? By now everybody knew that there was an attack planned. They still believed that it was aimed at Gaia, and she had done all she could to encourage that. But perhaps the search parties up on Aristarchus might realize what was going on. What if they came back, knowing that the base itself was in danger, and then started to search here at the Pole?

She mustn't give them enough time to find the bomb.

A short fuse, then.

Dana shivered. Better if she wasn't vaporized by the nuclear blast herself. Right now, her fingers were hovering over the control panel of a miracle of destructive technology which could turn Peary Crater into one of the circles of hell, sweeping away every trace of human presence as though it had never been. A good idea then to be as far away as possible, but when would the search parties return, when would the Charon set off? The safe option to make sure that she survived would be to set the detonator at twenty-four hours. But what if the communications jam failed prematurely, and they learned that the mini-nuke really was here at the Pole?

There was no way they could find that out.

But they could. The very fact that they knew that the bomb existed at all proved that they could find out anything. Callisto must have reached the Aristarchus Plateau by now. If they had found any survivors, then she could expect them back soon. If not, then they would keep searching for who knew how long. She couldn't decide based on what she thought the shuttles might do. She had to arm this bomb, hijack the Charon, and then fly to OSS. She'd have a lot of explaining to do once she got there; why she had flown off without the others, why she had flown off at all, how she could have known about the bomb. Especially if there were any survivors, who could bring all her carefully placed lies tumbling down.

But she would have to deal with that when it happened. She had been trained to deal with that sort of thing.

Her fingers twitched, indecisive.

Then she punched in a time code, piled the rocks up in front of the bomb again, and squirmed hastily backward. The inferno was set. Time to get out of here.

IGLOO 1

Wachowski was visibly startled.

"What are you doing here?"

Lynn looked down at him, mildly surprised to see herself in his eyes as he so clearly saw her, a pale phantom with wild hair, looming up silently as though driven into the room by a gust of wind, an apparition: Lady Madeline Usher, Elsa Lanchester as the Bride of Frankenstein, the very image of a B-movie. Quite astonishing, how clearly she could see all these pictures shining out in the darkness of her thoughts, now that her sanity had fled the scene—although it had obviously left a breadcrumb trail to guide the little girl lost back into the waking world.

Follow your thoughts, astral voices whispered to her. Go into the light, into the light, star-child, they muttered, higher intelligences without need of physical bodies but with a twisted sense of humor, who lured unsuspecting astronauts into monoliths, dumping them into bad copies of Louis Quatorze bedrooms, just as had happened to poor Bowman, who—

Bowman? Lady Madeline?

This is my mind, she screamed. My mind, Julian!

And her scream, that brave little scream, set out, bold little fellow, dragged itself the whole long way out to the event horizon, then lost its strength, lost its courage, tottered over backward and died.

"Are you all right?"

Wachowski cocked his head. Interesting. The way the snaking arteries at his temples busily pumped blood showed he was on edge, alert. Lynn could see the tiny submarines sailing through the flow.

"I didn't hear you come in."

Submarines in the blood. Dennis Quaid in *Inner Space*. No. Raquel Welch and Donald Pleasence, *Fantastic Voyage*. The o-o-o-o-riginal!

Oh yes. Sorry, Daddy.

She was contaminated ground. Poisoned by Julian. No mistake, there he was, teasing her, making a fool of her with his movie mania. Whenever she thought she had reached her real self, there she was in one of *his* worlds, Alice in Orley-Land, eternal heroine in *his* invention, *his* original creation.

You're mad, Lynn, she thought. You've ended up like Crystal. First depressive, then mad.

Or had Julian written *this* role for her as well?

His flashing eyes, his floating hands, whenever he took her and Tim into his private movie theater, where they had to watch every meter of celluloid or digital drama that ever a science-fiction author or director had dreamed up: Georges Méliès's *Voyage dans la lune*, Fritz Lang's *Woman in the Moon*, Nathan Juran's *First Men in the Moon*, *This Island Earth* with Jeff Morrow and Faith Domergue and the mutant—oh my word, that mutant!—*Star Trek*, *The Man Who Fell to Earth*, *A Space Odyssey*, *Star Wars*, *Alien*, *Independence Day*, *War of the Worlds*, *Perry Rhodan* with Finn O'Keefe, hey, Finn O'Keefe, wasn't he somewhere hereabouts, and always—fanfare!—Lynn Orley, the lead role in—

"You really gave me a shock."

Wachowski. All alone in the twilit control room, surrounded by screens and consoles. Shouldn't make such a fuss, the bastard. He looked unsettled himself.

"That's good," Lynn whispered.

She leaned down to him, put her hand to the back of his neck, and pressed her lips to his. Mmhm, warm, that was good. She was Grace Kelly. Wasn't she? And he—

"Miss Orley, Lynn—" Cary Grant stiffened.

Sorry, is this the right set for *To Catch a Thief*?

Funny. That wasn't even a science-fiction film. Julian liked it, though.

Click, hssss, verify.

You lost the hotel.

Another of those lit-up signposts. What was she doing here? What the hell was she doing in the control room, with her nose full of Wachowski's greasy smell? She pushed him away, started back, and wiped her lips in disgust.

"Are you okay?" he whispered, in fascinated horror.

"Yes, never better!" she snarled at him. "Do you have anything to drink?"

He jumped to his feet, nodding.

Glug, glug, and her thoughts were draining away once more, whirled down the drain. When he put the glass of water in her hand, she couldn't even remember having asked for it.

Hanna

He had given the residential towers a wide berth, trudging past them in an arc along the edge of the chasm. The canyon was a collapsed lava channel, and not all of its walls were sheer drops; rather they formed staircases and steps, so that Hanna could make his way down easily. To the west, the canyon opened out into a steep valley that cut through Peary Crater's flank, while to his right, toward the base, the chasm grew narrower. Standing on its floor, Hanna could just about see the tops of two residential towers, shining in the sunlight, and two bridges, not far apart, that spanned the canyon above. It was dark down here, and the canyon floor was strewn with rubble. He picked his way through under the first bridge, following a groove in the rock that led him like a path over the gently sloping ground, as far as the second bridge. Then he twisted to look upward.

About 10 meters above him, a hole yawned in the cliff face.

Several such holes dotted the rock where lava tubes opened up into the canyon, but this one in particular interested him. He clambered up, reached the opening, then switched on his helmet lamp and made his way into the twisting cave. The cave mouth was steep for a moment, and then leveled off. His headlamp caught the ragged gap through to where the bomb lay slumbering. For a moment he considered skipping the visit to the control room and programming the thing right away, but he had to speak to Dana first. A lot could have happened in the past few hours that would force them to make a whole new plan, and on top of that he urgently needed information to help him see where he stood personally. If all was going according to plan, the laser link between the base and Gaia would be functioning, but Dana would have fixed it so that all signals went straight through to her cell phone.

He ignored the crack and went to the air lock instead, and stepped into it. There was light coming through the tiny viewport. On the other side of the air lock was the room they called the Great Hall, a large natural cave leading off to the laboratories, greenhouses, and fish-tanks. An elevator from the Hall up to Igloo 1 led straight to the control room. Hanna glanced at his watch. Almost half past four. Could be that the control room wasn't even occupied. Nevertheless he drew his gun as he went into the Hall, scanned all around for threats, and then tapped the sensor that would bring the elevator down.

LAWRENCE

She was determined not to spend a second longer in the base than she had to. She'd glanced through the sickbay door in Igloo 2, heard the roomful of snoring sleepers like an orchestra playing softly, with Mukesh Nair taking the solo lead as far as she could tell. Minnie DeLucas, a African-American woman with dreadlocks, was working at a computer.

"How are they?" Dana asked, concern in her voice.

"They're as well as they can be." The medic put a finger to her lips and glanced over to the beds. "The smoke inhalation isn't so bad, but the tall German lady seems pretty traumatized, I'd say. She was telling me what happened in the elevator shafts at the hotel. How she couldn't save that woman."

"Yes," Dana whispered. "We saw some dreadful things. How is Miss Orley, though?"

"I would have had to strap her down to keep her here."

"She's gone then?"

"Wandering around somewhere. She can't sleep, or doesn't want to. I think she went over to Tommy in the control room. And you? Are you coping?"

"Oh yes. I've breathed in so much oxygen these past few hours that I don't think the smoke inhalation can touch me."

"I mean mentally."

"I cope." She shrugged her shoulders. "I try my best to do without mental traumas. I find they're something of a luxury."

"You should see a psychologist, in any case," DeLucas advised.

"Of course."

"I'm serious, Dana. Don't try burying it. There's no shame in asking for help."

"What makes you think I might be ashamed?"

"You just give the impression that you—" DeLucas hesitated. "That you're very hard on yourself. Yourself, and others."

"Oh." Dana raised her eyebrows, interested. "Do I?"

"There's nothing wrong with putting yourself on the couch," DeLucas smiled.

"Oh, there are some people who reckon I belong on the couch." She winked confidingly. "See you later. I'm going to run for a bit."

Igloo 1

In a lucid interval, Lynn had sought out the control room's coffee nook to put down her empty glass. It was a small space, half screened off from the rest of the room by a sheet of sand-blasted glass. Something inside her said that it was important to put things back where they belonged, after she'd spent weeks and months torturing herself with wild terrors, visions of destruction. Gaia was in ruins. She had wrecked it so often in her dreams that she felt a gnawing suspicion that she truly had destroyed it herself, but she wasn't really sure.

At the very moment that she put the glass down, suddenly all the pieces fell into place, and she remembered.

The rescue mission up on the crown of Gaia's head. Miranda's death.

She tried to cry. Turned down the corners of her mouth. Made a tearful face. But her tear ducts wouldn't do their job, and until she could cry, she would wander onward through the maze of her own soul, without hope of redemption. Undecided, she was staring dumbly at the glass when she heard the elevator humming.

Somebody was coming up here.

Her face twisted into a mask of rage. She didn't want anybody up here. She didn't want Tommy Wachowski anywhere near her. He'd kissed her, the pig! Hadn't he? How could he do a thing like that? As though she were some cheap slut! A slut in a space suit. There for anyone to fuck: a toy, an avatar, a plaything for other people's fantasies!

You can all go fuck yourselves, she thought.

Fuck you, Julian!

She leaned back a little, so that she could see past the edge of the frosted glass—and into the control room. The elevator shaft passed through the middle of the igloo like an axis. Somebody in a space suit came out of the elevator, helmet in one hand, gun in the other. It was quite obviously a gun, since he was pointing it at Wachowski, who jumped up and scurried backward in surprise.

"Who else is here?" the new arrival asked in a low voice.

"Nobody."

"Are you sure?"

Wachowski somehow managed not to glance toward the coffee nook.

"Just me," he said hoarsely.

"Anybody who might turn up anytime soon?"

Wachowski hesitated. He had been left as base commander. He hunched a little. He seemed to be considering whether to attack the other man, who was much bigger than him. Lynn was staring, paralyzed, at the shaven back of the big man's head, unable to move even a finger or turn away her gaze.

Carl Hanna!

"You never know who may just turn up," Wachowski said, playing for time. "It wouldn't be too smart to—"

There was a soft pop. The base commander dropped to the ground and didn't move.

Hanna turned around.

Nothing. Just the big, softly lit space of the control room. Deserted, save for the dead man at his feet.

Hanna put his helmet down on the console, kept his gun at the ready, and walked once around the elevator shaft. None of the other workstations was occupied. Faint light glowed from behind a frosted-glass screen, where he could see part of a shelf, full of packs of coffee, filters, and mugs.

He stopped dead, moved closer.

He heard a faint shuffling sound from where he had shot the other man. He spun around in an instant, trained the gun on the motion-less body, and then dropped the muzzle at the same moment when he realized that the man was dead as dead could be. It had just been his arm, slipping down to the side. He holstered his weapon and leaned over the console, studying its controls. His fingers scurried over the touchscreen, called up a connection with Gaia—or what ought to have been a connection, but there was no answer.

He tried again. The channel was dead.

What was happening over there?

"Dana, dammit," he hissed. "Pick up."

After he had tried one more time, it slowly dawned on him that it couldn't be Dana's fault. The computer was telling him that no connection could be made. In other words, there was no connection through to the hotel, even by laser link.

Gaia wasn't answering.

Lynn huddled against the sink, clenched like a fist, making herself smaller and smaller, pressing her face between her knees. She had overcome her paralysis at the last moment and pulled her head back in a flash—oh, the things you can do, thought little girl lost jubilantly, following the glowing trail of crumbs, amazed at her own miraculous reflexes, while the grown-up woman, the body she lived in, cramped up with tension and her lungs began to ache from holding her breath.

Another chasm yawned in her thoughts. That was Carl Hanna, the guy who would rather have been a pop star. Hanna, maybe a little standoffish, but pleasant enough for all that, popular with all, the man she'd chatted with one late evening in Gaia, the man whose muscular body she'd imagined—just for a moment—on hers, his strong hands passing skillfully across her, if only she could work up the nerve to drag him off to her suite. That hideous suite, oh hell, where the mirror held a hysteric, a notorious madwoman who gulped down green tablets; that was why she didn't like to spend time in that suite. Hanna had been cool and collected, and she had reined herself in, and after that there were a few chapters missing in the chronology, things were mixed up. Somebody had said that Hanna was a bad guy, that he wanted to blow up her hotel. Just a few words had turned her world topsy-turvy, and now the same nice guy she'd been flirting with in the Mama Quilla Club had shot poor Tommy Wachowski, and all of a sudden she felt a horror of his muscular body and his skilled hands. Fear bathed her brain in ice water, so that for a moment she could think clearly again, at least enough to know that she mustn't move a muscle, mustn't surrender to the urge to whimper helplessly and whistle the songs of a little girl lost, because if she did, the man who'd been calling himself Carl Hanna would kill her too.

She held her breath and listened, heard him curse, heard every word he spoke, heard his secrets.

HANNA

Change of plan. Dana was no longer a factor. Whatever had happened to her, he had to go on without her.

Those were the rules.

Hanna swung the dead man over his shoulders like a sack of Christmas toys and went back down to the Great Hall, dragged him out into the air lock, and watched his face distend in the vacuum. Then he pulled Wachowski into the cave beyond and didn't spare him another thought. He ran to the cleft, squirmed in, got down on his hands and knees, and slithered along like a snake until the passage opened out again and the familiar pile of rubble appeared in the torchlight. He shoveled the stones aside with both hands, opened up the control panel on the mini-nuke, lifted the cover—

And froze.

The detonator had been programmed.

For a moment, there was a vacuum in his mind. He refused to believe what he saw, but there was no doubt, somebody had activated the bomb. And that somebody could only be—

Dana Lawrence.

She was here! No, she was gone. As good as gone. If Dana Lawrence didn't want to risk being vaporized on the slopes of Peary Crater, she had to be leaving the base on board the Charon, probably at this very moment. Which meant—

He scrambled hastily backward out of the tunnel, stood up too soon, bashed his helmet on the roof, found his way out, and then ran along to the rift, following the bobbing light from his headlamp. He leaped down to the canyon floor, stumbled along the grooved path, climbed the cliff wall by the first bridge, and heaved himself over the edge. He loped along the road in long strides, past the residential towers, hurrying over the dusty regolith.

Igloo 2

Minnie DeLucas glided her fingers over the touchscreen and completed a set of four bases.

She had always argued that it would be possible to raise moon calves in the catacombs of Peary Base. Chickens could barely survive in the extremes of zero-g, but they did well enough in one-sixth of Earth's gravity, laying eggs that dropped neatly to the floor of their hutches. They also made a pretty good lunar chicken burger. So why shouldn't calves and lambs thrive at the Pole? Maybe even pigs, although the whole problem with the smell meant opening up some of the more distant caves. As a scientist, DeLucas was used to tackling problems from the practical and the theoretical side, and since right now there was no livestock to be had, she was busy experimenting with the genomes. Watching other people sleep wasn't exactly a challenge. As long as none of them fell out of bed, she could work undisturbed. Right now she had loaded data from some experiments with Galloway cattle embryos to the sickbay computer, and was so busy with the results that at first she didn't realize someone was talking to her.

"Peary, please come in. Io to Peary. This is Kyra Gore. Wachowski, why aren't you picking up?"

DeLucas looked at the clock: ten to five. Io was back within radio range. They'd got back surprisingly quickly, but why were they calling her?

"Minnie here," she said.

"Hey, what's up?" Gore asked urgently. "Where's Tommy kicking his heels?"

"No idea. Perhaps he's gone to the little boys' room."

"Tommy wouldn't go pee without taking his radio with him."

"He's not been by to talk to me. Where are—"

"We'll be with you in five minutes! Listen, Minnie, you've got to get the people out of there! Get out of the base! Bring them all to the landing field."

"What? Why?"

"The bomb's *in the base.*"

"In the base?"

"It's been hidden somewhere under our noses! The guy who's going to prime it is on his way to you. Get everybody into their space suits and bring them outside. And go look for Tommy."

The Landing Field, The Moon

Dana had switched her transceiver to pick up all frequencies, so that she heard Io's call as she went through the gate to the spaceport.

She stopped dead. What the hell were they doing back here already? At the very most, she'd have expected Tommy Wachowski to radio her to ask what she was up to, since she'd made no effort to stay out of sight as she dashed to the landing field, but now Io was coming in to land. And to make it even worse:

They knew about the bomb!

Now she really did have just a matter of minutes.

Dana began to run.

DeLucas

Fighting to remain calm, she ran next door and shook the German women awake, then the Indian couple. Which wasn't so easy, as she found out. Certainly Mukesh Nair started up from his sleep with one last trumpeting blast of snores, and Karla Kramp sat up straight, blinking curiously, but Eva Borelius and Sushma Nair both lay there as though in an enchanted slumber.

"What's going on?" asked Kramp.

"You'll have to get dressed," DeLucas said, her eyes skittering about. "Everyone into their space suits. We're leaving the base."

"Aha," said Kramp. "And why are we doing that?"

"It's a—precaution."

"Against?"

"Sushma?" Mukesh Nair was struggling visibly against the sedatives, and it looked as if he was losing. "Sushma, my love! Get up."

"I just want to know what's going on," Kramp said, but she was obediently gathering her belongings as she spoke.

"So do I," DeLucas said as she hurried out. "You just make sure that everyone here is ready to leave in five minutes."

Instead of taking the elevator, she ran up the stairs to the top floor, looked in the lounge, then sprang back down the steps and checked the fitness studio. Hadn't Dana said that she would be running? And where was Tommy lurking? Where was Lynn Orley? Her uneventful vigil had suddenly turned into herding cats. DeLucas dashed back up to the top floor, hurried along the passageway to Igloo 1, and went into the control room. It was lit only by the dim glow of computer screens, and seemed deserted.

"Tommy?" she called.

There was nobody here. The only noise in the room was the machines chattering away to one another, a faint humming of transistors and ventilation, whirring, clicking, beeping. She walked quickly around the room, looking at every screen in the hope that she might spot Wachowski, but he was nowhere to be seen. As she left she heard a new sound, a noise she couldn't quite recognize, a soft, high squeak. She paused on the threshold, hesitant, filled with dread, then turned around.

What was that?

Now she couldn't hear it.

Just as she was about to turn around again, she heard it once more. Not a squeak, more like a whimper. It was coming from somewhere toward the back of the room, and it was creepy. Her heart beat faster as she went back into the control room and circled the elevator shaft.

Halfway around it was closer, much closer: a thin, unhappy sound coming from the small recessed space of the coffee nook.

DeLucas drew a deep breath and looked inside.

Lynn Orley was squatting in front of the sink, her arms wrapped tightly around herself, making those forlorn sounds.

DeLucas squatted level with her.

"Miss Orley."

No reaction. The woman simply looked straight through her as though she wasn't there. DeLucas hesitated, put out her hand, and touched her shoulder gently.

She might just as well have pulled the ring on a hand grenade.

THE LANDING FIELD, THE MOON

Dana cursed. Why did the landing module have to be right at the other end of the spaceport? Every second that passed lessened her chances of being able to clear out of here.

She had to think of some alternatives.

What if she—?

"Wait."

Someone grabbed her upper arm.

Dana leaped to one side, turning. She saw a tall, well-built astronaut, barely recognizable behind his mirrored faceplate, but his height and voice left her in no doubt. She immediately switched to a secure channel.

"Where were you?" she hissed.

"You set the timer," Hanna stated, without answering her question. "Did you want to leave without me?"

"You weren't there."

"Now I'm here. Come along."

He started moving. Dana followed, just as the bulky shape of the Io came into sight on the other side of the blast walls. The next moment the shuttle was hanging over the landing field, dropping, its engines pumping, and blocked their way.

Hanna stopped dead, reached for his thigh, and drew his gun.

"Forget it," Dana whispered.

Io settled down, bouncing slightly, and the elevator shaft extended from its belly. There were two of them, facing Leland Palmer's troupe of five astronauts in peak physical condition and with excellent reflexes, admittedly unarmed but fast and with close-combat training. It might just be possible to take them down in a skirmish, but whatever happened, Dana's cover would be blown, and she couldn't allow that at any cost.

That made up her mind.

She switched back to the general broadcast channel, and unclipped the little pickax from its place on her suit. Everyone had one for emergencies, or to chip away little lumps of moon rock as souvenirs. Hanna had straddled his legs, taking up position, aiming. The air lock cabin traveled down the shaft to the landing pad. The doors opened. Astronauts emerged. She saw the pistol muzzle track upward, and she lifted the pickax over her head—

And brought it smashing down.

The point of the pick stabbed through the tough material of the suit and into the back of Hanna's hand, deep in between the bones and sinews. The Canadian groaned in pain. He spun around and struck out at Dana, knocking her off her feet.

"Help!" she yelled. "Help!"

There was a hubbub of voices. Incomprehensibly, Hanna was still holding his gun, the fingers of his left hand clenched over the hole in his space suit, and was aiming at Dana. She rolled, kicked out at his knee and made him stagger. The next moment, she had sprung to her feet and swung the pick again. This time the needle-sharp end hit Hanna's faceplate and made a tiny hole in the armored glass. He leaped backward and kicked her in the belly. The pickax was torn from her grasp and stayed where it was, lodged in his visor. She flew away and landed a few meters off, scrambling to her feet. Part of her chestplate splintered off, and she knew he had shot at her. The crew of Io were running toward them across the landing field in huge lunar leaps.

She had to finish this. Whatever happened, the astronauts mustn't take Hanna alive. She hurled herself at him with a great jump, knocked him to the ground, and grabbed hold of the pick-handle that jutted from his faceplate.

For a ghastly moment she thought that she could see his eyes, despite the mirrored glass.

"Dana," he whispered.

She wrenched at the pick and tore it free. Shards broke loose from the visor. Hanna dropped his gun and lifted both hands, but the air left his suit far faster than he could put his hands to his helmet. He lay there with his arms raised as though embracing a woman she could not see. Dana felt for his gun and slipped it into a pocket on her thigh— nobody could have seen her do it—then toppled ostentatiously to one side and called for help.

People hurried toward her. They helped her up. Jabbered at her.

"Hanna," she gasped. "It's Hanna. He—I think he was planning to escape with the Charon."

"Did he say anything?" Palmer asked urgently. "Did he say anything about the bomb?"

"He—" *Whatever you do, don't seem too unruffled, Dana!* Best to make a drama of the situation, so she staggered exaggeratedly, letting the others catch her. "I was outside. I saw him running from the base toward the spaceport. First I thought it was Wachowski, but from his size it could—it could only be Hanna—" She shook off the hands supporting her, took several deep breaths. "Then I ran after him, called him on the radio. He ran out onto the landing field—"

"Did he say anything?"

"Yes, when—when I caught up with him. I was trying to stop him, and he shouted that this whole place was about to blow up, and—that's when he attacked me. He just jumped at me, he was going to kill me, what could I have done?"

"Shit!" Palmer cursed.

"I had to defend myself," Dana wailed, putting a note of hysteria into her voice. Kyra Gore took her by the shoulders.

"You did good, Miss Lawrence, what you did was incredibly brave."

"Yes, it was," Palmer said, pacing back and forth for a moment, then he stopped dead and clenched his fists. "Crap! Damn the guy! He's dead now, the bastard. What are we going to do? *What are we going to do?*"

IGLOO 1

DeLucas felt carefully at her face. Glistening crimson liquid slicked her fingertips. Blood. Her blood.

The woman was mad!

Lynn Orley had unfolded like a switchblade and launched herself at her, swiping her fingernails across DeLucas's face and slicing her cheek open, then tried to run out of the control room. She had run after the fleeing woman, grabbed hold of her, and shoved her up against the elevator shaft.

"Miss Orley, stop it! It's me. Minnie!"

Then all of a sudden shouts for help were coming over the loudspeakers, fragments of words, Dana Lawrence, Palmer's voice.

Lynn tore free, swung an arm, and hit DeLucas on the nose so hard that for a moment all she saw was a red haze. When she could see clearly again, Lynn was just leaving the control room. Her head pounding, DeLucas ran after her, caught hold again, and clutched her tight, doing what she could to dodge the rain of blows from her fists. Lynn stumbled against Wachowski's empty chair, looked at the elevator shaft, and started backward, her eyes wide.

"Everything's okay," DeLucas said, coughing. "Everything's okay."

Lynn's lips opened. Her eyes darted from her to the elevator shaft, and back again.

"Can you understand me? Miss Orley? We have to get out of here."

Cautiously, she stretched out her right hand.

Lynn scurried backward.

"You have to come with me," DeLucas said firmly, even as she felt a thick trickle of something warm running down her upper lip. She put her tongue out, automatically, and licked at it. "Come next door. Put on your space suit."

All at once, there was sanity and comprehension in Lynn's eyes. She moved her lips again and put out a trembling finger.

"That's where he came from," she rasped.

DeLucas followed her gesture. The woman was obviously acutely frightened of the elevator shaft, or more exactly of someone who had come out of it.

"Who?" she asked. "Wachowski?"

Lynn shook her head. DeLucas felt a cold fear grip her.

"Who, Lynn? Who came out?"

"He just shot him," Lynn whispered. "Just like that. He could have shot me too." She began to hum a tune.

"Who, Lynn? Who shot who?"

"Minnie? Tommy!" Palmer's voice from the loudspeakers. "Please come in, we have a problem."

Lynn stopped humming and stared at DeLucas.

"What do you want from me anyway, you silly cow?" she snapped.

THE LANDING FIELD, THE MOON

"Leland, I'm having trouble with Lynn Orley."

"Oh great, that too! What about the rest of them?"

"They must be ready by now."

"Then get them out of there, Minnie!" Palmer paced up and down impatiently, with Hanna's corpse at his feet. "What are you waiting for?"

"Something seems to have happened to Tommy," DeLucas said. "Lynn claims that somebody appeared in the control room and shot some other person, she's scared out of her wits and—"

"Hanna," Palmer snarled.

"I think she's been trying to tell me that Tommy's been shot. But he's not here, nor is anybody else."

"Crap," murmured Gore.

"We have to make a decision," Palmer said. "Dana's managed to stop Hanna from escaping. She had to kill him to do it, but before that he said—"

"I caught what it was he'd said," DeLucas interrupted. "That this place is about to blow."

"So stop jabbering," Dana spat at her. "Will you kindly ensure that my guests are evacuated!"

"I can't be everywhere at once," DeLucas snapped back. "Tell her—"

"Listen, Minnie, I'm not going to give up the base as easy as that, but she's right; you have to get those people out of there."

Palmer stopped dead and gazed upward at the shimmering oceans of stars, fading out over to the east where the sun glowed low on the horizon. He simply couldn't imagine that all this might end.

"Could be we still have time," he said. "Hanna must have given himself long enough to get away in good time."

"He was in a hell of a hurry," Dana remarked.

"Whatever. We'll search the area while Kyra flies the guests to a safe distance on the Io."

"And where should I fly them to?" Gore asked.

"Take them to meet Callisto. Tell her to turn around right away. You should be in radio contact as soon as you're up there. Then go back to the Chinese base."

"That's madness," Dana said. "Forget it. How do you expect to find a bomb on a huge installation like this?"

"We'll look for it."

"Sheer idiocy! All you're doing is putting your people in danger."

"You'll be flying with the Io anyway." Palmer paid her no further attention, and turned to his crew. "Does anybody else want to fly with them? You have a free choice, we're not the army here. *I'm* going to look for the thing. The bastard must have given himself at least half an hour!"

Dana spread her arms to admit defeat.

"Leland?" Minnie DeLucas. "If what Lynn was telling me is true, maybe Hanna came up from underground. From the Great Hall."

"Good." Palmer nodded grimly. "Let's start there."

LONDON, GREAT BRITAIN

Had his suspicion been right, or did *MoonLight* really just mean "MoonLight"? There was uproar and disagreement in the Big O. The Moon was still besieged by the bot army, with no end in sight. No contact with Peary Base or Gaia. Merrick was hurrying, burrowing, scurrying from satellites to ground stations, but getting nowhere.

Meanwhile the MI6 delegation were in a feeding frenzy over the theory that China might be behind the attack. It was a beautiful theory, it fit everything so neatly, temptingly. Gaia, well indeed, why would China have Gaia in their sights, but Peary Base—if that were destroyed, a substantial part of America's lunar infrastructure would be knocked out. Not an attack on Orley, but on Washington's supremacy. Knock the enemy off his feet. Weaken the American helium-3 industry. It *had* to be China! Beijing, or Zheng, or both of them.

The CIA had barely joined the list of potential suspects than it was off again.

"Whatever the truth of it," Shaw said, "we've reached a whole new level of helplessness."

"Oh great," said Yoyo.

Security departments at Orley subsidiaries worldwide were reporting back to the London situation room, but there were no concrete leads on further attacks. Norrington insisted that the corporation had to take every precaution. He hadn't come up with any more information on Thorn. A photograph of Kenny Xin had been distributed which his own mother wouldn't have recognized. A shuttle had set out from the OSS to the Moon, but it would take more than two days to reach Peary Base.

"Norrington looks nervous to me," Jericho said. "Don't you think so?"

"Yes, he's fighting on too many fronts, opening up one campaign after another." Yoyo got to her feet. "If he carries on like this, he'll bring the whole operation to a grinding halt."

Just a few minutes ago, another crisis meeting with MI5 had broken up, since the agencies now reckoned that domestic security was threatened. There wasn't even a pause to draw breath. One discussion led straight into the next. The air twanged with the buzz of ideas, urgent purpose, and determination. But there was an undertone too, a feeling that all this to-do was deluded, based on the belief that being there and acting busy would lead to answers.

"So why's he doing that?" Jericho mused, following Yoyo outside. "Is he so worried?"

"You don't even believe that yourself. Norrington's not an idiot."

"Of course I don't believe it. He wants to put a wrench in the works."
Jericho looked around. Nobody was paying any attention to them.
Norrington was making phone calls in his room, and Shaw was doing
the same in hers. "I just haven't the first idea who we should trust to
talk to about him."

"You mean that they could all be in it together?"

"How would we know?"

"Hmm." Yoyo looked across at Shaw's open office door, dubious.
"She doesn't exactly look like a mole."

"Nobody looks like a mole, apart from moles."

"Also true." She fell silent for a while. "Good. Let's break in."

"Break in? Where?"

"The central computer. The drives we aren't authorized for. Norrington's patch of data."

Jericho stared at her. Somebody scurried past them, talking urgently
into a phone. Yoyo waited until he was out of earshot, and dropped her
voice in a conspiratorial fashion. "Simple enough, isn't it? If you know
your enemies and know yourself, you will not be imperiled in a hundred battles; if you know yourself but do not know your enemy, then
for every victory you gain you will suffer a defeat."

"Is that yours?"

"Sun Tzu, *Art of War*. Written two and a half thousand years ago,
and every word is as true as the day it was written. You want to know
who's pulling the strings? I'll tell you what we'll do, then. Your charming friend Diane will fish for Norrington's password, and we'll have a
look around his parlor."

"You're pulling my leg! How is she going to do that?"

"Why are you asking me?" Yoyo raised her eyebrows, all innocence.
"I thought you were the cyber-detective."

"And you're the cyber-dissident."

"True," she said, unruffled. "I'm better than you."

"How's that?" he asked, stung.

"Aren't I? Stop moaning, then, and give me some ideas."

Jericho glanced around. There was still no one paying them any
attention. He might just as well have gone off to sleep somewhere, popping up every couple of hours with more ominous news to set them all
scurrying.

"Right then," he hissed. "We only have one chance, if that."

"We'll do it, whatever it is."

Twelve minutes later Norrington left his glassed-in cubicle and
joined one of the working groups, that was busy making telescopic
observations of the Moon. He talked to them about this and that, and
then went to grab a coffee. Then he went to see Shaw in her office,
briefly, and went back to work at his own desk.

Access denied, said the computer.

Baffled, he clicked on the file again, with the same result. It was only then that he realized he wasn't logged on.

But he hadn't logged out when he left the room.

Or had he?

He glanced around the control room. Everybody was looking busy, except for the Chinese girl, who was standing not far from one of the workstations as though she didn't know where to go.

Norrington felt a gnawing doubt. Uneasy, he restarted the system to log himself in.

Yoyo watched him out of the corner of her eye. Nobody had noticed her slip into his office and log him out—it had only taken a few seconds. She pretended to be absorbed by one of the wall monitors, and pressed a button on her phone to send a signal up to the roof.

Jericho gave Diane the command to start recording.

Data coursed through the processors in the Big O. Nobody in the whole building had their own computer in the sense of an autonomous unit. All employees had a standardized hardware kit, a portable version of the boxy lavobots that Tu Technologies used. Everybody could access the Big O central computer from any jack or port, simply by logging in with name, eight-character password, and a thumbprint. But not everybody had access to all the drives. Even the powerful sysadmins who managed the superbrain and issued passwords couldn't access the whole machine. The ebb and flow of data in the Big O was like the roar and hum of traffic in a big city, and of course, the roar was loudest during normal working hours.

If you knew how, you could listen to the roar. Not by listening to every part of it at once. The information that coursed through the network was encoded of course, in bits and bytes. But if you knew the precise moment when a piece of information would be sent from A to B, you could record that transmission and then set to work painstakingly filtering out individual data packets; then you could apply powerful decoder programs to unlock the words and images inside. At the moment the system was fairly quiet, so that it was easy enough to isolate Norrington's data packet right at the moment when he logged on. And Diane began her calculations.

Six minutes later, she had the eight-character password. It took her another three minutes to crack the software that had carried Norrington's thumbscan to the central processors, and now she had his print as well.

Jericho stared at the prize. Now there was only one more hurdle to clear. Once logged on, nobody could log in again using the same personal data without raising a flag—no more than you could ring your own front doorbell while you were already inside in the living room.

They had to lock Norrington out again.

The chance came a little while later. Norrington was called to a pow-wow, but he spent a long time lingering near the workstations which gave him a view of his office. Edda Hoff chivvied him along. He hemmed and hawed, but finally gave up his watchpost and went into the room, not without casting one last, mistrustful look behind himself.

Jericho smiled at him.

He and Yoyo had switched places. One of the basic rules of sur-veillance was not to let the target see the same face the whole time. Now she was upstairs, waiting for *his* signal. The door to the confer-ence room clicked shut. Unhurriedly, Jericho was on his way across to Norrington's office when the conference room door opened again, and Shaw emerged.

"Owen," she called.

He stopped. He was ten, perhaps twelve steps from Norrington's office. He could be going anywhere.

"I think perhaps you should join the discussion. We've sifted some more data from Vogelaar's dossier, material which has to do with your friend Xin, and the Zheng Group." She glanced around. "By the way, where are your colleagues?"

Jericho went over to join her.

"Yoyo's on Vic Thorn's trail."

Her habitual scowl softened to a smile. "Could be that you'll be quicker about it than MI6 with your inquiries. And Tu Tian?"

"We've given him the day off. He has a business to run."

"Splendid. God forbid that the Chinese economy should falter. The American crash was quite enough. Are you coming?"

"Right away. Give me a minute."

Shaw went back inside without quite closing the door. Jericho strolled casually back to Norrington's office. Somebody at one of the workstations looked up at him, then back at the screen. Without stopping, Jericho stepped into the little room, logged Norrington out, and then walked purposefully across to the other side, and to the conference rooms. Just before he joined the others, he sent Yoyo the agreed signal.

Right away, she typed Norrington's name. The system asked for autho-rizations. She entered the eight-character password, squirted Nor-rington's thumbprint, and waited.

The screen filled with icons.

"There you go," Yoyo whispered, and told Diane to download Norrington's personal data.

"As you wish, Yoyo."

Yoyo? How nice. Owen must have stored her voiceprint. She watched eagerly as Diane's hard drive gulped down one data packet after another, holding her breath for the *Download complete* message.

Jericho was just as impatient, waiting for the signal that would tell him that the transfer had worked and that the false Norrington was now logged out. Once that happened, there was one more thing for him to do: leave the conference, go across to the office, and log the deputy head of security back in, so that Norrington would not notice the theft later.

At that moment, Norrington stood up.

"Excuse me," he said, smiled at the assembled talking heads, and left.

Jericho stared at his empty chair. Yoyo, he thought, what's going on? Why's it taking so long?

Should he leave too and catch up with Norrington? Stop him from going into his office? What would that look like? Norrington was already on edge at the idea that the central computer had simply shut him out, and if Jericho took any action, he would certainly suspect trickery. Ill at ease, he resisted the urge. He sat there hoping for the all-important signal, and tried to look interested.

Ever since he could remember, Norrington had suffered gut ache and stomach cramps whenever he was scared. He made for the toilet, sank down, grunting, and then left with a lighter step. He was at the door of the conference room, holding the handle in his hand, when all of a sudden he had the feeling that someone was staring at the back of his head. Not someone, something, some grinning, goggle-eyed bogey-man. He stopped dead, and whipped around toward his office.

Nobody there.

For a second he hesitated, but the whatever-it-was was still staring at him. Slowly he crossed the space, walked into his office, and around his desk. Everything seemed to be in order. He tapped the touchscreen and tried to open one of his files.

Access denied.

Norrington stumbled backward and looked around in a panic. What was happening here? A system error? Not on your life! He felt a trickle of ice creep up his spine as he remembered how Jericho had niggled at the matter of Vic Thorn, and what a stupid mistake he'd made in replying. Why hadn't he just admitted that they'd been friends? Good friends at that. What the hell would that prove, that he'd known Thorn, even if the guy turned out to be a terrorist a thousand times over?

He opened a login window and typed in his name.

The system told him that he was already logged in.

• • •

Download complete.
"At last," Yoyo said, logged Norrington out, and sent the message to Jericho's phone.

Norrington stared at his screen.
Somebody was helping themselves to his data.
His fingers trembling, he tried again. This time the system accepted his codes and let him in, but he knew all the same that they had been through his files. They had got hold of his access data and they'd been spying on him.
They were onto him.
Norrington steepled his index fingers and put them to his lips. He was fairly sure that he knew who "they" were, but what could he do to stop them? Demand that Jericho's computer be searched? Then the detective would cast his loyalty in doubt. Norrington would have to agree to a search of his own data if he didn't want to arouse suspicion, and that would be the beginning of the end. Once they started to piece together his deleted e-mails—
One moment though. Jericho was sitting in the conference room. It might have been Jericho who had logged him out, but he could hardly have anything to do with what had just happened. One of the others, either Tu Tian or Chen Yuyun, was sitting in front of Jericho's computer right now—what kind of stupid name had he given it? Diane? It was probably the girl. Hadn't she been roaming through the control room just a while back, looking as though she had nothing better to do?
Yoyo. He had to get rid of her.
"Andrew?"
He jumped. Edda Hoff. Pale and expressionless under her lacquered black pageboy cut. Expressionless? Really? Or wasn't there rather a gleam in her eye, the sly look of someone watching a trap to see who will walk into it?
"Jennifer rather urgently needs you to come back for the rest of the meeting." She drew her eyebrows together, infinitesimally. "Is everything all right? Are you not feeling well?"
"The stomach." Norrington got to his feet. "I'm fine."

The way he came back to the conference table set alarm bells ringing for Jericho. The man's face was a jaundiced yellow color, and his forehead was creased and lined with worry. There was no mistaking that Norrington knew exactly what was going on, but instead of pointing the finger at him and demanding an explanation, he sat down to suffer in silence. If any further proof of his perfidy were needed, Norrington had just supplied it.

"Possibly I should recap on the—" he began, when all of a sudden more faces appeared on the video wall, and the Xin working group broke in to have their say.

"Miss Shaw, Andrew, Tom—" One of the new arrivals held up a thin file. "You'll want to hear this."

"What have you got?" Shaw asked.

"It's about Julian Orley's good friend Carl Hanna. He's a Canadian investor, and he's worth fifteen billion, isn't that right?"

"That was his story," Norrington said, nodding.

"And you checked him out."

"You know that I did."

"Well, everybody makes mistakes. We asked around a little. In the end the CIA dug up his family tree."

Expectant silence.

"Hey." The man smiled at each of them in turn. "Anybody want to get to know the guy a little better? After all, this is somebody you people decided you could trust to go on a trip with Julian Orley."

"This is quite a build-up." Shaw gave them a razor-thin smile. "Is there going to be another advertisement break, or will you get to the point?"

The agent put the file down in front of him.

"From now on, you can call him Neil Gabriel. He's American, born in 1981 in Baltimore, Maryland. High school and US Navy, then after that he was with the police as an undercover detective. The CIA noticed him, recruited him, and sent him off to New Delhi for an operation. He did such good work there that they let him stay several years. He became something of an expert on the region, but also a bit of a lone wolf. So he was telling the truth about India, although that's about the only truth he did tell. In 2016 he left the good guys and signed up with African Protection Services."

"Hanna was with APS?" Jericho blurted out.

The man leafed through his pages. "Vogelaar mentions pretty nearly everybody in his dossier who was connected with the Mayé coup in 2017. There's a Neil Gabriel in that list, although he was only with the outfit for a little while and then went independent. It looks as though he did jobs for the Zhong Chan Er Bu as well, at least Vogelaar says that Xin liked his work. So now that we've talked to our American friends, we know who Neil Gabriel is. Clearly the APS must have split at the time. One part stuck with Vogelaar, while the others became Kenny Xin's creatures."

Jericho listened, fascinated, and kept an eye on Norrington at the same time. The security number two was visibly distressed by the barrage of facts.

"Right now we're busy trying to unravel Hanna's fake CV, pardon me, I mean Gabriel's. We hope to find out who set him up with shares in Light-years and Quantime. People with serious money. This won't be anywhere near as easy as it was to crack who he really is."

"You know one of them already," Jericho said. "Xin."

The agent turned toward him. "We don't hold out much hope of getting a glimpse of him. He seems to just melt away into thin air whenever you think you have him in your sights."

"Was it easy to crack Hanna's identity?" Shaw asked.

"Well, easy would be overstating the case. We have good contacts with our friends across the pond, and we couldn't have done it without them. But the bottom line is—" he paused, and looked at Norrington "—a quiet chat with the Central Intelligence Agency would have done the trick back at the start."

Norrington leaned forward.

"Do you really think we didn't talk to them?"

"I have absolutely no wish to question your competence," the agent said, cheerily. "I leave that to others."

Jericho's phone rang. He glanced at the screen, excused himself, and went outside, shutting the door behind him.

"Norrington knows," he said quietly.

"Crap." Yoyo was silent for a moment. "I thought—"

"Didn't work out as we expected. Were you able to download everything, at least?"

"I've been hard at work already! The search program can't find anything about Thorn in Norrington's data, but there's some stuff about Hanna. He was a long way from being the only one who could have taken Palstein's place. There was a regular line of candidates, Orley's business partners, it looks like, or people he wanted to do business with. Multi-billionaires, all of them, but Norrington always managed to find fault with something or other. Heart condition, high blood pressure, this one's been in therapy, that one might be flirting with the competition, the other's got close links with the Chinese government and he doesn't like the look of it, et cetera, et cetera. You can't help but think that he was being paid money to find reasons to rule them all out of going along."

"Maybe he *was* paid money."

"And after all that, Hanna's just smiles and sunshine. The perfect traveling companion for Julian Orley."

"And nobody double-checked?"

"Norrington's not just a line manager, Owen. He's deputy head of security. If somebody like him recommends Hanna, then Hanna flies. Orley must have trusted him, after all he pays him a lot of money for his expertise."

"All right, I'll talk to Shaw. Enough hide-and-seek."

She hesitated. "Are you sure that you can trust her?"

"Sure enough to take the risk. If the whole thing turns out to be flim-flam, she'll throw us out on our ear, but we'll chance it."

"Good. I'll spend some more time going through Norrington's sock drawers."

The door to the conference room opened. Norrington hurried over to his office. Shaw, Merrick, and the others got ready to go their separate ways.

"Jennifer." Jericho moved to intercept her. "Can I talk to you for a moment?"

She looked at him, her face expressionless.

Peary Base,
North Pole, The Moon

In the end DeLucas had given up caring and had marched Lynn up to the top floor by force, then along to Igloo 2, where she threw her a space suit, backpack, and helmet, and threatened to beat her up if she didn't pull herself together. She'd run out of patience, whether or not this was Julian Orley's beloved daughter. The woman was clearly two sandwiches short of a picnic. Sometimes she seemed to be perfectly lucid, then at the next moment DeLucas wouldn't have been surprised to see her crawling around on all fours, or stepping gaily into the air lock without putting her helmet on. She turfed the Ögis out of bed, who were mercifully cooperative and quick to understand the situation, but by the time she had got the whole crowd of them into one of the robot buses and over to the landing field, Palmer and his crew had already arrived and begun to search the caves. They turned the laboratories upside down as though carrying out a drug raid, tore the mattresses from the bunks in all the bedrooms, looked into all the lockers and behind the wall panels, in the aquaria, and the vegetable patches. Finally DeLucas, already in her space suit, her helmet under her arm, went into the Great Hall to join them. She hadn't the first idea what a mini-nuke looked like. All she knew was that it was small, and could be anywhere.

Where would *she* hide something like that? In the jungle of the greenhouses? In among the trout and the salmon?

In the ceiling?

She looked up at the Great Hall's basalt dome. She felt a feverish desire to get out of there, to go with the guests. What they were doing here was crazy! The fact that Hanna had showed up in the control room didn't remotely mean that the bomb had to be here in the underground. It could be anywhere in the whole vast complex.

She peered indecisively into the corridors.

What would make sense?

What did people do when nuclear attack threatened? They built bunkers, underground bases for protection. That was because an atom bomb exploding up on the surface would destroy everything for miles around, but there was some chance of survival if you were in a reinforced bunker. Did that mean that the underground would survive at Peary Base?

Hardly.

She looked at her watch. Twenty to five.

Think, Minnie! An atom bomb was an inferno, devouring everything in its path, but even a doomsday device could be deployed more or less optimally. Towns and cities were built on the surface, never mind all the tunnels, cellars, and sewers below ground. If you wanted to destroy New York with an atom bomb, your best bet was to drop it from above, but life on the Moon demanded a mole's-eye perspective once you'd lived there for a few months. If you wanted to destroy the base, *really* destroy it, it had to be done from inside. The bomb would have to tear apart the bowels of the plateau, and only then blaze up over the crater.

It *had* to be down in the catacombs. Between the aquaria, the greenhouses, the residential quarters, and the laboratories.

She glanced across at the air lock.

Hmm. She didn't need to search beyond the air lock. There was nothing there.

Wrong! That was where the unused part of the labyrinth began, and some of the passages led into the canyon.

How had Hanna even managed to get into the igloo? Through the surface-level air locks? It was possible. But if he had, wouldn't Wachowski have seen him on the screens? Well, maybe he had. Maybe Hanna had just strolled in, all aboveboard and official, but if so, why hadn't he gone from the ground floor to the control room on foot? It was only a couple of meters. Why had he taken the elevator?

Because he had come from underground.

"Nothing here," said a tense voice over her helmet link.

"Here neither," Palmer answered.

And how had he got into the catacombs unnoticed?

She walked toward the air lock. Hardly anybody ever went into the caves beyond. From here, the labyrinth burrowed endlessly into the massif and the crater wall beyond. It would have taken a whole army of astronauts weeks or months to search the labyrinth's full extent, but DeLucas knew that the only logical place to look for the bomb was nearby, somewhere central, below the habs, and that meant the Great Hall and its immediate surroundings.

She went into the air lock, put on her helmet, and pushed the button that would pump the air out. When the air lock door on the further side opened, she switched on her helmet lamp and stepped out into the forgotten corridor beyond.

Almost immediately, she stumbled across Tommy Wachowski's corpse.

"Tommy," she gasped. "Oh my God!"

Her knees trembling, she squatted down and played the cone of light over the body. His limbs were twisted as he lay there, his face deformed.

"Leland!" she called out. "Leland, Tommy's here, and—"

Then she realized that the interior radio network didn't work on this side of the bulkheads. She was in no-man's-land, cut off from the world.

She felt sick.

Gasping, she fell to all fours. Cold sweat broke out all over her body. It was only by a mighty effort of will that she succeeded in not throwing up inside her helmet. She crawled away from the dead man on all fours like an animal, into the corridor, where she closed her eyes and quickly took in a few deep breaths. Once she dared open her eyes again, she saw a shadow in the light from her helmet. It was just a few paces away.

For a second, her heart skipped a beat.

Then she realized that there was nobody standing there, that this was just a narrow gap in the cave wall. She squinted, her eyes still watering from the retching, then pulled herself together and stamped on her fear. She climbed to her feet like a puppet, walked across to the gap, and looked inside. She saw that it was more like a crack than a corridor. Not very inviting. Nowhere you would choose to go of your own accord.

And that, she thought, is exactly why you'll go in.

She drew in her shoulders and pushed her way in until the roof dipped sharply down and she had to crawl. Her breath caught and choked in her throat as the fear fought back. Then there wasn't even room to crawl. She had to lie flat on her belly, feeling her heart hammering against the rock below her like a jackhammer. She considered turning back. This was going nowhere. Dead end. She would go one more meter. Gasping, she pushed herself on, following the scurrying disc of light, imagining what it would be like to be buried alive here, and then all of a sudden the passage opened wide and her fingers were scrabbling in a heap of rubble.

That was it. End of the line.

Or was it? She hesitated. The rubble looked odd. Not a natural pile. DeLucas stooped, and the light scurried over the stones and reflected off something buried in among them. She began to clear the rocks away with one hand, and then saw the surface of something bulky and metallic, smooth, machine-tooled, sleek.

It couldn't be anything else but—

She shoveled the rubble aside madly, uncovering the thing. It was the size of a briefcase. She tugged it toward herself. There could be no doubt, now she saw the blinking display and the timecode running backward from—

"Oh no," she whispered.

So little time. So little time.

Frantic, clinging on to the bomb with both hands, she began to wriggle backward. Out, she had to get out of here, but the next moment her backpack was wedged against the low roof and she couldn't move another inch. She was stuck fast.

Waves of panic came crashing together over her head.

LONDON, GREAT BRITAIN

"You are crazy," said Shaw.

Her workspace was an identical copy of Norrington's office, modest and functional, the only difference being a few hints that she had a life beyond the Big O. Photographs showed that Shaw had a husband and grown-up children, that little kids somewhere called her grandma. Jericho thought of the exile of his own existence, and had a hard time imagining this flinty-featured security chief as someone with wants and needs, hormones, a woman who had whispered and moaned and cried out with pleasure, limbs entangled. Jennifer Shaw was in charge of the safety of the world's largest technology corporation. He wondered what her pet name was. At home, within her own four walls, between the TV set and the dental floss, was she Bunnikins or Mummy Bear? He glanced outside quickly, but Norrington's office was out of sight from here.

"Doesn't all that give you pause for thought?" he asked.

"What makes me pause is the thought that you've been abusing my trust," said Bunnikins, or Mother Bear, sternly.

"No, you're not looking at it right. We're trying to *stop* someone from abusing your trust." He drew up a chair and sat down. "Jennifer, I know we're on very thin ice here, but Norrington lied about his relationship to Vic Thorn. He obviously knew him better than he's letting on. Why would he do that if he had nothing to hide? He may have had perfectly understandable reasons to take Hanna under his wing, but given all the resources he has at his disposal, how come he couldn't identify an ex-CIA man? *Before* the moon trip! And once he noticed that we'd cracked his passcodes, well—what would *you* have done, in his place?"

She looked levelly at him with her gray-blue eyes.

"I would have nailed you to the wall."

"Quite!" Jericho slapped his hand down on the desk. "And what does he do? Comes slinking in, lets the MI6 fellows haul him over the coals and then rushes off again. Now, you told me that it was Edda Hoff who passed on my theory that Thorn had been supposed to arrange the attack, and that she told the security services too. Shouldn't we suppose that she told Norrington as well?"

"She's certain to have done so. Edda is extremely conscientious."

"But when I went into his office to talk to him about it, he acted as though it were a complete surprise! Even though by that point, he must have known we were thinking along those lines. And don't you get the feeling that all his activity is actually slowing down the Big O's attempts to find anything out, rather than helping?"

"I have told him that we're fighting on too many fronts at once."
Shaw gave him a level look. "And what should I do about that, in your
opinion? Relieve him of his duties because of one or two odd bits of
behavior? Have his data searched?"

"I think you know quite well what you should do."

Shaw was silent.

Two doors down, Norrington was dialing a number on his phone, his
fingers trembling.

He had made mistakes. He'd reacted without stopping to think.
The noose was tightening, since they would find proof, and once they
decided to put him through the wringer he would lose his nerve, he'd
break down, he'd spill the beans. He was an idiot to have got involved
in the whole thing to begin with, from the moment they offered him
money to suggest Thorn for a second mission. But it had been so much
money, so incredibly much, and there was the promise of much more
once Operation Mountains of Eternal Light was done with, once the
course of history had been changed. He had been a quick learner in the
school of corruption, and had risen to be one of Hydra's chief planners,
had fed the many-headed monster with information about the OSS,
about Gaia and Peary Base. He had even come up with the shadow
network which the conspirators used to communicate their murderous plans. A white-hot inferno, disguised as mere white noise. He had
met Hydra's immortal head, the brains behind the whole scheme, the
criminal mastermind whose identity only six other people knew. It had
been seven, but one of them had got cold feet. That was when Norrington had learned that if need be Hydra would sooner cut off one of
its own heads than let it turn blabbermouth.

He *mustn't* end up in secret service hands.

Xin picked up.

"We've been found out, Kenny! Just like I told you we would be."

"And I told you to keep your nerve."

"You go to hell with your know-it-all remarks! MI6 blew Gabriel's
identity. Jericho and the girl hacked into my data. I don't know when
Shaw's going to shut the trap on me; it could be that I already wouldn't
be allowed out of the building. Get me out of here."

Xin was silent for a moment.

"What about Ebola?" he asked. "Do they know about her, too?"

Norrington hesitated. For some reason, he just couldn't get used to
Dana's code name.

"They don't know anything about her, nor about the rest of it. They
just know that the bomb's at Peary. But of course the next thing they'll
do is make use of all my data, and then they'll take another look at
everybody whose appointment I approved."

"Are you sure that Jericho's been talking to Shaw about you?"

"No idea," he groaned. "I hope he hasn't yet. Under the circumstances, nothing's certain."

Xin thought.

"Good. I'll be on the flight deck in five minutes. Maybe you should try getting Jericho's computer out of the building."

"Maybe we should try painting the Moon yellow and putting a smiley face on it," Norrington snapped. "They mustn't get their hands on me, Kenny, don't you understand? *I have to get out of here!*"

"Everything's all right." Suddenly Xin's voice took on that soft, sibilant note. "Nobody's going to get their hands on you, Andrew. I promised to be there, and I keep my promises."

"You hurry up, damn you!"

While the street lights of London faded away under a magnificent dawn sky, Yoyo decided to call Jericho again. During the night, she and Diane had become fast friends. She'd never worked with such excellent search programs or selection parameters.

"I have some news," she said. "Where are you?"

"In Jennifer's office. We can speak openly. Wait a moment." He listened to a soft voice in the background, then said, "Look, the best thing to do is call again, direct to her number, okay?"

"You can tell her right away that—"

"Tell her yourself."

He hung up. Yoyo squirmed around impatiently on her chair. She was burning to tell him about the dossiers Norrington had put together on the guests and staff at Gaia. Diane had done a lightning search, comparing Norrington's supposed findings with publicly available biographies on the net and found no significant discrepancies, except perhaps for the fact that Evelyn Chambers was telling some whopping lies about her age. As for the staff at Gaia, two Germans, an Indian, and a Japanese, they had been chosen by the director of the hotel, Dana Lawrence, who in turn had got the job on the strength of a report from Norrington, knocking four other highly qualified candidates out of the running. Norrington hadn't actually turned any of these other four down flat, quite the opposite, it was rather that Lawrence's track record put all the others in the shade. Lynn Orley had made the final appointment, and she would have had to have been insane to refuse Lawrence the job, given such excellent references. It was only when you looked closer that you realized that Lawrence's official CV in the net was strangely different. Certain jobs that she had supposedly held made her just the right woman for the job in Gaia, but online they were missing, or didn't quite match up. It was certainly the career of a dedicated professional, but if you wanted to assume the worst, you could easily say that Norrington had massaged the facts to help Lynn make her decision. Yoyo saw nothing at all wrong in assuming the worst.

Eager to know what the others would make of her findings, she typed in Shaw's name and was just about to let the computer make the call when she heard a noise.

An elevator had stopped outside on the gallery. She heard the doors slide apart.

Yoyo froze. Nobody was supposed to be in the Big O right now except for the security patrols and the tireless crew down in the situation room. She strained her ears, becoming aware of her surroundings for the first time. She was sitting at somebody's workplace, an entirely interchangeable uniform cell; employees kept their personal possessions in the mobile units that let them log in anywhere needed, throughout the building. Diane lay to her left, beneath the holographic display, a slim, shimmering machine, while on her right was a wheeled set of drawers, probably containing all the clutter that a computer still couldn't replace, even in 2025.

She opened the top drawer, peered into it, opened the next one down.

She glanced at the panoramic windows. London's night was slowly giving way to early morning light, but over in the west it was stubbornly dark. She could see the office interior reflected in outline in the windowpane, the workstations, the door in the wall behind her that led through to the hallway and the gallery.

She could see a silhouette in the hallway.

Yoyo ducked. Whoever it was hesitated. A man, judging by the height. He was just standing there, staring.

He had to take her by surprise. It could be that Shaw still didn't know about the hacking. It would be one thing to overpower Yoyo and get hold of the computer, but then there would be Jericho to deal with. Perhaps there would be a way to lure him upstairs. Assuming that the two of them hadn't told Tu Tian what they were up to, it might be enough to get rid of them and then the computer as well. Then it would be as if none of this had ever happened; nobody would ever suspect that—

Garbage! This was wishful thinking from start to finish. How would he explain it once they were both dead? The surveillance system would show everything. Why grab Jericho's computer, when it didn't hold anything that wasn't also stored in the Big O mainframes? Shaw could get at his data any time she liked, which is what she *would* do if he killed two people up here—not to mention the fact that he'd never manage that, since in stark contrast to people like Xin, Hanna, Lawrence, and Gudmundsson, he wasn't a killer. It wasn't game over for Hydra yet, but for him it certainly was. Even making a break for it was as good as a confession of guilt, but if he stayed, he might just as well put the cuffs on himself. There wasn't any point cleaning up his trail now. He had to get out of here, drop out of sight!

He had enough money for a new life, quite a comfortable one at that.

The open-plan office lay in twilight.

How much had she learned? Had Jericho's computer been able to retrieve his deleted e-mails and reconstruct them?

Where was the girl?

He was torn between the urge to find out more and the need to get away. He looked across the room, then his feet carried him forward as though of their own accord. He stepped into the office. It looked empty. The overhead lights were dimmed. Two workstations away, monitor screens glowed, and he saw the modest little box that Yoyo had left there, the one they called Diane. He should search the office. The workstations offered various hiding places. Indecisive, he walked a little way into the room, paced this way and that, and looked at the clock. Xin must be here by now; he should get out, but the monitors glowed like the lights of some safe refuge.

He hurried across to the workstation, bent down, and had his hands on the little computer when the room burst into life behind him.

Petite though she might have been, Yoyo was also muscular and in good shape, so she had no trouble in picking up a fairly heavy office chair and taking a swing. As Norrington spun around to face her, the back of the chair caught him full-on, slamming into his head and his chest and knocking him backward onto the desk. He grunted, and scrabbled to gain his balance. Yoyo swung at him again, from the side this time, and he fell to the floor. Even as he landed there on his back next to Diane, she flung the chair aside and drew from her belt the scissors she had found in the drawer. She landed hard on his chest with both knees.

There was an audible crack. Norrington made a choking, hacking sound. His eyes bulged. Yoyo clamped the fingers of her left hand around his throat, leaned down low, and shoved the point of the scissors so hard against his balls that he could feel it poised there.

"One false move," she hissed, "and the Westminster Abbey Boys' Choir will be glad to make your acquaintance."

Norrington stared at her. Suddenly, he swung at her. She saw his clenched fist flying at her, ducked aside, and drove the scissors deeper into his crotch. He flinched with his whole body and then froze completely, simply staring at her again.

"What do you want from me, you madwoman?" he gasped.

"I want a little talk."

"You're crazy. I came up here to see whether everything's okay, whether you need anything, and you—"

"Andrew, hey, Andrew!" she interrupted. "That's crap. I don't want to hear any crap."

"I just wanted—"

"You wanted to swipe the computer, I saw that, thanks. I don't need any more proof, so get talking. Who are you working with, and what do they want? Were we right about Peary? Who's pulling the strings?"

"With the best will in the world, I don't know what you're—"

"Andrew, you're being foolish."

"—talking about."

Dark red swamped her vision, glowing and all-consuming. Utterly forgotten was any chance that the man beneath her might have had nothing to do with the deaths of her friends, with the agonies that Chen Hongbing had gone through while Xin had him trapped in front of the automatic rifle. Forgotten any idea that she might be wrong about him, that Norrington might have had nothing to do with any of this. Every cell of her body burned with hatred. She wanted, she *needed* a culprit, here, now, at last, anyone to blame before she lost her mind, a bad guy to stand in for the monsters who had tortured the people she loved, the people whose love she needed. Her loved ones, who had seen things that they couldn't talk about, things that clamped a mask over their faces. She jerked back her arm and rammed the scissors into Norrington's thigh, stabbing so hard that skin and flesh parted like butter before the blades, and the point scraped hard against the bone. Norrington screamed like a stuck pig. He raised both hands and tried to shove her away. Still wrapped in her red rage, she yanked the improvised weapon from the wound and set the point against Norrington's genitals again.

"It hurts, wherever I aim," she whispered. "But next time the consequences may be rather more permanent. Were we right about Peary?"

"Yes," he screamed.

"When? When's the bomb due to go off?"

"I don't know." He twisted and turned, his eyes stark with pain. "Sometime. Now. Soon. We're out of contact."

"You started the botnet."

"Yes."

"Can you stop it?"

"Yes, let me go, you're insane!"

"Is your organization called Hydra? Who's behind it all?"

Without warning Norrington's head jerked up, and Yoyo realized that it had been a mistake to crouch so low above him. There was a noise like two blocks of wood being slammed together as his forehead met hers. She was flung back. By reflex, she stabbed and heard him howl, then felt him grab hold and fling her aside. There were spots dancing in front of her eyes. Her head roared and her nose seemed to have swollen to several times its original size. She rolled swiftly out of Norrington's reach, holding the scissors out in front of her, but instead of launching himself at her, he hobbled away.

"You stay here," she gasped.

Norrington began to run, as much as his wounded leg would allow. Yoyo clambered to her feet, then fell down again right away and felt at her face. Blood was pouring from her nose. She felt sickeningly dizzy, but finally managed to stand up, staggered from the office out to the gallery, and saw Norrington climbing some stairs on the other side of the glass bridge between the Big O's western and eastern wings.

The shithead was making for the flight deck.

A quiet voice inside her warned her not to give way to her hatred, to consider that it might be dangerous up there. She didn't listen. Just as she could not doubt Norrington's guilt, right at this moment she couldn't think of anything but stopping him from getting away. She ran after him, glanced down at the dark glass canyon that yawned below the bridge, and felt a wave of nausea climb her throat. She fought it down.

Norrington was fighting his way up the last steps.

He was out of sight.

She shook herself. She resumed the chase, crossed the bridge at last, hurried up the steps two at a time, in constant danger of losing her balance. She made it to the top and saw one of the glass doors out to the roof gliding shut.

Norrington was outside.

Holding the scissors tightly, she went after him, and the glass doors glided open again. The flight deck stretched away before her eyes, with its helicopters and skycars. Norrington hobbled toward something without looking around, waving.

"Over here!" he called.

She quickened her pace. She was puzzled to note that there were airbikes up here as well, more exactly, *one* airbike. She hadn't noticed it the previous morning, and all of a sudden she knew why.

Because it hadn't been there.

She stopped. Her eyes skittered around the flight deck, and she saw two guards lying on the floor, their limbs outflung. A figure dismounted. Norrington staggered, recovered, and then dragged himself on toward the bike. The figure pointed a gun at him and he stopped, his hand pressed to his thigh.

"Kenny, what is this?" he asked, his voice wavering.

"We've classed you as a risk," Xin said. "You're stupid enough to get caught, and then you'll tell them what you mustn't tell anyone."

"No!" Norrington screamed. "No, I promise—"

He was flung upward a little into the air, and his body hung there for a moment like a puppet before he flew backward, his arms spread, and thudded at Yoyo's feet.

There was a only a mass of red where his face had been.

She froze. Sank to her knees, and dropped the scissors. Xin walked toward her and pressed the muzzle of the gun against her forehead.

"How nice," he whispered. "I had already given up all hope."

Yoyo stared dead ahead. She thought that if she ignored him perhaps he might just vanish, but he didn't, and her eyes filled slowly with tears, because it was over. Finally over. This time nobody would ride to her rescue. There was nobody who could turn up and take Xin by surprise.

Very softly, her voice hoarse, so that she could barely understand the word she spoke, she said, "Please."

Xin squatted down in front of her. Yoyo raised her eyes to the handsome, symmetrical mask of his face.

"You're pleading with me?"

She nodded. The gun's mouth pressed harder against her brow, as though boring a hole.

"For what? For your life?"

"For everyone's lives."

"How very exorbitant of you."

"I know." Fat tears rolled down her cheeks, and her lower lip began to tremble. And suddenly, curiously, she felt fear washed away with her tears, the fear that had been her constant companion for so long, leaving only a deep, painful sorrow behind. Sorrow that she would never learn now what had happened to Hongbing, why her life had been the way it was, why their lives hadn't been different. Xin couldn't scare her now, nor any of his kind. It wouldn't have taken much for her to fling her arms around his neck to sob on his shoulders. Why not?

"Yoyo?"

Someone was calling her name in the distance.

"Yoyo! Where are you?"

Jericho! Was that Owen?

Xin smiled. "Brave little Yoyo. Admirable. It's a shame. I would have liked the chance for a longer chat with you, but as you see, there's no rest for the wicked. They're looking for you, I'm afraid, so now I shall have to leave you."

He stood up, the gun still pointing straight at her forehead. Yoyo turned her face toward him. The dawn breeze was pleasant as it dried the tears on her cheeks. Caressing. Forgiving.

She heard Jericho shout, "Yoyo!"

Xin shook his head.

"I'm sorry about this, Yoyo."

Peary Base,
North Pole, The Moon

The evacuated guests took their seats in the Io and buckled themselves in. Kyra Gore was on her way to the cockpit when a call came through from Callisto. Nina Hedegaard's face appeared on the screen.

"Where are you?" Gore asked as she warmed up her engines.

"On our way to land soon."

"Turn around, right now! Orders from Palmer."

"What about our group?"

"They're all on board here with me." She modified thrust, aimed her jets, and lifted the shuttle slowly. "Here on Io."

"All of them?"

"The only ones left in the Base are Palmer and some of our crew. We had a visit from Carl Hanna. The whole place might blow up any moment now, so turn around and cover some ground away out of here!"

"What about Carl?" Julian Orley broke in. "Where is he?"

"Dead."

She cast her eyes over the control panel, from sheer force of habit. The landing field was dwindling away below the Io, and the whole scattered assembly, factories, pipelines, igloos, and corridors, were only toys, a bucket-and-spade set for scientists to muck around in the lunar sand. The roads ran across the regolith like grooves on a toybox lid. In the tiny hangars, little machines assembled other machines, not quite so little. The sunlight gleamed blindingly from the solar panels. Gore curved her flight path, climbed again, and steered Io across the crater wall to the west.

"Dead?" Orley snapped.

"Miss Lawrence killed him. She's with me, along with your daughter and your guests. They're all right."

"And the bomb? What are Palmer and his crew doing?"

"They're looking for it."

"We can't just leave them to—"

"Yes we can. Turn around. We're flying back to the Chinese."

DeLucas

Had only seconds passed? Or hours? DeLucas couldn't have said, but when she saw the timecode ticking backward on the bomb, she knew that the worst experience of her life had not even taken a minute. Kicking and screaming, she had finally managed to break free. Careful not to get stuck again, she pushed herself backward, less hastily this time. After a few meters, the bomb wedged against the rock. She had had enough of being afraid, so this time she simply yelled at the mini-nuke as though it were a snot-nosed kid who only heeded harsh words. Wonder of wonders, it actually listened to her, and the low box came free of the wall. A surge of adrenaline carried her along the corridor and past Tommy Wachowski's body into the air lock, where she hopped from one leg to the other as though the floor were electrified. As the air pumped slowly in, she saw through the viewport Palmer and Jagellovsk coming into the Great Hall, and she slammed her fists against the pane. Palmer spotted her and stopped dead in his tracks. The door glided open. DeLucas stumbled over the threshold and fell full-length on the floor, and the bomb skittered across to stop at the commander's feet.

"Six o'clock," she panted. "We still have thirty-five minutes."

Palmer grabbed the box with both hands and stared at it.

"Let's get it out of here," he said.

They went up with the elevator, left the igloo, and ran outside onto the bulldozed plain, out among the hangars. The Io was just disappearing off past the crater wall.

"What do we do with it now?"

"Disarm it!"

"Thanks, wise guy! Do you know how to do that?"

"Oh man, I must have seen it a thousand times in the movies. We just have to—"

"Red wire or green wire? Movies are movies, are you out of your mind?"

"Twenty-nine minutes!"

The mini-nuke lay there between them on the asphalt, a squat, malevolent box. The timecode ticked down mercilessly, a countdown to the end of creation, bringing a new Big Bang.

"Stop!" Palmer shouted, holding up both hands. "Everybody just shut up! Nobody's disarming a damn thing around here. Get it over to the landing field. We have to get rid of it."

"We'll never manage it," DeLucas said. "How do you intend to—"

Palmer switched over to the shuttle frequency.

"Io? Callisto? Leland Palmer here, can you hear me?"

"Kyra here. What's up, Leland?"

"We found the darn thing! It's going to blow in twenty-eight minutes, excuse me, twenty-seven. I need one of you back here, right now!"

"All right," Gore said. "We're turning around."

"We're nearer," Nina said.

"What? But you have to—"

"There!" called Jagellovsk.

DeLucas held her breath. Callisto broke free against the backdrop of the stars, curved around, and dropped down toward the base.

"I'm coming in to land," said Nina.

"Over to Igloo 1!" Palmer shouted. He leaped and danced like a dervish, waving his arms. "Igloo 1, you hear me? We're outside! Get the bomb on board and then dump it as far away as you can, in some goddamn crater!"

CALLISTO

"I see them," Nina said.

Julian bent down. "Once we've got the thing on board—"

"Once *I've* got the thing on board." She turned her head and looked at him. "You're getting out."

"What? Out of the question!"

"You are."

"We're flying together—"

"You're all getting out," she said, with an air of quiet command. "You too, Julian."

And then there it was.

For one deeply satisfying moment she saw fear in Julian's eyes. For just an instant, but an instant that would be with her forever, she saw at last what she knew she had earned, knew that she deserved from him, that she'd never asked for, in all the time by his side. He wasn't afraid for his guests, or his precious daughter, or for his hotel. He was afraid only for her, afraid that she might be hurt. Fearful of the hole she would leave in his life if she died, the hole in his heart.

She slowed, and let the shuttle sink down.

Down below, the astronauts were scurrying around and waving to her. She choked back on the thrust. The bulldozed patch down here was relatively small, full of vehicles and machinery. Carefully, she guided Callisto over to a spot near the igloo that offered just enough room for her to land, then settled with a bump, extended the air lock, and turned around to her passengers.

"Everybody out!" she shouted, clapping her hands. "Then bring the damn bomb in here. Quick!"

She looked at Julian. He hesitated. The storm clouds cleared on his face and she saw a beam of honest-to-goodness affection break through like the sun, and all of a sudden he was hugging her to himself, and gave her a scratchy kiss.

"Take care of yourself," he whispered.

"You won't get rid of me that easily." She smiled. "Watch out for the engines when you get out. Don't let them wander out under the thrusters."

He nodded, slid from his chair, and hurried to catch up with the others. Nina turned back to the controls. The lift control showed her that the group was going down to the ground. She watched through the cockpit window as an astronaut hurried across carrying something about the size of a suitcase in both hands. The figure disappeared under Callisto's belly, and then she heard Palmer's voice.

"It's in!"

"Got you."

"Get going then! Get the thing away from us! Twenty minutes to go!"

"You can say that again," she murmured, revving up. She brought the shuttle up a few meters even as the air lock was retracting, and turned. A shudder ran through Callisto.

"What happened?" she called.

"You struck the lock against one of the hangars here," Julian said. "Just brushed the roof."

Nina cursed, and lifted higher. She glanced around for any error message.

"Is it still retracting?"

"Yes! Seems fine."

The controls showed that the lock was fully inside Callisto. Nina climbed to 300 meters, then accelerated faster than she would ever have dared with passengers on board. The thrust pushed her back into her seat as Callisto shot off at more than 1,200 kilometers per hour. The base dropped away out of sight. Cliffs, chasms, and plateaus flew past below like a time-lapse landscape. She would have to make for lower ground as soon as she could, but the stark mountains below seemed to climb and climb forever where the edges of Peary Crater fused into Hermite to the west. Range reared up after range, ridges and plateaus marched on endlessly, but then at last she saw a ragged abyss yawn wide.

The bowl of Hermite Crater.

Still too close.

Even if the mountain ranges protected the base from the blast itself, there was no telling where the debris would rain down. Nina called up a polar map on her holographic display and looked for a suitable spot. The question was how far she could make the time left to her stretch out. If she waited too long to chuck the mini-nuke overboard, she was in danger of being caught in the nuclear furnace herself, but she didn't want to dump it out of the air lock too soon. The shadows of a sunlit plain rushed past below her, sown with impact craters from smaller meteorites. Flying as low as she was, she had lost radio contact with everyone. According to the dashboard clock she had been flying for eight minutes, and she still wasn't past the whole of Hermite. She could see the crater's western wall looming in the distance, a vast, curving cliff, growing fast, growing closer.

Twelve minutes left.

She looked back at her map. Further to the southwest was a smaller crater, in deep shadow, which suggested that it must be fairly deep. She asked the computer for more information, and a text field unrolled on top of the hologram.

Sylvester Crater, she read. 58 kilometers in diameter.

Depth: unknown.

She liked the look of it. It looked almost tailor-made to swallow the energy of a nuclear bomb, and all of a sudden she had to smile. Sylvester, how appropriate. A crater named for the father of industrial explosives, and it would see the biggest damn explosion the Moon had known for thousands of years. Grinning, she changed course a few degrees southwest, and Callisto tore over Hermit's western rim.

Eleven minutes.

The crater wall fell away beneath her, rugged, pocked by lesser impacts, and gave way to a broad, flat valley. The other side of the valley had to be Sylvester's outer wall. Nina leaped from the pilot's seat and ran to the air lock, suddenly scared that Palmer might have misread the timecode, but when she peered through the pane she saw the mini-nuke sitting on the cabin floor, its counter just ticking down from the ten-minute mark.

The sight of the bomb made her suddenly queasy.

09:57

09:56

09:55

Time to throw in her hand, she'd pushed her luck as far as she could. There was enough distance now between the bomb and the base. She ran back to the cockpit and gave the command to extend the air lock.

The computer gave her an error report.

Incredulous, she stared at the console. Suddenly the elevator symbol was blinking, fiery red. She tried again to extend the shaft, but without success.

Impossible. Just impossible!

She demanded a report.

Air lock not fully drawn up, it said. *Please draw up lock before attempting to extend.*

Her legs trembled wildly. Hastily she ordered the shaft to draw up, even though it was already drawn up—at least, it had seemed that way, but perhaps there was a centimeter or so still to go. But the display didn't stop blinking.

Air lock cannot be drawn up.

Cannot be drawn up?

Nine minutes.

Less than nine.

"Are you crazy?" she shouted at the control system. "Draw up, extend! How the hell am I supposed to—"

She stopped. You had to be completely crazy yourself to try arguing with a computer. The air lock wouldn't open, and that was that.

Which meant that she couldn't just spit the bomb out that way, and she couldn't grab it from the lock to throw it out of the rear hatch.

The rear hatch!

Her heart pounding, she raced to the stern, opened the bulkhead to the cargo hold, charged inside, and looked around. There were a few grasshoppers here, hanging in their brackets and ready to roam. It had hardly been eighteen hours since they had been using them to tour the legendary Apollo landing site. She loosened the clips on one of them, stood it up on its telescopic legs, and checked the fuel tank. Enough. All right then, back to the bridge, but as she drew level with the air lock she couldn't resist glancing inside. She hesitated, then looked in at the infernal device, saw the timecode running down—

06:44

06:43

—she tore herself away. Dashed into the cockpit.

Looked out.

Sylvester's crater wall, still a good way off but growing larger every moment. She had to make sure that the bomb would explode on the crater floor, deep inside. Otherwise she would be dead for sure. Her fingers leaped across the instrument panel like a virtuoso at the keyboard as she calculated the angle of approach she would need for a controlled crash, and the shuttle's nose dipped—no, that was too much, less!—there, that was it. A steady descent.

And now, out of here. Helmet on.

Her hands were trembling. Why were her hands trembling, now of all times?

05:59

The helmet wouldn't fit.

05:58

She had left it too late.

05:57

05:56

Now!

Cargo hold. Manual controls.

The loading hatch sank down, infuriatingly slowly, to reveal the stars and, far off, the Peary-Hermite range. Nina climbed up onto the grasshopper platform and kicked the thing up into the air, just a little. The hatch yawned wider. A hair's breadth was all she needed. Without waiting for it to open entirely, she steered the hopper along the cargo hold and through the shuttle's rear hatch as it tore down toward the ground.

It would be an illusion to think that she was safe now. The shuttle seemed to be standing still relative to her speed, which meant that she was still hurtling toward Sylvester at 1,200 kilometers per hour on her tiny craft, just as fast as Callisto itself. Realistically, her chances were just about as bad as could be, though she still had five minutes to achieve the impossible, maybe four. Somewhere between 250 and 300 seconds, at any rate. All her hopes hung on having calculated the proper angle of impact for the shuttle. She swung her nozzles to the horizontal and opened the throttle for as much thrust as the little machine could muster.

The hopper bucked and tried to throw her off.

Then it rushed for all its engines were worth away from Callisto, bravely doing its best against the murderous acceleration, and losing height all the while. The shuttle dwindled away rapidly in front of Nina's eyes. She swung the nozzles around a little further and went down to the ground, too close to the ground, as she established the next moment, since she was still going much too fast. She was in danger of being smashed to pieces, and she steered the hopper up again, wringing the last drop of thrust out of its jets, and saw Callisto speeding toward Sylvester's sunlit slopes. The dusty lunar surface was not racing past quite so fast beneath her now, as the hopper was battling against its own momentum and winning. It was slowing down, but would there be time to slow it to a safe landing speed?

And if she could? How much time did she still have?

Two minutes?

One?

A small crater rushed toward her, zipped by below, and then was lost to sight. An ideal spot to take shelter. Somehow she had to make her way back to the crater, but she was still traveling at considerable speed. Over on the horizon, Callisto hung above the sweeping wall of mountains, a gleaming point, so close to the rim that for a moment she was afraid that she had miscalculated and the shuttle would smash into the crater wall, that the bomb would explode there on the slopes, and that nothing would protect her from the fury of the blast.

Then the shining dot disappeared inside Sylvester, and she gave a victory whoop, since she'd won this point at least in the deadly game. Still whooping, she steered the hopper down, fought against her own headlong hurtle, and gradually, little by little, the contraption seemed to be bleeding off the speed that the shuttle had given it, even if it was still going too fast to land. She could forget about that little crater by now, it was already much too far behind her, but something about the same size sped toward her, maybe a little smaller. The ring wall was 2, perhaps 3 kilometers across but it was astonishingly high, so that all of a sudden she was afraid that the hopper wouldn't make it over the peaks, and would crash. Just before impact, she yanked the machine upward, scraping over the rim, and then looked down. The crater wall cast a threatening shadow into the cauldron, a curve of blackness like a scythe. She slowed further, flew over the opposite wall, then she could see the plain again and Sylvester, its peaks terrifyingly near, unsoftened by atmospheric haze.

There was something happening there.

Nina narrowed her eyes.

The sky above Sylvester blazed.

She held her breath.

From one moment to the next, the stars were swallowed up by a smear of blazing light as though a second sun were being born inside the crater. Instantly, she turned her eyes away, flew a 180-degree curve and realized that she now had full control of speed and direction. Her second little crater was some distance off by now, but the ground below was no longer hurtling past. She had won the battle against her acceleration and now she had to find shelter. All around, the slopes and cliffs, even the distant polar massif, were glowing in the light of the nuclear explosion, but that died away so suddenly that she couldn't resist her curiosity. She turned the hopper.

The light had vanished.

For a moment she thought that Sylvester had absorbed the energy of an entire nuclear explosion, but something was different now. At first she couldn't understand what she was seeing, but then the shock of recognition hit.

The ridge of the crater wall had vanished.

No, not vanished. It was hidden by a screen of dust that shrouded the upper slopes and fountained skyward, swallowing the stars, a plume many kilometers high, growing higher and higher, unreal, bizarre, a nightmare image—

Crawling down the slopes.

Crawling?

"Oh shit," whispered Nina.

All of a sudden, the wall of dust had become a huge wave, spilling over the crater wall in all directions and racing down toward the plain. Nina had no idea just how fast it was traveling, but it was certainly coming ten times faster than her little hopper could fly, twenty times, thirty. For a moment she was paralyzed, not able even to tear her eyes away, then she yanked the machine around and thrashed it back toward the nameless little crater. After the breakneck ride out of Callisto, it was as though the hopper was just creeping along. She risked another look. Sylvester had vanished completely. There was only the dust racing toward her, swallowing the sky and devouring all before it.

Faster. Faster!

The crater wall, her only hope of shelter!

Desperately, she yanked the grasshopper upward, and it hauled itself up the slope as though worn out by the excitement of the past few minutes. Its telescopic legs scrabbled across the rocks and it tottered from side to side, then with one leap it was over the ridge. Nina spread her arms and leaped from the platform. Her body slammed into the steep regolith and then she was rolling down, over a sudden edge. She fell in a long arc and landed quite a way further off, in the shadow of a sheer cliff face. From the corner of her eyes she could see the grasshopper tumbling end over end. She braced her feet in the scree slope and managed to stop her downward slide. She crawled into the shelter of an overhang and curled up into a ball.

Above her, the sky grew dark.

In the next moment, everything was gray. A hail of pebbles, tiny stones, pattered down into the crater's bowl. Nina cowered as small as she could, protected against the pressure wave and the rubble by her overhang, but the rocks falling in front of her sent up a spray of regolith in turn. She crossed her arms in front of her helmet for protection and hoped that the suit would hold up to the onslaught. She could see nothing at all, merely a thick gray cloud on a gray ground, and she shut her eyes.

The wall raced past her.

She had no idea how long she had been lying there. When she finally dared take her arms from her faceplate, the impacts had stopped and a hazy, shifting cloud of dust hung everywhere.

She clambered to her feet and stretched her limbs. She could hardly believe that she was still alive. That nothing had broken. Apparently, she was totally unharmed.

She had survived an atom bomb.

On the other hand, she was now stuck in a nameless crater miles from Peary Base with no means of getting away. Her own little crater, that had saved her life. She had an intact space suit, her radio, and enough oxygen for the next few hours until Io found her. At least, she hoped that they'd be looking for her and hadn't simply assumed that her death was inevitable.

First of all, she decided, she had to get out of this crater. Better for the radio reception once Io turned up.

Resigned, she set out on the long climb.

LONDON, GREAT BRITAIN

I'm sorry about this, Yoyo—

Whatever else Xin said after that reached her as mere wordsound, a voiceprint only, since at that moment her overloaded nerves gave way. The nervus vagus, that had survived so many lesser crises before now, simply stopped all regulatory function and left the organs under its command to their own devices, plunging them into chaos. Without higher functions to command them, arteries let the blood rush unhindered to her legs, her heart found nothing to pump, her brain waited in vain for the oxygen to arrive and Xin's next words were nothing more than a half-heard electrochemical impulse. "You lose." Maybe he said them, maybe he didn't. At that moment, all systems shut down. Her eyes turned up, and she slumped. Shot down by a bullet that never hit her.

That was how Jericho found her, as part of a collection of bodies scattered over the flight deck: two dead guards, the dead traitor, and Yoyo lying there as though dead, without a pulse, unbreathing, drenched in cold sweat. She hadn't picked up when Shaw called from her extension, nor when he tried his own phone. One look into Norrington's office told them that he wasn't there. This was enough to send him up to the sixty-eighth floor, worried, where he found Diane lying pitifully, her cables wrenched out, and clear signs of a fight. No sign at all of Yoyo but a trail of blood on the floor, on the gallery, the bridge, the steps up to the deck.

The rest was intuition.

He had burst out onto the roof just in time to see the airbike vanishing into the sky, and for a dreadful moment he thought that Yoyo was dead. He sank to his knees beside her, broken by his failure, seeing clearly the grief that would seize Tu and Chen Hongbing when he brought them the news. But then he heard a barely perceptible heartbeat, his ear pressed to her ribcage. Another followed. A slow, faltering rhythm that picked up speed and grew stronger, and then the blood flowed back to her brain and consciousness returned. When he propped her legs up she came to, groggy, confused, just about able to see and speak. Who am I? Headache, tired, sleep.

Xin had let her live.

Why?

Meanwhile Shaw was growing apoplectic. Norrington's guilt still had to be proved, even if she no longer doubted it. She was prey to a whole swarm of suspicions about what the deputy head of security could have done to damage Orley, and she ordered his data combed, his body searched. They found a datastick disguised as a house key, containing only a single program which uploaded as the image of a nine-headed snake, a shimmering, pulsing sign of his treachery.

That was the point when Jericho decided to give up.

They could fix their own problems. He couldn't do any more, didn't want to. It was as though he and Xin had some tacit agreement now that the killer had spared Yoyo's life and vanished, leaving a curt but unambiguous message: Mind your own business. Maybe Xin had simply recognized that by now, Yoyo's death was unnecessary, since so many other people knew her secret. It would have been pointless to kill her now, and somehow or other pointless actions simply didn't fit into Xin's . . . philosophy, if that was what it was.

Never mind.

He was a detective, and he had kept his promise. He had brought Yoyo back to his two clients, to Tu and Chen. Everything else was for Shaw and the British secret services to bother with, none of his business, and he was also horribly tired. At the same time, he knew that he wouldn't be able to sleep a wink, no matter how hard he was yawning now. Tu on the other hand hardly appeared to sleep at all, and the shock seemed to have jolted him into a state of unceasing wakefulness, driven by the guilt of not having been there at Yoyo's side. She had been asleep in her bed for two hours now—all the guest suites in the Big O had several rooms, and spectacular views—while he sat with Jericho in the living room, drinking tea and gobbling down the nuts and snacks like a maniac.

"I have to eat," he said half apologetically, belching loudly. "Food and sex are man's essential desires."

"Says who?" muttered Jericho.

"Confucius, since you ask, and he meant by it that we should be sure to eat well so that we can protect our women. Which means I have some catching up to do." A handful of Brazil nuts and jelly babies together. "And if I ever get my hands on that swine—"

"You won't."

Tu slapped the table. "We've got this far, *xiongdi*. Do you really think that I'll knuckle under and let the bastard get clean away? Think of what he did to Yoyo's friends, to Hongbing. The tortures he put him through!"

"Not so loud." Jericho glanced at the half-closed bedroom door. "No question that you're right to be angry, but perhaps you should just be grateful that you're not dead."

"All right, I'm grateful. What next?"

"Nothing next." Jericho spread his hands and rolled his eyes. "Live. Life goes on."

"It's not like you to take this attitude," Tu chided him. "The woodworm doesn't just sit around making comments on the carpentry."

"Thanks for the comparison."

"So why did we get involved in the first place?" Tu asked between gritted teeth. "So that the bastards could get away with it?"

"You listen to me." Jericho put down his teacup and leaned forward. "Maybe you're right, and maybe next week I'll see it all differently, but where has all this got us? Following leads in ever-widening circles, all these killers, mercenary armies, secret services, coups in West Africa, government ploys and corporation plots, today Equatorial Guinea, tomorrow the Moon, the day after tomorrow who knows, maybe Venus? Where has it got us? Corrupt oil cartels, Korean atom bombs, hotels on the Moon, rogue astronauts, oil managers getting shot at, Greenwatch wiped out, theories about China and the CIA, nine-headed monsters? Where? To a baking hot day and a man scared for his daughter. The furniture still in its packing and he's worried that she's disappeared, but first of all he has to help me get two chairs out of the bubble-wrap so that we have something to sit on. To be blunt, I couldn't give a shit about Xin and his Hydra. With the best will in the world, I have no idea what we have to do with Orley Enterprises. There's a girl in the next room, still breathing, we didn't have to lay out in a shroud, and to me that's worth all the global conspiracies you could pile up together, since it looks as though we're well out of this game, however the whole thing plays out. We've got those sods on the run, Tian, so much so that they can't see any point in killing us. The story will fizzle out of its own accord. It begins and ends on the Shanghai Pudong golf course when you asked me to bring your friend his daughter back, alive and in one piece. That's what I did. Thank you, next please."

Tian looked at him appraisingly, a handful of nuts raised halfway to his mouth.

"I'm very grate—"

"No, you're not following me." Jericho shook his head. "We're all grateful, all of us, to one another, but now we're going to fly off home, you can take care of your joint venture with Dao IT, Yoyo will carry on her studies, Hongbing will sell that silver Rolls that he was telling me about and enjoy his commission, and I'll wipe Xin's fingerprints from my furniture and try to fall in love with some woman who's not called Diane or Joanna. And won't it just be wonderful to be able to do all that! To lead a perfectly ordinary, boring life. We'll wake up from this hideous dream, we'll rub our eyes, and that will be that, because *this* isn't our life, Tian! These are other people's problems."

Tu scratched his belly. Jericho sank back into the depths of the sofa and wished he could believe what he'd just said.

"A perfectly ordinary, boring life," Tu echoed.

"Yes, Tian," he said. "Ordinary, boring. And if I can give you some advice, as a friend: talk to Yoyo. Both of you. Talking helps."

It was rude to talk this way in Chinese culture, even with a friend. But perhaps after all the last two days had brought—how much closer did you need to be before you allowed such trust? He looked out at London as the day began, and wondered whether he should leave Shanghai and come back here. Actually, he didn't much care either way.

"I'm sorry," he sighed. "I know it's nothing to do with me."

Tu let the nuts he was holding rattle back down into the bowl, and stirred them with his finger. For a while, neither of them said anything.

"Do you know what an ankang is?" he asked at last.

Jericho turned his head. "Yes."

"Would you like to hear a story about an ankang?" Tu smiled. "Of course you wouldn't. Nobody wants to hear a story about an ankang, but you've brought it upon yourself. This is a story which begins on January 12, 1968, in Zhejiang province, when a child is born, an only child. Nothing to do with the one child policy, by the way, that was only proclaimed years later, though of course you know that, since you're practically Chinese yourself."

January 12—

"Not your own birthday," Jericho said.

"No, besides which I was born in Shanghai, and this happened in a small town. The child's father was a teacher, meaning that he was under serious suspicion of harboring such heinous aims as wanting to educate people, or using his brain to develop an intellectual position. In other words, suspected of thought. Back in those days even knowing the rudiments of your own country's history was enough to have you beaten in the streets, but when Beijing's creatures began to destroy our culture in the name of revolutionizing it, this teacher of ours adapted to the new circumstances. At first. After all, the capital was a vipers' nest of Red Guards, but out in the provinces the local Party leaders were fighting the Guards. The peasants and workers out there were doing quite well from the policies of Deng Xiaoping and Liu Shaoqi. So our teacher worked in a tractor factory to avoid the suspicion of intellectualism, and he did what little he could to stop Deng and Liu from being toppled by the Maoists. There was a Red Guard faction established in his town that was openly sympathetic to Deng, the Coordinated Work Committee, and this teacher thought it would be a good idea to join them. Which it was. Until '68, when the committee broke up under pressure from the hard-liners, who didn't need to know more than that he had once *been* a teacher. The day that he began to fear for his life was the day his son was born."

Jericho sipped at his tea, and a suspicion stole over him.

"What was this teacher called, Tian?"

"Chen De." Tu tapped at a peanut with his finger, sending it skittering over the table. "You can probably guess his son's name for yourself."

"A name meant to show how faithful the father was. Red Soldier."

"Hongbing. A clever enough tactic, but it didn't help much. At the end of '68 they came to arrest Hongbing's mother for reactionary statements, supposedly, though it was actually because quite a few Guards had been practicing Cultural Revolution between her legs, and she wouldn't accept that it helped the poor peasant one bit if someone like that dragged her into bed. They took her off to a reeducation camp, where they, well, reeducated her. She came back home very ill, and broken, not the same person as she had been. Chen De started teaching again, sporadically, taking enormous risks to do so, but mostly he worked in the factory and did his best to teach his boy as much as he could, in secret, for instance telling him how to live an ethical life and why—highly dangerous propaganda, I can tell you! Then in the mid-seventies they noticed his links to the old committee. By now Mao liked to spend most of his time with the daughters of the Revolution, making sure that none of them were virgins. Chen De was accused of counterrevolutionary tendencies, seven years late, very quick trial, then prison. Hongbing was left behind, a child alone, looking after his sick mother, so he took over the job in the tractor factory."

Tu paused, pouring himself more tea.

"Well, various things changed, some for the better, some for the worse. His mother died, and then Mao soon after, Deng was rehabilitated from having been in disgrace, and Hongbing's father could teach again—as long as he stuck to the Party line, of course. The boy grows up caught between ideology and despair. Since he has no role models around him, he falls in love with cars, which were very rare indeed at the time. You can't make a living from something like that out in the country, so when he's seventeen he moves to Shanghai, which is as fun-loving as Beijing is sclerotic. He takes a string of odd jobs and falls in with a group of students who are tending the delicate shoots of democratic thought in postrevolutionary China, and they introduce him to books by Wei Jingsheng and Fang Lizhi—the Fifth Modernization, opening of society, all those enticing, forbidden thoughts."

"Hongbing was a democracy activist?"

"Oh yes!" Tu nodded enthusiastically. "He was up there on the front line, Owen my friend. A fighter! December 20, 1986, 70,000 people took to the streets in Shanghai to protest against the way the Party had manipulated appointments to the People's Congress, and Hongbing was at their head. It's a miracle that they didn't fling him behind bars right then. Meanwhile he'd also got a job at a repairs garage, fixing up cadre cars, making influential friends. This was where he lost the last of his illusions, since the new brand of Chinese managers could have invented corruption. Well, never mind that. Tell me, does April 15, 1989, mean anything to you?"

"June 4 does."

"Yes, but it all began earlier. Hu Yaobang died, a politician the students had always seen as their friend, especially after the Party made him their own internal scapegoat for the disturbances of '86. Thousands of people march in Beijing to remember him and pay their respects on Tiananmen Square, and the old demands come up again: democracy, freedom, all the stuff that enrages the old men in power. Then criticism of the regime spreads to other cities, Shanghai as well of course, and Hongbing raises a clenched fist once more and organizes protests. Deng refuses dialogue with the students, the demonstrators go on hunger strike, Tiananmen becomes the center of something like a huge carnival; there's something in the air, a mood of change, a happening, and Hongbing wants to see it for himself. By now there are a million people on the square. Journalists from all over the world, and the last straw comes when Mikhail Gorbachev arrives with his ideas of perestroika and glasnost. The Party is in a tight corner indeed."

"And Hongbing's in the thick of it."

"For all that, it could have ended peacefully. By the end of May most of the Beijing students want to wind the movement up, happy to have humiliated Deng, but the new arrivals like Hongbing insist that all demands must be met, and that escalates things. The rest is well known, I don't have to tell you about the Tiananmen Massacre. And once again, Hongbing has the most incredible luck. Nothing happens to him because his name's not on any of the blacklists. He went back to Shanghai, with the last of his illusions in shreds, decided to concentrate on his job instead and made it to deputy foreman. It's grown up to be a lovely big garage over all these years, the nouveaux riches have turned their backs on bicycles and nobody knows cars like Hongbing does. Every now and again he gets a trip to the brothel as a gift from a customer, the upper cadre invite him for meals, he's a good-looking kid, some fat cat functionaries wouldn't much mind if he got their daughters pregnant."

"So he's adapted to the times."

"Up until winter of '92, which is when Chen De hangs himself. He's spent all those years keeping his head down, and then he strings himself up. Depression. His wife had died, you see, and the Revolution had destroyed his family. Hongbing explodes with self-loathing. He hates his own name, he hates it when his drinking buddies boast and blather and yell *ganbei*, profiteers who used to be interested in the democracy movement but have sold out. He wants to make his voice heard. The year before, the dissident Wang Wanxing had been arrested for unfurling a banner on the anniversary of the Tiananmen Massacre, right in the middle of the Square. It called for the rehabilitation of the demonstrators who had been killed. So the Tiananmen anniversary comes around again, June 4, 1993, and Hongbing demonstrates for Wang's release along with a couple of like-minded souls. He reckons that this is a small thing to ask, modest enough, that it might have better chances of success than always pissing up the same tree and shouting that the whole system should change. And lo and behold, someone takes notice of him. The wrong kind, unfortunately."

"He's arrested."

"On the spot. And this is where things get really despicable, although you might say that it's all been quite despicable enough. You'd be wrong. So far, it's just been brutal."

Tu paused, while the sun climbed higher and flooded the Thames with light.

"For many years there was a pretty little Buddhist temple a few kilometers outside Hangzhou, in an idyllic spot between rice fields and tea plantations. Until they tore it down to build something in its place that was deemed more useful to Chinese society."

"An ankang."

Jericho felt his tiredness vanish. He had heard about the ankangs, though he had never seen one. The literal meaning of ankang was *safety, peace, and health,* but in fact these were the police psychiatric prisons.

"The ankang at Hangzhou was the first psychiatric clinic of its kind in China," Tu said. "Based on the belief that there is one perfect ideology, and that anybody who questions it must be suffering from some sort of mental illness, either acute or chronic. Just like you'd have to be mentally ill to believe that the Earth is a cube, or that your spouse is really a dog in disguise. Taking the Soviet Union as their example, China had always made a habit of declaring that its dissidents were crazy, but the Party only gave the psychiatric clinics that cute little name—*ankang*—at the end of the eighties. Up until then, they had operated in secret."

"Tell me, that dissident whom Hongbing was trying to get freed from prison, Wang Wanxing—wasn't he in an ankang as well?"

"For thirteen years, and then in the end he was deported in 2005. Up until then, there had only ever been rumors about the ankangs, dark mutterings that they had less to do with caring for the mentally ill than humiliating people who were of sound mind. That was when a debate began, very tentative at first, and it didn't stop the Party from opening more of these so-called clinics. There's a constant supply of people with paranoid delusions of human rights or schizophrenic beliefs about free elections. The world is full of lunatics, Owen, you just have to pay close attention: trade unionists, democrats, religious believers, people presenting petitions and lodging complaints about the demolitions and urban planning policy in Shanghai, for instance, and demanding outlandish things like citizen consultation. Not to mention the real crazies, the ones who think that our perfect society could harbor corruption."

Jericho kept quiet. Tu slurped at his tea, as though to wash the taste of the word ankang from his mouth.

"Well anyway, since Wanxing was deported in 2005 the victims have begun to speak up for themselves. Early 2005 the People's Congress even passed a law forbidding police torture, though this was a farce of course. It's still standard operating practice to work suspects over until they sign some kind of confession as proof of mental illness, then you can torture merrily away and call it medical treatment. There are about a hundred ankangs in China, and these days there's a lot of public debate and international pressure because of them, but back when Hongbing was admitted to the Hangzhou clinic it was still 1993 and there was no such thing as a right of appeal. There was a red banner hanging in the plane trees in the grounds, very pretty thing to look at, saying *A healthy mind in a healthy body means lifelong happiness*, the usual cynical vocabulary of the gulag. Hongbing gets a diagnosis: he's suffering from paranoid psychosis and political monomania. You won't find a doctor outside China who's heard of either of these conditions, they're not on any international list, but that's just more proof of how stupid foreigners are. The clinical assessment is all couched in the most harmless terms: it says that Hongbing makes a good impression, his mental condition is stable, he does as he's told, he listens to the radio, he likes reading, he's keen to help, it's just that—and I'm quoting word for word here—he displays *massive impairment in logical thought* as soon as talk turns to politics. He's quite obviously mentally disturbed and his thought processes display clear signs of megalomania, affective aggression, and a pathologically overdeveloped will. The doctors prescribe a course of pharmaceutical treatment and close supervision to bring poor Hongbing back to his wits, and with a stroke of their pen, he has no more rights."

"Couldn't he talk to a lawyer, at least?" Jericho asked, nonplussed. "There must have been some way to get his case heard."

"But Owen." Tu had started eating the nibbles again, scooping up another handful just as soon as he'd swallowed the first. "That would have been a nonsense. I mean, how can a madman contest the fact that he's mad, after all everybody knows that loonies always think they're the only sane ones. There's no way to appeal against a police finding that you're mad; the only people who decide how long you're detained are the police psychiatrists and functionaries. That's what makes it so unbearable for the victims. In a prison or a work camp, at least you know how long they've sent you down for, but when you're in an ankang it's entirely up to your tormentors. But do you know what's truly despicable here?"

Jericho shook his head.

"That most of the inmates really are mentally ill. That's cruel, eh? Just imagine how a healthy person suffers when he's surrounded by others who are seriously disturbed, criminals, threatening him the whole time. Not even half a year after admission, Hongbing sees two inmates murdered, and the staff stand by and watch. Night after night he forces himself to stay awake, for fear he could be next. Then there are other prisoners, pardon me, patients, who are perfectly sane, just like he is. Doesn't matter. They all have to go through the same hell. They're given regular therapy, the chemical assault, insulin shock, electroshock therapy. You'd never believe all the cures they have for a sick mind! They stub their cigarettes out on your skin, genitals preferably, they torture you with hot wires. Extreme heat, sleep deprivation, dunking in ice-cold water, and beatings, always the beatings. Troublemakers get chained to the bed and tortured until they pass out, for instance by sticking a needle into their upper lip and then passing a current through—they vary the voltage, switching from high to low so that you can't get used to the pain. Sometimes, if the doctors and nurses feel in the mood, all the inmates in a section have to submit to punishment, whether or not they've done anything wrong. Given this level of expert care, many patients die of heart attacks. One that Hongbing had befriended was so desperate that he went on hunger strike. So they chained him to the bed as well, and then the mentally ill inmates were told to force-feed him, under staff supervision. But how do you go about that? Since nobody actually taught them what to do, they just force the poor guy's jaws open and tip the liquid food into him until he suffocates, but at least he's eaten. The death certificate called it a heart attack. Nobody was charged. Hongbing was lucky, if you want to call it that: they didn't use the worst tortures on him. There are some car-crazy cadre members in Shanghai who put in a word on his behalf, discreetly, so that they wouldn't draw reprisals onto themselves, but it was enough to make sure he got relatively privileged treatment. He gets a cell to himself, he's allowed to read and watch television. Three times a day he gets a dose of narcoleptics, with very pronounced side effects, and all the while many of the doctors are quietly letting him know that they think he's entirely healthy. Hongbing hides the pills under his upper lip and then gets rid of them down the toilet, then he gets insulin shock therapy as punishment and lies in a coma for days. Another time, he's strapped down, the doctor puts on a pair of gloves with metal plates on them and puts his hand on his forehead, boom, there's an almighty bang and he can't see or hear. Electroshock therapy, this time as a punishment for being Hongbing. It's always booming and banging in the ankang; you can't get a wink of sleep for all the screams of pain. The patients hide under the beds, in the toilet, under the washbasin, no use any of it. If you've been chosen, they'll find you.—Oh, we're out of nibbles."

It took Jericho a moment to react. In a trance, he stood up, went to the bar, and came back with a couple of bags of chips.

"Cheese and onion," he read out. "Or would you like bacon?"

"All the same to me. In the second year, Hongbing tries to escape. He's almost out and then they catch him. He still dreams about that today, more than about all the rest of it. As a reward for showing so much initiative they dose him with scopolamine, which makes you listless, so that you don't spend your time thinking about silly things like escape. I hardly need mention that the stuff causes serious physical and psychological injury. In the third year of his stay, summer of '96, a young worker is admitted to the clinic who had reported her factory manager's son for taking bribes. The son beat her senseless, and she reported that as well, so the factory manager decided that anyone who could act with such a lack of decorum must be insane. The chief of police and the director of the ankang agreed. She's whisked away to the clinic without any medical diagnosis, without standing trial or being sentenced, while the ankang director's son-in-law is named a section manager in the factory. Coincidences do happen. Oh, and Hongbing? Falls in love with the lady, and looks after her until six months after her admission when she dies under insulin shock therapy. Which breaks the last of his resistance. On the day he lost that woman, Hongbing lost the last of his strength."

"That's dreadful, Tian," Jericho said softly.

Tu shrugged. "It's the story of a wrong turn, as so many of us have taken in life. A story of might-have-been and had-I-only. Then, spring '97, our merry band of madmen get a new member in their ranks, a well-to-do sort, pragmatic, self-assured. As you might expect, the first thing the doctors do is take care of that self-assurance. He's not exactly an unknown quantity in dissident circles, this man, he's something of a local hero for fighting against corruption. He was section head in an electronic components factory, and led thousands of employees in a protest against the management getting rich on the backs of the workers. Went to Beijing with proof, and was arrested and sectioned for his pains. In the ankang they give him all kinds of muck, he gets ill, his hair falls out, he has fits, can't sleep, his nerves are shot, and his memory's full of holes but they can't break his will to live. His only goal is to get out of there as quick as he can, and he has powerful friends in Shanghai, for instance his brother-in-law plays golf with the chief of police. This man likes Hongbing. He spends a lot of time with him, listens to what he has to say, slowly puts him back together again. Six months later he's back outside, gets a senior job at a software company, and makes plans to get rich and powerful. The year after that, when

Hongbing's finally free, he's thirty years old and he's spent five of those years in the clinic; his friend from the ankang fixes him a job with a car dealer and takes it upon himself to take care of him whenever and however he can."

The sun had climbed higher. Soft, rosy dawn light touched all the rooftops.

"You're the friend from the ankang," Jericho said softly.

"Yes." Tu took his glasses off and began to clean them on a corner of his shirt. "I'm the friend. That's the link between Hongbing and me."

Jericho was silent for a while.

"And Hongbing has never talked to Yoyo about this time?"

"Never." Tu held the glasses up to the light and looked thoughtfully at the lenses. "Have a look at your own life, Owen. You know it yourself, there are some experiences that just lock your vocal cords tight. You're tongue-tied by the shame, and also, you think that if you don't talk about it, it will fade with the years, but its power over you simply grows. After he was freed, Hongbing considered going to court. I told him, build your own life up first before you take any more steps. He had such a knack with cars! Whenever a new model came onto the market, he would know all there was to know about it within days. He listened to me, and worked up to being a salesman. In 1999 he got to know a girl from Ningbo and married her, in a great rush. They didn't suit one another, not one tiny bit, but he wanted to catch up on his five lost years, fast-forward, and start a family as soon as possible. Yoyo was born, the marriage broke up just as predicted, since Hongbing suddenly decided he wasn't able to love anymore. Truth was it was only himself he couldn't love, and he still can't today. The girl went back to Ningbo, Hongbing was given custody and tried to give Yoyo what he didn't have."

"Kindness."

"Hongbing's problem is that he thinks he doesn't deserve kindness. But Yoyo has got the wrong idea. She thinks that she's done something wrong. By saying nothing he's given her an enormous guilt complex, which is exactly the opposite of what he intended, but you've met him, you know what he's like by now. He's walled himself up in his own silence." Tu sighed. "The night before last, in Berlin, when I was out on the tiles with Yoyo and you were sulking in the hotel, I finally got around to telling her my story. She's clever, Yoyo, and right away she asked whether something like that had happened to Hongbing."

"What did you say?"

"Nothing."

"He'll have to talk to her."

"Yes." Tu nodded. "Once he can break out of his shell. I have to tell you that in secret, without her having the least idea, he's still fighting to be rehabilitated."

"And you? Were you ever rehabilitated?"

"In 2002, when I became manager at the software company, I decided to lodge an appeal. It was rejected nine times.—Then, totally out of the blue, I heard that it was all a dreadful mistake and that I had been the victim of misdiagnosis, even of a criminal conspiracy! My reputation was restored and that smoothed the path for my career. I put in a word for Hongbing and got him made technical director of a Mercedes dealership, which gave him enough of a livelihood that he could go to court at last, and he's been making his case ever since. He's gathered whole crates full of evidence, medical affidavits showing that he was never mentally ill, but so far his sentence has only ever been partially revised. I picked my fight with corrupt managers, but they'd broken the law after all. He took on the Party. And the Party's an elephant, Owen. He's a marked man, he's scarred for life. I think that if he were fully rehabilitated, he might even be able to confide in Yoyo, but as it is—"

Jericho turned his teacup around between his fingers.

"Yoyo has to learn the truth, Tian," he said. "If Hongbing won't talk to her, you'll have to."

"Ah well." Tu perched his glasses back on his nose and gave a wry grin. "After this morning, at least I have some practice."

"Thank you for telling me."

Tu gazed at the empty chip packets, lost in thought. Then he looked Jericho in the eyes.

"You're my friend, Owen. Our friend. You're one of us. You're part of it."

June 2, 2025
Lynn

LONDON, GREAT BRITAIN

The address 85 Vauxhall Cross in the southwest of the city, on Albert Embankment near Vauxhall Bridge, looked as if King Nebuchadnezzar II had tried to build a Babylonian ziggurat with Lego bricks. In fact, the sand-colored hulk with the green armored glass surfaces contained the beating heart of British security, the Secret Intelligence Service, also known as SIS or MI6. In spite of its playful appearance, it was a genuine bulwark against the enemies of the United Kingdom, last attacked by an IRA unit twenty-five years ago, when a missile had been fired at it from the opposite bank, although without doing much more than shake the cups and saucers in the secret service coffee lounge.

Jennifer Shaw was on her way to her son's birthday dinner when she received a call from a very senior authority. She switched to receive, and C's voice filled the leather-scented interior of her freshly restored Jaguar Mark II. In most people's eyes, the head of the British Foreign Secret Service was, after thirty-one James Bond films, called M, which was quite close to the reality, except that Sir Mansfield Smith-Cumming, the legendary first director, had introduced the letter C, and since then all directors had been called C—not least because it happened to stand for "control."

"Hello, Bernard," said Shaw, in the certain knowledge that her evening was stuffed.

"Jennifer. I hope I'm not disturbing you."

A set phrase. Bernard Lee, the current director, couldn't have cared less if he was disturbing her, and how. The only disturbance that he would have acknowledged was the disturbance to national security.

"I'm on my way to Bibendum," she said truthfully.

"Oh, always excellent. Especially the skate wing. I haven't been there for ages. Could you call in on me for a moment beforehand?"

"How long's a moment?"

"Only if you have time. On the other hand—"

"The traffic's not too bad. Give me ten minutes."

"Thanks."

She called her son from her cell phone and told him to go ahead and order a starter without her, but to get her a double portion of the iced lime soufflé.

"Which means that I won't see you before pudding," her son complained.

"I'll aim to be there for the main."

"Has this got anything to do with Orley's Moon trip?"

"No idea, darling."

"I thought the bomb went off and didn't do any harm, and they were all coming home safe and sound."

"I don't really know."

"Oh, well. I guess the Prime Minister's kids see their mother even more rarely."

"How nice to have brought positive-thinking people into the world. Don't be cross with me, sweetie, I'll call as soon as I can."

At Wellington Arch she turned from Piccadilly into Grosvenor Place and followed Vauxhall Bridge Road over the Thames. Soon she was sitting in full evening dress in Lee's office, with a glass of water in front of her.

"We've reconstructed Norrington's deleted e-mails," the director said without any preamble.

"And?" she asked excitedly.

"Well." Lee pursed his lips. "You know, all the clues pointed at him, but we didn't have any real evidence—"

"The fact that Kenny Xin shot him full in the face seems pretty convincing to me. Have you found any trace of Xin, by the way?"

"Not the slightest. But we have come across something alarming. Our American colleagues are worried too. Norrington's mails didn't make any sense at all at first, he had deleted nothing but white noise, so we tried it with the Hydra program. And suddenly we had a complex correspondence in front of our eyes. Unfortunately there's nothing to tell us who Hydra is, and it isn't clear who else received the mails. What is certain is that Norrington must have had access to a secret router, to which he sent encrypted e-mails."

"All from the central computer of the Big O?"

"Definitely. Without the mask, that snake-headed icon, we can't do a thing with the e-mails. It wouldn't have occurred to anybody that they are encoded, and he was too clever to install the decoding program on his work computer, and instead carried it around with him on a memory stick. However, we're getting some insights into the planning and construction of the launching pad in Equatorial Guinea, and learning some amazing things about the black market in Korean atom bombs, things that even we weren't aware of.—Okay, the bomb went off, as we know, without doing any damage."

"Indirectly it caused a lot of damage," said Jennifer. "But okay, Julian, Lynn, and most of the guests are on the way home. They should be at OSS in a few hours."

"You see; and now it's imperative that you talk to Julian."

"Will do."

"As soon as possible, I mean. Within the next hour. I need his assessment."

Shaw raised an eyebrow. "About what?"

"According to Norrington's correspondence, the whole business isn't quite over yet."

"Tell me quite clearly. I have to know that it's worth leaving my son to celebrate his thirtieth birthday without his mummy."

Lee nodded. "I think it's worth it, Jennifer. Last year, there wasn't just one mini-nuke sent to the Moon." He paused, sipped on his water and set the glass down carefully in front of him. "It was two."

"Two," echoed Jennifer.

"Yes. Kenny Xin bought two, and both were put on Maye's rocket. And now we're asking ourselves: where's the second one?"

Shaw stared at him. Lee was right, this *was* alarming. This meant *no* lime soufflé. What it did mean, she didn't want to think about.

CHARON, OUTER SPACE

Evelyn Chambers saw Olympiada Rogacheva floating from the sleeping area into the lounge with an expression of grim contentment. The spookily unreal aspect of her appearance had vanished. For the first time, the Russian seemed to see herself as the chief indicator of her own presence, as someone who didn't only exist thanks to her association with other people, but who would continue to be there even if her life's coordinators took their eyes off her.

"I told him to kiss my ass," she announced, and settled next to Heidrun.

"And how did he take that?"

"He said he wouldn't do that, exactly, but he wished me luck."

"Seriously," said Heidrun, amazed. "You told him you were leaving him?"

Olympiada Rogacheva looked down at herself with the shy sensuality of a teenager exploring the new territory of her body.

"Do you think I'm too old to—?"

"Nonsense," Heidrun said stoutly.

Olympiada smiled, looked up, and floated away. An imaginary Miranda Winter somersaulted weightlessly, shrieked and squeaked. Finn O'Keefe read his book, to keep from seeing her red lips forming a blossom of promise, or uttering words of breathtaking banality. They were hurrying through space in the constant presence of Rebecca Hsu, they heard Momoka Omura making her acid comments, and Warren Locatelli boasting, Chucky telling bad jokes even more badly than they deserved, Aileen making bouquets of brightly colored flowers of wisdom, Mimi Parker and Marc Edwards finding fulfillment in togetherness, and Peter Black telling the latest news from time and space. They even heard Carl Hanna playing guitar, the other Carl, who wasn't a terrorist, just a nice guy. Walo Ögi played chess under the ceiling and lost his third game against Karla Kramp, Eva Borelius was trapped in the hamster-wheel of her self-reproach, and Dana Lawrence, the self-declared heroine, was writing a report.

Evelyn Chambers said nothing, glad of the emptiness in her head. For the first time since leaving the Moon, she felt distinctly better. Looking back, that strange experience in the mining area had been too embarrassing for her to mention, but she would have to find words for it sooner or later. She felt a vague sense of dread, as if a monstrous presence in that sea of mist had become aware of her, and had been watching her since then, but even that she would deal with. She gently pushed herself away, left Olympiada to her own devices, and floated over to the bistro.

"How are you?" she asked.

"Fine." Rogachev, strapped into a harness, looked up from his computer. "You?"

"Better." She rubbed her temples with her index fingers. "The pressure is easing."

"Glad to hear it."

"But what if I yield to my professional curiosity?"

"You can ask anything you like." Rogachev's smile melted the ice between his blond eyelashes a little. "As long as you don't expect to get an answer to everything."

"What are you doing on that computer all the time?"

"Julian deserves a response. We had a fantastic week thanks to him. However it may have ended, we were given a lot. And now we've got to give something in return."

"You want to invest?" asked Mukesh Nair, floating over.

"Why not?"

"After this disaster?"

"So?" Oleg Rogachev shrugged. "Did people stop building ships just because the *Titanic* went down?"

"I'll admit, I'm uneasy."

"You know how failure works, Mukesh. It's always sparked by a fear of crisis. It starts with a soluble problem, but it drags a psychosis along behind it. A shark psychosis. It only takes one shark to paralyze the tourism of a whole region, because no one will go into the water even though the likelihood of being eaten tends to zero. The collapse of the economy, of the financial markets, has always involved psychoses. Not the individual terrorist attack, not the bankruptcy of an individual bank, the threat comes from the general paralysis that follows. Should I make my decision to invest in Julian's project, in the breakthrough of the global energy supply, dependent on a shark?"

"The shark was an *atom bomb*, Oleg!" Nair opened his eyes wide. "Possibly the start of a global conflict."

"Or not."

"At any rate, there was nothing Julian could have done about it," Evelyn confirmed. "We were the victim of an attack meant for somebody else. We were simply in the wrong place at the wrong time."

"But someone must know who was behind it!"

"And what are you going to do if they don't?" Rogachev asked ironically. "Suspend all space travel?"

"You know very well that's not what I think," Mukesh grumbled. "I just wonder if an investment would be *sensible*."

"I do too."

"And?"

Rogachev pointed at the computer screen. "I've worked it out. There's about 600,000 tons of helium-3 stored on the Moon, ten times the potential energy yield of all the oil, gas, and coal supplies on Earth. Perhaps even more, because the concentration of the isotope on the back of the Moon might be even higher than it is in the Earth's shadow. That's 5 meters of saturated regolith; the most interesting part is the first 2 to 3 meters, or exactly the depth plowed by the beetles." Rogachev typed on his computer. "Leaving out transport to Earth, the energy balance is as follows: one gram of regolith equals 1,750 Joules. Some of this is lost in heating and processing, leaving us with, let's say, 1,500 Joules. That's an area of 10,000 square kilometers that needs to be plowed and processed to cover the current energy needs of Earth. One thousandth of the Moon's surface. Where productivity is concerned, beetles work with sunlight, which means that they spend half the year without energy, meaning that we would need twice as many of the things as we have at present."

"And how many is that?"

"A few thousand."

"A few *thousand*?" cried Mukesh.

"Yes, of course," said Oleg, unmoved. "Assuming we're deploying that many, then supplies would last for around 4,000 years, always assuming that the world population stagnates and the Third World's energy needs remain lower than those of the developed countries. Neither of these two things will be the case. Realistically, we can expect a population of twenty-five billion people by the end of the century, and an overall increase in electricity usage. In that case the Moon will supply us with energy for 700 years at most."

"And then?" asked Evelyn Chambers.

"We'll have used up another fossil resource, and we'll be standing right where we are today. The Moon will have been leveled, uninteresting to hotels and pleasure trips, but may have been able to preserve a few conservation areas. Whether we'll be able to see them for dust is a whole other question."

"Thousands of mining machines." Nair shook his head. "That's crazy! We'll never be able to pay for them."

"We will," Rogachev snapped the computer shut. "We had a deficit problem with space travel, too. The elevator changed everything, and building a few thousand machines like that isn't such big news. Thousands of tanks will be built too, and a leveled moon is just a leveled moon."

"Shit," Chambers said to herself.

"Yes, shit. I know what you're thinking. Yet again we've destroyed a natural wonder for the sake of a short-term effect."

"But it's going to be worth it?"

"It'll be worth it for 700 years, and from a distance the Moon won't look much different from what it looks like today." Oleg pursed his lips. "So I think I'm going to invest part of the originally planned sum in Orley Space."

"Congratulations."

"Not least on *your* advice." He raised his eyebrows. "Have you forgotten? Isla de las Estrellas?"

"I hadn't been to the mining zone then."

"I understand. Shark psychosis."

"No, not at all. You've just expressed in words what I'd already worked out in the land of mists. The idiocy of the whole thing. When we talk about moon mining, most people think about a few lonely bulldozers lost in the vastness of the Moon. Instead, we're losing the Moon to the bulldozers." She shook her head. "Of course it's better to destroy the Moon than the Earth, aneutronic fusion is clean, and if it lasts 700 years, then fine. But I'm still allowed to think it's crap."

"I thought I'd put the other half of the money into buying up Warren Locatelli's Light-years."

"What?" Mukesh Nair rolled his eyes. "You want to—"

"I don't want to look ruthless." Rogachev raised both hands. "Warren's dead, but holding back won't bring him back to life. He was a little god, and like all gods he left a vacuum. In my view, Light-years is the best imaginable candidate for a buyout. Warren Locatelli did amazing things in solar technology, there's still much to come, and the best brains in the sector are working for his company. So let's be under no illusions: solar technology's going to be the only way of solving our energy problems in the long term!" He smiled. "So we may not even have to level the Moon."

"And you're sure that Light-years will simply allow itself to be swallowed up?" the Indian asked suspiciously.

"Hostile takeover."

"You'll have to offer a huge amount of money."

"I know. Are you in?"

"God Almighty, you ask some questions!" Nair rubbed his fleshy nose. "This isn't really my area. I'm just a simple—"

"Farmer's son, I know."

"I'll have to think about it, Oleg."

"Do that. I've already talked to Julian. He's with me. Walo too."

"One of them gets a leg, the other an arm," hummed Evelyn, as Nair floated off with solar cells in his eyes. Rogachev smiled his vulpine smile and remained silent for a moment.

"And you?" he asked. "What are you going to do?"

She looked at him. "About Julian?"

"You do administer the capital of public opinion, as you put it so nicely."

"Don't worry." Evelyn pulled a face. "I won't hurt him."

"A good friend," Rogachev chuckled.

"Friendship hasn't got much to do with it, Oleg. I was well disposed toward his projects *before* I went to the Moon, and I still am, regardless of what I think about the plundering that's going on up there. He's a pioneer, an innovator. No criminal gang is going to blow my sympathies for him out of my head just like that."

"So are you going to make a program about what happened?"

"Of course. Will you be on it?"

"If you like."

"In that case can I take the opportunity to ask you some questions about your private life?"

"No, you can only do that here." He winked at her. "As a *friend*."

"At the moment the word is that you're being abandoned."

"Ah, right." He glanced away. "Yes, I think Olympiada mentioned something along those lines."

"Christ, Oleg!"

He shrugged. "What do you expect? Since we got married she's left me every two weeks or so."

"She seems to mean it this time."

"I'd be glad if she would turn her thoughts into actions. Admittedly this is the first time she's left me without being falling-down drunk."

"You don't care?"

"No! It's way overdue."

"I'm sorry, but I don't get this at all. Why don't *you* just leave *her*, in that case?"

"I did, ages ago."

"Officially, I mean."

"Because I promised her father I wouldn't."

"I see. All that macho crap."

"What? Keeping your promises?" Rogachev studied her. "Shall I tell you the biggest reproach she levels at me, Evelyn? Do you want to know? What do you think?"

"No idea." She shrugged. "Infidelity? Cynicism?"

"No. That I've never taken the trouble to lie to her. Can you imagine that? *The trouble?*"

Confused, Evelyn said nothing.

"But I don't lie," said Rogachev. "You can accuse me of all sorts of things, probably rightly, but if there's something that I've never done and never will do, it's lying or breaking promises. Can you imagine that? Someone ignoring all your bad qualities and telling you off for your good one?"

"Perhaps she means it's more bearable—"

"For whom? For her? She could have gone, at any time. She should never have married me. She knew me, she knew exactly who I am, and that Ginsburg and I were just trying to marry our *fortunes* together. But Olympiada agreed because she couldn't think of anything better to do, and even today she can't think of anything to do but suffer." Rogachev shook his head. "Believe me, I'll never stop her. I'll never *force* her to leave me. She may think I've degraded her, but she's got to regain her own dignity. Olympiada says she's dying by my side. That's tough. But I can't save her life, she has to save her own life, by *going*."

Evelyn stared at her fingertips. Suddenly she saw the foot of the beetle coming down again, felt the creature's pale eye settling on her from the realm of the dead. I see you, it said. I'll watch you every day as you prepare yourself for death.

"You've saved *my* life," she said quietly. "Did I ever thank you for that?"

"I think you're trying to right now," said Rogachev.

She hesitated. Then she leaned across and kissed him on the cheek.

"I think you've got a few more positive characteristics," she said. "Even if you're pretty ignorant otherwise."

Rogachev nodded.

"I should have started sooner," he said. "My father was a brave man, braver than all of us put together, but I couldn't save his life. I try again every day, by pilling up money for him, buying companies for him, submitting people to my will and thus to his, but still he is shot over and over again. He will never come back to life, and I don't know how to deal with it. There's no middle way, Evelyn. Either you're too far away, or you're too close to it."

"You're not that far apart," hissed Amber. She was angry, because Julian and Tim could do nothing but bicker, and even angrier about the immovable persistence with which each clung to his resentment, while Lynn slept her time away as if under chloroform. "Both of you suspected her of being in a pact with Carl."

"Because that's how she behaved," said Tim.

"Ludicrous! As if Lynn would seriously have been capable of destroying her own hotel!"

"You saw her yourself," bellowed Julian. "It may seem weird to us in retrospect, but Lynn is mentally disturbed."

"Not much gets past you, does it?" sneered Tim.

"That's enough," Amber snapped at him. "This is kindergarten stuff. Either you learn to talk to each other sensibly, or it'll be me you're dealing with. Both of you!"

They had withdrawn into the landing module so as not to let the others see the spectacle of their rancor. Neither of them was any good at holding things back. The moldering corpse of their family life lay naked and repulsive before them, ready for the autopsy. After the Io had rescued Nina Hedegaard from a hell of dust, and the surviving members of the group had climbed aboard the landing module to get back to the mother ship, Lynn had collapsed in tears. Immediately after the coupling maneuver, she had regained consciousness, without recognizing anybody, faded away again, and set off on a horrific twenty-four-hour journey. Since then she had looked more or less composed, except that she couldn't remember most of what had happened on the Moon. A moment later she was asleep again.

"Just to clear up a few things—" Tim began.

"Stop." Amber shook her head.

"Why?"

"I said, stop!"

"You don't know what I—"

"I do, you want to attack your father! How long is this going to go on for? What are you actually accusing him of? Of making space travel economically viable? Of giving zillions of people jobs?"

"No."

"Of making people's dreams come true? Of fighting for clean energy, for a better world?"

"Of course not."

"Then what?" she yelled. "Oh, Christ, I'm so fed up with this wretched trench warfare. So fed up!"

"Amber." Tim crouched down. "He didn't care. When we—"

"Care about what?" she interrupted him. "Maybe he wasn't there for you very often. As I see it he cares day in, day out, for a weird cosmic phenomenon called humanity, which does all kinds of terrible, stupid things. Sorry, Tim, but I can't stand the peevish way young people talk about their parents, even if they produce miracles, all that in-an-ideal-world claptrap—I don't buy it, I'm afraid."

"It isn't just that he wasn't around," Tim defended himself. "But that on the few occasions when he should have been there, he wasn't! That Crystal lost her m—"

"You're completely unfair, you little shit," Julian snorted. "Your mother had a genetic predisposition."

"Crap!"

"She did! *Capito, hombre?* She'd have lost her mind even if I'd been there for her every hour of every day."

"You know very well that—"

"No, she was sick! It was in her genes, and before I married her she'd fried half of her brain on coke anyway. And where Lynn's concerned—"

"Where Lynn's concerned, you listen to me," Amber interrupted. "Because as a matter of fact, and Tim's completely right here, you can't look into anyone else's head. You think life's a film and you're directing it, and everyone acts and thinks according to the script. I don't know whether you really love Lynn, or only the part that she's supposed to play for you—"

"Of course I love her!"

"Okay, you've done everything for her, you've made sure she had the best possible career, but have you ever been *interested* in her? Are you sure you've ever really been interested in anyone?"

"Christ alive, why have I organized all this, in that case?"

"No, no." She raised a finger. "Listen, little Julian, to what your aunt says! You make films and you cast people in them. With ten billion extras and Lynn in the main part."

"That's not true!"

"Yes, it is. You can't see that your daughter is manic depressive, and that she threatens to suffer the same fate as her mother."

"Exactly," cried Tim. "Because you—"

"Shut it, Tim! Look, Julian, it's not that you don't want to see it, you just *don't* see it! Come down to earth. Lynn's unusually talented, she has brilliant qualities, just like you do, but unlike you she hasn't got power flowing through her veins, she's not a natural mover and shaker, and she doesn't have a buffalo hide. So stop selling her as perfect and beating up on her because she'll never dare to contradict you. Ease off on the pressure. Say after me: Lynn—is—not—like—me!"

"Erm—Julian?"

Amber looked up. Nina Hedegaard, visibly troubled, was hovering in the air lock leading to the habitation units. Julian turned his head and forced himself to assume a relaxed expression.

"Come in, come in. We were just swapping funny family stories and discussing our next Christmas party."

"I don't mean to bother you." She smiled shyly. "Hello, Amber. Hi, Tim."

Since the Charon had set off on its long trip back to the OSS, Julian had stopped trying to hide his relationship with the pilot. Amber liked Nina and felt sorry for her, particularly for the way she believed Julian when he hinted at their future together.

"What's up?" asked Julian.

"I've got Jennifer Shaw on the line."

"I'll be right there." He strolled to the air lock, all too willingly, it seemed to Amber.

"And then you come right back," she added. "I haven't finished with you yet."

"Yes," sighed Julian. "I'd been afraid of that."

Tim opened his mouth to make a disagreeable remark. Amber flashed a glance at him that made him think better of it.

Lynn was sharpening the blade of her suspicions.

What had happened on the Moon seemed like a single, painful dream sequence, and in fact she had difficulty remembering the last few hours in Gaia. But when Dana Lawrence floated past in her sleeping bag, at the same moment as she opened her eyes, cast her a glance, and asked her how she was, a synaptic firework exploded in her brain, and she couldn't help it. She said:

"Piss off to hell, you two-faced snake."

Dana paused, with her head thrown back, her eyelids heavy with arrogance. The voices of the others could be heard from the next sector along. Then she came closer.

"What's your problem with me, Lynn? I haven't done anything to you."

"You've questioned my authority."

"No, I was loyal. Do you think it was fun watching Kokoschka burn, even if he was in cahoots with Hanna? I had to order the evacuation."

The stupid thing was that she was right. By now Lynn knew that she had behaved in an extremely paranoid way, even though she wondered in what context it might have been. For example she hadn't understood why she hadn't wanted to show Julian certain films. And she couldn't remember her wild escape across the glass bridges, seconds before the fire had broken out, but she could remember Hanna's betrayal, the bomb, and the operation to rescue the people trapped in Gaia's head. For a moment she had regained her leadership qualities, before her mind had given in once and for all. That it was now working again seemed at first like a miracle, although she wasn't particularly pleased, since the generator of her emotions had clearly suffered some damage. Listless and depressed, she couldn't even remember what it was like to feel joy. On the other hand she knew what she definitely *hadn't* dreamed about in all that confusion. It was clearly in front of her eyes, it echoed in her ears, a matter in which Lawrence played an inglorious part.

"Leave me alone," she said.

"I did my job, Lynn," Dana said, insulted. "If shortcomings in the planning and construction of Gaia led to disaster, you can't blame me."

"There were no shortcomings. When will we actually get there?"

"In about three hours."

Lynn started unbuckling herself. She was thirsty. And for something specific, grapefruit juice. So she wasn't just thirsty, she'd got an appetite. An emotional reaction, almost.

"They should have put in more emergency exits," Dana Lawrence said, trickling acid into the wounds. "The throat was a bottleneck."

"Didn't I fire you?"

"You did."

"Then shut up."

Lynn pushed Lawrence aside and slipped over to the hatch leading to the next area. As always, everyone would be very nice and caring. Embarrassing, embarrassing; it should have been her task to ask Julian's guests what they would like. But she was ill. Gradually, in manageable portions, Tim had told her the full extent of the disaster, so by now she knew who had died and under what circumstances. And again she had struggled to feel anything, grief, or at the very least rage, and had come up with nothing but dull despair.

"What did she want?"

"What?" Julian took off his headphones.

"I said, what did she want?"

Tim tried not to sound unfriendly. Julian turned his head. The command panel of the Charon was in the back part of the sleeping area. Through the open bulkhead they could see into the adjacent lounge, where Heidrun, Sushma, and Olympiada were in conversation with Finn O'Keefe, while Walo Ögi was despairing over one of Karla Kramp's castling maneuvers.

"Something really strange," Julian said quietly. "She was asking how many bombs we found at the moon base."

"How *many*?"

"Clearly there were *two* mini-nukes aboard that rocket from Equatorial Guinea. There's another one of those things up there."

He said it in such a calm and matter-of-fact way that it took Tim a moment to understand the full import of the news.

"Shit," he whispered. "Does Palmer know about this?"

"They informed him right away. Panic must have broken out at the base. They want to inspect the caves again."

"You mean, in case a bomb is found—"

"Hanna may have hidden a second one."

"Pah."

"Mmhm." Julian rested a hand on Tim's shoulder. "Whatever, we don't want to tell the world about it."

"I don't know, Julian." Tim frowned. "Do you seriously think he put the second bomb in the caves as well?"

"You don't?"

"When there was already one in there? I'd find a different place for a second one."

"That's true too." Julian rubbed his beard. "And what if the mini-nuke isn't meant for the base?"

"Who else would it be meant for?"

"I've just got this idea. A bit crude, perhaps. But just imagine that someone's trying to stir the Chinese and Americans up against each other. Not hard, given that they mixed it up last year. So what if the second bomb—"

"Was meant for the Chinese?" Tim slowly exhaled. "You should write novels. But okay. There's a third possibility."

"Which is?"

"The mining zone."

"Yeah." Julian gnawed on his lower lip. "And there's nothing we can do about it."

"But how about I tell Amber?"

"Okay, but no one else. I'll have a talk to Jennifer and tell her what we think."

Orley Space Station (OSS),
Geostationary Orbit

They approached the space station at an angle, so that the massive 280-meter mushroom-shaped structure hung at a diagonal. By now they were all wearing their space suits again. Even though the Earth was still 36,000 kilometers away, seeing the OSS getting bigger on the screens was a bit like coming home: its five tori, the wide circle of its wharf, the extravagant modules of the Kirk and the Picard, the ring-shaped space harbor with its mobile air locks, manipulators, freight shuttles, and phalanxes of stumpy-winged evacuation pods. At 23:45 a hollow chime ran through the space-ship, along with a faint vibration as Nina Hedegaard docked on the ring.

"Please keep your suits on," said Nina. "The full kit. Your luggage—"

She fell silent. At that moment she had clearly realized that no one had any luggage. It had all been left in Gaia.

"From the Charon we go straight to the Picard, where a snack bar has already been set up. We haven't got much time, the elevator will be there at about a quarter past twelve, and will leave the OSS right away. We thought it—ahem, in your best interest to get back to Earth as quickly as possible. You can store your helmets and backpacks in Torus-2."

No one said anything. Gloomily, they left the spaceship by the air lock, said farewell to their cramped flying hotel, and in a sense, belatedly, to the Moon, which couldn't in the end do anything about what had happened. They floated one after the other down the corridor to Torus-2, the distributor ring that accommodated the lobby and hotel reception. From there, connecting tunnels branched out, leading down to the suites and up through the levels to the part of the station used by the research teams with its labs, observatories, and workshops. The two extendable air locks on the inside of the torus which led to elevator cabins were locked. Three astronauts were working on the consoles, checking the elevator systems, overseeing the unloading of a freighter, and repair work on a manipulator.

O'Keefe thought of the disc of the wharf, where spaceships were being built for bolder missions, of machines dashing through the silence of the universe, and solar panels sparkling in the cold, white sun. Heidrun had pushed him out of the air lock up there, she had made fun of him, and Warren Locatelli had puked in his helmet.

How long ago was that? A decade? A century?

He wouldn't be coming back, he knew that, as he set his helmet down on its shelf. Making brash science-fiction films, saving the universe, any time! Whatever the script called for. But no going back.

"No," he said to himself.

"No?"

Heidrun set her helmet down next to his. He turned his head and looked into her violet eyes. He studied her elfin face, saw her hair forming a flowing white fan in zero gravity, felt his heart like a lump in his chest.

"Would you come back?" he asked. "Here? To the Moon?"

She thought for a moment.

"Yes. I think I would."

"So you found something up here."

"A few things, Finn." She smiled. "Quite a lot, in fact. And you?"

Nothing, he wanted to say. I've just lost something. Before I had it. "Don't know."

He would never see her again either. He would stay out of everyone's way. The world was full of lonely places; it *was* a lonely place. You didn't have to go to the Moon to find one of those. Heidrun opened her lips and raised a hand as if to touch him.

"In our next life," she said quietly.

"But there's only this one here," he answered roughly.

She nodded, lowered her head, and slipped past him. A strand of her hair passed across his face and tickled his nose.

"*Mein Schatz*," he heard Walo say. "Are you coming?"

"Coming, sweetie!"

The lump was starting to hurt. Finn O'Keefe stared at his helmet, turned around, and drifted after the others, his mind a blank.

Midnight had just gone. It had been such an effort to quell the excitement of the last few days that no one felt much like reviving it with caffeine, so everyone pounced on fruit juice and tea in the Picard. Julian would have liked to have some soup, but because eating soup in microgravity was pretty much a no-no, there was lasagna. He sawed a piece of it off and disappeared into the tunnel that led down to the suites, to phone the Earth from there.

Dana Lawrence joined him.

"Not hungry?" he asked.

"No, I am. I just left my report in the Charon."

He stopped outside his cabin, balancing his lasagna. Did this woman make any sense at all? In Gaia, she had proved her mettle, she had challenged the traitor Kokoschka and finished off Carl Hanna. Lynn couldn't have made a better choice, and yet, thinking about it, it was the fact that any other choice was rationally unthinkable that unsettled him. Perhaps it was because of the image he had of women, of people in general, that he couldn't make heads or tails of her. He couldn't imagine her bursting into tears or bursting out laughing. Her

Madonna face with its heart-shaped mouth and piercing eyes made him think of a replicant, of Brooke Adams's postpod character in *Invasion of the Body Snatchers*, in the scene in which she opens her mouth and emits the hollow, unearthly scream of an alien. Clearly very intelligent and passably attractive, Dana Lawrence was miles away from any kind of passion.

"I must thank you," he said. "I know Lynn wasn't always—always quite up to it during the crisis."

"She fought remarkably well."

"But I also know that Lynn's initial enthusiasm for you turned into rejection. Don't blame her. Lynn's judgment was clouded during this trip. You were far-sighted and brave."

"I did my job." She mimicked a smile, making her features softer but no more sensual.

"Will you excuse me?"

"Of course." She floated past him and disappeared down the next side corridor.

Julian immediately forgot about her. He hungrily sniffed his lasagna, looked into the scanner, and slipped into his cabin.

Dana reached Torus-1, with its bars, libraries, and common rooms—then continued on and slipped into the long tunnel which led toward the upper level and connected the OSS Grand with Torus-2. Only two astronauts were still on duty at the terminal.

"I have to go to Charon for a minute," she said to them. "For some documents."

One of the men nodded. "Fine."

She turned away, disappeared into the corridor that linked Torus-2 with the outer ring of the space harbor, and drifted toward the air lock behind which the spaceship lay at anchor. Everything was still going to plan. Hydra still hadn't lost, quite the contrary. It was only Lynn's suspicion that unsettled her, as she couldn't work out how it had come about. But even that wasn't particularly important. Dana opened the bulkhead leading to the Charon and looked behind her, but no one had followed her down the corridor. In the Picard they were indulging in lasagna and homesickness. She sped into the landing unit and on into the habitation module, crossed the bistro, the lounge, and started working away at the wall covering.

Hanna had told her exactly where to do it.

And there she was.

The lightning flash of memory. Amazing how it appeared in the middle of heavy cloud cover. She couldn't remember exactly what she'd done in the igloo, but she could see Carl Hanna very clearly, before she had sunk

to the floor by the coffee machine, frozen with terror. She saw him mur-
dering Tommy Wachowski, heard his quiet, traitorous cursing:

Dana, for fuck's sake. Come on!

Dana.

Her suspicions had already been aroused a few hours before, when
Dana Lawrence had hypocritically asked her how she was, but now it
was certain. Hanna had tried to make contact with the bitch, in a way
that revealed that the contact had been prearranged. Why? Drawing
the necessary conclusions would have taken a considerable amount of
energy, too much to put Julian in the picture as well, particularly since
she didn't talk much to her father anymore. It had dawned on her that
she felt a lot better as soon as she banished him from the center of her
thoughts. At the same time she missed him, as a puppet misses the
hand that moves it, and she was already aware, at least on an intellectual level, that she actually idolized him. Maybe she no longer *felt* what
she felt, but at least she still *knew* what she felt.

Something had gone wrong in her life, and Dana Lawrence had
played an inglorious part in that.

Lynn peered down the corridor.

Determined not to let her enemy out of her sight, she had followed
Dana Lawrence when she had left the Picard with Julian. The cunning
of madness, she thought, *almost* with amusement, but the madness
had fled. A few seconds passed, then she slipped after Lawrence. At the
end of the corridor she saw that the Charon's bulkhead was open, and
knew that Lawrence was in the spaceship.

I'll get you, she thought. I will prove you're a snake, and the seething
hatred that I know you feel for me will be your downfall. You shouldn't
have allowed yourself to be dragged into all this, unapproachable, unassailable, controlled Dana, but you aren't unassailable after all. You didn't
try to shatter the others' confidence in me for nothing. You will pay.

She floated silently over the rim of the bulkhead, crossed the landing module, the bistro, the lounge. She glimpsed Dana in the sleeping
area, bent over something angular, the size of a briefcase, that she had
taken from the opened wall. Saw her fingers darting over a keyboard
and entering some data:

Nine hours: 09:00

The plan was so simple, so efficient at its core. Launching a rocket to
the Moon and detonating it above Peary Base might have worked, but
its trajectory would be immediately traceable, and the risk of missing
the base was great as well. To fire another missile at the OSS, whether
from Earth or a satellite, was practically impossible. The rocket would
have been intercepted, and here too the reconstruction of its flight path
would have led straight to its originator.

But Hydra had come up with the perfect solution. Two mini-nukes, disguised in a communication satellite, from which they could travel unnoticed to the Moon and land some distance from the base, to stay there until someone came to take them out of the capsule and put them in the right places. One in the base, the second in the spaceship that would bring the bomb and the killers back to the OSS. Immediately before leaving the base, set bomb one, then hide bomb two in the OSS, program that too, and travel quite officially back to Earth in the elevator before the timers set off both explosions, and destroyed both Peary Base and the OSS. The perfect double whammy.

A trajectory that couldn't be reconstructed.

Okay, they'd messed up Peary. They wouldn't mess up the OSS. At half past nine, when they had all arrived on Isla de las Estrellas long ago, or were back on the way to their own countries, the space station would vaporize, leaving only a few thousand kilometers of featherlight carbon rope to fall into the Pacific. They probably didn't even need to get the bomb out of the spaceship. The Charon was supposed to be at anchor for at least two days, as she had learned in the terminal. It didn't really make any difference whether she hid the mini-nuke in the ceiling cover of the air lock or just left it where it was.

08:59

08:58

She looked contentedly at the blinking box. And as she was savoring her triumph, the hairs on the back of her neck stood up.

There was someone there.

Right behind her.

Dana swung around.

That moment she felt a kick in the chest that threw her against the wall of the cabin. The mini-nuke slipped from her hands and sailed away. Lynn reached out for it, missed it, ended up at an angle, and started rotating on her own axis. Dana dashed after the spinning bomb, felt a hand gripping her ankle, and was pulled back. In front of her eyes Julian's daughter darted upward, grabbed the box, and fled, carried on her own momentum to the lounge and from there to the landing module.

She must not leave the Charon.

Dana hurried after her. Just before the air lock she caught up with Lynn, grabbed her by the collar, and dragged her back inside the unit. Lynn somersaulted, tightly gripping the bomb, and wedged herself, legs spread, in the passageway to the habitation module. Lawrence risked a glance over her shoulder. Through the open bulkhead she could see into the air lock and glimpse the connecting corridor. There was still no one to be seen, but she knew the air lock was under surveillance. She couldn't afford to let the silent struggle continue outside the Charon.

Julian's daughter stared at her, gripping the ticking atom bomb like a cherished object from which she never wanted to be parted.

"Indecisive?" she grinned.

"Give me that thing, Lynn." Dana was breathing heavily, less out of exertion than out of rage. "Right now."

"No."

"It's an expensive scientific device. I don't know what's got into you, but you're about to ruin a very high-level experiment. Your father will be furious."

"Oh, really?" Lynn rolled her eyes spookily. "Will he?"

"Lynn, please!"

"I know what this is, you bitch. It's a bomb, exactly like the one you and Carl hid in the base."

"You're confused, Lynn. You—"

"Don't you dare!" yelled Lynn. "I'm completely fine."

"Okay." Dana raised conciliatory hands. "You're completely fine. But that isn't a bomb."

"Then you won't have a problem letting me out!"

Dana clenched her fists and didn't move, as her thoughts did somersaults. She had to get hold of the mini-nuke, but what was she to do with the madwoman who clearly wasn't as crazy as all that? If she let Lynn live and go back to the others, she might just as well hand over the bomb and admit everything.

"Problems?" Lynn giggled. "Without me the elevator won't return to Earth, will it? They'll spend hours looking for me, and you'll have to join in. There's nothing you can do."

"Give me the box," Dana said, struggling to control herself, and floated closer.

Lynn lowered the bomb. For a moment it looked as if she was wondering whether she should comply with Dana's demand, then she suddenly threw herself back into the habitation module.

"And now?" she asked.

Dana bared her teeth.

And suddenly she lost her head, reached for the disguised pocket on her thigh, and brought out Carl Hanna's gun. Lynn's eyes widened. She leaped after the bomb. Her hand hit the sensor that controlled the bulkhead between the module and the habitation unit. Dana cursed, but the connecting door closed too quickly, no chance of getting through it, at best she'd be trapped. Through the narrowing gap she saw Lynn's torso, her flying, ash-blonde hair half covering her face, took aim, and shot.

The bulkhead thumped shut. She went straight to the control panel and tried to open it again, but it didn't budge. Lynn must have activated the emergency lock.

She hammered furiously against the steel door.
Too late.

Her body drifted somersaulting through the lounge.
Spirals turned before her eyes. With a great effort, Lynn focused her ideas on the command panel in the rear zone, straightened out, gripped the edge of the next passageway, and impelled herself forward to the control console.
The terminal. She had to call the terminal.
"Lynn Orley," she gasped. "Can anyone hear me?" Oops! Something wrong with her voice? Why did she sound so feeble, so crushed?
"Miss Orley, yes, I can hear you."
"Put me through to my father. He's in his—his suite. Quickly, get a move on!"
"Right away, Miss Orley."
Something had found its way through the crack. Something that hurt and dulled her senses. Everything went dark.
"Julian," she whispered. "Daddy?"

Dana was beside herself. She'd been duped. She'd let her feelings take control, rather than diplomacy. Flight was the only option now. It didn't matter whether she'd killed Lynn, wounded her, or even hit her at all, she had to get out of the OSS before the elevator arrived. She furiously catapulted herself out of the landing module, pelted down the corridor and into the torus, took aim, and shot one of the astronauts in the head.
The man tipped sideways and drifted slowly away. With her legs outstretched she braked herself and aimed the barrel of her gun at the other one. He stared at her in nameless horror, with his hands over the touchscreen.
"Get one of the evacuation pods!" she yelled. "Quickly!"
The man trembled.
"Go, now! Get it!"
Inflamed with rage, she whacked him in the face. He gripped the console to stay upright.
"I can't," he panted.
"Are you mad?" Of course he could, why couldn't he? "Do you want to die?"
"No—please—"
Stupid jerk! Trying to hold her up! All the docking ports could be relocated along the ring, she knew that. He would just park the Charon somewhere else, and instead take one of the pods to the air lock and anchor it there.
"Just do it," she hissed.

"I can't, I really can't." The astronaut gulped and licked his lips. "Not during the launching process."

"Why the launching process?"

"Wh-when a ship launches, I can't relocate the docking port, I have to wait until—"

"Launches?" she yelled at him. "What's launching?"

"The—" He closed his eyes. The movement of his lips was oddly out of time with what he said, as if he were praying at the same time. Spittle glistened at the corners of his mouth, and he was losing control of his bladder.

"Open your mouth, damn it!"

"The Charon. It's the Charon. It's—it's launching."

"Daddy?"

Julian gave a start. He had just been talking to Jennifer Shaw, when a second window had appeared in the holowall.

"Lynn," he said with surprise. "Sorry, Jennifer."

"Daddy, you've got to stop her."

Her face was right up against the camera, sunken and waxy, as if she were about to lose consciousness. He immediately switched Shaw to standby.

"Lynn, is everything okay?"

She shook her head feebly.

"Where are you?"

"In the spaceship. I've launched Charon."

"*What's going on?*"

"I'm flying away—I'm taking—the bomb away from here." Julian saw her eyelids fluttering and her head tipping over. "She's smuggled a second bomb on board, she or—Carl, I don't know—"

"Lynn!"

His hands gripped the console. Slow as snake venom the realization of what was happening seeped into his consciousness. Of course! It made horrible sense. This wasn't just a blow against the Americans, it was an attack on space travel!

"Lynn, don't do it!" he urged. "Bring Charon back! You can't do this!"

"You've got to stop her," she whispered. "Dana—it's Dana Lawrence. She's the—she's Hanna's—"

"Lynn! No!"

"I'm—I'm sorry, Daddy." Her words were barely audible, a breath. She closed her eyes. "So sorry."

The spaceship decoupled. The massive steel claws that connected it to the air lock opened to reveal the Charon.

It drifted slowly out into open space.

Julian's voice reached her ear. He called her name, over and over again, as if he had lost his mind.

Lynn lay down on her back.

Nonsense, of course, she was weightless. Just a matter of perspective whether she was lying on her back or her belly. She might even have been lying on her side, of course she was lying on her side, all at the same time, but from here she could see the bomb that floated above her, spinning listlessly.

The display blurred in front of her eyes.

08:47

No, not 8. Wasn't that two zeros? 00:47?

00:46

46 minutes? Minutes, of course, what else. Or seconds?

Not enough time. She needed thrust.

Thrust!

Before her eyes, little red spheres wobbled through space, some tiny, others as big as marbles. She reached for them, rubbed one to goo between her fingers, and suddenly she realized that the red bead curtain was coming out of her chest. There was something annoying there, eating away at her strength and restricting her movements, and she was terribly tired, but she couldn't lapse into unconsciousness. She had to pick up speed to put some distance between herself and the OSS. Then, once she was far enough away, get rid of the bomb. Somehow. Throw it overboard. Or escape into the landing module and decouple the habitation unit with the mini-nuke. And get back.

Something like that.

Her jaws opened and closed like a fish. She painfully pumped air into her lungs and rolled around.

"Haskin," yelled Julian. He'd tried to call the terminal, but there had been no answer. Now he was talking to the technical department. In fact, Haskin hadn't been on duty that night, but in the circumstances he'd been willing to assume charge of the standby team. Unfortunately he was in Torus-5, in the roof of OSS, far from the space harbor.

"My God, Julian, what—"

"Comb the station! Look for Dana Lawrence, arrest the woman. Possibly she's in the terminal!"

"Just a moment. I don't understand—"

"I don't care whether you understand it or not! Look for Dana Lawrence, the woman's a terrorist. No one's answering in the terminal. And stop the Charon. Stop it!"

He left Haskin's helpless, startled face on the screen, and whirled around to the cabin bulkhead.

"Open up!"

• • •

Dana stared at the controls, with the barrel of the gun pressed against the astronaut's temple, and listened to the radio traffic. She'd heard every word. The touching conversation between Lynn and her father, Julian's patriarchal bellow. Lynn sounded injured; she'd managed to hit the miserable spoilsport. Small consolation, but Haskin's men would be here soon.

"Block access to the Torus," she ordered.

"I can't," panted the astronaut.

"You can! I know you can."

"You don't know shit. I can close the entryways, but I can't lock them. They're going to get in, whether you like it or not."

"What about the pod?"

"The Charon's too close. I swear that's the truth!"

Then she would have to do something else. She didn't need the external air lock. There were emergency entrances to the pods themselves, wherever they happened to be parked, she just somehow had to get to the outer ring and grab one of them. That jabbering piece of humanity there couldn't help her, but she might still need the guy. Lawrence whacked him over the head again and left the toppling body to its own devices as she headed for the shelves of helmets.

Julian was consumed with anxiety. He bumped his shoulders and his head as he dashed through Torus-1 toward the corridor that led up to the terminal, tried to regain control of himself, and that wasn't good. He'd never found any of the distances in the station particularly great, but now he felt as if he were floating on the spot, and he kept crashing into things.

He was terribly worried.

She had looked as if the life was flowing out of her. Her voice had been getting more and more halting and thin, she must have been injured, seriously injured. But the worst thing was that Haskin had hardly any chance of getting the Charon back. It wasn't a drifting astronaut this time, it was a massive spaceship, and if Lynn—

Oh, no, he thought. Please not. Don't start the engine.

Lynn! Please don't—

—start the engine.

Again and again she had to fight the descending darkness, while her fingers groped around, but as long as she couldn't see anything it wasn't much use. She knew she was still too close to the OSS. For safety's sake she needed to get a lot further away, because otherwise there was a danger that the burning gases would damage parts of the construction.

With the best will in the world she couldn't remember the time span on the display of the mini-nuke, just that it was tight, very tight!

She coughed. All around her, weird and beautiful, drifted the sparkling red beads of her blood. Weightlessness had the advantage that you couldn't really collapse, you didn't need any energy to stay on your feet, so that her physical systems were able to mobilize one last, impossible reserve of energy. Her vision cleared. Her fingers, determined, albeit hesitant and straying, went traveling: stretched and bent. Indicators lit up, a soft, automatic voice began to speak. She forced her body into the pilot's seat, but she hadn't the strength to buckle herself in. Just to start the acceleration process.

Lynn stretched out her right arm. The tip of her index finger landed gently on the smooth surface of the touchscreen, and the jets ignited, developing maximum thrust. She was pressed into the padding and lost consciousness.

The Charon fired away.

Leave the torus. Via one of the internal passageways. Get to one of the massive lattice masts that formed the spine of the OSS, climb along the struts to the space harbor, prepare one of the pods, decouple, set course for Earth. The things worked a bit like old-fashioned space shuttles, which they also superficially resembled, except that unlike their predecessors they had generous fuel supplies, so that once the stolen vehicle had entered the Earth's atmosphere she could land anywhere in the world, where no one would find her.

That was the plan.

Lawrence floated to one of the two passageways, as her suit checked the life-support systems and made sure her helmet was on correctly. Behind the closed bulkhead lay a short tunnel, a mobile air lock whose segments were still telescoped together. When the space elevator reached the inside of the torus, they would stretch out to their full length and connect the torus with the cabin, so that the guests could transfer from there to the station, just as they had done on her arrival. She quickly opened the bulkhead. The opposite end of the air lock was sealed, with a porthole in the middle through which the external lights of the elevator cables shimmered.

She had been faster than Haskin. She no longer needed the unconscious astronaut. Just to pump the air out of the lock, open it, and get out, without any of those idiots stopping her. With her gun ready in its holster, she slipped into the tunnel.

Julian flew out of the corridor, bumped against the ceiling, ignored the pain, looked wildly in all directions. Someone drifted below him. Open eyes staring vacantly, liquid pearling from a small hole in his forehead. Where the bagel-shaped body of the torus curved away, a second body circulated slowly, impossible to say whether it was dead or unconscious. Julian pushed himself off, slid along just below the ceiling, and saw that a bulkhead was open on the inward-facing side, immediately below him.

One of the passageways branched off from it.

Dana?

Fury, hatred, fear, they all came together. He did a handstand, darted into the air lock, bumped against a person in a space suit who was about to operate the closing mechanism, pulled them away from the controls and deeper inside the air lock. He clearly recognized Dana Lawrence's surprised Madonna face, as her UV visor was still raised, then their bodies struck the outer portal, rebounded, and spun somersaulting back toward the torus. Dana fumbled for control, collided with the wall of the tunnel, pushed away, and threw herself against him. Julian saw her fist flying at him, tried in vain to dodge it. A galaxy exploded in his head. He was slung around, flailed with his arms, fought for control. Dana came flying after him. The second blow broke his nose. He should have put on a helmet, damn idiot, too late. Red and black mist floated in front of his eyes. He just managed to grab on to one of the hand-grips along the walls and kicked at random, hit Dana's helmet, and sent her flying around in circles.

"What have you done with Lynn?" he shouted. "What have you done with my daughter?"

His hatred exploded. Again he kicked, his hand gripping the butt of his gun. Dana was whirled around, turned upside down, caught herself, launched at him, and grabbed him by the shoulders. A moment later he flew off. Like a pinball he touched one side of the tunnel, then the other, and was carried out of the air lock.

Where was Haskin? Where was the dozy standby crew?

Lawrence was reaching for the control panel. She wanted to lock the air lock, to lock him out. What was her plan? Did she want to get out? What for? What did she want to do out there?

Clear out?

The blood was clotting in his nose, his head was swinging like a bell when he dashed back into the air lock at the last minute and managed to grab her arm. Lawrence's fingers couldn't reach the closing mechanism. Without letting go of her, and with blows drumming down on him from her one free hand, he pushed her back. They started spinning and collided against the outside portal. For a moment, through the porthole, Julian saw the brightly lit opposite side of the enormous ring module, the cables ending in the middle, only minutes to go until the cabin arrived—and then Lawrence rammed her knee into his stomach.

He felt a wave of nausea, he couldn't breathe. He let go of her arm and she hurled him against the wall, where he managed to grab onto a strut. Lawrence was floating upright by the outer portal, turned around and faced him. Her right hand wandered to her thigh and took something out of a sheath, a flat thing that looked like a pistol.

He had lost.

As in a stupor, Julian leaned his head to one side. It couldn't, mustn't end like this! His glance fell on a flap in the wall beside him. It took him a second to remember what it did, or more precisely what lay behind it, and then it came to him.

OSS handbook, Letter B:

Bulkhead emergency detonation.

In emergencies it may be necessary to blast open the outer portal of an air lock, regardless of whether a vacuum has been created inside it or not. This measure may be necessary if the bulkhead or air lock casing is caught or wedged in the rump of the elevator cabin or a docking spaceship and launch or departure are impeded, particularly when human lives are at stake. In the event of a detonation, care should be taken that the side of the air lock channel facing the habitation sector is closed and the person undertaking the detonation is wearing a space suit and is securely fastened to the wall of the air lock.

He wasn't securely fastened. He was just holding on with sheer muscle power, and the bulkhead to the torus was open. He wasn't even wearing a helmet.

The hell with it!

Holding tightly on to the bar, he pulled up the flap. A bright red handle became visible. Dana's eyes behind the visor widened as she worked out what he was planning. The barrel of her gun came flying up, but not fast enough. He pulled hard on the handle and brought it straight down.

Held his breath.

With a deafening crash the charges in the fixing pins went up and blew the bulkhead from its mooring. Tumbling over and over it whirled into open space, and at the same moment the suction began, a wailing, murderous storm, as the air flowed out, pulling Dana out of the air lock with it. Julian clung to the metal pole with both hands. More air streamed out of the torus, a hurricane now. That moment he realized all passageways to the adjacent corridors would close automatically, and he was unprotected, not even wearing a helmet. If he didn't make it out of the tunnel in the next few seconds and close the internal bulkhead, he would die in the vacuum, so he gritted his teeth, tensed his muscles, and tried to crawl his way back inside.

His fingers started sliding from the rail.

He panicked. He couldn't let go, but the hurricane was pulling at him, and most particularly it was pulling his leg. He turned his head and saw Dana Lawrence gripping onto one of his boots. The suction intensified, but she wouldn't let go, she hung horizontal in the roaring inferno, tried to aim her gun.

She pointed it at him.

Tiny muzzle, black.

Death.

And suddenly he'd just had enough of the damn woman. His rage, his fear, everything turned into pure strength.

"This is *my* space station," he yelled. "Now get *out!*"

And he kicked.

His boot crashed against her helmet. Lawrence's fingers slipped away. In a split second she had been swept outside, into the center of the torus, and even then she kept her gun pointed at him, took aim, and Julian waited for the end.

Her body passed the cable.

For a moment he didn't understand what he was seeing. Lawrence was flying in two directions at once. More precisely, her shoulder, part of her torso and the right arm holding the gun had separated themselves from the rest.

Because direct contact with the cable can cost you a body part in a fraction of a second. You must bear in mind that it's thinner than a razor blade, but incredibly hard.

His own words, down on the Isla de las Estrellas.

The storm raged around him. With an extreme effort of strength he pulled his way further along the rail, without any illusions of his own survival. He wasn't going to make it. He *couldn't* make it. His lungs hurt, his eyes watered, his head thumped like a jackhammer.

Lynn, he thought. My God, Lynn.

A figure appeared in his field of vision, wearing a helmet, secured with a safety line. Someone else. Hands grabbed him and pulled him back into the shelter of the torus. Gripped him tightly. The interior bulkhead slid shut.

Haskin.

Stars. Like dust.

Lynn is far away, far, far away. The spaceship silently plows the timeless, glittering night, an enclave of peace and refuge. When she briefly regains consciousness, she merely wonders why the bomb hasn't gone off, but perhaps she just hasn't been traveling for long enough. She vaguely remembers a plan she had to leave the mini-nuke in the habitation module and return to the OSS in the landing unit, to save herself.

Landing unit. Uning landit.

Mini-nuke. Nuki-Duke. Muki-Nuki-Duki, Mini-Something-Something.

Bruce Dern in *Silent Running*.

Great film. And at the end: *Boooooommmmmm!*

No, she'll stay here. And anyway, she's out of strength. So many things have gone wrong. Sorry, Julian. Didn't we want to go to the Moon? How is work going at the Stellar Island Hotel? What? Oh, shit, it's not finished, that's it, she knew it, she always knew, it's not finished! It will *never* be finished. Never, never, never!

Cold.

The little robot watering the flowers with Bruce Dern. He's sweet. On that platform in space, the last plants are on it before Dern blows himself up, and then there's a song by that eco-whore, Joan Baez; Julian says that every time he hears her he has the feeling somebody's chiseling his head open, and she messes up the whole great finale with her hysterical soprano.

"Lynn?"

There he is.

"Please answer! Lynn! Lynn!"

Oh! Is he crying? Why? Her fault? Did she do something wrong?

Don't cry, Julian. Come on, let's look at another one of those ropy old movies. *Armageddon*. No, he doesn't like that one, everything about it's wrong, he says, there's too much wrong, so how about Ed Wood, *Plan 9 from Outer Space*, or how about *It Came from Outer Space*? Come on, that one's cool! Jack Arnold, the old fairy-tale uncle. Always good for a joke or a horror story. The extraterrestrials with the big brains. That's what they really look like.

Really? Nonsense. They don't!

Do so too!

Daddy! Tim doesn't think they look like that.

"Lynn!"

Coming. I'm coming, Daddy.

I'm there.

June 3–8, 2025
Limit

Xintiandi, Shanghai, China

A perfectly normal life—

Hanging pictures, taking a step back, adjusting the angle. Sorting out books, arranging furniture, stepping back, rearranging. Making small changes, stepping back again, approaching things while remaining detached from them, establishing harmony, the universal Confucian formula against the powers of chaos.

If that was what constituted a normal life, Jericho had fitted himself back into normality without the slightest transition. Xin hadn't burned down his loft, everything was in its place or waiting to be assigned one. The television was on, a kaleidoscope of soundless world events, because he was less concerned with the content of information than with its decorative properties. He had an urgent need not to have to know anything anymore. He didn't want to understand any more connections, only to roll out the little carpet, which was to lie like *that*—or was it better like *that*? Jericho pulled it into a diagonal, took a step back, studied his work, and found it lacked balance, because it put a standard lamp in difficulties. Not harmonious, said Confucius, stressing the rights of lamps.

How was Yoyo?

At noon on the day of her rebirth thanks to Xin's mercy she had woken up, plagued by severe headaches, doubtless partly due to the encounter with Norrington's skull, also to an unaccustomed excess of Brunello di Montalcino, but finally also to the experience of having been practically shot. The resulting emotional hangover meant that she didn't talk much on the flight home. At around midday Tu had started the Aerion Supersonic, four hours later the jet had landed at Pudong Airport, and they had been home again. Of course, in the days that followed there was no escaping the news coverage. Once the Charon had come within range of terrestrial broadcasting, measurements had been confirmed corroborating that there had been a nuclear explosion in the no-man's-land of the lunar North Pole, and the outing of the tour group had ended in disaster, with some prominent fatalities. And although the secret services tried to spread a cloak of silence over the events, there were rumors of a conspiracy aimed at destroying the American lunar base, with China as a possible source—totally unconsidered assertions that buzzed cheerfully around the net.

Downwinds of suspicion blew anti-Chinese ideas all around the world. In fact there wasn't the slightest concrete evidence concerning the real masterminds behind it. Orley himself had taken the sting from the suspicions on the way back to OSS, announcing that it was only with

the help of the taikonaut Jia Keqiang and the Chinese space authorities
that it had been possible to prevent the attack at all. Regardless of this,
British, American, and Chinese media used the vocabulary of aggression. Not for the first time, China had attacked foreign networks, and
it was common knowledge that Beijing administered Kim Jong-un's
military legacy. Voices warning that the space-traveling nations should
finally pull together mingled with fears about the armament of space.
Zheng Pang-Wang found himself in a public relations crisis when
details emerged about the role of the Zheng Group in the construction of the launching pad in Equatorial Guinea. Rushing ahead, the
Zhong Chan Er Bu made clear that nothing was known about anyone
called Kenny Xin or an organization called Yü Shen, which supposedly
drew its recruits from psychiatric institutions and mental hospitals and
trained them up as killers. But if this man Xin did exist, he was operating unambiguously against the interests of the Party. And why were
Mr. Orley and the Americans really surprised, when they withheld
important technologies from the world and snubbed the international
community with continued violations of the treaty concerning the
Moon and space? This all sounded so familiar in terms of the lunar crisis that serious considerations about what the Chinese actually stood
to gain from the destruction of Peary Base (nothing at all, according to
seasoned analysts) faded into the background.

Standard lamp and carpet. Harmony refused to establish itself
between the two.

Although her shared apartment had gained an extra room after
Grand Cherokee Wang's demise, Yoyo had moved in with Tu. Temporarily, she stressed. Perhaps she wanted to stand by Hongbing, who was
also staying in the villa until his own apartment had been refurbished,
but Jericho suspected she was hoping for something like a confession
after the openness of the last few days. She was preparing to resume
her studies. Daxiong was working on his bike, disregarding medical
advice, as if he didn't have a freshly stitched wound in his back and
an even bigger one in his heart, Tu devoted himself to the steam-train
rhythm of his businesses, and pleasantly boring cases of web espionage
awaited Jericho. After Operation Mountains of Eternal Light had come
to such a bloody end, they had agreed that Hydra no longer posed a
threat. They still faced questioning by the Chinese police, but did not
feel obliged to reveal the circumstances under which Yoyo had come
across the message fragment, particularly since the secret services had
every reason to be grateful to them: in the end, what was more likely
to exonerate Beijing from the accusations that were flying around than
that the attack had been thwarted by the feisty actions of two Chinese
and an Englishman living in China? The first three days of June had
passed uneventfully, and Patrice Ho, Jericho's high-ranking policeman

friend from Shanghai, had called to announce his promotion and his move to Beijing.

"Of course I know that your investigations gave a great boost to my career," he said. "So if you have any idea of how I can pay you back—"

"Let's just see it as a credit," said Jericho.

"Hmm." Ho paused. "Perhaps I can come up with a way of increasing that credit."

"Aha."

"As you know, our investigations in Lanzhou were highly success-ful. We were able to take out a nest of pedophiles, and came across evidence that suggests—"

"Hang on a second! You want me to go on poking around in the pedophile scene?"

"Your experience might be very useful to us. Beijing places a lot of hope in me. After the double success in Shenzhen and Lanzhou, it might provoke irritation if our series of triumphs suddenly came to an end—"

"I understand," sighed Jericho. "At the risk of squandering my credit, I've decided not to take on any more jobs of that kind. A few days ago I moved into a larger apartment, and it's already too small for all the ghosts I have lodging with me."

"You won't have to go to the front line," Ho hurried to reassure him.

"You know one *always* ends up on the front line."

"Of course. Sorry if I've put you under extra pressure."

"You haven't. Can I think about it?"

"Of course! When are we going to go for a beer?"

"What about this week?"

"Wonderful."

Nothing was wonderful. The carpet and the standard lamp under-stood one another marvelously well. The point was that neither of them was in harmony with *him*. There was no harmony anywhere, and certainly no normality. As if by way of confirmation, Julian Orley's face appeared larger than life-size on the holowall, against the open sky and surrounded by people. He was saying something as he pushed his way through the crowd, followed by the actor Finn O'Keefe and a thrill-ingly weird-looking woman with snow-white hair. Clearly the tour group had come back to Earth. Jericho turned up the sound and heard the commentator say:

"—the explosion of the second mini-nuke at nine o'clock Central European time at a distance of 45,000 kilometers from the OSS, which it was clearly designed to destroy. Meanwhile fears are being raised that the series of nuclear attacks might resume. Julian Orley, who plans to leave Quito in the next few minutes, has so far refused—"

Jericho gave a start and turned the sound up again, but he seemed to have missed the most important bit. A news ticker along the bottom of the screen carried the message of an attempted nuclear attack on the OSS, and said that the number of victims was as yet unknown. Jericho zapped through the channels. Clearly there had been a second atom bomb hidden on the shuttle that had carried the survivors from Peary Base to the space station, but this had been discovered in time and detonated at a considerable distance from the OSS. Orley himself said that he didn't plan to comment in any way. Jericho thought he had aged several years.

Yoyo called. "Did you hear that? The stuff about the second bomb?"

He switched from CNN to a Chinese news channel, but it was running a story about university reform. Another one was trying to talk down new Uygur revolts in Xinjiang.

"Very strange," he said. "Vogelaar didn't mention a second bomb in his dossier."

"That means he only knew about one."

"Probably." The BBC was showing a special report on the event. "Luckily it's nothing to do with us anymore."

"Yeah, you're right. God, I'm glad we're out of that! And that they're leaving us in peace—On the other hand it's awesome, isn't it? It's *really* awesome!"

Jericho stared at the red strip of the news ticker.

"Mmhm," he said. "Everything else okay with you?"

"Yep, fine." She hesitated. "By the way, I'm sorry I haven't called, but there's so much happening at the moment, I'm—I'm just trying to get back in step. It's not that easy. I've got funerals of friends to go to, Daxiong is acting the hero, and my father—okay, we had a long talk, I think you know what about—"

These topics were always awkward. "And?" he asked cautiously.

"It's all right, Owen, we can talk openly about it. You can't tell me anything I haven't found out already. What can I say? I'm glad he told me."

She sounded oddly terse. She had suffered from Hongbing's silence all her life, and now all she could find to say was that she was *glad* that he was suddenly communicating openly with her.

"Hey!" she said suddenly. "You do understand that *we* prevented those attacks? Without us there would be no moon base, and no OSS."

A German channel. The same wobbly pictures of Orley and his group flickered across the holowall. A journalist with a microphone in his hand and the Pacific in the background claimed to have heard that a bomb had gone off on a spaceship, a moon shuttle, and that contrary to the initial reports there *had* been fatalities, at least one.

"Just think about it, that would have set American space travel back by decades," Yoyo observed. "Wouldn't it? What do you think? No space elevator, no helium-3. Orley could have mothballed his fusion reactors."

"It almost looks as if we're heroes," he said sourly.

"Yeah. So we can cautiously start being proud of ourselves, can't we? What are your plans for this evening?"

"Shifting furniture. Sleeping." Jericho glanced at his watch. Half past ten. "Hopefully. I've been exhausted for three days, and can't get to sleep. Only toward the morning, for two or three hours."

"I'm the same. Take a pill."

"Don't want to."

"Then it's your own fault. See you later."

After the call he no longer felt able to think in categories of Confucian interior design. Everything around him seemed to have lost its meaning, he could imagine any arrangement of furniture and none. A glass wall had appeared between him and the objects, harmony and normality became purely academic categories, as if a blind man were talking about colors. He turned off the television and found his jaws stretching into an endless, leonine yawn. According to Schopenhauer, the hero of his youth: *Yawning is one of the reflex movements. I suspect that its more distant cause may be a momentary depotentiation of the brain caused by boredom, mental slackness, or somnolence.*

Was he bored? Was his brain growing slack? Was he depotentiated? Not at all. He was unsettlingly wide awake. He lay down fully dressed on the couch, turned out the light, and tentatively closed his eyes. Perhaps if he avoided official actions like getting undressed or going to bed, he might trick his body and mind, which seemed to think that they had to resist sleep the more clearly he attempted to achieve it.

Half an hour later he knew better.

It wasn't over. Hydra still held him in its embrace, its poison would rage in him until he had finally understood its nature. He couldn't pretend that none of it concerned him any longer, just because no one was trying to kill him. You couldn't *decide* on normality. Things didn't come to an end just because you'd buried them in the past. The nightmare continued.

Who was Hydra?

He turned the lights back on. Yoyo was right. They'd found out a hell of a lot of things, they'd thwarted the plans of the conspirators, they had good reason to be proud. At the same time he felt as if they'd been looking through the wrong end of a telescope all along. The closest things had drifted into the distance, into supposed insignificance, but in fact all you had to do was turn the telescope around and the truth would move into the foreground. He opened a bottle of Shiraz, poured himself a glass, and systematically crossed all previous suspects off the list: Beijing, Zheng Pang-Wang, the CIA. On closer inspection all of these trails had turned in a circle, but there might have been one that he hadn't properly understood, one that carried straight on.

The Greenwatch massacre.

The complete leadership of the environmental broadcaster, all wiped out. Why? No one was able to say what Greenwatch had been working on most recently, even though there were several suggestions that there had been a report on environmental damage by oil companies. Loreena Keowa's ambition to clear up the Calgary attack had finally focused attention on the film that supposedly showed Gerald Palstein's attacker. But given how quickly these pictures had spread, the massacre could hardly have taken place in order to prevent their further dissemination.

He had Diane play through the film sequence once more. Toward the end, as the camera swung around toward the stage, you could see that the square was full of people with cell phones, and surrounded by television crews. A miracle, in fact, that Xin hadn't been captured more often, fat suit and all; at any rate Hydra should have predicted that and factored it in, but equally that might have been the first error of reasoning.

Perhaps they'd been *banking* on it!

The longer Jericho thought about the sequence, the more Xin's weird disguise and his stately way of creeping around seemed to be part of an act designed to present investigators with an Asian assassin just in case he was caught on camera—just as Zheng's visible presence in Equatorial Guinea had left an elephant track in the Middle Kingdom. There was a glimpse of Lars Gudmundsson with his double game; Palstein was still alive by happy chance, leaving the way open for Carl Hanna; Loreena Keowa got to the bottom of that, costing ten people their lives and Greenwatch its memory.

Did that make sense? Not really.

Unless she'd found out things at Greenwatch that *really* put the pressure on Hydra.

Loreena had traveled in from Calgary. Possibly in possession of explosive information. She had immediately gone to the editorial conference, a meeting that Hydra had been able to prevent at the last minute, although this meant that the conspirators still didn't know how much of the unwelcome research was already stored on the channel's hard drives, because Loreena might have sent e-mails in the run-up!

That was it.

Jericho got to work. While it was approaching midnight in Shanghai, the noon-day sun was shining on the other side of the Pacific. He had Diane draw up a list of all the relevant internet service providers and started phoning them, one after the other, always on the same pretext: he was calling on behalf of Loreena, because it was impossible to send or receive e-mails from her web address, and would they please be so kind as to take a look and see why that wasn't working. Eleven times he was told that no Loreena Keowa was stored as a customer, three of the people he spoke to knew Loreena from the net, had learned of her death and expressed their dismay, for which Jericho thanked them in his best funeral-director voice. He only struck gold with the twelfth call. He was asked to give a password, which meant that she was registered there. Jericho promised to call back. Then he hacked his way into the provider's system and put Diane to decoding Loreena's password. Every data transfer had been recorded, so that within a few minutes he received information about Loreena's mail provider. He rang back, gave the password, and asked if any e-mails sent over the last fourteen days were still stored in the system. They were stored for up to six weeks, he was told, and which ones did he wish to see?

All of them, he said.

Half an hour later he had viewed all the documents concerning the environmental scandal, which, under the title *Trash of the Titans*, had been supposed to form the core of that three-part broadcast. It named a lot of names, but Jericho didn't believe in a connection for a second. The massacre had occurred as a reaction to the last e-mail sent. It contained the answer to all the questions.

Hydra's identity.

Gerald Palstein

Director, Strategic Management, EMCO (USA), victim of an assassination attempt in Calgary on 21. 4. 2025, probable aim to prevent him from flying to the Moon (there are data on Palstein).
Assassin Asian, possibly Chinese.
(Chinese interests in EMCO? Oil-sand business?)

Alejandro Ruiz

Strategy manager (since July 2022) of Repsol YPF (Spanish-Argentinian). Nickname Ruiz El Verde, married, two children, conventional lifestyle, debt free.
Disappeared in Lima, 2022, during an inspection tour (crime?). Previously several days at conference in Beijing, incl. joint venture with Sinopec. Last meeting outside of Beijing on 1. 9. 2022: subject and participants unknown (Repsol wants to look through documents, I'm waiting to be called back). 2. 9. flew on to Lima, phone calls to his wife. Ruiz depressed and anxious. Cause probably previous day's meeting

Common factors Palstein, Ruiz:

Both men have tried to expand their companies' areas of business in new directions, e.g. solar power, Orley Enterprises. Ethical standpoints. Against oil-sand mining. Opponents in their own camp.
Appointed strategy managers when the threatened bankruptcy of their

companies leaves them with hardly any room to negotiate.
However: hardly any points of contact between EMCO and Repsol. Accord-
ing to Palstein, no personal contact between him and Ruiz.

Lars Gudmundsson
Palstein's bodyguard, freelance operative for Texan security company
Eagle Eye.
Career: Navy Seal, sniper training, moved to Africa to join Mamba private
army, from there to APS (African Protection Services), possible involvement
in coup d'état in West Africa, since 2000 back in the USA.
Playing false game: with his people, ensured that Palstein's attacker was
able to enter the building opposite Imperial Oil unimpeded (have informed
Palstein of Gudmundsson's betrayal and asked Eagle Eye about G. G. and
his team have since gone missing).

Gudmundsson—
The name sparked something in Jericho's mind. Following an intuition, he took out Vogelaar's dossier again, and there it was: Lars Gudmundsson had belonged to the special unit that had brought Mayé to
power—along with Neil Gabriel, aka Carl Hanna. They both seemed to
have got on particularly well with Kenny Xin, so well, in fact, that they
had worked for him in various ways and finally quit APS. Loreena's
e-mail also included the film from the crime scene, a direct line to Repsol and the private number of the presumably widowed Señora Ruiz.
He had Diane assemble further facts about the Spaniard, but didn't
come up with much more than the journalist had already put together.
In film sequences and pictures the man looked sympathetic, positive,
and energetic.
But after the meeting in Beijing he'd been worried.
And then he'd disappeared.
Why had that sudden change occurred? Because he'd experienced
or learned something at the meeting that stressed him? Right, but
more likely because he could no longer be sure of his life. If Alejandro
Ruiz had actually fallen victim to a crime, it was because someone had
wanted to keep the contents of that meeting from becoming public.
Had Hydra killed Ruiz because he knew about Operation Moun-
tains of Eternal Light? But in that case how was Palstein involved?
Loreena found striking factors in common between the two. Might
Palstein have been informed about Hydra's plans?
Jericho took a sip of Shiraz.
Nonsense. These were ludicrous hypotheses. Ruiz had disappeared
immediately after the meeting. Before he could open his mouth. Why
would they have given Palstein three years to bring his knowledge to
the people? Calgary had clearly served the purpose of slipping an agent

into Orley's tour group, and also Palstein was *alive*, even if it was only by chance. Since then there had been no more attempts on his life, even though opportunities had arisen. Gudmundsson, for example, constantly near him for professional reasons, could have killed him with a close-range bullet at any time.

And why hadn't he done it?

And why hadn't he done it *before*? Before Calgary?

Hydra had managed to infiltrate Palstein's inner circle, his security men. Why go to all that effort? A public event. Agents distracting the police. Kenny Xin, firing from an empty building? Why so *laborious*?

Because it was supposed to look like something that it wasn't.

No doubt about it: the connection between Lima and Calgary, between Ruiz and Palstein, existed. Loreena's research led directly to Hydra, otherwise the butchers of Vancouver wouldn't have murdered ten people and got rid of their computers. So what had *really* happened on April 21 in Canada?

The meeting in Beijing provided the key.

He was about to phone Repsol in Madrid when the doorbell rang. Startled, he looked at his watch. Twenty past one. Drunks? The bell rang again. For a moment he toyed with the idea of ignoring it, then he went to the intercom and looked at the screen.

Yoyo.

"What are you doing here?" he asked in a puzzled voice.

"How about you press the button," she snapped at him. "Or do I have to announce my visits in writing first?"

"It's not exactly the time of day when you expect visitors," he said as she stepped into his loft, her motorcycle helmet under her arm. Yoyo shrugged. She set the helmet down on the central kitchen counter, ambled into the living area, and glanced curiously around in all directions. He followed her.

"Pretty."

"Not quite finished."

"Still." She pointed at the open bottle of Shiraz. "Is there another glass?"

Jericho scratched himself irritably behind the ear as she slipped out of her leather jacket and threw herself on his sofa.

"Of course," he said. "Wait."

He looked across to her and brought out a second glass. In the gloom of the lounge a reddish glimmer indicated that she had lit a cigarette. After he had filled her glass, they sat there for a few minutes, drinking in silence, and Yoyo sent smoke signals issuing from the corners of her mouth, encoded explanations for her presence. She stared into the void. From time to time the heavy curtains of her eyelashes seemed to want to wipe away what they had seen, but whenever she looked up her gaze was as lost as before. More than ever they reminded him of the girl in the video film that Chen Hongbing had shown him a week and a half before.

A week and a half?

It could just as easily have been a year.

"And what are you up to at the moment?" she asked, glancing at Diane.

"Wondering what's brought you here."

"Didn't you want to go to bed? Get some sleep at last?"

"I've tried."

She nodded. "Me too. I thought it would be easier."

"Sleeping?"

"Carrying on from where you've left off. But it's like reaching into the void. A lot of things no longer exist. The control center at the steelworks. The Guardians. And then there's Grand Cherokee's room with all his stuff in it, as if he were about to come back. Spooky. On the other hand, college is college. The same professors, the same lecture halls. The same administration that makes sure you don't start thinking too independently. The same chicken coop, the same battles and trivia. I listen to music, I go out, watch television, remind myself that everyone else is even worse off than me, that I could be dead, and that the banality of everyday life has its good side. I try to convince myself that I should be feeling relieved."

Jericho crossed his legs. He sat in silence on the floor in front of her, his back resting against a chair.

"And then the thing I've been waiting for all my life happens. Hongbing takes me in his arms, tells me how much he loves me and showers me with tragedies. The whole terrible story. And I know I should be letting off fireworks for this moment, I should die of pity, go mad with joy, throw my arms around his neck, the bastards have no power over us now, it's all going to be okay, we can talk to each other at last, we're a family! Instead—" she blew smoke-snakes in the air "—my head feels like a chest of a thousand drawers, everyone stuffs whatever he feels like into it, and now my father's joining in! I think, Yoyo, you miserable little cripple, why don't you feel anything? Come on, now, you've got to *feel* something, after all, you wished—" She reached for her glass, downed the contents, and sucked the remaining life from her cigarette. "You so wished he would talk to you! Even when Kenny held his damn gun to my head, I thought, no! I don't want to die without finding out what threw *his* life so far off the rails. But now that I know, I just feel . . . full."

Jericho turned his glass around in his hand.

"And at the same time hollowed out," she went on. "That's crazy, isn't it? Nothing moves me! As if this isn't the world as I used to know it, but a mere copy of it. Everything looks as if it's made of cardboard."

"And you think it'll never be normal again."

"It scares me, Owen. Maybe everything's all right with the world, and *I'm* the copy. Maybe the real Yoyo was shot by Xin after all."

Jericho stared at his feet.

"In a sense she was."

"Xin stole something that night." She looked at him. "Took something. Took me away. I can no longer feel what I should be feeling. I'm no longer able to give my father the respect I should. Not even to burst dramatically into floods of tears."

"Because it isn't over yet."

"I want it back. I want to be me again."

She lit another cigarette. Again they were silent for a while, lost in smoke and thoughts.

"We haven't yet woken up, Yoyo." He threw his head back and looked at the ceiling. "That's our problem. For three days I've been trying to tell myself that I don't want to have anything more to do with Hydra. Or with Xin and all the freaks that frolic in my head when everyone else is asleep. I furnish my life with knick-knacks, I try and make it look as normal and unspectacular as possible, but it feels wrong. As if I'd ended up on a stage—"

"Yes, exactly!"

"And a little while ago, after we spoke on the phone, I understood. We're still trapped in this nightmare, Yoyo. It pretends we're awake, but we aren't. We're watching an illusion. It's far from over." He sighed. "I'm actually obsessed by Hydra! I have to go on working on this case. Clearing out the cellar in which I've been burying people alive for years. Hydra is turning into the model of my life and the question of how it's going to go on from here. I have to face up to these ghosts to get rid of them, even if it costs me my courage or my reason. I can't, won't go on like this. I can't bear living like this, do you understand? I want to wake up at last."

Otherwise we will be trapped forever in an imaginary world, he thought. Then we won't be real people, we'll only ever be the echoes of our unresolved past.

"And—have you kept on working on the case? On our case?"

"Yes." Jericho nodded. "Over the past two hours. When you arrived, I was about to phone Madrid."

"Madrid?"

"An oil company called Repsol."

He saw her face light up, so he told her about his research, familiarized her with Loreena's last e-mail, and introduced her to his theories. With every word Hydra slithered further into that dark loft, stretched her necks, fixed her pale yellow eyes on them. In their effort to shake the monster off, they had conjured it up, but something had changed. The monster didn't come to ambush and chase them, but because they had lured it, and for the first time Jericho felt stronger than the snake. Finally he dialed the number of the Spanish company.

"Of course!" a man's voice said. "Loreena Keowa! I tried to get through to her a number of times, why does she never answer?"

"She had an accident," said Jericho. "A fatal accident."

"How terrible." The man paused. When he went on speaking, there was an undertone of suspicion. "And you are—"

"A private detective. I'm trying to continue Miss Keowa's work and shed some light on the circumstances of her death."

"I see."

"She'd asked you for information, right?"

"Erm—that's right."

"About a meeting in Beijing that Alejandro Ruiz took part in before he disappeared?"

"Yes. Yes, exactly."

"I'm pursuing that trail. It might be the same people that have Ruiz and Loreena on their conscience. You would be doing me a big favor if you would let me have the information."

"Well—" The other man hesitated. Then he sighed. "Sure, why not. Will you keep us up to date? We'd very much like to know what happened to Ruiz."

"Of course."

"So, we've gone through the documents here. In 2022 Ruiz had just been appointed head of the strategy department. He was moving heaven and earth to open up new areas of business. Some of the oil multinationals were increasingly looking into joint ventures, so there were discussions in Beijing, for a whole week—"

"Why there?"

"No real reason. They could equally well have met in Texas or Spain. Perhaps because the most important was a project between Repsol, EMCO, and the Chinese oil company Sinopec, so they agreed on Beijing. The initiator of the joint venture suggested that it should be turned into a business summit. Almost all the big companies agreed to take part, which meant that discussions went on all week without interruption. Ruiz was happy about that. He thought something might change."

"Do you have any idea what he might have meant by that?"

"Not really, to be quite honest."

"And where did the summit meet?"

"At the Sinopec Congress Center on the edge of Chaoyang, a district to the north-east of Beijing."

"And Ruiz was in good spirits?"

"Most of the time, yes, although it turned out that the train had already pulled out. On the other hand, it could hardly have got worse.

On the last day of the summit he called and said that at least the week hadn't been wasted, and there was one last session that evening, more of an unofficial meeting. A few of them wanted to get together and discuss a few ideas."

"And the meeting was also held in the Congress Center?"

"No, further out. In the district of Shunyi, he said, at a private house. The next day he looked depressed and unwell. I asked him how the meeting had gone. He reacted oddly. He said nothing had come out of it, and he'd left early."

"Do you know who took part in it?"

"Not explicitly. Ruiz had hinted that representatives of the big companies had come together, I guess we were the smallest fish in the pond. Russians, Americans, Chinese, British, South Americans, Arabs. A normal summit. Not much seems to have come out of it."

I wouldn't be so sure of that, thought Jericho.

"I'd need a list of official participants at the summit," he said. "If such a thing still exists."

"I'll send it to you. Give me an e-mail address."

Jericho passed on his details and thanked the man. He promised to get in touch as soon as anything new came in, signed off, and looked at Yoyo.

"What do you think?"

"A meeting in which senior oil company representatives take part," she mused. "An unofficial one. Ruiz doesn't wait for the end. Why does he leave?"

"He might have felt unwell. That's the harmless explanation."

"That we don't believe."

"Of course not. He left because he'd come to the conclusion that the whole thing was going nowhere, because there was an argument, or because he didn't want to go along with whatever they decided."

"If he'd just been angry, he'd have told his people or his wife the reasons. Instead he said nothing."

"He felt threatened."

"He was afraid they might hush him up because he didn't want to play."

"As they did, by the look of it."

"And who are *they*?"

"Hmm." Jericho pursed his lips. "We're thinking along the same lines, aren't we?"

Yoyo stayed with him that night. Nothing happened except that they emptied another bottle of wine together and he held her in his arms, faintly surprised that he only wanted to console her: a girl overtaxed by adulthood, intelligent, talented, and beautiful who, at the age of only twenty-five, had already driven wedges of insecurity into the armor of the Party and at the same time preserved the attitude of a teenager, a punishing, immature crabbiness that was every bit as unerotic as her efforts to defy biology and keep from growing up. It seemed to him that Yoyo wanted to stay in adolescence forever, until circumstances calmed down enough to grant her a more peaceful youth than the one she had already had. He, on the other hand, wanted only to wipe out this phase of his life, those said transitional years. Small wonder, then, that neither of them felt what they should have felt, as Yoyo had put it.

He thought about this, and suddenly, quite unexpectedly, he felt lighter.

There was someone else with them in the room. He looked up, and that shy boy who had been hurt so often was sitting in the gloom of the loft, watching his fingers glide through Yoyo's hair. Numbed with red wine and worry, he stared straight ahead, while the boy's eyes filled with tears of disappointment that girls like Yoyo only ever used boys like him to talk to. His nose, disproportionately swollen by the beginnings of puberty, was still too big for his otherwise childish face. His hair needed washing, and of course he was wearing the stuff he always wore, a human being who loved everyone and everything more than he loved himself. How Jericho had hated the little bastard who couldn't understand why that adult man with the girl in his arms, the girl he could have had there and then, wasn't declaring his love—why he suddenly didn't desire her, when he had desired her, hadn't he?

Had he?

Jericho saw the boy sitting there, felt his paralyzing, nagging fear of being inadequate, failing, being rejected. And suddenly he didn't hate him anymore. Instead he drew him into the embrace, he granted him absolution and assured him that he wasn't to blame for anything, anything at all. He expressed his sympathy. Explained the necessity of finally disappearing from his life, since he had vanished from it in a purely physical sense long ago, and promised him that they would both find peace sooner or later.

The boy turned pale.

He would come back, that much was certain, but for that night at least they were reconciled. The world became more tangible, more colorful. Toward morning, when Yoyo lay snoring quietly on his belly, he still hadn't slept a wink, and yet he wasn't tired in the slightest. He carefully lifted her shoulders, slipped from the sofa, and let her drop back. She murmured, turned on her side, and rolled into a ball. Jericho looked at her. He wondered excitedly who would appear once she had shed the foolish costume of the eternal teenager. Someone very thrilling, he suspected. And she *would* be happy and adult. She just didn't know it yet.

She would be able to feel everything, not what she was supposed to feel, not what she wanted to feel, but just what she actually felt.

Just before nine. He picked up his phone, went into the kitchen area, and put on a strong pot of coffee. He knew what he had to do, and how they could nail those bastards.

Time to make a call.

"I've been thinking about your offer," he said.

"Oh." Patrice Ho seemed surprised. "I hadn't expected to hear from you so soon."

"Some decisions are quick to make."

"Owen, before you say something—" Ho hemmed and hawed. "I'm sorry if I behaved badly in any way. I didn't mean to put any pressure on you; you must think I'm never satisfied."

"I hope you aren't," said Jericho. "Not in terms of the results, anyway. So I will go on supporting you in this pedophile case."

"You will?" Short pause. "You're a friend! A true friend. I'm more obliged to you than ever."

"Good. Then I'd like to call in some of my credit."

"And I'll be happy to help you!"

"Just wait. It's possible that you're not going to like it."

"That's what I'm assuming," Ho said drily.

"Right, listen. In the last week of August 2022, in Beijing, or more precisely in the Sinopec Congress Center in the district of Chaoyang, there was a meeting of international oil companies. I'll send you the list of participants. On the last day of the summit, on the evening of September 1, some of these people met up unofficially in the district of Shunyi. I don't know who took part in that meeting, but it seems to have been an illustrious circle. And I don't know where the meeting took place."

"And that's what I'm to find out. I get it." Ho paused. "This sounds like a routine investigation. What wouldn't I like about it?"

"The second part of my request."

"Which would be?"

"I can only tell you once I've got the answer to part one."

"Fine. I'll figure it out."

Jericho felt the life flowing back into his veins. The prey had become the hunter! In tense expectation he viewed his e-mails and saw that the Repsol man had sent the whole schedule of the summit, and sure enough: everybody had met in Beijing, representatives of almost every company that was involved or ever had been involved in the oil and gas business, strategists almost to a man.

He went through the list and gave a start.

Of course! That was only to be expected. And yet—

He quickly passed on the details to Ho, looked in on Yoyo, who was fast asleep, sat back down at the kitchen counter, and started coming up with theories.

And all of a sudden everything fell into place.

Late that afternoon—Yoyo had groggily gone on her way, not without asking to be updated on the latest developments—Patrice Ho called him back.

"Three years is a long time," he said, trying to make it sound exciting. "But I may have found something. I can't tell you exactly who took part in the meeting, but I can tell you with some certainty where it took place and who the host was."

"A private house?"

"Correct. There are no Sinopec facilities in Shunyi, but the Strategy Manager of the company lives there. Big property. We looked into him just for a laugh, and found out that he lives notoriously beyond his means, but yes, lots of people do that. His name is Joe Song. He represented Sinopec during the summit. Can you do anything with that?"

"I think so, yeah." A name, another name! Now it would all depend on whether he was right. "Thanks! That's all fine."

"I get it. Now comes the bit I'm not going to like."

"Yes. You have to hack into Song's computer."

"Hmm."

"It could be that I'm mistaken and the guy has nothing to hide. But if—"

"Owen, listen. A promise is a promise, okay? But before I do that, I need more information. I've got to know where your investigations are leading."

Jericho hesitated. "Possibly to the retrieval of the Chinese government's honor."

"Aha."

"You promise to help me anyway?"

"As I said—"

"Okay, listen up. I'll give you the background. Then I'll tell you what you need to look for."

Twenty minutes later, when he could be certain that the Repsol man had drunk his first café con leche, he called Madrid again.

"Can I bother you again?"

"Of course."

"You mentioned that the joint venture planned between Sinopec, Repsol, and EMCO was based on an initiative. Can you remember who the initiator was?"

"Sure." The man told him the name. "By the way, he was the one who blew the whole thing up into a summit, and suggested holding the thing in Beijing. Sinopec liked that. The Chinese like the world being negotiated on their territory."

"Thanks. You've been a great help."

The initiator—

Jericho smiled grimly. He saw the Hydra stretching its necks, darting its heads forward, baring its fangs. It hissed at him, but its mighty serpentine body bent and started slowly retreating.

That night he slept a deep and dreamless sleep.

The next day, radio silence until lunchtime. Then Ho rang, and he sounded just as excited as he had two and a half weeks previously, when Jericho had passed on the news of the capture of Animal Ma Liping.

"Incredible," he said. "You were right."

Jericho's heartbeat did a drumroll.

"What exactly did you find?"

"The icon. That snaky thing, what's the creature called again?"

"Hydra."

"On Song's company computer! Hidden among other programs. To make his deleted e-mails visible again, however, we'll have to get at his hard disk."

"No problem. You have sufficient grounds to arrest him officially."

"Owen, that could—" Ho caught his breath. "That could make my promotion to Beijing—"

"I know," smiled Jericho. "Bust the guy. You'll find data that look like white noise, but using that icon you'll be able to get a message out of it without too much difficulty."

"I'll call you. I'll call you!"

"Wait!" Jericho started to pace back and forth, kept in motion by adrenaline. "We need the other participants in the meeting. It only looks like a plot by a business sector, but it's really a conspiracy by a small number of people. We've got to get to them. Focused and fast, so that none of them has a chance to get away. Perhaps you'll manage to wring a confession from our friend by pointing out the mitigating circumstances."

"Like him being able to keep his head attached to his neck," sniffed Ho.

"Oh come on. I thought the death penalty was abolished in 2021."

"So it was. But I can always threaten to bring it back specially for him. Soon we'll know who the other participants were, you can be sure of that!"

"Fine. If he doesn't talk, we'll have to check out every single alibi. I know that's going to be a big job."

"Not really. I'd say the companies will be very interested in getting the truth into the open. In times like these, they don't want to screw up their reputations."

"Whatever. It will have to be a concerted action. That means you'll have to bring in MI6 and the American secret service, as well as the secret services of all the countries affected. Then I'm going to phone Orley Enterprises, so promise me that the Chinese police won't stonewall. You're going to be bathed in glory."

"The glory will be yours, Owen!"

Jericho said nothing.

Did he want that? Did he want to be bathed in glory? A little bit proud, perhaps, as Yoyo had suggested. They'd earned that, Yoyo, Tian, and he. And apart from that, he just needed one more good night's sleep like the one he had just had.

Early in the afternoon, Joe Song, the oil strategist, was arrested in his office, looked completely dumbfounded, and the investigators went to work. Just as restorers work their way through layers of paint to reveal much older art, they brought to light Song's deleted e-mails, supposed white noise which, with the expert use of the decoding program, was shaped into a document whose contents were enough to put Song in jail for the rest of his life.

And yet he denied everything. For an evening and a night he denied having anything to do with the attacks, and nor did he know anything about an organization called Hydra, or how the icon and the message had found their way onto the Sinopec computer. Meanwhile a police unit was raging around his house before the eyes of his terrified wife, and found another gleaming, pulsing Hydra on Song's private computer, and the manager still claimed not to know anything. It took a night in jail and two consultations with his lawyers, before Patrice Ho, on the afternoon of June 6—in a soundproofed room—vividly presented him with the bleakness of the rest of his life, but not without suggesting a possible way out in the event that he admitted everything.

After that Joe Song couldn't stop talking.

Jericho listened ecstatically to what Ho went on to tell him. Immediately afterward he dialed Jennifer Shaw's number. It was nine in the morning in London, and he was almost pleased to be seeing her again.

"Owen! You keeping okay?"

"Pretty good now, thanks. You?"

"The Big O makes an ants' nest look like a Zen monastery. All the investigations get concentrated here; everyone unrolls the thread of his theory, so that you can't take so much as a step without getting hopelessly entangled."

"Doesn't necessarily sound as if you've achieved clarity."

"Still, by now we know that Gaia's hotel manager was a former Mossad agent. Good that you called, though. Julian seems to have triplicated himself. He's working around the clock, but I know he wanted to call you at the next possible opportunity."

"So is he there?"

"He's buzzing around the place. Shall I try to put you through?"

"I've got a much better suggestion, Jennifer. Bring him here."

Shaw raised a Mr. Spock eyebrow.

"I assume you have more on your mind than just saying hello."

He smiled. "You're going to like it."

A short time later they were all gathered in Jericho's loft, projected vivid and life-sized on Tu's holowall, and Jericho played his cards. Orley didn't interrupt him once, while his eyebrows drew together until they stood like craggy mountain ranges above his clear blue eyes, but when he finally turned his head toward Shaw, his voice sounded calm and relaxed.

"Prepare a helicopter to the airport," he said. "From there we'll take the jet. We'll pay him a visit."

"Now?" asked Shaw.

"When else do you suggest?"

"To be quite honest I haven't the faintest idea where he is right now. But okay, of course we can—"

"You don't need do." Orley smiled fiercely. "I know where he is. He told me, right after we got back. When he called to express his dismay."

"Of course," said Shaw devotedly. "When do you want to fly?"

"Give me an hour for hand luggage. Inform Interpol, MI6, but they're not to steal the show. Owen?" Orley stood up. "Do you want to come?"

Jericho hesitated. "Where to?"

Orley told him the name of the city. It really wasn't terribly far—for a well motorized Englishman.

Suddenly he burst out laughing.

"I'm in Shanghai, Julian."

"So?" Orley looked around, as if to prove that there were no problems in view. "This is *your* moment, Owen! Who cares about distances? I don't. Take the next high-speed jet, I'll book you a ticket."

"Very kind of you, but—"

"Kind?" Orley tilted his head. "Do you have any idea what I owe you? I'll carry you on my shoulders if I have to! No, here's what we'll do, have we got one of our Mach 4 jets anywhere in his vicinity? Find that out for me, Jennifer. I think there's one in Tokyo, isn't there? We'll collect you, Owen. And bring Tu Tian with you, and that wonderful girl—"

"Julian, wait."

"It's not a problem, it really isn't."

Jericho shook his head. I've got more important things to do, he was about to say. I have to marry a standard lamp and a carpet in a Confucian ceremony; that's *my* life, but he didn't want to insult Orley, particularly since, as Shaw had predicted, he actually liked him. The Englishman radiated something that made you unreservedly willing to plunge into the next adventure with him.

"I can't get away from here right now," he said. "I have clients, and you know how it is—you shouldn't leave anyone in the lurch."

"No, you're right." Orley stroked his beard, clearly displeased by the situation. Then he turned his sea-blue eyes back toward Jericho. "But perhaps there's a possibility of staying in Shanghai and still being in on it—but honestly, Owen, can you sleep peacefully without having brought all this to its conclusion?"

"No," said Jericho wearily. "But it's no longer my—"

He paused, searching for the right word.

"Campaign?" Orley nodded. "Okay, my friend. I know. You have to finish off your own story, not mine. Still, listen to my suggestion. It involves putting in a brief appearance, but you shouldn't miss out on that, Owen. You really shouldn't!"

VENICE, ITALY

The record for the biggest man-made mirror in the world was shared by the Large Binocular Telescope Observatory in Arizona on the top of Mount Graham—two individual mirrors, to be precise, each one 8.5 meters in diameter and sixteen tons in weight—and the Hobby Eberle Telescope in Texas, consisting of reflecting cells over a surface of 11 meters by 10 meters. On the other hand, there was no disputing the most beautiful mirror in the world. In times of global flooding, the Piazza San Marco in Venice surpassed anything that had ever been seen before.

Gerald Palstein sat outside the Caffè Florian, buffeted by the unceasing stream of tourists that repelled him just as much as the flooded Square of St. Mark's magically attracted him. For some years now the piazza had been continuously underwater. For the sake of it, he accepted the invasive spectacle, particularly since something was slowly changing in the behavior of the visitors. Even in Japanese tour groups, you could now detect a certain reluctance to cross the square on sunny days like this, and disturb the peace of the ankle-high standing water that perfectly reflected the Basilica di San Marco, the Campanile in front of it, and the surrounding Procuratie, a world based on water and at the same time commemorated in it, a symbolic glimpse of the future. As inexorably as the Lagoon rose, the city was sinking into the sea, like lovers seeking to unite even if it means that they merge together.

Apart from that, nothing in the city had changed. As ever, the clock tower diagonally opposite, with its passageway to the Merceria, showed the phases of the sun and moon and the star-signs on a background of lapis lazuli, and sent out bronze guardians to segment the earth and the universe into hours with its booming chimes, while faint breezes drifted across the one-and-a-half-square-kilometer mirror and rippled the architecture without dissolving it, as if the ghosts of Dalí and Hundertwasser were frolicking in the Square.

Palstein scraped the sticky and delicious crust of sugar from the bottom of his espresso cup. His wife hadn't wanted to come, and was preparing to leave for an Indian Ashram, which she had been visiting at increasingly short intervals ever since an exhibition opening where she had met a guru who had a knack of luring what he wanted from people's souls and bank balances. In point of fact Palstein preferred it that way. Alone, he didn't have to talk, or pretend to be interested, or see things that he would rather block out. He could live in the pleasant stillness of Venice reflected in the water, just as Alice had passed through the mirror to visit the world that lay on the other side.

Noise. Shouts. Laughter.

A moment later the illusion passed, as a group of teenagers splashed their way through the surface of the water and everything turned into a wild, splashing daub.

Idiots, destroying a masterpiece!

The illusion of a masterpiece.

Palstein watched after them, too tired to get angry. Wasn't that always the way? You took such trouble building something, brought it to a state of perfection, and then a few hooligans came along and destroyed it all. He paid the exorbitant cost of the espresso and chamber music, strolled through the arcades of the piazzetta to the Bacino di San Marco, where the Doge's Palace lay along the deeper water, and followed the footbridges to the Biennale Gardens. Near there, by a quiet canal in the tranquil sestiere of Castello, he had an early dinner at the Hosteria Da Franz, which experts held to be the best fish restaurant in Venice, had a chat with Gianfranco, the old proprietor, a man whose life was a Humboldt-style exploration of the world along paths both straight and winding, who would stir himself for nothing except perhaps the sight of a few empty glasses, hugged both him and Maurizio, his son, as he left, and boarded a water taxi that brought him to the Grand Canal and the Palazzo Loredan. EMCO had bought the magnificent early Renaissance building in better days, and had forgotten, during the insanity of its systematic decline, to get rid of it. The building still stood open to the company executives, though it had not been used for ages. But because Palstein loved Venice, and thought nothing was more appropriate to his position than the symbol of everything transient, he had come here for a week.

By now the sun was low over the Canal. The rattle and chug of the vaporetti and the barges mingled with the hum of elegant motorboats, the sound of accordions, and the tenor voices of the gondolieri, to form an aural backdrop unlike anything anywhere else in the world. Now that the ground floor was underwater, he entered the palazzo via a higher entrance, and climbed the wooden staircase to the piano nobile, the first floor. Where the late sunlight came in through the windows, sofas and armchairs were gathered around a low glass table.

In one of the chairs sat Julian Orley.

Palstein gave a start. Then he quickened his pace, hurried the cathedral-like width of the room and spread out his arms.

"Julian," he exclaimed. "What a surprise!"

"Gerald." Orley got to his feet. "You weren't expecting me, were you?"

"No, absolutely not." Palstein hugged the Englishman, who returned the embrace, a bit firmly, it seemed to him.

"How long have you been in Venice?"

"Got here an hour ago. Your concierge was kind enough to let me in, once I'd persuaded him I wasn't about to steal the Murano chandeliers."

"Why didn't you call? We could have gone for dinner. As it was I had to make do with the best turbot I've ever eaten, all by myself." Palstein walked over to a little bar, took out two glasses and a bottle, and turned around. "Grappa? *Prime uve*, soft in the mouth, and drinkable in large quantities."

"Bring it over." Julian sat back down. "We must clink glasses, my old friend. We have something to celebrate."

"Yes, your return." Palstein thoughtfully considered the label, half filled the glasses, and sat down opposite Julian. "Let's drink to survival," he smiled. "To *your* survival."

"Good idea." The Englishman raised his glass, took a good swig, and set his glass back down. Then he opened a bag, took out a laptop, flipped it open, and turned it on. "Because drinking to yours would be like drinking to the future of a hanged man. If you catch my meaning."

Palstein blinked, still smiling.

"Quite honestly, no."

The screen lit up. A camera showed the picture of a man who looked familiar to Palstein. A moment later he remembered. Jericho! Of course! That damned detective.

"Good evening, Gerald," Jericho said in a friendly voice.

Palstein hesitated.

"Hello, Owen. What can I do for you?"

"The same thing you once did in the Big O. Help us. You helped us a lot back then, you remember?"

"Of course. I'd have been happy to do even more."

"Fine. Now's your chance. Julian would like to know a lot of things, but first there's something I'd like to tell you. You'll be pleased to hear that we've solved the mystery of the Calgary shooting."

Palstein said nothing.

"Even though I was worried I would have a tough time of it." Jericho smiled, as if remembering a hurdle overcome. "Because you see, Gerald, if someone had wanted you out of the way, someone who had managed to infiltrate Lars Gudmundsson into your security men—why would he have needed a spectacle like Calgary? Why didn't Gudmundsson just quietly get on with it and shoot you? Even in the Big O it seemed to me that the whole assassination attempt was a big staged event, but who was it for? Eventually it occurred to me that Hydra—an organization I don't need to tell you anything more about—had decided to present the world with a Chinese assassin, if Xin was captured on camera in Calgary. And that was certainly one of the reasons, just as Hydra went on leaving trails back to China, on the one hand because the Chinese were the ideal scapegoat, but probably also because open conflict

would have further held up the lunar projects of the space powers after
the success of Operation Mountains of Eternal Light. But even seen
in this perspective the attack made no sense. Anyone as intimately
acquainted with Kenny Xin as we are knows, for example, that he is
infatuated with flechettes. In Quyu, in Berlin, on the roof of the Big
O, it's the ammunition he's always used. But in Calgary he settled for
decidedly smaller projectiles. Your injury will have been painful, but
entirely harmless, as a conversation with your doctors should confirm."
    Palstein stared into his glass.
    "Take this from someone who's managed to escape Xin several times.
He was ahead of us in London and Berlin, and he cost us a lot of lives. He's
a phenomenal marksman! Definitely not somebody who's going to miss a
target just because he trips, especially when he's got an unobstructed view.
But even if we were willing to accept that stumbling drew the first shot
to your shoulder rather than your head, the second would have got you
before you reached the ground." Jericho paused. "You were hit, nevertheless, Gerald. But certainly, however much you've risked and invested, it
can't have been in your interest to come away with a *serious* injury. And
I know very few marksmen who could pull off such a precision shot as
the one in Calgary: hitting a man while he pretends to slip, without giving him anything more than a completely harmless flesh wound that will
heal very quickly. A masterpiece, after which with the best will in the
world, no one could suspect that you'd cleared the way for Gabriel—or
shall we call him Hanna?—to join Julian's group. Even in the unlikely
event that someone discovered details about the operation, you'd covered
your tracks. Against this background, Loreena's discovery of the video
can hardly have troubled you that much, can it? It too was factored in."
    "I admired Loreena for her sharpness of mind," said Palstein. He
was listening with great interest to the lecture.
    "Of course you did," said the detective. "Except that you wouldn't
have predicted in a million years that she would dig out Ruiz and
establish a connection with a very particular meeting in Beijing three
years ago. At that point things got tight, very tight."
    "I warned Loreena," sighed Palstein. "Several times. You may not
believe it, but I was very keen to spare her that death. I liked her."
    "And Lynn?" Julian said, quietly severe. "What about Lynn? Didn't
you like her?"
    "I was prepared to make sacrifices."
    "My daughter."
    Palstein thoughtfully slipped his finger along the edge of his glass.
    "Seven people in Quyu," Jericho went on. "Ten people in Vancou-
ver, Vogelaar, Nyela. Even Norrington must have imagined that working with you wouldn't be quite like that. And purely out of interest,
who took care of Greenwatch?"

"Gudmundsson." Palstein stiffened. "We had to make sure that there was no editorial conference. I told him to disappear immediately after the operation."

"Which wonderfully confirmed your victim status once again. Gerald Palstein, betrayed by everybody. Might I also take the opportunity to ask you what happened to Alejandro Ruiz?"

"We had to disassociate ourselves from him."

Should he tell them how Xin and Gudmundsson had put the Spaniard on a boat while the city of Lima slept, and introduced him to the world of marine life? What sharks, crabs, and bacteria had left of him rested in the silent darkness of the Peruvian ocean trench. No, too many details. They'd never get out of here.

"He was a weakling," he said. "He was more than happy to do something about helium-3, convinced as he was that we were merely going to blow up a few digging machines. When Hydra met at Song's house on the evening of September 1, it turned out that I'd misjudged him. Unlike everyone else, by the way. I selected the heads of Hydra very carefully over a period of months. They had to have influence, and the power to divert large sums into fake projects without anyone asking any questions. But above all they had to be willing to do anything. As expected, when Xin and I presented Operation Mountains of Eternal Light, it only came as a surprise to Ruiz. He was completely horrified. Turned white as a sheet. Stormed out."

"He threatened to blow Hydra's cover?"

"His next step was predictable."

"Which meant that his fate was too."

Palstein ran his hands over his eyes. He was tired. Shockingly tired. "And how are you going to prove all this?" he asked.

"It's been proved already, Gerald. Joe Song's confessed. We know the heads of Hydra, and right at this very minute they're all getting visits from representatives of their national authorities. They will find snake icons and white noise on the computers of some of the world's biggest oil companies. Really titanic stuff, Gerald. Regardless of borders and ideologies. You were the initiator of the joint venture between Sinopec, Repsol, and EMCO, you turned the meeting in Beijing into a summit, but it's Hydra that'll make you go down in history." Jericho paused. "Except that your name will not be mentioned in very flattering contexts. By the way, how did you get hold of guys like Xin?"

"I wouldn't put it quite like that, Owen." Julian, who had until then been sitting with legs crossed, sat forward. "It should be: how did Xin get hold of people like Gerald."

"In Africa," Palstein said calmly. "In Equatorial Guinea, 2020, when Mayé was still of interest to EMCO."

"Why all this, Gerald?" Julian shook his head. "Why?"

"Why what?"

"Why did you go so far?"

"You're seriously asking me that?" Palstein stared at him listlessly. "To defend my interests. Just as you defend yours. The interests of my sector."

"With atom bombs?"

"Do you seriously imagine I wouldn't have done absolutely anything to solve the problems in a peaceful manner? Everybody knows how much I fought to steer the dinosaur in a different direction to the one it was cheerfully heading in, toward the hurtling meteorite that would seal its extinction. In most alternative sectors we could have held our own. But we missed all opportunities, we neglected to buy Light-years, to get Locatelli on our side, even though it was already clear that helium-3 would mean the end for us. And I even tried to get a foothold in the helium-3 business, as you know, except that I wasn't given permission to draw up an agreement with you."

"Which you were on the verge of doing."

"In the event of failure, yes. Not if two atom bombs had just destroyed the helium-3 mining infrastructure and set things back by decades."

And suddenly, enraged by the wasted potential of his plan, he jumped to his feet, fists clenched.

"I'd calculated everything, Julian! The consequences if we'd destroyed only the space elevator or only Peary Base, but it was only the double whammy that produced the best results. Like China, the Americans would have had to deploy conventional rockets to carry helium-3 to Earth, which would never have happened! Everyone knows that China's extraction is running at a loss. But even if they'd taken such a step, the extracted quantities would have remained pitiful enough. You would have had to build a new space elevator, a new space station, and that would have taken at least twenty years. You wouldn't have had it financed as quickly as you did the first time. And only if shuttle transports had been possible from the orbit to the Moon would you have been able to rebuild the infrastructure up there, and even that would have taken years, maybe decades."

"But in forty or fifty years it'll all be over anyway. Then you'll be finished, *because there'll be nothing left!*"

"Forty years, yes!" snorted Palstein. "Forty years of business left to us. Four decades of survival, in the course of which we could have made up for the mess made by all those idiots, my predecessors included. We could have reorganized. As long ago as 2020, I commissioned an analysis of all the possible scenarios of what would happen if helium-3 extraction were carried out successfully within a precise time frame. It meant our annihilation. We *had* to stand up to you!"

"We?" whispered Julian. "You and your gang of lunatics dare to speak for the whole sector? For thousands of decent people?"

"Thousands of people who would have lost their jobs," yelled Palstein. "A damaged global economy! Look around you! Wake up! How many countries, how many people who depend on oil will be damaged by your helium-3? Have you thought about that?"

"And you were once called the green conscience of the energy sector."

"Because I *am*!" Palstein cried. "But sometimes you have to go against your convictions. Do you think four more decades of oil economy would do more damage to the planet than it's done already? We might be a gang of lunatics, but—"

"No," said Jericho's voice from the laptop. "You're not insane, Gerald. You are calculating, and that's the worst thing about you. Like any other halfwit, you find a reason to blame your crimes on circumstances. You're not special."

Palstein said nothing. He slowly dropped back into his chair and stared at his feet.

"Why the flight to the Moon?" Julian asked quietly.

"Because something got in the way in 2024." Palstein shrugged. "An astronaut called Thorn was supposed to have—"

"I don't mean that. Why that one and not the next one? Why the one my children and I were on, people like Warren Locatelli, the Donoghues, Miranda Winter—"

"I didn't care about your guests, Julian," sighed Palstein. "It was the first opportunity that offered itself since Thorn's failure. When would the next trip have taken place? Only after the official opening. This year? Next year? How long would we have had to wait?"

"Perhaps you also factored in the possibility of Julian's death," said Jericho.

"Nonsense."

"His death would have strengthened the conservative forces at Orley. The people opposed to the idea of selling off technologies. The smaller the number of countries that can build a space elevator, the smaller the chance that a second—"

"You're fantasizing, Jericho. If you hadn't spoiled everything, Julian would have been back on Earth ages before the explosions took place. And his son and daughter too."

The muffled chugging and thudding of the boats reached them from outside. Right below their window someone was singing "O Sole Mio" with businesslike ardor.

"But we weren't on Earth," said Julian.

"That wasn't the plan."

"Fuck your plan. You went beyond the limit, Gerald. In every respect."

Palstein looked up.

"And you? You and your American friends? How is what you're doing any different from what we've been doing for decades? You

extract something from the ground until it's all gone and you find
you've destroyed a planet in the process. What limit do you people
go beyond? What limit do you in particular go beyond when you
run your company like a state that dictates the rules of play to real
states? Do you think you're being public-spirited? At least the oil companies served their countries. Who are you serving, apart from your
own vanity? There are no social states without state organizations,
but you're behaving like a modern Captain Nemo and spitting on the
world as it happens to work. We merely played the game that the circumstances required. Only look at mankind, their clean, just wars,
the cyclical collapse of their financial systems, the cynicism of their
profiteers, the unscrupulousness and stupidity of their politicians,
the perversion of their religious leaders, and don't talk to me about
limits."

Julian stroked his beard.

"You could be right, Gerald." He nodded and got to his feet. "But it
doesn't change anything. Owen, thanks for giving up your time. We're
going."

"Take care, Gerald," said Jericho. "Or not."

The picture on the screen went out. Julian snapped the laptop shut
and put it back in its bag.

"A little while ago," he said, "when I was stepping inside your lovely
residence, I noticed a little plaque: in the mezzanine of a building
across the courtyard from this palazzo, Richard Wagner died. You
know what? I liked that. I like the idea of great men dying in great
houses." He reached into his jacket, took out a pistol and set it down
on the table in front of Palstein. His clear blue eyes had a penetrating
expression, almost friendly and encouraging. "It's loaded. One shot is
generally enough, but you're a big man, Gerald. A very big man. You
might take two."

He turned around and crossed the room at a leisurely pace. Palstein
watched after him, until Julian's gray-blond ponytail had disappeared
beyond the landing. As if of their own accord, his fingers found their
way to his phone and keyed in a number.

"Hydra," he said mechanically.

"What can I do?"

"Get me out of here. I've been unmasked."

"Unma—" Xin fell silent for a moment. "You know, Gerald, I think
my contract's just run out."

"You're walking out on me?"

"I wouldn't put it like that. You know me, I'm loyal and I'm not
afraid to take risks, but in hopeless cases—and your case is unfortunately *completely* hopeless . . ."

"What—" Palstein gulped. "What are you going to do?"

"Hmm." Xin seemed to think for a moment. "Quite honestly, it's been rather tiring lately. I think I need a bit of a vacation. You take care."

Take care. The second person who'd said that to him.

Palstein froze. He slowly lowered his phone. Voices rose to him from below.

His eyes wandered to the gun.

The people from Interpol and MI6 were waiting for him in the stairwell. Shaw looked at him quizzically.

"Give him a minute," said Julian.

"Well, I'm not sure." One of the agents frowned. "He could do something to himself."

"Yes, exactly." Julian pushed past him. "Jennifer, let's go. I have to look after my daughter."

LONDON, GREAT BRITAIN

Stars like dust.

She had been lost in sleep, and the dream had put her back into the stillness of the spaceship dashing through the sparkling night, along with her and the bomb. She had lived through everything all over again. Again she had come up with the plan to stow the mini-nuke in the living module, uncouple it, and come back to the OSS with the landing unit. Back to Tim and Amber and Julian, who had cried so hard when he called her name. In her mind she had promised him never to leave him alone again, but her thoughts had been all that she was able to mobilize, and that wasn't much.

Then the moment when the spinning bomb, lit by the flickering of her dying consciousness, had revealed the truth, that there were still *hours* to go until detonation, not minutes or seconds as she had thought. That she would have had a chance.

She had gone to sleep in the pearly rain of her blood.

I'm coming. I'm coming, Daddy.

I'm there.

Clunk!

One of those noises that feel like a nuisance, even if they mean the salvation of *really* having made your peace. In the absence of choice, of course. But she *had* made her peace before the shuttle on which Julian, Nina, Tim, and Amber had followed her docked to the Charon—her lonely spaceship that had not had the chance of filling its tanks on the OSS, which was why it had finally run out of fuel. Even before it reached its top speed.

But she hadn't known anything about any of that.

Voices around her. People in space suits.

"Lynn? Lynn!"

Impotence. Scraps of words. As if through cotton balls.

"How long now?"

"Just over five hours. Enough time to bring both shuttles back."

"I think Lynn's stable." Nina. "She's lost a lot of blood, but it seems to me—"

Silence again. Then a voice on an endless loop:

"And now get the thing out of here!"

Thing out of here, thing out of here, thing out of here, thingoutofhere, thingoutofherethingout—

"Lynn."

She blinked. The hospital room. Back in the present. Hang on, wasn't there a film called—

Doesn't matter, what a film!

"How are you?" said Julian.

"Been dreaming." She sat up. Her left side hurt, but she was feeling better every day. Dana, the bitch, had missed taking her life by inches. "We were back in the spaceship." Christ, she was hungry. Incredibly hungry! She could have eaten the bed. "A nightmare, to be honest. Always the same nightmare."

"It's over."

"Hey, no big deal. It wasn't all that bad, either." She yawned. "Hopefully I'll dream something else eventually."

"No. It's *over*, Lynn." Julian took her hand and smiled, very much the magician of her childhood. "The nightmare is over."

Xintiandi, Shanghai, China

"Yoyo could really give us a call," Jericho complained.

Tu pulled a sticky strand of noodle from the cardboard box that stood in for his lunch plate.

"And you could *drop by* again," he said, chewing. "Instead of only ever phoning. Burying yourself away in your stupid loft."

"I'm busy. Honestly."

Tu gave him a disapproving look over the rim of his glasses. The bridge looked as if it was about to snap in two over his nose.

"You have friends to cultivate," he chided him. "What about this evening? A bunch of us are going out to eat. And drink, more importantly."

"Who's we?"

"Everyone you can think of. Yoyo too, once she's stopped crying. She's been sobbing away constantly; I'm thinking of installing a dam in the guest room. Terrible. Nothing but tears. A great big crybaby."

"And Hongbing?"

"He's crying too. They're closer than they've ever been."

"Sounds good."

"Yeah, great," growled Tu. "You just don't have to put up with it. What about tonight?"

"Fine."

"Good. I wouldn't have let you get away with anything else. *Xiongdi!*"

Jericho sat there for a while.

Then he went across to the kitchen area to magic a cappuccino from the coffee machine. His journey took him past the ensemble that he had now got used to calling "the odd couple," Jack Lemmon and Walter Matthau embodied by a standard lamp and a carpet, which failed, failed, failed to accomplish the ideal of Confucian harmony, in any imaginable arrangement.

He studied them for a moment.

Then he moved them aside, put them in the cellar, and looked at the corner. And finally, flooded only by light, clear and tidy, he liked it.

That had been important!

DRAMATIS PERSONAE

Anand, Ashwini Staff member at the Gaia moon hotel, responsible for accommodation, technology and logistics.

Black, Peter Tour guide at the Gaia moon hotel, pilot of the moon shuttle Charon. Knows all the moon craters by name.

Borelius, Eva Scientist and CEO of the German research company Borelius Pharmaceuticals. Northern German, dry character. Likes classical music, horses and chess. Married to the surgeon Karla Kramp. Member of the moon tour group.

Bruford, Sid Former oil worker at EMCO Imperial Oil, Canada, unemployed. Dreams of a career as an actor.

Chambers, Evelyn Most prominent and influential talk-show host in the USA, presenter of the show *Chambers*. Latina, whose bisexuality has turned her into a hate figure. Brilliant analyst, perceptive and curious. Member of the moon tour group.

Chen "Yoyo" Yuyun Student, daughter of Chen Hongbing, founder of the internet dissident group "the Guardians," member of the motorcycle club City Demons. Sings in a neo-prog band, loves parties and the excessive lifestyle. Beautiful and quite exhausting.

Chen Hongbing Car salesman, Yoyo's father. Polite, but reserved, with a murky past. Commissions Owen Jericho to find his missing daughter.

Crippen, Jan Technical director of the American Peary Base, lunar North Pole.

"Daxiong" Guan Guo Founder member and vice head of the internet dissident group "the Guardians," head of the motorcycle club City Demons and owner of the Demon Point motorcycle workshop. Giant with bear-like strength and French-style spleen.

DeLucas, Minnie   Doctor and specialist in life-support systems at the American Peary Base, lunar North Pole. Investigating the possibility of raising livestock on the Moon.

Diane   Owen Jericho's computer.

Donner, Andre   Owner of the Muntu African restaurant in Berlin. Murky past in Equatorial Guinea.

Donner, Nyela   West African, co-owner of the Muntu African restaurant in Berlin, Andre Donner's wife.

Donoghue, Chuck   Hotel mogul, founder and CEO of the Xanadu hotel and casino company. Amateur boxer and hard-line Republican. Loud and jovial. Cheerfully tells the world's worst jokes. Member of the moon tour group.

Donoghue, Aileen   CEO and artistic manager of the Xanadu hotel and casino company. Wife of Chuck Donoghue. Dominant-mother type. Member of the moon tour group.

Edwards, Marc   Founder and CEO of the microchip company Quantime Inc., extreme sports fanatic and diver, creationist view of the world. Husband of Mimi Parker, member of the moon tour group.

Funaki, Michio   Sous-chef and bartender in the Gaia moon hotel, sushi specialist.

Gore, Kyra   Shuttle pilot at the American Peary Base, lunar North Pole.

Gudmundsson, Lars   Bodyguard, employed with his team by the Eagle Eye security company to protect the oil manager Gerald Palstein.

Hanna, Carl   Canadian large-scale investor, main area alternative energies. Solitary type, macho, but likeable. Always has his guitar in his luggage. Member of the moon tour group.

Haskin, Ed   Chief technician, Orley Space Station OSS.

Hedegaard, Nina   Tour guide at the Gaia moon hotel, moon shuttle pilot. Capable and romantic. Involved in relationship with Julian Orley.

Ho, Patrice   Senior Shanghai police officer and careerist, friend of Owen Jericho. Jericho has supported Ho in several investigations, and is therefore owed a favor.

Hoff, Edda   Project manager, central security division, Orley Enterprises. Pale, expressionless and extremely reliable.

Holland, Sid   Political history editor at environmental broadcaster Greenwatch. Likes driving his friends and colleagues around in his old Thunderbird.

Hsu, Rebecca   Founder and CEO of the Taiwanese luxury company Rebecca Hsu, workaholic, incapable of being on her own. Fights a hopeless war with her obesity. Member of the moon tour group.

Hui Xiao-Tong   Member of the City Demons motorcycle club.

Hudsucker, Susan   Director of the environmental broadcaster Greenwatch and immediate superior of Loreena Keowva. Prudent, sometimes hesitant.

Intern   Colleague of Loreena Keowa at environmental broadcaster Greenwatch. Glutton and tireless researcher.

ISLAND-II   Psychotherapeutic aid program.

Jagellovsk, Annie   Astronomer and pilot at the American Peary Base, lunar North Pole.

Jericho, Owen   Cyber-detective from Great Britain, brought to Shanghai by an unhappy love affair. Outstanding investigator, lone wolf and linguistic genius. Suffers from loneliness and nightmares. Hired by his friend Tu Tian to find Yoyo.

Jia Keqiang   Commander of the Chinese helium-3 mining station, Sinus Iridum, Moon. Both a patriot and a supporter of international understanding.

Jin Jia Wei   Student, member of the internet dissident group "the Guardians" and of the City Demons motorcycle club.

Keowa, Loreena   Reporter for the environmental broadcaster Greenwatch, native American of the Tlingit tribe. Green views, elegant appearance. Determined to solve the assassination attempt on Gerald Palstein.

Kokoschka, Axel   Head chef, Gaia moon hotel. Genius at the stove, in the company of others shy, uncommunicative and awkward.

Karla Kramp   German surgeon, critical and analytic. Asks tough questions. Wife of Eva Borelius, member of moon tour group.

Lau Ye   Daxiong's right-hand man, mechanic at Demon Point motorcycle workshop and member of City Demons motorcycle club. Small, slight but intrepid and loyal.

Laurie, Jean-Jacques   Geologist at the American Peary Base, lunar North Pole.

Lawrence, Dana   Manager and head of security, Gaia moon hotel. Cool, unapproachable and thorough.

Lee, Bernard, "C"   Head of MI6, London.

Leto   Former mercenary, friend of Jan Kees Vogelaar, Berlin.

Liu, Naomi   Senior secretary at Tu Technologies; stylish appearance, with liking for strawberry tea.

Locatelli, Warren   Founder and CEO of photovoltaic manufacturer Light-years. American of Algerian-Italian descent, irascible and egocentric, although not without charm. Likes cursing, car-racing and sailing regattas. Winner of the America's Cup. Married to Momoka Omura. Member of moon tour group.

Lurkin, Laura   Fitness trainer, Orley Space Station OSS.

Ma "Animal" Liping   Violent pedophile, initiator of the child porn ring Paradise of the Little Emperors. In spite of hip and eye problems, extremely dangerous.

Ma Mak   Member of City Demons motorcycle club.

Maas, Svenja   Attractive postgraduate at the Charité Hospital, Berlin.

Mayé, Juan Alfonso Nguema   West African general and sometime leader of Equatorial Guinea. Successor to Teodoro Obiang, came to power in a coup in 2017. Corrupt and megalomaniac.

Merrick, Tom   Specialist in information and communication, central security division, Orley Enterprises. Introvert.

Moto, Severo   Opposition politician in Equatorial Guinea, during Teodoro Obiang's time in office.

Na Mou   Crew member, Chinese helium-3 extraction station, Sinus Iridum, Moon.

Nair, Mukesh   Founder and CEO of the Tomato food company. Wealthy son of a farmer, with a liking for the simple life, sees the beautiful and the good in everything. Member of moon tour group.

Nair, Sushma   Pediatrician, wife of Mukesh Nair, warm-hearted, sometimes a little fearful. Member of moon tour group.

Ndongo, Juan Aristide   Ruler of Equatorial Guinea after the fall of General Mayé. Trying to rebuild the country in a decent way.

Norrington, Andrew   Deputy head of the central security division, Orley Enterprises. Responsible for the safety of the moon tour group.

Obiang, Teodoro   Ruler of Equatorial Guinea until 2015.

O'Keefe, Finn   Irish actor, became global superstar with *Perry Rhodan*. Critics' favorite, sex symbol, solitary and shy, with a reckless past. Nurtures his rebel image. Member of moon tour group.

Omura, Momoka   Japanese actress, art film star, eccentric and arrogant. Wife of Warren Locatelli. Member of moon tour group.

Orley, Amber   Tim Orley's wife, teacher. Capable and uncomplicated, tries to act as go-between for Tim and his father. Member of moon tour group.

Orley, Julian   Former film producer, founder and CEO of technology empire Orley Enterprises and wealthiest man in the world. Unconventional, charismatic, with a pronounced instinct for power and a demonstrable dislike of nation states. Inventor of the space lift and host of moon tour group.

Orley, Lynn   Julian Orley's daughter and CEO of Orley Travel, the tourism group of Orley Enterprises. Perfectionist, psychologically unstable, architect of the Gaia moon hotel and member of the moon tour group.

Orley, Tim   Julian Orley's son, teacher, at loggerheads with his father. Tries to protect Lynn from collapse. Member of moon tour group.

Orley, Crystal   Julian Orley's late wife, spent the last months of her life in a state of mental derangement.

Ögi, Walo   Swiss investor, architect, man of the world and epicurean with a weakness for the music of the 1990s. Lovable, with tendency toward self-dramatization and grand gestures. Husband of Heidrun Ögi. Member of moon tour group.

Ögi, Heidrun Photographer, albino, former stripper and porn actress, calls a spade a spade. Wife of Walo Ögi and member of moon tour group.

Palmer, Leland Commander of the American Peary Base, lunar North Pole.

Palstein, Gerald Head of strategy at EMCO oil company. Aesthete, numerate, spent years fighting for his company to go into alternative energies. Narrowly escaped attempted assassination.

Parker-Edwards, Mimi Fashion designer and founder of the Mimi Kri label producing intelligent fashion. Diver, extreme sports fan, creationist views. Wife of Marc Edwards. Member of moon tour group.

Reardon, Mickey Ex-IRA man, specialist in alarm systems.

Rogachev, Oleg CEO of the Russian steel giant Rogamittal, with links to the Kremlin and the Russian Mafia. Martial arts and football enthusiast, places great stress on self-control, courteous, sometimes seems distant. Member of moon tour group.

Rogacheva, Olympiada Member of the Russian Parliament, daughter of the former Russian President Maxim Ginsburg and wife of Oleg Rogachev. Inconspicuous and dejected. Unhappy in her marriage, drinks. Member of moon tour group.

Ruiz, Alejandro Strategy manager of the Repsol oil company, vanished in South America, 2022.

Shaw, Jennifer Head of the central security division, Orley Enterprises. Competent and authoritarian, with a dry sense of humor.

Sina Editor, society and miscellaneous, at environmental broadcaster Greenwatch. Helps Loreena Keowa with her research.

Song, Joe Strategy manager of the Chinese oil company Sinopec, Beijing.

Sung, Tony Student, member of the internet dissident group "the Guardians" and of the City Demons motorcycle club.

Tautou, Bernard CEO of the Franco-British water company Suez, politician. Charmer with a tendency to complacency, member of moon tour group.

Tautou, Paulette Foreign language correspondent, wife of Bernard Tautou, condescending, weak stomach. Member of moon tour group.

Thiel, Sophie Deputy director of the Gaia moon hotel, responsible for housekeeping and life-support systems. Cheerful and open, detective instincts.

Thorn, Vic Commander of the first crew of the American Peary Base, lunar North Pole. Capable astronaut and playboy. Lost his life in an accident on OSS in 2024.

Tu, Joanna Painter, ex-girlfriend of Owen Jericho and wife of Tu Tian. Elegant and urbane, observes the world with sardonic detachment.

Tu Tian   Founder and CEO of Tu Technologies, a Shanghai company producing holograms and virtual environments. Skilled golfer and businessman, with unparalleled self-confidence. Confidant of Yoyo, companion of Chen Hongbing and close friend of Owen Jericho.

Vogelaar, Jan Kees   Mercenary, sometime member of the government of Equatorial Guinea under General Mayé. Extremely cunning. Special characteristic: glass eye.

Voss, Marika   Director of the Institute of Forensic Pathology at the Charité Hospital, Berlin.

Wachowski, Tommy   Deputy commander of the American Peary Base, lunar North Pole.

Wang, Grand Cherokee   Student, Yoyo's roommate, self-dramatist, weak character. Operates the Silver Dragon ride at the Shanghai World Financial Center (WFC).

Winter, Miranda   Ex-model, inheritor of billions and occasional actress. Naïve and uneducated, warm and strident. Has names for her breasts. Member of moon tour group.

Woodthorpe, Kay   Director of the biogenerative systems research group, Orley Space Station OSS.

Xiao "Maggie" Meiqi   Student, member of the internet dissident group "the Guardians" and of the City Demons motorcycle club.

Xin, Kenny   Agent, aesthete and neurotic.

Yin Ziyi   Student, member of the internet dissident group "the Guardians" and of the City Demons motorcycle club.

Zhang Li   Student, Yoyo's roommate.

Zhao Bide   Acquaintance and occasional helper of Owen Jericho from Quyu, like Jericho in search of Yoyo.

Zheng Pang-Wang   Founder and CEO of the Chinese technology company Zheng Group, great hope of Chinese space travel.

Zhou Jinping   Crew member of the Chinese helium-3 extraction station, Sinus Iridum, Moon.

Acknowledgments

Various textbooks, documentaries, photographs, and films were a great help to me when I was writing this book—so many that it would be impossible for me to list them all here. I should like to thank the authors, journalists, scientists, photographers, and directors whose discoveries flowed into my research all the more emphatically for their work.

But *Limit* would not have come into being if some remarkable people hadn't given up their time to me.

My knowledge of astronauts, space stations, spaceships, moon bases, satellites; of interplanetary communication; of the incidence of lunar helium-3 and the technology required for its extraction; of space law; of the Moon itself; and of the future of manned space travel was considerably enriched by:

Thomas Reiter, ISS and Mir astronaut, Chairman of the German
    Aerospace, DLR Porz
Kerstin Rogon, Thomas Reiter office, DLR Porz
Dr. Wolfgang Seboldt, Space missions and technology, DLR Porz
Dr. Reinhold Ewald, Mir astronaut and physicist
Professor Ernst Messerschmidt, astronaut and physicist
Dr. Eva Hassel-von Pock
Dr. Paolo Ferri, head of solar and planetary missions, ESA Space
    Operations Center, Darmstadt
Dr. Frank-Jürgen Dieckmann, Spacecraft Operations Manager for
    Envisat and ERS-2, ESA Space Operations Center Darmstadt
Dr. Manfred Warhaut, Head of Mission Operations, ESA Space
    Operations Center Darmstadt

Professor Dr. Tilman Spohn, Head of the Institute of Planetary Research Management, DLR, Berlin
Dr. Marietta Benkö, specialist in space law, Cologne
Ranga Yogeshwar, physicist and presenter

The oil and gas sector, business structures and prognoses, but also the growing market in alternative energies, was brought closer to me by:

Werner Breuers, Chairman of LANXESS AG
Wahida Hammond, Skywalker, Cologne—with extra thanks for contacts and *simply being Why*

I learned a lot about modern communication technology, the internet of tomorrow, IT security, holography and virtual environments from:

Dr. Manfred Bogen, Head of Virtual Environments at the Fraunhofer Institute for Intelligent Analysis and Information Systems, Sankt Augustin
Paul Friessem, Head of Department, Secure Processes and Infrastructures, at the Fraunhofer Institute for Secure Information Technology, Sankt Augustin
Thorsten Holtkämper, Project Manager, Virtual Environments, at the Fraunhofer Institute for Intelligent Analysis and Information Systems, Sankt Augustin
Roland Kuck, Project Manager, Virtual Environments, at the Fraunhofer Institute for Intelligent Analysis and Information Systems, Sankt Augustin
Thomas Tikwinski, Project Manager, NetMedia, at the Fraunhofer Institute for Intelligent Analysis and Information Systems, Sankt Augustin
Jochen Haas, Simply Net Data Services, Cologne

I was able to deepen my understanding of architecture and urban planning, particularly about urban development in China, but also about slums, thanks to:

Professor Dr. Eckhard Ribbeck, City Planning Institute, Stuttgart University
Ingeborg Junge-Reyer, mayor of Berlin and Senator for Urban Development

The present and future state of forensic medicine were brought to life for me by:

Dr. Michael Tsokos, Director of the Institute of Forensic Pathology at the Charité, Berlin

I was given information about the past, present, and future of China, about Chinese manners and names, and the status quo of Chinese pop music by:

Mian Mian, author and scene icon, Shanghai
Wei Butter, Master of Arts, Asian Languages, Bonn

Facts about mercenaries, private security services, arms technology, police and detective work were communicated to me by:

Peter Nasse, Head of Personal Security Management Services,
    Cologne
Uwe Steen, Public Relations, Cologne Police

Special thanks to:

Gisela Tolk, judge and passionate sinologist, who tirelessly collected
    material about China for me
Maren Steingross, who summarized my Chinese research and thus
    got it into my head
Jürgen Muthmann, who read more newspapers in a week than I do in
    a whole year, and drew my attention to a lot of things that I would
    otherwise have missed
Larissa Kranz for being such a great dining companion

You can get a bit unsociable when you're writing fat books, which is down to a perceived distortion of space and time. For example, you could swear you'd been out with your best friend only the previous week, until he points out on the phone that you haven't seen each other in six months. Dear people who are important to you engage in dialogue with each other about the question of which galaxy their physically and mentally absent friend, relation and husband may currently be traveling in. In fact I did go missing for a long time, but never heard a word of reproach. Instead I enjoyed two years of sympathy, support and patience. I owe my friends and family a debt of gratitude for that! More than anything else I'm glad to be able to spend more time with you all again—particularly since I hate sitting alone at my desk! If there were no laptops, high-performance batteries and extension leads, author would be the worst job imaginable for me. I like being around people too much, so I've got used to writing in public, surrounded by music, street noises and conversation. As a result, large parts of Limit were written in the establishments of restaurateur friends of mine, whose ministrations had considerable influence on the result.

   I am particularly grateful to Thomas Wippenbeck and his great team at Restaurant Fonda in Südstadt, Cologne, where I spent so much time that in the end I risked being mistaken for part of the furniture and stacked up with the chairs at night. I was also well looked after in the Spitz, whose friendly staff defended my regular table with knife and fork against all other guests. I was always given a welcome by the Sterns in the Vintage and Romain Wack in Wackes. Sometimes I simply had to get out of Cologne and headed for the island of Sylt, where I received perfect treatment both from Johannes King and his team at the Söl'ring Hof and from Herbert Seckler, Ivo Köster and their team at the Sansibar.

I would like to thank the brilliant, committed staff at my publishing house, and quite particularly you, Helge, for your friendship and invaluable confidence.

But my ultimate thanks is for you, Sabina. However much I may have enjoyed traveling to the Moon in my mind—the best thing was always looking back at the Earth. Because that's where you are.